THE BOOK OF THE NEW SUN

Other Books by Gene Wolfe

Operation ARES
The Fifth Head of Cerberus
Peace
The Devil in a Forest
The Island of Doctor Death and Other Stories
Gene Wolfe's Book of Days
The Wolfe Archipelago
The Castle of the Otter
Bibliomen
Free Live Free
Plan[e]t Engineering
Soldier of the Mist
Soldier of Arete
There Are Doors
The Urth of the New Sun
Storeys from the Old Hotel
Endangered Species
Pandora by Holly Holander
Castleview

The Book of the Long Sun

Nightside of the Long Sun
Lake of the Long Sun
Calde of the Long Sun
Exodus from the Long Sun

THE BOOK OF THE NEW SUN

The Shadow of the Torturer
The Claw of the Conciliator
The Sword of the Lictor
The Citadel of the Autarch

GENE WOLFE

First SFBC Science Fiction Printing: June 1998

Published by arrangement with:
Pocket Books
1230 Avenue of the Americas
New York, NY 10020

Visit our website at *http://www.sfbc.com*

ISBN 1-56865-807-9

PRINTED IN THE UNITED STATES OF AMERICA.

Contents

The Shadow of the Torturer

A thousand ages in thy sight
Are like an evening gone;
Short as the watch that ends the night
Before the rising sun.

I

Resurrection and Death

It is possible I already had some presentiment of my future. The locked and rusted gate that stood before us, with wisps of river fog threading its spikes like the mountain paths, remains in my mind now as the symbol of my exile. That is why I have begun this account of it with the aftermath of our swim, in which I, the torturer's apprentice Severian, had so nearly drowned.

"The guard has gone." Thus my friend Roche spoke to Drotte, who had already seen it for himself.

Doubtfully, the boy Eata suggested that we go around. A lift of his thin, freckled arm indicated the thousands of paces of wall stretching across the slum and sweeping up the hill until at last they met the high curtain wall of the Citadel. It was a walk I would take, much later.

"And try to get through the barbican without a safe-conduct? They'd send to Master Gurloes."

"But why would the guard leave?"

"It doesn't matter." Drotte rattled the gate. "Eata, see if you can slip between the bars."

Drotte was our captain, and Eata put an arm and a leg through the iron palings, but it was immediately clear that there was no hope of his getting his body to follow.

"Someone's coming," Roche whispered. Drotte jerked Eata out.

I looked down the street. Lanterns swung there among the fog-muffled sounds of feet and voices. I would have hidden, but Roche held me, saying, "Wait, I see pikes."

"Do you think it's the guard returning?"

He shook his head. "Too many."

"A dozen men at least," Drotte said.

Still wet from Gyoll we waited. In the recesses of my mind we stand shivering there even now. Just as all that appears imperishable tends toward its own destruction, those moments that at the time seem the most fleeting recreate themselves—not only in my memory (which in the final accounting loses nothing) but in the throbbing of my heart and the prickling of my hair, making themselves new just as our Commonwealth reconstitutes itself each morning in the shrill tones of its own clarions.

The men had no armor, as I could soon see by the sickly yellow light of the lanterns; but they had pikes, as Drotte had said, and staves and hatchets. Their leader wore a long, double-edged knife in his belt. What interested me more was the massive key threaded on a cord around his neck; it looked as if it might fit the lock of the gate.

Little Eata fidgeted with nervousness, and the leader saw us and lifted his lantern over his head. "We're waiting to get in, goodman," Drotte called. He was the taller, but he made his dark face humble and respectful.

"Not until dawn," the leader said gruffly. "You young fellows had better get home."

"Goodman, the guard was supposed to let us in, but he's not here."

"You won't be getting in tonight." The leader put his hand on the hilt of his knife before taking a step closer. For a moment I was afraid he knew who we were.

Drotte moved away, and the rest of us stayed behind him. "Who are you, goodman? You're not soldiers."

"We're the volunteers," one of the others said. "We come to protect our own dead."

"Then you can let us in."

The leader had turned away. "We let no one inside but ourselves." His key squealed in the lock, and the gate creaked back. Before anyone could stop him Eata darted through. Someone cursed, and the leader and two others sprinted after Eata, but he was too fleet for them. We saw his tow-colored hair and patched shirt zigzag among the sunken graves of paupers, then disappear in the thicket of statuary higher up. Drotte tried to pursue him, but two men grabbed his arms.

"We have to find him. We won't rob you of your dead."

"Why do you want to go in, then?" one volunteer asked.

"To gather herbs," Drotte told him. "We are physicians' gallipots. Don't you want the sick healed?"

The volunteer stared at him. The man with the key had dropped his lantern when he ran after Eata, and there were only two left. In their dim light the volunteer looked stupid and innocent; I suppose he was a laborer of some kind.

Drotte continued, "You must know that for certain simples to attain their highest virtues they must be pulled from grave soil by moonlight. It will frost soon and kill everything, but our masters require supplies for the winter. The three of them arranged for us to enter tonight, and I borrowed that lad from his father to help me."

"You don't have anything to put simples in."

I still admire Drotte for what he did next. He said, "We are to bind them in sheaves to dry," and without the least hesitation drew a length of common string from his pocket.

"I see," the volunteer said. It was plain he did not. Roche and I edged nearer the gate.

Drotte actually stepped back from it. "If you won't let us gather the herbs, we'd better go. I don't think we could ever find that boy in there now."

"No you don't. We have to get him out."

"All right," Drotte said reluctantly, and we stepped through, the volunteers following. Certain mystes aver that the real world has been constructed by the human mind, since our ways are governed by the artificial categories into which we place essentially undifferentiated things, things weaker than our words for them. I understood the principle intuitively that night as I heard the last volunteer swing the gate closed behind us.

A man who had not spoken before said, "I'm going to watch over my mother. We've wasted too much time already. They could have her a league off by now."

Several of the others muttered agreement, and the group began to scatter, one lantern moving to the left and the other to the right. We went up the center path (the one we always took in returning to the fallen section of the Citadel wall) with the remaining volunteers.

It is my nature, my joy and my curse, to forget nothing. Every rattling chain and whistling wind, every sight, smell, and taste, remains changeless in my mind, and though I know it is not so with everyone, I cannot imagine what it can mean to be otherwise, as if one had slept when in fact an experience is merely remote. Those few steps we took upon the whited path rise before me now: It was cold and growing colder; we had no light, and fog had begun to roll in from Gyoll in earnest. A few birds had come to roost in the pines and cypresses, and flapped uneasily from tree to tree. I remember the feel of my own hands as I rubbed my arms, and the lantern bobbing among the steles some distance off, and how the fog brought out the smell of the river water in my shirt, and the pungency of the new-turned earth. I had almost died that day, choking in the netted roots; the night was to mark the beginning of my manhood.

There was a shot, a thing I had never seen before, the bolt of violet energy splitting the darkness like a wedge, so that it closed with a thunderclap. Somewhere a monument fell with a crash. Silence then . . . in which everything around me seemed to dissolve. We began to run. Men were shouting, far off. I heard the ring of steel on stone, as if someone had struck one of the grave markers with a badelaire. I dashed along a path that was (or at least then seemed) completely unfamiliar, a ribbon of broken bone just wide enough for two to walk abreast that wound down into a little dale. In the fog I could see nothing but the dark bulk of the memorials to either side. Then, as suddenly as if it had been snatched away, the path was no longer beneath my feet—I suppose I must have failed to notice some turning. I swerved to dodge an oblesque that appeared to shoot up before me, and collided full tilt with a man in a black coat.

He was solid as a tree; the impact took me off my feet and knocked my breath away. I heard him muttering execrations, then a whispering sound as he swung some weapon. Another voice called, "What was that?"

"Somebody ran into me. Gone now, whoever he was."

I lay still.

A woman said, "Open the lamp." Her voice was like a dove's call, but there was urgency in it.

The man I had run against answered, "They would be on us like a pack of dholes, Madame."

"They will be soon in any case—Vodalus fired. You must have heard it."

"Be more likely to keep them off."

In an accent I was too inexperienced to recognize as an exultant's, the man who had spoken first said, "I wish I hadn't brought it. We shouldn't need it against this sort of people." He was much nearer now, and in a moment I could see him through the fog, very tall, slender, and hatless, standing near the heavier man I had run into. Muffled in black, a third figure was apparently the woman. In losing my wind I had also lost the strength of my limbs, but I managed to roll behind the base of a statue, and once secure there I peered out at them again.

My eyes had grown accustomed to the dark. I could distinguish the woman's heart-shaped face and note that she was nearly as tall as the slender man she had called Vodalus. The heavy man had disappeared, but I heard him say, "More rope." His voice indicated that he was no more than a step or two away from the spot where I crouched, but he seemed to have vanished like water cast into a well. Then I saw something dark (it must have been the crown of his hat) move near the slender man's feet, and understood that that was almost precisely what had become of him—there was a hole there, and he was in it.

The woman asked, "How is she?"

"Fresh as a flower, Madame. Hardly a breath of stink on her, and nothing to worry about." More agilely than I would have thought possible, he sprang out. "Now give me one end and you take the other, Liege, and we'll have her out like a carrot."

The woman said something I could not hear, and the slender man told her, "You didn't have to come, Thea. How would it look to the others if I took none of the risks?" He and the heavy man grunted as they pulled, and I saw something white appear at their feet. They bent to lift it. As though an amschaspand had touched them with his radiant wand, the fog swirled and parted to let a beam of green moonlight fall. They had the corpse of a woman. Her hair, which had been dark, was in some disorder now about her livid face; she wore a long gown of some pale fabric.

"You see," the heavy man said, "just as I told you, Liege, Madame, nineteen times of a score there's nothin' to it. We've only to get her over the wall now."

The words were no sooner out of his mouth than I heard someone shout. Three of the volunteers were coming down the path over the rim of the dale. "Hold them off, Liege," the heavy man growled, shouldering the corpse. "I'll take care of this, and get Madame to safety."

"Take it," Vodalus said. The pistol he handed over caught the moonlight like a mirror.

The heavy man gaped at it. "I've never used one, Liege . . ."

"Take it, you may need it." Vodalus stooped, then rose holding what appeared to be a dark stick. There was a rattle of metal on wood, and in place of the stick a bright and narrow blade. He called, *"Guard yourselves!"*

As if a dove had momentarily commanded an arctother, the woman took the shining pistol from the heavy man's hand, and together they backed into the fog.

The three volunteers had hesitated. Now one moved to the right and another to the left, so as to attack from three sides. The man in the center (still on the white path of broken bones) had a pike, and one of the others an ax.

The third was the leader Drotte had spoken with outside the gate.

"Who are you?" he called to Vodalus, "and what power of Erebus's gives you the right to come here and do something like this?"

Vodalus did not reply, but the point of his sword looked from one to another like an eye.

The leader grated, "All together now and we'll have him." But they advanced hesitantly, and before they could close Vodalus sprang forward. I saw his blade flash in the faint light and heard it scrape the head of the pike—a metallic slithering, as though a steel serpent glided across a log of iron. The pikeman yelled and jumped back; Vodalus leaped backward too (I think for fear the other two would get behind him), then seemed to lose his balance and fell.

All this took place in dark and fog. I saw it, but for the most part the men were no more than ambient shadows—as the woman with the heart-shaped face had been. Yet something touched me. Perhaps it was Vodalus's willingness to die to protect her that made the woman seem precious to me; certainly it was that willingness that kindled my admiration for him. Many times since then, when I have stood upon a shaky platform in some market-town square with *Terminus Est* at rest before me and a miserable vagrant kneeling at my feet, when I have heard in hissing whispers the hate of the crowd and sensed what was far less welcome, the admiration of those who find an unclean joy in pains and deaths not their own, I have recalled Vodalus at the graveside, and raised my own blade half pretending that when it fell I would be striking for him.

He stumbled, as I have said. In that instant I believe my whole life teetered in the scales with his.

The flanking volunteers ran toward him, but he had held onto his weapon. I saw the bright blade flash up, though its owner was still on the ground. I remember thinking what a fine thing it would have been to have had such a sword on the day Drotte became captain of apprentices, and then likening Vodalus to myself.

The axman, toward whom he had thrust, drew back; the other drove forward with his long knife. I was on my feet by then, watching the fight over the shoulder of a chalcedony angel, and I saw the knife come down, missing Vodalus by a thumb's width as he writhed away and burying itself to the hilt in the ground. Vodalus slashed at the leader then, but he was too near for the length of his blade. The leader, instead of backing off, released his weapon and clutched him like a wrestler. They were at the very edge of the opened grave—I suppose Vodalus had tripped over the soil excavated from it.

The second volunteer raised his ax, then hesitated. His leader was nearest him; he circled to get a clear stroke until he was less than a pace from where I hid. While he shifted his ground I saw Vodalus wrench the knife free and drive it into the leader's throat. The ax rose to strike; I grasped the helve just below the head almost by reflex, and found myself at once in the struggle, kicking, then striking.

Quite suddenly it was over. The volunteer whose bloodied weapon I held was dead. The leader of the volunteers was writhing at our feet. The pikeman was gone; his pike lay harmlessly across the path. Vodalus retrieved a black wand from the grass nearby and sheathed his sword in it. "Who are you?"

"Severian. I am a torturer. Or rather, I am an apprentice of the torturers, Liege. Of the Order of the Seekers for Truth and Penitence." I drew a deep breath. "I am a Vodalarius. One of the thousands of Vodalarii of whose existence you are unaware." It was a term I had scarcely heard.

"Here." He laid something in my palm: a small coin so smooth it seemed greased. I remained clutching it beside the violated grave and watched him stride away. The fog swallowed him long before he reached the rim, and a few moments later a silver flier as sharp as a dart screamed overhead.

The knife had somehow fallen from the dead man's neck. Perhaps he had pulled it out in his agony. When I bent to pick it up, I discovered that the coin was still in my hand and thrust it into my pocket.

We believe that we invent symbols. The truth is that they invent us; we are their creatures, shaped by their hard, defining edges. When soldiers take their oath they are given a coin, an asimi stamped with the profile of the Autarch. Their acceptance of that coin is their acceptance of the special duties and burdens of military life—they are soldiers from that moment, though they may know nothing of the management of arms. I did not know that then, but it is a profound mistake to believe that we must know of such things to be influenced by them, and in fact to believe so is to believe in the most debased and superstitious kind of magic. The would-be sorcerer alone has faith in the efficacy of pure knowledge; rational people know that things act of themselves or not at all.

Thus I knew nothing, as the coin dropped into my pocket, of the dogmas of the movement Vodalus led, but I soon learned them all, for they were in the air. With him I hated the Autarchy, though I had no notion of what might replace it. With him I despised the exultants who failed to rise against the Autarch and bound the fairest of their daughters to him in ceremonial concubinage. With him I detested the people for their lack of discipline and a common purpose. Of those values that Master Malrubius (who had been master of apprentices when I was a boy) had tried to teach me, and that Master Palaemon still tried to impart, I accepted only one: loyalty to the guild. In that I was quite correct—it was, as I sensed, perfectly feasible for me to serve Vodalus and remain a torturer. It was in this fashion that I began the long journey by which I have backed into the throne.

II

Severian

Memory oppresses me. Having been reared among the torturers, I have never known my father or my mother. No more did my brother apprentices know theirs. From time to time, but most particularly when winter draws on, poor wretches come clamoring to the Corpse Door, hoping to be admitted to our ancient guild. Often they regale Brother Porter with accounts of the torments they will willingly inflict in payment for warmth and food; occasionally they fetch animals as samples of their work.

All are turned away. Traditions from our days of glory, antedating the present degenerate age, and the one before it, and the one before that, an age whose name is hardly remembered now by scholars, forbid recruitment from such as they. Even at the time I write of, when the guild had shrunk to two masters and less than a score of journeymen, those traditions were honored.

From my earliest memory I remember all. That first recollection is of piling pebbles in the Old Yard. It lies south and west of the Witches' Keep, and is separated from the Grand Court. The curtain wall our guild was to help defend was ruinous even then, with a wide gap between the Red Tower and the Bear, where I used to climb the fallen slabs of unsmeltable gray metal to look out over the necropolis that descends that side of Citadel Hill.

When I was older, it became my playground. The winding paths were patrolled during daylight hours, but the sentries were largely concerned for the fresher graves on the lower ground, and knowing us to belong to the torturers, they seldom had much stomach for expelling us from our lurking places in the cypress groves.

Our necropolis is said to be the oldest in Nessus. That is certainly false, but the very existence of the error testifies to a real antiquity, though the autarchs were not buried there even when the Citadel was their stronghold, and the great families—then as now—preferred to inter their long-limbed dead in vaults on their own estates. But the armigers and optimates of the city favored the highest slopes, near the Citadel wall; and the poorer commons lay below them until the farthest reaches of the bottom lands, pressing against the tenements that came to line Gyoll, held potter's fields. As a boy I seldom went so far alone, or half so far.

There were always the three of us—Drotte, Roche, and I. Later Eata, the next oldest among the apprentices. None of us were born among the torturers, for none are. It is said that in ancient times there were both men and women in the guild, and that sons and daughters were born to them and brought up in the mystery, as is now the case among the lamp-makers and the goldsmiths and many other guilds. But Ymar the Almost Just, observing how cruel the women were and how often they exceeded the punishments he had decreed, ordered that there should be women among the torturers no more.

Since that time our numbers have been repaired solely from the children of those who fall into our hands. In our Matachin Tower, a certain bar of iron thrusts from a bulkhead at the height of a man's groin. Male children small enough to stand upright beneath it are nurtured as our own; and when a woman big with child is sent to us we open her and if the babe draws breath engage a wet-nurse if it be a boy. The females are rendered to the witches. So it has been since the days of Ymar, and those days are now by many hundreds of years forgotten.

Thus none of us knows our descent. Each would be an exultant if he could, and it is a fact that many persons of high lineage are given over to us. As boys each of us formed his own conjectures, and each attempted to question the older brothers among the journeymen, though they were locked in their own bitternesses and told us little. Eata, believing himself descended of that family, drew the arms of one of the great northern clans on the ceiling above his cot in the year of which I speak.

For my part, I had already adopted as my own the device graved in bronze above the door of a certain mausoleum. They were a fountain rising above waters, and a ship *volant*, and below these a rose. The door itself had been sprung long ago; two empty coffins lay on the floor. Three more, too heavy for me to shift and still intact, waited on the shelves along one wall. Neither the closed coffins nor the open ones constituted the attraction of the place, though I sometimes rested on what remained of the soft, faded padding of the latter. Rather, it was the smallness of the room, the thick walls of masonry, and the single, narrow window with its one bar, together with the faithless door (so massively heavy) that remained eternally ajar.

Through window and door I could look out unseen on all the bright life of tree and shrub and grass outside. The linnets and rabbits that fled when I approached could neither hear nor scent me there. I watched the storm crow build her nest and rear her young two cubits from my face. I saw the fox trot by with upraised brush; and once that giant fox, taller than all but the tallest hounds, that men call the maned wolf, loped by at dusk on some unguessable errand from the ruined quarters of the south. The caracara coursed vipers for me, and the hawk lifted his wings to the wind from the top of a pine.

A moment suffices to describe these things, for which I watched so long. The decades of a saros would not be long enough for me to write all they meant to the ragged apprentice boy I was. Two thoughts (that were nearly dreams) obsessed me and made them infinitely precious. The first was that at some not-distant time, time itself would stop . . . the colored days that had so long been drawn forth like a chain of conjuror's scarves come to an end, the sullen sun wink out at last. The second was that there existed somewhere a miraculous light—which I sometimes conceived of as a candle, sometimes as a flambeau—that engendered life in whatever objects it fell upon, so that a leaf plucked from a bush grew slender legs and waving feelers, and a rough brown brush opened black eyes and scurried up a tree.

Yet sometimes, particularly in the sleepy hours around noon, there was little to watch. Then I turned again to the blazon over the door and wondered what a ship, a rose, and a fountain had to do with me, and stared at the funeral bronze I had found and cleaned and set up in a corner. The dead man lay at full length, his heavy-lidded eyes closed. In the light that pierced the little window I examined his face and meditated on my own as I saw it in the polished metal. My straight nose, deep-set eyes, and sunken cheeks were much like his, and I longed to know if he too had dark hair.

In the winter I seldom came to the necropolis, but in summer that violated mausoleum and others provided me with places of observation and cool repose. Drotte and Roche and Eata came too, though I never guided them to my favorite retreat, and they, I knew, had secret places of their own. When we were together we seldom crept into tombs at all. Instead we made swords of sticks and held running battles, or threw pinecones at the soldiers, or scratched boards on the soil of new graves and played draughts with stones, and ropes and snails, and high-toss-cockle.

We amused ourselves in the maze that was the Citadel too, and swam in the great cistern under the Bell Keep. It was cold and damp there even in summer, under its vaulted ceiling beside the circular pool of endlessly deep, dark water. But it was hardly worse in winter, and it had the supreme advantage of being forbidden, so we could slip down to it with delicious stealth when we were assumed to be elsewhere, and not kindle our torches until we had closed the barred hatch behind us. Then, when the flames shot up from the burning pitch, how our shadows danced up those clammy walls!

As I have already mentioned, our other swimming place was in Gyoll, which winds through Nessus like a great, weary snake. When warm weather came, we trooped through the necropolis on our way there—first past the old exalted sepulchers nearest the Citadel wall, then between the vainglorious death houses of the optimates, then through the stony forest of common monuments (we trying to appear highly respectable when we had to pass the burly guards leaning on their polearms). And at last across the plain, bare mounds that marked the interments of the poor, mounds that sank to puddles after the first rain.

At the lowest margin of the necropolis stood the iron gate I have already described. Through it the bodies intended for the potter's field were borne. When we passed those rusting portals we felt we were for the first time truly outside the Citadel, and thus in undeniable disobedience of the rules that were supposed to govern our comings and goings. We believed (or pretended to believe) we would be tortured if our older brothers discovered the violation; in actuality, we would have suffered nothing worse than a beating—such is the kindness of the torturers, whom I was subsequently to betray.

We were in greater danger from the inhabitants of the many-storied tenements that lined the filthy street down which we walked. I sometimes think the reason the guild has endured so long is that it serves as a focus for the hatred of the people, drawing it from the Autarch, the exultants, and the army, and even in some degree from the pale cacogens who sometimes visit Urth from the farther stars.

The same presentment that told the guards our identity often seemed to inform the residents of the tenements; slops were thrown at us from upper windows occasionally, and an angry mutter followed us. But the fear that engendered this hatred also protected us. No real violence was done to us, and once or twice, when it was known that some tyrannical wildgrave or venal burgess had been delivered to the mercy of the guild, we received shouted suggestions as to his disposal—most of them obscene and many impossible.

At the place where we swam, Gyoll had lost its natural banks hundreds of years ago. Here it was a two-chain-wide expanse of blue nenuphars penned between walls of stone. Steps intended for boat landings led down into the river at several points; on a warm day each flight would be held by a gang of ten or fifteen brawling youths. The four of us lacked the strength to displace these groups, but they could not (or at least would not) deny us admission, though whichever we chose to join would threaten us as we approached and taunt us when we were in their midst. Soon, however, all would drift away, leaving us in sole possession until the next swimming day.

I have chosen to describe all this now because I never went again after the day on which I saved Vodalus. Drotte and Roche believed it was because I was afraid we would be locked out. Eata guessed, I think—before they come too near to being men, boys often have an almost female insight. It was because of the nenuphars.

The necropolis has never seemed a city of death to me; I know its purple roses (which other people think so hideous) shelter hundreds of small animals and birds. The executions I have seen performed and have performed myself so often are no more than a trade, a butchery of human beings who are for the most part less innocent and less valuable than cattle. When I think of my own death, or of the death of someone who has been kind to me, or even of the death of the sun, the image that comes to my mind is that of the nenuphar, with its glossy, pale leaves and azure flower. Under flower and leaves are black roots as fine and strong as hair, reaching down into the dark waters.

As young men we thought nothing of these plants. We splashed and floated among them, pushed them aside, and ignored them. Their perfume countered to some degree the foul odor of the water. On the day I was to save Vodalus I dove beneath their crowded pads as I had done a thousand times.

I did not come up. Somehow I had entered a region where the roots seemed far thicker than I had ever encountered them before. I was caught in a hundred nets at once. My eyes were open, but I could see nothing—only the black web of the roots. I swam, and could feel that though my arms and legs moved among their millions of fine tendrils, my body did not. I grasped them by the handful and tore them apart, but when I had torn them I was immobilized as ever. My lungs seemed to rise in my throat to choke me, as if they would burst of themselves out into the water. The desire to draw breath, to suck in the dark, cold fluid around me, was overwhelming.

I no longer knew in what direction the surface lay, and I was no longer conscious of the water as water. The strength had left my limbs. I was no longer afraid, though I knew I was dying, or perhaps already dead. There was a loud and very unpleasant ringing in my ears, and I began to see visions.

Master Malrubius, who had died several years before, was waking us by drumming on the bulkhead with a spoon: that was the metallic din I heard. I lay in my cot unable to rise, though Drotte and Roche and the younger boys were all up, yawning and fumbling for their clothes. Master Malrubius's cloak was thrown back; I could see the loose skin of his chest and belly where the muscle and fat had been destroyed by time. There was a triangle of hair there, and it was as gray as mildew. I tried to call to him to tell him I was awake, but I could make no sound. He began to walk along the bulkhead, still striking it with his spoon. After what seemed a very long time he reached the port, stopped and leaned out. I knew he was looking for me in the Old Yard below.

Yet he could not see far enough. I was in one of the cells below the examination room. I lay there on my back, looking up at the gray ceiling. A woman cried but I could not see her, and I was less conscious of her sobs than of the ringing, ringing, ringing of the spoon. Darkness closed over me, but out of the darkness came the face of a woman, as immense as the green face of the moon. It was not she who wept—I could hear the sobs still, and this face was untroubled, and indeed filled with that kind of beauty that hardly admits of expression. Her hands reached toward me, and I at once became a fledgling I had taken from its nest the year before in the hope of taming it to perch on my finger, for her hands were each as long as the coffins in which I sometimes rested in my secret mausoleum. They grasped me, pulled me up, then flung me down, away from her face and from the sound of sobbing, down into the blackness until at last I struck what I took to be the bottom mud and burst through it into a world of light rimmed with black.

Still I could not breathe. I no longer wished to, and my chest no longer moved of itself. I was sliding through the water, though I did not know how. (Later I learned that Drotte had seized me by the hair.) At once I lay on the cold, slimy stones with Roche, then Drotte, then Roche again, breathing into my mouth. I was enveloped in eyes as one is enveloped in the repetitious patterns of a kaleidoscope, and thought that some defect in my own vision was multiplying Eata's eyes.

At last I pulled away from Roche and vomited great quantities of black water. After that I was better. I could sit up, and breathe again in a crippled way, and though I had no strength and my hands shook, I could move my arms. The eyes around me belonged to real people, the denizens of the riverside tenements. A woman brought a bowl of some hot drink—I could not be sure if it was soup or tea, only that it was scalding and somewhat salty, and smelled of smoke. I pretended to drink it, and afterward found that I had slight burns on my lips and tongue.

"Were you trying to do that?" Drotte asked. "How did you come up?"

I shook my head.

Someone in the crowd said, "He shot right out of the water!"

Roche helped me steady my hand. "We thought you'd come up somewhere else. That you were playing a joke on us."

I said, "I saw Malrubius."

An old man, a boatman from his tar-stained clothes, took Roche by the shoulder. "Who's that?"

"Used to be Master of Apprentices. He's dead."

"Not a woman?" The old man was holding Roche but looking at me.

"No, no," Roche told him. "There are no women in our guild."

Despite the hot drink and the warmth of the day, I was cold. One of the youths we sometimes fought brought a dusty blanket, and I wrapped myself in it; but it was so long before I was strong enough to walk again that by the time we reached the gate of the necropolis, the statue of Night atop the khan on the opposite bank was a minute scratch of black against the sun's field of flame, and the gate itself stood closed and locked.

III

The Autarch's Face

It was midmorning of the next day before I thought to look at the coin Vodalus had given me. After serving the journeymen in the refectory we had breakfasted as usual, met Master Palaemon in our classroom, and after a brief preparatory lecture followed him to the lower levels to view the work of the preceding night.

But perhaps before I write further I should explain something more of the nature of our Matachin Tower. It is situated toward the back of the Citadel, upon the western side. At ground level are the studies of our masters, where consultations with the officers of justice and the heads of other guilds are conducted. Our common room is above them, with its back to the kitchen. Above that is the refectory, which serves us as an assembly hall as well as an eating place. Above it are the private cabins of the masters, in better days much more numerous. Above these are the journeymen's cabins, and above them the apprentices' dormitory and classroom, and a series of attics and abandoned cubicles. Near the very top is the gun room, whose remaining pieces we of the guild are charged with serving should the Citadel suffer attack.

The real work of our guild is carried out below all this. Just underground lies the examination room; beneath it, and thus outside the tower proper (for the examination room was the propulsion chamber of the original structure) stretches the labyrinth of the oubliette. There are three usable levels, reached by a central stairwell. The cells are plain, dry, and clean, equipped with a small table, a chair, and narrow bed fixed in the center of the floor.

The lights of the oubliette are of that ancient kind that is said to burn forever, though some have now gone out. In the gloom of those corridors, my feelings that morning were not gloomy but joyous—here I would labor when I became a journeyman, here I would practice the ancient art and raise myself to the rank of master, here I would lay the foundation for the restoration of our guild to its former glory. The very air of the place seemed to wrap me like a blanket that had been warmed before some cleanscented fire.

We halted before the door of a cell, and the journeyman on duty rattled his key in the lock. Inside, the client lifted her head, opening dark eyes very wide. Master Palaemon wore the sable-trimmed cloak and velvet mask of his rank; I suppose that these, or the protruding optical device that permitted him to see, must have frightened her. She did not speak, and of course none of us spoke to her.

"Here," Master Palaemon began in his driest tone, "we have something outside the routine of judicial punishment and well illustrative of modern technique. The client was put to the question last night—perhaps some of you heard her. Twenty minims of tincture were given before the excruciation, and ten after. The dose was only partially effective in preventing shock and loss of consciousness, so the proceedings were terminated after flaying the right leg, as you will see." He gestured to Drotte, who began unwrapping the bandages.

"Half boot?" Roche asked.

"No, full boot. She has been a maidservant, and Master Gurloes says he has found them strong-skinned. In this instance he was proved correct. A simple circular incision was made below the knee, and its edge taken with eight clamps. Careful work by Master Gurloes, Odo, Mennas, and Eigil permitted the removal of everything between the knee and the toes without further help from the knife."

We gathered around Drotte, the younger boys pushing in as they pretended they knew the points to look for. The arteries and major veins were all intact, but there was a slow, generalized welling of blood. I helped Drotte apply fresh dressings.

Just as we were about to leave the woman said, "I don't know. Only, oh, can't you believe I wouldn't tell you if I did? She's gone with Vodalus of the Wood, I don't know where." Outside, feigning ignorance, I asked Master Palaemon who Vodalus of the Wood was.

"How often have I explained that nothing said by a client under questioning is heard by you?"

"Many times, Master."

"But to no effect. Soon it will be masking day, and Drotte and Roche will be journeymen, and you captain of apprentices. Is this the example you'll set the boys?"

"No, Master."

Behind the old man's back, Drotte gave me a look that meant he knew much about Vodalus and would tell me at a convenient time.

"Once the journeymen of our guild were deafened. Would you have those days again? Take your hands from your pockets when I speak to you, Severian."

I had put them there because I knew it would distract his anger, but as I drew them out I realized I had been fumbling the coin Vodalus had given me the night before. In the remembered terror of the fight I had forgotten it; now I was in agony to look at it—and could not, with Master Palaemon's bright lens fixed on me.

"When a client speaks, Severian, you hear nothing. Nothing whatsoever. Think of mice, whose squeaking conveys no meaning to men."

I squinted to indicate that I was thinking of mice.

All the long, weary way up the stair to our classroom, I ached to look at the thin disc of metal I clutched; but I knew that if I were to do so the boy behind me (as it happened, one of the younger apprentices, Eusignius) would see it. In the classroom, where Master Palaemon droned over a ten-day corpse, the coin was like a coal of fire, and I dared not look.

It was afternoon before I found privacy, hiding myself in the ruins of the curtain wall among the shining mosses, then hesitating with my fist poised in a ray of sun because I was afraid that when I saw it at last the disappointment would be more than I could bear.

Not because I cared for its value. Though I was already a man, I had had so little money that any coin would have seemed a fortune to me. Rather it was that the coin (so mysterious now, but not likely to remain so) was my only link with the night before, my only connection with Vodalus and the beautiful, hooded woman and the heavy man who had struck at me with his shovel, my only booty from the fight at the opened grave. My life in the guild was the only life I had known, and it seemed as drab as my ragged shirt in comparison with the flash of the exultant's sword blade and the sound of the shot echoing among the stones. All that might be gone when I opened my hand.

In the end I looked, having drained the dregs of pleasant dread. The coin was a gold chrisos, and I closed my hand once more, fearing that I had only mistaken a brass orichalk, and waited until I found my courage again.

It was the first time I had ever touched a piece of gold. Orichalks I had seen in some plenty, and I had even possessed a few of my own. Silver asimi I had glimpsed once or twice. But chrisos I knew only in the same dim way I knew of the existence of a world outside our city of Nessus, and of continents other than our own to the north and east and west.

This one bore what I at first thought was a woman's face—a woman crowned, neither young nor old, but silent and perfect in the citrine metal. At last I turned my treasure over, and then indeed I caught my breath; stamped on the reverse was just such a flying ship as I had seen in the arms above the door of my secret mausoleum. It seemed beyond explanation—so much so that at the time I did not even trouble to speculate about it, so sure was I that any speculation would be fruitless. Instead, I thrust the coin back into my pocket and went, in a species of trance, to rejoin my fellow apprentices.

To carry the coin about with me was out of the question. As soon as there was an opportunity to do so, I slipped into the necropolis alone and sought out my mausoleum. The weather had turned that day—I pushed through drenching shrubbery and trudged over long, aged grass that had begun to flatten itself for winter. When I reached my retreat it was no longer the cool, inviting cave of summer but an icy trap where I sensed the nearness of enemies too vague for names, opponents of Vodalus who surely knew by now that I was his sworn supporter; as soon as I entered they would rush forward to swing the black door shut on newly oiled hinges. I knew that it was nonsense, of course. Yet I also knew there was truth in it, that it was a proximity in time I felt. In a few months or a few years I might reach the point at which those enemies waited for me; when I had swung the ax I had chosen to fight, a thing a torturer does not normally do.

There was a loose stone in the floor almost at the foot of my funeral bronze. I pried it up and put the chrisos under it, then muttered an incantation I had learned years before from Roche, a few lines of verse that would hold hidden objects safe:

"Where I put you, there you lie,
Never let a stranger spy,
Like glass grow to any eye,
Not of me.

Here be safe, never leave it,
Should a hand come, deceive it,
Let strange eyes not believe it,
Till I see."

For the charm to be really effective one had to walk around the spot at midnight carrying a corpse-candle, but I found myself laughing at the thought—which suggested Drotte's mummery about simples drawn at midnight from graves—and decided to rely on the verse alone, though I was somewhat astonished to discover that I was now old enough not to be ashamed of it.

Days passed, and the memory of my visit to the mausoleum remained vivid enough to dissuade me from making another to verify that my treasure was safe, though at times I longed to do so. Then came the first snow, turning the ruins of the curtain wall into an almost impassably slippery barrier, and the familiar necropolis into a strange wilderness of deceptive hummocks, in which monuments were suddenly too large under their coats of new snow, and the trees and bushes crushed to half size by theirs.

It is the nature of apprenticeship in our guild that, though easy at first, its burdens grow greater and greater as one comes to manhood. The smallest boys do no work at all. At the age of six, when work begins, it is at first no more than running up and down the stairs of the Matachin Tower with messages, and the little apprentice, proud of being entrusted with them, hardly feels the labor. As time progresses, however, his work becomes more and more onerous. His duties take him to other parts of the Citadel—to the soldiers in the barbican, where he learns that the military apprentices have drums and trumpets and ophicleides and boots and sometimes gilded cuirasses; to the Bear Tower, where he sees boys no older than himself learning to handle wonderful fighting animals of all kinds, mastiffs with heads as large as a lion's, diatrymae taller than a man, with beaks sheathed in steel; and to a hundred other such places where he discovers for the first time that his guild is hated and despised even by those (indeed, most of all by those) who make use of its services. Soon there is scrubbing and kitchen work. Brother Cook performs such cooking as might be interesting or pleasurable, and the apprentice is left to pare vegetables, serve the journeymen, and carry an endless succession of stacks of trays down the stairs to the oubliette.

I did not know it at the time, but soon this apprentice life of mine, which had been growing harder for as long as I could remember, would reverse its course and become less drudging and more pleasant. In the year before he is to become a journeyman, a senior apprentice does little but supervise the work of his juniors. His food and even his dress improve. The younger journeymen begin to treat him almost as an equal, and he has, above all, the elevating burden of responsibility and the pleasure of issuing and enforcing orders.

When his elevation comes, he is an adult. He does no work but that for which he has been trained; and he is free to leave the Citadel when his duties are over, for which recreation he is supplied with liberal funds. Should he eventually rise to mastership (an honor that requires the affirmative votes of all the living masters), he will be able to pick and choose such assignments as may interest or amuse him, and direct the affairs of the guild itself.

But you must understand that in the year I have been writing of, the year in which I saved the life of Vodalus, I was unconscious of all that. Winter (I was told) had ended the campaigning season in the north, and thus brought the Autarch and his chief officers and advisors back to the seats of justice. "And so," as Roche explained, "we have all these new clients. And more to come . . . dozens, maybe hundreds. We might have to reopen the fourth level." He waved a freckled hand to show that he at least was ready to do whatever might be necessary.

"Is he here?" I asked. "The Autarch? Here in the Citadel? In the Great Keep?"

"Of course not. If he ever came, you'd know it, wouldn't you? There'd be parades and inspections and all kinds of goings on. There's a suite for him there but the door hasn't been opened in a hundred years. He'll be in the hidden palace—the House Absolute—north of the city someplace."

"Don't you know where?"

Roche grew defensive. "You can't say where it is because there's nothing there except the House Absolute itself. It's where it is. To the north, on the other bank."

"Beyond the Wall?"

He smiled on my ignorance. "Far past it. Weeks, if you walked. Naturally the Autarch could get here by flier in an instant if he wanted to. The Flag Tower—that's where the flier would land."

But our new clients did not come in fliers. The less important arrived in coffles of ten to twenty men and women, chained one behind the other by the neck. They were guarded by dimarchi, hard-bitten troopers in armor that looked as if it had been made for use and used. Each client carried a copper cylinder supposedly containing his or her papers and thus his or her fate. All of them had broken the seals and read those papers, of course; and some had destroyed them or exchanged them for another's. Those who arrived without papers would be held until some further word concerning their disposition was received—probably for the remainder of their lives. Those who had exchanged papers with someone else had exchanged fates; they would be held or released, tortured or executed, in another's stead.

The more important arrived in armored carriages. The steel sides and barred windows of these vehicles were not intended to prevent escape so much as to thwart rescue, and no sooner had the first of them thundered around the east side of the Witches' Tower and entered the Old Yard than the whole guild was filled with rumors of daring raids contemplated or attempted by Vodalus. For all my fellow apprentices and most of the journeymen believed that many of these clients were his henchmen, confederates, and allies. I would not have released them for that reason—it would have brought disgrace on the guild, which for all my attachment to him and his movement I was unready to do, and would have been impossible anyway. But I hoped to provide those I considered my comrades-in-arms with such small comforts as lay within my power: extra food stolen from the trays of less deserving clients and occasionally a bit of meat smuggled from the kitchen.

One blustering day I was given the opportunity to learn who they were. I was scrubbing the floor in Master Gurloes's study when he was called away on some errand, leaving his table stacked with newly arrived dossiers. I hurried over as soon as the door had clanged behind him, and was able to skim most of them before I heard his heavy tread on the stair again. Not one—*not one*—of the prisoners whose papers I had read had been an adherent of Vodalus. There were merchants who had tried to make rich profits on supplies needed by the army, camp followers who had spied for the Ascians, and a sprinkling of sordid civil criminals. Nothing else.

When I carried my bucket out to empty in the stone sink in the Old Yard, I saw one of the armored carriages halted there with its long-maned team steaming and stamping, and the guards in their fur-trimmed helmets sheepishly accepting our smoking goblets of mulled wine. I caught the name Vodalus in the air; but at that moment it seemed I was the only one who heard it, and suddenly I felt Vodalus had been only an eidolon created by my imagination from the fog, and only the man I had slain with his own ax real. The dossiers I had fumbled through a moment before seemed blown like leaves against my face.

It was in this instant of confusion that I realized for the first time that I am in some degree insane. It could be argued that it was the most harrowing of my life. I had lied often to Master Gurloes and Master Palaemon, to Master Malrubius while he still lived, to Drotte because he was captain, to Roche because he was older and stronger than I, and to Eata and the other smaller apprentices because I hoped to make them respect me. Now I could no longer be sure my own mind was not lying to me; all my falsehoods were recoiling on me, and I who remembered everything could not be certain those memories were more than my own dreams. I recalled the moonlit face of Vodalus; but then, I had wanted to see it. I recalled his voice as he spoke to me, but I had desired to hear it, and the woman's voice too.

One freezing night, I crept back to the mausoleum and took out the chrisos again. The worn, serene, androgynous face on its obverse was not the face of Vodalus.

IV

Triskele

I had been poking a stick up a frozen drain as punishment for some petty infraction, and I found him where the keepers of the Bear Tower throw their refuse, the bodies of the torn animals killed in practice. Our guild buries its own dead beside the wall and our clients in the lower reaches of the necropolis, but the keepers of the Bear Tower leave theirs to be taken away by others. He was the smallest of those dead.

There are encounters that change nothing. Urth turns her aged face to the sun and he beams upon her snows; they scintillate and coruscate until each little point of ice hanging from the swelling sides of the towers seems the Claw of the Conciliator, the most precious of gems. Then everyone except the wisest believes that the snow must melt and give way to a protracted summer beyond summer.

Nothing of the sort occurs. The paradise endures for a watch or two, then shadows blue as watered milk lengthen on the snow, which shifts and dances under the spur of an east wind. Night comes, and all is at it was.

My finding Triskele was like that. I felt that it could have and should have changed everything, but it was only the episode of a few months, and when it was over and he was gone, it was only another winter passed and the Feast of Holy Katharine come again, and nothing had changed. I wish I could tell you how pitiful he looked when I touched him, and how cheerful.

He lay on his side, covered with blood. It was as hard as tar in the cold, and still bright red because the cold had preserved it. I went over and put my hand on his head—I don't know why. He seemed as dead as the rest, but he opened one eye then and rolled it at me, and there was a confidence in it that the worst was over now—I have carried my part, it seemed to say, and borne up, and done all I could do; now it is your turn to do your duty by me.

If it had been summer, I think I would have let him die. As it was I had not seen a living animal, not so much as a garbage-eating thylacodon, in some time. I stroked him again and he licked my hand, and I could not turn away after that.

I picked him up (surprised at how heavy he was) and looked about trying to decide what to do with him. He would be discovered in our dormitory before the candle had burned a finger's width, I knew. The Citadel is immense and immensely complicated, with little-visited rooms and passages in its towers, in the buildings that have been erected between the towers, and in the galleries delved under them. Yet I could not think of any such place that I could reach without being seen half a dozen times on the way, and in the end I carried the poor brute into the quarters of our own guild.

I then had to get him past the journeyman who stood guard at the head of the stair leading to the cell tiers. My first idea was to put him in the basket in which we took down the client's clean bedding. It was a laundry day, and it would have been easy enough to make one more trip than was actually required; the chance that the journeyman-guard would notice anything amiss seemed remote, but it would have involved waiting more than a watch for the scrubbed linen to dry and risking the questions of the brother on duty in the third tier, who would see me descending to the deserted fourth.

Instead I laid the dog in the examination room—he was too weak to move—and offered to take the guard's place at the head of the ramp. He was happy enough to seize the opportunity to relieve himself and handed over his wide-bladed carnificial sword (which I in theory was not supposed to touch) and his fuligin cloak (which I was forbidden to wear, though I was already taller than most of the journeymen) so that from a distance it would appear that there had been no substitution. I put on the cloak and as soon as he was gone stood the sword in a corner and got my dog. All our guild cloaks are voluminous, and this one was more so than most since the brother I had replaced was large of frame. Furthermore, the hue fuligin, which is darker than black, admirably erases all folds, bunchings, and gatherings so far as the eye is concerned, showing only a featureless dark. With the hood pulled up, I must have appeared to the journeymen at their tables in the tiers (if they looked toward the stair and saw me at all) as a brother somewhat more portly than most descending to the lower levels. Even the man on duty in the third, where the clients who had lost all reason howled and shook their chains, could have seen nothing unusual in another journeyman going down to the fourth when there were rumors that it was to be refurbished—or in an apprentice running down shortly after the journeyman went up again: no doubt he had forgotten something there and the apprentice had been sent to fetch it.

It was not a prepossessing place. About half of the old lights still burned, but mud had seeped into the corridors until it lay to the thickness of one's hand. A duty table stood where it had been left, perhaps, two hundred years before; the wood had rotted and the whole thing fell at a touch.

Yet the water had never been high here, and the farther end of the corridor I chose was free even of the mud. I laid my dog on a client's bed and cleaned him as well as I could with sponges I had carried down from the examination room.

Under the crusted blood his fur was short, stiff, and tawny. His tail had been cut so short that what remained was wider than it was long. His ears had been cut almost completely away, leaving only stiff points shorter than the first joint of my thumb. In his last fight his chest had been laid open. I could see the wide muscles like drowsy constrictors of pale red. His right foreleg was gone—the upper half crushed to a pulp. I cut it away after I had sutured up his chest as well as I could, and it began to bleed again. I found the artery and tied it, then folded the skin under (as Master Palaemon had taught us) to make a neat stump.

Triskele licked my hand from time to time as I worked, and when I had made the last stitch began slowly licking that, as if he were a bear and could lick a new leg into shape. His jaws were as big as an arctother's and his canines as long as my index finger, but his gums were white; there was no more strength in those jaws now than in a skeleton's hands. His eyes were yellow and held a certain clean madness.

That evening I traded tasks with the boy who was to bring the clients their meals. There were always extra trays because some clients would not eat, and now I carried two of these down to Triskele, wondering if he were still alive.

He was. He had somehow climbed out of the bed where I had laid him and crawled—he could not stand—to the edge of the mud, where a little water had gathered. That was where I found him. There was soup and dark bread and two carafes of water. He drank one bowl of soup, but when I tried to feed him the bread I found he could not chew it enough to swallow; I soaked it in the other bowl of soup for him, then filled the bowl again and again with water until both carafes were empty.

When I lay on my cot almost at the top of our tower, I thought that I could hear his labored breathing. Several times I sat up, listening; each time the sound faded away, only to return when I had lain flat for a time. Perhaps it was only the beating of my heart. If I had found him a year, two years, before, he would have been a divinity to me. I would have told Drotte and the rest, and he would have been a divinity to us all. Now I knew him for the poor animal he was, and yet I could not let him die because it would have been a breaking of faith with something in myself. I had been a man (if I was truly a man) such a short time; I could not endure to think that I had become a man so different from the boy I had been. I could remember each moment of my past, every vagrant thought and sight, every dream. How could I destroy that past? I held up my hands and tried to look at them—I knew the veins stood out on their backs now. It is when those veins stand out that one is a man.

In a dream I walked through the fourth level again, and found a huge friend there with dripping jaws. It spoke to me.

Next morning I served the clients again, and stole food to take down to the dog, though I hoped that he was dead. He was not. He lifted his muzzle and seemed to grin at me with a mouth so wide it appeared his head might fall in two halves, though he did not try to stand. I fed him and as I was about to leave was struck by the misery of his condition. He was dependent on me. Me! He had been valued; trainers had coached him as runners are coached for a race; he had walked in pride, his enormous chest, as wide as a man's, set on two legs like pillars. Now he lived like a ghost. His very name had been washed away in his own blood.

When I had time, I visited the Bear Tower and struck up such friendships as I could with the beast handlers there. They have their own guild, and though it is a lesser guild than ours, it has much strange lore. To a degree that astonished me, I found it to be the same lore, though I did not, of course, penetrate to their arcanum. In the elevation of their masters, the candidate stands under a metal grate trod by a bleeding bull; at some point in life each brother takes a lioness or bear-sow in marriage, after which he shuns human women.

All of which is only to say that there exists between them and the animals they bring to the pits a bond much like that between our clients and ourselves. Now I have traveled much farther from our tower, but I have found always that the pattern of our guild is repeated mindlessly (like the repetitions of Father Inire's mirrors in the House Absolute) in the societies of every trade, so that they are all of them torturers, just as we. His quarry stands to the hunter as our clients to us; those who buy to the tradesman; the enemies of the Commonwealth to the soldier;

the governed to the governors; men to women. All love that which they destroy.

A week after I had carried him down, I found only Triskele's hobbling footprints in the mud. He was gone, but I set out after him, sure that one of the journeymen would have mentioned it to me if he had come up the ramp. Soon the footprints led to a narrow door that opened on a welter of lightless corridors of whose existence I had been utterly unaware. In the dark I could no longer track him, but I pressed on nevertheless, thinking that he might catch my scent in the stale air and come to me. Soon I was lost, and went forward only because I did not know how to go back.

I have no way of knowing how old those tunnels are. I suspect, though I can hardly say why, that they antedate the Citadel above them, ancient though it is. It comes to us from the very end of the age when the urge to flight, the outward urge that sought new suns not ours, remained, though the means to achieve that flight were sinking like dying fires. Remote as that time is, from which hardly one name is recalled, we still remember it. Before it there must have been another time, a time of burrowing, of the creation of dark galleries, that is now utterly forgotten.

However that may be, I was frightened there. I ran—and sometimes ran into walls—until at last I saw a spot of pale daylight and clambered out through a hole hardly big enough for my head and shoulders.

I found myself crawling onto the ice-covered pedestal of one of those old, faceted dials whose multitudinous faces give each a different time. No doubt because the frost of these latter ages entering the tunnel below had heaved its foundation, it had slipped sidewise until it stood at such an angle that it might have been one of its own gnomons, drawing the silent passage of the short winter day across the unmarked snow.

The space about it had been a garden in summer, but not such a one as our necropolis, with half-wild trees and rolling, meadowed lawns. Roses had blossomed here in kraters set upon a tessellated pavement. Statues of beasts stood with their backs to the four walls of the court, eyes turned to watch the canted dial: hulking barylambdas; arctothers, the monarchs of bears; glyptodons; smilodons with fangs like glaives. All were dusted now with snow. I looked for Triskele's tracks, but he had not come here.

The walls of the court held high, narrow windows. I could see no light through them, and no motion. The spear-towers of the Citadel rose on every side, so that I knew I had not left it—instead, I seemed to be somewhere near its heart, where I had never been. Shaking with cold I crossed to the nearest door and pounded on it. I had the feeling that I might wander forever in the tunnels below without ever finding another way to the surface, and I was resolved to smash one of the windows if need be rather than return that way. There was no sound within, though I beat my fist against the door panels again and again.

There is really no describing the sensation of being watched. I have heard it called a prickling at the back of the neck, and even a consciousness of eyes that seem to float in darkness, but it is neither—at least, not for me. It is something akin to a sourceless embarrassment, coupled with the feeling that I must not turn around, because to turn will be to appear a fool, answering the promptings of baseless intuition. Eventually, of course, one does. I turned with the vague impression that someone had followed me through the hole at the base of the dial.

Instead I saw a young woman wrapped in furs standing before a door at the opposite side of the court. I waved to her and began to walk toward her (hurriedly, because I was so cold). She advanced toward me then, and we met on the farther side of the dial. She asked who I was and what I was doing there, and I told her as well as I could. The face circled by her fur hood was exquisitely molded, and the hood itself, and her coat and fur-trimmed boots, were soft-looking and rich, so that I was miserably conscious as I spoke to her of my own patched shirt and trousers and my muddy feet.

Her name was Valeria. "We do not have your dog here," she said. "You may search, if you do not believe me."

"I never thought you did. I only want to go back where I belong, to the Matachin Tower, without having to go down there again."

"You're very brave. I have seen that hole since I was a little girl, but I never dared go in."

"I'd like to go in," I said. "I mean, inside there."

She opened the door through which she had come and led me into a tapestried room where stiff, ancient chairs seemed as fixed in their places as the statues in the frozen court. A diminutive fire smoked in a grate against one wall. We went to it, and she took off her coat while I spread my hands to the warmth.

"Wasn't it cold in the tunnels?"

"Not as cold as outside. Besides, I was running and there was no wind."

"I see. How strange that they should come up in the Atrium of Time." She looked younger than I, but there was an antique quality about her metal-trimmed dress and the shadow of her dark hair that made her seem older than Master Palaemon, a dweller in forgotten yesterdays.

"Is that what you call it? The Atrium of Time? Because of the dials, I suppose."

"No, the dials were put there because we call it that. Do you like the dead languages? They have mottoes. *'Lux dei vitae viam monstrat,'* that's 'The beam of the New Sun lights the way of life.' *'Felicibus brevis, miseris hora longa.'* 'Men wait long for happiness.' *'Aspice ut aspiciar.'* "

I had to tell her with some shame that I knew no tongue beyond the one we spoke, and little of that.

Before I left we talked a sentry's watch or more. Her family occupied these towers. They had waited, at first, to leave Urth with the autarch of their era, then had waited because there was nothing left for them but waiting. They had given many castellans to the Citadel, but the last had died generations ago; they were poor now, and their towers were in ruins. Valeria had never gone above the lower floors.

"Some of the towers were built more strongly than others," I said. "The Witches' Keep is decayed inside too."

"Is there really such a place? My nurse told me of it when I was little—to frighten me—but I thought it was only a tale. There was supposed to be a Tower of Torment too, where all who enter die in agony."

I told her that, at least, was a fable.

"The great days of these towers are more fabulous to me," she said. "No one of my blood carries a sword now against the enemies of the Commonwealth, or stands hostage for us at the Well of Orchids."

"Perhaps one of your sisters will be summoned soon," I said, for I did not want, for some reason, to think of her going herself.

"I am all the sisters we breed," she answered. "And all the sons."

An old servant brought us tea and small, hard cakes. Not real tea, but the maté of the north, which we sometimes give our clients because it is so cheap.

Valeria smiled. "You see, you have found some comfort here. You are worried about your poor dog because he is lame. But he, too, may have found hospitality. You love him, so another may love him. You love him, so you may love another."

I agreed, but secretly thought that I would never have another dog, which has proved true.

I did not see Triskele again for almost a week. Then one day as I was carrying a letter to the barbican, he came bounding up to me. He had learned to run on his single front leg, like an acrobat who does handstands on a gilded ball.

After that I saw him once or twice a month for as long as the snow lasted. I never knew whom he had found, who was feeding him and caring for him; but I like to think it was someone who took him away with him in the spring, perhaps north to the cities of tents and the campaigns among the mountains.

V

The Picture-Cleaner and Others

The Feast of Holy Katharine is the greatest of days for our guild, the festival by which we are recalled to our heritage, the time when journeymen become masters (if they ever do) and apprentices become journeymen. I will leave my description of the ceremonies of that day until I have occasion to tell of my own elevation; but in the year I am recounting, the year of the fight by the graveside, Drotte and Roche were elevated, leaving me captain of apprentices.

The full weight of that office did not impress itself on me until the ritual was nearly over. I was sitting in the ruined chapel enjoying the pageantry and only just conscious (in the same pleasant way I was anticipating the feast) that I would be senior to all the rest when the last of it was done.

By slow degrees, however, a feeling of disquiet seized me. I was miserable before I knew I was no longer happy, and bowed with responsibility when I did not yet fully understand I held it. I remembered how much difficulty Drotte had encountered in keeping us in order. I would have to do it now without his strength, and with no one to be to me what Roche had been to him—a lieutenant of his own age. When the final chant crashed to a close and Master Gurloes and Master Palaemon in their gold-traced masks had slow-stepped through the door, and the old journeymen had hoisted Drotte and Roche, the new journeymen, on their shoulders (already fumbling in the sabretaches at their belts for the fireworks they would set off outside), I had steeled myself and even formed a rudimentary plan.

We apprentices were to serve the feast, and before we did so were to doff the relatively new and clean clothes we had been given for the ceremony. After the last cracker had popped and the matrosses, in their annual gesture of amity, had torn the sky with the largest piece of ordinance in the Great Keep, I hustled my charges—already, or so I thought, beginning to look at me resentfully—back to our dormitory, closed the door, and pushed a cot against it.

Eata was the oldest except for myself, and fortunately for me I had been friendly enough in the past that he suspected nothing until it was too late to make effective resistance. I got him by the throat and banged his head half a dozen times against the bulkhead, then kicked his feet from under him. ''Now,'' I said, ''are you going to be my second? Answer!''

He could not speak, but he nodded.

''Good. I'll get Timon. You take the next biggest.''

In the space of a hundred breaths (and very quick breaths they were) the boys had been kicked into submission. It was three weeks before any of them dared to disobey me, and then there was no mass rebellion, only individual malingering.

As captain of apprentices I had new functions, as well as more freedom than I had ever enjoyed before. It was I who saw that the journeymen on duty got their meals hot, and who supervised the boys who toiled under the stacks of trays intended for our clients. In the kitchen I drove my charges to their tasks, and in the classroom I coached them in their studies; I was employed to a much greater degree than previously in carrying messages to distant parts of the Citadel, and even in a small way in conducting the guild's business. Thus I became acquainted with all the thoroughfares and with many an unfrequented corner—granaries with lofty bins and demonic cats; wind-swept ramparts overlooking gangrenous slums; and the pinakotheken, with their great hallway topped by a vaulted roof of window-pierced brick, floored with flagstones strewn with carpets, and bound by walls from which dark arches opened to strings of chambers lined—as the hallway itself was—with innumerable pictures.

Many of these were so old and smoke-grimed that I could not discern their subjects, and there were others whose meaning I could not guess—a dancer whose wings seemed leeches, a silent-looking woman who gripped a double-bladed dagger and sat beneath a mortuary mask. After I had walked at least a league among these enigmatic paintings one day, I came upon an old man perched on a high ladder. I wanted to ask my way, but he seemed so absorbed in his work that I hesitated to disturb him.

The picture he was cleaning showed an armored figure standing in a desolate landscape. It had no weapon, but held a staff bearing a strange, stiff banner. The visor of this figure's helmet was entirely of gold, without eye slits or ventilation; in its polished surface the deathly desert could be seen in reflection, and nothing more.

This warrior of a dead world affected me deeply, though I could not say why or even just what emotion it was I felt. In some obscure way, I wanted to take down the picture and carry it—not into our necropolis but into one of those mountain forests of which our necropolis was (as I understood even then) an idealized but vitiated image. It should have stood among trees, the edge of its frame resting on young grass.

"—and so," a voice behind me said, "they all escaped. Vodalus had what he had come for, you see."

"You," snapped the other. "What are you doing here?"

I turned and saw two armigers dressed in bright clothes that came as near to exultants' as they dared have them. I said, "I have a communication for the archivist," and held up the envelope.

"Very well," said the armiger who had spoken to me. "Do you know the location of the archives?"

"I was about to ask, sieur."

"Then you are not the proper messenger to take the letter, are you? Give it to me and I'll give it to a page."

"I can't, sieur. It is my task to deliver it."

The other armiger said, "You needn't be so hard on this young man, Racho."

"You don't know what he is, do you?"

"And you do?"

The one called Racho nodded. "From what part of this Citadel are you, messenger?"

"From the Matachin Tower. Master Gurloes sends me to the archivist."

The other armiger's face tightened. "You are a torturer, then."

"Only an apprentice, sieur."

"I don't wonder then that my friend wants you out of his sight. Follow the gallery to the third door, make your turn and continue about a hundred paces, climb the stair to the second landing and take the corridor south to the double doors at the end."

"Thank you," I said, and took a step in the direction he had indicated.

"Wait a bit. If you go now, we'll have to look at you."

Racho said, "I'd as soon have him ahead of us as behind us."

I waited nonetheless, with one hand resting on the leg of the ladder, for the two of them to turn a corner.

Like one of those half-spiritual friends who in dreams address us from the clouds, the old man said, "So you're a torturer, are you? Do you know, I've never been to your place.'' He had a weak glance, reminding me of the turtles we sometimes frightened on the banks of Gyoll, and a nose and chin that nearly met.

''Grant I never see you there,'' I said politely.

''Nothing to fear now. What could you do with a man like me? My heart would stop like that!'' He dropped his sponge into his bucket and attempted to snap his wet fingers, though no sound came. ''Know where it is, though. Behind the Witches' Keep. Isn't that right?''

''Yes,'' I said, a trifle surprised that the witches were better known than we.

''Thought so. Nobody never talks about it, though. You're angry about those armigers and I don't blame you. But you ought to know how it is with them. They're supposed to be like exultants, only they're not. They're afraid to die, afraid to hurt, and afraid to act like it. It's hard on them.''

''They should be done away with,'' I said. ''Vodalus would set them quarrying. They're only a carryover from some past age—what possible help can they give the world?''

The old man cocked his head. ''Why, what help was they to begin? Do you know?''

When I admitted I did not, he scrambled down from the ladder like an aged monkey, seeming all arms and legs and wrinkled neck; his hands were as long as my feet, the crooked fingers laced with blue veins. ''I'm Rudesind the curator. You know old Ultan, I take it? No, course not. If you did, you'd know the way to the library.''

I said, ''I've never been in this part of the Citadel before.''

''Never been here? Why, this is the best part. Art, music, and books. We've a Fechin here that shows three girls dressing another one with flowers that's so real you expect the bees to come out of it. A Quartillosa, too. Not popular anymore, Quartillosa isn't, or we wouldn't have him here. But the day he was born he was a better draughtsman than the drippers and spitters they're wild for today. We get what the House Absolute don't want, you see. That means we get the old ones, and they're the best, mostly. Come in here dirty from having hung so long, and I clean them up. Sometimes I clean them again, after they've hung here a time. We've got a Fechin here. It's the truth! Or you take this one now. Like it?''

It seemed safe to say I did.

''*Third* time for it. When I was new come, I was old Branwallader's apprentice and he taught me how to clean. This was the one he used, because he said it wasn't worth nothing. He begun down here in this corner. When he'd dine about as much as you could cover with one hand, he turned it over to me and I did the rest. Back when my wife still lived I cleaned it again. That would be after our second girl was born. It wasn't all that dark, but I had things on my mind and wanted something to do. Today I took the notion to clean it again. And it needs it—see how nice it's brightening up? There's your blue Urth coming over his shoulder again, fresh as the Autarch's fish."

All this time the name of Vodalus was echoing in my mind. I felt certain the old man had come down from his ladder only because I had mentioned it, and I wanted to ask him about it. But try as I might, I could find no way to bring the conversation around to it. When I had been silent a moment too long and was afraid he was about to mount his ladder and begin cleaning again, I managed to say, "Is that the moon? I have been told it's more fertile."

"Now it is, yes. This was done before they got it irrigated. See that gray-brown? In those times, that's what you'd see if you looked up at her. Not green like she is now. Didn't seem so big either, because it wasn't so close in—that's what old Branwallader used to say. Now there's trees enough on it to hide Nilammon, as the saw goes."

I seized my opportunity. "Or Vodalus."

Rudesind cackled. "Or him, that's right enough. Your bunch must be rubbing their hands waiting to have him. Got something special planned?"

If the guild had particular excruciations reserved for specific individuals, I knew nothing of it; but I endeavored to look wise and said, "We'll think of something."

"I suppose you will. A bit ago, though, I thought you was for him. Still you'll have to wait if he's hiding in the Forests of Lune." Rudesind looked up at the picture with obvious appreciation before turning back to me. "I'm forgetting. You want to visit our Master Ultan. Go back to that arch you just come by—"

"I know the way," I said. "The armiger told me."

The old curator blew those directions to the winds with a puff of sour breath. "What he laid down would only get you to the Reading Room. From there it'd take you a watch to get to Ultan, if ever you did. No, step back to that arch. Go through and all the way to the end of the big room there, and down the stair. You'll come to a locked door pound till somebody lets you in. That's the bottom of the stacks, and that's where Ultan has his study."

Since Rudesind was watching I followed his directions, though I had not liked the part about the locked door, and steps downward suggested I might be nearing those ancient tunnels where I had wandered looking for Triskele.

On the whole I felt far less confident than when I was in those parts of the Citadel that I knew. I have learned since that strangers who visit it are awed by its size; but it is only a mote in the city spread about it, and we who grew up within the gray curtain wall, and have learned the names and relationships of the hundred or so landmarks necessary to those who would find their way in it, are by that very knowledge discomfited when we find ourselves away from the familiar regions.

So it was with me as I walked through the arch the old man had indicated. Like the rest of that vaulted hall it was of dull, reddish brick, but it was upheld by two pillars whose capitals bore the faces of sleepers, and I found the silent lips and pale, closed eyes more terrible than the agonized masks painted on the metal of our own tower.

Each picture in the room beyond contained a book. Sometimes they were many, or prominent; some I had to study for some time before I saw the corner of a binding thrusting from the pocket of a woman's skirt or realized that some strangely wrought spool held words spun like thread.

The steps were narrow and steep and without railings; they twisted as they descended, so that I had not gone down more than thirty before the light of the room above was nearly cut off. At last I was forced to put my hands before me and feel my way for fear I would break my head on the door.

My questing fingers never encountered it. Instead the steps ended (and I nearly fell in stepping off a step that was not there), and I was left to grope across an uneven floor in total darkness.

"Who's there?" a voice called. It was a strangely resonant one, like the sound of a bell tolled inside a cave.

VI

The Master of the Curators

"Who's there?" echoed in the dark. As boldly as I could, I said, "Someone with a message."

"Let me hear it then."

My eyes were growing used to the dark at last, and I could just make out a dim and very lofty shape moving among dark, ragged shapes that were taller still. "It is a letter, sieur," I answered. "Are you Master Ultan the curator?"

"None other." He was standing before me now. What I had at first thought was a whitish garment now appeared to be a beard reaching nearly to his waist. I was as tall already as many men who are called so, but he was a head and a half taller than I, a true exultant.

"Then here you are, sieur," I said, and held out the letter.

He did not take it. "Whose apprentice are you?" Again I seemed to hear bronze, and quite suddenly I felt that he and I were dead, and that the darkness surrounding us was grave soil pressing in about our eyes, grave soil through which the bell called us to worship at whatever shrines may exist below ground. The livid woman I had seen dragged from her grave rose before me so vividly that I seemed to see her face in the almost luminous whiteness of the figure who spoke. "Whose apprentice?" he asked again.

"No one's. That is, I am an apprentice of our guild. Master Gurloes sent me, sieur. Master Palaemon teaches us apprentices, mostly."

"But not grammar." Very slowly the tall man's hand groped toward the letter.

"Oh yes, grammar too." I felt like a child talking to this man, who had already been old when I was born. "Master Palaemon says we must be able to read and write and calculate, because when we are masters in our time, we'll have to send letters and receive the instructions of the courts, and keep records and accounts."

"Like this," the dim figure before me intoned. "Letters such as this."

"Yes, sieur. Just so."

"And what does this say?"

"I don't know. It's sealed, sieur."

"If I open it—" (I heard the brittle wax snap under the pressure of his fingers) "—will you read it to me?"

"It's dark in here, sieur," I said doubtfully.

"Then we'll have to have Cyby. Excuse me." In the gloom I could barely see him turn away and raise his hands to form a trumpet. *"Cy-by! Cy-by!"* The name rang through the dark corridors I sensed all about me as the iron tongue struck the echoing bronze on one side, then the other.

There was an answering call from far off. For some time we waited in silence.

At last I saw light down a narrow alley bordered (as it seemed) by precipitous walls of uneven stone. It came nearer—a five-branched candlestick carried by a stocky, very erect man of forty or so with a flat, pale face. The bearded man beside me said, "There you are at last, Cyby. Have you brought a light?"

"Yes, Master. Who is this?"

"A messenger with a letter." In a more ceremonious tone, Master Ultan said to me, "This is my own apprentice, Cyby. We have a guild too, we curators, of whom the librarians are a division. I am the only master librarian here, and it is our custom to assign our apprentices to our senior members. Cyby has been mine for some years now."

I told Cyby that I was honored to meet him, and asked, somewhat timidly, what the feast day of the curators was—a question that must have been suggested by the thought that a great many of them must have gone by without Cyby's being elevated to journeyman.

"It is now passed," Master Ultan said. He looked toward me as he spoke, and in the candlelight I could see that his eyes were the color of watered milk. "In early spring. It is a beautiful day. The trees put out their new leaves then, in most years."

There were no trees in the Grand Court, but I nodded; then, realizing he could not see me, I said, "Yes, beautiful with soft breezes."

"Precisely. You are a young man after my own heart." He put his hand on my shoulder—I could not help noticing that his fingers were dark with dust. "Cyby, too, is a young man after my heart. He will be chief librarian here when I am gone. We have a procession, you know, we curators. Down Iubar Street. He walks beside me then, the two of us robed in gray. What is the tinct of your own guild?''

''Fuligin,'' I told him. ''The color that is darker than black.''

''There are trees—sycamores and oaks, rock maples and duckfoot trees said to be the oldest on Urth. The trees spread their shade on either side of Iubar Street, and there are more on the esplanades down the center. Shopkeepers come to their doors to see the quaint curators, you know, and of course the booksellers and antique dealers cheer us. I suppose we are one of the spring sights of Nessus, in our little way.''

''It must be very impressive,'' I said.

''It is, it is. The cathedral is very fine too, once we reach it. There are banks of tapers, as though the sun were shining on the night sea. And candles in blue glass to symbolize the Claw. Enfolded in light, we conduct our ceremonies before the high altar. Tell me, does your own guild go to the cathedral?''

I explained that we used the chapel here in the Citadel, and expressed surprise that the librarians and other curators left its walls.

''We are entitled to, you see. The library itself does—doesn't it, Cyby?''

''Indeed it does, Master.'' Cyby had a high, square forehead, from which his graying hair was in retreat. It made his face seem small and a trifle babyish; I could understand how Ultan, who must occasionally have run his fingers over it as Master Palaemon sometimes ran his over mine, could think him still almost a boy.

''You are in close contact, then, with your opposite numbers in the city,'' I said.

The old man stroked his beard. ''The closest, for we are they. This library is the city library, and the library of the House Absolute too, for that matter. And many others.''

''Do you mean that the rabble of the city is permitted to enter the Citadel to use your library?''

''No,'' said Ultan. ''I mean that the library itself extends beyond the walls of the Citadel. Nor, I think, is it the only institution here that does so. It is thus that the contents of our fortress are so much larger than their container.''

He took me by the shoulder as he spoke, and we began to walk down one of the long, narrow paths between the towering bookcases. Cyby followed us holding up his candelabrum—I suppose more for his benefit than mine, but it permitted me to see well enough to keep from colliding with the dark oak shelves we passed. ''Your eyes have not yet failed you,'' Master Ultan said after a time. ''Do you apprehend any termination to this aisle?''

"No, sieur," I said, and in fact I did not. As far as the candlelight flew there was only row upon row of books stretching from the floor to the high ceiling. Some of the shelves were disordered, some straight; once or twice I saw evidence that rats had been nesting among the books, rearranging them to make snug two- and three-level homes for themselves and smearing dung on the covers to form the rude characters of their speech.

But always there were books and more books: rows of spines in calf, morocco, binder's cloth, paper, and a hundred other substances I could not identify, some flashing with gilt, many lettered in black, a few with paper labels so old and yellowed that they were as brown as dead leaves.

" 'Of the trail of ink there is no end,' " Master Ultan told me. "Or so a wise man said. He lived long ago—what would he say if he could see us now? Another said, 'A man will give his life to the turning over of a collection of books,' but I would like to meet the man who could turn over this one, on any topic."

"I was looking at the bindings," I answered, feeling rather foolish.

"How fortunate for you. Yet I am glad. I can no longer see them, but I remember the pleasure I once had in doing it. That would be just after I had become master librarian. I suppose I was about fifty. I had, you know, been an apprentice for many, many years."

"Is that so, sieur?"

"Indeed it is. My master was Gerbold, and for decades it appeared that he would never die. Year followed straggling year for me, and all that time I read—I suppose few have ever read so. I began, as most young people do, by reading the books I enjoyed. But I found that narrowed my pleasure, in time, until I spent most of my hours searching for such books. Then I devised a plan of study for myself, tracing obscure sciences, one after another, from the dawn of knowledge to the present. Eventually I exhausted even that, and beginning at the great ebony case that stands in the center of the room we of the library have maintained for three hundred years against the return of the Autarch Sulpicius (and into which, in consequence, no one ever comes) I read outward for a period of fifteen years, often finishing two books in one day."

Behind us, Cyby murmured, "Marvelous, sieur." I suspected that he had heard the story many times.

"Then the unlooked-for seized me by the coat. Master Gerbold died. Thirty years before I had been ideally suited by reason of predilection, education, experience, youth, family connections, and ambition to succeed him. At the time I actually did so, no one could have been less fit. I had waited so long that waiting was all I understood, and I possessed a mind suffocated beneath the weight of inutile facts. But I forced myself to take charge, and spent more hours than I could expect you to believe now in attempting to recall the plans and maxims I had laid down so many years ago for my eventual succession."

He paused, and I knew he was delving again in a mind larger and darker than even his great library. "But my old habit of reading dogged me still. I lost to books days and even weeks, during which I should have been considering the operations of the establishment that looked to me for leadership. Then, as suddenly as the striking of a clock, a new passion came to me, displacing the old. You will already have guessed what it was."

I told him I had not.

"I was reading—or so I thought—on the seat of that bow window on the forty-ninth floor that overlooks— I have forgotten, Cyby. What is it that it overlooks?"

"The upholsterers' garden, sieur."

"Yes, I recall it now—that little square of green and brown. I believe they dry rosemary there to put in pillows. I was sitting there, as I said, and had been for several watches, when it came to me that I was reading no longer. For some time I was hard put to say what I had been doing. When I tried, I could only think of certain odors and textures and colors that seemed to have no connection with anything discussed in the volume I held. At last I realized that instead of reading it, I had been observing it as a physical object. The red I recalled came from the ribbon sewn to the headband so that I might mark my place. The texture that tickled my fingers still was that of the paper on which the book was printed. The smell in my nostrils was old leather, still bearing the traces of birch oil. It was only then, when I saw the books themselves, that I began to understand their care."

His grip on my shoulder tightened. "We have books here bound in the hides of echidnes, krakens, and beasts so long extinct that those whose studies they are, are for the most part of the opinion that no trace of them survives unfossilized. We have books bound wholly in metals of unknown alloy, and books whose bindings are covered with thickset gems. We have books cased in perfumed woods shipped across the inconceivable gulf between creations—books doubly precious because no one on Urth can read them.

"We have books whose papers are matted of plants from which spring curious alkaloids, so that the reader, in turning their pages, is taken unaware by bizarre fantasies and chimeric dreams. Books whose pages are not paper at all, but delicate wafers of white jade, ivory, and shell; books too whose leaves are the desiccated leaves of unknown plants. Books we have also that are not books at all to the eye: scrolls and tablets and recordings on a hundred different substances. There is a cube of crystal here—though I can no longer tell you where—no larger than the ball of your thumb that contains more books than the library itself does. Though a harlot might dangle it from one ear for an ornament, there are not volumes enough in the world to counterweight the other. All these I came to know, and I made safeguarding them my life's devotion.

"For seven years I busied myself with that; and then, just when the pressing and superficial problems of preservation were disposed of, and we were on the point of beginning the first general survey of the library since its foundation, my eyes began to gutter in their sockets. He who had given all books into my keeping made me blind so that I should know in whose keeping the keepers stand."

"If you can't read the letter I brought, sieur," I said, "I will be glad to read it to you."

"You are right," Master Ultan muttered. "I had forgotten it. Cyby will read it—he reads well. Here, Cyby."

I held the candelabrum for him, and Cyby unfolded the crackling parchment, held it up like a proclamation, and began to read, the three of us standing in a little circle of candlelight while all the books crowded around.

" 'From Master Gurloes of the Order of the Seekers for Truth and Penitence—' "

"What," said Master Ultan. "Are you a torturer, young man?"

I told him I was, and there occurred a silence so long that Cyby began to read the letter a second time: " 'From Master Gurloes of the Order of the Seekers—' "

"Wait," Ultan said. Cyby paused again; I stood as I had, holding the light and feeling the blood mounting to my cheeks. At last Master Ultan spoke again, and his voice was as matter-of-fact as it had been in telling me Cyby read well. "I can hardly recall my own admission to our guild. You are familiar, I suppose, with the method by which we recruit our numbers?"

I admitted I was not.

"In every library, by ancient precept, is a room reserved for children. In it are kept bright picture books such as children delight in, and a few simple tales of wonder and adventure. Many children come to these rooms, and so long as they remain within their confines, no interest is taken in them."

He hesitated, and though I could discern no expression on his face,

I received the impression that he feared what he was about to say might cause Cyby pain.

"From time to time, however, a librarian remarks a solitary child, still of tender years, who wanders from the children's room . . . and at last deserts it entirely. Such a child eventually discovers, on some low but obscure shelf, *The Book of Gold.* You have never seen this book, and you will never see it, being past the age at which it is met."

"It must be very beautiful," I said.

"It is indeed. Unless my memory betrays me, the cover is of black buckram, considerably faded at the spine. Several of the signatures are coming out, and certain of the plates have been taken. But it is a remarkably lovely book. I wish that I might find it again, though all books are shut to me now.

"The child, as I said, in time discovers *The Book of Gold.* Then the librarians come—like vampires, some say, but others say like the fairy godparents at a christening. They speak to the child, and the child joins them. Henceforth he is in the library wherever he may be, and soon his parents know him no more. I suppose it is much the same among the torturers."

"We take such children as fall into our hands," I said, "and are very young."

"We do the same," old Ultan muttered. "So we have little right to condemn you. Read on, Cyby."

" 'From Master Gurloes of the Order of the Seekers for Truth and Penitence, to the Archivist of the Citadel: Greetings, Brother.

" 'By the will of a court we have in our keeping the exulted person of the Chatelaine Thecla; and by its further will we would furnish to the Chatelaine Thecla in her confinement such comforts as lie not beyond reason and prudence. That she may while away the moments until her time with us is come—or rather, as she has instructed me to say, until the heart of the Autarch, whose forebearance knows not walls nor seas, is softened toward her, as she prays—she asks that you, consonant with your office, provide her with certain books, which books are—' "

"You may omit the titles, Cyby," Ultan said. "How many are there?"

"Four, sieur."

"No trouble then. Proceed."

" 'For this, Archivist, we are much obligated to you.' Signed, 'Gurloes, Master of the Honorable Order commonly called the Guild of Torturers.' "

"Are you familiar with any of the titles on Master Gurloes's list, Cyby?"

"With three, sieur."

"Very good. Fetch them, please. What is the fourth?"

"*The Book of the Wonders of Urth and Sky,* sieur."

"Better and better—there is a copy not two chains from here. When you have your volumes, you may meet us at the door through which this young man, whom I fear we have already detained too long, entered the stacks."

I attempted to return the candelabrum to Cyby, but he indicated by a sign that I was to keep it and trotted off down a narrow aisle. Ultan was stalking away in the opposite direction, moving as surely as if he possessed vision. "I recollect it well," he said. "The binding is of brown cordwain, all edges are gilt, and there are etchings by Gwinoc, hand-tinted. It is on the third shelf from the floor, and leans against a folio in green cloth—I believe it is Blaithmaic's *Lives of the Seventeen Megatherians.*"

Largely to let him know I had not left him (though no doubt his sharp ears caught my footfalls behind him), I asked, "What is it, sieur? The Urth and sky book, I mean."

"Why," he said, "don't you know better than to ask that question of a librarian? Our concern, young man, is with the books themselves, not with their contents."

I caught the amusement in his tone. "I think you know the contents of every book here, sieur."

"Hardly. But *Wonders of Urth and Sky* was a standard work, three or four hundred years ago. It relates most of the familiar legends of ancient times. To me the most interesting is that of the Historians, which tells of a time in which every legend could be traced to half-forgotten fact. You see the paradox, I assume. Did that legend itself exist at that time? And if not, how came it into existence?"

"Aren't there any great serpents, sieur, or flying women?"

"Oh, yes," Master Ultan answered, stooping as he spoke. "But not in the legend of the Historians." Triumphantly, he held up a small volume bound in flaking leather. "Have a look at this, young man, and see if I've got the right one."

I had to set the candelabrum on the floor and crouch beside it. The book in my hands was so old and stiff and musty that it seemed impossible that it had been opened within the past century, but the title page confirmed the old man's boast. A subtitle announced: "Being a Collection from Printed Sources of Universal Secrets of Such Age That Their Meaning Has Become Obscured of Time."

"Well," asked Master Ultan, "was I right or no?"

I opened the book at random and read, ". . . by which means a picture might be graven with such skill that the whole of it, should it be destroyed, might be recreated from a small part, and that small part might be any part."

I suppose it was the word *graven* that suggested to me the events I had witnessed on the night I had received my chrisos. "Master," I answered, "you are phenomenal."

"No, but I am seldom mistaken."

"You, of all men, will excuse me when I tell you I tarried a moment to read a few lines of this book. Master, you know of the corpse-eaters, surely. I have heard it said that by devouring the flesh of the dead, together with a certain pharmacon, they are able to relive the lives of their victims."

"It is unwise to know too much about these practices," the archivist murmured, "though when I think of sharing the mind of a historian like Loman, or Hermas . . ." In his years of blindness he must have forgotten how nakedly our faces can betray our deepest feelings. By the light of the candles I saw his twisted in such an agony of desire that out of decency I turned away; his voice remained as calm as some solemn bell. "But from what I once read, you are correct, though I do not now recall that the book you hold treats of it."

"Master," I said, "I give you my word I would never suspect you of such a thing. But tell me this—suppose two collaborate in the robbing of a grave, and one takes the right hand for his share, and the other the left. Does he who ate the right hand have but half the dead man's life, and the other the rest? And if so, what if a third were to come and devour a foot?"

"It's a pity you are a torturer," Ultan said. "You might have been a philosopher. No, as I understand this noxious matter, each has the entire life."

"Then a man's whole life is in his right hand and in his left as well. Is it in each finger too?"

"I believe each participant must consume more than a mouthful for the practice to be effective. But I suppose that in theory at least, what you say is correct. The entire life is in each finger."

We were already walking back in the direction we had come. Since the aisle was too narrow for us to pass one another, I now carried the candelabrum before him, and a stranger, seeing us, would surely have thought I lighted his way. "But Master," I said, "how can that be? By the same argument, the life must reside in each joint of every finger, and surely that is impossible."

"How big is a man's life?" asked Ultan.

"I have no way of knowing, but isn't it larger than that?"

"You see it from the beginning, and anticipate much. I, recollecting it from its termination, know how little there has been. I suppose that is why the depraved creatures who devour the bodies of the dead seek more. Let me ask you this—are you aware that a son often strikingly resembles his father?"

"I have heard it said, yes. And I believe it," I answered. I could not help thinking as I did of the parents I would never know.

"Then it is possible, you will agree, since each son may resemble his father, for a face to endure through many generations. That is, if the son resembles the father, and *his* son resembles him, and that son's son resembles him, then the fourth in line, the great-grandson, resembles his great-grandfather."

"Yes," I said.

"Yet the seed of all of them was contained in a drachm of sticky fluid. If they did not come from there, from where did they come?"

I could make no answer to that, and walked along in puzzlement until we reached the door through which I had entered this lowest level of the great library. Here we met Cyby carrying the other books mentioned in Master Gurloes's letter. I took them from him, bade goodbye to Master Ultan, and very gratefully left the stifling atmosphere of the library stacks. To the upper levels of that place I returned several times; but I never again entered that tomblike cellar, or ever wished to.

One of the three volumes Cyby had brought was as large as the top of a small table, a cubit in width and a scant ell in height; from the arms impressed upon its saffian cover, I supposed it to be the history of some old noble family. The others were much smaller. A green book hardly larger than my hand and no thicker than my index finger appeared to be a collection of devotions, full of enameled pictures of ascetic pantocrators and hypostases with black halos and gemlike robes. I stopped for a time to look at them, sharing a little, forgotten garden full of winter sunshine with a dry fountain.

Before I had so much as opened any of the other volumes, I felt that pressure of time that is perhaps the surest indication we have left childhood behind. I had already been two watches at least on a simple errand, and soon the light would fade. I gathered up the books and hurried along, though I did not know it, to meet my destiny and eventually myself in the Chatelaine Thecla.

VII

The Traitress

It was already time for me to carry their meals to the journeymen on duty in the oubliette. Drotte was in charge of the first level, and I brought his last because I wanted to talk to him before I went up again. The truth was that my head was still swimming with thoughts engendered by my visit to the archivist, and I wanted to tell him about them.

He was nowhere to be seen. I put his tray and the four books on his table and shouted for him. A moment later I heard his answering call from a cell not far off. I ran there and looked through the grilled window set at eye level in the door; the client, a wasted-looking woman of middle age, was stretched on her cot. Drotte leaned over her, and there was blood on the floor.

He was too occupied to turn his head. "Is that you, Severian?"

"Yes. I've got your supper, and books for the Chatelaine Thecla. Can I do anything to help?"

"She'll be all right. Tore her dressings off and tried to bleed herself to death, but I got her in time. Leave my tray on my table, will you? And you might finish shoving their food at the rest for me, if you've got a moment."

I hesitated. Apprentices were not supposed to deal with those committed to the guild's care.

"Go ahead. All you have to do is poke the trays through the slots."

"I brought the books."

"Poke those through the slot too."

For a moment more I watched him as he bent over the livid woman on the cot; then I turned away, found the undistributed trays, and began to do as he had asked. Most of the clients in the cells were still strong enough to rise and take the food as I passed it through. A few were not, and I left their trays outside their doors for Drotte to carry in later. There were several aristocratic-looking women, but none who seemed likely to be the Chatelaine Thecla, a newly come exultant who was—at least for the time being—to be treated with deference.

As I should have guessed, she was in the last cell. It had been furnished with a carpet in addition to the usual bed, chair, and small table; in place of the customary rags she wore a white gown with wide sleeves. The ends of those sleeves and the hem of the skirt were sadly soiled now, but the gown still preserved an air of elegance as foreign to me as it was to the cell itself. When I first saw her, she was embroidering by the light of a candle brightened by a silver reflector; but she must have felt my eyes upon her. It would gratify me now to say there was no fear in her face, yet it would not be true. There was terror there, though controlled nearly to invisibility.

"It's all right," I said. "I've brought your food."

She nodded and thanked me, then rose and came to the door. She was taller even than I had expected, nearly too tall to stand upright in the cell. Her face, though it was triangular rather than heart-shaped, reminded me of the woman who had been with Vodalus in the necropolis. Perhaps it was her great violet eyes, with their lids shaded with blue, and the black hair that, forming a V far down her forehead, suggested the hood of a cloak. Whatever the reason, I loved her at once—loved her, at least, insofar as a stupid boy can love. But being only a stupid boy, I did not know it.

Her white hand, cold, slightly damp, and impossibly narrow, touched mine as she took the tray from me. "That's ordinary food," I told her. "I think you can get some that's better if you ask."

"You're not wearing a mask," she said. "Yours is the first human face I've seen here."

"I'm only an apprentice. I won't be masked until next year."

She smiled, and I felt as I had when I had been in the Atrium of Time and had come inside to a warm room and food. She had narrow, very white teeth in a wide mouth; her eyes, each as deep as the cistern beneath the Bell Keep, shone when she smiled.

"I'm sorry," I said. "I didn't hear you."

The smile came again and she tilted her lovely head to one side. "I told you how happy I was to see your face, and asked if you would bring my meals in the future, and what this was you brought me."

"No. No, I won't be. Only today, because Drotte is occupied." I tried to recall what her meal had been (she had put the tray on her little table, where I could not see its contents through the grill). I could not, though I nearly burst my brain with the effort. At last I said lamely,

"You'd probably better eat it. But I think you can get better food if you ask Drotte."

"Why, I intend to eat it. People have always complimented me on my slender figure, but believe me, I eat like a dire wolf." She picked up the tray and held it out to me, as though she knew I would need every help in unraveling the mystery of its contents.

"Those are leeks, Chatelaine," I said. "Those green things. The brown ones are lentils. And that's bread."

" 'Chatelaine'? You needn't be so formal. You're my jailer, and can call me anything you choose." There was merriment in the deep eyes now.

"I have no wish to insult you," I told her. "Would you rather I called you something else?"

"Call me Thecla—that's my name. Titles are for formal occasions, names for informal ones, and this is that or nothing. I suppose it will be very formal though, when I receive my punishment?"

"It is, usually, for exultants."

"There will be an exarch, I should think, if you will let him in. All in scarlet patches. Several others too—perhaps the Starost Egino. Are you certain this is bread?" She poked it with one long finger, so white I thought for a moment that the bread might soil it.

"Yes," I said. "The Chatelaine has eaten bread before, surely?"

"Not like this." She picked the meager slice up and tore it with her teeth, quickly and cleanly. "It isn't bad, though. You say they'll bring me better food if I ask for it?"

"I think so, Chatelaine."

"Thecla. I asked for books—two days ago when I came. But I haven't got them."

"I have them," I told her. "Right here." I ran back to Drotte's table and got them, and passed the smallest through the slot.

"Oh, wonderful! Are there others?"

"Three more." The brown book went through the slot as well, but the other two, the green book and the folio volume with arms on its cover, were too wide. "Drotte will open your door later and give them to you," I said.

"Can't you? It's terrible to look through this and see them, and not be able to touch them."

"I'm not even supposed to feed you. Drotte should do it."

"But you did. Besides, you brought them. Weren't you supposed to give them to me?"

I could argue only weakly, knowing she was right in principle. The rule against apprentices working in the oubliette was intended to prevent escapes; and I knew that tall though she was, this slender woman could never overpower me, and that should she do so she would have no chance of making her way out without being challenged. I went to the door of the cell where Drotte still labored over the client who had tried to take her own life, and returned with his keys.

Standing before her, with her own cell door closed and locked behind me, I found myself unable to speak. I put the books on her table beside the candlestand and her food pan and carafe of water; there was hardly room for them. When it was done I stood waiting, knowing I should leave and yet unable to go.

"Won't you sit down?"

I sat on her bed, leaving her the chair.

"If this were my suite in the House Absolute, I could offer you better comfort. Unfortunately, you never called while I was there."

I shook my head.

"Here I have no refreshment to offer you but this. Do you like lentils?"

"I won't eat that, Chatelaine. I'll have my own supper soon, and there's hardly enough for you."

"True." She picked up a leek, and then as if she did not know what else to do with it dropped it down her throat like a mountebank swallowing a viper. "What will you have?"

"Leeks and lentils, bread and mutton."

"Ah, the torturers get mutton—that's the difference. What's your name, Master Torturer?"

"Severian. It won't help, Chatelaine. It won't make any difference."

She smiled. "What won't?"

"Making friends with me. I couldn't give you your freedom. And I wouldn't—not if I had no friend but you in all the world."

"I didn't think you could, Severian."

"Then why do you bother to talk to me?"

She sighed, and all the gladness went out of her face, as the sunlight leaves the stone where a beggar seeks to warm himself. "Who else have I to talk to, Severian? It may be that I will talk to you for a time, for a few days or a few weeks, and die. I know what you're thinking—that if I were back in my suite I would never spare a glance for you. But you're wrong. One can't talk to everyone because there are so many everyones, but the day before I was taken I talked for some time with the man who held my mount. I spoke to him because I had to wait, you see, and then he said something that interested me."

"You won't see me again. Drotte will bring your food."

"And not you? Ask him if he will let you do it." She took my hands in hers, and they were like ice.

"I'll try," I said.

"Do. Do try. Tell him I want better meals than this, and you to serve me—wait, I'll ask him myself. To whom does he answer?"

"Master Gurloes."

"I'll tell the other—is it Drotte?—that I want to speak to him. You're right, they'll have to do it. The Autarch might release me—they don't know." Her eyes flashed.

"I'll tell Drotte you want to see him when he's not busy," I said, and stood up.

"Wait. Aren't you going to ask me why I'm here?"

"I know why you're here," I said as I swung back the door. "To be tortured, eventually, like the others." It was a cruel thing to say, and I said it without reflection as young men do, only because it was what was in my mind. Yet it was true, and I was glad in some way, as I turned the key in the lock, that I had said it.

We had had exultants for clients often before. Most, when they arrived, had some understanding of their situation, as the Chatelaine Thecla did now. But when a few days had passed and they were not put to torment, their hope cast down their reason and they began to talk of release—how friends and family would maneuver to gain their freedom, and of what they would do when they were free.

One would withdraw to his estates and trouble the Autarch's court no more. Another would volunteer to lead a muster of lansquenets in the north. Then the journeymen on duty in the oubliette would hear tales of hunting dogs and remote heaths, and country games, unknown elsewhere, played beneath immemorial trees. The women were more realistic for the most part, but even they in time spoke of highly placed lovers (cast aside now for months or years) who would never abandon them, and then of bearing children or adopting waifs. One knew when these never-to-be-born children were given names that clothing would not be far behind: a new wardrobe on their release, the old clothes to be burned; they talked of colors, of inventing new fashions and reviving old ones.

At last the time would come, to men and women alike, when instead of a journeyman with food, Master Gurloes would appear trailing three or four journeymen and perhaps an examiner and a fulgurator. I wanted to preserve the Chatelaine Thecla from such hopes if I could. I hung Drotte's keys on their accustomed nail in the wall, and when I passed the cell in which he was now swabbing blood from the floor told him that the chatelaine desired to speak with him.

* * *

On the next day but one, I was summoned to Master Gurloes. I had expected to stand, as we apprentices usually did, with hands behind back before his table; but he told me to sit, and removing his gold-traced mask, leaned toward me in a way that implied a common cause and friendly footing.

"A week ago, or a little less, I sent you to the archivist," he said.

I nodded.

"When you brought the books, I take it you delivered them to the client yourself. Is that right?"

I explained what had happened.

"Nothing wrong there. I don't want you to think I'm going to order extra fatigues for what you did, much less have you bent over a chair. You're nearly a journeyman yourself already—when I was your age, they had me cranking the alternator. The thing is, you see, Severian, the client is highly placed." His voice sank to a rough whisper. "Quite highly connected."

I said that I understood that.

"Not just an armiger family. High blood." He turned, and after searching the disorderly shelves behind his chair produced a squat book. "Have you any notion how many exulted families there are? This lists only the ones that are still going. A compendium of the extinguished ones would take an encyclopedia, I suppose. I've extinguished a few of them myself."

He laughed and I laughed with him.

"It gives about half a page to each. There are seven hundred and forty-six pages."

I nodded to show I understood.

"Most of them have nobody at court—can't afford it, or are afraid of it. Those are the small ones. The greater families must: the Autarch wants a concubine he can lay hands on if they start misbehaving. Now the Autarch can't play quadrille with five hundred women. There are maybe twenty. The rest talk to each other, and dance, and don't see him closer than a chain off once in a month."

I asked (trying to hold my voice steady) if the Autarch actually bedded these concubines.

Master Gurloes rolled his eyes and pulled at his jaw with one huge hand. "Well now, for decency's sake they have these khaibits, what they call the shadow women, that are common girls that look like the chatelaines. I don't know where they get them, but they're supposed to stand in place of the others. Of course they're not so tall." He chuckled. "I said stand in place, but when they're laying down the tallness probably doesn't make much difference. They do say, though, that oftentimes it works the other way than it's supposed to. Instead of those shadow girls doing duty for their mistresses, the mistresses do it for them. But the present Autarch, whose every deed, I may say, is sweeter than honey in the mouths of this honorable guild and don't you forget it—in his case, I may say, from what I understand it is more than somewhat doubtful if he has the pleasure of any of them."

Relief flooded my heart. "I never knew that. It's very interesting, Master."

Master Gurloes inclined his head to acknowledge that it was indeed, and laced his fingers over his belly. "Someday you may have the ordering of the guild yourself. You'll need to know these things. When I was your age—or a trifle younger, I suppose—I used to fancy I was of exulted blood. Some have been, you know."

It struck me, and not for the first time, that Master Gurloes and Master Palaemon too must have known whence all the apprentices and younger journeymen had come, having approved their admissions originally.

"Whether I am or no, I cannot say. I have the physique of a rider, I think, and I am somewhat over the average in height despite a hard boyhood. For it was harder, much harder, forty years ago, I'll tell you."

"So I have been told, Master."

He sighed, the kind of wheezing noise a leather pillow sometimes makes when one sits on it. "But with the passage of time I have come to understand that the Increate, in choosing for me a career in our guild, was acting for my benefit. Doubtless I had acquired merit in a previous life, as I hope I have in this one."

Master Gurloes fell silent, looking (it seemed to me) at the jumble of papers on his table, the instructions of jurists and the dossiers of clients. At last, when I was about to ask if he had anything further to tell me, he said, "In all my years, I have never known of a member of the guild put to torment. Of them, several hundred, I suppose."

I ventured the commonplace saying that it was better to be a toad hidden under a stone than a butterfly crushed beneath it.

"We of the guild are more than toads, I think. But I should have added that though I have seen five hundred or more exultants in our cells, I have never, until now, had charge of a member of that inner circle of concubines closest to the Autarch."

"The Chatelaine Thecla belonged to it? You implied that a moment ago, Master."

He nodded gloomily. "It wouldn't be so bad if she were to be put to torment at once, but that isn't to be. It may be years. It may be never."

"You believe she may be released, Master?"

"She's a pawn in the Autarch's game with Vodalus—even I know that much. Her sister, the Chatelaine Thea, has fled the House Absolute to become his leman. They will bargain with Thecla for a time at least, and while they do, we must give her good fare. Yet not too good."

"I see," I said. I was acutely uncomfortable not knowing what the Chatelaine Thecla had told Drotte, and what Drotte had told Master Gurloes.

"She's asked for better food, and I've made arrangements to supply it. She's asked for company as well, and when we told her visitors would not be permitted, she urged that one of us, at least, should keep her company sometimes."

Master Gurloes paused to wipe his shining face with the edge of his cloak. I said, "I understand." I was fairly certain that I indeed understood what was to come next.

"Because she had seen your face, she asked for you. I told her you'll sit with her while she eats. I don't ask your agreement—not only because you're subject to my instructions, but because I know you're loyal. What I do ask is that you be careful not to displease her, and not to please her too much."

"I will do my best." I was surprised to hear my own steady voice.

Master Gurloes smiled as if I had eased him. "You've a good head, Severian, though it's a young one yet. Have you been with a woman?"

When we apprentices talked, it was the custom to invent fables on this topic, but I was not among apprentices now, and I shook my head.

"You've never been to the witches? That may be for the best. They supplied my own instruction in the warm commerce, but I'm not sure I'd send them another such as I was. It's likely, though, that the Chatelaine wants her bed warmed. You're not to do it for her. Her pregnancy would be no ordinary one—it might force a delay in her torment and bring disgrace on the guild. You follow me?"

I nodded.

"Boys your age are troubled. I'll have somebody take you where such ills arc speedily cured."

"As you wish, Master."

"What? You don't thank me?"

"Thank you, Master," I said.

Gurloes was one of the most complex men I have known, because he was a complex man trying to be simple. Not a simple, but a complex man's idea of simplicity. Just as a courtier forms himself into something brilliant and involved, midway between a dancing master and a diplomacist, with a touch of assassin if needed, so Master Gurloes had shaped himself to be the dull creature a pursuivant or bailiff expected to see when he summoned the head of our guild, and that is the only thing a real torturer cannot be. The strain showed; though every part of Gurloes was as it should have been, none of the parts fit. He drank heavily and suffered from nightmares, but he had the nightmares when he had been drinking, as if the wine, instead of bolting the doors of his mind, threw them open and left him staggering about in the last hours of the night, trying to catch a glimpse of a sun that had not yet appeared, a sun that would banish the phantoms from his big cabin and permit him to dress and send the journeymen to their business. Sometimes he went to the top of our tower, above the guns, and waited there talking to himself, peering through glass said to be harder than flint for the first beams. He was the only one in our guild—Master Palaemon not excepted—who was unafraid of the energies there and the unseen mouths that spoke sometimes to human beings and sometimes to other mouths in other towers and keeps. He loved music, but he thumped the arm of his chair to it and tapped his foot, and did so most vigorously to the kind he liked best, whose rhythms were too subtle for any regular cadence. He ate too much and too seldom, read when he thought no one knew of it, and visited certain of our clients, including one on the third level, to talk of things none of us eavesdropping in the corridor outside could understand. His eyes were refulgent, brighter than any woman's. He mispronounced quite common words: *urticate, salpinx, bordereau.* I cannot well tell you how bad he looked when I returned to the Citadel recently, how bad he looks now.

VIII

The Conversationalist

Next day, for the first time, I carried Thecla's supper to her. For a watch I remained with her, frequently observed through the slot in the cell door by Drotte. We played word games, at which she was far better than I, and after a while talked of those things those who have returned are said to say lie beyond death, she recounting what she had read in the smallest of the books I had brought her—not only the accepted views of the hierophants, but various eccentric and heretic theories.

"When I am free," she said, "I shall found my own sect. I will tell everyone that its wisdom was revealed to me during my sojourn among the torturers. They'll listen to that."

I asked what her teachings would be.

"That there is no agathodaemon or afterlife. That the mind is extinguished in death as in sleep, yet more so."

"But who will you say revealed that to you?"

She shook her head, then rested her pointed chin upon one hand, a pose that showed off the graceful line of her neck admirably. "I haven't decided yet. An angel of ice, perhaps. Or a ghost. Which do you think best?"

"Isn't there a contradiction in that?"

"Precisely." Her voice was rich with the pleasure the question gave her. "In that contradiction will reside the appeal of this new belief. One can't found a novel theology on Nothing, and nothing is so secure a foundation as a contradiction. Look at the great successes of the past—they say their deities are the masters of all the universes, and yet that they require grandmothers to defend them, as if they were children frightened by poultry. Or that the authority that punishes no one while there exists a chance for reformation will punish everyone when there is no possibility anyone will become the better for it.''

I said, ''These things are too complex for me.''

''No they're not. You're as intelligent as most young men, I think. But I suppose you torturers have no religion. Do they make you swear to give it up?''

''Not at all. We've a celestial patroness and observances, just like any other guild.''

''We don't,'' she said. For a moment she seemed to brood on that. ''Only the guilds do, you know, and the army, which is a kind of guild. We'd be better off, I think, if we did. Still all the days of feast and nights of vigil have become shows, opportunities to wear new dresses. Do you like this?'' She stood and extended her arms to show the soiled gown.

''It's very pretty,'' I ventured. ''The embroidery, and the way the little pearls are sewed on.''

''It's the only thing I have here—what I was wearing when I was taken. It's for dinner, really. After late afternoon and before early evening.''

I said I was sure Master Gurloes would have others brought if she asked.

''I already have, and he says he sent some people to the House Absolute to fetch them for me, but they were unable to find it, which means that the House Absolute is trying to pretend I don't exist. Anyway, it's possible all my clothes have been sent to our chateau in the north, or one of the villas. He's going to have his secretary write them for me.''

''Do you know who he sent?'' I asked. ''The House Absolute must be nearly as big as our Citadel, and I would think it would be impossible for anyone to miss.''

''On the contrary, it's quite easy. Since it can't be seen, you can be there and never know it if you're not lucky. Besides, with the roads closed, all they have to do is alert their spies to give a particular party incorrect direction, and they have spies everywhere.''

I started to ask how it was possible for the House Absolute (which I had always imagined a vast palace of gleaming towers and domed halls) to be invisible; but Thecla was already thinking of something else altogether, stroking a bracelet formed like a kraken, a kraken whose tentacles wrapped the white flesh of her arm; its eyes were cabochon emeralds. ''They let me keep this, and it's quite valuable. Platinum, not silver. I was surprised.''

''There's no one here who can be bribed.''

"It might be sold in Nessus to buy clothing. Have any of my friends tried to see me? Do you know, Severian?"

I shook my head. "They would not be admitted."

"I understand, but someone might try. Do you know that most of the people in the House Absolute don't know this place exists? I see you don't believe me."

"You mean they don't know of the Citadel?"

"They're aware of that, of course. Parts of it are open to everyone, and anyway you can't miss seeing the spires if you get down into the southern end of the living city, no matter which side of Gyoll you're on." She slapped the metal wall of her cell with one hand. "They don't know of *this*—or at least, a great many of them would deny it still exists."

She was a great, great chatelaine, and I was something worse than a slave (I mean in the eyes of the common people, who do not really understand the functions of our guild). Yet when the time had passed and Drotte tapped the ringing door, it was I who rose and left the cell and soon climbed into the clean air of evening, and Thecla who stayed behind to listen to the moans and screams of the others. (Though her cell was some distance from the stairwell, the laughter from the third level was audible still when there was no one there to talk with her.)

In our dormitory that night I asked if anyone knew the names of the journeymen Master Gurloes had sent in search of the House Absolute. No one did, but my question stirred an animated discussion. Although none of the boys had seen the place or so much as spoken with anyone who had, all had heard stories. Most were of fabled wealth—gold plates and silk saddle blankets and that sort of thing. More interesting were the descriptions of the Autarch, who would have had to be a kind of monster to fit them all; he was said to be tall when standing, of common size seated, aged, young, a woman dressed as a man, and so on. More fantastic still were the tales of his vizier, the famous Father Inire, who looked like a monkey and was the oldest man in the world.

We had just begun trading wonders in good earnest when there was a knock at the door. The youngest opened it, and I saw Roche—dressed not in the fuligin breeches and cloak the regulations of the guild decree, but in common, though new and fashionable, trousers, shirt, and coat. He motioned to me, and when I came to the door to speak to him, he indicated that I was to follow him.

After we had gone some way down the stair, he said, "I'm afraid I frightened the little fellow. He doesn't know who I am."

"Not in those clothes," I told him. "He'd recall you if he saw you dressed the way you used to be."

That pleased him and he laughed. "Do you know, it felt so strange, having to bang on that door. Today is what? The eighteenth—it's been under three weeks. How are things going for you?"

"Well enough."

"You seem to have the gang in hand. Eata's your second, isn't he? He won't make a journeyman for four years, so he'll be captain for three after you. It's good for him to have the experience, and I'm sorry now you didn't have more before you had to take the job on. I stood in your way, but I never thought about it at the time."

"Roche, where are we going?"

"Well, first we're going down to my cabin to get you dressed. Are you looking forward to becoming a journeyman yourself, Severian?"

These last words were thrown over his shoulder as he clattered down the steps ahead of me, and he did not wait for an answer.

My costume was much like his, though of different colors. There were overcoats and caps for us too. "You'll be glad for them," he said as I put mine on. "It's cold out and starting to snow." He handed me a scarf and told me to take off my worn shoes and put on a pair of boots.

"They're journeymen's boots," I protested. "I can't wear those."

"Go ahead. Everyone wears black boots. Nobody will notice. Do they fit?"

They were too large, so he made me draw a pair of his stockings on over my own.

"Now, I'm supposed to keep the purse, but since there's always a chance we may be separated, it would be better if you have a few asimi." He dropped coins into my palm. "Ready? Let's go. I'd like to be back in time for some sleep if we can."

We left the tower, and muffled in our strange clothing rounded the Witches' Keep to take the covered walk leading past the Martello to the court called Broken. Roche had been right: it was starting to snow, fluffy flakes as big as the end of my thumb sifting so slowly through the air that it seemed they must have been falling for years. There was no wind, and we could hear the creaking our boots made in breaking through the familiar world's new, thin disguise.

"You're in luck," Roche told me. "I don't know how you worked this, but thank you."

"Worked what?"

"A trip to the Echopraxia and a woman for each of us. I know you know—Master Gurloes told me he'd already notified you."

"I had forgotten, and anyway I wasn't sure he meant it. Are we going to walk? It must be a long way."

"Not as long as you probably think, but I told you we have funds. There will be fiacres at the Bitter Gate. There always are—people are continually coming and going, though you wouldn't think it back in our little corner."

To make conversation, I told him what the Chatelaine Thecla had said: that many people in the House Absolute did not know we existed.

"That's so, I'm sure. When you're brought up in the guild it seems like the center of the world. But when you're a little older—this is what I've found myself, and I know I can rely on you not to tell tales—something pops in your head, and you discover it isn't the linchpin of this universe after all, only a well-paid, unpopular business you happen to have fallen into."

As Roche had predicted there were coaches, three of them, waiting in the Broken Court. One was an exultant's with blazonings painted on the doors and palfreniers in fanciful liveries, but the other two were fiacres, small and plain. The drivers in their low fur caps were bending over a fire they had kindled on the cobbles. Seen at a distance through the falling snow it seemed no bigger than a spark.

Roche waved an arm and shouted, and a driver vaulted into the seat, cracked his whip, and came rattling to meet us. When we were inside, I asked Roche if he knew who we were, and he said, "We're two optimates who had business in the Citadel and are bound now for the Echopraxia and an evening of pleasure. That's all he knows and all he needs to know."

I wondered if Roche were much more experienced at such pleasures than I was myself. It seemed unlikely. In the hope of discovering whether he had visited our destination before, I asked where the Echopraxia lay.

"In the Algedonic Quarter. Have you heard of it?"

I nodded and said that Master Palaemon had once mentioned that it was one of the oldest parts of the city.

"Not really. There are parts farther south that are older still, a waste of stone where only omophagists live. The Citadel used to stand some distance north of Nessus, did you know that?"

I shook my head.

"The city keeps creeping upriver. The armigers and optimates want purer water—not that they drink it, but for their fishponds, and for bathing and boating. Then too, anyone living too near the sea is always somewhat suspect. So the lowest parts, where the water's the worst, are gradually given up. In the end the law goes, and those who stay behind are afraid to kindle a fire for fear of what the smoke may draw down on them."

I was looking out the window. We had already passed through a gate unknown to me, dashing by helmeted guards; but we were still within the Citadel, descending a narrow close between two rows of shuttered windows.

"When you are a journeyman you can go into the city any time you want, provided you're not on duty."

I knew that already, of course; but I asked Roche if he found it pleasant.

"Not pleasant, exactly . . . I've only gone twice, to tell you the truth. Not pleasant, but interesting. They know who you are, naturally."

"You said the driver didn't."

"Well, he probably doesn't. Those drivers go all over Nessus. He may live anywhere, and not get to the Citadel more than once a year. But the locals know. The soldiers tell. They always know, and they always tell, that's what everybody says. They can wear their uniforms when they go out."

"These windows are all dark. I don't think there's anyone in this part of the Citadel at all."

"Everything's getting smaller. Not much anybody can do about that. Less food means fewer people until the New Sun comes."

Despite the cold, I felt stifled in the fiacre. "Is it much farther?" I asked.

Roche chuckled. "You're bound to be nervous."

"No, I'm not."

"Certainly you are. Just don't let it bother you. It's natural. Don't be nervous about being nervous, if you see what I mean."

"I'm quite calm."

"It can be quick, if that's what you want. You don't have to talk to the woman if you don't want to. She doesn't care. Of course, she'll talk if that's what you like. You're paying—in this case I am, but the principle's the same. She'll do what you want, within reason. If you strike her or use a grip, they'll charge more."

"Do people do that?"

"You know, amateurs. I didn't think you'd want to, and I don't think anybody in the guild does it, unless perhaps they're drunk." He paused. "The women are breaking the law, so they can't complain."

With the fiacre sliding alarmingly, we wheeled out of the close and into a still narrower one that ran crookedly east.

IX

The House Azure

Our destination was one of those accretive structures seen in the older parts of the city (but so far as I know, only there) in which the accumulation and interconnection of what were originally separate buildings produce a confusion of jutting wings and architectural styles, with peaks and turrets where the first builders had intended nothing more than rooftops. The snow had fallen more heavily here—or perhaps had only been falling while we rode. It surrounded the high portico with shapeless mounds of white, softened and blurred the outlines of the entrance, made pillows of the window ledges, and masking and robing the wooden caryatids who supported the roof, seemed to promise silence, safety, and secrecy.

There were dim yellow lights in the lower windows. The upper stories were dark. In spite of the drifted snow, someone within must have heard our feet outside. The door, large and old and no longer in the best condition, swung back before Roche could knock. We entered and found ourselves in a narrow little room like a jewel box, in which the walls and ceiling were covered with blue satin quilting. The person who had admitted us wore thick-soled shoes and a yellow robe; his short, white hair was smoothed back from a wide but rounded brow above a beardless and unlined face. As I passed him in the doorway, I discovered that I was looking into his eyes as I might have looked into a window. Those eyes could truly have been of glass, so unveined and polished they seemed—like a sky of summer drought.

"You are in good fortune," he said, and handed us each a goblet. "There is no one here but yourselves."

Roche answered, "I'm sure the girls are lonesome."

"They are. You smile . . . I see you do not believe me, but it is so.

They complain when too many attend their court, but they are sad, too, when no one comes. Each will try to fascinate you tonight. You'll see. They'll want to boast when you are gone that you chose them. Besides, you are both handsome young men.'' He paused, and though he did not stare, seemed to look at Roche more closely. ''You have been here previously, have you not? I remember your red hair and high color. Far to the south, in the narrow lands, the savages paint a fire spirit much like you. And your friend has the face of an exultant . . . that is what my young women like best of all. I see why you brought him here.'' His voice might have been a man's tenor or a woman's contralto.

Another door opened. It had a stained-glass insert showing the Temptation. We went into a room that seemed (no doubt in part because of the constriction of the one we had just left) more spacious than the building could well contain. The high ceiling was festooned with what appeared to be white silk, giving it the air of a pavilion. Two walls were lined with colonnades—these were false, the pretended columns being only half-round pilasters pressed against their blue-painted surfaces, and the architrave no more than a molding; but so long as we remained near the center, the effect was impressive and nearly perfect.

At the farther end of this chamber, opposite the windows, was a high-backed chair like a throne. Our host seated himself in it, and almost at once I heard a chime somewhere in the interior of the house. In two lesser chairs, Roche and I waited in silence while its clear echoes died. There was no sound from outside, yet I could sense the falling snow. My wine promised to hold the cold at bay, and in a few swallows I saw the bottom of the cup. It was as though I were awaiting the beginning of some ceremony in the ruined chapel, but at once less real and more serious.

''The Chatelaine Barbea,'' our host announced.

A tall woman entered. So poised was she, and so beautifully and daringly dressed, that it was several moments before I realized she could be no more than seventeen. Her face was oval and perfect, with limpid eyes, a small, straight nose, and a tiny mouth painted to appear smaller still. Her hair was so near to burnished gold that it might have been a wig of golden wires.

She posed herself a step or two before us and slowly began to revolve, striking a hundred graceful attitudes. At the time I had never seen a professional dancer; even now I do not believe I have seen one so beautiful as she. I cannot convey what I felt then, watching her in that strange room.

''All the beauties of the court are here for you,'' our host said. ''Here in the House Azure, by night flown here from the walls of gold to find their dissipation in your pleasure.''

Half hypnotized as I was, I thought this fantastic assertion had been put forward seriously. I said, ''Surely that's not true.''

''You came for pleasure, did you not? If a dream adds to your enjoyment, why dispute it?'' All this time the girl with the golden hair continued her slow, unaccompanied dance.

Moment flowed into moment.

''Do you like her?'' our host asked. ''Do you choose her?''

I was about to say—to shout rather, feeling everything in me that had ever yearned for a woman yearning then—that I did. Before I could catch my breath, Roche said, ''Let's see some of the others.'' The girl ended her dance at once, made an obeisance, and left the room.

''You may have more than one, you know. Separately or together. We have some very large beds.'' The door opened again. ''The Chatelaine Gracia.''

Though this girl seemed quite different, there was much about her that reminded me of the ''Chatelaine Barbea'' who had come before her. Her hair was as white as the flakes that floated past the windows, making her youthful face seem younger still, and her dark complexion darker. She had (or seemed to have) larger breasts and more generous hips. Yet I felt it was almost possible that it was the same woman after all, that she had changed clothing, changed wigs, dusked her face with cosmetics in the few seconds between the other's exit and her entrance. It was absurd, yet there was an element of truth in it, as in so many absurdities. There was something in the eyes of both women, in the expression of their mouths, their carriage and the fluidity of their gestures, that was one. It recalled something I had seen elsewhere (I could not remember where), and yet it was new, and I felt somehow that the other thing, that which I had known earlier, was to be preferred.

''That will do for me,'' Roche said. ''Now we must find something for my friend here.'' The dark girl, who had not danced as the other had, but had only stood, smiling very slightly, curtsying and turning in the center of the room, now permitted her smile to widen a trifle, went to Roche, seated herself on the arm of his chair, and began whispering to him.

As the door opened a third time, our host said, ''The Chatelaine Thecla.''

It seemed really she, just as I had remembered her—how she had escaped I could not guess. In the end it was reason rather than observation that told me I was mistaken. What differences I could have detected with the two standing side by side I cannot say, though certainly this woman was somewhat shorter.

"It is she you wish, then," our host said. I could not recall speaking.

Roche stepped forward with a leather burse, announcing that he would pay for both of us. I watched the coins as he drew them out, waiting to see the gleam of a chrisos. It was not there—there were only a few asimi.

The "Chatelaine Thecla" touched my hand. The scent she wore was stronger than the faint perfume of the real Thecla; still it was the same scent, making me think of a rose burning. "Come," she said.

I followed her. There was a corridor, dimly lit and not clean, then a narrow stair. I asked how many of the court were here, and she paused, looking down at me obliquely. Something there was in her face that might have been vanity satisfied, love, or that more obscure emotion we feel when what had been a contest becomes a performance. "Tonight, very few. Because of the snow. I came in a sleigh with Gracia."

I nodded. I thought I knew well enough that she had come only from one of the mean lanes about the house in which we were that night, and most likely on foot, with a shawl over her hair and the cold striking through old shoes. Yet what she said I found more meaningful than reality: I could sense the sweating destriers leaping through the falling snow faster than any machine, the whistling wind, the young, beautiful, jaded women bundled inside in sable and lynx, dark against red velvet cushions.

"Aren't you coming?"

She had already reached the top of the stair, nearly out of sight. Someone spoke to her, calling her "my dearest sister," and when I had gone up a few steps more I saw it was a woman very like the one who had been with Vodalus, she of the heart-shaped face and black hood. This woman paid no heed to me, and as soon as I gave her room to do so hurried down the stair.

"You see now what you might have had if you'd only waited for one more to come out." A smile I had learned to know elsewhere lurked at one corner of my paphian's mouth.

"I would have chosen you still."

"Now *that* is truly amusing—come on, come with me, you don't want to stand in this drafty hall forever. You kept a perfectly straight face, but your eyes rolled like a calf's. She's pretty, isn't she."

The woman who looked like Thecla opened a door, and we were in a tiny bedroom with an immense bed. A cold thurible hung from the ceiling by a silver-gilt chain; a lampstand supporting a pink-tinted light stood in one corner. There was a tiny dressing table with a mirror, a narrow wardrobe, and hardly room enough for us to move.

"Would you like to undress me?"

I nodded and reached for her.

"Then I warn you, you must be careful of my clothes." She turned away from me. "This fastens at the back. Begin at the top, at the back of my neck. If you get excited and tear something, he'll make you pay for it—don't say you haven't been told."

My fingers found a tiny catch and loosed it. "I would think, Chatelaine Thecla, that you would have plenty of clothes."

"I do. But do you think I want to return to the House Absolute in a torn gown?"

"You must have others here."

"A few, but I can't keep much in this place. Someone takes things when I'm gone."

The stuff between my fingers, which had looked so bright and rich in the colonnaded blue room below, was thin and cheap. "No satins, I suppose," I said as I unfastened the next catch. "No sables and no diamonds."

"Of course not."

I took a step away from her. (It brought my back almost to the door.) There was nothing of Thecla about her. All that had been a chance resemblance, some gestures, a similarity in dress. I was standing in a small, cold room looking at the neck and bare shoulders of some poor young woman whose parents, perhaps, accepted their share of Roche's meager silver gratefully and pretended not to know where their daughter went at night.

"You are not the Chatelaine Thecla," I said. "What am I doing here with you?"

There was surely more in my voice than I had intended. She turned to face me, the thin cloth of her gown sliding away from her breasts. I saw fear flicker across her face as though directed by a mirror; she must have been in this situation before, and it must have turned out badly for her. "I am Thecla," she said. "If you want me to be."

I raised my hand and she added quickly, "There are people here to protect me. All I have to do is scream. You may hit me once, but you won't hit me twice."

"No," I told her.

"Yes there are. Three men."

"There is no one. This whole floor is empty and cold—don't you think I've noticed how quiet it is? Roche and his girl stayed below, and perhaps got a better room there because he paid. The woman we saw at the top of the stair was leaving and wanted to speak to you first. Look.'' I took her by the waist and lifted her into the air. ''Scream. No one will come.'' She was silent. I dropped her on the bed, and after a moment sat down beside her.

''You are angry because I'm not Thecla. But I would have been Thecla for you. I will be still.'' She slipped the strange coat from my shoulders and let it fall. ''You're very strong.''

''No I'm not.'' I knew that some of the boys who were afraid of me were already stronger than I.

''Very strong. Aren't you strong enough to master reality, even for a little while?''

''What do you mean?''

''Weak people believe what is forced on them. Strong people what they wish to believe, forcing that to be real. What is the Autarch but a man who believes himself Autarch and makes others believe by the strength of it?''

''You are not the Chatelaine Thecla,'' I told her.

''But don't you see, neither is she. The Chatelaine Thecla, whom I doubt you've ever laid eyes on—No, I see I'm wrong. Have you been to the House Absolute?''

Her hands, small and warm, were on my own right hand, pressing. I shook my head.

''Sometimes clients say they have. I always find pleasure in hearing them.''

''Have they been? Really?''

She shrugged. ''I was saying that the Chatelaine Thecla is not the Chatelaine Thecla. Not the Chatelaine Thecla of your mind, which is the only Chatelaine Thecla you care about. Neither am I. What, then, is the difference between us?''

''None, I suppose.''

While I was undressing I said, ''Nevertheless, we all seek to discover what is real. Why is it? Perhaps we are drawn to the theo-center. That's what the hierophants say, that only that is true.''

She kissed my thighs, knowing she had won. ''Are you really ready to find it? You must be clothed in favor, remember. Otherwise you will be given over to the torturers. You wouldn't like that.''

''No,'' I said, and took her head between my hands.

X

The Last Year

I think it was Master Gurloes's intention that I should be brought to that house often, so I would not become too much attracted to Thecla. In actuality I permitted Roche to pocket the money and never went there again. The pain had been too pleasurable, the pleasure too painful; so that I feared that in time my mind would no longer be the thing I knew.

Then too, before Roche and I had left the house, the white-haired man (catching my eye) had drawn from the bosom of his robe what I had at first thought was an icon but soon saw to be a golden vial in the shape of a phallus. He had smiled, and because there had been nothing but friendship in his smile it had frightened me.

Some days passed before I could rid my thoughts of Thecla of certain impressions belonging to the false Thecla who had initiated me into the anacreontic diversions and fruitions of men and women. Possibly this had an effect opposite to that Master Gurloes intended, but I do not think so. I believe I was never less inclined to love the unfortunate woman than when I carried in my memory the recent impressions of having enjoyed her freely; it was as I saw it more and more clearly for the untruth it was that I felt myself drawn to redress the fact, and drawn through her (though I was hardly conscious of it at the time) to the world of ancient knowledge and privilege she represented.

The books I had carried to her became my university, she my oracle. I am not an educated man—from Master Palaemon I learned little more than to read, write, and cipher, with a few facts concerning the physical world and the requisites of our mystery. If educated men have sometimes thought me, if not their equal, at least one whose company did not shame them, that is owing solely to Thecla: the Thecla I remember, the Thecla who lives in me, and the four books.

What we read together and what we said of it to one another, I shall not tell; to recount the least of it would wear out this brief night. All that winter while snow whitened the Old Yard, I came up from the oubliette as if from sleep, and started to see the tracks my feet left behind me and my shadow on the snow. Thecla was sad that winter, yet she delighted in talking to me of the secrets of the past, of the conjectures formed of higher spheres, and of the arms and histories of heroes millennia dead.

Spring came, and with it the purple-striped and white-dotted lilies of the necropolis. I carried them to her, and she said my beard had shot up like them, and I should be bluer of cheek than the run of common men, and the next day begged my pardon for it, saying I was that already. With the warm weather and (I think) the blossoms I brought, her spirits lifted. When we traced the insignia of old houses, she talked of friends of her own station and the marriages they had made, good and bad, and how such and such a one had exchanged her future for a ruined stronghold because she had seen it in a dream; and how another, who had played at dolls with her when they were children, was the mistress now of so many thousands of leagues. "And there must be a new Autarch and perhaps an Autarchia sometime, you know, Severian. Things can go on as they have for a long while. But not forever."

"I know little of the court, Chatelaine."

"The less you know, the happier you will be." She paused, white teeth nibbling her delicately curved lower lip. "When my mother was in labor, she had the servants carry her to the Vatic Fountain, whose virtue is to reveal what is to come. It prophesied I should sit a throne. Thea has always envied me that. Still, the Autarch . . ."

"Yes?"

"It would be better if I didn't say too much. The Autarch is not like other people. No matter how I may talk sometimes, on all of Urth there is no one like him."

"I know that."

"Then that is enough for you. Look here," she held up the brown book. "Here it says, 'It was the thought of Thalelaeus the Great that the democracy'—that means the People—'desired to be ruled by some power superior to itself, and of Yrierix the Sage that the commonality would never permit one differing from themselves to hold high office. Notwithstanding this, each is called The Perfect Master.' "

I did not see what she meant, and said nothing.

"No one really knows what the Autarch will do. That's what it all comes down to. Or Father Inire either. When I first came to court I was told, as a great secret, that it was Father Inire who really determined the policy of the Commonwealth. When I had been there two years, a man very highly placed—I can't even tell you his name—said it was the Autarch who ruled, though to those in the House Absolute it might seem that it was Father Inire. And last year a woman whose judgment I trust more than any man's confided that it really made no difference, because they were both as unfathomable as the pelagic deeps, and if one decided things while the moon waxed and the other when the wind was in the east, no one could tell the difference anyway. I thought that was wise counsel until I realized she was only repeating something I had said to her myself half a year before.'' Thecla fell silent, reclining on the narrow bed, her dark hair spread on the pillow.

''At least,'' I said, ''you were right to have confidence in that woman. She had taken her opinions from a trustworthy source.''

As if she had not heard me, she murmured, ''But it's all true, Severian. No one knows what they may do. I might be freed tomorrow. It's quite possible. They must know by now that I am here. Don't look at me like that. My friends will speak with Father Inire. Perhaps some may even mention me to the Autarch. You know why I was taken, don't you?''

''Something about your sister.''

''My half-sister Thea is with Vodalus. They say she is his paramour, and I think it extremely likely.''

I recalled the beautiful woman at the top of the stairs in the House Azure and said, ''I think I saw your half-sister once. It was in the necropolis. There was an exultant with her who carried a cane-sword and was very handsome. He told me he was Vodalus. The woman had a heart-shaped face and a voice that made me think of doves. Was that she?''

''I suppose so. They want her to betray him to save me, and I know she won't. But when they discover that, why shouldn't they let me go?''

I spoke of something else until she laughed and said, ''You are so intellectual, Severian. When you're made a journeyman, you'll be the most cerebral torturer in history—a frightful thought.''

''I was under the impression you enjoyed such discussions, Chatelaine.''

''Only now, because I can't get out. Though it may come as a shock to you, when I was free I seldom devoted time to metaphysics. I went dancing instead, and pursued the peccary with pardine limers. The learning you admire was acquired when I was a girl, and sat with my tutor under the threat of the stick.''

"We need not talk of such things, Chatelaine, if you would rather we not."

She stood and thrust her face into the center of the bouquet I had picked for her. "Flowers are better theology than folios, Severian. Is it beautiful in the necropolis where you got these? You aren't bringing me the flowers from graves, are you? Cut flowers someone brought?"

"No. These were planted long ago. They come up every year."

At the slot in the door, Drotte said, "Time to go," and I stood up.

"Do you think you may see her again? The Chatelaine Thea, my sister?"

"I don't think so, Chatelaine."

"If you should, Severian, will you tell her about me? They may not have been able to communicate with her. There will be no treason in that—you'll be doing the Autarch's work."

"I will, Chatelaine." I was stepping through the doorway.

"She won't betray Vodalus, I know, but there may be some compromise."

Drotte closed the door and turned the key. It had not escaped me that Thecla had not asked how her sister and Vodalus had come to be in our ancient—and by such people as themselves, forgotten—necropolis. The corridor, with its lines of metal doors and cold-sweating walls, seemed dark after the lamp in the cell. Drotte began to talk of an expedition he and Roche had made to a lion pit across Gyoll; over the sound of his voice I heard Thecla calling faintly, "Remind her of the time we sewed Josepha's doll."

The lilies faded as lilies do, and the dark death roses came into bloom. I cut them and carried them to Thecla, nigrescent purple flecked with scarlet. She smiled and recited:

"Here Rose the Graced, not Rose the Chaste, reposes.
The scent that rises is no scent of roses."

"If their odor offends you, Chatelaine . . ."

"Not at all, it is very sweet. I was only quoting something my grandmother used to say. The woman was infamous when she was a girl, or so she told me, and all the children chanted that rhyme when she died. Actually I suspect it is much older, and lost in time, like the beginnings of all the good and bad things. Men are said to desire women, Severian. Why do they despise the women they obtain?"

"I don't believe all do, Chatelaine."

"That beautiful Rose gave herself, and suffered such mockery for it that I know of it, though her dreams long ago turned to dust with her smooth flesh. Come here and sit by me."

I did as I was told, and she slipped her hands under the frayed bottom of my shirt and drew it over my head. I protested, but found myself unable to resist.

"What are you ashamed of? You who have no breasts to hide. I've never seen such white skin coupled with dark hair . . . Do you think my own skin white?"

"Very white, Chatelaine."

"So do others, but it is dun next to yours. You must flee the sun when you're a torturer, Severian. You'll burn terribly."

Her hair, which she often let fall free, today was bound about her head in a dark aureole. She had never more closely resembled her half-sister Thea, and I felt such desire for her that I seemed to be spilling my blood upon the floor, growing weaker and fainter with each contraction of my heart.

"Why are you pounding on my door?" Her smile told me she knew.

"I must go."

"You'd better put your shirt back on before you leave—you wouldn't want your friend to see you like that."

That night, though I knew it was in vain, I went to the necropolis and spent several watches in wandering among the silent houses of the dead. The next night I returned, and the next, but on the fourth Roche took me into the city, and in a drinking den I heard someone who seemed to know say that Vodalus was far to the north, hiding among the frost-pinched forests and raiding kafilas.

Days passed. Thecla was certain now, since she had been held in safety so long, that she would never be put to torment, and had Drotte bring her materials for writing and drawing, with which she planned a villa she meant to build on the southern shore of Lake Diuturna, which is said to be the most remote part of the Commonwealth, as well as the most beautiful. I took parties of apprentices to swim, thinking that to be my duty, though I could never dive in deep water without fear.

Then, suddenly as it seemed, the weather was too cold for swimming; one morning there was sparkling frost on the worn flagstones of the Old Yard, and fresh pork appeared on our plates at dinner, a sure sign that the cold had reached the hills below the city. Master Gurloes and Master Palaemon summoned me.

Master Gurloes said, "From several quarters we have had good reports of you, Severian, and now your apprenticeship is nearly served."

Nearly whispering, Master Palaemon added, "Your boyhood is behind you, your manhood ahead of you.'' There was affection in his voice.

''Just so,'' Master Gurloes continued. ''The feast of our patroness draws near. I suppose you have given thought to it?''

I nodded. ''Eata will be captain after me.''

''And you?''

I did not understand what was meant; Master Palaemon, seeing that, asked gently, ''What will you be, Severian? A torturer? You may leave the guild, you know, if you prefer.''

I told him firmly—and as though I were slightly shocked by the suggestion—that I had never considered it. It was a lie. I had known, as all the apprentices knew, that one was not firmly and finally a member of the guild until one consented as an adult to the connection. Furthermore, though I loved the guild I hated it too—not because of the pain it inflicted on clients who must sometimes have been innocent, and who must often have been punished beyond anything that could be justified by their offenses; but because it seemed to me inefficient and ineffectual, serving a power that was not only ineffectual but remote. I do not know how better to express my feelings about it than by saying that I hated it for starving and humiliating me and loved it because it was my home, hated and loved it because it was the exemplar of old things, because it was weak, and because it seemed indestructible.

Naturally I expressed none of this to Master Palaemon, though I might have if Master Gurloes had not been present. Still, it seemed incredible that my profession of loyalty, made in rags, could be taken seriously; yet it was.

''Whether you have considered leaving us or not,'' Master Palaemon told me, ''it is an option open to you. Many would say that only a fool would serve out the hard years of apprenticeship and refuse to become a journeyman of his guild when his apprenticeship was past. But you may do so if you wish.''

''Where would I go?'' That, though I could not tell them so, was the real reason I was staying. I knew that a vast world lay outside the walls of the Citadel—indeed, outside the walls of our tower. But I could not imagine that I could ever have any place in it. Faced with a choice between slavery and the emptiness of freedom, I added, ''I have been reared in our guild,'' for fear they would answer my question.

''Yes,'' Master Gurloes said in his most formal manner. ''But you are no torturer yet. You have not put on fuligin.''

Master Palaemon's hand, dry and wrinkled as a mummy's, groped until it found mine. ''Among the initiates of religion it is said, 'You are an epopt always.' The reference is not only to knowledge but to their chrism, whose mark, being invisible, is ineradicable. You know our chrism.''

I nodded again.

''Less even than theirs can it be washed away. Should you leave now, men will only say, 'He was nurtured by the torturers.' But when you have been anointed they will say, 'He is a torturer.' You may follow the plow or the drum, but still you will hear, 'He is a torturer.' Do you understand that?''

''I wish to hear nothing else.''

''That is well,'' Master Gurloes said, and suddenly they both smiled, Master Palaemon showing his few old crooked teeth, and Master Gurloes his square yellow ones, like the teeth of a dead nag. ''Then it is time that we explained to you the final secret.'' (I can hear the emphasis his voice gave the words even as I write.) ''For it would be well for you to think upon it before the ceremony.''

Then he and Master Palaemon expounded to me that secret which lies at the heart of the guild and is the more sacred because no liturgy celebrates it, and it lies naked in the lap of the Pancreator.

And they swore me never to reveal it save—as they did—to one about to enter upon the mysteries of the guild. I have since broken that oath, as I have many others.

XI

The Feast

The day of our patroness falls in the fading of winter. Then do we make merry: the journeymen perform the sword dance in procession, leaping and fantastic; the masters light the ruined chapel in the Grand Court with a thousand perfumed candles, and we ready our feast.

In the guild, the annual observance is counted as *lofty* (in which a journeyman is elevated to mastership), *lesser* (in which one apprentice at least is created journeyman), or *least* (in which no elevation takes place). Since no journeyman rose to mastership in the year in which I was made a journeyman—which is not to be wondered at, since such occasions are rarer than the decades—the ceremony of my masking was a lesser feast.

Even so, weeks were spent in preparation. I have heard it said that no less than one hundred and thirty-five guilds have members laboring within the Citadel walls. Of these, some (as we have seen among the curators) are too few to keep their patron's feast in the chapel, but must join their brothers in the city. Those more numerous celebrate with such pomp as they may to raise the esteem in which they are held. Of this kind are the soldiers upon Hadrian's day, the matrosses on Barbara's, the witches on Mag's, and many others. By pageantry and wonders, and freely given food and drink, they seek to have as many as may be from outside their guilds attend their ceremonies.

Not so is it among the torturers. No one from without the guild has dined with us at Holy Katharine's feast for more than three hundred years, when a lieutenant of the guard (so it is said) dared to come for a wager. There are many idle tales of what befell him—as that we made him seat himself at our table upon a chair of glowing iron. None of them are true. By the lore of our guild, he was made welcome and well feasted; but because we did not, over our meat and Katharine cake, talk of the pain we had inflicted, or devise new modes of torment, or curse those whose flesh we had torn for dying too soon, he grew ever more anxious, imagining that we sought to lull his fears so we might entrap him subsequently. Thus thinking, he ate little and drank much, and returning to his own quarters fell and struck his head in such a way that he evermore upon occasion lost his wits and suffered great pain. In time he put the muzzle of his own weapon into his mouth, but it was none of our doing.

None but torturers, then, come to the chapel on Holy Katharine's day. Yet each year (knowing we are watched from high windows) we prepare as do all the rest, and more grandly. Outside the chapel our wines burn like gems in the light of a hundred flambeaux; our beeves steam and wallow in ponds of gravy, rolling baked-lemon eyes; capybaras and agoutis, posed in the stances of life and bearing fur in which toasted cocoanut mingles with their own flayed skin, clamber on logs of ham and scale boulders of new-baked bread.

Our masters, of whom, when I was made journeyman, there were only two, arrive in sedan chairs whose curtains are woven of blossoms, and tread carpets patterned of colored sands, carpets telling of the traditions of the guild and laid grain by grain by the journeymen in days of toil and destroyed at once by the feet of the masters.

Within the chapel wait a great spiked wheel, a maid, and a sword. That wheel I knew well, for as an apprentice I had several times assisted in setting it up and taking it down. It was stored in the topmost part of the tower, just under the gun room, when it was not in use. The sword—though it seemed a true headsman's blade from a pace or two away—was no more than a wooden batten provided with an old hilt and brightened with tinsel.

Of the maid I can tell you nothing. When I was very young, I did not even wonder about her; those are the earliest feasts I can remember. When I was a little older and Gildas (who was long since a journeyman at the time of which I write) was captain of apprentices, I thought her perhaps one of the witches. When I grew a year older, I knew such disrespect would not be tolerated.

Perhaps she was a servant from some remote part of the Citadel. Perhaps she was a resident of the city, who for gain or because of some old connection with our guild consented to play the part; I do not know. I only know that each feast found her in her place, and so far as I could judge, unchanged. She was tall and slender, though not so tall nor so slender as Thecla, dark of complexion, dark of eye, raven of hair. Hers was such a face as I have never seen elsewhere, like a pool of pure water found in the midst of a wood.

She stood between the wheel and the sword while Master Palaemon (as the older of our masters) told us of the founding of the guild, and of our precursors in the years before the ice came—this part was different each year, as his scholarship decided. Silent she stood too while we sang the Fearful Song, the hymn of the guild, which apprentices must get by heart but which is sung only on that one day of the year. Silent she stood too while we knelt among the broken pews and prayed.

Then Master Gurloes and Master Palaemon, aided by several of the older journeymen, began her legend. Sometimes one spoke alone. Sometimes all chanted together. Sometimes two spoke to different effect while the others played flutes they had carved of thighbones, or the three-stringed rebec that shrieks like a man.

When they reached that part of the narration at which our patroness is condemned by Maxentius, four masked journeymen rushed out to seize her. So silent and serene before, she resisted now, struggled and cried out. But as they bore her toward it, the wheel appeared to blur and change. In the light of the candles, it seemed at first that serpents, green pythons with jeweled heads of scarlet and citrine and white, writhed from it. Then it was seen that these were flowers, roses in the bud. When the maid was but a step away they bloomed (they were of paper, concealed, as I well knew, within the segments of the wheel). Feigning fear, the journeymen drew back; but the narrators, Gurloes, Palaemon, and the others, speaking together as Maxentius, urged them on.

Then I, still unmasked and in the dress of an apprentice, stepped forward and said: "Resistance avails nothing. You are to be broken on the wheel, but we would do you no further indignity."

The maid gave no answer but reached out and touched the wheel, which at once fell to pieces, collapsing with a clatter to the floor, all its roses gone.

"*Behead her,*" demanded Maxentius, and I took up the sword. It was very heavy.

She knelt before me. "You are a counselor of Omniscience," I said. "Though I must slay you, I beg you spare my life."

For the first time the maid spoke, saying, "Strike and fear not."

I lifted the sword. I remember that for a moment I feared it would overbalance me.

When I think back on that time, it is that moment I recall first; to remember more, I must work forward or backward from that. In memory it seems to me I stand always so, in gray shirt and ragged trousers, with the blade poised above my head. While I raised it, I was an apprentice; when it descended, I would be a journeyman of the Order of the Seekers for Truth and Penitence.

It is our rule that the executioner must stand between his victim and the light; the maid's head lay in shadow on the block. I knew that the sword in falling would do her no harm—I would direct it to one side, tripping an ingenious mechanism that would elevate a wax head smeared with blood while the maid draped her own with a fuligin cloth. Still I hesitated to give the blow.

She spoke again from the floor at my feet, and her voice seemed to ring in my ears. "Strike and fear not." With such strength as I was capable of, I sent the false blade down. For an instant it seemed to me that it met resistance; then it thudded into the block, which fell into two. The maid's head, all bloody, tumbled forward toward the watching brothers. Master Gurloes lifted it by the hair and Master Palaemon cupped his left hand to receive the blood.

"With this, our chrism," he said, "I anoint you, Severian, our brother forever." His index finger traced the mark upon my forehead.

"So be it," said Master Gurloes, and all the journeymen save I.

The maid stood. I knew even as I watched her that her head was only concealed in the cloth; but it seemed there was nothing there. I felt dizzy and tired.

She took the wax head from Master Gurloes and pretended to replace it on her shoulders, slipping it by some sleight into the fuligin cloth, then standing before us radiant and whole. I knelt before her, and the others withdrew.

She raised the sword with which I had so lately struck off her head; the blade was bloody now from some contact with the wax. "You are of the torturers," she said. I felt the sword touch either shoulder, and at once eager hands were drawing the head mask of the guild over my face and lifting me. Before I well knew what had occurred, I was on the shoulders of two journeymen—it was only afterward that I learned they were Drotte and Roche, though I should have guessed it. They were bearing me up the processional aisle through the center of the chapel, while everyone cheered and shouted.

We were no sooner outside than the fireworks began: crackers about our feet and even around our ears, torpedoes banging against the thousand-year-old walls of the chapel, rockets red and yellow and green leaping into the air. A gun from the Great Keep split the night.

All the brave meats I have described were on the tables in the court; I sat at the head between Master Palaemon and Master Gurloes, and drank too much (very little, for me, has always been too much), and was cheered and toasted. What became of the maid I do not know. She disappeared as she has each Katharine's Day I can remember. I have not seen her again.

How I reached my bed I have no notion. Those who drink much have told me that they sometimes forget all that befell them in the latter part of the night, and perhaps it was so with me. But I think it more likely that I (who never forget anything, who, if I may for once confess the truth, though I seem to boast, do not truly understand what others mean when they say *forget*, for it seems to me that all experience becomes a part of my being) only slept and was carried there.

However it may be, I woke not in the familiar low room that was our dormitory, but in a cabin so small it was much higher than wide, a journeyman's cabin, and because I was the most junior of the journeymen, the least desirable in the tower, a portless cubbyhole no longer than a cell.

My bed seemed to toss beneath me. I gripped the sides and sat up and it was still, but as soon as my head touched the pillow once more the swaying began again. I felt I was wide awake—then that I was awake again but had been sleeping only a moment before. I was conscious that someone was in the tiny cabin with me, and for some reason I could not have explained I thought it was the young woman who had taken the part of our patroness.

I sat up in the tossing bed. Dim light filtered beneath the door; there was no one there.

When I lay down again, the room was filled with Thecla's perfume. The false Thecla from the House Azure had come, then. I got out of bed, and nearly falling opened the door. There was no one in the passage outside.

A chamber pot waited beneath the bed, and I pulled it out and filled it with my spew, rich meats swimming in wine mixed with bile. Somehow I felt what I had done was treason, as if by casting out all that the guild had given me that night I had cast out the guild itself. Coughing and sobbing I knelt beside the bed, and at last, after wiping my mouth clean, lay down again.

No doubt I slept. I saw the chapel, but it was not the ruin I knew. The roof was whole and high and straight, and from it there hung ruby lamps. The pews were whole and gleamed with polish; the ancient stone altar was swatched in cloth of gold. Behind the altar rose a wonderful mosaic of blue; but it was blank, as if a fragment of sky without cloud or star had been torn away and spread upon the curving wall.

I walked toward it down the aisle, and as I did so I was struck by how much lighter it was than the true sky, whose blue is nearly black even on the brightest day. Yet how much more beautiful this was! It thrilled me to look at it. I felt I was floating in air, borne up by the beauty of it, looking down upon the altar, down into the cup of crimson wine, down upon shewbread and antique knife. I smiled . . .

And woke. In my sleep I had heard footsteps in the passage outside, and I knew I had recognized them, though I could not just then recall whose steps they were. Struggling, I brought back the sound; it was no human tread, only the padding of soft feet, and an almost imperceptible scraping.

I heard it again, so faint that for a time I thought I had confused my memory with reality; but it was real, slowly coming up the passage, slowly going back. The mere lifting of my head brought a wave of nausea; I let it fall again, telling myself that whoever might pace back and forth, it was no affair of mine. The perfume had vanished, and sick though I was, I felt I needed to fear unreality no longer—I was back in the world of solid objects and plain light. My door opened a trifle and Master Malrubius looked in as though to make certain I was all right. I waved to him and he shut the door again. It was some time before I recalled that he had died while I was still a boy.

XII

The Traitor

The next day my head ached and I was ill. But as I was (by a long-standing tradition) spared from the cleaning of the Grand Court and the chapel, where most of the brothers were, I was needed in the oubliette. For a few moments at least the morning calm of the corridors soothed me. Then the apprentices came clattering down (the boy Eata, not quite so small now, with a puffed lip and the gleam of triumph in his eye), bringing the clients' breakfast—cold meats mostly, salvage from the ruins of the banquet. I had to explain to several clients that this was the only day of the year on which they would get meat, and went along assuring one after another that there would be no excruciations—the feast day itself and the day after are exempt, and even when a sentence demands torment on those days, it is postponed. The Chatelaine Thecla was still asleep. I did not wake her, but unlocked her cell and carried her food in and put it on her table.

About midmorning I again heard the echoes of footsteps. Coming to the landing, I saw two cataphracts, an anagnost reading prayers, Master Gurloes, and a young woman. Master Gurloes asked if I had an empty cell, and I began to describe those that were vacant.

"Then take this prisoner. I have already signed for her."

I nodded and grasped the woman by the arm; the cataphracts released her and turned away like silver automata.

The elaboration of her sateen costume (somewhat dirty and torn now) showed that she was an optimate. An armigette would have worn finer stuffs in simpler lines, and no one from the poorer classes could have dressed so well. The anagnost tried to follow us down the corridor, but Master Gurloes prevented him. I heard the soldiers' steel-shod feet on the steps.

"When am I . . . ?" It had a rising, somehow terrorized inflection.

"To be taken to the examination room?"

She clung to my arm now as though I were her father or her lover. "Will I be?"

"Yes, Madame."

"How do you know?"

"All who are brought here are, Madame."

"Always? Isn't anybody ever released?"

"Occasionally."

"Then I might be too, mightn't I?" The hope in her voice now made me think of a flower growing in shadow.

"It's possible, but it's very unlikely."

"Don't you want to know what I've done?"

"No," I said. As it happened, the cell next to Thecla's was vacant; for a moment I wondered if I should put this woman there. She would be company (the two could speak through the slots in their doors), but her questions and the opening and closing of the cell might wake Thecla now. I decided to do it—the companionship, I felt, would more than compensate for a little lost sleep.

"I was affianced to an officer, and I found he was maintaining a jade. When he wouldn't give her up, I paid bravos to fire her thatch. She lost a featherbed, a few sticks of furniture, and some clothes. Is that a crime for which I should be tortured?"

"I don't know, Madame."

"My name is Marcellina. What is yours?"

I turned the key to her cell while I debated answering her. Thecla, whom I could hear stirring now, would doubtless tell her in any event. "Severian," I said.

"And you get your bread by breaking bones. It must give you good dreams by night."

Thecla's eyes, widely spaced and as deep as wells, were at the slot in her door. "Who is that with you, Severian?"

"A new prisoner, Chatelaine."

"A woman? I know she is—I heard her voice. From the House Absolute?"

"No, Chatelaine." Not knowing how long it might be before the two would be able to see each other again, I made Marcellina stand before Thecla's door.

"Another woman. Isn't that unusual? How many do you have, Severian?"

"Eight on this level now, Chatelaine."

"I would think you would often have more than that."

"We rarely have more than four, Chatelaine."

Marcellina asked, "How long will I have to stay here?"

"Not long. Few stay here long, Madame."

With an unhealthy seriousness, Thecla said, "I am about to be released, you understand. He knows."

Our guild's new client looked at what could be seen of her with increased interest. "Are you really about to be set free, Chatelaine?"

"He knows. He's mailed letters for me—haven't you, Severian? And he's been saying goodbye for these last few days. He's really rather a sweet boy in his way."

I said, "You must go in now, Madame. You may continue to talk, if you like."

I was relieved after I had served the clients their suppers. Drotte met me on the stair and suggested I go to bed.

"It's the mask," I told him. "You're not used to seeing me with it on."

"I can see your eyes, and that's all I need to see. Can't you recognize all the brothers by their eyes, and tell whether they're angry, or in the mood for a joke? You ought to go to bed."

I told him I had something to do first, and went to Master Gurloes's study. He was absent, as I had hoped he would be, and among the papers on his table I found what I had, in some fashion I cannot explain, known would be there: an order for Thecla's excruciation.

I could not sleep after that. Instead I went (for the last time, though I did not know it) to the tomb in which I had played as a boy. The funeral bronze of the old exultant was dull for lack of rubbing, and a few more leaves had drifted through the half-open door; otherwise it was unchanged. I had once told Thecla of the place, and now I imagined her with me. She had escaped by my aid, and I promised her that no one would find her here, and that I would bring her food, and when the hunt had cooled I would help her secure passage on a merchant dhow, by which she could make her way unnoticed down the winding coils of Gyoll to the delta and the sea.

Were I such a hero as we had read of together in old romances, I would have released her that very evening, overpowering or drugging the brothers on watch. I was not, and I possessed no drugs and no weapon more formidable than a knife taken from the kitchen.

And if the truth is to be known, between my inmost being and the desperate attempt there stood the words I had heard that morning—the morning after my elevation. The Chatelaine Thecla had said I was "rather a sweet boy," and some already mature part of me knew that even if I succeeded against all odds, I would still be *rather a sweet boy.* At the time I thought it mattered.

The next morning Master Gurloes ordered me to assist him in performing the excruciation. Roche came with us.

I unlocked her cell. She did not understand at first why we had come, and asked me if she had a visitor, or if she were to be discharged.

By the time we reached our destination she knew. Many men faint, but she did not. Courteously, Master Gurloes asked if she would like an explanation of the various mechanisms.

"Do you mean the ones you are going to employ?" There was a tremor in her voice, but it was not marked.

"No, no, I wouldn't do that. Just the curious machines you will be seeing as we pass through. Some are quite old, and most are hardly ever used."

Thecla looked about her before answering. The examination room—our workroom—is not divided into cells, but is a unified space, pillared with the tubes of the ancient engines and cluttered with the tools of our mystery. "The one to which I will be subjected—is that old too?"

"The most hallowed of all," Master Gurloes replied. He waited for her to say something more, and when she did not, proceeded with his descriptions. "The kite I'm certain you must be familiar with—everyone knows of it. Behind it there . . . if you'll take a step this way you'll be able to see it better . . . is what we call the apparatus. It is supposed to letter whatever slogan is demanded in the client's flesh, but it is seldom in working order. I see you're looking at the old post. It's no more than it seems, just a stake to immobilize the hands, and a thirteen-thonged scourge for correction. It used to stand in the Old Yard, but the witches complained, and the castellan made us move it down here. That was about a century ago."

"Who are the witches?"

"I'm afraid we don't have time to go into that now. Severian can tell you when you're back in your cell."

She looked at me as if to say "Am I really going back, eventually?" and I took advantage of my position on the side opposite Master Gurloes to clasp her icy hand.

"Beyond that—"

"Wait. Can I choose? Is there any way I can persuade you to . . . do one thing instead of another?" Her voice was still brave, but weaker now.

Gurloes shook his head. "We have no say in the matter, Chatelaine. Nor do you. We carry out the sentences that are delivered to us, doing no more than we are told, and no less, and making no changes." Embarrassed, he cleared his throat. "The next one's interesting, I think. We call it Allowin's necklace. The client is strapped into that chair, and the pad is adjusted against his breastbone. Each breath he draws thereafter tightens the chain, so that the more he breathes, the less breath he can take. In theory it can go on forever, with very shallow breaths and very small tightenings."

"How horrible. What is that behind it? That tangle of wire, and the great glass globe over the table?"

"Ah," said Master Gurloes. "We call this the revolutionary. The subject lies here. Will you, Chatelaine?"

For a long moment Thecla stood poised. She was taller than any of us, but with that terrible fear in her face, her height was no longer imposing.

"If you do not," Master Gurloes continued, "our journeymen will have to force you. You would not like that, Chatelaine."

Thecla whispered, "I thought you were going to show me all of them."

"Only until we reached this spot, Chatelaine. It's better if the client's mind is occupied. Now lie down, please. I won't be asking again."

She lay down at once, quickly and gracefully, as I had often seen her stretch herself in her cell. The straps Roche and I buckled about her were so old and cracked that I wondered if they would hold.

There were cables to be wound from one part of the examination room to another, rheostats and magnetic amplifiers to be adjusted. Antique lights like blood-red eyes gleamed on the control panel, and a droning like the song of some huge insect filled the entire chamber. For a few moments, the ancient engine of the tower lived again. One cable was loose, and sparks as blue as burning brandy played about its bronze fittings.

"Lightning," Master Gurloes said as he rammed the loose cable home. "There's another word for it, but I forget. Anyway, the revolutionary here runs by lightning. It's not as if you were going to be struck, of course, Chatelaine. But lightning's the thing that makes it go.

"Severian, push up your handle there until this needle's here." A coil that had been as cold as a snake when I had touched it a moment before was warm now.

"What does it do?"

"I couldn't describe it, Chatelaine. Anyway, I've never had it done, you see." Gurloes's hand touched a knob on the control panel and Thecla was bathed in white light that stole the color from all it fell upon. She screamed; I have heard screaming all my life, but that was the worst, though not the loudest; it seemed to go on and on like the shrieking of a cartwheel.

She was not unconscious when the white light died. Her eyes were open, staring upward; but she did not appear to see my hand, or to feel it when I touched her. Her breathing was shallow and rapid.

Roche asked, "Shall we wait until she can walk?" I could see he was thinking how awkward so tall a woman would be to carry.

"Take her now," Master Gurloes said. We got out the travail.

When all my other work was complete, I came into her cell to see her. She was fully aware by then, though she could not stand. "I ought to hate you," she said.

I had to lean over her to catch the words. "It's all right," I said.

"But I don't. Not for your sake . . . if I hate my last friend, what would be left?"

There was nothing to say to that, so I said nothing.

"Do you know what it was like? It was a long time before I could think of it."

Her right hand was creeping upward, toward her eyes. I caught it and forced it back.

"I thought I saw my worst enemy, a kind of demon. And it was me."

Her scalp was bleeding. I put clean lint there and taped it down, though I knew it would soon be gone. Curling, dark hairs were entangled in her fingers.

"Since then, I can't control my hands . . . I can if I think about it, if I know what they're doing. But it is so hard, and I'm getting tired." She rolled her head away and spat blood. "I bite myself. Bite the lining of my cheeks, and my tongue and lips. Once my hands tried to strangle me, and I thought oh good, I will die now. But I only lost consciousness, and they must have lost their strength, because I woke. It's like that machine, isn't it?"

I said, "Allowin's necklace."

"But worse. My hands are trying to blind me now, to tear my eyelids away. Will I be blind?"

"Yes," I said.

"How long before I die?"

"A month, perhaps. The thing in you that hates you will weaken as you weaken. The revolutionary brought it to life, but its energy is your energy, and in the end you will die together."

"Severian . . ."

"Yes?"

"I see," she said. And then, "It is a thing from Erebus, from Abaia, a fit companion for me. Vodalus . . ."

I leaned closer, but I could not hear. At last I said, "I tried to save you. I wanted to. I stole a knife, and spent the night watching for a chance. But only a master can take a prisoner from a cell, and I would have had to kill—"

"Your friends."

"Yes, my friends."

Her hands were moving again, and blood trickled from her mouth. "Will you bring me the knife?"

"I have it here," I said, and drew it from under my cloak. It was a common cook's knife with a span or so of blade.

"It looks sharp."

"It is," I said. "I know how to treat an edge, and I sharpened it carefully." That was the last thing I said to her. I put the knife into her right hand and went out.

For a time, I knew, her will would hold it back. A thousand times one thought recurred: I could reenter her cell, take back the knife, and no one would know. I would be able to live out my life in the guild.

If her throat rattled, I did not hear it; but after I had stared at the door of her cell for a long while, a little crimson rivulet crept from under it. I went to Master Gurloes then, and told him what I had done.

XIII

The Lictor of Thrax

For the next ten days I lived the life of a client, in a cell of the topmost level (not far, in fact, from that which had been Thecla's). In order that the guild should not be accused of having detained me without legal process, the door was left unlocked; but there were two journeymen with swords outside my door, and I never stepped from it save for a brief time on the second day when I was brought to Master Palaemon to tell my story again. That was my trial, if you like. For the remainder of the time, the guild pondered my sentence.

It is said that it is the peculiar quality of time to conserve fact, and that it does so by rendering our past falsehoods true. So it was with me. I had lied in saying that I loved the guild—that I desired nothing but to remain in its embrace. Now I found those lies become truths. The life of a journeyman and even that of an apprentice seemed infinitely attractive. Not only because I was certain I was to die, but truly attractive in themselves, because I had lost them. I saw the brothers now from the viewpoint of a client, and so I saw them as powerful, the active principles of an inimical and nearly perfect machine.

Knowing that my case was hopeless, I learned in my own person what Master Malrubius had once impressed on me when I was a child: that hope is a psychological mechanism unaffected by external realities. I was young and adequately fed; I was permitted to sleep and therefore I hoped. Again and again, waking and sleeping, I dreamed that just as I was to die Vodalus would come. Not alone as I had seen him fight in the necropolis, but at the head of an army that would sweep the decay of centuries away and make us once more the masters of the stars. Often I thought to hear tread of that army ringing in the corridors; sometimes

I carried my candle to the little slot in the door because I thought I had seen the face of Vodalus outside in the dark.

As I have said, I supposed I would be killed. The question that occupied my mind most during those slow days was that of means. I had learned all the arts of the torturer; now I thought of them—sometimes one by one, as we had been taught them, sometimes all together in a revelation of pain. To live day after day in a cell below ground, thinking of torment, is torment itself.

On the eleventh day I was summoned by Master Palaemon. I saw the red light of the sun again, and breathed that wet wind that tells in winter that spring is almost come. But, oh, how much it cost me to walk past the open tower door and looking out see the corpse door in the curtain wall, and old Brother Porter lounging there.

Master Palaemon's study seemed very large when I entered it and yet very precious to me—as though the dusty books and papers were my own. He asked me to sit. He was not masked and seemed older than I remembered him. "We have discussed your case," he said. "Master Gurloes and I. We have had to take the other journeymen into our confidence, and even the apprentices. It is better that they know the truth. Most agree that you are deserving of death."

He waited for me to comment, but I did not.

"And yet there was much said in your defense. Several of the journeymen urged in private meetings, to me and to Master Gurloes as well, that you be permitted to die without pain."

I cannot say why, but it became of central importance to me to know how many of these friends I had, and I asked.

"More than two, and more than three. The exact number does not matter. Do you not believe that you deserve to die painfully?"

"By the revolutionary," I said, hoping that if I asked that death as a favor it would not be granted.

"Yes, that would be fitting. But . . ."

And here he paused. The moment passed, then two. The first brass-backed fly of the new summer buzzed against the port. I wanted to crush it, to catch and release it, to shout at Master Palaemon to speak, to flee from the room; but I could do none of these things. I sat, instead, in the old wooden chair beside his table, feeling that I was already dead but still must die.

"We cannot kill you, you see. I have had a most difficult time convincing Gurloes of that, yet it is so. If we slay you without judicial order, we are no better than you: you have been false to us, but we will have been false to the law. Furthermore, we would be putting the guild in jeopardy forever—an Inquisitor would call it murder.''

He waited for me to comment, and I said, ''But for what I have done . . .''

''The sentence would be just. Yes. Still, we have no right in law to take life on our own authority. Those who have that right are properly jealous of it. If we were to go to them, the verdict would be sure. But were we to go, the repute of the guild would be publicly and irrevocably stained. Much of the trust now reposed in us would be gone, and permanently. We might confidently expect our affairs to be supervised by others in the future. Would you enjoy seeing our clients guarded by soldiers, Severian?''

The vision I had in Gyoll when I had so nearly drowned rose before me, and it possessed (as it had then) a sullen yet strong attraction. ''I would rather take my own life,'' I said. ''I will feign to swim, and die in mid-channel, far from help.''

The shadow of a sour smile crossed Master Palaemon's ruined face. ''I am glad you made that offer only to me. Master Gurloes would have taken far too much pleasure in pointing out that at least a month must pass before swimming can be made credible.''

''I am sincere. I sought a painless death, but it was death I sought, and not an extension of life.''

''Even if it were midsummer, what you propose could not be permitted. An Inquisitor might still conclude that we contrived your death. Fortunately for you, we have agreed upon a less incriminating solution. Do you know anything of the condition of our mystery in the provincial towns?''

I shook my head.

''It is but low. Nowhere but in Nessus—nowhere but here in the Citadel—is there a chapter of our guild. Lesser places have no more than a carnifex, who takes life and performs such excruciations as the judicators there decree. Such a man is universally hated and feared. Do you understand?''

''Such a position,'' I answered, ''is too high for me.'' There was no falsehood in what I said; I despised myself, at that moment, far more than I did the guild. Since then I have recalled those words often, though they were but my own, and they have been a comfort to me in many troubles.

''There is a town called Thrax, the City of Windowless Rooms,'' Master Palaemon continued. ''The archon there—his name is Abdiesus—has written the House Absolute. A marshall there has transmitted the letter to the Castellar, and from him I have it. They are in sore need in Thrax of the functionary I have described. In the past they have pardoned condemned men on the condition that they accept the post. Now the countryside is rotten with treachery, and since the position entails a certain degree of trust, they are reluctant to do so again."

I said, "I understand."

"Twice before members of the guild have been dispatched to outlying towns, though whether those were such cases as this the chronicles do not say. Nevertheless, they furnish a precedent now, and an escape from the maze. You are to go to Thrax, Severian. I have prepared a letter that will introduce you to the archon and his magistrates. It describes you as highly skilled in our mystery. For such a place, it will not be a falsehood."

I nodded, being already resigned to what I was to do. Yet while I sat there, maintaining the expressionless face of a journeyman whose only will is to obey, a new shame burned in me. Though it was not so hot as the one for the disgrace I had brought upon the guild, still it was fresher, and hurt the more because I had not yet grown accustomed to the sickness of it as I had the other. It was this: that I was glad to go—that my feet already longed for the feel of grass, my eyes for strange sights, my lungs for the new, clear air of far, unmanned places.

I asked Master Palaemon where the town of Thrax might be.

"Down Gyoll," he said. "Near the sea." Then he stopped as old men will, and said, "No, no, what am I thinking of? Up Gyoll, of course," and for me hundreds of leagues of marching waves, and the sand, and the seabirds' crying all faded away. Master Palaemon took a map from his cabinet and unrolled it for me, bending over it until the lens by which he saw such things nearly touched the parchment. "There," he said, and showed me a dot on the margin of the young river, at the lower cataracts. "If you had funds you might travel by boat. As it is, you must walk."

"I understand," I said, and though I remembered the thin piece of gold Vodalus had given me, safe in its hiding place, I knew I could not take advantage of whatever wealth it might represent. It was the guild's will to cast me out with no more money than a young journeyman might be expected to possess, and for prudence's sake as well as honor's, so I must go.

Yet I knew it was unfair. If I had not glimpsed the woman with the heart-shaped face and earned that small gold coin, it is more than possible I would never have carried the knife to Thecla and forfeited my place in the guild. In a sense, that coin had bought my life.

Very well—I would leave my old life behind me . . .

"Severian!" Master Palaemon exclaimed. "You are not listening to me. You were never an inattentive pupil in our classes."

"I'm sorry. I was thinking about a great many things."

"No doubt." For the first time he really smiled, and for an instant looked his old self, the Master Palaemon of my boyhood. "Yet I was giving you such good advice for your journey. Now you must do without it, but doubtless you would have forgotten everything anyway. You know of the roads?"

"I know they must not be used. Nothing more."

"The Autarch Maruthas closed them. That was when I was your age. Travel encouraged sedition, and he wished goods to enter and leave the city by the river, where they might be easily taxed. The law has remained in force since, and there is a redoubt, so I've heard, every fifty leagues. Still the roads remain. Though they are in poor repair, it is said some use them by night."

"I see," I said. Closed or not, the roads might make for an easier passage than traveling across the countryside as the law demanded.

"I doubt you do. I mean to warn you against them. They are patrolled by uhlans under orders to kill anyone found upon them, and since they have permission to loot the bodies of those they slay, they are not much inclined to ask excuses."

"I understand," I told him, and in private wondered how he came to know so much of travel.

"Good. The day is half spent now. If you like, you may sleep here tonight and depart in the morning."

"Sleep in my cell, you mean."

He nodded. Though I knew he could scarcely see my face, I felt that something in him was studying me.

"I will leave now, then." I tried to think of what I would have to do before I turned my back on our tower forever; nothing came to me, yet it seemed there must surely be something. "May I have a watch in which to prepare? When the time is up, I will go."

"That's easily granted. But before you leave, I want you to return here—I have something to give you. Will you do it?"

"Of course, Master, if you want me to."

"And Severian, be careful. There are many in the guild who are your friends—who wish this had never happened. But there are others who feel you have betrayed our trust and deserve agony and death."

"Thank you, Master," I said. "The second group is correct."

My few possessions were already in my cell. I bundled them together and found the whole bundle so small I could put it in the sabretache hanging from my belt. Moved by love, and regret for what had been, I went to Thecla's cell.

It was empty still. Her blood had been scrubbed from the floor, but a wide, dark spot of blood-rust had etched the metal. Her clothing was gone, and her cosmetics. The four books I had carried to her a year before remained, stacked with others on the little table. I could not resist the temptation to take one; there were so many in the library that they would never miss a single volume. My hand had stretched forth before I realized I did not know which to choose. The book of heraldry was the most beautiful, but it was too large by far to carry about the country. The book of theology was the smallest of all, but the brown book was hardly larger. In the end it was that I took, with its tales from vanished worlds.

I climbed the stair of our tower then, past the storeroom to the gun room where the siege pieces lounged in cradles of pure force. Then higher still to the room of the glass roof, with its gray screens and strangely contorted chairs, and up a slender ladder until I stood on the slippery panes themselves, where my presence scattered blackbirds across the sky like flecks of soot and our fuligin pennon streamed and snapped from the staff over my head.

Below me the Old Yard seemed small and even cramped, but infinitely comfortable and homey. The breach in the curtain wall was greater than I had ever realized, though to either side of it the Red Tower and the Bear Tower still stood proud and strong. Nearest our own, the witches' tower was slender, dark, and tall; for a moment the wind blew a snatch of their wild laughter to me and I felt the old fear, though we of the torturers have always been on the most friendly terms with the witches, our sisters.

Beyond the wall, the great necropolis rolled down the long slope toward Gyoll, whose waters I could glimpse between the half-rotted buildings on its banks. Across the flood of the river the rounded dome of the khan seemed no more than a pebble, the city about it an expanse of many-colored sand trodden by the master torturers of old.

I saw a caique, with high, sharp prow and stern, and a bellying sail, making south with the dark current; and against my will I followed it for a time—to the delta and the swamps, and at last to the flashing sea where that great beast Abaia, carried from the farther shores of the universe in anteglacial days, wallows until the moment comes for him and his kind to devour the continents.

Then I abandoned all thoughts of the south and her ice-choked sea and turned north to the mountains and the rising of the river. For a long time (I do not know how long, though the sun seemed in a new place when I took notice of its position again) I looked to the north. The mountains I could see with my mind's eye, but not with the body's: only the rolling expanse of the city with its million roofs. And to tell the truth, the great silver columns of the Keep and its surrounding spires blocked half my view. Yet I cared nothing for them, and indeed hardly saw them. North lay the House Absolute and the cataracts, and Thrax, City of Windowless Rooms. North lay the wide pampas, a hundred trackless forests, and the rotting jungles at the waist of the world.

When I had thought on all those things until I was half mad, I came down to Master Palaemon's study again and told him I was ready to depart.

XIV

Terminus Est

"I have a gift for you," Master Palaemon said. "Considering your youth and strength, I don't believe you will find it too heavy."

"I am deserving of no gifts."

"That is so. But you must recall, Severian, that when a gift is deserved, it is not a gift but a payment. The only true gifts are such as you now receive. I cannot forgive you for what you have done, but I cannot forget what you were. Since Master Gurloes rose to journeyman, I have had no better scholar." He rose and walked stiffly to the alcove, where I heard him say, "Ah, she is not overburdensome for me yet."

He was lifting something so dark it was swallowed by the shadows. I said, "Let me assist you, Master."

"No need, no need. Light to raise, weighty to descend. Such is the mark of a good one."

Upon his table he laid a night-black case nearly long enough for a coffin, but much narrower. When he opened its silver catches, they rang like bells.

"I am not giving you the casket, which would only impede you. Here is the blade, her sheath to protect her when you are traveling, and a baldric."

It was in my hands before I fully understood what it was he gave me. The sheath of sable manskin covered it nearly to the pommel. I drew it off (it was soft as glove leather), and beheld the sword herself.

I shall not bore you with a catalog of her virtues and beauties; you would have to see her and hold her to judge her justly. Her bitter blade was an ell in length, straight and square-pointed as such a sword's should be. Man-edge and woman-edge could part a hair to within a span of the guard, which was of thick silver with a carven head at either end.

Her grip was onyx bound with silver bands, two spans long and terminated with an opal. Art had been lavished upon her; but it is the function of art to render attractive and significant those things that without it would not be so, and so art had nothing to give her. The words *Terminus Est* had been engraved upon her blade in curious and beautiful letters, and I had learned enough of ancient languages since leaving the Atrium of Time to know that they meant *This Is the Line of Division.*

"She is well honed, I promise you," Master Palaemon said, seeing me test the man-edge with my thumb. "For the sake of those given over to you, see you keep her so. My question is whether she is not too ponderous a mate for you. Raise her and see."

I clasped *Terminus Est* as I had the false sword at my elevation, and lifted her above my head, taking care not to strike the ceiling. She shifted as though I wrestled a serpent.

"You have no difficulty?"

"No, Master. But she writhed when I poised her."

"There is a channel in the spine of her blade, and in it runs a river of hydrargyrum—a metal heavier than iron, though it flows like water. Thus the balance is shifted toward the hands when the blade is high, but to the tip when it falls. Often you will have to wait the completion of a final prayer, or a hand signal from the quaesitor. Your sword must not slack or tremble— But you know all that. I need not tell you to respect such an instrument. May the Moira favor you, Severian."

I took the whetstone from its pocket in the sheath and dropped it into my sabretache, folded the letter he had given me to the archon of Thrax, wrapped it in a scrap of oiled silk, and committed it to the sword's care. Then I took my leave of him.

With the broad blade slung behind my left shoulder, I made my way through the corpse door and out into the windy garden of the necropolis. The sentry at the lowest gate, nearest the river, allowed me to pass without challenge, though with many a strange look, and I threaded the narrow streets to the Water Way, that runs with Gyoll.

Now I must write something that still shames me, even after all that has occurred. The watches of that afternoon were the happiest of my life. All my old hatred of the guild had vanished, and my love for it, for Master Palaemon, my brothers, and even the apprentices, my love for its lore and usages, my love which had never wholly died, was all that remained. I was leaving all those things I loved, after having disgraced them utterly. I should have wept.

I did not. Something in me soared, and when the wind whipped my cloak out behind me like wings, I felt I might have flown. We are forbidden to smile in the presence of any but our masters, brothers, clients, and apprentices. I did not wish to wear my mask, but I had to pull up my hood and bow my head lest the passersby see my face. Wrongly I thought I would perish on the way. Wrongly I thought I should never return to the Citadel and our tower; but wrongly too I believed that there were many more such days to come, and I smiled.

In my ignorance, I had supposed that before dark I would have left the city behind me, and that I would be able to sleep in relative safety beneath some tree. In actuality, I had not so much as outwalked the older and poorer parts before the west was lifted to cover the sun. To ask hospitality in one of the tottering buildings that bordered the Water Way, or attempt to rest in some corner, would have been an invitation to death. And so I trudged along under stars brightened by the wind, no longer a torturer in the eyes of the few who passed me, but only a somberly clad traveler who shouldered a dark paterissa.

From time to time boats glided through the weed-choked water while the wind drew music from their rigging. The poorer sort showed no lights and seemed hardly more than floating debris; but several times I beheld rich thalamegii with bow and stern lamps to show off their gliding. These kept to the center of the channel for fear of attack, yet I could hear the song of their sweepsmen across the water:

Row, brothers, row!
The current is against us.
Row, brothers, row!
Yet God is for us.
Row, brothers, row!
The wind is against us.
Row, brothers, row!
Yet God is for us.

And so on. Even when the lamps were no more than sparks a league or more upriver, the sound came on the wind. As I was later to see, they pull the shaft with the refrain, and put it back again with the alternate phrases, and so make their way watch upon watch.

When it seemed that it must soon be day, I saw upon the broad, black ribbon of the river a line of sparks that were not the lights of vessels but fixed fires stretching from bank to bank. It was a bridge, and after tramping long through the dark I reached it. Leaving the lapping tongues of the river, I mounted a flight of broken steps from the Water Way to the more elevated street of the bridge, and at once found myself an actor in a new scene.

The bridge was as well lighted as the Water Way had been shadowed. There were flambeaux on staggering poles every ten strides or so, and at intervals of about a hundred strides, bartizans whose guardroom windows glared like fireworks clung to the bridge piers. Carriages with lanterns rattled along, and most of the people who thronged the walkway were accompanied by linkboys or carried lights themselves. There were vendors who shouted the wares they displayed in trays hung from their necks, externs who gabbled in rude tongues, and beggars who showed their sores, feigned to play flageolets and ophicleides, and pinched their children to make them weep.

I confess I was much interested by all this, though my training prohibited me from gawking at it. With my hood drawn well over my head, and my eyes resolutely to the front, I passed among the crowd as if indifferent to it; but for a short time at least I felt my fatigue melt away, and my strides were, I think, the longer and swifter because I wanted to remain where I was.

The guards in the bartizans were not city roundsmen but peltasts in half-armor, bearing transparent shields. I was almost at the western bank when two stepped forward to bar my way with their blazing spears. "It is a serious crime to wear the costume you affect. If you intend some jape or artifice, you endanger yourself for its sake."

I said, "I am entitled to the habit of my guild."

"You seriously claim you are a carnifex, then? Is that a sword you carry?"

"It is, but I am no such thing. I am a journeyman of the Order of the Seekers for Truth and Penitence."

There was a silence. A hundred people or so had surrounded us in the few moments required for them to ask, and me to answer, their question. I saw the peltast who had not spoken glance at the other as if to say *he means it,* and then at the crowd.

"Come inside. The lochage wishes to speak with you."

They waited while I preceded them through the narrow door. The interior boasted only one small room, with a table and a few chairs. I mounted a little stair much worn by booted feet. In the room above, a man in a cuirass was writing at a high desk. My captors had followed me up, and when we stood before him, the one who had spoken previously said, "This is the man."

"I am aware of that," the lochage answered without looking up.

"He calls himself a journeyman of the guild of torturers."

For a moment the quill, which had skated along steadily before, paused. "I had never thought to encounter such a thing outside the pages of some book, but I dare say he speaks no more than the truth."

"Ought we to release him then?" the soldier asked.

"Not quite yet."

Now the lochage wiped his quill, sanded the letter over which he had labored, and looked up at us. I said, "Your subordinates stopped me because they doubted my right to the cloak I wear."

"They stopped you because I ordered it, and I ordered it because you were creating a disturbance, according to the report of the eastern turrets. If you are of the guild of torturers—which to be honest I had supposed reformed out of existence long ago—you have spent your life in the—What do you call it?"

"The Matachin Tower."

He snapped his fingers, and looked as though he were both amused and chagrined. "I mean the place where your tower stands."

"The Citadel."

"Yes, the Old Citadel. It's east of the river, as I recall, and just at the northern edge of the Algedonic Quarter. I was taken there to see the Donjon when I was a cadet. How often have you gone out into the city?"

I thought of our swimming expeditions and said, "Often."

"Dressed as you are now?"

I shook my head.

"If you're going to do that, pull back that hood. I can only see the tip of your nose wiggle." The lochage slid from his stool and strode to a window overlooking the bridge. "How many people do you think there are in Nessus?"

"I have no idea."

"No more do I, Torturer. No more does anyone. Every attempt to count them has failed, as has every attempt to tax them systematically. The city grows and changes every night, like writing chalked on a wall. Houses are built in the streets by clever people who take up the cobbles in the dark and claim the ground—did you know that? The exultant Talarican, whose madness manifested itself as a consuming interest in the lowest aspects of human existence, claimed that the persons who live by devouring the garbage of others number two gross thousands. That there are ten thousand begging acrobats, of whom nearly half are women. That if a pauper were to leap from the parapet of this bridge each time we draw breath, we should live forever, because the city breeds and breaks men faster than we respire. Among such a throng, there is no alternative to peace. Disturbances cannot be tolerated, because disturbances cannot be extinguished. Do you follow me?"

"There is the alternative of order. But yes, until that is achieved, I understand."

The lochage sighed and turned to face me. "If you understand that at least, good. It will be necessary, then, for you to obtain more conventional clothing."

"I cannot return to the Citadel."

"Then get out of sight tonight and buy something tomorrow. Have you funds?"

"A trifle, yes."

"Good. Buy something. Or steal, or strip the clothes from the next unfortunate you shorten with that thing. I'd have one of my fellows take you to an inn, but that would mean more staring and whispering still. There's been some kind of trouble on the river, and they're telling each other too many ghost stories out there already. Now the wind's dying and a fog's coming in—that will make it worse. Where are you going?"

"I am appointed to the town of Thrax."

The peltast who had spoken before said, "Do you believe him, Lochage? He's shown no proof that he's what he claims."

The lochage was looking out the window again, and now I too saw the threads of ochre mist. "If you can't use your head, use your nose," he said. "What odors entered with him?"

The peltast smiled uncertainly.

"Rusting iron, cold sweat, putrescent blood. An impostor would smell of new cloth, or rags picked from a trunk. If you don't wake to your business soon, Petronax, you'll be north fighting the Ascians."

The peltast said, "But Lochage—" shooting such a look of hatred toward me that I thought he might attempt to do me some harm when I left the bartizan.

"Show this fellow you are indeed of the torturers' guild."

The peltast was relaxed, so there was no great difficulty. I knocked his shield aside with my right arm, putting my left foot on his right to pin him while I crushed that nerve in the neck that induces convulsions.

XV

Baldanders

The city at the western end of the bridge was very different from the one I had left. At first there were flambeaux at the corners, and nearly as much coming and going of coaches and drays as there had been on the bridge itself. Before quitting the bartizan, I had asked the lochage's advice about a place to spend what remained of the night; now, feeling the fatigue that had deserted me only briefly, I plodded along watching for the inn sign.

After a time the dark seemed to thicken with each step I took, and somewhere I must have taken the wrong turning. Unwilling to retrace my way, I tried to maintain a generally northerly route, comforting myself with the thought that though I might be lost, each stride carried me nearer Thrax. At last I discovered a small inn. I saw no sign and perhaps it had none, but I smelled cooking and heard the clink of tumblers, and I went in, throwing open the door and dropping into an old chair that stood near it without paying much attention to where I had come or whose company I had entered.

When I had been sitting there long enough to get my breath and was wishing for a place where I could take off my boots (though I was far from ready to get up to look for one), three men who had been drinking in a corner got up and left; and an old man, seeing, I suppose, that I was going to be bad for his business, came over and asked what I wanted. I told him I required a room.

"We have none."

I said, "That's just as well—I have no money to pay anyway."

"Then you will have to leave."

I shook my head. "Not yet. I'm too tired." (Other journeymen had told me of playing this trick in the city.)

"You're the carnifex, ain't you? You take their heads off."

"Bring me two of those fish I smell and you won't have anything but the heads left."

"I can call the City Guard. They'll have you out."

I knew from his tone that he did not believe what he said, so I told him to call away, but to bring me the fish in the meantime, and he went off grumbling. I sat up straighter then, with *Terminus Est* (which I had had to take from my shoulder to sit down) upright between my knees. There were five men still in the room with me, but none of them would meet my eye, and two soon left.

The old man returned with a small fish that had expired upon a slice of coarse bread, and said, "Eat this and go."

He stood and watched me while I had my supper. When I had finished it, I asked where I could sleep.

"No rooms. I told you."

If a palace had stood with open doors half a chain away, I do not think I could have driven myself to leave that inn to go to it. I said, "I'll sleep in this chair, then. You're not likely to have more trade tonight anyway."

"Wait," he said, and left me. I heard him talking to a woman in another room.

When I woke, he was shaking me by the shoulder. "Will you sleep three in a bed?"

"With whom?"

"Two optimates, I swear to you. Very nice men, traveling together."

The woman in the kitchen shouted something I could not understand.

"Did you hear that?" the old man continued. "One of them's not even come in yet. This time of night, he probably won't come at all. There'll be just the two of you."

"If these men have rented a bedchamber—"

"They won't object, I promise. Truth is, Carnifex, they're behind. Three nights here, and only paid for the first."

So I was to be used as an eviction notice. That did not disturb me much, and in fact it seemed somewhat promising—if the man sleeping there tonight left, I would have the room to myself. I clambered to my feet and followed the old man up a crooked stair.

The room we entered was not locked, but it was as dark as a tomb. I could hear heavy breathing. "Goodman!" the old fellow bawled, forgetting he had said his tenant was an optimate. "What-do-you-call-yourself? Baldy? Baldanders? I brought company for you. If you won't pay your rate, you got to take in boarders."

There was no reply.

"Here, Master Carnifex," the old man said to me, "I'll make you a light." He puffed at a bit of punk until it was bright enough to ignite a stub of candle.

The room was small, and held no furniture but a bed. In it, asleep on his side (as it appeared) with his back toward us and his legs drawn up, was the largest man I had ever seen—a man who might fairly have been called a giant.

"Aren't you going to wake, Goodman Baldanders, and see who your lodgemate might be?"

I wanted to go to bed and told the old man to leave us. He objected, but I pushed him out of the room and as soon as he was gone sat down on the unoccupied side of the bed and pulled off my boots and stockings. The weak light of the candle confirmed that I had developed several blisters. I took off my cloak and spread it on the worn counterpane. For a moment I considered whether I should take off my belt and trousers or sleep in them; prudence and weariness together urged the latter, and I noticed that the giant seemed fully dressed. With a feeling of inexpressible fatigue and relief I blew out the candle and lay down to spend the first night outside the Matachin Tower that I could recall.

"Never."

The tone was so deep and resonant (almost like the lowest notes of an organ) that I was not certain at first what the meaning of the word had been, or even if it had been a word at all. I mumbled, "What did you say?"

"Baldanders."

"I know—the innkeeper told me. I'm Severian." I was lying on my back, with *Terminus Est* (which I had brought into the bed for safekeeping) between us. In the dark, I could not tell whether my companion had rolled to face me or not, yet I was certain I would have felt any motion of that enormous frame.

"You—strike off."

"You heard us when we came in then. I thought you were asleep." My lips shaped themselves to say I was no carnifex, but a journeyman of the torturers' guild. Then I recalled my disgrace, and that Thrax has sent for an executioner. I said, "Yes, I'm a headsman, but you need not fear me. I only do what I am feed to do."

"Tomorrow, then."

"Yes, tomorrow will be time enough for us to meet and talk."

And then I dreamed, though it may have been that Baldanders' words, too, were a dream. Yet I do not think so, and if they were, it was a different dream.

I bestrode a great, leather-winged being under a lowering sky. Just equipoised between the rack of cloud and a twilit land we slid down a hill of air. Hardly once, it seemed to me, the finger-winged soarer flapped her long pinions. The dying sun was before us, and it seemed we matched the speed of Urth, for it stood unmoving at the horizon, though we flew on and on.

At last I saw a change in the land, and at first I thought it a desert. Far off, no cities or farms or woods or fields appeared, but only a level waste, a blackened purple in color, featureless and nearly static. The leathern-winged one observed it as well, or perhaps snatched some odor from the air. I felt iron muscles beneath me grow tense, and there were three wing strokes together.

The purple waste showed flecks of white. After a time I became aware that its seeming stillness was a sham born of uniformity—it was the same everywhere, but everywhere in motion—the sea—the World-River Uroboros—cradling Urth.

Then for the first time I looked behind me, seeing all the country of humankind swallowed in the night.

When it was gone, and there was everywhere beneath us the waste of rolling water and nothing more, the beast turned her head to regard me. Her beak was the beak of an ibis, her face the face of a hag; on her head was a miter of bone. For an instant we regarded each other, and I seemed to know her thought: *You dream; but were you to wake from your waking, I would be there.*

Her motion changed as a lugger's does when the sailors make it to come about on the opposite tack. One pinion dipped, the other rose until it pointed toward the sky, and I scrabbled at the scaled hide and plummeted into the sea.

The shock of the impact woke me. I twitched in every joint, and heard the giant mutter in his sleep. In much the same way I murmured too, and groped to find if my sword still lay at my side, and slept again.

The water closed over me, yet I did not drown. I felt I might breathe water, yet I did not breathe. Everything was so clear that I felt I fell through an emptiness more translucent than air.

Far off loomed great shapes—things hundreds of times larger than a man. Some seemed ships, and some clouds; one was a living head without a body; one had a hundred heads. A blue haze obscured them, and I saw below me a country of sand, carved by the currents. A palace stood there that was greater than our Citadel, but it was ruinous, its halls as unroofed as its gardens; through it moved immense figures, white as leprosy.

Nearer I fell, and they turned up their faces to me, faces such as I had seen once beneath Gyoll; they were women, naked, with hair of sea-foam green and eyes of coral. Laughing, they watched me fall, and their laughter came bubbling up to me. Their teeth were white and pointed, each a finger's length.

I fell nearer. Their hands reached up to me and stroked me as a mother strokes her child. The gardens of the palace held sponges and sea anemones and countless other beauties to which I could put no name. The great women circled me round, and I was only a doll before them. "Who are you?" I asked. "And what do you do here?"

"We are the brides of Abaia. The sweethearts and playthings, the toys and valentines of Abaia. The land could not hold us. Our breasts are battering rams, our buttocks would break the backs of bulls. Here we feed, floating and growing, until we are great enough to mate with Abaia, who will one day devour the continents."

"And who am I?"

Then they laughed all together, and their laughter was like surf upon a beach of glass. "We will show you," they said. "We will show you!" One took me by each hand, as sisters take their sister's child, and lifted me up, and swam with me through the garden. Their fingers were webbed, and as long as my arm from shoulder to elbow.

They halted, settling through the water like carracks sinking, until their feet and mine touched the strand. There stood before us a low wall, and on it a little stage and curtain, such as are used for children's entertainments.

Our roiling of the water seemed to flutter the kerchief-sized cloth. It rippled and swayed, and began to draw back as though teased by an unseen hand. At once there appeared the tiny figure of a man of sticks. His limbs were twigs, still showing bark and green bud. His body was a quarter-span of branch, big through as my thumb, and his head a knot whose whorls formed his eyes and mouth. He carried a club (which he brandished at us) and moved as if he were alive.

When the wooden man had jumped for us, and struck the little stage with his weapon to show his ferocity, there appeared the figure of a boy armed with a sword. This marionette was as finely finished as the other was crude—it might have been a real child reduced to the size of a mouse.

After both had bowed to us, the tiny figures fought. The wooden man performed prodigious leaps and seemed to fill the stage with the blows of his cudgel; the boy danced like a dust mote in a sunbeam to avoid it, darting at the wooden man to slash with his pin-sized blade.

At last the wooden figure collapsed. The boy strode over as if to set his foot upon its chest; but before he could do so, the wooden figure floated from the stage, and turning limply and lazily rose until it vanished from sight, leaving behind the boy, and the cudgel and the sword—both broken. I seemed to hear (no doubt it was really the squeaking of cartwheels on the street outside) a flourish of toy trumpets.

I woke because a third person had come into the room. He was a small, brisk man with fiery red hair, well and even foppishly dressed. When he saw me awake, he threw back the shutters that had covered the window, bringing red sunlight streaming in.

"My partner," he said, "sleeps soundly always. His snoring didn't deafen you?"

"I slept well myself," I told him. "And if he snored, I didn't hear him."

That seemed to please the small man, who showed a good many gold teeth when he smiled. "He does. He snores to shake Urth, I assure you. Happy you got your rest anyway." He extended a delicate, well-cared-for hand. "I am Dr. Talos."

"The Journeyman Severian." I threw off the thin coverings and stood up to take it.

"You wear black, I see. What guild is that?"

"It is the fuligin of the torturers."

"Ah!" He cocked his head to one side like a thrush, and hopped about to look at me from various angles. "You're a tall fellow—that's a shame—but all that sooty stuff is very impressive."

"We find it practical," I said. "The oubliette is a dirty place, and fuligin doesn't show bloodstains."

"You have humor! That's excellent! There are few advantages, I'll tell you, that profit a man more than humor. Humor will draw a crowd. Humor will calm a mob or reassure a nursery school. Humor will get you on and get you off, and pull in asimis like a magnet."

I had only the vaguest idea of what he was saying, but seeing that he was in an affable mood, I ventured, "I hope I didn't discommode you? The landlord said I was to sleep here, and there was room for another person in the bed."

"No, no, not at all! I never came back—found a better place to pass the night. I sleep very little, I may as well tell you, and I'm a light sleeper too. But I had a good night of it, an excellent night. Where are you going this morning, optimate?"

I was fumbling under the bed for my boots. "First to look for some breakfast, I suppose. After that, out of the city, to the north."

"Excellent! No doubt my partner would appreciate a breakfast—it will do him a world of good. And we're traveling north. After a most successful tour of the city, you know. Going back home now. Played the east bank down, and playing the west up. Perhaps we'll stop at the House Absolute on our way north. That's the dream, you know, in the profession. Play the Autarch's palace. Or come back, if you've already played there. Chrisos by the hatful."

"I've met one other person, at least, who dreamed of going back."

"Don't put on that long face—you must tell me about him sometime. But now, if we're to go to breakfast—*Baldanders!* Wake up! Come, Baldanders, come! Wake up!" He danced to the foot of the bed and grasped the giant by an ankle. "Baldanders! Don't take him by the shoulder, optimate!" (I had made no motion to do so.) "He thrashes about sometimes. BALDANDERS!"

The giant murmured and stirred.

"A new day, Baldanders! Still alive! Time to eat and defecate and make love—all that! Up now, or we'll never get home."

There was no sign that the giant had heard him. It was as if the murmur of the moment before had been only a protest voiced in a dream, or his death rattle. Dr. Talos seized the foul blankets with both hands and swept them back.

The monstrous shape of his partner lay revealed. He was even taller than I had supposed, nearly too tall for the bed, though he slept with his knees drawn almost to his chin. His shoulders were an ell across, high and hunched. His face I could not see; it lay buried in his pillow. There were strange scars about his neck and ears.

"Baldanders!"

His hair was grizzled, and despite the innkeeper's pretended error, very thick.

"Baldanders! Your pardon, optimate, but may I borrow that sword?"

"No," I said. "You may not."

"Oh, I'm not going to kill him, or anything of that sort. I only want to use the flat of it."

I shook my head, and when Dr. Talos saw I was still adamant, he began to rummage about the room. "Left my stick downstairs. Vile custom, they'll thieve it. I should learn to limp, I really should. There's nothing here at all."

He darted out the door, and was back in a moment carrying an ironwood walking stick with a gilt-brass knob. "Now then! *Baldanders!*"

The strokes fell upon the giant's broad back like the big raindrops that precede a thunderstorm.

Quite suddenly, the giant sat up. "I'm awake, Doctor." His face was large and coarse, but sensitive and sad as well. "Have you decided to kill me at last?"

"What are you talking about, Baldanders? Oh, you mean the optimate here. He's not going to do you any hurt—he shared the bed with you, and now he's going to join us at breakfast."

"He slept here, Doctor?"

Dr. Talos and I both nodded.

"Then I know whence my dreams rose."

I was still saturated with the sight of the huge women beneath the monstered sea, and so I asked what his dreams had been, though I was somewhat in awe of him.

"Of caverns below, where stone teeth dripped blood . . . Of arms dismembered found on sanded paths, and things that shook chains in the dark." He sat at the edge of the bed, cleaning sparse and surprisingly small teeth with one great finger.

Dr. Talos said, "Come on, both of you. If we're to eat and talk and get anything done today—why, we must be at it. Much to say and much to do."

Baldanders spat into the corner.

XVI

The Rag Shop

It was on that walk through the streets of still slumbering Nessus that my grief, which was to obsess me so often, first gripped me with all its force. When I had been imprisoned in our oubliette, the enormity of what I had done, and the enormity of the redress I felt sure I would make soon under Master Gurloes's hands, had dulled it. The day before, when I had swung down the Water Way, the joy of freedom and the poignancy of exile had driven it away. Now it seemed to me that there was no fact in all the world beyond the fact of Thecla's death. Each patch of darkness among the shadows reminded me of her hair; every glint of white recalled her skin. I could hardly restrain myself from rushing back to the Citadel to see if she might not still be sitting in her cell, reading by the light of the silver lamp.

We found a cafe whose tables were set along the margin of the street. It was still sufficiently early that there was very little traffic. A dead man (he had, I think, been suffocated with a lambrequin, there being those who practice that art) lay at the corner. Dr. Talos went through his pockets, but came back with empty hands.

"Now then," he said. "We must think. We must contrive a plan."

A waitress brought mugs of mocha, and Baldanders pushed one toward him. He stirred it with his forefinger.

"Friend Severian, perhaps I should elucidate our situation. Baldanders—he is my only patient—and I hail from the region about Lake Diuturna. Our home burned, and needing a trifle of money to set it right again we decided to venture abroad. My friend is a man of amazing strength. I assemble a crowd, he breaks some timbers and lifts ten men at once, and I sell my cures. Little enough, you will say. But there's more. I've a play, and we've assembled properties. When the situation is favorable, he and I enact certain scenes and even invite the participation of some of the audience. Now, friend, you say you are going north, and from your bed last night I take it you are not in funds. May I propose a joint venture?''

Baldanders, who appeared to have understood only the first part of his companion's speech, said slowly, ''It is not entirely destroyed. The walls are stone, very thick. Some of the vaults escaped.''

''Quite correct. We plan to restore the dear old place. But see our dilemma—we're now halfway on the return leg of our tour, and our accumulated capital is still far from sufficient. What I propose—''

The waitress, a thin young woman with straggling hair, came carrying a bowl of gruel for Baldanders, bread and fruit for me, and a pastry for Dr. Talos. ''What an attractive girl!'' he said.

She smiled at him.

''Can you sit down? We seem to be your only customers.''

After glancing in the direction of the kitchen, she shrugged and pulled over a chair.

''You might enjoy a bit of this—I'll be too busy talking to eat such a dry concoction. And a sip of mocha, if you don't object to drinking after me.''

She said, ''You'd think he'd let us eat for nothing, wouldn't you? But he won't. Charges everything at full price.''

''Ah! You're not the owner's daughter, then. I feared you were. Or his wife. How can he have allowed such a blossom to flourish unplucked?''

''I've only worked here about a month. The money they leave on the table's all I get. Take you three, now. If you don't give me anything, I will have served you for nothing.''

''Quite so, quite so! But what about this? What if we attempt to render you a rich gift, and you refuse it?'' Dr. Talos leaned toward her as he said this, and it struck me that his face was not only that of a fox (a comparison that was perhaps too easy to make because his bristling reddish eyebrows and sharp nose suggested it at once) but that of a stuffed fox. I have heard those who dig for their livelihood say there is no land anywhere in which they can trench without turning up the shards of the past. No matter where the spade turns the soil, it uncovers broken pavements and corroding metal; and scholars write that the kind of sand that artists call polychrome (because flecks of every color are mixed with its whiteness) is actually not sand at all, but the glass of the past, now pounded to powder by aeons of tumbling in the clamorous sea. If there are layers of reality beneath the reality we see, even as there are layers of history beneath the ground we walk upon, then in one of those more profound realities, Dr. Talos's face was a fox's mask on a wall, and I marveled to see it turn and bend now toward the woman, achieving by those motions, which made expression and thought appear to play across it with the shadows of the nose and brows, an amazing and realistic appearance of vivacity. "Would you refuse it?" he asked again, and I shook myself as though waking.

"What do you mean?" the woman wanted to know. "One of you is a carnifex. Are you talking about the gift of death? The Autarch, whose pores outshine the stars themselves, protects the lives of his subjects."

"The gift of death? Oh, no!" Dr. Talos laughed. "No, my dear, you've had that all your life. So has he. We wouldn't pretend to give you what is already yours. The gift we offer is beauty, with the fame and wealth that derive from it."

"If you're selling something, I haven't got any money."

"Selling? Not at all! Quite the contrary, we are offering you new employment. I am a thaumaturge, and these optimates are actors. Have you never wanted to go on the stage?"

"I thought you looked funny, the three of you."

"We stand in need of an ingenue. You may claim the position, if you wish. But you must come with us now—we've no time to waste, and we won't come this way again."

"Becoming an actress won't make me beautiful."

"I will make you beautiful because we require you as an actress. It is one of my powers." He stood up. "Now or not at all. Will you come?"

The waitress rose too, still looking at his face. "I have to go to my room . . ."

"What do you own but dross? I must cast the glamour and teach you your lines, all in a day. I will not wait."

"Give me the money for your breakfasts, and I'll tell him I'm leaving."

"Nonsense! As a member of our company, you must assist in conserving the funds we will require for your costumes. Not to mention that you ate my pastry. Pay for it yourself."

For an instant she hesitated. Baldanders said, "You may trust him. The doctor has his own way of looking at the world, but he lies less than people believe."

The deep, slow voice seemed to reassure her. "All right," she said, "I'll go."

In a few moments, the four of us were several streets away, walking past shops that were still for the most part shuttered. When we had gone some distance, Dr. Talos announced, "And now, my dear friends, we must separate. I will devote my time to the enhancement of this sylph. Baldanders, you must get our collapsing proscenium and the other properties from the inn where you and Severian spent the night—I trust that will present no difficulties. Severian, we will perform, I think, at Ctesiphon's Cross. Do you know the spot?"

I nodded, though I had no notion of where it might be. The truth was that I had no intention of rejoining them.

Now, as Dr. Talos quick-stepped away with the waitress trotting behind him, I found myself alone with Baldanders on the deserted street. Anxious that he leave too, I asked him where he meant to go. It was more like talking to a monument than speaking with a man.

"There is a park near the river where one may sleep by day, though not by night. When it is nearly dark, I will awaken and collect our belongings."

"I'm afraid I'm not sleepy. I'm going to look around the city."

"I will see you then, at Ctesiphon's Cross."

For some reason I felt he knew what was in my mind. "Yes," I said. "Of course."

His eyes were dull as an ox's as he turned away to lumber with long steps toward Gyoll. Since Baldanders's park lay east and Dr. Talos had taken the waitress west, I resolved to walk north and so continue my journey toward Thrax, the City of Windowless Rooms.

Meanwhile, Nessus, the City Imperishable (the city in which I had lived all my life, though I had seen so little of it), lay all about me. Along a wide, flint-paved avenue I walked, not knowing or caring whether it was a side street or the principal one of the quarter. There were raised paths for pedestrians at either side, and a third in the center, where it served to divide the northbound traffic from the southbound.

To the left and right, buildings seemed to spring from the ground like grain too closely planted, shouldering one another for a place; and what buildings they were—nothing so large as the Great Keep and nothing so old; none, I think, with walls like the metal walls of our tower, five paces through; yet the Citadel had nothing to compare with them in color or originality of conception, nothing so novel and fantastic as each of these structures was, though each stood among a hundred others. As is the fashion in some parts of the city, most of these buildings had shops in their lower levels, though they had not been built for the shops but as guildhalls, basilicas, arenas, conservatories, treasuries, oratories, artellos, asylums, manufacturies, conventicles, hospices, lazarets, mills, refectories, deadhouses, abattoirs, and playhouses. Their architecture reflected these functions, and a thousand conflicting tastes. Turrets and minarets bristled; lanterns, domes, and rotundas soothed; flights of steps as steep as ladders ascended sheer walls; and balconies wrapped facades and sheltered them in the par-terre privacies of citrons and pomegranates.

I was wondering at these hanging gardens amid the forest of pink and white marble, red sardonyx, blue-gray, and cream, and black bricks, and green and yellow and tyrian tiles, when the sight of a lansquenet guarding the entrance to a casern reminded me of the promise I had made the officer of the peltasts the night before. Since I had little money and was well aware that I would require the warmth of my guild cloak by night, the best plan seemed to be to buy a voluminous mantle of some cheap stuff that could be worn over it. Shops were opening, but those that sold clothing all appeared to sell what would not fit my purpose, and at prices greater than I could afford.

The idea of working at my profession before I reached Thrax had not yet occurred to me; if it had, I would have dismissed it, supposing that there would be so little call for a torturer's services that it would be impractical for me to seek out those who required them. I believed, in short, that the three asimis, and the orichalks and aes in my pocket would have to carry me all the way to Thrax; and I had no idea of the size of the rewards that would be proffered me. Thus I stared at balmacaans and surtouts, dolmans and jerkins of paduasoy, matelasse, and a hundred other costly fabrics without ever going into the places that displayed them, or even stopping to examine them.

Soon my attention was seduced by other goods. Though I knew nothing of it at the time, thousands of mercenaries were outfitting themselves for the summer campaign. There were bright military capes and saddle blankets, saddles with armored pommels to protect the loins, red forage caps, long-shafted khetens, fans of silver foil for signaling, bows curved and recurved for use by cavalry, arrows in matched sets of ten and twenty, bow cases of boiled leather decorated with gilt studs and mother-of-pearl, and archers' guards to protect the left wrist from the bowstring. When I saw all these, I remembered what Master Palaemon had said before my masking about following the drum; and although I had held the matrosses of the Citadel in some contempt, I seemed to hear the long rattle of the call to parade, and the bright challenge the trumpets sent from the battlements.

Just when I had been wholly distracted from my search, a slender woman of twenty or a little more came out of one of the dark shops to unfasten the gratings. She wore a pavonine brocade gown of amazing richness and raggedness, and as I watched her, the sun touched a rent just below her waist, turning the skin there to palest gold.

I cannot explain the desire I felt for her, then and afterward. Of the many women I have known, she was, perhaps, the least beautiful—less graceful than her I have loved most, less voluptuous than another, less reginal far than Thecla. She was of average height, with a short nose, wide cheekbones, and the elongated brown eyes that often accompany them. I saw her lift the grating, and I loved her with a love that was deadly and yet not serious.

Of course I went to her. I could no more have resisted her than I could have resisted the blind greed of Urth if I had tumbled over a cliff. I did not know what to say to her, and I was terrified that she would recoil in horror at the sight of my sword and fuligin cloak. But she smiled and actually seemed to admire my appearance. After a moment, when I said nothing, she asked what I wanted; and I asked if she knew where I might buy a mantle.

"Are you sure you need one?" Her voice was deeper than I had expected. "You've such a beautiful cloak now. May I touch it?"

"Please. If you wish to."

She took up the edge and rubbed the fabric gently between her palms. "I've never seen such a black—so dark you can't see folds in it. It makes my hand look as though it's disappeared. And that sword. Is that an opal?"

"Would you like to examine that too?"

"No, no. Not at all. But if you really want a mantle . . ." She gestured toward the window, and I saw that it was filled with articles of worn clothing of every kind, jelabs, capotes, smocks, cymars, and so on. "Very inexpensive. Really reasonable. If you'll just go in, I'm sure you'll find what you want." I entered through a jingling door, but the young woman did not (as I had so much hoped she would) follow me inside.

The interior was dim, yet as soon as I looked about I thought I understood why the woman had not been disturbed by my appearance. The man behind the counter was more frightening than any torturer. His face was a skeleton's or nearly so, a face with dark pits for eyes, shrunken cheeks, and a lipless mouth. If it had not moved and spoken, I would not have believed he was a living man at all, but a corpse left erect behind the counter in fulfilment of the morbid wish of some past owner.

XVII

The Challenge

Yet it did move, turning to look at me as I came in; and it did speak. "Very fine. Yes, very fine. Your cloak, optimate—may I see it?"

I walked across a floor of worn and uneven tiles to him. A slash of red sunshine alive with swarming dust stood stiff as a blade between us.

"Your garment, optimate." I caught up my cloak and extended my left hand, and he touched the fabric much as the young woman had outside. "Yes, very fine. Soft. Wool-like, yet softer, much softer. A blend of linen and vicuna? And wonderful color. A torturer's vesture. One doubts the real ones were half so fine, but who can argue with a textile like that?" He ducked beneath his counter and emerged with a handful of rags. "Might I examine the sword? I'll be extremely careful, I promise you."

I unsheathed *Terminus Est* and laid her on the rags. He bent over her, neither touching her nor speaking. By that time my eyes had become accustomed to the dimness of the shop, and I noticed a narrow black ribbon that stretched forward a finger's width from the hair above his ears. "You are wearing a mask," I said.

"Three chrisos. For the sword. Another for the cloak."

"I didn't come here to sell," I told him. "Take it off."

"If you like. All right, four chrisos for the sword." He lifted his hands and the death's-head fell into them. His real face, flat-cheeked and tanned, was remarkably like that of the young woman I had seen outside.

"I want to buy a mantle."

"Five chrisos for it. That's positively my last offer. You'll have to give me a day to raise the money."

"I told you, this sword is not for sale." I picked up *Terminus Est* and resheathed her.

"Six." Reaching across the counter, he took me by the arm. "That's more than it's worth. Listen, it's your last chance. I mean it. Six."

"I came in to buy a mantle. Your sister, as I would assume she was, said you would have one at a reasonable price."

He sighed. "All right, I'll sell you a mantle. Will you tell me first where you got that sword?"

"It was given me by a master of our guild." I saw an expression I could not quite identify flicker across his face, and I asked, "You don't believe me?"

"I do believe you, that's the trouble. Just what are you?"

"A journeyman of the torturers. We don't often get to this side of the river, or come this far north. But are you really so surprised?"

He nodded. "It's like encountering a psychopomp. Can I ask why you're in this quarter of the city?"

"You may, but it's the last question I'm going to answer. I'm on my way to Thrax, to take up an assignment there."

"Thank you," he said. "I won't pry any more. I don't have to, really. Now since you'll want to surprise your friends when you take off your mantle—am I right?—it ought to be of some color that will contrast with your vesture. White might be good, but it's a rather dramatic color itself, and terribly hard to keep clean. What about a dull brown?"

"The ribbons that held your mask," I said. "They're still there."

He was dragging down boxes from behind his counter and did not reply. After a moment or two we were interrupted by the tinkling of the bell above the door. The new customer was a youth whose face was hidden in an inlaid close helmet, of which down-curving and intertwined horns formed the visor. He wore armor of lacquered leather; a golden chimera with the blank, staring face of a madwoman fluttered on his breastplate.

"Yes, hipparch." The shopkeeper dropped his boxes to make a servile bow. "How may I assist you?"

A gauntleted hand reached toward me, the fingers pinched as though to give me a coin.

"Take it," the shopkeeper said in a frightened whisper. "Whatever it is."

I extended my own hand, and received a shining black seed the size of a raisin. I heard the shopkeeper gasp; the armored figure turned and went out.

When he was gone, I laid the seed on the counter. The shopkeeper squeaked, "Don't try to pass it to me!" and backed away.

"What is it?"

"You don't know? The stone of the avern. What have you done to offend an officer of the Household Troops?"

"Nothing. Why did he give me this?"

"You've been challenged. You're called out."

"To monomachy? Impossible. I'm not of the contending class."

His shrug was more eloquent than words. "You'll have to fight or they'll have you assassinated. The only question is whether you've really offended the hipparch, or if there's some highly placed official of the House Absolute behind this."

As clearly as I saw the shopkeeper, I saw Vodalus in the necropolis standing his ground against the three volunteer guards; and though all prudence told me to toss aside the avern stone and flee the city, I could not do it. Someone—perhaps the Autarch himself or shadowy Father Inire—had learned the truth about Thecla's death, and now sought to destroy me without disgracing the guild. Very well, I would fight. If I were victorious he might reconsider; if I were killed, that would be no more than just. Still thinking of Vodalus's slender blade, I said, "The only sword I understand is this one."

"You won't engage with swords—in fact, it would be best if you left that with me."

"Absolutely not."

He sighed again. "I see you know nothing about these matters, yet you are going to fight for your life at twilight. Very well, you are my customer, and I've never yet abandoned a customer. You wanted a mantle. Here." He strode to the back of his shop and came forward carrying a garment the color of dead leaves. "Try this one. It will be four orichalks if it fits."

A mantle so large and loose could not but fit unless it was grossly short or long. The price seemed excessive, but I paid, and in donning the mantle took one step further toward becoming the actor that day seemed to wish to force me to become. Indeed, I was already taking part in more dramas than I realized.

"Now then," the shopkeeper said, "I must stay here to look after things, but I'll send my sister to help you get your avern. She has often gone to the Sanguinary Field, so perhaps she can also teach you the rudiments of combat with it."

"Did someone speak of me?" The young woman I had met at the front of the shop now came from one of the dark storerooms at its rear. With her upturned nose and strangely tilted eyes, she looked so much like her brother I felt sure they were twins, but the slender figure and delicate features that seemed incongruent in him were compelling in her. Her brother must have explained what had befallen me. I do not know, because I did not hear it. I was looking only at her.

Now I begin again. It has been a long time (twice I have heard the guard changed outside my study door) since I wrote the lines you read only a moment before. I am not certain it is right to record these scenes, which perhaps are important only to me, in so much detail. I might easily have condensed everything: I saw a shop and went in; I was challenged by an officer of the Septentrions; the shopkeeper sent his sister to help me pluck the poisoned flower. I have spent weary days in reading the histories of my predecessors, and they consist of little but such accounts. For example, of Ymar:

> Disguising himself, he ventured into the countryside, where he spied a muni meditating beneath a plane tree. The Autarch joined him and sat with his back to the trunk until Urth had begun to spurn the sun. Troopers bearing an oriflamme galloped past, a merchant drove a mule staggering under gold, a beautiful woman rode the shoulders of eunuchs, and at last a dog trotted through the dust. Ymar rose and followed the dog, laughing.

Supposing this anecdote to be true, how easy it is to explain: the Autarch had demonstrated that he chose his active life by an act of will, and not because of the seductions of the world.

But Thecla had had many teachers, each of whom would explain the same fact in a different way. Here, then, a second teacher might say that the Autarch was proof against those things that attract common men, but powerless to control his love of the hunt.

And a third, that the Autarch wished to show his contempt for the muni, who had remained silent when he might have poured forth enlightenment and received more. That he could not do by leaving when there was none to share the road, since solitude has great attractions for the wise. Nor could he when the soldiers passed, nor the merchant with his wealth, nor the woman, for unenlightened men desire all those things, and the muni would have thought him one more such man.

And a fourth, that the Autarch accompanied the dog because it went forth alone, the soldiers having other soldiers, the merchant his mule and the mule his merchant, and the woman her slaves; while the muni did not go forth.

Yet why did Ymar laugh? Who shall say? Did the merchant follow the soldiers to buy their booty? Did the woman follow the merchant to sell her kisses and her loins? Was the dog of the hunting kind, or such a short-limbed one as women keep to bark lest someone fondle them while they sleep? Who now shall say? Ymar is dead, and such memories of his as lived for a time in the blood of his successors are long faded.

So mine in time shall fade too. Of this I feel sure: not one of the explanations for the behavior of Ymar was correct. The truth, whatever it may have been, was simpler and more subtle. Of me it might be asked why I accepted the shopkeeper's sister as my companion—I who in all my life had had no true companion. And who, reading only of "the shopkeeper's sister," would understand why I remained with her after what is, at this point in my own story, about to happen? No one, surely.

I have said that I cannot explain my desire for her, and it is true. I loved her with a love thirsty and desperate. I felt that we two might commit some act so atrocious that the world, seeing us, would find it irresistible.

No intellect is needed to see those figures who wait beyond the void of death—every child is aware of them, blazing with glories dark or bright, wrapped in authority older than the universe. They are the stuff of our earliest dreams, as of our dying visions. Rightly we feel our lives guided by them, and rightly too we feel how little we matter to them, the builders of the unimaginable, the fighters of wars beyond the totality of existence.

The difficulty lies in learning that we ourselves encompass forces equally great. We say, "I will," and "I will not," and imagine ourselves (though we obey the orders of some prosaic person every day) our own masters, when the truth is that our masters are sleeping. One wakes within us and we are ridden like beasts, though the rider is but some hitherto unguessed part of ourselves.

Perhaps, indeed, that is the explanation of the story of Ymar. Who can say?

However that may be, I let the shopkeeper's sister help me adjust the mantle. It could be drawn tightly about the neck, and when it was worn so, my fuligin guild cloak was invisible beneath it. Still without revealing myself, I could reach through the front or through slits at the sides. I unfastened *Terminus Est* from her baldric and carried her like a staff for as long as I wore that mantle, and because her sheath covered most of her guard and was tipped with dark iron, many of the people who saw me no doubt thought it was one.

It was the only time in my life when I have covered the habit of the guild with a disguise. I have heard it said that one always feels a fool in them, whether they succeed or not, and surely I felt a fool in that one. And yet it was hardly a disguise at all. Those wide, old-fashioned mantles originated with shepherds (who wear them still), and were passed from them to the military in the days when the fighting with the Ascians took place here in the cool south. From the army they were taken up by religious pilgrims, who no doubt found a garment that could be converted into a more-or-less-satisfactory little tent very practical. The decline of religion has no doubt done much to extinguish them in Nessus, where I never saw any other than the one I wore myself. If I had known more about them when I put on mine in the rag shop, I would have bought a soft, wide-brimmed hat to go with it; but I did not, and the shopkeeper's sister told me I looked a good palmer. No doubt she said it with that twinkle of mockery with which she said everything else, but I was concerned with my appearance and failed to notice it. I told her and her brother that I wished I knew more of religion.

Both smiled, and the brother said, ''If you mention it first, no one will want to talk about it. Besides, you can get the reputation of being a good fellow by wearing that and *not* talking about it. When you meet someone you don't want to talk to at all, beg alms.''

So I became, in appearance at least, a pilgrim bound for some vague northern shrine. Have I said that time turns our lies into truths?

XVIII

The Destruction of the Altar

The hush of early morning had vanished while I was in the rag shop. Wains and drays rumbled by in an avalanche of beasts, wood, and iron; the shopkeeper's sister and I had no more than stepped out of the door than I heard a flier skimming among the towers of the city. I looked up in time to see it, sleek as a raindrop on a windowpane.

"That's probably the officer who called you out," she remarked. "He'll be on his way back to the House Absolute. A hipparch of the Septentrion Guard—isn't that what Agilus said?"

"Is that your brother? Yes, something like that. What is your own name?"

"Agia. And you know nothing of monomachy? And have me for an instructor? Well, high Hypogeon help you. We'll have to go to the Botanic Gardens to begin with and cut you an avern. Fortunately they're not too far from here. Do you have enough money for us to take a fiacre?"

"I suppose so. If it is necessary."

"Then you're really not an armiger in costume. You're a—whatever you are."

"A torturer. Yes. When am I supposed to meet the hipparch?"

"Not until late afternoon, when the fighting begins at the Sanguinary Field and the avern opens its flower. We've plenty of time, but I think we'd better use it in getting you one and teaching you how to fight with it." A fiacre drawn by a pair of onegars was dodging toward us, and she waved to it. "You're going to be killed, you know."

"From what you say, it seems very likely."

"It's practically certain, so don't worry about your money." Agia stepped out into the traffic, looking for a moment (so finely chiseled was that delicate face, so graceful the curve of her body as she lifted an arm) like a memorial statue to the unknown woman on foot. I thought she was certain to be killed herself. The fiacre drew up to her with the skittish animals dancing to one side as though she were a thyacine, and she vaulted in. Light as she was, her weight made the little vehicle rock. I climbed in beside her, where we sat with our hips pressed together. The driver glanced back at us, Agia said, "The landing for the Botanic Gardens," and we jolted off. "So dying doesn't bother you—that's refreshing."

I braced myself with a hand on the back of the driver's bench. "Surely that's not unusual. There must be thousands, and perhaps millions of people like me. People accustomed to death, who feel that the only part of their lives that really mattered is over."

The sun was now just above the tallest spires, and the flooding light that turned the dusty pavement to red gold made me feel philosophical. In the brown book in my sabretache there was the tale of an angel (perhaps actually one of the winged women warriors who are said to serve the Autarch) who, coming to Urth on some petty mission or other, was struck by a child's arrow and died. With her gleaming robes all dyed by her heart's blood even as the boulevards were stained by the expiring life of the sun, she encountered Gabriel himself. His sword blazed in one hand, his great two-headed ax swung in the other, and across his back, suspended on the rainbow, hung the very battle horn of Heaven. "Where wend you, little one," asked Gabriel, "with your breast more scarlet than the robin's?" "I am killed," the angel said, "and I return to merge my substance once more with the Pancreator." "Do not be absurd. You are an angel, a pure spirit, and cannot die." "But I am dead," said the angel, "nevertheless. You have observed the wasting of my blood—do you not observe also that it no longer issues in straining spurtings, but only seeps sluggishly? Note the pallor of my countenance. Is not the touch of an angel warm and bright? Take my hand and you will imagine you hold a horror new dragged from some stagnant pool. Taste my breath—is it not fetid, foul, and nidorous?" Gabriel answered nothing, and at last the angel said, "Brother and better, even if I have not convinced you with all my proofs, I pray you stand aside. I would rid the universe of my presence." "I am convinced indeed," Gabriel said, stepping from the other's way. "It is only that I was thinking that had I known we might perish, I would not at all times have been so bold."

To Agia I said, "I feel like the archangel in the story—if I had known I could spend my life so easily and so soon, I would not—probably—have done it. Do you know the legend? But I have made my decisions now, and there's nothing more to say or do. This afternoon the Septentrion will kill me with what? A plant? A flower? In some way I don't understand. A short time ago, I thought I could go to a place called Thrax and live there whatever life there was to be lived. Well, last night I roomed with a giant. One is not more fantastical than the other."

She did not reply, and after a time I asked, "What is that building over there? The one with the vermilion roof and the forked columns? I think there's allspice pounded in the mortar. At least, I smell something of that sort from it."

"The mensal of the monachs. Do you know you are a frightening man? When you entered our shop, I thought you only another young armiger in motley. Then when I found you really were a torturer, I thought it couldn't really be so bad after all—that you were only a young man like other young men."

"And you have known a great many young men, I imagine." The truth was that I was hoping she had. I wanted her to be more experienced than I; and though I did not for an instant think myself pure, I wished to think her less pure still.

"But there is something more to you after all. You have the face of someone who stands to inherit two palatinates and an isle somewhere I never heard of, and the manners of a shoemaker, and when you say you're not afraid to die, you think you mean it, and under that you believe you don't. But you do, at the very bottom. It wouldn't bother you a bit to chop off my head either, would it?"

Around us swirled traffic of every sort: machines, wheeled and wheelless vehicles pulled by animals and slaves, walkers, and riders on the backs of dromedaries, oxen, metamynodons, and hackneys. Now an open fiacre like our own drew up beside us. Agia leaned toward the couple it carried and shouted, "We'll distance you!"

"Where bound?" the man called back, and I recognized Sieur Racho, whom I had once met when I had been sent to Master Ultan for books.

I gripped Agia by the arm. "Are you mad, or is he?"

"The Garden Landing, for a chrisos!"

The other vehicle tore away with ours behind it. "Faster!" Agia shouted to our driver. Then to me: "Have you a dagger? It's best to put the point to his back, so he can say he drove under threat of annihilation if we're stopped."

"Why are you doing this?"

"As a test. No one will believe your disguise. But everyone will believe you're an armiger in fancy dress. I've just proved it." (We careened about a dray loaded with sand.) "Besides, we'll win. I know this driver and his team's fresh. The other's been carting that whore for half the night.''

I realized then that I would be expected to give Agia the money if we won, and that the other woman would claim my (nonexistent) chrisos from Racho if they did. Yet how sweet to humble him! Speed and the nearness of death (for I felt certain I would indeed be slain by the hipparch) made me more reckless than I had ever been in my life. I drew *Terminus Est*, and thanks to the length of her blade I could reach the onegars easily. Their flanks were already soaked with sweat, and the shallow cuts I made there must have burned like flames. ''That's better than any dagger,'' I told Agia.

The crowd parted like water before the drivers' whips, mothers clasping their children as they fled, soldiers vaulting on their spears to the safety of windowsills. The conditions of the race favored us: the fiacre ahead to some extent cleared our path, and it was more impeded by other vehicles than we. Still we gained only slowly, and to get a few ells' advantage, our driver, who no doubt anticipated a rich tip if he won, sent the onegars hurtling up a flight of broad chalcedony steps. Marbles and monuments, pillars and pilasters, seemed thrown at our faces. We crashed through the green wall of a hedge as high as a house, overturned a cartload of comfits, dove through an arch and down a stair wound in a half turn, and were in the street again without ever knowing whose patio we had violated.

A baker's barrow drawn by sheep ambled into the narrow space between our vehicle and the other, and our big rear wheel jolted it, sending a shower of fresh bread into the street and throwing Agia's slight body against mine so pleasantly that I put an arm about it and held it there. I had clasped women so before—Thecla often, and hired bodies in the town. There was new bitter-sweetness in this, born of the cruel attraction Agia held for me. ''I'm glad you did that,'' she said in my ear. ''I hate men who grab me,'' and covered my face with kisses.

The driver looked back with a grin of triumph, letting the maddened team choose its own path. ''Gone down the Twisted Way—got them now—across the common and reach them by a hundred ells.''

The fiacre reeled and plunged into a narrow gateway in a barrier of shrubbery. An immense building loomed before us. The driver tried to turn his animals, but it was too late. We hit its side; it gave like the fabric of a dream, and we were in a cavernous space, dimly lit and smelling of hay. Ahead was a stepped altar as large as a cottage and dotted with blue lights. I saw it and realized I was seeing it too well—our driver had been swept out of his seat or had jumped clear. Agia shrieked.

We crashed into the altar. There was a confusion of flying objects impossible to describe, the sense of everything whirling and tumbling and never colliding, as in the chaos before creation. The ground seemed to leap at me; it struck with an impact that set my ears humming.

I had been holding *Terminus Est*, I think, while I flew through the air, but she was no longer in my hand. When I tried to get up to look for her, I had no breath and no strength. Somewhere far off, a man shouted. I rolled on my side, then managed to get my lifeless legs beneath me.

We seemed to be near the center of the building, which was as big around as the Great Keep and yet completely empty: without interior walls, stairs, or furniture of any kind. Through the golden, dusty air I could see crooked pillars that seemed of painted wood. Lamps, mere points of light, hung a chain or more overhead. Far above them, a many-colored roof rippled and snapped in a wind I could not feel.

I stood on straw, and straw was spread everywhere in an endless yellow carpet, like the field of a titan after harvest. All about me were the battens of which the altar had been constructed: fragments of thin wood braved with gold leaf and set with turquoises and violet amethysts. With some vague idea of finding my sword, I began to walk, stumbling almost at once over the smashed body of the fiacre. One onegar lay not far from it; I recall thinking it must have broken its neck. Someone called, "Torturer!" and I looked around and saw Agia—standing erect, though shakily. I asked if she were all right.

"Alive, anyway, but we must leave this place at once. Is that animal dead?"

I nodded.

"I could have ridden on it. Now you'll have to carry me if you can. I don't think my right leg will bear my weight." She tottered as she spoke, and I had to spring to her and catch her to keep her from falling. "Now we have to go," she said. "Look around . . . can you see a door? Quickly!"

I could not. "Why is it so urgent that we leave?"

"Use your nose if you can't use your eyes to see this floor."

I sniffed. The odor in the air was no longer straw, but straw burning; at almost the same instant I saw the flames, bright in the gloom, but still so small that a few moments before they must have been mere sparks. I tried to run, but could manage nothing better than a limping walk. "Where are we?"

"It's the Cathedral of the Pelerines—some call it the Cathedral of the Claw. The Pelerines are a band of priestesses who travel the continent. They never—"

Agia broke off because we were approaching a cluster of scarlet-clad people. Or perhaps they were approaching us, for they seemed to me to have appeared in the middle distance without warning. The men had shaven heads and held gleaming scimitars curved like the young moon and blazing with gilding; a woman with the towering height of an exultant cradled a sheathed two-handed sword: my own *Terminus Est*. She wore a hood and a narrow cape that trailed long tassels.

Agia began, "Our animals ran wild, Holy Domnicellae . . ."

"That is of no moment," the woman who held my sword said. There was much beauty in her, but it was not the beauty of women who quench desire. "This belongs to the man carrying you. Tell him to set you on your feet and take it. You can walk."

"A little. Do as she says, Torturer."

"Don't you know his name?"

"He told me, but I've forgotten."

I said, "Severian," and steadied her with one hand while I accepted *Terminus Est* with the other.

"Use it to end quarrels," the woman in scarlet said. "Not to begin them."

"The straw floor of this great tent is on fire, Chatelaine. Do you know it?"

"It will be extinguished. The sisters and our servants are crushing the embers now." She paused, her gaze flickering from Agia to me and back to Agia again. "In the remains of our high altar, which your vehicle destroyed, we found only one thing that seemed yours, and likely to be of value to you—that sword. We have returned it. Will you now also return to us anything of value to us you may have found?"

I remembered the amethysts. "I found nothing of value, Chatelaine." Agia shook her head, and I continued, "There were splinters of wood set with precious stones, but I left them where they had fallen."

The men shifted the hilts of their weapons in the hands and sought good footing, but the tall woman stood motionless, staring at me, then at Agia, then at me once more. "Come to me, Severian."

I came forward, a matter of three or four paces. It was a great temptation to draw *Terminus Est* as a defense against the men's blades, but I resisted it. Their mistress took my wrists in her hands and looked into my eyes. Her own were calm, and in the strange light seemed hard as beryls. "There is no guilt in him," she said.

One of the men muttered, "You are mistaken, Domnicellae."

"No guilt, I say. Step back, Severian, and let the woman come forward."

I did as she told me, and Agia limped to within a long pace of her.

When she would not come nearer, the tall woman came to her and took her wrists as she had mine. After a moment, she glanced toward the other women who had waited behind the swordsmen. Before I realized what was happening, two of them seized Agia's gown and drew it over her head and away. One said, "Nothing, Mother."

"I think this the day foretold."

Her hands crossed over her breasts, Agia whispered to me, "These Pelerines are insane. Everyone knows it, and if I had had more time I would have told you so."

The tall woman said, "Return her rags. The Claw has not vanished in living memory, but it does so at will and it would be neither possible nor permissible for us to stop it."

One of the women murmured, "We may find it in the wreckage still, Mother." A second added, "Should they not be made to pay?" "Let us kill them," a man said.

The tall woman gave no indication that she had heard any of them. She was already leaving us, seeming to glide across the straw. The women followed her, looking at one another, and the men lowered their gleaming blades and backed away.

Agia was struggling into her gown. I asked her what she knew of the Claw, and who these Pelerines were.

"Get me out of here, Severian, and I'll tell you. It isn't lucky to talk of them in their own place. Is that a tear in the wall over there?"

We walked in the direction she had indicated, stumbling sometimes in the soft straw. There was no opening, but I was able to lift the edge of the silken wall enough for us to slip under.

XIX

The Botanic Gardens

The sunlight was blinding; it seemed as if we had stepped from twilight into full day. Golden particles of straw swam in the crisp air about us.

"That's better," Agia said. "Wait a moment now and let me get my bearings. I think the Adamnian Steps will be to our right. Our driver wouldn't have gone down them—or perhaps he would, the fellow was mad—but they should take us to the landing by the shortest route. Give me your arm again, Severian. My leg's not quite recovered."

We were walking on grass now, and I saw that the tent-cathedral had been pitched on a champian surrounded by semi-fortified houses; its insubstantial belfries looked down upon their parapets. A wide, paved street bordered the open lawn, and when we reached it I asked again who the Pelerines were.

Agia looked sidelong at me. "You must forgive me, but I don't find it easy to talk of professional virgins to a man who's just seen me naked. Though under other circumstances it might be different." She drew a deep breath. "I don't really know a great deal about them, but we have some of their habits in the shop, and I asked my brother about them once, and after that paid attention to whatever I heard. It's a popular costume for masques—all that red.

"Anyway, they are an order of conventionals, as no doubt you've already discerned. The red is for the descending light of the New Sun, and they descend on landowners, traveling around the country with their cathedral and seizing enough to set it up. Their order claims to possess the most valuable relic in existence, the Claw of the Conciliator, so the red may be for the Wounds of the Claw as well."

Trying to be facetious I said, "I didn't know he had claws."

"It isn't a real claw—it's said to be a gem. You must have heard of it. I don't understand why it's called the Claw, and I doubt that those priestesses do themselves. But assuming it to have had some real association with the Conciliator, you can appreciate its importance. After all, our knowledge of him now is purely historical—meaning that we either confirm or deny that he was in contact with our race in the remote past. If the Claw is what the Pelerines represent it to be, then he once lived, though he may be dead now.''

A startled glance from a woman carrying a dulcimer told me the mantle I had bought from Agia's brother was in disarray, permitting the fuligin of my guild cloak (which must have looked like mere empty darkness to the poor woman) to be seen through the opening. As I rearranged it and reclasped the fibula I said, ''Like all these religious arguments, this one gets less significant as we continue. Supposing the Conciliator to have walked among us eons ago, and to be dead now, of what importance is he save to historians and fanatics? I value his legend as a part of the sacred past, but it seems to me that it is the legend that matters today, and not the Conciliator's dust.''

Agia rubbed her hands, seeming to warm them in the sunlight. ''Supposing him—we turn at this corner, Severian, you may see the head of the stair, if you'll look, there where the statues of the eponyms stand—supposing him to have lived, he was by definition the Master of Power. Which means the transcendence of reality, and includes the negation of time. Isn't that correct?''

I nodded.

''Then there is nothing to prevent him, from a position, say, of thirty thousand years ago, coming into what we call the present. Dead or not, if he ever existed, he could be around the next bend of the street or the next turn of the week.''

We had reached the beginning of the stair. The steps were of stone as white as salt, sometimes so gradual that several strides were needed to go from one descent to the next, sometimes almost as abrupt as a ladder. Confectioners, sellers of apes, and the like had set up their stands here and there. For whatever reason, it was very pleasant to discuss mysteries with Agia while descending these steps, and I said, ''All this because those women say they possess one of his glittering fingernails. I suppose it performs miraculous cures?''

''On occasion, so they claim. It also forgives injuries, raises the dead, draws new races of beings from the soil, purifies lust, and so on. All the things he is supposed to have done himself.''

''You're laughing at me now.''

''No, only laughing at the sunshine—you know what it is supposed to do to women's faces.''

"Make them brown."

"Make them ugly. To begin with, it dries the skin and creates wrinkles and so on. Then too, it shows up every little defect. Urvasi loved Pururavas, you know, before she saw him in a bright light. Anyway, I felt it on my face, and I was thinking, 'I don't care for *you*. I'm still too young to worry about you, and next year I'll get a wide hat from our stock.' "

Agia's face was far from perfect now in the clear sunshine, but she had nothing to fear from it. My hunger fed at least as ravenously upon her imperfections. She possessed the hopeful, hopeless courage of the poor, which is perhaps the most appealing of all human qualities; and I rejoiced in the flaws that made her more real to me.

"Anyway," she continued, squeezing my hand, "I have to admit I've never understood why people like the Pelerines always think ordinary people have to have their lust purified. In my experience, they control it well enough by themselves, and just about every day, too. What most of us need is to find someone we can unbottle it with."

"Then you care that I love you." I was only half joking.

"Every woman cares if she's loved, and the more men who love her, the better! But I don't choose to love you in return, if that's what you mean. It would be so easy today, going around the city with you like this. But then if you're killed this evening, I'll feel badly for a fortnight."

"So will I," I said.

"No you won't. You won't even care. Not about that or anything, not ever again. Being dead doesn't hurt, as you of all people should know."

"I'm almost inclined to think this whole affair is some trick of yours, or of your brother's. You were outside when the Septentrion came—did you tell him something to inflame him against me? Is he your lover?"

Agia laughed at that, her teeth flashing in the sun. "Look at me. I have a brocade gown, but you've seen what's beneath it. My feet are bare. Do you see rings or earrings? A silver lamia twined about my neck? Are my arms constricted with circlets of gold? If not, you may safely assume I have no officer of the Household Troops for my paramour. There's an old sailor, ugly and poor, who presses me to live with him. Other than that, well, Agilus and I own our shop. It was bequeathed to us by our mother, and it's free of debt only because we can find no one who's enough of a fool to lend anything on it. Sometimes we rip up something from our stock and sell it to the paper-makers so we can buy a bowl of lentils to divide between us."

"You should eat well tonight anyway," I told her. "I gave your brother a good price for this mantle."

"What?" Her good humor seemed to have returned. She took a step back and feigned astonishment with an open mouth. "You won't buy me a supper this evening? After I've spent the day counseling you and guiding you about?"

"Involving me in the destruction of the altar those Pelerines had erected."

"I'm sorry about that. I really am. I didn't want you to tire your legs—you'll need them when you fight. Then those others came up, and I thought I saw a chance for you to make some money."

Her look had left my face and come to rest on one of the brutal busts that flanked the stair. I asked, "Is that really all there was to it?"

"To confess the truth, I wanted them to go on thinking you might be an armiger. Armigers go about in fancy dress so much because they're always going to fetes and tournaments, and you have the face. That's why I thought so myself when I first saw you. And you see, if you were, then I was someone that somebody like that, an armiger and probably the bastard of an exultant, might care for. Even if it was only a kind of joke. I had no way of knowing what would happen."

"I understand," I said. Suddenly laughter overcame me. "What fools we must have looked, jolting along in the fiacre."

"If you understand, then kiss me."

I stared at her.

"Kiss me! How many chances have you left? I'll give you more, what you want—" She paused, then laughed too. "After supper, perhaps. If we can find a private spot, though it won't be good for your fighting." She threw herself into my arms then, rising on her toes to press my lips. Her breasts were firm and high, and I could feel the motion of her hips.

"There now." She pushed me away. "Look down there, Severian. Between the pylons. What do you see?"

Water glimmered like a mirror in the sun. "The river."

"Yes, Gyoll. Now to the left. Because there are so many nenuphars, the island is hard to see. But the lawn is a lighter, brighter green. Don't you see the glass? Where it catches the light?"

"I see something. Is the building all glass?"

She nodded. "That's the Botanic Gardens, where we're going. They'll let you cut your avern there—all you have to do is demand it as your right."

We made the rest of the descent in silence. The Adamnian Steps wind back and forth across a long hillside, and they are a favored place for strollers, who often hire a ride to the top and descend. I saw many couples finely dressed, men with the marks of old difficulties scarring their faces, and romping children. Saddening me more, I saw too from several points the dark towers of the Citadel on the opposite bank, and on the second or third such sighting it came to me that when I had swum from the eastern bank, diving from the water-stairs and fighting with the tenement children, I had once or twice noticed this narrow line of white on the other shore, so far upstream as to be nearly beyond sight.

The Botanic Gardens stood on an island near the bank, enclosed in a building of glass (a thing I had not seen before and did not know could exist). There were no towers or battlements: only the faceted tholus, climbing until it lost itself against the sky and its momentary brilliancies were confounded with the faint stars. I asked Agia if we would have time to see the gardens—and then, before she could reply, told her that I would see them whether there was time or not. The fact was that I had no compunction about arriving late for my death, and was beginning to have difficulty in taking seriously a combat fought with flowers.

"If you wish to spend your last afternoon visiting the gardens, so be it," she said. "I come here myself often. It's free, being maintained by the Autarch, and entertaining if you're not too squeamish."

We went up steps of glass, palely green. I asked Agia if the enormous building existed only to provide blooms and fruit.

She shook her head, laughing, and motioned toward the wide arch before us. "On either side of this corridor are chambers, and each chamber is a bioscape. I warn you though that because the corridor is shorter than the building itself, the chambers will widen as we go into them more deeply. Some people find that disconcerting."

We entered, and in so doing stepped into such silence as must have been in the morning of the world, before the fathers of men first hammered out brazen gongs, built squealing cartwheels, and splashed Gyoll with striding oars. The air was fragrant, damp, and a trifle warmer than it had been outside. The walls to either side of the tessellated floor were also of glass, but so thick that sight could scarcely penetrate them; leaves and flowers and even soaring trees seen through these walls wavered as though glimpsed through water. On one broad door I read:

THE GARDEN OF SLEEP

"You may enter whichever you like," an old man said, rising from his chair in a corner. "And as many as you like."

Agia shook her head. "We won't have time for more than one or two."

"Is it your first visit? Newcomers generally enjoy the Garden of Pantomime."

He wore a faded robe that reminded me of something I could not place. I asked if it were the habit of some guild.

"Indeed it is. We are the curators—have you never met one of our brotherhood previously?"

"Twice, I believe."

"There are only a few of us, but our charge is the most important that society boasts—the preservation of all that is gone. Have you seen the Garden of Antiquities?"

"Not yet," I said.

"You should! If this is your first visit, I would advise you to begin with the Garden of Antiquities. Hundreds and hundreds of extinct plants, including some that have not been seen for tens of millions of years."

Agia said, "That purple creeper you're so proud of—I met it growing wild on a hillside in Cobblers Common."

The curator shook his head sadly. "We lost spores, I'm afraid. We know about it . . . A roof pane broke, and they blew away." The unhappiness quickly left his lined face, draining away as the troubles of simple people do. He smiled. "It's likely to do well now. All its enemies are as dead as the disorders its leaves cured."

A rumbling made me turn. Two workmen were wheeling a cart through one of the doorways, and I asked what they were doing.

"That's the Sand Garden. They're rebuilding it. Cactuses and yucca—that kind of thing. I'm afraid there's not much to see there now."

I took Agia by the hand, saying, "Come on, I'd like to look at the work." She smiled at the curator and gave a half shrug, but followed docilely enough.

Sand there was, but no garden. We stepped into a seemingly unlimited space dotted with boulders. More stone rose in cliffs behind us, concealing the wall through which we had come. Just beside the doorway spread one large plant, half bush, half vine, with cruel, curved thorns; I assumed that it was the last of the old flora, not yet removed. There was no other vegetation, and no sign of the restocking the curator had implied except for the twin tracks of the workmen's cart, winding off among the rocks.

"This isn't much," Agia said. "Why don't you let me take you to the Garden of Delectation?"

"The door is open behind us—why is it I feel I can't leave this place?"

She looked at me sidelong. "Everyone feels like that in these gardens sooner or later, though usually not so quickly. It would be better for you if we stepped outside now." She said something else as well, something I could not catch. Far off, I seemed to hear surf pounding on the edge of the world.

"Wait . . ." I said. But Agia drew me out into the corridor again. Our feet carried away as much sand as a child might hold in the palm of one hand.

"We really don't have much time left now," Agia told me. "Let me show you the Garden of Delectation, then we'll pluck your avern and go."

"It can't be much later than midmorning."

"It's past noon. We were more than a watch just in the Sand Garden."

"Now I know you're lying to me."

For an instant I saw a flash of anger in her face. Then it was spread over with an unction of philosophical irony, the secretion of her injured self-esteem. I was far stronger than she, and poor though I was, richer; she told herself now (I felt I could almost hear her voice whispering in her own ear) that by accepting such insults she mastered me.

"Severian, you argued and argued, and in the end I had to drag you away. The gardens affect people like that—certain suggestible people. They say the Autarch wants some people to remain in each to accent the reality of the scene, and so his archimage, Father Inire, has invested them with a conjuration. But since you were so drawn to that one, it's not likely any of the others will affect you so much."

"I felt I belonged there," I said. "That I was to meet someone . . . and that a certain woman was there, nearby, but concealed from sight."

We were passing another door, on which was written:

THE JUNGLE GARDEN

When Agia did not answer me, I said, "You tell me the others won't affect me, so let's go in here."

"If we waste our time with that, we won't get to the Garden of Delectation at all."

"Only for a moment." Because she was so determined to take me into the garden she had selected, without seeing any of the others, I had grown frightened of what I might find there, or bring with me.

The heavy door of the Jungle Garden swung toward us, bringing a rush of steaming air. Beyond, the light was dim and green. Lianas half obscured the entrance, and a great tree, rotted to punk, had fallen across the path a few strides away. Its trunk still bore a small sign: *Caesalpinia sappan*.

"The real jungle is dying in the north as the sun cools," Agia said. "A man I know says it has been dying so for many centuries. Here, the old jungle stands preserved as it was when the sun was young. Come in. You wanted to see this place."

I stepped inside. Behind us the door swung shut and vanished.

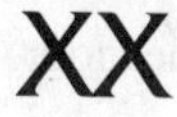

Father Inire's Mirrors

As Agia had said, the real jungles sickened far to the north. I had never seen them, yet the Jungle Garden made me feel I had. Even now, as I sit at my writing table in the House Absolute, some distant noise brings back to my ears the screams of the magenta-breasted, cynaeous-backed parrot that flapped from tree to tree, watching us with white-rimmed and disapproving eyes—though this is no doubt because my mind was already turned to that haunted place. Through its screaming, a new sound—a new voice—came from some red world still unconquered by thought.

"What is it?" I touched Agia's arm.

"A smilodon. But he's far away and only wants to frighten the deer so they'll blunder into his jaws. He'd run from you and your sword much faster than you could run from him." Her gown had been torn by a branch, exposing one breast. The incident had left her in no good mood.

"Where does the path lead? And how can the cat be so far off when all this is only one room of the building we saw from the top of the Adamnian Steps?"

"I've never gone so deeply into this garden. You were the one who wanted to come."

"Answer my questions," I said, and took her by the shoulder.

"If this path is like the others—I mean, in the other gardens—it runs in a wide loop that will eventually return us to the door by which we came in. There's no reason to be afraid."

"The door vanished when I shut it."

"Only trickery. Haven't you seen those pictures in which a pietist exhibits a meditating face when you're on one side of the room, but stares at you when you cross to the opposite wall? We'll see the door when we approach it from the other direction.''

A snake with carnelian eyes came gliding onto the path, lifted a venomous head to look at us, then slipped away. I heard Agia's gasp and said, ''Who's afraid now? Will that snake flee you as quickly as you would flee it? Now answer my question about the smilodon. Is it really far away? And if so, how can that be?''

''I don't know. Do you think there are answers to everything here? Is that true in the place you come from?''

I recalled the Citadel and the age-old usages of the guilds. ''No,'' I said. ''There are inexplicable offices and customs in my home, though in these decadent times they are falling out of use. There are towers no one has ever entered, too, and lost rooms, and tunnels whose entrances have not been seen.''

''Then can't you understand that it's the same way here? When we were at the top of the steps and you looked down and saw these gardens, could you make out the entire building?''

''No,'' I admitted. ''There were pylons and spires in the way, and the corner of the embankment.''

''And even so, could you delimit what you saw?''

I shrugged. ''The glass made it difficult to tell where the edges of the building were.''

''Then how can you ask the questions you do? Or if you have to ask them, can't you understand that I don't necessarily have the answers? From the sound of the smilodon's roar, I knew he was far off. Perhaps he is not here at all, or perhaps the distance is of time.''

''When I looked down on this building, I saw a faceted dome. Now when I look up, I see only the sky between the leaves and vines.''

''The surfaces of the facets are large. It may be that their edges are concealed by the limbs,'' Agia said.

We walked on, wading a trickle of water in which a reptile with evil teeth and a finned back soaked himself. I unsheathed *Terminus Est*, fearing he would dart at our feet. ''I grant,'' I told her, ''that the trees grow too thickly here to permit me to see far to either side. But look here, through the opening where this freshet runs. Upstream I can see only more jungle. Downstream there is the gleam of water, as though it empties into a lake.''

''I warned you that the rooms open out, and that you might find that disturbing. It is also said that the walls of these places are specula, whose reflective power creates the appearance of vast space.''

''I once knew a woman who had met Father Inire. She told me a tale about him. Would you like to hear it?''

"Suit yourself."

Actually it was I who wanted to hear the story, and I did suit myself: I told it to myself in the recesses of my mind, hearing it there hardly less than I had heard it first when Thecla's hands, white and cold as lilies taken from a grave filled with rain, lay clasped between my own.

"I was thirteen, Severian, and I had a friend named Domnina. She was a pretty girl who looked several years younger than she really was. Perhaps that's why he took a fancy to her.

"I know you know nothing of the House Absolute. You must take my word for it that at one place in the Hall of Meaning there are two mirrors. Each is three or four ells wide, and each extends to the ceiling. There's nothing between the two except a few dozen strides of marble floor. In other words, anyone who walks down the Hall of Meaning sees himself infinitely multiplied there. Each mirror reflects the images in its twin.

"Naturally, it's an attractive spot when you're a girl and fancy yourself something of a beauty. Domnina and I were playing there one night, turning around and around to show off new camisias. We had moved a couple of big candelabra so one was on the left of one mirror and the other on the left of the facing one—at opposite corners if you see what I mean.

"We were so busy looking at ourselves that we didn't notice Father Inire until he was only a step away. Ordinarily, you understand, we would have run and hidden when we saw him coming, though he was scarcely taller than we. He wore iridescent robes that seemed to fade into gray when I looked at them, as if they had been dyed in mist. 'You must be wary, children, of looking at yourselves like that,' he said. 'There's an imp who waits in silvered glass and creeps into the eyes of those who look into it.'

"I knew what he meant, and blushed. But Domnina said, 'I think I've seen him. Is he shaped like a tear, all gleaming?'

"Father Inire did not hesitate before he answered her, or even blink—still, I understood that he was startled. He said, 'No, that is someone else, dulcinea. Can you see him plainly? No? Then come into my presence chamber tomorrow a little after Nones, and I'll show him to you.'

"We were frightened when he left. Domnina swore a hundred times that she would not go. I applauded her resolution and tried to strengthen her in it. More to the point, we arranged that she should stay with me that night and the next day.

"It was all for nothing. A little before the appointed time, a servant in a livery neither of us had ever seen came for poor Domnina.

"A few days before I had been given a set of paper figures. There were soubrettes, columbines, coryphees, harlequinas, figurantes, and so on—the usual thing. I remember that I waited on the window seat all afternoon for Domnina, toying with these little people, coloring their costumes with wax pencils, arranging them in various ways and inventing games she and I would play when she came back.

"At last my nurse called me to supper. By that time I thought Father Inire had killed Domnina, or that he had sent her back to her mother with an order that she must never visit us again. Just as I was finishing my soup there was a knock. I heard mother's servitrix go to answer the door, then Domnina burst in. I'll never forget her face—it was as white as the faces of the dolls. She cried and my nurse comforted her, and eventually we got the story out of her.

"The man who had been sent for her had taken her through halls she hadn't known existed. That, you understand, Severian, was frightening in itself. We both thought ourselves perfectly familiar with our wing of the House Absolute. Eventually he had led her into what must have been the presence chamber. She said it was a large room with hangings of a solid, dark red and almost no furniture except for vases taller than a man and wider than she could spread her arms.

"In the center was what she at first took to be a room within the room. The walls were octagonal and painted with labyrinths. Over it, just visible from where she stood at the entrance to the presence chamber, burned the brightest lamp she had ever seen. It was blue-white, she said, and so brilliant an eagle could not have kept his eyes on it.

"She had heard the click of the bolt when the door had been closed behind her. There was no other exit she could see. She ran to the curtains hoping to find another door behind them, but as soon as she pulled one aside, one of the eight walls painted with labyrinths opened and Father Inire stepped out. Behind him she saw what she called a bottomless hole filled with light.

" 'There you are,' he said. 'You've come just in time. Child, the fish is nearly caught. You can watch the setting of the hook, and learn by what means his golden scales are to be meshed in our landing net.' He took her arm and led her into the octagonal enclosure."

At this point I was forced to interrupt my tale to help Agia through a section of the path almost completely overgrown. "You're talking to yourself," she said. "I can hear you muttering behind me."

"I'm telling myself the story I mentioned to you. You seemed to have no wish to hear it, and I wanted to listen to it again—besides, it concerns the specula of Father Inire, and may contain hints useful to us.''

''Domnina drew away. In the center of the enclosure, just under the lamp, was a haze of yellow light. It was never still, she said. It moved up and down and from side to side with rapid flickerings, never leaving a space that might have been four spans high and four long. It did indeed remind her of a fish. Much more than the faint flagae she had glimpsed in the mirrors of the Hall of Meaning ever had—a fish swimming in air, confined to an invisible bowl. Father Inire drew the wall of the octagon closed behind them. It was a mirror in which she could see his face and hand and shining, indefinite robes reflected. Her own form too, and the fish's . . . but there seemed to be another girl—her own face peering over her shoulder; then another and another and another, each with a smaller face behind it. And so on *ad infinitum*, an endless chain of fainter Domnina-faces.

''She realized when she saw them that the wall of the octagonal enclosure through which she had passed faced another mirror. In fact, all the others were mirrors. The light of the blue-white lamp was caught by them all and reflected from one to another as boys might pass silver balls, interlacing and intertwining in an interminable dance. In the center, the fish flickered to and fro, a thing formed, as it seemed, by the convergence of the light.

'' 'Here you see him,' Father Inire said. 'The ancients, who knew this process at least as well as we and perhaps better, considered the Fish the least important and most common of the inhabitants of specula. With their false belief that the creatures they summoned were ever present in the depths of the glass, we need not concern ourselves. In time they turned to a more serious question: By what means may travel be effected when the point of departure is at an astronomical distance from the place of arrival?'

'' 'Can I put my hand through him?'

'' 'At this stage you may, child. Later I would not advise it.'

''She did so, and felt a sliding warmth. 'Is this how the cacogens come?'

'' 'Has your mother ever taken you riding in her flier?'

'' 'Of course.'

'' 'And you have seen the toy fliers older children make on the pleasance at night, with paper hulls and parchment lanterns. What you see here is to the means used to travel between suns as those toy fliers are to real ones. Yet we can call up the Fish with these, and perhaps other things too. And just as the boys' fliers sometimes set the roof of a pavilion ablaze, so our mirrors, though their concentration is not powerful, are not without danger.'

" 'I thought that to travel to the stars you'd have to sit on the mirror.'

"Father Inire smiled. It was the first time she had seen him smile, and though she knew he meant only that she had amused and pleased him (perhaps more than a grown woman could have) it was not pleasant. 'No, no. Let me outline the problem to you. When something moves very, very fast—as fast as you see all the familiar things in your nursery when your governess lights your candle—it grows heavy. Not larger, you understand, but only heavier. It is attracted to Urth or any other world more strongly. If it were to move swiftly enough, it would become a world itself, pulling other things to it. Nothing ever does, but if something did, that is what would happen. Yet even the light from your candle does not move swiftly enough to travel between the suns.'

"(The Fish flickered up and down, forward and back.)

" 'Couldn't you make a bigger candle?' I feel sure Domnina was thinking of the paschal candle she saw each spring, thicker than a man's thigh.

" 'Such a candle could be made, but its light would fly no more swiftly. Yet even though light is so weightless we have given its name to that condition, it presses against what it falls on, just as wind, which we cannot see, pushes the arms of a mill. See now what happens when we provide light to mirrors set face to face: The image they reflect travels from one to the other and returns. Suppose it meets itself in returning—what do you suppose happens then?'

"Domnina laughed despite her fear, and said she could not guess.

" 'Why it cancels itself. Think of two little girls running across a lawn without looking where they're going. When they meet, there are no more little girls running. But if the mirrors are well made and the distances between them are correct, the images do not meet. Instead, one comes behind the other. That has no effect when the light comes from a candle or a common star, because both the earlier light and the later light that would otherwise tend to drive it forward are only random white light, like the random waves a little girl might make by flinging a handful of pebbles into a lily pond. But if the light is from a coherent source, and forms the image reflected from an optically exact mirror, the orientation of the wave fronts is the same because the image is the same. Since nothing can exceed the speed of light in our universe, the accelerated light leaves it and enters another. When it slows again, it reenters ours—naturally at another place.'

" 'Is it just a reflection?' Domnina asked. She was looking at the Fish.

" 'Eventually it will be a real being, if we do not darken the lamp or shift the mirrors. For a reflected image to exist without an object to originate it violates the laws of our universe, and therefore an object will be brought into existence.' "

"Look," Agia said, "we're coming to something."

The shade of the tropical trees was so intense that spots of sunshine on the path seemed to blaze like molten gold. I squinted to peer beyond their burning shafts of light.

"A house set on stilts of yellow wood. It's thatched with palm fronds. Can't you see it?"

Something moved, and the hut seemed to spring at my eyes as it emerged from the pattern of greens, yellows, and blacks. A shadowed splotch became a doorway; two sloping lines, the angle of the roof. A man in light-colored clothes stood on a tiny veranda looking down the path at us. I straightened my mantle.

"You don't have to do that," Agia said. "It doesn't matter in here. If you're hot, take it off."

I removed the mantle and folded it over my left arm. The man on the veranda turned with an expression of unmistakable terror and went into the hut.

XXI

The Hut in the Jungle

A ladder led to the veranda. It was made of the same knobby-jointed wood as the hut, lashed together with vegetable fiber. "You're not going up that?" Agia protested.

"If we're going to see what's to be seen here we must," I said. "And recalling the state of your undergarments, I thought you might feel more comfortable if I preceded you."

She surprised me by blushing. "It will only lead to such a house as was used in the hot parts of the world in ancient days. You'll soon be bored, believe me."

"Then we can come down, and we will have lost very little time." I swung myself up the ladder. It sagged and creaked alarmingly, but I knew that in a public pleasureground it was impossible that it should be really dangerous. When I was halfway up, I felt Agia behind me.

The interior was hardly larger than one of our cells, but there all resemblance ceased. In our oubliette, the overwhelming impression was of solidity and mass. The metal plates of the walls echoed even the slightest sounds; the floors rang beneath the tread of the journeymen and gave not a hairsbreadth under the walker's weight; the ceiling could never fall—but if it should, it would crush everything below it.

If it is true that each of us has an antipolaric brother somewhere, a bright twin if we are dark, a dark twin if we are bright, then that hut was surely such a changeling to one of our cells. There were windows on all sides save the one through which we entered by the open door, and they had neither bars nor panes nor any other sort of closing. Floor and walls and window frames were of the branches of the yellow tree; branches not planed to boards but left in the round so that I could, in places, see sunlight through the walls, and if I had dropped a worn orichalk, it would very likely have come to rest on the ground below. There was no ceiling, only a triangular space beneath the roof where pans and food bags hung.

A woman was reading aloud in a corner, with a naked man crouched at her feet. The man we had seen from the path stood at the window opposite the door, looking out. I felt that he knew we had come (and even if he had not seen us a few moments before, he must certainly have felt the hut shake when we climbed the ladder), but that he wished to pretend he did not. There is something in the line of the back when a man turns so as not to see, and it was evident in his.

The woman read: "Then he went up from the plain to Mt. Nebo, the headland that faces the city, and the Compassionating showed him the whole country, all the land as far as the Western Sea. Then he said to him: 'This is the land I swore to your fathers I should give their sons. You have seen it, but you shall not set your feet upon it.' So there he died, and was buried in the ravine."

The naked man at her feet nodded. "It is even so with our own masters, Preceptress. With the smallest finger it is given. But the thumb is hooked into it, and a man has only to take the gift, and dig in the floor of his house, and cover all with a mat, than the thumb begins to pull and bit by bit the gift rises from the earth and ascends into the sky and is seen no more."

The woman seemed impatient with this, and began, "No, Isangoma—" But the man at the window interrupted her without turning around. "Be quiet, Marie. I want to hear what he has to say. You can explain later."

"A nephew of mine," the naked man continued, "a member of my own fire circle, had no fish. And so he took up his gowdalie and went to a certain pool. So quietly did he lean over the water he might have been a tree." The naked man leaped up as he said this, and posed his sinewy frame as though to spear the woman's feet with a shaft of air. "Long, long he stood . . . until the monkeys no longer feared him and returned to drop sticks in the water, and the hesperorn fluttered to her nest. A big fish came out of his den in the sunken trunks. My nephew watched him circle, slowly, slowly. He swam near the surface, and then when my nephew was about to drive home the three-toothed spear, there was no longer a fish to be seen, but a lovely woman. At first my nephew thought the fish was the fish-king, who had changed his form that he might not be speared. Then he saw the fish moving beneath the woman's face, and knew that he saw a reflection. He looked up at once, but there was nothing to be seen but the whisk of the vines. The woman was gone!" The naked man looked up, mimicking very well the amazement of the fisherman. "That night my nephew went to the Numen, the Proud One, and slit the throat of a young oreodont, saying—"

Agia whispered to me, "In the name of the Theoanthropos, how long do you mean to stay here? This could go on all day."

"Let me look about the hut," I whispered back, "and we'll go."

"Mighty is the Proud One, sacred all his names. Everything found beneath leaves is his, the storms are carried in his arms, the poison holds no death unless his curse is pronounced over it!"

The woman said, "I don't think we need all these praises of your fetish, Isangoma. My husband wishes to hear your story. Very well, but tell it and spare us your litanies."

"The Proud One protects his supplicant! Would not he be shamed if one who adores him were to die?"

"Isangoma!"

From the window, the man said, "He's afraid, Marie. Can't you hear it in his voice?"

"There is no fear for those who wear the sign of the Proud One! His breath is the mist that hides the infant uakaris from the claws of the margay!"

"Robert, if you won't do something about this, I will. Isangoma, be silent. Or leave and never return here again."

"The Proud One knows Isangoma loves the Preceptress. He would save her if he could."

"Save me from what? Do you think there's one of your dreadful beasts here? If there were, Robert would shoot it with his gun."

"The tokoloshe, Preceptress. The tokoloshe come. But the Proud One in his condensation will protect us. He is the mighty commander of all tokoloshe! When he roars, they hide beneath the fallen leaves."

"Robert, I think he's lost his mind."

"He has eyes, Marie, and you don't."

"What do you mean by that? And why do you keep looking out that window?"

Quite slowly, the man turned to face us. For a moment he looked at Agia and me, then he turned away. His expression was the one I have seen our clients wear when Master Gurloes showed them the instruments to be used in their anacrisis.

"Robert, for goodness' sake tell me what's wrong with you."

"As Isangoma says, the tokoloshe are here. Not his, I think, but ours. Death and the Lady. Have you heard of them, Marie?"

The woman shook her head. She had risen from her seat and opened the lid of a small chest.

"You wouldn't have, I suppose. It's a picture—an artistic theme, rather. Pictures by several artists. Isangoma, I don't think your Proud One has much authority over these tokoloshe. These come from Paris, where I used to be a student, to remonstrate with me for giving up art for this.''

The woman said, ''You have a fever, Robert. That's obvious. I'm going to give you something, and you'll feel better soon.''

The man looked toward us again, at Agia's face and my own, as though he did not wish to do so but found himself unable to control the motion of his eyes. ''If I am ill, Marie, then the diseased know things the well have overlooked. Isangoma knows they're here too, don't forget. Didn't you feel the floor tremble while you were reading to him? That was when they came in, I think.''

''I've just poured you a glass of water so you can swallow your quinine. There are no ripples in it.''

''What are they, Isangoma? Tokoloshe—but what are tokoloshe?''

''Bad spirits, Preceptor. When man think bad thought or woman do bad thing, there is another tokoloshe. He stay behind. Man think: *No one know, everyone dead.* But tokoloshe remain until end of world. Then everyone will see, know what that man did.''

The woman said, ''What a horrible idea.''

Her husband's hands clenched the yellow stick of the windowsill. ''Don't you see they are only the results of what we do? They are the spirits of the future, and we make them ourselves.''

''They are a lot of pagan nonsense, that's what I see, Robert. Listen. Your vision is so sharp, can't you listen for a moment?''

''I am listening. What do you want to say?''

''Nothing. I only want you to listen. What do you hear?''

The hut fell silent. I listened too, and could not have not listened if I had wanted to. Outside the monkeys chattered, and the parrots screamed as before. Then I heard, over the jungle noises, a faint humming, as though an insect as large as a boat were flying far away.

''What is it?'' the man asked.

''The mail plane. If you're lucky, you should be able to see it soon.''

The man craned his neck out the window, and I, curious to see what he was looking for, went to the window on his left and looked out as well. The foliage was so thick that at first it seemed impossible to see anything, but he was staring almost straight up past the edge of the thatch, and I found a patch of blue there.

The humming grew louder. Into view came the strangest flier I have ever seen. It was winged, as if it had been built by some race that had not yet realized that since it would not flap wings like a bird in any case, there was no reason its lift, like a kite's, could not come from its hull. There was a bulbous swelling on each argent pinion, and a third at the front of the hull; the light seemed to glimmer before these swellings.

"In three days we could be at the landing strip, Robert. The next time it comes, we would be waiting."

"If the Lord has sent us here—"

"Yes, Preceptor, we must do what the Proud One wishes! There is none like he! Preceptress, let me dance to the Proud One, and sing his song. Then it may be the tokoloshe will depart."

The naked man snatched her book from the woman and began to beat it with the flat of his hand—rhythmic claps as though he played a tambour. His feet scraped the uneven floor, and his voice, beginning with a melodic stridulation, became the voice of a child:

"In the night when all is silent,
  Hear him screaming in the treetops!
  See him dancing in the fire!
He lives in the arrow poison,
  Tiny as a yellow firefly!
  Brighter than a falling star!
Hairy men walk in the forest—"

Agia said, "I'm leaving, Severian," and stepped through the doorway behind us. "If you want to stay and watch this, you can. But you'll have to get your avern yourself, and find your way to the Sanguinary Fields. Do you know what will happen if you fail to appear?"

"They'll employ assassins, you said."

"And the assassins will employ the snake called yellowbeard. Not on you, at first. On your family, if you have any, and your friends. Since I've been with you all over our quarter of the city, that probably means me."

"He comes when the sun is setting,
  See his feet upon the water!
  Tracks of flame across the water!"

The chant continued, but the chanter knew we were going: his singsong held a note of triumph. I waited until Agia had reached the ground, then followed her.

She said, "I thought you'd never leave. Now that you're here, do you really like this place so much?" The metallic colors of her torn gown seemed as angry as she herself against the cool green of the unnaturally dark leaves.

"No," I said. "But I find it interesting. Did you see their flier?"

"When you and the inmate looked out the windows? I wasn't such a fool."

"It was like no other I've ever seen. I should have been looking at the roof facets of this building, but instead I saw the flier *he* expected to see. At least, that's what it seemed like. Something from somewhere else. A little while ago I wanted to tell you about a friend of a friend of mine who was caught in Father Inire's mirrors. She found herself in another world, and even when she returned to Thecla—that was my friend's name—she wasn't quite sure she had found her way back to her real point of origin. I wonder if we aren't still in the world those people left, instead of them in ours."

Agia had already started down the path. Flecks of sunlight seemed to turn her brown hair to dark gold as she looked over her shoulder to say, "I told you certain visitors are attracted to certain bioscapes."

I trotted to catch up with her.

"As time goes on, their minds bend to conform to their surroundings, and it may be they bend ours as well. It was probably an ordinary flier you saw."

"He saw us. So did the savage."

"From what I've heard, the further an inhabitant's consciousness must be warped, the more residual perceptions are likely to remain. When I meet monsters, wild men, and so forth in these gardens, I find they're a lot more likely to be at least partially aware of me than the others are."

"Explain the man," I said.

"I didn't build this place, Severian. All I know is that if you turn around on the path now, that last place we saw probably won't be there. Listen, I want you to promise me that when we get out of here, you'll let me take you straight to the Garden of Endless Sleep. We don't have time left for anything else, not even the Garden of Delectation. And you're not really the kind of person who ought to go sightseeing in here."

"Because I wanted to stay in the Sand Garden?"

"Partly, yes. You're going to make trouble for me here sooner or later, I think."

As she said that, we rounded one of the path's seemingly endless sinuosities. A log tagged with a small white rectangle that could only be a species sign lay across the path, and through the crowding leaves on our left I could see the wall, its greenish glass forming an unobtrusive backdrop for the foliage. Agia had already taken a step past the door when I shifted *Terminus Est* to the other hand and opened it for her.

XXII

Dorcas

When I had first heard of the flower, I had imagined averns would be grown on benches, in rows like those in the conservatory of the Citadel. Later, when Agia had told me more about the Botanic Gardens, I conceived of a place like the necropolis where I had frolicked as a boy, with trees and crumbling tombs, and walkways paved with bones.

The reality was very different—a dark lake in an infinite fen. Our feet sank in sedge, and a cold wind whistled past with nothing, as it seemed, to stop it before it reached the sea. Rushes grew beside the track on which we walked, and once or twice a water bird passed overhead, black against a misted sky.

I had been telling Agia about Thecla. Now she touched my arm. "You can see them from here, though we'll have to go half around the lake to pluck one. Look where I'm pointing . . . that smudge of white."

"They don't look dangerous from here."

"They've done for a great many people, I can assure you. Some of them are interred in this garden, I imagine."

So there were graves after all. I asked where the mausolcums stood.

"There aren't any. No coffins either, or mortuary urns, or any of that clutter. Look at the water slopping at your boots."

I did. It was as brown as tea.

"It has the property of preserving corpses. The bodies are weighed by forcing lead shot down their throats, then sunk here with their positions mapped so they can be fished up again later if anyone wants to look at them."

I would readily have sworn that there was no one within a league of where we stood. Or at least (if the segments of the glass building really confined the spaces they enclosed as they were supposed to do) within the borders of the Garden of Endless Sleep. But Agia had no sooner said what she did than the head and shoulders of an old man appeared over the top of some reeds a dozen paces off. " 'Tis not true," he called. "I know they say so, but 'tisn't right."

Agia, who had allowed the torn bodice of her gown to hang as it would, quickly drew it up again. "I didn't know I was talking to anyone but my escort here."

The old man ignored the rebuke. No doubt his thoughts were already too involved with the remark he had overheard for him to pay much heed. "I've the figure here—would you like to see it? You, young sieur—you've an education, anyone can tell that. Will you look?" He appeared to be carrying a staff. I watched its head rise and fall several times before I understood that he was poling toward us.

"More trouble," Agia said. "We'd better go."

I asked if it might not be possible for the old man to ferry us across the lake, thus saving us the long walk around.

He shook his head. "Too heavy for my little boat. There's but room for Cas and me here. You great folk would capsize us."

The prow came into sight, and I saw that what he said was true: the skiff was so small it seemed almost too much to ask of it that it keep the old man himself afloat, though he was bowed and shrunken by age (he appeared older even than Master Palaemon) until he could hardly have weighed more than a boy of ten. There was no one in it with him.

"Your pardon, sieur," he said. "But I can't come no nearer. Wet she may be, but she gets too dry for me, or you couldn't walk upon it. Can you step here by the edge so's I can show you my figure?"

I was curious to see what it was he wanted of us, so I did as he asked, Agia following me reluctantly.

"Here now." Reaching into his tunic he pulled out a small scroll. "Here is the position. Have a look, young sieur."

The scroll was headed with some name and a long description of where this person had lived, whose wife she was, and what her husband had done for a living; all of which I only pretended to glance at, I am afraid. Below the description were a crude map and two numbers.

"Now you see, sieur, it ought to be easy enough. First number there, that's paces *over* from the Fulstrum. Second number's paces *up*. Now would you believe that for all these years I've been trying to find her, and never found her yet?" Looking at Agia, he drew himself up until he stood almost normally.

"I'd believe it," Agia said. "And if it will satisfy you, I'm sorry to hear it. But it has nothing to do with us."

She turned to go, but the old man thrust out his pole to prevent my following her. "Don't you heed what they say. They put them where the figure shows, but they don't stay there. Some has been see'd in the river, even." He looked vaguely toward the horizon. "Out there."

I told him I doubted that was possible.

"All the water here, where'd you think it come from? There's a conduit underground that brings it, and if it didn't this whole place'd dry out. When they get to moving about, what's to prevent one from swimming through? What's to prevent twenty? Can't be any current to speak of. You and her—you come to get a avern, did you? You know why they planted 'em here to begin with?"

I shook my head.

"For the manatees. They're in the river, and used to swim in through the conduit. It scared the kin to see their faces bobbing in the lake, so Father Inire had the gardeners plant the averns. I was here and saw it. Just a little man he is, with a wry neck and bow legs. If a manatee comes now, those flowers kill it in the night. One morning I come looking for Cas like I always do unless I've something else I have to take care of, and there was two curators on the shore with a harpoon. Dead manatee in the lake, they said. I went out with my hook and got it, and it wasn't no manatee, but a man. He'd spit up his lead, or they hadn't put enough in. Looked as good as you or her, and better than me."

"Had he been dead long?"

"No way of telling, for the water here pickles them. You'll hear it said it turns their skin to leather, and so it does. But don't think of the sole of your boot when you hear it. More like a woman's glove."

Agia was far ahead of us, and I began to walk after her. The old man followed us, poling his skiff parallel to the floating path of sedge.

"I told them I'd had better luck in one day for them than I've had in forty years for myself. Here's what I use." He held up an iron grapple on a length of rope. "Not that I haven't caught aplenty, all kinds. But not Cas. I started where the figure showed, year after she died. She wasn't there, so I kept working my way out. After five years of that I was a ways far away—that's what I thought then—from what it said. I got to be afraid she might be there after all, so I begun over. First where it said, then working out. Ten years of that. I got to be afraid again, so what I do now is start in the morning where it says, and make my first cast there. After that I go to where I stopped the last time, and circle out some more. She's not where it says—I know that, I know everyone that's there now, and some of them I've pulled up a hundred times. But she's wandering, and I keep thinking maybe she'll come home."

"She was your wife?"

The old man nodded, and to my surprise said nothing.

"Why do you want to recover her body?"

Still he said nothing. His pole made no sound as it slipped in and out of the water; the skiff left only the faintest of wakes behind it, tiny ripples that lapped the side of the sedge track like the tongues of kittens.

"Are you sure you would know her, after so long a time, if you found her?"

"Yes . . . yes." He nodded, slowly at first, then vigorously. "You're thinking I may have hooked her already. Drug her up, looked her in the face, and throwed her back in. Ain't you? It ain't possible. Not know Cas? You wondered why I want her back. One reason is the memory I have of her—the one that's strongest—is of this brown water closing over her face. Her eyes shut. Do you know about that?"

"I'm not certain I know what you mean."

"They've a cement they put on the lids. It's supposed to hold them down forever, but when the water hit them, they opened. Explain that. It's what I remember, what comes into my mind when I try to sleep. This brown water rolling over her face, and her eyes opening blue through the brown. I have to go to sleep five, six times every night, what with the waking up. Before I lie down here myself I'd like to have another picture there—her face coming back up, even if it's only on the end of my hook. You follow what I say?"

I thought of Thecla and the trickle of blood from beneath the door of her cell, and I nodded.

"Then there's the other thing. Cas and I, we had a little shop. Cloisonné-work, mostly. Her father and brother had the trade of making it, and they set us up on Signal Street, just past the middle, next to the auction house. The building's still there, though nobody lives in it. I'd go over to the inlaws and carry the boxes home on my back, and pull them open, and put the pieces on our shelves. Cas priced 'em, sold, and kept everything so clean! You know how long we did that? Run our little place?"

I shook my head.

"Four years, less a month and a week. Then she died. Cas died. It wasn't long before it was all gone, but it was the biggest part of my life. I've got a place to sleep in a loft now. A man I knew years before, though that was years after Cas was gone, he lets me sleep there. There isn't a piece of cloisonné in it, or a garment, or so much as a nail from the old shop. I tried to keep a locket and Cas's combs, but everything's gone. Tell me this, now. How am I to know it wasn't no dream?"

It seemed to me that the old man might be spell-caught, as the people in the house of yellow wood had been; so I said, "I have no way of knowing. Perhaps, as you say, it was a dream. I think you torment yourself too much.''

His mood changed in an instant, as I have seen the moods of young children do, and he laughed. ''It's easy to see, sieur, that despite the outfit under that mantle, you're no torturer. I do truly wish I could ferry you and your doxie. Since I can't, there's a fellow farther along that has a bigger boat. He comes here pretty often, and he talks to me sometimes like you did. Tell him I hope he'll take you across.''

I thanked him and hurried after Agia, who by this time was a great distance ahead. She was limping, and I recalled how far she had walked today after wrenching her leg. As I was about to overtake her and give her my arm, I made one of those missteps that seem disastrous and enormously humiliating at the time, though one laughs at them afterward; and in so doing I set in motion one of the strangest incidents of my admittedly strange career. I began to run, and in running came too near the inner side of a curve in the track.

At one moment I was bounding along on the springy sedge—at the next I was floundering in icy brown water, much impeded by my mantle. For the space of a breath I knew again the terror of drowning; then I righted myself and got my face above water. The habits developed on all those summer swims in Gyoll reasserted themselves: I blew the water from my nose and mouth, took a deep breath, and pushed my sopping hood back from my face.

I was no sooner calm than I realized that I had dropped *Terminus Est*, and at that moment losing that blade seemed more terrible than the chance of death. I dove, not even troubling to kick off my boots, forcing my way through an umber fluid that was not water purely, but water laced and thickened with the fibrous stems of the reeds. These stems, though they multiplied the threat of drowning many times, saved *Terminus Est* for me—she would surely have outraced me to the bottom and buried herself in the mud there despite the meager air retained in her sheath, if her fall had not been obstructed. As it was, eight or ten cubits beneath the surface one frantically groping hand encountered the blessed, familiar shape of her onyx grip.

At the same instant, my other hand touched an object of a completely different kind. It was another human hand, and its grasp (for it had seized my own the moment I touched it) coincided so perfectly with the recovery of *Terminus Est* that it seemed the hand's owner was returning my property to me, like the tall mistress of the Pelerines. I felt a surge of lunatic gratitude, then fear returned tenfold: the hand was pulling my own, drawing me down.

XXIII

Hildegrin

With what must surely have been the last strength I possessed, I managed to throw *Terminus Est* onto the floating track of sedge and grasp its ragged margin before I sank again.

Someone caught me by the wrist. I looked up expecting Agia; it was not she but a woman younger still, with streaming yellow hair. I strove to thank her, but water, not words, poured from my mouth. She tugged and I struggled, and at last I lay wholly supported on the sedge, so weak I could do nothing more.

I must have rested there at least as long as it takes to say the angelus, and perhaps longer. I was conscious of the cold, which grew worse, and of the sagging of the whole fabric of rotting plants, which bent beneath my weight until I was half submerged again. I breathed in great gasps that failed to satisfy my lungs, and coughed water; water trickled from my nostrils too. Someone (it was a man's voice, a loud one I seemed to have heard a long time before) said, "Pull him over or he'll sink." I was lifted by my belt. In a few moments more I was able to stand, though my legs trembled so I feared I would fall.

Agia was there, and the blond girl who had helped me onto the sedge, and a big, beef-faced man. Agia asked what had happened, and half-conscious though I was I noticed how pale she was.

"Give him time," the big man said. "He'll be all right soon enough." And then, "Who in Phlegethon are you?"

He was looking at the girl, who seemed as dazed as I felt. She made a stammering sound, "D-d-d-d," then hung her head and was silent. From hair to heels she was smeared with mud, and what clothing she had seemed no better than rags.

The big man asked Agia, "Where did that one come from?"

"I don't know. When I looked back to see what was keeping Severian, she was pulling him onto this floating path."

"Good thing she did, too. Good for him, anyway. Is she mad? Or chant-caught here, you think?"

I said, "Whatever she is, she saved me. Can't you give her something to cover herself with? She must be freezing." I was freezing myself, now that I was alive enough to notice it.

The big man shook his head, and seemed to draw his heavy coat about him more closely. "Not unless she gets clean I won't. And she won't unless she's put back in the water, and stirred around, too. But I've something here that's the next best thing, and maybe better." From one of his coat pockets he took a metal flask shaped like a dog, which he handed to me.

A bone in the dog's mouth proved to be the stopper. I offered the flask to the blond girl, who at first seemed not to know what to do with it. Agia took it from her and held it to her lips until she had taken several swallows, then handed it back to me. The contents seemed to be plum brandy; its fiery impact washed away the bitterness of the fen water very pleasantly. By the time I replaced the bone in the dog's mouth, his belly was, I think, better than half empty.

"Now then," said the big man, "I think you people ought to tell me who you are and what you're doing here—and don't none of you say you've just come to see the sights of the garden. I see enough gawkers these days to know them before they come in hailing distance." He looked at me. "That's a good big whittle you've got there, to begin with."

Agia said, "The armiger is in costume. He has been challenged, and has come to cut an avern."

"He's in costume and you aren't, I suppose. Do you think I don't know stage brocade? And bare feet too, when I see them?"

"I never said I was not in costume, nor that I was of his rank. As for my shoes, I left them outside so as not to ruin them in this water."

The big man nodded in a way that gave no clue as to whether he believed her or not. "Now you, goldy-hair. The embroidered baggage here has already said she don't know you. And from the look of him, I don't believe her fish—that you pulled out for her, and a good piece of work that was, too—knows any more than I do. Maybe not that much. So who are you?"

The blond girl swallowed. "Dorcas."

"And how'd you get here, Dorcas? And how'd you get in the water? For that's where you've been, plainly. You couldn't of got that wet just pulling out our young friend."

The brandy had brought a flush to the girl's cheeks, but her face was as vacant and bewildered as before, or nearly so. "I don't know," she whispered.

Agia asked, "You don't remember coming here?"

Dorcas shook her head.

"Then what's the last thing you do remember?"

There was a long silence. The wind seemed to be blowing harder than ever, and despite the drink, I was miserably cold. At last Dorcas murmured, "Sitting by a window . . . There were pretty things in the window. Trays and boxes, and a rood."

The big man said, "Pretty things? Well, if you was there, I'm assured there was."

"She's mad," Agia said. "Either someone's been taking care of her and she's wandered away, or no one is taking care of her, which seems more likely from the state of her clothes, and she wandered in here when the curators weren't looking."

"It may be somebody's cracked her over the head, took her things, and threw her in here thinking she was gone. There's more ways in, Mistress Slops, than the curator knows of. Or maybe somebody brought her in to be sunk when she was only sick and sleepin'. In a com'er, as they call it, and the water woke her up."

"Surely whoever brought her in would have seen her."

"They can stay under a long time in a com'er, so I've heard. But whichever way it was, it don't much matter now. Here she is, and it's up to her, I should say, to find out where she come from and who she is."

I had dropped the brown mantle and was trying to wring my guild cloak dry; but I looked up when Agia said, "You've been asking all of us who we are. Who are you?"

"You've every right to know," the big man said. "Every right in the world, and I'll give you better bona fides than any of you have given me. Only after I does so, I must be about my own business. I come because I saw the young armiger here drowning, like any good man would. But I've my own affairs to take care of, the same as the next."

With that he pulled off his tall hat, and reaching inside produced a greasy card about twice the size of the calling cards I had occasionally seen in the Citadel. He handed it to Agia, and I peered over her shoulder. In florid script, the legend read:

HILDEGRIN THE BADGER
Excavations of *all* kinds, by a single
digger or 20 score.

Stone is not too hard nor mud too soft.
Ask on *Argosy* Street at the sign of the
BLIND SHOVEL
Or inquire at the Alticamelus around
the corner on Velleity.

"And that's who I am, Mistress Slops and young sieur—which I hope you won't mind my calling you, firstly because you're younger than me, and secondly because you're a sight younger than what she is, for all you was probably born only a couple years sooner. And I'll be on my way."

I stopped him. "Before I fell in, I met an old man in a skiff who told me there was someone farther down the track who could ferry us across the lake. I think you must be the man he referred to. Will you take us?"

"Ah, the one what's lookin' for his wife, poor soul. Well, he's been a good friend to me many a time, so if he recommends you, I suppose I'd better do it. My scow will hold four in a pinch."

He strode off motioning for us to follow; I noticed that his boots, which seemed to have been greased, sank in the sedge even deeper than my own. Agia said, "She's not coming with us." Still it was obvious that she (Dorcas) was, trailing along behind Agia and looking so forlorn that I dropped behind to try to comfort her. "I'd lend you my mantle," I whispered to her, "if it weren't so wet it would make you colder than you are already. But if you'll go along this track the other way, you'll come out of here altogether and into a corridor where it's warmer and drier. Then if you'll look for a door with *Jungle Garden* on it, that will let you into a place where the sun is warm and you'll be quite comfortable."

I had no sooner spoken than I remembered the pelycosaur we had seen in the jungle. Fortunately, perhaps, Dorcas showed no sign of having heard what I said. Something in her face conveyed that she was afraid of Agia, or at least aware, in a helpless way, of having displeased her; but there was no other indication she was any more alert to her surroundings than a somnambulist.

Conscious that I had failed to relieve her misery, I began again. "There's a man in the corridor, a curator. I'm sure he'll at least try to find some clothes and a fire for you."

The wind whipped Agia's chestnut hair as she looked back at us. "There are too many of these beggar girls for anyone to be worried about one, Severian. Including yourself."

At the sound of Agia's voice, Hildegrin glanced over his shoulder. "I know a woman might take her in. Yes, and clean her up and give her some clothes. There's a high-bred shape under that mud, thin though she is."

"What are you doing here, anyway?" Agia snapped. "You contract laborers, according to your card, but what's your business here?"

"Just what you said, Mistress. My business."

Dorcas had begun to shiver. "Honestly," I told her, "all you have to do is go back. It's much warmer in the corridor. Don't go in the Jungle Garden. You might go into the Sand Garden, it's sunny and dry in there."

Something in what I had said seemed to touch a chord in her. "Yes," she whispered. "Yes."

"The Sand Garden? You'd like that?"

Very softly: "Sun."

"Here's the old scow now," Hildegrin announced. "With so many, we're going to have to be particular about the seatin'. And there's to be no movin' about—she'll be low in the water. One of the women in the bow, please, and the other and the young armiger in the stern."

I said, "I'd be happy to take an oar."

"Ever rowed before? I thought not. No, you'd best sit in the stern like I told you. It ain't much harder pullin' two oars than one, and I've done it many a time, believe me, though there was half a dozen in her with me."

His boat was like himself, wide, rough, and heavy-looking. Bow and stern were square, so much so that there was hardly any horizontal taper from the waist, where the rowlocks were, though the hull was shallower at the ends. Hildegrin got in first, and standing with one leg to either side of the bench, used an oar to nudge the boat closer to shore for us.

"You," Agia said, taking Dorcas by the arm. "You sit up there in front."

Dorcas seemed willing to obey, but Hildegrin stopped her. "If you don't mind, Mistress," he said to Agia, "I'd sooner it was you in the bow. I won't be able to keep my eye on her, you see, when I'm rowin', unless she sits behind. She's not right, which even you and me can agree on, and low as we'll be I'd like to know if she starts friskin' around."

Dorcas surprised us all by saying, "I'm not mad. It's just . . . I feel as if I've just been wakened."

Hildegrin made her sit in the stern with me nonetheless. "Now this," he said as he pushed us off, "this is something you're not likely to forget if you've never done it before. Crossin' the Lake of Birds here in the middle of the Garden of Everlastin' Sleep." His oars dipping into the water made a dull and somehow melancholy sound.

I asked why it was called the Lake of Birds.

"Because so many's found dead in the water, is what some say. But it might only be that that's because there's so many here. There's a great deal said against Death. I mean by the people that has to die, drawin' her picture like a crone with a sack, and all that. But she's a good friend to birds, Death is. Wherever there's dead men and quiet, you'll find a good many birds, that's been my experience."

Recalling how the thrushes sang in our necropolis, I nodded.

"Now if you'll look past my shoulder, you'll have a clear view of the shore ahead of us and be able to see a lot of things you couldn't before, because of the rushes growin' all around you back there. You'll notice, if it's not too misty, that the land rises farther on. The bogginess stops there, and the trees begin. Can you see 'em?"

I nodded again, and beside me Dorcas nodded as well.

"That's because this whole peep show is meant to look like the mouth of a dead volcaner. The mouth of a dead man is what some say, but that's not really so. If it was, they'd of put in teeth. You'll remember, though, that when you come in here you come up through a pipe in the ground."

Once more, Dorcas and I nodded together. Though Agia was no more than two strides from us, she was nearly out of sight behind Hildegrin's broad shoulders and fearnought coat.

"Over there," he continued, jerking his square chin to show the direction, "you ought to be able to see a spot of black. Just about halfway up, it is, between the bog and the rim. Some sees it and thinks it's where they come out of, but that's behind you and lower down, and a whole lot smaller. This that you see now is the Cave of the Cumaean—the woman that knows the future and the past and everything else. There's some that say this whole place was built only for her, though I don't believe it."

Softly, Dorcas asked, "How could that be?" and Hildegrin misunderstood her, or at least pretended to do so.

"The Autarch wants her here, so they say, so he can come and talk without travelin' to the other side of the world. I wouldn't know about that, but sometimes I see somebody walkin' around up there, and metal or maybe a jewel or two flashin'. Who it is I wouldn't know, and since I don't want to know my future—and I know my past, I should think, better than her—I don't go near the cave. People come sometimes hopin' to know when they'll be married, or about success in trade. But I've observed they don't often come back."

We had nearly reached the center of the lake. The Garden of Endless Sleep rose around us like the sides of a vast bowl, mossy with pines toward the lip, scummed with rushes and sedge below. I was still very cold, more so because of the inactivity of sitting in the boat while another rowed; I was beginning to worry about what the immersion in water might do to the blade of *Terminus Est* if I did not dry and oil it soon, yet even so, the spell of the place held me. (A spell there was, surely, in this garden. I could almost hear it humming over the water, voices chanting in a language I did not know but understood.) I think it held everyone, even Hildegrin, even Agia. For some time we rowed in silence; I saw geese, alive and content for all I could tell, bobbing a long way off; and once, like something in a dream, the nearly human face of a manatee looking into my own through a few spans of brownish water.

XXIV

The Flower of Dissolution

Beside me, Dorcas plucked a water hyacinth and put it in her hair. Except for the vague spot of white on the bank some distance ahead, it was the first flower I had seen in the Garden of Endless Sleep; I looked for others, but saw none.

Is it possible the flower came into being only because Dorcas reached for it? In daylight moments, I know as well as the next that such things are impossible; but I am writing by night, and then, when I sat in that boat with the hyacinth less than a cubit from my eyes, I wondered at the dim light and recalled Hildegrin's remark of a moment before, a remark that implied (though quite possibly he did not know it) that the seeress's cave, and thus this garden, was on the opposite side of the world. There, as Master Malrubius had taught us long ago, all was reversed: warmth to the south, cold to the north; light at night, dark by day; snow in summer. The chill I felt would be appropriate then, for it would be summer soon, with sleet riding the wind; the darkness that stood even between my eyes and the blue flowers of the water hyacinth would be appropriate then too, for it would soon be night, with light already in the sky.

The Increate maintains all things in order surely; and the theologicans say light is his shadow. Must it not be then that in darkness order grows ever less, flowers leaping from nothingness into a girl's fingers just as by light in spring they leap from mere filthiness into the air? Perhaps when night closes our eyes there is less order than we believe. Perhaps, indeed, it is this lack of order we perceive as darkness, a randomization of the waves of energy (like a sea), the fields of energy (like a farm) that appear to our deluded eyes—set by light in an order of which they themselves are incapable—to be the real world.

Mist was rising from the water, reminding me first of the swirling motes of straw in the insubstantial cathedral of the Pelerines, then of steam from the soup kettle when Brother Cook carried it into the refectory on a winter afternoon. The witches were said to stir such kettles; but I had never seen one, though their tower stood hardly a chain from ours. I remembered that we rowed across the crater of a volcano. Might it not have been the Cumaean's kettle? Urth's fires were long dead, as Master Malrubius had taught us; it was more than possible that they had cooled long before men had risen from the position of the beasts to cumber her face with their cities. But witches, it was said, raised the dead. Might not the Cumaean raise the dead fires to boil her pot? I dipped my fingers into the water; it was as cold as snow.

Hildegrin leaned toward me as he rowed, then drew away as he pulled his oars. "Goin' to your death," he said. "That's what you're thinkin'. I can see it in your face. To the Sanguin'ry Field, and he'll kill you, whoever he is."

"Are you?" Dorcas asked, and gripped my hand.

When I did not answer, Hildegrin nodded for me. "Don't have to, you know. There's them that doesn't follow the rules, and yet runs free."

"You're mistaken," I said. "I wasn't thinking about monomachy—or dying either."

In my ear, too softly, I think, even for Hildegrin to hear, Dorcas said, "Yes, you were. Your face was full of beauty, of a kind of nobility. When the world is horrible, then thoughts are high, full of grace and greatness."

I looked at her, thinking she was mocking me, but she was not.

"The world is filled half with evil and half with good. We can tilt it forward so that more good runs into our minds, or back, so that more runs into this." A movement of her eyes took in all the lake. "But the quantities are the same, we change only their proportion here or there."

"I would tilt it as far back as I can, until at last the evil runs out altogether," I said.

"It might be the good that would run out. But I am like you; I would bend time backward if I could."

"Nor do I believe that beautiful thoughts—or wise ones—are engendered by external troubles."

"I did not say beautiful thoughts, but thoughts of grace and greatness, though I suppose that is a kind of beauty. Let me show you." She lifted my hand and slipping it inside her rags pressed it to her right breast. I could feel the nipple, as firm as a cherry, and the warmth of the gentle mound beneath it, delicate, feather-soft and alive with racing blood.

"Now," she said, "what are your thoughts? If I have made the external world sweet to you, aren't they less than they were?"

"Where did you learn all this?" I asked. Her face was drained of its wisdom, which condensed in crystal drops at the corners of her eyes.

The shore on which the averns grew was less marshy than the other. It seemed strange, after having walked on buoyant sedge and floated on water for so long, to set foot again on soil that was no worse than soft. We had landed at some distance from the plants; but we were near enough now that they were no longer a mere bank of white, but growths of definite color and shape, whose size could be readily estimated. I said, "They are not from here, are they? Not from our Urth." No one replied; I think I must have spoken too softly for any of the others (except perhaps Dorcas) to hear.

They had a stiffness, a geometrical precision, surely born under some other sun. The color of their leaves was that of a scarab's back, but infused with tints at once deeper and more translucent. It seemed to imply the existence of light somewhere, some inconceivable distance away, of a spectrum that would have withered or perhaps ennobled the world.

As we walked nearer, Agia leading the way—I following her with Dorcas behind me, and Hildegrin following us—I saw that each leaf was like a dagger blade, stiff and pointed, with edges sharp enough to satisfy even Master Gurloes. Above these leaves, the half-closed white blossoms we had seen from across the lake seemed creations of pure beauty, virginal fantasies guarded by a hundred knives. They were wide and lush, and their petals curled in a way that should have seemed tousled if it had not formed a complex swirling pattern that drew the eye like a spiral limned on a revolving disc.

Agia said, "Good form requires that you pick the plant yourself, Severian. But I'll go with you and show you how. The trick is to put your arm under the lowest leaves, and snap the stem off at the ground."

Hildegrin caught her by the shoulder. "That you won't, Mistress," he said. And then to me, "You go forward since you're of a mind to, young sieur. I'll take the females to safety."

I was already several strides past him, but I stopped for an instant when he spoke. Luckily Dorcas called out, "Be careful!" at that moment, and I was able to pretend it was her warning that had halted me.

The truth was otherwise. From the time we had met Hildegrin, I had felt certain I had encountered him before, though the shock of recognition that had come so swiftly when I saw Sieur Racho again was in this instance long delayed. Now it had come at last, with paralyzing force.

As I have said, I remember everything; but often I can find a fact, face, or feeling only after a long search. I suppose that in this case, the problem was that from the moment he had bent over me on the sedge track I could see him clearly, and previously I had hardly seen him at all. It was only when he said, "*I'll take these females to safety*," that my memory closed upon his voice.

"The leaves are poisoned," Agia called. "Twisting your mantle tight about your arm will give you some protection, but try not to touch them. And watch out—you are always closer to an avern than you think."

I nodded to show I understood.

Whether the avern is deadly to the life of its own world I have no way of knowing. It may be that it is not, that it is only dangerous to us by reason of a nature accidentally inimical to our own. Whether that is so or not, the ground between and beneath the plants was covered with short and very fine grass, grass quite different from the coarse growth elsewhere; and this short grass was littered with the curled bodies of bees and dotted with the white bones of birds.

When I was no more than a couple of paces from the plants, I stopped, suddenly aware of a problem I had given no thought to previously. The avern I selected would be my weapon in the contest to come—yet because I knew nothing as yet of the way it would be fought, I had no means of judging which plant might be best adapted to it. I could have gone back and questioned Agia, but I would have felt absurd examining a woman on such a matter, and in the end I decided to trust my judgment, since she would no doubt send me back for another if my first choice were wholly unsuitable.

The averns varied in height from seedlings of hardly more than a span to old plants of three cubits or a little less. These older plants had fewer, though larger, leaves. Those of the smaller ones were narrower, and so closely spaced that the stems were completely hidden; those of the big plants were much broader in proportion to their length, and somewhat separated on the fleshy-looking stems. If (as seemed likely) the Septentrion and I were to use our plants as maces, the largest possible plant with the longest possible stem and the stoutest possible leaves would be the best. But these all grew well away from the edges of the planting, so that it would be necessary to break down a number of smaller plants to reach them; and to do that by the method Agia had advised was clearly impossible, because the leaves of many of the smaller plants grew nearly to the ground.

In the end I chose one about two cubits high. I had knelt beside it and was reaching toward it when as though a veil had been snatched away I realized that my hand, which I had thought still several spans from the needlelike point of the nearest leaf, was about to be impaled. I drew it back hurriedly; the plant seemed almost out of reach—indeed, I was not certain I could touch its stem even by lying prone. The temptation to use my sword was very great, but I felt it would disgrace me before Agia and Dorcas to do so, and I knew I would have to handle the plant during the combat in any case.

I advanced my hand again, cautiously, this time keeping my forearm in contact with the ground, and discovered that though I had to press my shoulder against the grass as well to prevent my upper arm from being stabbed by the lowest leaves, I could touch the stem quite readily. A point that appeared to be half a cubit from my face trembled with my breath.

It was while I was snapping off the stem—no easy task—that I saw the reason only the short, soft grass flourished beneath the averns. One of the leaves of the plant I was breaking had cut half through a blade of coarse marsh grass, and the entire grass plant, almost an ell across, had begun to wither.

Once picked, the plant was an enormous nuisance, as I ought to have anticipated. It would plainly have been impossible to carry it in Hildegrin's boat as it was without killing one or more of us, so before we reembarked I had to climb the slope and cut a sapling. When the twigs had been lopped, Agia and I bound the avern to one end of its spindly trunk, so that as we made our way through the city later, I appeared to be bearing some grotesque standard.

Then Agia explained the use of the plant as a weapon; and I broke a second plant (although she objected, and at even greater risk, I fear, than before, since I was somewhat too confident) and practiced what she had told me.

The avern is not, as I had assumed, merely a viper-toothed mace. Its leaves can be detached by twisting them between the thumb and forefinger in such a way that the hand does not contact the edges or the point. The leaf is then in effect a handleless blade, envenomed and razor-sharp, ready to throw. The fighter holds the plant in his left hand by the base of the stem and plucks the lower leaves to throw with his right. Agia cautioned me, however, to keep my own plant out of my opponent's reach, since as the leaves are removed an area of bare stem appears, and this he might grasp and use to wrest my plant from me.

When I flourished the second plant and practiced striking out with it and picking and throwing the leaves, I found that my own avern was likely to be almost as great a danger to me as the Septentrion's. If I held it near me, there was a grave risk of pricking my arm or chest with the long lower leaves; and the flower with its swirling pattern held my gaze whenever I glanced down to tear off a leaf, and with the dry lust of death sought to draw me to it. All this seemed unpleasant enough; but when I had learned to keep my eyes away from the half-closed blossom, I reflected that my opponent would be exposed to the same dangers.

Throwing the leaves was easier than I had supposed. Their surfaces were glossy, like the leaves of many of the plants I had seen in the Jungle Garden, so that they left the fingers readily, and they were heavy enough to fly far and true. They could be thrown point-foremost like any knife, or made to spin in flight to cut down anything in their path with their deadly edges.

I was eager, of course, to question Hildegrin about Vodalus; but no opportunity to do so came until he had rowed us back across the silent lake. Then for a moment Agia became so intent on driving Dorcas away that I was able to draw him to one side and whisper that I, too, was a friend to Vodalus.

"You've mistaken me, young sieur, for somebody else—do you refer to Vodalus the outlaw?"

"I never forget a voice," I told him, "or anything else." And then in my eagerness, I impulsively added what was perhaps the worst thing I could have said: "You tried to brain me with your shovel." His face became masklike at once, and he stepped back into his boat and rowed out onto the brown water.

When Agia and I left the Botanic Gardens, Dorcas was still with us. Agia was anxious to make her go away, and for a time I permitted her to try. I was moved in part by the fear that with Dorcas near it would be impossible for me to persuade Agia to lie with me; but even more by a vague appreciation of the pain Dorcas would feel, lost and dismayed as she was already, if she should see me die. Only a short time before, I had poured out to Agia all my sorrow at the death of Thecla. Now these new concerns had replaced it, and I found I had poured it out indeed, as a man might spill sour wine on the ground. By the use of the language of sorrow I had for the time being obliterated my sorrow—so powerful is the charm of words, which for us reduces to manageable entities all the passions that would otherwise madden and destroy us.

Whatever my motives may have been, and whatever Agia's may have been, and whatever Dorcas's may have been for following us, nothing Agia did succeeded. And in the end, I threatened to strike her if she did not desist, and called to Dorcas, who was then fifty paces or so behind us.

After that we three trudged along in silence, drawing many strange looks. I was soaked to soddenness, and no longer cared whether my mantle covered my fuligin torturer's cloak. Agia in her torn brocade must have looked nearly as strange as I. Dorcas was still smeared with mud—it dried on her in the warm spring wind that now wrapped the city, caking in her golden hair and leaving smears of powdery brown on her pale skin. Above us the avern brooded like a gonfalon; from it there drifted a myrrhic perfume. The half-closed flower still shone as white as bone, but its leaves looked nearly black in the sunlight.

XXV

The Inn of Lost Loves

It has been my good fortune—or evil fortune, as it may be—that the places with which my life has been largely associated have been, with very few exceptions, of the most permanent character. I might tomorrow, if I wished, return to the Citadel and (I think) to the very cot on which I slept as an apprentice. Gyoll still rolls past my city of Nessus; the Botanic Gardens still glitter in the sun, faceted with those strange enclosures wherein a single mood is preserved for all time. When I think of the ephemera of my life, they are likely to be men and women. But there are a few houses as well, and first among these stands the inn at the margin of the Sanguinary Field.

We had walked away the afternoon, down broad avenues and up narrow byways, and always the buildings that hemmed us round were of stone and brick. At last we came to grounds that seemed no grounds at all, for there was no exalted villa at their center. I remember I warned Agia that a storm was brewing—I could feel the closeness of the air, and I saw a line of bitter black along the horizon.

She laughed at me. "What you see and what you feel too is nothing more than the City Wall. It's always like this here. The Wall impedes the movement of the air."

"That line of dark? It goes halfway to the sky."

Agia laughed again, but Dorcas pressed herself against me. "I am afraid, Severian."

Agia heard her. "Of the Wall? It won't hurt you unless it falls on you, and it has stood through a dozen ages." I looked questioningly at her, and she added, "At least it looks that old, and it may be older. Who knows?"

"It could wall out the world. Does it stretch completely around the city?"

"By definition. The city is what is enclosed, though there's open country to the north, so I've heard, and leagues and leagues of ruins in the south, where no one lives. But now, look between those poplars. Do you see the inn?"

I did not, and said so.

"Under the tree. You've promised me a meal, and that's where I want it. We should just have time to eat before you have to meet the Septentrion."

"Not now," I said. "I'll be happy to feed you when my duel is over. I'll make the arrangements now, if you like." I could still find no building, but I had come to see that there was something strange about the tree: a stair of rustic wood twined up the trunk.

"Do so. If you're killed, I'll invite the Septentrion—or if he won't come, that broken sailor who is forever inviting me. We'll drink to you."

A light kindled high in the branches of the tree, and now I saw that a path led up to the stair. Before it, a painted sign showed a weeping woman dragging a bloody sword. A monstrously fat man in an apron stepped out of the shadow and stood beside it, rubbing his hands while he waited our coming. Faintly now, I could hear the clinking of pots.

"Abban at your command," said the fat man when we reached him. "What is your wish?" I noticed he kept a nervous eye on my avern.

"We'll have dinner for two, to be served at . . ." I looked at Agia.

"The new watch."

"Good, good. But it cannot be so soon, sieur. It will take longer to prepare. Unless you'll settle for cold meats, a salad, and a bottle of wine?"

Agia looked impatient. "We'll have a roast fowl—a young one."

"As you wish. I'll have the cook begin his preparations now, and you can amuse yourselves with baked stuff after the sieur's victory until the bird is done." Agia nodded, and a look flashed between the two that made me feel certain they had met previously. "Meanwhile," the innkeeper continued, "if you've yet time, I could provide a basin of warm water and a sponge for this other young lady, and perhaps you might all enjoy a glass of Medoc and some biscuits?"

I was suddenly conscious of having fasted since my breakfast at dawn with Baldanders and Dr. Talos, and conscious too that Agia and Dorcas might have had nothing all day. When I nodded, the innkeeper conducted us up the broad, rustic stair; the trunk it circled was a full ten paces around.

"Have you visited us before, sieur?"

I shook my head. "I was about to ask you what manner of inn this is. I've never seen anything like it."

"Nor will you, sieur, except here. But you ought to have come before—we keep a famous kitchen, and dining in the open air gives one the best appetite."

I thought that it must indeed if he maintained such a girth in a place where every room was reached by steps, but I kept the reflection to myself.

"The law, you see, sieur, forbids all buildings so near the Wall. We are permitted, having neither walls nor a roof. Those who attend the Sanguinary Field come here, the famous combatants and heroes, the spectators and physicians, even the ephors. Here's your chamber now."

It was a circular and perfectly level platform. Around and above it, pale green foliage shut out sight and sound. Agia sat in a canvas chair, and I (very tired, I confess) threw myself down beside Dorcas on a couch made of leather and the linked horns of lechwes and waterbucks. When I had laid the avern behind it, I drew *Terminus Est* and began to clean her blade. A scullion brought water and a sponge for Dorcas and, when she saw what I was doing, rags and oil for me. I was soon tapping at the pommel so I could strip the blade from its furniture for a real cleaning.

"Can't you wash yourself?" Agia asked Dorcas.

"I'd like a bath, yes, but not with you watching me."

"Severian will turn his head if you ask him. He did very well in a place where we were this morning."

"And you, madame," Dorcas said softly. "I'd rather you didn't watch. I'd like a private place, if I might have one."

Agia smiled at that, but I called the scullion again and gave her an orichalk to bring a folding screen. When it was set up, I told Dorcas I would buy her a gown if there were one to be had at the inn.

"No," she said. In a whisper, I asked Agia what she thought was the matter with her.

"She likes what she has, clearly. I must walk with a hand up to hold my bodice if I wouldn't be shamed for life." She let her hand fall, so that her high breasts gleamed in the dying sunlight. "But those rags let her show just leg and chest enough. There's a rent at the groin too, though I dare say you haven't noticed it."

The innkeeper interrupted us, leading in a waiter who carried a plate of pastries, a bottle, and glasses. I explained that my clothing was wet, and he had a brazier brought in—then proceeded to warm himself by it, for all the world as if he stood in his private apartment. "Feels good, this time of year," he said. "The sun's dead and don't know it yet, but we do. If you're killed, you'll get to miss next winter, and if you're hurt bad, you'll get to stay inside. That's what I always tell them. Of course, most of the fights are around midsummer's eve, so it's more appropriate then, so to speak. I don't know if it comforts them or not, but it does no harm."

I took off the brown mantle and my guild cloak, put my boots on a stool near the brazier, and stood beside him to dry my breeches and hose, asking if all those who came this way on monomachy stopped to refresh themselves with him. Like every man who feels himself likely to die, I would have been happy to know that I was taking part in some established tradition.

"*All?* Oh, no," he said. "May moderation and St. Amand bless you, sieur. If everyone who came tarried at my inn, why it wouldn't be my inn—I'd have sold it, and be living comfortable in a big, stone house with atroxes at the door and a few young fellows with knives hanging about me to settle my enemies. No, there's many a one goes by here without a glance, never thinking that when he comes past next time, it may be too late to drink my wine."

"Speaking of which," said Agia, and handed me a glass. It was full to the brim with a dark, crimson vintage. Not a good wine, perhaps—it made my tongue prickle, and carried with its delicious taste something of harshness. But a wonderful wine, a wine better than good, in the mouth of someone as fatigued and cold as I. Agia held a full glass of her own, but I saw by her flaming cheeks and sparkling eyes that she had already downed one other at least. I told her to save something for Dorcas, and she said, "That milk and water virgin? She won't drink it, and it's you who'll need courage—not she."

Not quite honestly, I said I was not afraid.

The innkeeper exclaimed, "That's the way! Don't you be feared, and don't fill your head with no noble thoughts about death and last days and all that. The ones that do is the ones that never come back, you may be sure. Now you was going to order a meal, I think, for you and your two young women afterward?"

"We have ordered it," I said.

"Ordered, but not paid nothing toward, that was my meaning. Also there's the wine and these here *gâteaux secs*. Those must be paid for here and now as they're eaten here and now, and drank up too. For the dinner I'll require a deposit of three orichalks, with two more to be paid when you come to eat it."

"And if I don't come?"

"Then there's no more charge, sieur. That's how I'm able to offer my dinners at such low prices."

The man's complete insensibility disarmed me; I handed over the money and he left us. Agia peeped around the side of the screen behind which Dorcas was cleansing herself with the aid of the scullion, and I sat down again on the couch and took a pastry to go with what remained of my wine.

"If we could make the hinges in this thing lock, Severian, we might enjoy ourselves for a few moments without interruption. We could put a chair against it, but no doubt those two would choose the worst possible moment to squall and knock everything over."

I was about to make some bantering reply when I noticed a scrap of paper, folded many times, that had been put beneath the waiter's tray in such a fashion that it could be seen only by someone sitting where I was. "This is really too much," I said. "A challenge, and now the mysterious note."

Agia came to look. "What are you talking about? Are you drunk already?"

I put my hand on the rounded fullness of her hip, and when she made no objection, used that pleasant handle to draw her toward me until she could see the paper. "What do you suppose it says? 'The Commonwealth has need of you—ride at once . . .' 'Your friend is he who shall say to you, camarilla . . . ' 'Beware of the man with pink hair . . .' "

Falling in with the joke, Agia offered, " 'Come when you hear three pebbles tap the window . . .' The *leaves*, I should say here. 'The rose hath stabbed the iris, who nectar affords . . .' That's your avern killing me, clearly. 'You will know your true love by her red pagne . . .' " She bent to kiss me, then sat in my lap. "Aren't you going to look?"

"I *am* looking." Her torn bodice had fallen again.

"Not there. Cover that with your hand, and then you can look at the note."

I did as she told me, but left the note where it was. "It's really too much, as I said a moment ago. The mysterious Septentrion and his challenge, then Hildegrin, and now this. Have I mentioned the Chatelaine Thecla to you?"

"More than once, while we were walking."

"I loved her. She read a great deal—there was really nothing for her to do when I was gone but read and sew and sleep—and when I was with her we used to laugh at the plots of some of the stories. This sort of thing was always happening to the people in them, and they were incessantly involved in high and melodramatic affairs for which they had no qualifications."

Agia laughed with me and kissed me again, a lingering kiss. When our lips parted, she said, "What's this about Hildegrin? He seemed ordinary enough."

I took another pastry, touched the note with it, then put a corner into her mouth. "Some time ago I saved the life of a man called Vodalus—"

Agia pulled away from me, spewing crumbs. "Vodalus? You're joking!"

"Not at all. That's what his friend called him. I was still hardly more than a boy, but I held back the haft of an ax for a moment. The blow would have killed him, and he gave me a chrisos."

"Wait. What has this to do with Hildegrin?"

"When I first saw Vodalus, he had a man and a woman with him. Enemies came upon them, and Vodalus remained behind to fight while the other man took the woman to safety." (I had decided it was wiser to say nothing about the corpse, or my killing of the axman.)

"I'd have fought myself—then there'd have been three fighters instead of one. Go on."

"Hildegrin was the man with Vodalus, that's all. If we had met him first, I would have had some idea, or thought I had some idea, of why a hipparch of the Septentrion Guard would want to fight me. And for that matter why someone has chosen to send me some sort of furtive message. You know, all the things the Chatelaine Thecla and I used to laugh about, spies and intrigue, masked trysts, lost heirs. What's the matter, Agia?"

"Do I revolt you? Am I so ugly?"

"You're beautiful, but you look as if you're about to be sick. I think you drank too fast."

"Here." A quick twist took Agia out of her pavonine gown; it lay about her brown, dusty feet like a heap of precious stones. I had seen her naked in the cathedral of the Pelerines, but now (whether because of the wine I had drunk or the wine she had drunk, because the light was dimmer now, or brighter, or only because she had been frightened and shamed then, covering her breasts and hiding her womanhood between her thighs) she drew me far more. I felt stupid with desire, thick-headed and thick-tongued as I pressed her warmth against my own cold flesh.

"Severian, wait. I'm not a strumpet, whatever you may think. But there's a price."

"What?"

"You must promise me you won't read that note. Throw it into the brazier."

I let go of her and stepped back.

Tears appeared in her eyes, rising as springs do among rocks. "I wish you could see the way you're looking at me now, Severian. No, I don't know what it says. It's just that—have you never heard of some women having supernatural knowledge? Premonitions? Knowing things they could not possibly have learned?''

The longing I had felt was nearly gone. I was frightened as well as angry, though I did not know why. I said, ''We have a guild of such women, our sisters, in the Citadel. Neither their faces nor their bodies are like yours.''

''I know I'm not like that. But that's why you must do what I advise. I've never in my life had a premonition of any strength, and I have one now. Don't you see that must mean it's something so true and so important to you that you can't and mustn't ignore it? Burn the note.''

''Someone is trying to warn me, and you don't want me to see it. I asked you if the Septentrion was your lover. You told me he was not, and I believed you.''

She started to speak, but I silenced her.

''I believe you still. Your voice had truth in it. Yet you are laboring to betray me in some way. Tell me now that isn't so. Tell me you are acting in my best interests, and nothing beyond.''

''Severian . . .''

''Tell me.''

''Severian, we met this morning. I hardly knew you and you hardly know me. What can you expect, and what would you expect if you had not just left the shelter of your guild? I've tried to help you from time to time. I'm trying to help you now.''

''Put on your dress.'' I took the note from under the tray. She rushed at me, but it was not difficult to hold her off with one hand. The note had been penned with a crow quill, in a straggling scrawl; in the dim light I could decipher only a few words.

''I could have distracted you, and thrown it into the fire. That's what I ought to have done. Severian, let me go—''

''Be quiet.''

''I had a knife, only last week. A misericorde with an ivy-root handle. We were hungry, and Agilus put it in pawn. If I had it still, I could stab you now!''

''It would be in your gown, and your gown is over there on the floor.'' I gave her a push that sent her staggering backward (there was wine enough in her stomach that it was not entirely from the violence of my motion) into the canvas chair, and carried the note to a spot where the last light of the sun penetrated the crowding leaves.

The woman with you has been here before.
Do not trust her. Trudo says the man is
a torturer. You are my mother come again.

XXVI

Sennet

I had just had time to absorb the words when Agia jumped from her chair, snatched the note from my hand, and threw it over the edge of the platform. For a moment she stood before me, looking from my face to *Terminus Est*, which by this time leaned, reassembled, against an arm of the couch. I think she feared I was going to strike off her head and throw it after the note. When I did nothing, she said, "Did you read it? Severian, say you didn't!"

"I read it, but I don't understand it."

"Then don't think about it."

"Be calm for a moment. It wasn't even meant for me. It may have been for you, but if it was, why was it put where no one but I could see it? Agia, have you had a child? How old are you?"

"Twenty-three. That's plenty old enough, but no, I haven't. I'll let you look at my belly if you don't believe me."

I tried to make a mental calculation and discovered I did not know enough about the maturation of women. "When did you menstruate first?"

"Thirteen. If I'd got pregnant, I would have been fourteen when the baby came. Is that what you're trying to find out?"

"Yes. And the child would be nine now. If it were bright, it might be able to write a note like that. Do you want me to tell you what it said?"

"No!"

"How old would you say Dorcas is? Eighteen? Nineteen, perhaps?"

"You shouldn't think about it, Severian. Whatever it was."

"I won't play games with you now. You're a woman—how old?"

Agia pursed her full lips. "I'd say your drab little mystery's sixteen or seventeen. Hardly more than a child."

Sometimes, as I suppose everyone has noticed, talking of absent persons seems to summon them up like eidolons. So it was now. A panel of the screen swung back and Dorcas came out, no longer the muddy creature we had become accustomed to, but a round-breasted, slender girl of singular grace. I have seen skin whiter than hers, but that was not a healthy whiteness. Dorcas seemed to glow. Freed of filth, her hair was pale gold; her eyes were as they had always been: the deep blue of the world-river Uroboros in my dream. When she saw that Agia was naked, she tried to return to the shelter of the screen, but the thick body of the scullion prevented her.

Agia said, "I had better put my rags on again before your pet faints."

Dorcas murmured, "I won't look."

"I don't care if you do," Agia told her, but I noticed she turned her back to us while she put on her gown. Speaking to the wall of leaves, she added, "Now we really must go, Severian. The trumpet will sound at any moment."

"And what will that mean?"

"You don't know?" She swung about to face us. "When the machionations of the City Wall appear to touch the edge of the solar disc, a trumpet—the first—is sounded on the Sanguinary Field. Some think it's only to regulate the combats there, though that's not so. It is a signal to the guards inside the Wall to close the gates. It's also the signal to begin the fighting, and if you're there when it blows, that's when your contest will start. When the sun is below the horizon and true night comes, a trumpeter on the Wall sounds tattoo. That means the gates will not be opened again even for those who carry special passes and also that anyone who, having given or received a challenge, has not yet come to the Field is assumed to have refused satisfaction. He can be assaulted wherever he is found, and an armiger or an exultant can engage assassins without soiling his honor."

The scullion, who had been standing by the stair listening to all this and nodding, moved aside for her master, the innkeeper. "Sieur," he said, "if you indeed have a mortal appointing, I—"

"That is just what my friend was saying," I told him. "We must go."

Dorcas asked then if she might have some wine. Somewhat surprised, I nodded; the innkeeper poured her a glass, which she held in both hands like a child. I asked him if he supplied writing implements for his guests.

"You wish to make a testament, sieur? Come with me—we have a bower reserved for that purpose. There's no charge, and if you like, I will engage a boy who'll carry the document to your executor."

I picked up *Terminus Est* and followed him, leaving Agia and Dorcas to keep watch on the avern. The bower our host boasted of was perched on a small limb and hardly big enough to hold a desk, but there was a stool there, several crow-quill pens, paper, and a pot of ink. I sat down and wrote out the words of the note; so far as I could judge, the paper was the same as that on which it had been written, and the ink gave the same faded black line. When I had sanded my scribble, folded it, and tucked it away in a compartment of my sabretache I seldom used, I told the innkeeper no messenger would be required, and asked if he knew anyone named Trudo.

"Trudo, sieur?" He looked puzzled.

"Yes. It's a common enough name."

"Surely it is, sieur, I know that. It's just that I was trying to think of somebody that might be known to me and somebody, if you understand me, sieur, in your exalted position. Some armiger or—"

"Anyone," I said. "Anyone at all. It would not, for example, be the name of the waiter who served us, would it?"

"No, sieur. His name's Ouen. I had a neighbor once named Trudo, sieur, but that was years ago, before I bought this place. I don't suppose it would be him you're after? Then there's my ostler here—his name's Trudo."

"I'd like to speak to him."

The innkeeper nodded, his chin vanishing in the fat that circled his neck. "As you wish, sieur. Not that he's likely to be able to tell you much." The steps creaked beneath his weight. "He's from far south, I warn you." (He meant the southern regions of the city, not the wild and largely treeless lands abutting on the ice.) "And from across the river to boot. You're not likely to get much sense from him, though he's a hard-working fellow."

I said, "I suspect I know what part of the city he comes from."

"Do you now? Well, that's interesting, sieur. Very interesting. I've heard one or two say they could tell such things by the way a man dressed or how he spoke, but I wasn't aware you'd laid eyes on Trudo, as the saying is." We were nearing the ground now, and he bawled, "*Trudo! Tr-u-u-do!*" And then, "REINS!"

No one appeared. A single flagstone the size of a large tabletop had been laid at the foot of the stair, and we stepped out upon it.

It was just at that moment when lengthening shadows cease to be shadows at all and become instead pools of blackness, as if some fluid darker even than the waters of the Lake of Birds was rising from the ground. Hundreds of people, some alone, some in small groups, were hurrying over the grass from the direction of the city. All seemed intent, bowed by an eagerness they carried upon their backs and shoulders like a pack. Most bore no weapons I could see, but a few had cases of rapiers, and at some distance off I made out the white blossom of an avern, carried, it seemed, on a pole or staff just as mine was.

"Pity they won't stop here," the innkeeper said. "Not that I won't get some of them coming back, but a dinner before is where the money is. I speak frankly, for I can see that young as you are, sieur, you're too sensible not to know that every business is run to make a profit. I try to give good value, and as I've said, we've a famous kitchen. *Tr-u-do!* I have to have one, for no other sort of food will agree with me—I'd starve, sieur, if I had to eat what most do. *Trudo you louse farm, where are you?"*

A dirty boy appeared from somewhere behind the trunk, wiping his nose on his arm. "He's not back there, Master."

"Well, where is he? Go look for him."

I was still watching the streaming hundreds. "They are all going to the Sanguinary Field then?" For the first time, I think, I fully realized that I was liable to die before the moon shone. Accounting for the note seemed futile and childish.

"Not all to fight, you understand. Most are only going to watch, there's some come only once, because somebody they know's fighting, or just because they were told about it, or read about it, or heard a song. Usually those get taken ill, because they come here and generally put away a bottle or so when they're getting over it.

"But there's others that come every night, or anyway four or five nights out of the week. They're specialists, and only foller one weapon, or perhaps two, and they pretend to know more about those than them that use them, which perhaps some do. After your victory, sieur, two or three will want to buy you a round. If you let them, they'll tell you what you did wrong and what the other man did wrong, but you'll find they don't agree."

I said, "Our dinner is to be private," and as I spoke I heard the whisper of bare feet on the steps behind us. Agia and Dorcas were coming down, Agia carrying the avern, which seemed to me to have grown larger in the failing light.

I have already told how strongly I desired Agia. When we are talking to women, we talk as though love and desire are two separate entities; and women, who often love us and sometimes desire us, maintain the same fiction. The fact is that they are aspects of the same thing, as I might have talked to the innkeeper of the north side of his tree and the south. If we desire a woman, we soon come to love her for her condescension in submitting to us (this, indeed, had been the original foundation of my love for Thecla), and since if we desire her she always submits in imagination at least, some element of love is ever present. On the other hand, if we love her, we soon come to desire her, since attraction is one of the attributes a woman should possess, and we cannot bear to think she is without any of them; in this way men come to desire even women whose legs are locked in paralysis, and women to desire those men who are impotent save with men like themselves.

But no one can say from what it is that what we call (almost at our pleasure) *love* or *desire* is born. As Agia came down the stair, one side of her face was lit by the last light of day, and the other thrown into shadow; her skirt, split nearly to the waist, permitted a flash of silken thigh. And all I had lost in feeling for her a few moments before when I had pushed her away came back doubled and doubled again. She saw that in my face, I know, and Dorcas, hardly a step behind her, saw it too and looked away. But Agia was angry with me still (as perhaps she had a right to be), so although she smiled for policy's sake and could not have concealed the ache in her loins if she would, yet she withheld much.

I think it is in this that we find the real difference between those women to whom if we are to remain men we must offer our lives, and those who (again—if we are to remain men) we must overpower and outwit if we can, and use as we never would a beast: that the second will never permit us to give them what we give the first. Agia enjoyed my admiration and would have been moved to ecstasy by my caresses; but even if I were to pour myself into her a hundred times, we would part strangers. I understood all this as she descended the last few steps, one hand closing the bodice of her gown, the other upholding the avern, whose pole she used as a staff and carried like a baculus. And yet I loved her still, or would have loved her if I could.

The boy came running up. "Trudo's gone, cook says. She was out fetchin' water 'cause the girl was gone, and seen him runnin' off, and his things is gone from the mews too."

"Gone for good, then," the innkeeper said. "When did he go? Just now?"

The boy nodded.

"He heard you were looking for him, sieur, that's what I'm afraid of. One of the others must have heard you asking me about the name, and run and told him. Did he steal from you?"

I shook my head. "He did me no harm, and I suspect he was trying to do good in whatever he did do. I'm sorry I cost you a servant."

The innkeeper spread his hands. "He'd some wages coming, so I won't lose by it."

As he turned away, Dorcas whispered. "And I am sorry to have taken your joy from you upstairs. I would not have deprived you. But, Severian, I love you."

From somewhere not far off, the silver voice of a trumpet called to the renascent stars.

XXVII

Is He Dead?

The Sanguinary Field, of which all my readers will have heard, though some, I hope, will never have visited it, lies northwest of the built sections of our capital of Nessus, between a residential enclave of city armigers and the barracks and stables of the Xenagie of the Blue Dimarchi. It is near enough the Wall to seem very near to someone like myself, who had never been near it at all, yet still leagues of hard walking by twisted avenues from the actual base. How many combats can be accommodated I do not know. It may be that the railings that delimit the grounds of each—upon which the spectators lean or sit as the fancy takes them—can be moved, and are adjusted to suit the evening's needs. I have only visited the spot once, but it seemed to me, with its trampled grass and silent, languid watchers, a strange and melancholy one.

During the brief time I have occupied the throne, many issues have been of more immediate concern than monomachy. Whether it is good or evil (as I am inclined to think), it is surely ineradicable in a society such as ours, which must for its own survival hold the military virtues higher than any others, and in which so few of the armed retainers of the state can be spared to police the populace.

Yet is it evil?

Those ages that have outlawed it (and many hundreds have, by my reading) have replaced it largely with murder—and with just such murders, by and large, as monomachy seems designed to prevent: murders resulting from quarrels among families, friends, and acquaintances. In these cases two die instead of one, for the law tracks down the slayer (a person not by disposition a criminal but by chance) and slays him, as though his death would restore his victim's life. Thus if, say, a thousand legal combats between individuals resulted in a thousand deaths (which is very unlikely, since most such combats do not terminate in death) but prevented five hundred murders, the state would be no worse.

Further, the survivor of such a combat is likely to be the individual most suited to defending the state, and also the most suited to engendering healthy children; while there is no survivor of most murders, and the murderer (were he to survive) is likely to be only vicious, and not strong, quick, or intelligent.

And yet how readily this practice lends itself to intrigue.

We heard the shouted names when we were still a hundred strides away, loudly and formally announced above the trilling of the hylas.

"Cadroe of the Seventeen Stones!"

"Sabas of the Parted Meadow!"

"Laurentia of the House of the Harp!" (This in a woman's voice.)

"Cadroe of the Seventeen Stones!"

I asked Agia who it was who thus called.

"They have given challenges, or have been challenged themselves. By bawling their names—or having a servant do it for them—they advertise that they have come, and to the world that their opponent has not."

"Cadroe of the Seventeen Stones!"

The vanishing sun, whose disc was now a quarter concealed behind the impenetrable blackness of the Wall, had dyed the sky with gamboge and cerise, vermillion and lurid violet. These colors, falling upon the throng of monomachists and loungers much as we see the aureate beams of divine favor fall on hierarchs in art, lent them an appearance insubstantial and thaumaturgic, as though they had all been produced a moment before by the flourish of a cloth and would vanish into the air again at a whistle.

"Laurentia of the House of the Harp!"

"Agia," I said, and from somewhere nearby we heard the choking death makes in a man's throat. "Agia, you are to call out, 'Severian of the Matachin Tower.' "

"I'm not your servant. Bawl it yourself if you want it bawled."

"Cadroe of the Seventeen Stones!"

"Don't look at me like that, Severian. I wish we hadn't come! *Severian! Severian of the Torturers! Severian of the Citadel! Of the Tower of Pain! Death! Death is come!*" My hand caught her just below the ear and she went sprawling, the avern on its pole beside her.

Dorcas gripped my arm. "You ought not have done that, Severian."

"It was only the flat of my hand. She'll be all right."

"She will hate you even more."

"Then you think she hates me now?"

Dorcas did not answer, and a moment later I myself forgot for the time being that I had asked the question—some distance away among the crowd, I had seen an avern.

The ground was a level circle some fifteen strides across, railed off save for an entrance at either end.

The ephor called: "The adjudication of the avern has been offered and accepted. Here is the place. The time is now. It only remains to be decided whether you will engage as you are, naked, or otherwise. How say you?"

Before I could speak, Dorcas called, "Naked. That man is in armor."

The Septentrion's grotesque helm swung from side to side in negation. Like most cavalry helmets it left the ears bare to better hear the graisle and the shouted orders of the wearer's superiors; in the shadow behind the cheekpiece I thought I saw a narrow band of black, and tried to recall where I had seen such a thing before.

The ephor asked, "You refuse, hipparch?"

"The men of my country do not go naked save in the presence of women alone."

"He wears armor," Dorcas called again. "This man has not even a shirt." Her voice, always so soft before, rang in the twilight like a bell.

"I will remove it." The Septentrion threw back his cape and raised a gauntleted hand to the shoulder of his cuirass. It slipped from him and fell at his feet. I had expected a chest as massive as Master Gurloes's, but the one I saw was narrower than my own.

"The helmet also."

Again the Septentrion shook his head, and the ephor asked, "Your refusal is absolute?"

"It is." There was a barely perceptible hesitation. "I can only say that I am instructed not to remove it."

The ephor turned to me. "We none of us would desire, I think, to embarrass the hipparch, and still less the personage—I do not say whom it may be—that he serves. I believe the wisest course would be to allow you, sieur, some compensating advantage. Have you one to suggest?"

Agia, who had been silent since I had struck her, said, "Refuse the combat, Severian. Or reserve your advantage until you need it."

Dorcas, who was loosening the strips of rag that bound the avern, said also, "Refuse the combat."

"I've come too far to turn back now."

The ephor asked pointedly, "Have you decided, sieur?"

"I think I have." My mask was in my sabretache. Like all those used in the guild it was of thin leather stiffened with strips of bone. Whether it would keep out the thrown leaves of the avern I had no way of knowing—but it was satisfying to hear the lookers-on draw breath when I snapped it open.

"You are ready now? Hipparch? Sieur? Sieur, you must give that sword to someone to hold for you. No weapon but the avern may be carried."

I looked about for Agia, but she had vanished into the crowd. Dorcas handed me the deadly blossom, and I gave her *Terminus Est.*

"Begin!"

A leaf whizzed close to my ear. The Septentrion was advancing with an irregular motion, his avern gripped beneath the lowest leaves by his left hand, and his right thrust forward as though to wrestle mine from me. I recalled that Agia had warned me of the danger of this, and clasped it as close as I dared.

For the space of five breaths we circled. Then I struck at his outstretched hand. He countered with his plant. I raised my own above my head like a sword, and as I did so realized the position was an ideal one—it put the vulnerable stem out of my opponent's reach, permitted me to slash downward with the whole plant at will, yet allowed me to detach leaves with my right hand.

This last discovery I put to the test at once, snapping off a leaf and sending it skimming toward his face. Despite the protection his helm gave him he ducked, and the crowd behind him scattered to avoid the missile. I followed it with another. And then another, which struck his own in flight.

The result was remarkable. Instead of absorbing the other's momentum and clattering down together as inanimate blades would, the leaves appeared to writhe and wind their edged lengths about each other, slashing and striking with their points so rapidly that before they had fallen a cubit they were no more than ragged strips of blackish-green that turned to a hundred colors and spun like a child's top . . .

Something, or someone, was pressing against my back. It was as though an unknown stood close behind me, his spine against mine, exerting a slight pressure. I felt cold, and was grateful for the warmth of his body.

"Severian!" The voice was Dorcas's, but she seemed to have wandered away.

"Severian! Won't anyone help him? Let me go!"

The peal of a carillon. The colors, which I had taken to be those of the struggling leaves, were in the sky instead, where a rainbow unrolled beneath the aurora. The world was a great paschal egg, crowded with all the colors of the palette. Near my head a voice inquired, *"Is he dead?"* and someone answered matter-of-factly, *"That's it. Those things always kill. Unless you want to see them drag him off?"*

The Septentrion's voice (oddly familiar) said, "I claim victor right to his clothing and weapons. Give me that sword."

I sat up. The leaves were still faintly struggling wisps a few paces from my boots. The Septentrion stood beyond them, still holding his avern. I drew breath to ask what had happened, and something fell from my chest to my lap; it was a leaf with a bloodstained tip.

Seeing me, the Septentrion whirled and lifted his avern. The ephor stepped between us, arms extended. From the railings some spectator called, *"Gentle right! Gentle right, soldier! Let him stand up and get his weapon."*

My legs would hardly bear me. I looked around stupidly for my own avern, and found it at last only because it lay near the feet of Dorcas, who was struggling with Agia. The Septentrion shouted, "He should be dead!" The ephor said, "He is not, hipparch. When he regains his weapon, you may pursue the combat."

I touched the stem of my avern, and for an instant felt I had grasped the tail of some cold-blooded but living animal. It seemed to stir in my hand, and the leaves rattled. Agia was shouting, *"Sacrilege!"* and I paused to look at her, then picked up the avern and turned to face the Septentrion.

His eyes were shadowed by his helmet, but there was terror in every line of his body. For a moment he seemed to look from me to Agia. Then he turned and fled toward the opening in the rails at his end of the arena. The spectators blocked his way and he used his avern like a scourge, striking to right and left. There was a scream, then a crescendo of screams. My own avern was pulling me backward, or rather, my avern was gone and someone gripped me by the hand. Dorcas. Somewhere far away Agia shrieked, *"Agilus!"* and another woman called, *"Laurentia of the House of the Harp!"*

XXVIII

Carnifex

I woke the next morning in a lazaret, a long, high-ceilinged room where we, the sick, the injured, lay upon narrow beds. I was naked, and for a long time, while sleep (or perhaps it was death) tugged at my eyelids, I moved my hands slowly over my body, searching it for injuries while I wondered, as I might have wondered of someone in a song, how I would live without clothing or money, how I should explain to Master Palaemon the loss of the sword and cloak he had given me.

For I was sure they were lost—or rather, that I was myself in some way lost from them. An ape with the head of a dog ran down the aisle, paused at my bed to look at me, then ran on. That seemed no stranger to me than the light that, passing through a window I could not see, fell upon my blanket.

I woke again, and sat up. For a moment I truly thought I was in our dormitory again, that I was captain of apprentices, that everything else, my masking, the death of Thecla, the combat of the averns, had been only a dream. This was not the last time this was to happen. Then I saw that the ceiling was of plaster and not our familiar metal one, and that the man in the bed next to my own was swathed in bandages. I threw back the blanket and swung my feet to the floor. Dorcas sat, asleep, with her back to the wall at the head of my bed. She had wrapped herself in the brown mantle; *Terminus Est* lay across her lap, the hilt and scabbard-tip protruding from either side of my heaped belongings. I managed to get my boots and hose, my breeches, my cloak, and my belt with its sabretache without waking her, but when I tried to take my sword she murmured and clung to it, so I left it with her.

Many of the sick were awake and stared at me, but none spoke. A door at the end of the room opened onto a flight of steps, and these descended to a courtyard where destriers stamped. For a moment I thought I was dreaming still: the cynocephalus was climbing upon the crenelations of the wall. But it was an animal as real as the champing steeds, and when I threw a bit of rubbish at it, it bared teeth as impressive as Triskele's.

A trooper in a hauberk came out to get something from his saddlebag, and I stopped him and asked where I was. He supposed that I meant in what part of the fortress, and pointed out a turret behind which, he said, was the Hall of Justice; then told me that if I would come with him I could probably get something to eat.

As soon as he spoke, I realized I was famished. I followed him down a dark hallway into a room much lower and darker than the lazaret, where two or three score dimarchi like himself were bent over a midday meal of fresh bread, beef, and boiled greens. My new friend advised me to take a plate and tell the cooks I had been instructed to come here for my dinner. I did so, and though they looked a trifle surprised at my fuligin cloak, they served me without objection.

If the cooks were incurious, the soldiers were curiosity itself. They asked my name, and where I came from, and what my rank was (for they assumed our guild was organized like the military). They asked where my ax was, and when I told them we used the sword, where that was; and when I explained that I had a woman with me who was watching it, they cautioned me that she might run away with it, and then counseled me to carry out bread for her under my cloak, since she would not be permitted to come where we were to eat. I discovered that all the older men had supported women—camp followers of what is perhaps the most useful and least dangerous kind—at one time or another, though few had them now. They had spent the summer before in fighting in the north and had been sent to winter in Nessus, where they served to maintain order. Now they expected to go north again within a week. Their women had returned to their own villages to live with parents or relatives. I asked if the women would not have preferred to follow them south.

"Prefer it?" said my friend. "Of course they'd prefer it. But how would they do it? It's one thing to follow cavalry that's fighting its way north with army, for that doesn't make more than a league or two on the best days, and if it clears three in a week, you can bet it will lose two the next. But how would they keep up on the way back to the city? Fifteen leagues a day. And what would they eat on the way? It's better for them to wait. If a new xenagie comes to our old sector, they'll have some new men. Some new girls will come too, and some of the old ones drop out, and it gives everyone a chance to change off if they want. I heard they brought in one of you carnifexes last night, but he was nearly dead himself. Have you been to see him?''

I said I had not.

''One of our patrols reported him, and when the chiliarch heard of it he sent them back to bring him, seeing we were sure to need one in a day or so. They swear they didn't touch him, but they had to bring him back on a litter. I don't know if he's one of your comrades, but you might want to take a look.''

I promised I would, and after thanking the soldiers for their hospitality, left them. I was worried about Dorcas, and their questioning, though it was clearly well meant, had made me uneasy. There were too many things I could not explain—how I had come to be injured, for example, if I had admitted I was the man who had been carried in the night before, and where Dorcas had come from. Not really understanding those things myself bothered me at least as much, and I felt, as we always feel when there is a whole sector of our lives that cannot bear light, that no matter how far the last question had been from one of the forbidden subjects, the next would pierce to the heart of it.

Dorcas was awake and standing by my bed, where someone had left a cup of steaming broth. She was so delighted to see me that I felt happy myself, as though joy were as contagious as a pestilence. ''I thought you were dead,'' she told me. ''You were gone, and your clothes were gone, and I thought they had taken them to bury you in.''

''I'm all right,'' I said. ''What happened last night?''

Dorcas became serious at once. I made her sit on the bed with me and eat the bread I had brought and drink the broth while she answered. ''You remember fighting with the man who wore that strange helmet, I'm sure. You put on a mask and went into the arena with him, although I begged you not to. Almost at once he hit you in the chest, and you fell. I remember seeing the leaf, a horrible thing like a flatworm made of iron, half in your body and turning red as it drank your blood.

''Then it fell away. I don't know how to describe it. It was as though everything I had seen had been *wrong*. But it wasn't wrong—I remember what I saw. You got up again, and you looked . . . I don't know. As if you were lost, or some part of you was far away. I thought he was going to kill you at once, but the ephor protected you, saying he had to allow you to get your avern. His was quiet, the way yours had been when you pulled it up in that awful place, but yours had begun to writhe and open its flower—I thought it had been open before, the white thing with the swirl of petals, only now I believe I was thinking too much of roses, and it had not been open at all. There was something underneath, something else, a face like the face poison would have, if poison had a face.

"You didn't notice. You picked it up and it began to curl toward you, slowly, as though it were only half awake. But the other man, the hipparch, couldn't believe what he had seen. He was staring at you, and that woman Agia was shouting to him. And all at once he turned and ran away. The people who were watching didn't want him to, they wanted to see someone killed. So they tried to stop him, and he . . ."

Her eyes were brimming with tears; she turned her head to keep me from seeing them. I said, "He struck several of them with his avern, and I suppose killed them. Then what happened?"

"It wasn't just that he struck them. It struck *at* them, after the first two, like a snake. The ones who were cut with the leaves didn't die at once, they screamed, and some of them ran and fell and got up and ran again, as if they were blind, knocking other people down. And at last a big man struck him from behind and a woman who had been fighting somewhere else came with a braquemar. She cut the avern—not sidewise but down the stem so it split. Then some of the men held the hipparch and I heard her blade clash on his helmet.

"You were just standing there. I wasn't sure you even knew he was gone, and your avern was bending back toward your face. I thought of what the woman had done and hit at it with your sword. It was heavy, so very heavy at first, and then it was hardly heavy at all. But when I slashed down with it I felt as if I could have struck the head from a bison. Only I had forgotten to take off the sheath. But it knocked the avern out of your hand, and I took you and led you away . . ."

"Where?" I asked.

She shivered and dipped a piece of bread in the steaming broth. "I don't know. I didn't care. It was just so good to be walking with you, to know I was taking care of you the way you had taken care of me before we got the avern. But I was cold, terribly cold, when night came. I put your cloak all around you and fastened it in front, and you didn't seem to be cold, so I took this mantle and wrapped myself in it. My dress was falling to pieces. It still is."

I said, "I wanted to buy you another one when we were at the inn."

She shook her head, chewing the tough crust. "Do you know, I think this is the first food I've had in a long, long time. I have pains in my stomach—that's why I drank the wine there—but this makes it feel better. I hadn't realized how weak I was getting.

"But I didn't want a new dress from there because I would have had to wear it for a long time, and it would always have reminded me of that day. You can buy me a dress now, if you like, because *it* will remind me of this day, when I thought you were dead when you were really well.

"Anyway, we got back into the city somehow. I was hoping to find a place to stop where you could lie down, but there were only big houses with terraces and balustrades. That sort of thing. Some soldiers came galloping up and asked if you were a carnifex. I didn't know the word, but I remembered what you had told me and so I told them you were a torturer, because soldiers have always seemed to me to be a kind of torturer and I knew they would help us. They tried to get you to ride, but you fell off. So some of them tied their capes between two lances and laid you on that, and put the ends of the lances in the stirrup straps of two destriers. One of them wanted to take me up into his saddle, but I wouldn't do it. I walked beside you all the way and sometimes I talked to you, but I don't think you heard me."

She drained the last of the broth. "Now I want to ask you a question. When I was washing myself behind the screen, I could hear you and Agia whispering about a note. Later you were looking for someone in the inn. Will you tell me about that?"

"Why didn't you ask before?"

"Because Agia was with us. If you had found out anything, I didn't want her to hear what it was."

"I'm sure Agia could discover anything I discovered," I said. "I don't know her well, and in fact I don't feel I know her as well as I know you. But I know her well enough to realize that she's much clev-erer than I am."

Dorcas shook her head again. "She's the sort of woman who's good at making puzzles for other people, but not at solving ones she didn't make herself. I think she thinks—I don't know—side-wise. So no one else can follow it. She's the kind of woman people say thinks like a man, but those women don't think like real men at all, in fact, they think less like real men than most women do. They just don't think like women. The way they do think is hard to follow, but that doesn't mean it's clear, or deep."

I told her about the note, and what it said, and mentioned that although it had been destroyed I had copied it out on the inn's paper and found it to be the same paper, and the same ink.

"So someone wrote it there," she said pensively. "Probably one of the inn servants, because he called the ostler by name. But what does it mean?"

"I don't know."

"I can tell you why it was put where it was. I sat there, on that horn settee, before you sat down. It made me happy, I recall, because you sat beside me. Do you remember if the waiter—he must have carried the note, whether he wrote it or not—put the tray there before I got up to bathe?''

"I can remember everything,'' I said, "except last night. Agia sat in a folding canvas chair, you sat on the couch, that's right, and I sat down beside you. I had been carrying the avern on the pole as well as my sword, and I laid the avern flat behind the couch. The kitchen girl came in with water and towels for you, then she went out and got oil and rags for me.''

Dorcas said, "We ought to have given her something.''

"I gave her an orichalk to bring the screen. That's probably as much as she's paid for a week. Anyway, you went behind it, and a moment later the host led the waiter in with the tray and wine.''

"That's why I didn't see it, then. But the waiter must have known where I was sitting, because there was no place else. So he left it under the tray, hoping I'd see it when I came out. What was the first part again?''

" 'The woman with you has been here before. Do not trust her.' ''

"It must have been for me. If it had been for you, it would have distinguished between Agia and me, probably by hair color. And if it had been meant for Agia, it would have been out on the other side of the table where she would have seen it instead.''

"So you reminded someone of his mother.''

"Yes.'' Once more there were tears in her eyes.

"You're not old enough to have had a child who could have written that note.''

"I don't remember,'' she said, and buried her face in the loose folds of the brown mantle.

XXIX

Agilus

When the physician in charge had examined me and found I had no need of treatment, he asked us to leave the lazaret, where my cloak and sword were, as he said, upsetting to his patients.

On the opposite side of the building in which I had eaten with the troopers, we found a shop that catered to their needs. Together with false jewelry and trinkets of the sort such men give their paramours, it carried a certain amount of women's clothing; and though my money had been much depleted by the dinner we had never returned to the Inn of Lost Loves to enjoy, I was able to buy Dorcas a simar.

The entrance to the Hall of Justice was not far from this shop. A crowd of a hundred or so was milling before it, and since the people pointed and elbowed one another when they caught sight of my fuligin, we retreated again to the courtyard where the destriers were tethered. A portreeve from the Hall of Justice found us there—an imposing man with a high, white forehead like the belly of a pitcher. ''You are the carnifex,'' he said. ''I was told you are well enough to perform your office.''

I told him I could do whatever was necessary today, if his master required it.

''Today? No, no, that's not possible. The trial won't be over until this afternoon.''

I remarked that since he had come to make certain I was well enough to carry out the execution, he must have felt certain the prisoner would be found guilty.

''Oh, there's no question of that—not the least. Nine persons died, after all, and the man was apprehended on the spot. He's of no consequence, so there's no possibility of pardon or appeal. The tribunal will reconvene at midmorning, but you won't be required until noon.''

Because I had had no direct experience with judges or courts (at the Citadel, our clients had always been sent to us, and Master Gurloes dealt with those officials who occasionally came to inquire about the disposition of some case or other), and because I was eager to actually perform the act in which I had been drilled for so long, I suggested that the chiliarch might wish to consider a torchlight ceremony that same night.

''That would be impossible. He must meditate his decision. How would it look? A great many people feel already that the military magistrates are hasty and even capricious. And to be frank, a civil judge would probably have waited a week, and the case would be all the better for it, since there would have been ample time, then, for someone to come forward with fresh evidence, which of course no one will actually do.''

''Tomorrow afternoon then,'' I said. ''We'll require quarters for the night. Also I'll want to examine the scaffold and block, and ready my client. Will I need a pass to see him?''

The portreeve asked if we could not stay in the lazaret, and when I shook my head, we—the portreeve, Dorcas, and I—went there to permit him to argue with the physician in charge, who, as I had predicted, refused to have us. That was followed by a lengthy discussion with a noncommissioned officer of the xenagie, who explained that it was impossible for us to stay in the barracks with the troopers, and that if we were to use one of the rooms set aside for the higher ranks, no one would want to occupy it in the future. In the end a little, windowless storeroom was cleared out for us, and two beds and some other furniture (all of which had seen hard use) brought in. I left Dorcas there, and after assuring myself that I was unlikely to step through a rotten board at the critical moment, or to have to saw the client's head off while I held him across my knee, I went to the cells to make the call that our traditions demand.

Subjectively at least, there is a great difference between detention facilities to which one has become accustomed and those to which one has not. If I had been entering our own oubliette, I would have felt I was, quite literally, coming home—perhaps coming home to die, but coming home nevertheless. Although I would have realized in the abstract that our winding metal corridors and narrow gray doors might hold horror for the men and women confined there, I would have felt nothing of that horror myself, and if one of them had suggested I should, I would have been quick to point out their various comforts—clean sheets and ample blankets, regular meals, adequate light, privacy that was scarcely ever interrupted, and so on.

Now, going down a narrow and twisted stone stair into a facility a hundredth the size of ours, my feelings were precisely the reverse of what I would have felt there. I was oppressed by the darkness and stench as if by a weight. The thought that I might myself be confined there by some accident (a misunderstood order, for example, or some unsuspected malice on the part of the portreeve) recurred no matter how often I pushed it aside.

I heard the sobbing of a woman, and because the portreeve had spoken of a man, assumed that it came from a cell other than the one that held my client. That, I had been told, was the third from the right. I counted: one, two, and three. The door was merely wood bound with iron, but the locks (such is military efficiency!) had been oiled. Within, the sobbing hesitated and almost ceased as the bolt fell back.

Inside a naked man lay upon straw. A chain ran from the iron collar about his neck to the wall. A woman, naked too, bent over him, her long, brown hair falling past her face and his so that it seemed to unite them. She turned to look at me, and I saw that it was Agia.

She hissed, "Agilus!" and the man sat up. Their faces were so nearly alike that Agia might have been holding a mirror to her own.

"It was you," I said. "But that isn't possible." Even while I spoke, I was recalling the way Agia had behaved at the Sanguinary Field, and the strip of black I had seen by the hipparch's ear.

"You," Agia said. "Because you lived, he has to die."

I could only answer, "Is it really Agilus?"

"Of course." My client's voice was an octave lower than his twin's, though less steady. "You still don't understand, do you?"

I could only shake my head.

"It was Agia in the shop. In the Septentrion costume. She came in through the rear entrance while I was speaking to you, and I made a sign to her when you wouldn't even talk of selling the sword."

Agia said, "I couldn't speak—you would have known it for a woman's voice—but the cuirass hid my breasts and the gauntlets my hands. Walking like a man isn't as hard as men think."

"Have you ever *looked* at that sword? The tang should be signed." Agilus's hands lifted for a moment, as though he would have taken it still if he could. Agia added in a toneless voice, "It is. By Jovinian. I saw it in the inn."

There was a tiny window high up in the wall behind them, and from it, suddenly, as though the ridge of a roof, or a cloud, had now fallen below the sun, a beam of light came to bathe them both. I looked from one aureate face to the other. "You tried to kill me. Just for my sword."

Agilus said, "I hoped you would leave it—don't you remember? I tried to persuade you to leave, to flee in disguise. I would have given the clothes to you, and as much money as I could."

"Severian, don't you understand? It was worth ten times more than our shop, and the shop was all we had."

"You've done this before. You must have. Everything went too smoothly. A legal murder, with no body to weight for Gyoll."

"You're going to kill Agilus, aren't you? That must be why you're here—but you didn't know it was us until you opened the door. What have we done that you're not going to do?"

Less stridently, her brother's voice followed Agia's. "It was a fair combat. We were equally armed, and you agreed to the conditions. Will you give me such a fight tomorrow?"

"You knew that when evening came the warmth of my hands would stimulate the avern, and that it would strike at my face. You wore gloves and you only had to wait. In reality, you didn't even have to do that, because you had thrown the leaves often before."

Agilus smiled. "So the business of the gauntlets was a side issue after all." He spread his hands. "I won. But in reality you won, by some concealed art neither my sister nor I understand. I have been wronged by you three times now, and the old law said that a man three times wronged might claim any boon of his oppressor. I grant that the old law is no longer in force, but my darling tells me you have an attachment to times past, when your guild was great and your fortress the center of the Commonwealth. I claim the boon. Set me free."

Agia rose, brushing the straw from her knees and rounded thighs. As though she realized only now that she was naked, she picked up the blue-green brocade gown I remembered so well and clasped it to her.

I said, "How have I wronged you, Agilus? It seems to me that you have wronged me, or tried to."

"First by entrapment. You carried an heirloom worth a villa about the city without knowing what it was you had. As owner it was your duty to know, and your ignorance threatens to cost me my life tomorrow unless you free me tonight. Secondly, by refusing to entertain any offer to buy. In our commercial society, one may set one's price as high as one wishes, but to refuse to sell at any price is treason. Agia and I wore the gaudy armor of a barbarian—you wore his heart. Thirdly, by the sleight with which you won our combat. Unlike you, I found myself contesting powers greater than I could comprehend. I lost my nerve, as any man would, and here I am. I call on you to free me."

Laughter came unwished-for, carrying with it the taste of gall. "You're asking me to do for you, whom I have every reason to despise, what I wouldn't do for Thecla, whom I loved almost more than my own life. No. I'm a fool, and if I was not one before, surely your darling sister has made one of me. But not such a fool as that."

Agia dropped her gown and threw herself toward me with such violence that I thought for an instant she was attacking me. Instead she covered my mouth with kisses, and seizing my hands put one on her breast and the other upon her velvet hip. There were bits of rotten straw there still, and on her back, to which I shifted both hands a moment later.

"Severian, I love you! I longed for you when we were together, and tried to give myself to you a score of times. Don't you remember the Garden of Delectation? How much I wanted to take you there? It would have been rapture for us both, but you wouldn't go. For once be honest." (She spoke as if honesty were an abnormality like mania.) "Don't you love me? Take me now . . . here. Agilus will turn his face away, I promise you." Her fingers had slid between my waistband and my belly, and I was not aware that her other hand had lifted the flap of my sabretache until I heard the rustle of paper there.

I slapped her wrist, perhaps harder than I should, and she flew at me, clawing for my eyes as Thecla used sometimes to do when she could no longer bear the thoughts of imprisonment and pain. I pushed her away—not into a chair this time but against the wall. Her head struck the stone, and though it must have been padded by her abundant hair, the sound was as sharp as the tap of a mason's hammer. All the strength seemed to leave her knees; she slid down until she was sitting on the straw. I would never have guessed that Agia was capable of weeping, but she wept.

Agilus asked, "What did she do?" There was no emotion beyond curiosity in the question.

"You must have seen her. She tried to reach into my sabretache." I scooped what coins I possessed out of their compartment: two brass orichalks and seven copper aes. "Or perhaps she wanted to steal the letter I have to the archon of Thrax. I told her about that once, but I don't carry it in here."

"She wanted the coins, I am sure. They've fed me, but she must be dreadfully hungry."

I picked Agia up and thrust her torn gown into her arms, then opened the door and led her out. She was still dazed, but when I gave her an orichalk she threw it down and spat at it.

When I reentered the cell, Agilus was sitting cross-legged, his back propped by the wall. "Don't ask me about Agia," he said. "Everything you suspect is true—is that enough? I will be dead tomorrow, and she will wed the old man who dotes on her, or someone else. I wanted her to do it sooner. He couldn't have prevented her from seeing me, her brother. Now I will be gone, and she won't have even that to worry about."

"Yes," I said, "you will die tomorrow. That's what I've come to talk to you about. Do you care how you look on the scaffold?"

He stared at his hands, slender and rather soft, where they lay in the narrow beam of sunlight that had given his head, and Agia's, an aureole a few moments before. "Yes," he said. "She may come. I hope she won't, but yes, I care."

I told him then (as I had been taught) to eat little in the morning so that he would not be ill when the time came, and cautioned him to empty his bladder, which relaxes at the stroke. I drilled him too in that false routine we teach to all who must die, so they will think the moment is not quite come when in fact it has come, the false routine that lets them die with something less of fear. I do not know if he believed me, though I hope he did; if ever a lie is justified in the sight of the Pancreator, it is that one.

When I left him, the orichalk was gone. In its place—and no doubt with its edge—a design had been scratched on the filthy stones. It might have been the snarling face of Jurupari, or perhaps a map, and it was wreathed with letters I did not know. I rubbed it away with my foot.

XXX

Night

There were five of them, three men and two women. They waited outside the door, in a sense, but not near it, grouped a dozen strides away. Waiting, they talked among themselves, two or three talking together, almost shouting, laughing, waving arms, nudging one another. I watched them from the shadows for a time. They could not see me there, or did not, wrapped as I was in my fuligin cloak, and I was able to pretend I did not know what they were; they might have been at a party, all a little drunk.

They came eagerly yet hesitantly, afraid of being repulsed and determined to make the advance. One man was taller than I, surely the illegitimate son of some exultant, fifty or more, and nearly as fat as the host at the Inn of Lost Loves. A thin woman of twenty or so walked beside him, almost pressing against him; she had the hungriest eyes I have ever seen. When the fat man stepped in front of me, blocking my way with his bulk, she nearly (yet not quite) embraced me, coming so close it seemed almost magical that we did not touch, her long-fingered hands moving at the opening of my cloak with the desire to stroke my chest, but never quite doing so, so that I felt I was about to fall prey to some blood-drinking ghost, a succubus or lamia. The others crowded around me, hemming me against the building.

"It's tomorrow, isn't it? How does it feel?" "What's your real name?" "He's a bad one, isn't he? A monster?" None of them waited for answers to their questions, or, so far as I could see, expected or wanted any. They sought propinquity, and the experience of having spoken to me. "Will you break him first? Will there be a branding?" "Have you ever killed a woman?"

"Yes," I said. "Yes, I did, once."

One of the men, short and slight, with the high, bumpy forehead of an intellectual, was putting an asimi into my hand. "I know you fellows don't get much, and I hear he's a pauper, can't tip." A woman, gray hair straggling over her face, tried to make me take a lace-trimmed handkerchief. "Get blood on it. As much as you want, or even only a little. I'll pay you afterward."

All of them stirred me to pity even as they revolted me; but one man most of all. He was even smaller than the one who had given me the money, grayer than the gray-haired woman; and there was a madness in his dull eyes, a shadow of some half-suppressed concern that had worn itself out in the prison of his mind until all its eagerness was gone and only its energy remained. He seemed to be waiting until the other four had finished speaking, and since that time clearly would never come, I quieted them with a gesture and asked him what he wanted.

"M-m-master, when I was on the *Quasar* I had a paracoita, a doll, you see, a genicon, so beautiful with her great pupils as dark as wells, her i-irises purple like asters or pansies blooming in summer, Master, whole beds of them, I thought, had b-been gathered to make those eyes, that flesh that always felt sun-warmed. Wh-wh-where is she now, my own scopolagna, my poppet? Let h-h-hooks be buried in the hands that took her! Crush them, Master, beneath stones. Where has she gone from the lemon-wood box I made for her, where she never slept at all, for she lay with me all night, not in the box, the lemon-wood box where she waited all day, watch-and-watch, Master, smiling when I laid her in so she might smile when I drew her out. How soft her hands were, her little hands. Like d-d-doves. She might have flown with them about the cabin had she not chosen instead to lie with me. W-w-wind their guts about your w-windlass, stuff their eyes into their mouths. Unman them, shave them clean below so their doxies may not know them, their lemans may rebuke them, leave them to the brazen laughter of the brazen mouths of st-st-strumpets. Work your will upon those guilty. Where was their mercy on the innocent? When did they tremble, when weep? What kind of men could do as they have done—thieves, false friends, betrayers, bad shipmates, no shipmates, murderers and kidnappers. W-without you, where are their nightmares, where are their restitutions, so long promised? Where are their chains, fetters, manacles, and cangues? Where are their abacinations, that shall leave them blind? Where are the defenestrations that shall break their bones, where is the estrapade that shall grind their joints? Where is she, the beloved whom I lost?"

Dorcas had found a daisy for her hair; but as we walked about outside the walls (I wrapped in my cloak, so that to anyone more than a few paces off it must have seemed that she walked alone), it folded its petals in sleep, and she plucked instead one of those white, trumpet-shaped blossoms that are called moonflowers because they appear green in the moon's green light. Neither of us had much to say other than that we would be utterly alone save for the other. Our hands spoke of that, clasping each other tightly.

Victuallers came and went, for the soldiers were making ready to depart. To north and east the Wall hemmed us round, making the wall that enclosed the barracks and administrative buildings seem no more than children's work, a wall of sand that might be trodden down by accident. To south and west extended the Sanguinary Field. We heard the trumpet blown there, and the cries of the new monomachists who sought their foes. Both of us, I think, for a time dreaded that the other would suggest we walk there and watch the combats. Neither did.

When the last curfew had come drifting down from the Wall, we returned, with a borrowed candle, to our windowless and fireless room. There was no bolt for the door, but we put the table against it and stood the candlestick on that. I had told Dorcas she was free to go, and that forever afterward it would be said of her that she was a torturer's woman, who gave herself under the scaffold for money spotted with blood.

She had said, "That money has clothed and fed me." Now she drew off the brown mantle (which hung to her heels—and beyond, when she was not careful of it, so the hem dragged in the dust) and smoothed the raw, yellow-brown linen of her simar.

I asked if she were frightened.

"Yes," she said. Then quickly, "Oh, not of you."

"Of what then?" I was taking off my clothes. If she had asked me, I would not have touched her throughout the night. But I wanted her to ask—indeed, I wanted her to beg; and the pleasure I would have had in abstinence would then have been at least as great (as I thought) as I would have had in possession, with the additional pleasure of knowing that on the next night she would feel the more obliged because I had spared her.

"Of myself. Of what thoughts may return to me when I lie again with a man."

"Again? Do you remember a time before?"

Dorcas shook her head. "But I am certain I am no virgin. I have desired you often, yesterday and today. For whom did you believe I washed myself? Last night I held your hand while you slept, and I dreamed we sated ourselves and lay in each other's arms. But I know satiety as well as desire—so I have known one man at least. Do you wish me to remove this before I blow out the candle?''

She was slender, high-breasted and narrow-hipped, strangely childlike to me, though fully a woman. ''You seem so small,'' I said, and held her to me.

''And you are so big.''

I knew then that however much I tried not to I would hurt her, that night and afterward. I knew too that I was incapable of sparing her. A moment before I would have refrained if she had asked. Now I could not; and just as I would have thrust forward though it had plunged my body on a spike, I would follow her later and try to cleave her to me.

But it was not my body that was impaled, but hers. We had been standing while I ran my hands over her and kissed her breasts, that were like round fruits sliced in two. Now I lifted her, and together we fell on one of the beds. She cried out, half in delight, half in pain, and pushed me away before she clutched at me. ''I'm glad,'' she said. ''I'm so glad,'' and bit me on the shoulder. Her body bent backward like a bow.

Later we pushed the beds together so we could lie side by side. Everything was slower the second time; she would not agree to a third. ''You'll need your strength tomorrow,'' she said.

''Then you don't care.''

''If we could have our way, no man would have to go roving or draw blood. But women did not make the world. All of you are torturers, one way or another.''

It rained that night, so hard we could hear it drumming on the tiles over our heads, a cleansing, crashing, unending downpour of water. I dozed, and dreamed that the world had been turned upside down. Gyoll was overhead now, decanting all its flood of fish and filth and flowers over us. I saw the great face I had seen under the water when I had nearly drowned—a portent of coral and white seen in the sky, smiling with needle teeth.

Thrax is called the City of Windowless Rooms. This windowless room of ours, I thought, is a preparation for Thrax. Thrax will be like this. Or perhaps Dorcas and I are already there, it was not so far north as I thought, so far north as I was led to believe . . .

Dorcas got up to go out, and I went with her, knowing it would not be safe for her to go alone at night in a place where there were so many soldiers. The corridor outside our room ran along an outer wall pierced with embrasures; water splashed through each in a fine spray. I wanted to keep *Terminus Est* in her sheath, but so large a sword is slow to draw. When we were back in our room again, with the table against the door, I took out the whetstone and sharpened the man-side of the blade, honing its edge until the endmost third, the part I would use, would divide a thread tossed into the air. Then I wiped and oiled the whole blade and stood the sword against the wall near my head.

Tomorrow would be my first appearance on the scaffold, unless the chiliarch decided at the last moment to exercise clemency. That was always a possibility, always a risk. History shows that every age has some unquestioned neurosis, and Master Palaemon had taught me that clemency is ours, a way of saying that one less one is more than nothing, that since human law need not be self-consistent, justice need not be so either. There is a dialogue in the brown book somewhere between two mystes, in which one argues that culture was an outgrowth of the vision of the Increate as logical and just, bound by interior consistency to fulfill his promises and threats. If that was the case, I thought, surely we will perish now, and the invasion from the north, that so many have died to resist, is no more than the wind that topples a tree already rotten.

Justice is a high thing, and that night, when I lay beside Dorcas listening to the rain, I was young, so that I desired high things only. That, I think, was why I so desired that our guild regain the position and regard it had once possessed. (And I still desired that, even then, when I had been cast out of it.) Perhaps it was for the same reason that the love of living things, which I had felt so strongly as a child, had declined until it was hardly more than a memory when I found poor Triskele bleeding outside the Bear Tower. Life, after all, is not a high thing, and in many ways is the reverse of purity. I am wise now, if not much older, and I know it is better to have all things, high and low, than to have the high only.

Unless the chiliarch decided, then, to grant clemency, tomorrow I would take Agilus's life. No one can say what that means. The body is a colony of cells (I used to think of our oubliette when Master Palaemon said that). Divided into two major parts, it perishes. But there is no reason to mourn the destruction of a colony of cells: such a colony dies each time a loaf of bread goes into the oven. If a man is no more than such a colony, a man is nothing; but we know instinctively that a man is more. What happens, then, to that part that is more?

It may be that it perishes as well, though more slowly. There are a great many haunted buildings, tunnels, and bridges; yet I have heard that in those cases in which the spirit is that of a human being and not an elemental, its appearances grow less and less frequent and at last cease. Historiographers say that in the remote past men knew only this one world of Urth, and had no fear of such beasts as were on it then, and traveled freely from this continent to the north; but no one has ever seen even the ghosts of such men.

It may be that it perishes at once—or that it wanders among the constellations. This Urth, surely, is less than a village in the immensity of the universe. And if a man lives in a village and his neighbors burn his house, he leaves the place if he does not die in it. But then we must ask how he came.

Master Gurloes, who has performed a great many executions, used to say that only a fool worried about making some failure of ritual: slipping in the blood, or failing to perceive that the client wore a wig and attempting to lift the head by the hair. The greater dangers were a loss of nerve that would make one's arms tremble and give an awkward blow and a feeling of vindictiveness that would transform the act of justice into mere revenge. Before I slept again, I tried to steel myself against both.

XXXI

The Shadow of the Torturer

It is a part of our office to stand uncloaked, masked, sword bared, upon the scaffold for a long time before the client is brought out. Some say this is to symbolize the unsleeping omnipresence of justice, but I believe the real reason is to give the crowd a focus, and the feeling that something is about to take place.

A crowd is not the sum of the individuals who compose it. Rather it is a species of animal, without language or real consciousness, born when they gather, dying when they depart. Before the Hall of Justice, a ring of dimarchi surrounded the scaffold with their lances, and the pistol their officer carried could, I suppose, have killed fifty or sixty before someone could snatch it from him and knock him to the cobblestones to die. Still it is better to have a focus, and some open symbol of power.

The people who had come to see the execution were by no means all, or even mostly, poor. The Sanguinary Field is near one of the better quarters of the city, and I saw plenty of red and yellow silk, and faces that had been washed with scented soap that morning. (Dorcas and I had splashed ourselves at the well in the courtyard.) Such people are much slower to violence than the poor, but once roused are far more dangerous because they are not accustomed to being overawed by force, and despite the demagogues, have a good deal more courage.

And so I stood with my hands resting on the quillions of *Terminus Est*, and turned this way and that, and adjusted the block so that my shadow would fall across it. The chiliarch was not visible, though I discovered later that he was watching from a window. I looked for Agia in the crowd but could not find her; Dorcas was on the steps of the Hall of Justice, a position reserved for her at my request by the portreeve.

The fat man who had waylaid me the day before was as near the scaffold as he could get, with a lance-fire threatening his bulging coat. The woman of the hungry eyes was on his right and the gray-haired woman on his left; I had her handkerchief in my boot top. The short man who had given me an asimi and the dull-eyed man who stammered and talked so strangely were nowhere to be seen. I looked for them on the rooftops where they could have had a good view despite their small stature, and though I did not find them, perhaps they were there.

Four sergeants in high dress helmets led Agilus forth. I saw the crowd opening for them like the water behind Hildegrin's boat before I could see them at all. Then came the scarlet plumes, then the flash of armor, and at last Agilus's brown hair and his wide, boyish face held uptilted because the chains that bound his arms forced his shoulder blades together. I remembered how elegant he had looked in the armor of a guards officer, with the golden chimera splashed across his chest. It seemed tragic that he could not be accompanied now by men of the unit that had in some sense been his, instead of these scarred regulars in laboriously polished steel. He had been stripped of all his finery now, and I waited to receive him wearing the fuligin mask in which I had fought him. Silly old women believe the Panjudicator punishes us with defeats and rewards us with victory: I felt I had been given more reward than I desired.

A few moments later he mounted the scaffold and the brief ceremony began. When it was over, the soldiers forced him to his knees and I lifted my sword, forever blotting out the sun.

When the blade is as sharp as it should be, and the stroke is given correctly, one feels only a slight hesitation as the spinal column parts, then the solid bite of the edge into the block. I would take an oath that I smelled Agilus's blood on the rain-washed air before his head banged into the basket. The crowd drew back, then surged forward against the leveled lances. I heard the fat man's exhalation distinctly, precisely the sound he might have made at climax when he sweated over some hired woman. From far away came a scream, Agia's voice as unmistakable as a face seen by lightning. Something in its timbre made me feel she had not been watching at all, but had known nevertheless when her twin died.

The aftermath is often more troublesome than the act itself. As soon as the head has been exhibited to the crowd, it can be dropped back into the basket. But the headless body (which remains capable of losing a good deal of blood for a long time after the action of the heart has ceased) must be taken away in a manner dignified yet dishonorable.

Furthermore, it must be not just taken "away," but taken to some specific spot where it will be safe from molestation. An exultant can, by custom, be laid across the saddle of his own destrier, and his remains are surrendered to his family at once. Persons of lesser rank, however, must be provided with some resting place secure from the eaters of the dead; and at least until they are safely out of sight, they must be dragged. The executioner cannot perform this task because he is already burdened with the head and with his weapon, and it is rare for anyone else involved—soldiers, officers of the court, and so on—to be willing to do so. (At the Citadel it was done by two journeymen and thus presented no difficulty.)

The chiliarch, a cavalryman by training and no doubt by inclination, had solved the problem by ordering that the body should be pulled behind a baggage sumpter. The animal had not been consulted, however, and being more of the laborer than the warrior kind, took fright at the blood and tried to bolt. We had an interesting time of it before we were able to get poor Agilus into a quadrangle from which the public was excluded.

I was cleaning off my boots when the portreeve met me there. When I saw him I supposed he had come to give me my fee, but he indicated that the chiliarch wished to pay me himself. As I told him, it was an unexpected honor.

"He watched everything," the portreeve said. "And he was quite pleased. He instructed me to tell you that you and the woman who travels with you are welcome to spend the night here, if you wish."

"We'll leave at twilight," I told him. "I believe that will be safer."

He took thought for a moment, then nodded, showing more intelligence than I would have anticipated. "The miscreant will have a family, I suppose, and friends—though no doubt you know no more of them than I. Still, it's a difficulty you must face frequently."

"I have been warned by more experienced members of my guild," I said.

I had said that we would leave at twilight, but in the event we waited until it was fully dark, in part for safety's sake and in part because it seemed wise to eat the evening meal before we left.

We could not, of course, make directly for the Wall and Thrax. The gate (of whose location I had only a vague idea in any event) would be shut, and I had been told by everyone that there were no inns between the barracks and the Wall. What we had to do, then, was first to lose ourselves, and then to find a place where we could spend the night and from which we could go without difficulty to the gate the next day. I had gotten detailed directions from the portreeve, and though we missed our way, it was some time before we realized it, and we began our walk quite cheerfully. The chiliarch had tried to hand me my fee instead of casting it on the ground at my feet (as is customary), and I had had to dissuade him for the sake of his own reputation. I gave Dorcas a detailed account of this incident, which had amused me nearly as much as it had flattered me. When I had finished, she asked practically, "He paid you well then, I suppose?"

"More than twice what he should have given for the services of a single journeyman. A master's fee. And of course I got a few tips in connection with the ceremony. Do you know, despite all I spent while Agia was with me, I have more money now than I did when I left our tower? I'm beginning to think that by practicing the mystery of our guild while you and I are traveling, I'll be able to support us."

Dorcas seemed to draw the brown mantle closer about her. "I was hoping you wouldn't have to practice it again at all. At least, not for a long time. You were so ill afterward, and I don't blame you."

"It was only nerves—I was afraid that something would go wrong."

"You pitied him. I know you did."

"I suppose so. He was Agia's brother, and like her, I think, in everything except sex."

"You miss Agia, don't you? Did you like her so much?"

"I only knew her for a day—much less time than I have known you already. If she had had her way, I'd be dead now. One of those two averns would have been the end of me."

"But the leaf didn't kill you."

I still recall the tone she used when she told me that; indeed, if I close my eyes now, I can hear her voice again and renew the shock I felt as I realized that ever since I had sat up to see Agilus still grasping his plant, I had been avoiding the thought. The leaf had not killed me, but I had turned my mind from my survival just as a man suffering from a deadly sickness manages by a thousand tricks never to look at death squarely; or rather, as a woman alone in a large house refrains from looking into mirrors, and instead busies herself with trivial errands, so that she may catch no glimpse of the thing whose feet she hears at times on the stairs.

I had survived, and I should be dead. I was haunted by my own life. I thrust one hand into my cloak and stroked my flesh, gingerly at first. There was something like a scar, and a little caked blood still adhered to the skin; but there was no bleeding and no pain. "They don't kill," I said. "That's all."

"She said they did."

"She told a great many lies." We were mounting a gentle hill bathed in pale green moonlight. Ahead of us, seeming as mountains do to be nearer than it was or could possibly be, was the pitch-black line of the Wall. Behind us the lights of Nessus created a false dawn that died bit by bit as the night advanced. I stopped at the top of the hill to admire them, and Dorcas took my arm. "So many homes. How many people are there in the city?"

"No one knows."

"And we will be leaving them all behind. Is it far to Thrax, Severian?"

"A long way, as I've told you already. At the foot of the first cataract. I'm not compelling you to go. You know that."

"I want to. But suppose . . . Severian, just suppose I wanted to go back later. Would you try and stop me?"

I said, "It would be dangerous for you to try to make the trip alone, so I might try to persuade you not to. But I wouldn't bind or imprison you, if that's what you mean."

"You told me you'd written out a copy of the note someone left for me in that inn. Do you remember? But you never showed it to me. I'd like to see it now."

"I told you exactly what it said, and it's not the real note, you know. Agia threw that away. I'm sure she thought that someone—Hildegrin, perhaps—was trying to warn me." I had already opened my sabretache; as I grasped the note, my fingers touched something else as well, something cold and strangely shaped.

Dorcas saw my expression and asked, "What is it?"

I drew it out. It was larger than an orichalk, but not by much, and only a trifle thicker. The cold material (whatever it was) flashed celestine beams back at the frigid rays of the moon. I felt I held a beacon that could be seen all over the city, and I thrust it back and dropped the closure of my sabretache.

Dorcas was clasping my arm so tightly that she might have been a bracelet of ivory and gold grown woman-sized. "What was that?" she whispered.

I shook my head to clear my thoughts. "It isn't mine. I didn't even know I had it. A gem, a precious stone . . ."

"It couldn't be. Didn't you feel the warmth? Look at your sword there—that's a gem. But what was that thing you just took out?"

I looked at the dark opal on the pommel of *Terminus Est*. It glowed in the moonlight, but it was no more like the object I had drawn from my sabretache than a lady's glass is like the sun. "The Claw of the Conciliator," I said. "Agia put it there. She must have, when we broke the altar, so it would not be found on her person if she were searched. She and Agilus would have got it again when Agilus claimed victor-right, and when I didn't die, she tried to steal it in his cell."

Dorcas was no longer staring at me. Her face was lifted and turned toward the city and the sky-glow of its myriad lamps. "Severian," she said. "It can't be."

Hanging over the city like a flying mountain in a dream was an enormous building—a building with towers and buttresses and an arched roof. Crimson light poured from its windows. I tried to speak, to deny the miracle even as I saw it; but before I could frame a syllable, the building had vanished like a bubble in a fountain, leaving only a cascade of sparks.

XXXII

The Play

It was only after the vision of that great building hanging, then vanishing, above the city, that I knew I had come to love Dorcas. We walked down the road—for we had found a new road just over the top of the hill—into darkness. And because our thoughts were entirely of what we had seen, our spirits embraced without hindrance, each passing through those few seconds of vision as if through a door never previously opened and never to be opened again.

I do not know just where it was we walked. I recall a winding road down the hillside, an arched bridge at the bottom, and another road, bordered for a league or so by a vagabond wooden fence. Wherever it was we went, I know we talked about ourselves not at all, but only of what we had seen and what its meaning might be. And I know that at the beginning of that walk I looked on Dorcas as no more than a chance-met companion, however desirable, however to be pitied. And at the end of it I loved Dorcas in a way that I have never loved another human being. I did not love her because I had come to love Thecla less—rather by loving Dorcas I loved Thecla more, because Dorcas was another self (as Thecla was yet to become in a fashion as terrible as the other was beautiful), and if I loved Thecla, Dorcas loved her also.

"Do you think," she asked, "that anyone saw it but us?"

I had not considered that, but I said that although the suspension of the building had endured for only a moment, yet it had taken place above the greatest of cities; and that if millions and tens of millions had failed to see it, yet hundreds must still have seen.

"Isn't it possible it was only a vision, meant only for us?"

"I have never had a vision, Dorcas."

"And I don't know whether I've had any or not. When I try to recall the time before I helped you out of the water, I can only remember being in the water myself. Everything before that is like a vision shattered to pieces, only small bright bits, a thimble I saw laid on velvet once, and the sound of a small dog barking outside a door. Nothing like this. Nothing like what we've seen."

What she said made me remember the note, which I had been searching for when my fingers touched the Claw, and that in turn suggested the brown book, which lay in the pleat of my sabretache next to it. I asked Dorcas if she would not like to see the book that had once been Thecla's, when we found a place to stop.

"Yes," she said. "When we are seated by a fire again, as we were for a moment at that inn."

"Finding that relic—which of course I will have to return before we can leave the city—and what we have been saying too, remind me of something I read there once. Do you know of the key to the universe?"

Dorcas laughed softly. "No, Severian, I who scarcely know my name do not know anything about the key to the universe."

"I didn't say that as well as I should have. What I meant was, are you familiar with the idea that the universe has a secret key? A sentence, or a phrase, some say even a single word, that can be wrung from the lips of a certain statue, or read in the firmament, or that an anchorite on a world across the seas teaches his disciples?"

"Babies know it," Dorcas said. "They know it before they learn to speak, but by the time they're old enough to talk, they have forgotten most of it. At least, someone told me that once."

"That's what I mean, something like that. The brown book is a collection of the myths of the past, and it has a section listing all the keys of the universe—all the things people have said were The Secret after they had talked to mystagogues on far worlds or studied the *popul vuh* of the magicians, or fasted in the trunks of holy trees. Thecla and I used to read them and talk about them, and one of them was that everything, whatever happens, has three meanings. The first is its practical meaning, what the book calls, 'the thing the plowman sees.' The cow has taken a mouthful of grass, and it is real grass, and a real cow—that meaning is as important and as true as either of the others. The second is the reflection of the world about it. Every object is in contact with all others, and thus the wise can learn of the others by observing the first. That might be called the soothsayers' meaning, because it is the one such people use when they prophesy a fortunate meeting from the tracks of serpents or confirm the outcome of a love affair by putting the elector of one suit atop the patroness of another."

"And the third meaning?" Dorcas asked.

"The third is the transsubstantial meaning. Since all objects have their ultimate origin in the Pancreator, and all were set in motion by him, so all must express his will—which is the higher reality."

"You're saying that what we saw was a sign."

I shook my head. "The book is saying that everything is a sign. The post of that fence is a sign, and so is the way the tree leans across it. Some signs may betray the third meaning more readily than others."

For perhaps a hundred paces we were both silent. Then Dorcas said, "It seems to me that if what the Chatelaine Thecla's book says is true, then people have everything backward. We saw a great structure leap into the air and fall to nothing, didn't we?"

"I only saw it suspended over the city. Did it leap?"

Dorcas nodded. I could see the glimmer of her pale hair in the moonlight. "It seems to me that what you call the third meaning is very clear. But the second meaning is harder to find, and the first, which ought to be the easiest, is impossible."

I was about to say I understood her—at least about the first meaning—when I heard from some distance off a rumbling roar that might have been a long roll of thunder. Dorcas exclaimed, "What's that?" and took my hand in her own small, warm one, which I found very pleasant.

"I don't know, but I think it came from the copse up ahead."

She nodded. "Now I hear voices."

"Your hearing is better than mine then."

The rumbling sounded again, louder and more prolonged; and this time, perhaps only because we were a trifle nearer, I thought I saw the gleam of lights through the trunks of the grove of young beeches ahead of us.

"There!" Dorcas said, and pointed in a direction somewhat to the north of the trees. "That can't be a star. It's too low and too bright, and moves too quickly."

"It's a lantern, I think. On a wagon, perhaps, or carried in someone's hand."

The rumble came once more, and this time I knew it for what it was, the rolling of a drum. I could hear voices now myself, very faintly, and particularly one voice that sounded deeper than the drum and almost as loud.

As we rounded the edge of the copse, we saw about fifty people gathered around a small platform. On it, between flaring torches, stood a giant who held a kettledrum beneath one arm like a tom-tom. A much smaller man, richly dressed, stood on his right, and on his left, nearly naked, the most sensuously beautiful woman I have ever seen.

"Everyone is here," the small man was saying, loudly and very rapidly. "Everyone is here. What would you have? Love and beauty?" He pointed to the woman. "Strength? Courage?" He waved the stick he carried toward the giant. "Deception? Mystery?" He tapped his own chest. "Vice?" He pointed toward the giant again. "And look here—see who's just come! It's our old enemy Death, who always comes sooner or later." With this he pointed to me, and every face in the audience turned to stare.

It was Dr. Talos and Baldanders; their presence seemed inevitable as soon as I had recognized them. So far as I knew, I had never seen the woman.

"Death!" Dr. Talos said. "Death has come. I doubted you these past two days, old friend; I ought to have known better."

I expected the audience to laugh at this grim humor, but they did not. A few muttered to themselves, and a crone spat into her palm and pointed two fingers toward the ground.

"And who is it he has brought with him?" Dr. Talos leaned forward to peer at Dorcas in the torchlight. "Innocence, I believe it is. Yes, it's Innocence. Now everyone is here! The show will begin in a moment or two. Not for the faint of heart! You have never seen anything like it, anything at all! Everyone is here now."

The beautiful woman was gone, and such was the magnetism of the doctor's voice that I had not noticed when she left.

If I were to describe Dr. Talos's play now, as it appeared to me (a participant), the result could only be confusion. When I describe it as it appeared to the audience (as I intend to do at a more appropriate point in this account), I will not, perhaps, be believed. In a drama with a cast of five, of whom two on this first night had not learned their parts, armies marched, orchestras played, snow fell, and Urth trembled. Dr. Talos demanded much from the imagination of his audience; but he assisted that imagination with narration, simple yet clever machinery, shadows cast upon screens, holographic projectors, recorded noises, reflecting backdrops, and every other conceivable sleight, and on the whole he succeeded admirably, as evidenced by the sobs, shouts, and sighs that floated toward us from time to time out of the dark.

Triumphing in all this, he yet failed. For his desire was to communicate, to tell a great tale that had being only in his mind and could not be reduced to common words; but no one who ever witnessed a performance—and still less we who moved across his stage and spoke at his bidding—ever left it, I think with any clear understanding of what that tale was. It could only (Dr. Talos said) be expressed in the ringing of bells and the thunder of explosions, and sometimes by the postures of ritual. Yet as it proved in the end it could not be expressed even by these. There was a scene in which Dr. Talos fought Baldanders until the blood ran down both their faces; there was another in which Baldanders searched for a terrified Jolenta (that was the name of the most beautiful woman in the world) in a room of an underground palace, and at last seated himself on the chest where she lay hidden. In the final part I held the center of the stage, presiding over a chamber of inquiry in which Baldanders, Dr. Talos, Jolenta, and Dorcas were bound in various apparatuses. As the audience watched, I inflicted the most bizarre and ineffective (had they been real) torments on each in turn. In this scene, I could not help but notice how strangely the audience began to murmur while I was preparing, as it seemed, to wrench Dorcas's legs from their sockets. Though I was unaware of it, they had been permitted to see that Baldanders was freeing himself. Several women screamed when his chain clattered to the stage; I looked covertly toward Dr. Talos for directions, but he was already springing toward the audience, having freed himself with far less effort.

"Tableau," he called. "Tableau, everyone." I froze in position, having learned that was what was meant. "Gracious people, you have watched our little show with admirable attention. Now we ask a bit of your purse as well as your time. At the conclusion of the play you will see what occurs now that the monster has freed himself at last." Dr. Talos was holding out his tall hat to the audience, and I heard several coins clink into it. Unsatisfied, he leaped from the stage and began to move among the people. "Remember that once he is free, nothing stands between him and the consummation of his brutal desires. Remember that I, his tormentor, am bound now and at his mercy. Remember that you have never as yet learned—thank you, sieur—the identity of the mysterious figure seen by the Contessa through the curtained windows. Thank you. That above the dungeon you see now the weeping statue—thank you—still digs under the rowan tree. Come now, you have been very generous with your time. We ask only that you will not be penurious with your money. A few, truly, have treated us well, but we will not perform for a few. Where are the shining asimi that should have showered into my poor hat long ago from the rest of you? The few shall not pay for the multitude! If you've no asimis, then orichalks; if you have none, surely there is no one here without an aes!"

Eventually a sufficient sum was gathered, and Dr. Talos vaulted back into his place and deftly reaffixed the fastenings that seemed to hold him in an embrace of spikes. Baldanders roared and stretched forth his long arms as though to grasp me, allowing the audience to observe that a second chain, unnoticed previously, still constrained him. "See him," Dr. Talos prompted me *sotto voce*. "Hold him off with one of the flambeaux."

I pretended to discover for the first time that Baldanders's arms were free, and plucked one of the torches from its socket at the corner of the stage. At once both torches guttered; the flames, which had been of clear yellow above scarlet, now burned blue and pale green, spitting sparks and sputtering, doubling and tripling in size with a fearful hiss, only to sink at once as if on the point of going out. I thrust the one I had uprooted at Baldanders, shouting, "No! No! Back! Back!" prompted again by Dr. Talos. Baldanders responded by roaring more furiously than ever. He strained at the chain in a way that made the scenery wall to which he was bound creak and snap, and his mouth began quite literally to foam, a thick white liquid running from the corners of his lips to bedew his huge chin and fleck his rusty black clothes as though with snow. Someone in the audience screamed, and the chain broke with a report like the snapping of a drover's whip. By this time the giant's face was hideous in its madness, and I would no more have attempted to stand in his way than to stop an avalanche; but before I could move a step to escape him, he had wrested the torch from me and knocked me down with its iron shaft.

I got my head up in time to see him jerk the other torch from its place and make for the audience with both. The shrieking of men drowned the shrilling of women—it sounded as if our guild were exercising a hundred clients together. I pulled myself up and was about to seize Dorcas and dash for the cover of the copse when I saw Dr. Talos. He seemed filled with what I can only call malignant good humor, and though he was freeing himself from his fastenings, he was taking his time about it. Jolenta was setting herself free as well, and if there were any expression at all on that perfect face, it was one of relief.

"Very well!" Dr. Talos exclaimed. "Very well indeed. You may come back now, Baldanders. Don't leave us in the dark." To me: "Did you enjoy your maiden experience of the boards, Master Torturer? For a beginner acting without rehearsal, you played nicely enough."

I managed to nod.

"Except when Baldanders knocked you down. You must forgive him, he could see you didn't know enough to drop. Come with me now. Baldanders has his talents, but a fine eye for minutiae lost in grass isn't one of them. I have some lights backstage, and you and Innocence shall help us pick up."

I did not understand what he meant, but in a few moments the torches were back in place and we were hunting through the trampled area in front of the stage with dark lanterns. "It's a gambling proposition," Dr. Talos explained. "And I confess to loving them. The money in the hat is a sure thing—by the close of the first act I can predict to an orichalk how much it will be. But the dropsies! They may be no more than two apples and a turnip, or as much as the imagination can encompass. We have found a baby pig. Delicious, so Baldanders told me when he ate it. We have found a baby baby. We have found a gold-headed stick, and I retain it. Antique brooches. Shoes . . . We frequently find shoes of all kinds. Just now I have found a woman's parasol." He held it up. "This will be just the thing to keep the sun from our fair Jolenta when we go strolling tomorrow."

Jolenta straightened up as people do who are straining not to stoop. Above the waist her creamy amplitude was such that her spine must have been curved backward to balance the weight. "If we're going to an inn tonight, I'd like to go now," she said. "I'm very tired, Doctor."

I was exhausted myself.

"An inn? Tonight? A criminal waste of funds. Look at it this way, my dear. The nearest is a league away at the very least, and it would take Baldanders and me a watch to pack the scenery and properties, even with the help of this friendly Angel of Torment. By the time we reached the inn at that rate the horizon would be under the sun, the cocks would be crowing, and like as not a thousand fools would be rising, banging their doors and throwing their slops."

Baldanders grunted (I thought in confirmation), then struck with his boot as if at some venomous thing he had discovered in the grass.

Dr. Talos threw wide his arms to embrace the universe. "While here, my dear, beneath stars that are the personal and cherished property of the Increate, we have all anyone could wish for the most salubrious rest. There's just chill enough in the air tonight to make sleepers grateful for the warmth of their coverings and the heat of the fire, and not a hint of rain. Here we will camp, here we will break our fast in the morning, and from here we will walk renewed in the joyful hours when the day is young."

I said, "You mentioned something about breakfast. Is there any food now? Dorcas and I are hungry."

"Of course there is. I see Baldanders has just picked up a basket of yams."

Several members of our erstwhile audience must have been farm people returning from a market with whatever produce they had been unable to sell. Besides the yams we had, eventually, a pair of squabs and several stalks of young sugar cane. There was not much bedding, but there was some, and Dr. Talos himself used none of it, saying he would sit up and watch the fire, and perhaps nap, later, in the chair that had been the Autarch's throne and the Inquisitor's bench a short time before.

XXXIII

Five Legs

For perhaps a watch I lay awake. I soon realized that Dr. Talos was not going to sleep, but I clung to the hope that he would leave us for one reason or another. He sat for a time as if deep in thought, then stood and began to pace up and down before the fire. His was an immobile yet expressive face—a slight movement of one eyebrow or the cocking of his head could change it utterly, and as he passed back and forth before my half-closed eyes I saw sorrow, glee, desire, ennui, resolution, and a score of other emotions that have no names flicker across that vulpine mask.

At last he began to swing his cane at the blossoms of wild flowers. In a short time he had decapitated all those within a dozen steps of the fire. I waited until I could no longer see his erect, energetic figure and only faintly hear the whistling strokes of his cane. Then slowly I drew forth the gem.

It was as if I held a star, a thing that burned in the light. Dorcas was asleep, and though I had hoped that we could examine the gem together, I forbore from waking her. The icy blue radiance waxed until I was afraid Dr. Talos would see it, far off as he was. I held the gem to my eye with some childish idea of viewing the fire through it as through a lens, then snatched it away—the familiar world of grass and sleepers had become no more than a dance of sparks, slashed by a scimitar blade.

I am not sure how old I was when Master Malrubius died. It was a number of years before I became captain, so I must have been quite a small boy. I remember very well, however, how it was when Master Palaemon succeeded him as master of apprentices; Master Malrubius had held that position ever since I had been aware that such a thing existed, and for weeks and perhaps months it seemed to me that Master Palaemon (though I liked him as well or better) could not be our real master in the sense that Master Malrubius had been. The atmosphere of dislocation and unreality was heightened by the knowledge that Master Malrubius was not dead or even away . . . that he was, in fact, merely lying in his cabin, lying in the same bed he had slept in each night when he was still teaching and disciplining us. There is a saying that unseen is as good as unbeen; but in this case it was otherwise—unseen, Master Malrubius was more palpably present than ever before. Master Palaemon refused to assert that he would never return, and so every act was weighed in double scales: *''Would Master Palaemon permit it?''* and *''What would Master Malrubius say?''*

(In the end he said nothing. Torturers do not go to the Tower of Healing, no matter how ill; there is a belief—whether true or not I cannot say—that old scores are settled there.)

If I were writing this history to entertain or even to instruct, I would not digress here to discuss Master Malrubius, who must, at the moment when I thrust away the Claw, have been dust for long years. But in a history, as in other things, there are necessities and necessities. I know little of literary style; but I have learned as I have progressed, and find this art not so much different from my old one as might be thought.

Many scores and sometimes many hundreds of persons come to watch an execution, and I have seen balconies torn from their walls by the weight of the watchers, killing more in their single crash than I in my career. These scores and hundreds may be likened to the readers of a written account.

But there are others besides these spectators who must be satisfied: the authority in whose name the carnifex acts; those who have given him money so that the condemned may have an easy (or a hard) death; and the carnifex himself.

The spectators will be content if there are no long delays, if the condemned is permitted to speak briefly and does it well, if the upraised blade gleams in the sun for a moment before it descends, thus giving them time to catch breath and nudge one another, and if the head falls with a satisfactory gout of blood. Similarly you, who will some day delve in Master Ultan's library, will require of me no long delays; personages who are permitted to speak only briefly yet do it well; certain dramatic pauses which shall signal to you that something of import is about to occur; excitement; and a sating quantity of blood.

The authorities for whom the carnifex acts, the chiliarchs or archons (if I may be permitted to prolong my figure of speech), will have little complaint if the condemned is prevented from escaping, or much inflaming the mob; and if he is undeniably dead at the conclusion of the proceedings. That authority, as it seems to me, in my writing is the impulse that drives me to my task. Its requirements are that the subject of this work must remain central to it—not escaping into prefaces or indexes or into another work entirely; that the rhetoric not be permitted to overwhelm it; and that it be carried to a satisfactory conclusion.

Those who have paid the carnifex to make the act a painless or a painful one may be likened to the literary traditions and accepted models to which I am compelled to bow. I recall that one winter day, when cold rain beat against the window of the room where he gave us our lessons, Master Malrubius—perhaps because he saw we were too dispirited for serious work, perhaps only because he was dispirited himself—told us of a certain Master Werenfrid of our guild who in olden times, being in grave need, accepted remuneration from the enemies of the condemned and from his friends as well; and who by stationing one party on the right of the block and the other on the left, by his great skill made it appear to each that the result was entirely satisfactory. In just this way, the contending parties of tradition pull at the writers of histories. Yes, even at autarchs. One desires ease; the other, richness of experience in the execution . . . of the writing. And I must try, in the dilemma of Master Werenfrid but lacking his abilities, to satisfy each. This I have attempted to do.

There remains the carnifex himself; I am he. It is not enough for him to earn praise from all. It is not enough, even, for him to perform his function in a way he knows to be entirely creditable and in keeping with the teaching of his masters and the ancient traditions. In addition to all this, if he is to feel full satisfaction at the moment when Time lifts his own severed head by the hair, he must add to the execution some feature however small that is entirely his own and that he will never repeat. Only thus can he feel himself a free artist.

When I shared a bed with Baldanders, I dreamed a strange dream; and in composing this history I did not hesitate to relate it, the relation of dreams being entirely in the literary tradition. At the time I write of now, when Dorcas and I slept under the stars with Baldanders and Jolenta, and Dr. Talos sat by, I experienced what may have been less or greater than a dream; and that is outside that tradition. I give warning to you who will later read this that it has little bearing on what will soon follow; I give it only because it puzzled me at the time and it will provide me with satisfaction to relate it. Yet it may be that insofar as it entered my mind and has remained there from that time to this, it affected my actions during the latter part of my narrative.

With the Claw safely hidden away, I lay stretched on an old blanket near the fire. Dorcas lay with her head near mine; Jolenta with her feet to mine; Baldanders on his back on the opposite side of the fire, his thick-soled boots among the embers. Dr. Talos's chair stood near the giant's hand, but it was turned away from the fire. Whether or not he did sit in it with his face to the night I cannot say; for parts of the time I am going to relate I seemed conscious of his presence in the chair, at other times I sensed that he was absent. The sky was growing lighter, I believe, than it is at full dark.

Footfalls reached my ears yet hardly disturbed my rest, heavy, yet softly pattering; then the sound of breath, the snuffling of an animal. If I was awake, my eyes were open; but I was still so nearly in sleep that I did not turn my head. The animal approached me and sniffed at my clothes and my face. It was Triskele, and Triskele lay down with his spine pressed against my body. It did not seem odd then that he had found me, though I recall feeling a certain pleasure at seeing him again.

Once more I heard footsteps, now the slow, firm tread of a man; I knew at once that it was Master Malrubius—I could recall his step in the corridors under the tower on the days when we made the rounds of the cells; the sound was the same. He came into the circle of my vision. His cloak was dusty, as it always was save on the most formal occasions; he drew it about him in the old way as he seated himself on a box of properties. "Severian. Name for me the seven principles of governance."

It was an effort for me to speak, but I managed (in my dream, if it was a dream) to say, "I do not recall that we have studied such a thing, Master."

"You were always the most careless of my boys," he told me, and fell silent.

A foreboding grew on me; I sensed that if I did not reply, some tragedy would occur. At last I began weakly, "Anarchy . . ."

"That is not governance, but the lack of it. I taught you that it precedes all governance. Now list the seven sorts."

"Attachment to the person of the monarch. Attachment to a bloodline or other sequence of succession. Attachment to the royal state. Attachment to a code legitimizing the governing state. Attachment to the law only. Attachment to a greater or lesser board of electors, as framers of the law. Attachment to an abstraction conceived as including the body of electors, other bodies giving rise to them, and numerous other elements, largely ideal."

"Tolerable. Of these, which is the earliest form, and which the highest?"

"The development is in the order given, Master," I said. "But I do not recall that you ever asked before which was highest."

Master Malrubius leaned forward, his eyes burning brighter than the coals of the fire. "Which is highest, Severian?"

"The last, Master?"

"You mean attachment to an abstraction conceived as including the body of electors, other bodies giving rise to them, and numerous other elements, largely ideal?"

"Yes, Master."

"Of what kind, Severian, is your own attachment to the Divine Entity?"

I said nothing. It may have been that I was thinking; but if so, my mind was too much filled with sleep to be conscious of its thought. Instead, I became profoundly aware of my physical surroundings. The sky above my face in all its grandeur seemed to have been made solely for my benefit, and to be presented for my inspection now. I lay upon the ground as upon a woman, and the very air that surrounded me seemed a thing as admirable as crystal and as fluid as wine.

"Answer me, Severian."

"The first, if I have any."

"To the person of the monarch?"

"Yes, because there is no succession."

"The animal that rests beside you now would die for you. Of what kind is his attachment to you?"

"The first?"

There was no one there. I sat up. Malrubius and Triskele had vanished, yet my side felt faintly warm.

XXXIV

Morning

"You are awake," Dr. Talos said. "I trust you slept well?"

"I had a strange dream." I stood and looked about.

"There's no one here but ourselves." As though he were reassuring a child, Dr. Talos gestured toward Baldanders and the sleeping women.

"I dreamed my dog—he has been lost for years now—came back and lay beside me. I could still feel the warmth of his body when I woke."

"You were lying beside a fire," Dr. Talos pointed out. "There has been no dog here."

"A man, dressed much as I am."

Dr. Talos shook his head. "I could not have failed to see him."

"You might have dozed."

"Only earlier in the evening. I have been awake for the past two watches."

"I'll guard the stage and properties for you," I said, "if you'd like to sleep now." The truth was that I was afraid to lie down again.

Dr. Talos seemed to hesitate, then said, "That's very kind of you," and stiffly lowered himself onto my now dew-soaked blanket.

I took his chair, turning it so I could watch the fire. For some time I was alone with my thoughts, which were at first of my dream, then of the Claw, the mighty relic chance had dropped into my hands. I felt very glad when Jolenta began to stir and at last rose and stretched her lush limbs against the scarlet-shot sky. "Is there water?" she asked. "I want to wash."

I told her that I thought Baldanders had carried the water for our supper from the direction of the copse, and she nodded and went off to look for a stream. Her appearance, at least, distracted my thoughts; I found myself glancing from her retreating figure to Dorcas's prone one. Jolenta's beauty was perfect. No other woman I have ever seen could approach it—Thecla's towering stateliness made her seem coarse and mannish in comparison, Dorcas's blond delicacy as meager and childlike as Valeria, the forgotten girl I had encountered in the Atrium of Time.

Yet I was not attracted to Jolenta as I had been to Agia; I did not love her as I had loved Thecla; and I did not desire the intimacy of thought and feeling that had sprung up between Dorcas and me, or think it possible. Like every man who ever saw her I desired her, but I wanted her as one wants a woman in a painting. And even while I admired her, I could not help but notice (as I had on the stage the night before) how clumsily she walked, she who appeared so graceful in repose. Those round thighs chafed one another, that admirable flesh weighed her until she carried her voluptuousness as another woman would have carried a child in her belly. When she returned from the copse with drops of clear water shining in her lashes, and her face as pure and perfect as the curve of the rainbow, I felt still almost as though I were alone.

". . . I said, there's fruit if you want it. The doctor had me save some last night so we'd have something for breakfast." Her voice was husky and slightly breathless. One listened as if to music.

"I'm sorry," I told her. "I was thinking. Yes, I'd like some fruit. That's very kind of you."

"I won't get it for you, you'll have to fetch it yourself. It's there, behind that stand of armor."

The armor to which she pointed was actually of cloth stretched over a wire frame and painted silver. Behind it I found an old basket containing grapes, an apple, and a pomegranate.

"I'd like something too," Jolenta said. "Those grapes, I think."

I gave her the grapes, and considering that Dorcas would probably prefer the apple, put it near her hand and took the pomegranate for myself.

Jolenta held up her grapes. "Grown under glass by some exultant's gardener—it's too soon for natural ones. I don't think this strolling life's going to be too bad. And I get a third of the money."

I asked if she had not trouped with the doctor and his giant before.

"You don't remember me, do you? I didn't think so." She popped a grape into her mouth and so far as I could see swallowed it whole. "No, I haven't. I did have a rehearsal, although with that girl thrust into the story so suddenly we had to change everything."

"I must have disturbed things more than she did. She was on stage much less."

"Yes, but you were supposed to be there. Dr. Talos took your roles when we practiced as well as his own, and told me what you were supposed to say."

"He depended on my meeting him, then."

The doctor himself sat up at that, almost with a snap. He looked wide awake. "Of course, of course. We told you where we'd be when we were at breakfast, and if you hadn't appeared last night, we would've presented 'Great Scenes From' and waited another day. Jolenta, you won't be getting a third of the receipts now, but a quarter—it's only fair that we share with the other woman."

Jolenta shrugged and swallowed another grape.

"Wake her now, Severian. We should be going. I'll rouse Baldanders, and we can divide the money and pack."

"I won't be going with you," I said.

Dr. Talos looked at me quizzically.

"I have to return to the city. I have business with the Order of Pelerines."

"You can remain with us until we reach the main road, then. It will be your most expeditious route back." Perhaps because he refrained from questioning me, I felt he knew more than what he had said indicated.

Ignoring our talk, Jolenta smothered a yawn. "I'll have to have more sleep before tonight, or my eyes won't look as good as they should."

I said, "I will, but when we reach the road, I must go."

Dr. Talos had already turned away to wake the giant, shaking him and striking his shoulders with his slender cane. "As you wish," he said, and I could not be sure whether he was addressing Jolenta or me. I stroked Dorcas's forehead and whispered that we would have to move on now.

"I wish you hadn't done that. I was having the most wonderful dream . . . Very detailed, very real."

"So was I—before I woke, I mean."

"You've been awake a long time then? Is this apple mine?"

"All the breakfast you'll get, I'm afraid."

"All I need. Look at it, how round it is, how red. What is it they say? 'Red as the apples of . . .' I can't think of it. Would you like a bite?"

"I've eaten already. I had a pomegranate."

"I should have known from the stains on your mouth. I thought you'd been sucking blood all night." I must have looked shocked when she said this, because she added, "Well, you did look like a black bat bending over me."

Baldanders was sitting up now, rubbing his eyes with his hands like an unhappy child. Dorcas called across the fire, "Terrible to have to rise so early, isn't it, goodman? Were you dreaming too?"

"No dreams," Baldanders answered. "I never dream." (Dr. Talos looked toward me and shook his head as if to say, *Most unhealthy*.)

"I'll give you some of mine then. Severian says he has plenty of his own."

Though he seemed thoroughly awake, Baldanders stared at her. "Who are you?"

"I'm . . ." Dorcas turned toward me, frightened.

"Dorcas," I said.

"Yes, Dorcas. Don't you remember? We met behind the curtain last night. You . . . your friend introduced us, and said I shouldn't be afraid of you, because you would only pretend to hurt people. In the show. I said I understood, because Severian does terrible things but is really so kind." Dorcas looked to me again. "You remember, Severian, don't you?"

"Of course. I don't think you have to be anxious about Baldanders just because he's forgotten. He's big, I know, but his size is like my fuligin clothes—it makes him look much worse than he is."

Baldanders told Dorcas, "You have a wonderful memory. I wish I could recall everything like that." His voice was like the rolling of heavy stones.

While we were talking, Dr. Talos had produced the money box. He jingled it now to interrupt us. "Come, friends, I have promised you a fair and equitable distribution of the proceeds of our performance, and when that is complete, it will be time to be moving. Turn around, Baldanders, and spread your hands in your lap. Sieur Severian, ladies, will you gather around me as well?"

I had observed, of course, that when the doctor spoke earlier of dividing the contributions he had collected the night before, he had specified division into four parts; but I had assumed it was Baldanders, who seemed to be his slave, who would receive nothing. Now, however, after rummaging in the box, Dr. Talos dropped a shining asimi into the giant's hands, gave another to me, a third to Dorcas, and a fistful of orichalks to Jolenta; then he began to distribute orichalks singly. "You will notice that everything thus far is good money," he said. "I regret to report that there are a fair number of dubious coins here as well. When the undoubted specie is exhausted, you will each come in for a share of them."

Jolenta asked, "Have you already taken yours, Doctor? I think the rest of us ought to have been present."

For a moment Dr. Talos's hands, which had been darting from one of us to another as he counted out the coins, paused. ''I take no share from this,'' he said.

Dorcas glanced toward me as if to confirm her judgment and whispered, ''That doesn't seem fair.''

I said, ''It isn't fair. Doctor, you took as large a part in the show last night as any of us, and collected the money, and from what I have seen, you provided the stage and scenery as well. If anything, you should have a double share.''

''I take nothing,'' Dr. Talos said slowly. It was the first time I had seen him abashed. ''It is my pleasure to direct what I may now call the company. I wrote the play we perform, and like . . .'' (he looked around as if at a loss for a simile) ''. . . that armor there I play my part. These things are my pleasure, and all the reward I require.

''Now, friends, you will have observed that we are reduced to single orichalks, and there are not enough to make the circle again. To be specific, only two are left. Whoever wishes may have both by renouncing claim to the aes and doubtful stuff remaining. Severian? Jolenta?''

Somewhat to my surprise, Dorcas announced, ''I'll take them.''

''Very good. I will not presume to judge among the rest, but simply hand it out. I warn you who receive it to be careful in passing it. There are penalties for such things, though outside the Wall— What's this?''

I followed the direction of his eyes and saw a man in shabby gray advancing toward us.

XXXV

Hethor

I do not know why it should be humiliating to receive a stranger while sitting on the ground, but it is so. Both the women stood as the gray figure approached, and so did I. Even Baldanders lumbered to his feet, so that by the time the newcomer was within speaking distance, only Dr. Talos, who had reoccupied our one chair, remained seated.

Yet a less impressive figure would have been difficult to imagine. He was small of stature, and because his clothes were too large for him, seemed smaller still. His weak chin was covered with stubble; as he approached, he pulled a greasy cap away to show a head on which the hair had retreated at either side to leave a single wavering line like the crest of an old and dirty burginot. I knew I had seen him elsewhere, but it was a moment before I recognized him.

"Lords," he said. "O lords and mistresses of creation, silken-capped, silken-haired women, and man commanding empires and the armies of the F-f-foemen of our Ph-ph-photosphere! Tower strong as stone is strong, strong as the o-o-oak that puts forth leaves new after the fire! And my master, dark master, death's victory, viceroy over the n-night! Long I signed on the silver-sailed ships, the hundred-masted whose masts reached out to touch the st-st-stars, I, floating among their shining jibs with the Pleiades burning beyond the top-royal sp-sp-spar, but never have I seen ought like you! He-he-hethor am I, come to serve you, to scrape the mud from your cloak, whet the great sword, c-c-carry the basket with the eyes of your victims looking up at me, Master, eyes like the dead moons of Verthandi when the sun has gone out. When the sun has g-g-gone out! Where are they then, the bright players? How long will the torches burn? The f-f-freezing hands grope toward them, but the torch bowls are colder than any ice, colder than the moons of Verthandi, colder than the dead eyes! Where is the strength then that beats the lake to foam? Where is the empire, where the Armies of the Sun, long-lanced and golden-bannered? Where are the silken-haired women we loved only l-l-last night?''

''You were in our audience, I take it,'' said Dr. Talos. ''I can well sympathize with your desire to see the performance again. But we won't be able to oblige you until evening, and by then we hope to be some distance from here.''

Hethor, whom I had met outside Agilus's prison with the fat man, the hungry-eyed woman and the others, did not seem to have heard him. He was staring at me, with occasional glances toward Baldanders and Dorcas. ''He hurt you, didn't he? Writhing, writhing. I saw you with the blood running, red as pentecost. Wh-wh-what honor for you! You serve him too, and your calling is higher than mine.''

Dorcas shook her head and turned her face away. The giant only stared. Dr. Talos said, ''Surely you understand that what you saw was a theatrical performance.'' (I remember thinking that if most of the audience had had a firmer grip on that idea, we would have found ourselves in an embarrassing dilemma when Baldanders jumped from the stage.)

''I u-understand more than you think, I the old captain, the old lieutenant, the old c-c-cook in his old kitchen, cooking soup, cooking broth for the dying pets! My master is real, but where are your armies? Real, and where are your empires? Sh-shall false blood run from a true wound? Where is your strength when the b-b-blood is gone, where is the luster of the silken hair? I w-will catch it in a cup of glass, I, the old c-captain of the old limping sh-ship, with its crew black against the silver sails, and the C-c-coalstack behind it.''

Perhaps I should say here that at the time I paid little attention to the rush and stumble of Hethor's words, though my ineradicable memory enables me to recreate them on paper now. He spoke a gobbling singsong, with a fine spray of spittle flying through the gaps in his teeth. In his slow way, Baldanders may have understood him. Dorcas, I feel sure, was too repelled by him to hear much of what he said. She turned aside as one turns from the mutterings and cracking bones when an alzabo savages a carcass, and Jolenta listened to nothing that did not concern herself.

''You can see for yourself that the young woman is unharmed.'' Dr. Talos rose and put away his money box. ''It's always a pleasure to speak to someone who has appreciated our performance, but I'm afraid we've work to do. We must pack. If you'll excuse us?''

Now that his conversation had become one with Dr. Talos exclusively, Hethor put his cap on again, pulling it down until it nearly covered his eyes. ''Stowage? There's no one better for it than I, the old s-supercargo, the old chandler and steward, the old st-stevedore. Who else shall put the kernels back on the cob, fit the f-fledgling into the egg again? Who shall fold the solemn-winged m-moth, with w-wings each like stuns'ls, into the broken cocoon left h-hanging like a s-s-sarcophagus? And for the love of the M-master, I'll do it, for the sake of the M-master, I'll do it. And f-f-f-follow anywhere, anywhere he goes.''

I nodded, not knowing what to say. Just at the moment, Baldanders—who had apparently caught the references to packing if he had caught nothing else—scooped a backdrop from the stage and began to wind it on its pole. Hethor vaulted up with unexpected agility to fold the set for the Inquisitor's chamber and reel in the projector wires. Dr. Talos turned to me as if to say, *He's your responsibility after all, just as Baldanders is mine.*

''There are a good many of them,'' I told him. ''They find pleasure in pain, and want to associate with us just as a normal man might want to be around Dorcas and Jolenta.''

The doctor nodded. ''I wondered. One can imagine an ideal servant who serves out of pure love for his master, just as one can an ideal rustic who remains a ditcher from a love of nature, or an ideal fricatrice who spreads her legs a dozen times a night from a love of copulation. But one never encounters these fabulous creatures in reality.''

In about a watch we were on the road. Our small theater packed itself quite neatly into a huge barrow formed from parts of the stage, and Baldanders, who wheeled this contraption, also carried a few odds and ends on his back. Dr. Talos, with Dorcas, Jolenta, and me behind him, led the way, and Hethor followed Baldanders at a distance of perhaps a hundred paces.

''He's like me,'' Dorcas said, glancing back. ''And the doctor is like Agia, only not as bad. Do you remember? She couldn't make me go away, and eventually you made her stop trying.''

I did remember, and asked why she had followed us with such determination.

''You were the only people I knew. I was more afraid of being alone than I was of Agia.''

''Then you *were* afraid of Agia.''

''Yes, very much. I still am. But . . . I don't know where I've been, but I think I've been alone, wherever I was. For a long time. I didn't want to do that anymore. You won't understand this—or like it—but . . ."

"Yes?"

"If you had hated me as much as Agia did, I would have followed you anyway."

"I don't think Agia hated you."

Dorcas stared up at me, and I can see that piquant face now as well as if it were reflected in the quiet well of vermillion ink. It was, perhaps, a trifle pinched and pale, too childlike for great beauty; but the eyes were bits of the azure firmament of some hidden world waiting for Man; they could have vied with Jolenta's own. "She hated me," Dorcas said softly. "She hates me more now. Do you remember how dazed you were after the fight? You never looked back when I led you away. I did, and I saw her face."

Jolenta had been complaining to Dr. Talos because she had to walk. Baldanders's deep, dull voice came from behind us now. "I will carry you."

She glanced back at him. "What? On top of all the rest?"

He did not reply.

"When I say I want to ride, I don't mean, as you seem to think, like a fool at a flogging."

In my imagination, I saw the giant's sad nod.

Jolenta was afraid of looking foolish, and what I am going to write now will sound foolish indeed, though it is true. You, my reader, may enjoy yourself at my expense. It struck me then how fortunate I was, and how fortunate I had been since leaving the Citadel. Dorcas I knew was my friend—more than a lover, a true companion, though we had been together only a few days. The giant's heavy tread behind me reminded me of how many men there are who wander Urth utterly alone. I knew then (or thought I did) why Baldanders chose to obey Dr. Talos, bending his mighty strength to whatever task the red-haired man laid on him.

A touch at my shoulder took me from my revery. It was Hethor, who must have come up silently from his position in the rear. "Master," he said.

I told him not to call me that, and explained that I was only a journeyman of my guild, and would probably never attain to mastership.

He nodded humbly. Through his open lips I could glimpse the broken incisors. "Master, where do we go?"

"Out the gate," I said, and told myself I said it because I wanted him to follow Dr. Talos and not me; the truth was that I was thinking of the preternatural beauty of the Claw, and how sweet it would be to carry it to Thrax with me, instead of retracing my steps to the center of Nessus. I gestured toward the Wall, which now rose in the distance as the walls of a common fortress must rise before a mouse. They were black as thunderheads, and held certain clouds captive at their summit.

"I will carry your sword, Master."

The offer seemed honestly made, though I was reminded that the plot Agia and her brother had conceived against me had been born of their desire for *Terminus Est*. As firmly as I could, I said, "No. Not now or ever."

"I feel pity for you, Master, seeing you walk with it on your shoulder so. It must be very heavy."

I was explaining, quite truthfully, that it was not as burdensome as it appeared, when we rounded the side of a gentle hill and saw half a league off a straight highway running toward an opening in the Wall. It was crowded with carts and wagons and traffic of all kinds, all dwarfed by the Wall and the towering gate until the people looked like mites and the beasts like ants pulling at little crumbs. Dr. Talos turned until he was walking backward and waved at the Wall as proudly as if he had built it himself.

"Some of you, I think, have never seen this. Severian? Ladies? Have you been this near before?"

Even Jolenta shook her head, and I said, "No. I've spent my life so near the middle of the city that the Wall was no more than a dark line on the northern horizon when we looked from the glass-roofed room at the top of our tower. I am astounded, I admit."

"The ancients built well, did they not? Think—after so many millennia, all the open area through which we have passed today yet remains for the growth of the city. But Baldanders is shaking his head. Don't you see, my dear patient, that all these bosquets and pleasant meadows among which we have journeyed this morning will one day be displaced by buildings and streets?"

Baldanders said, "They were not for the growing of Nessus."

"Of course, of course. I'm sure you were there, and know all about it." The doctor winked at the rest of us. "Baldanders is older than I, and so believes he knows everything. Sometimes."

We were soon within a hundred paces or so of the highway, and Jolenta's attention became fixed on its traffic. "If there's a litter for hire, you must get it for me," she told Dr. Talos. "I won't be able to perform tonight if I have to walk all day."

He shook his head. "You forget, I have no money. Should you see a litter and wish to engage it, you are of course free to do so. If you cannot appear tonight, your understudy will take your role."

"My understudy?"

The doctor gestured toward Dorcas. "I'm certain she is eager to try the starring part, and that she will do famously. Why do you think I permitted her to join us and share in the proceeds? Less rewriting will be necessary than if we have two women."

"She will go with Severian, you fool. Didn't he say this morning he was going back to look for—" Jolenta wheeled on me, more beautiful than ever for being angry. "What did you call them? Pelisses?"

I said, "Pelerines." And at this a man riding a merychip at the edge of the concourse of people and animals reined his diminutive mount over. "If you're looking for the Pelerines," he said, "your way lies with mine—out the gate, not toward the city. They passed along this road last night."

I quickened my step until I could grasp the cantle of his saddle, and asked if he were sure of his information.

"I was disturbed when the other patrons of my inn rushed into the road to receive their blessing," the man on the merychip said. "I looked out the window and saw their procession. Their servants carried deeses illuminated with candles but reversed, and the priestesses themselves had torn their habits." His face, which was long and worn and humorous, split in a wry grin. "I don't know what was wrong, but believe me, their departure was impressive and unmistakable—that's what the bear said, you know, about the picnickers."

Dr. Talos whispered to Jolenta, "I think the angel of agony there, and your understudy, will remain with us a while longer."

As it proved, he was half in error. No doubt you, who have perhaps seen the Wall many times, and perhaps passed often through one or another of its gates, will be impatient with me; but before I continue this account of my life, I find I must for my own peace spend a few words on it.

I have already spoken of its height. There are few sorts of birds, I think, that would fly over it. The eagle and the great mountain teratornis, and possibly the wild geese and their allies; but few others. This height I had come to expect by the time we reached the base: the Wall had been in plain view then for many leagues, and no one who saw it, with the clouds moving across its face as ripples do across a pond, could fail to realize its altitude. It is of black metal, like the walls of the Citadel, and for this reason it seemed less terrible to me than it would have otherwise—the buildings I had seen in the city were of stone or brick, and to come now on the material I had known from earliest childhood was no unpleasant thing.

Yet to enter the gate was to enter a mine, and I could not suppress a shudder. I noticed too that everyone around me except for Dr. Talos and Baldanders seemed to feel as I did. Dorcas clasped my hand more tightly, and Hethor hung his head. Jolenta seemed to consider that the doctor, with whom she had been quarreling a moment before, might protect her; but when he paid no heed to her touch at his arm and continued to swagger forward and pound the pavement with his stick just as he had in the sunlight, she left him and to my astonishment took the stirrup strap of the man on the merychip.

The sides of the gate rose high above us, pierced at wide intervals by windows of some material thicker, yet clearer, than glass. Behind these windows we could see the moving figures of men and women, and of creatures that were neither men nor women. Cacogens, I think, were there, beings to whom the avern was but what a marigold or a marguerite is to us. Others seemed beasts with too much of men about them, so that horned heads watched us with eyes too wise, and mouths that appeared to speak showed teeth like nails or hooks. I asked Dr. Talos what these creatures were.

"Soldiers," he said. "The pandours of the Autarch."

Jolenta, whose fear made her press the side of one full breast against the thigh of the man on the merychip, whispered, "Whose perspiration is the gold of his subjects."

"Within the Wall itself, Doctor?"

"Like mice. Although it is of immense thickness, it's honey-combed everywhere—so I am given to understand. In its passages and galleries there dwell an innumerable soldiery, ready to defend it just as termites defend their ox-high earthen nests on the pampas of the north. This is the fourth time Baldanders and I have passed through, for once, as we told you, we came south, entering Nessus by this gate and going out a year afterward through the gate calling Sorrowing. Only recently we returned from the south with what little we had won there, passing in at the other southern gate, that of Praise. On all these passages we beheld the interior of the Wall as you see it now, and the faces of these slaves of the Autarch looked out at us. I do not doubt that there are among them many who search for some particular miscreant, and that if they were to see the one they seek, they would sally out and lay hold of him."

At this the man on the merychip (whose name was Jonas, as I learned later) said, "I beg your pardon, optimate, but I could not help overhearing what you said. I can enlighten you further, if you wish."

Dr. Talos glanced at me, his eyes sparkling. "Why that would be pleasant, but we must make one proviso. We will speak only of the

Wall, and those who dwell in it. Which is to say, we will ask you no questions concerning yourself. And you, likewise, will return that courtesy to us.''

The stranger pushed back his battered hat, and I saw that in place of his right hand he wore a jointed contrivance of steel. ''You have understood me better than I wanted, as the man said when he looked in the mirror. I admit I'd hoped to ask you why you traveled with the carnifex, and why this lady, the loveliest I've ever seen, is walking in the dust.''

Jolenta released his stirrup strap and said, ''You're poor, goodman, from the look of you, and no longer young. It hardly suits you to inquire of me.''

Even in the shadow of the gate, I saw the flush of blood creep into the stranger's cheeks. All she had said was true. His clothes were worn and travel-stained, though not so dirty as Hethor's. His face had been lined and coarsened by the wind. For perhaps a dozen steps he did not reply, but at last he began. His voice was flat and neither high nor deep, but possessed of a dry humor.

''In the old times, the lords of this world feared no one but their own people, and to defend themselves against them built a great fortress on a hilltop to the north of the city. It was not called Nessus then, for the river was unpoisoned.

''Many of the people were angry at the building of that citadel, holding it to be their right to slay their lords without hindrance if they so desired. But others went out in the ships that ply between the stars, returning with treasure and knowledge. In time there returned a woman who had gained nothing among them but a handful of black beans.''

''Ah,'' said Dr. Talos. ''You are a professional tale-teller. I wish you had informed us of it from the beginning, for we, as you must have seen, are something the same.''

Jonas shook his head. ''No, this is the only tale I know—or nearly so.'' He looked down at Jolenta. ''May I continue, most marvelous of women?''

My attention was distracted by the sight of daylight ahead of us, and by the disturbance among the vehicles that clogged the road as many sought to turn back, flailing their teams and trying to clear a path with their whips.

''—she displayed the beans to the lords of men, and told them that unless she were obeyed she would cast them into the sea and so put an end to the world. They had her seized and torn to bits, for they were a hundred times more complete in their domination than our Autarch.''

''May he endure to see the New Sun,'' Jolenta murmured.

Dorcas tightened her grip on my arm and asked, "Why are they so frightened?" Then screamed and buried her face in her hands as the iron tip of a lash flicked her cheek. I pressed past the merychip's head, seized the ankle of the wagoneer who had struck her, and pulled him from his seat. By that time all the gate was ringing with bawling and swearing, and the cries of the injured, and the bellowings of frightened animals; and if the stranger continued his tale I could not hear it.

The driver I pulled down must have died at once. Because I had wished to impress Dorcas, I had hoped to perform the excruciation we call *two apricots*; but he had fallen under the feet of the travelers and the heavy wheels of the carts. Even his screams were lost.

Here I pause, having carried you, reader, from gate to gate—from the locked and fog-shrouded gate of our necropolis to this gate with its curling wisps of smoke, this gate which is perhaps the largest in existence, perhaps the largest ever to exist. It was by entering that first gate that I set my feet upon the road that brought me to this second gate. And surely when I entered this second gate, I began again to walk a new road. From that great gate forward, for a long time, it was to lie outside the City Imperishable and among the forests and grasslands, mountains and jungles of the north.

Here I pause. If you wish to walk no farther with me, reader, I cannot blame you. It is no easy road.

Appendix

A Note on the Translation

In rendering this book—originally composed in a tongue that has not yet achieved existence—into English, I might easily have saved myself a great deal of labor by having recourse to invented terms; in no case have I done so. Thus in many instances I have been forced to replace yet undiscovered concepts by their closest twentieth-century equivalents. Such words as *peltast, androgyn*, and *exultant* are substitutions of this kind, and are intended to be suggestive rather than definitive. *Metal* is usually, but not always, employed to designate a substance of the sort the word suggests to contemporary minds.

When the manuscript makes reference to animal species resulting from biogenetic manipulation or the importation of extrasolar breeding stock, the name of a similar extinct species has been freely substituted. (Indeed, Severian sometimes seems to assume that an extinct species has been restored.) The nature of the riding and draft animals employed is frequently unclear in the original text. I have scrupled to call these creatures *horses*, since I am certain the word is not strictly correct. The "destriers" of *The Book of the New Sun* are unquestionably much swifter and more enduring animals than those we know, and the speed of those used for military purposes seems to permit the delivering of cavalry charges against enemies supported by high-energy armament.

Latin is once or twice employed to indicate that inscriptions and the like are in a language Severian appears to consider obsolete. What the actual language may have been, I cannot say.

To those who have preceded me in the study of the posthistoric world, and particularly to those collectors—too numerous to name here—who have permitted me to examine artifacts surviving so many centuries of futurity, and most especially to those who have allowed me to visit and photograph the era's few extant buildings, I am truly grateful.

G. W.

The Claw of the Conciliator

But strength still goes out from your thorns,
and from your abysses the sound of music.
Your shadows lie on my heart like roses
and your nights are like strong wine.

I

The Village of Saltus

Morwenna's face floated in the single beam of light, lovely and framed in hair dark as my cloak; blood from her neck pattered to the stones. Her lips moved without speech. Instead I saw framed within them (as though I were the Increate, peeping through his rent in Eternity to behold the World of Time) the farm, Stachys her husband tossing in agony upon his bed, little Chad at the pond, bathing his fevered face.

Outside, Eusebia, Morwenna's accuser, howled like a witch. I tried to reach the bars to tell her to be quiet, and at once became lost in the darkness of the cell. When I found light at last, it was the green road stretching from the shadow of the Piteous Gate. Blood gushed from Dorcas's cheek, and though so many screamed and shouted, I could hear it pattering to the ground. Such a mighty structure was the Wall that it divided the world as the mere line between their covers does two books; before us now stood such a wood as might have been growing since the founding of Urth, trees as high as cliffs, wrapped in pure green. Between them lay the road, grown up in fresh grass, and on it were the bodies of men and women. A burning cariole tainted the clean air with smoke.

Five riders sat destriers whose hooked tushes were encrusted with lazulite. The men wore helmets and capes of indanthrene blue and carried lances whose heads ran with blue fire; their faces were more akin than the faces of brothers. On these riders, the tide of travelers broke as a wave on a rock, some turning left, some right. Dorcas was torn from my arms, and I drew *Terminus Est* to cut down those between us and found I was about to strike Master Malrubius, who stood calmly, my dog Triskele at his side, in the midst of the tumult. Seeing him so,

I knew I dreamed, and from that knew, even while I slept, that the visions I had had of him before had not been dreams.

I threw the blankets aside. The chiming of the carillon in the Bell Tower was in my ears. It was time to rise, time to run to the kitchen pulling on my clothes, time to stir a pot for Brother Cook and steal a sausage—a sausage bursting, savory, and nearly burned—from the grill. Time to wash, time to serve the journeymen, time to chant lessons to myself before Master Palaemon's examination.

I woke in the apprentices' dormitory, but everything was in the wrong place: a blank wall where the round port should have been, a square window that should have been a bulkhead. The row of hard, narrow cots was gone, and the ceiling too low.

Then I was awake. Country smells—much like the pleasant odors of flower and tree that used to float across the ruined curtain wall from the necropolis, but mixed now with the hot reek of a stable—drifted through the window. The bells began again, ringing in some campanile not far away, calling the few who retained their faith to beseech the coming of the New Sun, though it was very early still, the old sun had hardly dropped Urth's veil from his face, and save for the bells the village lay silent.

As Jonas had discovered the night before, our water-ewer held wine. I used some to rinse my mouth, and its astringency made it better than water; but I still wanted water to splash on my face and smooth my hair. Before sleeping I had folded my cloak, with the Claw at the center, to use for a pillow. I spread it now, and remembering how Agia had once tried to slip her hand into the sabretache on my belt, thrust the Claw into my boot top.

Jonas still slept. In my experience, people asleep look younger than they do awake, but Jonas seemed older—or perhaps only ancient; he had the face, with straight nose and straight forehead, that I have often noted in old pictures. I buried the smoldering fire in its own ashes and left without waking him.

By the time I had finished refreshing myself from the bucket of the innyard well, the street before the inn was no longer silent, but alive with hooves that splashed through the puddles left by the previous night's rain, and the clacking of scimitar horns. Each animal was taller than a man, black or piebald, rolling-eyed and half blinded by the coarse hair that fell across its face. Morwenna's father, I remembered, had been a drover; it was possible this herd was his, though it seemed unlikely. I waited until the last lumbering beast had passed and watched the men ride by. There were three, dusty and common looking, flourishing iron-tipped goads longer than themselves; and with them, their hard, watchful, low-bred dogs.

Inside the inn once more, I ordered breakfast and got bread warm from the oven, newly churned butter, pickled duck's eggs, and peppered chocolate beaten to a froth. (This last a sure sign, though I did not know it then, that I was among people who drew their customs from the north.) Our hairless gnome of a host, who had no doubt seen me in conversation with the alcalde the night before, hovered over my table wiping his nose on his sleeve, inquiring about the quality of each dish as it was served—though they were all, in truth, very good—promising better food at supper, and condemning the cook, who was his wife. He called me *sieur*, not because he thought as they sometimes had in Nessus that I was an exultant incognito, but because a torturer here, as the efficient arm of the law, was a great person. Like most peons, he could conceive of no more than one social class higher than his own.

"The bed, it was comfortable? Plenty of quilts? We will bring more."

My mouth was full, but I nodded.

"Then we shall. Will three be enough? You and the other sieur, are you comfortable together?"

I was about to say that I would prefer separate rooms (I thought Jonas no thief, but I was afraid the Claw might be too much of a temptation for any man, and I was unused, moreover, to sleeping double) when it occurred to me that he might have difficulty paying for a private accommodation.

"You will be there today, sieur? When they break through the wall? A mason could take down the ashlars, but Barnoch's been heard moving inside and may have strength left. Perhaps he's found a weapon. Why, he could bite the masons' fingers, if nothing else!"

"Not in an official capacity. I may watch if I can."

"Everyone's coming." The bald man rubbed his hands, which slithered together as if they had been oiled. "There's to be a fair, you know. The alcalde announced it. He's got a good head for business, our alcalde has. You take the average man—he'd see you here in my parlor and never think of a thing. Or at least, no more than to have you put an end to Morwenna. Not ours! He sees things. He sees the possibilities of them. You might say that in the wink of an eye the whole fair sprang up out of his head, colored tents and ribbons, roast meat and spun sugar, all together. Today? Why today we'll open the sealed house and pull Barnoch out like a badger. That will warm them up, that will draw them for leagues around. Then we'll watch you do for Morwenna and that country fellow. Tomorrow you'll begin on Barnoch—hot irons you start with usually, don't you? And everybody will want to be there. The day after, finish him off and fold the tents. It doesn't do to let them hang about too long after they've spent their money, or they begin to beg and fight and so on. All well planned, all well thought out! There's an alcalde for you!"

I went out again after breakfast and watched the alcalde's enchanted thoughts take shape. Countryfolk were stumping into the village with fruits and animals and bolts of home-woven cloth to sell; among them were a few autochthons carrying fur pelts and strings of black and green birds killed with the cerbotana. Now I wished I still had the mantle Agia's brother had sold me, for my fuligin cloak drew some odd looks. I was about to step inside once more when I heard the quickstep of marching feet, a sound familiar to me from the drilling of the garrison in the Citadel, but which I had not heard since I had left it.

The cattle I had watched earlier that morning had been going down to the river, there to be herded into barges for the remainder of their trip to the abattoirs of Nessus. These soldiers were coming the other way, up from the water. Whether that was because their officers felt the march would toughen them, or because the boats that had brought them were needed elsewhere, or because they were destined for some area remote from Gyoll, I had no way of knowing. I heard the shouted order to sing as they came into the thickening crowd, and almost together with it the thwacks of the vingtners' rods and the howls of the unfortunates who had been hit.

The men were kelau, each armed with a sling with a two-cubit handle and each carrying a painted leather pouch of incendiary bullets. Few looked older than I and most seemed younger, but their gilded brigandines and the rich belts and scabbards of their long daggers proclaimed them members of an elite corps of the erentarii. Their song was not of battle or women as most soldiers' songs are, but a true slingers' song. Insofar as I heard it that day, it ran thus:

"When I was a lad, my mother said,
 'You dry your tears and go to bed;
I know my son will travel far,
 Born beneath a shooting star.'

"In after years, my father said,
 As he pulled my hair and knocked my head,
'They mustn't whimper at a scar,
 Who're born beneath a shooting star.'

"A mage I met, and the mage he said,
 'I see for you a future red,

Fire and riot, raid and war,
O born beneath a shooting star.'

"A shepherd I met, and the shepherd said,
'We sheep must go where we are led,
To Dawn-Gate where the angels are,
Following the shooting star.' "

And so on, verse after verse, some cryptic (as it seemed to me), some merely comic, some clearly assembled purely for the sake of the rhymes, which were repeated again and again.

"A fine sight, aren't they?" It was the innkeeper, his bald head at my shoulder. "Southerners—notice how many have yellow hair and dotted hides? They're used to cold down there, and they'll need to be in the mountains. Still, the singing almost makes you want to join 'em. How many, would you say?"

The baggage mules were just coming into view, laden with rations and prodded forward with the points of swords. "Two thousand. Perhaps twenty-five hundred."

"Thank you, sieur. I like to keep track of them. You wouldn't believe how many I've seen coming up our road here. But precious few going back. Well, that's what war is, I believe. I always try to tell myself they're still there—I mean, wherever it was they went—but you know and I know there's a lot that have gone to stay. Still, the singing makes a man want to go with 'em."

I asked if he had news of the war.

"Oh, yes, sieur. I've followed it for years and years now, though the battles they fight never seem to make much difference, if you understand me. It never seems to get much closer to us, or much farther off either. What I've always supposed was that our Autarch and theirs appoints a spot to fight in, and when it's over they both go home. My wife, fool that she is, don't believe there's a real war at all."

The crowd had closed behind the last mule driver, and it thickened with every word that passed between us. Bustling men set up stalls and pavilions, narrowing the street and making the press of people greater still; bristling masks on tall poles seemed to have sprouted from the ground like trees.

"Where does your wife think the soldiers are going, then?" I asked the innkeeper.

"Looking for Vodalus, that's what *she says*. As if the Autarch—

whose hands run with gold and whose enemies kiss his heel—would send his whole army to fetch a bandit!''

I scarcely heard a word beyond *Vodalus*.

Whatever I possess I would give to become one of you, who complain every day of memories fading. My own do not. They remain always, and always as vivid as at their first impression, so that once summoned they carry me off spellbound.

I think I turned from the innkeeper and wandered into the crowd of pushing rustics and chattering vendors, but I saw neither them nor him. Instead I felt the bone-strewn paths of the necropolis under my feet, and saw through the drifting river fog the slender figure of Vodalus as he gave his pistol to his mistress and drew his sword. Now (it is a sad thing to have become a man) I was struck by the extravagance of the gesture. He who had professed in a hundred clandestine placards to be fighting for the old ways, for the ancient high civilization Urth has now lost, has discarded the effectual weapon of that civilization.

If my memories of the past remain intact, perhaps it is only because the past exists only in memory. Vodalus, who wished as I did to summon it again, yet remained a creature of the present. That we are capable only of being what we are remains our unforgivable sin.

No doubt if I had been one of you whose memories fade, I would have rejected him on that morning as I elbowed my way through the crowd, and so in some fashion would have escaped this death in life that grips me even as I write these words. Or perhaps I would not have escaped at all. Yes, more likely not. And in any case, the old, recalled emotions were too strong. I was trapped in admiration for what I had once admired, as a fly in amber remains the captive of some long-vanished pine.

II

The Man in the Dark

The bandit's house had differed in no way from the common houses of the village. It was of broken mine-stone, single storied, with a flattish, solid-looking roof of slabs of the same material. The door and the only window I could see from the street had been closed with rough masonry. A hundred or so fair-goers stood before the house now, talking and pointing; but there was no sound from within, and no smoke issuing from the chimney.

"Is this commonly done hereabouts?" I asked Jonas.

"It's traditional. You've heard the saying, 'A legend, a lie, and a likelihood make a tradition'?"

"It seems to me it would be easy enough to get out. He could break through a window or the wall itself by night, or dig a passage. Of course, if he expected something like this—and if it's common and he was really engaged in spying for Vodalus, there's no reason he shouldn't—he could have supplied himself with tools as well as a quantity of food and drink."

Jonas shook his head. "Before they close the openings, they go though the house and take everything they can find in the way of food and tools and lights, besides whatever else may be of value."

A resonant voice said, "Having good sense, as we flatter ourselves, we do indeed." It was the alcalde, who had come up behind us without either of us noticing his presence in the crowd. We wished him a good day, and he returned the courtesy. He was a solid, square-built man whose open face was marred by something too clever about the eyes. "I thought I recognized you, Master Severian, bright clothes or no. Are these new? They look it. If they don't give satisfaction, speak out to me about it. We try to keep the traders honest that come to our fairs.

It's only good business. If he doesn't make them right for you, whoever he is, we'll duck him in the river, you may be sure. One or two ducked a year keep the rest from feeling too comfortable."

He paused to step back and examine me more carefully, nodding to himself as though greatly impressed. "They become you. I must say, you've a fine figure. A handsome face too, save perhaps for a bit too much pallor, which our hot northern weather will soon make right. Anyway, they become you and look to wear well. If you're asked where you had them, you might say Saltus Fair. Such talk does no harm."

I promised I would, though I was far more concerned about the safety of *Terminus Est*, which I had left hidden in our room at the inn, than about my own appearance or the durability of the lay clothes I had bought from a slopman.

"You and your assistant have come to see us draw out the miscreant, I suppose? We'll be at him as soon as Mesmin and Sebald bring the post. A battering ram is what we called it when we passed the word of what was intended, but I'm afraid the truth is that it's nothing more than a tree trunk, and not a big one either—otherwise the village would have had to fee too many men to handle it. Yet it should do the work. I don't suppose you've heard of the case we had here eighteen years gone?"

Jonas and I shook our heads.

The alcalde threw out his chest, as politicians do whenever they see an opportunity to speak for more than a couple of sentences. "I recall it well enough, though I wasn't more than a stripling. A woman. I've forgotten her name, but we called her Mother Pyrexia. The stones were put up on her, just like what you see here, for it's largely the same ones doing it, and they did it in the same way. But it was the other end of summer, just at apple-picking time, and that I recall very well because of the people drinking new cider in the crowd, and myself with a fresh apple to eat while I watched.

"Next year when the corn was up, someone wanted to buy the house. Property becomes the property of the town, you know. That's how we finance the work, the ones that do it take what they can find for their share, and the town takes the house and ground.

"To shorten a lengthy tale, we cut a ram and broke through the door in fine fashion, thinking to sweep up the old woman's bones and turn the place over to the new owner." The alcalde paused and laughed, throwing back his head. There was something ghostly in that laughter, possibly only because it blended with the noise of the crowd, and so seemed silent.

I asked, "Wasn't she dead?"

"It depends on what you mean by that. I'll say this—a woman sealed in the dark long enough can become something very strange, just like the strange things you find in rotten wood, back among the big trees. We're miners, mostly, here in Saltus, and used to things found underground, but we took to our heels and came back with torches. It didn't like the light, or the fire either."

Jonas touched me on the shoulder and pointed to a swirl in the crowd. A group of purposeful-looking men were shouldering their way down the street. None had helmets or body armor, but several carried narrow-headed piletes, and the rest had brass-bound staves. I was strongly reminded of the volunteer guards who had admitted Drotte, Roche, Eata, and me to the necropolis so long ago. Behind these armed men were four who carried the tree trunk the alcalde had mentioned, a rough log about two spans across and six cubits long.

A collective indrawn breath greeted them; it was followed by louder talk and some good-natured cheering. The alcalde left us to take charge, directing the men with staves to clear a space about the door of the sealed house and using his authority, when Jonas and I pushed forward to get a better view, to make the crowd give way for us.

I had supposed that when all the breakers-in were in position they would proceed without ceremony. In that, I had reckoned without the alcalde. At the last possible moment he mounted the doorstep of the sealed house, and waving his hat for silence, addressed the crowd.

"Welcome visitors and fellow villagers! In the time it takes to draw breath thrice, you will see us smash this barrier and drag out the bandit Barnoch. Whether he be dead, or, as we have good reason to believe—for he hasn't been in there that long—alive. You know what he has done. He has collaborated with the traitor Vodalus's cultellarii, informing them of the arrivals and departures of those who might become their victims! All of you are thinking now, and rightly!, that such a vile crime deserves no mercy. Yes, I say! Yes, we all say! Hundreds and maybe thousands lie in unmarked graves because of this Barnoch. Hundreds and maybe thousands have met a fate far worse!

"Yet for a moment, before these stones come down, I ask you to reflect. Vodalus has lost a spy. He will be seeking another. On some still night not long, I think, from now, a stranger will come to one of you. It is certain he will have much talk—"

"Like you!" someone shouted, to general laughter.

"Better talk than mine—I'm only a rough miner, as many of you know. Much smooth, persuasive talk, I ought to have said, and possibly some money. Before you nod your head at him, I want you to remember this house of Barnoch's the way it looks now, with those ashlars where the door should be. Think about your own house with no doors and no windows, but with you inside it.

"Then think about what you're going to see done to Barnoch when we take him out. Because I'm telling you—you strangers particularly—what you're about to see here is only the beginning of what you'll be seeing at our fair in Saltus! For the events of the next few days we have employed one of the finest professionals from Nessus! You will see *at least* two persons executed here in the formal style, with the head struck off at a single blow. One's a woman, so we'll be using the chair! That's something a lot of people who boast of their sophistication and the cosmopolitan tincture of their educations have never seen. And you will see this man," pausing, the alcalde struck the sunlit door-stones with the flat of his hand, "this Barnoch, led to Death by an expert guide! It may be that he has made some sort of small hole in the wall by now. Frequently they do, and if so he may be able to hear me."

He lifted his voice to a shout. "If you can, Barnoch, cut your throat now! Because if you don't, you're going to wish you had starved long ago!"

For a moment there was silence. I was in agony at the thought that I should soon have to practice the Art on a follower of Vodalus's. The alcalde raised his right arm over his head, then brought it down in an emphatic gesture. "All right, lads, at it with a will!"

The four who had brought the ram counted *one, two, three* to themselves as if by prearrangement and ran at the walled-up door, losing some of their impetuosity when the two in front mounted the step. The ram struck the stones with a loud thump, but with no other result.

"All right, lads," the alcalde repeated. "Let's try it again. Show them the kind of men Saltus breeds."

The four charged a second time. At this attempt, those in front handled the step more skillfully; the stones plugging the doorway seemed to shudder under the impact, and a fine dust issued from the mortar. A volunteer from the crowd, a burly, black-bearded fellow, joined the original ramsmen, and all five charged; the thump of the ram was not noticeably louder, but it was accompanied by a cracking like the breaking of bones. "One more," the alcalde said.

He was right. The next blow sent the stone it struck into the house, leaving a hole the size of a man's head. After that, the ramsmen no longer bothered with a running start; they knocked the remaining stones out by swinging the ram with their arms until the aperture was large enough for a man to step through.

Someone I had not noticed previously had brought torches, and a boy ran to a neighboring house to kindle them at the kitchen fire. The men with piletes and staves took them from him. Showing more courage than I would have credited to those clever eyes, the alcalde drew a short truncheon from under his shirt and entered first. We spectators crowded after the armed men, and because Jonas and I had been in the forefront of the onlookers, we reached the opening almost at once.

The air was foul, far worse than I had anticipated. Broken furniture lay on every side, as though Barnoch had locked his chests and cupboards when the sealers came, and they had smashed them to get at his household goods. On a crippled table, I saw the guttered wax of a candle that had burned to the wood. The people behind me were pushing to go in farther; and I, as I discovered somewhat to my surprise, was pushing back.

There was a commotion at the rear of the house—hurried and confused footsteps—a shout—then a high, inhuman scream.

"They've got him!" someone behind me called, and I heard the news being passed to those outside.

A fattish man who might have been a smallholder came running out of the dark, a torch in one hand and a stave in the other. "Out of the way! Get back, all of you! They're bringing him out!"

I do not know what I expected to see. . . . Perhaps a filthy creature with matted hair. What came instead was a ghost. Barnoch had been tall; he was tall still, but stooped and very thin, with skin so pale it seemed to glow as decayed wood does. He was hairless, bald, and beardless; I learned that afternoon from his guards that he had formed the habit of plucking his hairs out. Worst of all were his eyes: protuberant, seemingly blind, and dark as the black abscess of his mouth. I turned away from him as he spoke, but I knew the voice was his. "I will be free," it said. "Vodalus! Vodalus will come!"

How I wished then that I had never been imprisoned myself, for his voice brought back to me all those airless days when I waited in the oubliette beneath our Matachin Tower. I too had dreamed of rescue by Vodalus, of a revolution that would sweep away the animal stench and degeneracy of the present age and restore the high and gleaming culture that was once Urth's.

And I had been saved not by Vodalus and his shadowy army, but by the advocacy of Master Palaemon—and no doubt of Drotte and Roche and a few other friends—who had persuaded the brothers that it would be too dangerous to kill me and too disgraceful to bring me before a tribunal.

Barnoch would not be saved at all. I, who should have been his comrade, would brand him, break him on the wheel, and at last sever his head. I tried to tell myself that he had acted, perhaps, only to get money; but as I did so some metal object, no doubt the steel head of a pilete, struck stone, and I seemed to hear the ringing of the coin Vodalus had given me, the ringing as I dropped it into the space beneath the floor-stone of the ruined mausoleum.

Sometimes when all our attention is thus focused on memory, our eyes, unguided by ourselves, will distinguish from a mass of detail some single object, presenting it with a clarity never achieved by concentration. So it was with me. Out of all the struggling tide of faces beyond the doorway, I saw one, upturned, illuminated by the sun. It was Agia's.

III

The Showman's Tent

The instant was frozen as though we two, and all those about us, stood in a painting. Agia's uptilted face, my own wide eyes; so we remained amid the cloud of countryfolk with their bright clothes and bundles. Then I moved, and she was gone. I would have run to her if I could; but I could only push my way through the onlookers, taking perhaps a hundred poundings of my heart to reach the spot where she had stood.

By then she had vanished utterly, and the crowd was swirling and changing like the water under the bow of a boat. Barnoch had been led forth, screaming at the sun. I took a miner by the shoulder and shouted a question to him, but he had paid no attention to the young woman beside him and had no notion of where she might have gone. I followed the throng who followed the prisoner until I was sure she was not among them, then, knowing nothing better to do, began to search the fair, peering into tents and booths, and making inquiries of the farmwives who had come to sell their fragrant cardamom-bread, and of the hot-meat vendors.

All this, as I write it, slowly convoluting a thread of the vermilion ink of the House Absolute, sounds calm and even methodical. Nothing could be further from the truth. I was gasping and sweating as I did these things, shouting questions to which I hardly stayed for an answer. Like a face seen in dream, Agia's floated before my imagination: wide, flat cheeks and softly rounded chin, freckled, sun-browned skin and long, laughing, mocking eyes. Why she had come, I could not imagine; I only knew she had, and that my glimpse of her had reawakened the anguish of my memory of her scream.

"*Have you seen a woman so tall, with chestnut hair?*" I repeated it again and again, like the duelist who had called out "Cadroe of Seventeen Stones,'' until the phrase was as meaningless as the song of the cicada.

''Yes. Every country maid who comes here.''

''Do you know her name?''

''A woman? Certainly I can get you a woman.''

''Where did you lose her?''

''Don't worry, you'll soon find her again. The fair's not big enough for anybody to stay lost long. Didn't the two of you arrange a place to meet? Have some of my tea—you look so tired.''

I fumbled for a coin.

''You don't have to pay, I sell enough as it is. Well, if you insist. It's only an aes. Here.''

The old woman rummaged in her apron pocket and produced a flood of little coins, then splashed the tea, hissing hot, from her kettle into an earthenware cup and offered me a straw of some dimly silver metal. I waved it away.

''It's clean. I rinse everything after each customer.''

''I'm not used to them.''

''Watch the rim then—it'll be hot. Have you looked by the judging? There'll be a lot of people there.''

''Where the cattle are? Yes.'' The tea was maté, spicy and a trifle bitter.

''Does she know you're looking for her?''

''I don't think so. Even if she saw me, she wouldn't have recognized me. I . . . am not dressed as I usually am.''

The old woman snorted and pushed a straggling lock of gray hair back under her kerchief. ''At Saltus Fair? Of course not! Everybody wears his best to a fair, and any girl with sense would know that. How about down by the water where they've got the prisoner chained?''

I shook my head. ''She seems to have disappeared.''

''But you haven't given up. I can tell from the way you look at the people going past instead of me. Well, good for you. You'll find her yet, though they do say all manner of strange things have been happening round and about of late. They caught a green man, do you know that? Got him right over there where you see the tent. Green men know everything, people say, if you can but make them talk. Then there's the cathedral. I suppose you've heard about that?''

''The cathedral?''

''I've heard tell it wasn't what cityfolk call a real one—I know you're from the city by the way you drink your tea—but it's the only cathedral most of us around Saltus ever saw, and pretty too, with all the hanging lamps and the windows in the sides made of colored silk. Myself, I don't believe—or rather, I think that if the Pancreator don't care nothing for me, I won't care nothing for him, and why should I? Still, it's a shame what they did, if they did what's told against them. Set fire to it, you know."

"Are you talking about the Cathedral of the Pelerines?"

The old woman nodded sagely. "There, you said it yourself. You're making the same mistake they did. It wasn't the Cathedral of the Pelerines, it was the Cathedral of the Claw. Which is to say, it wasn't theirs to burn."

To myself I muttered, "They rekindled the fire."

"I beg pardon." The old woman cocked an ear. "I didn't hear that."

"I said they burned it. They must have set fire to the straw floor."

"That's what I heard too. They just stood back and watched it burn. It went up to the Infinite Meadows of the New Sun, you know."

A man on the opposite side of the alleyway began to pound a drum. When he paused I said, "I know that certain persons have claimed to have seen it rise into the air."

"Oh, it rose all right. When my grandson-in-law heard about it, he was fairly struck flat for half a day. Then he pasted up a kind of hat out of paper and held it over my stove, and it went up, and then he thought it was nothing that the cathedral rose, no miracle at all. That shows what it is to be a fool—it never came to him that the reason things were made so was so the cathedral would rise just like it did. He can't see the Hand in nature."

"He didn't see it himself?" I asked. "The cathedral, I mean."

She failed to understand. "Oh, he's seen it when they've been through here, at least a dozen times."

The chant of the man with the drum, similar to that I had once heard Dr. Talos use, but more hoarsely delivered and bereft of the doctor's malicious intelligence, cut through our talk. "*Knows everything! Knows everybody! Green as a gooseberry! See for yourself!*"

(The insistent voice of the drum: BOOM! BOOM! BOOM!)

"Do you think the green man would know where Agia is?"

The old woman smiled. "So that's her name, is it? Now I'll know, if anybody should mention her. He might. You've money, why not try him?"

Why not indeed, I thought.

"*Brought from the jun-gles of the North! Never eats! A-kin to the bush-es and the grass-es!*" BOOM! BOOM! "*The fu-ture and the remote past are one to him!*"

When he saw me approaching the door of his tent, the drummer stopped his clamor. ''Only an aes to see him. Two to speak with him. Three to be alone with him.''

''Alone for how long?'' I asked as I selected three copper aes. A wry grin crossed the drummer's face. ''For as long as you wish.'' I handed him his money and stepped inside.

It had been plain he had not thought I would want to stay long, and I expected a stench or something equally unpleasant. There was nothing beyond a slight odor as of hay curing. In the center of the tent, in a dust-spangled shaft of sunlight admitted by a vent in the canvas roof, was chained a man the color of pale jade. He wore a kilt of leaves, now fading; beside him stood a clay pot filled to the brim with clear water.

For a moment we were silent. I stood looking at him. He sat looking at the ground. ''That's not paint,'' I said. ''Nor do I think it dye. And you have no more hair than the man I saw dragged from the sealed house.''

He looked up at me, then down again. Even the whites of his eyes held a greenish tint.

I tried to bait him. ''If you are truly vegetable, I would think your hair should be grass.''

''No.'' He had a soft voice, saved from womanishness only by its depth.

''You *are* vegetable then? A speaking plant?''

''You are no countryman.''

''I left Nessus a few days ago.''

''With some education.''

I thought of Master Palaemon, then of Master Malrubius and my poor Thecla, and I shrugged. ''I can read and write.''

''Yet you know nothing about me. I am not a talking vegetable, as you should be able to see. Even if a plant were to follow the one evolutionary way, out of some many millions, that leads to intelligence, it is impossible that it should duplicate in wood and leaf the form of a human being.''

''The same thing might be said of stones, yet there are statues.''

For all his aspect of despair (and his was a sadder face by far than my friend Jonas's), something tugged at the corners of his lips. ''That is well put. You have no scientific training, but you are better taught than you realize.''

''On the contrary, all my training has been scientific—although it had nothing to do with these fantastic speculations. What are you?''

''A great seer. A great liar, like every man whose foot is in a trap.''

''If you'll tell me what you are, I'll endeavor to help you.''

He looked at me, and it was as if some tall herb had opened eyes and shown a human face. "I believe you," he said. "Why is it that you, of all the hundreds who come to this tent, know pity?"

"I know nothing of pity, but I have been imbued with a respect for justice, and I am well acquainted with the alcalde of this village. A green man is still a man; and if he is a slave, his master must show how he came to that state, and how he himself came into possession of him."

The green man said, "I'm a fool, I suppose, to put any confidence in you. And yet I do. I am a free man, come from your own future to explore your age."

"That is impossible."

"The green color that puzzles your people so much is only what you call pond scum. We have altered it until it can live in our blood, and by its intervention have at last made our peace in humankind's long struggle with the sun. In us, the tiny plants live and die, and our bodies feed from them and their dead and require no other nourishment. All the famines, and all the labor of growing food, are ended."

"But you must have sun."

"Yes," the green man said. "And I have not enough here. Day is brighter in my age."

That simple remark thrilled me in a way that nothing had since I had first glimpsed the unroofed chapel in the Broken Court of our Citadel. "Then the New Sun comes as prophesied," I said, "and there is indeed a second life for Urth—if what you say is the truth."

The green man threw back his head and laughed. Much later I was to hear the sound the alzabo makes as it ranges the snowswept tablelands of the high country; its laughter is horrible, but the green man's was more terrible, and I drew away from him. "You're not a human being," I said. "Not now, if you ever were."

He laughed again. "And to think I hoped in you. What a poor creature I am. I thought I had resigned myself to dying here among a people who are no more than walking dust; but at the tiniest gleam, all my resignation fell from me. I am a true man, friend. You are not, and in a few months I will be dead."

I remembered his kin. How often I had seen the frozen stalks of summer flowers dashed by the wind against the sides of the mausoleums in our necropolis. "I understand you. The warm days of sun are coming, but when they are gone, you will go with them. Grow seed while you can."

He sobered. "You do not believe me or even understand that I am a man like yourself, yet you still pity me. Perhaps you are right, and for us a new sun has come, and because it has come we have forgotten it.

If I am ever able to return to my own time, I will tell them there of you."

"If you are indeed of the future, why cannot you go forward to your home, and so escape?"

"Because I am chained, as you see." He held out his leg so that I could examine the shackle about his ankle. His berylline flesh was swollen about it, as I have seen the bark of a tree swollen that had grown through an iron ring.

The tent flap opened, and the drummer thrust his head through. "Are you still here? I have others outside." He looked significantly at the green man and withdrew.

"He means that I must drive you off, or he will close the vent through which my sunlight falls. I drive away those who pay to see me by foretelling their futures, and I will foretell yours. You are young now, and strong. But before this world has wound itself ten times more about the sun you shall be less strong, and you shall never regain the strength that is yours now. If you breed sons, you will engender enemies against yourself. If—"

"Enough!" I said. "What you are telling me is only the fortune of all men. Answer one question truthfully for me, and I will go. I am looking for a woman called Agia. Where will I find her?"

For a moment his eyes rolled upward until only a narrow crescent of pale green showed beneath their lids. A faint tremor seized him; he stood and extended his arms, his fingers splayed like twigs. Slowly he said, "Above ground."

The tremor ceased, and he sat again, older looking and paler than before.

"You are only a fraud then," I told him as I turned away. "And I was a simpleton to believe in you even by so little."

"No," the green man whispered. "Listen. In coming here, I have passed through all your future. Some parts of it remain with me, no matter how clouded. I told you only the truth—and if you are indeed a friend of the alcalde of this place, I will tell you something further that you may tell him, something I have learned from the questions of those who have come to question me. Armed men are seeking to free a man called Barnoch."

I took my whetstone from the sabretache at my belt, broke it on the top of the chain-stake, and gave half to him. For a moment he did not comprehend what it was he held. Then I saw the knowledge growing in him, so that he seemed to unfold in his great joy, as though he were already basking in the brighter light of his own day.

IV

The Bouquet

As I left the showman's tent, I glanced up at the sun. The western horizon had already climbed more than half up the sky; in a watch or less it would be time for me to make my appearance. Agia was gone, and any hope of overtaking her had been lost in the frantic time I had spent dashing from one end of the fair to the other; yet I took comfort from the green man's prophecy, which I took to mean that Agia and I should meet again before either of us died, and from the thought that since she had come to watch Barnoch drawn into the light, so, equally, might she come to observe the executions of Morwenna and the cattle thief.

These speculations occupied me at first as I made my way back to the inn. But before I reached the room I shared with Jonas, they had been displaced by recollections of Thecla and my elevation to journeyman, both occasioned by the need to change from my new lay clothes into the fuligin of the guild. So strong is the power of association that it could be exercised by that habit while it was still out of sight on the pegs in the room, and by *Terminus Est* while she remained concealed beneath the mattress.

It used to entertain me, while I was still attendant upon Thecla, to find that I could anticipate much of her conversation, and particularly the first of it, from the nature of the gift I carried when I entered her cell. If it were some favorite food thieved from the kitchen, for example, it would elicit a description of a meal at the House Absolute, and the kind of food I brought even governed the nature of the repast described: flesh, a sporting dinner with the shrieking and trumpeting of game caught alive drifting up from the abattoir below and much talk of brachets, hawks, and hunting leopards; sweets, a private repast given by one of the great Chatelaines for a few friends, deliciously intimate, and soaked in gossip; fruit, a twilit garden party in the vast park of the House Absolute, lit by a thousand torches and enlivened by jugglers, actors, dancers, and pyrotechnic displays.

She ate standing as often as sitting, walking the three strides that took her from one end of her cell to the other, holding the dish in her left hand while she gestured with her right. "Like this, Severian, they all spring into the ringing sky, showering green and magenta sparks, while the maroons boom like thunder!"

But her poor hand could hardly show the rockets rising higher than her towering head, for the ceiling was not much taller than she.

"But I'm boring you. A moment ago, when you brought me these peaches, you looked so happy, and now you won't smile. It's just that it does me good, here, to remember those things. How I'll enjoy them when I see them again."

I was not bored, of course. It was only that it saddened me to see her, a woman still young and endowed with a terrible beauty, so confined. . . .

Jonas was uncovering *Terminus Est* for me when I came into our room. I poured myself a cup of wine. "How do you feel?" he asked.

"What of you? It's your first time, after all."

He shrugged. "I only have to fetch and carry. You've done it before? I wondered, because you look so young."

"Yes, I've done it before. Never to a woman."

"You think she's innocent?"

I was taking off my shirt; when I had my arms freed I mopped my face with it and shook my head. "I'm sure she's not. I went down and talked to her last night—they have her chained at the edge of the water, where the midges are bad. I told you about it."

Jonas reached for the wine himself, his metal hand clinking when it met the cup. "You told me that she was beautiful, and that she had black hair like—"

"Thecla. But Morwenna's is straight. Thecla's curled."

"Like Thecla, whom you seem to have loved as I love your friend Jolenta. I confess you had a great deal more time to fall in love than I did. And you told me she said her husband and child had died of some sickness, probably from bad water. The husband had been quite a bit older than she."

I said, "About your age, I think."

"And there was an older woman there who had wanted him too, and now she was tormenting the prisoner."

"Only with words." Among the guild, apprentices alone wear shirts. I drew on my trousers and put my cloak (which was of fuligin, the color darker than black) around my bare shoulders. "Clients who have been exposed by the authorities like that have usually been stoned. When we see them they're bruised, and often they've lost a few teeth. Sometimes they have broken bones. The women have been raped."

"You say she's beautiful. Perhaps people think she's innocent. Perhaps they took pity on her."

I picked up *Terminus Est*, drew her, and let the soft sheath fall away. "The innocent have enemies. They are afraid of her."

We went out together.

When I had entered the inn, I had to push my way through the mob of drinkers. Now it opened before me. I wore my mask and carried *Terminus Est* unsheathed across my shoulder. Outside, the sounds of the fair stilled as we went forward until nothing remained but a whispering, as though we strode through a wilderness of leaves.

The executions were to take place at the very center of the festivities, and a dense crowd had already gathered there. A caloyer in red stood beside the scaffold clutching his little formulary; he was an old man, as most of them are. The two prisoners waited beside him, surrounded by the men who had taken forth Barnoch. The alcalde wore his yellow gown of office and his gold chain.

By ancient custom, we must not use the steps (although I have seen Master Gurloes assist his vault to the scaffold with his sword, in the court before the Bell Tower). I was, very possibly, the only person present who knew of the tradition; but I did not break it, and a great roar, like the voice of some beast, escaped the crowd as I leaped up with my cloak billowing about me.

"Increate," read the caloyer, *"it is known to us that those who will perish here are no more evil in your sight than we. Their hands run with blood. Ours also."*

I examined the block. Those used outside the immediate supervision of the guild are notoriously bad: "Wide as a stool, dense as a fool, and dished, as a rule." This one fulfilled the first two specifications in the proverbial description only too well, but by the mercy of Holy Katharine it was actually slightly convex, and though the idiotically hard wood would be sure to dull the male side of my blade, I was in the fortunate position of having before me one subject of either sex, so that I could use a fresh edge on each.

". . . by thy will they may, in that hour, have so purified their spirits as to gain thy favor. We who must confront them then, though we spill their blood today . . ."

I posed, legs wide as I leaned upon my sword as if I were in complete control of the ceremony, though the truth was that I did not know which of them had drawn the short ribbon.

"You, the hero who will destroy the black worm that devours the sun; you for whom the sky parts as a curtain; you whose breath shall wither vast Erebus, Abaia, and Scylla who wallow beneath the wave; you that equally live in the shell of the smallest seed in the farthest forest, the seed that hath rolled into the dark where no man sees."

The woman Morwenna was coming up the steps, preceded by the alcalde and followed by a man with an iron spit who used it to prod her. Someone in the crowd shouted an obscene suggestion.

". . . have mercy on those who had no mercy. Have mercy on us, who shall have none now."

The caloyer was finished, and the alcalde began. "Most hatefully and unnaturally . . ."

His voice was high, quite different both from his normal speaking voice and the rhetorical tone he had adopted for the speech outside Barnoch's house. After listening absently for a few moments (I was looking for Agia in the crowd), it struck me that he was frightened. He would have to witness everything that was done to both prisoners at close range. I smiled, though my mask concealed it.

". . . of respect for your sex. But you shall be branded on the right cheek and the left, your legs broken, and your head struck from your body."

(I hoped they had had sense enough to remember that a brazier of coals would be required.)

"Through the power of the high justice laid upon my unworthy arm by the condescension of the Autarch—whose thoughts are the music of his subjects—I do now declare . . . I do now declare . . ."

He had forgotten it. I whispered the words: "That your moment has come upon you."

"I do now declare that your moment has come on you, Morwenna."

"If you have pleas for the Conciliator, speak them in your heart."

"If you have pleas for the Conciliator, speak them."

"If you have counsels for the children of women, there will be no voice for them after this."

The alcalde's self-possession was returning, and he got it all: "If you have counsels for the children of women, there will be no voice for them after this."

Clearly but not loudly, Morwenna said, "I know that most of you think me guilty. I am innocent. I would never do the horrible things you have accused me of."

The crowd drew closer to hear her.

"Many of you are my witnesses that I loved Stachys. I loved the child Stachys gave me."

A patch of color caught my eye, purple-black in the strong spring sunshine. It was such a bouquet of threnodic roses as a mute might carry at a funeral. The woman who held them was Eusebia, whom I had met when she tormented Morwenna at the riverside. As I watched her, she inhaled their perfume rapturously, then employed their thorny stems to open a path for herself through the crowd, so that she stood just at the base of the scaffold. "These are for you, Morwenna. Die before they fade."

I hammered the planks with the blunt tip of my blade for silence. Morwenna said, "The good man who read the prayers for me, and who has talked to me before I was brought here, prayed that I would forgive you if I achieved bliss before you. I have never until now had it in my power to grant a prayer, but I grant his. I forgive you now."

Eusebia was about to speak again, but I silenced her with a look. The gap-toothed, grinning man beside her waved, and with something of a start I recognized Hethor.

"Are you ready?" Morwenna asked me. "I am."

Jonas had just set a bucket of glowing charcoal on the scaffold. From it thrust what was presumably the handle of a suitable inscribed iron; but there was no chair. I gave the alcalde a glance I intended to be significant.

I might have been looking at a post. At last I said, "Have we a chair, Your Worship?"

"I sent two men to fetch one. And some rope."

"When?" (The crowd was beginning to stir and murmur.)

"A few moments ago."

The evening before he had assured me that everything would be in readiness, but there was no point in reminding him of that now. There is no one, as I have since found, so liable to fluster on the scaffold as the average rural official. He is torn between an ardent desire to be the center of attention (a position closed to him at an execution) and the quite justified fear that he lacks the ability and training that might enable him to comport himself well. The most cowardly client, mounting the steps in the full knowledge that his eyes are to be plucked out, will in nineteen cases from a score conduct himself better. Even a shy cenobite, unused to the sounds of men and diffident to the point of tears, can be better relied on.

Someone called, "Get it over with!"

I looked at Morwenna. With her famished face and clear complexion, her pensive smile and large, dark eyes, she was a prisoner likely to arouse quite undesirable feelings of sympathy in the crowd.

"We could seat her on the block," I told the alcalde. I could not resist adding, "It's more suited to that anyway."

"There's nothing to tie her with."

I had permitted myself a remark too many already, so I forbore giving my opinion of those who require their prisoners bound.

Instead, I laid *Terminus Est* flat behind the block, made Morwenna sit down, lifted my arms in the ancient salute, took the iron in my right hand, and, gripping her wrists with my left, administered the brand to either cheek, then held up the iron still glowing almost white. The scream had silenced the crowd for an instant; now they roared.

The alcalde straightened himself and seemed to become a new man. "Let them see her," he said.

I had been hoping to avoid that, but I helped Morwenna to rise. With her right hand in mine, as though we were taking part in a country dance, we made a slow, formal circuit of the platform. Hethor was beside himself with delight, and though I tried to shut out the sound of his voice, I could hear him boasting of his acquaintance with me to the people around him. Eusebia held up her bouquet to Morwenna, calling, "Here, you'll need these soon enough."

When we had gone once around, I looked at the alcalde, and after the pause necessitated by his wondering at the occasion for the delay, received the signal to proceed.

Morwenna whispered, "Will it be over soon?"

"It is almost over now." I had seated her on the block again, and was picking up my sword. "Close your eyes. Try to remember that almost everyone who has ever lived has died, even the Conciliator, who will rise as the New Sun."

Her pale, long-lashed eyelids fell, and she did not see the upraised sword. The flash of steel silenced the crowd again, and when the full hush had come, I brought the flat of the blade down upon her thighs; over the smack of it on flesh, the sound of the femurs breaking came as clear as the *crack, crack* of a winning boxer's left-hand, right-hand blows. For an instant Morwenna remained poised on the block, fainted but not fallen; in that instant I took a backward step and severed her neck with the smooth, horizontal stroke that is so much more difficult to master than the downward.

To be candid, it was not until I saw the up-jetting fountain of blood and heard the thud of the head striking the platform that I knew I had carried it off. Without realizing it, I had been as nervous as the alcalde.

That is the moment when, again by ancient tradition, the customary dignity of the guild is relaxed. I wanted to laugh and caper. The alcalde was shaking my shoulder and babbling as I wished to myself; I could not hear what he said—some happy nonsense. I held up my sword, and taking the head by the hair held it up too, and paraded the scaffold. Not a single circuit this time, but again and again, three times, four times. A breeze had sprung up; it dotted my mask and arm and bare chest with scarlet. The crowd was shouting the inevitable jests: "Will you cut my wife's (husband's) hair too?" "Half a measure of sausage when you're done with that." "Can I have her hat?"

I laughed at them all and was feigning to toss the head to them when someone plucked at my ankle. It was Eusebia, and I knew before her first word that she was under that compulsion to speak I had often observed among the clients in our tower. Her eyes were sparkling with excitement, and her face was twisted by her attempt to get my attention, so that she looked simultaneously older and younger than she had appeared before. I could not make out what she was shouting and bent to listen.

"Innocent! She was innocent!"

This was no time to explain that I had not been Morwenna's judge. I only nodded.

"She took Stachys—from me! Now she's dead. Do you understand? She was innocent after all, but I am so glad!"

I nodded again and made another circuit of the scaffold, holding up the head.

"I killed her!" Eusebia screamed. *"Not you—!"*

I called down to her: "If you like!"

"Innocent! I knew her—so careful. She would have kept something back—poison for herself! She would have died before you got her."

Hethor grasped her arm and pointed to me. *"My master! Mine! My own!"*

"So it was somebody else. Or sickness after all—"

I shouted: "To the Demiurge alone belongs all justice!" The crowd was still noisy, though it had quieted a trifle by this time.

"But she stole my Stachys, and now she's gone." Louder than ever: *"Oh, wonderful! She's gone!"* With that, Eusebia plunged her face into the bouquet as though to fill her lungs to bursting with the roses' cloying perfume. I dropped Morwenna's head into the basket that awaited it and wiped my sword blade with the piece of scarlet flannel Jonas handed me. When I noticed Eusebia again she was lifeless, sprawled among a circle of onlookers.

At the time I thought little of it, only supposing that her heart had failed in her excess of joy. Later that afternoon the alcalde had her bouquet examined by an apothecary, who found among the petals a strong but subtle poison he could not identify. Morwenna must, I suppose, have had it in her hand when she mounted the steps, and must have cast it into the blossoms when I led her around the scaffold after the branding.

Allow me to pause here and speak to you as one mind to another, though we are separated, perhaps, by the abyss of eons. Though what I have already written—from the locked gate to the fair at Saltus—embraces most of my adult life, and what remains to be recorded concerns a few months only, I feel I am less than half concluded with my narrative. In order that it shall not fill a library as great as old Ultan's, I will (I tell you now plainly) pass over many things. I have recounted the execution of Agia's twin brother Agilus because of its importance to my story, and that of Morwenna because of the unusual circumstances surrounding it. I will not recount others unless they hold some special interest. If you delight in another's pain and death, you will gain little satisfaction from me. Let it be sufficient to say that I performed the prescribed operations on the cattle thief, which terminated in his execution; in the future, when I describe my travels, you are to understand that I practiced the mystery of our guild where it was profitable to do so, though I do not mention the specific occasions.

V

The Bourne

That evening, Jonas and I dined alone in our room. It is a very pleasant thing, I found, to be popular with the mob and known to everyone; but it is tiring too, and after a time one grows weary of answering the same simple-minded questions again and again, and of politely refusing invitations to drink.

There had been a slight disagreement with the alcalde concerning the compensation I was to receive for my work, my understanding having been that in addition to the quarter-payment made when I was engaged, I would receive full payment for each client upon death, while the alcalde had intended, so he said, that full payment should be made only after all three were attended to. I would never have agreed to that, and liked it less than ever in the light of the green man's warning (which out of loyalty to Vodalus I had kept to myself). But after I had threatened not to appear on the following afternoon I was paid, and everything peaceably resolved.

Now Jonas and I were settled over a smoking platter and a bottle of wine, the door was shut and bolted, and the innkeeper had been instructed to deny that I was in his establishment. I would have been completely at ease if the wine in my cup had not recalled to me so vividly the much better wine Jonas had discovered in our ewer the night before, after I had examined the Claw in secret.

Jonas, observing me, I think, as I stared at the pale red fluid, poured a cup of his own and said, "You must remember that you are not responsible for the sentences. If you had not come here, they would have been punished eventually anyway, and probably would have suffered worse in less skilled hands."

I asked him what he thought he was talking about.

"I can see it troubles you . . . what happened today."

"I thought it went well," I said.

"You know what the octopus remarked when he got out of the mermaid's kelp bed: 'I'm not impugning your skill—quite the opposite. But you look as if you could use a little cheering up.' "

"We're always a little despondent afterward. That's what Master Palaemon always said, and I've found it true in my own case. He called it a purely mechanical psychological function, and at the time that seemed to me an oxymoron, but now I'm not sure he wasn't right. Could you see what happened, or did they keep you too busy?"

"I was standing on the steps behind you most of the time."

"You had a good view then, so you must have seen how it was—everything proceeded smoothly after we decided not to wait for the chair. I exercised my skills to applause, and I was the focus of admiration. There's a feeling of lassitude afterward. Master Palaemon used to talk of crowd melancholy and court melancholy, and said that some of us have both, some have neither, and some have one but not the other. Well, I have crowd melancholy; I don't suppose I'll ever have the chance, in Thrax, of discovering whether I also have court melancholy or not."

"And what is that?" Jonas was looking down into his wine cup.

"A torturer, let's say a master at the Citadel, is occasionally brought into contact with exultants of the highest degree. Suppose there's some exceedingly sensitive prisoner who's thought to possess important information. An official of lofty standing is likely to be delegated to attend such a prisoner's examination. Very often he will have had little experience with the more delicate operations, so he will ask the master questions and perhaps confide in him certain fears he has concerning the subject's temperament or health. A torturer under those circumstances feels himself to be at the center of things—"

"Then feels let down when it's over with. Yes, I suppose I can see that."

"Have you ever seen one of these affairs when it was badly botched?"

"No. Aren't you going to eat any of this meat?"

"Neither have I, but I've heard about them, and that's why I was tense. Times when the client has broken away and fled into the crowd. Times when several strokes were needed to part the neck. Times when a torturer lost all confidence and was unable to proceed. When I vaulted onto that scaffold, I had no way of knowing that none of those things was going to happen to me. If they had, I might have been finished for life."

"'Still, it's a terrible way to earn a living.' That's what the thornbush said to the shrike, you know."

"I really don't—" I broke off because I had seen something move on the farther side of the room. At first I thought it was a rat, and I have a pronounced dislike of them; I have seen too many clients bitten in the oubliette under our tower.

"What is it?"

"Something white." I walked around the table to see. "A sheet of paper. Someone has slipped a note under our door."

"Another woman wanting to sleep with you," Jonas said, but by that time I had already picked it up. It was indeed a woman's delicate script, written in grayish ink upon parchment. I held it close to the candle to read.

Dearest Severian:

From one of the kind men who are assisting me, I have learned you are in the village of Saltus, not far away. It seems too good to be true, but now I must discover whether you can forgive me.

I swear to you that any suffering you have endured for my sake was not by my choice. From the first, I wanted to tell you everything, but the others would not hear of it. They judged that no one should know but those who had to know (which meant no one but themselves), and at last told me outright that if I did not obey them in *everything* they would forgo the plan and leave me to die. I knew you would die for me, and so I dared to hope that you would have chosen, if you could choose, to suffer for me too. Forgive me.

But now I am away and almost free—my own mistress so long as I obey the simple and humane instructions of good Father Inire. And so I will tell you everything, in the hope that when you have heard it all you will indeed forgive me.

You know of my arrest. You will remember too how anxious your Master Gurloes was for my comfort, and how frequently he visited my cell to talk to me, or had me brought to him so that he and the other masters might question me. That was because my patron, the good Father Inire, had charged him to be strictly attentive to me.

At length, when it became clear that the Autarch would not free me, Father Inire arranged to do so himself. I do not know what threats were made to Master Gurloes, or what bribes were offered him. But they were sufficient, and a few days before my death—as you thought, dearest Severian—he explained to me how the matter was to be arranged. It was not enough, of course, that I be freed. I must be freed in such a way that no search should be made for me. That meant it needs appear that I was dead;

yet the instructions Master Gurloes had received had charged him strictly not to let me die.

You will now be able to fathom for yourself how we cut through this tangle of obstructions. It was arranged that I should be subjected to a device whose action was internal only, and Master Gurloes first so disarmed it that I should suffer no real harm. When you thought me in agony, I was to ask you for means of terminating my wretched life. All went as planned. You provided the knife, and I made a shallow cut on my arm, crouched near the door so some blood would run beneath it, then smeared my throat and fell across the bed for you to see when you looked into my prison.

Did you look? I lay as still as death. My eyes were closed, but I seemed to feel your pain when you saw me there. I nearly wept, and I recall how frightened I was that you might see the tears welling up. At last I heard your footsteps, and I bandaged my arm and washed my face and neck. After a time Master Gurloes came and took me away. Forgive me.

Now I would see you again, and if Father Inire wins a pardon for me as he has solemnly pledged himself to do, there is no reason why we need ever part again. But come to me at once—I am awaiting his messenger, and if he arrives I must fly to the House Absolute to cast myself at the feet of the Autarch, whose name be thrice-blessed balm upon the scorched brows of his slaves.

Speak to *no one* of this, but go northeast from Saltus until you encounter a brook that winds its way to Gyoll. Trace it against the current, and you will find it to issue from the mouth of a mine.

Here I must impart to you a grave secret, which you must by no means reveal to others. This mine is a treasure house of the Autarch's, and in it he has stored great sums of coined money, bullion, and gems against a day in which he may be forced from the Phoenix Throne. It is guarded by certain servitors of Father Inire's, but you need have no fear of them. They have been instructed to obey me, and I have told them of you, and ordered them to permit you to pass without challenge. Entering the mine, then, follow the water-course until you reach the end, where it issues from a stone. Here I wait, and here I write, in the hope that you will forgive your

THECLA

I cannot describe the surge of joy I felt as I read and reread this letter. Jonas, who saw my face, at first leaped from his chair—I think he supposed I was on the point of fainting—then drew away as he might have from a lunatic. When at last I folded the letter and thrust it in my sabretache, he asked no questions (for Jonas was indeed a friend) but showed by his look that he stood ready to help me.

"I need your animal," I said. "May I take her?"

"Gladly. But—"

I was already unbolting the door. "You cannot come. If all goes well, I'll see that she is returned to you."

As I raced down the stair and into the innyard, the letter spoke in my mind in Thecla's very voice; and by the time I entered the stable I was a lunatic indeed. I looked for Jonas's merychip, but instead saw before me a great destrier, his back higher than my eyes. I had no notion who might have ridden him into this peaceful village, and I gave it no thought. Without hesitating an instant I sprang onto his back, drew *Terminus Est,* and with a stroke severed the reins that tethered him.

I have never seen a better mount. He was out of the stable in one bound, and in two, lunging into the village street. For the space of a breath I feared he would trip on some tent rope, but he was sure-footed as a dancer. The street ran east toward the river; as soon as we were clear of the houses, I urged him to the left. He leaped a wall as a boy might skip across a stick, and I found myself galloping full tilt over a meadow where bulls lifted their horns in the green moonlight.

I am no great rider now, and was still less one then. Despite the high saddle, I think I would have tumbled from the back of an inferior animal before we had covered half a league; but my stolen destrier moved, for all his speed, as smoothly as a shadow. A shadow indeed we must have appeared, he with his black hide, I in my fuligin cloak. He had not slacked his pace before we splashed across the brook mentioned in the letter. I checked him there—partly by grasping his halter, more by speech, to which he harkened as a brother might. There was no path on either side of the water, and we had not traced it far before trees rimmed the banks. I guided him into the brook then (though he was loath to go) where we made our way up foaming races as a man climbs steps, and swam deep pools.

For more than a watch, we waded this brook through a forest much like the one through which Jonas and I had passed after being separated from Dorcas, Dr. Talos, and the rest at the Piteous Gate. Then the banks grew higher and more rugged, the trees smaller, and twisted. There were boulders in the stream; from their squared edges I knew they were the work of hands, and that we were in the region of the mines, with the wreck of some great city below us. Our way was steeper, and for all his mettle he faltered sometimes on sliding stones, so that I was forced to dismount and lead him. In this way we passed through a series of little, dreaming hollows, each dark in the shadows of its high sides, but each flecked in places with green moonlight, each ringing with the sound of water—but with that sound only, and otherwise wrapped in silence.

At last we entered a vale smaller and narrower than any of the others; and at the end of it, a chain or so off where the moonlight spilled upon a sheer elevation, I saw a dark opening. The brook had its origin there, flooding out like saliva from the lips of petrified titan. I found a patch of ground beside the water sufficiently level for my mount to stand and contrived to tie him there, knotting what remained of his reins around a dwarfish tree.

Once, no doubt, a timber trestle had provided access to the mine, but it had rotted away long ago. Though the climb looked impossible in the moonlight, I was able to find a few footholds in the ancient wall and scaled it to one side of the descending jet.

I had my hands inside the opening when I heard, or thought I heard, some sound from the vale behind me. I paused, and turned my head to look back. The rush of the water would have drowned any noise less commanding than a bugle call or an explosion, and it had drowned this, yet still I had sensed something—the note of stone falling upon stone, perhaps, or the splash of something plunging into the water.

The vale seemed peaceful and silent. Then I saw my destrier shift his stance, his proud head and forward-cocked ears coming for an instant into the light. I decided that what I had heard was nothing more than the striking of his steel-shod feet against the rock as he stamped in discontent at being so closely tethered. I drew my body into the mine entrance, and by doing so, as I later learned, saved my life.

A man of any wit, setting out as I had and knowing he must enter such a place, would have brought a lantern and a plentiful supply of candles. I had been so wild at the thought that Thecla still lived that I had none. Thus I crept forward in the dark, and had not taken a dozen steps before the moonlight of the vale had vanished behind me. My boots were in the stream, so I walked as I had when I had led the destrier up it. *Terminus Est* was slung over my left shoulder, and I had no fear that the tip of her sheath might be wet by the stream, for the ceiling of the tunnel was so low that I walked bent double. So I proceeded for a long time, fearing always that I had come wrong, and that Thecla waited for me elsewhere, and would wait in vain.

VI

Blue Light

I grew so accustomed to the sound of the icy water that had you asked me I should have said I walked in silence; but it was not so, and when, most suddenly, the constricted tunnel opened into a large chamber equally dark, I knew it at once from the change in the music of the stream. I took another step, and then another, and raised my head. There was no ragged stone now to strike it. I lifted my arms. Nothing. I grasped *Terminus Est* by her onyx hilt and waved her blade, still in the protection of its sheath. Nothing still.

Then I did something that you, reading this record, will find foolish indeed, though you must recall that I had been told that such guards as might be in the mine had been warned of my arrival and instructed to do me no harm. I called Thecla's name.

And the echoes answered: "*Thecla . . . Thecla . . . Thecla . . .*"

Then silence again.

I remembered that I was to have followed the water until it welled from a rock, and that I had not done so. Possibly it trickled through as many galleries here beneath the hill as it had through dells outside it. I began to wade again, feeling my way at each step for fear I might plunge over my head with the next.

I had not taken five strides when I heard something, far off yet distinct, above the whispering of the now smoothly flowing water. I had not taken five more when I saw light.

It was not the emerald reflection of the fabled forests of the moon, nor was it such a light as guards might carry with them—the scarlet flame of a torch, the golden radiance of a candle, or even the piercing white beam I had sometimes glimpsed by night when the fliers of the Autarch soared over the Citadel. Rather, it was a luminous mist, sometimes seeming of no color, sometimes of an impure yellowish green. It was impossible to say how far it was, and it seemed to possess no shape. For a time it shimmered before my sight; and I, still following the stream, splashed toward it. Then it was joined by another.

It is difficult for me to concentrate on the events of the next few minutes. Perhaps everyone holds in his subconscious certain moments of horror, as our oubliette held, in its lowest inhabited level, those clients whose minds had long ago been destroyed or transformed into consciousness no longer human. Like them, these memories shriek and lash the walls with their chains, but are seldom brought high enough to see the light.

What I experienced under the hill remains with me as they remained with us, something I endeavor to lock within the furthest recesses of my mind but am from time to time made conscious of. (Not long ago, when the *Samru* was still near the mouth of Gyoll, I looked over the sternrail by night; there I saw each dipping of the oars appear as a spot of phosphorescent fire, and for a moment imagined that those from under the hill had come for me at last. They are mine to command now, but I have small comfort in that.)

The light I had seen was joined by a second, as I have described, then the first two by a third, and the first three by a fourth, and still I went on. Soon there were too many of the lights to count; but not knowing what they were, I was actually comforted and encouraged by the sight of them, imagining each perhaps to be a spark from a torch of some kind not known to me, a torch held by one of the guards mentioned in the letter. When I had taken a dozen more steps, I saw that these flecks of light were coalescing into a pattern, and that the pattern was a dart or arrowhead pointed toward myself. Then I heard, very faintly, such a roaring as I used to hear from the tower called the Bear when the beasts were given their food. Even then, I think, I might have escaped if I had turned and fled.

I did not. The roaring grew—not quite any noise of animals, yet not the shouting of the most frenzied human mob. I saw that the flecks of light were not shapeless, as I had imagined before. Rather, each was of that figure called in art a star, having five unequal points.

It was then, much too late, that I halted.

By this time the uncertain, hueless light these stars shed had increased enough for me to see as looming shadows the shapes about me. To either side were masses whose angular sides suggested that they were works of men—it seemed I walked in the buried city (here not collapsed under the weight of the overlaying soil) from which the miners of Saltus delved their treasures. Among these masses stood squat pillars of an ordered irregularity such as I have sometimes noticed in ricks of firewood, from which every stick protrudes yet goes to make the whole. These glinted softly, throwing back the corpse light of the moving stars as something less sinister, or at least more beautiful, than they had received.

For a moment I wondered at these pillars; then I looked at the star-shapes again, and for the first time saw them. Have you ever toiled by night toward what seemed a cottage window, and found it to be the balefire of a great fortress? Or climbing, slipped, and caught yourself, and looked below, and seen the fall a hundred times greater than you had believed? If you have, you will have some notion of what I felt. The stars were not sparks of light, but shapes like men, small only because the cavern in which I stood was more vast than I had ever conceived that such a place could be. And the men, who seemed not men, being thicker of shoulder and more twisted than men, were rushing toward me. The roar I heard was the sound of their voices.

I turned, and when I found I could not run through the water mounted the bank where the dark structures stood. By that time they were almost upon me, and some were moving wide to my right and left and cut me off from the outer world.

They were terrible in a fashion I am not certain I can explain—like apes in that they had hairy, crooked bodies, long-armed, short-legged, and thick-necked. Their teeth were like the fangs of smilo-dons, curved and saw-edged, extending a finger's length below their massive jaws. Yet it was not any of these things, nor the noctilucent light that clung to their fur, that brought the horror I felt. It was something in their faces, perhaps in the huge, pale-irised eyes. It told me they were as human as I. As the old are imprisoned in rotting bodies, as women are locked in weak bodies that make them prey for the filthy desires of thousands, so these men were wrapped in the guise of lurid apes, and knew it. As they ringed me, I could see that knowledge, and it was the worse because those eyes were the only part of them that did not glow.

I gulped air to shout *Thecla* once more. Then I knew, and closed my lips, and drew *Terminus Est*.

One, larger or at least bolder than the rest, advanced on me. He carried a short-hafted mace whose shaft had once been a thigh bone. Just out of sword-reach he threatened me with it, roaring and slapping the metal head of his weapon in a long hand.

Something disturbed the water behind me, and I turned in time to see one of the glowing man-apes fording the stream. He leaped backward as I slashed at him, but the square blade-tip caught him below the armpit. So fine was that blade, so magnificently tempered and perfectly edged, that it cut its way out through the breastbone.

He fell and the water carried his corpse away, but before the stroke went home I had seen that he waded in the stream with distaste, and that it had slowed his movements at least as much as it had slowed mine. Turning to keep all my attackers in view, I backed into it and began slowly to move toward the point where it ran to the outside world. I felt that if I could once reach the constricted tunnel I would be safe; but I knew too that they would never permit me to do so.

They gathered more thickly around me until there must have been several hundred. The light they gave was so great then that I could see that the squared masses I had glimpsed earlier were indeed buildings, apparently of the most ancient construction, built of seamless gray stone and soiled everywhere by the dung of bats.

The irregular pillars were stacks of ingots in which each layer was laid across the last. From their color I judged them to be silver. There were a hundred in each stack, and surely many hundreds of stacks in the buried city.

All this I saw while taking a half-dozen steps. At the seventh they came for me, twenty at least, and from all sides. There was no time for clean strokes through the neck. I swung my blade in circles, and its singing filled that underground world and echoed from the stony walls and ceiling, audible over the bellowing and the screams.

One's sense of time goes mad at such moments. I recall the rush of the attack and my own frantic blows, but in retrospect everything seems to have happened in a breath. Two and five and ten were down, until the water around me was blood-black in the corpse light, choked with dying and dead; but still they came. A blow on my shoulder was like the smash of a giant's fist. *Terminus Est* slipped out of my hand, and the weight of the bodies bore me down until I was grappling blind under water. My enemy's fangs slashed my arm as two spikes might, but he feared drowning too much, I think, to fight as he would have otherwise. I thrust fingers into his wide nostrils and snapped his neck, though it seemed tougher than a man's.

If I could have held my breath then until I worked my way to the tunnel, I might have escaped. The man-apes seemed to have lost sight of me, and I drifted underwater some small distance downstream. By then my lungs were bursting; I lifted my face to the surface, and they were upon me.

No doubt there comes a time for every man when by rights he should die. This, I have always felt, was mine. I have counted all the life I have held since as pure profit, an undeserved gift. I had no weapon, and my right arm was numbed and torn. The man-apes were bold now. That boldness gave me a moment more of life, for so many crowded forward to kill me that they obstructed one another. I kicked one in the face. A second grasped my boot; there was a flash of light, and I (moved by what instinct or inspiration I do not know) snatched at it. I held the Claw.

As though it gathered to itself all the corpse light and dyed it with the color of life, it streamed forth a clear azure that filled the cavern. For one heartbeat the man-apes halted as though at the stroke of a gong, and I lifted the gem overhead; what frenzy of terror I hoped for (if I really hoped at all) I cannot say now.

What happened was quite different. The man-apes neither fled shrieking nor resumed their attack. Instead they retreated until the nearest were perhaps three strides off, and squatted with their faces pressed against the floor of the mine. There was silence again as there had been when I had first entered it, with no sound but the whispering of the stream; but now I could see everything, from the stacks of tarnished silver ingots near to which I stood, to the very end where the man-apes had descended a ruined wall, appearing to my sight then like flecks of pale fire.

I began to back away. The man-apes looked up at that, and their faces were the faces of human beings. When I saw them thus, I knew of the eons of struggles in the dark from which their fangs and saucer eyes and flap ears had come to be. We, so the mages say, were apes once, happy apes in forests swallowed by deserts so long ago they have no names. Old men return to childish ways when at last the years becloud their minds. May it not be that mankind will return (as an old man does) to the decayed image of what once was, if at last the old sun dies and we are left scuffling over bones in the dark? I saw our future—one future at least—and I felt more sorrow for those who had triumphed in the dark battles than for those who had poured out their blood in that endless night.

I took a step backward (as I have said), and then another, and still none of the man-apes moved to stop me. Then I remembered *Terminus Est*. Were I to have made my escape from the most frantic battle, I would have despised myself if I had left her behind. To walk out unmolested without her was more than I could bear. I began to advance again, watching by the light of the Claw for her gleaming blade.

At this the faces of those strange, twisted men seemed to brighten, and I saw by their looks that they hoped I meant to remain with them, so that the Claw and its blue radiance would be theirs always. How terrible it seems now when I set the words on paper; yet it would not,

I think, have been terrible in fact. Bestial though they appeared, I could see adoration on every brute face, so that I thought (as I think now) that if they are worse in many ways than we are, these people of the hidden cities beneath Urth are better in others, blessed with an ugly innocence.

From side to side I searched, from bank to bank; but I saw nothing, though it seemed to me that the light shone from the Claw more brightly, and more brightly still, until at last each tooth of stone that hung from the ceiling of that cavernous space cast behind it a sharp-sided shadow of pitch black. At last I called out to the crouching men, "My sword . . . Where is my sword? Did one of you take her?"

I would not have spoken to them if I had not been half frantic with the fear of losing her; but it seemed they understood. They began to mutter among themselves and to me, and to make signs to me—without rising—to show they would fight no more, extending their bludgeons and spears of pointed bone for me to take.

Then above the murmuring of the water and the muttering of the man-apes, I heard a new sound, and at once they fell silent. If an ogre were to eat of the very legs of the world, the grinding of his teeth would make just such a noise. The bed of the stream (where I still stood) trembled under me, and the water, which had been so clear, received a fine burden of silt, so that it looked as though a ribbon of smoke wound through it. From far below I heard a step that might have been the walking of a tower on the Final Day, when it is said all the cities of Urth will stride forth to meet the dawn of the New Sun.

And then another.

At once the man-apes rose, and crouching low fled toward the farther end of the gallery, silent now and swift as so many flitting bats. The light went with them, for it seemed, as I had somehow feared, that the Claw had flamed for them and not for me.

A third step came from underground, and with it the last gleam winked out; but at that instant, in that final gleam, I saw *Terminus Est* lying in the deepest water. In the dark I bent, and putting the Claw back into the top of my boot, took up my sword; and in so doing I discovered that the numbness had left my arm, which now seemed as strong as it had before the fight.

A fourth step sounded and I turned and fled, groping before me with the blade. What creature it was we had called from the roots of the continent I think I now know. But I did not know then, and I did not know whether it was the roaring of the man-apes, or the light of the Claw, or some other cause that had waked it. I only knew that there was something far beneath us before which the man-apes, with all the terror of their appearance and their numbers, scattered like sparks before a wind.

VII

The Assassins

When I recall my second passage through the tunnel that led to the outer world, I feel it occupied a watch or more. My nerves have never, I suppose, been fully sound, tormented as they have always been by a relentless memory. Then they were keyed to the highest pitch, so that to take three strides seemed to exhaust a lifetime. I was frightened, of course. I have never been called a coward since I was a small boy, and on certain occasions various persons have commented on my courage. I have performed my duties as a member of the guild without flinching, fought both privately and in war, climbed crags, and several times nearly drowned. But I believe there is no other difference between those who are called courageous and those who are branded craven than that the second are fearful before the danger and the first after it.

No one can be much frightened, certainly, during a period of great and immanent peril—the mind is too much concentrated on the thing itself, and on the actions necessary to meet or avoid it. The coward is a coward, then, because he has brought his fear with him; persons we think cowardly will sometimes amaze us by their bravery, if they have had no forewarning of their danger.

Master Gurloes, whom I had supposed to be of the most dauntless courage when I was a boy, was unquestionably a coward. During the period when Drotte was captain of apprentices, Roche and I used to alternate, turn and turn about, in serving Master Gurloes and Master Palaemon; and one night, when Master Gurloes had retired to his cabin but instructed me to stay to fill his cup for him, he began to confide in me.

"Lad, do you know the client Ia? An armiger's daughter and quite good-looking."

As an apprentice I had few dealings with clients; I shook my head.

"She is to be abused."

I had no idea what he meant, so I said, "Yes, Master."

"That's the greatest disgrace that can befall a woman. Or a man either. To be abused. By the torturer." He touched his chest and threw back his head to look at me. He had a remarkably small head for so large a man; if he had worn a shirt or jacket (which of course he never did), one would have been tempted to believe it padded.

"Yes, Master."

"Aren't you going to offer to do it for me? A young fellow like you, full of juice. Don't tell me you're not hairy yet."

At last I understood what he meant, and I told him that I had not realized it would be permissible, since I was still an apprentice; but that if he gave the order, I would certainly obey.

"I imagine you would. She's not bad, you know. But tall, and I don't like them tall. There's an exultant's bastard in that family a generation or so back, you may be sure. Blood will confess itself, as they say, though only we know all that means. Want to do it?"

He held out his cup and I poured. "If you wish me to, Master." The truth was that I was excited at the thought. I had never possessed a woman.

"You can't. I must. What if I were to be questioned? Then too, I must certify it—sign the papers. A master of the guild for twenty years, and I've never falsified papers. I suppose you think I can't do it."

The thought had never crossed my mind, just as the opposite thought (that he might still retain some potency) had never occurred to me with regard to Master Palaemon, whose white hair, stooped shoulders, and peering lens made him seem like one who had been decrepit always.

"Well, look here," Master Gurloes said, and heaved himself out of his chair.

He was one of those who can walk well and speak clearly even when they are very drunk, and he strode over to a cabinet quite confidently, though I thought for a moment that he was going to drop the blue porcelain jar he took down.

"This is a rare and potent drug." He took the lid off and showed me a dark brown powder. "It never fails. You'll have to use it someday, so you ought to know about it. Just take as much as you could get under your fingernail on the end of a knife, you follow me? If you take too much, you won't be able to appear in public for a couple of days."

I said, "I'll remember, Master."

"Of course it's a poison. They all are, and this is the best—a little more than *that* would kill you. And you mustn't take it again until the moon changes, understand?"

"Perhaps you'd better have Brother Corbinian weigh the dose, Master." Corbinian was our apothecary; I was terrified that Master Gurloes might swallow a spoonful before my eyes.

"Me? I don't need it." Contemptuously, he put the lid on the jar again and banged it down on its shelf in the cabinet.

"That's well, Master."

"Besides" (he winked at me), "I'll have this." From his sabretache he took an iron phallus. It was about a span and a half long and had a leather thong through the end opposite the tip.

It must seem idiotic to you who read this, but for an instant I could not imagine what the thing was for, despite the somewhat exaggerated realism of its design. I had a wild notion that the wine had rendered him childish, as a little boy is who supposes there is no essential difference between his wooden mount and a real animal. I wanted to laugh.

"'Abuse,' that's their word. That, you see, is where they've left us an out." He had slapped the iron phallus against his palm—the same gesture, now that I think of it, that the man-ape who had threatened me had made with his mace. Then I had understood and had been gripped by revulsion.

But even that revulsion was not the emotion I would feel now in the same situation. I did not sympathize with the client, because I did not think of her at all; it was only a sort of repugnance for Master Gurloes, who with all his bulk and great strength was forced to rely on the brown powder, and still worse, on the iron phallus I had seen, an object that might have been sawed from a statue, and perhaps had been. Yet I saw him on another occasion, when the thing had to be done immediately for fear the order could not otherwise be carried out before the client died, act at once, and without powder or phallus, and without difficulty.

Master Gurloes was a coward then. Still, perhaps his cowardice was better than the courage I would have possessed in his position, for courage is not always a virtue. I had been courageous (as such things are counted) when I had fought the man-apes, but my courage was no more than a mixture of foolhardiness, surprise, and desperation; now, in the tunnel, when there was no longer any cause for fear, I was afraid and nearly dashed my brains out against the low ceiling; but I did not pause or even slacken speed before I saw the opening before me, made visible by the blessed sheen of moonlight. Then, indeed, I halted; and considering myself safe wiped my sword as well as I might with the ragged edge of my cloak, and sheathed her.

That done, I slung her over my shoulder and swung myself out and down, feeling with the toes of my sodden boots for the ledges that had supported me in the ascent. I had just gained the third when two quarrels struck the rock near my head. One must have wedged its point in some flaw in the ancient work, for it remained in place, blazing with white fire. I recall how astonished I was, and also how I hoped, in the few moments before the next struck nearer still and nearly blinded me, that the arbalests were not of the kind that bring a new projectile to the string when cocked, and thus are so swift to shoot again.

When the third exploded against the stone, I knew they were, and dropped before the marksmen who had missed could fire yet again.

There was, as I ought to have known there would be, a deep pool where the stream fell from the mouth of the mine. I got another ducking, but since I was already wet it did no harm, and in fact quenched the flecks of fire that had clung to my face and arms.

There could be no question here of cannily remaining below the surface. The water seized me as if I were a stick and flung me to the top where it willed. This, by the greatest good luck, was some distance from the rock face, and I was able to watch my attackers from behind as I clambered onto the bank. They and the woman who stood between them were staring at the place where the cascade fell.

As I drew *Terminus Est* for the final time that night, I called, "Over here, Agia."

I had guessed earlier that it was she, but as she turned (more swiftly than either of the men with her) I glimpsed her face in the moonlight. It was a terrible face to me (though for all her self-depreciation so lovely) because the sight of it meant that Thecla was surely dead.

The man nearest me was fool enough to try to bring his arbalest to his shoulder before he pulled the trigger. I ducked and cut his legs from under him, while the other's quarrel whizzed over my head like a meteor.

By the time I had straightened up again, the second man had dropped his arbalest and was drawing his hanger. Agia was quicker, making a cut at my neck with an athame before his weapon was free of the scabbard. I dodged her first stroke and parried her second, though *Terminus Est*'s blade was not made for fencing. My own attack made her bound back.

"Get behind him," she called to the second arbalestier. "I can front him."

He did not answer. Instead, his mouth swung open and his point swung wide. Before I realized that it was not at me that he was looking, something feverishly gleaming bounded past me. I heard the ugly sound of a breaking skull. Agia turned as gracefully as any cat and would have spitted the man-ape, but I struck the poisoned blade from her hand and sent it skittering into the pool. She tried to flee then; I caught her by the hair and jerked her off her feet.

The man-ape was mumbling over the body of the arbalestier he had killed—whether he sought to loot it or was merely curious about its appearance I have never known. I set my foot on Agia's neck, and the man-ape straightened and turned to face me, then dropped in the crouching posture I had seen in the mine and held up his arms. One hand was gone; I recognized the clean cut of *Terminus Est*. The man-ape mumbled something I could not understand.

I tried to reply. "Yes, I did that. I am sorry. We are at peace now."

The beseeching look remained, and he spoke again. Blood still seeped from the stump, though his kind must possess a mechanism for pinching shut the veins, as thylacodons are said to do; without the attentions of a surgeon, a man would have bled to death from that wound.

"I cut it," I said. "But it was while we were still fighting, before you people saw the Claw of the Conciliator." Then it came to me that he must have followed me outside for another glimpse of the gem, braving the fear engendered by whatever we had waked below the hill. I thrust my hand into the top of my boot and pulled out the Claw, and the instant I had done so realized what a fool I had been to put the boot and its precious cargo so close to Agia's reach, for her eyes went wide with cupidity at the moment that the man-ape abased himself further and stretched forth his piteous stump.

For a moment we were posed, all three, and a strange group we must have looked in that eerie light. An astonished voice—Jonas's—called "Severian!" from the heights above. Like the trumpet note in a shadow play that dissolves all feigning, that shout ended our tableau. I lowered the Claw and concealed it in my palm. The man-ape bolted for the rock face, and Agia began to struggle and curse beneath my foot.

A rap with the flat of my blade quieted her, but I kept my boot on her until Jonas had joined me and there were two of us to prevent her escape.

"I thought you might need help," he said. "I perceive I was mistaken." He was looking at the corpses of the men who had been with Agia.

I said, "This wasn't the real fight."

Agia was sitting up, rubbing her neck and shoulders. "There were four, and we would have had you, but the bodies of those things, those firefly tiger-men, started pitching out of the hole, and two were afraid and slipped away."

Jonas scratched his head with his steel hand, a sound like the currying of a charger. "I saw what I thought I saw, then. I had begun to wonder."

I asked what he thought he had seen.

"A glowing being in a fur robe making an obeisance to you. You were holding up a cup of burning brandy, I think. Or was it incense? What's this?" He bent and picked up something from the edge of the bank, where the man-ape had crouched.

"A bludgeon."

"Yes, I see that." There was a loop of sinew at the end of the bone handle, and Jonas slipped it over his wrist. "Who are these people who tried to kill you?"

"We would have," Agia said, "if it hadn't been for that cloak. We saw him coming out of the hole, but it covered him when he started to climb down, and my men couldn't see the target, only the skin of his arms."

I explained as briefly as I could how I had become involved with Agia and her twin, and described the death of Agilus.

"So now she's come to join him." Jonas looked from her to the crimson length of *Terminus Est* and gave a little shrug. "I left my merychip up there, and perhaps I ought to go and look after her. That way I can say afterward that I saw nothing. Was this woman the one who sent the letter?"

"I should have known. I had told her about Thecla. You don't know about Thecla, but she did, and that was what the letter was about. I told her while we were going through the Botanic Gardens in Nessus. There were mistakes in the letter and things Thecla would never have said, but I didn't stop to think of them when I read it."

I stepped away and replaced the Claw in my boot, thrusting it deep. "Maybe you had better attend to your animal, as you say. My own seems to have broken loose, and we may have to take turns riding yours."

Jonas nodded and began to climb back the way he had come.

"You were waiting for me, weren't you?" I asked Agia. "I heard something, and the destrier cocked his ears at the sound. That was you. Why didn't you kill me then?"

"We were up there." She gestured toward the heights. "And I wanted the men I'd hired to shoot you when you came wading up the brook. They were stupid and stubborn as men always are, and said they wouldn't waste their quarrels—that the creatures inside would kill you. I rolled down a stone, the biggest I could move, but by then it was too late."

"They had told you about the mine?"

Agia shrugged, and the moonlight turned her bare shoulders to something more precious and more beautiful than flesh. ''You're going to kill me now, so what does it matter? All the local people tell stories about this place. They say those things come out at night during storms and take animals from the cowsheds, and sometimes break into the houses for children. There's also a legend that they guard treasure inside, so I put that in the letter too. I thought if you wouldn't come for your Thecla, you might for that. Can I stand with my back to you, Severian? If it's all the same, I don't want to see it coming.''

When she said that, I felt as though a weight had been lifted from my heart: I had not been certain I could strike her if I had to look into her face.

I raised my own iron phallus, and as I did so felt there was one more thing I wanted to ask Agia; but I could not recall what it might be.

''Strike,'' she said. ''I am ready.''

I sought good footing, and my fingers found the woman's head at one end of the guard, the head that marked the female edge.

And a little later, again, ''Strike!''

But by that time I had climbed out of the vale.

VIII

The Cultellarii

We returned to the inn in silence, and so slowly that the eastern sky was gray before we reached the town. Jonas was unsaddling the merychip when I said, ''I didn't kill her.''

He nodded without looking at me. ''I know.''

''Did you watch? You said you wouldn't.''

''I heard her voice when you were practically standing beside me. Will she try again?''

I waited, thinking, while he carried the little saddle into the tack room. When he came out, I said, ''Yes, I'm sure she will. I didn't exact a promise from her, if that's what you mean. She wouldn't have kept one in any case.''

''I would have killed her then.''

''Yes,'' I said. ''That would have been the right thing to do.''

We walked out of the stable together. There was light enough in the innyard now for us to see the well, and the wide doors that led into the inn.

''I don't think it would have been right—I'm only saying that I would have done it. I would have imagined myself stabbed in my sleep, dying on a dirty bed somewhere, and I would have swung that thing. It wouldn't have been right.'' Jonas lifted the mace the man-ape had left behind, and chopped with it in a parody, brutal and graceless, of a sword cut. The head caught the light and both of us gasped.

It was of pounded gold.

Neither of us felt any desire to join the festivities the fair still proffered to those who had caroused all night. We retired to the room we shared, and prepared for sleep. When Jonas offered to share his gold with me, I refused. Earlier, I had had money in plenty and the advance on my fee, and he had been living, as it were, upon my largess. Now I was happy that he would no longer feel himself in my debt. I was ashamed, too, when I saw how completely he trusted me with his gold, and remembered how carefully I had concealed (in fact, still concealed) the existence of the Claw from him. I felt bound to tell him of it; but I did not, and contrived instead to slip my foot from my wet boot in such a way that the Claw fell into the toe.

I woke about noon, and after satisfying myself that the Claw was still there, roused Jonas as he had asked me. "There should be jewelers at the fair who'll give me some sort of price for this," he said. "At least, I can bargain with them. Want to come with me?"

"We should have something to eat, and by the time we're through, I'll be due at the scaffold."

"Back to work then."

"Yes." I had picked up my cloak. It was sadly torn, and my boots were dull and still slightly damp.

"One of the maids here can sew that for you. It won't be as good as new, but it will be a lot better than it is now." Jonas swung open the door. "Come along, if you're hungry. What are you looking so thoughtful about?"

In the inn's parlor, with a good meal between us, and the innkeeper's wife exercising her needle on my cloak in another room, I told him what had happened under the hill, ending with the steps I had heard far below ground.

"You're a strange man," was all he said.

"You are stranger than I. You don't want people to know it, but you're a foreigner of some kind."

He smiled. "A cacogen?"

"An outlander."

Jonas shook his head, then nodded. "Yes, I suppose I am. But you—you have this talisman that lets you command nightmares, and you have discovered a hoard of silver. Yet you talk about it to me as someone else might talk about the weather."

I took a bit of bread. "It is strange, I agree. But the strangeness resides in the Claw, the thing itself, and not in me. As for talking about it to you, why shouldn't I? If I were to steal your gold, I could sell it and spend the money, but I don't think things would go well for someone who stole the Claw. I don't know why I think that, but I do, and of course Agia stole it. As for the silver—"

"And she put it in your pocket?"

"In the sabretache that hangs from my belt. She thought her brother would kill me, remember. Then they were going to claim my body—they had planned that already, so they'd get *Terminus Est* and my habit. She would have had my sword and clothes and the gem too, and meanwhile, if it were found, I would be blamed and not she. I remember . . ."

"What?"

"The Pelerines. They stopped us as we were trying to get out. Jonas, do you think it's true that some people can read the thoughts of others?"

"Of course."

"Not everyone is so sure. Master Gurloes used to speak favorably of the idea, but Master Palaemon wouldn't hear of it. Still, I think the chief priestess of the Pelerines could, at least to some degree. She knew Agia had taken something, and that I had not. She made Agia strip so they could search her, but they didn't search me. Later they destroyed their cathedral, and I think that must have been because of the loss of the Claw—it was the Cathedral of the Claw, after all."

Jonas nodded thoughtfully.

"But none of this is what I wanted to ask you about. I'd like your opinion of the footsteps. Everyone knows about Erebus and Abaia and the other beings in the sea who will come to land someday. Nevertheless, I think you know more about them than most of the rest of us."

Jonas's face, which had been so open before, was closed and guarded now. "And why do you think that?"

"Because you've been a sailor, and because of the story about the beans—the story you told at the gate. You must have seen my brown book when I was reading it upstairs. It tells all the secrets of the world, or at least what various mages have said they were. I haven't read it all or even half of it, though Thecla and I used to read an entry every few days and spend the time between readings arguing about it. But I've noticed that all the explanations in that book are simple, and seemingly childish."

"Like my story."

I nodded. "Your story might have come out of the book. When I first carried it to Thecla, I supposed it was intended for children, or for adults who enjoyed childish things. But when we had talked about some of the thoughts in it, I understood that they had to be expressed in that way or they couldn't be expressed at all. If the writer had wanted to describe a new way to make wine or the best way to make love, he could have used complex and accurate language. But in the book he really wrote he had to say, 'In the beginning was only the hexaemeron,' or 'It is not to see the icon standing still, but to see the still standing.' The thing I heard underground . . . was that one of them?"

"I didn't see it." Jonas rose. "I'm going out now to sell the mace, but before I go I'm going to tell you what all housewives sooner or later tell their husbands: 'Before you ask more questions, think about whether you really want to know the answers.' "

"One last question," I said, "and then I promise I won't ask you anything more. When we were going through the Wall, you said the things we saw in there were soldiers, and you implied they had been stationed there to resist Abaia and the others. Are the man-apes soldiers of the same kind? And if they are, what good can human-sized fighters do when our opponents are as large as mountains? And why didn't the old autarchs use human soldiers?"

Jonas had wrapped the mace in a rag and stood now shifting it from one hand to the other. "That's three questions, and the only one I can answer for certain is the second. I'll guess at the other two, but I'm going to hold you to your promise; this is the last time we're going to speak of these things.

"The last question first. The old autarchs, who were not autarchs or called so, did use human soldiers. But the warriors they had created by humanizing animals, and perhaps, in secret by bestializing men, were more loyal. They had to be, since the populace—who hated their rulers—hated these inhuman servitors more still. Thus the servitors could be made to endure things that human soldiers would not. That may have been why they were used in the Wall. Or there may be some other explanation entirely."

Jonas paused and walked to the window, looking not into the street but up at the clouds. "I don't know whether your man-apes are the same kind of hybrid. The one I saw looked quite human to me except for his pelt, so I would be inclined to agree with you that they are human beings who have undergone some change in their essential nature as a result of their life in the mines and their contact with the relics of the city buried there. Urth is very old now. It's very old, and no doubt there have been many treasures hidden in bygone times. Gold and silver do not alter, but their guardians can suffer metamorphoses stranger than those that turn grapes to wine and sand to pearls."

I said, "But we outside endure the dark each night, and the treasures carried up from the mines are brought to us. Why haven't we changed too?"

Jonas did not answer, and I remembered my promise to ask him nothing more. Still, when he turned to face me there was something in his eyes that told me I was being a fool, that we *had* changed. He turned away again and stared out and up once more.

"All right," I conceded, "you don't have to answer that. But what about the other question you pledged yourself to answer? How can human soldiers resist the monsters from the seas?"

"You were correct when you said Erebus and Abaia are as great as mountains, and I admit that I was surprised you knew it. Most people lack the imagination to conceive of anything so large, and think them no bigger than houses or ships. Their actual size is so great that while they remain on this world they can never leave the water—their own weight would crush them. You mustn't think of them battering at the Wall with their fists, or tossing boulders about. But by their thoughts they enlist servants, and they fling them against all rules that rival their own."

Jonas opened the inn's door then and slipped out into the bustle of the street; I remained where I was, resting an elbow on what had been our breakfast table, and recalled the dream I had experienced when I had shared Baldanders's bed. *The land could not hold us*, the monstrous women had said.

Now I am come to a part of my story where I cannot help but write of something I have largely avoided mentioning before. You that read it cannot but have noticed that I have not scrupled to recount in great detail things that transpired years ago, and to give the very words of those who spoke to me, and the very words with which I replied; and you must have thought this only a conventional device I had adopted to make my story flow more smoothly. The truth is that I am one of those who are cursed with what is called perfect recollection. We cannot, as I have sometimes heard foolishly alleged, remember everything. I cannot recall the ordering of the books on the shelves in the library of Master Ultan, for example. But I can remember more than many would credit: the position of each object on a table I walked past when I was a child, and even that I have recalled some scene to mind previously, and how that remembered incident differed from the memory of it I have now.

It was my power of recollection that made me the favorite pupil of Master Palaemon, and so I suppose it can be blamed for the existence of this narrative, for if he had not favored me, I would not have been sent to Thrax bearing his sword.

Some say this power is linked to weak judgement—of that I am no judge. But it has another danger, one I have encountered many times. When I cast my mind into the past, as I am doing now and as I did then when I sought to recall my dream, I remember it so well that I seem to move again in the bygone day, a day old-new, and unchanged each time I draw it to the surface of my mind, its eidolons as real as I.

I can even now close my eyes and walk into Thecla's cell as I did one winter evening; and soon my fingers will feel the heat of her garment while the perfume of her person fills my nostrils like the perfume of lilies warmed before a fire. I lift her gown from her and embrace that ivory body, feeling her nipples pressed to my face. . . .

You see? It is very easy to waste hours and days in such rememberings, and sometimes I fall so deeply into them that I am drugged and drunken. So it was now. The footfalls I had heard in the man-apes' cavern still echoed in my mind, and seeking some explanation I returned to my dream, certain now that I knew from whom it had come, and hoping it had revealed more than its shaper apprehended.

Again I bestride the mitred, leather-winged steed. Pelicans fly below us with stiffly formal strokes, and gulls wheel and keen.

Again I fall, tumbling through the abyss of air, whistling toward the sea, yet suspended, for a time, between wave and cloud. I arch my body, bring down my head, let my legs trail behind me like a banner, and so cleave the water and see floating in clear azure the head with hair of snakes and the many-headed beast, and then the swirling sand-garden far below. The giantesses lift arms like the trunks of sycamores, each finger tipped with an amaranthine talon. Then very suddenly, I who had been blind before understood why it was that Abaia had sent me this dream, and had sought to enlist me in the great and final war of Urth.

But now the tyranny of memory overwhelmed my will. Though I could see the titan odalisques and their garden and knew them to be no more than dream-stuff recalled, I could not escape from their fascination and the memory of the dream. Hands grasped me like a doll, and as I dandled thus between the meretrices of Abaia, I was lifted from my broad-armed chair in the inn of Saltus; yet still, for perhaps a hundred heartbeats more, I could not rid my mind of the sea and its green-haired women.

"He sleeps."

"His eyes are open."

A third voice: "Shall we bring the sword?"

"Bring it—there may be work for it."

The titanesses faded. Men in deerskin and rough wool held me on either side, and one with a scarred face held the point of his dirk at my throat. The man on my right had picked up *Terminus Est* with his free hand; he was the black-bearded volunteer who had helped break open the sealed house.

"Someone's coming."

The man with the scarred face glided away. I heard the door rattle, and Jonas's exclamation as he was drawn inside.

"This is your master, isn't it? Well, don't move, my friend, or cry out. We'll kill you both."

IX

The Liege of Leaves

They forced us to stand with our faces to the wall while they bound our hands. Our cloaks were draped over our shoulders afterward to hide the thongs, so that we appeared to walk with our hands clasped behind us, and we were led out into the innyard, where a huge baluchither shifted from foot to foot under a plain howdah of iron and horn. The man who held my left arm reached up and struck the beast at the hollow of the knee with the shaft of a goad to make him kneel, and we were driven onto his back.

When Jonas and I had come to Saltus, our path had threaded hills of debris from the mines, hills composed largely of broken stone and brick. When I had ridden on the false errand of Agia's letter, I had galloped past more of these, though my route had lain chiefly through the forest at its nearest approach to the village. Now we went among the heaps of tailings where there was no path. Here, in addition to much rubble, the miners had cast all they had brought forth from the buried past that might otherwise have defamed their village and occupation. Everything foul lay in tumbled heaps ten times and more the height of the baluchither's lofty back—obscene statues, canted and crumbling, and human bones to which strips of dry flesh and hanks of hair still clung. And with them ten thousand men and women; those who, in seeking a private resurrection, had rendered their corpses forever imperishable lay here like drunkards after their debauch, their crystal sarcophagi broken, their limbs relaxed in grotesque disarray, their clothing rotted or rotting, and their eyes blindly fixed upon the sky.

At first Jonas and I had attempted to question our captors, but they had silenced us with blows. Now that the baluchither wound his way among this desolation, they seemed easier of mind, and I asked again where they were taking us. The man with the scarred face replied, "To the wild, the home of free men and lovely women."

I thought of Agia and asked if he served her; he laughed and shook his head. "My master is Vodalus of the Wood."

"Vodalus!"

"Ah," he said. "You know him then." And he nudged the black-bearded man, who rode in the howdah with us. "Very kindly Vodalus will treat you, no doubt, for offering so blithely to rack one of his servants."

"I know him indeed," I said, and was about to tell the scarred man of my connection with Vodalus, whose life I had preserved in the last year before I became captain of apprentices. But then I came to doubt if Vodalus would remember it, and only said that if I had known Barnoch to be a servant of Vodalus, I would on no account have agreed to perform his excruciation. I lied, of course; for I had known, and had justified accepting my fee by the thought that I would be able to spare Barnoch some suffering. The lie did me no good; all three chortled, even the trainer who bestrode the baluchither's neck.

When their merriment had subsided, I said, "Last night I rode out of Saltus to the northeast. Are we going that way now?"

"So that's where you were. Our master came seeking you, and came back empty-handed." The scarred man smiled, and I could see that it was not an unpleasant thought that he returned now successful where Vodalus himself had failed.

Jonas whispered, "We go north, as you can see by the sun."

"Yes," said the scarred man, who must have been sharp-eared. "North, but not for long." And then, to pass the time, he described to me the means by which his master dealt with captives, most of which were primitive in the extreme, and more productive of theatrical effects than of true agony.

As if some invisible hand had spread a curtain over us, the shadows of the trees fell upon the howdah. The glitter of billions of shards of glass was left behind with the staring of the dead eyes, and we entered into the coolness and green shade of the high forest. Among those mighty trunks even the baluchither, though he stood three times the height of a man, seemed no more than a little, scurrying beast; and we who rode his back might have been pygmies from some children's tale, bound for the anthill stronghold of a pixie monarch.

And it came to me that these trees had been hardly smaller when I was yet unborn, and had stood as they stood now when I was a child playing among the cypresses and peaceful tombs of our necropolis, and that they would stand yet, drinking in the last light of the dying sun, even as now, when I had been dead as long as those who rested there. I saw how little it weighed on the scale of things whether I lived or died, though my life was precious to me. And of those two thoughts I forged a mood by which I stood ready to grasp each smallest chance to live, yet in which I cared not too much whether I saved myself or not. By that mood, as I think, I did live; it has been so good a friend to me that I have endeavored to wear it ever since, succeeding not always, but often.

"Severian, are you all right?"

It was Jonas who spoke. I looked at him, I think, in some wonder. "Yes. Did I seem ill?"

"For a moment."

"I was only reflecting on the familiarity of this place, seeking to understand it. I think it recalls to me many summer days in our Citadel. These trees are nearly as large as the towers there, and many of the towers are wrapped in ivy, so that in quiet summer weather the light between them has this emerald quality. Too, it is quiet here, as there. . . ."

"Yes?"

"You must have ridden many times in boats, Jonas."

"Occasionally, yes."

"It is something I had long wanted to do, and did for the first time only when Agia and I were ferried to the island where the Botanic Gardens stands, and then later when we crossed the Lake of Birds. The motion is much like the motion of this beast, and it is as silent, save for a splashing, sometimes, when the oar goes into the water. I feel now that I'm traveling through the Citadel in a flood, solemnly rowed."

At that Jonas looked so grave that I burst out laughing at the sight of his face, and stood up, meaning (I think) to look over the side of the howdah and show by some remark about the forest floor that I was merely indulging my fancy.

I had no sooner stood, however, than the scarred man rose too, and holding his dirk's point within a thumb of my throat told me to sit again. To spite him I shook my head.

He flourished his weapon. "Get down or I'll rip your belly open!"

"And lose the glory of bringing me back? I don't think so. Wait until the others tell Vodalus that you had me, and you stabbed me when my hands were tied."

Now came the turn of fate. The bearded man who held *Terminus Est* tried to draw her, and not being acquainted with the proper way to bare so long a sword—which is to grip the quillons in one hand and the throat of the sheath with the other, and by opening the arms to the right and left draw the blade clear—sought to free it by pulling up, as if he were jerking a weed from a field. In this clumsy business he was taken off guard by one of the baluchither's rolling steps, and lurched against the man with the scarred face. The edges of the blade, keen enough to part a hair, cut them both; the man with the scarred face threw himself backward, and Jonas, by hooking one of his feet behind the scarred man's and pressing his leg with the sole of the other, managed to tumble him over the railing of the howdah.

Meantime, the black-bearded man had dropped *Terminus Est* and was staring at his wound, which was very long, though no doubt shallow. I knew that weapon as I know my own hand, and it took only a moment to turn and crouch and grasp the hilt, and then, wedging it between my heels, to cut the thongs that bound my wrists. The black-bearded man drew a dagger then and might have killed me had not Jonas kicked him between the legs.

He bent double, and long before he could straighten himself I was up, with *Terminus Est* ready.

The contraction of his muscles snapped him erect, as often happens when the subject is not made to kneel; I think the spray of blood was the first sign the trainer had (so swiftly had it all taken place) that something was amiss. He looked back at us, and I was able to take him very neatly, swinging the blade one-handed in the horizontal stroke, as I leaned out of the howdah.

His head had no more than struck the ground when the baluchither stepped between two great trees growing so close together that he seemed to squeeze himself like a mouse through a crevice in a wall. Beyond lay a glade more open than anything I had seen in that forest—where grass grew as well as fern, and spots of sunlight, unshaded with green and rich as orpiment, played over the turf. Here Vodalus had caused to be erected his throne, beneath a canopy woven of flowering vines; and here, as it chanced, he sat with the Chatelaine Thea beside him just as we entered, judging and rewarding his followers.

Jonas saw nothing of that, being still sprawled on the floor of the howdah, where he was cutting his hands free with the dagger. I made up for him, for I beheld everything as I stood upright, balanced against the pitching of the baluchither's back and holding up my sword, red now to the hilt. A hundred faces turned toward us, with the face of the exultant on the throne among them, and the heart-shaped face of his consort; and in their eyes I saw what they must have seen at that moment: the great animal bestridden by a headless man, its forequarters dyed with his blood; myself standing erect upon its back, with my sword and fuligin cloak.

Had I slipped down and sought to flee, or tried to goad the baluchither to greater speed, I would have died. Instead, by the virtue of the spirit that had entered me when I saw the long-dead bodies among the refuse of the mines and the eternal trees, I remained as I was; and the baluchither, with no one to guide him, trod forward steadily (Vodalus's followers dodging aside to make a path for him) until the dais supporting the throne and canopy were before him. Then he halted, and the dead man pitched forward and fell on the dais at Vodalus's feet; and I, leaning far out of the howdah, struck the beast behind one leg and the other with the flat of my blade, and he knelt.

Vodalus smiled a thin smile that held many things, but amusement was one of them, and perhaps the foremost. "I sent my men to fetch the headsman," he said. "I perceive they succeeded."

I saluted with my sword, holding the hilt before my eyes as we were taught to do when an exultant came to observe an execution in the Grand Court. "Sieur, they have brought you the anti-heads-man—there was a time when your own would have rolled on fresh-turned soil if it had not been for me."

He looked at me more closely then, at my face instead of at my sword and cloak, and after a moment he said, "Yes, you were the youth. Has it been that long?"

"Just long enough, sieur."

"We will talk of this in private, but I have public business to do now. Stand here." He pointed to the ground at the left of the dais.

I climbed from the baluchither with Jonas following me, and two grooms led the beast away. There we waited and heard Vodalus give his orders and transmit his plans, reward and punish, for perhaps a watch. All the boasted human panoply of pillars and arches is no more than an imitation in sterile stone of the boles and vaulting branches of the forest, and here it seemed to me that there was scarcely any difference between the two except that the one was gray or white, and the other brown and pale green. Then I believed I understood why all the soldiers of the Autarch and all the thronging retainers of the exultants could not subdue Vodalus—he occupied the mightiest fortress of Urth, greater far than our Citadel, to which I had likened it.

At length he dismissed the crowd, each man and woman to his or her own place, and came down from the dais to talk to me, bending over me as I might have bent above a child.

"You served me once," he said. "For that I will spare your life whatever else befalls, though it may be necessary that you remain my guest for a time. Knowing that your life is no longer in danger, will you serve me again?''

The oath to the Autarch I had taken on the occasion of my elevation had not the strength to resist the memory of that misty evening with which I have begun this account of my life. Oaths are only mere weak things of honor compared to the benefits we give to others, which are things of the spirit; let us once save another, and we are his for life. I have often heard it said that gratitude is not to be found. That is not true—those who say so have always looked in the mistaken place. One who truly benefits another is for a moment at a level with the Pancreator, and in gratitude for that elevation will serve the other all his days; and so I told Vodalus.

''Good!'' he said, and clapped me on the shoulder. ''Come. Not far from here we have a meal prepared. If you and your friend will sit with me and eat, I will tell you what must be done.''

''Sieur, I have disgraced my guild once. I only ask that I may not be made to disgrace it again.''

''Nothing you do will be known,'' Vodalus said. And that satisfied me.

X

Thea

With a dozen or so others we left the glade on foot, and half a league away found a table set among the trees. I was placed at Vodalus's left hand, and while the others ate, I feigned to and feasted my eyes on him and his lady, whom I had so often recalled as I lay on my cot among the apprentices in our tower.

When I had saved him, mentally at least I had still been a boy, and to a boy all grown men appear lofty unless they are of very low stature indeed. I saw now that Vodalus was as tall as Thecla or taller, and that Thecla's half-sister Thea was as tall as she. Then I knew them to be truly of the exalted blood, and not armigers merely, such as Sieur Racho had been.

It was with Thea that I had first fallen in love, worshipping her because she belonged to the man I had saved. Thecla I had loved, in the beginning, because she recalled Thea. Now (as autumn dies, and winter and spring, and summer comes again, the end of the year as it is its beginning) I loved Thea once more—because she recalled Thecla.

Vodalus said, "You are an admirer of women," and I lowered my eyes.

"I have been little in polite company, sieur. Please forgive me."

"I share your admiration, so there is nothing to forgive. But you were not, I hope, studying that slender throat with the thought of parting it?"

"Never, sieur."

"I am delighted to hear it." He picked up a platter of thrushes, selected one, and put it upon my plate. It was a sign of special favor. "Still, I own I am a trifle surprised. I would have thought that a man in your profession would look on us poor human beings much as a butcher does on cattle."

"Of that I cannot inform you, sieur. I have not been bred a butcher."

Vodalus laughed. "A touch! I am almost sorry now that you have consented to serve me. If you had only elected to remain my prisoner, we would have had many delightful conversations while I used you—as I had intended to—to cheap for the unfortunate Barnoch's life. As it is, you will be away by morning. Yet I think I have an errand for you that will consort well with your own inclinations."

"If it is your errand, sieur, it must."

"You are wasted on the scaffold." He smiled. "We will find better work for you before long. But if you are to serve me well, you must understand something of the position of the pieces on the board, and the goal of the game we play. Call the sides white and black, and in honor of your garments—so that you shall know where your interests lie—we shall be black. No doubt you have been told that we blacks are mere bandits and traitors, but have you any notion of what it is we strive to do?"

"To checkmate the Autarch, sieur?"

"That would be well enough, but it is only a step and not our final goal. You have come from the Citadel—I know, you see, something of your journeyings and history—that great fortress of bygone days, so you must possess some feeling for the past. Has it never struck you that mankind was richer by far, and happier too, a chiliad gone than it is now?"

"Everyone knows," I said, "that we have fallen far from the brave days of the past."

"As it was then, so shall it be again. Men of Urth, sailing between the stars, leaping from galaxy to galaxy, the masters of the daughters of the sun."

The Chatelaine Thea, who must have been listening to Vodalus though she had showed no sign of it, looked across him to me and said in a sweet, cooing voice, "Do you know how our world was renamed, torturer? The dawn-men went to red Verthandi, who was then named War. And because they thought that had an ungracious sound that would keep others from following them, they renamed it, calling it Present. That was a jest in their tongue, for the same word meant *Now* and *The Gift*. Or so one of our tutors once explained the matter to my sister and me, though I do not see how any language could endure such confusion."

Vodalus listened to her as though he were impatient to speak himself, yet was too well mannered to interrupt her.

"Then others—who would have drawn a people to the innermost habitable world for their own reasons—took up the game as well, and called that world Skuld, the World of the Future. Thus our own became Urth, the World of the Past."

"You are wrong in that, I fear," Vodalus told her. "I have it on good authority that this world of ours has been called by that name from the utmost reaches of antiquity. Still, your error is so charming that I would rather have it that you are correct and I mistaken."

Thea smiled at that, and Vodalus turned again toward me. "Though it does not explain why Urth is called as she is, my dear Chatelaine's tale makes the vital point well, which is that in those times mankind traveled by his own ships from world to world, and mastered each, and built on them the cities of Man. Those were the great days of our race, when our fathers' fathers' fathers strove for the mastery of the universe."

He paused, and because he seemed to expect some comment from me, I said, "Sieur, we are much diminished in wisdom from that age."

"Ah, now you strike to the heart. Yet with all your perspicacity, you mistake it. No, we are not diminished in wisdom. We are diminished in power. Study has advanced without letup, but even as men have learned all that is needful for mastery, the strength of the world has been exhausted. We exist now, and precariously, upon the ruin of those who preceded us. While some skim the air in their fliers, ten thousand leagues in a day, we others creep upon the skin of Urth, unable to go from one horizon to the next before the westernmost has lifted itself to veil the sun. You spoke a moment ago of checkmating that mewling fool the Autarch. I want you to conceive now of two autarchs—two great powers striving for mastery. The white seeks to maintain things as they are, the black to set Man's foot on the road to domination again. I called it the black by chance, but it would be well to remember that it is by night that we see the stars strongly; they are remote and all but invisible in the red light of day. Now, of those two powers, which would you serve?"

The wind was stirring in the trees, and it seemed to me that everyone at the table had fallen silent, listening to Vodalus and waiting for my reply. I said, "The black, surely."

"Good! But as a man of sense you must understand that the way to reconquest cannot be easy. Those who wish no change may sit hugging their scruples forever. *We* must do everything. *We* must dare everything!"

The others had begun to talk and eat again. I lowered my voice until only Vodalus could hear me. "Sieur, there is something I have not told you. I dare not conceal it longer for fear you should think me faithless."

He was a better intriguer than I, and turned away before he answered, pretending to eat. ''What is it? Out with it.''

''Sieur,'' I said, ''I have a relic, the thing they say is the Claw of the Conciliator.''

He was biting the roasted thigh of a fowl as I spoke. I saw him pause; his eyes turned to look at me, though he did not move his head.

''Do you wish to see it, sieur? It is very beautiful, and I have it in the top of my boot.''

''No,'' he whispered. ''Yes, perhaps, but not here. . . . No, better not at all.''

''To whom should I give it, then?''

Vodalus chewed and swallowed. ''I had heard from friends I have in Nessus that it was gone. So you have it. You must keep it until you can dispose of it. Do not try to sell it—it would be identified at once. Hide it somewhere. If you must, throw it into a pit.''

''But surely, sieur, it is very valuable.''

''It is beyond value, which means it is worthless. You and I are men of sense.'' Despite his words, there was a tinge of fear in his voice. ''But the rabble believe it to be sacred, a performer of all manner of wonders. If I were to possess it, they would think me a desecrator and an enemy of the Theologoumenon. Our masters would think me turned traitor. You must tell me—''

Just at that moment, a man I had not seen previously came running up to the table with a look that indicated he bore urgent news. Vodalus rose and walked a few paces away with him, looking very much, I thought, like a handsome schoolmaster with a boy, for the messenger's head was no higher than his shoulder.

I ate, thinking he would soon return; but after a long questioning of the messenger he walked away with him, disappearing among the broad trunks of the trees. One by one the others rose too, until no one remained but the beautiful Thea, Jonas and me, and one other man.

''You are to join us,'' Thea said at last in her cooing voice. ''Yet you do not know our ways. Have you need of money?''

I hesitated, but Jonas said, ''That's something that's always welcome, Chatelaine, like the misfortunes of an older brother.''

''Shares will be set aside for you, from this day, of all we take. When you return to us, they will be given to you. Meanwhile I have a purse for each of you to speed you on your way.''

''We are going, then?'' I asked.

''Were you not told so? Vodalus will instruct you at the supper.''

I had supposed the meal we were eating would be the final one of the day, and the thought must have been reflected in my face.

"There will be a supper tonight, when the moon is bright," Thea said. "Someone will be sent to fetch you." Then she quoted a scrap of verse:

> "Dine at dawn to open your eyes,
> Dine at noon that you be strong.
> Dine at eve, and then talk long,
> Dine by night, if you'd be wise. . . .

But now my servant Chuniald will take you to a place where you can rest for your journey."

The man, who had been silent until now, stood and said, "Come with me."

I told Thea, "I would speak with you, Chatelaine, when we have more leisure. I know something that concerns your schoolmate."

She saw that I was serious in what I said, and I saw that she had seen. Then we followed Chuniald through the trees for a distance, I suppose, of a league or more, and at length reached a grassy bank beside a stream. "Wait here," he said. "Sleep if you can. No one will come until after dark."

I asked, "What if we were to leave?"

"There are those all through this wood who know our liege's will concerning you," he said, and turning on his heel, walked away.

Then I told Jonas what I had seen beside the opened grave, just as I have written it here.

"I see," he remarked when I was finished, "why you will join this Vodalus. But you must realize that I am your friend, not his. What I desire is to find the woman you call Jolenta. You want to serve Vodalus, and to go to Thrax and begin a new life in exile, and to wipe out the stain you say you have made on the honor of your guild—though I confess I don't understand how such a thing can be stained—and to find the woman called Dorcas, and to make peace with the woman called Agia while returning something we both know of to the women called Pelerines."

He was smiling by the time he finished this list, and I was laughing.

"And though you remind me of the old man's kestrel, that sat on a perch for twenty years and then flew off in all directions, I hope you achieve these things. But I trust you realize that it is possible—just barely possible, perhaps, but possible—that one or two of them may get in the way of four or five of the others."

"What you're saying is very true," I admitted. "I'm striving to do all those things, and although you won't credit it, I am giving all my strength and as much of my attention as can be of any benefit to all of them. Yet I have to admit things aren't going as well as they might. My divided ambitions have landed me in no better place than the shade of this tree, where I am a homeless wanderer. While you, with your single-minded pursuit of one all-powerful objective . . . look where you are.''

In such talk we passed the watches of late afternoon. Birds twittered overhead, and it was very pleasant to have such a friend as Jonas, loyal, reasonable, tactful, and filled with wisdom, humor, and prudence. At that time I had no hint of his history, but I sensed that he was being less than candid about his background, and I sought, without venturing direct questions, to draw him out. I learned (or rather, I thought I did) that his father had been a craftsman; that he had been raised by both parents in what he called the usual way, though it is, in fact, rather rare; and that his home had been a seacoast town in the south, but that when he had last visited it he had found it so much changed that he had no desire to remain.

From his appearance, when I had first encountered him beside the Wall, I had supposed him to be about ten years my elder. From what he said now (and to a lesser extent from some earlier talks we had had) I decided he must be somewhat older; he seemed to have read a good deal of the chronicles of the past, and I was still too naive and unlettered myself, despite the attention Master Palaemon and Thecla had given my mind, to think that anyone much below middle age could have done so. He had a slightly cynical detachment from mankind that suggested he had seen a great deal of the world.

We were still talking when I glimpsed the graceful figure of the Chatelaine Thea moving among the trees some distance away. I nudged Jonas, and we fell silent to watch her. She was coming toward us without having seen us, so that she moved in the blind way people do who are merely following directions. At times a shaft of sunlight fell upon her face, which, if it chanced to be in profile, suggested Thecla's so strongly that the sight of it seemed to tear at my chest. She had Thecla's walk as well, the proud phororhacos stalk that should never have been caged.

''It must be a truly ancient family,'' I whispered to Jonas. ''Look at her! Like a dryad. It might be a willow walking.''

''Those ancient families are the newest of all,'' he answered. ''In ancient times there was nothing like them.''

I do not believe she was near enough to make out our words, but she seemed to hear his voice, and looked toward us. We waved and she quickened her pace, not running yet coming very rapidly because of the length of her stride. We stood, then sat again when she had reached us and seated herself upon her scarf with her face toward the brook.

"You said you had something to tell me about my sister?" Her voice made her seem less formidable, and seated she was hardly taller than we.

"I was her last friend," I said. "She told me they would try to make you persuade Vodalus to give himself up to save her. Did you know she was imprisoned?"

"Were you her servant?" Thea seemed to weigh me with her eyes. "Yes, I heard they took her to that horrible place in the slums of Nessus, where I understand she died very quickly."

I thought of the time I had spent waiting outside Thecla's door before the scarlet thread of blood came trickling from under it, but I nodded.

"How was she arrested—do you know?"

Thecla had told me the details, and I recounted them just as I had got them from her, omitting nothing.

"I see," Thea said, and was silent for a moment, staring at the moving water. "I have missed the court, of course. Hearing about those people and that business of muffling her with a tapestry—that's so very characteristic—calls up the reasons I left it."

"I think she missed it sometimes too," I said. "At least, she talked of it a great deal. But she told me that if she were ever freed she would not go back. She spoke about the country house from which she took her title, and told me how she would refurnish it and give dinners there for the leading persons of the region, and hunt."

Thea's face twisted in a bitter smile. "I have had enough of hunting now for ten lifetimes. But when Vodalus is Autarch, I will be his consort. Then I shall walk beside the Well of Orchids again, this time with the daughters of fifty exultants in my train to amuse me with their singing. Enough of that; it is some months off at least. For the present I have—what I have."

She looked somberly at Jonas and me, and rose very gracefully, indicating by a gesture that we were to remain where we were. "I was happy to hear something now of my half-sister. That house you spoke of is mine now, you know, though I can't claim it. To recompense you, I warn you of the supper we will soon share. You didn't seem receptive of the hints Vodalus flung you. Did you understand them?"

When Jonas said nothing, I shook my head.

"If we, and our allies and masters who wait in the countries beneath the tides, are to triumph, we must absorb all that can be learned of the past. Do you know of the analeptic alzabo?"

I said, "No, Chatelaine, but I have heard tales of the animal of that name. It is said it can speak, and that it comes by night to a house where a child has died, and cries to be let in."

Thea nodded. "That animal was brought from the stars long ago, as were many other things for the benefit of Urth. It is a beast having no more intelligence than a dog, and perhaps less. But it is a devourer of carrion and a clawer at graves, and when it has fed upon human flesh it knows, at least for a time, the speech and ways of human beings. The analeptic alzabo is prepared from a gland at the base of the animal's skull. Do you understand me?"

When she had gone, Jonas would not look at me, nor I at his face; we both knew what feast it was we were to attend that night.

XI

Thecla

After we had sat, so it seemed to me, for a long time (though it was probably no more than a few moments), I could tolerate what I felt no longer. I went to the margin of the brook, and kneeling there on the soft earth spewed out the dinner I had eaten with Vodalus; and when there was nothing more to come forth, I remained where I was, retching and shivering, and rinsing my face and mouth, while the cold, clear water washed away the wine and half-digested meat I had brought up.

When at last I was able to stand, I returned to Jonas and told him, "We must go."

He looked at me as though he pitied me, and I suppose he did. "Vodalus's fighting men are all around us."

"You were not sick, I see, the way I was. But you heard who their allies are. Perhaps Chuniald was lying."

"I've heard our guards walking among the trees—they're not as silent as all that. You have your sword, Severian, and I have a knife, but Vodalus's men will have bows. I noticed that most of those who sat with us at table did. We can try to hide behind the trunks like alouattes. . . ,"

I understood what he meant, and said, "Alouattes are shot every day."

"Still, no one hunts them by night. It would be dark in a watch or less."

"You will go with me if we wait until then?" I thrust out my hand.

Jonas clasped it. "Severian, my poor friend, you told me of seeing Vodalus—and this Chatelaine Thea and another man—beside a violated grave. Didn't you know what it was they planned to do with what they got there?"

I had known, of course, but it had been a remote and seemingly irrelevant knowledge then. Now I found I had nothing to say, and indeed almost no thoughts at all outside the hope that night would come quickly.

The men Vodalus sent for us came more quickly still: four burly fellows who might have been peasants and carried berdiches, and a fifth, with something of the armiger about him, who wore an officer's spadroon. Perhaps these men were in the crowd before the dais who had watched us arrive; at any rate, they seemed determined to take no risks with us and surrounded us with their weapons at the ready even while they hailed us as friends and comrades in arms. Jonas put as brave a face on it as a man could, and chatted with them while they escorted us down the forest paths; I could think of nothing but the ordeal ahead, and walked as I might have to the end of the world.

Urth turned her face from the sun's as we traveled. No glimmer of starlight seemed to penetrate the thronging leaves, yet our guides knew the way so well they hardly slowed. With each step I took, I wanted to ask if we would be forced to join in the meal to which we were led, but I knew without asking that to refuse—or even to seem to wish to refuse—would destroy whatever confidence Vodalus had in me, endangering my freedom and perhaps my life.

Our five guards, who had talked only reluctantly at first in response to Jonas's jests and queries, grew more cheerful as I became more desperate, gossiping as if they were on the way to a drinking bout or a brothel. Yet though I recognized the note of anticipation in their voices, the gibes they made were as unintelligible to me as the banter of libertines is to a little child: "Going far this time? Going to drown yourself again?" (This from the man at the back of our party, a mere disembodied voice in the dark.)

"By Erebus, I'm going to sink so far you won't see me until winter."

A voice I recognized as belonging to the armiger asked, "Have any of you seen her yet?" The others had sounded merely boastful, but there was hunger of a kind I had never heard before behind his simple words. He might have been some lost traveler asking about his home.

"No, Waldgrave."

(Another voice.) "Alcmund says a good one, not old or too young."

"Not another tribade, I hope."

"I don't . . ."

The voice broke off, or perhaps I only stopped attending to what it said. I had seen a glimmer through the trees.

After a few strides more, I could make out torches, and hear the sound of many voices. Someone ahead called for us to halt, and the armiger went forward and gave a password softly.

Soon I found myself sitting on forest duff, with Jonas on my right and a low chair of carved wood at my left. The armiger had taken a position on Jonas's right, and the rest of the people present (almost as though they had been waiting for our arrival) had formed a circle whose center was a smokey orange lantern suspended from the boughs of a tree.

No more than a third of those who had been at the audience in the glade were there, but from their dress and weapons it seemed to me that they were largely those of highest rank, together, perhaps, with members of certain favored fighting cadres. There were four or five men to every woman; but the women seemed as warlike as the men, and if anything more eager for the feast to begin.

We had been waiting for some time when Vodalus stepped dramatically out of the darkness and strode across the circle. All present stood, then resumed their seats as he dropped into the carved chair beside me.

Almost at once, a man in the livery of an upper servant in some great house came forward to stand in the center of the circle beneath the orange light. He carried a salver with a large and a small bottle on it, and a crystal goblet. A murmuring began—not a thing for words, I thought, but the sound of a hundred little noises of satisfaction, of quick breathings and tongues on lips. The man with the salver stood motionless until this had run its course, then advanced toward Vodalus with measured steps.

Behind me the cooing voice of Thea said, "The alzabo, of which I told you, is in the smaller bottle. The other holds a compound of herbs that soothe the stomach. Take one full swallow of the mixture."

Vodalus turned to look at her with an expression of surprise.

She entered the circle, passing between Jonas and me, and then between Vodalus and the man who bore the salver, and at last took a place at Vodalus's left. Vodalus leaned toward her and would have spoken, but the man with the salver had begun to mix the contents of the bottles in the goblet, and he seemed to think the moment inappropriate.

The salver was moved in circles to impart a gentle swirling motion to the liquid. "Very good," Vodalus said. He took the goblet from the salver with both hands and raised it to his lips, then passed it to me. "As the Chatelaine told you, you must take one full swallow. If you take less, the amount will be insufficient, and there will be no sharing. If you take more, it will be of no benefit to you, and the drug, which is very precious, will be wasted."

I drank from the goblet as he had directed. The mixture was as bitter as wormwood and seemed cold and fetid, recalling a winter day long before when I had been ordered to clean the exterior drain that carried wastes away from the journeymen's quarters. For a moment I felt that my gorge would rise as it had beside the brook, though in truth nothing remained in my stomach to come up. I choked and swallowed and passed the goblet to Jonas, then discovered that I was salivating rapidly.

He had as much difficulty as I, or more, but he managed it at last and passed the goblet to the Waldgrave who had captained our guards. After that I watched it make its slow way around the circle. It appeared to hold enough for ten drinkers; when it was emptied, the man in livery wiped the rim, filled the goblet again from the bottles on the salver, and started it once more.

Gradually, he seemed to lose the solid form natural to a rounded object and become a silhouette only, a mere colored figure sawn from wood. I was reminded of the marionettes I had seen in my dream on the night I had shared Baldanders's bed.

The circle, too, in which we sat, though I knew it to contain thirty or forty persons, seemed to have been cut from paper and bent like a toy crown. Vodalus on my left and Jonas at my right were normal; but the armiger appeared already half pictured, as did Thea.

As the man in livery reached her, Vodalus rose, and moving so effortlessly that he might have been propelled by the night breeze, floated toward the orange lantern. In the orange light he seemed far away, yet I could feel his gaze as one feels the heat from the brazier that readies the irons.

"There is an oath to be sworn before the sharing," he said, and the trees above us nodded solemnly. "By the second life you are to receive, do you swear you will never betray those gathered here? And that you will consent to obey, without hesitation or scruple, to death if need be, Vodalus as your chosen leader?"

I tried to nod with the trees, and when that seemed insufficient I said, "I consent," and Jonas, "Yes."

"And that you will obey as you would Vodalus, any person whatsoever whom Vodalus sets over you?"

"Yes."

"Yes."

"And that you will put this oath above all other oaths, whether sworn before this time or after it?"

"We will," said Jonas.

"Yes," I said.

The breeze was gone. It was as if some unquiet spirit had haunted the gathering, then suddenly vanished. Vodalus was once more in his chair beside me. He leaned toward me. If his voice was slurred, I did not observe it; but something in his eyes told me he was under the influence of the alzabo, perhaps as deeply as I was myself.

"I am no scholar," he began, "but I know it has been said that the greatest causes are often joined by the basest means. Nations are united by trade, the fair ivory and rare woods of altars and reliquaries by the boiled offal of ignoble animals, men and women by the organs of elimination. So we are joined—you and I. So will we both be joined, a few moments hence, to a fellow mortal who will live again—strongly, for a time—in us, by the effluvia pressed from the sweetbreads of one of the filthiest beasts. So blossoms spring from muck."

I nodded.

"This was taught us by our allies, those who wait until man is purified again, ready to join with them in the conquest of the universe. It was brought by the others for foul purposes they hoped to keep secret. I mention this to you because you, when you go to the House Absolute, may meet them, whom the common people call cacogens and the cultured Extrasolarians or Hierodules. You must be careful in no way to bring yourself to their notice, because if they observe you closely they will know by certain signs that you have used alzabo."

"The House Absolute?" Though only for an instant, the thought dispersed the mists of the drug.

"Indeed. I've a fellow there to whom I must transmit certain instructions, and I have learned that the troupe of players to which you once belonged will be admitted there for a thiasus a few days hence. You will rejoin them and take the opportunity to give what I shall give you," he fumbled in his tunic, "to the one who shall say to you, 'The pelagic argosy sights land.' And should he give you any message in return, you may entrust it to whoever says to you, 'I am from the quercine penetralia.' "

"Liege," I said, "my head is swimming." (Then, lying,) "I cannot remember those words—truly, I have forgotten them already. Did I hear you say that Dorcas and the other will be in the House Absolute?"

Vodalus now pressed into my hand a small object that was not a knife, yet was shaped something like one. I stared at it; it was a steel, such as flint is struck against to kindle fire. "You will remember," he said. "And you will never forget your oath to me. Many of those you see here came, as they believed, only once."

"But, sieur, the House Absolute . . ."

The fluting notes of a upanga sounded from the trees behind the farther side of the circle.

"I must go soon to escort the bride, but have no fear. Some time past you encountered a certain badger of mine—"

"Hildegrin! Sieur, I understand nothing."

"He uses that name among others, yes. He thought it sufficiently unusual to see a torturer so far from the Citadel—and talking of me—as to make it worthwhile to have you watched, though he had no notion you had saved me that night. Unfortunately, the watchers lost you at the Wall; since then they have observed the movements of your traveling companions in the hope you would rejoin them. I supposed that an exile might choose to side with us and so save my poor Barnoch long enough for us to free him. Last night I myself rode into Saltus to speak with you, but I had my mount stolen for my pains and accomplished not a straw. Today, then, it was necessary that we take you by whatever means to prevent you from exercising your skills on my servant; but I still hoped you would make cause with us, and for that reason instructed the men I sent for you to bring you living to me. That cost me three and gained two. The question now is whether the two will outweigh the three."

Vodalus stood then, a little unsteadily; I thanked Holy Katharine that I did not have to stand as well, for I was sure my legs would not hold me. Something dim and white and twice the height of a man was sailing among the trees to the twittering of the upanga. Every neck craned to look at it, and Vodalus drifted to meet it. Thea leaned across his empty chair to speak to me. "Lovely, is she not? They have accomplished wonders."

It was a woman seated on a silver litter borne on the shoulders of six men. For a moment I thought it was Thecla—it looked so like her in the orange light. Then I realized that it was rather her image, made, perhaps, of wax.

"It is said to be perilous," Thea cooed, "when one has known the shared in life; memories held together may amaze the mind. Yet I who loved her will risk that confusion, and knowing from your look when you spoke of her that you would desire it as well, I said nothing to Vodalus."

He had reached up to touch the figurine's arm as it was borne through the circle; with it entered a sweet and unmistakable odor. I recalled the agoutis served at our masking banquets, with their fur of spiced coconut and their eyes of preserved fruits, and knew that what I saw was just such a re-creation of a human being in roasted flesh.

I think I would have gone mad at that moment if it had not been for the alzabo. It stood between my perception and reality like a giant of mist, through which everything could be seen but nothing apprehended.

I had another ally as well: it was the knowledge growing in me, the certainty that if I were to consent now and swallow some part of Thecla's substance, the traces of her mind that must otherwise soon fade in decay would enter me and endure, however attenuated, as long as I.

Consent came. What I was about to do no longer seemed filthy or frightening. Instead I opened every part of myself to Thecla, and decked the essence of my being with welcome. Desire came too, born of the drug, a hunger on other food could satisfy, and when I looked around the circle I saw that hunger on every face.

The liveried servant, who I think must have been one of Vodalus's old household gone into exile with him, joined the six who had borne Thecla into the circle and helped lower the litter to the ground. For the space of a few breaths their backs blocked my view. When they parted, she was gone; nothing remained but smoking meats laid upon what might have been a white tablecloth. . . .

I ate and waited, begging forgiveness. She deserved the most magnificent sepulcher, priceless marble of exquisite harmony. In its place she was to be entombed in my torturer's workroom, with the floor scrubbed and the devices half disguised under garlands of flowers. The night air was cool, but I was sweating. I waited for her to come, feeling the drops roll down my bare chest and staring at the ground because I was afraid I would see her in the faces of the others before I felt her presence in myself.

Just when I despaired—she was there, filling me as a melody fills a cottage. I was with her, running beside the Acis when we were a child. I knew the ancient villa moated by a dark lake, the view through the dusty windows of the belvedere, and the secret space in the odd angle between two rooms where we sat at noon to read by candlelight. I knew the life of the Autarch's court, where poison waited in a diamond cup. I learned what it was for one who had never seen a cell or felt a whip to be a prisoner of the torturers, what dying meant, and death.

I learned that I had been more to her than I had ever guessed, and at last fell into a sleep in which my dreams were all of her. Not memories merely—memories I had possessed in plenty before. I held her poor, cold hands in mine, and I no longer wore the rags of an apprentice, nor the fuligin of a journeyman. We were one, naked and happy and clean, and we knew that she was no more and that I still lived, and we struggled against neither of those things, but with woven hair read from a single book and talked and sang of other matters.

XII

The Notules

I came from my dreams of Thecla directly to the morning. At one instant we walked mutely together in what surely must have been the paradise the New Sun is said to open to all who, in their final moments, call upon him; and though the wise teach that it is closed to those who are their own executioners, yet I cannot but think that he who forgives so much must sometimes forgive that as well. At the next, I was aware of cold and unwelcome light, and the piping of birds.

I sat up. My cloak was soaked with dew, and dew lay like sweat upon my face. Beside me, Jonas had just begun to stir. Ten paces off two great destriers—one the color of white wine, one of unspotted black—champed their bits and stamped with impatience. Of feast and feasters there was no more sign than of Thecla, whom I have never seen again and now no longer hope to see in this existence.

Terminus Est lay beside me in the grass, secure in her tough, well oiled sheath. I picked her up and made my way downhill until I found a stream, where I did what I might to refresh myself. When I returned, Jonas was awake. I directed him to the water, and while he was gone I made my farewell to dead Thecla.

Yet some part of her is with me still; at times I who remember am not Severian but Thecla, as though my mind were a picture framed behind glass, and Thecla stands before that glass and is reflected in it. Too, ever since that night, when I think of her without thinking also of a particular time and place, the Thecla who rises in my imagination stands before a mirror in a shimmering gown of frost-white that scarcely covers her breasts but falls in ever changing cascades below her waist. I see her poised for a moment there; both hands reach up to touch our face.

Then she is whirled away in a room whose walls and ceiling and floor are all of mirrors. No doubt it is her own memory of her image in those mirrors that I see, but after a step or two she vanishes into the dark and I see her no more.

By the time Jonas returned I had mastered my grief and was able to make a show of examining our mounts. "The black for you," he said, "and the cream for me, obviously. Both of them look like they outvalue either of us, though, as the sailor told the surgeon who took off his legs. Where are we going?"

"To the House Absolute." I saw the incredulity in his face. "Did you overhear me talking with Vodalus last night?"

"I caught the name, but not that we were to go there."

I am no rider, as I have said before, but I got one foot into the black's stirrup and swung myself up. The mount I had stolen from Vodalus two nights before had worn a lofty war saddle, fiendishly uncomfortable but very difficult to fall out of; this black carried a nearly flat affair of padded velvet that was both luxurious and treacherous. I had no sooner got my legs around him than he began to dance with eagerness.

It was the worst possible time, perhaps; but it was also the only time. I asked, "How much do you remember?"

"About the woman last night? Nothing." Jonas dodged the black, loosed the cream's reins, and vaulted up. "I didn't eat. Vodalus was watching you, but after they had swallowed the drug, no one was watching me, and anyway I have learned the art of appearing to eat without actually doing it."

I looked at him in astonishment.

"I've practiced several times with you—at breakfast yesterday, for example. I don't have much appetite, and I find it socially useful." As he urged the cream down a forest path, he called over his shoulder, "As it happens, I know the route fairly well, at least for most of the way. But would you mind telling me why we're going?"

"Dorcas and Jolenta will be there," I said. "And I have to do an errand for our liege, Vodalus." Because we were almost certainly watched, I thought it better not to say that I had no intention of performing it.

Here, lest this account of my career run forever, I must pass very quickly over the events of several days. As we rode, I told Jonas all that Vodalus had told me, and much more. We halted at villages and towns as we found them, and where we halted I practiced such of my craft as was in demand—not because the money I earned was strictly necessary to us (for we had the purses the Chatelaine Thea had given us, much of my fee from Saltus, and the money Jonas had obtained for the man-ape's gold) but in order to allay suspicion.

Our fourth morning found us still pressing northward. Gyoll sunned itself to our right like a sluggish dragon guarding the forbidden road that returned to grass upon its bank. The day before, we had seen uhlans on patrol, men mounted much as we were and bearing lances like those that had killed the travelers at the Piteous Gate.

Jonas, who had been ill at ease since we had set out, muttered, "We must hurry if we're to be near the House Absolute tonight. I wish Vodalus had given you the date that celebration begins and some indication of how long it's to last."

I asked, "Is the House Absolute still far off?"

He pointed out an isle in the river. "I think I recall that, and when I was two days from it, some pilgrims told me the House Absolute was nearby. They warned me of the praetorians, and seemed to know what they were talking about."

Following his example, I had allowed my mount to break into a trot. "You were walking."

"Riding my merychip—I suppose I'll never see the poor creature again. She was slower at her best than these animals at their worst, I'll grant you. But I'm not certain they're twice as fast."

I was about to say I did not believe Vodalus would have dispatched us when he did if he had not thought it possible for us to reach the House Absolute in time, when something that at first seemed a great bat came skimming within a handsbreadth of my head.

If I did not know what it was, Jonas did. He shouted words I could not understand and lashed my destrier with the ends of his reins. It bounded forward and nearly threw me, and in an instant we were galloping madly. I remember shooting between two trees with not a span to spare on either side and seeing the thing silhouetted against the sky like a fleck of soot. A moment later it was rattling among the branches behind us.

When we cleared the margin of the wood and entered the dry gully beyond, it was not to be seen; but as we reached the bottom and began to climb the farther side, it emerged from the trees, more ragged than ever.

For the space of a prayer it seemed to have lost sight of us, soaring at an angle to our own path, then swooping toward us again in a long, flat glide. I had *Terminus Est* clear of her sheath, and I neck-reined the black between the flying thing and Jonas.

Swift though our destriers were, it came far more swiftly. If I had possessed a pointed blade, I think I could have spitted it as it dove; had I done so I would surely have perished. As it was, I caught it with a two-handed stroke. It was like cutting air, and I thought the thing too light and tough for even that bitter edge. An instant later it parted like a rag; I felt a brief sensation of warmth, as though the door of an oven had been opened, then soundlessly shut.

I would have dismounted to examine it, but Jonas shouted and waved. We had left the lofty forest about Saltus far behind, and were entering a broken country of steep hills and ragged cedars. A grove of these stood at the top of the slope; we plunged into their tangled growth like madmen, flattened against the necks of our mounts.

Soon the foliage grew so thick they could move no faster than a walk. Almost at once we reached a sheer rock face and were forced to halt. When we were no longer smashing through the tangled limbs, I could hear something else behind us—a dry rustling, as though a wounded bird were fluttering among the treetops. The medicinal fragrance of the cedars oppressed my lungs.

"We must get out," Jonas panted, "or at least keep moving." The splintered end of a branch had gouged his cheek; a trickle of blood coursed down it as he spoke. After looking in both directions he chose the right, toward the river, and lashed his mount to force it into what appeared to be an impenetrable thicket.

I let him break a trail for me, reflecting that if the dark thing caught us I might be able to make some sort of defense against it. Soon I saw it through the gray-green foliage; a few moments later there was another, much like the first and only a short distance behind it.

The wood ended, and we were able to flog our mounts to a gallop again. The fluttering scraps of night came after us, but though their smaller size made them appear swifter, they were slower than the single large entity had been.

"We have to find a fire," Jonas shouted above the drumming of the destriers' hooves. "Or a big animal we can kill. If you slashed the belly of one of these beasts, that would probably do it. But if it didn't, we couldn't get away."

I nodded to show that I also opposed killing one of the destriers, though it crossed my mind that my own might soon drop from exhaustion. Jonas was having to allow his to slow now to keep from distancing me. I asked, "Is it blood they want?"

"No. Heat."

Jonas swung his destrier to the right and slapped its flank with his steel hand. It must have been a good blow, for the animal leaped ahead as though stung. We jumped a dry water course, careened sliding and stumbling down a dusty hillside, then struck open, rolling ground where the destriers could show their best speed.

Behind us fluttered the rags of black. They flew at twice the height of a tall tree and seemed to be blown along by the wind, though the rippling of the grass showed that they faced it.

Ahead, the lay of the ground changed as subtly and yet as abruptly as cloth alters at a seam. A sinuous ribbon of green lay as flat as if it had been rolled, and I swung the black down it, shouting in his ears and belaboring him with the flat of my blade. He was drenched with sweat now and streaked with blood from the broken twigs of the cedars. Behind us I could hear Jonas's shouted warnings, but I gave them no heed.

We rounded a curve, and through a break in the trees I saw the gleam of the river. Another curve, with the black beginning to flag again—then, far off, the sight I had been waiting for. Perhaps I should not tell it, but I lifted my sword to Heaven then, to the diminished sun with the worm in his heart; and I called, "His life for mine, New Sun, by your anger and my hope!"

The uhlan (and there was only one alone) must surely have thought me threatening him, as indeed I was. The blue radiance at the tip of his lance increased as he spurred toward us.

Winded though he was, the black swerved for me like a hunted hare. A twitch of the reins, and he was sliding and turning, his hooves scarring the green verdure of the road. In no more than a breath, we had reversed our track and were pounding back toward the things that pursued us. Whether Jonas understood my plan then I do not know, but he fell in with it as though he did, never slackening his own pace.

One of the fluttering creatures swooped, looking for all Urth like a hole torn in the universe, for it was true fuligin, as lightless as my own habit. It was trying for Jonas, I believe, but it came within sword reach, and I parted it as I had before, and again felt a gust of warmth. Knowing from where that heat came, it seemed more evil to me than any vile odor could; the mere sensation on my skin made me ill. I reined sharply away from the river, fearing a bolt from the uhlan's lance at any moment. We had no more than left the road when it came, searing the ground and setting a dead tree ablaze.

I pulled my mount's head up, making him rear and roar. For a moment I looked for the three dark things around the burning tree. They were not there. I glanced toward Jonas then, fearing they had overtaken him after all and were attacking him in some way I could not comprehend.

They were not there either, but his eyes showed me where they had gone: they flitted about the uhlan, and he, as I watched, sought to defend himself with his lance. Bolt after bolt split the air, so that there was a continual crashing like thunder. With each bolt the brightness of the sun was washed away, but the very energies with which he sought to destroy them seemed to give them strength. To my eyes they no longer flew, but flickered as beams of darkness might, appearing first in one place then in another, and always nearer the uhlan, until in less time than I have taken to write of it all three were at his face. He tumbled from his saddle, and the lance fell from his hand and went out.

XIII

The Claw of the Conciliator

I called, "Is he dead?", and saw Jonas nod in reply. I would have ridden away then, but he motioned for me to join him and dismounted. When we met by the uhlan's body, he said, "We may be able to destroy those things so they can't be flown against us again or be used to harm anyone else. They're sated now, and I think we might handle them. We need something to put them in—something water-tight, of metal or glass."

I had nothing of that kind and told him so.

"Neither have I." He knelt beside the uhlan and turned out his pockets. Aromatic smoke from the blazing tree wreathed everything like incense, and I had the sensation of being once more in the Cathedral of the Pelerines. The litter of twigs and last summer's leaves on which the uhlan lay might have been the straw strewn floor; the trunks of the scattered trees, the supporting poles.

"Here," Jonas said, and picked up a brass vasculum. Unscrewing the lid he emptied it of herbs, then rolled the dead uhlan on his back.

"Where are they?" I asked. "Has the body absorbed them?"

Jonas shook his head, and after a moment began, very carefully and delicately, to draw one of the dark things from the uhlan's left nostril. Save for being absolutely opaque, it was like the finest tissue paper.

I wondered at his caution. "If you tear it, won't it just become two?"

"Yes, but it is sated now. Divided, it would lose energy and might be impossible to handle. A lot of people have died, by the way, because they found they could cut these creatures, and choose to stand their ground doing it until they were surrounded by too many to fend off."

One of the uhlan's eyes was half open. I had seen corpses often before, but I could not escape the eerie feeling that he was in some sense watching me, the man who had killed him to save himself. To turn my mind to other things, I said, "After I cut the first one, it seemed to fly more slowly."

Jonas had placed the horror he had drawn out in the vasculum and was extracting a second from the right nostril; he murmured, "The speed of any flying thing depends on its wing area. If that weren't the case, the adepts who use these creatures would tear them into scraps before they sent them forth, I suppose."

"You sound as though you've encountered them before."

"We docked once at a port where they're used in ritual murders. I suppose it was inevitable that someone would bring them home, but these are the first I've seen here." He opened the brass lid and laid the second fuligin thing on the first, which stirred sluggishly. "They'll recombine in there—this is what the adepts do to get them back together. I doubt if you noticed it, but they were torn somewhat in going through the wood and healed themselves in flight."

"There's one more," I said.

He nodded and used his steel hand to force open the dead man's mouth; instead of holding teeth and livid tongue and gums it appeared to be a bottomless gulf, and for a moment my stomach churned. Jonas drew out the third creature, streaked with the dead man's saliva.

"Wouldn't he have had a nostril open, or his mouth, if I hadn't cut the thing a second time?"

"Until they worked their way into his lungs. We're lucky, actually, to have been able to get to him so quickly. Otherwise you would have had to slice the body open to get them out."

A wisp of smoke called to mind the burning cedar. "If it was heat they wanted . . ."

"They prefer life's heat, though they can sometimes be distracted by a fire of living vegetable matter. It's something more than heat, I think, really. Perhaps some radiant energy characteristic of growing cells." Jonas stuffed the third creature into the vasculum and snapped it shut. "We called them notules, because they usually came after dark, when they could not be seen, and the first warning we had was a breath of warmth; but I have no idea what the natives call them."

"Where is this island?"

He looked at me curiously.

"Is it far from the coast? I've always wanted to see Uroboros, though I suppose it is dangerous."

"Very far," Jonas said in a flat voice. "Very far indeed. Wait a moment."

I waited, watching, as he strode to the riverbank. He threw the vasculum hard—it had almost reached midstream when it dropped into the water. When he returned I asked, "Couldn't we have used those things ourselves? It doesn't seem likely that whoever sent them is going to give up now, and we might have need of them."

" 'They would not obey us, and the world is better without them anyway,' as the butcher's wife told him when she cut away his manhood. Now we'd best be going. There's somebody coming down the road."

I looked where Jonas had pointed, and saw two figures on foot. He had caught his destrier by the halter as it drank and was ready to climb into the saddle. "Wait," I said. "Or go on a chain or two and wait for me there." I was thinking of the man-ape's bleeding stump, and I seemed to see the dim votive lights of the cathedral hanging, crimson and magenta, among the trees. I reached into my boot, far down where I had pushed it for safety, and drew out the Claw.

It was the first time I had seen it by full daylight. It caught the sun and flashed like a New Sun itself, not blue only but with every color from violet to cyan. I laid it on the uhlan's forehead, and for an instant tried to will him alive.

"Come on," Jonas called. "What are you doing?"

I did not know how to answer him.

"He's not quite dead," Jonas called. "Get off the road before he finds his lance!" He lashed his mount.

Faintly, a voice I seemed to recognize called, "Master!" I turned my head to look down the grass-grown highway.

"Master!" One of the travelers waved an arm, and both began to run.

"It's Hethor," I said; but Jonas had gone. I looked back at the uhlan. Both his eyes were open now, and his chest rose and fell. When I took the Claw from his forehead and thrust it back into my boot top, he sat up. I shouted to Hethor and his companion to leave the road, but they did not appear to understand.

"Who are you?"

"A friend," I said.

Though the uhlan was feeble, he tried to rise. I gave him my hand and pulled him up. For a moment he stared at everything—myself, the two men running toward him, the river, and the trees. The destriers appeared to frighten him, even his own, which stood patiently awaiting its rider. "What is this place?"

"Only a stretch of the old road beside Gyoll."

He shook his head and pressed it with his hands.

Hethor came panting up, like an ill-bred dog that has run when called and now expects a petting for it. His companion, whom he had outreached by a hundred strides or so, wore the gaudy clothes and greasy look of a small trader.

"M-m-master," Hethor said, "you can have no idea how much t-t-trouble, how much deadly loss and difficulty we have had in overtaking you across the mountains, across the wide-blown seas and c-c-creaking plains of this fair world. What am I, your s-slave, but an abandoned sh-shell, the sport of a thousand tides, cast up here in this lonely place because I cannot r-r-rest without you? H-how could you, the red-clawed master, know of the endless labor you've cost us?"

"Since I left you in Saltus afoot and have been well mounted these past few days, I should think a good deal."

"Exactly," he said. "Exactly." He looked significantly at his companion as if my remark had confirmed something he had told him earlier, and sank down to rest upon the ground.

The uhlan said slowly, "I am Cornet Mineas. Who are you?"

Hethor bobbed his head as though he would have bowed. "M-m-master is the noble Severian, servant of the Autarch—whose urine is the wine of his subjects—in the Guild of the Seekers for Truth and Penitence. H-h-hethor is his humble servant. Beuzec is also his humble servant. I suppose the man who rode away is his servant too."

I gestured for him to be quiet. "We are all only poor travelers, Cornet. We saw you lying here stunned and sought to help you. A moment ago, we thought you dead; it must have been a near thing."

"What is this place?" the uhlan asked again.

Hethor answered eagerly. "The road north of Quiesco. M-m-master, we were on a boat, sailing the wide waters of Gyoll in the blind night. We di-d-disembarked at Quiesco. On her deck and at her sails we worked our p-passage, Beuzec and me. So slowly upriver, while the lucky ones whizzed above on their way to the H-h-house Absolute, but she m-m-made h-h-headway whether we woke or slept, and thus we caught up to you."

"The House Absolute?" the uhlan muttered.

I said, "It's not far from here, I think."

"I am to be especially vigilant."

"I feel sure one of your comrades will be along soon." I caught my mount and clambered onto his lofty back.

"M-m-master, you're not going to l-l-leave us again? Beuzec has seen you perform but twice."

I was about to answer Hethor when I caught sight of a flash of white among the trees across the highway. Something huge was moving there. At once, the thought that the sender of the notules might have other weapons at hand filled my mind, and I dug my heels into the black's flanks.

He sprang away. For half a league or more we raced along the narrow strip of ground that separated the road from the river. When at last I saw Jonas, I galloped across to warn him, and told him what I had seen.

While I spoke he seemed lost in reflection. When I had finished, he said, "I know of nothing like the being you describe, but there may be many importations I know nothing of."

"But surely such a thing wouldn't be wandering free like a strayed cow!"

Instead of replying, Jonas pointed toward the ground a few strides ahead.

A graveled path hardly more than a cubit wide wound among the trees. It was bordered with more wild flowers than I have ever seen growing naturally in company, and it was of pebbles so uniform in size, and of such shining whiteness, that they must surely have been carried from some secret and far off beach.

After riding a bit closer to examine it, I asked Jonas what such a path here could possibly mean.

"Only one thing, surely—that we are already on the grounds of the House Absolute."

Quite suddenly, I recalled the spot. "Yes," I said. "Once Josepha and I, with some others, made up a fishing party and came here. We crossed by the twisted oak . . ."

Jonas looked at me as though I were mad, and for a moment I felt that I was. I had ridden hunting often before, but this was a charger I sat, and no hunter. My hands raised themselves like spiders to pluck out my eyes—and would have done so if the ragged man beside me had not struck them down with his own hand, which was of steel. "You are not the Chatelaine Thecla," he said. "You are Severian, a journeyman of the torturers, who was unfortunate enough to love her. See yourself!" He held up the steel hand so that I could see a stranger's face, narrow, ugly, and bewildered, reflected in its work-polished balm.

I remembered our tower then, the curved walls of smooth, dark metal. "I am Severian," I said.

"That is correct. The Chatelaine Thecla is dead."

"Jonas . . ."

"Yes?"

"The uhlan is alive now—you saw him. The Claw gave him life again. I laid it on his forehead, but perhaps it was just that he saw it with his dead eyes. He sat up. He breathed and spoke to me, Jonas."

"He was not dead."

"You saw him," I said again.

"I am much older than you are. Older than you think. If there is one thing I have learned in so many voyages, it is that the dead do not rise, nor the years turn back. What has been and is gone does not come again."

Thecla's face was before me still, but it was blown by a dark wind until it fluttered and went out. I said, "If I had only used it, called on the power of the Claw when we were at the banquet of the dead . . ."

"The uhlan had nearly suffocated, but was not quite dead. When I got the notules away from him he was able to breathe, and after a time he regained consciousness. As for your Thecla, no power in the universe could have restored her to life. They must have dug her up while you were still imprisoned in the Citadel and stored her in an ice cave. Before we saw her, they had gutted her like a partridge and roasted her flesh." He gripped my arm. "Severian, don't be a fool!"

At that moment I wanted only to perish. If the notule had reappeared, I would have embraced it. What did appear, far down the path, was a white shape like that I had seen nearer the river. I tore myself away from Jonas and galloped toward it.

XIV

The Antechamber

There are beings—and artifacts—against which we batter our intelligence raw, and in the end make peace with reality only by saying, "It was an apparition, a thing of beauty and horror."

Somewhere among the swirling worlds I am so soon to explore, there lives a race like and yet unlike the human. They are no taller than we. Their bodies are like ours save that they are perfect, and that the standard to which they adhere is wholly alien to us. Like us they have eyes, a nose, a mouth; but they use these features (which are, as I have said, perfect) to express emotions we have never felt, so that for us to see their faces is to look upon some ancient and terrible alphabet of feeling, at once supremely important and utterly unintelligible.

Such a race exists, yet I did not encounter it there at the edge of the gardens of the House Absolute. What I had seen moving among the trees, and what I now—until I at last saw it clearly—flung myself toward, was rather the giant image of such a being kindled to life. Its flesh was of white stone, and its eyes had the smoothly rounded blindness (like sections cut from eggshells) we see in our own statues. It moved slowly, like one drugged or sleeping, yet not unsteadily. It seemed sightless, yet it gave the impression of awareness, however slow.

I have just paused to reread what I have written of it, and I see that I have failed utterly to convey the essence of the thing. Its spirit was that of sculpture. If some fallen angel had overheard my conversation with the green man, he might have contrived such an enigma to mock me. In its every movement it carried the serenity and permanency of art and stone; I felt that each gesture, each position of the head and limbs and torso, might be the last. Or that each might be repeated interminably, as the poses of the gnomens of Valeria's many-faceted dial were repeated down the curving corridors of the instants.

My initial terror, after the white statue's strangeness had washed away my will toward death, was the instinctive one that it would do me hurt. My second was that it would not attempt to. To be as frightened of something as I was of that silent, inhuman figure, and then to discover that it meant no harm, would have been unbearably humiliating. Forgetting for a moment the ruin it would bring her blade to strike that living stone, I drew *Terminus Est* and reined in the black. The breeze itself seemed to pause as we stood there, the black hardly quivering, myself with sword upraised, as still almost ourselves as statues. The real statue came toward us, its three or four times life-size face stamped with inconceivable emotion and its limbs wrapped in terrible and perfect beauty.

I heard Jonas shout, and the sound of a blow. I had just time to see him on the ground grappling with men in tall, crested helmets that vanished and reappeared even as I looked at them, when something whizzed past my ear; another struck my wrist, and I found myself struggling in a web of cords that constricted like little boas. Someone seized my leg and pulled, and I fell.

When I had recovered enough to be aware of what was taking place, I had a wire noose about my neck, and one of my captors was rummaging through my sabretache. I could see his hands clearly, darting like brown sparrows. His face was visible too, an impassive mask that might have been suspended above me on a conjuror's thread. Once or twice, as he moved, the extraordinary armor he wore gleamed; then I saw it as one sees a crystal beaker immersed in clear water. It was reflective, I think, burnished beyond any merely human skill, so that its own material was invisible and only the greens and browns of the wood could be seen, twisted by the shapes of cuirass, gorget, and greaves.

Despite my protest that I was a member of the guild, the praetorian took all the money I had (though he left me Thecla's brown book, my fragment of whetstone, oil and flannel, and the other miscellaneous objects in my sabretache). Then he skillfully drew off the cords that entangled me and thrust them (as nearly as I could tell) into the armhole of his breastplate, though not before I had seen them. They reminded me of the whip we used to call a "cat," and were a bundle of thongs joined at one end and weighted at the other; I have learned since that this weapon is called the *achico*.

My captor now lifted the wire noose until I stood. I was conscious, as I have been on several similar occasions, that we were in some sense playing a game. We were pretending that I was totally in his power, when in fact I might have refused to rise until he had either strangled me or called over some of his comrades to carry me. I could have done several other things as well—seized the wire and tried to wrest it from him, struck him in the face. I might have escaped, been killed, been rendered unconscious, or plunged into agony; but I could not actually be forced to do as I did.

At least I knew it was a game, and I smiled as he sheathed *Terminus Est* and led me to where Jonas stood.

Jonas said, "We've done no harm. Return my friend's sword and give us back our animals, and we will go."

There was no reply. In silence two praetorians (four fluttering sparrows, as it seemed) caught our destriers and led them away. How like us those animals were, walking patiently they knew not where, their massive heads following thin strips of leather. Nine-tenths of life, so it seems to me, consists of these surrenders.

We were made to go with our captors out of the wood and onto a rolling meadow that soon became a lawn. The statue walked after us, and others of his kind joined him until there were a dozen or more, all huge, all different, and all beautiful. I asked Jonas who the soldiers were and where they were taking us; but he did not answer, and I was nearly throttled for my pains.

So far as I could tell, they were armored from head to foot, yet the perfect polish of the metal imparted to it a seeming softness, an almost liquid yielding, that was profoundly disturbing to the eye and that permitted it to fade into sky and grass at a distance of a few paces. When we had walked half a league across the sward, we entered a grove of flowering plums, and at once the crested helms and flaring pauldrons danced with pink and white.

There we struck a path that curved and curved again. Just as we were on the point of emerging from the grove we halted, and Jonas and I were pushed violently back. I heard the feet of the stony figures that followed us grate on the gravel as they too stopped short; one of the soldiers warned them off with what seemed to me a wordless cry. I peered through the blossoms as well as I could to see what lay ahead.

Before us was a walk much broader than the one we trod. It was, in fact, a garden path grown until it had become a magnificent processional way. The pavement was of white stone, and marble balustrades flanked it to either side. Down it marched a motley company. Most were on foot, but some rode beasts of various sorts. One led a shaggy arctother;

another perched upon the neck of a ground sloth greener than the lawns. No sooner had this group passed than other groups followed them. While they were still too far for me to distinguish their faces, I noticed one in which the bowed head of a single individual was lifted above the rest by at least three cubits. A moment later I had recognized another as Dr. Talos, strutting along with his chest thrown out and his head well back. My own dear Dorcas followed close behind him, looking more than ever like a forlorn child wandered from some higher sphere. Fluttering with veils and sparkling with bijoux under her parasol, Jolenta rode a diminutive jennet sidesaddle; and behind them all, patiently wheeling such properties as he could not shoulder, lumbered he whom I had identified first, the giant, Baldanders.

If it was painful for me to see them pass without being able to call out, it must have been torment for Jonas. When Jolenta was nearly opposite us, she turned her head. To me, at that moment, it seemed she must have winded his desire, as among the mountains certain unclean spirits are said to be attracted by the odor of meat that has been cast upon a fire for them. No doubt it was really only the flowering trees among which we stood that caught her attention. I heard the inhalation of Jonas's breath; but the first syllable of her name was cut short by the thud of the blow that followed, and he pitched at my feet. When I recall that scene now, the rattle of his metal hand on the gravel of the path is as vivid as the perfume of the plum blossoms.

After all the troupes of performers had gone, two praetorians picked up poor Jonas and carried him. They did it as easily as they might have carried a child; but I at the time attributed that only to their strength. We crossed the road down which the performers had come and penetrated a hedge of roses higher than a man, covered with immense white blossoms and filled with nesting birds.

Beyond it lay the gardens proper. If I should try to describe them, I should seem only to have borrowed the mad, stammering eloquence of Hethor. Every hill and tree and flower seemed to have been arranged by some master intelligence (which I have since learned is that of Father Inire) to form a breathtaking vision. The observer feels that he is at the center, that everything he sees has been directed toward the point at which he stands; but after he has walked a hundred paces, or a league, he finds himself at the center still; and every vision seems to convey some incommunicable truth, like one of the unutterable insights granted eremites.

So beautiful were these gardens that we had been in them for some time before I realized that no towers were lifted above them. Only the birds and the clouds, and beyond them the old sun and the pale stars, rose higher than their treetops; we might have been wandering through some divine wilderness. Then we reached the crest of a wave of land more lovely than any cobalt wave of Uroboros's, and with breathtaking suddenness a pit opened at our feet. I have called it a pit, but it was not at all like the dark abyss usually associated with that word. Rather, it was a grotto filled with fountains and night flowers, and dotted with people more brilliant than any flowers, people who loitered beside its waters and gossiped among its shades.

At once, as though a wall had collapsed to let light into a tomb, many of the memories of the House Absolute, mine by absorption now from the life of Thecla, coalesced. I understood something that had been implicit in the doctor's play and in many of the stories Thecla had told me as well, though she had never mentioned it directly: The whole of this great palace lay underground—or rather, its roofs and walls were heaped with soil planted and landscaped, so that we had been walking all this time over the seat of the Autarch's power, which I had thought still some distance away.

We did not go down into that grotto, which no doubt opened onto chambers quite unsuited to the detention of prisoners, or into any of the next score or so we passed. At last, however, we came upon one far more grim, though no less beautiful. The stair by which we entered it had been carved to resemble a natural formation of dark rock, irregular and sometimes treacherous. Water dripped from above, and ferns and dark ivy grew in the upper parts of this artificial cavern, where a little sunlight still found its way. In the lower regions, a thousand steps down, the walls were studded with blind fungi; some of these were luminous; some strewed the air with strange, musty odors; some suggested fantastic phallic fetishes.

In the center of this dark garden, supported by scaffolding and green with verdigris, hung a set of gongs. It appeared to me that they were intended to be rung by the wind; yet it seemed impossible that any wind should ever reach them.

So I thought, at least, until one of the praetorians opened a heavy door of bronze and worm-scarred wood in one of the dark stone walls. Then a draft of cold, dry air blew through that doorway and set the gongs to swaying and clashing, so well tuned that their chiming seemed the purposeful composition of some musician, whose thoughts were now in exile here.

In looking up at the gongs (which the praetorians did not prevent me from doing) I saw the statues, forty at least, who had followed us all the way across the gardens. They now rimmed the pit, motionless at last, and looked down on us like a frieze of cenotaphs.

* * *

I had expected to be the only occupant of a small cell, I suppose because I unconsciously transferred the practices of our own oubliette to this unknown place. Nothing more different from the actual arrangement could have been imagined. The entrance opened on no corridor of narrow doors, but to a spacious and carpeted one with a second entrance opposite. Hastarii with flaming spears stood as sentries before this second set of doors. At a word from one of the praetorians, they swung them open; beyond lay a vast, shadowy, bare room with a very low ceiling. Several dozen persons, men and women and a few children, were scattered in diverse parts of it—most singly, but some in couples or groups. Families occupied alcoves, and in some places screens of rags had been erected to provide privacy.

Into this we were thrust. Or rather, I was thrust and the unfortunate Jonas was thrown. I tried to catch him as he fell, and I at least prevented his head from striking the floor; as I did so, I heard the doors slam shut behind me.

XV

Fool's Fire

I was ringed by faces. Two women took Jonas from me, and promising to care for him carried him away. The rest began to ply me with questions. What was my name? What clothes were those I wore? Where had I come from? Did I know such a one, or such a one, or such a one? Had I ever been to this town or that? Was I of the House Absolute? Of Nessus? From the east bank of Gyoll or the west? What quarter? Did the Autarch still live? What of Father Inire? Who was archon in the city? How went the war? Had I news of so-and-so, a commander? Of so-and-so, a trooper? Of so-and-so, a chiliarch? Could I sing, recite, play an instrument?

As may be imagined, in such a welter of inquiries I was able to answer almost none. When the first flurry was spent, an old, gray-bearded man and a woman who seemed almost equally old silenced the others and drove them away. Their method, which would surely have succeeded nowhere but here, was to clap each by the shoulder, point to the most remote part of the room, and say distinctly, "*Plenty of time.*" Gradually the others fell silent and walked to what seemed the limits of hearing, until at last the low room was as still as it had been when the doors opened.

"I am Lomer," the old man said. He cleared his throat noisily. "This is Nicarete."

I told him my name, and Jonas's.

The old woman must have heard the concern in my voice. "He will be safe, rest assured. Those girls will treat him as well as they can, in the hope that he'll soon be able to talk to them." She laughed, and something in the way she threw back her well shaped head told me she had once been beautiful.

I began to question them in my turn, but the old man interrupted me. "Come with us," he said, "to our corner. We will be able to sit at ease there, and I can offer you a cup of water."

As soon as he pronounced the word, I realized that I was terribly thirsty. He led us behind the rag screen nearest the doors and poured water for me from an earthenware jug into a delicate porcelain cup. There were cushions there, and a little table not more than a span high.

"Question for question," he said. "That's the old rule. We have told you our names and you have told us yours, and so we begin again. Why were you taken?"

I explained that I did not know, unless it were merely for violating the grounds.

Lomer nodded. His skin was of that pale color peculiar to those who never see the sun; with his straggling beard and uneven teeth, he would have been repulsive in any other setting; but he belonged here as much as the half-obliterated tiles of the floor did. "I am here by the malice of the Chatelaine Leocadia. I was seneschal to her rival the Chatelaine Nympha, and when she brought me here to the House Absolute with her in order that we might review the accounts of the estate while she attended the rites of the philomath Phocas, the Chatelaine Leocadia entrapped me by the aid of Sancha, who—"

The old woman, Nicarete, interrupted him. "Look!" she exclaimed. "He knows her."

And so I did. A chamber of pink and ivory had risen in my mind, a room of which two walls were clear glass exquisitely framed. Fires burned there on marble hearths, dimmed by the sunbeams streaming through the glass but filling the room with a dry heat and the odor of sandalwood. An old woman wrapped in many shawls sat in a chair that was like a throne; a decanter of cut crystal and several brown phials stood on an inlaid table at her side. "An elderly woman with a hooked nose," I said. "The Dowager of Fors."

"You do know her then." Lomer's head nodded slowly, as though it were answering the question put by its own mouth. "You are the first in many years."

"Let us say that I remember her."

"Yes." The old man nodded. "They say she is dead now. But in my day she was a fine, healthy young woman. The Chatelaine Leocadia persuaded her to it, then caused us to be discovered, as Sancha knew she would. She was but fourteen, and no crime was charged to her. We had done nothing in any case; she had only begun to undress me."

I said, "You must have been quite a young man yourself."

He did not answer, so Nicarete replied for him. "He was twenty-eight."

"And you," I asked. "Why are you here?"

"I am a volunteer."

I looked at her in some surprise.

"Someone must make amends for the evil of Urth, or the New Sun will never come. And someone must call attention to this place and the others like it. I am of an armiger family that may yet remember me, and so the guards must be careful of me, and of all the others while I remain here."

"Do you mean that you can leave, and will not?"

"No," she said, and shook her head. Her hair was white, but she wore it flowing about her shoulders as young women do. "I will leave, but only on my own terms, which are that all those who have been here so long that they have forgotten their crimes be set free as well."

I remembered the kitchen knife I had stolen for Thecla, and the ribbon of crimson that had crept from under the door of her cell in our oubliette, and I said, "Is it true that prisoners really forget their crimes here?"

Lomer looked up at that. "Unfair! Question for question—that's the rule, the old rule. We still keep the old rules here. We're the last of the old crop, Nicarete and me, but while we last, the old rules still stand. Question for question. Have you friends who may strive for your release?"

Dorcas would, surely, if she knew where I was. Dr. Talos was as unpredictable as the figures seen in clouds, and for that very reason might seek to have me freed, though he had no real motive for doing so. Most importantly, perhaps, I was Vodalus's messenger, and Vodalus had at least one agent in the House Absolute—him to whom I was supposed to deliver his message. I had tried to cast away the steel twice while Jonas and I were riding north, but had found that I could not; the alzabo, it seemed, had laid yet another spell upon my mind. Now I was glad of that.

"Have you friends? Relations? If you have, you may be able to do something for the rest of us."

"Friends, possibly," I said. "They may try to help me if they ever learn what has happened to me. Is it likely they may succeed?"

In that way we talked for a long time; if I were to write it all here, there would be no end to this history. In that room, there is nothing to do but talk and play a few simple games, and the prisoners do those things until all the savor has gone out of them, and they are left like gristle a starving man has chewed all day. In many respects, these prisoners are better off than the clients beneath our own tower; by day they have no fear of pain, and none is alone. But because most of them have been there so long, and few of our clients had been long confirmed, ours were, for the most part, filled with hope, while those in the House Absolute are despairing.

After what must have been ten watches or more, the glowing lamps in the ceiling began to fade, and I told Lomer and Nicarete I could remain awake no longer. They led me to a spot far from the door, where it was very dark, and explained that it would be mine until one of the other prisoners died and I succeeded to a better position.

As they left, I heard Nicarete say, "Will they come tonight?" Lomer made some reply, but I could not say what that reply was, and I was too fatigued to ask. My feet told me there was a thin pallet on the floor; I sat down and had begun to stretch myself full length when my hand touched a living body.

Jonas's voice said, "You needn't jerk back. It's only me."

"Why didn't you say something? I saw you walking about, but I couldn't break away from the two old people. Why didn't you come over?"

"I didn't say anything because I was thinking. And I didn't come over because I couldn't break away from the women who had me, at first. Afterward, those people couldn't break away from me. Severian, I must escape from here."

"Everyone wants to, I suppose," I told him. "Certainly I do."

"But I *must*." His thin, hard hand—his left hand of flesh—gripped mine. "If I don't, I will kill myself or lose my reason. I've been your friend, haven't I?" His voice dropped to the faintest of whispers. "Will the talisman you carry . . . the blue gem . . . set us free? I know the praetorians didn't find it; I watched while they searched you."

"I don't want to take it out," I said. "It gleams so in the dark."

"I'll turn one of these mats on its side and hold it to shield us."

I waited until I could feel the pallet in position, then drew out the Claw. Its light was so faint I might have shaded it with my hand.

"Is it dying?" Jonas asked.

"No, it's often like this. But when it is active—when it transmuted the water in our carafe and when it awed the man-apes—it shines brightly. If it can procure our escape at all, I don't believe it will do so now."

"We must take it to the door. It might spring the lock." His voice was shaking.

"Later, when the others are all asleep. I'll free them if we can get free ourselves; but if the door doesn't open—and I don't think it will—I don't want them to know I have the Claw. Now tell me why you must escape at once.''

"While you were talking to the old people I was being questioned by a whole family,'' Jonas began. "There were several old women, a man of about fifty, another about thirty, three other women, and a flock of children. They had carried me to their own little niche in the wall, you see, and the other prisoners couldn't come there unless they were invited, which they weren't. I expected that they'd ask me about friends on the outside, or politics, or the fighting in the mountains. Instead I seemed to be only a kind of amusement for them. They wanted to hear about the river, and where I had been, and how many people dressed the way I did. And the food outside—there were a great many questions about food, some of them quite ludicrous. Had I ever seen butchering? And did the animals plead for their lives? And was it true that the ones who make sugar carried poisoned swords and would fight to defend it? . . .

"They had never seen bees, and seemed to think they were about the size of rabbits.

"After a time I began to ask questions of my own and found that none of them, not even the oldest woman, had ever been free. Men and women are put into this room alike, it seems, and in the course of nature they produce children. And though some are taken away, most remain here throughout their lives. They have no possessions and no hope of release. Actually, they don't know what freedom is, and although the older man and one girl told me seriously that they would like to go outside, I don't think they meant to stay. The old women are seventh-generation prisoners, so they said—but one let it slip that her mother had been a seventh-generation prisoner as well.

"They are remarkable people in some respects. Externally they have been shaped completely by this place where they have spent all their lives. Yet beneath that are . . .'' Jonas paused, and I could feel the silence pressing in all about us. "Family memories, I suppose you could call them. Traditions from the outside world that have been handed down to them, generation to generation, from the original prisoners from whom they are descended. They don't know what some of the words mean any longer, but they cling to the traditions, to the stories, because those are all they have; the stories and their names.''

He fell silent. I had thrust the tiny spark of the Claw back into my boot, and we were in perfect darkness. His labored breathing was like the pumping of the bellows at a forge.

"I asked them the name of the first prisoner, the most remote from whom they counted their descent. It was Kimleesoong. . . . Have you heard that name?''

I told him I had not.

''Or anything like it? Suppose it were three words.''

''No, nothing like that,'' I said. ''Most of the people I have known have had one-word names like you, unless a part of the name was a title, or a nickname of some sort that had been attached to it because there were too many Bolcans or Altos or whatever.''

''You told me once that you thought I had an unusual name. Kim Lee Soong would have been a very common kind of name when I was . . . a boy. A common name in places now sunk beneath the sea. Have you ever heard of my ship, Severian? She was the *Fortunate Cloud.*''

''A gambling ship? No, but—''

My eye was caught by a gleam of greenish light so faint that even in that darkness it was scarcely visible. At once there came a murmur of voices echoing and reechoing throughout the wide, low, crooked room. I heard Jonas scrambling to his feet. I did the same, but I was no sooner up than I was blinded by a flash of blue fire. The pain was as severe as I have ever felt; it seemed as though my face were being torn away. I would have fallen if it had not been for the wall.

Somewhere farther off the blue fire flashed again, and a woman cried out.

Jonas was cursing—at least, the tone of his voice told me he was cursing, though the words came in tongues unknown to me. I heard his boots on the floor. There was another flash, and I recognized the lightning-like sparks I had seen the day Master Gurloes, Roche, and I administered the revolutionary to Thecla. No doubt Jonas screamed as I had, but by that time there was such bedlam I could not distinguish his voice.

The greenish light grew stronger, and while I watched, still more than half paralyzed with pain and wracked by as much fear as I can recall ever having experienced, it gathered itself into a monstrous face that glared at me with saucer eyes, then quickly faded to mere dark.

All this was more terrifying than my pen could ever convey, though I were to slave over this part of my account forever. It was the fear of blindness as well as of pain, but we were all, for all that mattered, already blind. There was no light, and we could make none. There was not one of us who could light a candle or so much as strike fire to tinder. All around that cavernous room, voices screamed, wept, and prayed. Over the wild din I heard the clear laughter of a young woman; then it was gone.

XVI

Jonas

I hungered then for light as a starving man for meat, and at last I risked the Claw. Perhaps I should say that it risked me; it seemed I had no control of the hand that slid into my boot top and grasped it.

At once the pain faded, and there came a rush of azure light. The hubbub redoubled as the other wretched inhabitants of the place, seeing that radiance, feared some new terror was to be thrust among them. I pushed the gem down into my boot once more, and when its light was no longer visible began to grope for Jonas.

He was not unconscious, as I had supposed, but lay writhing, some twenty steps from where we had rested. I carried him back (finding him astonishingly light) and when I had covered us both with my cloak touched his forehead with the Claw.

In a short time he was sitting up. I told him to rest, that whatever it was that had been in the prison chamber with us was gone.

He stirred and muttered, "We must get power to the compressors before the air goes bad."

"It's all right," I told him. "Everything is all right, Jonas." I despised myself for it, but I was talking to him as if he were the youngest of apprentices, just as, years before, Master Malrubius had spoken to me.

Something hard and cold touched my wrist, moving as if it were alive. I grasped it, and it was Jonas's steel hand; after a moment I realized he had been trying to clasp my own hand with it. "I feel weight!" His voice was growing louder. "It must be only the lights." He turned, and I heard his hand ring and scrape as it struck the wall. He began talking to himself in a nasal, monosyllabic language I did not understand.

Greatly daring, I drew out the Claw again and touched him with it once more. It was as dull as it had been when we had first examined it that evening, and Jonas became no better; but in time I was able to calm him. At last, long after the remainder of the room had grown quiet, we lay down to sleep.

When I woke, the dim lamps were burning again, though I somehow felt that it was yet night outside, or at least no more than earliest morning.

Jonas lay beside me, still asleep. There was a long tear in his tunic, and I saw where the blue fire had branded him. Recalling the man-ape's severed hand, I made certain no one was observing us and began to trace the burn with the Claw.

It sparkled in the light much more brightly than it had the evening before; and though the black scar did not vanish, it seemed narrower, and the flesh to either side less inflamed. To reach the lower end of the wound, I lifted the cloth a trifle. When I thrust in my hand, I heard a faint note; the gem had struck metal. Drawing back the cloth more, I saw that my friend's skin ended as abruptly as grass does where a large stone lies, giving way to shining silver.

My first thought was that it was armor; but soon I saw that it was not. Rather, it was metal standing in the place of flesh, just as metal stood in the place of his right hand. How far it continued I could not see, and I was afraid to touch his legs for fear of waking him.

Concealing the Claw again, I rose. And because I wanted to be alone and think for a few moments, I walked away from Jonas and into the center of the room. It had been a strange enough place the day before, when everyone was awake and active. Now it seemed stranger still, a ragged blot of a room, frayed with odd corners and crushed under its lowering ceiling. Hoping that exercise would set my mind in motion (as it often does), I decided to pace off the room's length and width, treading softly so as not to wake the sleepers.

I had not gone forty paces when I saw an object that seemed completely out of place in that collection of ragged people and filthy canvas pallets. It was a woman's scarf woven of some rich, smooth material the color of a peach. There is no describing the scent of it, which was not that of any fruit or flower that grows on Urth, but was very lovely.

I was folding this beautiful thing to put in my sabretache when I heard a child's voice say, "It's bad luck. Terrible luck. Don't you know?"

Looking around, then down, I saw a little girl with a pale face and sparkling midnight eyes that seemed too large for it; and I asked, "What's bad luck, Mistress?"

"Keeping findings. They come back for them later. Why do you wear those black clothes?"

"They're fuligin, the hue that is darker than black. Hold out your hand and I'll show you. Now, do you see how it seems to disappear when I trail the edge of my cloak across it?"

Her little head, which small though it was seemed much too big for the shoulders below it, nodded solemnly. "Burying people wear black. Do you bury people? When the navigator was buried there were black wagons and people in black clothes walking. Have you ever seen a burying like that?"

I crouched to look more easily into the solemn face. "No one wears fuligin clothes at funerals, Mistress, for fear they might be mistaken for members of my guild, which would be a slander of the dead—in most cases. Now here is the scarf. See how pretty it is? Is it what you call a finding?"

She nodded. "The whips leave them, and what you ought to do is push them out through the space under the doors. Because they'll come and take their things back." Her eyes were no longer on mine. She was looking at the scar that ran across my right cheek.

I touched it. "These are the whips? The ones who do this? Who are they? I saw a green face."

"So did I." Her laughter held the notes of little bells. "I thought it was going to eat me."

"You don't sound frightened now."

"Mama says the things you see in the dark don't mean anything—they're different almost every time. It's the whips that hurt, and she held me behind her, between her and the wall. Your friend is waking up. Why are you looking so funny?"

(I recalled laughing with other people; three were young men, two were women of about my own age. Guibert handed me a scourge with a heavy handle and a lash of braided copper. Lollian was preparing the firebird, which he would twirl on a long cord.)

"*Severian!*" It was Jonas, and I hurried over. "I'm glad you're here," he said when I was squatting beside him. "I . . . thought you'd gone away."

"I could hardly do that, remember?"

"Yes," he said. "I remember now. Do you know what this place is called, Severian? They told me yesterday. It's the antechamber. I see you already knew."

"No."

"You nodded."

"I recalled the name when you pronounced it, and I knew it was the right one. I . . . Thecla was here, I think. She never considered it a strange place for a prison, I suppose because it was the only one she had seen before she was taken to our tower, but I find I do. Individual cells, or at least several separate rooms, seem more practical to me. Perhaps I'm only prejudiced.''

Jonas pulled himself up until he was sitting with his back to the wall. His face had gone pale under the brown, and it shone with perspiration as he said, ''Can't you imagine how this place came to be? Look around you.''

I did so, seeing no more than I had seen before: the sprawling room with its dim lamps.

''This used to be a suite—several suites, probably. The walls have been torn away, and a uniform floor laid over all the old ones. I'm sure that's what we used to call a drop ceiling. If you were to lift one of those panels, you'd see the original structure above it.''

I stood and tried; but though the tips of my fingers brushed the rectangular panes, I was not tall enough to exert much force on them. The little girl, who had been watching us from a distance of ten paces or so, and listening, I feel sure, to every word, said, ''Hold me up and I'll do it.''

She ran toward us. I lifted her and found that with my hands around her waist I could easily raise her over my head. For a few seconds her small arms struggled with the square of ceiling above her. Then it went up, showering dust. Beyond it I saw a network of slender metal bars, and through them a vaulted ceiling with many moldings and a flaking painting of clouds and birds. The girl's arms weakened, the panel sunk again, with more dust, and my view was cut off.

When she was safely down, I turned back to Jonas. ''You're right. There was an old ceiling above this one, for a room much smaller than this. How did you know?''

''Because I talked to those people. Yesterday.'' He raised his hands, the hand of steel as well as the hand of flesh, and appeared to rub his face with both. ''Send that child away, will you?''

I told the little girl to go to her mother, though I suspect she only crossed the room, then made her way back along the wall until she was within earshot of us.

''I feel as if I were waking up,'' Jonas said. ''I think I said yesterday that I was afraid I would go mad. I think perhaps I'm going sane, and that is as bad or worse.'' He had been sitting on the canvas pad where we had slept. Now he slumped against the wall just as I have since seen a corpse sit with its back to a tree. ''I used to read, aboard ship. Once

I read a history. I don't suppose you know anything about it. So many chiliads have elapsed here.''

I said, ''I suppose not.''

''So different from this, but so much like it too. Queer little customs and usages . . . some that weren't so little. Strange institutions. I asked the ship and she gave me another book.''

He was still perspiring, and I thought his mind was wandering. I used the square of flannel I carried to wipe my sword blade to dry his forehead.

''Hereditary rulers and hereditary subordinates, and all sorts of strange officials. Lancers with long, white mustaches.'' For an instant the ghost of his old humorous smile appeared. ''The White Knight is sliding down the poker. He balances very badly, as the King's notebook told him.''

There was a disturbance at the farther end of the room. Prisoners who had been sleeping, or talking quietly in small groups, were rising and walking toward it. Jonas seemed to assume that I would go as well, and gripped my shoulder with his left hand; it felt as weak as a woman's. ''None of it began so.'' There was a sudden intensity in his quavering voice. ''Severian, the king was elected at the Marchfield. Counts were appointed by the kings. That was what they called the dark ages. A baron was only a freeman of Lombardy.''

The little girl I had lifted to the ceiling appeared as if from nowhere and called to us, ''There's food. Aren't you coming?'' and I stood up and said, ''I'll get us something. It might make you feel better.''

''It became ingrained. It all endured too long.'' As I walked toward the crowd, I heard him say, ''The people didn't know.''

Prisoners were walking back with small loaves cradled in one arm. By the time I reached the doorway the crowd had thinned, and I was able to see that the doors were open. Beyond it, in the corridor, an attendant in a miter of starched white gauze watched over a silver cart. The prisoners were actually leaving the antechamber to circle around this man. I followed them, feeling for a moment that I had been set free.

The illusion was dispelled soon enough. Hastarii stood at either end of the corridor to bar it, and two more crossed their weapons before the door leading to the Well of Green Chimes.

Someone touched my arm, and I turned to see the white-haired Nicarete. ''You must get something,'' she said. ''If not for yourself, then for your friend. They never bring enough.''

I nodded, and by reaching over the heads of several persons I was able to pick up a pair of sticky loaves. ''How often do they feed us?''

"Twice a day. You came yesterday just after the second meal. Everyone tries not to take too much, but there is never quite enough."

"These are pastries," I said. The tips of my fingers were coated with sugar icing flavored with lemon, mace, and turmeric.

The old woman nodded. "They always are, though they vary from day to day. That silver biggin holds coffee, and there are cups on the lower tier of the cart. Most of the people confined here don't like it and don't drink it. I imagine a few don't even know about it."

All the pastries were gone now, and the last of the prisoners, save for Nicarete and me, had drifted back into the low-ceilinged room. I took a cup from the lower tier and filled it. The coffee was very strong and hot and black, and thickly sweetened with what seemed to me thyme honey.

"Aren't you going to drink it?"

"I'm going to carry it back to Jonas. Will they object if I take the cup?"

"I doubt it," Nicarete said, but as she spoke she jerked her head toward the soldiers.

They had advanced their spears to the position of guard, and the fires at the spearheads burned more brightly. With her I stepped back into the antechamber, and the doors swung closed behind us.

I reminded Nicarete that she had told me the day before that she was here by her will, and asked if she knew why the prisoners were fed on pastries and southern coffee.

"You know yourself," she said. "I hear it in your voice."

"No. It's only that I think Jonas knows."

"Perhaps he does. It is because this prison is not supposed to be a prison at all. Long ago—I believe before the reign of Ymar—it was the custom for the Autarch himself to judge anyone accused of a crime committed within the precincts of the House Absolute. Perhaps the autarchs felt that by hearing such cases they would be made aware of plots against them. Or perhaps it was only that they hoped that by dealing justly with those in their immediate circle they might shame hatred and disarm jealousy. Important cases were dealt with quickly, but the offenders in less serious ones were sent here to wait—"

The doors, which had closed such a short time ago, were opening again. A little, ragged, gap-toothed man was pushed inside. He fell sprawling, then picked himself up and threw himself at my feet. It was Hethor.

Just as they had when Jonas and I had come, the prisoners swarmed around him, lifting him up and shouting questions. Nicarete, soon joined by Lomer, forced them away and asked Hethor to identify himself. He clutched his cap (reminding me of the morning when he had found me camping on the grass by Ctesiphon's Cross) and said, "I am the slave of my master, far-traveled, m-m-map-worn Hethor am I, dust-choked and doubly deserted," looking at me all the while with bright, deranged eyes, like one of the Chatelaine Lelia's hairless rats, rats that ran in circles and bit their own tails when one clapped one's hands.

I was so disgusted by the sight of him, and so concerned about Jonas, that I left at once and went back to the spot where we had slept. The image of a shaking, gray-fleshed rat was still vivid as I sat down; then, as though it had itself recalled that it was no more than an image purloined from the dead recollections of Thecla, it flicked out of existence like Domnina's fish.

"Something wrong?" Jonas asked. He appeared to be a trifle stronger.

"I'm troubled by thoughts."

"A bad thing for a torturer, but I'm glad of the company."

I put the sweet loaves in his lap and set the cup by his hand. "City coffee—no pepper in it. Is that the way you like it?"

He nodded, picked up the cup, and sipped. "Aren't you having any?"

"I drank mine there. Eat the bread; it's very good."

He took a bit of one of the loaves. "I have to talk to somebody, so it has to be you even though you'll think I'm a monster when I'm done. You're a monster too, do you know that, friend Severian? A monster because you take for your profession what most people only do as a hobby."

"You're patched with metal," I said. "Not just your hand. I've known that for some time, friend monster Jonas. Now eat your bread and drink your coffee. I think it will be another eight watches or so before they feed us again."

"We crashed. It had been so long, on Urth, that there was no port when we returned, no dock. Afterward my hand was gone, and my face. My shipmates repaired me as well as they could, but there were no parts anymore, only biological material." With the steel hand I had always thought scarcely more than a hook, he picked up the hand of muscle and bone as a man might lift a bit of filth to cast it away.

"You're feverish. The whip hurt you, but you'll recover and we'll get out and find Jolenta."

Jonas nodded. "Do you remember how, when we neared the end of the Piteous Gate, in all that confusion, she turned her head so that the sun shone on one cheek?"

I told him I did.

"I have never loved before, never in all the time since our crew scattered."

"If you can't eat anything more, you ought to rest now."

"Severian." He gripped my shoulder as he had before, but this time with his steel hand; it felt as strong as a vise. "You must talk to me. I cannot bear the confusion of my own thoughts."

For some time I spoke of whatever came into my head, without receiving any reply. Then I remembered Thecla, who had often been oppressed in much the same way, and how I had read to her. Taking out her brown book, I opened it at random.

XVII

The Tale of the Student and His Son

Part I

The Redoubt of the Magicians

Once, upon the margin of the unpastured sea, there stood a city of pale towers. In it dwelt the wise. Now that city had both law and curse. The law was this: That for all who dwelt there, life held but two paths: they might rise among the wise and walk clad with hoods of myriad colors, or they must leave the city and go into the friendless world.

Now one there was who had studied long all the magic known in the city, which was most of the magic known in the world. And he grew near the time at which he must choose his path. In high summer, when flowers with yellow and careless heads thrust even from the dark walls overlooking the sea, he went to one of the wise who had shaded his face with myriad colors for longer than most could remember, and for long had taught the student whose time was come. And he said to him: "How may I—even I who know nothing—have a place among the wise of the city? For I wish to study spells that are *not* sacred all my days, and not go into the friendless world to dig and carry for bread."

Then the old man laughed and said, "Do you recall how, when you were hardly more than a boy, I taught you the art by which we flesh sons from dream stuff? How skillful you were in those days, surpassing all the others! Go now, and flesh such a son, and I will show it to the hooded ones, and you will be as we."

But the student said: "Another season. Let pass another season, and I will do everything you advise."

Autumn came, and the sycamores of the city of pale towers, that were sheltered from the sea winds by its high wall, dropped leaves like the gold manufactured by their owners. And the wild salt geese streamed among the pale towers, and after them the ossifrage and the lammergeir.

Then the old man sent again for him who had been his student, and said: ''Now, surely, you must flesh for yourself a creation of dream as I have instructed you. For the others among the hooded ones grow impatient. Save for us, you are the eldest in the city, and it may be that if you do not act now they will turn you out by winter.''

But the student answered: ''I must study further, that I may achieve what I seek. Can you not for one season protect me?'' And the old man who had taught him thought of the beauty of the trees that had for so many years delighted his eyes like the white limbs of women.

At length the golden autumn wore away, and Winter came stalking into the land from his frozen capital, where the sun rolls along the edge of the world like a trumpery gilded ball and the fires that flow between the stars and Urth kindle the sky. His touch turned the waves to steel, and the city of the magicians welcomed him, hanging banners of ice from its balconies and heaping its roofs with glaces of snow. The old man summoned his student again, and the student answered as before.

Spring came and with it gladness to all nature, but at spring the city was hung with black; and hatred, and the loathing of one's own powers—that eats like a worm at the heart—fell on the magicians. For the city had but one law and one curse, and though the law held sway all the year, the curse ruled the spring. In spring, the most beautiful maidens of the city, the daughters of the magicians, were clothed in green; and while the soft winds of spring teased their golden hair, they walked unshod through the portal of the city, and down the narrow path that led to the quay, and boarded the black-sailed ship that waited them. And because of their golden hair, and their gowns of green faille, and because it seemed to the magicians that they were reaped like grain, they were called Corn Maidens.

When the man who had long been the student of the old man but was yet unhooded heard the dirges and laments, and looking from his window saw the maidens filing by, he set aside all his books and began to draw such figures as no man had ever seen, and to write in many languages, as his master had taught him aforetime.

Part II

The Fleshing of the Hero

Day after day he labored. When the first light came at the window, his pen had been a drudge already many hours; and when the moon tangled her crooked back among the pale towers, his lamp shone bright. At first it seemed to him that all the skill his master had taught him of old had deserted him, for from the first light to the moonlight he was alone in his chambers save for the moth that fluttered sometimes to show the insignia of Death at his undaunted candle flame.

Then there crept into his dreams, when sometimes he nodded over the table, another; and he, knowing who that other was, welcomed him, though the dreams were fleeting and soon forgotten.

He labored on, and that which he strove to create gathered about him as smoke collects about the new fuel thrown upon a fire almost dead. At times (and particularly when he worked early or late, and when having at long last laid aside all the implements of his art, he stretched himself at length upon the narrow bed provided for those who had not yet earned the many colored hood) he heard the step, always in another room, of the man he hoped to call into life.

In time these manifestations, originally rare, and, indeed, at first limited almost entirely to those nights when thunder rumbled among the pale towers, became common, and there were unmistakable signs of the other's presence: a book he had not unshelved in decades lying beside a chair; windows and doors that unlocked, as it seemed, of themselves; an ancient alfange, for years past an ornament hardly more deadly than a trompe l'œil picture, found cleansed of its patina, gleaming and newly sharp.

One golden afternoon, when the wind played the innocent games of childhood with the fresh-fledged sycamores, there came a knock at the door of his study. Not daring to turn or express even the smallest part of what he felt by his voice, or even to desist from his work, he called: "Enter."

As doors open at midnight though no living thing stirs, the door began, a thread's width at a time, to swing back. Yet as it moved it seemed to gather strength, so that when it was open (as he judged by the sound) enough that a hand might have been thrust into the room, it seemed that the playful breeze had come in by the window to push life into its wooden heart. And when it was open, as he judged again, wider still, so much so that a diffident helot might have entered with a tray, it seemed a very sea storm seized it and flung it back against the wall. Then he heard strides behind him—quick and resolute—and a voice respectful and youthful, yet deep with a cleanly manhood, addressed him, saying: "Father, I little like to vex you when you are deep in your art. But my heart is sorely troubled and has been so these several days, and I beg you by the love you have for me to suffer my intrusion and counsel me in my difficulties."

Then the student dared turn himself where he sat, and he saw standing before him a youth haughty of port, wide of shoulder, and mighty of thew. Command was in his firm mouth, knowing wit in his bright eyes, and courage in all his face. Upon his brow sat that crown that is invisible to every eye, but can be seen even by the blind; the crown beyond price that draws brave men to a paladin, and makes weak men brave. Then the student said: "My son, have no fear of disturbing me, now or ever, for there is nothing under Heaven that I should rather see than your face. What is it that troubles you?"

"Father," the young man said, "every night for many nights my sleep has been rent with the screams of women, and often I have seen, like a green serpent called by the notes of a pipe, a column of green slip down the cliff below our city to the quay. And sometimes it is vouchsafed me in my dream to go near, and then I see that all who walk in that column are fair women, and that they weep and scream and stagger as they walk, so that I might think them a field of young grain beaten by a moaning wind. What is the meaning of this dream?"

"My son," said the student, "the time has come when I must tell you what I have concealed from you until now, fearing that in the rashness of your youth you might dare too much before the time was ripe. Know that this city is oppressed by an ogre, who each year demands of it its fairest daughters, even as you have seen in your dream."

At this the young man's eyes flashed, and he demanded: "Who is this ogre, and what form has he, and where does he dwell?"

"His name no man knows, for no man can approach near enough. His form is that of a naviscaput, which is to say that to men he appears a ship having upon its deck—which is in truth his shoulders—a single castle, which is his head, and in the castle a single eye. But his body swims in the deep waters with the skate and the shark, with arms longer than the most lofty masts and legs like pilings that reach even to the floor of the sea. His harbor is an isle to the west, where a channel with many a twist and bend, dividing and redividing, reaches far inland. It is on this isle, so my lore teaches me, that the Corn Maidens are made to dwell; and there he rides at anchor in the midst of them, turning his eye ever to left and right to watch them in their despair."

Part III

The Encounter with the Princess

Then the young man fared forth and gathered to him other young men of the city of the magicians to be his crew, and from those who wore the colored hoods he obtained a stout ship, and all that summer he and the young men he had gathered to him armored her, and mounted on her sides the mightiest artillery, and a hundred times practiced the making of sail, and the reefing of sail, and the firing of the guns, until she answered as a blooded mare does to the rein. For the pity they felt for the Corn Maidens, they christened her *Land of Virgins.*

At last, when the golden leaves fell from the sycamores (even as the gold manufactured by magicians falls at last from the hands of men), and the gray salt geese streamed among the pale towers of the city with the lammergeir and the ossifrage screaming after them, the youths set sail. Much befell them on the whale road to the isle of the ogre that has no place here; but at the end of those adventures the lookouts saw before them a country of tawny hills dotted with green; and even as they shaded their eyes to see it, the green grew greater, and greater still. Then the young man whom the student had fleshed from dreams knew that it was indeed the isle of the ogre, and that the Corn Maidens were hastening to the shore for the sight of his sail.

Then were the great guns readied, and the flags of the city of the magicians, that are all of yellow and black, were hung in the rigging. Near they came and nearer, until fearing to run aground they put about and beat along the coast. The Corn Maidens followed them, and following attracted more of their sisterhood until they covered all the land like grain indeed. But the young man did not forget what he had been told: that the ogre lived among the Corn Maidens.

After a half day's sailing, they rounded a point and saw that the coast fell away as a deep channel that did not end, but wound its way among the low hills of the country until it was lost to sight. At the entrance to this channel stood a calotte of white marble surrounded by gardens, and here the young man ordered his companions to cast anchor, and went ashore.

He had no more than set foot on the soil of the isle than there came to meet him a woman of great beauty, swart of skin, black of hair, and luminous of eye. He bowed before her, saying: "Princess or Queen, I see that you are not of the Corn Maidens. Their robes are green; yours is sable. Yet were you to wear a dress of green, I should know you still, for your eyes sorrow not, and the light that is in them is not of Urth."

"You speak truly," the princess said. "For I am Noctua, the daughter of the Night, and the daughter too of him whom you have come to slay."

"Then we cannot be friends, Noctua," said the young man. "But let us not be enemies." For though he did not know why, being of the stuff of dreams he was drawn to her; and she, whose eyes held starlight, to him.

At this the princess spread her hands and declared: "Know that my father took my mother by force, and here holds me against my wishes where I would soon go mad were it not that she comes to me at each day's end. If you do not see sorrow in my eyes, it is only because it lies upon my heart. That I may be free, I shall willingly counsel you how you may engage my father and triumph."

All the young men of the city of the magicians grew quiet and gathered to listen to her.

"First you must understand that the waterways of this isle turn and turn again, in such a way that they can never be charted. You can by no means use sail as you wander them, but must kindle your furnaces ere you go farther."

"I have no fear of that," said the young man fleshed from dreams. "Half a forest was laid waste to fill our bins, and those great wheels you see shall walk these waters with the tread of giants."

At that the princess trembled and said: "Oh, speak not of giants, for you know not what you say. Many ships have come as you have, until the oozy bottoms of all these measureless channels are white with skulls. For it is the custom of my father to allow them to wander among the islets and straits until their fuel is spent—however much it may be—and then, coming upon them by night when he can see them by the glow of their dying fires and they not see him, slay them."

Then the heart of the young man fleshed from dreams was troubled, and he said: "We will seek him as we are sworn, but is there no way in which we may escape the fate of those others?"

At this the princess took pity on him, for all who have the stuff of dreams about them seem fair in some degree at least to the daughters of Night, and he fairest of all. Thus she said: "To find my father before your last stick is burned, you need only search out the darkest water, for wherever he passes his great body raises a foul mud, and by observing it you may discover him. But each day you must begin the search at dawn, and at noon desist; for otherwise you may come upon him by twilight, and it will go evilly with you."

"For this counsel I would have given my life," said the young man, and all his companions who had come ashore with him raised a cheer. "For now we will surely overcome the ogre."

At this the solemn face of the princess became more sober yet, and she said: "No, not surely, for he is a dread antagonist in any sea fight. But I know a stratagem that may aid you. You have said that you came well supplied. Have you tar to pay your ship, should she leak?"

"Many barrels," said the young man.

"Then when you fight, see that the wind blows from yourself to him. And when the fight is hottest—which will not be long after you have joined—have your men cast tar into your furnaces. I cannot promise that it will give you the victory, but it will aid you greatly."

At this all the young men thanked her most extravagantly, and the Corn Maidens, who had stood shyly by while the young man fleshed from dreams and the daughter of Night spoke, raised such a cheer as maidens raise, a cheer not strong, but filled with joy.

Then the young men made ready to depart, kindling the fires in the great furnaces amidships until the white specter was born that drives good ships ahead no matter what wind may blow. And the princess watched them from the strand and gave them her blessing.

But just as the great wheels began to turn, so slowly at first that they appeared scarcely to move, she called the young man fleshed from dreams to the railing, saying: "It may be that you shall find my father. Should you find him, it may be that you shall defeat him, laying low even such prowess as his. Yet even so, you may be sorely vexed to find your way to the sea once more, for the channels of this isle are most wondrously wrought. Yet there is a way. From my father's right hand you must flay the tip of the first finger. There you will see a thousand tangled lines. Be not discouraged, but study it closely; for it is the map he followed in webbing the waterways, that he himself might always have it by him."

Part IV

The Battle with the Ogre

Inland they turned their bow, and even as the princess had foretold, the channel they followed soon divided, and divided again, until there were a thousand forking channels and ten thousand islets. When the shadow of the mainmast was no larger than a hat, the young man fleshed from dreams gave orders that the anchors be cast, and the fires banked, and there, for a long afternoon, they waited, oiling the guns, and readying the powder, and preparing all that might be needful in the hardest fought battle.

At length Night came, and they saw her striding from islet to islet with her bats about her shoulders and her dire wolves dogging her steps. No more than an easy carronade shot from their anchorage she seemed, yet they all observed that she passed not before Hesperus or even Sirius; but they before her. For a moment only she turned her face toward them, and none could be certain what her look conveyed. But all of them wondered if indeed the ogre had taken her without her will as her daughter had said; and if so, if she had not lost the resentment she might be imagined to have felt.

With the first light, the trumpet sounded from the quarterdeck and the banked fires were fed new fuel; but as the dawn breeze stood fair for the channel they held, the young man ordered all plain sail set before the great wheels were ready to take their first step. And when the white specter wakened, the ship pressed forward at double speed.

For many leagues that channel ran, not straight, but near enough that there was no need to furl the sails or even put about. A hundred others crossed it, and at each they studied the water; but each was translucent as crystal. To tell the strange sights they beheld on the islets they passed would require a dozen tales as long as this—women stem-grown like flowers overhung the ship, and in kissing them sought to smear their faces with the powder from their cheeks; men to whom wine had brought death long before lay by springs of wine and drank still, too stupefied to know their lives were past; beasts that would be omens to future times, with twisted limbs and fur of colors never seen, waited the nearer approach of battles, earthquakes, and the murders of kings.

At last the youth who stood first mate to the young man fleshed from dreams approached him where he waited near the steersman, saying: "Far we have traveled on this channel already, and the sun, that had not shown his face when we bent our sails, approaches his zenith. Following it, we have crossed a thousand others, and none has shone a trace of the ogre. May it not be that it is an unlucky course we take? Would not it be wiser to turn aside soon and try another?"

Then the young man answered: "Even now we pass a channel to starboard. Look down, and tell me if its waters are more soiled than our own."

The youth did as he was bid, and said: "Nay, clearer."

"Soon now, another opens to port. To what depth can you see?"

The youth waited until the ship stood opposite the channel of which the young man spoke, and then he answered: "To the utmost. I see the wreck of a ship of long time past, many a fathom down."

"And can you see so far in this channel we sail now?"

Then the youth looked at the waters they cleaved, and they were become as ink; and the very splatters that flew from the laboring wheels might have been rooks and ravens. At once understanding came to him, and he shouted to all the others to stand by the guns, for he could not tell them to make ready, who had made ready so long before.

Ahead lay an islet higher than most, crowned with tall and somber trees; and here the channel bent gently, so that the wind, that had been dead astern, was at the quarter. The steersman shifted his grip on the wheel, and the watch payed out certain sheets and tightened others, and the ship's prow came around the quick curve of the cliff, and there before them lay a long hull of narrow beam, with a single castle of iron amidships and a single gun larger than any they carried thrusting from its one embrasure.

Then the young man fleshed from dreams opened his lips to shout to the bow-chaser crews that they should fire. Before the words could be spoken, the great gun of their enemy roared, and its sound was not as thunder or as any other sound familiar to the ears of men; but rather, it seemed that they had stood in a tall tower of stone, and it had fallen all around them in a moment.

And the ball of that shot struck the breech of the first gun of their starboard battery, and striking it broke it to pieces and shattered itself as well, so that the fragments of the breaking of both scattered through the ship like dark leaves before a great wind, and many died thereby.

Then the steersman, waiting no order, swung the ship about until her port battery bore, and the guns fired each by the will of the man that pointed it, as wolves howl at the moon. And their shots flew about the single castle of the enemy to either side, and some struck it so that it tolled knells for those who had perished a moment before, and some struck the water before the hull that bore it, and some struck the deck (which was of iron also) and at that contact fled shrieking into the sky.

Then the single gun of their enemy spoke again.

And so it continued, in moments that seemed whole years of time. At last the young man bethought him of the advice of the princess, the daughter of Night; but though the wind blew strong, it was hardly more than astern of his ship, and if he were to shift until it blew from him to his enemy (as the princess had counseled) for many moments no gun would bear but the bow chasers, and then when a battery might be brought to bear, it would be the starboard, of which one gun was destroyed and so many men dead.

But it came to him in that moment that they fought as a hundred others had fought, and that these hundred others were all dead, their ships sunk and their bones scattered among the myriad channels that whorled and tangled the face of the isle of the ogre. Then he gave his order to the steersman; but none answered, for he was dead, and the wheel he had held, held him. So seeing, the young man fleshed from dreams took the spokes in his own hands and presented to their enemy the ship's narrow bow. Then it was seen how the three sisters favor the bold, for the next shot from their enemy, that might have raked her from stem to stern, went to port by the length of an oar. And the next, to starboard by the width of a boat.

Now their enemy, who had stood fast before, neither seeking to fly nor to close, swung about. Seeing that he would escape them if he could, the crew raised a great shout as though already they had won the victory. But marvelous to see, the single castle, which all had until then believed fixed, swung about the other way, so that its great gun, that was greater than any of their own, still bore.

A moment later and its ball had struck them amidships, dashing a gun of the starboard battery from its truck as a drunken man might fling an infant from its cradle and sending it skittering across the deck and smashing everything in its path. Then the guns of the battery—those that remained—spoke all in a chorus of fire and iron. And because the distance was now less than half what it had been (or perhaps only because their enemy, having shown fear, had weakened the fabric of his being), their shot no longer struck his castle with an empty clanging, but with a cracking as though the bell that will toll the end of the world were breaking; and ragged flaws sprang to life on the oiled blackness of the iron.

Then the young man shouted into the gosport to those who had remained faithfully in the engine room feeding the furnaces with treewrack, telling them to cast tar into the flames as the princess had counseled them. At first he feared that all there were dead, then that the order was not understood in the din of battle. But a shadow fell upon the sun-brightened water that stretched between their enemy and himself, and he looked upward.

In ancient times, so it is said, a tattered child, the daughter of a fisherman, found on the sand a stoppered flask, and by breaking the seal and drawing forth the cork became queen from ice to ice. Just so, it seemed, an elemental being, strong with the strength of the forging of creation, debouched from the tall smokestacks of their ship, tumbling over himself in dark joy and growing with a rush, as the wind comes.

And the wind came indeed, and it seized him with its uncounted hands and bore him as a solid mass down upon their enemy. Even when nothing more could be seen—neither the long, dark hull with its deck of iron, nor the single guns whose mouth had spoken words to doom them—they wasted no moment, but fell to their guns and fired into the blackness. And from time to time they heard the gun of their enemy also firing; but no flash did they see, and where those shots struck they could not say.

It may be they have struck nothing yet, and still circle round the world seeking their target.

They fired until the barrels shone like ingots newly come from the crucible. Then the smoke that had poured forth so long diminished, and those below shouted by the gosport that all the tar was consumed, and the young man fleshed from dreams ordered that firing cease, and the men who had worked the guns fell upon the deck like so many corpses, too exhausted even to beg water.

The black cloud melted. Not as fog melts in the sun, but as an army strong to evil dissolves before repeated charges, giving here, stubbornly standing there, still mustering a wisp of skirmishers when it seems all has given way.

In vain then they searched the new-polished waves for their enemy. Nothing could they see: not his hull, nor his castle, nor his gun, nor any plank or spar.

Slowly, so cautiously it might have been thought they feared an unseen foe, they advanced to the very spot where he had lain at anchor, noting the shattered trees and furrowed ground of the islet beyond, where their shot had spent its energies. When they were over the point at which that long iron hull had lain, the young man fleshed from dreams ordered the great wheels reversed, and at last halted, so that they rested as quietly as their opponent had. Then he strode to the rail and looked down; but with such an expression that no one, not even the most brave, dared to look at him.

When he lifted his eyes at last, his face was set and grim, and with no word to any man he took himself to his cabin and barred the door. Then the youth that was second to him ordered the ship put about, that they might return to the white calotte of the princess; and he ordered also that wounds be bandaged, and pumps set in motion, and such repairs as could be made begun. But the dead he kept with them, that they might be buried on the high sea.

Part V

The Death of the Student

It may be that the channel was not so straight as they believed. Or that they had lost their bearings in the fight, without being aware thereof. Or that the channels twisted (as some alleged) like worms in a litch, when no eye was upon them. Whatever the truth might be, all day they steamed—for the wind had died away—and by the last light saw only that they cruised among islets unknown.

All night they lay to. When morning came, the youth called to him such others as he felt might offer the most valuable counsel; but none of them could suggest anything save calling upon the young men fleshed from dreams (which they were loath to do) or pressing onward until they reached open waters or the calotte of the princess.

That they did all day, striving to hold a straight course, but winding against their will among the many turnings of the channels. And when night came again, their position was no better than before.

But on the morning of the third day, the young man fleshed from dreams came out of his cabin and began to walk up and down the decks as he was wont to do, examining such repairs as they had made to their damage and asking those wounded who by the pain of their wounds were awake early how they fared. Then the youth and those who had advised him came to him, and they explained all that they had done and asked how they might find the sea again, that they might bury the dead and return to their homes in the city of the magicians.

At this he looked up into the very vault of the firmament. And some thought he prayed, and some that he sought to restrain the anger he felt against them, and some only that he hoped to gain inspiration there. But so long did he stare that they waxed afraid, even as they had when he had peered into the water, and one or two began to creep away. Then he said to them: "Behold! Do you not see the sea birds? From every corner of the sky they stream. Follow them."

Until morning was nearly done, they followed the birds insofar as the winding channels permitted. And at last they saw them wheeling and diving at the water ahead, so their white wings and ebon heads seemed a cloud low hung in their course, a cloud fair without but thunderous within. Then the young man fleshed from dreams told them to load a carronade with powder only, and to fire it; and at the crash of the gun all those sea birds rose mewing and crying. And where they had been, the crew saw a great piece of carrion floating, which seemed to them to have been a beast of the land, for it had, as they thought, a head and legs four. But it was greater than many elephants.

When they were near, the young man ordered the boat put into the water, and when he climbed aboard they saw that he had thrust into his belt a great alfange whose blade caught the sun. For a time he labored over the carrion, and when he returned he carried a chart, the largest any of them had seen, drawn upon untanned hide.

By dark they reached the calotte of the princess. All waited on board while her mother visited her; but when that terrible woman was gone, all who could walk went ashore, and the Corn Maidens crowded about them, a hundred to each youth, and the young man fleshed from dreams took the daughter of Night into his arms and led them all in dances. None of them ever forgot that night.

The dew found them beneath the trees of the princess' garden, half smothered in flowers. For a time they slept so, but when afternoon threw backward the shadows of their masts they were awake. Then the princess bade farewell to the isle and swore that though she might visit every country over which her mother strode, she never would return there; and the Corn Maidens swore likewise. Too many of them there were, perhaps, for the ship to hold; yet it held them, so that all the decks were green with their gowns and gold with their hair. Many adventures they had in making their way back to the city of the magicians. This tale might tell how they cast their dead into the sea with prayers, yet afterward saw them in the rigging by night; or how certain of the Corn Maidens wed those princes who, having spent years so long enchanted that they are loath to leave that life (and have in that time learned much of gramary), build palaces on lily pads and are seldom seen by men.

But all those things have no place here. Be it sufficient to say that as they neared the cliff at whose top stands the city of the magicians, the student who had fleshed the young man from dreams stood on the battlements, watching for them over the sea. And when he beheld their dark sails, smutted by the burning tar that had blinded their enemy, he believed them blackened in mourning for the young man, and he threw himself down, and so perished. For no man lives long when his dreams are dead.

XVIII

Mirrors

As I read this idle tale I looked at Jonas from time to time, but I never saw the least flicker of expression on his face, though he did not sleep. When it was complete, I said, ‘‘I’m not certain I understand why the student at once assumed his son was dead when he saw the black sails. The ship the ogre sent had black sails, but it came only once a year, and had already come.’’

‘‘I know,’’ Jonas said. His voice held a flatness I had not heard before.

‘‘Do you mean you know the answers to those questions?’’

He did not reply, and for a time we sat in silence, I with the brown book (so insistently evocative of Thecla and the evenings we had shared) still held open by a forefinger, he with his back to the cold wall of the prison room, and his hands, one of metal, one of flesh, lying to either side as though he had forgotten them.

At last a small voice ventured to say, ‘‘That must be a really old story.’’ It was the little girl who had lifted the ceiling tile for me.

I was so concerned for Jonas that for a moment I was angry at her for interrupting us; but Jonas muttered, ‘‘Yes, it is a very old story, and the hero had told the king, his father, that if he failed he would return to Athens with black sails.’’ I am not sure what that remark meant, and it may have been delirium; but since it was almost the last thing I heard Jonas say, I feel I should record it here, as I have transcribed the wonder-tale that prompted it.

For a time both the girl and I endeavored to persuade him to speak again. He would not, and at last we desisted. I spent the remainder of the day sitting beside him, and after a watch or so Hethor (whose small store of wit—as I supposed—had soon been exhausted by the prisoners) came to join us. I had a word with Lomer and Nicarete, and they arranged that his sleeping place should be on the opposite side of the room.

Whatever we may say, all of us suffer from disturbed sleep at times. Some in truth hardly sleep, though some who sleep copiously swear that they do not. Some are disquieted by incessant dreams, and a fortunate few are visited often by dreams of delightful character. Some will say they were at one time troubled in sleeping but have "recovered" from it, as though awareness were a disease, as perhaps it is.

My own case is that I usually sleep without memorable dreams (though I sometimes have them, as the reader who has gone this far with me will know) and seldom wake before morning. But on this night my sleep was so different from its usual nature that I have sometimes wondered if it should be called sleep at all. Perhaps it was some other state posing as sleep, as alzabos, when they have eaten of men, pose as men.

If it was the result of natural causes, I attribute it to a combination of unfortunate circumstances. I, who had all my life been accustomed to hard work and violent exercise, had for that day been confined without either. The tale from the brown book had affected my imagination—which was still more stimulated by the book itself and its associations with Thecla, and by the knowledge that I was now within the walls of the House Absolute itself, of which I had heard her speak so often. Possibly most important, my thoughts were oppressed by worry for Jonas, and by the feeling (which had been growing on me all day) that this place was the end of my journey; that I would never reach Thrax; that I would never rejoin poor Dorcas; that I would never restore the Claw, or even rid myself of it; that in fact the Increate, whom the owner of the Claw had served, had decreed that I who had seen so many prisoners die should end my own life as one.

I slept, if it may be called sleep, only for a moment. I had the sensation of falling; a spasm, the instinctive stiffening of a victim cast from a high window, wrenched all my limbs. When I sat up, I could see nothing but darkness. I heard Jonas's breathing, and my fingers told me he was still sitting as I had left him, his back propped by the wall. I lay down and slept again.

Or rather, I tried to sleep, and passed into that vague state that is neither sleeping nor waking. At other times I have found it pleasant, but it was not so now—I was conscious of the need for sleep, and conscious that I was not sleeping. Yet I was not "conscious" in the usual meaning of that term. I heard faint voices in the innyard, and felt, somehow, that soon the bells of the campanile would chime, and it would be day. My limbs jerked again, and I sat up.

For a moment I imagined I had seen a flash of green fire, but there was nothing. I had covered myself with my cloak; I threw it off, and in the instant it took to do so remembered that I was in the antechamber of the House Absolute, and that I had left the inn of Saltus far behind, though Jonas lay beside me still, on his back, his good hand behind his head. The pale blur I saw was the white of his right eye, though the sighing of his breath was that of one who slept. I was still too much asleep myself to wish to talk, and I had a presentiment that he would not answer me in any case.

Lying down again, I surrendered myself to my irritation at being unable to sleep. I thought of the herd driven through Saltus and counted them from memory: one hundred and thirty-seven. Then there were the soldiers who had come singing up from Gyoll. The innkeeper had asked me how many there were and I had guessed at a figure, but I had never counted them until now. He might, or might not, have been a spy.

Master Palaemon, who had taught us so much, had never taught us how to sleep—no apprentice had ever needed to learn that after a day of errands and scrubbing and kitchen work. We had rioted each night for half a watch in our quarters, then slept like the citizens of the necropolis until he came to wake us to polishing floors and emptying slops.

There is a rack of knives over the table where Brother Aybert slices meat. One, two, three, four, five, six, seven knives, all with plainer blades than Master Gurloes's. One with a rivet missing from its handle. One with a handle a little burned because Brother Aybert had once laid it on the stove. . . .

I was wide awake again, or thought I was, and I did not know why. Beside me Drotte slumbered undisturbed. I closed my eyes once more and tried to sleep as he did.

Three hundred and ninety steps from the ground to our dormitory. How many more to the room where the guns throbbed at the top of the tower? One, two, three, four, five, six guns. One, two, three levels of cells in use in the oubliette. One, two, three, four, five, six, seven, eight wings on each level. One, two, three, four, five, six, seven, eight, nine, ten, eleven, twelve, thirteen, fourteen, fifteen, sixteen, seventeen cells in each wing. One, two, three bars on the little window of my cell's door.

I woke with a start and a sensation of cold, but the sound that had disturbed me was only the slamming of one of the hatches far down the corridor. Beside me, my boy lover, Severian, lay in the easy sleep of youth. I sat up thinking I would light my candle and look for a moment at the fresh coloring of that chiseled face. Each time he returned to me, he carried a speck of freedom glowing on that face. Each time I took it and blew upon it, and held it to my breast, and each time it pined and died; yet sometime it would not, and then instead of sinking deeper under this load of earth and metal, I would rise through metal and earth to the wind and the sky.

Or so I told myself. If it was not true, still the only joy remaining to me was to gather in that speck.

But when I groped for the candle it was gone, and my eyes and my ears and the very skin of my face told me that my cell itself had vanished with it. There was dim light here—very dim, but not the light from the candle of the torturer in the corridor, the light that filtered through the three bars of my cell's hatch. Faint echoes proclaimed that I was in an area larger than a hundred such cells; my cheeks and forehead, which had worn themselves away in signaling the nearness of my walls, confirmed it.

I stood and smoothed my gown, and began to walk almost as a somnambulist might . . . One, two, three, four, five, six, seven strides, then the odor of close-kept bodies and confined air told me where I was. It was the antechamber! I felt a wrench of dislocation. Had the Autarch ordered me carried here while I slept? Would the others spare their lashes when they saw me? The door! The door!

My confusion was so great I nearly fell, borne down by the jumble of my mind.

I wrung my hands, but the hands I wrung were not my own. My right hand felt a hand too large and too strong, and at the same instant my left hand felt a similar hand.

Thecla fell from me like a dream. Or I should say, dwindled to nothing, and in dwindling vanished within me until I was myself again, and nearly alone.

Yet I had caught it. The location of the door, the secret door through which the young exultants came by night with their energized lashes of braided wire, was still in my memory. With everything else I have seen or thought. I could escape tomorrow. Or now.

"Please," a voice beside me said, "where did the lady go?"

It was the child again, the little girl with the dark hair and the staring eyes. I asked her if she had seen a woman.

She took my hand in her own tiny one. "Yes, a tall lady, and I'm scared. There's a horrible thing in the dark. Did it find her?"

"You're not afraid of horrible things, remember? You laughed at the green face."

"This is different, a black thing that snuffles in the dark." There was real terror in her voice, and the hand that held mine shook.

"What did the lady look like?"

"I don't know. I could only see her because she was darker than the shadows, but I could tell she was a lady by the way she walked. When I came to see who it was, there was nobody here but you."

"I understand," I told her, "though I doubt that you ever will. Now you must return to your mother and go to sleep."

"It's coming along the wall," she said. Then she released my hand and vanished, but I am sure she did not do as I told her. Instead, she must have followed Jonas and me, for I have glimpsed her twice since I returned here to the House Absolute, where no doubt she exists on stolen food. (It is possible she used to return to the antechamber to eat, but I have ordered that all the people confined there are to be freed, even if it is necessary—as I think it will be—to drive most of them forth at pike point. I have also ordered that Nicarete be brought to me, and when I was writing of our capture, a moment ago, my chamberlain entered to say she waited my pleasure.)

Jonas lay as I had left him, and again I saw the whites of his eyes in the dark. "You said it was necessary to go if you were to remain sane," I told him. "Come. The sender of the notules, whoever that may be, has laid his hands upon another weapon. I have found the way out, and we are going now."

He did not move, and at last I had to take him by the arm and lift him up. Many of those parts of him that were metal must have been forged from those white alloys that deceive the hand by their lightness, for it was like lifting a boy; but the metal parts, and his flesh as well, had been wetted with some thin slime. My foot found the same filthy dampness on the floor nearby and on the wall itself. Whatever it was the child had warned me of had come and gone while I spoke with her, and it had not been for Jonas that it had searched.

The door by which the tormentors entered was not far from our sleeping place, in the center of the rearmost wall of the antechamber. It was unlocked by a word of power, as such ancient things almost always are. I whispered, and we passed through the hidden portal and left it standing open, poor Jonas striding beside me like a thing wholly metal.

A narrow stairway, festooned with the webs of pale spiders and carpeted with dust, led by circuitous turnings downward. That much I recalled, but beyond the stair I could remember nothing. Whatever might come, the stale air tasted of freedom, so that merely to breathe it was pleasure. Worried though I was, I could have laughed aloud.

Secret doors opened at many landings, but there seemed a chance and more than a chance that we might encounter someone as soon as we entered one, and the stair seemed deserted. Before I was seen by any resident of the House Absolute, I wished to be as far from the antechamber as possible.

We had descended perhaps a hundred steps when we reached a door painted with a crimson teratoid sign that appeared to me to be a glyph from some tongue beyond the shores of Urth. At that moment I heard a tread upon the stair. There was neither knob nor latch, but I threw myself against the door, and after an initial resistance it flew open. Jonas followed me; it shut behind us so quickly that it seemed it should have made a great noise, though there was none.

The chamber beyond the door was dim, but the light grew brighter when he had entered. After I had made certain there was no one present but ourselves, I made use of this light to examine him. His face was still fixed, as it had been when he sat with the wall of the antechamber at his back, yet it was not the lifeless thing I had feared. It was the face, almost, of a man about to wake, and tears had left moist furrows down his cheeks.

"Do you know me?" I asked, and he nodded without speaking. "Jonas, I must recover *Terminus Est*, if I can. I've run like any coward, but now that I've had a chance to think, I see I must go back for her. My letter to the archon of Thrax is in her scabbard pocket, and I couldn't bear to part with her anyway. But if you want to try to escape this place, I'll understand. You're not bound to me."

He did not appear to have heard. "I know where we are," he said, and raised one arm stiffly to point toward something I had taken to be a folding screen.

I was delighted to hear his voice, and largely in the hope that he would speak again, I asked, "Where are we, then?"

"On Urth," he answered, and strode across the room to the folded panels. Their backs were set with clustered diamonds, as I now saw, and enameled with such twisted signs as had been on the door. Yet these signs were no stranger than the actions of my friend Jonas when he threw the panels open. The rigidity I had remarked in him only a moment before was gone—yet he had not returned to his old self.

It was then that I knew. We have all watched someone who has lost one hand (as he had) and replaced it with a hook or some other artificial contrivance perform some task that involves both his real hand and the artificial one. So it was with Jonas when I watched him pull back the panels; but the prosthetic hand was the hand of flesh. When I understood that, I understood what he had said much earlier:that in the wreck of his ship his face had been destroyed.

I said, "The eyes . . . They could not replace your eyes. Is that right? And so they gave you that face. Was he killed too?"

He looked about at me in a way that told me he had forgotten I was present. "He was on the ground," he said. "We killed him by accident, coming in. I needed his eyes and larynx, and I took some other parts."

"That was why you were able to tolerate me, a torturer. You are a machine."

"You are no worse than the rest of your kind. Remember that for years before I met you, I had become one of you. Now I am worse than you. You would not have left me, but I am leaving you. Now I have the chance, and it is the chance I sought for years as I went up and down the seven continents of this world seeking the Hierodules and tinkering with clumsy mechanisms."

I thought of all that had happened since I had carried the knife to Thecla; and though I did not follow everything he had said, I told him, "If it is your only chance, then go, and good luck. If I ever see Jolenta, I will tell her you once loved her, and nothing more."

Jonas shook his head. "Don't you understand? I will come back for her when I have been repaired. When I am sane and whole."

Then he stepped into the circle of panels, and a brilliant light kindled in the air above his head.

How foolish to call them mirrors. They are to mirrors as the enveloping firmament is to a child's balloon. They reflect light indeed; but that, I think, is no part of their true function. They reflect reality, the metaphysical substance that underlies the material world.

Jonas closed the circle and moved to its center. For perhaps the time of the briefest prayer, something of wires and flashing, metallic dust danced above the tops of the panels before all was gone and I was alone.

XIX

Closets

I was alone, and I had not been truly alone since I had entered his room in the tumbledown city inn and seen Baldanders's broad shoulders above the blankets. There had been Dr. Talos, then Agia, then Dorcas, then Jonas. The disease of memory gained upon me, and I saw the sharp silhouette of Dorcas, the giant, and the others as I had seen them when Jonas and I were being led through the plum grove. There had been men with animals as well and performers of other kinds, all of them no doubt going to that part of the grounds where (as Thecla had often told me) the outdoor entertainments were held.

I began to search the room with some vague hope of finding my sword. It was not there, and it struck me that there was probably some repository near the antechamber where the goods of the prisoners were kept—most likely on the same level. The stair I had come down would only lead me into the antechamber itself again; the exit from the room of the mirrors took me only to another room, one in which curious objects were stored. Eventually I found a door that opened onto a dark and quiet corridor, carpeted and hung with paintings. I put on my mask and drew my cloak about me, thinking that though the guards who had seized us in the wood had not seemed to know of the existence of the guild, those I might encounter in the halls of the House Absolute itself might not be so ignorant.

In the event, I was never challenged. A man in rich and elaborate clothing drew aside, and several lovely women stared at me curiously; I felt Thecla's memories stirring at the sight of their faces. At last I found another stair—not narrow and secretive like the one that had taken Jonas and me to the chamber of mirrors, but a broad, open flight of wide steps.

I ascended some distance, reconnoitered the corridor there until I was certain I was still lower than the antechamber, then began to climb again when I saw a young woman hurrying down the stair toward me.

Our eyes met.

In that moment, I feel sure, she was as conscious as I that we had exchanged glances thus before. In memory I heard her say again, "My dearest sister," in that cooing voice, and the heartshaped face sprang into place. It was not Thea, the consort of Vodalus, but the woman who looked like her (and no doubt borrowed her name) whom I had passed on the stair in the House Azure—she descending and I climbing, just as we were now. Harlots then, as well as entertainers, had been summoned for whatever fete was being organized.

Almost purely by chance, I discovered the level of the antechamber. I had no sooner left the stair than I realized I was standing almost precisely where the hastarii had stood while Nicarete and I talked beside the silver cart. This was the point of greatest danger, and I was careful to walk slowly. The wall on my right held a dozen or more doors, each framed in carved woodwork, and each (as I saw when I stopped to examine them) spiked to its frame and sealed with the varnish of years. On my left, the only door was the great one of worm-gnawed oak through which the soldiers had dragged Jonas and me. Opposite it was the entrance to the antechamber, and beyond that stretched another row of spiked doors like the first, at the end of which was another stair. It appeared that the antechamber had grown to occupy all of this level of this wing of the House Absolute.

If there had been anyone in sight, I would not have dared to pause; but since the corridor was empty, I ventured to lean for a moment against the newel post of the second stair. While two soldiers had guarded me, a third had carried *Terminus Est*. It was reasonable to suppose that as Jonas and I were being put through the doorway of the antechamber, this third man would have taken the first few steps at least toward wherever it was that such captured weapons were kept. But I could remember nothing; the soldier had dropped behind when we descended the steps of the grotto, and I had not seen him again. It was possible, even, that he had not come in with us.

In desperation, I returned to the worm-gnawed door and opened it. The musty odor of the well entered the corridor at once, and I heard the song of the green gongs begin. Outside, the world was plunged in night. Save for the corpse candles of the fungi, the rugged walls were invisible, and only a circle of stars overhead showed where the well dropped into the earth.

I closed the door; no sooner had it grated shut than I heard the sound of footsteps on the stair up which I myself had come. There was no place to hide, and if I had darted for the second stair I would have had little chance of reaching it before I was seen. Rather than attempt to duck out through the heavy oak door and close it once more, I decided to remain where I was.

The newcomer was a plump man of fifty or so dressed in livery. Even down the length of the corridor, I saw his face pale at the sight of me. He came hurrying toward me, however, and when he was still twenty or thirty paces off he began to bow, saying, "Can I help you, your honor? I am Odilo, the steward here. You, I can see, are on a mission of some confidence to . . . Father Inire?"

"Yes," I said. "But first I must require my sword of you."

I had hoped that he had seen *Terminus Est* and would produce her for me, but he looked blank.

"I was escorted here earlier. At that time I was told that I would have to surrender my sword, but that it would be restored to me before Father Inire required me to use it."

The little man was shaking his head. "I assure you, in my position I would have been informed if any of the other servants—"

"I was told this by a praetorian," I said.

"Ah, I ought to have known. They've been everywhere, answering to no one. We have an escaped prisoner, your honor, as I suppose you've heard."

"No."

"A man called Beuzec. They say he's not dangerous, but he and another fellow were found lurking in an arbor. This Beuzec made a dash for it before they locked him up, and got away. They say they'll take him soon; I don't know. I'll tell you, I've lived in our House Absolute all my life, and it has some strange corners—some very strange corners."

"Possibly my sword is in one of them. Will you look?"

He took a half step back, as though I had raised my hand to him. "Oh, I will, Your Honor, I will. I was only trying to make a bit of conversation. It's probably down here. If you'll just follow me . . ."

We walked toward the other stair, and I saw that in my hasty search I had overlooked one door, a narrow one beneath the staircase. It was painted white, so that it was almost of the same shade as the stone.

The steward produced a heavy ring of keys and opened this door. The triangular room inside was much larger than I would have guessed, reaching far back beneath the steps and boasting a sort of loft, accessible by a shaky ladder, toward the rear. Its lamp was of the same type as those I had noticed in the antechamber, but dimmer.

"Do you see it?" the steward asked. "Wait, there's a candle about here somewhere, I think. That one light's not much use, the shelves throw such heavy shadows."

I was examining the shelves as he spoke. They were piled with clothing, with here and there a pair of shoes, a pocket fork, a pen case, a pommander ball.

"When I was just a lad myself, the kitchen boys used to pick the lock and come in here to rummage about. I put a stop to that—got a good lock—but I'm afraid the best things disappeared long ago."

"What is this place?"

"A closet for petitioners, originally. Coats, hats, and boots—you know. Those places always fill up with the things the lucky ones forget to take with them when they go, and then this wing has always been Father Inire's, and I suppose there's always been some that came to see him that never came back out, as well as the ones that come out what never came in." He paused and glanced around. "I had to give the soldiers keys to keep them from kicking down the doors when they were searching for this Beuzec, so I suppose they might have put your sword in here. If they didn't, they probably took it up to their guardroom. This wouldn't be it, I don't imagine?" From a corner he drew out an ancient spadone.

"Hardly."

"It seems to be the only sword here, I'm afraid. I can give you directions for getting to the guardroom. Or I can wake up one of the pages to go and ask, if you like."

The ladder to the loft was shaky, but I scrambled up it after borrowing the steward's candle. Though it seemed exceedingly improbable that the soldier had put *Terminus Est* there, I wanted a few moments to think over the courses of action open to me.

As I climbed I heard a slight noise from above that I supposed was the scurrying of some rodent; but when I thrust my head and the candle above the level of the loft's floor, I saw the small man who had been with Hethor on the road kneeling in an attitude of intense supplication. That was Beuzec, of course; I had failed to recall the name until I saw him.

"Anything up there, your honor?"

"Rags. Rats."

"Just as I thought," the steward said as I stepped from the last rung. "I should have a look myself sometime, but one isn't anxious to climb a thing like that at my age. Would you like to go to the guardroom yourself, or shall I rouse one of the boys?"

"I'll go."

He nodded sagaciously. "That's best, I think. They might not hand it over to a page, or even admit they had it. You're in the Hypogeum Apotropaic now, as I suppose you know. If you don't want to be stopped by the patrols, you had better go indoors, so the best plan would be to go up this stairway we're standing under for three flights, then left. Follow the gallery around for about a thousand paces until you come to the hypethral. With it dark out you might miss it, so keep an eye open for the plants. Turn right in there and go another two hundred paces. There's always a sentry at the door."

I thanked him and managed to get ahead of him on the stair by leaving while he was still fumbling with the lock, then stepped into a corridor off the first landing I reached and allowed him to go past me. When he was well out of the way, I went down again to the corridor of the antechamber.

It seemed to me that if my sword had indeed been carried off to some guardroom, it was very unlikely that I could recover it save by stealth or violence, and I wished to assure myself that it had not been left in some more accessible place before I attempted either. Then too, it seemed possible that Beuzec had seen it in the course of his creeping and hiding, and I wanted to question him about it.

At the same time, I was very much concerned about the prisoners of the antechamber. By that time (as I imagined) they would have discovered the door Jonas and I had left open for them, and would be spreading through this wing of the House Absolute. It could not be long before one was recaptured and a search began for the others.

When I reached the door of the closet beneath the stair, I pressed my ear to the panel hoping to hear Beuzec moving about. There was no sound. I called him softly by name without eliciting a response, then tried to push the door open with my shoulder. It would not budge, and I was afraid to make noise by running against it. At last I managed to wedge the steel Vodalus had given me between the door and the jamb, and so split out the lock.

Beuzec was gone. After a short search I discovered a hole in the back of the closet that opened into the hollow center of some wall. From there he must have crept into the closet looking for a place large enough for him to stretch his limbs, and to there he had fled again. It is said that in the House Absolute such recesses are inhabited by a species of white wolf that slunk in from the surrounding forests long ago. Perhaps he fell prey to these creatures; I have not seen him since.

That night I did not seek to follow him, but pulled the closet door into place and concealed the damage to the lock as well as I could. It was only then that I noticed the symmetry of the corridor: the entrance to the antechamber in the center, the sealed doors to either side of it, the staircases at either end. If this hypogeum had been set aside for Father Inire (as the steward had said and its name indicated) its selection might have been due, at least in part, to this mirror-image quality. If that were so, then there should certainly be a second closet beneath the other stair.

XX

Pictures

The question was why Odilo the steward had not taken me there; but I did not pause to think on it while I sprinted along the corridor, and when I arrived the answer was plain enough. That door had been broken long before—not just the socket of the lock, but the entire thing smashed so that only two discolored fragments of wood clinging to the hinges showed there had ever been a door there. The lamp within had gone out, leaving the interior to darkness and spiders.

I had actually turned away from it and taken a step or two before I stopped, under the influence of that consciousness of error that often comes to us before we understand in the least in what the error consists. Jonas and I had been thrust into the antechamber late in the afternoon. That night the young exultants had come with their whips. The next morning Hethor had been taken, and at that time, it seemed, Beuzec had bolted from the praetorians, who had been given keys by the steward so they might search the hypogeum for him. When the same steward, Odilo, had met me a few moments before, and I had told him that *Terminus Est* had been taken from me by a praetorian, he had assumed I had come during the day, after Beuzec's escape.

In point of fact, I had not; and therefore, the praetorian who had been carrying *Terminus Est* could not have put her in the locked closet beneath the second stair.

I went back to the closet with the broken door again. By the scant light that filtered in from the corridor, it was apparent that it had once been lined with shelves like its twin; its interior was bare now, the shelving having been stripped away to serve some new use, leaving the shelf brackets to thrust fruitlessly from the walls. I could see no other object of any kind, but I could also see that no guardsman who had to stand inspection would willingly have set foot among its dust and cobwebs. Without bothering to thrust my own head inside, I reached around the jamb of the broken door, and—with an indescribable mingling of triumph and familiarity—felt my hand close upon the beloved hilt.

I was a whole man again. Or rather, more than a man: a journeyman of the guild. There in the corridor I verified that my letter remained in the pocket of the sheath, then drew the shining blade, wiped it, oiled it, and wiped it again, testing its edges with finger and thumb as I walked along. Now let the hunter in the dark appear.

My next objective was to rejoin Dorcas, but I knew nothing of the location of Dr. Talos's company except that they were to perform at a thiasus held in a garden—no doubt one of many gardens. If I went outside now, by night, it would perhaps be as difficult for the praetorians to see me in my fuligin as for me to see them. But I was unlikely to find any aid; and when the eastern horizon dropped below the sun, I would no doubt be apprehended as promptly as Jonas and I had been when we rode onto the grounds. If I stayed within the House Absolute itself, my experience with the steward indicated I might well pass unchallenged, and I might even come across someone who would give me information; indeed, I hit upon the plan of telling anyone I met that I had been summoned to the celebration myself (I supposed it was not unlikely that an excruciation would be a part of the festivities) and that I had left the sleeping quarters assigned to me and lost my way. In that fashion, I might discover where Dorcas and the rest were staying.

Thinking upon this plan I mounted the stair, and at the second landing turned off down a corridor I had not seen previously. It was far longer and more sumptuously furnished than the one before the antechamber. Dark pictures in gold frames hung on the walls, and urns and busts and objects for which I knew no names stood on pedestals between them. The doors opening off the corridor were a hundred or more paces apart, indicating huge rooms beyond; but all were locked, and when I tried their handles I found that they were of a form and metal unknown to me, not shaped to be grasped by human fingers.

When I had walked down this corridor for what seemed at least half a league, I saw someone ahead of me sitting (as I first thought) upon a high stool. As I drew nearer, I found that what I had taken to be a stool was a stepladder, and that the old man perched on it was cleaning one of the pictures. "Excuse me," I said.

He turned and peered down at me in puzzlement. "Know your voice, don't I?"

Then I knew his, and his face as well. It was Rudesind the curator, the old man I had met so long before, when Master Gurloes had first sent me to fetch books for the Chatelaine Thecla.

"While ago you come looking for Ultan. Didn't you find him?"

"Yes, I found him," I said. "But it wasn't a short time ago."

He seemed to grow angry at that. "I didn't mean today! But it wasn't long. Why, I recollect the landscape I was working on, so it couldn't have been that long."

"So do I," I told him. "Brown desert reflected in the gold visor of a man in armor."

He nodded, and his anger seemed to melt away. Gripping the sides of the ladder, he began to descend, his sponge still in his hand. "Exactly. Exactly the one. Want me to show it to you? It come out very nice."

"We're not in the same place, Master Rudesind. That was in the Citadel. This is the House Absolute."

The old man ignored that. "Come out nice . . . It's down here a ways, somewhere. Those old artists—you couldn't beat 'em for drawing, though their colors has gone off now. And let me tell you, I know art. I've seen armigers, and exultants too, that come and look at them and say this and that, but they don't know a thing. Who's looked at every little bit of these pictures up close?" He thumped his own bosom with the sponge, then bent close to me, whispering though there was no one but ourselves in the long corridor. "Now I'll tell you a secret they don't none of them know—one of these is me!"

To be polite, I said I would like to see it.

"I'm looking for it, and when I find it I'll tell you where. They don't know, but that's why I clean them all the time. Why, I could have retired. But I'm still here, and I work longer than any, except maybe Ultan. He can't see the watchglass." The old man gave a long, cracked laugh.

"I wonder if you could help me. There are performers here who have been summoned for the thiasus. Do you know where they're quartered?"

"I've heard tell of it," he said doubtfully. "The Green Room is what they call it."

"Can you take me there?"

He shook his head. "There's no picturers there, so I've never been, though there's a picture of it. Come and walk a ways with me. I'll find the picture and point it out to you."

He pulled the edge of my cloak, and I followed him.

"I'd rather you took me to someone who could guide me there."

"I can do that too. Old Ultan has a map somewhere in his library. That boy of his will get it for you."

"This isn't the Citadel," I reminded him again. "How did you come to be here, anyway? Did they bring you here to clean these?"

"That's right. That's right." He leaned on my arm. "There's a logical explanation for everything, and don't you forget it. That must have been the way. Father Inire wanted me to clean his, so here I am." He paused, considering. "Wait a bit, I've got it wrong. I had talent as a boy, that's what I'm supposed to say. My parents, you know, always encouraged me, and I'd draw for hours. I recollect one time I spent all one sunny day sketching in chalk on the back of our house."

A narrower corridor had opened to our left, and he pulled me down it. Though it was less well lit (nearly dark, in fact) and so cramped that one could not stand at anything like the proper distance from them, it was lined with pictures much larger than those in the main corridor, pictures that stretched from floor to ceiling, and that were far wider than my outstretched arms. From what I could see of them, they appeared very bad—mere daubs. I asked Rudesind who it was who had told him he must tell me about his childhood.

"Why, Father Inire," he said, cocking his head up to look at me. "Who do you suppose?" He dropped his voice. "Senile. That's what they say. Been vizier to I don't know how many autarchs since Ymar. Now you be quiet and let me talk. I'll find old Ultan for you.

"An artist—a real one—came by where we lived. My mother, being so proud of me, showed him some of the things I'd done. It was Fechin, Fechin himself, and the portrait he made of me hangs here to this day, looking out at you with my brown eyes. I'm at a table with some brushes and a tangerine on it. I'd been promised them when I was through sitting."

I said, "I don't think I have time to look at it right now."

"So I became an artist myself. Pretty soon, I took to cleaning and restoring the works of the great ones. Twice I've cleaned my own picture. It's strange, I tell you, for me to wash my own little face like that. I keep wishing somebody would wash mine now, make the dirt of the years come off with his sponge. But that's not what I'm taking you to see—it's the Green Room you're after, ain't it?"

"Yes," I said eagerly.

"Well, we've a picture of it right here. Have a look. Then when you see it, you'll know it."

He indicated one of the wide, coarse paintings. It was not of a room at all, but seemed to show a garden, a pleasance bordered by high hedges, with a lily pond and some willows swept by the wind. A man in the fantastic costume of a llanero played a guitar there, as it appeared for no ear but his own. Behind him, angry clouds raced across a sullen sky.

"After this you can go to the library and see Ultan's map," the old man said.

The painting was of that irritating kind which dissolves into mere blobs of color unless it can be seen as a whole. I took a step backward to get a better perspective of it, then another. . . .

With the third step, I realized I should have made contact with the wall behind me, and that I had not. I was standing instead inside the picture that had occupied the opposite wall: a dark room of ancient leather chairs and ebony tables. I turned to look at it, and when I turned back, the corridor where I had stood with Rudesind had vanished, and a wall covered with old and faded paper stood in its place.

I had drawn *Terminus Est* without consciously willing to do so, but there was no enemy to strike. Just as I was on the point of trying the room's single door, it opened and a figure in a yellow robe entered. Short, white hair was brushed back from his rounded brow, and his face might almost have served a plump woman of forty; about his neck, a phallus-shaped vial I remembered hung on a slender chain.

"Ah," he said. "I wondered who had come. Welcome, Death."

With as much composure as I could muster, I said, "I am the Journeyman Severian—of the guild of torturers, as you see. My entrance was entirely involuntary, and to be truthful, I would be very grateful to you if you could explain just how it happened. When I was in the corridor outside, this room appeared to be no more than a painting. But when I took a step or two back to view the one on the other wall, I found myself in here. By what art was that done?"

"No art," the man in the yellow robe said. "Concealed doors are scarcely an original invention, and the constructor of this room did no more than devise a means of concealing an open door. The room is shallow, as you see; indeed, it is shallower than you perceive even now, unless you're already aware that the angles of the floor and ceiling converge, and that the wall at the end is not so high as the one through which you came."

"I see," I said, and in fact I did. As he spoke that crooked room, which my mind, accustomed always to ordinary ones, had tricked me into believing of normal shape, became itself, with a slanted and trapezoidal ceiling and a trapezoidal floor. The very chairs that faced the wall through which I had come were things of little depth, so that one could hardly have sat on them; the tables were no wider than boards.

"The eye is deceived in a picture by such converging lines," the man in the yellow robe continued. "So that when it encounters them in reality, with little actual depth and the additional artificiality of monochromatic lighting, it believes it sees another picture—particularly when it has been conditioned by a long succession of true ones. Your entrance with that great weapon caused a real wall to rise behind you to detain you until you had been examined. I need hardly add that the other side of the wall is painted with the picture you believed you saw."

I was more astounded than ever. "But how could the room know I carried my sword?"

"That is more complex than I can well explain . . . far more so than this poor room. I can only say that the door is wrapped with metal strands, and that these know when the other metals, their brothers and sisters, pass their circle."

"Did you do all this?"

"Oh, no. All these things . . ." He paused. "And a hundred more like them, make up what we call the Second House. They are the work of Father Inire, who was called by the first Autarch to create a secret palace within the walls of the House Absolute. You or I, my son, would no doubt have built a mere suite of concealed rooms. He contrived that the hidden house should be everywhere coextensive with the public one."

"But you aren't he," I said. "Because now I know who you are! Do you recognize me?" I drew off my mask so he could see my face.

He smiled and said, "You came but once. The khaibit did not please you, then."

"She pleased me less than the woman she counterfeited—or rather, I loved the other more. Tonight I have lost a friend, yet it seems to be a time for meeting old acquaintances. May I ask how you've come here from your House Azure? Were you summoned for the thiasus? I saw one of your women earlier tonight."

He nodded absently. An oddly angled mirror set above a trumeau at one side of the strange, shallow room caught his profile, delicate as a cameo, and I decided he must be an androgyne. Pity welled up in me, with a sense of helplessness, as I thought of him opening the door to men, night after night, at his establishment in the Algedonic Quarter. "Yes," he said. "I will remain here for the celebration, then go."

My mind was full of the picture old Rudesind had shown me in the corridor outside, and I said, "Then you can show me where the garden is."

I sensed at once that he had been caught off guard, possibly for the first time in many years. There was pain in his eyes, and his left hand moved (though only slightly) toward the vial at his throat. ''So you have heard of that . . .'' he said. ''Even supposing that I knew the way, why should I reveal it to you? Many will seek to flee by that road if the pelagic argosy sights land.''

XXI

Hydromancy

Several seconds passed before I rightly understood what it was the androgyne had said. Then the remembered scent of Thecla's roasted flesh rose sickening-sweet in my nostrils, and I seemed to feel the unquiet of the leaves. Forgetting in the stress of the moment how futile such precautions must be in that deception-filled room, I looked about, seeking to assure myself that no one could overhear us, then found that without my having willed it (consciously, I had intended to question him before betraying my connection with Vodalus) my hand had taken the knife-shaped steel from the innermost compartment of my sabretache.

The androgyne smiled. "I felt you might be the one. For days now I have been expecting you, and I have kept the old man outside and many others under instructions to bring promising strangers to me."

"I was imprisoned in the antechamber," I said. "And so lost time."

"But you escaped, I see. It isn't likely you'd be released before my man came to search it. It's well you did—there isn't much time left . . . the three days of the thiasus, then I must go. Come, and I will show you the way to the Garden, though I am by no means sure you will be permitted to enter."

He opened the door by which he had come in, and this time I saw that it was not truly rectangular. The room beyond was hardly larger than the one we had left; but its angles seemed normal, and it was richly furnished.

"You came to the correct part of the Secret House at least," the androgyne said. "Otherwise we would have had to walk a weary way. Your pardon, while I read the message you brought."

He crossed to what I at first supposed was a glass-topped table, and put the steel under it on a shelf. At once a light kindled, shining down from the glass, though there was no light above it. The steel grew until it seemed a sword, and its striations, in place of mere teeth on which to strike sparks from a flint, I saw to be lines of flowing script.

"Stand back," the androgyne said. "If you have not read this before, you must not read it now."

I did as he bid, and for some time watched him bending over the little object I had carried away from Vodalus's glade. At last he said, "There is no help for it then . . . we must fight on two flanks. But this is none of your affair. Do you see that cabinet with the eclipse carved in its door? Open it and lift down the book you find there. Here, you may put it on this stand."

Although I feared some trap, I opened the door of the cabinet he had indicated. It held one monstrous book—a thing nearly as tall as I and a good two cubits wide—that stood with its cover of mottled blue-green leather facing me much as a corpse might had I opened the lid of an upright casket. Sheathing my sword, I gripped this great volume with both hands and placed it on the stand. The androgyne asked if I had seen it previously, and I told him I had not.

"You looked fearful of it, and tried . . . as it appeared to me . . . to keep your face from it when you carried it." He threw back the cover as he spoke. The first page, thus revealed, was written in red in a character I did not know. "This is a warning to the seekers of the path," he said. "Shall I read it to you?"

I blurted, "It seemed to me that I saw a dead man in the leather, and that he was myself."

He closed the cover again and ran his hand over it. "These pavonine dyeings are but the work of craftsmen long gone . . . the lines and swirls beneath them, only the scars of the suffering animals' backs, the marks of ticks and whips. But if you are fearful, you need not go."

"Open it," I said. "Show me the map."

"There is no map. This is the thing itself," he said, and with that he threw back the cover and the first page as well.

I was blinded, almost, as I have been on dark nights by a discharge of lightning. The inner pages seemed of pure silver, beaten and polished, that caught every wisp of illumination in the room and flung it back amplified a hundred times. "They're mirrors," I said, and in saying it realized that they were not, but those things for which we have no word but *mirrors*, those things that less than a watch before had returned Jonas to the stars. "But how can they have power, when they do not face each other?"

The androgyne answered, "Consider how long they faced each other when the book was closed. Now the field will withstand the tension we put on it for some time. Go, if you dare.''

I did not dare. As he spoke, something shaped itself in shining air above the open pages. It was neither a woman nor a butterfly, but it partook of both, and just as we know when we look at the painted figure of a mountain in the background of some picture that it is in reality as huge as an island, so I knew that I saw the thing only from far off—its wings beat, I think, against the proton winds of space, and all Urth might have been a mote disturbed by their motion. Then as I had seen it, so it saw me, much as the androgyne a moment before had seen the swirls and loops of writing on the steel through his glass. It paused and turned to me and opened its wings that I might observe them. They were marked with eyes.

The androgyne closed the book with a crash, like a door slammed shut. ''What did you see?'' he asked.

I could think only that I no longer had to look into the pages, and said, ''Thank you, sieur. Whoever you may be, I am your servant from this time forward.''

He nodded. ''Perhaps sometime I may remind you of that. But I will not ask you again what it was you saw. Here, wipe your forehead. The sight has marked you.''

He handed me a clean cloth as he spoke, and I wiped my brow with it as he told me, because I could feel the moisture running down my face. When I looked at the cloth, it was crimson with blood.

As though he had read my thoughts, he said, ''You are not wounded. The physicians' term is haematidrosis, I believe. Under the stress of strong emotion, minute veins in the skin of the afflicted part . . . of the skin everywhere, sometimes . . . rupture during a profuse sweating. You will have a nasty bruise there, I'm afraid.''

''Why did you do that?'' I asked. ''I thought you were going to show me a map. I only want to find the Green Room, as old Rudesind out there says it's called, where the players are quartered. Did Vodalus's message say you were to kill the bearer?'' I was fumbling for my sword as I spoke, but when my hands gripped the familiar hilt, I found I was too weak to draw the blade.

The androgyne laughed. It was pleasant laughter at first, wavering somewhere between a woman's and a boy's, but it trailed off into tittering, as a drunken man's sometimes does. Thecla's memories stirred in me; almost, they woke. ''Was that all you wished?'' he said when he had control of himself again. ''You asked me for a light for your candle, and I tried to give you the sun, and now you are burned. The fault was mine . . . I sought, perhaps, to postpone my time, yet even so

I would not have let you travel so far had I not read in the message that you have carried the Claw. And now I am most truly sorry, but I cannot help but laugh. Where will you go, when you have found the Green Room, Severian?''

''Where you send me. As you remind me, I have sworn service to Vodalus.'' (In fact, I feared him, and feared that the androgyne would inform him if I professed disobedience.)

''But if I have no orders for you? Have you already disposed of the Claw?''

''I could not,'' I said.

There was a pause. He did not speak.

''I'll go to Thrax,'' I said. ''I have a letter to the archon there; he's supposed to have work for me. For the honor of my guild, I would like to go.''

''That is well. How great, in truth, is your love of Vodalus?''

Again I felt the haft of the ax in my hand. For you others, as I am told, memory dies; mine scarcely dims. The mist that shrouded the necropolis that night blew against my face again, and everything I had felt when I received the coin from Vodalus and watched him walk away to a place where I could not follow returned to me. ''I saved him once,'' I said.

The androgyne added, ''Then here is what you are to do. You must go to Thrax as you planned, telling everyone . . . even yourself . . . that you are going to fill the position that waits you there. The Claw is perilous. Are you aware of it?''

''Yes. Vodalus told me that if it became known we possess it, we might lose the support of the populace.''

For a moment the androgyne stood silent again. Then he said, ''The Pelerines are in the north. If you are given the opportunity, you must restore the Claw to them.''

''That is what I had hoped to do.''

''Good. There is something else you must do as well. The Autarch is here, but long before you reach Thrax he will be in the north too, with the army. If he comes near Thrax, you are able to go to him. In time you will discover the way in which you must take his life.''

His tone betrayed him as much as Thecla's thoughts. I wanted to kneel, but he clapped his hands, and a bent little man slipped silently into the room. He wore a cowled habit like a cenobite's. The Autarch spoke to him, something I was too distracted to understand.

In all the world, there can be few sights more beautiful than that of the sun at dawn seen through the thousand sparkling waters of the Vatic

Fountain. I am no esthete, but my first sight of its dance (of which I had so often heard), must have acted as a restorative. I still recall it for my pleasure, just as I saw it when the cowled servitor opened a door for me—after so many leagues of the contrived corridors of the Second House—and I watched the silver streams trace ideographs across the solar disc.

"Straight ahead," the cowled figure murmured. "Follow the path through the Gate of Trees. You will be safe among the players." The door shut behind me and became the grassy slope of a hillock.

I stumbled toward the fountain, which refreshed me with windblown spray. I was surrounded by a pavement of serpentine; for a time I stood there, seeking to read my fortune in the dancing shapes, and at last I fumbled in my sabretache for an offering. The praetorians had taken all my money, but while I felt among the few possessions I yet carried there (a flannel, the fragment of whetstone, and a flask of oil for *Terminus Est*; a comb and the brown book for myself) I spied a coin wedged between the green blocks at my feet. After only a little effort I was able to draw it out—a single asimi, worn so thin that hardly a trace of the imprint remained. With a whispered wish, I threw it into the very center of the fountain. A jet caught it there and tossed it skyward, so that it flashed for a moment before it fell. I began to read the symbols the water made against the sun.

A sword. That seemed clear enough. I would continue a torturer.

A rose then, and beneath it a river. I would climb Gyoll as I had planned, since that was the road to Thrax.

Now angry waves, becoming soon a long, sullen swell. The sea, perhaps; but one could not reach the sea, I thought, by climbing toward the source of the river.

A rod, a chair, a multitude of towers, and I began to think the oracular powers of the fountain, in which I had never greatly believed, to be wholly false. I turned away; but as I turned, I glimpsed a many-pointed star, growing ever larger.

Since I have returned to the House Absolute, I have twice revisited the Vatic Fountain. Once I came at the first light, approaching it through the same door through which I first glimpsed it. But I have never again dared to ask it questions.

My servants, who confess one and all that they have dropped their orichalks into it when the garden was clear of guests, tell me one and all that they have received no true prophecy for their money. Yet I am unsure, recalling the green man, who drove off his visitors with his accounts of their futures. May it not be that these servants of mine, seeing only a lifetime of trays and brooms and ringing bells, reject it? I have asked my ministers as well, who doubtless cast in chrisos by the handful, but their answers are doubtful and mixed.

It was hard indeed to keep my back to the fountain and its lovely, cryptic messages and walk toward the old sun. Huge as a giant's face and darkly red it showed as the horizon dropped away. The poplars of the grounds were silhouetted against it, making me think of the figure of Night atop the khan on this western bank of Gyoll, which I had so often seen with the sun behind it at the close of one of our swimming parties.

Not realizing that I was now deep within the bounds of the House Absolute and well away from the patrols about the periphery, I feared I might be stopped at any moment, and perhaps cast back into the antechamber—whose secret door, I felt sure, would have been discovered and sealed by now. Nothing of the kind occurred. So far as I could see, no one stirred in all the leagues of hedge and velvet lawn, flower and trickling water, except myself. Lilies far taller than I, their star-shaped faces spangled with unshaken dew, overhung the path; its perfect surface showed behind me only the disturbance of my own feet. Nightingales, some free, some suspended from the branches of trees in golden cages, were singing still.

Once I saw before me, with something of the old feeling of horror, one of the walking statues. Like a colossal man (though it was not a man) too graceful and too slow to be human, it came across a small secretive lawn as if moving to the inaudible notes of some strange processional. I confess I hung back until it had passed, wondering if it could sense me where I stood in the shadow, and if it cared that I stood so.

Just when I had despaired of finding the Gate of Trees, I saw it. There was no mistaking it. Even as lesser gardeners espalier pears against a wall, the greater gardeners of the House Absolute, who have generations in which to complete their work, had molded the huge limbs of oaks until every twig conformed to an inspiration wholly architectural, and I, walking on the rooftops of the greatest palace of Urth, with not a stone in sight, saw looming to one side that great, green entranceway built of living wood as if of masonry.

I ran then.

XXII

Personifications

Through the wide, dripping arch of the Gate of Trees I ran, and out onto a broad expanse of grass, now spangled with tents. Somewhere a megathere roared and shook its chain. There seemed to be no other sound. I halted and listened, and the megathere, no longer disturbed by my footfalls, settled back into the death-like sleep of its kind. I could hear the dew running from the leaves, and the faint, interrupted twitter of birds.

Something else there was as well. A faint *whick, whick*, quick and irregular, that grew louder as I listened for it. I began to thread a path among the silent tents, following the sound. I must have misjudged it, however, for Dr. Talos saw me before I saw him.

"My friend! My partner! They are all asleep—your Dorcas and the rest. All but you and I. Over here!"

He flourished his cane as he spoke; the *whick, whick* had been his chopping at the heads of flowers.

"You have rejoined us just in time. Just in time! We perform tonight, and I would have been forced to hire one of these fellows to take your part. I'm delighted to see you! I owe you some money—do you recall? Not much, and between you and I, I think it false. But it is owed just the same, and I always pay."

"I'm afraid I don't recall," I said, "so it can't be a great sum. If Dorcas is all right I'm quite willing to forget it, provided you'll give me something to eat and show me where I can sleep for a couple of watches."

The doctor's sharp nose dipped for an instant to express regret. "Sleep you may have in plenty until the others wake you. But I'm afraid we've no food. Baldanders, you know, eats like a fire. The Thiasus

Marshal has promised to bring something today for all of us.'' He waved his stick vaguely at the irregular city of tents. ''But I'm afraid that won't be before midmorning at the earliest.''

''It's probably just as well. I'm really too tired to eat, but if you'll show me where I can lie down—''

''What got your head? Never mind—we'll mask it with greasepaint. This way!'' He was already trotting before me. I followed him through a maze of tent ropes to a heliotrope dome. Baldanders's barrow stood at the door, and at last I felt certain I had found Dorcas again.

When I woke, it was as though we had never been separated. Dorcas's delicate loveliness was unchanged; Jolenta's radiance threw it into shadow as always, yet made me wish, when the three of us were together, that she would leave so that I might rest my eyes on Dorcas. I took Baldanders to one side, an hour or so after we were all awake, and asked him why he had left me in the forest beyond the Piteous Gate.

''I was not with you,'' he said slowly. ''I was with my Dr. Talos.''

''And so was I. We might have sought him together and been of help to each other.''

There was a long hesitation; I seemed to feel the weight of those dull eyes on my face, and thought in my ignorance what a terrible thing it would be if Baldanders possessed energy and the will to anger. At last he said, ''Were you with us when we left the city?''

''Of course. Dorcas and Jolenta and I were all with you.''

Another hesitation. ''We found you there, then.''

''Yes, don't you remember?''

He shook his head slowly, and I noticed that his thatch of coarse black hair was touched with gray. ''I woke one morning and there you were. I was thinking. You left me soon.''

''The circumstances were different then—we had arranged to meet again.'' (I felt a pang of guilt when I recalled that I had never intended to honor that promise.)

''We have met again,'' Baldanders said dully; and then, seeing that the answer failed to satisfy me, added, ''There is nothing here real to me but Dr. Talos.''

''Your loyalty is very commendable, but you might have remembered that he wanted me with him as well as yourself.'' I found it impossible to be angry with this dim, gentle giant.

''We will collect money here in the south, and then we will build again, as we have built before, when they have forgotten.''

''This is the north. But that's right, your house was destroyed, wasn't it?''

"Burned," Baldanders said. I could almost see the flames reflected in his eyes. "I am sorry if you came to harm. For so long I have thought only of the castle and my work."

I left him sitting there and went to inspect the properties of our theater—not that they seemed in need of it, or that I could have detected any but the most obvious lacks. A number of showmen were gathered around Jolenta, and Dr. Talos drove them away and ordered her to go into the tent. A moment later, I heard the smack of his cane on flesh; he came out grinning but still angry.

"It isn't her fault," I said. "You know how she looks."

"Too gaudy. Too gaudy by far. Do you know what I like about you, Sieur Severian? You prefer Dorcas. Where is she, by the way? Have you seen her since you came back?"

"I warn you, Doctor. Don't strike her."

"I wouldn't think of it. I'm only afraid she may be lost."

His surprised expression convinced me that he was telling the truth. I told him, "We only got to talk for a moment. She's gone to fetch water."

"That's courageous of her," he said, and when I looked puzzled he added, "She's afraid of it. Surely you've noticed. She's clean, but even when she washes, the water is only thumb deep; when we cross bridges, she holds onto Jolenta and trembles."

Dorcas returned then, and if the doctor said anything more I did not hear it. When she and I had met that morning, neither of us had been able to do much more than smile, and touch with incredulous hands. Now she came to me, putting down the pails she carried, and seemed to devour me with her eyes. "I have missed you so," she said. "I've been so lonely without you."

I laughed to think of anyone missing me, and held up the edge of my fuligin cloak. "You missed this?"

"Death, you mean. Did I miss death? No, I missed you." She took the cloak from my hand and used it to draw me toward the line of poplars that formed one wall of the Green Room. "There is a bench I found where there are beds of herbs. Come and sit with me. They can spare us for a while after so many days, and eventually Jolenta will come out and find the water, which was for her anyway."

As soon as we were away from the bustle of the tents, where jugglers tossed their knives and acrobats their children, we were wrapped in the stillness of the gardens. They are perhaps the largest tract of land anywhere planned and planted for beauty, save for those wildernesses that are the gardens of the Increate and whose cultivators are invisible to us. Overlapping hedges formed a narrow door. We passed into a grove of trees with white, perfumed boughs that reminded me sadly of the flowering plums through which the praetorians had dragged Jonas and me, though those had seemed planted for ornament, and these, I thought, for the sake of their fruit. Dorcas had broken a twig bearing half a dozen of the blossoms and thrust it into her pale golden hair.

Beyond the orchard was a garden so old that I felt sure it had been forgotten by everyone save the servants who tended it. The stone seat there had been carved with heads, but they had worn away until they were almost featureless. A few beds of simple flowers remained, and with them fragrant rows of kitchen herbs—rosemary, angelica, mint, basil, and rue, all growing in a soil black as chocolate from the labor of countless years.

There was a little stream too, where Dorcas had no doubt drawn her water. Its source may once have been a fountain—now it was only a species of spring, rising in a shallow stone bowl to splash over the lip and eventually wind its way through little canals lined with rough masonry to water the fruit trees. We sat in the stone seat, I leaned my sword against its arm, and she took my hands in hers.

"I am afraid, Severian," she said. "I have such terrible dreams."

"Since I've been gone?"

"All the time."

"When we slept side by side in the field, you told me you had awakened from a good dream. You said it was very detailed and seemed real."

"If it was good, I have forgotten it now."

I had already noticed that she was careful to keep her eyes away from the water spilling from the ruined fountain.

"Every night, I dream I am walking through streets of shops. I am happy, or at least content. I have money to spend, and there is a long list of things I wish to buy. Again and again I recite the list to myself, and I try to decide in what parts of the quarter I can get each in the best quality for the lowest price.

"But gradually, as I go from shop to shop, I grow aware that everyone who sees me hates me and holds me in contempt, and I am aware that it is because they believe me to be an unclean spirit who has wrapped itself in the woman's body they see. At last I enter a tiny shop conducted by an old man and an old woman. She sits making lace while he spreads their wares on the counter for me. I hear the sound her thread makes behind me as it is pulled through the work."

I asked, "What is it you have come to buy?"

"Tiny clothes." Dorcas held her small, white hands half a span apart. "Doll's clothing, perhaps. I particularly remember little shirts of fine wool. At last I choose one and hand the old man money. But it is not money at all—only a lump of filth.''

Her shoulders were shaking, and I put my arm about her to comfort her.

''I want to scream then that they are wrong, that I am not the foul specter they take me for. Yet I know that if I do, whatever I may say will be taken as the final proof that they are right, and the words choke me. The worst part is that just then the hissing of the thread stops.'' She had taken my free hand again, and now she gripped it as though to drive her meaning into me. ''I know that no one could understand who has not had the same dream, but it is terrible. Terrible.''

''Perhaps now that I am here with you again, these dreams will end.''

''And then I sleep, or at least fall into blackness. If I do not wake then, there is a second dream. I am in a boat poled across a spectral lake—''

''There is no mystery in that, at least,'' I said. ''You rode in such a boat with Agia and me. It belonged to a man named Hildegrin. Surely you must remember that trip.''

Dorcas shook her head. ''It is not that boat but a much smaller one. An old man poles it, and I lie at his feet. I am awake, but I cannot move. My arm trails in the black water. Just as we are about to touch shore, I fall from the boat, but the old man does not see me, and as I sink through the water I know that he has never known I was there at all. Soon the light is gone, and I am very cold. Far above me, I hear a voice I love calling my name, but I cannot remember whose voice it is.''

''It's my voice, calling to wake you.''

''Perhaps.'' The whip mark Dorcas had carried from the Piteous Gate burned on her cheek like a brand.

For a while we sat without speaking. The nightingales were silent now, but linnets were singing in all the trees, and I saw a parrot, clad in scarlet and green like a little messenger in livery, flash among the branches.

At last Dorcas said, ''What a frightful thing water is. I should not have brought you here, but it was the only place nearby where I could think to go. I wish we had sat on the grass under those trees.''

''Why do you hate it? It seems beautiful to me.''

''Because it is here in the sunshine, but by its own nature it runs down and down forever, away from the light.''

''But it rises again,'' I said. ''The rain we see in spring is the same water we saw running the gutters the year before. Or so Master Malrubius taught us.''

Dorcas's smile flashed like a star. "That is good to believe, whether it's true or not. Severian, it's silly for me to say you're the best person I know, because you're the only good person I know. But I think if I met a thousand others, you would still be the best. That was what I wanted to talk to you about."

"If you need my protection, you have it. You know that."

"It isn't that at all," Dorcas said. "In a way I want to give you mine. Now *that* sounds silly, doesn't it? I have no family, I have no one except you, and yet I think I can protect you."

"You know Jolenta, and Dr. Talos and Baldanders."

"They are no one. Don't you feel that, Severian? Even I am no one, but they are less than I. The five of us were in the tent last night, and yet you were alone. You told me once that you don't have much imagination, but you must have sensed that."

"Is that what you want to protect me from—loneliness? I would welcome such protection."

"Then I will give you all I can, for as long as I can. But most of all, I want to protect you from the opinion of the world. Severian, do you remember what I told you of my dream? How all the people in the shops, and on the street, believed that I was only some hideous ghost? They may be right."

She was shaking, and I held her.

"That is part of the reason the dream is so painful. The other part comes from knowing that in some other way they are wrong. The foul specter is in me. It is me. But there are other things in me too, and they are what I am as much as it is."

"You could never be a foul specter, or anything foul."

"Oh, yes," she said seriously, and looked up at me. Her small, tilted face was never more beautiful than it was then in the sunlight, or more pure. "Oh, yes I could, Severian. Just as you can be what they call you. What you sometimes are. Do you remember how we saw the cathedral leap into the sky and burn away in an instant? And how we went walking down a road between trees until we saw a light ahead, and it was Dr. Talos and Baldanders, ready to put on their show with Jolenta?"

"You held my hand," I said. "And we talked about philosophy. How could I forget?"

"When we came to the light and Dr. Talos saw us—do you remember what he said?"

I cast my mind back to that evening, the end of the day on which I had executed Agilus. In memory I heard the roar of the crowd, Agia's scream, and then the roll of Baldanders's drum. "He said that everyone had come now, and that you were Innocence, and I was Death."

Dorcas nodded solemnly. "That's right. But you're not really Death, you know, no matter how often he calls you that. You're no more Death than a butcher is because he cuts the throats of steers all day. To me you're Life, and you're a young man named Severian, and if you wanted to put on different clothes and become a carpenter or a fisherman, no one could stop you."

"I have no desire to leave my guild."

"But you could. Today. That's the thing to remember. People don't want other people to be people. They throw names over them and lock them in, but I don't want you to let them lock you in. Dr. Talos is worse than most. In his own way, he's a liar . . ."

She left the accusation unfinished, and I ventured, "I once heard Baldanders say he seldom lied."

"In his own way, I said. Baldanders is right, Dr. Talos doesn't lie the way other people understand lying. Calling you Death wasn't a lie, it was a . . . a . . ."

"Metaphor," I suggested.

"But it was a dangerous, *bad* metaphor, and it was aimed at you like a lie."

"Do you think Dr. Talos hates me, then? I would have said he was one of the few people who've showed me real kindness since I left the Citadel. You, Jonas—who's gone now—an old woman I met while I was imprisoned, a man in a yellow robe—who also called me Death, by the way—and Dr. Talos. It's a short list, actually."

"I don't think he hates in the way we understand it," Dorcas replied softly. "Or for that matter, that he loves. He wants to manipulate everything he comes upon, to change it with his will. And since tearing down is easier than building, that's what he does most often."

"Baldanders seems to love him, though," I said. "I used to have a crippled dog, and I've seen Baldanders look at the doctor the way Triskele used to look at me."

"I understand you, but it doesn't strike me that way. Have you ever thought of how you must have looked, when you looked at your dog? Do you know anything about their past?"

"Only that they lived together near Lake Diurturna. The people there appear to have set fire to their house to drive them away."

"Do you think Dr. Talos could be Baldanders's son?"

The idea was so absurd that I laughed, happy to have the release from tension.

"Just the same," Dorcas said, "that's how they act. Like a slow-thinking, hard-working father with a brilliant, erratic son. At least so it seems to me."

It was not until we had left the bench and were walking back to the Green Room (which no more resembled the picture Rudesind had shown me than any other garden would have) that it occurred to me to wonder whether Dr. Talos's calling Dorcas "Innocence" had not been a metaphor of the same kind.

XXIII

Jolenta

The old orchard and the herb garden beyond it had been so silent, so freighted with oblivion, that they had recalled to me the Atrium of Time, and Valeria with her exquisite face framed in furs. The Green Room was pandemonium. Everyone was awake now, and sometimes it seemed that everyone was shouting. Children climbed the trees to free the caged birds, pursued by their mothers' brooms and their fathers' missiles. Tents were being struck even while rehearsals continued, so that I saw a seemingly solid pyramid of striped canvas collapse like a flag thrown down and reveal beyond it the grass-green megathere rearing on his hind legs while a dancer pirouetted on his forehead.

Baldanders and our tent were gone, but in a moment Dr. Talos came rushing up and hurried us away down twisted walks, past balustrades and waterfalls and grottoes filled with raw topazes and flowering moss, to a bowl of clipped lawn where the giant labored to erect our stage under the eyes of a dozen white deer.

It was to be a much more elaborate stage than the one I had played upon within the Wall of Nessus. Servants from the House Absolute, it seemed, had brought timbers and nails, tools and paint and cloth in quantities much greater than we could possibly make use of. Their generosity had waked the doctor's bent toward the grandoise (which never slumbered deeply) and he alternated between assisting Baldanders and me with the heavier constructions and making frantic additions to the manuscript of his play.

The giant was our carpenter, and though he moved slowly, he worked so steadily, and with such great strength—driving a spike as thick as my forefinger with a blow or two and cutting a timber it would have taken me a watch to saw through with a few strokes of his ax—that he might have been ten slaves toiling under the whip.

Dorcas found a talent for painting that I at least was surprised by. Together, we erected the black plates that drink the sun, not only to gather energy for the night's performance, but to power the projectors now. These contrivances can provide a backdrop of a thousand leagues as easily as the interior of a hut, but the illusion is complete only in total darkness. It is best, therefore, to strengthen it with painted scenes behind, and Dorcas created those with skill, standing waist high in mountains as she thrust her brushes through the daylight-faded images.

Jolenta and I were of less value. I had no painter's hand, and too little understanding of the necessities of the play even to assist the doctor in arranging our properties. Jolenta, I think, rebelled physically and psychically against any kind of work, and certainly against this. Those long legs, so slender below the knees, so rounded to bursting above them, were inadequate to bear much weight beyond that of her own body; her jutting breasts were in constant danger of having their nipples crushed between lumber or smeared with paint. Nor had she any of that spirit that animates the members of a group forwarding the group's purpose. Dorcas had said that I had been alone the night before, and perhaps she had been more nearly correct than I supposed, but Jolenta was more solitary still. Dorcas and I had each other, Baldanders and the doctor their crooked friendship, and we came together in the performance of the play. Jolenta had only herself, the incessant performance whose sole goal was to garner admiration.

She touched my arm, and without speaking rolled enormous emerald eyes to indicate the edge of our natural amphitheater, where a grove of chestnuts lifted white candles among their pale leaves.

I saw that none of the others were looking at us and nodded. After Dorcas, Jolenta walking beside me seemed nearly as tall as Thecla, though she took small steps instead of Thecla's swinging strides. She was a head taller than Dorcas at least, her coiffure made her seem taller still, and she wore boots with high, riding heels.

"I want to see it," she said. "It's the only chance I shall ever have."

That was a palpable lie, but as though I believed it I said, "The opportunity is symmetric. Today and only today the House Absolute has the opportunity to see you."

She nodded; I had enunciated a profound truth. "I need someone—someone the ones I don't want to talk to will be afraid of. I mean all these showmen and mummers. When you were gone, no one but Dorcas would go with me, and no one is afraid of her. Could you draw that sword and carry it over your shoulder?"

I did so.

"If I don't smile, make them leave. Understand?"

Grass much longer than that in the natural amphitheater, but softer than fern, grew among the chestnuts; the path was of quartz pebbles shot with gold.

"If only the Autarch saw me, he would desire me. Do you think he will come to our play?"

To please her I nodded, but added, "I have heard he has little use for women, however beautiful, save as advisors, spies, and shield maids."

She stopped and turned, smiling. "That's just it. Don't you see? I can make anyone desire me, and so he, the One Autarch, whose dreams are our reality, whose memories are our history, will desire me too, unmanned or not. You have wanted women other than me, haven't you? Wanted them badly?"

I admitted I had.

"And so you think you desire me as you wished for them." She turned and began to walk again, hobbling a little, as it seemed she always did, but invigorated for the moment by her own argument. "But I make every man stiffen and every woman itch. Women who have never loved women wish to love me—did you know that? The same ones come to our performances again and again, and send me their food and their flowers, scarfs, shawls, and embroidered kerchiefs with oh, such sisterly, motherly notes. They're going to *protect* me, protect me from my physician, from his giant, from their husbands and sons and neighbors. And the *men!* Baldanders has to throw them in the river."

I asked if she were lame, and as we emerged from the chestnuts, I looked about for some conveyance for her, but there was nothing.

"My thighs are chafed and it hurts to walk. I have an unguent for them that helps a bit, and a man bought a jennet for me to ride, but I don't know where it's pastured now. I'm really only comfortable when I can keep my legs apart."

"I could carry you."

She smiled again, displaying perfect teeth. "We'd both enjoy that, wouldn't we? But I'm afraid it wouldn't look dignified. No, I'll walk—I just hope I don't have to walk far. I *won't* walk far, in fact, no matter what happens. No one seems to be about but the mummers anyway. Perhaps the important people are sleeping late to prepare for the night's festivities. I'll have to sleep myself, four watches at least, before I go on."

I heard the sound of water sliding over stones, and having no better goal to seek made for it. We passed through a hawthorn hedge whose spotted white blossoms seemed from a distance to present an insurmountable barrier, and saw a river hardly wider than a street, on which swans sailed like sculptures of ice. There was a pavilion there, and beside it three boats, each shaped like the wide flower of the nenuphar. Their interiors were lined with the thickest silk brocade, and when I stepped into one I found that they exuded the odor of spices.

"Wonderful," Jolenta said. "They won't mind if we take one, will they? Or if they do, I'll be brought before someone important, just as it is in the play, and when he sees me he'll never let me leave. I'll make Dr. Talos stay with me, and you if you want. They'll have some use for you."

I told her I would have to continue my journey north and lifted her into the boat, putting my arm about a waist quite as slender as Dorcas's.

She lay down at once upon the cushions, where the uplifted petals gave her perfect complexion shade. It made me think of Agia, laughing in the sun as we descended the Adamnian Steps and boasting of the wide-brimmed hat she would wear next year. Agia had no feature that was not inferior to Jolenta's; she had been hardly taller than Dorcas, with hips over-wide and breasts that would have seemed meager beside Jolenta's overflowing plenitude; her long, brown eyes and high cheekbones were more expressive of shrewdness and determination than passion and surrender. Yet Agia had engendered a healthy rut in me. Her laughter, when it came, was often tinged with spite; but it was real laughter. She had sweated with her heat; Jolenta's desire was no more than the desire to be desired, so that I wished, not to comfort her loneliness as I had wished to comfort Valeria's, nor to find expression for an aching love like the love I had felt for Thecla, nor to protect her as I wished to protect Dorcas; but to shame and punish her, to destroy her self-possession, to fill her eyes with tears and tear her hair as one burns the hair of corpses to torment the ghosts that have fled them. She had boasted that she made tribadists of women. She came near to making an algophilist of me.

"This is my last performance, I know. I feel it. The audience is sure to hold someone . . ." She yawned and stretched. It appeared so certain her straining bodice would be unable to contain her that I averted my eyes. When I looked again, she was sleeping.

A slender oar trailed behind the boat. I took it and found that despite the circularity of the hull above the water, there was a keel below. In the center of the river the current ran strongly enough that I needed only to steer our slow progress along a series of gracefully sweeping meanders. Just as the hooded servant and I had passed unseen through suites and alcoves and arcades when he had escorted me along the hidden ways of the Second House, so now the sleeping Jolenta and I passed without noise or effort, almost completely unobserved, through leagues of garden. Couples lay on the soft grass beneath the trees and in the more refined comfort of summerhouses and seemed to think our craft hardly more than a decoration sent idly downstream for their delectation, or if they saw my head above the curved petals assumed us intent upon our own affairs. Lone philosophers meditated on rustic seats, and parties, not invariably erotic, proceeded undisturbed in clerestories and arboriums.

Eventually I came to resent Jolenta's sleep. I abandoned the oar and knelt beside her on the cushions. There was a purity in her sleeping face, however artificial, that I had never observed when she was awake. I kissed her, and her large eyes, hardly open, seemed almost Agia's long eyes, as her red-gold hair appeared almost brown. I loosened her clothing. She seemed half drugged, whether by some soporific in the heaped cushions or merely by the fatigue induced by our walk in the open and the burden of so great a quantity of voluptuous flesh. I freed her breasts, each nearly as large as her own head, and those wide thighs, which seemed to hold a new-hatched chick between them.

When we returned, everyone knew where we had been, though I doubt that Baldanders cared. Dorcas wept in private, vanishing for a time only to emerge with inflamed eyes and a heroine's smile. Dr. Talos, I think, was simultaneously enraged and delighted. I received the impression (which I hold to this day) that he had never enjoyed Jolenta, and that it was only to him, of all the men of Urth, that she would have given herself entirely willingly.

We spent the watches that remained before nightfall in listening to Dr. Talos chaffer with various officials of the House Absolute, and in rehearsal. Since I have already said something of what it was to act in Dr. Talos's play, I propose to give an approximation of the text here—not as it existed on the fragments of soiled paper we passed from hand to hand that afternoon, which often contained no more than hints for improvisations, but as it might have been recorded by some diligent clerk in the audience; and as it was, in fact, recorded by the demonic witness who dwells behind my eyes.

But first you must visualize our theater. Urth's laboring margin has climbed once more above the red disc; long-winged bats flit overhead, and a green quarter moon hangs low in the eastern sky. Imagine the slightest of valleys, a thousand paces or more from lip to lip, set among the gentlest turf-covered rolling hills. There are doors in these hills, some no wider than the entrance to an ordinary private room, some as wide as the doors of a basilica. These doors are open, and a mist-tinged light spills from them. Flagged paths wind down toward the tiny arch of our proscenium; they are dotted with men and women in the fantastic costumes of a masque—costumes drawn largely from remote ages, so that I, with no more than the smattering of history furnished me by Thecla and Master Palaemon, scarcely recognize one of them. Servants move among these masquers carrying trays loaded with cups and tumblers, heaped with delicious-smelling meats and pastries. Black seats of velvet and ebony, as delicate as crickets, face our stage, but many in the audience prefer to stand, and throughout our performance the spectators come and go without interruption, many remaining to hear no more than a dozen lines. Hylas sing in the trees, the nightingales trill, and atop the hills the walking statues move slowly through many poses. All the parts in the play are taken by Dr. Talos, Baldanders, Dorcas, Jolenta, or me.

XXIV

Dr. Talos's Play: Eschatology and Genesis

Being a dramatization (as he claimed) of certain parts of the lost Book of the New Sun

Persons in the Play:
- Gabriel
- The Giant Nod
- Meschia, the First Man
- Meschiane, the First Woman
- Jahi
- The Autarch
- The Contessa
- Her Maid
- Two Soldiers
- A Statue
- A Prophet
- The Generalissimo
- Two Demons (disguised)
- The Inquisitor
- His Familiar
- Angelic Beings
- The New Sun
- The Old Sun
- The Moon

The back of the stage is dark. GABRIEL *appears bathed in golden light and carrying a crystal clarion.*

GABRIEL: Greetings. I have come to set the scene for you—after all, that is my function. It is the night of the last day, and the night before the first. The Old Sun has set. He will appear in the sky no more. Tomorrow the New Sun will rise, and my siblings and I will greet him. Tonight . . . tonight no one knows. Everyone sleeps.

Footsteps, heavy and slow. Enter NOD.

GABRIEL: Omniscience! Defend your servant!

NOD: Do you serve him? So do we Nephilim. I will not harm you, then, unless he suggests it.

GABRIEL: You are of his household? How does he communicate with you?

NOD: To tell the truth, he doesn't. I'm forced to guess at what he wishes me to do.

GABRIEL: I was afraid of that.

NOD: Have you seen Meschia's son?

GABRIEL: Have I seen him? Why, you great ninny, he isn't even born yet. What do you want with him?

NOD: He is to come and dwell with me, in my land east of this garden. I will give him one of my daughters to wife.

GABRIEL: You have the wrong creation, my friend—you're fifty million years too late.

NOD: (*Nods slowly, not understanding.*) If you should see him—

Enter MESCHIA *and* MESCHIANE, *with* JAHI *following. All are naked, but* JAHI *wears jewelry.*

MESCHIA: What a lovely place! Delightful! Flowers, fountains, and statues—isn't it wonderful?

MESCHIANE: (*Timidly.*) I saw a tame tiger with fangs longer than my hand. What shall we call him?

MESCHIA: Whatever he wants. (*To* GABRIEL:) Who owns this beautiful spot?

GABRIEL: The Autarch.

MESCHIA: And he permits us to live here. That's very gracious of him.

GABRIEL: Not exactly. There's someone following you, my friend. Do you know it?

MESCHIA: (*Not looking.*) There's something behind you too.

GABRIEL: (*Flourishing the clarion that is his badge of office.*) Yes, *He* is behind me!

MESCHIA: Close, too. If you're going to blow that horn to call help, you'd better do it now.

GABRIEL: Why, how perceptive of you. But the time is not quite ripe.

The golden light fades, and GABRIEL *vanishes from the stage.* NOD *remains motionless, leaning on his club.*

MESCHIANE: I'll start a fire, and you had better begin to build us a house. It must rain often here—see how green the grass is.

MESCHIA: (*Examining* NOD.) Why, it's only a statue. No wonder he wasn't afraid of it.

MESCHIANE: It might come to life. I heard something once about raising sons from stones.

MESCHIA: Once! Why you were only born just now. Yesterday, I think.

MESCHIANE: Yesterday! I don't remember it. . . . I'm such a child, Meschia. I don't remember anything until I walked out into the light and saw you talking to a sunbeam.

MESCHIA: That wasn't a sunbeam! It was . . . to tell the truth, I haven't thought of a name for what it was yet.

MESCHIANE: I fell in love with you then.

Enter the AUTARCH.

AUTARCH: Who are you?

MESCHIA: As far as that goes, who are *you*?

AUTARCH: The owner of this garden.

MESCHIA *bows, and* MESCHIANE *curtsies, though she has no skirt to hold.*

MESCHIA: We were speaking to one of your servants only a moment ago. Now that I come to think of it, I am astonished at how much he resembled your august Self. Save that he was . . . ah . . .

AUTARCH: Younger?

MESCHIA: In appearance, at least.

AUTARCH: Well, it is inevitable, I suppose. Not that I am attempting to excuse it now. But I was young, and though it would be better to confine oneself to women nearer one's own station, still there are times—as you would understand, young man, if you had ever been in my position—when a little maid or country girl, who can be wooed with a handful of silver or a bolt of velvet, and will not demand, at the most inconvenient moment, the death of some rival or an ambassadorship for her husband . . . Well, when a little person like that becomes a most enticing proposition.

While the AUTARCH *has been speaking*, JAHI *has been creeping up behind* MESCHIA. *Now she lays a hand on his shoulder.*

JAHI: Now you see that he, whom you have esteemed your divinity, would countenance and advise all I have proposed of you. Before the New Sun rises, let us make a new beginning.

AUTARCH: Here's a lovely creature. How is it, child, that I see the bright flames of candles reflected in each eye, while your sister there still puffs cold tinder?

JAHI: She is no sister of mine!

AUTARCH: Your adversary then. But come with me. I will give these two my leave to camp here, and you shall wear a rich gown this night, and your mouth shall run with wine, and that slender figure shall be rendered a shade less graceful, perhaps, by larks stuffed with almonds and candied figs.

JAHI: Go away, old man.

AUTARCH: What! Do you know who I am?

JAHI: I am the only one here who does. You are a ghost and less, a column of ashes upheld by the wind.

AUTARCH: I see, she is mad. What does she want you to do, friend?

MESCHIA: (*Relieved.*) You hold no resentment toward her? That is good of you.

AUTARCH: None at all! Why, a mad mistress should be a most interesting experience—I am looking forward to it, believe me, and there are few things to look forward to when you've seen and done all I have. She doesn't bite, does she? I mean, not hard?

MESCHIANE: She does, and her fangs run with venom.

JAHI *springs forward to claw her.* MESCHIANE *darts offstage, pursued.*

AUTARCH: I shall have my piquenaires search the garden for them.

MESCHIA: Don't worry, they'll both be back soon. You'll see. Meanwhile I am, actually, glad to have a moment alone with you like this. There are some things I've been wanting to ask you.

AUTARCH: I grant no favors after six—that's a rule I've had to make to keep my sanity. I'm sure you understand.

MESCHIA: (*Somewhat taken aback.*) That's good to know. But I wasn't going to ask for something, really. Only for information, for divine wisdom.

AUTARCH: In that case, go ahead. But I warn you, you must pay a price. I mean to have that demented angel for my own to night.

MESCHIA *drops to his knees.*

MESCHIA: There is something I have never understood. Why must I talk to you when you know my every thought? My first question was: Knowing her to be of that brood you have banished, should I not still do what she proposes? For she knows I know, and it is in my heart to believe that she puts forward right action in the thought that I will spurn it because it comes from her.

AUTARCH: (*Aside.*) He is mad too, I see, and because of my yellow robes thinks me divine. (*To* MESCHIA:) A little adultery never hurt any man. Unless of course it was his wife's.

MESCHIA: Then mine would hurt her? I—

Enter the CONTESSA *and her* MAID.

CONTESSA: My Sovereign Lord! What do you do here?

MESCHIA: I am at prayer, daughter. Take off your shoes at least, for this is holy ground.

CONTESSA: Liege, who is this fool?

AUTARCH: A madman I found wandering with two women as mad as he.

CONTESSA: Then they outnumber us, unless my maid be sane.

MAID: Your Grace—

CONTESSA: Which I doubt. This afternoon she laid out a purple stole with my green capote. I was to look like a post decked with morning-glories, it would seem.

MESCHIA, *who has been growing angrier as she speaks, strikes her, knocking her down. Unseen behind him, the* AUTARCH *flees.*

MESCHIA: Brat! Don't trifle with holy things when I am near, or dare do anything but what I tell you.

MAID: Who are you, sir?

MESCHIA: I am the parent of the human race, my child. And you *are* my child, as she is.

MAID: I hope you will forgive her—and me. We had heard you were dead.

MESCHIA: That requires no apology. Most are, after all. But I have come round again, as you see, to welcome the new dawn.

NOD: (*Speaking and moving after his long silence and immobility.*) We have come too early.

MESCHIA: (*Pointing.*) A giant! A giant!

CONTESSA: Oh! Solange! Kyneburga!

MAID: I'm here, Your Grace. Lybe is here.

NOD: Too early for the New Sun by some time still.

CONTESSA: (*Beginning to weep.*) The New Sun is coming! We shall melt like dreams.

MESCHIA: (*Seeing that* NOD *intends no violence.*) Bad dreams. But it will be the best thing for you, you understand that, don't you?

CONTESSA: (*Recovering a little.*) What I don't understand is how you, who suddenly seem so wise, could mistake the Autarch for the Universal Mind.

MESCHIA: I know that you are my daughters in the old creation. You must be, since you are human women, and I have had none in this.

NOD: His son will take my daughter to wife. It is an honor our family has done little to deserve—we are only humble people, the children of Gea—but we will be exulted. I will be . . . What will I be, Meschia? The father-in-law of your son. It may be, if you don't object, that someday my wife and I will visit our daughter on the same day you come to see him. You wouldn't refuse us, would you, a place at the table? We would sit on the floor, naturally.

MESCHIA: Of course not. The dog does that already—or will, when we see him. (*To the* CONTESSA:) Has it not struck you that I may know more of him you call the Universal Mind than your Autarch does of himself? Not only your Universal Mind, but many lesser powers wear our humanity like a cloak when they will, sometimes only as concerns two or three of us. We who are worn are seldom aware that, seeming ourselves to ourselves, we are yet Demiurge, Paraclete, or Fiend to another.

CONTESSA: That is wisdom I have gained late, if I must fade with the New Sun's rising. Is it past midnight?

MAID: Nearly so, Your Grace.

CONTESSA: (*Pointing to the audience.*) All these fair folk—what will befall them?

MESCHIA: What befalls leaves when their year is past, and they are driven by the wind?

CONTESSA: If—

MESCHIA *turns to watch the eastern sky, as though for the first sign of dawn.*

CONTESSA: If—

MESCHIA: If what?

CONTESSA: If my body held a part of yours—drops of liquescent tissue locked in my loins . . .

MESCHIA: If it did, you might wander Urth for a time longer, a lost thing that could never find its way home. But I will not bed you. Do you think that you are more than a corpse? You are less.

MAID *faints.*

CONTESSA: You say you are the father of all things human. It must be so, for you are death to woman.

The stage darkens. When the light returns, MESCHIANE *and* JAHI *are lying together beneath a rowan tree. There is a door in the hillside behind them.* JAHI*'s lip is split and puffed, giving her a pouting look. Blood trickles from it to her chin.*

MESCHIANE: How strong I would be still to search for him, if only I knew you would not follow me.

JAHI: I move with the strength of the World Below, and will follow you to the second ending of Urth, if need be. But if you strike me again you will suffer for it.

MESCHIANE *lifts her fist, and* JAHI *cowers back.*

MESCHIANE: Your legs were shaking worse than mine when we decided to rest here.

JAHI: I suffer far more than you. But the strength of the World Below is to endure past endurance—even as I am more beautiful than you, I am a more tender creature by far.

MESCHIANE: We've seen that, I think.

JAHI: I warn you again, and there will be no third warning. Strike me at your peril.

MESCHIANE: What will you do? Summon up Erinys to destroy me? I have no fear of that. If you could, you would have done it long before.

JAHI: Worse. If you strike me again, you will come to enjoy it.

Enter FIRST SOLDIER *and* SECOND SOLDIER, *armed with pikes.*

FIRST SOLDIER: Look here!

SECOND SOLDIER: (*To the women:*) Down, down! Don't stand, or like a heron I'll skewer you. You're coming with us.

MESCHIANE: On our hands and knees?

FIRST SOLDIER: None of your insolence!

He prods her with his pike, and as he does there is a groaning almost too deep for hearing. The stage vibrates in sympathy with it, and the ground shakes.

SECOND SOLDIER: What was that?

FIRST SOLDIER: I don't know.

JAHI: The end of Urth, you fool. Go ahead and spear her. It's the end of you anyway.

SECOND SOLDIER: Little you know! It's the beginning for us. When the order came to search the garden, special mention was made of you two, and orders given to bring you back. Ten chrisos you'll be worth, or I'm a cobbler.

He seizes JAHI, *and as soon as he does so,* MESCHIANE *darts off into the darkness.* FIRST SOLDIER *runs after her.*

SECOND SOLDIER: Bite me, will you!

He strikes JAHI *with the shaft of his weapon. They struggle.*

JAHI: Fool! She's escaping!

SECOND SOLDIER: That's Ivo's worry. I've got my prisoner, and he let his escape, if he doesn't catch her. Come on, we're going to see the chiliarch.

JAHI: Will you not love me before we leave this winsome spot?

SECOND SOLDIER: And have my manhood cut off and shoved into my mouth? Not I!

JAHI: They'd have to find it first.

SECOND SOLDIER: What's that? (*Shakes her.*)

JAHI: You take the office of Urth, who will not trouble herself for me. But wait—release me only for a moment and I will show you wonderful things.

SECOND SOLDIER: I can see them now, for which I give all thanks to the moon.

JAHI: I can make you rich. Ten chrisos will be as nothing to you. But I have no power while you grasp my body.

SECOND SOLDIER: Your legs are longer than the other woman's, but I've seen that you don't move so readily on them. Indeed, I think that you can scarcely stand.

JAHI: No more can I.

SECOND SOLDIER: I'll hold your necklace—the chain looks stout enough. If that's sufficient, show me what you can do. If it's not, come with me. You'll be no freer while I have you.

JAHI *raises both hands, with the little fingers, index fingers, and thumbs extended. For a moment there is silence, then a strange, soft music filled with trillings. Snow falls in gentle flakes.*

SECOND SOLDIER: Stop that!

He seizes one arm and jerks it down. The music stops abruptly. A few last snowflakes settle on his head.

SECOND SOLDIER: That was not gold.

JAHI: Yet you saw.

SECOND SOLDIER: There's an old woman in my home village who can work the weather too. She's not as quick as you, I admit, but then she's a lot older, and feeble.

JAHI: Whoever she may be, she is not a thousandth part as old as I.

Enter the STATUE, *moving slowly and as though blind.*

JAHI: What is that thing?

SECOND SOLDIER: One of Father Inire's little pets. It can't hear you or make a sound. I'm not even sure it's alive.

JAHI: Why, neither am I, for all of that.

As the STATUE *passes near her, she strokes its cheek with her free hand.*

JAHI: Lover . . . lover . . . lover. Have you no greeting for me?

STATUE: E-e-e-y!

SECOND SOLDIER: What's this? Stop! Woman, you said you had no power while I held you.

JAHI: Behold my slave. Can you fight him? Go ahead—break your spear on that broad chest.

The STATUE *kneels and kisses* JAHI*'s foot.*

SECOND SOLDIER: No, but I can outrun him.

He throws JAHI *across his shoulder and runs. The door in the hill opens. He enters, and it slams shut behind him. The* STATUE *hammers it with mighty blows, but it does not yield. Tears stream down his face. At last he turns away and begins to dig with his hands.*

GABRIEL: (*Offstage.*) Thus stone images keep faith with a departed day, Alone in the desert when man has fled away.

As the STATUE *continues to dig, the stage grows dark. When the lights come up again, the* AUTARCH *is seated on his throne. He is alone on stage, but silhouettes projected on screens to either side of him indicate that he is surrounded by his court.*

AUTARCH: Here I sit as though the lord of a hundred worlds. Yet not master even of this.

The tramp of marching men is heard offstage. There is a shouted order.

AUTARCH: Generalissimo!

Enter a PROPHET. *He wears a goat skin and carries a staff whose head has been rudely carved into a strange symbol.*

PROPHET: A hundred portents are abroad. At Incusus, a calf was dropped that had no head, but mouths in its knees. A woman of known propriety has dreamed she is with child by a dog, last night a shower of stars fell hissing onto the southern ice, and prophets walk abroad in the land.

AUTARCH: You yourself are a prophet.

PROPHET: The Autarch himself has seen them!

AUTARCH: My archivist, who is most learned in the history of this spot, once informed me that over a hundred prophets have been slain here—stoned, burned, torn by beasts, and drowned. Some have even been nailed like vermin to our doors. Now I would learn of you something of the coming of the New Sun, so long prophesied. How is it to come about? What does it mean? Speak, or we shall give the old archivist another mark for his tally, and train the pale moonflower to climb that staff.

PROPHET: I despair of satisfying you, but I shall attempt it.

AUTARCH: Do you not know?

PROPHET: I know. But I know you for a practical man, concerned with the affairs of this universe alone, who seldom looks higher than the stars.

AUTARCH: For thirty years I have prided myself on that.

PROPHET: Yet even you must know that cancer eats the heart of the old sun. At its center, matter falls in upon itself, as though there were there a pit without bottom, whose top surrounds it.

AUTARCH: My astronomers have long told me so.

PROPHET: Think on an apple rotten from the bud. Fair still without, until it collapses into foulness at last.

AUTARCH: Every man who finds himself still strong in the latter half of life has thought on that fruit.

PROPHET: So much then for the old sun. But what of its cancer? What know we of that, save that it deprives Urth of heat and light, and at last of life?

Sounds of struggle are heard offstage. There is a scream of pain, and a crash as though a large vase had been knocked from its pedestal.

AUTARCH: We will learn what that commotion is soon enough, Prophet. Continue.

PROPHET: We know it to be far more, for it is a discontinuity in our universe, a rent in its fabric bound by no law we know. From it nothing comes—all enters in, nought escapes. Yet from it anything may appear, for it alone of all the things we know is no slave to its own nature.

Enter NOD, *bleeding, prodded by pikes held offstage.*

AUTARCH: What is this miscreation?

PROPHET: The very proof of those portents I spoke to you. In future times, so it has long been said, the death of the old sun will destroy Urth. But from its grave will rise monsters, a new people, and the New Sun. Old Urth will flower then as a butterfly from its dry husk, and the New Urth shall be called Ushas.

AUTARCH: Yet all we know will be swept aside? This ancient house in which we stand? Yourself? Me?

NOD: I have no wisdom. Yet I heard a wise man—soon to be a relative of marriage—say not long ago that all that is for the best. We are but dreams, and dreams possess no life by their own right. See, I am wounded. (*Holds out his hand.*) When my wound heals, it will be gone. Should it with its bloody lips say it is sorry to heal? I am only trying to explain what another said, but that is what I think he meant.

Deep bells toll offstage.

AUTARCH: What's that? You, Prophet, go and see who's ordered that clamor, and why. *Exit* PROPHET.

NOD: I feel sure your bells have begun the welcome of the New Sun. It is what I came to do myself. It is our custom, when an honored guest arrives, to roar and beat our chests, and pound the ground and the trunks of trees all about with gladness, and lift the greatest rocks we can, and send them down the gorges in honor of him. I will do that this morning, if you will set me free, and I feel sure Urth herself will join me. The very mountains will leap into the sea when the New Sun rises up today.

AUTARCH: And from where did you come? Tell me, and I'll release you.

NOD: Why, from my own country, to the east of Paradise.

AUTARCH: And where is that?

NOD *points to the east.*

AUTARCH: And where is Paradise? In the same direction?

NOD: Why, this is Paradise—we are in Paradise, or at least under it.

Enter the GENERALISSIMO, *who marches to the throne and salutes.*

GENERALISSIMO: Autarch, we have searched all the land above this House Absolute, as you ordered. The Contessa Carina has been found, and, her injuries not being serious, escorted to her apartments. We have also found the colossus you see before you, the bejeweled woman you described, and two merchants.

AUTARCH: What of the other two, the naked man and his wife?

GENERALISSIMO: There is no trace of them.

AUTARCH: Repeat your search, and this time look well.

GENERALISSIMO: (*Salutes.*) As my Autarch wills.

AUTARCH: And have the jeweled woman sent to me.

NOD *begins to walk offstage, but is stopped by pikes. The* GENERALISSIMO *draws his pistol.*

NOD: Am I not free to leave?

GENERALISSIMO: By no means!

NOD: (*To* AUTARCH.) I told you where my country lies. Just east of here.

GENERALISSIMO: More than your country lies. I know that area well.

AUTARCH: (*Fatigued.*) He has told the truth as he knows it. Perhaps the only truth there is.

NOD: Then I am free to go.

AUTARCH: I think that he whom you came to welcome will arrive whether you are free or not. Yet there is a chance—and such creatures as you cannot be allowed to roam abroad in any case. No, you are not free, nor ever again will be.

NOD *rushes from the stage, pursued by the* GENERALISSIMO. *Shots, screams, and crashes. The figures around the* AUTARCH *fade. In the midst of the uproar, the bells toll again.* NOD *reenters with a laser burn across one cheek. The* AUTARCH *strikes him with his scepter; each blow produces an explosion and a burst of sparks.* NOD *seizes the* AUTARCH *and is about to dash him to the stage when two*DEMONS *disguised as merchants enter, throw him down, and restore the* AUTARCH *to his throne.*

AUTARCH: Thank you. You will be richly rewarded. I had given up hope of being rescued by my guards, and I see I thought rightly. May I ask who you are?

FIRST DEMON: Your guards are dead. That giant has smashed their skulls against your walls and broken their spines upon his knees.

SECOND DEMON: We are two traders merely. Your soldiers took us up.

AUTARCH: Would that they were traders, and in their places I had such soldiers as you! And yet, you are in appearance so slight I would think you incapable of even ordinary strength.

FIRST DEMON: (*Bowing.*) Our strength is inspired by the master we serve.

SECOND DEMON: You will wonder why we—two commonplace traders in slaves—should have been found wandering your grounds by night. The fact is that we came to warn you. Our travels but lately took us to the northern jungles, and there, in a temple older than man, a shrine overgrown with rank vegetation until it seemed hardly more than a leafy mound, we spoke to an ancient shaman who foretold great peril to your realm.

FIRST DEMON: With that intelligence we hastened here to give you the alarm before it should be too late, arriving at the very wince of time.

AUTARCH: What must I do?

SECOND DEMON: This world that you and we treasure has now been driven round the sun so often that the warp and woof of its space grow threadbare and fall as dust and feeble lint from the loom of time.

FIRST DEMON: The continents themselves are old as raddled women, long since stripped of beauty and fertility. The New Sun comes—

AUTARCH: I know!

FIRST DEMON: —and he will send them crashing into the sea like foundered ships.

SECOND DEMON: And from the sea lift new—glittering with gold, silver, iron, and copper. With diamonds, rubies, and turquoises, lands wallowing in the soil of a million millennia, so long ago washed down to the sea.

FIRST DEMON: To people these lands, a new race is prepared. The humankind you know will be shouldered aside even as the grass, that has prospered on the plain so long, yields to the plow and so gives way to wheat.

SECOND DEMON: But what if the seed were burned? What then? The tall man and the slight woman you met not long ago are such seed. Once it was hoped that it might be poisoned in the field, but she who was dispatched to accomplish it has lost sight of the seed now among the dead grass and broken clods, and for a few sleights of hand has been handed over to your Inquisitor for strict examination. Yet the seed might be burned still.

AUTARCH: The thought you suggest has already passed through my own mind.

FIRST & SECOND DEMON: (*In chorus.*) Of course!

AUTARCH: But would the death of those two truly halt the coming of the New Sun?

FIRST DEMON: No. But would you wish it? The new lands shall be yours.

The screens grow radiant. Wooded hills and cities of spires appear. The AUTARCH *turns to face them. There is a pause. He draws a communicator from his robes.*

AUTARCH: May never the New Sun see what we do here. . . . Ships! Sweep over us with flame till all is sere.

As the two DEMONS *vanish,* NOD *sits up. The cities and hills fade, and the screens show the image of the* AUTARCH *multiplied many times. The stage does dark.*

When the lights go up again, the INQUISITOR *sits at a high desk in the center of the stage. His* FAMILIAR, *dressed as a torturer and masked, stands beside the desk. To either side are various instruments of torment.*

INQUISITOR: Bring in the woman said to be a witch, Brother.

FAMILIAR: The Contessa waits outside, and as she is of exalted blood, and a favorite of our sovereign's, I beg you see her first.

Enter the CONTESSA.

CONTESSA: I heard what was said, and as I could not think you would be deaf, Inquisitor, to such an appeal, I have made bold to come in at once. Do you think me bold for that?

INQUISITOR: You toy with words. But yes, I own I do.

CONTESSA: Then you think wrongly. Eight years since my girlhood have I abode in this House Absolute. When first the blood seeped from out my loins and my mother brought me here, she warned me never to come near these apartments of yours, where the blood has trickled from so many, caring nothing for the phases of the fickle moon. And never have I come till now, and now, trembling.

INQUISITOR: Here the good need have no fear. Yet even so, I think you grown bold by your own testimony.

CONTESSA: And am I good? Are you? Is he? My confessor would tell you I am not. What does yours tell you, or is he in fear? And is your familiar a better man than you?

FAMILIAR: I would not wish to be.

CONTESSA: No, I am not bold—nor safe here, as I know. It is fear that drives me to these grim chambers. They have told you of the naked man who struck me. Has he been taken?

INQUISITOR: He has not been brought before me.

CONTESSA: Scarcely a watch ago some soldiers found me moaning in the garden, where my maid sought to comfort me. Because I feared to be outside by dark, they carried me to my own suite by way of that gallery called the Road of Air. Do you know it?

INQUISITOR: Well.

CONTESSA: Then you know too that it is everywhere overhung with windows, so that all the chambers and corridors that abut on it may receive the benefit. As we passed by, I saw in one the figure of a man, tall and clean-limbed, wide of shoulder and slender of waist.

INQUISITOR: There are many such men.

CONTESSA: So I thought. But in a little time, the same figure appeared in another window—and another. Then I appealed to the soldiers who carried me to fire upon it. They thought me mad and would not, but the party they sent to take that man returned with empty hands. Still he looked at me through the windows, and appeared to sway.

INQUISITOR: And you believe this man you saw to be the man who struck you?

CONTESSA: Worse. I fear it was not he, though it resembled him. Besides, he would be kind to me, I am sure, if only I treated his madness with respect. No, on this strange night, when we, who are the winter-killed stalks of man's old sprouting, find ourselves so mixed with next year's seed, I fear that he is something more we do not know.

INQUISITOR: That may be so, but you will not find him here, nor the man who struck you. (*To his* FAMILIAR:) Bring in the witch-woman, Brother.

FAMILIAR: Such are they all—though some are worse than others.

He exits and returns leading MESCHIANE *by a chain.*

INQUISITOR: It is alleged against you that you so charmed seven of the soldiers of our sovereign the Autarch that they betrayed their oath and turned their weapons upon their comrades and their officers. (*He rises, and lights a large candle at one side of his desk.*) I now most solemnly adjure you to confess this sin, and if you have so sinned, what power aided you to accomplish it, and the names of those who taught you to call upon that power.

MESCHIANE: The soldiers only saw I meant no harm, and were afraid for me. I—

FAMILIAR: Silence!

INQUISITOR: No weight is given to the protestations of the accused unless they are made under duress. My familiar will prepare you.

FAMILIAR *seizes* MESCHIANE *and straps her into one of the contrivances.*

CONTESSA: With so little time left to the world, I shall not waste it in watching this. Are you a friend to the naked man of the garden?

I am going to seek him, and I will tell him what has become of you.

MESCHIANE: Oh, do! I hope that he will come before it is too late.

CONTESSA: And *I* hope he will accept me, in your stead. No doubt both hopes are equally forlorn, and we shall soon be sisters in despair.

Exit the CONTESSA.

INQUISITOR: I go too, to speak to those that were her rescuers. Prepare the subject, for I shall return shortly.

FAMILIAR: There is another, Inquisitor. Of similar crimes, but less, perhaps, in potency.

INQUISITOR: Why did you not tell me? I might have instructed both together. Bring her in.

FAMILIAR *exits and returns leading* JAHI. *The* INQUISITOR *searches among the papers on his desk.*

INQUISITOR: It is alleged against you that you so charmed seven of the soldiers of our sovereign the Autarch that they betrayed their oath and turned their weapons upon their comrades and their officers. I now most solemnly adjure you to confess this sin, and if you have so sinned, what power aided you to accomplish it, and the names of those who taught you to call upon that power.

JAHI: (*Proudly.*) I have done all you accuse me of and more than you know. The power I dare not name lest this upholstered rathole be blasted to bits. Who taught me? Who teaches a child to call upon her father?

FAMILIAR: Her mother?

INQUISITOR: I would not know. Prepare her. I shall return soon.

Exit the INQUISITOR.

MESCHIANE: They fought for you too? How sad that so many had to die!

FAMILIAR: (*Locking* JAHI *in a contrivance on the other side of the desk.*) He had your paper again. I'll point his error out to him—diplomatically, you may be sure—when he comes back.

JAHI: You charmed the soldiers? Then charm this fool, and free us.

MESCHIANE: I have no chant of power, and I charmed but seven of fifty.

Enter NOD, *bound, driven by* FIRST SOLDIER *with a pike.*

FAMILIAR: What's this?

FIRST SOLDIER: Why, such a prisoner as you've never had before. He's killed a hundred men as we might puppies. Have you shackles big enough for him?

FAMILIAR: I'll have to link several pairs together, but I'll contrive something.

NOD: I am no man, but less and more—being born of the clay, of Mother Gea, whose pets are the beasts. If your dominion is over men, then you must let me go.

JAHI: We're not men either. Let us go too!

FIRST SOLDIER: (*Laughing.*) We can see you're not. I wasn't in doubt for a moment.

MESCHIANE: She's no woman. Don't let her trick you.

FAMILIAR: (*Snapping the last fetter on* NOD.) She won't. Believe me, the time of tricks is over.

FIRST SOLDIER: You'll have some fun, won't you, when I'm gone.

He reaches for JAHI, *who spits like a cat.*

FIRST SOLDIER: I don't suppose you'd be a good fellow and turn your back for a moment?

FAMILIAR: (*Preparing to torture* MESCHIANE.) If I were such a good fellow as that, I'd find myself broken on my own wheel soon enough. But if you wait here until my master the Inquisitor returns, you may find yourself lying beside her as you wish.

FIRST SOLDIER *hesitates, then realizes what is meant, and hurries out.*

NOD: That woman will be the mother of my son-in-law. Do not harm her. (*He strains at his chains.*)

JAHI: (*Stifling a yawn.*) I've been up all night, and though the spirit is as willing as ever, this flesh is ready for rest. Can't you hurry with her and get to me?

FAMILIAR: (*Not looking.*) There is no rest here.

JAHI: So? Well, it's not quite as homelike as I would expect.

JAHI *yawns again, and when she moves a hand to cover her mouth, the shackle falls away.*

MESCHIANE: You have to hold her—don't you understand? The soil has no part in her, so iron has no power over her.

FAMILIAR: (*Still looking at* MESCHIANE, *whom he is torturing.*) She is held, never fear.

MESCHIANE: Giant! Can you free yourself? The world depends on it!

NOD *strains at his bonds, but cannot break them.*

JAHI: (*Walking out of her shackles.*) Yes! It is I who answer, because in the world of reality I am far larger than any of you. (*She walks around the desk and leans over the* FAMILIAR'S *shoulder.*) How interesting! Crude, but interesting.

The FAMILIAR *turns and gapes at her, and she flees, laughing. He runs clumsily after her, and a moment later returns crestfallen.*

FAMILIAR: (*Panting.*) She's gone.

NOD: Yes. Free.

MESCHIANE: Free to pursue Meschia and ruin everything, as she did before.

FAMILIAR: You don't realize what this means. My master will return soon, and I am a dead man.

NOD: The world is dead. So she has told you.

MESCHIANE: Torturer, you have one chance yet—listen to me. You must free the giant as well.

FAMILIAR: And he will kill me and release you. I will consider it. At least it will be a quick death.

MESCHIANE: He hates Jahi, and though he isn't clever he knows her ways, and he is very strong. What's more, I can tell you an oath that he will never break. Give him the key to his shackles, then stand by me with your sword at my neck. Make him swear to find Jahi, return her here, and bind himself again.

The FAMILIAR *hesitates.*

MESCHIANE: You've nothing to lose. Your master doesn't even know he's supposed to be here. But if she's gone when he returns . . .

FAMILIAR: I'll do it! (*He detaches a key from the ring at his belt.*)

NOD: I swear as I hope to be linked by marriage to the family of Man, so that we giants may be called the Sons of the Father, that I will capture the succubus for you, and return her here, and hold her so that she shall not escape again, and bind myself as I am bound now.

FAMILIAR: Is that the oath?

MESCHIANE: Yes!

The FAMILIAR *throws the key to* NOD, *then draws his sword and holds it ready to strike* MESCHIANE.

FAMILIAR: Can he find her?

MESCHIANE: He *must* find her!

NOD: (*Unlocking himself.*) I will catch her. That body weakens, as she said. She may whip it far, but she will never learn that whipping will not do everything. (*Exits.*)

FAMILIAR: I must continue with you. I hope you understand. . . .

The FAMILIAR *tortures* MESCHIANE, *who screams.*

FAMILIAR: (*Sotto voce.*) How fair she is! I wish that we . . . were met when better things might be.

The stage darkens; JAHI*'s running feet are heard. After a time, a faint light shows* NOD *loping through the corridors of the House Absolute. Moving images of urns, pictures, and furniture behind him show his progress.* JAHI *appears among them, and he exits stage right in pursuit.* JAHI *enters stage left, with* SECOND DEMON *walking in lockstep behind her.*

JAHI: Where can he have gone? The gardens are burned black. You have no flesh beyond a seeming—cannot you make yourself an owl and seek him out for me?

SECOND DEMON: (*Mocking.*) Who-o-o?

JAHI: Meschia! Wait until the Father hears how you have treated me, and betrayed all our efforts.

SECOND DEMON: From you? It was you who left Meschia, lured away by the woman. What will you say? "The woman tempted me?" We have done with that so long ago that no one remembers it save you and I, and now you have spoiled the lie by making it come true.

JAHI: (*Turning on him.*) You little foul sniveler! You scrabbler at windows!

SECOND DEMON: (*Jumping back.*) And now you are exiled to the land of Nod, east of Paradise.

NOD'*s footfalls are heard offstage.* JAHI *hides behind a clepsydra, and* SECOND DEMON *produces a pike and stands with it in the attitude of a soldier as* NOD *enters.*

NOD: How long have you been standing there?

SECOND DEMON: (*Saluting.*) As long as you want, sieur.

NOD: What news is there?

SECOND DEMON: All you want, sieur. A giant as high as a steeple has killed the throne-guards, and the Autarch's missing. We've searched the gardens so often that if only we'd been carrying dung instead of spears, the daisies'd be as big as umbrellas. Ducks' clothes is down and hopes is up—so's the turnips. Tomorrow should be fair, warm, and bright . . . *looks significantly toward the clepsydra*) and a woman with no clothes on has been running through the halls.

NOD: What is that thing?

SECOND DEMON: A water clock, sieur. See, you, knowing what time it is, can tell by that how much water's flowed.

NOD: (*Examining the clepsydra.*) There is nothing like this in my land. Do these puppets move by water?

SECOND DEMON: Not the big one, sieur.

JAHI *bolts offstage, pursued by* NOD, *but before he is fully out of sight of the audience, she dives between his legs, reentering. He continues off, giving her time to hide in a chest. Meanwhile,* SECOND DEMON *has disappeared.*

NOD: (*Reentering.*) Ho! Stop! (*Runs to opposite side of stage and returns.*) My fault! My fault! In the garden there—she passed close by me once. I could have reached out and crushed her like a cat—a worm—a mouse—a snake. (*Turns on audience.*) Don't laugh at me! I could kill you all! The whole poisoned race of you! Oh, to strew the valleys with your white bones! But I am done—I am done! And Meschiane, who trusted in me, is undone!

NOD *strikes the clepsydra, sending brass pans and water flying across the stage.*

NOD: What good is this gift of speech, except that I can curse myself. Good mother of all the beasts, take it from me. I would be as I was, and shout wordless among the hills. Reason shows reason can only bring pain—how wise to forget and be happy again!

NOD *seats himself on the chest in which* JAHI *hides, and buries his face in his hands. As the lights dim, the chest begins to splinter beneath his weight.*

When the lights come up again, the scene is once more the INQUISITOR*'s chamber.* MESCHIANE *is on the rack. The* FAMILIAR *is turning the wheel. She screams.*

FAMILIAR: That made you feel better, didn't it? I told you it would. Besides, it lets the neighbors know we're awake in here. You wouldn't believe it, but this whole wing is full of empty rooms and sinecures. Here the master and I do our business still. We do it still, and that's why the Commonwealth stands. And we want them to know it.

Enter the AUTARCH. *His robes are torn and stained with blood.*

AUTARCH: What place is this? (*He sits on the floor, his head in his hands in an attitude reminiscent of* NOD*'s.*)

FAMILIAR: What place? Why, the Chambers of Mercy, you jackass. Can you come here without knowing where you are?

AUTARCH: I have been so hunted through my house this night that I might be anywhere. Bring me some wine—or water, if you've no wine here—and bar the door.

FAMILIAR: We have claret, but no wine. And I can hardly bar the door, since I expect my master back.

AUTARCH: (*More forcefully.*) Do as I tell you.

FAMILIAR: (*Very softly.*) You are drunk, friend. Go out.

AUTARCH: I am—What does it matter? The end is here. I am a man neither worse nor better than you.

NOD*'s heavy tread is heard in the distance.*

FAMILIAR: He has failed—I know it!

MESCHIANE: He has succeeded! He would not come back so soon with empty hands. The world may yet be saved!

AUTARCH: What do you mean?

Enter NOD. *The madness he prayed for is upon him, but he drags* JAHI *behind him. The* FAMILIAR *runs forward with shackles.*

MESCHIANE: Someone must hold her, or she will escape as she did before.

The FAMILIAR *drapes chains on* NOD *and snaps closed the locks, then chains one of* NOD*'s arms across his body in such a way that he holds* JAHI. NOD *tightens the grip.*

FAMILIAR: He's killing her! Let go, you great booby!

The FAMILIAR *snatches up the bar with which he has been tightening the rack and belabors* NOD *with it.* NOD *roars, tries to grasp him, and lets the unconscious* JAHI *slip down. The* FAMILIAR *seizes her by the foot and pulls her to where the* AUTARCH *sits.*

FAMILIAR: Here, you, you'll do.

He jerks the AUTARCH *erect and swiftly imprisons him in such a way that one hand is clamped about* JAHI*'s wrist, then returns to torture* MESCHIANE. *Unseen behind him,* NOD *is freeing himself of his chains.*

XXV

The Attack on the Hierodules

Though we were outdoors, where sounds are so easily lost against the immensity of the sky, I could hear the clatter Baldanders made as he feigned to struggle with his bonds. There were conversations in the audience, and I could hear those as well—one about the play, which discovered in it significances I had never guessed and which Dr. Talos, I would say, had never intended; and another about some legal case that a speaker with the drawling intonation of an exultant seemed certain the Autarch was about to judge wrongly. As I turned the windlass of the rack, letting the pawl drop with a satisfying clack, I risked a sidelong look at those who watched us.

No more than ten chairs were in use, but lofty figures stood at the sides of the seating area, and behind it. There were a few women in court dresses much like the ones I had once seen in the House Azure, dresses with very low décolletages and full skirts that were often slit, or relieved with panels of lace. Their hair was simply dressed, but it was set off with flowers, jewels, or brilliantly luminous larvae.

Most of those in our audience seemed men, and more arrived momentarily. Many were as tall as or taller than Vodalus. They stood wrapped in their cloaks as though they were chilled by the soft spring air. Their faces were shadowed beneath broad-brimmed, low-crowned petasoses.

Baldanders's chains fell with a crash, and Dorcas shrieked to let me know he was free. I turned toward him, then cowered away, wrenching the nearest flambeau from its socket to fend him off. It guttered as the oil in its bowl nearly drowned the flame, sputtering to renewed life when the brimstone and mineral salts Dr. Talos had gummed around the rim took fire.

The giant was feigning madness, as his role required. His coarse hair hung about his eyes; and they, behind its screen, blazed so wildly I could see them despite it. His mouth hung slack, drooling spittle and showing his yellowed teeth. Arms twice the length of my own groped toward me.

What frightened me—and I was frightened, I admit, and wished heartily I had *Terminus Est* in my hands instead of the iron flambeau—was what I can only call the expression beneath the lack of expression on his face. It was there like the black water we sometimes glimpse moving beneath the ice when the river freezes. Baldanders had found a terrible joy now in being as he was; and when I faced him I realized for the first time that he was not so much feigning madness on the stage as feigning sanity and his dim humility off it. I wondered then how much he had influenced the writing of the play, though it may be only that Dr. Talos had (as he surely had) understood his patient better than I.

We were not, of course, to terrify the Autarch's courtiers as we had the country people. Baldanders would wrest the flambeau from me, pretend to break my back, and end the scene. He did not. Whether he was as mad as he pretended or was genuinely enraged at our growing audience, I cannot say. Perhaps both those explanations are correct.

However that might be, he jerked the flambeau from me and turned on them, flourishing it so the burning oil flew about him in a shower of fire. My sword, with which I had threatened Dorcas's head a few moments before, lay near my feet, and I stooped for it instinctively. By the time I had straightened up again, Baldanders was in the midst of the audience. The flambeau had gone out, and he swung it like a mace.

Someone fired a pistol. The bolt set his costume afire, but must have missed his body. Several exultants had drawn their swords, and someone—I could not see who—possessed that rarest of all weapons, a dream. It moved like tyrian smoke, but very much faster, and in an instant it had enveloped the giant. It seemed then that he stood wrapped in all that was past and much that had never been: a gray-haired woman sprouted from his side, a fishing boat hovered just over his head, and a cold wind whipped the flames that wreathed him.

Yet the visions, which are said to leave soldiers dazed and helpless, a burden to their cause, did not seem to affect Baldanders. He strode forward still, and the flambeau smashed clear a path for him.

Then, in the moment more that I watched (for I soon recovered enough self-command to flee that mad fight) I saw several figures throw aside their capes and—as it appeared—their faces too. Under those faces, which when they were no longer worn seemed of a tissue as insubstantial as that of the notules, were such monstrosities as I had not thought existence could support: a circular mouth rimmed with needle teeth; eyes that were themselves a thousand eyes, clustered like the scales of a pine cone; jaws like tongs. These things have remained in my memory as everything remains, and I have stared again at them in the dark watches of the night. I am very glad, when at last I rouse myself to turn my face toward the stars and moon-drenched clouds instead, that I could see only those nearest our footlights.

I have already said that I fled. But that slight delay, during which I picked up *Terminus Est* and stood observing Baldanders's mad attack, almost cost me dearly; by the time I turned to take Dorcas to safety, she was gone.

I ran then not so much from Baldanders's fury, or from the cacogens in the audience, or from the Autarch's praetorians (who I felt would surely arrive soon), but in pursuit of Dorcas. Searching for her and calling her name as I went, I found nothing but the groves and fountains and abrupt wells of that endless garden; and at last, winded and with aching legs, I slowed to a walk.

It is impossible for me to set down on paper all the bitterness I felt then. To have found Dorcas and lost her so soon seemed more than I could bear. Women believe—or at least often pretend to believe—that all our tenderness for them springs from desire; that we love them when we have not for a time enjoyed them, and dismiss them when we are sated, or to express it more precisely, exhausted. There is no truth in this idea, though it may be made to appear true. When we are rigid with desire, we are apt to pretend a great tenderness in the hope of satisfying that desire; but at no other time are we in fact so liable to treat women brutally, and so unlikely to feel any deep emotion but one. As I wandered through the nighted gardens, I felt no physical need for Dorcas (though I had not enjoyed her since we had slept in the fortress of the dimarchi, beyond the Sanguinary Fields) because I had poured out my manhood again and again with Jolenta in the nenuphar boat. Yet if I had found Dorcas I would have smothered her with kisses; and for Jolenta, whom I had been prone to dislike, I now had conceived a certain affection.

Neither Dorcas nor Jolenta appeared, nor did I see hastening soldiers or even the revelers we had come to entertain. The thiasus, it seemed clear, had been confined to some certain part of the grounds; and I was now far from that part. Even now, I am unsure how far the House Absolute extends. There are maps, but they are incomplete and contradictory. There are no maps of the Second House, and even Father Inire tells me that he has long ago forgotten many of its mysteries. In wandering its narrow corridors, I have seen no white wolves; but I have found stairs leading to domes beneath the river, and hatches opening into what appears to be untouched forest. (Some of these are marked above ground by ruinous, half-overgrown marble steles; some are not.) When I have closed such hatches and retreated regretfully into an artificial air still laced with the odors of vegetable growth and decay, I have often wondered whether some passage or other does not reach the Citadel. Old Ultan hinted once that his library stacks extended to the House Absolute. What is that but to say that the House Absolute extended to his library stacks? There are parts of the Second House that are not unlike the blind corridors in which I searched for Triskele; perhaps they are the same corridors, though if they are, I ran a greater risk than I then knew.

Whether these speculations of mine are rooted in fact or not, I had no notion of them at the time of which I write now. In my innocence I supposed that the borders of the House Absolute, which extended both in space and in time so much further than the uninformed would guess, could be strictly delimited; and that I was approaching, or would soon approach, or had already passed them. Thus I walked all that night, directing my course northward by the stars. And as I walked, I reviewed my life in just the way I have so often attempted to prevent myself from doing while I waited for sleep. Again Drotte and Roche and I swam in the clammy cistern beneath the Bell Keep; again I replaced Josephina's toy imp with the stolen frog; again I stretched forth my hand to grasp the haft of the ax that would have slain the great Vodalus and so saved a Thecla not yet imprisoned; again I saw the ribbon of crimson creep from under Thecla's door, Malrubius bending over me, Jonas vanishing into the infinity between dimensions. I played again with pebbles in the courtyard beside the fallen curtain wall, as Thecla dodged the hooves of my father's mounted guard.

Long after I had seen the last balustrade, I feared the soldiers of the Autarch; but after some time, when I had not so much as glimpsed a distant patrol, I grew contemptuous of them, believing their ineffectiveness to be a part of that general disorganization I had observed in the Commonwealth so often. With or without my help, Vodalus, I felt, would surely destroy such bunglers—indeed, could do so now, if he would only strike.

And yet the androgyne in the yellow robe, who had known Vodalus's password and received his message as if expecting it, was unquestionably the Autarch, the master of those soldiers and in fact of the entire Commonwealth insofar as it recognized a master. Thecla had seen him often; those memories of Thecla's were now my own, and it was he. If Vodalus had won already, why did he remain in hiding? Or was Vodalus merely a creature of the Autarch's? (If so, why did Vodalus refer to the Autarch as though he were a servitor?) I tried to persuade myself that everything that had passed in the chamber of the picture and the rest of the Second House had been a dream; but I knew it was not so, and the steel was gone.

Thinking of Vodalus reminded me of the Claw, which the Autarch himself had urged me to return to the order of priestesses called Pelerines. I drew it out. Its light was soft now, neither flashing as it had been in the mine of the man-apes nor dull as it had been when Jonas and I had examined it in the antechamber. Though it lay upon the palm of my hand, it seemed to me now a great pool of blue water, purer than the cistern, purer far than Gyoll, into which I might dive . . . though in doing so I should in some incomprehensible fashion be diving *up*. It was at once comforting and disquieting, and I pushed it into my boot top again and walked on.

Dawn found me on a narrow path that straggled through a forest more sumptuous in its decay even than that outside the Wall of Nessus. The cool fern arches I had seen there were absent here, but fleshy-fingered vines clung to the great mahoganies and rain-trees like hetaerae, turning their long limbs to clouds of floating green and lowering rich curtains spangled with flowers. Birds unknown to me called overhead, and once a monkey who might, save for his four hands, have been a wizened, red-bearded man in fur, spied on me from a fork as high as a spire. When I could walk no farther, I found a dry, well shaded spot between pillar-thick roots and wrapped myself in my cloak.

Often I have had to hunt down sleep as though it were the most elusive of chimeras, half legend and half air. Now it sprang upon me. I had no sooner closed my eyes than I faced the maddened giant again. This time I held *Terminus Est*, but she seemed no more than a wand. Instead of the stage, we stood upon a narrow parapet. To one side flamed the torches of an army. On the other a sheer drop terminated in a spreading lake that at once was and was not the azure pool of the Claw. Baldanders lifted his terrible flambeau, and I had somehow become the childish figure I had seen beneath the sea. The gigantic women, I felt, could not be far away. The mace crashed down.

It was broad afternoon, and flame-colored ants were making a caravan across my chest. After two or three watches spent in walking among the pale leaves of that noble yet doomed forest, I struck a broader path, and in another watch (when the shadows were lengthening) I halted, sniffed the air, and found that the odor I had detected was indeed the reek of smoke. I was wracked with hunger by that time, and I hurried forward.

XXVI

Parting

Where the path crossed another, four people sat on the ground around a tiny fire. I recognized Jolenta first—her aura of beauty made the clearing seem a paradise. At almost the same moment, Dorcas recognized me and came running to kiss me, and I glimpsed Dr. Talos's fox-like face over Baldanders's massive shoulder.

The giant, whom I ought to have known at once, was changed almost out of recognition. His head was swathed in dirty bandages, and in place of the baggy black coat he had worn, his wide back was covered with a sticky ointment that resembled clay and smelled like stagnant water.

"Well met, well met," Dr. Talos called. "We've all been wondering what became of you." Baldanders indicated with a slight inclination of his head that it was actually Dorcas who had been wondering, which I think I might have guessed without the hint.

"I ran," I said. "So did Dorcas, I know. I'm surprised the rest of you weren't killed."

"We very nearly were," the doctor admitted, nodding.

Jolenta shrugged, making the simple movement seem an exquisite ceremony. "I ran away too." She cupped her huge breasts with her hands. "But I don't think I'm well suited to running, do you? Anyway, in the dark I soon bumped against an exultant who told me I would have to run no farther, that he would protect me. But then some spahis came—I would like to have their animals harnessed to my carriage someday, they were very fine—and they had with them a high official of the sort that cares nothing for women. I hoped then that I would be taken to the Autarch—whose pores outshine the stars themselves—the way it nearly happens in the play. But they made my exultant leave, and instead it was back to the theater where he," she gestured toward

Baldanders, "and the doctor were. The doctor was putting salve on him, and the soldiers were going to kill us, although I could see they didn't really want to kill me. Then they let us go, and here we are."

Dr. Talos added, "We found Dorcas at daybreak. Or rather, she found us, and we have been traveling slowly toward the mountains ever since. Slowly, because ill though he is, Baldanders is the only one of us with the strength to carry our baggage, and though we have discarded much of it, there remain certain items we must keep."

I said I was surprised to hear Baldanders was merely ill, since I had been certain he was dead.

"Dr. Talos stopped him," Dorcas said. "Isn't that right, Doctor? That's how he was captured. It's surprising that both of them weren't killed."

"Yet as you see," Dr. Talos said, smiling, "we yet walk among the living. And though we are somewhat the worse for wear, we are rich. Show Severian our money, Baldanders."

Painfully, the giant shifted his position and took out a bulging leather purse. After looking at the doctor as though for additional instructions, he loosened the strings and poured into his huge hand a shower of new-minted chrisos.

Dr. Talos took one of the coins and held it up so it caught the light. "How long do you think a man from one of the fishing villages about Lake Diuturna would build walls for that?"

I said, "At least a year, I should imagine."

"Two! Every day, winter and summer, rain or shine, provided we dole it out in bits of copper, as we shall. We'll have fifty such men to help rebuild our home. Wait until you see it next!"

Baldanders added in his heavy voice, "If they will work."

The red-haired doctor whirled on him. "They'll work! I've learned something since last time, let me tell you!"

I interposed. "I assume that a part of that money is mine, and that a part belongs to these women—does it not?"

Dr. Talos relaxed. "Oh, yes. I had forgotten. The women have already had their shares. Half of this is yours. After all, we wouldn't have had it without you." He scooped the coins out of the giant's hand and began to create two stacks on the ground before him.

I supposed that he meant only that I had contributed to the success of his play, such as it was. But Dorcas, who must have sensed that something more lay behind the credit he had given me, asked, "Why do you say that, Doctor?"

The fox-face smiled. "Severian has friends in high places. I own I have thought so for some time—a torturer wandering the roads like a vagrant was a bit too much even for Baldanders to swallow, and I have, I fear, an excessively narrow throat.''

''If I have such friends,'' I said, ''I am unaware of them.''

The stacks were level now, and the doctor pushed one toward me and the other back to the giant. ''At first, when I found you abed with Baldanders, I thought you might have been sent to warn us against performing my play—in some respects it is, as you may have observed, at least in appearance critical of the Autarchy.''

''Somewhat,'' Jolenta lisped sarcastically.

''Yet surely, to send a torturer from the Citadel to frighten a couple of strolling mountebanks would be an absurd overreaction. Then I realized that we, by the very fact that we were staging the play, served to conceal you. Few would suspect that a servant of the Autarch would associate himself with such an enterprise. I wrote in the Familiar's part so that we should hide you better by giving your habit a reason for existence.''

''I know nothing of this,'' I said.

''Of course. I have no desire to force you to violate your trust. But as we were setting up our theater yesterday, a highly placed servant from the House Absolute—an agamite, I think, and they are always close to the ear of authority—came asking if our troupe was the one in which you performed, and if you were with us. You and Jolenta had absented yourselves, but I answered in the affirmative. He asked then how great a share you had of what we made, and when I told him, said that he was instructed to pay us now for the night's performance. Very fortunate that proved, since this great ninny went charging out into our audience.''

It was one of the few times I saw Baldanders appear hurt by his physician's jibes. Though it clearly cost him pain to do so, he swung his big body about until he faced away from us.

Dorcas had told me that when I had slept in Dr. Talos's tent, I had slept alone. Now I sensed that the giant felt so; that for him the clearing held only himself and certain small animals, pets of whom he was tiring.

''He has paid for his rashness,'' I said. ''He looks badly burned.''

The doctor nodded. ''Actually, Baldanders was fortunate. The Hierodules dialed down their beams and tried to turn him back instead of killing him. He lives now through their forbearance, and will regenerate.''

Dorcas murmured, ''Heal, you mean? I trust so. I feel more pity for him than I can say.''

''Yours is a tender heart. Too tender, perhaps. But Baldanders is still growing, and growing children have great recuperative powers.''

"Still growing?" I asked. "His hair is partly gray."

The doctor laughed. "Then perhaps he is growing grayer. But now, dear friends," he rose and dusted his trousers, "now we have come, as some poet aptly puts it, to the place where men are pulled apart by their destinations. We had halted here, Severian, not only because we were fatigued, but because it is here that the route toward Thrax, where you are going, and that toward Lake Diuturna and our own country diverge. I was loath to pass this point, the last at which I had hopes of seeing you, without making a fair division of our gains—but that is accomplished now. Should you communicate again with your benefactors in the House Absolute, will you own that you have been equitably dealt with?"

The stack of chrisos was still on the ground before me. "There is a hundred times more here than I ever expected to receive," I said. "Yes. Certainly." I picked up the coins and put them into my sabretache.

A glance passed between Dorcas and Jolenta, and Dorcas said, "I am going to Thrax with Severian, if that is where Severian is going."

Jolenta held up a hand to the doctor, obviously expecting that he would help her to rise.

"Baldanders and I will be traveling alone," he said, "and we will walk all night. We will miss all of you, but the time of parting is upon us. Dorcas, my child, I am delighted that you will have a protector." (Jolenta's hand was by this time on his thigh.) "Come, Baldanders, we must be away."

The giant lumbered to his feet, and though he made no moan, I could see how much he suffered. His bandages were wet with mingled sweat and blood. I knew what I had to do, and said, "Baldanders and I must speak privately for a moment. Could I ask the rest of you to move off a hundred paces or so?"

The women began to do as I had asked, Dorcas walking down one path and Jolenta (whom Dorcas had helped up) down another; but Dr. Talos remained where he was until I repeated my request that he go.

"You wish me to leave as well? It's quite useless. Baldanders will tell me anything you tell him as soon as we are together again. Jolenta! Come here, dear."

"She is leaving at my request, just as I asked you to."

"Yes, but she's going the wrong way, and I cannot have it. Jolenta!"

"Doctor, I only wish to help your friend—or your slave, or whatever he is."

Quite unexpectedly, Baldanders's deep voice issued from beneath his swirl of bandages. "I am his master."

"Exactly so," said the doctor, as taking up the stack of chrisos he had pushed toward Baldanders, he dropped it into the giant's trousers pocket.

Jolenta had hobbled back to us with tears streaking her lovely face. "Doctor, can't I go with you?"

"Of course not," he said as coolly as if a child had asked for a second slice of cake. Jolenta collapsed at his feet.

I looked up at the giant. "Baldanders, I can help you. A friend of mine was burned as much as you are not long ago, and I was able to help him. But I won't do it while Dr. Talos and Jolenta look on. Will you come with me, only a short way, back down the path toward the House Absolute?"

Slowly, the giant's head swung from side to side.

"He knows the lenitive you offer," Dr. Talos said, laughing. "He himself has provided it to many, but he loves life too much."

"Life is what I offer—not death."

"Yes?" The doctor raised an eyebrow. "Where is your friend?"

The giant had picked up the handles of his barrow. "Baldanders," I said, "do you know who the Conciliator was?"

"That was long ago," Baldanders answered. "It does not matter." He started down the path Dorcas had not taken. Dr. Talos followed him for a few strides, with Jolenta clinging to his arm, then stopped.

"Severian, you have guarded a good many prisoners, according to what you've told me. If Baldanders were to give you another chrisos, would you hold this creature until we are well gone?"

I was still sick with the thought of the giant's pain and my own failure; but I managed to say, "As a member of the guild, I can accept commissions only from the legally constituted authorities."

"We will kill her then, when we are out of your sight."

"That is a matter between you and her," I said, and started after Dorcas.

I had hardly caught up with her before we heard Jolenta's screams. Dorcas halted and grasped my hand more tightly, asking what the sound was; I told her of the doctor's threat.

"And you let her go?"

"I didn't believe he meant it."

As I said that, we had turned and were already retracing our way. We had not gone a dozen strides before the screams were succeeded by a silence so profound we could hear the rustling of a dying leaf. We hurried on; but by the time we reached the crossing, I felt certain we were too late, and so I was, if the truth be known, only hurrying because I knew Dorcas would be disappointed in me if I did not.

I was wrong in thinking Jolenta dead. As we rounded a turn in the path we saw her running toward us, her knees together as if her legs were hampered by her generous thighs, her arms crossed over her breasts to steady them. Her glorious red-gold hair fell across her eyes, and the thin organza shift she wore had been slashed to tatters. She fainted when Dorcas embraced her. "Those devils, they've beaten her," Dorcas said.

"A moment ago we were afraid they would kill her." I looked at the welts on the beautiful woman's back. "These are the marks of the doctor's cane, I think. She's lucky he didn't set Baldanders on her."

"But what can we do?"

"We can try this." I fished the Claw from my boot top and showed it to her. "Do you remember the thing we found in my sabretache? That you said was no true gem? This is what it was, and it seems to help injured people, sometimes. I wanted to use it on Baldanders, but he wouldn't let me."

I held the Claw over Jolenta's head, then ran it along the bruises on her back, but it flamed no brighter and she seemed no better. "It isn't working," I said. "I'll have to carry her."

"Put her over your shoulder, or you'll be holding her just where she's been hurt worst."

Dorcas carried *Terminus Est*, and I did as she suggested, finding Jolenta nearly as heavy as a man. For a long while we trudged thus beneath the pale green canopy of the leaves before Jolenta's eyes opened. Even then she could hardly walk or stand without help, however, or so much as comb back that extraordinary hair with her fingers to let us better see the tear-stained oval of her face.

"The doctor won't let me come with him," she said.

Dorcas nodded. "It seems not." She might have been talking to someone far younger than herself.

"I will be destroyed."

I asked why she said that, but she only shook her head. After a time she said, "May I go with you, Severian? I don't have any money. Baldanders took away what the doctor had given me." She shot a sidelong glance at Dorcas. "She has money too—more than I got. As much as the doctor gave you."

"He knows that," Dorcas said. "And he knows any money I have is his, if he wants it."

I changed the subject. "Perhaps both of you should know that I may not be going to Thrax, or at least, not directly. Not if I can discover the whereabouts of the order of Pelerines."

Jolenta looked at me as if I were mad. "I've heard they roam the whole world. Besides, they accept only women."

"I don't want to join them, only to find them. The last news I had was that they were on the way north. But if I can find out where they are, I'll have to go there—even if it means turning south again."

"I'm going where you go," Dorcas declared. "Not to Thrax."

"And I'm going nowhere," Jolenta sighed.

As soon as we no longer had to support Jolenta, Dorcas and I drew somewhat ahead of her. When we had been walking for some time, I turned to look back at her. She was no longer weeping, but I hardly recognized the beauty who had once accompanied Dr. Talos. She had held her head proudly, and even arrogantly. Her shoulders had been thrown back and her magnificent eyes had flashed like emeralds. Now her shoulders drooped with weariness and she looked at the ground.

"What was it you spoke of with the doctor and the giant?" Dorcas asked as we walked.

"I've already told you," I said.

"Once you called out so loudly that I could hear what you said. It was 'Do you know who the Conciliator was?' But I couldn't tell if you didn't know yourself, or were only seeking to discover if they knew."

"I know very little—nothing, really. I've seen pictures that are supposed to be of him, but they differ so much they can hardly be of the same man."

"There are legends."

"Most of them I've heard sound very foolish. I wish Jonas were here; he would take care of Jolenta, and he would know about the Conciliator. Jonas was the man we met at the Piteous Gate, the man who rode the merychip. For a time he was a good friend to me."

"Where is he now?"

"That's what Dr. Talos wanted to know. I don't know, and I don't wish to speak of it. Tell me about the Conciliator, if you want to talk."

No doubt it was foolish, but as soon as I mentioned that name, I felt the silence of the forest like a weight. The sighing of a little wind somewhere among the uppermost branches might have been the sigh from a sickbed; the pale green of the light-starved leaves suggested the pallid faces of starved children.

"No one knows much about him," Dorcas began, "and I probably know less than you do. I don't even remember now how I learned what I know. Anyway some people say he was hardly more than a boy. Some say he was not a human being at all—not a cacogen, but the thought, tangible to us, of some vast intelligence to whom our actuality is no more real than the paper theaters of the toy sellers. The story goes that he once took a dying woman by the hand and a star by the other, and from that time forward he had the power to reconcile the universe with humanity, and humanity with the universe, ending the old breach. He had a way of vanishing, then reappearing when everyone thought he was dead—reappearing sometimes after he had been buried. He might be encountered as an animal, speaking the human tongue, and he appeared to some pious woman or other in the form of roses."

I recalled my masking. "Holy Katharine, I suppose, at her execution."

"There are darker legends, too."

"Tell them to me."

"They frightened me," Dorcas said. "Now I don't even remember them. Doesn't that brown book you carry with you make any mention of him?"

I drew it out and saw that it did, and then, since I could not comfortably read while we walked, I thrust it back in my sabretache again, resolving to read that section when we camped, as we would have to soon.

XXVII

Toward Thrax

Our path ran through the stricken forest for as long as the light lasted; a watch after dark we reached the edge of a river smaller and swifter than Gyoll, where by moonlight we could see broad cane fields on the farther side waving in the night wind. Jolenta had been sobbing with weariness for some distance, and Dorcas and I agreed to halt. Since I would never have risked *Terminus Est*'s honed blade on the heavy limbs of the forest trees, we would have had little firewood there; such dead branches as we had come across had been soaked with moisture and were already spongy with decay. The riverbank provided an abundance of twisted, weathered sticks, hard and light and dry.

We had broken a good many and laid our fire before I remembered I no longer had my striker, having left it with the Autarch, who must also, I felt certain, have been the ''highly placed servant'' who had filled Dr. Talos's hands with chrisos. Dorcas had flint, steel, and tinder among her scant baggage, however, and we were soon comforted by a roaring blaze. Jolenta was fearful of wild beasts, though I labored to explain to her how unlikely it was that the soldiers would permit anything dangerous to live in a forest that ran up to the gardens of the House Absolute. For her sake we burned three thick brands at one end only, so that if need arose we could snatch them from the fire and threaten the creatures she dreaded.

No beasts came, our fire drove off the mosquitoes, and we lay upon our backs and watched the sparks mount into the air. Far higher, the lights of fliers passed to and fro, filling the sky for a moment or two with a ghostly false dawn as the ministers and generals of the Autarch returned to the House Absolute or went forth to war. Dorcas and I speculated about what they might think when they looked down—for only an instant as they were whirled away—and saw our scarlet star; and we decided that they must wonder about us much as we wondered about them, pondering who we might be, and where we went, and why. Dorcas sang a song for me, a song about a girl who wanders through a grove in spring, lonely for her friends of the year before, the fallen leaves.

Jolenta lay between our fire and the water, I suppose because she felt safer there. Dorcas and I were on the opposite side of the fire, not only because we wanted to be out of her sight as nearly as possible, but because Dorcas, as she told me, disliked the sight and sound of the cold, dark stream slipping by. "Like a worm," she said. "A big ebony snake that is not hungry now, but knows where we are and will eat us by and by. Aren't you afraid of snakes, Severian?"

Thecla had been; I felt the shade of her fear stir at the question and nodded.

"I've heard that in the hot forests of the north, the Autarch of All Serpents is Uroboros, the brother of Abaia, and that hunters who discover his burrow believe they have found a tunnel under the sea, and descending it enter his mouth and all unknowing climb down his throat, so that they are dead while they still believe themselves living; though there are others who say that Uroboros is only the great river there that flows to its own source, or the sea itself, that devours its own beginnings."

Dorcas edged closer as she recounted all this, and I put my arm about her, knowing that she wanted me to make love to her, though we could not be sure Jolenta was asleep on the other side of the fire. Indeed, from time to time she stirred, seeming because of her full hips, narrow waist, and billowing hair, to undulate like a serpent herself. Dorcas lifted her small, tragically clean face to mine, and I kissed her and felt her press herself to me, trembling with desire.

"I am so cold," she whispered.

She was naked, though I had not seen her undress. When I put my cloak about her, her skin felt flushed—as my own was—from the heat of the blaze. Her little hands slipped under my clothes, caressing me.

"So good," she said. "So smooth." And then (though we had coupled before), "Won't I be too small?", like a child.

When I woke, the moon (it was almost beyond belief that it was the same moon that had guided me through the gardens of the House Absolute) had nearly been overtaken by the mounting horizon of the west. Its berylline light streamed down the river, giving to every ripple the black shadow of a wave.

I felt uneasy without knowing why. Jolenta's fears of beasts no longer seemed so foolish as they had, and I got up and, after making certain she and Dorcas were unharmed, found more wood for our dying fire. I remembered the notules, which Jonas had told me were often sent forth by night, and the thing in the antechamber. Night birds sailed overhead—not only owls, such as we had in plenty nesting in the ruined towers of the Citadel, birds marked by their round heads and short, broad, silent wings, but birds of other kinds with two-forked and three-forked tails, birds that stooped to skim the water and twittered as they flew. Occasionally, moths vastly larger than any I had seen before passed from tree to tree. Their figured wings were as long as a man's arms, and they spoke among themselves as men do, but in voices almost too high for hearing.

After I had stirred the fire, made sure of my sword, and looked for a time on Dorcas's innocent face with its great, tender eyelashes closed in sleep, I lay down again to watch the birds voyage among the constellations and enter that world of memory that, no matter how sweet or how bitter it may be, is never wholly closed to me.

I sought to recall that celebration of Holy Katharine's day that fell the year after I became captain of apprentices; but the preparations for the feast were hardly begun before other memories came crowding unbidden around it. In our kitchen I lifted a cup of stolen wine to my lips—and found it had become a breast running with warm milk. It was my mother's breast then, and I could hardly contain my elation (which might have wiped the memory away) at having reached back at last to her, after so many fruitless attempts. My arms sought to clasp her, and I would, if only I could, have lifted my eyes to look into her face. My mother certainly, for the children the torturers take know no breasts. The grayness at the edge of my field of vision, then, was the metal of her cell wall. Soon she would be led away to scream in the Apparatus or gasp in Allowin's Necklace. I sought to hold her back, to mark the moment so I might return to it when I chose; she faded even as I tried to bind her to me, dissolving as mist does when the wind rises.

I was a child again . . . a girl . . . Thecla. I stood in a magnificent chamber whose windows were mirrors, mirrors that at once illuminated and reflected. Around me were beautiful women twice my height or more, in various stages of undress. The air was thick with scent. I was searching for someone, but as I looked at the painted faces of the tall women, lovely and indeed perfect, I began to doubt if I should know her. Tears rolled down my cheeks. Three women ran to me and I stared from one to another. As I did, their eyes narrowed to points of light, and a heart-shaped patch beside the lips of the nearest spread web-fingered wings.

"Severian."

I sat up, uncertain of the point at which memory had become dream. This voice was sweet, yet very deep, and though I was conscious of having heard it before, I could not at once recall where. The moon was nearly behind the western horizon now, and our fire was dying a second death. Dorcas had thrown aside her ragged bedding, so that she slept with her sprite's body exposed to the night air. Seeing her thus, her pale skin rendered more pale still by the waning moonlight, save where the glow of the embers flushed it with red, I felt such desire as I had never known—not when I had clasped Agia to me on the Adamnian Steps, not when I had first seen Jolenta on Dr. Talos's stage, not even on the innumerable occasions when I had hastened to Thecla in her cell. Yet it was not Dorcas I desired; I had enjoyed her only a short time ago, and though I fully believed she loved me, I could not be certain she would have given herself so readily if she had not more than suspected I had entered Jolenta on the afternoon before the play, and if she had not believed Jolenta to be watching us across the fire.

Nor did I desire Jolenta, who lay upon her side and snored. Instead I wanted them both, and Thecla, and the nameless meretrix who had feigned to be Thecla in the House Azure, and her friend who had taken the part of Thea, the woman I had seen on the stair in the House Absolute. And Agia, Valeria, Morwenna, and a thousand more. I recalled the witches, their madness and their wild dancing in the Old Court on nights of rain; the cool, virginal beauty of the red-robed Pelerines.

"Severian."

It was no dream. Sleepy birds, perched on branches at the margin of the forest, had stirred at the sound. I drew *Terminus Est* and let her blade catch the cold dawn light, so that whoever had spoken should know me armed.

All was quiet again—quieter now than it had ever been by night. I waited, turning my head slowly in my attempt to locate the one who had called my name, though I was conscious it would have been better if I could have appeared to know the correct direction already. Dorcas stirred and moaned, but neither she nor Jolenta woke; there was no other sound but the crackling of the fire, the dawn wind among the leaves, and the lapping water.

"Where are you?" I whispered, but there was no reply. A fish jumped with a silver splash, and all was silent again.

"Severian."

However deep, it was a woman's voice, throbbing with passion, moist with need; I remembered Agia and did not sheathe my sword.

"The sandbar . . ."

Though I feared it was merely a trick to make me turn my back on the trees, I let my eyes search the river until I saw it, about two hundred paces from our fire.

"Come to me."

It was no trick, or at least not the trick I had at first feared. It was from downstream that the voice spoke.

"Come. Please. I cannot hear you where you stand."

I said, "I did not speak," but there was no reply. I waited, reluctant to leave Dorcas and Jolenta alone.

"Please. When the sun reaches this water, I must go. There may be no other chance."

The little river was wider at the sandbar than below or above it, and I could walk upon the yellow sand itself, dryshod, nearly to the center. To my left the greenish water gradually narrowed and deepened. To my right lay a deep pool perhaps twenty paces wide, from which water flowed swiftly yet smoothly. I stood on the sand with *Terminus Est* gripped in both hands, her square point buried between my feet. "I'm here," I said. "Where are you? Can you hear me now?"

As though the river itself were replying, three fish leaped at once, then leaped again, making a series of soft explosions on the surface. A moccasin, his brown back marked with linked rings of gold and black, glided up almost at my boot toes, turned as if to menace the jumping fish and hissed, then entered the ford on the upper side of the bar and swam away in long undulations. Through the body, he had been as thick as my forearm.

"Do not fear. Look. See me. Know that I will not harm you."

Green though the water had been, it grew greener still. A thousand jade tentacles writhed there, never breaking the surface. As I watched, too fascinated to be afraid, a disc of white three paces across appeared among them, rising slowly toward the surface.

It was not until it was within a few spans of the ripples that I understood what it was—and then only because it opened eyes. A face looked through the water at me, the face of a woman who might have dandled Baldanders like a toy. Her eyes were scarlet, and her mouth was bordered by full lips so darkly crimson I had not at first thought them lips at all. Behind them stood an army of pointed teeth; the green tendrils that framed her face were her floating hair.

"I have come for you, Severian," she said. *"No, you are not dreaming."*

XXVIII

The Odalisque of Abaia

I said, "Once before I dreamed of you." Dimly, I could see her naked body in the water, immense and gleaming.

"We watched the giant, and so found you. Alas, we lost sight of you too soon, when you and he separated. You believed then that you were hated, and did not know how much you were loved. The seas of the whole world shook with our mourning for you, and the waves wept salt tears and threw themselves despairing upon the rocks."

"And what is it you want of me?"

"Only your love. Only your love."

Her right hand came to the surface as she spoke, and floated there like a raft of five white logs. Here, truly, was the hand of the ogre, whose fingertip held the map of his domain.

"Am I not fair? Where have you beheld skin clearer than mine, or redder lips?"

"You are breathtaking," I said truthfully. "But may I ask why you were observing Baldanders when I met him? And why you were not observing me, though it seems you wished to?"

"We watch the giant because he grows. In that he is like us, and like our father-husband, Abaia. Eventually he must come to the water, when the land can bear him no longer. But you may come now, if you will. You will breathe—by our gift—as easily as you breathe the thin, weak wind here, and whenever you wish you shall return to the land and take up your crown. This river Cephissus flows to Gyoll, and Gyoll to the peaceful sea. There you may ride dolphin-back through current-swept fields of coral and pearl. My sisters and I will show you the forgotten cities built of old, where a hundred trapped generations of your kin bred and died when they had been forgotten by you above."

"I have no crown to take up," I said. "You mistake me for someone else."

"All of us will be yours there, in the red and white parks where the lionfish school."

As the undine spoke, she slowly lifted her chin, allowing her head to fall back until the whole plane of face lay at an equal depth, and only just submerged. Her white throat followed, and crimson-tipped breasts broke the surface, so that little lapping waves caressed their sides. A thousand bubbles sparkled in the water. In the space of a few breaths she lay at full length upon the current, forty cubits at least from alabaster feet to twining hair.

No one who reads this, perhaps, will understand how I could be drawn to so monstrous a thing; yet I wanted to believe her, to go with her, as a drowning man wants to gasp air. If I had fully credited her promises, I would have plunged into the pool at that moment, forgetting everything else.

"You have a crown, though you know not of it yet. Do you think that we, who swim in so many waters—even between the stars—are confined to a single instant? We have seen what you will become, and what you have been. Only yesterday you lay in the hollow of my palm, and I lifted you above the clotted weed lest you die in Gyoll, saving you for this moment."

"Give me the power to breathe water," I said, "and let me test it on the other side of the sandbar. If I find you have told the truth, I will go with you."

I watched those huge lips part. I cannot say how loudly she spoke in the river that I should hear her where I stood in air; but again fish leaped at her words.

"It is not so easily done as that. You must come with me, trusting, though it is only a moment. Come."

She extended her hand toward me, and at the same moment I heard Dorcas's agonized voice crying for help.

I turned to run to her. Yet if the undine had waited, I think I might have turned back. She did not. The river itself seemed to heave from its bed with a roar like breaking surf. It was as though a lake had been flung at my head, and it struck me like a stone and tumbled me in its wash like a stick. A moment later, when it receded, I found myself far up the bank, soaked and bruised and swordless. Fifty paces away the undine's white body rose half out of the river. Without the support of the water her flesh sagged on bones that seemed ready to snap under its weight, and her hair hung lank to the soaking sand. Even as I watched, water mingled with blood ran from her nostrils.

I fled, and by the time I reached Dorcas at our fire, the undine was gone save for a swirl of silt that darkened the river below the sandbar.

Dorcas's face was nearly as white. "What was that?" she whispered. "Where were you?"

"You saw her then. I was afraid . . ."

"How horrible." Dorcas had thrown herself into my arms, pressing her body to mine. "Horrible."

"That wasn't why you called, though, was it? You couldn't have seen her from here until she rose out of the pool."

Dorcas pointed mutely toward the farther side of the fire, and I saw the ground was soaked with blood where Jolenta lay.

There were two narrow cuts in her left wrist, each about the length of my thumb; and though I touched them with the Claw, it seemed the blood that welled from them would not clot. When we had soaked several bandages torn from Dorcas's scant store of clothing, I boiled thread and needle in a little pan she had and sewed the edges of the wounds shut. Through all this Jolenta seemed less than half conscious; from time to time her eyes opened, but they closed again almost immediately, and there was no recognition in them. She spoke only once, saying, "Now you see that he, whom you have esteemed your divinity, would countenance and advise all I have proposed to you. Before the New Sun rises, let us make a new beginning." At the time, I did not recognize it as one of her lines.

When her wound no longer bled, and we had shifted her to clean ground and washed her, I went back to the place where I had found myself when the water receded, and after some searching discovered *Terminus Est* with only her pommel and two fingers' width of hilt protruding from the wet sand.

I cleaned and oiled the blade, and Dorcas and I discussed what we should do. I told her of my dream, the night before I met Baldanders and Dr. Talos, and then about hearing the undine's voice while she and Jolenta slept, and what she had said.

"Is she still there, do you think? You were down there when you found your sword. Could you have seen her through the water if she were near the bottom?"

I shook my head. "I don't believe she is. She injured herself in some way when she tried to leave the river to stop me, and from the pallor of her skin, I doubt she would stay long in any water shallower than Gyoll's under the sun of a clear day. But no, if she had been there I don't think I would have seen her—the water was too roiled."

Dorcas, who had never looked more charming than at this moment, sitting on the ground with her chin propped on one knee, was silent for a time, and seemed to watch the eastern clouds, dyed cerise and flame by the eternal mysterious hope of dawn. At length she said, "She must have wanted you very badly."

"To have come up out of the water like that? I think she must have been on land before she had become so large, and she forgot for a moment at least that she could no longer do it."

"But before that she swam up filthy Gyoll, and then up this narrow little river. She must have been hoping to seize you when we crossed, but she found she could not get above the sandbar, and so she called you down. Altogether, it can't have been a pleasant trip for someone accustomed to swimming between the stars."

"You believe her, then?"

"When I was with Dr. Talos and you were gone, he and Jolenta used to tell me what a simple-minded person I was for believing people we met on the road, and things that Baldanders said, and things they said themselves, too. Just the same, I think that even the people who are called liars tell the truth much more often than they lie. It's so much easier! If that story about saving you wasn't true, why tell it? It could only frighten you when you thought back on it. And if she *doesn't* swim between stars, what a useless thing to say. Something's bothering you, though. I can see it. What is it?"

I did not want to describe my meeting with the Autarch in detail, so I said, "Not long ago I saw a picture—in a book—of a being who lives in the gulf. She was winged. Not like birds' wings, but enormous continuous planes of thin, pigmented material. Wings that could beat against the starlight."

Dorcas looked interested. "Is it in your brown book?"

"No, another book. I don't have it here."

"Just the same, it reminds me that we were going to see what your brown book has to say about the Conciliator. Do you still have it?"

I did, and I drew it out. It was damp from my wetting, so I opened it and laid it where the sun would strike its leaves, and the breezes that had sprung up as Urth's face looked on his again would play over them. After that, the pages turned gently as we talked, so that pictures of men and women and monsters took my eye between our words, and thus engraved themselves on my mind, so that they are there yet. Occasionally too, phrases, and even short passages, glowed and faded as the light caught, then released, the sheen of the metallic ink: "soulless warrior!" "lucid yellow," "by noyade." Later: "These times are the ancient times, when the world is ancient." And: "Hell has no limits, nor is circumscribed; for where we are is Hell, and where Hell is, there we must be."

"You don't want to read it now?" Dorcas asked.

"No. I want to hear what happened to Jolenta."

"I don't know. I was sleeping and dreaming of . . . the kind of thing I always do. And I went into a toy shop. There were shelves along the wall with dolls on them, and a well in the center of the floor with dolls sitting on the coping. I remember thinking that my baby was too young for dolls, but they were so pretty, and I had not had one since I was a little girl, so I would buy one and keep it for the baby, and meanwhile I could take it out sometimes and look at it, and perhaps make it stand before the mirror in my room. I pointed to the most beautiful one, which was one of those on the coping, and when the shopman picked it up for me I saw it was Jolenta, and it slipped from his hands. I saw it falling down very far, toward the black water. Then I woke up. Naturally I looked to see if she was all right . . ."

"And you found her bleeding?"

Dorcas nodded, her pale golden hair glinting in the light. "So I called for you—twice—and then I saw you down by the sandbar, and that thing came out of the water after you."

"There's no reason for you to look so pale," I told her. "Jolenta was bitten by an animal, that's clear. I've no idea of what kind, but judging from the bite it was a fairly small one, and no more to be feared than any other little animal with sharp teeth and a bad disposition."

"Severian, I remember being told that there were blood bats farther north. When I was just a child, someone used to frighten me by telling me about them. And then when I was older, once a common bat got into the house. Somebody killed it, and I asked my father if it were a blood bat, and if there were really any such things. He said there were, but they lived in the north, in the steaming forests at the center of the world. They bit sleeping people and grazing animals by night, and their spittle was poisoned so that the wounds of their teeth bled on."

Dorcas paused, looking up into the trees. "My father said that the city had been creeping northward along the river for all of history, having begun as an autochthon village where Gyoll joins the sea, and how terrible it would be when it entered the region where the blood bats fly and they could roost in the derelict buildings. It must be terrible already for the people of the House Absolute. We cannot have walked so very far from there."

"The Autarch has my sympathy," I said. "But I don't think I have ever heard you talk so much about your past life before. Do you remember your father now, and the house where the bat was killed?"

She stood; though she tried to look brave, I could see that she was trembling. "I remember more each morning, after my dreams. But, Severian, we must go now. Jolenta will be weak. She must have food, and clean water to drink. We can't stay here."

I was ravenously hungry myself. I put the brown book back into my sabretache and sheathed *Terminus Est*'s freshly oiled blade. Dorcas packed her little bundle of belongings.

Then we set out, fording the river well above the sandbar. Jolenta was unable to walk alone; we had to support her on either side. Her face was drawn, and though she had regained consciousness when we lifted her, she seldom spoke. When she did it was only a word or two. For the first time, I noticed how thin her lips were, and now the lower lip had lost its firmness and hung away from her teeth, showing the livid gums. It seemed to me that her entire body, yesterday so opulent, had softened like wax, so that instead of appearing (as she once had) a woman to Dorcas's child, she seemed a flower too long blown, the very end of summer to Dorcas's spring.

As we walked thus along a narrow, dusty track with sugarcane already higher than my head to either side, I found myself thinking over and over of how I had desired her in the short time I had known her. Memory, so perfect and vivid as to be more compelling than any opiate, showed me the woman as I had believed I had seen her first, when Dorcas and I had come around a grove of trees by night to find Dr. Talos's stage gleaming with lights in a pasture. How strange it had seemed to see her by daylight as perfect as she had appeared in the flattering glow of the flambeaux the night before, when we set off northward on the most glorious morning I can remember.

Love and desire are said to be no more than cousins, and I had found it so until I walked with Jolenta's flaccid arm about my neck. But it is not really true. Rather, the love of women was the dark side of a feminine ideal I had nourished for myself on dreams of Valeria and Thecla and Agia, of Dorcas and Jolenta and Vodalus's leman of the heart-shaped face and cooing voice, the woman I now knew to be Thecla's half-sister Thea. So that as we trudged between the walls of cane, when desire had fled and I could only look at Jolenta with pity, I found that though I had believed I cared only for her importunate, rose-flushed flesh and the awkward grace of her movements, I loved her.

XXIX

The Herdsmen

For most of the morning we walked through the cane, meeting no one. Jolenta grew neither stronger nor weaker, so far as I could judge; but it seemed to me that hunger, and the fatigue of supporting her, and the pitiless glare of the sun were telling upon me, for twice or thrice, when I glimpsed her from the corner of an eye, it seemed that I was not seeing Jolenta at all, but someone else, a woman I recalled but could not identify. If I turned my head to look at her, this impression (which was always very slight) vanished altogether.

So we walked, talking little. It was the only time since I had received her from Master Palaemon that *Terminus Est* seemed burdensome to me. My shoulder grew raw under the baldric.

I cut cane for us, and we chewed it for the sweet juice. Jolenta was always thirsty, and since she could not walk unless we aided her, and could not hold her stalk of cane when we did, we were forced to stop often. It was strange to see those long legs, so beautifully molded, with their slender ankles and ripe thighs, so useless.

In a day we reached the end of the cane and emerged onto the edge of the true pampa, the sea of grass. Here there were still a few trees, though they were so widely scattered that each was in sight of no more than two or three others. To each of these trees the body of some beast of prey was lashed with rawhide, its forepaws outspread like arms. They were mostly the spotted tigers common in that part of the country; but I saw atroxes too, with hair like man's, and sword-toothed smilodons. Most were hardly more than bones, but some lived and made those sounds that, as the people believe, serve to frighten other tigers, atroxes, and smilodons which, if they were not so frightened, would prey upon the cattle.

These cattle represented a far greater danger to us than the cats did. The herd bulls will charge anything that comes near them, and we were forced to give each herd we came across as much room as would prevent their short-sighted eyes from seeing us, and to move downwind of each. On these occasions, I was forced to let Dorcas prop Jolenta's weight as best she could, so I could walk ahead of them and somewhat nearer the animals. Once I had to leap aside and strike off the head of a bull as it charged. We built a fire of dry grass and roasted some of the meat.

The next time I recalled the Claw, and the way in which it had ended the attack of the man-apes. I drew it out, and the fierce black bull trotted to me and nuzzled my hand. We put Jolenta on his back with Dorcas to hold her on, and I walked beside his head, holding the gem where he could see its blue light.

A living smilodon was bound to the next tree we reached, which was nearly the last we saw, and I was afraid he would frighten the bull. Yet when we passed him I seemed to feel his eyes upon my back, yellow eyes as large as pigeon's eggs. My own tongue was swollen with his thirst. I gave Dorcas the gem to hold and went back and cut him down, thinking all the while that he would surely attack me. He fell to the ground too weak to stand, and I, who had no water to give him, could only walk away.

A little after noon, I noticed a carrion bird circling high above us. It is said they smell death, and I remembered that once or twice when the journeymen were very busy in the examination room, it was necessary for us apprentices to turn out to throw stones at those who settled on the ruined curtain wall, lest they give the Citadel a reputation more evil than it already possessed. The thought that Jolenta might die was repugnant to me, and I would have given much for a bow, so that I might perhaps pick the bird out of the air; but I had nothing of the kind, and could only wish.

After an interminable time, this first bird was joined by two much smaller ones, and from their bright head color, occasionally visible even from so far below, I knew them to be Cathartidae. Thus the first, whose wings had three times the spread of theirs, was a mountain teratornis, the breed that is said to attack climbers, raking their faces with poisoned talons and striking them with the elbows of its great pinions until they fall to their deaths. From time to time the other two approached it too closely, and it turned upon them. When that occurred, we sometimes heard a shrill cry come drifting down from the ramparts of their castle of air. Once, in a macabre mood, I gestured for the birds to join us. All three dove, and I brandished my sword at them and gestured no more.

When the western horizon had climbed nearly to the sun, we reached a low house, scarcely more than a hut, built of turf. A wiry man in leather leggings sat on a bench before it, drinking maté and pretending to watch the colors in the clouds. In truth, he must have seen us long before we saw him, for he was small and brown and blended well with his small, brown home, while we had been silhouetted against the sky.

I thrust away the Claw when I saw this herdsman, though I was not certain what the bull would do when it was no longer in his sight. In the event he did nothing, plodding ahead with the two women on his back as before. When we reached the sod house I lifted them down, and he raised his muzzle and sniffed the wind, then looked at me from one eye. I waved toward the undulating grass, both to show him I had no more need of him and to let him see that my hand was empty. He wheeled and trotted away.

The herdsman took his pewter straw from between his lips. "That was an ox," he said.

I nodded. "We needed him to carry this poor woman, who is ill, and so we borrowed him. Is he yours? We hoped you wouldn't mind, and after all, we did him no harm."

"No, no." The herdsman made a vaguely deprecating gesture. "I only asked because when I first saw you I thought he was a destrier. My eyes are not as good as they once were." He told us how good they once were, which was very good indeed. "But as you say, it was an ox."

This time Dorcas and I nodded together.

"You see what it is to become old. I would have licked the blade of this knife," he slapped the metal hilt that protruded above his broad belt, "and pointed it to the sun to swear that I saw something between the ox's legs. But if I were not such a fool I would know that no one can ride the bulls of the pampas. The red panther does it, but then he holds on with his claws, and sometimes he dies even so. No doubt it was an udder the ox inherited from his mother. I knew her, and she had one."

I said I was a city man, and very ignorant of everything that concerned cattle.

"Ah," he said, and sucked his maté. "I am a man more ignorant than you. Everyone around here but me is one ignorant eclectic. You know these people they call eclectics? They don't know anything—how can a man learn with neighbors like that?"

Dorcas said, "Please, won't you let us take this woman inside where she can lie down? I am afraid she's dying."

"I told you I don't know nothing. You should ask this man here—he can lead an ox—I almost said a bull—like a dog."

"But he can't help her! Only you can."

The herdsman cocked an eye at me, and I understood that he had established to his own satisfaction that it was I, and not Dorcas, who had tamed the bull. "I'm very sorry for your friend," he said, "who I can see must have been a lovely woman once. But even though I've been sitting here cracking jokes with you, I have a friend of my own, and right now he's lying inside. You're afraid your friend is dying. I know mine is, and I'd like to let him go with no one to bother him."

"We understand, but we won't disturb him. We may even be able to help him."

The herdsman looked from Dorcas to me and back again. "You are strange people—what do I know? No more than one of those ignorant eclectics. Come in, then. But be quiet, and remember you're my guests."

He rose and opened the door, which was so low I had to stoop to get through it. A single room constituted the house, and it was dark and smelled of smoke. A man much younger and, I thought, much taller than our host lay on a pallet before the fire. He had the same brown skin, but there was no blood beneath the pigment; his cheeks and forehead might have been smeared with dirt. There was no bedding beyond that on which the sick man lay, but we spread Dorcas's ragged blanket on the earthen floor and laid Jolenta on it. For a moment her eyes opened. There was no consciousness in them, and their once clear green had faded like shoddy cloth left in the sun.

Our host shook his head and whispered, "She won't last longer than that ignorant eclectic Manahen. Maybe not as long."

"She needs water," Dorcas told him.

"In back, in the catch barrel. I'll get it."

When I heard the door shut behind him, I drew out the Claw. This time it flashed with such searing, cyaneous flame that I feared it would penetrate the walls. The young man who lay on the pallet breathed deeply, then released his breath with a sigh. I put the Claw away again at once.

"It hasn't helped her," Dorcas said.

"Perhaps the water will. She's lost a great deal of blood."

Dorcas reached down to smooth Jolenta's hair. It must have been falling out, as the hair of old women and of people who suffer high fevers often does; so much clung to Dorcas's damp palm that I could see it plainly despite the dimness of the light. "I think she's always been ill," Dorcas whispered. "Ever since I've known her. Dr. Talos gave her something that made her better for a time, but now he has driven her away—she used to be very demanding, and he has had his revenge.''

''I can't believe he meant it to be as severe as this.''

''Neither can I, really. Severian, listen; he and Baldanders will surely stop to perform and spy out the land. We might be able to find them.''

''To spy?'' I must have looked as surprised as I felt.

''At least, it always seemed to me that they wandered as much to discover what passed in the world as to get money, and once Dr. Talos as much as admitted that to me, though I never learned just what they were looking for.''

The herdsman came in with a gourd of water. I lifted Jolenta to a sitting position, and Dorcas held it to her lips. It spilled and soaked Jolenta's tattered shift, but some of it went down her throat as well, and when the gourd was empty and the herdsman filled it again, she was able to swallow. I asked him if he knew where Lake Diuturna lay.

''I am only an ignorant man,'' he said. ''I have never ridden so far. I have been told that way,'' pointing, ''to the north and the west. Do you wish to go there?''

I nodded.

''You must pass through a bad place, then. Perhaps through many bad places, but surely through the stone town.''

''There is a city near here, then?''

''There is a city, yes, but no people. The ignorant eclectics who live near there believe that no matter which way a man goes, the stone town moves itself to wait in his path.'' The herdsman laughed softly, then sobered. ''That is not so. But the stone town bends the way a man's mount walks, so he finds it before him when he thinks he will go around it. You understand? I think you do not.''

I remembered the Botanic Gardens and nodded. ''I understand. Go on.''

''But if you are going north and west, you must pass through the stone town anyway. It will not even have to bend the way you walk. Some find nothing there but the fallen walls. I have heard that some find treasures. Some come back with fresh stories and some do not come back. Neither of these women are virgins, I think.''

Dorcas gasped. I shook my head.

''That is well. It is they who most often do not return. Try to pass through by day, with the sun over the right shoulder by morning and later in the left eye. If night comes, do not stop or turn to one side. Keep the stars of the Ihuaivulu before you when they first grow bright.''

I nodded and was about to ask for further information when the sick man opened his eyes and sat up. His blanket fell away, and I saw there was a bloodstained bandage over his chest. He started, stared at me, and shouted something. Instantly, I felt the cold blade of the herdsman's knife at my throat. "He won't harm you," he told the sick man. He used the same dialect, but because he spoke more slowly I was able to understand him. "I don't believe he knows who you are."

"I tell you, Father, it is the new lictor of Thrax. They have sent for one, and the clavigers say he's coming. Kill him! He'll kill all of them who haven't died already."

I was astounded to hear him mention Thrax, which was still so far away, and wanted to question him about it. I believe I could have talked to him and his father and made some sort of peace, but Dorcas struck the older man on the ear with the gourd—a futile, woman's blow that did nothing more than smash the gourd and cause little pain. He slashed at her with his crooked, two-edged knife, but I caught his arm and broke it, then broke the knife too under the heel of my boot. His son, Manahen, tried to rise; but if the Claw had restored his life it had, at least, not made him strong, and Dorcas pushed him down on his pallet again.

"We will starve," the herdsman said. His brown face was twisted by the effort he made not to cry out.

"You cared for your son," I told him. "Soon he will be well enough to care for you. What was it he did?"

Neither man would tell.

I set the bone and splinted it, and Dorcas and I ate and slept outside that night after telling father and son that we would kill them if we so much as heard the door open, or if any harm was done Jolenta. In the morning, while they were still asleep, I touched the herdsman's broken arm with the Claw. There was a destrier picketed not far from the house, and riding him I was able to catch another for Dorcas and Jolenta. As I led it back, I noticed the sod walls had turned green overnight.

XXX

The Badger Again

Despite what the herdsman had told me, I hoped for some place like Saltus, where we might find pure water and a few aes would buy us food and rest. What we found instead was scarcely the remnant of a town. Coarse grass grew between the enduring stones that had been its pavements, so that from a distance it seemed hardly different from the surrounding pampa. Fallen columns lay among this grass like the trunks of trees in a forest devastated by some frenzied storm; a few others still stood, broken and achingly white beneath the sun. Lizards with bright, black eyes and serrated backs lay frozen in the light. The buildings were mere hillocks from which more grass sprouted in soil caught from the wind.

There was no reason I could see to turn from our course, and so we continued northwest, urging our destriers forward. For the first time I became conscious of the mountains ahead. Framed in a ruined arch, they were no more than a faint line of blue on the horizon; yet they were a presence, as the mad clients on the third level of our oubliette were a presence though they were never taken up a single step, or even out of their cells. Lake Diuturna lay somewhere in those mountains. So did Thrax; the Pelerines, so far as I had been able to discover, wandered somewhere among their peaks and chasms, nursing the wounded of the endless war against the Ascians. That too lay in the mountains. There hundreds of thousands perished for the sake of a pass.

But now we had come to a town where no voice sounded but the raven's. Although we had carried water in skin bags from the herdsman's house, it was nearly gone. Jolenta was weaker, and Dorcas and I agreed that if we did not find more by nightfall, it was likely she would die. Just as Urth began to roll across the sun, we came upon a broken sacrificial table whose basin still caught rain. The water was stagnant and stinking, but in our desperation we allowed Jolenta to drink a few swallows, which she immediately vomited. Urth's turning revealed the moon, now well past the full, so that we gained her weak greenish gleam as we lost the sunlight.

To have come upon a simple campfire would have seemed a miracle. What we actually saw was stranger but less startling. Dorcas pointed to the left. I looked, and a moment later beheld, as I thought, a meteor. "It's a falling star," I said. "Did you see one before? They come in showers sometimes."

"No! That's a building—can't you see it? Look for the dark place against the sky. It must have a flat roof, and someone's up there with flint and steel."

I was about to tell her that she imagined too much, when a dull red glow no bigger, it seemed, than the head of a pin, appeared where the sparks had fallen. Two breaths more, and there was a tiny tongue of flame.

It was not far, but the dark and the broken stones we rode over made it seem so, and by the time we reached the building the fire was bright enough for us to see that three figures crouched about it. "We need your help," I called. "This woman is dying."

All three raised their heads, and a crone's screech asked, "Who speaks? I hear a man's voice, but I see no man. Who are you?"

"Here," I called, and threw back my fuligin cloak and hood. "On your left. I've dark clothes, that's all."

"So you do . . . so you do. Who's dying? Not little pale hair . . . big red-gold. We've wine here and a fire, but no other physic. Go around, that's where the stair is."

I led our animals around the corner of the building as she had indicated. The stone walls cut off the low moon and left us in blind darkness, but I stumbled on rough steps that must have been made by piling stones from fallen structures against the side of the building. After hobbling the two destriers, I carried Jolenta up, Dorcas going before us to feel the way and warn me of danger.

The roof, when we reached it, was not flat; and the pitch was great enough for me to fear falling at every step. Its hard, uneven surface seemed to be of tiles—once one loosened, and I heard it grating and clattering against the others until it fell over the edge and smashed on the uneven slabs below.

When I was an apprentice and too young to be entrusted with any but the most elementary tasks, I was given a letter to take to the witches' tower, across the Old Court from our own. (I learned much later that there was a good reason for selecting only boys well below the age of puberty to carry the messages our proximity to the witches required.) Now, when I know of the horror our own tower inspired not only in the people of the quarter but to an equal or greater degree in the other residents of the Citadel itself, I find a flavor of quaint naïveté in the recollection of my own fear; yet to the small and unattractive boy I was, it was very real. I had heard terrible stories from the older apprentices, and I had seen that boys unquestionably braver than I were afraid. In that most gaunt of all the Citadel's myriad towers, strangely colored lights burned by night. The screams we heard through the ports of our dormitory came not from some underground examination room like our own, but from the highest levels; and we knew that it was the witches themselves who screamed thus and not their clients, for in the sense we used that word, they had none. Nor were those screams the howlings of lunacy and the shrieks of agony, as ours were.

I had been made to wash my hands so they would not soil the envelope, and I was very conscious of their dampness and their redness as I picked my way among the puddles of freezing water that dotted the courtyard. My mind conjured up a witch who should be immensely dignified and humiliating, who would not shrink from punishing me in some particularly repulsive way for daring to carry a letter to her in red hands and would send me back with a scornful report to Master Malrubius as well.

I must have been very small indeed: I had to jump to reach the knocker. The smack of the witches' deeply worn doorstep against the thin soles of my shoes remains with me still.

"Yes?" The face that looked into mine was hardly higher than my own. It was one of those—outstanding of its kind among all the hundreds of thousands of faces I have seen—that are at once suggestive of beauty and disease. The witch to whom it belonged seemed old to me and must actually have been about twenty or a little less; but she was not tall, and she carried herself in the bent-backed posture of extreme age. Her face was so lovely and so bloodless that it might have been a mask carved in ivory by some master sculptor.

Mutely, I held up my letter.

"Come with me," she said. Those were the words I had feared, and now that they had actually been given voice, they seemed as inevitable as the procession of the seasons.

I entered a tower very different from our own. Ours was oppressively solid, of plates of metal so closely fitted that they had, ages ago, diffused into one another to become one mass, and the lower floors of our tower were warm and dripping. Nothing seemed solid in the witches' tower, and few things were. Much later, Master Palaemon explained to me that it was far older than most other parts of the Citadel, and had been built when the design of towers was still little more than the imitation in inanimate materials of human physiology, so that skeletons of steel were used to support a fabric of flimsier substances. With the passing of the centuries, that skeleton had largely corroded away—until at last the structure it had once stiffened was held up only by the piecemeal repairs of past generations. Oversized rooms were separated by walls not much thicker than draperies; no floor was level, and no stair straight; each bannister and railing I touched seemed ready to come off in my hand. Gnostic designs in white, green, and purple had been chalked on the walls, but there was little furniture, and the air seemed colder than that outside.

After climbing several stairs and a ladder lashed together from the unpeeled saplings of some fragrant tree, I was ushered into the presence of an old woman who sat in the only chair I had yet seen there, staring through a glass tabletop at what appeared to be an artificial landscape inhabited by hairless, crippled animals. I gave her my letter and was led away; but for a moment she had glanced at me, and her face, like the face of the young-old woman who had brought me to her, has of course remained graven in my mind.

I mention all this now because it seemed to me, as I laid Jolenta on the tiles beside the fire, that the women who crouched over it were the same. It was impossible; the old woman to whom I had handed my letter was almost certainly dead, and the young one (if she were still living) would be changed beyond recognition, as I was myself. Yet the faces that turned toward me were the faces I recalled. Perhaps there are but two witches in the world, who are born into it again and again.

"What is the matter with her?" the younger woman asked, and Dorcas and I explained as well as we could.

Long before we finished, the older one had Jolenta's head in her lap and was forcing wine from a clay bottle into her throat. "It would harm her if it were strong to harm," she said. "But this is three parts pure water. Since you do not wish to see her die, you are fortunate, possibly, to have come across us so. Whether she is also fortunate, I cannot say."

I thanked her, and inquired where the third person who had been at their fire had gone.

The old woman sighed, and stared at me for a moment before returning her attention to Jolenta.

"There were only the two of us," the younger woman said. "You saw three?"

"Very clearly, in the firelight. Your grandmother—if that is who she is—looked up and spoke to me. You and whoever was with you lifted your heads, then bowed them again."

"She is the Cumaean."

I had heard the word before, but for a moment I could not remember where, and the younger woman's face, immobile as an oread's in a picture, gave me no clue.

"The seeress," Dorcas supplied. "And who are you?"

"Her acolyte. My name is Merryn. It is significant, possibly, that you, who are three, saw three of us at the fire, while we who are two at first saw but two of you." She looked to the Cumaean as if for confirmation, and then, as if she had received it, back to us, though I saw no glance pass between them.

"I'm quite sure I saw a third person who was larger than either of you," I said.

"This is a strange evening, and there are those who ride the night air who sometimes choose to borrow a human seeming. The question is why such a power would wish to show itself to you."

The effect of her dark eyes and serene face was so great that I think I might have believed her if it had not been for Dorcas, who suggested with an almost imperceptible movement of her head that the third member of the group about the fire might have escaped our observation by crossing the roof and hiding on the farther side of the ridge.

"She may live," the Cumaean said without lifting her gaze from Jolenta's face. "Though she does not wish it."

"It's a good thing for her that the two of you had so much wine," I said.

The old woman did not rise to the bait, saying only, "Yes, it is. For you and possibly even for her."

Merryn picked up a stick and stirred the fire. "There is no death."

I laughed a little, mostly, I think, because I was no longer quite so worried about Jolenta. "Those of my trade think otherwise."

"Those of your trade are mistaken."

Jolenta murmured, *"Doctor?"* It was the first time she had spoken since morning.

"You do not need a physician now," Merryn said. "Someone better is here."

The Cumaean muttered, "She seeks her lover."

"Who is not this man in fuligin then, Mother? I thought he seemed too common for her."

"He is but a torturer. She seeks a worse."

Merryn nodded to herself, then said to us, "You will not wish to move her farther tonight, but we must ask that you do. You will find a hundred better camping places on the other side of the ruins, and it would be dangerous for you to stay here."

"A danger of death?" I asked. "But you tell me there is none—so if I believe you, why should I fear? And if I cannot believe you, why should I believe you now?" Nevertheless, I rose to go.

The Cumaean looked up. "She's right," she croaked. "Though she does not know it, and only speaks by rote like a starling in a cage. Death is nothing, and for that reason you must fear it. What is more to be feared?"

I laughed again. "I can't argue with someone as wise as you. And because you gave us what help you could, we will go now because you wish it."

The Cumaean permitted me to take Jolenta from her, but said, "I do not wish it. My acolyte still believes the universe hers to command, a board where she can move counters to form whatever patterns suit her. The Magi see fit to number me among themselves when they write their short roll, and I should lose my place on it if I did not know that people like ourselves are only little fish, who must swim with unseen tides if we are not to exhaust ourselves without finding sustenance. Now you must wrap this poor creature in your cloak and lay her by my fire. When this place passes out of the shadow of Urth, I will look to her wound again."

I remained standing, holding Jolenta, uncertain whether we should go or stay. The Cumaean's intentions seemed friendly enough, but her metaphor had carried an unpleasant reminder of the undine; and as I studied her face I had come to doubt that she was an old woman at all, and to recall only too clearly the hideous faces of the cacogens who had removed their masks when Baldanders had rushed among them.

"You shame me, Mother," Merryn said. "Shall I call to him?"

"He has heard us. He will come without your call."

She was right. I already detected the scrape of boots on the tiles of the other side of the roof.

"You are alarmed. Would it not be better to put down the woman as I instructed you, so you might take up your sword to defend your paramour? But there will be no need."

By the time she had finished speaking, I could see a tall hat and a big head and broad shoulders silhouetted against the night sky. I laid Jolenta near Dorcas and drew *Terminus Est*.

''No need of that,'' a deep voice said. ''No need at all, young fellow. I'd have come out sooner to renew our acquaintance, but I didn't know the Chatelaine here wanted it. My master—and yours—sends his greetings.'' It was Hildegrin.

XXXI

The Cleansing

"You may tell your master I delivered his message," I said.

Hildegrin smiled. "And have you a message to return, armiger? Remember, I'm from the quercine penetralia."

"No," I said. "None."

Dorcas looked up. "I do. A person I met in the gardens of the House Absolute told me I would encounter someone who identified himself thus, and that I was to say to him, 'When the leaves are grown, the wood is to march north.' "

Hildegrin laid a finger beside his nose. "*All* the wood? Is that what he said?"

"He gave me the words I have already recited to you, and nothing more."

"Dorcas," I asked, "why didn't you tell me this?"

"I've hardly had an opportunity to talk to you alone since we met at the crossing of the paths. And besides, I could see it was a dangerous thing to know. I couldn't see any reason to put that danger on you. It was the man who gave Dr. Talos all that money who told me. But he didn't give Dr. Talos the message—I know because I listened when they talked. He only said that he was your friend, and told me."

"And told you to tell me."

Dorcas shook her head.

Hildegrin's thick-throated chuckle might almost have come from underground. "Well, it don't hardly matter now, does it? It's been delivered, and for myself I don't mind tellin' you I wouldn't have minded if it had waited a little longer. But we're all friends here, except maybe for the sick girl, and I don't think she can hear what's said, or understand what we're talkin' about if she could. What did you say her name was? I couldn't hear you too clear when I was over there on the other side.''

''That was because I didn't say it at all,'' I told him. ''But her name is Jolenta.'' As I pronounced *Jolenta*, I looked at her, and seeing her in the firelight realized she was Jolenta no longer—nothing of the beautiful woman Jonas had loved remained in that haggard face.

''And a bat bite did it? They've grown uncommon strong lately then. I've been bit a couple of times myself.'' I looked at Hildegrin sharply, and he added, ''Oh yes, I've seen her before, young sieur, as well as yourself and little Dorcas. You didn't think I let you and that other gal leave the Botanic Gardens alone, did you? Not with you talkin' of goin' north and fightin' a officer of the Septentrions. I saw you fight and saw you take that fellow's head off—I helped to catch him, by the bye, because I thought he might be from the House Absolute for true—and I was in the back of the people that watched you on the stage that night. I didn't lose you till the affair at the gate the next day. I seen you and I seen her, though there's not much left of her now except the hair, and I think even that's changed.''

Merryn asked the Cumaean, ''Shall I tell them, Mother?''

The old woman nodded. ''If you can, child.''

''She has been imbued with a glamour that rendered her beautiful. It is fading fast now because of the blood she lost, and because she has had a great deal of exercise. By morning only traces will remain.''

Dorcas drew back. ''Magic, you mean?''

''There is no magic. There is only knowledge, more or less hidden.''

Hildegrin was staring at Jolenta with a thoughtful expression. ''I didn't know looks could be changed so much. That might be useful, that might. Can your mistress do it?''

''She could do much more than this, if she willed it.''

Dorcas whispered, ''But how was this done?''

''There have been substances drawn from the glands of beasts added to her blood, to change the pattern in which her flesh was deposited. Those gave her a slender waist, breasts like melons, and so on. They may have been used to add calf to her legs as well. Cleaning and the application of healthening broths to the skin freshened her face. Her teeth were cleaned too, and some were ground down and given false crowns—one has fallen away now, if you'll look. Her hair was dyed, and thickened by sewing threads of colored silk into her scalp. No doubt much body hair was killed as well, and that at least will remain so. Most important, she was promised beauty while entranced. Such promises are believed with faith greater than any child's, and her belief compelled yours.''

"Can nothing be done for her?" Dorcas asked.

"Not by me, and it is not a task of the kind the Cumaean undertakes, save in great need."

"But she will live?"

"As the Mother told you—though she will not wish it."

Hildegrin cleared his throat and spat over the side of the roof. "That's settled then. We've done what we can for her, and it's all we can do. So what I say is let's get on with what we come for. Like you said, Cumaean, it's good these others showed up. I got the message I was supposed to, and they're friends of the Liege of Leaves, just like me. The armiger here can help me fetch up this Apu-Punchau, and what with my two fellows bein' killed on the road, I'll be glad to have him. So what's to keep us from goin' ahead?"

"Nothing," the Cumaean murmured. "The star is in the ascendant."

Dorcas said, "If we're going to assist you with something, shouldn't we know what it is?"

"Bringin' back the past," Hildegrin told her grandly. "Divin' back into the time of old Urth's greatness. There was somebody who used to live in this here place we're sittin' on that knew things that could make a difference. I intend to have him up. It'll be the high point, if I may say it, of a career that's already considered pretty spectacular in knowin' circles."

I asked, "You're going to open the tomb? Surely, even with alzabo—"

The Cumaean reached out to smooth Jolenta's forehead. "We may call it a tomb, but it was not his. His house, rather."

"You see what with me workin' so near," Hildegrin explained, "I've been in the way to do this Chatelaine a favor now and again. More than one, if I may say it, and more than two. Finally I figured the time had come for me to collect. I mentioned my little plan to the Master of the Wood, you may be sure. And here we are."

I said, "I had been given to understand that the Cumaean served Father Inire."

"She pays her debts," Hildegrin announced smugly. "Quality always does. And you don't have to be a wise woman to know it might be wise to have a few friends on the other side, just in case that's the side that wins."

Dorcas asked the Cumaean, "Who was this Apu-Punchau, and why is his palace still standing when the rest of the town is only tumbled stones?"

When the old woman did not reply, Merryn said, "Less than a legend, for not even scholars now remember his story. The Mother has told us that his name means the Head of Day. In the earliest eons he appeared among the people here and taught them many wonderful secrets. Often he vanished, but always he returned. At last he did not return, and invaders laid waste to his cities. Now he shall return for the last time."

"Indeed. Without magic?"

The Cumaean looked up at Dorcas with eyes that seemed as bright as the stars. "Words are symbols. Merryn chooses to delimit magic as that which does not exist . . . and so it does not exist. If you choose to call what we are about to do here magic, then magic lives while we do it. In ancient days, in a land far off, there stood two empires, divided by mountains. One dressed its soldiers in yellow, the other in green. For a hundred generations they struggled. I see that the man with you knows the tale."

"And after a hundred generations," I said, "an eremite came among them and counseled the emperor of the yellow army to dress his men in green, and the master of the green army that he should clothe it in yellow. But the battle continued as before. In my sabretache, I have a book called *The Wonders of Urth and Sky*, and the story is told there."

"That is the wisest of all the books of men," the Cumaean said. "Though there are few who can gain any benefit from reading it. Child, explain to this man, who will be a sage in time, what we do tonight."

The young witch nodded. "All time exists. That is the truth beyond the legends the epopts tell. If the future did not exist now, how could we journey toward it? If the past does not exist still, how could we leave it behind us? In sleep the mind is encircled by its time, which is why we so often hear the voices of the dead there, and receive intelligence of things to come. Those who, like the Mother, have learned to enter the same state while waking live surrounded by their own lives, even as the Abraxas perceives all of time as an eternal instant."

There had been little wind that night, but I noticed now that such wind as there had been had died utterly. A stillness hung in the air, so that despite the softness of Dorcas's voice her words seemed to ring. "Is that what this woman you call the Cumaean will do, then? Enter that state, and speaking with the voice of the dead tell this man whatever it is he wishes to know?"

"She cannot. She is very old, but this city was devastated whole ages before she came to be. Only her own time rings her, for that is all her mind comprehends by direct knowledge. To restore the city, we must make use of a mind that existed when it was whole."

"And is there anyone in the world that old?"

The Cumaean shook her head. "In the world? No. Yet such a mind exists. Look where I point, child, just above the clouds. The red star there is called the Fish's Mouth, and on its one surviving world there dwells an ancient and acute mind. Merryn, take my hand, and you, Badger, take the other. Torturer, take the right hand of your sick friend, and Hildegrin's. Your paramour must take the sick woman's other hand, and Merryn's. . . . Now we are linked, men to one side, women to the other.''

''And we'd best do somethin' quick,'' Hildegrin grumbled. ''There's a storm comin', I would say.''

''We shall, as quickly as may be. Now I must use all your minds, and the sick woman's will be of little help. You will feel me guiding your thought. Do as I bid you.''

Releasing Merryn's hand for a moment, the old woman (if she were in truth a woman at all) reached into her bodice and drew out a rod whose tips vanished into the night as if they were at the borders of my field of vision, though it was hardly longer than a dagger. She opened her mouth; I thought she meant to hold the rod between her teeth, but she swallowed it. A moment later I could detect its glowing image, muted and tinged with crimson, below the sagging skin of her throat.

''Close eyes, all of you. . . . There is a woman here I do not know, a high woman chained . . . never mind, Torturer, I know her now. Do not shrink from my hand. . . . None of you shrink from my hand. . . .''

In the stupor that had followed Vodalus's banquet, I had known what it was to share my mind with another. This was different. The Cumaean did not appear as I had seen her, or as a young version of herself, or (as it seemed to me) as anything. Rather, I found my thought surrounded by hers, as a fish in a bowl floats in a bubble of invisible water. Thecla was there with me, but I could not see her whole; it was as if she were standing behind me and I saw her hand over my shoulder at one moment, and felt her breath on my cheek at the next.

Then she was gone and everything with her. I felt my thought hurled off into the night, lost among the ruins.

When I recovered, I was lying on the tiles near the fire. My mouth was wet with the foam of my spittle mixed with my own blood, for I had bitten my lips and tongue. My legs were too weak to stand, but I raised myself to a sitting posture again.

At first I thought the others were gone. The roof was solid under me, but they had become, to my sight, as vaporous as ghosts. A phantom Hildegrin sprawled on my right—I thrust my hand into his chest and felt his heart beat against it like a moth that struggled to escape. Jolenta was dimmest of all, hardly present. More had been done to her than Merryn had guessed; I saw wires and bands of metal beneath her flesh, though even they were dim. I looked to myself then, at my legs and feet, and found I could see the Claw burning like a blue flame through the leather of my boot. I grasped it, but there was no strength in my fingers; I could not take it forth.

Dorcas lay as if in sleep. There was no foam flecking her lips, and she was more solid in appearance than Hildegrin. Merryn had collapsed into a black-clad doll, so thin and dim that slender Dorcas seemed robust beside her. Now that intelligence no longer animated that ivory mask, I saw that it was no more than parchment over bone.

As I had suspected, the Cumaean was not a woman at all; yet neither was she one of the horrors I had beheld in the gardens of the House Absolute. Something sleekly reptilian coiled about the glowing rod. I looked for the head but found none, though each of the patternings on the reptile's back was a face, and the eyes of each face seemed lost in rapture.

Dorcas woke while I looked from one to another. "What has happened to us?" she said. Hildegrin was stirring.

"I think we are seeing ourselves from a perspective longer than a single instant's."

Her mouth opened, but there was no cry.

Although the threatening clouds had brought no wind, dust was swirling through the streets below us. I do not know how to describe it except by saying that it seemed as if an uncountable host of minute insects a hundredth the size of midges had been concealed in the crevices of the rough pavement, and now were drawn by the moonlight to their nuptial flight. There was no sound, and no regularity in their motions, but after a time the undifferentiated mass formed swarms that swept to and fro, growing always larger and more dense, and at last sank again to the broken stones.

It seemed then that the insects no longer flew, but crawled over one another, each trying to reach the center of the swarm. "They are alive," I said.

But Dorcas whispered, "Look, they are dead."

She was correct. The swarms that had seethed with life a moment before now showed bleached ribs; the dust motes, linking themselves just as scholars piece together shards of ancient glass to re-create for us a colored window shattered thousands of years before, formed skulls that gleamed green in the moonlight. Beasts—aelurodons, lumbering spelaeae, and slinking shapes to which I could put no name, all fainter than we who watched from the rooftop—moved among the dead.

One by one they rose, and the beasts vanished. Feebly at first, they began to rebuild their town; stones were lifted again, and timbers molded of ashes were laid into sockets in the restored walls. The people, who had seemed hardly more than ambulant corpses when they rose, gathered strength from their work and became a bandylegged race who walked like sailors and rolled cyclopean stones with the might of their wide shoulders. Then the town was complete, and we waited to see what would happen next.

Drums broke the stillness of the night; by their tone I knew that when they had last beat a forest had stood about the town, for they reverberated as sounds only reverberate among the boles of great trees. A shaman with a shaven head paraded the street, naked and painted with pictographs in a script I had never seen, so expressive that the mere shapes of the words seemed to shout their meanings.

Dancers followed him, a hundred or more capering in lockstep, single file, the hands of each on the head of the dancer before him. Their faces were upturned, making me wonder (as I wonder still) if they did not dance in imitation of the hundred-eyed serpent we called the Cumaean. Slowly they coiled and twined, up and down the street, around the shaman and back again until at last they reached the entrance to the house from which we watched them. With a crash like thunder, the stone slab of the door fell. There was an odor as of myrrh and roses.

A man came forth to greet the dancers. If he had possessed a hundred arms, or had worn his head beneath his hands, I could not have been more astonished, for his was a face I had known since childhood, the face of the funeral bronze in the mausoleum where I played as a boy. There were massive gold bracelets on his arms, bracelets set with jacinths and opals, carnelians and flashing emeralds. With measured strides he advanced until he stood in the center of the procession, with the dancers swaying about him. Then he turned toward us and lifted his arms. He was looking at us, and I knew that he, alone of all the hundreds there, truly saw us.

I had been so entranced by the spectacle below me that I had not noticed when Hildegrin left the roof. Now he darted—if so large a man can be said to dart—into the crowd and laid hold of Apu-Punchau.

What followed I hardly know how to describe. In a way it was like the little drama in the house of yellow wood in the Botanic Gardens; yet it was far stranger, if only because I had known then that the woman and her brother, and the savage, were chant-caught. And now it seemed almost that it was Hildegrin, Dorcas, and I who were wrapped in magic. The dancers, I am sure, could not see Hildegrin; but they were somehow aware of him, and cried out against him, and slashed the air with stone-toothed cudgels.

Apu-Punchau, I felt certain, *did* see him, just as he had seen us on the rooftop and as Isangoma had seen Agia and me. Yet I do not believe he saw Hildegrin as I saw him, and it may be that what he saw seemed as strange to him as the Cumaean had to me. Hildegrin held him, but he could not subdue him. Apu-Punchau struggled, but he could not break free. Hildegrin looked up to me and shouted for help.

I do not know why I responded. Certainly I no longer consciously desired to serve Vodalus and his purposes. Perhaps it was the lingering effect of the alzabo, or only the memory of Hildegrin's rowing Dorcas and me across the Lake of Birds.

I tried to push the bandylegged men away, but one of their random blows caught the side of my head and knocked me to my knees. When I rose again, I seemed to have lost sight of Apu-Punchau among the leaping, shrieking dancers. Instead there were two Hildegrins, one who grappled with me, one who fought something invisible. Wildly, I threw off the first and tried to come to the aid of the second.

"Severian!"

Rain beating upon my upturned face awakened me—big drops of cold rain that stung like hail. Thunder rolled across the pampas. For a moment I thought I had gone blind; then a flash of lightning showed me wind-lashed grass and tumbled stones.

"Severian!"

It was Dorcas. I started to rise, and my hand touched cloth as well as mud. I seized it and pulled it free—a long, narrow strip of silk tipped with tassels.

"Severian!" There was terror in the cry.

"Here!" I called. "I'm down here!" Another flash showed me the building and Dorcas's frantic figure silhouetted on the roof. I circled the blind walls and found the steps. Our mounts were gone. On the roof, so were the witches; Dorcas, alone, bent over the body of Jolenta. By lightning, I saw the the dead face of the waitress who had served Dr. Talos, Baldanders, and me in the café in Nessus. It had been washed clean of beauty. In the final reckoning there is only love, only that divinity. That we are capable only of being what we are remains our unforgivable sin.

Here I pause again, having taken you, reader, from town to town—from the little mining village of Saltus to the desolate stone town whose very name had long ago been lost among the whirling years. Saltus was for me the gateway to the world beyond the City Imperishable. So too, the stone town was a gateway, a gateway to the mountains I had glimpsed through its ruined arches. For a long way thereafter, I was to journey among their gorges and fastnesses, their blind eyes and brooding faces.

Here I pause. If you wish to walk no farther with me, reader, I do not blame you. It is no easy road.

Appendixes

Social Relationships in the Commonwealth

One of the translator's most difficult tasks is the accurate expression of matter concerned with caste and position in terms intelligible to his own society. In the case of *The Book of the New Sun*, the lack of supportive material renders it doubly difficult, and nothing more than a sketch is presented here.

So far as can be determined from the manuscripts, the society of the Commonwealth appears to consist of seven basic groups. Of these, one at least seems completely closed. A man or woman must be born an *exultant*, and if so born, remains an exultant throughout life. Although there may well be gradations within this class, the manuscripts indicate none. Its women are called "Chatelaine," and its men by various titles. Outside the city I have chosen to call Nessus, it carries on the administration of day-to-day affairs. Its hereditary assumption of power is deeply at variance with the spirit of the Commonwealth, and sufficiently accounts for the tension evident between the exultants and the autarchy; yet it is difficult to see how local governance might be better arranged under the prevailing conditions—democracy would inevitably degenerate into mere haggling, and an appointive bureaucracy is impossible without a sufficient pool of educated but relatively unmoneyed executives to fill its offices. In any case, the wisdom of the autarchs no doubt includes the principle that an entire sympathy with the ruling class is the most deadly disease of the state. In the manuscripts, Thecla, Thea, and Vodalus are unquestionably exultants.

The *armigers* seem much like exultants, though on a lesser scale. Their name indicates a fighting class, but they do not appear to have monopolized the major roles in the army; no doubt their position could be likened to that of the samurai who served the daimyos of feudal Japan. Lomer, Nicarete, Racho, and Valeria are armigers.

The *optimates* appear to be more or less wealthy traders. Of all the seven, they make the fewest appearances in the manuscripts, though there are some hints that Dorcas originally belonged to this class.

As in every society, the *commonality* constitute the vast bulk of the population. Generally content with their lot, ignorant because their nation is too poor to educate them, they resent the exultants' arrogance and stand in awe of the Autarch, who is, however, in the final analysis their own apotheosis. Jolenta, Hildegrin, and the villagers of Saltus all belong to this class, as do countless other characters in the manuscripts.

Surrounding the Autarch—who appears to distrust the exultants, and no doubt with good reason—are the *servants of the throne*. They are his administrators and advisors, both in military and civil life. They appear to be drawn from the commonality, and it is noteworthy that they treasure such education as they have obtained. (For contrast, see Thecla's contemptuous rejection of it.) Severian himself and the other inhabitants of the Citadel, with the exception of Ultan, might be said to belong to this class.

The *religious* are almost as enigmatic as the god they serve, a god that appears fundamentally solar, but not Apollonian. (Because the Conciliator is given a Claw, one is tempted to make the easy association of the eagle of Jove with the sun; it is perhaps too pat.) Like the Roman Catholic clergy of our own day, they appear to be members of various orders, but unlike them they seem subject to no uniting authority. At times there is something suggestive of Hinduism about them, despite their obvious monotheism. The Pelerines, who play a larger part in the manuscripts than any other holy community, are clearly a sisterhood of priestesses, accompanied (as such a roving group would have to be in their place and time) by armed male servants.

Lastly, the *cacogens* represent, in a way we can hardly more than sense, that foreign element that by its very foreignness is most universal, existing in nearly every society of which we have knowledge. Their common name seems to indicate that they are feared, or at least hated, by the commonality. Their presence at the Autarch's festival would seem to show that they are accepted (though perhaps under duress) at court. Although the populace of Severian's time appears to consider them a homogeneous group, it appears likely that they are in fact diverse. In the manuscripts, the Cumaean and Father Inire represent this element.

The honorific I have translated as *sieur* would seem to belong only to the highest classes, but to be widely misapplied at the lower levels of society. *Goodman* properly indicates a householder.

Money, Measures, and Time

I have found it impossible to derive precise estimates of the values of the coins mentioned in the original of *The Book of the New Sun*. In the absence of certainty, I have used *chrisos* to designate any piece of gold stamped with the profile of an autarch; although these no doubt differ somewhat in weight and purity, it appears they are of roughly equal value.

The even more various silver coins of the period I have lumped together as *asimi*.

The large brass coins (which appear from the manuscripts to furnish the principal medium of exchange among the common people) I have called *orichalks*.

The myriad small brass, bronze, and copper tokens (not struck by the central government, but by the local archons at need, and intended only for provincial circulation) I have called *aes*. A single aes buys an egg; an orichalk, a day's work from a common laborer; an asimi, a well made coat suitable for an optimate; a chrisos, a good mount.

It is important to remember that measures of length or distance are not, strictly speaking, commensurable. In this book, *league* designates a distance of about three miles; it is the correct measure for distances between cities, and within large cities such as Nessus.

The *span* is the distance between the extended thumb and forefinger—about eight inches. A *chain* is the length of a measuring chain of 100 links, in which each link measures a span; it is thus roughly 70 feet.

An *ell* represents the traditional length of the military arrow; five spans, or about 40 inches.

The *pace*, as used here, indicates a single step, or about two and a half feet. The *stride* is a double step.

The most common measure of all, the distance from a man's elbow to the tip of his longest finger (about 18 inches), I have given as a *cubit*. (It will be observed that throughout my translation I have preferred modern words that will be understandable to every reader in attempting to reproduce—in the Roman alphabet—the original terms.)

Words indicative of duration seldom occur in the manuscripts; one sometimes intuits that the writer's sense of the passage of time, and that of the society to which he belongs, has been dulled by dealings with intelligences who have been subjected to, or have surmounted, the Einsteinian time paradox. Where they occur, a *chiliad* designates a period of 1,000 years. An *age* is the interval between the exhaustion of some mineral or other resource in its naturally occurring form (for example, sulfur) and the next. The *month* is the (then) lunar one of 28 days, and the *week* is thus precisely equal to our own week: a quarter of the lunar month, or seven days. A *watch* is the duty period of a sentry: one-tenth of the night, or approximately one hour and 15 minutes.

G. W.

The Sword of the Lictor

Into the distance disappear the mounds of human heads.
I dwindle—go unnoticed now.
But in affectionate books, in children's games,
I will rise from the dead to say: the sun!
Osip Mandelstam

I

Master of the House of Chains

"It was in my hair, Severian," Dorcas said. "So I stood under the waterfall in the hot stone room—I don't know if the men's side is arranged in the same way. And every time I stepped out, I could hear them talking about me. They called you the black butcher, and other things I don't want to tell you about."

"That's natural enough," I said. "You were probably the first stranger to enter the place in a month, so it's only to be expected that they would chatter about you, and that the few women who knew who you were would be proud of it and perhaps tell some tales. As for me, I'm used to it, and you must have heard such expressions on the way here many times; I know I did."

"Yes," she admitted, and sat down on the sill of the embrasure. In the city below, the lamps of the swarming shops were beginning to fill the valley of the Acis with a yellow radiance like the petals of a jonquil, but she did not seem to see them.

"Now you understand why the regulations of the guild forbid me from taking a wife—although I will break them for you, as I have told you many times, whenever you want me to."

"You mean that it would be better for me to live somewhere else, and only come to see you once or twice a week, or wait till you came to see me."

"That's the way it's usually done. And eventually the women who talked about us today will realize that sometime they, or their sons or husbands, may find themselves beneath my hand."

"But don't you see, this is all beside the point. The thing is . . ." Here Dorcas fell silent, and then, when neither of us had spoken for some time, she rose and began to pace the room, one arm clasping the other. It was something I had never seen her do before, and I found it disturbing.

"What is the point, then?" I asked.

"That it wasn't true then. That it is now."

"I practiced the Art whenever there was work to be had. Hired myself out to towns and country justices. Several times you watched me from a window, though you never liked to stand in the crowd—for which I hardly blame you."

"I didn't watch," she said.

"I recall seeing you."

"I didn't. Not when it was actually going on. You were intent on what you were doing, and didn't see me when I went inside or covered my eyes. I used to watch, and wave to you, when you first vaulted onto the scaffold. You were so proud then, and stood just as straight as your sword, and looked so fine. You were honest. I remember watching once when there was an official of some sort up there with you, and the condemned man and a hieromonach. And yours was the only honest face."

"You couldn't possibly have seen it. I must surely have been wearing my mask."

"Severian, I didn't have to see it. I know what you look like."

"Don't I look the same now?"

"Yes," she said reluctantly. "But I have been down below. I've seen the people chained in the tunnels. When we sleep tonight, you and I in our soft bed, we will be sleeping on top of them. How many did you say there were when you took me down?"

"About sixteen hundred. Do you honestly believe those sixteen hundred would be free if I were no longer present to guard them? They were here, remember, when we came."

Dorcas would not look at me. "It's like a mass grave," she said. I could see her shoulders shake.

"It should be," I told her. "The archon could release them, but who could resurrect those they've killed? You've never lost anyone, have you?"

She did not reply.

"Ask the wives and the mothers and the sisters of the men our prisoners have left rotting in the high country whether Abdiesus should let them go."

"Only myself," Dorcas said, and blew out the candle.

Thrax is a crooked dagger entering the heart of the mountains. It lies in a narrow defile of the valley of the Acis, and extends up it to Acies

Castle. The harena, the pantheon, and the other public buildings occupy all the level land between the castle and the wall (called the Capulus) that closes the lower end of the narrow section of the valley. The private buildings of the city climb the cliffs to either side, and many are in large measure dug into the rock itself, from which practice Thrax gains one of its sobriquets—the City of Windowless Rooms.

Its prosperity it owes to its position at the head of the navigable part of the river. At Thrax, all goods shipped north on the Acis (many of which have traversed nine tenths of the length of Gyoll before entering the mouth of the smaller river, which may indeed be Gyoll's true source) must be unloaded and carried on the backs of animals if they are to travel farther. Conversely, the hetmans of the mountain tribes and the landowners of the region who wish to ship their wool and corn to the southern towns bring them to take boat at Thrax, below the cataract that roars through the arched spillway of Acies Castle.

As must always be the case when a stronghold imposes the rule of law over a turbulent region, the administration of justice was the chief concern of the archon of the city. To impose his will on those without the walls who might otherwise have opposed it, he could call upon seven squadrons of dimarchi, each under its own commander. Court convened each month, from the first appearance of the new moon to the full, beginning with the second morning watch and continuing as long as necessary to clear the day's docket. As chief executor of the archon's sentences, I was required to attend these sessions, so that he might be assured that the punishments he decreed should be made neither softer nor more severe by those who might otherwise have been charged with transmitting them to me; and to oversee the operation of the Vincula, in which the prisoners were detained, in all its details. It was a responsibility equivalent on a lesser scale to that of Master Gurloes in our Citadel, and during the first few weeks I spent in Thrax it weighed heavily upon me.

It was a maxim of Master Gurloes's that no prison is ideally situated. Like most of the wise tags put forward for the edification of young men, it was inarguable and unhelpful. All escapes fall into three categories—that is, they are achieved by stealth, by violence, or by the treachery of those set as guards. A remote place does most to render escapes by stealth difficult, and for that reason has been favored by the majority of those who have thought long upon the subject.

Unfortunately, deserts, mountaintops, and lone isles offer the most fertile fields for violent escape—if they are besieged by the prisoners' friends, it is difficult to learn of the fact before it is too late, and next to impossible to reinforce their garrisons; and similarly, if the prisoners rise in rebellion, it is highly unlikely that troops can be rushed to the spot before the issue is decided.

A facility in a well-populated and well-defended district avoids these difficulties, but incurs even more severe ones. In such places a prisoner needs, not a thousand friends, but one or two; and these need not be fighting men—a scrubwoman and a street vendor will do, if they possess intelligence and resolution. Furthermore, once the prisoner has escaped the walls, he mingles immediately with the faceless mob, so that his reapprehension is not a matter for huntsmen and dogs but for agents and informers.

In our own case, a detached prison in a remote location would have been out of the question. Even if it had been provided with a sufficient number of troops, in addition to its clavigers, to fend off the attacks of the autochthons, zoanthrops, and cultellarii who roamed the countryside, not to mention the armed retinues of the petty exultants (who could never be relied upon), it would still have been impossible to provision without the services of an army to escort the supply trains. The Vincula of Thrax is therefore located by necessity within the city—specifically, about halfway up the cliffside on the west bank, and a half league or so from the Capulus.

It is of ancient design, and always appeared to me to have been intended as a prison from the beginning, though there is a legend to the effect that it was originally a tomb, and was only a few hundred years ago enlarged and converted to its new purpose. To an observer on the more commodious east bank, it appears to be a rectangular bartizan jutting from the rock, a bartizan four stories high at the side he sees, whose flat, merloned roof terminates against the cliff. This visible portion of the structure—which many visitors to the city must take for the whole of it—is in fact the smallest and least important part. At the time I was lictor, it held no more than our administrative offices, a barracks for the clavigers, and my own living quarters.

The prisoners were lodged in a slanted shaft bored into the rock. The arrangement used was neither one of individual cells such as we had for our clients in the oubliette at home, nor the common room I had encountered while I was myself confined in the House Absolute. Instead, the prisoners were chained along the walls of the shaft, each with a stout iron collar about his neck, in such a way as to leave a path down the center wide enough that two clavigers could walk it abreast without danger that their keys might be snatched away.

This shaft was about five hundred paces long, and had over a thousand positions for prisoners. Its water supply came from a cistern sunk into the stone at the top of the cliff, and sanitary wastes were disposed of by flushing the shaft whenever this cistern threatened to overflow. A sewer drilled at the lower end of the shaft conveyed the wastewater to a conduit at the cliff base that ran through the wall of the Capulus to empty into the Acis below the city.

The rectangular bartizan clinging to the cliff, and the shaft itself, must originally have constituted the whole of the Vincula. It had subsequently been complicated by a confusion of branching galleries and parallel shafts resulting from past attempts to free prisoners by tunneling from one or another of the private residences in the cliff face, and from countermines excavated to frustrate such attempts—all now pressed into service to provide additional accommodations.

The existence of these unplanned or poorly planned additions rendered my task much more difficult than it would otherwise have been, and one of my first acts was to begin a program of closing unwanted and unnecessary passages by filling them with a mixture of river stones, sand, water, burned lime, and gravel, and to start widening and uniting those passages that remained in such a way as to eventually achieve a rational structure. Necessary though it was, this work could be carried forward only very slowly, since no more than a few hundred prisoners could be freed to work at a time, and they were for the most part in poor condition.

For the first few weeks after Dorcas and I arrived in the city, my duties left me time for nothing else. She explored it for us both, and I charged her strictly to inquire about the Pelerines for me. On the long journey from Nessus the knowledge that I carried the Claw of the Conciliator had been a heavy burden. Now, when I was no longer traveling and could no longer attempt to trace the Pelerines along the way or even reassure myself that I was walking in a direction that might eventually bring me in contact with them, it became an almost unbearable weight. While we were traveling I had slept under the stars with the gem in the top of my boot, and with it concealed in the toe on those few occasions when we were able to stop beneath a roof. Now I found that I could not sleep at all unless I had it with me, so I could assure myself, whenever I woke in the night, that I retained possession of it. Dorcas sewed a little sack of doeskin for me to hold it, and I wore it about my neck day and night. A dozen times during those first weeks I dreamed I saw the gem aflame, hanging in the air above me like its own burning cathedral, and woke to find it blazing so brightly that a faint radiance showed through the thin leather. And once or twice each night I awakened to discover that I was lying on my back with the sack on my chest seemingly grown so heavy (though I could lift it with my hand without effort) that it was crushing out my life.

Dorcas did everything in her power to comfort and assist me; yet I could see she was conscious of the abrupt change in our relationship and disturbed by it even more than I. Such changes are always, in my experience, unpleasant—if only because they imply the likelihood of further change. While we had been journeying together (and we had been traveling with greater or lesser expedition from the moment in the Garden of Endless Sleep when Dorcas helped me clamber, half-drowned, onto the floating walkway of sedge) it had been as equals and companions, each of us walking every league we covered on our own feet or riding our own mount. If I had supplied a measure of physical protection to Dorcas, she had equally supplied a certain moral shelter to me, in that few could pretend for long to despise her innocent beauty, or profess horror at my office when in looking at me they could not help but see her as well. She had been my counselor in perplexity and my comrade in a hundred desert places.

When we at last entered Thrax and I presented Master Palaemon's letter to the archon, all that was by necessity ended. In my fuligin habit I no longer had to fear the crowd—rather, they feared me as the highest official of the most dreaded arm of the state. Dorcas lived now, not as an equal but as the paramour the Cumaean had once called her, in the quarters in the Vincula set aside for me. Her counsel had become useless or nearly so because the difficulties that oppressed me were the legal and administrative ones I had been trained for years to wrestle with and about which she knew nothing; and moreover because I seldom had the time or the energy to explain them to her so that we might discuss them.

Thus, while I stood for watch after watch in the archon's court, Dorcas fell into the habit of wandering the city, and we, who had been incessantly together throughout the latter part of the spring, came now in summer to see each other hardly at all, sharing a meal in the evening and climbing exhausted into a bed where we seldom did more than fall asleep in each other's arms.

At last the full moon shone. With what joy I beheld it from the roof of the bartizan, green as an emerald in its mantle of forest and round as the lip of a cup! I was not yet free, since all the details of excruciations and administration that had been accumulating during my attendance on the archon remained to be dealt with; but I was now at least free to devote my full attention to them, which seemed then nearly as good a thing as freedom itself. I had invited Dorcas to go with me on the next day, when I made an inspection of the subterranean parts of the Vincula.

It was an error. She grew ill in the foul air, surrounded by the misery of the prisoners. That night, as I have already recounted, she told me she had gone to the public baths (a rare thing for her, whose fear of water was so great that she washed herself bit by bit with a sponge dipped in a bowl no deeper than a dish of soup) to free her hair and skin from the odor of the shaft, and that she had heard the bath attendants pointing her out to the other patrons.

II

Upon the Cataract

The following morning, before she left the bartizan, Dorcas cut her hair until she almost seemed a boy, and thrust a white peony through the circulet that confined it. I labored over documents until afternoon, then borrowed a layman's jelab from the sergeant of my clavigers and went out hoping to encounter her.

The brown book I carry says there is nothing stranger than to explore a city wholly different from all those one knows, since to do so is to explore a second and unsuspected self. I have found a thing stranger: to explore such a city only after one has lived in it for some time without learning anything of it.

I did not know where the baths Dorcas had mentioned stood, though I had surmised from talk I had heard in court that they existed. I did not know where the bazaar where she bought her cloth and cosmetics was located, or even if there were more than one. I knew nothing, in short, beyond what I could see from the embrasure, and the brief route from the Vincula to the archon's palace. I had, perhaps, a too-ready confidence in my own ability to find my way about in a city so much smaller than Nessus; even so I took the precaution of making certain from time to time, as I trod the crooked streets that straggled down the cliff between cave-houses excavated from the rock and swallow-houses jutting out from it, that I could still see the familiar shape of the bartizan, with its barricaded gate and black gonfalon.

In Nessus the rich live toward the north where the waters of Gyoll are purer, and the poor to the south where they are foul. Here in Thrax that custom no longer held, both because the Acis flowed so swiftly that the excrement of those upstream (who were, of course, but a thousandth part as numerous as those who lived about the northern reaches of

Gyoll) hardly affected its flood, and because water taken from above the cataract was conveyed to the public fountains and the homes of the wealthy by aqueducts, so that no reliance had to be put upon the river save when the largest quantities of water—as for manufacturing or wholesale washing—were required.

Thus in Thrax the separation was by elevation. The wealthiest lived on the lowest slopes near the river, within easy reach of the shops and public offices, where a brief walk brought them to piers from which they could travel the length of the city in slave-rowed caiques. Those somewhat less well off had their houses higher, the middle class in general had theirs higher still, and so on until the very poorest dwelt just below the fortifications at the cliff tops, often in jacals of mud and reeds that could be reached only by long ladders.

I was to see something of those miserable hovels, but for the present I remained in the commercial quarter near the water. There the narrow streets were so thronged with people that I at first thought a festival was in progress, or perhaps that the war—which had seemed so remote while I remained in Nessus but had become progressively more immediate as Dorcas and I journeyed north—was now near enough to fill the city with those who fled before it.

Nessus is so extensive that it has, as I have heard said, five buildings for each living inhabitant. In Thrax that ratio is surely reversed, and on that day it seemed to me at times that there must have been fifty for each roof. Too, Nessus is a cosmopolitan city, so that although one saw many foreigners there, and occasionally even cacogens come by ship from other worlds, one was always conscious that they *were* foreigners, far from their homes. Here the streets swarmed with diverse humanity, but they merely reflected the diverse nature of the mountain setting, so that when I saw, for example, a man whose hat was made from a bird's pelt with the wings used for ear flaps, or a man in a shaggy coat of kaberu skin, or a man with a tattooed face, I might see a hundred more such tribesmen around the next corner.

These men were eclectics, the descendants of settlers from the south who had mixed their blood with that of the squat, dark autochthons, adopted certain of their customs, and mingled these with still others acquired from the amphitryons farther north and those, in some instances, of even less-known peoples, traders and parochial races.

Many of these eclectics favor knives that are curved—or as they are sometimes called, bent—having two relatively straight sections, with an elbow a little toward the point. This shape is said to make it easier to pierce the heart by stabbing beneath the breastbone; the blades are stiffened with a central rib, are sharpened on both sides, and are kept very sharp; there is no guard, and their hafts are commonly of bone. (I have described these knives in detail because they are as characteristic of the region as anything can be said to be, and because it is from them that Thrax takes another of its names: the City of Crooked Knives. There is also the resemblance of the plan of the city to the blade of such a knife, the curve of the defile corresponding to the curve of the blade, the River Acis to the central rib, Acies Castle to the point, and the Capulus to the line at which the steel vanishes into the haft.)

One of the keepers of the Bear Tower once told me that there is no animal so dangerous or so savage and unmanageable as the hybrid resulting when a fighting dog mounts a she-wolf. We are accustomed to think of the beasts of the forest and mountain as wild, and to think of the men who spring up, as it seems, from their soil as savage. But the truth is that there is a wildness more vicious (as we would know better if we were not so habituated to it) in certain domestic animals, despite their understanding so much human speech and sometimes even speaking a few words; and there is a more profound savagery in men and women whose ancestors have lived in cities and towns since the dawn of humanity. Vodalus, in whose veins flowed the undefiled blood of a thousand exultants—exarchs, ethnarchs, and starosts—was capable of violence unimaginable to the autochthons that stalked the streets of Thrax, naked beneath their huanaco cloaks.

Like the dog-wolves (which I never saw, because they were too vicious to be useful), these eclectics took all that was most cruel and ungovernable from their mixed parentage; as friends or followers they were sullen, disloyal, and contentious; as enemies, fierce, deceitful, and vindictive. So at least I had heard from my subordinates at the Vincula, for eclectics made up more than half the prisoners there.

I have never encountered men whose language, costume, or customs are foreign without speculating on the nature of the women of their race. There is always a connection, since the two are the growths of a single culture, just as the leaves of a tree, which one sees, and the fruit, which one does not see because it is hidden by the leaves, are the growths of a single organism. But the observer who would venture to predict the appearance and flavor of the fruit from the outline of a few leafy boughs seen (as it were) from a distance, must know a great deal about leaves and fruit if he is not to make himself ridiculous.

Warlike men may be born of languishing women, or they may have sisters nearly as strong as themselves and more resolute. And so I, walking among crowds composed largely of these eclectics and the townsmen (who seemed to me not much different from the citizens of Nessus, save that their clothing and their manners were somewhat rougher) found myself speculating on dark-eyed, dark-skinned women, women with glossy black hair as thick as the tails of the skewbald mounts of their brothers, women whose faces I imagined as strong yet delicate, women given to ferocious resistance and swift surrender, women who could be won but not bought—if such women exist in this world.

From their arms I traveled in imagination to the places where they might be found, the lonely huts crouched by mountain springs, the hide yurts standing alone in the high pastures. Soon I was as intoxicated with the thought of the mountains as I had been once, before Master Palaemon had told me the correct location of Thrax, with the idea of the sea. How glorious are they, the immovable idols of Urth, carved with unaccountable tools in a time inconceivably ancient, still lifting above the rim of the world grim heads crowned with mitres, tiaras, and diadems spangled with snow, heads whose eyes are as large as towns, figures whose shoulders are wrapped in forests.

Thus, disguised in the dull jelab of a townsman, I elbowed my way down streets packed with humanity and reeking with the odors of ordure and cookery, with my imagination filled with visions of hanging stone, and crystal streams like carcanets.

Thecla must, I think, have been taken at least into the foothills of these heights, no doubt to escape the heat of some particularly torrid summer; for many of the scenes that rose in my mind (as it seemed, of their own accord) were noticeably childlike. I saw rock-loving plants whose virginal flowers I beheld with an immediacy of vision no adult achieves without kneeling; abysses that seemed not only frightening but shocking, as though their existence were an affront to the laws of nature; peaks so high they appeared to be literally without summit, as though the whole world had been falling forever from some unimaginable Heaven, which yet retained its hold on these mountains.

Eventually I reached Acies Castle, having walked almost the entire length of the city. I made my identity known to the postern guards there and was permitted to enter and climb to the top of the donjon, as I had once climbed our Matachin Tower before taking my leave of Master Palaemon.

When I had gone there to make my farewell to the only place I had known, I had stood at one of the loftiest points of the Citadel, which was itself poised atop one of the highest elevations in the whole area of Nessus. The city had been spread before me to the limits of vision, with Gyoll traced across it like the green slime of a slug across a map; even the Wall had been visible on the horizon at some points, and nowhere was I beneath the shadow of a summit much superior to my own.

Here the impression was far different. I bestrode the Acis, which leaped toward me down a succession of rocky steps each twice or three times the height of a tall tree. Beaten to a foaming whiteness that glittered in the sunlight, it disappeared beneath me and reappeared as a ribbon of silver racing through a city as neatly contained in its declivity as one of those toy villages in a box that I (but it was Thecla) recalled receiving on a birthday.

Yet I stood, as it were, at the bottom of a bowl. On every side the walls of stone ascended, so that to look at any one of them was to believe, for a moment at least, that gravity had been twisted until it stood at right angles to its proper self by some sorcerer's multiplication with imaginary numbers, and the height I saw was properly the level surface of the world.

For a watch or more, I think, I stared up at those walls, and traced the spidery lines of the waterfalls that dashed down them in thunder and clean romance to join the Acis, and watched the clouds trapped among them that seemed to press softly against their unyielding sides like sheep bewildered and dismayed among pens of stone.

Then I grew weary at last of the magnificence of the mountains and my mountain dreams—or rather, not weary, but dizzied by them until my head reeled with vertigo, and I seemed to see those merciless heights even when I closed my eyes, and felt that in my dreams, that night and for many nights, I would fall from their precipices, or cling with bloody fingers to their hopeless walls.

Then I turned in earnest to the city and reassured myself with the sight of the bartizan of the Vincula, a very modest little cube now, cemented to a cliff that was hardly more than a ripple among the incalculable waves of stone around it. I plotted the courses of the principal streets, seeking (as in a game, to sober myself from my long gazing on the mountains) to identify those I had walked in reaching the castle, and to observe from this new perspective the buildings and market squares I had seen on the way. By eye I looted the bazaars, finding that there were two, one on either side of the river; and I marked afresh the familiar landmarks I had learned to know from the embrasure of the Vincula—the harena, the pantheon, and the archon's palace. Then, when everything I had seen from the ground had been confirmed from my new vantage point, and I felt I understood the spatial relationship of the place at which I stood to what I had known earlier of the plan of the city, I began to explore the lesser streets, peering along the twisted paths that climbed the upper cliffs and probing narrow alleys that often seemed no more than mere bands of darkness between buildings.

In seeking them out, my gaze came at last to the margins of the river again, and I began to study the landings there, and the storehouses, and even the pyramids of barrels and boxes and bales that waited there to be carried aboard some vessel. Now the water no longer foamed, save when it was obstructed by the piers. Its color was nearly indigo, and like the indigo shadows seen at evening on a snowy day, it seemed to slip silently along, sinuous and freezing; but the motion of the hurrying caiques and laden feluccas showed how much turbulence lay concealed beneath that smooth surface, for the larger craft swung their long bowspirits like fencers, and both yawed crabwise at times while their oars threshed the racing eddies.

When I had exhausted all that lay farther downstream, I leaned from the parapet to observe the closest reach of the river and a wharf that was no more than a hundred strides from the postern gate. Looking down at the stevedores there who toiled to unburden one of the narrow river boats, I saw near them, unmoving, a tiny figure with bright hair. At first I thought her a child because she seemed so small beside the burly, nearly naked laborers; but it was Dorcas, sitting at the very edge of the water with her face in her hands.

III

Outside the Jacal

When I reached Dorcas I could not make her speak. It was not simply that she was angry with me, although I thought so at the time. Silence had come upon her like a disease, not injuring her tongue and lips but disabling her will to use them and perhaps even her desire to, just as certain infections destroy our desire for pleasure and even our comprehension of joy in others. If I did not lift her face to mine, she would look at nothing, staring at the ground beneath her feet without, I think, seeing even that, or covering her face with her hands, as she had been covering it when I found her.

I wanted to talk to her, believing—then—that I could say something, though I was not certain what, that would restore her to herself. But I could not do so there on the wharf, with stevedores staring at us, and for a time I could find no place to which I could lead her. On a little street nearby that had begun to climb the slope east of the river, I saw the board of an inn. There were patrons eating in its narrow common room, but for a few aes I was able to rent a chamber on the floor above it, a place with no furniture but a bed and little space for any, with a ceiling so low that at one end I could not stand erect. The hostess thought we were renting her chamber for a tryst, naturally enough under the circumstances—but thought too, because of Dorcas's despairing expression, that I had some hold on her or had bought her from a procurer, and so gave her a look of melting sympathy that I do not believe she noticed in the least, and me one of recrimination.

I shut and bolted the door and made Dorcas lie on the bed; then I sat beside her and tried to cajole her into conversation, asking her what was wrong, and what I might do to right whatever it was that troubled her, and so on. When I found that had no effect, I began to talk about myself, supposing that it was only her horror of the conditions in the Vincula that had moved her to sever herself from discourse with me.

"We are despised by everyone," I said. "And so there is no reason why I should not be despised by you. The surprising thing is not that you should have come to hate me now, but that you could go this long before coming to feel as the rest do. But because I love you, I am going to try to state the case for our guild, and thus for myself, hoping that perhaps afterward you won't feel so badly about having loved a torturer, even though you don't love me any longer.

"We are not cruel. We take no delight in what we do, except in doing it well, which means doing it quickly and doing neither more nor less than the law instructs us. We obey the judges, who hold their offices because the people consent to it. Some individuals tell us we should do nothing of what we do, and that no one should do it. They say that punishment inflicted with cold blood is a greater crime than any crime our clients could have committed.

"There may be justice in that, but it is a justice that would destroy the whole Commonwealth. No one could feel safe and no one could be safe, and in the end the people would rise up—at first against the thieves and the murderers, and then against anyone who offended the popular ideas of propriety, and at last against mere strangers and outcasts. Then they would be back to the old horrors of stoning and burning, in which every man seeks to outdo his neighbor for fear he will be thought tomorrow to hold some sympathy for the wretch dying today.

"There are others who tell us that certain clients are deserving of the most severe punishment, but that others are not, and that we should refuse to perform our office upon those others. It certainly must be that some are more guilty than the rest, and it may even be that some of these who are handed over to us have done no wrong at all, neither in the matter in which they are accused, nor in any other.

"But the people who urge these arguments are doing no more than setting themselves up as judges over the judges appointed by the Autarch, judges with less training in the law and without the authority to call witnesses. They demand that we disobey the real judges and listen to them, but they cannot show that they are more deserving of our obedience.

"Others yet hold that our clients should not be tortured or executed, but should be made to labor for the Commonwealth, digging canals, building watchtowers, and the like. But with the cost of their guards and chains, honest workers might be hired, who otherwise would want for bread. Why should these loyal workers starve so that murderers shall not die, nor thieves feel any pain? Furthermore, these murderers and thieves, being without loyalty to the law and without hope of reward, would not work save under the lash. What is that lash but torture again, going under a new name?

"Still others say that all those judged guilty should be confined, in comfort and without pain, for many years—and often for as long as they will live. But those who have comfort and no pain live long, and every orichalk spent to maintain them so would have to be taken from better purposes. I know little of the war, but I know enough to understand how much money is needed to buy weapons and pay soldiers. The fighting is in the mountains to the north now, so that we fight as if behind a hundred walls. But what if it should reach the pampas? Would it be possible to hold back the Ascians when there was so much room to maneuver? And how would Nessus be fed if the herds there were to fall into their hands?

"If the guilty are not to be locked away in comfort, and are not to be tortured, what remains? If they are all killed, and all killed alike, then a poor woman who steals will be thought as bad as a mother who poisons her own child, as Morwenna of Saltus did. Would you wish that? In time of peace, many might be banished. But to banish them now would only be to deliver a corps of spies to the Ascians, to be trained and supplied with funds and sent back among us. Soon no one could be trusted, though he spoke our own tongue. Would you wish that?"

Dorcas lay so silent upon the bed that I thought for a moment she had fallen asleep. But her eyes, those enormous eyes of perfect blue, were open; and when I leaned over to look at her, they moved, and seemed for a time to watch me as they might have watched the spreading ripples in a pond.

"All right, we are devils," I said. "If you would have it so. But we are necessary. Even the powers of Heaven find it necessary to employ devils."

Tears came into her eyes, though I could not tell whether she wept because she had hurt me or because she found that I was still present. In the hope of winning her back to her old affection for me, I began to talk of the times when we were still on the way to Thrax, reminding her of how we had met in the clearing after we had fled the grounds of the House Absolute, and of how we had talked in those great gardens before Dr. Talos's play, walking through the blossoming orchard to sit on an old bench beside a broken fountain, and of all she had said to me there, and of all that I had said to her.

And it seemed to me that she became a trifle less sorrowful until I mentioned the fountain, whose waters had run from its cracked basin to form a little stream that some gardener had sent wandering among the trees to refresh them, and there to end by soaking the ground; but then a darkness that was nowhere in the room but on Dorcas's face came to settle there like one of those strange things that had pursued Jonas and me through the cedars. Then she would no longer look at me, and after a time she truly slept.

I got up as silently as I could, unbolted the door, and went down the crooked stair. The hostess was still working in the common room below, but the patrons who had been there were gone. I explained to her that the woman I had brought was ill, paid the rent of the room for several days, and promising to return and take care of any other expenses, asked her to look in on her from time to time, and to feed her if she would eat.

"Ah, it will be a blessing to us to have someone sleeping in the room," the hostess said. "But if your darling's sick, is the Duck's Nest the best place you can find for her? Can't you take her home?"

"I'm afraid living in my house is what has made her ill. At least, I don't want to risk the chance that returning there will make her worse."

"Poor darling!" The hostess shook her head. "So pretty too, and doesn't look more than a child. How old is she?"

I told her I did not know.

"Well, I'll have a visit with her and give her some soup when she's ready for it." She looked at me as if to say that the time would come soon enough once I was away. "But I want you to know that I won't hold her a prisoner for you. If she wants to leave, she'll be free to go."

When I stepped out of the little inn, I wished to return to the Vincula by the most direct route; but I made the mistake of supposing that since the narrow street on which the Duck's Nest stood ran almost due south, it would be quicker to continue along it and cross the Acis lower down than to retrace the steps Dorcas and I had already taken and go back to the foot of the postern wall of Acies Castle.

The narrow street betrayed me, as I would have expected if I had been more familiar with the ways of Thrax. For all those crooked streets that snake along the slopes, though they may cross one another, on the whole run up and down; so that to reach one cliff-hugging house from another (unless they are quite close together or one above the other) it is necessary to walk down to the central strip near the river, and then back up again. Thus before long I found myself as high up the eastern cliff as the Vincula was on the western one, with less prospect of reaching it than I had when I left the inn.

To be truthful, it was not a wholly unpleasant discovery. I had work to do there, and no particular desire to do it, my mind being still full of thoughts of Dorcas. It felt better to wear out my frustrations by the use of my legs, and so I resolved to follow the capering street to the top if need be and see the Vincula and Acies Castle from that height, and then to show my badge of office to the guards at the fortifications there and walk along them to the Capulus and so cross the river by the lowest way.

But after half a watch of strenuous effort, I found I could go no farther. The street ended against a precipice three or four chains high, and perhaps had properly ended sooner, for the last few score paces I had walked had been on what was probably no more than a private path to the miserable jacal of mud and sticks before which I stood.

After making certain there was no way around it, and no way to the top for some distance from where I stood, I was about to turn away in disgust when a child slipped out of the jacal, and sidling toward me in a half bold, half fearful way, watching me with its right eye only, extended a small and very dirty hand in the universal gesture of beggars. Perhaps I would have laughed at the poor little creature, so timid and so importunate, if I had felt in a better mood; as it was, I dropped a few aes into the soiled palm.

Encouraged, the child ventured to say, "My sister is sick. Very sick, sieur." From the timbre of its voice I decided it was a boy; and because he turned his head almost toward me when he spoke, I could see that his left eye was swollen shut by some infection. Tears of pus had run from it to dry on the cheek below. "Very, very sick."

"I see," I told him.

"Oh, no, sieur. You cannot, not from here. But if you wish you can look in through the door—you will not bother her."

Just then a man wearing the scuffed leather apron of a mason called, "What is it, Jader? What does he want?" He was toiling up the path in our direction.

As anyone might have anticipated, the boy was only frightened into silence by the question. I said, "I was asking the best way to the lower city."

The mason answered nothing, but stopped about four strides from me and folded arms that looked harder than the stones they broke. He seemed angry and distrustful, though I could not be sure why. Perhaps my accent had betrayed that I came from the south; perhaps it was only because of the way I was dressed, which though it was by no means rich or fantastic, indicated that I belonged to a social class higher than his own.

"Am I trespassing?" I asked. "Do you own this place?"

There was no reply. Whatever he felt about me, it was plain that in his opinion there could be no communication between us. When I spoke to him, it could only be as a man speaks to a beast, and not even to intelligent beasts at that, but only as a drover shouts at kine. And on his side, when I spoke it was only as beasts speak to a man, a sound made in the throat.

I have noticed that in books this sort of stalemate never seems to occur; the authors are so anxious to move their stories forward (however wooden they may be, advancing like market carts with squeaking wheels that are never still, though they go only to dusty villages where the charm of the country is lost and the pleasures of the city will never be found) that there are no such misunderstandings, no refusals to negotiate. The assassin who holds a dagger to his victim's neck is eager to discuss the whole matter, and at any length the victim or the author may wish. The passionate pair in love's embrace are at least equally willing to postpone the stabbing, if not more so.

In life it is not the same. I stared at the mason, and he at me. I felt I could have killed him, but I could not be sure of it, both because he looked unusually strong and because I could not be certain he did not have some concealed weapon, or friends in the miserable dwellings close by. I felt he was about to spit onto the path between us, and if he had I would have flung my jelab over his head and pinned him. But he did not, and when we had stared at each other for several moments, the boy, who perhaps had no idea of what was taking place said again, "You can look through the door, sieur. You won't bother my sister." He even dared to tug a little at my sleeve in his eagerness to show he had not lied, not seeming to realize that his own appearance justified any amount of begging.

"I believe you," I said. But then I understood that to say I believed him was to insult him by showing that I did not have faith enough in what he said to put it to the test. I bent and peered, though at first I could see little, looking as I was from the bright sunshine into the shadowy interior of the jacal.

The light was almost squarely behind me. I felt its pressure on the nape of my neck, and I was conscious that the mason could attack me with impunity now that my back was toward him.

Tiny as it was, the room inside was not cluttered. Some straw had been heaped against the wall farthest from the door, and the girl lay upon it. She was in that state of disease in which we no longer feel pity for the sick person, who has instead become an object of horror. Her face was a death's head over which was stretched skin as thin and translucent as the head of a drum. Her lips could no longer cover her teeth even in sleep, and under the scythe of fever, her hair had fallen away until only wisps remained.

I braced my hands on the mud and wattle wall beside the door and straightened up. The boy said, "You see she is very sick, sieur. My sister." He held out his hand again.

I saw it—I see it before me now—but it made no immediate impression on my mind. I could think only of the Claw; and it seemed to me that it was pressing against my breastbone, not so much like a weight as like the knuckles of an invisible fist. I remembered the uhlan who had appeared dead until I touched his lips with the Claw, and who now seemed to me to belong to the remote past; and I remembered the man-ape, with his stump of arm, and the way Jonas's burns had faded when I ran the Claw along their length. I had not used it or even considered using it since it had failed to save Jolenta.

Now I had kept its secret so long that I was afraid to try it again. I would have touched the dying girl with it, perhaps, if it had not been for her brother looking on; I would have touched the brother's diseased eye with it if it had not been for the surly mason. As it was, I only labored to breathe against the force that strained my ribs, and did nothing, walking away downhill without noticing in what direction I walked. I heard the mason's saliva fly from his mouth and smack the eroded stone of the path behind me; but I did not know what the sound was until I was almost back at the Vincula and had more or less returned to myself.

IV

In the Bartizan of the Vincula

"You have company, Lictor," the sentry told me, and when I only nodded to acknowledge the information, he added, "It might be best for you to change first, Lictor." I did not need then to ask who my guest was; only the presence of the archon would have drawn that tone from him.

It was not difficult to reach my private quarters without passing through the study where I conducted the business of the Vincula and kept its accounts. I spent the time it took to divest myself of my borrowed jelab and put on my fuligin cloak in speculating as to why the archon, who had never come to me before, and whom, for that matter, I had seldom even seen outside his court, should find it necessary to visit the Vincula—so far as I could see, without an entourage.

The speculation was welcome because it kept certain other thoughts at a distance. There was a large silvered glass in our bedroom, a much more effective mirror than the small plates of polished metal to which I was accustomed; and on it, as I saw for the first time when I stood before it to examine my appearance, Dorcas had scrawled in soap four lines from a song she had once sung for me:

Horns of Urth, you fling notes to the sky,
Green and good, green and good.
Sing at my step; a sweeter glade have I.
Lift, oh, lift me to the fallen wood!

There were several large chairs in the study, and I had anticipated finding the archon in one of them (though it had also crossed my mind that he might be availing himself of the opportunity to go through my papers—something he had every right to do if he chose). He was standing at the embrasure instead, looking out over his city much as I myself had looked out at it from the ramparts of Acies Castle earlier that afternoon. His hands were clasped behind him, and as I watched I saw them move as if each possessed a life of its own, engendered by his thoughts. It was some time before he turned and caught sight of me.

"You are here, Master Torturer. I did not hear you come in."

"I am only a journeyman, Archon."

He smiled and seated himself on the sill, his back to the drop. His face was coarse, with a hook nose and large eyes rimmed with dark flesh, but it was not a masculine face; it might almost have been the face of an ugly woman. "Charged by me with the responsibility for this place, you remain a mere journeyman?"

"I can bc clevated only by the masters of our guild, Archon."

"But you are the best of their journeymen, judging from the letter you carried, from their choosing you to send here, and from the work you've done since you arrived. Anyway, no one here would know the difference if you chose to put on airs. How many masters are there?"

"I would know, Archon. Only two, unless someone has been elevated since I've been gone."

"I'll write them and ask them to elevate you *in absentia*."

"I thank you, Archon."

"It's nothing," he said, and turned to stare out the embrasure as though the situation embarrassed him. "You should have word of it, I suppose, in a month."

"They will not elevate me, Archon. But it will make Master Palaemon happy to hear you think so well of me."

He swung around again to look at me. "We need not be so formal, surely. My name is Abdiesus, and there is no reason you should not use it when we're alone. You're Severian, I believe?"

I nodded.

He turned away again. "This is a very low opening. I was examining it before you came in, and the wall hardly reaches above my knees. It would be easy, I'm afraid, for someone to fall out of it."

"Only for someone as tall as yourself, Abdiesus."

"In the past, were not executions performed, occasionally, by casting the victim from a high window or from the edge of a precipice?"

"Yes, both those methods have been employed."

"Not by you, I suppose." Once more he faced me.

"Not within living memory, so far as I know, Abdiesus. I have performed decollations—both with the block and with the chair—but that is all."

"But you would have no objection to the use of other means? If you were instructed to employ them?"

"I am here to carry out the archon's sentences."

"There are times, Severian, when public executions serve the public good. There are others when they would only do harm by inciting public unrest."

"That is understood, Abdiesus," I said. As sometimes I have seen in the eyes of a boy the worry of the man he will be, I could see the future guilt that had already come (perhaps without his being aware of it) to settle on the archon's face.

"There will be a few guests at the palace tonight. I hope that you will be among them, Severian."

I bowed. "Among the divisions of administration, Abdiesus, it has long been customary to exclude one—my own—from the society of the others."

"And you feel that is unjust, which is wholly natural. Tonight, if you wish to think of it in that way, we will be making some restitution."

"We of the guild have never complained of injustice. Indeed, we have gloried in our unique isolation. Tonight, however, the others may feel they have reason to protest to you."

A smile twitched at his mouth. "I'm not concerned about that. Here, this will get you onto the grounds." He extended his hand, holding delicately, as though he feared it would flutter from his fingers, one of those disks of stiff paper, no bigger than a chrisos and lettered in gold leaf with ornate characters, of which I had often heard Thecla speak (she stirred in my mind at the touch of it), but which I had never before seen.

"Thank you, Archon. Tonight, you said? I will try to find suitable clothing."

"Come dressed as you are. It's to be a ridotto—your habit will be your costume." He stood and stretched himself with the air, I thought, of one who nears the completion of a long and disagreeable task. "A moment ago we spoke of some of the less elaborate ways that you might perform your function. It might be well for you to bring whatever equipment you will require tonight."

I understood. I would need nothing beyond my hands, and told him so; then, feeling I had already been remiss in my duties as his host, I invited him to take what refreshment we had.

"No," he said. "If you knew how much I am forced to eat and drink for courtesy's sake, you'd know how much I relish the company of someone whose hospitable offers I can refuse. I don't suppose your fraternity has ever considered using food as a torment, instead of starvation?''

''It is called planteration, Archon.''

''You must tell me about it sometime. I can see your guild is far ahead of my imagination—no doubt by a dozen centuries. After hunting, yours must be the oldest science of them all. But I cannot stay longer. We will see you at evening?''

''It is nearly evening now, Archon.''

''At the end of the next watch then.''

He went out; it was not until the door closed behind him that I detected the faint odor of the musk that had perfumed his robe.

I looked at the little circle of paper I held, turning it over in my hand. Pictured on the back were a falsity of masks, in which I recognized one of the horrors—a face that was no more than a mouth ringed with fangs—I had seen in the Autarch's garden when the cacogens tore away their disguises, and a man-ape's face from the abandoned mine near Saltus.

I was tired from my long walk as well as from the work (almost a full day's, for I had risen early) that had preceded it; and so before going out again I undressed and washed myself, ate some fruit and cold meat, and sipped a glass of the spicy northern tea. When a problem troubles me deeply, it remains in my mind even when I am unaware of it. So it was with me then; though I was not conscious of them, the thought of Dorcas lying in her narrow, slant-ceilinged room in the inn and the memory of the dying girl on her straw bound my eyes and stopped my ears. It was because of them, I think, that I did not hear my sergeant, and did not know, until he entered, that I had been taking up kindling from its box beside the fireplace and breaking the sticks with my hands. He asked if I were going out again, and since he was responsible for the operation of the Vincula in my absence I told him I was, and that I could not say when I would return. Then I thanked him for the loan of his jelab, which I said I would not need again.

''You are welcome to it anytime, Lictor. But that was not what concerned me. I wanted to suggest that you take a couple of our clavigers when you go down to the city.''

''Thank you,'' I said. ''But it is well policed, and I will be in no danger.''

He cleared his throat. ''It's a matter of the prestige of the Vincula, Lictor. As our commander, you should have an escort.''

I could see he was lying, but I could also see that he was lying for what he believed to be my good, and so I said, ''I will consider it, assuming you have two presentable men you can spare.''

He brightened at once.

"However," I continued, "I don't want them to carry weapons. I'm going to the palace, and it would be insulting to our master the archon if I were to arrive with an armed guard."

At that he began to stammer, and I turned on him as though I were furious, throwing down the splintered wood so that it crashed against the floor. "Out with it! You think I am threatened. What is it?"

"Nothing, Lictor. Nothing that concerns you, particularly. It is just . . ."

"Just what?" Knowing he was going to speak now, I went to the sideboard and poured us two cups of rosolio.

"There have been several murders in the city, Lictor. Three last night, two the night before. Thank you, Lictor. To your health."

"To yours. But murders are nothing unusual, are they? The eclectics are forever stabbing one another."

"These men were burned to death, Lictor. I really don't know much about it—no one seems to. Possibly you know more yourself." The sergeant's face was as expressionless as a carving of coarse, brown stone; but I saw him look quickly at the cold fireplace as he spoke, and I knew he attributed my breaking of the sticks (the sticks that had been so hard and dry in my hands but that I had not felt there until long after he entered, just as Abdiesus had not, perhaps, realized he was contemplating his own death until long after I had come to watch him) to something, some dark secret, the archon had imparted to me, when in fact it was nothing more than the memory of Dorcas and her despair, and of the beggar girl, whom I confused with her. He said, "I have two good fellows waiting outside, Lictor. They're ready to go whenever you are, and they will wait for you until you're ready to come back."

I told him that was very good, and he turned away at once so I would not guess he knew, or believed he knew, more than he had reported to me; but his stiff shoulders and corded neck, and the quick steps he took toward the door, conveyed more information than his stony eyes ever could.

My escorts were beefy men chosen for their strength. Flourishing their big, iron claves, they accompanied me as I shouldered *Terminus Est* down the winding streets, walking to either side when the way was wide enough, before and behind me when it was not. At the edge of the Acis I dismissed them, making them the more eager to leave me by telling them they had my permission to spend the remainder of the evening as they saw fit, and hired a narrow little caique (with a gaily painted canopy I had no need of now that the day's last watch was over) to carry me upriver to the palace.

It was the first time I had actually ridden on the Acis. As I sat in the stern, between the steersman-owner and his four oarsmen, with the clear, icy river rushing by so near that I could have trailed both hands in it if I wished, it seemed impossible that this frail wooden shell, which from the embrasure of our bartizan must have appeared no more than a dancing insect, could hope to gain a span against the current. Then the steersman spoke and we were off—hugging the bank to be sure, but seeming almost to skip over the river like a thrown stone, so rapid and perfectly timed were the strokes of our eight oars and so light and narrow and smooth were we, traveling more in the air above the water than in the water itself. A pentagonal lantern set with panes of amethyst glass hung from the sternpost; just at the moment when I, in my ignorance, thought we were at the point of being caught amidships by the current, capsized, and swept sinking down to the Capulus, the steersman let the tiller hang by its lashings while he lit the wick.

He was right, of course, and I wrong. As the little door of the lantern shut upon the butter-yellow flame within and the violet beams leaped forth, an eddy caught us, spun us about, whirled us upstream a hundred strides or more while the rowers shipped their oars, and left us in a miniature bay as quiet as a millpond and half-filled with gaudy pleasure boats. Water stairs, very similar to the steps from which I had swum in Gyoll as a boy though much cleaner, marched out of the depths of the river and up to the brilliant torches and elaborate gates of the palace grounds.

I had often seen this palace from the Vincula, and thus I knew that it was not the subterranean structure modeled on the House Absolute that I might otherwise have expected. No more was it any such grim fortress as our Citadel—apparently the archon and his predecessors had considered the strongpoints of Acies Castle and the Capulus, doubly linked as they were by the walls and forts strung along the crests of the cliffs, sufficient security for the safety of the city. Here the ramparts were mere box hedges intended to exclude the gaze of the curious and perhaps to give a check to casual thieves. Buildings with gilded domes were scattered over a pleasance that seemed intimate and colorful; from my embrasure they had looked much like peridots broken from their string and dropped upon a figured carpet.

There were sentries at the filigree gates, dismounted troopers in steel corselets and helmets, with blazing lances and long-bladed cavalry spathae; but they had the air of minor and amateur actors, good-natured, hard-bitten men enjoying a respite from running fights and wind-swept patrols. The pair to whom I showed my circle of painted paper no more than glanced at it before waving me inside.

V

Cyriaca

I was one of the first guests to arrive. There were more bustling servants still than masquers, servants who seemed to have begun their work only a moment before, and to be determined to complete it at once. They lit candelabra with crystal lenses and coronas lucis suspended from the upper limbs of the trees, carried out trays of food and drink, positioned them, shifted them, then carried them back to one of the domed buildings again—the three acts being performed by three servants, but occasionally (no doubt because the others were busy elsewhere) by one.

For a time I wandered about the grounds, admiring the flowers by the fast fading twilight. Then, glimpsing people in costume between the pillars of a pavilion, I strolled inside to join them.

What such a gathering could be in the House Absolute, I have already described. Here, where the society was entirely provincial, it had, rather, the atmosphere of children playing dress-up in their parents' old clothing; I saw men and women costumed as autochthons, with their faces stained russet and dabbed with white, and even one man who was an autochthon and yet was dressed like one, in a costume no more and no less authentic than the others, so that I was inclined to laugh at him until I realized that though he and I might be the only ones who knew it, he was in fact costumed more originally than any of the rest, as a citizen of Thrax in costume. Around all these autochthons, real and self-imagined, were a score of other figures not less absurd—officers dressed as women and women dressed as soldiers, eclectics as fraudulent as the autochthons, gymnosophists, ablegates and their acolytes, eremites, eidolons, zoanthrops half beast and half human, and deodands and remontados in picturesque rags, with eyes painted wild.

I found myself thinking how strange it would be if the New Sun, the

Daystar himself, were to appear now as suddenly as he had appeared so long ago when he was called the Conciliator, appearing here because it was an inappropriate place and he had always preferred the least appropriate places, seeing these people through fresher eyes than we ever could; and if he, thus appearing here, were to decree by theurgy that all of them (none of whom I knew and none of whom knew me) should forever after live the roles they had taken up tonight, the autochthons hunching over smoky fires in mountain huts of stone, the real autochthon forever a townsman at a ridotto, the women spurring toward the enemies of the Commonwealth with sword in hand, the officers doing needlepoint at north windows and looking up to sigh over empty roads, the deodands mourning their unspeakable abominations in the wilderness, the remontados burning their own homes and setting their eyes upon the mountains; and only I unchanged, as it is said the velocity of light is unchanged by mathematical transformations.

Then, while I was grinning to myself behind my mask, it seemed that the Claw, in its soft leathern sack, drove against my breastbone to remind me that the Conciliator had been no jest, and that I bore some fragment of his power with me. At that moment, as I looked across the room over all the feathered and helmeted and wild-haired heads, I saw a Pelerine.

I made my way across to her as quickly as I could, pushing aside those who did not stand aside for me. (They were but few, for though not one of them thought I was what I seemed, my height made them take me for an exultant, with no true exultants near.)

The Pelerine was neither young nor old; beneath her narrow domino her face seemed a smooth oval, refined and remote like the face of the chief priestess who had permitted me to pass in the tent cathedral after Agia and I had destroyed the altar. She held a little glass of wine as if to toy with it, and when I knelt at her feet she set it on a table so she could give me her fingers to kiss.

"Shrive me, Domnicellae," I begged her. "I have done you and all your sisters the greatest harm."

"Death does us all harm," she answered.

"I am not he." I looked up at her then, and the first doubt struck me.

Over the chatter of the crowd I heard the hiss of her indrawn breath. "You are not?"

"No, Domnicellae." And though I doubted her already, I feared she would flee from me, and I reached out to catch the cincture that dangled from her waist. "Domnicellae, forgive me, but are you a true member of the order?"

Without speaking she shook her head, then fell to the floor.

It is not uncommon for a client in our oubliette to feign unconsciousness, but the imposture is easily detected. The false fainter deliberately closes his eyes and keeps them closed. In a true faint, the victim, who is almost as likely to be a man as a woman, first loses control of his eyes, so that for an instant they no longer look in precisely the same direction; sometimes they tend to roll up under their lids. These lids, in turn, seldom entirely close, since their closing is not a deliberate action but a mere relaxation of their muscles. One can usually see a slender crescent of the sclera between the upper and lower lids, as I did when this woman fell.

Several men helped me carry her to an alcove, and there was a good deal of foolish talk about heat and excitement, neither of which had been present. For a time it was impossible to drive the onlookers away—then the novelty was gone, and it would have been almost equally impossible for me to have kept them there had I desired to do so. By then the woman in scarlet was beginning to stir, and I had learned from a woman of about the same age who was dressed as a child that she was the wife of an armiger whose villa stood at no great distance from Thrax, but who had gone to Nessus on some business or other. I went back to the table then and fetched her little glass and touched her lips with the red liquid it contained.

"No," she said weakly. "I don't want it . . . It's sangaree and I hate it—I—I only chose it because the color matches my costume."

"Why did you faint? Was it because I thought you were a real conventual?"

"No, because I guessed who you are," she said, and we were silent for a moment, she still half-reclining on the divan to which I had helped carry her, I sitting at her feet.

I brought the moment when I had knelt before her to life again in my mind; I have, as I have said, the power to so reconstruct every instant of my life. And at last I had to say, "How did you know?"

"Anyone else in those clothes, asked if he were Death, would have said he was . . . because he would be in costume. I sat in the archon's court a week ago, when my husband charged one of our peons with theft. That day I saw you standing to one side, with your arms folded on the guard of the sword you carry now, and when I heard you say what you did, when you had just kissed my fingers, I recognized you, and I thought . . . Oh, I don't know what I thought! I suppose I thought you had knelt to me because you intended to kill me. Just from the way you stood, you always looked, when I saw you in court, like someone who would be gallant to the poor people whose heads he was going to lop off, and particularly to women.''

''I only knelt to you because I am anxious to locate the Pelerines, and your costume, like my own, did not seem to be a costume.''

''It isn't. That is to say, I'm not entitled to wear it, but it isn't just something I had my maids run up for me. It's a real investiture.'' She paused. ''Do you know I don't even know your name?''

''Severian. Yours is Cyriaca—one of the women mentioned it while we were taking care of you. May I ask how you came to have those clothes, and if you know where the Pelerines are now?''

''This isn't a part of your duty, is it?'' For a moment she stared into my eyes, then she shook her head. ''Something private. I was nurtured by them. I was a postulant, you know. We traveled up and down the continent, and I used to have wonderful botany lessons just looking at the trees and flowers as we passed. Sometimes when I think back on it, it feels as if we went from palms to pines in a week, though I know that can't be true.

''I was going to take final vows, and the year before you're to be invested they make the investiture so you can try it on and get the fit right, and then so that you'll see it among your ordinary clothes each time you unpack. It's like a girl's looking at her mother's wedding dress, when it was her grandmother's too and she knows she'll be married in it, if she is ever married. Only I never wore my investiture, and when I went home, after a long time of waiting until we passed close by since there would be no one to escort me, I took it with me.

''I hadn't thought of it for a long time. Then when I got the archon's invitation I got it out again and decided to wear it tonight. I'm proud of my figure, and we only had to let it out a little here and there. It becomes me, I think, and I have the face for a Pelerine, though I don't have their eyes. Actually I never had the eyes, though I used to think I'd get them when I took my vows, or afterward. Our director of postulants had that look. She could sit sewing, and to look at her eyes you would believe they were seeing to the ends of Urth where the perischii live, staring right through the old, torn skirt and the walls of the tent, staring through everything. No, I don't know where the Pelerines are now—I doubt if they do themselves, though perhaps the Mother does.''

I said, ''You must have had some friends among them. Didn't some of your fellow postulants stay?''

Cyriaca shrugged. ''None of them ever wrote to me. I really don't know.''

''Do you feel well enough to go back to the dance?'' Music was beginning to filter into our alcove.

Her head did not move, but I saw her eyes, which had been tracing the corridors of the years when she talked of the Pelerines, swing around to look at me sidelong. "Is that what you want to do?"

"I suppose not. I'm never completely at ease among crowds, unless the people are my friends."

"You have some, then?" She seemed genuinely astonished.

"Not here—well, one friend here. In Nessus I used to have the brothers of our guild."

"I understand." She hesitated. "There's no reason we have to go. This affair will wear out the night, and at dawn, if the archon is still enjoying himself, they'll let down the curtains to exclude the light, and perhaps even raise the celure over the garden. We can sit here as long as we wish, and every time one of the servers comes around we'll get what we like to eat and drink. When someone we want to talk with goes by, we'll make him stop and entertain us."

"I'm afraid I would begin to bore you before the night was much worn," I said.

"Not at all, because I have no intention of allowing you to talk much. I'm going to talk myself, and make you listen to me. To begin—do you know you are very handsome?"

"I know that I am not. But since you've never seen me without this mask, you can't possibly know what I look like."

"On the contrary."

She leaned forward as though to examine my face through the eyeholes. Her own mask, which was the color of her gown, was so small that it was hardly more than a convention, two almond-shaped loops of fabric about her eyes; yet it lent her an exotic air she would not otherwise have possessed, and lent her too, I think, a feeling of mystery, of a concealment that lifted from her the weight of responsibility.

"You are a very intelligent man I am sure, but you haven't been to as many of these things as I have, or you would have learned the art of judging faces without seeing them. It's hardest, of course, when the person you're looking at has on a wooden vizard that doesn't conform to the face, but even then you can tell a great deal. You have a sharp chin, don't you? With a little cleft."

"Yes to the sharp chin," I said. "No to the cleft."

"You're lying to throw me off, or else you've never noticed it. I can judge chins by looking at waists, particularly in men, which is where my chief interest lies. A narrow waist means a sharp chin, and that leather mask leaves just enough showing to confirm it. Even though your eyes are deeply set, they're large and mobile, and that means a cleft chin in a man, particularly when the face is thin. You have high cheekbones—their outlines show a trifle through the mask, and your flat cheeks will make them look higher. Black hair, because I can see it on the backs of your hands, and thin lips that show through the mouth of the mask. Since I can't see all of them, they curve and curl about, which is a most desirable thing in a man's lips.''

I did not know what to say, and to tell the truth I would have given a great deal to leave her just then; at last I asked, ''Do you want me to take my mask off so you can check the accuracy of your assessments?''

''Oh, no, you mustn't. Not until they play the aubade. Besides, you should consider my feelings. If you did and I found you weren't handsome after all, I should be deprived of an interesting night.'' She had been sitting up. Now she smiled and leaned back on the divan again, her hair spreading about her in a dark aureole. ''No, Severian, instead of unmasking your face, you must unmask your spirit. Later you will do that by showing me everything you would do were you free to do whatever you wished, and now by telling me everything I want to know about you. You come from Nessus—I've learned that much. Why are you so eager to find the Pelerines?''

VI

The Library of the Citadel

As I was about to answer her question, a couple strolled by our alcove, the man robed in a sanbenito, the woman dressed as a midinette. They only glanced at us as they passed, but something—the inclination, perhaps, of the two heads together, or some expression of the eyes—told me that they knew, or at least suspected, I was not in masquerade. I pretended I had noticed nothing, however, and said, "Something that belongs to the Pelerines came into my hands by accident. I want to return it to them."

"You're not going to do them harm then?" Cyriaca asked. "Can you tell me what it is?"

I did not dare to tell the truth, and I knew I would be asked to produce whatever object I named, and so I said, "A book—an old book, beautifully illustrated. I don't pretend to know anything about books, but I feel sure it's of religious importance and quite valuable," and from my sabretache I drew the brown book from Master Ultan's library that I had carried away when I left Thecla's cell.

"Old, yes," Cyriaca said. "And more than a little water-stained, I see. May I look at it?"

I handed it to her and she fanned the pages, then stopped at a picture of the sikinnis, holding it up until it caught the gleam of a lamp burning in a niche above our divan. The horned men seemed to leap in the flickering light, the sylphs to writhe.

"I don't know anything about books either," she said, handing it back. "But I have an uncle who does, and I think he might give a great deal for this one. I wish he were here tonight so he could see it—though perhaps it's all for the best, because I'd probably try to get it from you in some way. In every pentad he travels as far as I ever did when I was with the Pelerines, just to seek out old books. He's even gone to the lost archives. Have you heard about those?''

I shook my head.

''All I know is what he told me once when he had drunk a little more of our estate cuvee than he usually takes, and it may be that he didn't tell me everything, because as I talked to him I had the feeling he was a bit afraid I might try to go myself. I never have, though I've regretted it sometimes. Anyway, in Nessus, a long way south of the city most people visit, so far down the great river in fact that most people think the city would have ended long before, there stands an ancient fortress. Everyone save perhaps for the Autarch himself—may his spirit live in a thousand successors—has forgotten it long ago, and it's supposed to be haunted. It stands upon a hill overlooking Gyoll, my uncle told me, staring out over a field of ruined sepulchers, guarding nothing.''

She paused and moved her hands, shaping the hill and its stronghold in the air before her. I had the feeling that she had told the story many times, perhaps to her children. It made me conscious that she was indeed old enough to have them, children old enough themselves to have listened to this and other tales many times. No years had marked her smooth, sensuous face; but the candle of youth that burned so brightly still in Dorcas and had shed its clear, unworldly light even about Jolenta, that had shone so hard and bright behind Thecla's strength and had lit the mist-shrouded paths of the necropolis when her sister Thea took Vodalus's pistol at the grave side, had in her been extinguished so long that not even the perfume of its flame remained. I pitied her.

''You must know the story of how the race of ancient days reached the stars, and how they bargained away all the wild half of themselves to do so, so that they no longer cared for the taste of the pale wind, nor for love or lust, nor to make new songs nor to sing old ones, nor for any of the other animal things they believed they had brought with them out of the rain forests at the bottom of time—though in fact, so my uncle told me, those things brought them. And you know, or you should know, that those to whom they sold those things, who were the creations of their own hands, hated them in their hearts. And truly they had hearts, though the men who had made them never reckoned with that. Anyway, they resolved to ruin their makers, and they did it by returning, when mankind had spread to a thousand suns, all that had been left with them long before.

''So much, at least, you should know. My uncle once told it to me as I have told it to you, and he found all that and more recorded in a book in his collection. It was a book no one had opened, as he believed, for a chiliad.

"But how they did what they did is less well known. I remember that when I was a child, I imagined the bad machines digging—digging by night until they had cleared away the twisted roots of old trees and laid bare an iron chest they had buried when the world was very young, and that when they struck off the lock of that chest, all the things we've spoken of came flying out like a swarm of golden bees. That's foolish, but even now I can hardly imagine what the reality of those thinking engines can have been like."

I recalled Jonas, with the light, bright metal where the skin of his loins ought to have been, but I could not picture Jonas setting free a plague to trouble mankind, and shook my head.

"But my uncle's book, he said, made clear what it was they did, and the things they let go free were no swarm of insects but a flood of artifacts of every kind, calculated by them to revive all those thoughts that people had put behind them because they could not be written in numbers. The building of everything from cities to cream pitchers was in the hands of the machines, and after a thousand lifetimes of building cities that were like great mechanisms, they turned to building cities that were like banks of cloud before a storm, and others like the skeletons of dragons."

"When was this?" I asked.

"A very long time ago—long before the first stones of Nessus were laid."

I had put an arm about her shoulders, and now she let her hand creep into my lap; I felt its heat and slow search.

"And they followed the same principle in all they did. In the shaping of furniture, for example, and the cutting of clothing. And because the leaders who had decided so long before that all the thoughts symbolized by the clothes and furniture, and by the cities, should be put behind mankind forever were long dead, and the people had forgotten their faces and their maxims, they were delighted with the new things. Thus all that empire, which had been built only upon order, passed away.

"But though the empire dissolved, the worlds were a long time dying. At first, so that the things they were returning to humans would not be rejected again, the machines conceived of pageants and phantasmagoria, whose performances inspired those who watched them to think on fortune or revenge or the invisible world. Later they gave each man and woman a companion, unseen by all other eyes, as an advisor. The children had such companions long before.

"When the powers of the machines had weakened further—as the machines themselves wished—they could no longer maintain these phantoms in the minds of their owners, nor could they build more cities, because the cities that remained were already nearly empty.

"They had reached, so my uncle told me, that point at which they had hoped mankind would turn on them and destroy them, yet no such thing had occurred, because by this time they who had been despised as slaves or worshiped as devils before were greatly loved.

"And so they called all who loved them best around them, and for long years taught them all the things their race had put away, and in time they died.

"Then all those whom they had loved, and who had loved them, took counsel together as to how their teachings could be preserved, for they well knew their kind would not come again upon Urth. But bitter quarrels broke out among them. They had not learned together, but rather each of them, man or woman, had listened to one of the machines as if there were no one in the world but those two. And because there was so much knowledge and only a few to learn it, the machines had taught each differently.

"Thus they divided into parties, and each party into two, and each of those two into two again, until at last every individual stood alone, misunderstood and reviled by all the others and reviling them. Then each went away, out of the cities that had held the machines or deeper into them, save for a very few who by habit remained in the palaces of the machines to watch beside their bodies."

A sommelier brought us cups of wine almost as clear as water, and as still as water until some motion of the cup woke it. It perfumed the air like those flowers no man can see, the flowers that can be found only by the blind; and to drink it was like drinking strength from the heart of a bull. Cyriaca took her cup eagerly, and draining it cast it ringing into a corner.

"Tell me more," I said to her, "of this story of the lost archives."

"When the last machine was cold and still and each of those who had learned from them the forbidden lore mankind had cast aside was separated from all the rest, there came dread into the heart of each. For each knew himself to be only mortal, and most, no longer young. And each saw that with his own death the knowledge he loved best would die. Then each of them—each supposing himself the only one to do so—began to write down what he had learned in the long years when he had harkened to the teachings of the machines that spilled forth all the hidden knowledge of wild things. Much perished but much more survived, sometimes falling into the hands of those who copied it enlivened by their own additions or weakened by omissions . . . Kiss me, Severian."

Though my mask hampered us, our lips met. As she drew away, the shadow memories of Thecla's old bantering love affairs, played out among the pseudothyrums and catachtonian boudoirs of the House Absolute welled up within me, and I said, "Don't you know this kind of thing requires a man's undivided attention?"

Cyriaca smiled. "That's why I did it—I wanted to see if you were listening.

"Anyway, for a long time—no one knows quite how long, I suppose, and anyway the world was not as near the sun's failing then and its years were longer—these writings circulated or else lay moldering in cenotaphs where their authors had concealed them for safekeeping. They were fragmentary, contradictory, and eisegesistic. Then when some autarch (though they were not called autarchs then) hoped to recapture the dominion exercised by the first empire, they were gathered up by his servants, white-robed men who ransacked cocklofts and threw down the androsphinxes erected to memorialize the machines and entered the cubicula of moiraic women long dead. Their spoil was gathered into a great heap in the city of Nessus, which was then newly built, to be burned.

"But on the night before the burning was to begin, the autarch of that time, who had never dreamed before the wild dreams of sleep but only waking dreams of dominion, dreamed at last. And in his dream he saw all the untamed worlds of life and death, stone and river, beast and tree slipping away from his hands forever.

"When morning came, he ordered that the torches not be kindled, but that there should be a great vault built to house all the volumes and scrolls the white-robed men had gathered. For he thought that if the new empire he planned should fail him at last, he would retire to that vault and enter the worlds that, in imitation of the ancients, he was determined to cast aside.

"His empire did fail him, as it had to. The past cannot be found in the future where it is not—not until the metaphysical world, which is so much larger and so much slower than the physical world, completes its revolution and the New Sun comes. But he did not retire as he had planned into that vault and the curtain wall he had caused to be built about it, for when once the wild things have been put behind a man for good and all, they are trap-wise and cannot be recaptured.

"Nevertheless, it is said that before all he gathered was sealed away, he set a guardian over it. And when that guardian's time on Urth was done, he found another, and he another, so that they continue ever faithful to the commands of that autarch, for they are saturated in the wild thoughts sprung from the lore saved by the machines, and such faith is one of those wild things."

I had been disrobing her as she spoke, and kissing her breasts; but I said, "Did all those thoughts of which you spoke go out of the world when the autarch locked them away? Haven't I ever heard of them?"

"No, because they had been passed from hand to hand for a long time, and had entered into the blood of all the peoples. Besides, it is said that the guardian sometimes sends them out, and though they always return to him at last, they are read, whether by one or many, before they sink once more into his dark."

"It is a wonderful story," I said. "I think that perhaps I know more of it than you, but I had never heard it before." I found that her legs were long, and smoothly tapered from thighs like cushions of silk to slender ankles; all her body, indeed, was shaped for delight.

Her fingers touched the clasp that held my cloak about my shoulders. "Need you take this off?" she asked. "Can't it cover us?"

"It can," I said.

VII

Attractions

Almost I drowned in the delight she gave me, for though I did not love her as I had once loved Thecla, nor as I loved Dorcas even then, and she was not beautiful as Jolenta had once been beautiful, I felt a tenderness for her that was no more than in part born of the unquiet wine, and she was such a woman as I had dreamed of as a ragged boy in the Matachin Tower, before I had ever beheld Thea's heart-shaped face by the side of the opened grave; and she knew far more of the arts of love than any of the three.

When we rose we went to a flowing basin of silver to wash. There were two women there who had been lovers as we had been, and they stared at us and laughed; but when they saw I would not spare them because they were women, they fled shrieking.

Then we cleansed each other. I know Cyriaca believed that I would leave her then, as I believed that she would leave me; but we did not separate (though it would, perhaps, have been better if we had), but went out into the silent little garden, which was full of night, and stood beside a lonely fountain.

She held my hand, and I held hers as children do. ''Have you ever visited the House Absolute?'' she asked. She was watching our reflections in the moon-drenched water, and her voice was so low I could scarcely hear her.

I told her that I had, and at the words her hand tightened on mine.

''Did you visit the Well of Orchids there?''

I shook my head.

''I have been to the House Absolute also, but I have never seen the Well of Orchids. It is said that when the Autarch has a consort—as ours does not—she holds her court there, in the most beautiful place in the world. Even now, only the loveliest are permitted to walk in that spot. When I was there we stayed, my lord and I, in a certain small room appropriate to our armigerial rank. One evening when my lord was gone and I did not know where, I went out into the corridor, and as I stood there looking up and down, a high functionary of the court passed by. I did not know his name or his office, but I stopped him and asked if I might go to the Well of Orchids.''

She paused. For the space of three or four breaths there was no sound but the music from the pavilions and the tinkling of the fountain.

''And he stopped and looked at me, I think in some surprise. You cannot know how it feels to be a little armigette from the north, in a gown sewn by your own maids, and provincial jewels, and be looked at so by someone who has spent all his life among the exultants of the House Absolute. Then he smiled.''

She gripped my hand very tightly now.

''And he told me. Down such and such a corridor and turn at such a statue, up certain steps and along the ivory path. Oh, Severian, my lover!''

Her face was radiant as the moon itself. I knew the moment she had described had been the crown of her life, and that she now treasured the love I had given her partially, and perhaps largely, because it had recalled to her that moment, when her beauty had been weighed by one she felt fit to rule upon it, and had not been found wanting. My reason told me I should take offense at that, but I could find no resentment in me.

''He went away, and I began to walk as he had said—a score of strides, perhaps two score. Then I met my lord, and he ordered me to return to our little room.''

''I see,'' I said, and shifted my sword.

''I think you do. Is it wrong then for me to betray him like this? What do you think?''

''I am no magistrate.''

''Everyone judges me . . . all my friends . . . all my lovers, of whom you are neither the first nor the last; even those women in the caldarium just now.''

''We are trained from childhood not to judge, but only to carry out the sentences handed down by the courts of the Commonwealth. I will not judge you or him.''

''I judge,'' she said, and turned her face toward the bright, hard light of the stars. For the first time since I had glimpsed her across the crowded ballroom I understood how I could have mistaken her for a monial of the order whose habit she wore. ''Or at least, I tell myself I judge. And I find myself guilty, but I can't stop. I think I draw men like you to myself. Were you drawn? There were women there lovelier than I am now, I know."

"I'm not certain," I said. "While we were coming here to Thrax . . ."

"You have a story too, don't you? Tell me, Severian. I've already told you almost the only interesting thing that has ever happened to me."

"On the way here, we—I'll explain some other time who I was traveling with—fell in with a witch and her famula and her client, who had come to a certain place to reinspirit the body of a man long dead."

"Really?" Cyriaca's eyes sparkled. "How wonderful! I've heard of such things but I've never seen them. Tell me all about it, but make sure you tell me the truth."

"There really isn't anything much to tell. Our path lay through a deserted city, and when we saw their fire, we went to it because we had someone with us who was ill. When the witch brought back the man she had come to revive, I thought at first that she was restoring the whole city. It wasn't until several days afterward that I understood . . ."

I found I could not say what it was I understood; that it was in fact on the level of meaning above language, a level we like to believe scarcely exists, though if it were not for the constant discipline we have learned to exercise upon our thoughts, they would always be climbing to it unaware.

"Go on."

"I didn't really understand, of course. I still think about it, and I still don't. But I know somehow that she was bringing him back, and *he* was bringing the stone town back with him, as a setting for himself. Sometimes I have thought that perhaps it had never had any reality apart from him, so that when we rode over its pavements and the rubble of its walls, we were actually riding among his bones."

"And did he come?" she asked. "Tell me!"

"Yes, he returned. And then the client was dead, and the sick woman who had been with us also. And Apu-Punchau—that was the dead man's name—was gone again. The witches ran away, I think, though perhaps they flew. But what I wanted to say was that we went on the next day on foot, and stayed the next night in the hut of a poor family. And that night while the woman who was with me slept, I talked to the man, who seemed to know a great deal about the stone town, though he did not know its original name. And I spoke with his mother, who I think knew something more than he, though she would not tell me as much."

I hesitated, finding it hard to speak of such things to this woman. "At first I supposed their ancestors might have come from that town, but they said it had been destroyed long before the coming of their race. Still, they knew much lore of it, because the man had sought for treasures there since he had been a boy, though he had never found anything, he said, save for broken stones and broken pots, and the tracks of other searchers who had been there long before him.

" 'In ancient days,' his mother told me, 'they believed that you could draw buried gold by putting a few coins of your own in the ground, with thispell or that. Many a one did it, and some forgot the place, or were kept from digging their own up again. That's what my son finds. That is the bread we eat.' "

I remembered her as she had been that night, old and stooped as she warmed her hands at a little fire of turf. Perhaps she resembled one of Thecla's old nurses, for something about her brought Thecla closer to the surface of my mind than she had been since Jonas and I had been imprisoned in the House Absolute, so that once or twice when I caught sight of my hands, I was startled to see the thickness of the fingers, and their brown color, and to see them bare of rings.

"Go on, Severian," Cyriaca said again.

"Then the old woman told me there was something in the stone town that truly drew its like to it. 'You have heard tales of necromancers,' she said, 'who fish for the spirits of the dead. Do you know there are vivimancers among the dead, who call to them those who can make them live again? There is such a one in the stone town, and once or twice in each saros one of those he has called to him will sup with us.' And then she said to her son, 'You will recall the silent man who slept beside his staff. You were only a child, but you will remember him, I think. He was the last until now.' Then I knew that I, too, had been drawn by the vivimancer Apu-Punchau, though I had felt nothing."

Cyriaca gave me a sidelong look. "Am I dead then? Is that what you're saying? You told me there was a witch who was the necromancer, and that you only stumbled upon her fire. I think that you yourself were the witch you spoke of, and no doubt the sick person you mentioned was your client, and the woman your servant."

"That's because I have neglected to tell you all the parts of the story that have any importance," I said. I would have laughed at being thought a witch; but the Claw pressed against my breastbone, telling me that by its stolen power I was a witch indeed in everything except knowledge; and I understood—in the same sense that I had "understood" before—that though Apu-Punchau had brought it to his hand, he could not (or would not?) take it from me. "Most importantly," I went on, "when the revenant vanished, one of the scarlet capes of the

Pelerines, like the one you're wearing now, was left behind in the mud. I have it in my sabretache. Do the Pelerines dabble in necromancy?''

I never heard the answer to my question, for just as I spoke, the tall figure of the archon came up the narrow path that led to the fountain. He was masked, and costumed as a barghest, so that I would not have known him if I had seen him in a good light; but the dimness of the garden stripped his disguise from him as effectively as human hands could have, so that as soon as I saw the loom of his height, and his walk, I knew him at once.

''Ah,'' he said. ''You have found her. I ought to have anticipated that.''

''I thought so,'' I told him, ''but I wasn't sure.''

VIII

Upon the Cliff

I left the palace grounds by one of the landward gates. There were six troopers on guard there, with nothing of the air of relaxation that had characterized the two at the river stairs a few watches before. One, politely but unmistakably barring the way, asked me if I had to leave so early. I identified myself and said that I was afraid I must—that I still had work to do that night (as indeed I did) and would have a hard day facing me the next morning as well (as indeed I would).

"You're a hero then." The soldier sounded slightly more friendly. "Don't you have an escort, Lictor?"

"I had two clavigers, but I dismissed them. There's no reason I can't find my way back to the Vincula alone."

Another trooper, who had not spoken previously, said, "You can stay inside until morning. They'll find you a quiet place to bunk down."

"Yes, but my work wouldn't get done. I'm afraid I must leave now."

The soldier who had been blocking my way stood aside. "I'd like to send a couple of men with you. If you'll wait a moment, I'll do it. I have to get permission from the officer of the guard."

"That won't be necessary," I told him, and left before they could say more. Something—presumably the committer of the murders my sergeant had told me of—was clearly stirring in the city; it seemed almost certain that another death had occurred while I was in the archon's palace. The thought filled me with a pleasant excitement—not because I was such a fool as to imagine myself superior to any attack, but because the idea of being attacked, of risking death that night in the dark streets of Thrax, lifted some part of the depression I would otherwise have felt. This unfocused terror, this faceless menace of the night, was the earliest of all my childhood fears; and as such, now that childhood was behind me, it had the homey quality of all childhood things when we are fully grown.

I was already on the same side of the river as the jacal I had visited that afternoon, and had no need to take boat again; but the streets were strange to me and in the dark seemed almost a labyrinth built to confound me. I made several false starts before I found the narrow way I wanted, leading up the cliff.

The dwellings to either side of it, which had stood silent while they waited for the mighty wall of stone opposite them to rise and cover the sun, were murmurous with voices now, and a few windows glowed with the light of grease lamps. While Abdiesus reveled in his palace below, the humble folk of the high cliff celebrated too, with a gaiety that differed from his chiefly in that it was less riotous. I heard the sounds of love as I passed, just as I had heard them in his garden after leaving Cyriaca for the last time, and the voices of men and women in quiet talk, and bantering too, here as there. The palace garden had been scented by its flowers, and its air was washed by its own fountains and by the great fountain of cold Acis, which rushed by just outside. Here those odors were no more; but a breeze stirred among the jacals and the caves with their stoppered mouths, bringing sometimes the stench of ordure, and sometimes the aroma of brewing tea or some humble stew, and sometimes only the clean air of the mountains.

When I was high up the cliff face, where no one dwelt who was rich enough to afford more light than a cooking fire would give, I turned and looked back at the city much as I had looked down upon it—though with an entirely different spirit—from the ramparts of Acies Castle that afternoon. It is said that there are crevices in the mountains so deep that one can see stars at their bottoms—crevices that pass, then, entirely through the world. Now I felt I had found one. It was like looking into a constellation, as though all of Urth had fallen away, and I was staring into the starry gulf.

It seemed likely that by this time they were searching for me. I thought of the archon's dimarchi cantering down the silent streets, perhaps carrying flambeaux snatched up in the garden. Far worse was the thought of the clavigers I had until now commanded fanning out from the Vincula. Yet I saw no moving lights and heard no faint, hoarse cries, and if the Vincula was disturbed, it was not a disturbance that affected the dim streets webbing the cliff across the river. There should have been a winking gleam too where the great gate opened to let out the freshly roused men, closed, then opened again; but there was none. I turned at last and began to climb once more. The alarm had not yet been given. Still, it would soon sound.

* * *

There was no light in the jacal and no noise of speech. I took the Claw from its little bag before I entered, for fear I would lack the nerve to do so once I was inside. Sometimes it blazed like a firework, as it had in the inn at Saltus. Sometimes it possessed no more light than a bit of glass. That night in the jacal it was not brilliant, but it glowed with so deep a blue that the light itself seemed almost a clearer darkness. Of all the names of the Conciliator, the one that is, I believe, least used, and which has always seemed the most puzzling to me, is that of Black Sun. Since that night, I have felt myself almost to comprehend it. I could not hold the gem in my fingers as I had done often before and was yet to do afterward; I laid it flat on the palm of my right hand so that my touch would commit no more sacrilege than was strictly necessary. With it held thus before me, I stooped and entered the jacal.

The girl lay where she had lain that afternoon. If she still breathed I could not hear her, and she did not move. The boy with the infected eye slept on the bare earth at her feet. He must have bought food with the money I had given him; corn husks and fruit peels were scattered over the floor. For a moment I dared to hope that neither of them would wake.

The deep light of the Claw showed the girl's face to be a weaker and more horrible thing than I had seen it by day, accentuating the hollows under her eyes, and her sunken cheeks. I felt I should say something, invoke the Increate and his messengers by some formula, but my mouth was dry and more empty of words than any beast's. Slowly I lowered my hand toward her until the shadow of it cut off all the light that had bathed her. When I lifted my hand again there had been no change, and remembering that the Claw had not helped Jolenta, I wondered if it were possible that it could have no good effect on women, or if it were necessary that a woman hold it. Then I touched the girl's forehead with it, so that for a moment it seemed a third eye in that deathlike face.

Of all the uses I made of it, that was the most astounding, and perhaps the only one in which it was not possible that any self-deception on my part, or any coincidence no matter how farfetched, could account for what occurred. It may have been that the man-ape's bleeding was staunched by his own belief, that the uhlan on the road by the House Absolute was merely stunned and would have revived in any event, that the apparent healing of Jonas's wounds had been no more than a trick of the light.

But now it was as though some unimaginable power had acted in the interval between one chronon and the next to wrench the universe from its track. The girl's real eyes, dark as pools, opened. Her face was no longer the skull mask it had been, but only the worn face of a young woman. "Who are you in those bright clothes?" she asked. And then, "Oh, I am dreaming."

I told her I was a friend, and that there was no reason for her to be afraid.

"I am not afraid," she said. "I would be if I were awake, but I am not now. You look as if you have fallen from the sky, but I know you are only the wing of some poor bird. Did Jader catch you? Sing for me . . ."

Her eyes closed again; this time I could hear the slow sighing of her breath. Her face remained as it had been while they were open—thin and drawn, but with the stamp of death rubbed away.

I took the gem from her forehead and touched the boy's eye with it as I had touched his sister's face, but I am not sure it was necessary that I do so. It appeared normal before it ever felt the kiss of the Claw, and it may be that the infection was already vanquished. He stirred in his sleep and cried out as though in some dream he were running ahead of slower boys and urging them to follow him.

I put the Claw back into its little bag and sat on the earthen floor among the husks and peels, listening to him. After a time he grew quiet again. Starlight made a dim pattern near the door; other than that, the jacal was utterly dark. I could hear the sister's regular breathing, and the boy's own.

She had said that I, who had worn fuligin since my elevation to journeyman, and gray rags before that, was dressed in bright clothing. I knew she had been dazzled by the light at her forehead—anything, any clothing, would have appeared bright to her then. And yet, I felt that in some sense she was correct. It was not that (as I have been tempted to write) I came to hate my cloak and trousers and boots after that moment; but rather that I came in some sense to feel they were indeed the disguise they had been taken to be when I was at the archon's palace, or the costume they had appeared to be when I took part in Dr. Talos's play. Even a torturer is a man, and it is not natural for a man to dress always and exclusively in that hue that is darker than black. I had despised my own hypocrisy when I had worn the brown mantle from Agilus's shop; perhaps the fuligin beneath it was a hypocrisy as great or greater.

Then the truth began to force itself upon my mind. If I had ever truly been a torturer, a torturer in the sense that Master Gurloes and even Master Palaemon were torturers, I was one no longer. I had been given a second chance here in Thrax. I had failed in that second chance as well, and there would be no third. I might gain employment by my skills and my clothing, but that was all; and no doubt it would be better for me to destroy them when I could, and try to make a place for myself among the soldiers who fought the northern war, once I had succeeded—if I ever succeeded—in returning the Claw.

The boy stirred and called a name that must have been his sister's. She murmured something still in sleep. I stood and watched them for a moment more, then slipped out, fearful that the sight of my hard face and long sword would frighten them.

IX

The Salamander

Outside, the stars seemed brighter, and for the first time in many weeks the Claw had ceased to drive itself against my chest.

When I descended the narrow path, it was no longer necessary to turn and halt to see the city. It spread itself before me in ten thousand twinkling lights, from the watchfire of Acies Castle to the reflection of the guard-room windows in the water that rushed through the Capulus.

By now all the gates would be closed against me. If the dimarchi had not already ridden forth, they would do so before I reached the level land beside the river; but I was determined to see Dorcas once more before I left the city, and, somehow, I had no doubt of my ability to do so. I was just beginning to turn over plans for escaping the walls afterward when a new light flared out far below.

It was small at that distance, no more than a pinprick like all the others; yet it was not like them at all, and perhaps my mind only registered it as light because I knew nothing else to liken it to. I had seen a pistol fired at full potential that night in the necropolis when Vodalus resurrected the dead woman—a coherent beam of energy that had split the mists like lightning. This fire was not like that, but it was more nearly like that than like anything else I could call to mind. It flared briefly and died, and a heartbeat afterward I felt the wash of heat upon my face.

Somehow I missed the little inn called the Duck's Nest in the dark. I have never known if I took a wrong turning or merely walked past the shuttered windows without glimpsing the sign hanging overhead. However it happened, I soon found myself farther from the river than I should have been, striding along a street that ran for a time at least parallel to the cliff, with the smell of scorched flesh in my nostrils as at a branding. I was about to retrace my steps when I collided in the dark with a woman. So hard and unexpectedly did we strike each other that I nearly fell, and as I went reeling back, I heard the thud of her body on the stone.

"I didn't see you," I said as I reached down for her.

"Run! Run!" she gasped. And then, "Oh, help me up." Her voice was faintly familiar.

"Why should I run?" I pulled her to her feet. In the faint light I could see the blur of her face, and even, I thought, something of the fear there.

"It killed Jurmin. He burned alive. His staff was still on fire when we found him. He . . ." Whatever she had begun to say after that trailed off into sobs.

"What burned Jurmin?" When she did not answer, I shook her, but that only made her weep the harder. "Don't I know you? Talk, woman! You're the mistress of the Duck's Nest. Take me there!"

"I can't," she said. "I'm afraid. Give me your arm, please, sieur. We ought to get inside."

"Fine. We'll go to the Duck's Nest. It can't be far—now what is this?"

"Too far!" She wept. "Too far!"

There was something in the street with us. I do not know whether I had failed to detect its approach, or it had been undetectable until then; but it was suddenly present. I have heard people who have a horror of rats say they are aware of them the moment they enter a house, even if the animals are not visible. It was so now. There was a feeling of heat without warmth; and though the air held no odor, I sensed that its power to support life was being drained away.

The woman seemed still unaware of it. She said, "It burned three last night near the harena, and one tonight, they said, close by the Vincula. And now Jurmin. It's looking for somebody—that's what they say."

I recalled the notules and the thing that had snuffled along the walls of the antechamber of the House Absolute, and I said, "I think it has found him."

I let her go and turned, then turned again, trying to discover where it was. The heat grew, but no light showed. I was tempted to take out the Claw so as to see by its glow; then I recalled how it had waked whatever slept beneath the mine of the man-apes, and I feared the light would only permit this thing—whatever it might be—to locate me. I was not sure my sword would be more effective against it than it had been against the notules when Jonas and I had fled them through the cedar wood; nevertheless, I drew it.

Almost at once there was a clatter of hooves and a yell as two dimarchi thundered round a corner no more than a hundred strides away. Had there been more time I would have smiled to see how closely they corresponded to the figures I had imagined. As it was, the firework glare of their lances outlined something dark and crooked and stooped that stood between us.

It turned toward the light, whatever it was, and seemed to open as a flower might, growing tall more swiftly, almost, than the eye could follow it, thinning until it had become a creature of glowing gauze, hot yet somehow reptilian, as those many-colored serpents we see brought from the jungles of the north are reptilian still, though they seem works of colored enamel. The mounts of the soldiers reared and screamed, but one of the men, with more presence of mind that I would have shown, fired his lance into the heart of the thing that faced him. There was a flare of light.

The hostess of the Duck's Nest slumped against me, and I, not wishing to lose her, supported her with my free arm. "I think it's seeking living heat," I told her. "It should go for the destriers. We'll get away."

Just as I spoke, it turned toward us.

I have already said that from behind, when it opened itself toward the dimarchi, it seemed a reptilian flower. That impression persisted now when we saw it in its full terror and glory, but it was joined by two others. The first was the sensation of intense and otherworldly heat; it seemed a reptile still, but a reptile that burned in a way never known on Urth, as though some desert asp had dropped into a sphere of snow. The second was of raggedness fluttering in a wind that was not of air. It seemed a blossom still, but it was a blossom whose petals of white and pale yellow and flame had been tattered by some monstrous tempest born in its own heart.

In all these impressions, surrounding them and infusing them, was a horror I cannot describe. It drew all resolution and strength from me, so that for that moment I could neither flee nor attack it. The creature and I seemed fixed in a matrix of time that had nothing to do with anything that had gone before or since, and that, since it held us who were its only occupants immobile, could be altered by nothing.

A shout broke the spell. A second party of dimarchi had galloped into the street behind us, and seeing the creature were lashing their mounts to the charge. In less than the space of a breath they were boiling around us, and it was only by the intercession of Holy Katharine that we were not ridden down. If I had ever doubted the courage of the Autarch's soldiery I lost those doubts then, for both parties hurled themselves upon the monster like hounds upon a stag.

It was useless. There came a blinding flash and the sensation of fearful heat. Still holding the half-unconscious woman, I sprinted down the street.

I meant to turn where the dimarchi had entered it, but in my panic (and it was panic, not only my own, but that of Thecla screaming in my mind) I rounded the corner too late or too soon. Instead of the steep descent to the lower city I expected, I found myself in a little, stub-end court built on a spur of rock jutting from the cliff. By the time I realized what was wrong, the creature, now again a twisted, dwarfish thing but radiating a terrible and invisible energy, was at the mouth of the court.

In the starlight it might have been only an old, hunched man in a black coat, but I have never felt more terror than I did at the sight of it. There was a jacal at the back of the court: a larger structure than the hovel in which the sick girl and her brother had suffered, but built of sticks and mud in the same fashion. I kicked its door in and ran into a little warren of odious rooms, bolting through the first and into another, through that into a third where a half dozen men and women lay sleeping, through that into a fourth—only to see a window that looked out over the city much as my own embrasure in the Vincula did. It was the end, the farthest room of the house, hanging like a swallow's nest over a drop that seemed at that moment to go down forever.

From the room we had just left I could hear the angry voices of the people I had wakened. The door flew open, but whoever had come to expel the intruder must have seen the gleam of *Terminus Est*; he stopped short, swore, and turned away. A moment later someone screamed and I knew the creature of fire was in the jacal.

I tried to set the woman upright, but she fell in a heap at my feet. Outside the window there was nothing—the wattled wall ended a few cubits down, and the supports of the floor did not extend beyond it. Above, an overhanging roof of rotten thatch offered no more purchase to my hand than gossamer. As I struggled to grasp it, there came a flood of light that destroyed all color and cast shadows as dark as fuligin itself, shadows like fissures in the cosmos. I knew then that I must fight and die as the dimarchi had, or jump, and I swung about to face the thing that had come to kill me.

It was still in the room beyond, but I could see it through the doorway, opened again now as it had been in the street. The half-consumed corpse of some wretched crone lay before it on the stone floor, and while I watched, it seemed to bend over her in what was, I would almost swear, an attitude of inquiry. Her flesh blistered and cracked like the fat of a roast, then fell away. In a moment even her bones were no more than pale ashes the creature scattered as it advanced.

Terminus Est I believe to have been the best blade ever forged, but I knew she could accomplish nothing against the power that had routed so many cavalrymen; I cast her to one side in the vague hope that she might be found and eventually returned to Master Palaemon, and took the Claw from its little bag at my throat.

It was my last, faint chance, and I saw at once that it had failed me. However the creature sensed the world about it (and I had guessed from its movements that it was nearly blind on our Urth), it could make out the gem clearly, and it did not fear it. Its slow advance became a rapid and purposeful flowing forward. It reached the doorway—there was a burst of smoke, a crash, and it was gone. Light from below flashed through the hole it had burned in the flimsy floor that began where the stone of the outcrop ended; at first it was the colorless light of the creature, then a rapid alternation of chatoyant pastels—peacock blue, lilac, and rose. Then only the faint, reddish light of leaping flames.

X

Lead

There was a moment when I thought I would fall into the gaping hole in the center of the little room before I could regain *Terminus Est* and carry the mistress of the Duck's Nest to safety, and another when I was certain everything was going to fall—the trembling structure of the room itself and us together.

Yet in the end we escaped. When we reached the street, it was clear of dimarchi and townsfolk alike, the soldiers no doubt having been drawn to the fire below, and the people frightened indoors. I propped the woman with my arm, and though she was still too terrified to answer my questions intelligibly, I let her choose our way; as I had supposed she would, she led us unerringly to her inn.

Dorcas was asleep. I did not wake her, but sat down in the dark on a stool near the bed where there was now also a little table sufficient to hold the glass and bottle I had taken from the common room below. Whatever the wine was, it seemed strong in my mouth and yet no more than water after I had swallowed it; by the time Dorcas woke, I had drunk half the bottle and felt no more effect from it than I would have if I had swallowed so much sherbet.

She started up, then let her head fall upon the pillow again. "Severian. I should have known it was you."

"I'm sorry if I frightened you," I said. "I came to see how you were."

"That's very kind. It always seems, though, that when I wake up you're bending over me." For a moment she closed her eyes again. "You walk so very quietly in those thick-soled boots of yours, do you know that? It's one reason people are afraid of you."

"You said I reminded you of a vampire once, because I had been eating a pomegranate and my lips were stained with red. We laughed about it. Do you remember?'' (It had been in a field within the Wall of Nessus, when we had slept beside Dr. Talos's theater and awakened to feast on fruit dropped the night before by our fleeing audience.)

''Yes,'' Dorcas said. ''You want me to laugh again, don't you? But I'm afraid I can't ever laugh anymore.''

''Would you like some wine? It was free, and it's not as bad as I expected.''

''To cheer me? No. One ought to drink, I think, when one is cheerful already. Otherwise nothing but more sorrow is poured into the cup.''

''At least have a swallow. The hostess here says you've been ill and haven't eaten all day.''

I saw Dorcas's golden head move on the pillow then as she turned it to look at me; and since she seemed fully awake, I ventured to light the candle.

She said, ''You're wearing your habit. You must have frightened her out of her wits.''

''No, she wasn't afraid of me. She's pouring into her cup whatever she finds in the bottle.''

''She's been good to me—she's very kind. Don't be hard on her if she chooses to drink so late at night.''

''I wasn't being hard on her. But won't you have something? There must be food in the kitchen here, and I'll bring you up whatever you want.''

My choice of phrase made Dorcas smile faintly. ''I've been bringing up my own food all day. That was what she meant when she told you I'd been ill. Or did she tell you? Spewing. I should think you could smell it yet, though the poor woman did what she could to clean up after me.''

Dorcas paused and sniffed. ''What is it I do smell? Scorched cloth? It must be the candle, but I don't suppose you can trim the wick with that great blade of yours.''

I said, ''It's my cloak, I think. I've been standing too near a fire.''

''I'd ask you to open the window, but I see it's open already. I'm afraid it's bothering you. It does blow the candle about. Do the flickering shadows make you dizzy?''

''No,'' I said. ''It's all right as long as I don't actually look at the flame.''

''From your expression, you feel the way I always do around water.''

''This afternoon I found you sitting at the very edge of the river.''

''I know,'' Dorcas said, and fell silent. It was a silence that lasted so long that I was afraid she was not going to speak again at all, that the pathological silence (as I now was sure it had been) that had seized her then had returned.

At last I said, "I was surprised to see you there—I remember that I looked several times before I was sure it was you, although I had been searching for you."

"I spewed, Severian. I told you that, didn't I?"

"Yes, you told me."

"Do you know what I brought up?"

She was staring at the low ceiling, and I had the feeling that there was another Severian there, the kind and even noble Severian who existed only in Dorcas's mind. All of us, I suppose, when we think we are talking most intimately to someone else, are actually addressing an image we have of the person to whom we believe we speak. But this seemed more than that; I felt that Dorcas would go on talking if I left the room. "No," I answered. "Water, perhaps?"

"Sling-stones."

I thought she was speaking metaphorically, and only ventured, "That must have been very unpleasant."

Her head rolled on the pillow again, and now I could see her blue eyes with their wide pupils. In their emptiness they might have been two little ghosts. "Sling-stones, Severian my darling. Heavy little slugs of metal, each about as big around as a nut and not quite so long as my thumb and stamped with the word *strike*. They came rattling out of my throat into the bucket, and I reached down—put my hand down into the filth that came up with them and pulled them up to see. The woman who owns this inn came and took the bucket away, but I had wiped them off and saved them. There are two, and they're in the drawer of that table now. She brought it to put my dinner on. Do you want to see them? Open it."

I could not imagine what she was talking about, and asked if she thought someone was trying to poison her.

"No, not at all. Aren't you going to open the drawer? You're so brave. Don't you want to look?"

"I trust you. If you say there are sling-stones in the table, I'm sure they're there."

"But you don't believe I coughed them up. I don't blame you. Isn't there a story about a hunter's daughter who was blessed by a pardal, so that beads of jet fell from her mouth when she spoke? And then her brother's wife stole the blessing, and when she spoke toads hopped from her lips? I remember hearing it, but I never believed it."

"How could anyone cough up lead?"

Dorcas laughed, but there was no mirth in it. "Easily. So very easily.

Do you know what I saw today? Do you know why I couldn't talk to you when you found me? And I couldn't, Severian, I swear it. I know you thought I was just angry and being stubborn. But I wasn't—I had become like a stone, wordless, because nothing seemed to matter, and I'm still not sure anything does. I'm sorry, though, for what I said about your not being brave. You are brave, I know that. It's only that it seems not brave when you're doing things to the poor prisoners here. You were so brave when you fought Agilus, and later when you would have fought with Baldanders because we thought he was going to kill Jolenta . . ."

She fell silent again, then sighed. "Oh, Severian, I'm so tired."

"I wanted to talk to you about that," I said. "About the prisoners. I want you to understand, even if you can't forgive me. It was my profession, the thing I was trained to do from boyhood." I leaned forward and took her hand; it seemed as frail as a songbird.

"You've said something like this before. Truly, I understand."

"And I could do it well. Dorcas, that's what you *don't* understand. Excruciation and execution are arts, and I have the feel, the gift, the blessing. This sword—all the tools we use live when they're in my hands. If I had remained at the Citadel, I might have been a master. Dorcas, are you listening? Does this mean anything at all to you?"

"Yes," she said. "A bit, yes. I'm thirsty, though. If you're through drinking, pour me a little of that wine now, please."

I did as she asked, filling the glass no more than a quarter full because I was afraid she might spill it on her bedclothes.

She sat up to drink, something I had not been certain until then that she was capable of, and when she had swallowed the last scarlet drop hurled the glass out the window. I heard it shatter on the street below.

"I don't want you to drink after me," she told me. "And I knew that if I didn't do that you would."

"You think whatever is wrong with you is contagious, then?"

She laughed again. "Yes, but you have it already. You caught it from your mother. Death. Severian, you never asked me what it was I saw today."

XI

The Hand of the Past

As soon as Dorcas said, "You never asked me what I saw today," I realized that I had been trying to steer the conversation away from it. I had a premonition that it would be something quite meaningless to me, to which Dorcas would attach great meaning, as madmen do who believe the tracks of worms beneath the bark of fallen trees to be a supernatural script. I said, "I thought it might be better to keep your mind off it, whatever it was."

"No doubt it would, if only we could do it. It was a chair."

"A chair?"

"An old chair. And a table, and several other things. It seems that there is a shop in the Turners' Street that sells old furniture to the eclectics, and to those among the autochthons who have absorbed enough of our culture to want it. There is no source here to supply the demand, and so two or three times a year the owner and his sons go to Nessus—to the abandoned quarters of the south—and fill their boat. I talked to him, you see; I know all about it. There are tens of thousands of empty houses there. Some have fallen in long ago, but some are still standing as their owners left them. Most have been looted, yet they still find silver and bits of jewelry now and then. And though most have lost most of their furniture, the owners who moved almost always left some things behind."

I felt that she was about to weep, and I leaned forward to stroke her forehead. She showed me by a glance that she did not wish me to, and laid herself on the bed again as she had been before.

"In some of those houses, all the furnishings are still there. Those are the best, he said. He thinks that a few families, or perhaps only a few people living alone, remained behind when the quarter died. They were too old to move, or too stubborn. I've thought about it, and I'm sure some of them must have had something there they could not bear to leave. A grave, perhaps. They boarded their windows against the marauders, and they kept dogs, and worse things, to protect them. Eventually they left—or they came to the end of life, and their animals devoured their bodies and broke free; but by that time there was no one there, not even looters or scavengers, not until this man and his sons."

"There must be a great many old chairs," I said.

"Not like that one. I knew everything about it—the carving on the legs and even the pattern in the grain of the arms. So much came back then. And then here, when I vomited those pieces of lead, things like hard, heavy seeds, then I knew. Do you remember, Severian, how it was when we left the Botanic Garden? You, Agia, and I came out of that great, glass vivarium, and you hired a boat to take us from the island to the shore, and the river was full of nenuphars with blue flowers and shining green leaves. Their seeds are like that, hard and heavy and dark, and I have heard that they sink to the bottom of Gyoll and remain there for whole ages of the world. But when chance brings them near the surface they sprout no matter how old they may be, so that the flowers of a chiliad past are seen to bloom again."

"I have heard that too," I said. "But it means nothing to you or me."

Dorcas lay still, but her voice trembled. "What is the power that calls them back? Can you explain it?"

"The sunshine, I suppose—but no, I cannot explain it."

"And is there no source of sunlight except the sun?"

I knew then what it was she meant, though something in me could not accept it.

"When that man—Hildegrin, the man we met a second time on top of the tomb in the ruined stone town—was ferrying us across the Lake of Birds, he talked of millions of dead people, people whose bodies had been sunk in that water. How were they made to sink, Severian? Bodies float. How do they weight them? I don't know. Do you?"

I did. "They force lead shot down the throats."

"I thought so." Her voice was so weak now that I could scarcely hear her, even in that silent little room. "No, I knew so. I knew it when I saw them."

"You think that the Claw brought you back."

Dorcas nodded.

"It has acted, sometimes, I'll admit that. But only when I took it out, and not always then. When you pulled me out of the water in the Garden of Endless Sleep, it was in my sabretache and I didn't even know I had it.''

''Severian, you allowed me to hold it once before. Could I see it again now?''

I pulled it from its soft pouch and held it up. The blue fires seemed sleepy, but I could see the cruel-looking hook at the center of the gem that had given it its name. Dorcas extended her hand, but I shook my head, remembering the wineglass.

''You think I will do it some harm, don't you? I won't. It would be a sacrilege.''

''If you believe what you say, and I think you do, then you must hate it for drawing you back . . .''

''From death.'' She was watching the ceiling again, now smiling as if she shared some deep and ludicrous secret with it. ''Go ahead and say it. It won't hurt you.''

''From sleep,'' I said. ''Since if one can be recalled from it, it is not death—not death as we have always understood it, the death that is in our minds when we say *death*. Although I have to confess it is still almost impossible for me to believe that the Conciliator, dead now for so many thousands of years, should act through this stone to raise others.''

Dorcas made no reply. I could not even be sure she was listening.

''You mentioned Hildegrin,'' I said, ''and the time he rowed us across the lake in his boat, to pick the avern. Do you remember what he said of death? It was that she was a good friend to the birds. Perhaps we ought to have known then that such a death could not be death as we imagine it.''

''If I say I believe all that, will you let me hold the Claw?''

I shook my head again.

Dorcas was not looking at me, but she must have seen the motion of my shadow; or perhaps it was only that her mental Severian on the ceiling shook his head as well. ''You are right, then—I was going to destroy it if I could. Shall I tell you what I really believe? I believe I have been dead—not sleeping, but dead. That all my life took place a long, long time ago when I lived with my husband above a little shop, and took care of our child. That this Conciliator of yours who came so long ago was an adventurer from one of the ancient races who outlived the universal death.'' Her hands clutched the blanket. ''I ask you, Severian, when he comes again, isn't he to be called the New Sun? Doesn't that sound like it? And I believe that when he came he brought with him something that had the same power over time that Father Inire's mirrors are said to have over distance. It is that gem of yours.''

She stopped and turned her head to look at me defiantly; when I said nothing, she continued. "Severian, when you brought the uhlan back to life it was because the Claw twisted time for him to the point at which he still lived. When you half healed your friend's wounds, it was because it bent the moment to one when they would be nearly healed. And when you fell into the fen in the Garden of Endless Sleep, it must have touched me or nearly touched me, and for me it became the time in which I had lived, so that I lived again. But I have been dead. For a long, long time I was dead, a shrunken corpse preserved in the brown water. And there is something in me that is dead still."

"There is something in all of us that has always been dead," I said. "If only because we know that eventually we will die. All of us except the smallest children."

"I'm going to go back, Severian. I know that now, and that's what I've been trying to tell you. I have to go back and find out who I was and where I lived and what happened to me. I know you can't go with me . . ."

I nodded.

"And I'm not asking you to. I don't even want you to. I love you, but you are another death, a death that has stayed with me and befriended me as the old death in the lake did, but death all the same. I don't want to take death with me when I go to look for my life."

"I understand," I said.

"My child may still be alive—an old man, perhaps, but still alive. I have to know."

"Yes," I said. But I could not help adding, "There was a time when you told me I was not death. That I must not let others persuade me to think of myself in that way. It was behind the orchard on the grounds of the House Absolute. Do you remember?"

"You have been death to me," she said. "I have succumbed to the trap I warned you of, if you like. Perhaps you are not death, but you will remain what you are, a torturer and a carnifex, and your hands will run with blood. Since you remember that time at the House Absolute so well, perhaps you . . . I can't say it. The Conciliator, or the Claw, or the Increate, has done this to me. Not you."

"What is it?" I asked.

"Dr. Talos gave us both money afterward, in the clearing. The money he had got from some court official for our play. When we were traveling, I gave everything to you. May I have it back? I'll need it. If not all of it, at least some of it."

I emptied the money in my sabretache onto the table. It was as much as I had received from her, or a trifle more.

"Thank you," she said. "You won't need it?"

"Not as badly as you will. Besides, it is yours."

"I'm going to leave tomorrow, if I feel strong enough. The day after tomorrow whether I feel strong or not. I don't suppose you know how often the boats put out, going downriver?"

"As often as you want them to. You push them in, and the river does the rest."

"That's not like you, Severian, or at least not much. More the sort of thing your friend Jonas would have said, from what you've told me. Which reminds me that you're not the first visitor I've had today. Our friend—your friend, at least—Hethor was here. That's not funny to you, is it? I'm sorry, I just wanted to change the subject."

"He enjoys it. Enjoys watching me."

"Thousands of people do when you perform in public, and you enjoy doing it yourself."

"They come to be horrified, so they can congratulate themselves later on being alive. And because they like the excitement, and the suspense of not knowing whether the condemned will break down, or if some macabre accident will occur. I enjoy exercising my skill, the only real skill I have—enjoy making things go perfectly. Hethor wants something else."

"The pain?"

"Yes, the pain, but something more too."

Dorcas said, "He worships you, you know. He talked with me for some time, and I think he would walk into a fire if you told him to." I must have winced at that, because she continued, "All this about Hethor is making you ill, isn't it? One sick person is enough. Let's speak of something else."

"Not ill as you are, no. But I can't think of Hethor except as I saw him once from the scaffold, with his mouth open and his eyes . . ."

She stirred uncomfortably. "Yes, those eyes—I saw them tonight. Dead eyes, though I suppose I shouldn't be the one to say that. A corpse's eyes. You have the feeling that if you touched them they would be as dry as stones, and never move under your finger."

"That isn't it at all. When I was on the scaffold in Saltus and looked down and saw him, his eyes danced. You said, though, that the dull eyes he has at most times reminded you of a corpse's. Haven't you ever looked into the glass? Your own eyes are not the eyes of a dead woman."

"Perhaps not." Dorcas paused. "You used to say they were beautiful."

"Aren't you glad to live? Even if your husband is dead, and your child is dead, and the house you once lived in is a ruin—if all those things are true—aren't you full of joy because you are here again? You're not a ghost, not a revenant like those we saw in the ruined town. Look in the glass as I told you. Or if you won't, look into my face or any man's and see what you are."

Dorcas sat up even more slowly and painfully than she had risen to drink the wine, but this time she swung her legs over the edge of the bed, and I saw that she was naked under the thin blanket. Before her illness Jolenta's skin had been perfect, with the smoothness and softness of confectionery. Dorcas's was flecked with little golden freckles, and she was so slender that I was always aware of her bones; yet she was more desirable in her imperfection than Jolenta had ever been in the lushness of her flesh. Conscious of how culpable it would be to force myself on her or even to persuade her to open to me now, when she was ill and I was on the point of leaving her, I still felt desire for her stir in me. However much I love a woman—or however little—I find I want her most when I can no longer have her. But what I felt for Dorcas was stronger than that, and more complex. She had been, though only for so brief a time, the closest friend I had known, and our possession of each other, from the frantic desire in our converted storeroom in Nessus to the long and lazy playing in the bedchamber of the Vincula, was the characteristic act of our friendship as well as our love.

"You're crying," I said. "Do you want me to leave?"

She shook her head, and then, as though she could no longer contain the words that seemed to force themselves out, she whispered, "Oh, won't you go too, Severian? I didn't mean it. Won't you come? Won't you come with me?"

"I can't."

She sank back into the narrow bed, smaller now and more childlike. "I know. You have your duty to your guild. You can't betray it again and face yourself, and I won't ask you. It's only that I never quite gave up hoping you might."

I shook my head as I had before. "I have to flee the city—"

"Severian!"

"And to the north. You'll be going south, and if I were with you, we would have courier boats full of soldiers after us."

"Severian, what happened?" Dorcas's face was very calm, but her eyes were wide.

"I freed a woman. I was supposed to strangle her and throw her body into the Acis, and I could have done it—I didn't feel anything for her, not really, and it should have been easy. But when I was alone with her, I thought of Thecla. We were in a little summerhouse screened with shrubbery, that stood at the edge of the water. I had my hands around her neck, and I thought of Thecla and how I had wanted to free her. I couldn't find a way to do it. Have I ever told you?''

Almost imperceptibly, Dorcas shook her head.

''There were brothers everywhere, five to pass by the shortest route, and all of them knew me and knew of her.'' (Thecla was shrieking now in some corner of my mind.) ''All I really would have had to do would have been to tell them Master Gurloes had ordered me to bring her to him. But I would have had to go with her then, and I was still trying to devise some way by which I could stay in the guild. I did not love her enough.''

''It's past now,'' Dorcas said. ''And, Severian, death is not the terrible thing you think it.'' We had reversed our roles, like lost children who comfort each other alternately.

I shrugged. The ghost I had eaten at Vodalus's banquet was nearly calm again; I could feel her long, cool fingers on my brain, and though I could not turn inside my own skull to see her, I knew her deep and violet eyes were behind my own. It required an effort not to speak with her voice. ''At any rate, I was there with the woman, in the summer-house, and we were alone. Her name was Cyriaca. I knew or at least suspected that she knew where the Pelerines were—she had been one of them for a time. There are silent means of excruciation that require no equipment, and although they are not spectacular, they are quite effective. One reaches into the body, as it were, and manipulates the client's nerves directly. I was going to use what we call Humbaba's Stick, but before I had touched her she told me. The Pelerines are near the pass of Orithyia caring for the wounded. This woman had a letter, she said, only a week ago, from someone she had known in the order . . .''

XII

Following the Flood

The summerhouse had boasted a solid roof, but the sides were mere latticework, closed more by the tall forest ferns planted against them than by their slender laths. Moonbeams leaked through. More came in at the doorway, reflected from the rushing water outside. I could see the fear in Cyriaca's face, and the knowledge that her only hope was that I retained some love for her; and I knew that she was thus without hope, for I felt nothing.

"At the Autarch's camp," she repeated. "That was what Einhildis wrote. In Orithyia, near the springs of Gyoll. But you must be careful if you go there to return the book—she said too that cacogens had landed somewhere in the north."

I stared at her, trying to determine whether she were lying.

"That's what Einhildis told me. I suppose they must have wished to avoid the mirrors at the House Absolute so they could escape the eyes of the Autarch. He's supposed to be their servitor, but sometimes he acts as if they were his."

I shook her. "Are you joking with me? The Autarch serves them?"

"Please! Oh, please . . ."

I dropped her.

"Everyone . . . Erebus! Pardon me." She sobbed, and though she lay in shadow I sensed that she was wiping her eyes and nose with the hem of her scarlet habit. "Everyone knows it except the peons, and the good men and the good women. All the armigers and even most of the optimates, and of course the exultants have always known. I've never seen the Autarch, but I'm told that he, the Viceroy of the New Sun, is scarcely taller than I am. Do you think our proud exultants would permit someone like that to rule if there weren't a thousand cannon behind him?''

''I've seen him,'' I said, ''and I wondered about that.'' I sought among Thecla's memories for confirmation of what Cyriaca said, but I found only rumor.

''Would you tell me about him? Please, Severian, before—''

''No, not now. But why should the cacogens be a danger to me?''

''Because the Autarch will surely send scouts to locate them, and I suppose the archon here will too. Anyone found near them will be assumed to have been spying for them, or what's worse, seeking them out in the hope of enlisting them in some plot against the Phoenix Throne.''

''I understand.''

''Severian, don't kill me. I beg you. I'm not a good woman—I've never been a good woman, never since I left the Pelerines, and I can't face dying now.''

I asked her, ''What have you done, anyway? Why does Abdiesus want you killed? Do you know?'' It is simplicity itself to strangle an individual whose neck muscles are not strong, and I was already flexing my hands for the task; yet at the same time I wished it had been permissible for me to use *Terminus Est* instead.

''Only loved too many men, men other than my husband.''

As if moved by the memory of those embraces, she rose and came toward me. Again the moonlight fell upon her face; her eyes were bright with unshed tears.

''He was cruel to me, so cruel, after our marriage . . . and so I took a lover, to spite him, and afterwards, another . . .''

(Her voice dropped until I could hardly hear the words.)

''And at last taking a new lover becomes a habit, a way of pushing back the days and showing yourself that all your life has not run between your fingers already, showing yourself that you are still young enough for men to bring gifts, young enough that men still want to stroke your hair. That was what I had left the Pelerines for, after all.'' She paused and seemed to gather her strength. ''Do you know how old I am? Did I tell you?''

''No,'' I said.

''I won't, then. But I might almost be your mother. If I had conceived within a year or two of the time it became possible for me. We were far in the south, where the great ice, all blue and white, sails on black seas. There was a little hill where I used to stand and watch, and I dreamed of putting on warm clothes and paddling out to the ice with food and a trained bird I never really had but only wanted to have, and so riding my own ice island north to an isle of palms, where I would discover the ruins of a castle built in the morning of the world. You would have been born then, perhaps, while I was alone on the ice. Why shouldn't an imaginary child be born on an imaginary trip? You would have grown up fishing and swimming in water warmer than milk."

"No woman is killed for being unfaithful, except by her husband," I said.

Cyriaca sighed, and her dream fell from her. "Among the landed armigers hereabout, he is one of the few who support the archon. The others hope that by disobeying him as much as they dare and fomenting trouble among the eclectics they can persuade the Autarch to replace him. I have made my husband a laughing stock—and by extension his friends and the archon."

Because Thecla was within me, I saw the country villa—half manor and half fort, full of rooms that had scarcely changed in two hundred years. I heard the tittering ladies and the stamping hunters, and the sound of the horn outside the windows, and the deep barking of the boarhounds. It was the world to which Thecla had hoped to retreat; and I felt pity for this woman, who had been forced into that retreat when she had never known any wider sphere.

Just as the room of the Inquisitor in Dr. Talos's play, with its high judicial bench, lurked somewhere at the lowest level of the House Absolute, so we have each of us in the dustiest cellars of our minds a counter at which we strive to repay the debts of the past with the debased currency of the present. At that counter I tendered Cyriaca's life in payment for Thecla's.

When I led her from the summerhouse, she supposed, I know, that I intended to kill her at the edge of the water. Instead, I pointed to the river.

"This flows swiftly south until it meets the flood of Gyoll, which then runs more slowly to Nessus, and at last to the southern sea. No fugitive can be found in the maze of Nessus who does not wish it, for there are streets and courts and tenements there without number, and all the faces of all lands are seen a hundred times over. If you could go there, dressed as you are now, without friends or money, would you do so?"

She nodded, one pale hand at her throat.

"There is no barrier to boats yet at the Capulus; Abdiesus knows he need not fear any attack made against the current there until midsummer. But you will have to shoot the arches, and you may drown. Even if you reach Nessus, you will have to work for your bread—wash for others, perhaps, or cook."

"I can dress hair and sew. Severian, I have heard that sometimes, as the last and most terrible torture, you tell your prisoner she will be freed. If that is what you're doing to me now, I beg you to stop. You've gone far enough."

"A caloyer does that, or some other religious functionary. No client would believe us. But I want to be certain there will be no foolishness of returning to your home or seeking a pardon from the archon."

"I am a fool," Cyriaca said. "But no. Not even such a fool as I am would do that, I swear."

We skirted the water's edge until we came to the stairs where the sentries stood to admit the archon's guests, and the little, brightly hued pleasure boats were moored. I told one of the soldiers we were going to try the river, and asked if we would have any difficulty hiring rowers to take us back upstream. He said we might leave the boat at the Capulus if we wished, and return in a fiacre. When he turned away to resume his conversation with his comrade, I pretended to inspect the boats, and slipped the painter of the one farthest from the torches of the guard post.

Dorcas said, "And so now you are going north as a fugitive, and I have taken your money."

"I won't need much, and I will get more." I stood up.

"Take back half at least." When I shook my head, she said, "Then take back two chrisos. I can whore, if worst comes to worst, or steal."

"If you steal, your hand will be struck off. And it is better that I strike off hands for my dinner than that you give your hands for yours."

I started to go, but she sprang out of bed and held my cloak. "Be careful, Severian. There is something—Hethor called it a salamander—loose in the city. Whatever it is, it burns its victims."

I told her I had much more to fear from the archon's soldiers than from the salamander, and left before she could say more. But as I toiled up a narrow street on the western bank that my boatmen had assured me would lead to the cliff top, I wondered if I would not have more to fear from the cold of the mountains, and their wild beasts, than from either. I wondered too about Hethor, and how he had followed me so far into the north, and why. But more than I thought on any of those things, I thought about Dorcas, and what she had been to me, and I to her. It was to be a long time before I would so much as glimpse her again, and I believe that in some way I sensed that. Just as when I had first left the Citadel I had pulled up my hood so that the passersby might not observe my smiles, so now I hid my face to conceal the tears running down my cheeks.

* * *

I had seen the reservoir that supplied the Vincula twice before by day, but never by night. It had appeared small then, a rectangular pond no larger than the foundation of a house and no deeper than a grave. Under the waning moon it seemed almost a lake, and might have been as deep as the cistern below the Bell Tower.

It lay no more than a hundred paces from the wall that defended the western margin of Thrax. There were towers on that wall—one quite near the reservoir—and no doubt the garrisons had by that time been ordered to apprehend me if I tried to escape from the city. At intervals, as I had walked along the cliff, I had glimpsed the sentries who patrolled the wall; their lances were unkindled, but their crested helms showed against the stars, and sometimes faintly caught the light.

Now I crouched, looking out over the city and relying on my fuligin cloak and hood to deceive their eyes. The barred iron portcullises of the arches of the Capulus had been lowered—I could detect the roiling of the Acis where it battered against them. That removed all doubt: Cyriaca had been stopped—or more probably, simply seen and reported. Abdiesus might or might not make strenuous efforts to capture her; it seemed most probable to me that he would allow her to vanish, and so avoid drawing attention to her. But he would surely apprehend me if he could, and execute me as the traitor to his rule that I was.

From the water I looked to water again, from the rushing Acis to the still reservoir. I had the word for the sluice gate, and I used it. The ancient mechanism ground up as though moved by phantom slaves, and then the still waters rushed too, rushed faster than the raging Acis at the Capulus. Far below, the prisoners would hear their roar, and those nearest the entrance would see the white foam of the flood. In a moment those who stood would be up to their ankles in water, and those who had slept would be scrambling to their feet. In another moment, all would be waist deep; but they were chained in their places, and the weaker would be supported by the stronger—none, I hoped, would drown. The clavigers at the entrance would leave their posts and hurry up the steep trail to the cliff top to see who had tampered with the reservoir there.

And as the last water drained away, I heard the stones dislodged by their feet rattling down the slope. I closed the sluice gate again and lowered myself into the slimy and nearly vertical passage that the water had just traversed. Here my progress would have been far easier if I had not been carrying *Terminus Est.* To brace my back against one side of that crooked, chimneylike pipe, I had to unsling her; yet I could not spare a hand to hold her. I put her baldric around my neck, let her blade and sheath hang down, and managed her weight as well as I could.

Twice I slipped, but each time I was saved by a turn of the narrowing sluice; and at last, after so long a time that I was certain the clavigers would have returned, I saw the gleam of red torchlight and drew forth the Claw.

I was never to see it flame so bright again. It was blinding, and I carrying it upraised down the long tunnel of the Vincula, could only wonder that my hand was not reduced to ashes. No prisoner, I think, saw *me*. The Claw fascinated them as a lantern by night does the deer of the forest; they stood motionless, their mouths open, their raddled, bearded faces uplifted, their shadows behind them as sharp as silhouettes cut in metal and dark as fuligin.

At the very end of the tunnel, where the water ran out into the long, sloping sewer that carried it below the Capulus, were the weakest and most diseased prisoners; and it was there that I saw most clearly the strength the Claw lent them all. Men and women who had not stood straight in the memory of the oldest claviger now seemed tall and strong. I waved in salute to them, though I am sure none of them observed it. Then I put the Claw of the Conciliator back into its little pouch, and we were plunged into a night beside which the night of the surface of Urth would be day.

The rush of water had swept the sewer clean, and it was easier to descend than the sluice had been, for though it was narrower, it was less steep, and I could crawl rapidly down headforemost. There was a grill at the bottom; but as I had noted on one of my inspection tours, it was nearly rusted through.

XIII

Into the Mountains

Spring had ended and summer begun when I crept away from the Capulus in the gray light, but even so it was never warm in the high lands except when the sun was near the zenith. Yet I did not dare to go into the valleys where the villages huddled, and all day I walked up, into the mountains, with my cloak furled across one shoulder to make it look as nearly as possible like the garment of an eclectic. I also dismounted the blade of *Terminus Est* and reassembled it without the guard, so that the sheathed sword seen from a distance would have the appearance of a staff.

By noon the ground was all of stone, and so uneven that I did as much climbing as walking. Twice I saw the glint of armor far below me, and looking down beheld little parties of dimarchi cantering down trails most men could scarcely have persuaded themselves to walk, their scarlet military capes billowing behind them. I found no edible plants and sighted no game other than high soaring birds of prey. Had I seen any, I would have had no chance of taking it with my sword, and I possessed no other weapon.

All that sounds desperate enough, but the truth was that I was thrilled by the mountain views, the vast panorama of the empire of air. As children we have no appreciation of scenery because, having not yet stored similar scenes in our imagination, with their attendant emotions and circumstances, we perceive it without psychic depth. I now looked at the cloud-crowned summits with my view of Nessus from the nose cone of our Matachin Tower and my view of Thrax from the battlements of Acies Castle before me as well, and miserable though I was, I was ready to faint with pleasure.

* * *

That night I spent huddled in the lee of a naked rock. I had not eaten since I had changed clothes in the Vincula, which now seemed weeks, if not years, before. In actuality, it had been only months since I had smuggled a worn kitchen knife to poor Thecla, and seen her blood seeping, a groping worm of crimson, from beneath her cell door.

I had chosen my stone well, at least. It blocked the wind, so that as long as I remained behind it I might almost have rested in the quiet, frigid air of some ice cave. A step or two to either side brought me into the full blast, so that I was chilled to the bone in a single frosty moment.

I slept for about a watch, I think, without any dreams that outlived my sleep, then woke with the impression—which was not a dream, but the sort of foundationless knowledge or pseudo-knowledge that comes to us at times when we are weary and fearful—that Hethor was leaning over me. I seemed to feel his breath, stinking and icy cold, upon my face; his eyes, no longer dull, blazed into mine. When I was fully awake, I saw that the points of light I had taken for their pupils were in fact two stars, large and very bright in the thin, clean air.

I tried to sleep again, closing my eyes and forcing myself to remember the warmest and most comfortable places I had known: the journeyman's quarters I had been given in our tower, which had then seemed so palatial with their privacy and soft blankets after the apprentices' dormitory; the bed I had once shared with Baldanders, into which his broad back had projected heat like a stove's; Thecla's apartments in the House Absolute; the snug room in Saltus where I had lodged with Jonas.

Nothing helped. I could not sleep again, and yet I dared not to try to walk farther for fear that I would fall over some precipice in the dark. I spent the remainder of the night staring at the stars; it was the first time I had ever really experienced the majesty of the constellations, of which Master Malrubius had taught us when I was the smallest of the apprentices. How strange it is that the sky, which by day is a stationary ground on which the clouds are seen to move, by night becomes the backdrop for Urth's own motion, so that we feel her rolling beneath us as a sailor feels the running of the tide. That night the sense of this slow turning was so strong that I was almost giddy with its long, continued sweep.

Strong too was the feeling that the sky was a bottomless pit into which the universe might drop forever. I had heard people say that when they looked at the stars too long they grew terrified by the sensation of being drawn away. My own fear—and I felt fear—was not centered on the remote suns, but rather on the yawning void; and at times I grew so frightened that I gripped the rock with my freezing fingers, for it seemed to me that I must fall off Urth. No doubt everyone feels some touch of this, since it is said that there exists no climate so mild that people will consent to sleep in unroofed houses.

I have already described how I woke thinking that Hethor's face (I suppose because Hethor had been much in my mind since I talked to Dorcas) was staring into mine, yet discovered when I opened my eyes that the face retained no detail except the two bright stars that had been its own. So it was with me at first when I tried to pick out the constellations, whose names I had often read, though I had only the most imperfect idea of the part of the sky in which each might be found. At first all the stars seemed a featureless mass of lights, however beautiful, like the sparks that fly upward from a fire. Soon, of course, I began to see that some were brighter than others, and that their colors were by no means uniform. Then, quite unexpectedly, when I had been staring at them for a long time, the shape of a peryton seemed to spring out as distinctly as if the bird's whole body had been powdered with the dust ground from diamonds. In a moment it was gone again, but it soon returned, and with it other shapes, some corresponding to constellations of which I had heard, others that were, I am afraid, entirely of my own imagining. An amphisbaena, or snake with a head at either end, was particularly distinct.

When these celestial animals burst into view, I was awed by their beauty. But when they became so strongly evident (as they quickly did) that I could no longer dismiss them by an act of will, I began to feel as frightened of them as I was of falling into that midnight abyss over which they writhed; yet this was not a simple physical and instinctive fear like the other, but rather a sort of philosophical horror at the thought of a cosmos in which rude pictures of beasts and monsters had been painted with flaming suns.

After I covered my head with my cloak, which I was forced to do lest I go mad, I fell to thinking of the worlds that circled those suns. All of us know they exist, many being mere endless plains of rock, others spheres of ice or of cindery hills where lava rivers flow, as is alleged of Abaddon; but many others being worlds more or less fair, and inhabited by creatures either descended from the human stock or at least not wholly different from ourselves. At first I thought of green skies, blue grass, and all the rest of the childish exotica apt to inflict the mind that conceives of other than Urthly worlds. But in time I tired of those puerile ideas, and began in their place to think of societies and ways of thought wholly different from our own, worlds in which all the people, knowing themselves descended from a single pair of colonists, treated one another as brothers and sisters, worlds where there was no currency but honor, so that everyone worked in order that he might be entitled to associate himself with some man or woman who had saved the community, worlds in which the long war between mankind and the beasts was pursued no more. With these thoughts came a hundred or more new ones—how justice might be meted out when all loved all, for example; how a beggar who retained nothing but his humanity might beg for honor, and the ways in which people who would kill no sentient animal might be shod and fed.

When I had first come to realize, as a boy, that the green circle of the moon was in fact a sort of island hung in the sky, whose color derived from forests, now immemorially old, planted in the earliest days of the race of Man, I had formed an intention of going there, and had added to it all the other worlds of the universe as I came in time to realize their existence. I had abandoned that wish as a part (I thought) of growing up, when I learned that only people whose positions in society appeared to me unattainably high ever succeeded in leaving Urth.

Now that old longing was rekindled again, and though it seemed to have grown more absurd still with the passage of the years (for surely the little apprentice I had been had more chance of flashing between the stars at last than the hunted outcast I had become) it was immensely firmer and stronger because I had learned in the intervening time the folly of limiting desire to the possible. I would go, I was resolved. For the remainder of my life I would be sleeplessly alert for any opportunity, however slight. Already I had found myself once alone with the mirrors of Father Inire; then Jonas, wiser by far than I, had without hesitation cast himself on the tide of photons. Who could say that I would never find myself before those mirrors again?

With that thought, I snatched my cloak away from my head, resolved to look upon the stars once more, and found that the sunlight had come lancing over the crowns of the mountains to dim them almost to insignificance. The titan faces that loomed above me now were only those of the long-dead rulers of Urth, haggard by time, their cheeks fallen away in avalanches.

I stood and stretched. It was clear that I could not spend the day without food, as I had spent the day before; and clearer still that I could not spend the next night as I had spent this, with no shelter but my cloak. Thus, though I did not dare yet go down into the peopled valleys, I shaped my path to take me to the high forest I could see marching over the slopes below me.

It took most of the morning to reach it. When at last I scrambled down to stand among the scrub birches that were its outriders, I saw that although it was more steeply pitched than I had supposed, it contained, toward its center where the ground was somewhat more level and the sparse soil thus a trifle richer, trees of very considerable height, so closely spaced that the apertures between their trunks were hardly wider than the trunks themselves. They were not, of course, the glossy-leaved hardwoods of the tropical forest we had left behind on the south bank of the Cephissus. These were shaggy-barked conifers for the most part, tall, straight trees that leaned, even in their height and strength, away from the shadow of the mountain, and showed plainly in at least a quarter of their number the wounds of their wars with wind and lightning.

I had come hoping to find woodcutters or hunters from whom I might claim the hospitality that everyone (as city people fondly believe) offers to strangers in the wilds. For a long time, however, I was disappointed in that hope. Again and again I paused to listen for the ringing of an ax or the baying of hounds. There was only silence, and indeed, though the trees would have provided a great quantity of lumber, I saw no signs that any had ever been cut.

At last I came across a little brook of ice-cold water that wandered among the trees, fringed with dwarfed and tender bracken and grass as fine as hair. I drank my fill, and for perhaps half a watch followed the water down the slope through a succession of miniature falls and tarns, wondering, as no doubt others have for countless chiliads, to observe it grown slowly larger, though it had recruited no others of its kind that I could see.

Eventually it was swollen until the trees themselves were no longer safe from it, and I saw ahead the trunk of one, four cubits thick at least, that had fallen across it, its roots undermined. I approached it with no great care, for there was no sound to warn me, and bracing myself on a projecting stub vaulted to the top.

Almost I tumbled into an ocean of air. The battlement of Acies Castle, from which I had seen Dorcas in her dejection, was a balustrade compared to that height. Surely the Wall of Nessus is the only work of hands that could rival it. The brook fell silently upon a gulf that blew it to spray, so that it vanished into a rainbow. The trees below might have been toys made for a boy by an indulgent father, and at the edge of them, with a little field beyond, I saw a house no bigger than a pebble, with a wisp of white smoke, the ghost of the ribbon of water that had fallen and died, curling up to disappear like it into nothingness.

To descend the cliff appeared at first only too easy, for the momentum of my vault had nearly carried me over the fallen trunk, which itself hung half over the edge. When I had regained my balance, however, it seemed close to impossible. The rock face was sheer over large areas, so far as I could see, and though perhaps if I had carried a rope I could have let myself down and so reached the house well before night, I of course had none, and in any case would have been very slow to trust a rope of such immense length as would have been required.

I spent some time exploring the top of the cliff, however, and eventually discovered a path that, though very precipitous and very narrow, showed unmistakable signs of use. I will not recount the details of the climb down, which really have little to do with my story, although they were as may be imagined deeply absorbing at the time. I soon learned to watch only the path and the face of the cliff, to my right or left as the path wound back and forth. For most of its length it was a steep descent about a cubit wide or a little less. Occasionally it became a series of descending steps cut into the living rock, and at one point there were only hand and foot holes, which I descended like a ladder. These were far easier—viewed objectively—than the crevices to which I had clung by night at the mouth of the mine of the man-apes, and at least I was spared the shock of crossbow quarrels exploding about my ears; but the height was a hundred times greater, and dizzying.

Perhaps because I was forced to labor so hard to ignore the drop on the opposite side, I became acutely conscious of the vast, sectioned sample of the world's crust down which I crawled. In ancient times—so I read once in one of the texts Master Palaemon sent me—the heart of Urth herself was alive, and the shifting motions of that living core made plains erupt like fountains, and sometimes opened seas in a night between islands that had been one continent when last seen by the sun. Now it is said she is dead, and cooling and shrinking within her stony mantle like the corpse of an old woman in one of those abandoned houses Dorcas had described, mummifying in the still, dry air until her clothing falls in upon itself. So it is, it is said, with Urth; and here half a mountain had dropped away from its mating half, falling a league at least.

XIV

The Widow's House

In Saltus, where Jonas and I stayed for a few days and where I performed the second and third public decollations of my career, the miners rape the soil of metals, building stones, and even artifacts laid down by civilizations forgotten for chiliads before the Wall of Nessus ever rose. This they do by narrow shafts bored into the hillsides until they strike some rich layer of ruins, or even (if the tunnelers are particularly fortunate) a building that has preserved some part of its structure so that it serves them as a gallery already made.

What was done with so much labor there might have been accomplished on the cliff I descended with almost none. The past stood at my shoulder, naked and defenseless as all dead things, as though it were time itself that had been laid open by the fall of the mountain. Fossil bones protruded from the surface in places, the bones of mighty animals and of men. The forest had set its own dead there as well, stumps and limbs that time had turned to stone, so that I wondered as I descended, if it might not be that Urth is not, as we assume, older than her daughters the trees, and imagined them growing in the emptiness before the face of the sun, tree clinging to tree with tangled roots and interlacing twigs until at last their accumulation became our Urth, and they only the nap of her garment.

Deeper than these lay the buildings and mechanisms of humanity. (And it may be that those of other races lay there as well, for several of the stories in the brown book I carried seemed to imply that colonies once existed here of those beings whom we call the cacogens, though they are in fact of myriad races, each as distinct as our own.) I saw metals there that were green and blue in the same sense that copper is said to be red or silver white, colored metals so curiously wrought that

I could not be certain whether their shapes had been intended as works of art or as parts for strange machines, and it may be indeed that among some of those unfathomable peoples there is no distinction.

At one point, only slightly less than halfway down, the line of the fault had coincided with the tiled wall of some great building, so that the windy path I trod slashed across it. What the design was those tiles traced, I never knew; as I descended the cliff I was too near to see it, and when I reached the base at last it was too high for me to discern, lost in the shifting mists of the falling river. Yet as I walked, I saw it as an insect may be said to see the face in a portrait over whose surface it creeps. The tiles were of many shapes, though they fit together so closely, and at first I thought them representations of birds, lizards, fish and suchlike creatures, all interlocked in the grip of life. Now I feel that this was not so, that they were instead the shapes of a geometry I failed to comprehend, diagrams so complex that the living forms seemed to appear in them as the forms of actual animals appear from the intricate geometries of complex molecules.

However that might be, these forms seemed to have little connection with the picture or design. Lines of color crossed them, and though they must have been fired into the substance of the tiles in eons past, they were so willful and bright that they might have been laid on only a moment before by some titanic artist's brush. The shades most used were beryl and white, but though I stopped several times and strove to understand what might be depicted there (whether it was writing, or a face, or perhaps a mere decorative design of lines and angles, or a pattern of intertwined verdure) I could not; and perhaps it was each of those, or none, depending on the position from which it was seen and the predisposition the viewer brought to it.

Once this enigmatic wall was passed, the way down grew easier. It was never necessary again for me to climb down a sheer drop, and though there were several more flights of steps, they were not so steep or so narrow as before. I reached the bottom before I expected it, and looked up at the path down which I had traveled with as much wonder as if I had never set foot on it—indeed, I could see several points at which it appeared to have been broken by the spalling away of sections of the cliff, so that it seemed impassable.

The house I had beheld so clearly from above was invisible now, hidden among trees; but the smoke of its chimney still showed against the sky. I made my way through a forest less precipitous than the one through which I had followed the brook. The dark trees seemed, if anything, older. The great ferns of the south were absent there, and in fact I never saw them north of the House Absolute, except for those under cultivation in the gardens of Abdiesus; but there were wild violets with glossy leaves and flowers the exact color of poor Thecla's eyes growing between the roots of the trees, and moss like the thickest green velvet, so that the ground seemed carpeted, and the trees themselves all draped in costly fabric.

Some time before I could see the house or any other sign of human presence, I heard the barking of a dog. At the sound, the silence and wonder of the trees fell back, present still but infinitely more distant. I felt that some mysterious life, old and strange, yet kindly too, had come to the very moment of revealing itself to me, then drawn away like some immensely eminent person, a master of the musicians, perhaps, whom I had struggled for years to attract to my door but who in the act of knocking had heard the voice of another guest who was unpleasing to him and had put down his hand and turned away, never to come again.

Yet how comforting it was. For almost two long days I had been utterly alone, first upon the broken fields of stone, then among the icy beauty of the stars, and then in the hushed breath of the ancient trees. Now that harsh, familiar sound made me think once more of human comfort—not only think of it, but imagine it so vividly that I seemed to feel it already. I knew that when I saw the dog himself he would be like Triskele; and so he was, with four legs instead of three, somewhat longer and narrower in the skull, and more brown than lion-colored, but with the same dancing eyes and wagging tail and lolling tongue. He began with a declaration of war, which he rescinded as soon as I spoke to him, and before I had gone twenty strides he was presenting his ears to be scratched. I came into the little clearing where the house stood with the dog romping about me.

The walls were of stone, hardly higher than my head. The thatched roof was as steep as I have ever seen, and dotted with flat stones to hold down the thatch in high winds. It was, in short, the home of one of those pioneering peasants who are the glory and despair of our Commonwealth, who in one year produce a surplus of food to support the population of Nessus, but who must themselves be fed in the next lest they starve.

When there is no paved path before a door, one can judge how often feet go out and in by the degree to which the grass encroaches on the trodden ground. Here there was only a little circle of dust the size of a kerchief before the stone step. When I saw it, I supposed that I might frighten the person who lived in that cabin (for I supposed there could only be one) if I were to appear at the door unannounced, and so since the dog had long ago ceased to bark, I paused at the edge of the clearing and shouted a greeting.

The trees and the sky swallowed it, and left only silence.

I shouted again and advanced toward the door with the dog at my heels, and had almost reached it when a woman appeared there. She had a delicate face that might easily have been beautiful had it not been for her haunted eyes, but she wore a ragged dress that differed from a beggar's only by being clean. After a moment, a round-faced little boy, larger-eyed even than his mother, peeped past her skirt.

I said, "I am sorry if I startled you, but I have been lost in these mountains."

The woman nodded, hesitated, then drew back from the door, and I stepped inside. Her house was even smaller within its thick walls than I had supposed, and it reeked with the smell of some strong vegetable boiling in a kettle suspended on a hook over the fire. The windows were few and small, and because of the depth of the walls seemed rather boxes of shadow than apertures of light. An old man sat upon a panther skin with his back to the fire; his eyes were so lacking in focus and intelligence that at first I thought him blind. There was a table at the center of the room, with five chairs about it, of which three seemed to have been made for adults. I remembered what Dorcas had told me about furniture from the abandoned houses of Nessus being brought north for eclectics who had adopted more cultivated fashions, but all the pieces showed signs of having been made on the spot.

The woman saw the direction of my glance and said, "My husband will be here soon. Before supper."

I told her, "You don't have to worry—I mean you no harm. If you'll let me share your meal and sleep here tonight out of the cold, and give me directions in the morning, I'll be glad to help with whatever work there is to be done."

The woman nodded, and quite unexpectedly the little boy piped, "Have you seen Severa?" His mother turned on him so quickly that I was reminded of Master Gurloes demonstrating the grips used to control prisoners. I heard the blow, though I hardly saw it, and the little boy shrieked. His mother moved to block the door, and he hid himself behind a chest in the corner farthest from her. I understood then, or thought I understood, that Severa was a girl or woman whom she considered more vulnerable than herself, and whom she had ordered to hide (probably in the loft, under the thatch) before letting me in. But I reasoned that any further protestation of my good intentions would be wasted on the woman, who however ignorant was clearly no fool, and that the best way to gain her confidence was to deserve it. I began by asking her for some water so that I could wash, and said that I would gladly carry it from whatever source they had if she would permit me to heat it at her fire. She gave me a pot, and told me where the spring was.

At one time or another I have been in most of the places that are conventionally considered romantic—atop high towers, deep in the bowels of the world, in palatial buildings, in jungles, and aboard a ship—yet none of these have affected me in the same way as that poor cabin of stones. It seemed to me the archetype of those caves into which, as scholars teach, humanity has crept again at the lowest point of each cycle of civilization. Whenever I have read or heard a description of an idyllic rustic retreat (and it was an idea of which Thecla was very fond) it has dwelt on cleanliness and order. There is a bed of mint beneath the window, wood stacked by the coldest wall, a gleaming flagstone floor, and so on. There was nothing of that here, no ideality; and yet the house was more perfect for all its imperfection, showing that human beings might live and love in such a remote spot without the ability to shape their habitat into a poem.

"Do you always shave with your sword?" the woman asked. It was the first time she had spoken to me unguardedly.

"It is a custom, a tradition. If the sword were not sharp enough for me to shave with, I would be ashamed to bear it. And if it is sharp enough, what need do I have of a razor?"

"Still it must be awkward, holding such a heavy blade up like that, and you must have to take great care not to cut yourself."

"The exercise strengthens my arms. Besides, it's good for me to handle my sword every chance I get, so that it becomes as familiar as my limbs."

"You're a soldier, then. I thought so."

"I am a butcher of men."

She seemed taken aback at that, and said, "I didn't mean to insult you."

"I'm not insulted. Everyone kills certain things—you killed those roots in your kettle when you put them into the boiling water. When I kill a man, I save the lives of all the living things he would have destroyed if he had continued to live himself, including, perhaps, many other men, and women and children. What does your husband do?"

The woman smiled a little at that. It was the first time I had seen her smile, and it made her look much younger. "Everything. A man has to do everything up here."

"You weren't born here then."

"No," she said. "Only Severian . . ." The smile was gone.

"Did you say *Severian*?"

"That's my son's name. You saw him when you came in, and he's spying on us now. He is a thoughtless boy sometimes."

"That is my own name. I am Master Severian."

She called to the boy, "Did you hear that? The goodman's name is the same as yours!" Then to me again, "Do you think it's a good name? Do you like it?"

"I'm afraid I've never thought much about it, but yes, I suppose I do. It seems to suit me." I had finished shaving, and seated myself in one of the chairs to tend the blade.

"I was born in Thrax," the woman said. "Have you ever been there?"

"I just came from there," I told her. If the dimarchi were to question her after I left, her description of my habit would give me away in any case.

"You didn't meet a woman called Herais? She's my mother."

I shook my head.

"Well, it's a big town, I suppose. You weren't there long?"

"No, not long at all. While you have been in these mountains, have you heard of the Pelerines? They're an order of priestesses who wear red."

"I'm afraid not. We don't get much news here."

"I'm trying to locate them, or if I can't, to join the army the Autarch is leading against the Ascians."

"My husband could give you better directions than I can. You shouldn't have come up here so high, though. Becan—that's my husband—says the patrols never bother soldiers moving north, not even when they use the old roads."

While she spoke of soldiers moving north, someone else, much nearer, was moving as well. It was a movement so stealthy as to be scarcely audible above the crackling of the fire and the harsh breathing of the old man, but it was unmistakable nonetheless. Bare feet, unable to endure any longer the utter motionlessness that silence commands, had shifted almost imperceptibly, and the planks beneath them had chirped with the new distribution of weight.

XV

He Is Ahead of You!

The husband who was supposed to have come before supper did not come, and the four of us—the woman, the old man, the boy, and I—ate the evening meal without him. I had at first thought his wife's prediction a lie intended to deter me from whatever criminality I might otherwise have committed; but as the sullen afternoon wore on in that silence that presages a storm, it became apparent that she had believed what she had said, and was now sincerely worried.

Our supper was as simple, almost, as such a meal can be; but my hunger was so great that it was one of the most gratifying I recall. We had boiled vegetables without salt or butter, coarse bread, and a little meat. No wine, no fruit, nothing fresh and nothing sweet; yet I think I must have eaten more than the other three together.

When our meal was over, the woman (whose name, I had learned, was Casdoe) took a long, iron-shod staff out of a corner and set off to look for her husband, first assuring me that she required no escort and telling the old man, who seemed not to hear her, that she would not go far and would soon return. Seeing him remain as abstracted as ever before his fire, I coaxed the boy to me, and after I had won his confidence by showing him *Terminus Est* and permitting him to hold her hilt and attempt to lift her blade, I asked him whether Severa should not come down and take care of him now that his mother was away.

"She came back last night," he told me.

I thought he was referring to his mother and said, "I'm sure she'll come back tonight too, but don't you think Severa ought to take care of you now, while she's gone?"

As children who are not sufficiently confident of language to argue sometimes do, the boy shrugged and tried to turn away.

I caught him by the shoulders. "I want you to go upstairs now, little Severian, and tell her to come down. I promise I won't hurt her."

He nodded and went to the ladder, though slowly and reluctantly. "Bad woman," he said.

Then, for the first time since I had been in the house, the old man spoke. "Becan, come over here! I want to tell you about Fechin." It was a moment before I understood that he was addressing me under the impression that I was his son-in-law.

"He was the worst of us all, that Fechin. A tall, wild boy with red hair on his hands, on his arms. Like a monkey's arms, so that if you saw them reaching around the corner to take something, you'd think, except for the size, that it was a monkey taking it. He took our copper pan once, the one Mother used to make sausage in, and I saw his arm and didn't tell who had done it, because he was my friend. I never found it again, never saw it again, though I was with him a thousand times. I used to think he had made a boat of it and sailed it on the river, because that was what I had always wanted to do with it myself. I walked down the river trying to find it, and the night came before I ever knew it, before I had even turned around to go home. Maybe he polished the bottom to look in—sometimes he drew his own likeness. Maybe he filled it with water to see his reflection."

I had gone across the room to listen to him, partly because he spoke indistinctly and partly out of respect, for his aged face reminded me a little of Master Palaemon's, though he had his natural eyes. "I once met a man of your age who had posed for Fechin," I said.

The old man looked up at me; as quickly as the shadow of a bird might cross some gray rag thrown out of the house upon the grass, I saw the realization that I was not Becan come and go. He did not stop speaking, however, or in any other way acknowledge the fact. It was as if what he was saying were so urgent that it had to be told to someone, poured into any ears before it was lost forever.

"His face wasn't a monkey's face at all. Fechin was handsome—the handsomest around. He could always get food or money from a woman. He could get anything from women. I remember once when we were walking down the trail that led to where the old mill stood then. I had a piece of paper the schoolmaster had given me. Real paper, not quite white, but with a touch of brown to it, and little speckles here and there, so it looked like a trout in milk. The schoolmaster gave it to me so I could write a letter for Mother—at the school we always wrote on boards, then washed them clean with a sponge when we had to write again, and when nobody was looking we'd hit the sponge with the board and send it flying against the wall, or somebody's head. But Fechin loved to draw, and while we walked I thought about that, and how his face would look if he had paper to make a picture he could keep.

"They were the only things he kept. Everything else he lost, or gave away, or threw away, and I knew what Mother wanted to tell pretty much, and I decided if I wrote small I could get it on half the paper. Fechin didn't know I had it, but I took it out and showed it to him, then folded it and tore it in two."

Over our heads, I could hear the fluting voice of the little boy, though I could not understand what he was saying.

"That was the brightest day I've ever seen. The sun had new life to him, the way a man will when he was sick yesterday and will be sick tomorrow, but today he walks around and laughs so that if a stranger was to come he'd think there was nothing wrong, no sickness at all, that the medicines and the bed were for somebody else. They always say in prayers that the New Sun will be too bright to look at, and I always up until that day had taken it to be just the proper way of talking, the way you say a baby's beautiful, or praise whatever a good man has made for himself, that even if there were two suns in the sky you could look at both. But that day I learned it was all true, and the light of it on Fechin's face was more than I could stand. It made my eyes water. He said thank you, and we went farther along and came to a house where a girl lived. I can't remember what her name was, but she was truly beautiful, the way the quietest are sometimes. I never knew up till then that Fechin knew her, but he asked me to wait, and I sat down on the first step in front of the gate."

Someone heavier than the boy was walking overhead, toward the ladder.

"He wasn't inside long, but when he came out, with the girl looking out the window, I knew what they had done. I looked at him, and he spread those long, thin, monkey arms. How could he share what he'd had? In the end, he made the girl give me half a loaf of bread and some fruit. He drew my picture on one side of the paper and the girl's on the other, but he kept the pictures."

The ladder creaked, and I turned to look. As I had expected, a woman was descending it. She was not tall, but full-figured and narrow-waisted; her gown was nearly as ragged as the boy's mother's, and much dirtier. Rich brown hair spilled down her back. I think I recognized her even before she turned and I saw the high cheekbones and her long, brown eyes—it was Agia. "So you knew I was here all along," she said.

"I might make the same remark to you. You seem to have been here before me."

"I only guessed that you would be coming this way. As it happened,

I arrived a little before you, and I told the mistress of this house what you would do to me if she did not hide me,'' she said. (I supposed she wished me to know she had an ally here, if only a feeble one.)

''You've been trying to kill me ever since I glimpsed you in the crowd at Saltus.''

''Is that an accusation? Yes.''

''You're lying.''

It was one of the few times I have ever seen Agia caught off balance. ''What do you mean?''

''Only that you were trying to kill me before Saltus.''

''With the avern. Yes, of course.''

''And afterward. Agia, I know who Hethor is.''

I waited for her to reply, but she said nothing.

''On the day we met, you told me there was an old sailor who wanted you to live with him. Old and ugly and poor, you called him, and I could not understand why you, a lovely young woman, should even consider his offer when you were not actually starving. You had your twin to protect you, and a little money coming in from the shop.''

It was my turn to be surprised. She said, ''I should have gone to him and mastered him. I have mastered him now.''

''I thought you had only promised yourself to him, if he would kill me.''

''I have promised him that and many other things, and so mastered him. He is ahead of you, Severian, waiting word from me.''

''With more of his beasts? Thank you for the warning. That was it, wasn't it? He had threatened you and Agilus with the pets he had brought from other spheres.''

She nodded. ''He came to sell his clothes, and they were the kind worn on the old ships that sailed beyond the world's rim long ago, and they weren't costumes or forgeries or even tomb-tender old garments that had lain for centuries in the dark, but clothes not far from new. He said his ships—all those ships—became lost in the blackness between the suns, where the years do not turn. Lost so that even Time cannot find them.''

''I know,'' I said. ''Jonas told me.''

''After I learned that you would kill Agilus, I went to him. He is iron-strong in some ways, weak in many others. If I had withheld my body I could have done nothing with him, but I did all the queer things he wished me to, and made him believe I love him. Now he will do anything I ask. He followed you for me after you killed Agilus; with his silver I hired the men you killed at the old mine, and the creatures he commands will kill you for me yet, if I don't do it here myself.''

"You meant to wait until I slept, and then come down and murder me, I suppose."

"I would have waked you first, when I had my knife at your throat. But the child told me you knew I was here, and I thought this might be more pleasant. Tell me though—how did you guess about Hethor?"

A breath of wind stirred through the narrow windows. It made the fire smoke, and I heard the old man, who sat there in silence once more, cough, and spit onto the coals. The little boy, who had climbed down from the loft while Agia and I talked, watched us with large, uncomprehending eyes.

"I should have known it long before," I said. "My friend Jonas had been just such a sailor. You will remember him, I think—you glimpsed him at the mine mouth, and you must have known of him."

"We did."

"Perhaps they were from the same ship. Or perhaps it was only that each would have known the other by some sign, or that Hethor at least feared they would. However that may be, he seldom came near me when I was traveling with Jonas, though he had been so eager to be in my company before. I saw him in the crowd when I executed a woman and a man at Saltus, but he did not try to join me there. On the way to the House Absolute, Jonas and I saw him behind us, but he did not come running up until Jonas had ridden off, though he must have been desperate to get back his notule. When he was thrown into the antechamber of the House Absolute, he made no attempt to sit with us, even though Jonas was nearly dead; but something that left a trail of slime was searching the place when we left it."

Agia said nothing, and in her silence she might have been the young woman I had seen on the morning of the day after I left our tower unfastening the gratings that had guarded the windows of a dusty shop.

"You two must have lost my trail on the way to Thrax," I continued, "or been delayed by some accident. Even after you discovered we were in the city, you must not have known that I had charge of the Vincula, because Hethor sent his creature of fire prowling the streets to find me. Then, somehow, you found Dorcas at the Duck's Nest—"

"We were lodging there ourselves," Agia said. "We had only arrived a few days before, and we were out looking for you when you came. Afterward when I realized that the woman in the little garret room was the mad girl you had found in the Botanic Gardens, we still didn't guess it was you who had put her there, because that hag at the inn said the man had worn common clothes. But we thought she might know where you were, and that she would be more apt to talk to Hethor. His name isn't really Hethor, by the way. He says it's a much older one, that hardly anyone has heard of now.''

''He told Dorcas about the fire creature,'' I said, ''and she told me. I had heard of the thing before, but Hethor had a name for it—he called it a salamander. I didn't think anything of it when Dorcas mentioned it, but later I remembered that Jonas had a name for the black thing that flew after us outside the House Absolute. He called it a notule, and said the people on the ships had named them that because they betrayed themselves with a gust of warmth. If Hethor had a name for the fire creature, it seemed likely that it was a sailor's name too, and that he had something to do with the creature itself.''

Agia smiled thinly. ''So now you know all, and you have me where you want me—provided you can swing that big blade of yours in here.''

''I have you without it. I had you beneath my foot at the mine mouth, for that matter.''

''But I still have my knife.''

At that moment the boy's mother came through the doorway, and both of us paused. She looked in astonishment from Agia to me; then, as though no surprise could pierce her sorrow or alter what she had to do, she closed the door and lifted the heavy bar into place.

Agia said, ''He heard me upstairs, Casdoe, and made me come down. He intends to kill me.''

''And how am I to prevent that?'' the woman answered wearily. She turned to me. ''I hid her because she said you meant her harm. Will you kill me too?''

''No. Nor will I kill her, as she knows.''

Agia's face distorted with rage, as the face of another lovely woman, molded by Fechin himself perhaps in colored wax, might have been transformed with a gout of flame, so that it simultaneously melted and burned. ''You killed Agilus, and you gloried in it! Aren't I as fit to die as he was? We were the same flesh!'' I had not fully believed her when she said she was armed with a knife, but without my having seen her draw it, it was out now—one of the crooked daggers of Thrax.

For some time the air had been heavy with an impending storm. Now the thunder rolled, booming among the peaks above us. When its echoings and reechoings had almost died away, something answered them. I cannot describe that voice; it was not quite a human shout, nor was it the mere bellow of a beast.

All her weariness left the woman Casdoe, replaced by the most desperate haste. Heavy wooden shutters stood against the wall beneath each of the narrow windows; she seized the nearest, and lifting it as if it weighed no more than a pie pan sent it crashing into place. Outside, the dog barked frantically then fell silent, leaving no sound but the pattering of the first rain.

"So soon," Casdoe cried. "So soon!" To her son: "Severian, get out of the way."

Through one of the still open windows, I heard a child's voice call, *"Father, can't you help me?"*

XVI

The Alzabo

I tried to assist Casdoe, and in the process turned my back on Agia and her dagger. It was an error that almost cost me my life, for she was upon me as soon as I was encumbered with a shutter. Women and tailors hold the blade beneath the hand, according to the proverb, but Agia stabbed up to open the tripes and catch the heart from below, like an accomplished assassin. I turned only just in time to block her blade with the shutter, and the point drove through the wood to show a glint of steel.

The very strength of her blow betrayed her. I wrenched the shutter to one side and threw it across the room, and her knife with it. She and Casdoe both leaped for it. I caught Agia by an arm and jerked her back, and Casdoe slammed the shutter into place with the knife out, toward the gathering storm.

"You fool," Agia said. "Don't you realize you're giving a weapon to whomever it is you're afraid of?" Her voice was calm with defeat.

"It has no need of knives," Casdoe told her.

The house was dark now except for the ruddy light of the fire. I looked around for candles or lanterns, but there were none in sight; later I learned that the few the family owned had been carried to the loft. Lightning flashed outside, outlining the edges of the shutters and making a broken line of stark light at the bottom of the door—it was a moment before I realized that it had been a broken line, when it should have been a continuous one. "There's someone outside," I said. "Standing on the step."

Casdoe nodded. "I closed the window just in time. It has never come so early before. It may be that the storm wakened it."

"You don't think it might be your husband?"

Before she could answer me, a voice higher than the little boy's called, *''Let me in, Mother.''*

Even I, who did not know what it was that spoke, sensed a fearful wrongness in the simple words. It was a child's voice, perhaps, but not a human child's.

''Mother,'' the voice called again. *''It is beginning to rain.''*

''We had better go up,'' Casdoe said. ''If we pull the ladder after us, it cannot reach us even if it should get inside.''

I had gone to the door. Without lightning, the feet of whatever it was that stood on the doorstep were invisible; but I could hear a hoarse, slow breathing above the beating of the rain, and once a scraping sound, as though the thing that waited there in the dark had shifted its footing.

''Is this your doing?'' I asked Agia. ''Some creature of Hethor's?''

She shook her head; the narrow, brown eyes were dancing. ''They roam wild in these mountains, as you should know much better than I.''

''Mother?''

There was a shuffle of feet—with that fretful question, the thing outside had turned from the door. One of the shutters was cracked, and I tried to look through the slit; I could see nothing in the blackness outside, but I heard a soft, heavy tread, precisely the sound that sometimes came through the barred ports of the Tower of the Bear at home.

''It took Severa three days ago,'' Casdoe said. She was trying to get the old man to rise; he did so slowly, reluctant to leave the warmth of the fire. ''I never let her or Severian go among the trees, but it came into the clearing here, a watch before twilight. Since then it has returned every night. The dog wouldn't track it, but Becan went to hunt it today.''

I had guessed the beast's identity by that time, though I had never beheld one of its kind. I said, ''It is an alzabo, then? The creature from whose glands the analept is made?''

''It is an alzabo, yes,'' Casdoe answered. ''I know nothing of any analept.''

Agia laughed. ''But Severian does. He has tasted the creature's wisdom, and carries his beloved about within himself. I understand one hears them whispering together by night, in the very heat and sweat of love.''

I struck at her; but she dodged nimbly, then put the table between herself and me. ''Aren't you delighted, Severian, that when the animals came to Urth to replace all those our ancestors slew, the alzabo was among them? Without the alzabo, you would have lost your dearest Thecla forever. Tell Casdoe here how happy the alzabo has made you.''

To Casdoe I said, "I am truly sorry to hear of your daughter's death. I will defend this house from the animal outside, if it must be done."

My sword was standing against the wall, and to show that my will was as good as my words, I reached for it. It was fortunate I did so, for just at that instant a man's voice at the door called, *"Open, darling!"*

Agia and I sprang to stop Casdoe, but neither of us was swift enough. Before we could reach her, she had lifted the bar. The door swung back.

The beast that waited there stood upon four legs; even so, its hulking shoulders were as high as my head. Its own head was carried low, with the tips of its ears below the crest of fur that topped its back. In the firelight, its teeth gleamed white and its eyes glowed red. I have seen the eyes of many of these creatures that are supposed to have come from beyond the margin of the world—drawn, as certain philonoists allege, by the death of those whose genesis was here, even as tribes of enchors come slouching with their stone knives and fires into a countryside depopulated by war or disease; but their eyes are the eyes of beasts only. The red orbs of the alzabo were something more, holding neither the intelligence of humankind nor the innocence of the brutes. So a fiend might look, I thought, when it had at last struggled up from the pit of some dark star; then I recalled the man-apes, who were indeed called fiends, yet had the eyes of men.

For a moment it seemed the door might be shut again. I saw Casdoe, who had recoiled in horror, try to swing it to. The alzabo appeared to advance slowly and even lazily, yet it was too swift for her, and the edge of the door struck its ribs as it might have struck a stone.

"Let it stay open," I called. "We'll need whatever light there is." I had unsheathed *Terminus Est*, so that her blade caught the firelight and seemed itself a bitter fire. An arbalest like the ones Agia's henchmen had carried, whose quarrels are ignited by the friction of the atmosphere and burst when they strike like stones cast into a furnace, would have been a better weapon; but it would not have seemed an extension of my arm as *Terminus Est* did, and perhaps after all an arbalest would have permitted the alzabo to spring on me while I sought to recock it, if the first quarrel missed.

The long blade of my sword did not wholly obviate that danger. Her square, unpointed tip could not impale the beast, should it spring. I would have to slash at it in air, and though I had no doubt that I could strike the head from that thick neck while it flew toward me, I knew that to miss would be death. Furthermore, I needed space enough to make the stroke, for which that narrow room was scarcely adequate; and though the fire was dying, I needed light.

The old man, the boy Severian, and Casdoe were all gone—I was not certain if they had climbed the ladder to the loft while my attention had been fixed on the eyes of the beast, or if some of them, at least, had not fled through the doorway behind it. Only Agia remained, pressed into a corner with Casdoe's iron-tipped climbing stick to use as a weapon, as a sailor might, in desperation, try to fend off a galleass with a boat hook. I knew that to speak to her would be to call attention to her; yet it might be that if the beast so much as turned its head toward her, I would be able to sever its spine.

I said, "Agia, I must have light. It will kill me in the dark. You once told your men you would front me, if only they would kill me from behind. I will front this for you now, if you will only bring a candle."

She nodded to show she understood, and as she did the beast moved toward me. It did not spring as I had expected, however, but sidled lazily yet adroitly to the right, coming nearer while contriving to keep just beyond blade reach. After a moment of incomprehension I realized that by its position near the wall it cramped further any attack I might make, and that if it could circle me (as it nearly did) to gain a position between the fire and my own, much of the benefit I had from the firelight would be lost.

So we began a careful game, in which the alzabo sought to make what use it could of the chairs, the table, and the walls, and I tried to get as much space as I could for my sword.

Then I leaped forward. The alzabo avoided my cut, as it seemed to me, by no more than the width of a finger, lunged at me, and drew back just in time to escape my return stroke. Its jaws, large enough to bite a man's head as a man bites an apple, had snapped before my face, drenching me in the reek of its putrid breath.

The thunder boomed again, so near that after its roar I could hear the crashing fall of the great tree whose death it had proclaimed; the lightning flash, illuminating every detail in its paralyzing glare, left me dazzled and blinded. I swung *Terminus Est* in the rush of darkness that followed, felt her bite bone, sprang to one side, and as the thunder rumbled out slashed again, this time only sending some stick of furniture flying into ruin.

Then I could see once more. While the alzabo and I had shifted ground and feinted, Agia had been moving too, and she must have made a dash for the ladder when the lightning struck. She was halfway up, and I saw Casdoe reach down to help her. The alzabo stood before me, as whole, so it seemed, as ever; but dark blood dribbled into a pool at its forefeet. Its fur looked red and ragged in the firelight, and the nails of its feet, larger and coarser than a bear's, were darkly red as well, and seemed translucent. More hideous than the speaking of a corpse could ever be, I heard the voice that had called, *''Open darling,''* at the door. It said: *''Yes, I am injured. But the pain is nothing much, and I can stand and move as before. You cannot bar me from my family forever.''* From the mouth of a beast, it was the voice of a stern, stamping honest man.

I took out the Claw and laid it on the table, but it was no more than a spark of blue. ''Light!'' I shouted to Agia. No light came, and I heard the rattle of the ladder on the loft's floor as the women drew it up.

''Your escape is cut off, you see,'' the beast said, still in the man's voice.

''So is your advance. Can you jump so high, with a wounded leg?''

Abruptly the voice became the plaintive treble of the little girl. *''I can climb. Do you think I won't think to move the table over there under the hole? I, who can talk?''*

''You know yourself a beast, then.''

The man's voice came again. *''We know we are within the beast, just as once we were within the cases of flesh the beast has devoured.''*

''And you would consent to its devouring your wife and your son, Becan?''

''I would direct it. I do direct it. I want Casdoe and Severian to join us here, just as I joined Severa today. When the fire dies, you die too—joining us—and so shall they.''

I laughed. ''Have you forgotten that you got your wound when I couldn't see?'' Holding *Terminus Est* at the ready, I crossed the room to the ruin of the chair, snatched up what had been its back, and threw it into the fire, making a cloud of sparks. ''That was well-seasoned wood, I think, and it has been rubbed with bees' wax by some careful hand. It should burn brightly.''

''Just the same, the dark will come.'' The beast—Becan—sounded infinitely patient. *''The dark will come, and you will join us.''*

''No. When all the chair has burned and the light is failing, I will advance on you and kill you. I only wait now to let you bleed.''

There was silence, the more eerie because nothing in the beast's expression hinted of thought. I knew that even as the wreck of Thecla's neural chemistry had been fixed in the nuclei of certain of my own frontal cells by a secretion distilled from the organs of just such a creature, so the man and his daughter haunted the dim thicket of the beast's brain and believed they lived; but what that ghost of life might be, what dreams and desires might enter it, I could not guess.

At last the man's voice said, *''In a watch or two, then, I will kill you or you will kill me. Or we will destroy each other. If I turn now and go out into the night and the rain, will you hunt me down when Urth turns toward the light once more? Or remain here to keep me from the woman and child that are mine?"*?

"No," I said.

"On such honor as you have? Will you swear on that sword, though you cannot point it to the sun?"

I took a step backward and reversed *Terminus Est*, holding her by the blade in such a way that her tip was directed toward my own heart. "I swear by this sword, the badge of my Art, that if you do not return this night I will not hunt you tomorrow. Nor will I remain in this house."

As swiftly as a gliding snake it turned. For an instant I might, perhaps, have cut at its thick back. Then it was gone, and no trace of its presence remained save for the open door, the shattered chair, and the pool of blood (darker, I think, than the blood of the animals of this world) that soaked into the scrubbed planks of the floor.

I went to the door and barred it, returned the Claw to the little sack suspended from my neck, and then, as the beast had suggested, shifted the table until I could climb upon it and easily pull myself into the loft. Casdoe and the old man waited at the farther end with the boy called Severian, in whose eyes I saw the memories this night might hold for him twenty years hence. They were bathed in the vacillating radiance of a lamp suspended from one of the rafters.

"I have survived," I told them, "as you see. Could you hear what we said below?"

Casdoe nodded without speaking.

"If you had brought me the light I asked for, I would not have done what I did. As it was, I felt I owed you nothing. If I were you, I would leave this house as soon as it is day, and go to the lowlands. But that is up to you."

"We were afraid," Casdoe muttered.

"So was I. Where is Agia?"

To my surprise, the old man pointed, and looking at the place he indicated, I saw that the thick thatch had been parted to make an opening large enough for Agia's slender body.

That night I slept before the fire, after warning Casdoe that I would kill anyone who came down from the loft. In the morning, I walked around the house; as I had expected, Agia's knife had been pulled from the shutter.

XVII

The Sword of the Lictor

"We are leaving," Casdoe told me. "But I will make breakfast for us before we go. You will not have to eat it with us if you do not wish to do so."

I nodded and waited outside until she brought out a wooden bowl of plain porridge and a wooden spoon; then I took them to the spring and ate. It was screened by rushes, and I did not come out; it was, I suppose, a violation of the oath I had given the alzabo, but I waited there, watching the house.

After a time Casdoe, her father, and little Severian emerged. She carried a pack and her husband's staff, and the old man and the boy had each their little sack. The dog, which must have crawled beneath the floor when the alzabo came (I cannot say I blame him, but Triskele would not have done that) was frisking about their heels. I saw Casdoe look around for me. When she failed to find me, she put down a bundle on the doorstep.

I watched them walk along the edge of their little field, which had been plowed and sown only a month or so before, and now would be reaped by birds. Neither Casdoe nor her father glanced behind them; but the boy, Severian, stopped and turned before going over the first ridge, to see once more the only home he had ever known. Its stone walls stood as stoutly as ever, and the smoke of the breakfast fire still curled from its chimney. His mother must have called to him then, because he hurried after her and so disappeared from view.

I left the shelter of the rushes and went to the door. The bundle on the step held two blankets of soft guanaco and dried meat wrapped in a clean rug. I put the meat into my sabretache and refolded the blankets so I could wear them across my shoulder.

The rain had left the air fresh and clean, and it was good to know that I would soon leave the stone cabin and its smells of smoke and food behind me. I looked around inside, seeing the black stain of the alzabo's blood and the broken chair. Casdoe had moved the table back to its old place, and the Claw, that had gleamed so feebly there, had left no mark upon its surface. There was nothing left that seemed worth the carrying; I went out and shut the door.

Then I set off after Casdoe and her party. I did not forgive her for having failed to give me light when I fought the alzabo—she might easily have done so by lowering her lamp from the loft. Yet I could not greatly blame her for having sided with Agia, a woman alone among the staring faces and icy crowns of the mountains; and the child and the old man, neither of whom could be said to have much guilt in the matter, were at least as vulnerable as she.

The path was soft, so much so that I could track them in the most literal sense, seeing Casdoe's small footprints, the boy's even smaller ones beside them taking two strides to her one, and the old man's, with the toes turned out. I walked slowly in order not to overtake them, and though I knew my own danger increased with each step I took, I dared to hope that the archon's patrols, in questioning them, would warn me. Casdoe could not betray me, since whatever honest information she might tender the dimarchi would lead them astray; and if the alzabo were about, I hoped to hear or smell it before it attacked—I had not sworn, after all, to leave its prey undefended, but only not to hunt it, or to remain in the house.

The path must have been no more than a game trail enlarged by Becan; it soon vanished. The scenery here was less stark than it had been above the timberline. South-facing slopes were often covered with small ferns and mosses, and conifers grew from the cliffs. Falling water was seldom out of earshot. In me Thecla recalled coming to a place much like this to paint, accompanied by her teacher and two gruff bodyguards. I began to feel that I would soon come across the easel, palette, and untidy brush case, abandoned beside some cascade when the sun no longer lingered in the spray.

Of course I did not, and for several watches there was no sign of humanity at all. Mingled with the footprints of Casdoe's party were the tracks of deer, and twice the pug marks of one of the tawny cats that prey on them. These had been made, surely, just at dawn, when the rain had stopped.

Then I saw a line of impressions left by a naked foot larger than the old man's. Each was as large, in fact, as my own booted print, and its maker's stride had been, if anything, longer. The tracks crossed at right angles to those I followed, but one imprint fell over one of the boy's, showing that their maker had passed between us.

I hurried forward.

I assumed that the footprints were those of an autochthon, though even then I wondered at his long stride—those savages of the mountains are normally rather small. If it was indeed an autochthon, he was unlikely to do Casdoe and the others any real harm, though he might pillage the goods she carried. From all I had heard of them, the autochthons were clever hunters, but not warlike.

The impressions of bare feet resumed. Two or three more individuals, at least, had joined the first.

Deserters from the army would be another matter; about a quarter of our prisoners in the Vincula had been such men and their women, and many of them had committed the most atrocious crimes. Deserters would be well armed, but I would have expected them to be well shod too, certainly not barefoot.

A steep climb rose ahead of me. I could see the gouges made by Casdoe's staff, and the branches broken where she and the old man had used them to pull themselves up—some broken, possibly, by their pursuers as well. I reflected that the old man must be exhausted by now, that it was surprising that his daughter could still urge him on; perhaps he, perhaps all of them, knew by now that they were pursued. As I neared the crest I heard the dog bark, and then (at the same time it seemed almost an echo of the night before) a wild, wordless yell.

Yet it was not the horrible, half-human cry of the alzabo. It was a sound I had heard often before, sometimes, faintly, even while I lay in the cot next to Roche's, and often when I had carried their meals and the clients' to the journeymen on duty in our oubliette. It was precisely the shout of one of the clients on the third level, one of those who could no longer speak coherently and for that reason were never, for practical purposes, brought again to the examination room.

They were zoanthrops, such as I had seen feigned at Abdiesus's ridotto. When I reached the top I could see them, as well as Casdoe with her father and son. One cannot call them men; but they seemed men at that distance, nine naked men who circled the three, bounding and crouching. I hurried forward until I saw one strike with his club, and the old man fall.

Then I hesitated, and it was not Thecla's fear that stopped me but my own.

I had fought the man-apes of the mine bravely, perhaps, but I had to fight them. I had stood against the alzabo to stalemate, but there had been nowhere to run but the darkness outside, where it would surely have killed me.

Now there was a choice, and I hung back.

Living where she had, Casdoe must have known of them, though possibly she had never encountered them before. While the boy clung to her skirt she slashed with the staff as though it were a sabre. Her voice carried to me over the yells of the zoanthrops, shrill, unintelligible, and seemingly remote. I felt the horror one always feels when a woman is attacked, but beside it or perhaps beneath it lay the thought that she who would not fight beside me must now fight alone.

It could not last, of course. Such creatures are either frightened away at once or not frightened away at all. I saw one snatch the staff from her hand, and I drew *Terminus Est* and began to run down the long slope toward her. The naked figure had thrown her to the ground and was (as I supposed) preparing to rape her.

Then something huge plunged out of the trees to my left. It was so large and moved so swiftly that I at first thought it a red destrier, riderless and saddleless. Only when I saw the flash of its teeth and heard the scream of a zoanthrop did I realize it was the alzabo.

The others were upon it at once. Rising and falling, the heads of their ironwood bludgeons seemed for a moment grotesquely like the heads of feeding hens when corn has been scattered on the ground for them. Then a zoanthrop was thrown into the air, and he, who had been naked before, now appeared to be wrapped in a cloak of scarlet.

By the time I joined the fight, the alzabo was down, and for a moment I could give no attention to it. *Terminus Est* sang in orbit about my head. One naked figure fell, then another. A stone the size of a fist whizzed past my ear, so close that I could hear the sound; if it had struck, I would have died a moment afterward.

But these were not the man-apes of the mine, so numerous they could not, in the end, be overcome. I cut one from shoulder to waist, feeling each rib part in turn and rattle across my blade, slashed at another, split a skull.

Then there was only silence and the whimpering of the boy. Seven zoanthrops lay upon the mountain grass, four killed by *Terminus Est*, I think, and three by the alzabo. Casdoe's body was in its jaws, her head and shoulders already devoured. The old man who had known Fechin lay crumpled like a doll; that famous artist would have made something wonderful of his death, showing it from a perspective no one else could have found, and embodying the dignity and futility of all human life in the misshapen head. But Fechin was not here. The dog lay beside the old man, its jaws bloodied.

I looked about for the boy. To my horror, he was huddled against the alzabo's back. No doubt the thing had called to him in his father's voice, and he had come. Now its hindquarters trembled spasmodically and its eyes were closed. As I took him by the arm, its tongue, wider and thicker than a bull's, emerged as though to lick his hand; then its shoulders shuddered so violently that I started back. The tongue was never wholly returned to its mouth, but lay flaccid on the grass.

I drew the boy away and said, "It is over now, little Severian. Are you all right?"

He nodded and began to cry, and for a long time I held him and walked up and down.

For a moment I considered using the Claw, though it had failed me in Casdoe's house as it had failed me at times before. Yet if it had succeeded, who could say what the result might have been? I had no wish to give the zoanthrops or the alzabo new life, and what life might be granted Casdoe's headless corpse? As for the old man, he had been sitting at the doors of death already; now he had died, and swiftly. Would he have thanked me for summoning him back, to die again in a year or two? The gem flashed in the sunlight, but its flashing was mere sunshine and not the light of the Conciliator, the gegenschein of the New Sun, and I put it away again. The boy watched me with wide eyes.

Terminus Est had been bloodied to her guard and beyond. I sat upon a fallen tree and cleaned her with the rotting wood while I debated what to do, then whetted and oiled her blade. I cared nothing for the zoanthrops or the alzabo, but to leave Casdoe's body, and the old man's, to be dismembered by beasts seemed a vile thing.

Prudence warned against it as well. What if another alzabo should come, and when it had glutted itself upon Casdoe's flesh set off after the boy? I considered carrying them both back to the cabin. It was a considerable distance, however; I could not carry the two together, and it seemed sure that whichever I left behind would be violated by the time I returned for it. Drawn by the sight of so much blood, the carrion-eating teratornises were already circling overhead, each borne on wings as wide as the main yard of a caravel.

For a time I probed the ground, seeking some place soft enough that I might dig it with Casdoe's staff; in the end, I carried both bodies to a stretch of rocky ground near a watercourse, and there built a cairn over them. Under it they would lie, I hoped, for nearly a year, until the melting of the snows, at about the time of the feast of Holy Katharine, should sweep the bones of daughter and father away.

Little Severian, who had only watched at first, had himself carried small stones before the cairn was complete. When we were washing ourselves of grit and sweat in the stream, he asked, "Are you my uncle?"

I told him, "I'm your father—for now, at least. When someone's father dies, he must have a new one, if he's as young as you are. I'm the man."

He nodded, lost in thought; and quite suddenly I recalled how I had dreamed, only two nights before, of a world in which all the people knew themselves bound by ties of blood, being all descended from the same pair of colonists. I, who did not know my own mother's name, or my father's, might very well be related to this child whose name was my own, or for that matter to anyone I met. The world of which I had dreamed had been, for me, the bed on which I had lain. I wish I could describe how serious we were there by the laughing stream, how solemn and clean he looked with his wet face and the droplets sparkling in the lashes of his wide eyes.

XVIII

Severian and Severian

I drank as much water as I could, and told the boy that he must do so as well, that there were many dry places in the mountains, and that we might not drink again until next morning. He had asked if we would not go home now; and though I had planned until then to retrace our route back to the house that had been Casdoe's and Becan's, I said we would not, because I knew it would be too terrible for him to see that roof again, and the field and the little garden, and then to leave them for a second time. At his age he might even suppose that his father and his mother, his sister and his grandfather were somehow still inside.

Yet we could not descend much farther—we were already well below the level at which travel was dangerous for me. The arm of the archon of Thrax stretched a hundred leagues and more, and now there was every chance that Agia would put his dimarchi on my trail.

To the northeast stood the highest peak I had yet seen. Not only its head but its shoulders too bore a shroud of snow, which descended nearly to its waist. I could not say, and perhaps no one now could, what proud face it was that stared westward over so many lesser summits; but surely he had ruled in the earliest of the greatest days of humanity, and had commanded energies that could shape granite as a carver's knife does wood. Looking at his image, it seemed to me that even the hard-bitten dimarchi, who knew the wild uplands so well, might stand in awe of him. And so we made for him, or rather for the high pass that linked the folded drapery of his robe to the mountain where Becan had once established a home. For the time being, the climbs were not severe, and we spent far more effort in walking than in climbing.

The boy Severian held my hand often when there was no need of my support. I am no great judge of the ages of children, but he seemed to me to be about of that growth when, if he had been one of our apprentices, he would first have entered Master Palaemon's schoolroom—that is to say, he was old enough to walk well, and to talk sufficiently to understand and to make himself understood.

For a watch or more he said nothing beyond what I have already related. Then, as we were descending an open, grassy slope bordered by pines, a place much like that in which his mother had died, he asked, "Severian, who were those men?"

I knew whom he meant. "They were not men, although they were once men and still resemble men. They were zoanthrops, a word that indicates those beasts that are of human shape. Do you understand what I am saying?"

The little boy nodded solemnly, then asked, "Why don't they wear clothes?"

"Because they are no longer human beings, as I told you. A dog is born a dog and a bird is born a bird, but to become a human being is an achievement—you have to think about it. You have been thinking about it for the past three or four years at least, little Severian, even though you may never have thought about the thinking."

"A dog just looks for things to eat," the boy said.

"Exactly. But that raises the question of whether a person should be forced to do such thinking, and some people decided a long time ago that he should not. We may force a dog, sometimes, to act like a man—to walk on his hind legs and wear a collar and so forth. But we shouldn't and couldn't force a man to act like a man. Did you ever want to fall asleep? When you weren't sleepy or even tired?"

He nodded.

"That was because you wanted to put down the burden of being a boy, at least for a time. Sometimes I drink too much wine, and that is because for a while I would like to stop being a man. Sometimes people take their own lives for that reason. Did you know that?"

"Or they do things that might hurt them," he said. The way he said it told me of arguments overheard; Becan had very probably been that kind of man, or he would not have taken his family to so remote and dangerous a place.

"Yes," I told him. "That can be the same thing. And sometimes certain men, and even women, come to hate the burden of thought, but without loving death. They see the animals and wish to become as they are, answering only to instinct, and not thinking. Do you know what makes you think, little Severian?"

"My head," the boy said promptly, and grasped it with his hands.

"Animals have heads too—even very stupid animals like crayfish and oxen and ticks. What makes you think is only a small part of your head, inside, just above your eyes.'' I touched his forehead. ''Now if for some reason you wanted one of your hands taken off, there are men you can go to who are skilled in doing that. Suppose, for example, your hand had suffered some hurt from which it would never be well. They could take it away in such a fashion that there would be little chance of any harm coming to the rest of you.''

The boy nodded.

''Very well. Those same men can take away that little part of your head that makes you think. They cannot put it back, you understand. And even if they could, you couldn't ask them to do it, once that part was gone. But sometimes people pay these men to take that part away. They want to stop thinking forever, and often they say they wish to turn their backs on all that humanity has done. Then it is no longer just to treat them as human beings—they have become animals, though animals who are still of human shape. You asked why they did not wear clothes. They no longer understand clothes, and so they would not put them on, even if they were very cold, although they might lie down on them or even roll themselves up in them.''

''Are you like that, a little bit?'' the boy asked, and pointed to my bare chest.

The thought he was suggesting had never occurred to me before, and for a moment I was taken aback. ''It's the rule of my guild,'' I said. ''I haven't had any part of my head taken away, if that's what you're asking, and I used to wear a shirt . . . But, yes, I suppose I am a little like that, because I never thought of it, even when I was very cold.''

His expression told me I had confirmed his suspicions. ''Is that why you're running away?''

''No, that's not why I'm running away. If anything, I suppose you could say it is the other side of it. Perhaps that part of my head has grown too large. But you're right about the zoanthrops, that is why they are in the mountains. When a man becomes an animal, he becomes a dangerous animal, and animals like that cannot be tolerated in more settled places, where there are farms and many people. So they are driven to these mountains, or brought here by their old friends, or by someone they paid to do it before they discarded the power of human thought. They can still think a little, of course, as all animals can. Enough to find food in the wild, though many die each winter. Enough to throw stones as monkeys throw nuts, and use their clubs, and even to hunt for mates, for there are females among them as I said. Their sons and daughters seldom live long, however, and I suppose that is for the best, because they are born just as you were—and I was—with the burden of thought."

That burden lay heavily on me when we had finished speaking; so heavily indeed that for the first time I truly understood that it could be as great a curse to others as memory has sometimes been to me.

I have never been greatly sensitive to beauty, but the beauty of the sky and the mountainside were such that it seemed they colored all my musings, so that I felt I nearly grasped ungraspable things. When Master Malrubius had appeared to me after our first performance of Dr. Talos's play—something I could not then understand and still could not understand, though I grew more confident that it had occurred, and not less—he had spoken to me of the circularity of governance, though I had no concern with governance. Now it struck me that the will itself was governed, and if not by reason, then by things below or above it. Yet it was very difficult to say on what side of reason these things lay. Instinct, surely, lay below it; but might it not be above it as well? When the alzabo rushed at the zoanthrops, its instinct commanded it to preserve its prey from others; when Becan did so, his instinct, I believe, was to preserve his wife and child. Both performed the same act, and they actually performed it in the same body. Did the higher and the lower instinct join hands at the back of reason? Or is there but one instinct standing behind all reason, so that reason sees a hand to either side?

But is instinct truly that "attachment to the person of the monarch" which Master Malrubius implied was at once the highest and the lowest form of governance? For clearly, instinct itself cannot have arisen out of nothing—the hawks that soared over our heads built their nests, doubtless, by instinct; yet there must have been a time in which nests were not built, and the first hawk to build one cannot have inherited its instinct to build from its parents, since they did not possess it. Nor could such an instinct have developed slowly, a thousand generations of hawks fetching one stick before some hawk fetched two; because neither one stick nor two could be of the slightest use to the nesting hawks. Perhaps that which came before instinct was the highest as well as the lowest principle of the governance of the will. Perhaps not. The wheeling birds traced their hieroglyphics in the air, but they were not for me to read.

As we approached the saddle that joined the mountain to that other even loftier one I have described, we seemed to move across the face of all Urth, tracing a line from pole to equator; indeed the surface over which we crawled like ants might have been the globe itself turned inside out. Far behind us and far ahead of us loomed the broad, gleaming fields of snow. Below them lay stony slopes like the shore of the ice-bound southern sea. Below these were high meadows of coarse grass, now dotted with wildflowers; I remembered well those over which I had passed the day before, and beneath the blue haze that wreathed the mountain ahead I could discern their band upon the chest, like a green fourragere; beneath it the pines shone so darkly as to appear black.

The saddle to which we descended was quite different, an expanse of montane forest where glossy-leaved hardwoods lifted sickly heads three hundred cubits toward the dying sun. Among them their dead brothers remained upright, supported by the living and wrapped in winding sheets of lianas. Near the little stream where we halted for the night the vegetation had already lost most of its mountain delicacy and was acquiring something of the lushness of the lowlands; and now that we were sufficiently near the saddle for him to have a clear view of it, and his attention was no longer monopolized by the need to walk and climb, the boy pointed and asked if we were going down there.

"Tomorrow," I said. "It will be dark soon, and I would like to get through that jungle in a day."

His eyes widened at the word *jungle*. "Is it dangerous?"

"I don't really know. From what I heard in Thrax, the insects shouldn't be nearly as bad as they are in lower places, and we're not likely to be troubled by blood bats there—a friend of mine was bitten by a blood bat once, and it's not very pleasant. But that's where the big apes are, and there will be hunting cats and so on."

"And wolfs."

"And wolves, of course. Only there are wolves high up too. As high as your house was, and much higher."

The moment I mentioned his old home I regretted it, for something of the joy in living that had been returning to his face went out of it with the word. For a moment he seemed lost in thought. Then he said, "When those men—"

"Zoanthrops."

He nodded. "When the zoanthrops came and hurt Mama, did you come to help as quick as you could?"

"Yes," I said. "I came as quickly as I could make myself come." It was true, at least in some sense, but nevertheless it was painful to say.

"Good," he said. I had spread a blanket for him, and he lay down on it now. I folded it over him. "The stars got brighter, didn't they? They get brighter when the sun goes away."

I lay beside him looking up. "It doesn't go away, really. Urth just swings her face away, so that we think it does. If you don't look at me, I don't go away, even though you don't see me."

"If the sun is still there, why do the stars shine harder?"

His voice told me he was pleased with his own cleverness in argument, and I was pleased with it too; I suddenly understood why Master Palaemon had enjoyed talking with me when I was a child. I said, "A candle flame is almost invisible in bright sunshine, and the stars, which are really suns themselves, seem to fade in the same way. Pictures painted in the ancient days, when our sun was brighter, appear to show that the stars could not be seen at all until twilight. The old legends—I have a brown book in my sabretache that tells many of them—are full of magic beings who vanish slowly and reappear in the same way. No doubt those stories are based on the look of the stars then."

He pointed. "There's the hydra."

"I think you're right," I said. "Do you know any others?"

He showed me the cross and the great bull, and I pointed out my amphisbaena, and several others.

"And there's the wolf, over by the unicorn. There's a little wolf too, but I can't find him."

We discovered it together, near the horizon.

"They're like us, aren't they? The big wolf and the little wolf. We're big Severian and little Severian."

I agreed that was so, and he stared up at the stars for a long time, chewing the piece of dried meat I had given him. Then he said, "Where is the book with stories in it?"

I showed it to him.

"We had a book too, and sometimes Mama would read to Severa and me."

"She was your sister, wasn't she?"

He nodded. "We were twins. Big Severian, did you ever have a sister?"

"I don't know. My family is all dead. They've been dead since I was a baby. What kind of story would you like?"

He asked to see the book, and I gave it to him. After he had turned a few pages he returned it to me. "It's not like ours."

"I didn't think it was."

"See if you can find a story with a boy in it who has a big friend, and a twin. There should be wolfs in it."

I did the best I could, reading rapidly to outrace the fading light.

XIX

The Tale of the Boy Called Frog

Part I

Early Summer and Her Son

On a mountaintop beyond the shores of Urth there once lived a lovely woman named Early Summer. She was the queen of that land, but her king was a strong, unforgiving man, and because she was jealous of him he was jealous of her in turn, and killed any man he believed to be her lover.

One day Early Summer was walking in her garden when she saw a most beautiful blossom of a kind wholly new to her. It was redder than any rose and more sweetly perfumed, but its strong stalk was thornless and smooth as ivory. She plucked it and carried it to a secluded spot, and as she reclined there contemplating it, it grew to seem to her no blossom at all but such a lover as she had longed for, powerful and yet as tender as a kiss. Certain of the juices of the plant entered her and she conceived. She told the king, however, that the child was his, and since she was well guarded, he believed her.

It was a boy, and by his mother's wish he was called Spring Wind. At his birth all those who study the stars were gathered to cast his horoscope, not only those who lived upon the mountaintop, but many of the greatest of Urth's magi. Long they labored over their charts, and nine times met in solemn conclave; and at last they announced that in battle Spring Wind would be irresistible, and that no child of his would die before it had reached full growth. These prophecies pleased the king much.

As Spring Wind grew, his mother saw with secret pleasure that he delighted most in field and flower and fruit. Every green thing thrived under his hand, and it was the pruning knife he desired to hold, and not the sword. But when he was grown a young man, war came, and he took up his spear and his shield. Because he was quiet in demeanor and obedient to the king (whom he believed to be his father, and who believed himself to be the father), many supposed the prophecy would prove false. It was not so. In the heat of battle he fought coolly, his daring well judged and his caution sober; no general was more fertile of stratagems and sleights than he was, and no officer more attentive to every duty. The soldiers he led against the king's enemies were drilled until they seemed men of bronze quickened with fire, and their loyalty to him was such that they would have followed him to the World of Shadows, the realm farthest from the sun. Then men said it was the spring wind that threw down towers, and the spring wind that capsized ships, though that was not what Early Summer had intended.

Now it happened that the chances of war often brought Spring Wind to Urth, and there he came to know of two brothers who were kings. Of these, the elder had several sons, but the younger only a single daughter, a girl named Bird of the Wood. When this girl became a woman, her father was slain; and her uncle, in order that she might never breed sons who would claim their grandfather's kingdom, entered her name on the roll of the virgin priestesses. This displeased Spring Wind, because the princess was beautiful and her father had been his friend. One day it happened that he had gone alone into the world of Urth, and there he saw Bird of the Wood sleeping beside a stream, and woke her with his kisses.

Of their coupling were engendered twin sons, but though the priestesses of her order had aided Bird of the Wood in concealing their growth in her womb from the king, her uncle, they could not hide the babes. Before Bird of the Wood ever saw them, the priestesses placed them in a winnowing basket lined with blankets of featherwork and carried them to the bank of that same stream where Spring Wind had surprised her, and launching the basket in the water went away.

Part II

How Frog Found a New Mother

Far that basket sailed, over fresh waters and salt. Other children would have died, but the sons of Spring Wind could not die, because they were not yet grown. The armored monsters of the water splashed about their basket and the apes threw sticks and nuts into it, but it drifted ever onward until at last it came to a bank whereon two poor sisters were washing clothes. These good women saw it and shouted, and when shouting availed nothing, tucked their skirts into their belts and waded into the river and brought it to shore.

Because they had been found in the water, the boys were named Fish and Frog, and when the sisters had showed them to their husbands, and it was seen that they were children of remarkable strength and handsomeness, each sister chose one. Now the sister who chose Fish was the wife of a herdsman, and the husband of the sister who chose Frog was a woodcutter.

This sister cared well for Frog and suckled him at her own breast, for it so happened that she had recently lost a child of her own. She carried him slung behind her in a shawl when her husband went into the wild lands to cut firewood, and thus it is said by the weavers of lore that she was the strongest of all women, for she carried an empire on her back.

A year passed, and at the end of it, Frog had learned to stand upright and take a few steps. One night the woodcutter and his wife were sitting beside their own little fire in a clearing in the wild lands; and while the woodcutter's wife prepared their supper, Frog walked naked to the fire and stood warming himself before the flames. Then the woodcutter, who was a gruff, kindly man, asked him, "Do you like that?" and though he had never spoken before, Frog nodded and answered, "Red flower." At that, it is said, Early Summer stirred upon her bed on the mountaintop beyond the shores of Urth.

The woodcutter and his wife were astonished, but they had no time to tell each other what had happened, or to try to persuade Frog to speak again, or even to rehearse what they would say to the herdsman and his wife when next they met them. For there came then into the clearing a dreadful sound—those who have listened say it is the most frightening on the world of Urth. So few who have heard it have lived that it has no name, but it is something like the hum of bees, and something like the sound a cat might make if a cat were larger than a cow, and something like the noise the voice-throwers learn first to make, a droning in the throat that seems to come from everywhere at once. It was the song a smilodon sings when he has crept close to his prey, the song that frightens even mastodons so much they often charge in the wrong direction and are stabbed from behind.

Surely the Pancreator knows all mysteries. He spoke the long word that is our universe, and few things happen that are not a part of that word. By his will, then, there rose a knoll not far from the fire, where there had been a great tomb in the most ancient days; and though the poor woodcutter and his wife knew nothing of it, two wolves had built their home there, a house low of roof and thick of wall, with galleries lit by green lamps descending among the ruined memorials and broken urns, a house, that is, such as wolves love. There the he-wolf sat sucking at the thigh-bone of a coryphodon, and the she-wolf, his wife, held her cubs to her breasts.

From near they heard the smilodon's song and cursed it in the Gray Language as wolves can curse, for no lawful beast hunts near the home of another of the hunting kind, and wolves are on good terms with the moon.

When the curse was finished, the she-wolf said, "What prey can that be, that the Butcher, that stupid killer of river-horses, has found, when you, O my husband, who wind the lizards that frisk on the rocks of the mountains that lie beyond Urth, have been content to worry a parched stick?"

"I do not devour carrion," the he-wolf answered shortly. "Nor do I pull worms from the morning grass, nor angle for frogs in the shallows."

"No more does the Butcher sing for them," said his wife.

Then the he-wolf raised his head and sniffed the air. "He hunts the son of Meschia and the daughter of Meschiane, and you know no good can come of such meat." At this the she-wolf nodded, for she knew that alone among the living creatures, the sons of Meschia kill all when one of their own is slain. That is because the Pancreator gave Urth to them, and they have rejected the gift.

His song ended, the Butcher roared so as to shake the leaves from the trees; then he screamed, for the curses of wolves are strong curses so long as the moon shines.

"How has he come to grief?" asked the she-wolf, who was licking the face of one of her daughters.

The he-wolf sniffed again. "Burnt flesh! He has leaped into their fire." He and his wife laughed as wolves do, silently, showing all their teeth; their ears stood up as tents stand in the desert, for they were listening to the Butcher as he blundered through the thickets looking for his prey.

Now the door of the wolves' house stood open, because when either of the grown wolves were at home they did not care who entered, and fewer departed than came in. It had been full of moonlight (for the moon is always a welcome guest in the houses of wolves) but it grew dark. A child stood there, somewhat fearful, it may be, of the darkness, but smelling the strong smell of milk. The he-wolf snarled, but the she-wolf called in her most motherly voice, "Come in, little son of Meschia. Here you may drink, and be warm and clean. Here are the bright-eyed, quick-footed playmates, the best in all the world."

Hearing this, the boy entered, and the she-wolf put down her milk-gorged cubs and took him to her breast.

"What good is such a creature?" said the he-wolf.

The she-wolf laughed. "You can suck at a bone of the last moon's kill and ask that? Do you not remember when war raged hereabouts, and the armies of Prince Spring Wind scoured the land? Then no son of Meschia hunted us, for they hunted one another. After their battles we came out, you and I and all the Senate of Wolves, and even the Butcher, and He Who Laughs, and the Black Killer, and we moved among the dead and dying, choosing what we wished."

"That is true," said the he-wolf. "Prince Spring Wind did great things for us. But that cub of Meschia's is not he."

The she-wolf only smiled and said, "I smell the battle smoke in the fur of his head, and upon his skin." (It was the smoke of the Red Flower.) "You and I shall be dust when the first column marches from the gate of his wall, but that first shall breed a thousand more to feed our children and their children, and their children's children."

The he-wolf nodded to this, for he knew that the she-wolf was wiser than he, and even as he could sniff out things that lay beyond the shores of Urth, so could she see the days beyond the next year's rains.

"I shall call him Frog," said the she-wolf. "For indeed the Butcher angled for frogs, as you said, O my husband." She believed that she said this in compliment to the he-wolf, because he had so readily acquiesced to her wishes; but the truth was that the blood of the people of the mountaintop beyond Urth ran in Frog, and the names of those who bear the blood cannot be concealed for long.

Outside wild laughter pealed. It was the voice of He Who Laughs, calling, "It is there, Lord! There, there, there! Here, here, here is the spoor! It went in at the door!"

"You see," the he-wolf remarked, "what comes of mentioning evil. To name is to call. That is the law." And he got down his sword and fingered the edge.

The doorway was darkened again. It was a narrow doorway, for none but fools and temples have wide doors, and wolves are no fools; Frog had filled most of it. Now the Butcher filled it all, turning his shoulders to get in, and stooping his great head. Because the wall was so thick, the doorway was like a passage.

"What seek you?" asked the he-wolf, and he licked the flat of his blade.

"What is my own, and only that," said the Butcher. Smilodons fight with a curved knife in either hand, and he was much larger than the he-wolf, but he did not wish to have to engage him in that close place.

"It was never yours," said the she-wolf. Setting Frog on the floor, she came so near the Butcher that he might have struck at her if he dared. Her eyes flashed fire. "The hunt was unlawful, for an unlawful prey. Now he has drunk of me and is a wolf forever, sacred to the moon."

"I have seen dead wolves," said the Butcher.

"Yes, and eaten their flesh, though it were too foul for the flies, I dare say. It may be you shall eat mine, if a falling tree kill me."

"You say he is a wolf. He must be brought before the Senate." The Butcher licked his lips, but with a dry tongue. He would have faced the he-wolf in the open, perhaps; but he had no heart to face the pair together, and he knew that if he gained the doorway they would snatch up Frog and retreat to the passages below ground among the tumbled ashlars of the tomb, where the she-wolf would soon be behind him.

"And what have you to do with the Senate of Wolves?" the she-wolf asked.

"Perhaps as much as he," said the Butcher, and went to look for easier meat.

Part III

The Black Killer's Gold

The senate of wolves meets under each full moon. All come who can, for it is assumed that any who do not come plot treachery, offering, perhaps, to guard the cattle of the sons of Meschia in return for scraps. The wolf who is absent for two Senates must stand trial when he returns, and he is killed by the she-wolves if the Senate finds him guilty.

Cubs too must come before the Senate, so that any grown wolf who wishes may inspect them to assure himself that their father was a true wolf. (Sometimes a she-wolf lies with a dog for spite, but though the sons of dogs often look much like wolf cubs, they have always a spot of white on them somewhere, for white was the color of Meschia, who remembered the pure light of the Pancreator; and his sons leave it still for a brand on all they touch.)

Thus the she-wolf stood before the Senate of Wolves at the full moon, and her cubs played before her feet, and Frog—who looked a frog indeed when the moonlight through the windows stained his skin green—stood beside her and clung to the fur of her skirt. The President of the Pack sat in the highest seat, and if he was surprised to see a son of Meschia brought before the Senate, his ears did not show it. He sang:

> ''Here are the five!
> The sons and daughters born alive!
> If they be false, say how-ow-ow!
> If ye would speak, speak now-ow-ow!''

When the cubs are brought before the Senate, their parents may not defend them if they are challenged; but at any other time it is murder if any other seek to harm them.

''Speak NOW-OW-OW!'' The walls echoed it back, so that in the huts in the valley the sons of Meschia barricaded their doors, and the daughters of Meschiane clutched their own children.

Then the Butcher, who had been waiting behind the last wolf, came forward. ''Why do you delay?'' he said. ''I am not clever—I am too strong for cleverness, as you well understand. But there are four wolf cubs here, and a fifth that is not a wolf but my prey.''

At this the he-wolf asked, ''What right has *he* to speak here? Surely *he* is no wolf.''

A dozen voices answered, ''Anyone may speak, if a wolf asks his testimony. Speak, Butcher!''

Then the she-wolf loosened her sword in the scabbard and prepared for her last fight if it came to fighting. A demon she looked with her gaunt face and blazing eyes, for an angel is often only a demon who stands between us and our enemy.

''You say I am no wolf,'' continued the Butcher. ''And you say rightly. We know how a wolf smells, and the sound and look of a wolf. That wolf has taken this son of Meschia for her cub, but we all know that having a wolf for a mother does not make a cub a wolf.''

The he-wolf shouted, ''Wolves are those whose mothers and fathers are wolves! I take this cub as my son!''

There was laughter at that, and when it died, one strange voice laughed on. It was He Who Laughs, come to advise the Butcher before the Senate of Wolves. He called, ''Many have talked so, ho, ho! But their cubs have fed the pack.''

The Butcher said, ''They were killed for their white fur. The skin is under the fur. How can this live? Give it to me!''

''Two must speak,'' the President announced. ''That is the law. Who speaks for the cub here? It is a son of Meschia, but is it also a wolf? Two who are not its parents must speak for it.''

Then the Naked One, who is counted a member of the Senate for teaching the young wolves, rose. ''I have never had a son of Meschia to teach,'' he said. ''I may learn something from it. I speak for him.''

''Another,'' said the President. ''Another must also speak.''

There was only silence. Then the Black Killer strode from the back of the hall. Everyone fears the Black Killer, for though his cloak is as soft as the fur of the youngest cub, his eyes burn in the night. ''Two who are no wolves have spoken here already,'' he said. ''May I not speak also? I have gold.'' He held up a purse.

''Speak! Speak!'' called a hundred voices.

''The law says also that a cub's life may be bought,'' said the Black Killer, and he poured gold into his hand, and so ransomed an empire.

Part IV

The Plowing of the Fish

If all the adventures of Frog were told—how he lived among the wolves, and learned to hunt and fight, it would fill many books. But those who bear the blood of the people of the mountaintop beyond Urth always feel its call at last; and the time came when he carried fire into the Senate of Wolves and said, ''Here is the Red Flower. In his name I rule.'' And when no one opposed him he led forth the wolves and called them the people of his kingdom, and soon men came to him as well as wolves, and though he was still only a boy, he seemed always taller than the men about him, for he bore the blood of Early Summer.

One night when the wild roses were opening, she came to him in a dream and told him of his mother, Bird of the Wood, and of her father and her uncle, and of his brother. He found his brother, who had become a herdsman, and with the wolves and the Black Killer and many men they went to the king and demanded their heritage. He was old and his sons had died without sons, and he gave it to them, and of it Fish took the city and the farmlands, and Frog the wild hills.

But the number of the men who followed him grew. They stole women from other peoples, and bred children, and when the wolves were no longer needed and returned to the wilds, Frog judged his people should have a city to dwell in, with walls to protect them when the men were at war. He went to the herds of Fish and took a white cow and a white bull therefrom and harnessed them to a plow, and with them plowed a furrow that should mark the wall. Fish came to seek the return of his cattle while the people were preparing to build. When Frog's people showed him the furrow and told him it was to be their wall, he laughed and jumped over it; and they, knowing that small things mocked can never grow large, slew him. But he was then a man grown, so the prophecy made at the birth of Spring Wind was fulfilled.

When Frog saw the dead Fish, he buried him in the furrow to assure the fertility of the land. For so he had been taught by the Naked One, who was also called the Savage, or Squanto.

XX

The Circle of the Sorcerers

By the first light of morning we entered the mountain jungle as one enters a house. Behind us the sunlight played on grass and bushes and stones; we passed through a curtain of tangled vines so thick I had to cut it with my sword and saw before us only shadow and the towering boles of the trees. No insect buzzed within, and no bird chirped. No wind stirred. At first the bare soil we trod was almost as stony as the mountain slopes, but before we had walked a league it grew smoother, and at last we came to a short stair that had surely been carved with the spade. "Look," said the boy, and he pointed to something red and strangely shaped that lay upon the uppermost step.

I stopped to look at it. It was a cock's head; needles of some dark metal had been run through its eyes, and it held a strip of cast snakeskin in its bill.

"What is it?" The boy's eyes were wide.

"A charm, I think."

"Left here by a witch? What does it mean?"

I tried to recall what little I knew of the false art. As a child, Thecla had been in the care of a nursemaid who tied and untied knots to speed childbirth and claimed to see the face of Thecla's future husband (was it mine, I wonder?) at midnight, reflected in a platter that had held bridal cake.

"The cock," I told the boy, "is the herald of day, and in a magical sense his crow at dawn can be said to bring the sun. He has been blinded, perhaps, so that he will not know when dawn appears. A snake's casting of his skin means cleansing or rejuvenation. The blinded cock holds onto the old skin."

"But what does it mean?" the boy asked again.

I said I did not know; but in my heart I felt sure it was a charm against the coming of the New Sun, and it somehow pained me to find that renewal, for which I had hoped so fervently when I was a boy myself, but in which I hardly believed, should be opposed by anyone. At the same time, I was conscious that I bore the Claw. Enemies of the New Sun would surely destroy the Claw, should it fall into their hands.

Before we had gone another hundred paces, there were strips of red cloth suspended from the trees; some of these were plain, but others had been written over in black in a character I did not understand—or as seemed more likely, with symbols and ideographs of the sort those who pretend to more knowledge than they possess use in imitation of the writing of the astronomers.

''We had better go back,'' I said. ''Or go around.''

I had no sooner spoken than I heard a rustling behind me. For a moment I truly thought the figures that stepped onto the path were devils, huge-eyed and striped with black, white, and scarlet; then I saw that they were only naked men with painted bodies. Their hands were fitted with steel talons, which they held up to show me. I drew *Terminus Est*.

''We will not hinder you,'' one said. ''Go. Leave us, if you wish.'' It seemed to me that beneath the paint he had the pale skin and fair hair of the south.

''You would be well advised not to. With this long blade I could kill you both before you touched me.''

''Go, then,'' the blond man told me. ''If you have no objection to leaving the child with us.''

At that I looked around for little Severian. He had somehow vanished from my side.

''If you wish him returned to you, however, you will surrender your sword to me and come with us.'' Showing no sign of fear, the painted man walked up to me and extended his hands. The steel talons emerged from between his fingers, being fastened to a narrow bar of iron he held in his palm. ''I will not ask again,'' he said.

I sheathed the blade, then took off the baldric that held the sheath and handed the whole to him.

He closed his eyes. Their lids had been painted with dark dots rimmed with white, like the markings of certain caterpillars that would have the birds think them snakes. ''This has drunk much blood.''

''Yes,'' I said.

His eyes opened again, and he regarded me with an unblinking stare. His painted face—like that of the other, who stood just behind him—

was as expressionless as a mask. "A newly forged sword would have little power here, but this might do harm."

"I trust it will be returned to me when my son and I leave. What have you done with him?"

There was no reply. The two walked around me, one to either side, and went down the path in the direction the boy and I had been going. After a moment I followed them.

I might call the place to which they led me a village, but it was not a village in the ordinary sense, not such a village as Saltus, or even a place like the clusters of autochthon huts that are sometimes called villages. Here the trees were greater, and farther separated, than I had ever seen forest trees before, and the canopy of their leaves formed an impenetrable roof several hundred cubits overhead. So great indeed were these trees that they seemed to have been growing for whole ages; a stair led to a door in the trunk of one, which had been pierced for windows. There was a house of several stories built upon the branches of another, and a thing like a great oriole's nest swung from the limbs of a third. Open hatches showed that the ground at our feet was mined.

I was taken to one of these hatches and told to descend a crude ladder that led into darkness. For a moment (I do not know why) I feared that it might go very far, into such deep caverns as lay beneath the man-apes' nighted treasure house. It was not so. After descending what was surely not more than four times my height and clambering through what then seemed to be ruined matting, I found myself in a subterranean room.

The hatch had been shut over my head, leaving everything dark. Groping, I explored the place and found it to be about three paces by four. The floor and walls were of earth, and the ceiling of unpeeled logs; there were no furnishings whatsoever.

We had been taken at about mid morning. In seven watches more, it would be dark. Before that time it might be that I would find myself led into the presence of someone in authority. If so, I would do what I could to persuade him that the child and I were harmless and should be let go in peace. If not, then I would climb the ladder again and see if I could not break out of the hatch. I sat down to wait.

I am certain I did not sleep; but I used the facility I have for calling forth past time, and so, at least in spirit, left that dark place. For a time I watched the animals in the necropolis beyond the Citadel wall, as I had as a boy. I saw the geese shape arrowheads against the sky, and the comings and goings of fox and rabbit. They raced across the grass for me once more, and in time left their tracks in snow. Triskele lay dead, as it seemed, on the refuse behind the Bear Tower; I went to him, saw him shudder and lift his head to lick my hand. I sat with Thecla in her narrow cell, where we read aloud to each other and stopped to argue what we had read. "The world runs down like a clock," she said. "The Increate is dead, and who will recreate him? Who could?"

"Surely clocks are supposed to stop when their owners die."

"That's superstition." She took the book from my hands so she could hold them in her own, which were long-fingered and very cold. "When the owner is on his deathbed, no one pours in fresh water. He dies, and his nurses look at the dial to note the time. Later they find it stopped, and the time is the same."

I told her, "You're saying that it stops before the owner; so if the universe is running down now, that does not mean that the Increate is dead—only that he never existed."

"But he is ill. Look around you. See this place, and the towers above you. Do you know, Severian, that you never have?"

"He could still tell someone else to fill the mechanism again," I suggested, and then, realizing what I had said, blushed.

Thecla laughed. "I haven't seen you do that since I took off my gown for you the first time. I laid your hands on my breasts, and you went red as a berry. Do you remember? Tell somebody to fill it? Where is the young atheist now?"

I put my hand upon her thigh. "Confused, as he was then, by the presence of divinity."

"You don't believe in me then? I think you're right. I must be what you young torturers dream of—a beautiful prisoner, as yet unmutilated, who calls on you to slake her lust."

Trying to be gallant I said, "Such dreams as you lie beyond my power."

"Surely not, since I am in your power now."

Something was in the cell with us. I looked at the barred door and Thecla's lamp with its silver reflector, then into all the corners. The cell grew darker, and Thecla and even I myself vanished with the light, but the thing that had intruded upon my memory of us did not.

"Who are you," I asked, "and what do you wish with us?"

"You know well who we are, and we know who you are." The voice was cool and, I think, perhaps the most authoritative I have ever heard. The Autarch himself did not speak so.

"Who am I, then?"

"Severian of Nessus, the lictor of Thrax."

"I am Severian of Nessus," I said. "But I am no longer lictor of Thrax."

"So you would have us believe."

There was silence again, and after a time I understood that my interrogator would not question me, but rather would force me, if I desired my freedom, to explain myself to him. I wanted greatly to seize him—he could not have been more than a few cubits away—but I knew that in all likelihood he was armed with the steel talons the guards on the path had shown me. I wanted also, as I had for some time, to draw the Claw from its leathern sack, though nothing could have been more foolish. I said, "The archon of Thrax wished me to kill a certain woman. I freed her instead, and had to flee the city."

"By magic passing the posts of the soldiers."

I had always believed all self-proclaimed wonder-workers to be frauds; now something in my interrogator's voice suggested that even as they attempted to deceive others, so they might deceive themselves. There was mockery in it, but it was mockery of me, not of magic. "Perhaps," I said. "What do you know of my powers?"

"That they are insufficient to free you from this place."

"I have not attempted to free myself, and yet I have already been free."

That disturbed him. "You were not free. You merely brought the woman here in spirit!"

I let my breath out, trying to keep the sigh inaudible. In the antechamber of the House Absolute, a little girl had once mistaken me for a tall woman, when Thecla had for a time displaced my own personality. Now, it seemed, the remembered Thecla must have spoken through my mouth. I said, "Surely I am a necromancer then, who can command the spirits of the dead. For that woman is dead."

"You told us you freed her."

"Another woman, who only slightly resembled that one. What have you done to my son?"

"He does not call you his father."

"He suffers fancies," I said.

There was no reply. After a time I rose and ran my hands once more over the walls of my underground prison; they were of plain earth, as before. I had seen no light and heard no sound, but it seemed to me that it would have been possible to cover the hatch with some portable structure to exclude the day, and if the hatch were skillfully constructed, it might be lifted silently. I mounted the first rung of the ladder; it creaked beneath my weight.

I climbed a step up, and another, and it creaked at each. I tried to rise to the fourth rung, and felt my scalp and shoulders prodded as though with the points of daggers. A trickle of blood from my right ear wet my neck.

I retreated to the third rung and groped overhead. The thing that had seemed like a torn mat when I entered the underground chamber proved to be a score or more of sharp bamboo splittings, anchored somehow in the shaft with their points directed down. I had descended with ease because my body had forced them to one side; now they prevented me from ascending much as the barbs on a fish spear prevent the fish from getting away. I took hold of one and tried to break it, but though I might have done so with both hands, it was impossible with one. Given light and time I might have worked my way through them; light perhaps I might have had, but I did not dare to take the risk. I jumped to the floor again.

Another circuit of the room told me no more than I had known before, yet it seemed beyond credence that my questioner had climbed the ladder without making a sound, though he might perhaps possess some special knowledge that would permit him to pass through the bamboo. I went about the floor on my hands and knees, and learned no more than before.

I attempted to move the ladder, but it was fixed in position; so beginning at the corner nearest the shaft, I jumped and touched the wall at a point as high as I could reach, then moved half a step to one side and jumped again. When I had arrived at a place that must have been more or less opposite the spot where I had been sitting, I found it: a rectangular hole perhaps a cubit high and two across, with its lower edge slightly higher than my head. My interrogator might have climbed from it silently, perhaps with the aid of a rope, and returned the same way; but it seemed more likely that he had merely thrust his head and shoulders through, so that his voice had sounded as if he were truly in the room with me. I gripped the edge of the hole as well as I could, jumped, and pulled myself up.

XXI

The Duel of Magic

The chamber beyond the one in which I had been imprisoned seemed much like it, though its floor was higher. It was, of course, utterly dark; but now that I was confident I was no longer being observed, I took the Claw from its sack and looked about me by its light which was, though not bright, sufficient.

There was no ladder, but a narrow door gave access to what I assumed was a third subterranean room. Concealing the Claw again, I stepped through it, but found myself instead in a tunnel no wider than the doorway, which turned and turned again before I had taken half a dozen strides. At first I supposed it was simply a baffled passage to prevent light from betraying the opening in the wall of the room where I had been confined. But no more than three turns should have been necessary. The walls seemed to bend and divide; yet I remained in impenetrable darkness. I took out the Claw once more.

Perhaps because of the confined space in which I stood, it seemed somewhat brighter; but there was nothing to see beyond what my hands had already told me. I was alone. I stood in a maze with earthen walls and a ceiling (now just above my head) of rough poles; its narrow turnings quickly defeated the light.

I was about to thrust the Claw away again when I detected an odor at once pungent and alien. My nose is by no means the sensitive one of the he-wolf in the tale—if anything, I have rather a poorer sense of smell than most people. I thought I recognized the scent, but it was several moments before I placed it as the one I had experienced in the antechamber on the morning of our escape, when I returned for Jonas after talking to the little girl. She had said that something, some nameless seeker, had been snuffling among the prisoners there; and I had found a viscous substance on the floor and wall where Jonas lay.

I did not put the Claw back in its sack after that; but though I crossed a fetid trail several times as I wandered in the maze, I never glimpsed the creature that left it. After what must have been a watch or more of wandering, I reached a ladder that led up a short, open shaft. The square of daylight at its top was at once blinding and delightful. For a time I basked in it without even setting foot on the ladder. If I were to climb it, it seemed almost certain I would be recaptured at once; and yet I was so hungry and thirsty by then that I could hardly keep myself from doing so, and the thought of the foul thing that sought for me—it was surely one of Hethor's pets—made me want to bolt up it at once.

At last I climbed cautiously up and thrust my head above the level of the ground. I was not (as I had supposed) in the village I had seen; the windings of the maze had carried me beyond it to some secret exit. The great, silent trees stood closer here, and the light that had appeared so brilliant to me was the filtered green shade of their leaves. I emerged and found that I had left a hole between two roots, a place so obscure that I might have walked within a pace of it and yet not seen it. If I could, I would have blocked it with some weight to prevent or at least delay the escape of the creature that hunted me; but there was no stone or other object to hand that would serve such a purpose.

By the old trick of observing the slope of the ground and in so far as possible always walking downhill, I soon discovered a small stream. There was a little open sky above it, and as nearly as I could judge, the day appeared eight or nine watches over. Guessing that the village would not lie far from the source of the good water I had found, I soon found that as well. Wrapped in my fuligin cloak and standing in the deepest shade, I observed it for some time. Once a man—not painted like the two who had stopped us on the path—crossed the clearing. Once another left the suspended hut, went to the spring and drank, then returned to the hut.

It grew darker, and the strange village woke. A dozen men left the suspended hut and began to pile wood in the center of the clearing. Three more, robed and bearing forked staffs, emerged from the house of the tree. Still others, who must have been watching the jungle paths, slipped out of the shadows soon after the fire was kindled and spread a cloth before it.

One of the robed men stood with his back to the fire while the other two crouched at his feet; there was something extraordinary about them all, but I was reminded of the bearing of exultants, rather than of the Hierodules I had seen in the gardens of the House Absolute—it was the carriage that the consciousness of leadership confers, even as it severs the leader from common humanity. Painted and unpainted men sat cross-legged on the ground, facing the three. I heard the murmur of voices and the strong speech of the standing man, but I was too far to understand what was said. After a time the crouching men rose. One opened his robe like a tent, and Becan's son, whom I had made my own, stepped forth. The other produced *Terminus Est* in the same manner and drew her, displaying her bright blade and the black opal in her hilt to the crowd. Then one of the painted men rose, came some distance toward me (so that I feared he was about to see me, though I had covered my face with my mask) and lifted a door set into the ground. Soon afterward he emerged from another nearer the fire, and moving somewhat more rapidly went to the robed men to report.

There could be little doubt of what he was saying. I squared my shoulders and walked into the firelight. "I am not there," I said. "I am here."

There was an inrush of many breaths, and though I knew I might soon die, it was good to hear.

The midmost of the robed men said, "As you see, you cannot escape us. You were free, yet we drew you back." It was the voice that had interrogated me in my underground cell.

I said, "If you have walked far in The Way, you know you have less authority over me than the ignorant may believe." (It is not difficult to ape the way such people talk, for it is itself an aping of the speech of ascetics, and such priestesses as the Pelerines.) "You stole my son, who is also son to The Beast Who Speaks, as you must know by this time if you have much questioned him. To gain his return, I surrendered my sword to your slaves, and for a time submitted myself to you. I will take it up again now."

There is a place in the shoulder that, when pressed firmly with the thumb, paralyzes the entire arm. I laid my hand on the shoulder of the robed man who held *Terminus Est*, and he dropped it at my feet. With more presence of mind than I would have credited in a child, the boy Severian picked it up and handed it to me. The midmost robed man lifted his staff and shouted, "Arms!" and his followers rose as one man. Many had the talons I have described, and many of the others drew knives.

I fastened *Terminus Est* over my shoulder in her accustomed place and said, "You surely do not suppose that I require this ancient sword as a weapon? She has higher properties, as you of all people should know."

The robed man who had produced little Severian said hurriedly, "So Abundantius has just told us." The other man was still rubbing his arm.

I looked at the midmost robed man, who was clearly the one referred to. His eyes were clever, and as hard as stones. "Abundantius is wise," I said. I was trying to think of some way in which I could kill him without drawing the others down on us. "He knows too, I think, of the curse that afflicts those who harm the person of a magus."

"You are a magus then," Abundantius said.

"I, who took the archon's prey from out of his hands and passed invisible through the midst of his army? Yes, I have been called so."

"Prove then that you are a magus and we will hail you as a brother. But if you fail the test or refuse it—we are many, and you have but one sword."

"I will fail no fair assay," I said. "Though neither you nor your followers have authority to make one."

He was too clever to be drawn into such a debate. "The test is known to all here except yourself, and known, too, to be just. Everyone you see about you has succeeded in it, or hopes to."

They took me to a hall I had not seen before, a place substantially built of logs, and hidden among the trees. It had no windows, and only a single entrance. When torches were carried inside, I saw that its one chamber was unfurnished but for a carpet of woven grass, and so long in proportion to its width that it seemed almost a corridor.

Abundantius said, "Here you will have your combat with Decuman." He indicated the man whose arm I had numbed, who was, perhaps, a trifle surprised at being thus singled out. "You bested him by the fire. Now he must best you, if he can. You may sit here, nearest the door, so that you may be assured we cannot enter to give him aid. He will sit at the farther end. You shall not approach one another, or touch one another as you touched him by the fire. You must weave your spells, and in the morning we shall come to see who has mastered."

Taking little Severian by the hand, I led him to the blind end of that dark place. "I'll sit here," I said. "I have every confidence that you will not come to Decuman's aid, but you have no way of knowing whether I have confederates in the jungle outside. You have offered to trust me, and so I shall trust you."

"It would be better," Abundantius said, "if you were to leave the child in our keeping."

I shook my head. "I must have him with me. He is mine, and when you robbed me of him on the path, you robbed me too of half my power. I will not be separated from him again."

After a moment, Abundantius nodded. "As you wish. We but desired that he might come to no harm."

"No harm will come to him," I said.

There were iron brackets on the walls, and four of the naked men thrust their torches into them before they left. Decuman seated himself cross-legged near the door, his staff upon his lap. I sat too, and drew the boy to me. "I'm scared," he said; he buried his little face in my cloak.

"You have every right to be. The past three days have been bad ones for you."

Decuman had begun a slow, rhythmic chant.

"Little Severian, I want you to tell me what happened to you on the path. I looked around and you were gone."

It took some comforting and coaxing, but at last his sobs ceased. "They came out—the three-colored men with claws, and I was afraid and ran away."

"Is that all?"

"And then more three-colored men came out and caught me, and they made me go into a hole in the ground, where it was dark. And then they woke me and lifted me up, and I was inside a man's coat, and then you came and got me."

"Didn't anyone ask you questions?"

"A man in the dark."

"I see. Little Severian, you mustn't ever run away again, the way you did on the path—do you understand? Only run if I run too. If you hadn't run away when we met the three-colored men, we wouldn't be here."

The boy nodded.

"Decuman," I called. "Decuman, can we talk?"

He ignored me, save perhaps that his murmured chant grew a trifle louder. His face was lifted so that he appeared to be staring at the roof poles, but his eyes were closed.

"What is he doing?" the boy asked.

"He is weaving an enchantment."

"Will it hurt us?"

"No," I said. "Such magic is mostly fakery—like lifting you up through a hole so it would look as if the other one had made you appear under his robe."

Yet even as I spoke, I was conscious there was something more. Decuman was concentrating his mind on me as few minds can be concentrated, and I felt I was naked in some brightly lit place where a thousand eyes watched. One of the torches flickered, guttered, and went out. As the light in the hall dimmed, the light I could not see seemed to grow brighter.

I rose. There are ways of killing that leave no mark, and I reviewed them mentally as I stepped forward.

At once, pikes sprang from the walls, an ell on either side. They were not such spears as soldiers have, energy weapons whose heads strike bolts of fire, but simple poles of wood tipped with iron, like the pilets the villagers of Saltus had used. Nevertheless, they could kill at close range, and I sat down again. The boy said, "I think they're outside watching us through the cracks between the logs."

"Yes, I know that now too."

"What can we do?" he asked. And then when I did not reply, "Who are these people, Father?"

It was the first time he had called me that. I drew him closer, and it seemed to weaken the net Decuman was knotting about my mind. I said, "I'm only guessing, but I would say this is an academy of magicians—of those cultists who practice what they believe are secret arts. They are supposed to have followers everywhere—though I choose to doubt that—and they are very cruel. Have you heard of the New Sun, little Severian? He is the man who prophets say will come and drive back the ice and set the world right."

"He will kill Abaia," the boy answered, surprising me.

"Yes, he is supposed to do that as well, and many other things. He is said to have come once before, long ago. Did you know that?"

He shook his head.

"Then his task was to forge a peace between humanity and the Increate, and he was called the Conciliator. He left behind a famous relic, a gem called the Claw." My hand went to it as I spoke, and though I did not loosen the drawstrings of the little sack of human skin that held it, I could feel it through the soft leather. As soon as I touched it, the invisible glare Decuman had created in my mind fell almost to nothing. I cannot say now just why I had presumed for so long that it was necessary for the Claw to be taken from its place of concealment for it to be effective. I learned that night that it was not so, and I laughed.

For a moment Decuman halted his chant, and his eyes opened. Little Severian clutched me more tightly. "Aren't you afraid anymore?"

"No," I said. "Could you see that I was frightened?"

He nodded solemnly.

"What I was going to tell you was that the existence of that relic seems to have given some people the idea that the Conciliator used claws as weapons. I have sometimes doubted that he existed; but if such a person ever lived, I'm sure that he used his weapons largely against himself. Do you understand what I am saying?''

I doubt that he did, but he nodded.

''When we were on the path, we found a charm against the coming of the New Sun. The three-colored men, who I think are the ones who have passed this test, use claws of steel. I think they must want to hold back the coming of the New Sun so they can take his place and perhaps usurp his powers. If—''

Outside, someone screamed.

XXII

The Skirts of the Mountain

My laugh had broken Decuman's concentration, if only for a moment. The scream from outside did not. His net, so much of which had fallen in ruins when I gripped the Claw, was being knotted again, more slowly but more tightly.

It is always a temptation to say that such feelings are indescribable, though they seldom are. I felt that I hung naked between two sentient suns, and I was somehow aware that these suns were the hemispheres of Decuman's brain. I was bathed in light, but it was the glare of furnaces, consuming and somehow immobilizing. In that light, nothing seemed worthwhile; and I myself infinitely small and contemptible.

Thus my concentration too, in a sense, remained unbroken. Yet I was aware, however dimly, that the scream might signal an opportunity for me. Much later than I should have, after perhaps a dozen breaths had passed my nostrils, I stumbled to my feet.

Something was coming through the doorway. My first thought, absurd as it may sound, was that it was mud—that a convulsion had rocked Urth, and the hall was about to be inundated in what had been the bottom of some fetid marsh. It flowed around the doorposts blindly and softly, and as it did, another torch went out. Soon it was about to touch Decuman, and I shouted to warn him.

I am not sure whether it was the touch of the creature or my voice, but he recoiled. I was conscious again of the breaking of the spell, the ruin of the snare that had held me between the twin suns. They flew apart and dimmed as they vanished, and I seemed to expand, and to turn in a direction neither up nor down, left nor right, until I stood wholly in the hall of testing, with little Severian clinging to my cloak.

Decuman's hand flashed with talons then. I had not even realized he had them. Whatever that black and nearly shapeless creature was, its side cut as fat does under the lash. Its blood was black too, or perhaps darkly green. Decuman's was red; when the creature flowed over him, it seemed to melt his skin like wax.

I lifted the boy and made him cling to my neck and clasp my waist with his legs, then jumped with all my strength. But though my fingertips touched a roof pole, I could not grasp it. The creature was turning, blindly but purposefully. Perhaps it hunted by scent, yet I have always felt it was by thought—that would explain why it was so slow to find me in the antechamber, where I had dreamed myself to Thecla, and so swift in the hall of testing, when Decuman's mind was focused on mine.

I jumped again, but this time I missed the pole by a span at least. To get one of the two remaining torches, I had to run toward the creature. I did and seized the torch, but it went out as I took it from its bracket.

Holding the bracket with one hand, I jumped a third time, assisting my legs with the strength of my arm; and now I caught a smooth, narrow pole with my left hand. The pole bent beneath my weight, but I was able to draw myself up, with the boy on my shoulders, until I could get one foot on the bracket.

Below me, the dark, shapeless creature reared, fell, and lifted itself again. Still holding the pole, I drew *Terminus Est*. A slash bit deep into the oozing flesh, but the blade was no sooner clear than the wound seemed to close and knit. I turned my sword on the roof thatch then, an expedient I confess to stealing from Agia. It was thick, of jungle leaves bound with tough fibers; my first frantic strokes seemed to make little impression on it, but at the third a great swath fell. Part of it struck the remaining torch, smothering it, then sending up a gout of flame. I vaulted through the gap and into the night.

Leaping blindly as I did with that sharp blade drawn, it is a wonder that I did not kill both the boy and myself. I dropped it and him when I struck the ground, and fell to my knees. The red blaze of the thatch grew brighter with the passing of every moment. I heard the boy whimper and called to him not to run, then pulled him to his feet with one hand and snatched up *Terminus Est* with the other and ran myself.

All the rest of that night we fled blindly through the jungle. In so far as I could, I tried to direct our steps uphill—not only because our way north would mean climbing, but because I knew we were less likely to tumble over some drop. When morning came, we were in the jungle still, with no more idea than we had before of where we were. I carried the boy then, and he fell asleep in my arms.

In another watch there could be no doubt the ground was rising steeply before us, and at last we came to a curtain of vines such as I had cut through the day before. Just as I was ready to try to put down the boy without waking him, so that I could draw my sword, I saw bright daylight streaming through a rent to my left. I went to it, walking as quickly as I could, almost running; then through it, and out onto a rocky upland of coarse grass and shrubs. A few more steps brought me to a clear stream that sang over rocks—unquestionably the stream beside which the boy and I had slept two nights before. Not knowing or caring whether the shapeless creature was on our track still, I lay down beside it and slept again.

I was in a maze, like and yet unlike the dark underground maze of the magicians. The corridors were wider here, and sometimes seemed galleries as mighty as those of the House Absolute. Some, indeed, were lined with pier glasses, in which I saw myself with ragged cloak and haggard face, and Thecla, half-transparent in a lovely, trailing gown, close beside me. Planets whistled down long, oblique, curving tracks that only they could see. Blue Urth carried the green moon like an infant, but did not touch her. Red Verthandi became Decuman, his skin eaten away, turning in his own blood.

I fled and fell, jerking all my limbs. I saw true stars in the sun-drenched sky for a moment, but sleep drew me as irresistibly as gravity. Beside a wall of glass, I walked; and through it I saw the boy, running and frightened, in the old, patched, gray shirt I had worn as an apprentice, running from the fourth level, I thought, to the Atrium of Time. Dorcas and Jolenta came hand in hand, smiling at each other, and did not see me. Then autochthons, copper-skinned and bowlegged, feathered and jeweled, were dancing behind their shaman, dancing in the rain. The undine swam in air, vast as a cloud, blotting out the sun.

I woke. Soft rain pattered on my face. Beside me, little Severian slept still. I wrapped him as well as I could in my cloak and carried him again to the rent in the curtain of vines. Beyond that curtain under the wide-boughed trees, the rain hardly penetrated; and there we lay and slept once more. This time there were no dreams, and when I woke we had slept a day and a night, and the pale light of dawn lay everywhere.

The boy was already up, wandering among the boles of the trees. He showed me where the brook was in this place, and I washed, and shaved as well as I could without hot water, which I had not done since the first afternoon in the house beneath the cliff. Then we found the familiar path and made our way north again.

"Won't we meet the three-colored men?" he asked, and I told him not to worry and not to run—that I would handle the three-colored men.

The truth was that I was far more concerned about Hethor and the creature he had set upon my track. If it had not perished in the fire, it might be moving toward us now; for though it had seemed an animal that would fear the sun, the dimness of the jungle was the very stuff of twilight.

Only one painted man stepped into the path, and he did so not to bar the way but to prostrate himself. I was tempted to kill him and be done with it; we are taught strictly to kill and maim only at the order of a judge, but that training had been weakening in me as I moved farther and farther from Nessus and toward the war and the wild mountains. Some mystics hold that the vapors arising from battles affect the brain, even a long way downwind; and it may be so. Nevertheless, I lifted him up, and merely told him to stand aside.

''Great Magus,'' he said, ''what have you done with the creeping dark?''

''I have sent it back to the pit, from which I drew it,'' I told him, for since we had not encountered the creature, I was fairly certain Hethor had recalled it, if it was not dead.

''Five of us transmigrated,'' the painted man said.

''Your powers, then, are greater than I would have credited. It has killed hundreds in a night.''

I was far from sure he would not attack us when our backs were to him, but he did not. The path down which I had walked as a prisoner the day before seemed deserted now. No more guards appeared to challenge us; some of the strips of red cloth had been torn down and trampled under foot, though I could not imagine why. I saw many footprints on the path, which had been smooth (perhaps raked smooth) before.

''What are you looking for?'' the boy asked.

I kept my voice low, still not sure there were no listeners behind the trees. ''The slime of the animal we ran away from last night.''

''Do you see it?''

I shook my head.

For a time, the boy was silent. Then he said, ''Big Severian, where did it come from?''

''Do you remember the story? From one of the mountaintops beyond the shores of Urth.''

''Where Spring Wind lived?''

''I don't think it was the same one.''

''How did he get here?''

''A bad man brought him,'' I said. ''Now be quiet for a while, little Severian.''

If I was short with the boy, it was because I had been troubled by the same thought. Hethor must have smuggled his pets aboard the ship on which he served, that seemed clear enough; and when he had followed me out of Nessus, he might easily have carried the notules in some small, sealed container on his person—terrible though they were, they were no thicker than tissue, as Jonas had known.

But what of the creature we had seen in the hall of testing? It had appeared in the antechamber of the House Absolute too, after Hethor had come, but how? And had it followed Hethor and Agia like a dog as they journeyed north to Thrax? I summoned the memory of it, as I had seen it when it killed Decuman, and tried to estimate its weight: it must have been as heavy as several men, and perhaps as heavy as a destrier. A large cart, surely, would have been required to transport and conceal it. Had Hethor driven such a cart through these mountains? I could not believe it. Had the viscid horror we had seen shared such a cart with the salamander I had seen destroyed in Thrax? I could not believe that either.

The village seemed deserted when we reached it. Some parts of the hall of testing still stood and smoldered. I looked in vain for the remains of Decuman's body there, though I found his half-burned staff. It had been hollow, and from the smoothness of its interior, I suspected that with the head removed it had formed a sabarcane for shooting poisoned darts. No doubt it would have been used if I had proved overly resistant to the spell he wove.

The boy must have been following my thoughts from my expression and the direction of my glance. He said, "That man really was magic, wasn't he? He almost magicked you."

I nodded.

"You said it wasn't real."

"In some ways, little Severian, I am not much wiser than you. I didn't think it was. I had seen so much fakery—the secret door into the underground room where they kept me, and the way they made you appear under the other man's robe. Still, there are dark things everywhere, and I suppose that those who look hard enough for them cannot help but find some. Then they become, as you said, real magicians."

"They could tell everybody what to do, if they know real magic."

I only shook my head to that, but I have thought much about it since. It seems to me there are two objections to the boy's idea, though expressed in a more mature form it must appear more convincing.

The first is that so little knowledge is passed from one generation to the next by the magicians. My own training was in what may be called the most fundamental of the applied sciences; and I know from it that the progress of science depends much less upon either theoretical considerations or systematic investigation than is commonly believed, but rather on the transmittal of reliable information, gained by chance or insight, from one set of men to their successors. The nature of those who hunt after dark knowledge is to hoard it even in death, or to transmit it so wrapped in disguise and beclouded with self-serving lies that it is of little value. At times, one hears of those who teach their lovers well, or their children; but it is the nature of such people seldom to have either, and it may be that their art is weakened when they do.

The second is that the very existence of such powers argues a counterforce. We call powers of the first kind dark, though they may use a species of deadly light as Decuman did; and we call those of the second kind bright, though I think that they may at times employ darkness, as a good man nevertheless draws the curtains of his bed to sleep. Yet there is truth to the talk of darkness and light, because it shows plainly that one implies the other. The tale I read to little Severian said that the universe was but a long word of the Increate's. We, then, are the syllables of that word. But the speaking of any word is futile unless there are other words, words that are not spoken. If a beast has but one cry, the cry tells nothing; and even the wind has a multitude of voices, so that those who sit indoors may hear it and know if the weather is tumultuous or mild. The powers we call dark seem to me to be the words the Increate did *not* speak, if the Increate exists at all; and these words must be maintained in a quasi-existence, if the other word, the word spoken, is to be distinguished. What is not said can be important—but what is said is more important. Thus my very knowledge of the existence of the Claw was almost sufficient to counter Decuman's spell.

And if the seekers after dark things find them, may not the seekers after bright find them as well? And are they not more apt to hand their wisdom on? So the Pelerines had guarded the Claw, from generation unto generation; and thinking of this, I became more determined than ever to find them and restore it to them; for if I had not known it before, the night with the alzabo had brought home to me that I was only flesh, and would die in time certainly, and perhaps would die soon.

Because the mountain we approached stood to the north and thus cast its shadow toward the saddle of jungle, no curtain of vines grew on that side. The pale green of the leaves only faded to one more pale still, and the number of dead trees increased, though all the trees were smaller. The canopy of leaves beneath which we had walked all day broke, and in another hundred strides broke again, and at last vanished altogether.

Then the mountain rose before us, too near for us to see it as the image of a man. Great folded slopes rolled down out of a bank of cloud;

they were, I knew, but the sculptured drapery of his robes. How often he must have risen from sleep and put them on, perhaps without reflecting that they would be preserved here for the ages, so huge as almost to escape the sight of humankind.

XXIII

The Cursed Town

At about noon of the next day we found water again, the only water the two of us were to taste upon that mountain. Only a few strips of the dried meat Casdoe had left for me remained. I shared them out, and we drank from the stream, which was no more than a trickle the size of a man's thumb. That seemed strange, because I had seen so much snow on the head and shoulders of the mountain; I was to discover later that the slopes below the snow, where snow might have melted with the coming of summer, were blown clear by the wind. Higher, the white drifts might accumulate for centuries.

Our blankets were damp with dew, and we spread them there on stones to dry. Even without the sun, the dry gusts of mountain air dried them in a watch or so. I knew that we would be spending the coming night high up the slopes, much as I had spent the first night after leaving Thrax. Somehow, the knowledge was powerless to depress my spirits. It was not so much that we were leaving the dangers we had found in the saddle of jungle, as that we were leaving behind a certain sordidness there. I felt that I had been befouled, and that the cold atmosphere of the mountain would cleanse me. For a time that feeling remained with me almost unexamined; then, as we began to climb in earnest, I realized that what disturbed me was the memory of the lies I had told the magicians, pretending, as they did, to command great powers and be privy to vast secrets. Those lies had been wholly justifiable—they had helped to save my life and little Severian's. Nevertheless, I felt myself somewhat less of a man because I had resorted to them. Master Gurloes, whom I had come to hate before I left the guild, had lied frequently; and now I was not sure whether I had hated him because he lied, or hated lying because he did it.

And yet Master Gurloes had possessed as good an excuse as I did, and perhaps a better one. He had lied to preserve the guild and advance its fortunes, giving various officials and officers exaggerated accounts of our work, and when necessary concealing our mistakes. In doing that, he, the de facto head of the guild, had been advancing his own position, to be sure; yet he had also been advancing mine, and that of Drotte, Roche, Eata, and all the other apprentices and journeymen who would eventually inherit it. If he had been the simple, brutal man he wished everyone to believe he was, I could have been certain now that his dishonesty had been for his benefit alone. I knew that he was not; perhaps for years he had seen himself as I now saw myself.

And yet I could not be certain I had acted to save little Severian. When he had run and I had surrendered my sword, it might have been more to his advantage if I had fought—I myself was the one whose immediate advantage had been served by my docile capitulation, since if I had fought I might have been killed. Later, when I had escaped, I had surely returned as much for *Terminus Est* as for the boy; I had returned for her in the mine of the man-apes, when he had not been with me; and without her, I would have become a mere vagabond.

A watch after I entertained these thoughts, I was scaling a rock face with both the sword and the boy on my back, and with no more certainty concerning how much I cared for either than I had before. Fortunately I was fairly fresh, it was not a difficult climb as such things go, and at the top we struck an ancient highway.

Although I have walked in many strange places, I have walked in none that gave me so great a sensation of anomaly. To our left, no more than twenty paces off, I could see the termination of this broad road, where some rockslide had carried its lower end away. Before us it stretched as perfect as on the day it was completed, a ribbon of seamless black stone winding up toward that immense figure whose face was lost above the clouds.

The boy gripped my hand when I put him down. "My mother said we couldn't use the roads, because of the soldiers."

"Your mother was right," I told him. "But she was going to go down, where the soldiers are. No doubt there were soldiers on this road once, but they died a long time before the biggest tree in the jungle down there was a seed." He was cold, and I gave him one of the blankets and showed him how to wrap it about him and hold it closed to make a cloak. If anyone had seen us then, we would have appeared a small, gray figure followed by a disproportionate shadow.

* * *

We entered a mist, and I thought it strange to find one that high up. It was only after we had climbed above it and could look down upon its sunlit top that I realized it had been one of the clouds that had seemed so remote when I had looked up at them from the saddle.

And yet that saddle of jungle, so far below us now, was itself no doubt thousands of cubits above Nessus and the lower reaches of Gyoll. I thought then how far I must have come, that jungles could exist at such altitudes—nearly to the waist of the world, where it was always summer, and only height produced any difference in the climate. If I were to journey to the west, out of these mountains, then from what I had learned from Master Palaemon, I would find myself in a jungle so pestilential as to make the one we had left seem a paradise, a coastal jungle of steaming heat and swarming insects; and yet there too I would see the evidences of death, for though that jungle received as much of the sun's strength as any spot on Urth, still it was less than it had received in times past, and just as the ice crept forward in the south and the vegetation of the temperate zone fled from it, so the trees and other plants of the tropics died to give the newcomers space.

While I looked down at the cloud, the boy had been walking ahead. Now he looked back at me with shining eyes and called, "Who made this road?"

"No doubt the workers who carved the mountain. They must have had great energies at their command and machines more powerful than any we know about. Still, they would have had to carry the rubble away in some fashion. A thousand carts and wains must have rolled here once." And yet I wondered, because the iron wheels of such vehicles score even the hard cobbles of Thrax and Nessus, and this road was as smooth as a processional way. Surely, I thought, only the sun and wind have passed here.

"Big Severian, look! Do you see the hand?"

The boy was pointing toward a spur of the mountain high above us. I craned my neck, but for a moment I saw nothing but what I had seen before: a long promontory of inhospitable gray rock. Then the sunlight flashed on something near the end. It seemed, unmistakably, the gleam of gold; when I had seen that, I saw also that the gold was a ring, and under it I saw the thumb lying frozen in stone along the rock, a thumb perhaps a hundred paces long, with the fingers above it hills.

We had no money, and I knew how valuable money might be when we were forced, as eventually we must be, to reenter the inhabited lands. If I was still searched for, gold might persuade the searchers to look elsewhere. Gold might also buy little Severian an apprenticeship in some worthy guild, for it was clear he could not continue to travel with me.

It seemed most probable that the great ring was only gold leaf over stone; even so, so vast a quantity of gold leaf, if it could be peeled away and rolled up, must amount to a considerable total. And though I made an effort not to, I found myself wondering if mere gold leaf could have endured so many centuries. Would it not have loosened and fallen away long ago? If the ring were of solid gold, it would be worth a fortune; but all the fortunes of Urth could not have bought this mighty image, and he who had ordered its construction must have possessed wealth incalculable. Even if the ring were not solid through to the finger beneath, there might be some substantial thickness of metal.

As I considered all this, I toiled upward, my long legs soon outstripping the boy's short ones. At times the road climbed so steeply I could hardly believe vehicles burdened with stone had ever traversed it. Twice we crossed fissures, one so wide that I was forced to throw the boy across it before leaping over it myself. I was hoping to find water before we halted; I found none, and when night fell we had no better shelter than a crevice of stone where we wrapped ourselves in the blankets and my cape and slept as well as we could.

In the morning we were both thirsty. Although the rainy season would not come until autumn, I told the boy I thought it might rain today, and we started forward again in good spirits. Then too, he showed me how carrying a small stone in the mouth helps to quench thirst. It is a mountain trick, one I had not known. The wind was colder now than it had been before, and I began to feel the thinness of the air. Occasionally the road twisted to some point where we received a few moments of sunshine.

In doing so, it wound farther and farther from the ring, until at last we found ourselves in full shadow, out of sight of the ring altogether and somewhere near the knees of the seated figure. There was a last steep climb, so abrupt that I would have been grateful for steps. And then, ahead of us where they seemed to float in the clear air, a cluster of slender spires. The boy called out "Thrax!" so happily that I knew his mother must have told him tales of it, and told him too, when she and the old man took him from the house where he had been born, that she would bring him there.

"No," I said. "It is not Thrax. This looks more like my own Citadel—our Matachin Tower, and the witches' tower, and the Bear Tower and the Bell Tower."

He looked at me, wide-eyed.

"No, it isn't that either, of course. Only I have been to Thrax, and Thrax is a city of stone. Those towers are of metal, as ours were."

"They have eyes," little Severian said.

So they did. At first I thought my imagination was deceiving me, particularly since not all the towers possessed them. At last I came to realize that some faced away from us, and that the towers had not only eyes but shoulders and arms as well; that they were, in fact, the metallic figures of cataphracts, warriors armored from head to toe. "It isn't a real city," I told the boy. "What we have found are the guardsmen of the Autarch, waiting in his lap to destroy those who would harm him."

"Will they hurt us?"

"It's a frightening thought, isn't it? They could crush you and me beneath their feet like mice. I'm sure they won't, however. They're only statues, spiritual guards left here as memorials to his powers."

"There are big houses too," the boy said.

He was right. The buildings were no more than waist-high to the towering metal figures, so that we had overlooked them at first. That again reminded me of the Citadel, where structures never meant to brave the stars are mingled with the towers. Perhaps it was merely the thin air, but I had a sudden vision of these metal men rising slowly, then ever more swiftly, lifting hands toward the sky as they dove into it as we used to dive down to the dark waters of the cistern by torchlight.

Although my boots must have grated on the wind-swept rock, I find I have no memory of such a sound. Perhaps it was lost in the immensity of the mountaintop, so that we approached the standing figures as silently as if we walked over moss. Our shadows, which had spread behind us and to our left when they had first appeared, were contracted into pools about our feet; and I noticed that I could see the eyes of every figure. I told myself that I had overlooked some at first, yet they glittered in the sun.

At last we threaded a path among them, and among the buildings that surrounded them. I had expected these buildings to be ruinous, like those in the forgotten city of Apu-Punchau. They were closed, secretive, and silent; but they might have been constructed only a few years before. No roofs had fallen in; no vines had dislodged the square gray stones of their walls. They were windowless, and their architecture did not suggest temples, fortresses, tombs, or any other type of structure with which I was familiar. They were utterly without ornament and without grace; yet their workmanship was excellent, and their differing forms seemed to indicate differences in function. The shining figures stood among them as if they had been halted in their places by some sudden, freezing wind, not as monuments stand.

I selected a building and told the boy we would break into it, and that if we were fortunate we might find water there, and perhaps even preserved food. It proved a foolish boast. The doors were as solid as the walls, the roof as strong as the foundation. Even if I had possessed an ax, I do not think I could have smashed my way in, and I dared not hew with *Terminus Est*. Poking and prying for some weakness, we wasted several watches. The second and third buildings we attempted proved no easier than the first.

"There's a round house over there," the boy said at last. "I'll go and look at it for you."

Because I felt sure there was nothing in this deserted place that could harm him, I told him to go ahead.

Soon he was back. "The door's open!"

XXIV

The Corpse

I had never discovered what uses the other buildings had served. No more did I understand this one, which was circular and covered by a dome. Its walls were metal—not the darkly lustrous metal of our Citadel towers, but some bright alloy like polished silver.

This gleaming building stood atop a stepped pedestal, and I wondered to see it there when the great images of the cataphracts in their antique armor stood plainly in the streets. There were five doorways about its circumference (for we walked around it before venturing inside), and all of them stood open. By examining them and the floor before them, I tried to judge whether they had stood so for so many years; there was little dust at this elevation, and in the end I could not be certain. When we had completed our inspection, I told the boy to let me go first, and stepped inside.

Nothing happened. Even when the boy followed me, the doors did not close, no enemy rushed at us, no energy colored the air, and the floor remained firm beneath our feet. Nevertheless, I had the feeling that we had somehow entered a trap: that outside on the mountain we had been free, however hungry and thirsty we were, and that here we were free no longer. I think I would have turned and run if he had not been with me. As it was, I did not want to appear superstitious or afraid, and I felt an obligation to try to find food and water.

There were many devices in that building to which I can give no name. They were not furniture, nor boxes, nor machines as I understand the term. Most were oddly angled; I saw some that appeared to have niches in which to sit, though the sitter would have been cramped, and would have faced some part of the device instead of his companions.

Others contained alcoves where someone might once, perhaps, have rested.

These devices stood beside aisles, wide aisles that ran toward the center of the structure as straight as the spokes of a wheel. Looking down the one we had entered, I could see, dimly, some red object, and upon it, much smaller, something brown. At first, I did not pay great attention to either, but when I had satisfied myself that the devices I have described were of no value and no danger to us, I led the boy toward them.

The red object was a sort of couch, a very elaborate one, with straps so that a prisoner might be confined upon it. Around it were mechanisms that seemed intended to provide for nourishment and elimination. It stood upon a small dais, and on it lay what had once been the body of a man with two heads. The thin, dry air of the mountain had desiccated that body long ago—like the mysterious buildings, it might have been a year old or a thousand. He had been a man taller than I, perhaps even an exultant, and powerfully muscled. Now I might, I thought, tear one of his arms from its socket with a gesture. He wore no loincloth, or any other garment, and though we are accustomed to sudden changes in the size of the organs of procreation, it was strange to see them so shriveled here. Some hair remained upon the heads, and it appeared to me that the hair of the right had been black; that of the head on the left was yellowish. The eyes of both were closed, and the mouths open, showing a few teeth. I noticed that the straps that might have bound this creature to the couch were not buckled.

At the time, however, I was far more concerned with the mechanism that had once fed him. I told myself that ancient machines were often astoundingly durable, and though it had long been abandoned, it had enjoyed the most favorable conditions for its preservation; and I twisted every dial I could find, and shifted each lever, in an attempt to make it produce some nutriment. The boy watched me, and when I had been moving things here and there for some time asked if we were going to starve.

"No," I told him. "We can go a great deal longer without food than you would think. Getting something to drink is a great deal more urgent, but if we can't find anything here, there is sure to be snow further up the mountain."

"How did he die?" For some reason I had never brought myself to touch the corpse; now the boy ran his plump fingers along one withered arm.

"Men die. The wonder is that such a monster lived. Such things usually perish at birth."

"Do you think the others left him here when they went away?" He asked.

"Left him here alive, you mean? I suppose they could have. There would have been no place for him, perhaps, in the lands below. Or perhaps he did not want to go. Maybe they confined him here on this couch when he misbehaved. Possibly he was subject to madness, or fits of violent rage. If any of those things are true, he must have spent his last days wandering over the mountain, returning here to eat and drink, and dying when the food and water he depended on were exhausted."

"Then there isn't any water in there," the boy said practically.

"That's true. Still, we don't know it happened like that. He may have died for some other reason before his supplies ran out. Then too, the kind of thing we've been saying would seem to assume that he was a sort of pet or mascot for the people who carved the mountain. This is a very elaborate place in which to keep a pet. Just the same, I don't think I'm ever going to be able to reactivate this machine."

"I think we ought to go down," the boy announced as we were leaving the circular building.

I turned to look behind us, thinking how foolish all my fears had been. Its doors remained open; nothing had moved, nothing had changed. If it had ever been a trap, it seemed certain it was a trap that had rusted open centuries before.

"So do I," I said. "But the day is nearly over—see how long our shadows are now. I don't want to be overtaken by the night when we're climbing down the other side, so I'm going to find out whether I can reach the ring we saw this morning. Perhaps we'll find water as well as gold. Tonight we'll sleep in that round building out of the wind, and tomorrow we'll start down the north side by the first light."

He nodded to show that he understood, and accompanied me willingly enough as I set off to look for a path to the ring. It had been on the southern arm, so that we were in some sense returning to the side we had first climbed, though we had approached the cluster of sculptured cataphracts and buildings from the southeast. I had feared that the ascent to the arm would be a difficult climb; instead, just where the vast height of the chest and upper arm rose before us, I found what I had been wishing for much earlier: a narrow stair. There were many hundreds of steps, so it was a weary climb still, and I carried the boy up much of it.

The arm itself was smooth stone, yet so wide there seemed to be little danger that the boy would fall off as long as we kept to the center. I made him hold my hand and strode along quite eagerly, my cloak snapping in the wind.

To our left lay the ascent we had begun the day before; beyond it was the saddle between the mountains, green under its blanket of jungle. Beyond even that, hazy now with distance, rose the mountain where Becan and Casdoe had built their home. As I walked, I tried to distinguish their cabin, or at least the area in which it stood, and at last I found what seemed to me the cliff face I had descended to reach it, a tiny fleck of color on the side of that less lofty mountain, with the glint of the falling water in its center like an iridescent mote.

When I had seen it, I halted and turned to look up at the peak on whose slope we walked. I could see the face now and its mitre of ice, and below it the left shoulder, where a thousand cavalrymen might have been exercised by their chiliarch.

Ahead of me, the boy was pointing and shouting something I could not understand, pointing down toward the buildings and the standing figures of the metal guardsmen. It was a moment before I realized what he meant—their faces were turned three-quarters toward us, as they had been turned three-quarters toward us that morning. Their heads had moved. For the first time, I followed the direction of their eyes—and found that they were looking at the sun.

I nodded to the boy and called, "I see!"

We were on the wrist, with the little plain of the hand spread before us, broader and safer even than the arm. As I strode over it, the boy ran ahead of me. The ring was on the second finger, a finger larger than a log cut from the greatest tree. Little Severian ran out upon it, balancing himself without difficulty on the crest, and I saw him throw out his hands to touch the ring.

There was a flash of light—bright, yet not blindingly so in the afternoon sunshine; because it was tinted with violet, it seemed almost a darkness.

It left him blackened and consumed. For a moment, I think, he still lived; his head jerked back and his arms were flung wide. There was a puff of smoke, carried away at once by the wind. The body fell, its limbs contracting as the legs of a dead insect do, and rolled until it had tumbled out of sight in the crevice between the second and third fingers.

I, who had seen so many brandings and abacinations, and had even used the iron myself (among the billion things I recall perfectly is the flesh of Morwenna's cheeks blistering), could scarcely force myself to go and look at him.

There were bones there, in that narrow place between the fingers, but they were old bones that broke beneath my feet when I leaped down like the bones strewn upon the paths in our necropolis, and I did not trouble to examine them. I took out the Claw. When I had cursed myself for not using it when Thecla's body was brought forth at Vodalus's banquet, Jonas had told me not to be a fool, that whatever powers the Claw might possess could not possibly have restored life to that roasted flesh.

And I could not help but think that if it acted now and restored little Severian to me, for all my joy I would take him to some safe place and slash my own throat with *Terminus Est*. Because if the Claw would do that, it would have called Thecla back too, if only it had been used; and Thecla was a part of myself, now forever dead.

For a moment it seemed that there was a glimmering, a bright shadow or aura; then the boy's corpse crumbled to black ash that stirred in the unquiet air.

I stood, and put the Claw away, and began to walk back, vaguely wondering how much trouble I would have in leaving that narrow place and regaining the back of the hand. (In the end, I had to stand *Terminus Est* on the tip of her own blade and put one foot on a quillion to get up, then crawl back, head down, until I could grasp her pommel and pull her up after me.) There was no confusion of memory, but for a time a confusion of mind, in which the boy was merged in that other boy, Jader, who had lived with his dying sister in the jacal upon the cliff in Thrax. The one, who had come to mean so much to me, I could not save; the other, who had meant little, I had cured. In some way, it seemed to me they were the same boy. No doubt that was merely some protective reaction of my mind, a shelter it sought from the storm of madness; but it seemed to me somehow that so long as Jader lived, the boy his mother had named Severian could not truly perish.

I had meant to halt upon the hand and look back; I could not—the truth is that I feared I would go to the edge and throw myself over. I did not actually stop until I had nearly regained the narrow stair that led down so many hundreds of steps to the broad lap of the mountain. Then I seated myself and once more found that fleck of color that was the cliff below which Casdoe's home had stood. I remembered the barking of the brown dog as I had come through the forest toward it. He had been a coward, that dog, when the alzabo came, but he had died with his teeth in the defiled flesh of a zoanthrop, while I, a coward too, had hung back. I remembered Casdoe's tired, lovely face, the boy peeping from behind her skirt, the way the old man had sat cross-legged with his back to the fire, talking of Fechin. They were all dead now, Severa and Becan, whom I had never seen; the old man, the dog, Casdoe, now little Severian, even Fechin, all dead, all lost in the mists that obscure our days. Time itself is a thing, so it seems to me, that stands solidly like a fence of iron palings with its endless row of years; and we flow past like Gyoll, on our way to a sea from which we shall return only as rain.

I knew then, on the arm of that giant figure, the ambition to conquer time, an ambition beside which the desire of the distant suns is only the lust of some petty, feathered chieftain to subjugate some other tribe.

There I sat until the sun was nearly hidden by the rising of the mountains in the west. It should have been easier to descend the stair than it had been to climb it, but I was very thirsty now, and the jolt of each step hurt my knees. The light was nearly gone, and the wind like ice. One blanket had been burned with the boy; I unfolded the other and wrapped my chest and shoulders in it under my cloak.

When I was perhaps halfway down, I paused to rest. Only a thin crescent of reddish brown remained of the day. That narrowed, then vanished; and as it did, each of the great metal cataphracts below me raised a hand in salute. So quiet they were, and so steady, that I could almost have believed them sculptured with lifted arms, as I saw them.

For a time the wonder of it washed all my sorrow from me, and I could only marvel. I remained where I was, staring at them, not daring to move. Night rushed across the mountains; in the last, dim twilight I watched the mighty arms come down.

Still dazed, I reentered the silent cluster of buildings that stood in the figure's lap. If I had seen one miracle fail, I had witnessed another; and even a seemingly purposeless miracle is an inexhaustible source of hope, because it proves to us that since we do not understand everything, our defeats—so much more numerous than our few and empty victories—may be equally specious.

By some idiotic error, I contrived to lose my way when I tried to return to the circular building where I had told the boy we would spend the night, and I was too fatigued to search for it. Instead I found a sheltered spot well away from the nearest metal guardsman, where I rubbed my aching legs and wrapped myself against the cold as well as I could. Although I must have fallen asleep almost at once, I was soon awakened by the sound of soft footsteps.

XXV

Typhon and Piaton

When I heard the footsteps, I had risen and drawn my sword, and I waited in a shadow for what seemed a watch at least, though it was no doubt much less. Twice more I heard them, quick and soft, yet somehow suggestive of a large man—a powerful man hurrying, almost running, light-footed and athletic.

Here the stars were in all their glory; as bright as they must be seen by the sailors whose ports they are, when they go aloft to spread the golden gauze that would wrap a continent. I could see the motionless guardsmen almost as if by day, and the buildings around me, bathed in the many-colored lights of ten thousand suns. We think with horror of the frozen plains of Dis, the outermost companion of our sun—but of how many suns are we the outermost companion? To the people of Dis (if such exist) it is all one long, starry night.

Several times, standing there under the stars, I nearly slept; and at the borders of sleep I worried about the boy, thinking that I had probably awakened him when I rose and wondering where I should find food for him when the sun could be seen again. After such thoughts, the memory of his death would come to my mind as night had come to the mountain, a wave of blackness and despair. I knew then how Dorcas had felt when Jolenta died. There had been no sexual play between the boy and me, as I believe there had at some time been between Dorcas and Jolenta; but then it had never been their fleshly love that had aroused my jealousy. The depth of my feeling for the boy had been as great as Dorcas's for Jolenta, surely (and surely greater far than Jolenta's for Dorcas). If Dorcas had known of it, she would have been as jealous as I had sometimes been, I thought, if only she had loved me as I had loved her.

* * *

At last, when I heard the footsteps no longer, I concealed myself as well as I could and lay down and slept. I half expected I would not wake from that sleep, or that I would wake with a knife at my throat, but no such thing happened. Dreaming of water, I slept well past the dawn and woke alone, cold and stiff in every limb.

I cared nothing then for the secret of the footsteps, or the guardsmen, or the ring, or for anything else in that accursed place. My only wish was to leave it, and as quickly as possible; and I was delighted—though I could not have explained why—when I found that I would not have to repass the circular building on my way to the northwestern side of the mountain.

There have been many times when I have felt I have gone mad, for I have had many great adventures, and the greatest adventures are those that act most strongly upon our minds. So it was then. A man, larger than I and far broader of shoulder, stepped from between the feet of a cataphract, and it was as though one of the monstrous constellations of the night sky had fallen to Urth and clothed itself in the flesh of humankind. For the man had two heads, like an ogre in some forgotten tale in *The Wonders of Urth and Sky*.

Instinctively, I put my hand on the sword hilt at my shoulder. One of the heads laughed; I think it was the only laughter I was ever to hear at the baring of that great blade.

"Why are you alarmed?" he called. "I see you are as well equipped as I am. What is your friend's name?"

Even in my surprise, I admired his boldness. "She is *Terminus Est,*" I said, and I turned the sword so he could see the writing on the steel.

" 'This is the place of parting.' Very good. Very good indeed, and particularly good that it should be read here and now, because this time will truly be a line between old and new such as the world has not seen. My own friend's name is Piaton, which I fear means nothing much. He is an inferior servant to that you have, though perhaps a better steed."

Hearing its name, the other head opened wide its eyes, which had been half closed, and rolled them. Its mouth moved as though to speak, but no sound emerged. I thought it a species of idiot.

"But now you may put up your weapon. As you see, I am unarmed, though already be-headed, and in any case, I mean you no hurt."

He raised his hands as he spoke, and turned to one side and then the other, so that I might see that he was entirely naked, something that was already clear enough.

I asked, "Are you perhaps the son of the dead man I saw in the round building back there?"

I had sheathed *Terminus Est* as I spoke, and he took a step nearer, saying, "Not at all. I am the man himself."

Dorcas rose in my thoughts as if through the brown waters of the Lake of Birds, and I felt again her dead hand clutch mine. Before I knew that I was speaking, I blurted, "I restored you to life?"

"Say rather that your coming awakened me. You thought me dead when I was only dry. I drank, and as you see, I live again. To drink is to live, to be bathed in water is to have a new birth."

"If what you tell me is true, it is wonderful. But I am too much in need of water myself to think much about it now. You say that you have drunk, and the way you say it implies at least that you're friendly toward me. Prove it, please. I haven't eaten or drunk for a long time."

The head that spoke smiled. "You have the most marvelous way of falling in with whatever I plan—there is an appropriateness about you, even to your clothing, that I find delightful. I was just about to suggest that we go where there is food and drink in plenty. Follow me."

At that time, I think I would have followed anyone who promised me water anywhere. Since then I have tried to convince myself that I went out of curiosity, or because I hoped to learn the secret of the great cataphracts; but when I recall those moments and search my mind as it was then, I find nothing other than despair and thirst. The waterfall above Casdoe's house wove its silver columns before my eyes, and I remembered the Vatic Fountain of the House Absolute, and the rush of water from the cliff top in Thrax when I opened the sluice gate to flood the Vincula.

The two-headed man walked before me as if he were confident I would follow him, and equally confident that I would not attack him. When we rounded a corner, I realized for the first time that I had not been, as I had thought, on one of the radiating streets that led to the circular building. It stood before us now. A door—though it was not the one through which little Severian and I had passed—was open as before, and we entered.

"Here," the head that spoke said. "Get in."

The thing toward which he gestured was like a boat, and padded everywhere within as the nenuphar boat in the Autarch's garden had been; yet it floated not on water but in air. When I touched the gunwale, the boat rocked and bobbed beneath my hand, though the motion was almost too small to be seen. I said, "This must be a flyer. I've never seen one so close before."

"If a flyer were a swallow, this would be—I don't know—a sparrow, perhaps. Or a mole, or the toy bird that children strike with paddles to make it fly back and forth between them. Courtesy, I fear, demands that you enter first. I assure you there is no danger.''

Still, I hung back. There seemed something so mysterious about that vessel that for the moment I could not bring myself to set foot in it. I said, ''I come from Nessus and from the eastern bank of Gyoll, and we were taught there that the place of honor in any craft is to be the last to enter and the first to leave.''

''Precisely,'' the head that spoke replied, and before I realized what was happening, the two-headed man seized me about the waist and tossed me into the boat as I might have tossed the boy. It dipped and rolled under the impact of my body, and a moment later yawed violently as the two-headed man sprang in beside me. ''You didn't think, I hope, that you were to take precedence over me?''

He whispered something and the vessel began to move. It glided forward slowly at first, but it was picking up speed.

''True courtesy,'' he continued, ''earns the name. It is courtesy that is truthful. When the plebeian kneels to the monarch, he is offering his neck. He offers it because he knows his ruler can take it if he wishes. Common people like that say—or rather, they used to say, in older and better times—that I have no love of truth. But the truth is that it is precisely truth that I love, an open acknowledgment of fact.''

All this time we were lying at full length, with hardly the width of a hand between us. The idiotic head the other had called Piaton goggled at me and moved its lips as he spoke, making a confused mumbling.

I tried to sit up. The two-headed man caught me with an arm of iron and pulled me down again, saying, ''It's dangerous. These things were built to lie in. You wouldn't want to lose your head, would you? It's nearly as bad, believe me, as getting an extra one.''

The boat nosed down and plunged into the dark. For a moment I thought we were going to die, but the sensation became one of exhilarating speed, the kind of feeling I had known as a boy when we used to slide on evergreen boughs among the mausoleums in winter. When I had become somewhat accustomed to it, I asked, ''Were you born as you are? Or was Piaton actually thrust upon you in some way?'' Already, I think, I had begun to realize that my life would depend on finding out as much as I could about this strange being.

The head that spoke laughed. ''My name is Typhon. You might as well call me by it. Have you heard of me? Once I ruled this planet, and many more.''

I was certain he lied, so I said, ''Rumors of your might echo still . . . Typhon.''

He laughed again. ''You were on the point of calling me Imperator or something of the sort, weren't you? You shall yet. No, I was not born as I am, or born at all, as you meant it. Nor was Piaton grafted to me. I was grafted to him. What do you think of that?"

The boat moved so rapidly now that the air was whistling above our heads, but the descent seemed less steep than it had been. As I spoke, it became nearly level. "Did you wish it?"

"I commanded it."

"Then I think it very strange. Why should you desire to have such a thing done?"

"That I might have life, of course." It was too dark now for me to see either face, though Typhon's was less than a cubit from my own. "All life acts to preserve its life—that is what we call the Law of Existence. Our bodies, you see, die long before we do. In fact, it would be fair to say that we only die because they do. My physicians, of whom I naturally had the best of many worlds, told me it might be possible for me to take a new body, their first thought being to enclose my brain in the skull previously occupied by another. You see the flaw in that?"

Wondering if he were serious, I said, "No, I'm afraid I do not."

"The face—the face! The face would be lost, and it is the face that men are accustomed to obey!" His hand gripped my arm in the dark. "I told them it wouldn't do. Then one came who suggested that the entire head might be substituted. It would even be easier, he said, because the complex neural connections controlling speech and vision would be left intact. I promised him a palatinate if he should succeed."

"It would appear to me—" I began.

Typhon laughed once more. "That it would be better if the original head were removed first. Yes, I always thought so myself. But the technique of making the neural connections was difficult, and he found that the best way—all this was with experimental subjects I provided for him—was to transfer only the voluntary functions by surgery. When that was done, the involuntary ones transferred themselves, eventually. Then the original head could be removed. It would leave a scar, of course, but a shirt would cover it."

"But something went wrong?" I had already moved as far from him as I could in the narrow boat.

"Mostly it was a matter of time." The terrible vigor of his voice, which had been unrelenting, now seemed to wane. "Piaton was one of my slaves—not the largest, but the strongest of all. We tested them. It never occurred to me that someone with his strength might be strong, too, in holding to the action of the heart . . ."

"I see," I said, though in truth I saw nothing.

"It was a period of great confusion as well. My astronomers had told me that this sun's activity would decay slowly. Far too slowly, in fact, for the change to be noticeable in a human lifetime. They were wrong. The heat of the world declined by nearly two parts in a thousand over a few years, then stabilized. Crops failed, and there were famines and riots. I should have left then."

"Why didn't you?" I asked.

"I felt a firm hand was needed. There can only be one firm hand, whether it is the ruler's or someone else's . . .

"Then too, a wonder-worker had arisen, as such people do. He wasn't really a troublemaker, though some of my ministers said he was. I had withdrawn here until my treatment should be complete, and since diseases and deformities seemed to flee from him, I ordered him brought to me."

"The Conciliator," I said, and a moment later could have opened my own wrist for it.

"Yes, that was one of his names. Do you know where he is now?"

"He has been dead for many chiliads."

"And yet he remains, I think?"

That remark startled me so that I looked down at the sack suspended from my neck to see if azure light were not escaping from it.

At that moment, the vessel in which we rode lifted its prow and began to ascend. The moaning of the air about us became the roaring of a whirlwind.

XXVI

The Eyes of the World

Perhaps the boat was controlled by light—when light flashed about us, it stopped at once. In the lap of the mountain I had suffered from the cold, but that was nothing to what I felt now. No wind blew, but it was colder than the bitterest winter I could recall, and I grew dizzy with the effort of sitting up.

Typhon sprang out. "It's been a long time since I was here last. Well, it's good to be home again."

We were in an empty chamber hewn from solid rock, a place as big as a ballroom. Two circular windows at the far end admitted the light; Typhon hastened toward them. They were perhaps a hundred paces apart, and each was some ten cubits wide. I followed him until I noticed that his bare feet left distinct, dark prints. Snow had drifted through the windows and spilled upon the stone floor. I fell to my knees, scooped it up, and stuffed my mouth with it.

I have never tasted anything so delicious. The heat of my tongue seemed to melt it to nectar at once; I truly felt that I could remain where I was all my life, on my knees devouring the snow. Typhon turned back, and seeing me, laughed. "I had forgotten how thirsty you were. Go ahead. We have plenty of time. What I wanted to show you can wait."

Piaton's mouth moved too as it had before, and I thought I caught an expression of sympathy on the idiot face. That brought me to myself again, possibly only because I had already gulped several mouthfuls of the melting snow. When I had swallowed again, I remained where I was, scraping a new heap together, but I said, "You told me about Piaton. Why can't he speak?"

"He can't get his breath, poor fellow," Typhon said. Now I saw that he had an erection, which he nursed with one hand. ''As I told you, I control all the voluntary functions—I will control the involuntary ones too, soon. So although poor Piaton can still move his tongue and shape his lips, he is like a musician who fingers the keys of a horn he cannot blow. When you've had enough of that snow, tell me, and I'll show you where you can get something to eat.''

I filled my mouth again and swallowed. ''This is enough. Yes, I am very hungry.''

''Good,'' he said, and turning away from the windows went to the wall at one side of the chamber. When I neared it, I saw that it, at least, was not (as I had thought) plain stone. Instead, it seemed a kind of crystal, or thick, smoky glass; through it I could see loaves and many strange dishes, as still and perfect as food in a painting.

''You have a talisman of power,'' Typhon told me. ''Now you must give it to me, so that we can open this cupboard.''

''I'm afraid I don't understand what you mean. Do you want my sword?''

''I want the thing you wear at your neck,'' he said, and stretched out a hand for it.

I stepped back. ''There is no power in it.''

''Then you lose nothing. Give it to me.'' As Typhon spoke, Piaton's head moved almost imperceptibly from side to side.

''It is only a curio,'' I said. ''Once I thought it had great power, but when I tried to revive a beautiful woman who was dying, it had no effect, and yesterday it could not restore the boy who traveled with me. How did you know of it?''

''I was watching you, of course. I climbed high enough to see you well. When my ring killed the child and you went to him, I saw the sacred fire. You don't have to actually put it in my hand if you don't want to—just do what I tell you.''

''You could have warned us, then,'' I said.

''Why should I? At that time you were nothing to me. Do you want to eat or not?''

I took out the gem. After all, Dorcas and Jonas had seen it, and I had heard the Pelerines had displayed it in a monstrance on great occasions. It lay on my palm like a bit of blue glass, all fire gone.

Typhon leaned over it curiously. ''Hardly impressive. Now kneel.''

I knelt.

''Repeat after me: I swear by all this talisman represents that for the food I shall receive, I shall be the creature of him I know as Typhon, evermore—''

A snare was closing beside which Decuman's net was a primitive first attempt. This one was so subtle I scarcely knew it was there, and yet I sensed that every strand was of hard-drawn steel.

"—rendering to him all I have and all I shall be, what I own now and what I shall own in days to come, living or dying at his pleasure."

"I have broken oaths before," I said. "If I took it, I should break that one."

"Then take it," he said. "It is no more than a form we must follow. Take it, and I can release you as soon as you have finished eating."

I stood instead. "You said you loved truth. Now I see why—it is truth that binds men." I put the Claw away.

If I had not done so, it would have been lost forever a moment later. Typhon seized me, pinning my arms to my sides so I could not draw *Terminus Est*, and ran with me to one of the windows. I struggled, but it was as a puppy struggles in the hands of a strong man.

As we approached it, the great size of the window made it seem not a window at all; it was as though a part of the outer world had intruded itself into the chamber, and it was a part consisting not of the fields and trees at the mountain's base, which was what I had expected, but of mere extension, a fragment of the sky. The chamber's rock wall, less than a cubit thick, floated backward at the corner of my vision like the muddled line we see, swimming with open eyes, that is the demarcation between the water and the air.

Then I was outside. Typhon's hold had shifted to my ankles, but whether because of the thickness of my boots or merely because of my panic, for a moment I felt I was not held at all. My back was to the mass of the mountain. The Claw, in its soft bag, dangled below my head, held by my chin. I remember feeling a sudden, absurd fear that *Terminus Est* would slip from her sheath.

I pulled myself up with my belly muscles, as a gymnast does when he hangs from the bar by his feet. Typhon released one of my ankles to strike my mouth with his fist, so that I fell back again. I cried out, and tried to wipe my eyes clear of the blood trickling into them from my lips.

The temptation to draw my sword, raise myself again, and strike with it was almost too great to resist. Yet I knew that I could not do so without giving Typhon ample time to see what I intended and let me fall. Even if I succeeded, I would die.

"I urge you now . . ." Typhon's voice came above me, seeming distant in that golden immensity. ". . . to require of your talisman such help as it can provide you."

He paused, and every moment seemed Eternity itself.

"Can it aid you?"

I managed to call, "No."

"Do you understand where you are?"

"I saw. On the face. The mountain autarch."

"It is my face—did you see that? I was the autarch. It is I who come again. You are at my eyes, and it is the iris of my right eye that is to your back. Do you comprehend? You are a tear, a single black tear I weep. In an instant, I may let you fall away to stain my garment. Who can save you, Talisman-bearer?"

"You. Typhon."

"Only I?"

"Only Typhon."

He pulled me back up, and I clung to him as the boy had once clung to me, until we were well inside the great chamber that was the cranial cavity of the mountain.

"Now," he said, "we will make one more attempt. You must come with me to the eye again, and this time you must go willingly. Perhaps it will be easier for you if we go to the left eye instead of the right."

He took my arm. I suppose I could be said to have gone by my own will, since I walked; but I think I have never in my life walked with less heart. It was only the memory of my recent humiliation that kept me from refusing. We did not halt until we stood upon the very rim of the eye; then with a gesture, Typhon forced me to look out. Below us lay an ocean of undulating cloud, blue with shadow where it was not rose with sunlight.

"Autarch," I said, "how are we here, when the vessel in which we rode plunged down so long a tunnel?"

He shrugged my question aside. "Why should gravity serve Urth, when it can serve Typhon? Yet Urth is fair. Look! You see the robe of the world. Is it not beautiful?"

"Very beautiful," I agreed.

"It can be your robe. I have told you that I was autarch on many worlds. I shall be autarch again, and this time on many more. This world, the most ancient of all, I made my capital. That was an error, because I lingered too long when disaster came. By the time I would have escaped, escape was no longer open to me—those to whom I had given control of such ships as could reach the stars had fled in them, and I was besieged on this mountain. I shall not make that mistake again. My capital will be elsewhere, and I will give this world to you, to rule as my steward."

I said, "I have done nothing to deserve so exalted a position."

"Talisman-bearer, no one, not even you, can require me to justify my acts. Instead, view your empire."

Far below us, a wind was born as he spoke. The clouds seethed under its lash and gathered themselves like soldiers into serried ranks moving eastward. Beneath them I saw mountains, and the coastal plains, and beyond the plains the faint, blue line of the sea.

"Look!" Typhon pointed, and as he did so, a pinprick of light appeared in the mountains to the northeast. "Some great energy weapon has been used there," he said. "Perhaps by the ruler of this age, perhaps by his foes. Whichever it may be, its location is revealed now, and it will be destroyed. The armies of this age are weak. They will fly before our flails as chaff at the harvest."

"How can you know all this?" I asked. "You were as dead, until my son and I came upon you."

"Yes. But I have lived almost a day and have sent my thought into far places. There are powers in the seas now who would rule. They will become our slaves, and the hordes of the north are theirs."

"What of the people of Nessus?" I was chilled to the bone; my legs trembled under me.

"Nessus shall be your capital, if you wish it. From your throne in Nessus you will send me tribute of fair women and boys, of the ancient devices and books, and all the good things this world of Urth produces."

He pointed again. I saw the gardens of the House Absolute like a shawl of green and gold cast upon a lawn, and beyond it the Wall of Nessus, and the mighty city itself, the City Imperishable, spreading for so many hundreds of leagues that even the towers of the Citadel were lost in that endless expanse of roofs and winding streets.

"No mountain is so high," I said. "If this one were the greatest in all the world, and if it stood upon the crown of the second greatest, a man could never see as far as I do now."

Typhon took me by the shoulder. "This mountain is as lofty as I wish it to be. Have you forgotten whose face it bears?"

I could only stare at him.

"Fool," he said. "You see through my eyes. Now get out your talisman. I will have your oath upon it."

I drew forth the Claw—for the last time, as I thought—from the leathern bag Dorcas had sewn for it. As I did, there was some slight stirring far below me. The sight of the world from out of the window of the chamber was still grand beyond imagining, but it was only what a man might discern from a mighty peak: the blue dish of Urth. Through the clouds below I could glimpse the lap of the mountain, with many rectangular buildings, the circular building in the center, and the cataphracts. Slowly they were turning their faces away from the sun, upward, to look at us.

"They honor me," Typhon said. Piaton's mouth moved too, but not with his. This time I heeded it.

"You were at the other eye, previously," I told Typhon, "and they did not honor you then. They salute the Claw. Autarch, what of the New Sun, if at last he comes? Will you be his enemy too, as you were the enemy of the Conciliator?"

"Swear to me, and believe me, when he comes I shall be his master, and he my most abject slave."

I struck then.

There is a way of smashing the nose with the heel of one's hand so that the splintered bone is driven into the brain. One must be very quick, however, because without the need for thought a man will lift his hands to protect his face when he sees the blow. I was not so swift as Typhon, but it was his own face his hands were thrown up to guard. I struck at Piaton, and felt the small and terrible cracking that is the sigil of death. The heart that had not served him for so many chiliads ceased to beat.

After a moment, I pushed Typhon's body over the drop with my foot.

XXVII

On High Paths

The floating boat would not obey me, for I had not the word for it. (I have often thought that its word may have been among the things Piaton had tried to tell me, as he had told me to take his life; and I wish I had come to heed him sooner.) In the end, I was forced to climb from the right eye—the worst climb of my life. In this overlong account of my adventures, I have said often that I forget nothing; but I have forgotten much of that, because I was so exhausted that I moved as though in sleep. When I staggered at last into the silent, sealed town that stood among the feet of the cataracts, it must have been nearly night, and I lay down beside a wall that gave me shelter from the wind.

There is a terrible beauty in the mountains, even when they bring one near to death; indeed, I think it is most evident then, and that the hunters who enter the mountains well clothed and well fed and leave them well fed and well clothed seldom see them. There all the world can seem a natural basin of clear water, still and icy cold.

I descended far that day, and found high plains that stretched for leagues, plains filled with sweet grass and such flowers as are never seen at lower altitudes, flowers small and quick to bloom, perfect and pure as roses can never be.

These plains were bordered as often as not by cliffs. More than once I thought I could not go north anymore and would have to retrace my steps; but I always found a way in the end, up or down, and so pressed on. I saw no soldiers riding or marching below me, and though that was in some sense a relief—for I had been afraid the archon's patrol might still be tracking me—it was also unsettling, because it showed I was no longer near the routes by which the army was supplied.

The memory of the alzabo returned to haunt me; I knew that there must be many more of its kind in the mountains. Then too, I could not feel certain it was truly dead. Who could say what recuperative powers such a creature might possess? Though I could forget it by daylight, forcing it, so to speak, away from my consciousness with worries about the presence or absence of soldiers, and the thousand lovely images of peak and cataract and swooping valley that assailed my eyes on every side, it returned by night, when, huddled in my blanket and cloak and burning with fever, I believed I heard the soft padding of its feet, the scraping of its claws.

If as is often said, the world is ordered to some plan (whether one formed prior to its creation or one derived during the billion aeons of its existence by the inexorable logic of order and growth makes no difference) then in all things there must be both the miniature representation of higher glories and the enhanced depiction of smaller matters. To hold my circling attention from the recollection of its horror, I tried sometimes to fix it on that facet of the nature of the alzabo that permits it to incorporate the memories and wills of human beings into its own. The parallel to smaller matters gave me little difficulty. The alzabo might be likened to certain insects, that cover their bodies with twigs and bits of grass, so that they will not be discovered by their enemies. Seen in one way, there is no deception—the twigs, the fragments of leaves are there and are real. Yet the insect is within. So with the alzabo. When Becan, speaking through the creature's mouth, told me he wished his wife and the boy with him, he believed himself to be describing his own desires, and so he was; yet those desires would serve to feed the alzabo, who was within, whose needs and consciousness hid behind Becan's voice.

Not surprisingly, the problem of correlating the alzabo with some higher truth was more difficult; but at last I decided that it might be likened to the absorption by the material world of the thoughts and acts of human beings who, though no longer living, have so imprinted it with activities that in the wider sense we may call works of art, whether buildings, songs, battles, or explorations, that for some time after their demise it may be said to carry forward their lives. In just this fashion the child Severa suggested to the alzabo that it might shift the table in Casdoe's house to reach the loft, though the child Severa was no more.

I had Thecla, then, to advise me, and though I had little hope when I called on her, and she little advice to give, yet she had been warned often against the dangers of the mountains, and she urged me up and onward, and down, always down to lower lands and warmth, at the first light.

I hungered no longer, for hunger is a thing that passes if one does not eat. Weakness came instead, bringing with it a pristine clarity of mind. Then, in the evening of the second day after I had climbed from the pupil of the right eye, I came upon a shepherd's bothy, a sort of beehive of stone, and found in it a cooking pot and a quantity of ground corn.

A mountain spring was only a dozen steps away, but there was no fuel. I spent the evening collecting the abandoned nests of birds from a rock face a half league distant, and that night I struck fire from the tang of *Terminus Est* and boiled the coarse meal (which took a long time to cook, because of the altitude) and ate it. It was, I think, as good a dinner as I have ever tasted, and it had an elusive yet unmistakable flavor of honey, as if the nectar of the plant had been retained in the dry grains as the salt of seas that only Urth herself recalls is held within the cores of certain stones.

I was determined to pay for what I had eaten, and went through my sabretache looking for something of at least equal value that I might leave for the shepherd. Thecla's brown book I would not give up; I soothed my conscience by reminding myself that it was unlikely the shepherd could read in any case. Nor would I surrender my broken whetstone—both because it recalled the green man, and because it would be only a tawdry gift here, where stones nearly as good lay among the young grass on every side. I had no money, having left every coin I had possessed with Dorcas. At last I settled on the scarlet cape she and I had found in the mud of the stone town, long before we reached Thrax. It was stained and too thin to provide much warmth, but I hoped that the tassels and bright color would please him who had fed me.

I have never fully understood how it came to be where we found it, or even whether the strange individual who had called us to him so that he might have that brief period of renewed life had left it behind intentionally or accidentally when the rain dissolved him again to that dust he had been for so long. The ancient sisterhood of priestesses beyond question possesses powers it seldom or never uses, and it is not absurd to suppose that such raising of the dead is among them. If that is so, he may have called them to him as he called us, and the cape may have been left behind by accident.

Yet even if that is so, some higher authority may have been served. It is in such fashion most sages explain the apparent paradox that though we freely choose to do this or the other, commit some crime or by altruism steal the sacred distinction of the Empyrian, still the Increate commands the entirety and is served equally (that is, totally) by those who would obey and those who would rebel.

Not only this. Some, whose arguments I have read in the brown book and several times discussed with Thecla, have pointed out that fluttering in the Presence there abide a multitude of beings that though appearing minute—indeed, infinitely small—by comparison are correspondingly vast in the eyes of men, to whom their master is so gigantic as to be invisible. (By this unlimited size he is rendered minute, so that we are in relation to him like those who walk upon a continent but see only forests, bogs, hills of sand, and so on, and though feeling, perhaps, some tiny stones in their shoes, never reflect that the land they have overlooked all their lives is there, walking with them.)

There are other sages too, who doubting the existence of that power these beings, who may be called the amschaspands, are said to serve, nonetheless assert the fact of their existence. Their assertions are based not on human testimony—of which there is much and to which I add my own, for I saw such a being in the mirror-paged book in the chambers of Father Inire—but rather on irrefutable theory, for they say that if the universe was not created (which they, for reasons not wholly philosophical, find it convenient to disbelieve), then it must have existed forever to this day. And if it has so existed, time itself extends behind the present day without end, and in such a limitless ocean of time, all things conceivable must of necessity have come to pass. Such beings as the amschaspands are conceivable, for they, and many others, have conceived of them. But if creatures so mighty once entered existence, how should they be destroyed? Therefore they are still extant.

Thus by the paradoxical nature of knowledge, it is seen that though the existence of the Ylem, the primordial source of all things, may be doubted, yet the existence of his servants may not be doubted.

And as such beings certainly exist, may it not be that they interfere (if it can be called interference) in our affairs by such accidents as that of the scarlet cape I left in the bothy? It does not require illimitable might to interfere with the internal economy of a nest of ants—a child can stir it with a stick. I know of no thought more terrible than this. (That of my own death, which is popularly supposed to be so awful as to be inconceivable, does not much trouble me; it is of my life that I find, perhaps because of the perfection of my memory, that I cannot think.)

Yet there is another explanation: It may be that all those who seek to serve the Theophany, and perhaps even all those who allege to serve him, though they appear to us to differ so widely and indeed to wage a species of war upon one another, are yet linked, like the marionettes of the boy and the man of wood that I once saw in a dream, and who, although they appeared to combat each other, were nevertheless under the control of an unseen individual who operated the strings of both. If this is the case, then the shaman we saw may have been the friend and ally of those priestesses who range so widely in their civilization across the same land where he, in primitive savagery, once sacrificed with liturgical rigidity of drum and crotal in the small temple of the stone town.

In the last light of the day after I slept in the shepherd's bothy, I came to the lake called Diuturna. It was that, I think, and not the sea, that I had seen on the horizon before my mind was enchained by Typhon's—if indeed my encounter with Typhon and Piaton was not a vision or a dream, from which I awoke of necessity at the spot where I began it. Yet Lake Diuturna is nearly a sea itself, for it is sufficiently vast to be incomprehensible to the mind; and it is the mind, after all, that creates the resonances summoned by that word—without the mind there is only a fraction of Urth covered with brackish water. Though this lake lies at an altitude substantially higher than that of the true sea, I spent the greater part of the afternoon descending to its shore.

The walk was a remarkable experience, and one I treasure even now, perhaps the most beautiful I can recall, though I now hold in my mind the experiences of so many men and women, for as I descended I strode through the year. When I left the bothy, I had above me, behind me, and to my right great fields of snow and ice, through which showed dark crags colder even than they, crags too wind-swept to retain the snow, which sifted down to melt on the tender meadow grass I trod, the grass of earliest spring. As I walked, the grass grew coarser, and of a more virile green. The sounds of insects, of which I am seldom conscious unless I have not heard them in some time, resumed, with a noise that reminded me of the tuning of the strings in the Blue Hall before the first cantilena began, a noise I sometimes used to listen to when I lay on my pallet near the open port of the apprentices' dormitory.

Bushes, which for all their appearance of wiry strength had not been able to endure the heights where the tender grasses lived, appeared now; but when I examined them with care, I found that they were not bushes at all, but plants I had known as towering trees, stunted here by the shortness of the summer and the savagery of the winter, and often split by that ill use into severe straggling trunks. In one of these dwarfed trees, I found a thrush upon a nest, the first bird I had seen in some time except for the soaring raptors of the peaks. A league farther on, and I heard the whistling of cavies, who had their holes among the rocky outcrops, and who thrust up brindled heads with sharp black eyes to warn their relatives of my coming.

A league farther on, and a rabbit went skipping ahead of me in dread of the whirling astara I did not possess. I was descending rapidly at this point, and I became aware of how much strength I had lost, not only to hunger and illness, but to the thinness of the air. It was as though I had been afflicted with a second sickness, of which I had been unaware until the return of trees and real shrubs brought its cure.

At this point, the lake was no longer a line of misted blue; I could see it as a great and almost featureless expanse of steely water, dotted by a few boats I was later to learn were built for the most part of reeds, with a perfect little village at the end of a bay only slightly to the right of my present line of travel.

Just as I had not known my weakness, until I saw the boats and the rounded curves of the thatched roofs of the village I had not known how solitary I had been since the boy died. It was more than mere loneliness, I think. I have never had much need for companionship, unless it was the companionship of someone I could call a friend. Certainly I have seldom wished the conversation of strangers or the sight of strange faces. I believe rather that when I was alone I felt I had in some fashion lost my individuality; to the thrush and the rabbit I had been not Severian, but Man. The many people who like to be utterly alone, and particularly to be utterly alone in a wilderness, do so, I believe, because they enjoy playing that part. But I wanted to be a particular person again, and so I sought the mirror of other persons, which would show me that I was not as they were.

XXVIII

The Hetman's Dinner

It was nearly evening before I reached the first houses. The sun spread a path of red gold across the lake, a path that appeared to extend the village street to the margin of the world, so that a man might have walked down it and out into the larger universe. But the village itself, small and poor though I saw it to be when I reached it, was good enough for me, who had been walking so long in high and remote places.

There was no inn, and since none of the people who peered at me over the sills of their windows seemed at all eager to admit me, I asked for the hetman's house, pushed aside the fat woman who answered the door, and made myself comfortable. By the time the hetman arrived to see who had appointed himself his guest, I had my broken stone and my oil out and was leaning over the blade of *Terminus Est* as I warmed myself before his fire. He began by bowing, but he was so curious about me that he could not resist looking up as he bowed; so that I had difficulty in refraining from laughing at him, which would have been fatal to my plans.

"The optimate is welcome," the hetman said, blowing out his wrinkled cheeks. "Most welcome. My poor house—all our poor little settlement—is at his disposal."

"I am not an optimate," I told him. "I am the Grand Master Severian, of the Order of the Seekers for Truth and Penitence, commonly called the guild of torturers. You, Hetman, will address me as *Master*. I have had a difficult journey, and if you will provide me with a good dinner and a tolerable bed, it is not likely I will have to trouble you or your people for much else before morning."

"You will have my own bed," he said quickly. "And such food as we can provide."

"You must have fresh fish here, and waterfowl. I'll have both. Wild rice, too." I remembered that once, when Master Gurloes was discussing our guild's relations with the others in the Citadel, he had told me that one of the easiest ways to dominate a man is to demand something he cannot supply. "Honey, new bread, and butter should do it, except for the vegetable and the salad, and since I'm not particular about those, I will let you surprise me. Something good, and something I haven't had before, so that I'll have a tale to carry back to the House Absolute."

The hetman's eyes had been growing rounder and rounder as I spoke, and at the mention of the House Absolute, which was doubtless no more than the most distant of rumors in his village, they seemed about to pop out of his skull. He tried to murmur something about cattle (presumably that they could not live to supply butter at these altitudes) but I waved him out, then caught him by the scruff of the neck for not closing the door behind him.

When he was gone, I risked taking off my boots. It never pays to appear relaxed around prisoners (and he and his village were mine now, I thought, though they were not confined), but I felt sure no one would dare enter the room until some sort of meal was ready. I finished cleaning and oiling *Terminus Est*, and gave her enough strokes with the whetstone to restore her edges.

That done, I withdrew my other treasure (though it was not in fact mine) from its bag and examined it in the light of the hetman's pungent fire. Since I had left Thrax it no longer pressed against my chest like a finger of iron—indeed, while I tramped in the mountains I had sometimes forgotten for half a day that I wore it, and once or twice I had clasped it in panic, thinking, when I recalled it at last, that I had lost it. In this low-ceilinged, square room of the hetman's, where the rounded stones in the walls seemed to warm their bellies like burgesses, it did not flash as it had in the one-eyed boy's jacal; but neither was it so lifeless as it had been when I showed it to Typhon. Now, rather, it seemed to glow, and I could almost have imagined that its energies played upon my face. The crescent-shaped mark in its heart had never appeared more distinct, and though it was dark, a star-point of light emanated from it.

I put away the gem at last, a little ashamed of having toyed with so entheal a thing as if it were a bauble. I took out the brown book and would have read from it if I could; but though my fever seemed to have left me, I was still very fatigued, and the flickering firelight made the cramped, old-fashioned letters dance on the page and soon defeated my eyes, so that the story I was reading appeared at some times to be no more than nonsense, and at others to deal with my own concerns—

endless journeyings, the cruelty of crowds, streams running with blood. Once I thought I saw Agia's name, but when I looked a second time it had become the word *again*: "Agia she leaped, and twisting round the columns of the carapace . . ."

The page seemed luminous yet indecipherable, like the reflection of a looking glass seen in a quiet pool. I closed the book and put it back in my sabretache, not certain I had in fact seen any of the words I had thought an instant ago I had read. Agia must indeed have leaped from the thatched roof of Casdoe's house. Certainly she twisted, for she had twisted the execution of Agilus into murder. The great tortoise that in myth is said to support the world and is thus an embodiment of the galaxy, without whose swirling order we would be a lonely wanderer in space, is supposed to have revealed in ancient times the Universal Rule, since lost, by which one might always be sure of acting rightly. Its carapace represented the bowl of heaven, its plastron the plains of all the worlds. The columns of the carapace would then be the armies of the Theologoumenon, terrible and gleaming . . .

Yet I was not sure I had read any of this, and when I took out the book again and tried to find the page, I could not. Though I knew my confusion was only the result of fatigue, hunger, and the light, I felt the fear that has always come upon me on the many occasions of my life when some small incident has made me aware of an incipient insanity. As I stared into the fire, it seemed more possible than I would have liked to believe that someday, perhaps after a blow on the head, perhaps for no discernible cause, my imagination and my reason might reverse their places—just as two friends who come every day to the same seats in some public garden might at last decide for novelty's sake to exchange them. Then I would see as if in actuality all the phantoms of my mind, and only perceive in that tenuous way in which we behold our fears and ambitions the people and things of the real world. These thoughts, occurring at this point in my narrative, must seem prescient; I can only excuse them by saying that tormented as I am by my memories, I have meditated in the same way very often.

A faint knock at the door ended my morbid revery. I pulled on my boots and called, "Come in!"

A person who took care to remain out of my sight, though I am fairly sure it was the hetman, pushed back the door; and a young woman entered carrying a brass tray heaped with dishes. It was not until she set it down that I realized she was quite naked except for what I at first took to be rude jewelry, and not until she bowed, lifting her hands to her head in the northern fashion, that I saw that the dully shining bands about her wrists, which I had taken for bracelets, were in fact gyves of watered steel joined by a long chain.

"Your supper, Grand Master," she said, and backed toward the door until I could see the flesh of her rounded hips flattened where they pressed against it. With one hand she attempted to lift the latch; but though I heard its faint rattle, the door did not give. No doubt the person who had admitted her was holding it closed from the outside.

"It smells delicious," I told her. "Did you cook it yourself?"

"A few things. The fish, and the fried cakes."

I stood, and leaning *Terminus Est* against the rough masonry of the wall so as not to frighten her, went over to examine the meal: a young duck, quartered and grilled, the fish she had mentioned, the cakes (which later proved to be of cattail flour mixed with minced clams), potatoes baked in the embers of a fire, and a salad of mushrooms and greens.

"No bread," I said. "No butter and no honey. They will hear of this."

"We hoped, Grand Master, that the cakes would be acceptable."

"I realize it isn't your fault."

It had been a long time since I had lain with Cyriaca, and I had been trying not to look at this slave girl, but I did so now. Her long, black hair hung to her waist and her skin was nearly the color of the tray she held, yet she had a slender waist, a thing seldom found in autochthon women, and her face was piquant and even a trifle sharp. Agia, for all her fair skin and freckles, had broader cheeks by far.

"Thank you, Grand Master. He wants me to stay here to serve you while you eat. If you do not want that, you must tell him to open the door and let me out."

"I will tell him," I said, raising my voice, "to go away from the door and cease eavesdropping on my conversation. You are speaking of your owner, I suppose? Of the hetman of this place?"

"Yes, of Zambdas."

"And what is your own name?"

"Pia, Grand Master."

"And how old are you, Pia?"

She told me, and I smiled to find her precisely the same age as myself.

"Now you must serve me, Pia. I'm going to sit over here at the fire, where I was before you came in, and you can bring me the food. Have you served at table before?"

"Oh, yes, Grand Master. I serve at every meal."

"Then you should know what you're doing. What do you recommend first—the fish?"

She nodded.

"Then bring that over, and the wine, and some of your cakes. Have you eaten?"

She shook her head until the black hair danced. "Oh, no, but it would not be right for me to eat with you."

"Still I notice I can count a good many ribs."

"I would be beaten for it, Grand Master."

"Not while I am here, at least. But I won't force you. Just the same, I would like to assure myself that they haven't put anything in any of this that I wouldn't give my dog, if I still had him. The wine would be the most likely place, I think. It will be rough but sweet, if it's like most country wines." I poured the stone goblet half full and handed it to her. "You drink that, and if you don't fall to the floor in fits, I'll try a drop too."

She had some difficulty in getting it down, but she did so at last and, with watering eyes, handed the goblet back to me. I poured some wine for myself and sipped it, finding it every bit as bad as I expected.

I made her sit beside me then, and fed her one of the fish she herself had fried in oil. When she had finished it, I ate a couple too. They were so much superior to the wine as her own delicate face was to the old hetman's—caught that day, I felt sure, and in water much colder and cleaner than the muddy lower reaches of Gyoll, from which the fish I had been accustomed to in the Citadel had come.

"Do they always chain slaves here?" I asked her as we divided the cakes. "Or have you been particularly unruly, Pia?"

She said, "I am of the lake people," as though that answered my question, as no doubt it would have if I had been familiar with the local situation.

"I would think these are the lake people." I gestured to indicate the hetman's house and the village in general.

"Oh, no. These are the shore people. Our people live in the lake, on the islands. But sometimes the wind blows our islands here, and Zambdas is afraid I will see my home then and swim to it. The chain is heavy—you can see how long it is—and I can't take it off. And so the weight would drown me."

"Unless you found a piece of wood to bear the weight while you paddled with your feet."

She pretended not to have heard me. "Would you like some duck, Grand Master?"

"Yes, but not until you eat some of it first, and before you have any, I want you to tell me more about those islands. Did you say the wind blew them here? I confess I have never heard of islands that were blown by the wind."

Pia was looking longingly toward the duck, which must have been a delicacy in that part of the world. "I have heard that there are islands that do not move. That must be very inconvenient, I suppose, and I have never seen any. Our islands travel from one place to another, and sometimes we put sails in their trees to make them go faster. But they will not sail across the wind very well, because they do not have wise bottoms like the bottoms of boats, but foolish bottoms like the bottoms of tubs, and sometimes they turn over."

"I want to see your islands sometime, Pia," I told her. "I also want to get you back to them, since that seems to be where you want to go. I owe something to a man with a name much like yours, and so I'll try to do that before I leave this place. Meanwhile, you had better build up your strength with some of that duck."

She took a piece, and after she had swallowed a few mouthfuls began to peel off slivers for me that she fed me with her fingers. It was very good, still hot enough to steam and imbued with a delicate flavor suggestive of parsley, which perhaps came from some water plant on which these ducks fed; but it was also rich and somewhat greasy, and when I had eaten the better part of one thigh, I took a few bites of salad to clear my palate.

I think I ate some more of the duck after that, then a movement in the fire caught my eye. A fragment of almost-consumed wood glowing with heat had fallen from one of the logs into the ashes under the grate, but instead of lying there and becoming dim and eventually black, it seemed to straighten up, and in doing so became Roche, Roche with his fiery red hair turned to real flames, Roche holding a torch as he used to when we were boys and went to swim in the cistern beneath the Bell Keep.

It seemed so extraordinary to see him there, reduced to a glowing micromorph, that I turned to Pia to point him out to her. She appeared to have seen nothing; but Drotte, no taller than my thumb, was standing on her shoulder, half concealed in her flowing black hair. When I tried to tell her he was there, I heard myself speaking in a new tongue, hissing, grunting, and clicking. I felt no fear at any of this, only a detached wonder. I could tell that what I was saying was not human speech, and observe the horrified expression on Pia's face as though I were contemplating some ancient painting in old Rudisind's gallery in the Citadel; yet I could not turn my noises into words, or even halt them. Pia screamed.

The door flew open. It had been closed for so long that I had almost forgotten it could not be locked; but it was open now, and two figures stood there. When the door opened they were men, men whose faces had been replaced by smooth pelts of fur like the backs of two otters, but men still. An instant later they had become plants, tall stalks of viridian from which protruded the razor-sharp, oddly angled leaves of the avern. Spiders, black and soft and many-legged, had been hiding there. I tried to rise from my chair, and they leaped at me trailing webs of gossamer that shone in the firelight. I had only time to see and remember Pia's face, with its wide eyes and its delicate mouth frozen in a circle of horror before a peregrine with a beak of steel stooped to tear the Claw from my neck.

XXIX

The Hetman's Boat

After that I was locked in the dark for what I later found had been the night and the greater part of the following morning. Yet though it was dark where I lay, it was not at first dark to me, for my hallucinations needed no candle. I can recall them still, as I can recall everything; but I will not bore you, my ultimate reader, with the entire catalog of phantoms, though it would be easy enough for me to describe them here. What is not easy is the task of expressing my feelings concerning them.

It would have been a great relief for me to believe that they were all in some way contained in the drug I had swallowed (which was, as I guessed then and learned later, when I could question those who treated the wounded of the Autarch's army, nothing more than the mushrooms that had been chopped into my salad) just as Thecla's thoughts and Thecla's personality, comforting at times and troubling at others, had been contained in the fragment of her flesh I had eaten at Vodalus's banquet. Yet I knew it could not be so, and that all the things I saw, some amusing, some horrible and terrifying, some merely grotesque, were the product of my own mind. Or of Thecla's, which was now a part of my own.

Or rather, as I first began to realize there in the dark as I watched a parade of women from the court—exultants immensely tall and imbued with the stiff grace of costly porcelains, their complexions powdered with the dust of pearls or diamonds and their eyes made large as Thecla's had been by the application of minute amounts of certain poisons in childhood—products of the mind that now existed in the combination of the minds that had been hers and mine.

Severian, the apprentice I had been, the young man who had swum beneath the Bell Keep, who had once nearly drowned in Gyoll, who had idled alone on summer days in the ruined necropolis, who had handed the Chatelaine Thecla, in the nadir of his despair, the stolen knife, was gone.

Not dead. Why had he thought that every life must end in death, and never in anything else? Not dead, but vanished as a single note vanished, never to reappear, when it becomes an indistinguishable and inseparable part of some extemporized melody. That young Severian had hated death, and by the mercy of the Increate, whose mercy indeed (as is wisely said in many places) confounds and destroys us, he did not die.

The women turned long necks to look down at me. Their oval faces were perfect, symmetrical, expressionless yet lewd; and I understood quite suddenly that they were not—or at least no longer were—the courtiers of the House Absolute, but had become the courtesans of the House Azure.

For some while, as it seemed to me, the parade of those seductive and inhuman women continued, and at each beat of my heart (of which I was conscious at that time as I have seldom been before or since, so that it seemed as if a drum throbbed in my chest) they reversed their roles without changing the least detail of their appearance. Just as I have sometimes known in dreams that a certain figure was in fact someone whom it did not in the least resemble, so I knew at one instant that these women were the ornaments of the Autarchial presence, and at the next that they were to be sold for the night for a handful of orichalks.

During all this time, and all the much longer periods that preceded and followed it, I was acutely uncomfortable. The spiders' webs, which I came gradually to perceive were common fishing nets, had not been removed; but I had been bound with ropes as well, so that one arm was tightly pinioned by my side and the other bent until the fingers of my hand, which soon grew numb, almost touched my face. At the height of the action of the drug I had become incontinent, and now my trousers were soaked with urine, cold and stinking. As my hallucinations grew less violent and the intervals between them longer, the misery of my circumstances afflicted me more, and I became fearful of what would happen to me when I was eventually taken from the windowless storeroom into which I had been cast. I supposed that the hetman had learned from some estafette that I was not what I had pretended to be, and no doubt also that I was fleeing the archon's justice; for I assumed that he would not otherwise have dared to treat me as he had. Under these circumstances, I could only wonder whether he would dispose of me himself (doubtless by noyade, in such a place), deliver me to some petty ethnarch, or return me to Thrax. I resolved to take my own life should the opportunity be afforded me, but it seemed so improbable that I should be given the chance that I was ready to kill myself in my despair.

At last the door opened. The light, though it was only that of a dim room in that thick-walled house, seemed blinding. Two men dragged me forth as they might have pulled out a sack of meal. They were heavily bearded, and so I suppose it was they who had appeared, when they burst in upon Pia and me, to have the pelts of animals for faces. They set me upon my feet, but my legs would not hold, and they were forced to untie me and to remove the nets that had taken me when the net of Typhon had failed. When I could stand again, they gave me a cup of water and a strip of salt fish.

After a time the hetman came in. Although he stood as importantly as he was no doubt accustomed to stand when he directed the affairs of his village, he could not keep his voice from quavering. Why he should still be frightened of me I could not understand, but plainly he still was. Since I had nothing to lose and everything to gain by the attempt, I ordered him to release me.

"That I cannot do, Grand Master," he said. "I am acting under instructions."

"May I ask who has dared tell you to act in this fashion toward the representative of your Autarch?"

He cleared his throat. "Instructions from the castle. My messenger bird carried your sapphire there last night, and another bird came this morning, with a sign that means we are to bring you."

At first I supposed he meant Acies Castle, where one of the squadrons of dimarchi had its headquarters, but after a moment I realized that here, two score leagues at least from the fortifications of Thrax, it was most unlikely that he would be so specific. I said, "What castle is that? And do your instructions preclude my cleaning myself before I present myself there? And having my clothing washed?"

"I suppose that might be done," he said uncertainly; then to one of his men: "How stands the wind?"

The man addressed gave a half shrug that meant nothing to me, though it seemed to convey information to the hetman.

"All right," he told me. "We can't set you free, but we'll wash your clothes and give you something to eat, if you wish it." As he was leaving, he turned back with an expression that was almost apologetic. "The castle is near, Grand Master, the Autarch far. You understand. We have had great difficulties in the past, but now there is peace."

I would have argued with him, but he gave me no chance. The door shut behind him.

Pia, now dressed in a ragged smock, came in a short time later. I was forced to submit to the indignity of being stripped and washed by her; but I was able to take advantage of the process to whisper to her, and I asked her to see that my sword was sent wherever I was—for I was hoping to escape, if only by confessing to the master of the mysterious castle and offering to join forces with him. Just as she had ignored me when I had suggested that she might float the weight of her chain on a stick of firewood, she gave no indication of having heard me now; but a watch or so later, when, dressed once more, I was being paraded to a boat for the edification of the village, she came running after our little procession with *Terminus Est* cradled in her arms. The hetman had apparently wanted to retain such a fine weapon, and remonstrated with her; but I was able to warn him as I was being dragged on board that when I arrived at the castle I would inform whoever received me there of the existence of my sword, and in the end he surrendered.

The boat was a kind I had never seen before. In form it might have been a xebec, sharp fore and aft, wide amidships, with a long, overhanging stern and an even longer prow. Yet the shallow hull was built of bundles of buoyant reeds tied together in a sort of wickerwork. There could be no step for a conventional mast in such a frail hull, and in its place stood a triangular lash-up of poles. The narrow base of the triangle ran from gunwale to gunwale; its long isosceles sides supported a block used, just as the hetman and I clambered aboard, to hoist a slanting yard that trailed a widely striped linen sail. The hetman now held my sword, but just as the painter was cast off, Pia leaped into the boat with her chain jangling.

The hetman was furious and struck her; but it is not an easy matter to take in the sail of such a craft and turn it about with sweeps, and in the end, though he sent her weeping to the bow, he permitted her to stay. I ventured to ask him why she had wanted to come, though I thought I knew.

"My wife is hard on her when I am not at home," he told me. "Beats her and makes her scrub all day. It's good for the child, naturally, and it makes her happy to see me when I come back. But she would rather go with me, and I don't greatly blame her."

"Nor do I," I said, trying to turn my face away from his sour breath. "Besides, she will get to see the castle, which I suppose she has never seen before."

"She's seen the walls a hundred times. She comes of the landless lake people, and they are blown about by the wind and so see everything."

If they were blown by the wind, so were we. Air as pure as spirit filled the striped sail, made even that broad hull heel over, and sent us scudding across the water until the village vanished below the rim of the horizon—though the white peaks of the mountains were still visible, rising as it seemed from the lake itself.

XXX

Natrium

So primitively armed were these lakeshore fisherfolk—indeed, far more primitively than the actual autochthonous primitives I had seen about Thrax—that it was some time before I understood that they were armed at all. There were more on board than were needed to steer and make sail, but I assumed at first that they had come merely as rowers, or to add to the prestige of their hetman when he brought me to his master at the castle. In their belts they carried knives of the straight, narrow-bladed kind fishermen everywhere use, and there was a sheaf of barb-headed fishing spears stowed forward, but I thought nothing of that. It was not until one of the islands I had been so eager to see came into view and I noticed one of the men fingering a club edged with animal teeth that I realized they had been brought as a guard, and there was in fact something to guard against.

The little island itself appeared unexceptional until one saw that it truly moved. It was low and very green, with a diminutive hut (built like our boat of reeds and thatched with the same material) at its highest point. A few willows grew upon it, and a long narrow boat, again built of reeds, was tied at the water's edge. When we were closer, I saw that the island was of reeds too, but of living ones. Their stems gave it its characteristic verdescence; their interlaced roots must have formed its raftlike base. Upon their massed, living tangle, soil had accumulated or been stored up by the inhabitants. The trees had sprouted there to trail their roots in the waters of the lake. A little patch of vegetables flourished.

Because the hetman and all the others on board except Pia scowled at it, I regarded this tiny land with favor; and seeing it as I saw it then, a spot of green against the cold and seemingly infinite blue of the face of Diuturna and the deeper, warmer, yet truly infinite blue of the sun-crowned, star-sprinkled sky, it was easy to love it. If I had looked upon this scene as I might have upon a picture, it would have seemed more heavily symbolic—the level line of the horizon dividing the canvas into equal halves, the dot of green with its green trees and brown hut—than those pictures critics are accustomed to deride for their symbolism. Yet who could have said what it meant? It is impossible, I think, that all the symbols we see in natural landscapes are there only because we see them. No one hesitates to brand as mad the solipsists who truly believe that the world exists only because they observe it and that buildings, mountains, and even ourselves (to whom they have spoken only a moment before) all vanish when they turn their heads. Is it not equally mad to believe that the meaning of the same objects vanishes in the same way? If Thecla had symbolized love of which I felt myself unworthy, as I know now that she did, then did her symbolic force disappear when I locked the door of her cell behind me? That would be like saying that the writing in this book, over which I have labored for so many watches, will vanish into a blur of vermilion when I close it for the last time and dispatch it to the eternal library maintained by old Ultan.

The great question, then, that I pondered as I watched the floating island with longing eyes and chafed at my bonds and cursed the hetman in my heart, is that of determining what these symbols mean in and of themselves. We are like children who look at print and see a serpent in the last letter but one, and a sword in the last.

What message was intended for me in the little homey hut and its green garden suspended between two infinities I do not know. But the meaning I read into it was that of freedom and home, and I felt then a greater desire for freedom, for the liberty to rove the upper and the lower worlds at will, carrying with me such comforts as would suffice me, than I had ever felt before—even when I was a prisoner in the antechamber of the House Absolute, even when I was client of the torturers in the Old Citadel.

Then, just at the time when I desired most to be free and we were as near the island as our course would take us, two men and a boy of fifteen or so came out of the hut. For a moment they stood before their door, looking at us as though they were taking the measure of boat and crew. There were five villagers on board in addition to the hetman, and it seemed clear the islanders could do nothing against us, but they put out in their slender craft, the men paddling after us while the boy rigged a crude sail of matting.

The hetman, who turned from time to time to look back at them, was seated beside me with *Terminus Est* across his lap. It seemed to me that at every moment he was about to set her aside and go astern to speak to the man at the tiller, or go forward to talk to the other four who lounged in the bow. My hands were tied in front of me, and it would have taken only an instant to draw the blade a thumb's width clear of her sheath and cut the cords, but the opportunity did not come.

A second island hove into view, and we were joined by another boat, this bearing two men. The odds were slightly worse now, and the hetman called one of his villagers to him and went a step or two astern, carrying my sword. They opened a metal canister that had been concealed under the steersman's platform there and took out a weapon of a type I had not seen before, a bow made by binding two slender bows, each of which carried its own string, to spacers that held them half a span apart. The strings were lashed together at their centers as well, so that the lashings made a sling for some missile.

While I was looking at this curious contrivance, Pia edged closer. "They're watching me," she whispered. "I can't untie you now. But perhaps . . ." She looked significantly toward the boats that followed ours.

"Will they attack?"

"Not unless there are more to join them. They have only fish spears and pachos." Seeing my look of incomprehension she added, "Sticks with teeth—one of these men has one too."

The villager the hetman had summoned was taking what appeared to be a wadded rag from the canister. He unwrapped it on the open lid and disclosed several silver-gray, oily-looking slugs of metal.

"Bullets of power," Pia said. She sounded frightened.

"Do you think more of your people will come?"

"If we pass more islands. If one or two follow a landboat, then all do, to share in what there is to be gotten from it. But we will be in sight of the shore again soon—" Under her ragged smock, her breasts heaved as the villager wiped his hand on his coat, picked up one of the silvery slugs, and fitted it into the sling of the double bow.

"It's only like a heavy stone—" I began. He drew the strings to his ear and let fly, sending the slug whizzing through the space between the slender bows. Pia had been so frightened that I half expected it to undergo some transformation as it flew, perhaps becoming one of those spiders I still half believed I had seen when, drugged, I had been caught in these fishermen's nets.

Nothing of the sort occurred. The slug flew—a shining streak—across the water and splashed into the lake a dozen paces or so before the bow of the nearer boat.

For the space of a breath, nothing more happened. Then there was a sharp detonation, a fireball, and a geyser of steam. Something dark, apparently the missile itself, still intact and flung up by the explosion it had caused, was thrown into the air only to fall again, this time between the two pursuing boats. A new explosion followed, only slightly less intense than the first, and one of the boats was nearly swamped. The other veered away. A third explosion came, and a fourth, but the slug, whatever other powers it might possess, seemed incapable of tracking the boats the way Hethor's notules had followed Jonas and me. Each blast carried it farther off, and after the fourth it appeared spent. The two pursuing boats fell back out of range, but I admired their courage in keeping up the chase at all.

"The bullets of power bring fire from water," Pia told me.

I nodded. "So I see." I was getting my legs set under me, finding secure footing among the bundles of reeds.

It is no great trick to swim even when your hands are bound behind you—Drotte, Roche, Eata and I used to practice swimming while gripping our own thumbs at the small of the back, and with my hands tied before me, I knew I could stay afloat for a long time if necessary; but I was worried about Pia, and told her to go as far forward as she could.

"But then I will not be able to untie you."

"You'll never be able to while they're watching us," I whispered. "Go forward. If this boat breaks up, hang onto a bunch of reeds. They'll still float. Don't argue."

The men in the bow did not stop her, and she halted only when she had reached the point at which a cable of woven reeds formed the vessel's stem. I took a deep breath and leaped overboard.

If I had wished to I could have dived with hardly a ripple, but I hugged my knees to my chest instead to make as great a splash as I could, and thanks to the weight of my boots I sank far deeper than I would have if I had been stripped for swimming. It was that point that had worried me; I had seen when the hetman's archer had fired his missile that there was a distinct pause before the explosion. I knew that as well as drenching both men, I must have wet every slug lying on the oiled rag—but I could not be certain they would go off before I came to the surface.

The water was cold and grew colder as I went down. Opening my eyes, I saw a marvelous cobalt color that grew darker as it swirled about me. I felt a panicky urge to kick off my boots; but that would have brought me up quickly, and I filled my mind instead with the wonder of the color and the thought of the indestructible corpses I had seen littering the refuse heaps about the mines of Saltus—corpses sinking forever in the blue gulf of time.

Slowly I revolved without effort until I could make out the brown hull of the hetman's boat suspended overhead. For a while that spot of brown and I seemed frozen in our positions; I lay beneath it as dead men lie below a carrion bird that, filling its wings with the wind, appears to hover only just below the fixed stars.

Then with bursting lungs I began to rise.

As if it had been a signal I heard the first explosion, a dull and distant boom. I swam upward as a frog does, hearing another explosion and another, each sounding sharper than the last.

When my head broke water, I saw that the stern of the hetman's boat had opened, the reed bundles spreading like broomstraws. A secondary explosion to my left deafened me for a moment and dashed my face with spray that stung like hail. The hetman's archer was floundering not far from me, but the hetman himself (still, I was delighted to see, gripping *Terminus Est*), Pia, and the others were clinging to what remained of the bow, and thanks to the buoyancy of the reeds it yet floated, though the lower end was awash. I tore at the cords on my wrists with my teeth until two of the islanders helped me climb into their craft, and one of them cut me free.

XXXI

The People of the Lake

Pia and I spent the night on one of the floating islands, where I, who had entered Thecla so often when she was unchained but a prisoner, now entered Pia when she was still chained but free. She lay upon my chest afterward and wept for joy—not so much the joy she had of me, I think, but the joy of her freedom, though her kinsmen the islanders, who have no metal but that they trade or loot from the people of the shore, had no smith to strike off her shackles.

I have heard it said by men who have known many women that at last they come to see resemblances in love between certain ones, and now for the first time I found this to be true in my own experience, for Pia with her hungry mouth and supple body recalled Dorcas. But it was false too in some degree; Dorcas and Pia were alike in love as the faces of sisters are sometimes alike, but I would never have confused one with the other.

I had been too exhausted when we reached the island to fully appreciate the wonder of it, and night had been nearly upon us. Even now, all I recall is dragging the little boat to shore and going into a hut where one of our rescuers kindled a tiny blaze of driftwood, and I oiled *Terminus Est*, which the islanders had taken from the captured hetman and returned to me. But when Urth turned her face to the sun again, it was a wondrous thing to stand with one hand on the willow's graceful trunk and feel the whole of the island rock beneath me!

Our hosts cooked fish for our breakfast; before we had finished them, a boat arrived bearing two more islanders with more fish and root vegetables of a kind I had never tasted before. We roasted these in the ashes and ate them hot. The flavor was more like a chestnut's than anything else I can think of. Three more boats came, then an island with four trees and bellying, square sails rigged in the branches of each, so that when I saw it from a distance I thought it a flotilla. The captain was an elderly man, the closest thing the islanders had to a chief. His name was Llibio. When Pia introduced me to him, he embraced me as fathers do their sons, something no one had ever done to me previously.

After we separated, all the others, Pia included, drew far enough away to permit us to speak privately if we kept our voices low—some men going into the hut, and the rest (there were now about ten in all) to the farther side of the island.

"I have heard that you are a great fighter, and a slayer of men," Llibio began.

I told him that I was indeed a slayer of men, but not great.

"That is so. Every man fights backward—to kill others. Yet his victory comes not in the killing of others but in the killing of certain parts of himself."

To show that I understood him, I said, "You must have killed all the worst parts of your own being. Your people love you."

"That is also not to be trusted." He paused, looking out over the water. "We are poor and few, and had the people listened to another in these years . . ." He shook his head.

"I have traveled far, and I have observed that poor people usually have more wit and more virtue than rich ones."

He smiled at that. "You are kind. But our people have so much wit and virtue now that they may die. We have never possessed great numbers, and many perished in the winter just past, when much water froze."

"I had not thought how difficult winter must be for your people, without wool or furs. But I can see, now that you have pointed it out to me, that it must be hard indeed."

The old man shook his head. "We grease ourselves, which does much, and the seals give us finer cloaks than the shore people have. But when the ice comes, our islands cannot move, and the shore people need no boats to reach them, and so can come against us with all their force. Each summer we fight them when they come to take our fish. But each winter they kill us, coming across the ice for slaves."

I thought then of the Claw, which the hetman had taken from me and sent to the castle, and I said, "The land people obey the master of the castle. Perhaps if you made peace with him, he would stop them from attacking you."

"Once, when I was a young man, these quarrels took two or three lives in a year. Then the builder of the castle came. Do you know the tale?"

I shook my head.

"He came from the south, whence, as I am told, you come as well. He had many things the shore people wanted, such as cloth, and silver, and many well-forged tools. Under his direction they built his castle. Those were the fathers and grandfathers of those who are the shore people now. They used the tools for him, and as he had promised, he permitted them to keep them when the work was done, and he gave them many other things. My mother's father went to them while they labored, and asked if they did not see that they were setting up a ruler over themselves, since the builder of the castle could do as he chose with them, then retire behind the strong walls they had built for him where no one could reach him. They laughed at my mother's father and said they were many, which was true, and the builder of the castle only one, which was also true."

I asked if he had ever seen the builder, and if so what he looked like.

"Once. He stood on a rock talking to shore people while I passed in my boat. I can tell you he was a little man, a man who would not, had you been there, have reached higher than your shoulder. Not such a man as inspires fear." Llibio paused again, his dim eyes seeing not the waters of his lake but times long past. "Still, fear came. The outer wall was complete, and the shore people returned to their hunting, their weirs and their herds. Then their greatest man came to us and said we had stolen beasts and children, and that they would destroy us if we did not return them."

Llibio stared into my face and gripped my hand with his own, which was as hard as wood. Seeing him then, I saw the vanished years as well. They must have seemed grim enough at the time, though the future they had spawned—the future in which I sat with him, my sword across my lap, hearing his story—was grimmer than he could have known at the time. Yet there was joy in those years for him; he had been a strong young man, and though he was not, perhaps, thinking of that, his eyes remembered.

"We told them we did not devour children and had no need of slaves to fish for us, nor any pasturage for beasts. Even then, they must have known it was not we, because they did not come in war against us. But when our islands neared the shore, we heard their women wailing through the night.

"In those times, each day after the full moon was a trading day, when those of us who wished came to the shore for salt and knives. When the next trading day came, we saw that the shore people knew where their children had gone, and their beasts, and whispered it among themselves. Then we asked why they did not go to the castle and carry it by storm, for they were many. But they took our children instead, and men and women of all ages, and chained them outside their doors so that their own people might not be taken—or even marched them to the gates and bound them there.''

I ventured to ask how long this had gone on.

''For many years—since I was a young man, as I told you. Sometimes the shore people fought. More often, they did not. Twice warriors came from the south, sent by the proud people of the tall houses of the southern shore. While they were here, the fighting stopped, but what was said in the castle I do not know. The builder, of whom I told you, was seen by no one once his castle was complete.''

He waited for me to speak. I had the feeling, which I have often had when talking with old people, that the words he said and the words I heard were quite different, that there was in his speech a hoard of hints, clues, and implications as invisible to me as his breath, as though Time were a species of white spirit who stood between us and with his trailing sleeves wiped away before I had heard it the greater part of all that was said. At last I ventured, ''Perhaps he is dead.''

''An evil giant dwells there now, but no one has seen him.''

I could hardly repress a smile. ''Still, I would think his presence must do a great deal to prevent the shore people from attacking the place.''

''Five years past, and they swarmed over it by night like the fingerlings that crowd a dead man. They burned the castle, and slew those they found there.''

''Do they continue to make war on you by habit, then?''

Llibio shook his head. ''After the melting of the ice this year, the people of the castle returned. Their hands were full of gifts—riches, and the strange weapons you turned against the shore people. There are others who come there too, but whether as servants or masters, we of the lake do not know.''

''From the north or the south?''

''From the sky,'' he said, and pointed up to where the faint stars hung dimmed by the majesty of the sun; but I thought he meant only that the visitors had come in fliers, and inquired no further.

All day the lake dwellers arrived. Many were in such boats as had followed the hetman's; but others chose to sail their islands to join Llibio's, until we were in the midst of a floating continent. I was never asked directly to lead them against the castle. Yet as the day wore on, I came to realize that they wished it, and they to understand that I would so lead them. In books, I think, these things are conventionally done with fiery speeches; reality is sometimes otherwise. They admired my height and my sword, and Pia told them I was the representative of the

Autarch, and that I had been sent to free them. Llibio said, "Though it is we who suffer most, the shore people were able to make the castle their own. They are stronger in war than we, but not all they burned has been rebuilt, and they had no leader from the south." I questioned him and others about the lands near the castle, and told them we should not attack until night made it difficult for sentries on the walls to see our approach. Though I did not say so, I also wanted to wait for darkness to make good shooting impossible; if the master of the castle had given the bullets of power to the hetman, it seemed probable that he had kept much more effective weapons for himself.

When we sailed, I was at the head of about one hundred warriors, though most of them had only spears pointed with the shoulder bones of seals, pachos, or knives. It would swell my self-esteem now to write that I had consented to lead this little army out of a feeling of responsibility and concern for their plight, but it would not be true. Neither did I go because I feared what might be done to me if I refused, though I suspected that unless I did so diplomatically, feigning to delay or to see some benefit to the islanders in not fighting, it might have gone hard with me.

The truth was that I felt a coercion stronger than theirs. Llibio had worn a fish carved from a tooth about his neck; and when I had asked him what it was, he had said that it was Oannes, and covered it with his hand so that my eyes could not profane it, for he knew that I did not believe in Oannes, who must surely be the fish-god of these people.

I did not, yet I felt I knew everything about Oannes that mattered. I knew that he must live in the darkest deeps of the lake, but that he was seen leaping among the waves in storms. I knew he was the shepherd of the deep, who filled the nets of the islanders, and that murderers could not go on the water without fear, lest Oannes appear alongside, with his eyes as big as moons, and overturn the boat.

I did not believe in Oannes or fear him. But I knew, I thought, whence he came—I knew that there is an all-pervasive power in the universe of which every other is the shadow. I knew that in the last analysis my conception of that power was as laughable (and as serious) as Oannes. I knew that the Claw was his, and I felt it was only of the Claw that I knew that, only of the Claw among all the altars and vestments of the world. I had held it in my hand many times, I had lifted it above my head in the Vincula, I had touched the Autarch's uhlan with it, and the sick girl in the jacal in Thrax. I had possessed infinity, and I had wielded its power; I was no longer certain I could turn it over tamely to the

Pelerines, if I ever found them, but I knew with certainty that I would not lose it tamely to anyone else.

Moreover, it seemed to me that I had somehow been chosen to hold—if only for a brief time—that power. It had been lost to the Pelerines through my irresponsibility in allowing Agia to goad our driver into a race; and so it had been my duty to care for it, and use it, and perhaps return it, and surely my duty to rescue it from the hands, monstrous hands by all accounts, into which it had now fallen through my carelessness.

I had not thought, when I began this record of my life, to reveal any of the secrets of our guild that were imparted to me by Master Palaemon and Master Gurloes just before I was elevated, at the feast of Holy Katharine, to the rank of journeyman. But I will tell one now, because what I did that night on Lake Diuturna cannot be understood without understanding it. And the secret is only that we torturers obey. In all the lofty order of the body politic, the pyramid of lives that is immensely taller than any material tower, taller than the Bell Keep, taller than the Wall of Nessus, taller than Mount Typhon, the pyramid that stretches from the Autarch on the Phoenix Throne to the most humble clerk grubbing for the most dishonorable trader—a creature lower than the lowest beggar—we are the only sound stone. No one truly obeys unless he will do the unthinkable in obedience; no one will do the unthinkable save we.

How could I refuse to the Increate what I had willingly given the Autarch when I struck off Katharine's head?

XXXII

To the Castle

The remaining islands were separated now, and though the boats moved among them and sails were bent to every limb, I could not but feel that we were stationary under the streaming clouds, our motion only the last delusion of a drowning land.

Many of the floating islands I had seen earlier that day had been left behind as refuges for women and children. Half a dozen remained, and I stood upon the highest of Llibio's, the largest of the six. Besides the old man and me, it carried seven fighters. The other islands bore four or five apiece. In addition to the islands we had about thirty boats, each crewed by two or three.

I did not deceive myself into thinking that our hundred men, with their knives and fish spears, constituted a formidable force; a handful of Abdiesus's dimarchi would have scattered them like chaff. But they were my followers, and to lead men into battle is a feeling like no other.

Not a glimmer showed upon the waters of the lake, save for the green, reflected light that fell from the myriad leaves of the Forest of Lune, fifty thousand leagues away. Those waters made me think of steel, polished and oiled. The faint wind brought no white foam, though it moved them in long swells like hills of metal.

After a time a cloud obscured the moon, and I wondered briefly whether the lake people would lose their bearings in the dark. It might have been broad noon, however, from the way they handled their vessels, and though boats and islands were often close together, I never in all that voyage saw two that were in the slightest danger of fouling each other.

To be conveyed as I was, by starlight and in darkness, in the midst of my own archipelago, with no sound but the whisper of the wind and the dipping of paddles that rose and fell as regularly as the ticking of a clock, with no motion that could be felt beyond the gentle swelling of the waves, might have been calming and even soporific, for I was tired, though I had slept a little before we set out; but the chill of the night air and the thought of what we were going to do kept me awake.

Neither Llibio nor any of the other islanders had been able to give me more than the vaguest information about the interior of the castle we were to storm. There was a principal building and a wall. Whether or not the principal building was a true keep—that is, a fortified tower high enough to look down upon the wall—I had no idea. Nor did I know whether there were other buildings in addition to the principal one (a barbican, for example), or whether the wall was strengthened with towers or turrets, or how many defenders it might have. The castle had been built in the space of two or three years with native labor; so it could not be as formidable as, say, Acies Castle; but a place a quarter of its strength would be impregnable to us.

I was acutely conscious of how little fitted I was to lead such an expedition. I had never so much as seen a battle, much less taken part in one. My knowledge of military architecture came from my upbringing in the Citadel and some casual sightseeing among the fortifications of Thrax, and what I knew—or thought I knew—of tactics had been gleaned from equally casual reading. I remembered how I had played in the necropolis as a boy, fighting mock skirmishes with wooden swords, and the thought made me almost physically ill. Not because I feared much for my own life, but because I knew that an error of mine might result in the deaths of most of these innocent and ignorant men, who looked to me for leadership.

Briefly the moon shone again, crossed by the black silhouettes of a flight of storks. I could see the shoreline as a band of denser night on the horizon. A new mass of cloud cut off the light, and a drop of water struck my face. It made me feel suddenly cheerful without knowing why—no doubt the reason was that I unconsciously recalled the rain outside on the night when I stood off the alzabo. Perhaps I was thinking too of the icy waters that spewed from the mouth of the mine of the man-apes.

Yet leaving aside all these chance associations, the rain might be a blessing indeed. We had no bows, and if it wet our opponents' bowstrings, so much the better. Certainly it would be impossible to use the bullets of power the hetman's archer had fired. Besides, rain would favor an attack by stealth, and I had long ago decided that it was only by stealth that our attack could hope to succeed.

I was deep in plans when the cloud broke again, and I saw that we were on a course parallel to the shore, which rose in cliffs to our right. Ahead, a peninsula of rock higher still jutted into the lake, and I walked to the point of the island to ask the man stationed there if the castle was situated on it. He shook his head and said, "We will go about."

So we did. The clews of all the sails were loosed, and retied on new limbs. Leeboards weighted with stones were lowered into the water on one side of the island while three men strained at the tiller bar to bring the rudder around. I was struck by the thought that Llibio must have ordered our present landfall, wisely enough, to escape the notice of any lookouts who might keep watch over the waters of the lake. If that were the case, we would still be in danger of being seen when we no longer had the peninsula between the castle and our little fleet. It also occurred to me that since the builder of the castle had not chosen to put it on the high spur of rock we were skirting now, which looked very nearly invulnerable, it was perhaps because he had found a place yet more secure.

Then we rounded the point and sighted our destination no more than four chains down the coast—an outthrust of rock higher still and more abrupt, with a wall at its summit and a keep that seemed to have the impossible shape of an immense toad-stool.

I could not believe my eyes. From the great, tapering central column, which I had no doubt was a round tower of native stone, spread a lens-shaped structure of metal ten times its diameter and apparently as solid as the tower itself.

All about our island, the men in the boats and on the other islands were whispering to one another and pointing. It seemed that this incredible sight was as novel to them as to me.

The misty light of the moon, the younger sister's kiss upon the face of her dying elder, shone on the upper surface of that huge disk. Beneath it, in its thick shadow, gleamed sparks of orange light. They moved, gliding up or down, though their movement was so slow that I had watched them for some time before I was conscious of it. Eventually, one rose until it appeared to be immediately under the disk and vanished, and just before we came to shore, two more appeared in the same spot.

A tiny beach lay in the shadow of the cliff. Llibio's island ran aground before we reached it, however; I had to jump into the water once more, this time holding *Terminus Est* above my head. Fortunately there was no surf, and though rain still threatened, it had not yet come. I helped some of the lake men drag their boats onto the shingle while others moored islands to boulders with sinew hawsers.

After my trip through the mountains, the narrow, treacherous path would have been easy if I had not had to climb it in the dark. As it was, I would rather have made the descent past the buried city to Casdoe's house, though that had been five times farther.

When we reached the top we were still some distance from the wall, which was screened from us by a grove of straggling firs. I gathered the islanders about me and asked—a rhetorical question—if they knew from where the sky ship above the castle had come. And when they assured me they did not, I explained that I did (and so I did, Dorcas having warned me of them, though I had never seen such a thing before), and that because of its presence here it would be better if I were to reconnoiter the situation before we proceeded with the assault.

No one spoke, but I could sense their feeling of helplessness. They had believed they had found a hero to lead them, and now they were going to lose him before the battle was joined.

“I am going inside if I can,” I told them. “I will come back to you if that is possible, and I will leave such doors as I may open for you.”

Llibio asked, “But suppose you cannot come back. How shall we know when the moment to draw our knives has come?”

“I will make some signal,” I said, and strained my wits to think what signal I might make if I were pent in that black tower. “They must have fires on such a night as this. I'll show a brand at a window, and drop it if I can so that you'll see the streak of fire. If I make no signal and cannot return to you, you may assume they have taken me prisoner—attack when the first light touches the mountains.”

A short time later I stood at the gate of the castle, banging a great iron knocker shaped (so far as I could determine with my fingers) like the head of a man against a plate of the same metal set in oak.

There was no response. After I had waited for the space of a score of breaths, I knocked again. I could hear the echoes waked inside, an empty reverberation like the throbbing of a heart, but there was no sound of voices. The hideous faces I had glimpsed in the Autarch's garden filled my mind and I waited in dread for the noise of a shot, though I knew that if the Hierodules chose to shoot me—and all energy weapons came ultimately from them—I would probably never hear it. The air was so still it seemed the atmosphere waited with me. Thunder rolled to the east.

At last there were footsteps, so quick and light I could have thought them the steps of a child. A vaguely familiar voice called, “Who's there? What do you want?”

And I answered, “Master Severian of the Order of the Seekers for Truth and Penitence—I come as the arm of the Autarch, whose justice is the bread of his subjects.”

"Do you indeed!" exclaimed Dr. Talos, and threw open the gate.

For a moment I could only stare at him.

"Tell me, what does the Autarch want with us? The last time I saw you, you were on your way to the City of Crooked Knives. Did you ever get there?"

"The Autarch wanted to know why your vassals laid hold of one of his servants," I said. "That is to say, myself. This puts a slightly different light on the matter."

"It does! It does! From our point of view too, you understand. I didn't know you were the mysterious visitor at Murene. And I'm sure poor old Baldanders didn't either. Come in and we'll talk about it."

I stepped through the gateway in the wall, and the doctor pushed the heavy gate closed behind me and fitted an iron bar into place.

I said, "There really isn't much to talk about, but we might begin with a valuable gem that was taken from me by force, and as I have been informed, sent to you."

Even while I spoke, however, my attention was drawn from the words I pronounced to the vast bulk of the ship of the Hierodules, which was directly overhead now that I was past the wall. Staring up at it gave me the same feeling of dislocation I have sometimes had on looking down through the double curve of a magnifying glass; the convex underside of that ship had the look of something alien not only to the world of human beings, but to all the visible world.

"Oh, yes," Dr. Talos said. "Baldanders has your trinket, I believe. Or rather, he had it and has stuck it away somewhere. I'm sure he'll give it back to you."

From inside the round tower that appeared (though it could not possibly have done so) to support the ship, there came faintly a lonely and terrible sound that might have been the howling of a wolf. I had heard nothing like it since I had left our own Matachin Tower; but I knew what it was, and I said to Dr. Talos, "You have prisoners here."

He nodded. "Yes. I'm afraid I've been too busy to feed the poor creatures today, what with everything." He waved vaguely toward the ship overhead. "You don't object to meeting cacogens, I hope, Severian? If you want to go in and ask Baldanders for your jewel, I'm afraid you'll have to. He's in there talking to them."

I said I had no objection, though I am afraid I shuddered inwardly as I said it.

The doctor smiled, showing above his red beard the line of sharp, bright teeth I recalled so well. "That's wonderful. You were always a wonderfully unprejudiced person. If I may say so, I suppose your training has taught you to take every being as he comes."

XXXIII

Ossipago, Barbatus, and Famulimus

As is common in such pele towers, there was no entrance at ground level. A straight stair, narrow, steep, and without railings, led to an equally narrow door some ten cubits above the pavement of the courtyard. This door stood open already, and I was delighted to see that Dr. Talos did not close it after us. We went through a short corridor that was, no doubt, no more than the thickness of the tower wall and emerged into a room that appeared (like all the rooms I saw within that tower) to occupy the whole of the area available at its level. It was filled with machines that seemed to be at least as ancient as those we had in the Matachin Tower at home, but whose uses were beyond my conjecture. At one side of this room another narrow stair ascended to the floor above, and at the opposite side a dark stairwell gave access to whatever place it was in which the howling prisoner was confined, for I heard his voice floating from its black mouth.

"He has gone mad," I said, and inclined my head toward the sound.

Dr. Talos nodded. "Most of them are. At least, most of those I've examined. I administer decoctions of hellebore, but I can't say they seem to do much good."

"We had clients like that in the third level of our oubliette, because we were forced to retain them by the legalities; they had been turned over to us, you see, and no one in authority would authorize their release."

The doctor was leading me toward the ascending stair. "I sympathize with your predicament."

"In time they died," I continued doggedly. "Either by the aftereffects of their excruciations or from other causes. No real purpose was served by confining them."

"I suppose not. Watch out for that gadget with the hook. It's trying to catch hold of your cloak."

"Then why do you keep him? You aren't a legal repository in the sense we were, surely."

"For parts, I suppose. That's what Baldanders has most of this rubbish for." With one foot on the first step, Dr. Talos turned to look back at me. "You remember to be on your good behavior now. They don't like to be called cacogens, you know. Address them as whatever it is they say their names are this time, and don't refer to slime. In fact, don't talk of anything unpleasant. Poor Baldanders has worked so hard to patch things up with them after he lost his head at the House Absolute. He'll be crushed if you spoil everything just before they leave."

I promised to be as diplomatic as I could.

Because the ship was poised above the tower, I had supposed that Baldanders and its commanders would be in the uppermost room. I was wrong. I heard the murmur of voices as we ascended to the next floor, then the deep tones of the giant, sounding, as they so often had when I was traveling with him, like the collapse of some ruinous wall far off.

This room held machines too. But these, though they might have been as old as those below, gave the impression of being in working order; and moreover, of standing in some logical though impenetrable relation to one another, like the devices in Typhon's hall. Baldanders and his guests were at the farther end of the chamber, where his head, three times the size of any ordinary man's, reared above the clutter of metal and crystal like that of a tyrannosaur over the topmost leaves of a forest. As I walked toward them, I saw what remained of a young woman who might have been a sister of Pia's lying beneath a shimmering bell jar. Her abdomen had been opened with a sharp blade and certain of her viscera removed and positioned around her body. It appeared to be in the early stages of decay, though her lips moved. Her eyes opened as I passed her, then closed again.

"Company!" Dr. Talos called. "You won't guess who."

The giant's head swung slowly around, but he regarded me, I thought, with as little comprehension as he had when Dr. Talos had awakened him that first morning in Nessus.

"Baldanders you know," the doctor continued to me, "but I must introduce you to our guests."

Three men, or what appeared to be men, rose graciously. One, if he had been truly a human being, would have been short and stout. The other two were a good head taller than I, as tall as exultants. The masks all three wore gave them the faces of refined men of middle age, thoughtful and poised; but I was aware that the eyes that looked out through the slits in the masks of the two taller figures were larger than human eyes, and that the shorter figure had no eyes at all, so that only darkness was visible there. All three were robed in white.

"Your Worships! Here's a great friend of ours, Master Severian of the torturers. Master Severian, let me present the honorable Hierodules Ossipago, Barbatus, and Famulimus. It's the labor of these noble personages to inculcate wisdom in the human race—here represented by Baldanders, and now, yourself."

The being Dr. Talos had introduced as Famulimus spoke. His voice might have been wholly human save that it was more resonant and more musical than any truly human voice I have ever heard, so that I felt I might have been listening to the speech of some stringed instrument called to life. "Welcome," it sang. "There is no greater joy for us, than greeting you, Severian. You bow to us in courtesy, but we to you will bend our knees." And he did briefly kneel, as did both the others.

Nothing he could possibly have said or done could have astounded me more, and I was too much taken by surprise to offer any reply.

The other tall cacogen, Barbatus, spoke as a courtier might to fill the silence of an otherwise embarrassing gap in the conversation. His voice was deeper than Famulimus's, and seemed to have something soldierly in it. "You are welcome here—very welcome, as my dear friend has said, and all of us have tried to indicate. But your own friends must remain outside as long as we are here. You know that, of course. I mention it only as a matter of form."

The third cacogen, in a tone so deep that one felt rather than heard it, muttered, "It doesn't matter," and as though he feared I might see the empty eye slits of his mask, turned and made a show of staring out the narrow window behind him.

"Perhaps it doesn't, then," Barbatus said. "Ossipago knows best, after all."

"You have friends here then?" Dr. Talos whispered. It was a peculiarity of his that he seldom spoke to a group as most people do, but either addressed a single individual in it almost as though he and the other were alone, or else orated as if to an assembly of thousands.

"Some of the islanders gave me an escort," I said, trying to put the best face I could on things. "You must know of them. They live on the floating masses of reeds in the lake."

"They are rising against you!" Dr. Talos told the giant. "I warned you this would happen." He rushed to the window through which the being called Ossipago seemed to look, shouldering him to one side, and stared out into the night. Then, turning toward the cacogen, he knelt, seized his hand, and kissed it. This hand was quite plainly a glove of some flexible material painted to resemble flesh, with something in it that was not a hand.

"You will help us, Worship, will you not? You have fantassins aboard your ship, surely. Once line the walls with horrors, and we will be safe for a century."

In his slow voice, Baldanders said, "Severian will be the victor. Else why did they kneel to him? Though he may die, and we may not. You know their ways, Doctor. The looting may disseminate knowledge."

Dr. Talos turned upon him furiously. "Did it before? I ask you!"

"Who can say, Doctor?"

"You know it did not. They are the same ignorant, superstitious brutes they have always been!" He whirled again. "Noble Hierodules, answer me. You must know, if anyone does."

Famulimus gestured, and I was never more aware of the truth behind his mask than I was at that moment, for no human arm could have made the motion his did, and it was a meaningless motion, conveying neither agreement nor disagreement, neither irritation nor consolation.

"I will not speak of all the things you know," he said. "That those you fear have learned to overcome you. It may be true that they are simple still; still, something carried home may make them wise."

He was addressing the doctor, but I could contain myself no longer and said, "May I ask what you're talking about, sieur?"

"I speak of you, of all of you, Severian. It cannot harm you now, that I should speak."

Barbatus interjected, "Only if you don't do it too freely."

"There is a mark they use upon some world, where sometimes our worn ship finds rest at last. It is a snake with heads at either end. One hand is dead—the other gnaws at it."

Without turning from the window, Ossipago said, "That is this world, I think."

"No doubt Camoena could reveal its home. But then, it doesn't matter if you know it. You will understand me the more clearly The living head stands for destruction. The head that does not live, for building. The former feeds upon the latter; and feeding, nourishes its food. A boy might think that if the first should die, the dead, constructive thing would triumph, making his twin now like himself. The truth is both would soon decay."

Barbatus said, "As so often, my good friend is less than clear. Are you following him?"

"I am not!" Dr. Talos announced angrily. He turned away as if in disgust and hurried down the stair.

"That does not matter," Barbatus told me, "since his master does."

He paused as though waiting for Baldanders to contradict him, then continued, still addressing me. "Our desire, you see, is to advance your race, not to indoctrinate it."

"Advance the shore people?" I asked.

All this time, the waters of the lake were murmuring their night-grief through the window. Ossipago's voice seemed to blend with it as he said, "All of you . . ."

"It is true then! What so many sages have suspected. We are being guided. You watch over us, and in the ages of our history, which must seem no more than days to you, you have raised us from savagery." In my enthusiasm, I drew out the brown book, still somewhat damp from the wetting I had given it earlier in the day, despite its wrappings of oiled silk. "Here, let me show you what this says: 'Man, who is not wise, is yet the object of wisdom. If wisdom finds him a fit object, is it wise in him to make light of his folly?' Something like that."

"You are mistaken," Barbatus told me. "Ages are aeons to us. My friend and I have dealt with your race for less than your own lifetime."

Baldanders said, "These things live only a score of years, like dogs." His tone told me more than is written here, for each word fell like a stone dropped down some deep cistern.

I said, "That cannot be."

"You are the work for which we live," Famulimus explained. "That man you call Baldanders lives to learn. We see that he hoards up past lore—hard facts like seeds to give him power. In time he'll die by hands that do not store, but die with some slight gain for all of you. Think of a tree that splits a rock. It gathers water, the sun's life-bringing heat . . . and all the stuff of life for its own use. In time it dies and rots to dress the earth, that its own roots have made from stone. Its shadow gone, fresh seeds spring up; in time a forest flourishes where it stood."

Dr. Talos emerged again from the stairwell, clapping slowly and derisively.

I asked, "You have left them these machines, then?" I was acutely conscious, as I spoke, of the eviscerated woman mumbling beneath her glass somewhere behind me, a thing that once would not have bothered the torturer Severian in the least.

Barbatus said, "No. Those he found, or constructed for himself. Famulimus said that he wished to learn, and that we saw to it that he did, not that we taught him. We teach no one anything, and only trade such devices as are too complex for your people to duplicate."

Dr. Talos said, "These monsters, these horrors, do nothing for us. You've seen them—you know what they are. When my poor patient ran wild through them in the theater of the House Absolute, they nearly killed him with their pistols.''

The giant shifted in his great chair. ''You need not feign sympathy, Doctor. It suits you badly. Playing the fool while they looked on . . .'' His immense shoulders rose and fell. ''I shouldn't have let it overcome me. They've agreed now to forget.''

Barbatus said, ''We could have killed your creator easily that night, as you know. We burned him only enough to turn aside his charges.''

I recalled then what the giant had told me when we parted in the forest beyond the Autarch's gardens—that he was the doctor's master. Now, before I had time to consider what I was doing, I seized the doctor's hand. Its skin seemed as warm and living as my own, though curiously dry. After a moment he jerked away.

''What are you?'' I demanded, and when he did not answer, I turned to the beings who called themselves Famulimus and Barbatus. ''Once, sieurs, I knew a man who was only partly human flesh . . .''

They looked toward the giant instead of replying, and though I knew their faces were only masks, I felt the force of their demand.

''A homunculus,'' Baldanders rumbled.

XXXIV

Masks

The rain came as he spoke, a cold rain that struck the rude, gray stones of the castle with a million icy fists. I sat down, clamping *Terminus Est* between my knees to keep them from shaking.

"I had already concluded," I said with as much self-possession as I could summon, "that when the islanders told me of a small man who paid for the building of this place, they were speaking of the doctor. But they said that you, the giant, had come afterward."

"I was the small man. The doctor came afterward."

A cacogen showed a dripping, nightmare face at the window, then vanished. Possibly he had conveyed some message to Ossipago, though I heard nothing. Ossipago spoke without turning. "Growth has its disadvantages, though for your species it is the only method by which youth can be reinstated."

Dr. Talos sprang to his feet. "We will overcome them! He has put himself in my hands."

Baldanders said, "I was forced to. There was no one else. I created my own physician."

I was still attempting to regain my mental balance as I looked from one to the other; there was no change in the appearance or manner of either. "But he beats you," I said. "I have seen him."

"Once I overheard you while you confided in the smaller woman. You destroyed another woman, whom you loved. Yet you were her slave."

Dr. Talos said, "I must get him up, you see. He must exercise, and it is a part of what I do for him. I'm told that the Autarch—whose health is the happiness of his subjects—has an isochronon in his sleeping chamber, a gift from another autarch from beyond the edge of the world. Perhaps it is the master of these gentlemen here. I don't know. Anyway, he fears a dagger at his throat and will let no one near him when he sleeps, so this device tells the watches of his night. When dawn comes, it rouses him. How then should he, the master of the Commonwealth, permit his sleep to be disturbed by a mere machine? Baldanders created me as his physician, as he told you. Severian, you've known me some time. Would you say I was much afflicted with the infamous vice of false modesty?''

I managed a smile as I shook my head.

''Then I must tell you that I am not responsible for my virtues, such as they are. Baldanders wisely made me all that he is not, so that I might counterweight his deficiencies. I am not fond of money, for example. That's an excellent thing for the patient, in a personal physician. And I am loyal to my friends, because he is the first of them.''

''Still,'' I said, ''I have always been astounded that he did not slay you.'' It was so cold in the room that I drew my cloak closer about me, though I felt sure that the present deceptive calm could not long endure.

The giant said, ''You must know why I keep my temper in check. You have seen me lose it. To have them sitting there, watching me, as though I were a bear on a chain—''

Dr. Talos touched his hand; there was something womanly in the gesture. ''It's his glands, Severian. The endocrine system and the thyroid. Everything must be managed so carefully, otherwise he would grow too fast. And then I must see that his weight doesn't break his bones, and a thousand other things.''

''The brain,'' the giant rumbled. ''The brain is the worst of all, and the best.''

I said, ''Did the Claw help you? If not, perhaps it will, in my hands. It has performed more for me in a short time than it did for the Pelerines in many years.''

When Baldanders's face showed no sign of comprehension, Dr. Talos said, ''He means the gem the fishermen sent. It is supposed to perform miraculous cures.''

At that Ossipago turned to face us at last. ''How interesting. You have it here? May we see it?''

The doctor looked anxiously from the cacogen's expressionless mask to Baldanders's face and back again as he said, ''Please, Your Worships, it is nothing. A fragment of corundum.''

In all the time since I had entered this level of the tower, none of the cacogens had shifted his place by more than a cubit; now Ossipago crossed to my chair with short, waddling steps. I must have recoiled from him, for he said, ''You need not fear me, though we do your kind much hurt. I want to hear about this Claw, which the homunculus tells us is only a mineral specimen.''

When I heard him say that, I was afraid that he and his companions would take the Claw from Baldanders and carry it to their own home beyond the void, but I reasoned that they could not do so unless they forced him to produce it, and that if they did that, it might be possible for me to gain possession of it, which I might fail to do otherwise. So I told Ossipago all the things the Claw had accomplished while it had been in my keeping—about the uhlan on the highway, and the man-apes, and all the other instances of its power that I have already recorded here. As I spoke, the giant's face grew harder, and the doctor's, I thought, more anxious.

When I had finished, Ossipago said, ''And now we must see the wonder itself. Bring it out, please,'' and Baldanders rose and stalked across the wide room, making all his machines appear mere toys by his size, and at last pulled out the drawer of a little, white-topped table and took out the gem. It was more dull in his hand than I had ever seen it; it might have been a bit of blue glass.

The cacogen took it from him and held it up in his painted glove, though he did not turn up his face to look at it as a man would. There it seemed to catch the light from the yellow lamps that sprouted downward from above, and in that light it flashed a clear azure. ''Very beautiful,'' he said. ''And most interesting, though it cannot have performed the feats ascribed to it.''

''Obviously,'' Famulimus sang, and made another of those gestures that so recalled to me the statues in the gardens of the Autarch.

''It is mine,'' I told them. ''The shore people took it from me by force. May I have it back?''

''If it is yours,'' Barbatus said, ''where did you get it?''

I began the task of describing my meeting with Agia and the destruction of the altar of the Pelerines, but he cut me short.

''All this is speculation. You did not see this jewel upon the altar, nor did you feel the woman's hand when she gave it to you, if in fact she did. *Where did you get it?*''

''I found it in a compartment of my sabretache.'' It seemed that there was nothing else to say.

Barbatus turned away as though disappointed. ''And you . . .'' He looked toward Baldanders. ''Ossipago has the jewel now, and he got it from you. Where did you get it?''

Baldanders rumbled, ''You saw me. From the drawer of that table.''

The cacogen nodded by moving his mask with his hands. ''You see then, Severian, his claim has become as good as yours.''

"But the gem is mine and not his."

"It is not our task to judge between you; you must settle that when we are gone. But out of curiosity, which torments even such strange creatures as you believe us to be—Baldanders, will you keep it?"

The giant shook his head. "I would not have such a monument to superstition in my laboratory."

"Then there should be little difficulty in effecting a settlement," Barbatus declared. "Severian, would you like to watch our craft rise? Baldanders always comes to see us off, and though he is not the type to rhapsodize over views artificial or natural, I should think myself that it must be worth seeing." He turned away, adjusting his white robes.

"Worshipful Hierodules," I said, "I would very much like to, but I want to ask you something before you go. When I arrived, you said you had no greater joy than seeing me, and you knelt. Did you mean what you said, or anything like it? Were you confusing me with someone else?"

Baldanders and Dr. Talos had risen to their feet when the cacogen first mentioned his departure. Now, though Famulimus remained to listen to my questions, the others had already begun to move away; Barbatus was mounting the stair that led to the level above, with Ossipago, still carrying the Claw, not far behind him.

I began to walk too, because I feared to be separated from it, and Famulimus walked with me. "Though you did not now pass our test, I meant no less than what I said to you." His voice was like the music of some wonderful bird, bridging the abyss from a wood unattainable. "How often we have taken counsel, Liege. How often we have done each other's will. You know the water women, I believe. Are Ossipago, brave Barbatus, I, to be so much less sapient than they?"

I drew a deep breath. "I don't know what you mean. But somehow I feel that though you and your kind are hideous, you are good. And that the undines are not, though they are so lovely, as well as so monstrous, that I can scarcely look at them."

"Is all the world a war of good and bad? Have you not thought it might be something more?"

I had not, and could only stare.

"And you will kindly tolerate my looks. Without offense may I remove this mask? We both know it for one and it is hot. Baldanders is ahead and will not see."

"If you wish, Worship," I said. "But won't you tell—"

With a quick flick of one hand, as though with relief, Famulimus stripped away the disguise. The face revealed was no face, only eyes in a sheet of putrescence. Then the hand moved again as before, and that too fell away. Beneath it was the strange, calm beauty I had seen carved in the faces of the moving statues in the gardens of the House Absolute, but differing from that as the face of a living woman differs from her own life mask.

"Did you not ever think, Severian," she said, "that he who wore a mask might wear another? But I who wore the two do not wear three. No more untruths divide us now, I swear. Touch, Liege—your fingers on my face."

I was afraid, but she took my hand and lifted it to her cheek. It felt cool and yet living, the very opposite of the dry heat of the doctor's skin.

"All of the monstrous masks you've seen us wear are but your fellow citizens of Urth. An insect, lamprey, now a dying leper. All are your brothers, though you may recoil."

We were already close to the uppermost level of the tower, treading charred wood at times—the ruin left by the conflagration that had driven forth Baldanders and his physician. When I took my hand away, Famulimus put on her mask again. "Why do you do this?" I asked.

"So that your folk will hate and fear us all. How long, Severian, if we did not, would common men abide a reign not ours? We would not rob your race of your own rule; by sheltering your kind from us, does not your Autarch keep the Phoenix Throne?"

I felt as I sometimes had in the mountains on waking from a dream, when I sat up wondering, looked about and saw the green moon pinned to the sky with a pine, and the frowning, solemn faces of the mountains beneath their broken diadems instead of the dreamed-of walls of Master Palaemon's study, or our refectory, or the corridor of cells where I sat at the guard table outside Thecla's door. I managed to say, "Then why did you show me?"

And she answered, "Though you see us, we will not see you more. Our friendship here begins and ends, I fear. Call it a gift of welcome from departing friends."

Then the doctor, ahead of us, threw open a door, and the drumming of the rain became a roaring, and I felt the cold, deathlike air of the tower invaded by icy but living air from outside. Baldanders had to stoop and turn his shoulders to pass the doorway, and I was struck by the realization that in time he would be unable to do so, whatever care he received from Dr. Talos—the door would have to be widened, and the stairs too, perhaps, for if he fell he would surely perish. Then I understood what had puzzled me before: the reason for the huge rooms and high ceilings of this, his tower. And I wondered what the vaults in the rock were like, where he confined his starving prisoners.

XXXV

The Signal

The ship, which from below had appeared to rest upon the structure of the tower itself, did not. Rather it seemed to float half a chain or more above us—too high to provide much shelter from the lashing rain that made the smooth curve of its hull gleam like black nacre. As I stared up at it, I could not help but speculate on the sails such a vessel might spread to catch the winds that blow between the worlds; and then, just as I was wondering if the crew did not ever peer down to see us, the mermen, the strange, uncouth beings who for a time walked the bottom below their hull, one of them indeed came down, head foremost like a squirrel, wreathed in orange light and clinging to the hull with hands and feet, though it was wet as any stone in a river and polished like the blade of *Terminus Est*. He wore such a mask as I have often described, but I now knew it to be one. When he saw Ossipago, Barbatus, and Famulimus below, he descended no farther, and in a moment a slender line, glowing orange too so that it seemed a thread of light, was cast down from somewhere above.

"Now we must go," Ossipago told Baldanders, and he handed him the Claw. "Think well on all the things we have not told you, and remember what you have not been shown."

"I will," Baldanders said, his voice as grim as I was ever to hear it.

Then Ossipago caught the line and slid up it until it bent around the curve of the hull and he disappeared from sight. But it somehow seemed that he did not in fact slide up, but down, as if that ship were a world itself and drew everything belonging to it to itself with a blind hunger, as Urth does; or perhaps it was only that he was to become lighter than our air, like a sailor who dives from his ship into the sea, and rose as I had risen after I leaped from the hetman's boat.

However that may be, Barbatus and Famulimus followed him. Famulimus waved just as the swell of the hull blocked her from view; no doubt the doctor and Baldanders thought she bade them farewell; but I knew she had waved to me. A sheet of rain struck my face, blinding my eyes despite my hood.

Slowly at first, then faster and faster, the ship lifted and receded, vanishing not upwards or to the north or the south or the east or west, but dwindling into a direction to which I could no longer point when it was gone.

Baldanders turned to me. "You heard them."

I did not understand, and said, "I spoke with them, yes. Dr. Talos invited me to when he opened the door in the wall for me."

"They told me nothing. They have shown me nothing."

"To have seen their ship," I said, "and to have spoken to them—surely those things are not nothing."

"They are driving me forward. Always forward. They drive me as an ox to slaughter."

He went to the battlement and stared out over the vast expanse of the lake, whose rain-churned waters made it seem a sea of milk. The merlons were several spans higher than my head, but he put his hands on them as upon a railing, and I saw the blue gleam of the Claw in one closed fist. Dr. Talos pulled at my cloak, murmuring that it would be better if we were to go inside out of the storm, but I would not leave.

"It began long before you were born. At first they helped me, though it was only by suggesting thoughts, asking questions. Now they only hint. Now they only let slip enough to tell me a certain thing may be done. Tonight there was not even that."

Wanting to urge that he no longer take the islanders for his experiments, but without knowing how to do so, I said that I had seen his explosive bullets, which were surely very wonderful, a very great achievement.

"Natrium," he said, and turned to face me, his huge head lifted to the dark sky. "You know nothing. Natrium is a mere elemental substance spawned by the sea in endless profusion. Do you think I'd have given it to the fishermen if it were more than a toy? No, I am my own great work. And I am my only great work!"

Dr. Talos whispered, "Look about you—don't you recognize this? It is just as he says!"

"What do you mean?" I whispered in return.

"The castle? The monster? The man of learning? I only just thought of it. Surely you know that just as the momentous events of the past cast their shadows down the ages, so now, when the sun is drawing toward the dark, our own shadows race into the past to trouble mankind's dreams.''

''You're mad,'' I said. ''Or joking.''

''Mad?'' Baldanders rumbled. ''*You* are mad. You with your fantasies of theurgy. How they must be laughing at us. They think all of us barbarians . . . I, who have labored three lifetimes.''

He extended his arm and opened his hand. The Claw blazed for him now. I reached for it, and with a sudden motion he threw it. How it flashed in the rain-swept dark! It was as if bright Skuld herself had fallen from the night sky.

I heard the yell, then, of the lake people who waited outside the wall. I had given them no signal; yet the signal had been given by the only act, save perhaps for an attack on my person, that could have induced me to give it. *Terminus Est* left her sheath while the wind still carried their battle cry. I lifted her to strike, but before I could close with the giant, Dr. Talos sprang between us. I thought the weapon he raised to parry was only his cane; if my heart had not been torn by the loss of the Claw, I would have laughed as I hewed it. My blade rang on steel, and though it drove his own back upon himself he was able to contain the blow. Baldanders rushed past me before I could recover and dashed me against the parapet.

I could not dodge the doctor's thrust, but he was deceived, I think, by my fuligin cloak, and though his point grazed my ribs, it rattled on stone. I clubbed him with the hilt and sent him reeling.

Baldanders was nowhere to be seen. After a moment I realized that his headlong charge must have been for the door behind me, and the blow he had given me no more than an afterthought, as a man intent on other things may snuff a candle before he leaves the room.

The doctor sprawled on the stone pavement that was the roof of the tower—stones that were, perhaps, merely gray in sunlight, but now appeared a rain-drowned black. His red hair and beard were visible still, permitting me to see that he lay belly down, his head twisted to one side. It had not seemed to me that I had struck him so hard, though it may be I am stronger than I know, as others have sometimes said. Still I felt that beneath all his cocksure strutting Dr. Talos had been weaker than any of us except Baldanders would have guessed. I could have slain him easily then, swinging *Terminus Est* so the corner of her blade would bury itself in his skull.

Instead I picked up his weapon, the faint line of silver that had fallen from his hand. It was a single-edged blade about as wide as my forefinger, very sharp—as befitted a surgeon's sword. After a moment I realized that the grip was only the handle of his walking stick, which I had seen so often; it was a sword cane, like the sword Vodalus had drawn in our necropolis once, and I smiled there in the rain to think of the doctor carrying his sword thus for so many leagues, unknown to me, who had labored along with my own slung over my back. The tip had shattered on the stones when he thrust at me; I flung the broken blade over the parapet, as Baldanders had flung the Claw, and went down into his tower to kill him.

When we had climbed the stair, I had been too deep in conversation with Famulimus to pay much heed to the rooms through which we passed. The uppermost I recalled only as a place where it seemed that everything was draped in scarlet cloth. Now I saw red globes, lamps that burned without a flame like the silver flowers that sprouted from the ceiling of the wide room where I had met the three beings I could no longer call cacogens. These globes stood on ivory pedestals that seemed as light and slender as the bones of birds, rising from a floor that was no floor but only a sea of fabrics, all red, but of varying shades and textures. Over this room stretched a canopy supported by atlantes. It was scarlet, but sewn with a thousand plates of silver, so well polished that they were mirrors nearly as perfect as the armor of the Autarch's praetorians.

I had nearly descended the height of the stair before I understood that what I saw was no more than the giant's bedchamber, the bed itself, five times the expanse of a normal one, being sunk level with the floor, and its cerise and carmine coverings scattered about upon the crimson carpet. Just then, I saw a face among these twisted bedclothes. I lifted my sword and the face vanished, but I left the stair to drag away one of the downy cloths. The catamite beneath (if catamite he was) rose and faced me with the boldness small children sometimes show. Indeed he was a small child, though he stood nearly as tall as I, a naked boy so fat his distended paunch obscured his tiny generative organs. His arms were like pink pillows bound with cords of gold, and his ears had been pierced for golden hoops strung with tiny bells. His hair was golden too, and curled; beneath it he looked at me with the wide, blue eyes of an infant.

Large though he was, I have never been able to believe that Baldanders practiced pederasty as that term is usually understood, though it may well be that he had hoped to do so when the boy grew larger still. Certainly it must have been that just as he held his own growth in check, permitting only as much as needed to save his mountainous body from the ravages of the years, so he had accelerated the growth of this poor boy in so far as was possible to his anthroposophic knowledge. I say that because it seemed certain that he had not had him under his control until some time after he and Dr. Talos had parted from Dorcas and me.

(I left this boy where I had found him, and to this day I have no notion of what may have become of him. It is likely enough that he perished; but it is possible also that the lake men may have preserved and nourished him, or that the hetman and his people finding him at a somewhat later time, did so.)

I had no sooner descended to the floor below than what I saw there wiped all thought of the boy from my mind. This room was as wreathed in mist (which I am certain had not been present when I had passed through before) as the other had been in red cloth; it was a living vapor that seethed as I might have imagined the logos to writhe as it left the mouth of the Pancreator. While I watched it, a man of fog, white as a grave worm, rose before me brandishing a barbed spear. Before I realized he was a mere phantom, the blade of my sword went through his wrist as it might have penetrated a column of smoke. At once he began to shrink, the fog seeming to fall in upon itself, until he stood hardly higher than my waist.

I went forward, down more steps, until I stood in the cold, roiling whiteness. Then there came bounding across its surface a hideous creature formed, like the man, of the fog itself. In dwarfs I have seen, the head and torso are of normal size or larger, but the limbs, however muscled, remain childlike; this was the reverse of such a dwarf, with arms and legs larger than my own issuing from a twisted, stunted body.

The anti-dwarf brandished an estoc, and opening its mouth in a soundless cry, it thrust its weapon into the man's neck, utterly heedless of his spear, which was plunged into its own chest.

I heard a laugh then, and though I had seldom heard him merry, I knew whose laugh it was.

"Baldanders!" I called.

His head rose from the mist, just as I have seen the mountain-tops lifted above it at dawn.

XXXVI

The Fight in the Bailey

"Here is a real enemy," I said. "With a real weapon." I walked down into the mist, groping ahead of me with my sword blade.

"You see in my cloud chamber real enemies too," Baldanders rumbled, his voice quite calm. "Save that they are outside, in the bailey. The first was one of your friends, the second one of my foes."

As he spoke, the mist dispersed, and I saw him near the center of the room, sitting in a massive chair. When I turned toward him, he rose from it and seizing it by the back sent it hurtling toward me as easily as he might have thrown a basket. It missed me by no more than a span.

"Now you will attempt to kill me," he said. "And all for a foolish charm. I ought to have killed you, that night when you slept in my bed."

I could have said the same thing, but I did not bother to reply. It was clear that by feigning helplessness he was hoping to lure me into a careless attack, and though he appeared to be without a weapon, he was still twice my height and, as I had reason to believe, of four times or more my strength. Then too I was conscious, as I drew nearer him, that we were reenacting here the performance of the marionettes I had seen in a dream on the night of which he had reminded me, and in that dream, the wooden giant had been armed with a bludgeon. He retreated from me step by step as I advanced; yet he seemed always ready to come to grips.

Quite suddenly, when we were perhaps three quarters across the room from the stair, he turned and ran. It was astonishing, like seeing a tree run.

It was also very quick Ungainly though he was, he covered two paces with every step, and he reached the wall—where there was just such a slit of window as Ossipago had stared from—long before me.

For an instant I could not think what he meant to do. The window was far too narrow for him to climb through. He thrust both his great hands into it, and I heard the grinding of stone upon stone.

Just in time I guessed, and managed a few steps back. A moment later he held a block of stone wrenched from the wall itself. He lifted it above his head and hurled it at me.

As I leaped aside, he tore free another, and then another. At the third I had to roll desperately, still clutching my sword, to avoid the fourth, the stones coming quicker and quicker as the lack of those already torn away weakened the structure of the wall. By the purest chance, that roll brought me close to a casket, a thing no bigger than a modest housewife might have for her rings, lying on the floor.

It was ornamented with little knobs, and something in their form recalled to me those Master Gurloes had adjusted at Thecla's excruciation. Before Baldanders could pry out another stone, I scooped the casket up and twisted one of its knobs. At once the vanished mist came boiling out of the floor again, quickly reaching the level of my head, so that I was blinded in its sea of white.

"You have found it," Baldanders said in his deep, slow tones. "I should have turned it off. Now I cannot see you, but you cannot see me."

I kept silent because I knew he was standing with a block of stone poised to throw, waiting for the sound of my voice. After I had drawn perhaps two dozen breaths, I began to edge toward him as silently as I could. I was certain that despite all his cunning he could not walk without my hearing him. When I had taken four steps, the stone crashed on the floor behind me, and there was the noise of another being torn from the wall.

It was one stone too many; there came a deafening roar, and I knew a whole section of the wall above the window must have gone crashing down. Briefly I dared to hope it had killed him; but the mist began to thin at once, pouring through the rent in the wall and out into the night and the rain outside, and I saw him still standing beside the gaping hole.

He must have dropped the stone he had wrenched loose when the wall fell; he was empty-handed. I dashed toward him hoping to attack him before he realized I was upon him. Once again he was too quick. I saw him grasp the wall that remained and swing himself out, and by the time I had reached the opening he was some distance below. What he had done seemed impossible; but when I looked more carefully at that part of the tower illuminated by the lights of the room in which I stood, I saw that the stones were roughly cut and laid without mortar, so there were often sizable crevices between them, and that the wall sloped inward as it rose.

I was tempted to sheathe *Terminus Est* and follow him, but I would have been utterly vulnerable if I had done so, since Baldanders would be certain to reach the ground before me. I flung the casket at him and soon lost sight of him in the rain. With no other choice left to me, I groped my way back to the stair and descended to the level I had seen when I first entered the castle.

It had been silent then, uninhabited save by its ancient mechanisms. Now it was pandemonium. Over and under and through the machines swarmed scores of hideous beings akin to the ghostly thing whose phantom I had seen in the room Baldanders called his chamber of clouds. Like Typhon, some wore two heads; some had four arms; many were cursed with disproportionate limbs—legs twice the length of their bodies, arms thicker than their thighs. All had weapons, and so far as I could judge, were mad, for they struck at one another as freely as at the islanders who fought with them. I remembered then what Baldanders had told me: that the courtyard below was filled with my friends and his foes. He had surely been correct; these creatures would have attacked him on sight, just as they attacked each other.

I cut down three before I reached the door, and I was able to rally the lake men who had entered the tower to me as I went, telling them that the enemy we sought was outside. When I saw how much they dreaded the lunatic monsters who leaped still from the dark stairwell (and whom they failed to recognize for what they undoubtedly were—the ruins of their brothers and their children) I was surprised they had dared to enter the castle at all. It was wonderful, however, to see how my presence stiffened them; they let me take the lead, but by the look of their eyes I knew that wherever I led they would follow. That was the first time, I think, that I truly understood the pleasure his position must have given Master Gurloes, which until then I had supposed must have consisted merely in a celebration of his ability to impose his will on others. I understood too why so many of the young men at court forsook their fiancees, my friends in the life I had as Thecla, to accept commissions in obscure regiments.

The rain had slackened, though it still fell in silver sheets. Dead men, and many more of the giant's creatures, lay on the steps—I was compelled to kick several over the side for fear I would fall if I tried to walk over them. Below in the bailey there was still much fighting, but none of the creatures there came up to attack us, and the lake men held the stair against those we had left behind in the tower. I saw no sign of Baldanders.

Fighting, I have found, though it is exciting in the sense that it takes one out of oneself, is difficult to describe. And when it is over, what one best remembers—for the mind is too full at the time of struggle to do much recording—is not the cuts and parries but the hiatuses between engagements. In the bailey of Baldanders's castle I traded frantic blows with four of the monsters he had forged, but I cannot now say when I fought well and when badly.

The darkness and the rain favored the style of wild combat forced on me by the design of *Terminus Est*. Not only formal fencing but any sword or spear play that resembles it requires a good light, since each antagonist must see the other's weapon. Here there was hardly light at all. Furthermore, Baldanders's creatures possessed a suicidal courage that served them badly. They tried to leap over or duck under the cuts I made at them, and for the most part they were caught by the backhand that followed. In each of these piecemeal fights, the warriors of the islands took some part, and in one case actually dispatched my opponent for me. In the others, they distracted him, or had wounded him before I engaged him. None of these encounters was satisfactory in the sense that a well-performed execution is.

After the fourth there were no more, though their dead and dying lay everywhere. I gathered the islanders about me. We were all in that euphoric state that rides with victory, and they were willing enough to attack any giant, no matter how huge; but even those who had been in the bailey when the stones fell swore they had seen none. Just as I was beginning to think they were blind, and they were no doubt ready to believe I was mad, we were saved by the moon.

How strange it is. Everyone looks for knowledge in the sky, whether in studying the influence of the constellations upon events, or like Baldanders in seeking to wrest it from those the ignorant call cacogens, or only, in the case of farmers, fishermen, and the like, in searching for weather signs; yet no one looks for immediate help there, though we often receive it, as I did that night.

It was no more than a break in the clouds. The rain, which had already grown fitful, did not truly cease; but for a very short time the light of the waning moon (high overhead and, though hardly more than half full, very bright) fell upon the giant's courtyard just as the light from one of the largest luminaries in the odeum in the oneiric level of the House Absolute used to fall upon the stage. Beneath it the smooth, wet stones of the pavement shone like pools of still, dark water; and in them I saw reflected a sight so fantastic that I wonder now that I was able to do more than stare at it until I perished—which would not have been long.

For Baldanders was falling upon us; but he was falling slowly.

XXXVII

Terminus Est

There are pictures in the brown book of angels swooping down upon Urth in just that posture, the head thrown back, the body inclined so that the face and the upper part of the chest are at the same level. I can imagine the wonder and horror of beholding that great being I glimpsed in the book in the Second House descending in that way; yet I do not think it could be more frightful. When I recall Baldanders now, it is thus that I think of him first. His face was set, and he held upraised a mace tipped with a phosphorescent sphere.

We scattered as the sparrows do when an owl drops among them at twilight. I felt the wind of his blow at my back and turned in time to see him alight, catching himself with his free hand and bounding from it upright as I have watched street acrobats do; he wore a belt I had not noticed before, a thick affair of linked metal prisms. I never found out, however, how he had contrived to reenter his tower to get the mace and the belt while I thought him descending the wall; perhaps there was a window somewhere larger than those I saw, or even a door that had provided access to some structure that the burning of the castle by the shore people had destroyed. It is even possible that he only reached through some window with one arm.

But, oh, the silence as he came floating down, the grace as he, who was large as the huts of so many poor folk, caught himself on that hand and turned upright. The best way to describe silence is to say nothing—but what grace!

I whirled then with my cloak wind-whipped behind me and my sword, as I had so often held it, lifted for the stroke; and I knew then what I had never troubled to think upon before—why my destiny had sent me wandering half across the continent, facing dangers from fire and the depths of Urth, from water and now from air, armed with this weapon, so huge, so heavy that fighting any ordinary man with it was like cutting lilies with an ax. Baldanders saw me and raised his mace, its head shining yellow-white; I think it was a kind of salute.

Five or six of the lake men hedged him about with spears and toothed clubs, but they did not close with him. It was as though he were the center of some hermetic circle. As we came together, we two, I discovered the reason: a terror I could neither understand nor control gripped me. It was not that I was afraid of him or of death, but simply that I was *afraid.* I felt the hair of my head moving as if beneath the hand of a ghost, a thing I had heard of but always dismissed as an exaggeration, a figure of speech grown into a lie. My knees were weak and trembled—so much so that I was glad of the dark because they could not be seen. But we closed.

I knew very well from the size of that mace and the size of the arm behind it that I would never survive a blow from it; I could only dodge and jump back. Baldanders, equally, could not endure a stroke from *Terminus Est*, for though he was large and strong enough to wear armor as thick as a destrier's bardings, he had none, and so heavy a blade, with so fine an edge, easily capable of cleaving an ordinary man to the waist, could deal him his death wound with a single cut.

This he knew, and so we fenced much as players do upon a stage, with sweeping blows but without actually coming to grips. All that time the terror held me, so that it seemed that if I did not run my heart would burst. There was a singing in my ears, and as I watched the mace-head, whose pale nimbus made it, indeed, too easy to watch, I became aware that it was from there that the singing came. The weapon itself hummed with that high, unchanging note, like a wineglass struck with a knife and immobilized in crystalline time.

No doubt the discovery distracted me, even though it was only for a moment. Instead of a quartering stroke, the mace drove downward like a mallet hammering a tent peg. I moved to one side just in time, and the singing, shimmering head flashed past my face and crashed into the stone at my feet, which cracked and flew to pieces like a clay pot. One of its shards laid open a corner of my forehead, and I felt my blood streaming down.

Baldanders saw it, and his dull eyes lit with triumph. From that time forward he struck a stone at every stroke, and at every stroke stone shattered. I had to back away, and back away again, and soon I found myself with the curtain wall at my back. As I retreated along it, the giant used his weapon to greater advantage than ever, swinging it horizontally and striking the wall again and again. Often the stone shards, as sharp as flints, missed me; but often too they did not, and soon blood was running into my eyes, and my chest and arms were crimson.

As I leaped away from the mace for perhaps the hundredth time, something struck my heel and I nearly fell. It was the lowest step of a flight that climbed the wall. I went up, gaining a bit of advantage from the height but not enough to let me halt my retreat. There was a narrow walkway along the top of the wall. I was driven backward along it step by step. Now indeed I would have turned to run if I had dared, but I recalled how quickly the giant had moved when I surprised him in the chamber of clouds, and I knew that he would be upon me in a leap, just as I had, as a boy, overtaken the rats in the oubliette below our tower, breaking their spines with a stick.

But not every circumstance favored Baldanders. Something white flashed between us, then there was a bone-tipped spear thrust into one huge arm, like an ylespil's quill in the neck of a bull. The lake men were now far enough from the singing mace that the terror it waked no longer prevented them from throwing their weapons. Baldanders hesitated for a moment, stepping back to pull the spear out. Another struck him, grazing his face.

Then I knew hope and leaped forward, and in leaping lost my footing on a broken, rain-slick stone. I nearly went over the edge, but at the last instant caught hold of the parapet—in time to see the luminous head of the giant's mace descending. Instinctively I raised *Terminus Est* to ward off the blow.

There was such a scream as might have been made if all the specters of all the men and women she had slain were gathered on the wall—then a deafening explosion.

I lay stunned for a moment. But Baldanders was stunned as well, and the lake men, with the spell of the mace broken, were swarming along the walkway toward him from either side. Perhaps the steel of her blade, which had its own natural frequency and, as I had often observed, chimed with miraculous sweetness if tapped with a finger, was too much for whatever mechanism lent its strange powers to the giant's mace. Perhaps it was only that her edge, sharper than a surgeon's knife and as hard as obsidian, had penetrated the mace-head. Whatever had occurred, the mace was gone, and I held in my hands only the sword's hilt, from which protruded less than a cubit of shattered metal. The hydrargyrum that had labored so long in the darkness there ran from it now in silver tears.

Before I could rise, the lake men were springing over me. A spear plunged into the giant's chest, and a thrown club struck him in the face. At a sweep of his arm, two of the lake warriors tumbled screaming from the wall. Others were upon him at once, but he shook them off. I struggled to my feet, still only half comprehending what had taken place.

For an instant, Baldanders stood poised upon the parapet; then he leaped. No doubt he received great aid from the belt he wore, but the strength of his legs must have been enormous. Slowly, heavily, he arched out and out, down and down. Three who had clung to him too long fell to their deaths on the rocks of the promontory.

At last he fell too, hugely, as if he were—alone and in himself—some species of flying ship out of control. White as milk, the lake erupted, then closed over him. Something that writhed like a serpent and sometimes caught the light rose from the water and into the sky, until at last it vanished among the sullen clouds; no doubt it was the belt. But though the islanders stood with spears poised, his head never showed above the waves.

XXXVIII

The Claw

That night the lake men ransacked the castle; I did not join them, nor did I sleep inside its walls. In the center of the grove of pines where we had held our council, I found a spot so sheltered by the boughs that its carpet of fallen needles was still dry. There, when my wounds had been washed and bandaged, I lay down. The hilt of the sword that had been mine, and Master Palaemon's before me, lay beside me, so that I felt I slept with a dead thing; but it brought me no dreams.

I woke with the fragrance of the pines in my nostrils. Urth had turned almost her full face to the sun. My body was sore, and the cuts I had received from the flying shards of stone smarted and burned, but it was the warmest day I had experienced since I had left Thrax and mounted into the high lands. I walked out of the grove and saw Lake Diuturna sparkling in the sun and fresh grass growing between the stones.

I sat down on a projecting rock, with the wall of Baldanders's castle rising behind me and the blue lake spread at my feet, and for the last time removed the tang of the ruined blade that had been *Terminus Est* from the lovely hilt of silver and onyx. It is the blade that is the sword, and *Terminus Est* is no more; but I carried that hilt with me for the rest of my journey, though I burned the manskin sheath. The hilt will hold another blade someday, even if it cannot be as perfect and will not be mine.

What remained of my blade I kissed and cast into the water.

Then I began my search among the rocks. I had only a vague idea of the direction in which Baldanders had hurled the Claw, but I knew his throw had been toward the lake, and though I had seen the gem clear the top of the wall, I felt that even such an arm as his might have failed to send so small an object far from shore.

I soon found, however, that if it had gone into the lake at all, it was lost utterly, for the water was many ells deep everywhere. Yet it still seemed possible that it had not reached the lake and was lodged in a crevice where its radiance was invisible.

And so I searched, afraid to ask the lake men to assist me, and afraid also to give up the search to rest or eat for fear someone else would take it up. Night came, and the cry of the loon at the dying of the light, and the lake men offered to take me to their islands, but I refused. They feared that shore people would come, or that they were already organizing an attack that would revenge Baldanders (I did not dare to tell them that I suspected he was not dead, but remained alive beneath the waters of the lake), and so at last, at my urging they left me alone, still crawling among the sharp-cornered rocks of the promontory.

Eventually I grew too weary to hunt more in the dark and settled myself upon a shelving slab to wait for day. From time to time it seemed that I saw azure gleaming from some crack near where I lay or from the waters below; but always when I stretched out my hand to grasp it or tried to stand to walk to the edge of the slab to look down at it, I woke with a start and found I had been dreaming.

A hundred times I wondered if someone else had not found the gem while I slept under the pine, which I cursed myself for doing. A hundred times, also, I reminded myself how much better it would be for it to be found by anyone than for it to be lost forever.

Just as summer-killed meat draws flies, so the court draws spurious sages, philosophists, and acosmists who remain there as long as their purses and their wits will maintain them, in the hope (at first) of an appointment from the Autarch and (later) of obtaining a tutorial position in some exalted family. At sixteen or so, Thecla was attracted, as I think young women often are, to their lectures on theogony, thodicy, and the like, and I recall one particularly in which a phoebad put forward as an ultimate truth the ancient sophistry of the existence of three Adonai, that of the city (or of the people), that of the poets, and that of the philosophers. Her reasoning was that since the beginning of human consciousness (if such a beginning ever was) there have been vast numbers of persons in the three categories who have endeavored to pierce the secret of the divine. If it does not exist, they should have discovered that long before; if it does, it is not possible that Truth itself should mislead them. Yet the beliefs of the populace, the insights of the rhapsodists, and the theories of the metaphysicians have so far diverged that few of them can so much as comprehend what the others say, and someone who knew nothing of any of their ideas might well believe there was no connection at all between them.

May it not be, she asked (and even now I am not certain I can answer), that instead of traveling, as has always been supposed, down three roads to the same destination, they are actually traveling toward three quite different ones? After all, when in common life we behold three roads issuing from the same crossing, we do not assume they all proceed toward the same goal.

I found (and find) this suggestion as rational as it is repellent, and it represents for me all that monomaniacal fabric of argument, so tightly woven that not even the tiniest objection or spark of light can escape its net, in which human minds become enmeshed whenever the subject is one in which no appeal to fact is possible.

As a fact the Claw was thus an incommensurable. No quantity of money, no piling up of archipelagoes or empires could approach it in value any more than the indefinite multiplication of horizontal distance could be made to equal vertical distance. If it was, as I believed, a thing from outside the universe, then its light, which I had seen shine faintly so often, and a few times brightly, was in some sense the only light we had. If it were destroyed, we were left fumbling in the dark.

I thought I had valued it highly in all the days in which I had carried it, but as I sat there upon that shelving stone overlooking the benighted waters of Lake Diuturna, I realized what a fool I had been to carry it at all, through all my wild scrapes and insane adventures, until I lost it at last. Just before sunrise I vowed to take my own life if I did not find it before the dark came again.

Whether or not I could have kept that vow I cannot say. I have loved life so long as I can remember. (It was, I believe, that love of life that gave me whatever skill I possessed at my art, because I could not bear to see the flame I cherished extinguished other than perfectly.) Surely I loved my own life, now mingled with Thecla's, as much as others. If I had broken that vow, it would not have been the first.

There was no need to. About mid morning of one of the most pleasant days I have ever experienced, when the sunlight was a warm caress and the lapping of the water below a gentle music, I found the gem—or what remained of it.

It had shattered on the rocks; there were pieces large enough to adorn a tetrarchic ring and flecks no bigger than the bright specks we see in mica, but nothing more. Weeping, I gathered the fragments bit by bit, and when I knew them to be as lifeless as the jewels miners delve up every day, the plundered finery of the long dead, I carried them to the lake and cast them in.

I made three of those climbs down to the water's edge with a tiny heap of bluish chips held in the hollow of one hand, each time returning to the place where I had found the broken gem to search for more; and after the third I found, wedged deep between two stones so that I had, in the end, to return to the pine grove to break twigs with which to free it and fish it up, something that was neither azure nor a gem, but that shone with an intense white light, like a star.

It was with curiosity rather than reverence that I drew it out. It was so unlike the treasure I had sought—or at least, unlike the broken bits of it I had been finding—that it hardly occurred to me until I held it that the two might be related. I cannot say how it is possible for an object in itself black to give light, but this did. It might have been carved in jet, so dark it was and so highly polished; yet it shone, a claw as long as the last joint of my smallest finger, cruelly hooked and needle-pointed, the reality of that dark core at the heart of the gem, which must have been no more than a container for it, a lipsanotheca or pyx.

For a long time I knelt with my back to the castle, looking from this strange, gleaming treasure to the waves and back again while I tried to grasp its significance. Seeing it thus without its case of sapphire, I felt profoundly an effect I had never noticed at all during the days before it had been taken from me in the hetman's house. Whenever I looked at it, it seemed to erase thought. Not as wine and certain drugs do, by rendering the mind unfit for it, but by replacing it with a higher state for which I know no name. Again and again I felt myself enter this state, rising always higher until I feared I should never return to the mode of consciousness I call normality; and again and again I tore myself from it. Each time I emerged, I felt I had gained some inexpressible insight into immense realities.

At last, after a long series of these bold advances and fearful retreats, I came to understand that I should never reach any real knowledge of the tiny thing I held, and with that thought (for it was a thought) came a third state, one of happy obedience to I knew not what, an obedience without reflection because there was no longer anything to reflect upon, and without the least tincture of rebellion. This state endured all that day and a large part of the next, by which time I was already deep into the hills.

Here I pause, having carried you, reader, from fortress to fortress—from the walled city of Thrax, dominating the upper Acis, to the castle of the giant, dominating the northern shore of remote Lake Diuturna. Thrax was for me the gateway to the wild mountains. So too, this lonely tower was to prove a gateway—the very threshold of the war, of which a single far-flung skirmish had taken place here. From that time to this, that war has engaged my attention almost without cease.

Here I pause. If you have no desire to plunge into the struggle beside me, reader, I do not condemn you. It is no easy one.

Appendix

A Note on Provincial Administration

Severian's brief record of his career in Thrax is the best (though not the only) evidence we have concerning the business of government in the age of the Commonwealth, as it is carried out beyond the shining corridors of the House Absolute and the teeming streets of Nessus. Clearly, our own distinctions between the legislative, executive, and judicial branches do not apply—no doubt administrators like Abdiesus would laugh at our notion that laws should be made by one set of people, put into effect by a second, and judged by a third. They would consider such a system unworkable, as indeed it is proving to be.

At the period of the manuscripts, archons and tetrarchs are appointed by the Autarch, who as the representative of the people has all power in his hands. (See, however, Famulimus's remark on this topic to Severian.) These officials are expected to enforce the commands of the Autarch and to administer justice in accordance with the received usages of the populations they govern. They are also empowered to make local laws—valid only over the area governed by the lawmaker and only during his term of office—and to enforce them with the threat of death. In Thrax, as well as in the House Absolute and the Citadel, imprisonment for a fixed term—our own most common punishment—seems unknown. Prisoners in the Vincula are held awaiting torture or execution, or as hostages for the good behavior of their friends and relatives.

As the manuscript clearly shows, the supervision of the Vincula ("the house of chains") is only one of the duties of the lictor ("he who binds"). This officer is the chief subordinate of the archon involved with the administration of criminal justice. On certain ceremonial occasions he walks before his master bearing a naked sword, a potent reminder of the archon's authority. During sessions of the archon's court (as Severian complains) he is required to stand at the left of the bench. Executions and other major acts of judicial punishment are personally performed by him, and he supervises the activities of the clavigers ("those with keys").

These clavigers are not only the guards of the Vincula; they act also as a detective police, a function made easier by their opportunities for extorting information from their prisoners. The keys they bear seem sufficiently large to be used as bludgeons, and are thus their weapons as well as their tools and their emblems of authority.

The dimarchi ("those who fight in two ways") are the archon's uniformed police as well as his troops. However, their title does not appear to refer to this dual function, but to equipment and training that permits them to act as cavalry or infantry as the need arises. Their ranks appear to be filled by professional soldiers, veterans of the campaigns in the north and nonnatives of the area.

Thrax itself is clearly a fortress city. Such a place could scarcely be expected to stand for more than a day at most against the Ascian enemy—rather, it seems designed to fend off raids by brigands and rebellions by the local exultants and armigers. (Cyriaca's husband, who would have been a person almost beneath notice in the House Absolute, is clearly of some importance, and even some danger, in the neighborhood of Thrax.) Although the exultants and armigers seem to be forbidden private armies, there appears little doubt that many of their followers, though called huntsmen, stewards, and the like, are fundamentally fighting men. They are presumably essential to protect the villas from marauders and to collect rents, but in the event of civil unrest they would be a potent source of danger to such as Abdiesus. The fortified city straddling the headwaters of the river would give him an almost irresistible advantage in any such conflict.

The route chosen by Severian for his escape indicates how closely egress from the city could be controlled. The archon's own fortress, Acies Castle ("the armed camp of the point"), guards the northern end of the valley. It appears to be entirely separate from his palace in the city proper. The southern end is closed by the Capulus ("the sword halt''), apparently an elaborate fortified wall, a scaled-down imitation of the Wall of Nessus. Even the cliff tops are protected by forts linked by walls. Possessing, as it does, an inexhaustible supply of fresh water, the city appears capable of withstanding a protracted siege by any force not provided with heavy armament.

G. W.

The Citadel of the Autarch

At two o'clock in the morning, if you open your window and listen,
You will hear the feet of the Wind that is going to call the sun.
And the trees in the shadow rustle and the trees in the moonlight glisten,
And though it is deep, dark night, you feel that the night is done.

Rudyard Kipling

I

The Dead Soldier

I had never seen war, or even talked of it at length with someone who had, but I was young and knew something of violence, and so believed that war would be no more than a new experience for me, as other things—the possession of authority in Thrax, say, or my escape from the House Absolute—had been new experiences.

War is not a new experience; it is a new world. Its inhabitants are more different from human beings than Famulimus and her friends. Its laws are new, and even its geography is new, because it is a geography in which insignificant hills and hollows are lifted to the importance of cities. Just as our familiar Urth holds such monstrosities as Erebus, Abaia, and Arioch, so the world of war is stalked by the monsters called battles, whose cells are individuals but who have a life and intelligence of their own, and whom one approaches through an ever-thickening array of portents.

One night I woke long before dawn. Everything seemed still, and I was afraid some enemy had come near, so that my mind had stirred at his malignancy. I rose and looked about. The hills were lost in the darkness. I was in a nest of long grass, a nest I had trampled flat for myself. Crickets sang.

Something caught my eye far to the north: a flash, I thought, of violet just on the horizon. I stared at the point from which it seemed to have come. Just as I had convinced myself that what I believed I had seen was no more than a fault of vision, perhaps some lingering effect of the drug I had been given in the hetman's house, there was a flare of magenta a trifle to the left of the point I had been staring at.

I continued to stand there for a watch or more, rewarded from time to time with these mysteries of light. At last, having satisfied myself that they were a great way off and came no nearer, and that they did not appear to change in frequency, coming on the average with each five hundredth beat of my heart, I lay down again. And because I was then thoroughly awake, I became aware that the ground was shaking, very slightly, beneath me.

When I woke again in the morning it had stopped. I watched the horizon diligently for some time as I walked along, but saw nothing disturbing.

It had been two days since I had eaten, and I was no longer hungry, though I was aware that I did not have my normal strength. Twice that day I came upon little houses falling to ruin, and I entered each to look for food. If anything had been left, it had been taken long before; even the rats were gone. The second house had a well, but some dead thing had been thrown down it long ago, and in any case there was no way to reach the stinking water. I went on, wishing for something to drink and also for a better staff than the succession of rotten sticks I had been using. I had learned when I had used *Terminus Est* as a staff in the mountains how much easier it is to walk with one.

About noon I came upon a path and followed it, and a short time afterward heard the sound of hoofs. I hid where I could look down the road; a moment later a rider crested the next hill and flashed past me. From the glimpse I had of him, he wore armor somewhat in the fashion of the commanders of Abdiesus's dimarchi, but his wind-stiffened cape was green instead of red and his helmet seemed to have a visor like the bill of a cap. Whoever he was, he was magnificently mounted: His destrier's mouth was bearded with foam and its sides drenched, yet it flew by as though the racing signal had dropped only an instant before.

Having encountered one rider on the path, I expected others. There were none. For a long while I walked in tranquillity, hearing the calls of birds and seeing many signs of game. Then (to my inexpressible delight) the path forded a young stream. I walked up a dozen strides to a spot where deeper, quieter water flowed over a bed of white gravel. Minnows skittered away from my boots—always a sign of good water—and it was still cold from the mountain peaks and sweet with the memory of snow. I drank and drank again, and then again, until I could hold no more, then took off my clothes and washed myself, cold though it was. When I had finished my bath and dressed and returned to the place where the path crossed the stream, I saw two pug marks on the other side, daintily close together, where the animal had crouched to drink. They overlay the hoofprints of the officer's mount, and each was as big as a dinner plate, with no claws showing beyond the soft pads of the toes. Old Midan, who had been my uncle's huntsman when I was the girl-child Thecla, had told me once that smilodons drink only after they have gorged themselves, and that when they have gorged and drunk they are not dangerous unless molested. I went on.

The path wound through a wooded valley, then up into a saddle between hills. When I was near the highest point, I noticed a tree two spans in diameter that had been torn in half (as it appeared) at about the height of my eyes. The ends of both the standing stump and the felled trunk were ragged, not at all like the smooth chipping of an ax. In the next two or three leagues I walked, there were several score like it. Judging from the lack of leaves, and in some cases of bark, on the fallen parts, and the new shoots the stumps had put forth, the damage had been done at least a year ago, and perhaps longer.

At last the path joined a true road, something I had heard of often, but never trodden except in decay. It was much like the old road the uhlans had been blocking when I had become separated from Dr. Talos, Baldanders, Jolenta, and Dorcas when we left Nessus, but I was unprepared for the cloud of dust that hung about it. No grass grew upon it, though it was wider than most city streets.

I had no choice except to follow it; the trees about it were thick set, and the spaces between them choked with brush. At first I was afraid, remembering the burning lances of the uhlans; still, it seemed probable that the law that prohibited the use of roads no longer had force here, or this one would not have seen as much traffic as it clearly had; and when, a short time later, I heard voices and the sound of many marching feet behind me, I only moved a pace or two into the trees and watched openly while the column passed.

An officer came first, riding a fine, champing blue whose fangs had been left long and set with turquoise to match his bardings and the hilt of his owner's estoc. The men who followed him on foot were antepilani of the heavy infantry, big shouldered and narrow waisted, with sunbronzed, expressionless faces. They carried three-pointed korsekes, demilunes, and heavy headed voulges. This mixture of armaments, as well as certain discrepancies among their badges and accouterments, led me to believe that their mora was made up of the remains of earlier formations. If that were so, the fighting they must have seen had left them phlegmatic. They swung along, four thousand or so in all, without excitement, reluctance, or any sign of fatigue, careless in their bearing but not slovenly, and seemed to keep step without thought or effort.

Wagons drawn by grunting, trumpeting trilophodons followed. I edged nearer the road as they came, for much of the baggage they carried was clearly food; but there were mounted men among the wagons, and one called to me, asking what unit I belonged to, then ordering me to him. I fled instead, and though I was fairly sure he could not ride among the trees and would not abandon his destrier to pursue me on foot, I ran until I was winded.

When I stopped at last, it was in a silent glade where greenish sunlight filtered through the leaves of spindly trees. Moss covered the ground so thickly that I felt as if I walked upon the dense carpet of the hidden picture-room where I had encountered the Master of the House Absolute. For a while I rested my back against one of the thin trunks, listening. There came no sound but the gasping of my own breath and the tidal roar of my blood in my ears.

In time I became aware of a third note: the faint buzzing of a fly. I wiped my streaming face with the edge of my guild cloak. That cloak was sadly worn and faded now, and I was suddenly conscious that it was the same one Master Gurloes had draped about my shoulders when I became a journeyman, and that I was likely to die in it. The sweat it had absorbed felt cold as dew, and the air was heavy with the odor of damp earth.

The buzzing of the fly ceased, then resumed—perhaps a trifle more insistently, perhaps merely seeming so because I had my breath again. Absently, I looked for it and saw it dart through a shaft of sunlight a few paces off, then settle on a brown object projecting from behind one of the thronging trees.

A boot.

I had no weapon whatsoever. Ordinarily I would not have been much afraid of confronting a single man with my hands alone, especially in such a place, where it would have been impossible to swing a sword; but I knew much of my strength was gone, and I was discovering that fasting destroys a part of one's courage as well—or perhaps it is only that it consumes a part of it, leaving less for other exigencies.

However that might be, I walked warily, sidelong and silently, until I saw him. He layed sprawled, with one leg crumpled under him and the other extended. A falchion had fallen near his right hand, its leather lanyard still about his wrist. His simple barbute had dropped from his head and rolled a step away. The fly crawled up his boot until it reached the bare flesh just below the knee, then flew again, with the noise of a tiny saw.

I knew, of course, that he was dead, and even as I felt relief my sense of isolation came rushing back, though I had not realized that it had departed. Taking him by the shoulder, I turned him over. His body had not yet swelled, but the smell of death had come, however faint. His face had softened like a mask of wax set before a fire; there was no telling now with what expression he had died. He had been young and blond—one of those handsome, square faces. I looked for a wound but found none.

The straps of his pack had been drawn so tight that I could neither pull it off nor even loosen the fastenings. In the end I took the coutel from his belt and cut them, then drove the point into a tree. A blanket, a scrap of paper, a fire-blackened pan with a socket handle, two pairs of rough stockings (very welcome), and, best of all, an onion and a half loaf of dark bread wrapped in a clean rag, and five strips of dried meat and a lump of cheese wrapped in another.

I ate the bread and cheese first, forcing myself, when I found I could not eat slowly, to rise after every third bite and walk up and down. The bread helped by requiring a great deal of chewing; it tasted precisely like the hard bread we used to feed our clients in the Matachin Tower, bread I had stolen, more from mischief than from hunger, once or twice. The cheese was dry and smelly and salty, but excellent all the same; I thought that I had never tasted such cheese before, and I know I have never tasted any since. I might have been eating life. It made me thirsty, and I learned how well an onion quenches thirst by stimulating the salivary glands.

By the time I reached the meat, which was heavily salted too, I was satiated enough to begin debating whether I should reserve it against the night, and I decided to eat one piece and save the other four.

The air had been still since early that morning, but now a faint breeze blew, cooling my cheeks, stirring the leaves, and catching the paper I had pulled from the dead soldier's pack and sending it rattling across the moss to lodge against a tree. Still chewing and swallowing, I pursued it and picked it up. It was a letter—I assume one he had not had the opportunity to send, or perhaps to complete. His hand had been angular, and smaller than I would have anticipated, though it may be that its smallness only resulted from his wish to crowd many words onto the small sheet, which appeared to have been the last he possessed.

> O my beloved, we are a hundred leagues north of the place from which I last wrote you, having come by hard marches. We have enough to eat and are warm by day, though sometimes cold at night. Makar, of whom I told you, has fallen sick and was permitted to remain behind. A great many others claimed then to be ill and were made to march before us without weapons and carrying double packs and under guard. In all this time we have seen no sign of the Ascians, and we are told by the lochage that they are still several days' march off. The seditionists killed sentries for three nights, until we put three men on each post and kept patrols moving outside

our perimeter. I was assigned to one of these patrols on the first night and found it very discomforting, since I feared one of my comrades would cut me down in the dark. My time was spent tripping over roots and listening to the singing at the fire—

"Tomorrow night's sleep
Will be on stained ground,
So tonight all drink deep,
Let the friend-cup go round.
Friend, I hope when they shoot,

Every shot will fly wide,
And I wish you good loot,
And myself at your side.
Let the friend-cup go round,
For we'll sleep on stained ground."

Naturally, we saw no one. The seditionists call themselves the Vodalarii after their leader and are said to be picked fighters. And well paid, receiving support from the Ascians. . . .

II

The Living Soldier

I put aside the half-read letter and stared at the man who had written it. Death's shot had not flown wide for him; now he stared at the sun with lusterless blue eyes, one nearly winking, the other fully open.

Long before that moment I should have recalled the Claw, but I had not. Or perhaps I had only suppressed the thought in my eagerness to steal the rations in the dead man's pack, never reasoning that I might have trusted him to share his food with the rescuer who had recalled him from death. Now, at the mention of Vodalus and his followers (who I felt would surely assist me if only I were able to find them), I remembered it at once and took it out. It seemed to sparkle in the summer sunlight, brighter indeed than I had ever seen it without its sapphire case. I touched him with it, then, urged by I cannot say what impulse, put it into his mouth.

When this, too, effected nothing, I took it between my thumb and first finger and pushed its point into the soft skin of his forehead. He did not move or breathe, but a drop of blood, fresh and sticky as that of a living man, welled forth and stained my fingers.

I withdrew them, wiped my hand with some leaves, and would have gone back to his letter if I had not thought I heard a stick snap some distance away. For a moment I could not choose among hiding, fleeing, and fighting; but there was little chance of successfully doing the first, and I had already had enough of the second. I picked up the dead man's falchion, wrapped myself in my cloak, and stood waiting.

No one came—or at least, no one visible to me. The wind made a slight sighing among the treetops. The fly seemed to have gone. Perhaps I had heard nothing more than a deer bounding through the shadows. I had traveled so far without any weapon that would permit me to hunt that I had almost forgotten the possibility. Now I examined the falchion and found myself wishing it had been a bow.

Something behind me stirred, and I turned to look.

It was the soldier. A tremor seemed to have seized him—if I had not seen his corpse, I would have thought him dying. His hands shook, and there was a rattling in his throat. I bent and touched his face; it was as cold as ever, and I had the impulsive need to kindle a fire.

There had been no fire-making gear in his pack, but I knew every soldier must carry such things. I searched his pockets and found a few aes, a hanging dial with which to tell time, and a flint and striking bar. Tinder lay in plenty under the trees—the danger was that I might set fire to all of it. I swept a space clear with my hands, piling the sweepings in the center, set them ablaze, then gathered a few rotten boughs, broke them, and laid them on the fire.

Its light was brighter than I had expected—day was almost done, and it would soon be dark. I looked at the dead man. His hands no longer shook; he was silent. The flesh of his face seemed warmer. But that was, no doubt, no more than the heat of the fire. The spot of blood on his forehead had nearly dried, yet it seemed to catch the light of the dying sun, shining as some crimson gem might, some pigeon's blood ruby spilled from a treasure hoard. Though our fire gave little smoke, what there was seemed to me fragrant as incense, and like incense it rose straight until it was lost in the gathering dark, suggesting something I could not quite recall. I shook myself and found more wood, breaking and stacking it until I had a pile I thought large enough to last the night.

Evenings were not nearly so cold here in Orithyia as they had been in the mountains, or even in the region about Lake Diuturna, so that although I recalled the blanket I had found in the dead man's pack, I felt no need of it. My task had warmed me, the food I had eaten had invigorated me, and for a time I strode up and down in the twilight, brandishing the falchion when such warlike gestures accorded with my thoughts but taking care to keep the fire between the dead man and myself.

My memories have always appeared with the intensity, almost, of hallucinations, as I have said often in this chronicle. That night I felt I might lose myself forever in them, making of my life a loop instead of a line; and for once I did not resist the temptation but reveled in it. Everything I have described to you came crowding back to me, and a thousand things more. I saw Eata's face and his freckled hand when he sought to slip between the bars of the gate of the necropolis, and the storm I had once watched impaled on the towers of the Citadel, writhing and lashing out with its lightnings; I felt its rain, colder and fresher far than the morning cup in our refectory, trickle down my face. Dorcas's voice whispered in my ears: "Sitting in a window . . . trays and a rood. What will you do, summon up some Erinys to destroy me?"

Yes. Yes, indeed, I would have if I could. If I had been Hethor, I would have drawn them from some horror behind the world, birds with the heads of hags and the tongues of vipers. At my order they would have threshed the forests like wheat and beaten cities flat with their great wings . . . and yet, if I could, I would have appeared at the final moment to save her—not walking coldly off afterward in the way we all wish to do when, as children, we imagine ourselves rescuing and humiliating the loved one who has given us some supposed slight, but raising her in my arms.

Then for the first time, I think, I knew how terrible it must have been for her, who had been hardly more than a child when death had come, and who had been dead so long, to have been called back.

And thinking of that, I remembered the dead soldier whose food I had eaten and whose sword I held, and I paused and listened to hear if he drew breath or stirred. Yet I was so lost in the worlds of memory that it seemed to me the soft forest earth under my feet had come from the grave Hildegrin the Badger had despoiled for Vodalus, and the whisper of the leaves was the soughing of the cypresses in our necropolis and the rustle of the purple-flowered roses, and that I listened, listened in vain for breath from the dead woman Vodalus had lifted with the rope beneath her arms, lifted in her white shroud.

At last, the croaking of a nightjar brought me to myself. I seemed to see the soldier's white face staring at me, and went around the fire and searched until I found the blanket, and draped his corpse with it.

Dorcas belonged, as I now realized, to that vast group of women (which may, indeed, include all women) who betray us—and to that special type who betray us not for some present rival but for their own pasts. Just as Morwenna, whom I had executed at Saltus, must have poisoned her husband and her child because she recalled a time in which she was free and, perhaps, virginal, so Dorcas had left me because I had not existed (had, as she must unconsciously have seen it, failed to exist) in that time before her doom fell upon her.

(For me, also, that is the golden time. I think I must have treasured the memory of the crude, kindly boy who fetched books and blossoms to my cell largely because I knew him to be the last love before the doom, the doom that was not, as I learned in that prison, the moment at which the tapestry was cast over me to muffle my outcry, nor my arrival at the Old Citadel in Nessus, nor the slam of the cell door behind me, nor even the moment when, bathed in such a light as never shines on Urth, I felt my body rise in rebellion against me—but that instant in which I drew the blade of the greasy paring knife he had brought, cold and mercifully sharp, across my own neck. Possibly we all come to such a time, and it is the will of the Caitanya that each damn herself for what she has done. Yet can we be hated so much? Can we be hated at all? Not when I can still remember his kisses on my breasts, given, not breathing to taste the perfume of my flesh—as Aphrodisius's were, and that young man's, the nephew of the chiliarch of the Companions—but as though he were truly hungry for my flesh. Was something watching us? He has eaten of me now. Awakened by the memory, I lift my hand and run fingers through his hair.)

I slept late, wrapped in my cloak. There is a payment made by Nature to those who undergo hardships; it is that the lesser ones, at which people whose lives have been easier would complain, seem almost comfortable. Several times before I actually rose, I woke and congratulated myself to think how easily I had spent this night compared to those I had endured in the mountains.

At last the sunlight and the singing birds brought me to myself. On the other side of our dead fire, the soldier shifted and, I think, murmured something. I sat up. He had thrown the blanket aside and lay with his face to the sky. It was a pale face with sunken cheeks; there were dark shadows beneath the eyes and deeply cut lines running from the mouth; but it was a living face. The eyes were truly closed, and breath sighed in the nostrils.

For a moment I was tempted to run before he woke. I had his falchion still—I started to replace it, then took it back for fear he would attack me with it. His coutel still protruded from the tree, making me think of Agia's crooked dagger in the shutter of Casdoe's house. I thrust it back into the sheath at his belt, mostly because I was ashamed to think that I, armed with a sword, should fear any man with a knife.

His eyelids fluttered, and I drew away, remembering a time when Dorcas had been frightened to find me bending over her when she woke. So that I should not appear a dark figure, I pushed back my cloak to show my bare arms and chest, browned now by so many days' suns. I could hear the sighing of his breath; and when it changed from sleep to waking, it seemed to me a thing almost as miraculous as the passage from death to life.

Empty-eyed as a child, he sat up and looked about him. His lips moved, but only sound without sense came forth. I spoke to him, trying to make my tone friendly. He listened but did not seem to understand,

and I recalled how dazed the uhlan had been, whom I had revived on the road to the House Absolute.

I wished that I had water to offer him, but I had none. I drew out a piece of the salt meat I had taken from his pack, broke it into two, and shared that with him instead.

He chewed and seemed to feel a little better. "Stand up," I said. "We must find something to drink." He took my hand and allowed me to pull him erect, but he could hardly stand. His eyes, which had been so calm at first, grew wilder as they became more alert. I had the feeling that he feared the trees might rush upon us like a pride of lions, yet he did not draw his coutel or attempt to reclaim the falchion.

When we had taken three or four steps, he tottered and nearly fell. I let him lean upon my arm, and together we made our way through the wood to the road.

III

Through Dust

I did not know whether we should turn north or south. Somewhere to the north lay the Ascian army, and it was possible that if we came too near the lines we would be caught up in some swift maneuver. Yet the farther south we went, the less likely we were to find anyone who would help us, and the more probable it became that we would be arrested as deserters. In the end I turned northward; no doubt I acted largely from habit, and I am still not sure if I did well or ill.

The dew had already dried upon the road, and its dusty surface showed no footprints. To either side, for three paces or more, the vegetation was a uniform gray. We soon passed out of the forest. The road wound down a hill and over a bridge that vaulted a small river at the bottom of a rock-strewn valley.

We left it there and went down to the water to drink and bathe our faces. I had not shaved since I had turned my back on Lake Diuturna, and though I had noticed none when I took the flint and striker from the soldier's pocket, I ventured to ask him if he carried a razor.

I mention this trifling incident because it was the first thing I said to him that he seemed to comprehend. He nodded, then reaching under his hauberk produced one of those little blades that country people use, razors their smiths grind from the halves of worn oxshoes. I touched it up on the broken whetstone I still carried and stropped it on the leg of my boot, then asked if he had soap. If he did, he failed to understand me, and after a moment he seated himself on a rock from which he could stare into the water, reminding me very much of Dorcas. I longed to question him about the fields of Death, to learn all that he remembered of that time that is, perhaps, dark only to us. Instead, I washed my face in the cold river water and scraped my cheeks and chin as well as I could. When I sheathed his razor and tried to return it to him, he did not seem to know what to do with it, so I kept it.

For most of the rest of that day we walked. Several times we were stopped and questioned; more often we stopped others and questioned them. Gradually I developed an elaborate lie: I was the lictor of a civil judge who accompanied the Autarch; we had encountered this soldier on the road, and my master had ordered me to see that he was cared for; he could not speak, and so I did not know what unit he was from. That last was true enough.

We crossed other roads and sometimes followed them. Twice we reached great camps where tens of thousands of soldiers lived in cities of tents. At each, those who tended the sick told me that though they would have bandaged my companion's wounds had he been bleeding, they could not take responsibility for him as he was. By the time I spoke to the second, I no longer asked the location of the Pelerines but only to be directed to a place where we might find shelter. It was nearly night.

"There is a lazaret three leagues from here that may take you in." My informant looked from one of us to the other, and seemed to have almost as much sympathy for me as for the soldier, who stood mute and dazed. "Go west and north until you see a road to the right that passes between two big trees. It is about half as wide as the one you will have been following. Go down that. Are you armed?"

I shook my head; I had put the soldier's falchion back in his scabbard. "I was forced to leave my sword behind with my master's servants—I couldn't have carried it and managed this man too."

"Then you must beware of beasts. It would be better if you had something that would shoot, but I can't give you anything."

I turned to go, but he stopped me with a hand on my shoulder.

"Leave him if you're attacked," he said. "And if you're forced to leave him, don't feel too badly about it. I've seen cases like his before. He's not likely to recover."

"He has already recovered," I told him.

Although this man would not allow us to stay or lend me a weapon, he did provide us with something to eat; and I departed with more cheerfulness than I had felt for some time. We were in a valley where the western hills had risen to obscure the sun a watch or more before. As I walked along beside the soldier, I discovered that it was no longer necessary for me to hold his arm. I could release it, and he continued to walk at my side like any friend. His face was not really like Jonas's, which had been long and narrow, but once when I saw it sidelong I caught something there so reminiscent of Jonas that I felt almost that I had seen a ghost.

The gray road was greenish-white in the moonlight; the trees and brush to either side looked black. As we strode along I began to talk. Partially, I admit, it was from sheer loneliness; yet I had other reasons as well. Unquestionably there are beasts, like the alzabo, who attack men as foxes do fowls, but I have been told that there are many others who will flee if they are warned in time of human presence. Then too, I thought that if I spoke to the soldier as I might have to any other man, any ill-intentioned persons who heard us would be less apt to guess how unlikely he was to resist them.

"Do you recall last night?" I began. "You slept very heavily."

There was no reply.

"Perhaps I never told you this, but I have the facility of recalling everything. I can't always lay hands on it when I want, but it is always there; some memories, you know, are like escaped clients wandering through the oubliette. One may not be able to produce them on demand, but they are always there, they cannot get away.

"Although, come to think of it, that isn't entirely true. The fourth and lowest level of our oubliette has been abandoned—there are never enough clients to fill the topmost three anyway, and perhaps eventually Master Gurloes will give up the third. We only keep it open now for the mad ones that no official ever comes to see. If they were in one of the higher levels, their noise would disturb the others. Not all of them are noisy, of course. Some are as quiet as yourself."

Again there was no reply. In the moonlight I could not tell if he was paying attention to me, but remembering the razor I persevered.

"I went that way myself once. Through the fourth level, I mean. I used to have a dog, and I kept him there, but he ran away. I went after him and found a tunnel that left our oubliette. Eventually I crawled out of a broken pedestal in a place called the Atrium of Time. It was full of sundials. I met a young woman there who was really more beautiful than anyone I've ever seen since—more lovely even than Jolenta, I think, though not in the same way."

The soldier said nothing, yet now something told me he heard me; perhaps it was no more than a slight movement of his head seen from a corner of my eye.

"Her name was Valeria, and I think she was younger than I, although she seemed older. She had dark, curling hair, like Thecla's, but her eyes were dark too. Thecla's were violet. She had the finest skin I have ever seen, like rich milk mixed with the juice of pomegranates and strawberries.

"But I didn't set out to talk about Valeria, but about Dorcas. Dorcas is lovely too, though she is very thin, almost like a child. Her face is a peri's, and her complexion is flecked with freckles like bits of gold. Her hair was long before she cut it; she always wore flowers there."

I paused again. I had continued to talk of women because that seemed to have caught his attention. Now I could not say if he were still listening or not.

"Before I left Thrax I went to see Dorcas. It was in her room, in an inn called the Duck's Nest. She was in bed and naked, but she kept the sheet over herself, just as if we had never slept together—we who had walked and ridden so far, camping in places where no voice had been heard since the land was called up from the sea, and climbing hills where no feet had ever walked but the sun's. She was leaving me and I her, and neither of us really wished it otherwise, though at the last she was afraid and asked me to come with her after all.

"She said she thought the Claw had the same power over time that Father Inire's mirrors are said to have over distance. I didn't think much of the remark then—I'm not really a very intelligent man, I suppose, not a philosopher at all—but now I find it interesting. She told me, 'When you brought the uhlan back to life it was because the Claw twisted time for him to the point at which he still lived. When you half-healed your friend's wounds, it was because it bent the moment to one when they would be nearly healed.' Don't you think that's interesting? A little while after I pricked your forehead with the Claw, you made a strange sound. I think it may have been your death rattle."

I waited. The soldier did not speak, but quite unexpectedly I felt his hand on my shoulder. I had been talking almost flippantly; his touch brought home to me the seriousness of what I had been saying. If it were true—or even some trifling approximation to the truth—then I had toyed with powers I understood no better than Casdoe's son, whom I had tried to make my own, would have understood the giant ring that took his life.

"No wonder then that you're dazed. It must be a terrible thing to move backward in time, and still more terrible to pass backward through death. I was about to say that it would be like being born again; but it would be much worse than that, I think, because an infant lives already in his mother's womb." I hesitated. "I . . . Thecla, I mean . . . never bore a child."

Perhaps only because I had been thinking of his confusion, I found I was confused myself, so that I scarcely knew who I was. At last I said lamely, "You must excuse me. When I'm tired, and sometimes when I'm near sleep, I come near to becoming someone else." (For whatever reason, his grip on my shoulder tightened when I said that.) "It's a long story that has nothing to do with you. I wanted to say that in the Atrium of Time, the breaking of the pedestal had tilted the dials so their gnomons no longer pointed true, and I have heard that when that happens, the watches of day stop, or run backward for some part of each day. You carry a pocket dial, so you know that for it to tell time truly you must direct its gnomon toward the sun. The sun remains stationary while Urth dances about him, and it is by her dancing that we know the time, just as a deaf man might still beat out the rhythm of a tarantella by observing the swaying of the dancers. But what if the sun himself were to dance? Then, too, the march of the moments might become a retreat.

"I don't know if you believe in the New Sun—I'm not sure I ever have. But if he will exist, he will be the Conciliator come again, and thus *Conciliator* and *New Sun* are only two names for the same individual, and we may ask why that individual should be called the New Sun. What do you think? Might it not be for this power to move time?"

Now I felt indeed that time itself had stopped. Around us the trees rose dark and silent; night had freshened the air. I could think of nothing more to say, and I was ashamed to talk nonsense, because I felt somehow that the soldier had been listening attentively to all I had said. Before us I saw two pines far thicker through their trunks than the others lining the road, and a pale path of white and green that threaded its way between them. "There!" I exclaimed.

But when we reached them, I had to halt the soldier with my hands and turn him by the shoulders before he followed me. I noticed a dark splatter in the dust and bent to touch it.

It was clotted blood. "We are on the right road," I told him. "They have been bringing the wounded here."

IV

Fever

I cannot say how far we walked, or how far worn the night was before we reached our destination. I know that I began to stumble some time after we turned aside from the main road, and that it became a sort of disease to me; just as some sick men cannot stop coughing and others cannot keep their hands from shaking, so I tripped, and a few steps farther on tripped again, and then again. Unless I thought of nothing else, the toe of my left boot caught at my right heel, and I could not concentrate my mind—my thoughts ran off with every step I took.

Fireflies glimmered in the trees to either side of the path, and for a long time I supposed that the lights ahead of us were only more such insects and did not hurry my pace. Then, very suddenly as it seemed to me, we were beneath some shadowy roof where men and women with yellow lamps moved up and down between long rows of shrouded cots. A woman in clothes I supposed were black took charge of us and led us to another place where there were chairs of leather and horn, and a fire burned in a brazier. There I saw that her gown was scarlet, and she wore a scarlet hood, and for a moment I thought that she was Cyriaca.

"Your friend is very ill, isn't he?" she said. "Do you know what is the matter with him?"

And the soldier shook his head and answered, "No. I'm not even sure who he is."

I was too stunned to speak. She took my hand, then released it and took the soldier's. "He has a fever. So do you. Now that the heat of summer is come, we see more disease each day. You should have boiled your water and kept yourselves as clean of lice as you could."

She turned to me. "You have a great many shallow cuts too, and some of them are infected. Rock shards?"

I managed to say, ''I'm not the one who is ill. I brought my friend here.''

''You are both ill, and I suspect you brought each other. I doubt that either of you would have reached us without the other. Was it rock shards? Some weapon of the enemy's?''

''Rock shards, yes. A weapon of a friend's.''

''That is the worst thing, I am told—to be fired upon by your own side. But the fever is the chief concern.'' She hesitated, looking from the soldier to me and back. ''I'd like to put you both in bed now, but you'll have to go to the bath first.''

She clapped her hands to summon a burly man with a shaven head. He took our arms and began to lead us away, then stopped and picked me up, carrying me as I had once carried little Severian. In a few moments we were naked and sitting in a pool of water heated by stones. The burly man splashed more water over us, then made us get out one at a time so he could crop our hair with a pair of shears. After that we were left to soak awhile.

''You can speak now,'' I said to the soldier.

I saw him nod in the lamplight.

''Why didn't you, then, when we were coming here?''

He hesitated, and his shoulders moved a trifle. ''I was thinking of many things, and you didn't talk yourself. You seemed so tired. Once I asked if we shouldn't stop, but you didn't answer.''

I said, ''It seemed to me otherwise, but perhaps we are both correct. Do you recall what happened to you before you met me?''

Again there was a pause. ''I don't even remember meeting you. We were walking down a dark path, and you were beside me.''

''And before that?''

''I don't know. Music, perhaps, and walking a long way. In sunshine at first but later through the dark.''

''That walking was while you were with me,'' I said. ''Don't you recall anything else?''

''Flying through the dark. Yes, I was with you, and we came to a place where the sun hung just above our heads. There was a light before us, but when I stepped into it, it became a kind of darkness.''

I nodded. ''You weren't wholly rational, you see. On a warm day it can seem that the sun's just overhead, and when it is down behind the mountains it seems the light becomes darkness. Do you recall your name?''

At that he thought for several moments, and at last smiled ruefully. ''I lost it somewhere along the way. That's what the jaguar said, who had promised to guide the goat.''

The burly man with the shaven head had come back without either of us noticing. He helped me out of the pool and gave me a towel with which to dry myself, a robe to wear, and a canvas sack containing my possessions, which now smelled strongly of the smoke of fumigation. A day earlier it would have tormented me nearly to frenzy to have the Claw out of my possession for an instant. That night I had hardly realized it was gone until it was returned to me, and I did not verify that it had indeed been returned until I lay on one of the cots under a veil of netting. The Claw shone in my hand then, softly as the moon; and it was shaped as the moon sometimes is. I smiled to think that its flooding light of pale green is the reflection of the sun.

On the first night I slept in Saltus, I had awakened thinking I was in the apprentices' dormitory in our tower. Now I had the same experience in reverse: I slept and found in sleep that the shadowy lazaret with its silent figures and moving lamps had been no more than a hallucination of the day.

I sat up and looked around. I felt well—better, in fact, than I had ever felt before; but I was warm. I seemed to glow from within. Roche was sleeping on his side, his red hair tousled and his mouth slightly open, his face relaxed and boyish without the energy of his mind behind it. Through the port I could see snow drifts in the Old Court, new-fallen snow that showed no tracks of men or their animals; but it occurred to me that in the necropolis there would be hundreds of footprints already as the small creatures who found shelter there, the pets and the playmates of the dead, came out to search for food and to disport themselves in the new landscape Nature had bestowed on them. I dressed quickly and silently, holding my finger to my own lips when one of the other apprentices stirred, and hurried down the steep stair that wound through the center of the tower.

It seemed longer than usual, and I found I had difficulty in going from step to step. We are always aware of the hindrance of gravity when we climb stairs, but we take for granted the assistance it gives us when we descend. Now that assistance had been withdrawn, or nearly so. I had to force each foot down, but do it in a way that prevented it from sending me shooting up when it struck the step, as it would have if I had stamped. In that uncanny way we know things in dreams, I understood that all the towers of the Citadel had risen at last and were on their voyage beyond the circle of Dis. I felt happy in the knowledge, but I still desired to go into the necropolis and track the coatis and foxes. I was hurrying down as fast as I could when I heard a groan. The stairway no longer descended as it should but led into a cabin, just as the stairs in Baldanders's castle had stretched down the walls of its chambers.

This was Master Malrubius's sickroom. Masters are entitled to spacious quarters; still, this was larger by far than the actual cabin had been. There were two ports just as I remembered, but they were enormous—the eyes of Mount Typhon. Master Malrubius's bed was very large, yet it seemed lost in the immensity of the room. Two figures bent over him. Though their clothing was dark, it struck me that it was not the fuligin of the guild. I went to them, and when I was so near I could hear the sick man's labored breathing, they straightened up and turned to look at me. They were the Cumaean and her acolyte Merryn, the witches we had met atop the tomb in the ruined stone town.

''Ah, sister, you have come at last,'' Merryn said.

As she spoke, I realized that I was not, as I had thought, the apprentice Severian. I was Thecla as she had been when she was his height, which is to say at about the age of thirteen or fourteen. I felt an intense embarrassment—not because of my girl's body or because I was wearing masculine clothes (which indeed I rather enjoyed) but because I had been unaware of it previously. I also felt that Merryn's words had been an act of magic—that both Severian and I had been present before, and that she had by some means driven him into the background. The Cumaean kissed me on the forehead, and when the kiss was over wiped blood from her lips. Although she did not speak, I knew this was a signal that I had in some sense become the soldier too.

''When we sleep,'' Merryn told me, ''we move from temporality to eternity.''

''When we wake,'' the Cumaean whispered, ''we lose the facility to see beyond the present moment.''

''She never wakes,'' Merryn boasted.

Master Malrubius stirred and groaned, and the Cumaean took a carafe of water from the table by his bed and poured a little into a tumbler. When she set down the carafe again, something living stirred in it. I, for some reason, thought it the undine; I drew back, but it was Hethor, no higher than my hand, his gray, stubbled face pressed against the glass.

I heard his voice as one might hear the squeaking of mice: ''Sometimes driven aground by the photon storms, by the swirling of the galaxies, clockwise and counterclockwise, ticking with light down the dark sea-corridors lined with our silver sails, our demon-haunted mirror sails, our hundred-league masts as fine as threads, as fine as silver needles sewing the threads of starlight, embroidering the stars on black velvet, wet with the winds of Time that goes racing by. The bone in her teeth!

The spume, the flying spume of Time, cast up on these beaches where old sailors can no longer keep their bones from the restless, the unwearied universe. Where has she gone? My lady, the mate of my soul? Gone across the running tides of Aquarius, of Pisces, of Aries. Gone. Gone in her little boat, her nipples pressed against the black velvet lid, gone, sailing away forever from the star-washed shores, the dry shoals of the habitable worlds. She is her own ship, she is the figurehead of her own ship, and the captain. Bosun, Bosun, put out the launch! Sailmaker, make a sail! She has left us behind. We have left her behind. She is in the past we never knew and the future we will not see. Put out more sail, Captain, for the universe is leaving us behind. . . .''

There was a bell on the table beside the carafe. Merryn rang it as though to overpower Hethor's voice, and when Master Malrubius had moistened his lips with the tumbler, she took it from the Cumaean, flung what remained of its water on the floor, and inverted it over the neck of the carafe. Hethor was silenced, but the water spread over the floor, bubbling as though fed by a hidden spring. It was icy cold. I thought vaguely that my governess would be angry because my shoes were wet.

A maid was coming in answer to the ring—Thecla's maid, whose flayed leg I had inspected the day after I had saved Vodalus. She was younger, as young as she must have been when Thecla was actually a girl, but her leg had been flayed already and ran with blood. ''I am so sorry,'' I said. ''I am so sorry, Hunna. I didn't do it—it was Master Gurloes, and some journeymen.''

Master Malrubius sat up in bed, and for the first time I observed that his bed was in actuality a woman's hand, with fingers longer than my arm and nails like talons. ''You're well!'' he said, as though I were the one who had been dying. ''Or nearly well, at least.'' The fingers of the hand began to close upon him, but he leaped from the bed and into water that was now knee high to stand beside me.

A dog—my old dog Triskele—had apparently been hiding beneath the bed, or perhaps only lying on the farther side of it, out of sight. Now he came to us, splashing the water with his single forepaw as he drove his broad chest through it and barking joyously. Master Malrubius took my right hand and the Cumaean my left; together they led me to one of the great eyes of the mountain.

I saw the view I had seen when Typhon had led me there: The world rolled out like a carpet and visible in its entirety. This time it was more magnificent by far. The sun was behind us; its beams seemed to have multiplied their strength. Shadows were alchemized to gold, and every green thing grew darker and stronger as I looked. I could see the grain ripening in the fields and even the myriad fish of the sea doubling and redoubling with the increase of the tiny surface plants that sustained them. Water from the room behind us poured from the eye and, catching the light, fell in a rainbow.

Then I woke.

While I slept, someone had wrapped me in sheets packed with snow. (I learned later that it was brought down from the mountaintops by sure-footed sumpters.) Shivering, I longed to return to my dream, though I was already half-aware of the immense distance that separated us. The bitter taste of medicine was in my mouth, the stretched canvas felt as hard as a floor beneath me, and scarlet-clad Pelerines with lamps moved to and fro, tending men and women who groaned in the dark.

V

The Lazaret

I do not believe I really slept again that night, though I may have dozed. When dawn came, the snow had melted. Two Pelerines took the sheets away, gave me a towel with which to dry myself, and brought dry bedding. I wanted to give the Claw to them then—my possessions were in the bag under my cot—but the moment seemed inappropriate. I lay down instead, and now that it was daylight, slept.

I woke again about noon. The lazaret was as quiet as it ever became; somewhere far off two men were talking and another cried out, but their voices only emphasized the stillness. I sat up and looked around, hoping to see the soldier. On my right lay a man whose close-cropped scalp made me think at first that he was one of the slaves of the Pelerines. I called to him, but when he turned his head to look at me, I saw I had been mistaken.

His eyes were emptier than any human eyes I had ever seen, and they seemed to watch spirits invisible to me. ''Glory to the Group of Seventeen,'' he said.

''Good morning. Do you know anything about the way this place is run?''

A shadow appeared to cross his face, and I sensed that my question had somehow made him suspicious. He answered, ''All endeavors are conducted well or ill precisely in so far as they conform to Correct Thought.''

''Another man was brought in at the same time I was. I'd like to talk to him. He's a friend of mine, more or less.''

''Those who do the will of the populace are friends, though we have never spoken to them. Those who do not do the will of the populace are enemies, though we learned together as children.''

The man on my left called, ''You won't get anything out of him. He's a prisoner.''

I turned to look at him. His face, though wasted nearly to a skull, retained something of humor. His stiff, black hair looked as though it had not seen a comb for months.

''He talks like that all the time. Never any other way. *Hey, you!* We're going to beat you!''

The other answered, ''For the Armies of the Populace, defeat is the springboard of victory, and victory the ladder to further victory.''

''He makes a lot more sense than most of them, though,'' the man on my left told me.

''You say he's a prisoner. What did he do?''

''Do? Why, he didn't die.''

''I'm afraid I don't understand. Was he selected for some kind of suicide mission?''

The patient beyond the man on my left sat up—a young woman with a thin but lovely face. ''They all are,'' she said. ''At least, they can't go home until the war is won, and they know, really, that it will never be won.''

''External battles are already won when internal struggles are conducted with Correct Thought.''

I said, ''He's an Ascian, then. That's what you meant. I've never seen one before.''

''Most of them die,'' the black-haired man told me. ''That's what I said.''

''I didn't know they spoke our language.''

''They don't. Some officers who came here to talk to him said they thought he'd been an interpreter. Probably he questioned our soldiers when they were captured. Only he did something wrong and had to go back to the ranks.''

The young woman said, ''I don't think he's really mad. Most of them are. What's your name?''

''I'm sorry, I should have introduced myself. I'm Severian.'' I almost added that I was a lictor, but I knew neither of them would talk to me if I told them that.

''I'm Foila, and this is Melito. I was of the Blue Huzzars, he a hoplite.''

''You shouldn't talk nonsense,'' Melito growled. ''I am a hoplite. You are a huzzar.''

I thought he appeared much nearer death than she.

''I'm only hoping we will be discharged when we're well enough to leave this place,'' Foila said.

"And what will we do then? Milk somebody else's cow and herd his pigs?" Melito turned to me. "Don't let her talk deceive you—we were volunteers, both of us. I was about to be promoted when I was wounded, and when I'm promoted I'll be able to support a wife."

Foila called, "I haven't promised to marry you!"

Several beds away, someone said loudly, "Take her so she'll shut up about it!"

At that, the patient in the bed beyond Foila's sat up. "She will marry me." He was big, fair skinned, and pale haired, and he spoke with the deliberation characteristic of the icy isles of the south. "I am Hallvard."

Surprising me, the Ascian prisoner announced, "United, men and women are stronger; but a brave woman desires children, and not husbands."

Foila said, "They fight even when they're pregnant—I've seen them dead on the battlefield."

"The roots of the tree are the populace. The leaves fall, but the tree remains."

I asked Melito and Foila if the Ascian were composing his remarks or quoting some literary source with which I was unfamiliar.

"Just making it up, you mean?" Foila asked. "No. They never do that. Everything they say has to be taken from an approved text. Some of them don't talk at all. The rest have thousands—I suppose actually tens or hundreds of thousands—of those tags memorized."

"That's impossible," I said.

Melito shrugged. He had managed to prop himself up on one elbow. "They do it, though. At least, that's what everybody says. Foila knows more about them than I do."

Foila nodded. "In the light cavalry, we do a lot of scouting, and sometimes we're sent out specifically to take prisoners. You don't learn anything from talking to most of them, but just the same the General Staff can tell a good deal from their equipment and physical condition. On the northern continent, where they come from, only the smallest children ever talk the way we do."

I thought of Master Gurloes conducting the business of our guild. "How could they possibly say something like 'Take three apprentices and unload that wagon'?"

"They wouldn't *say* that at all—just grab people by the shoulder, point to the wagon, and give them a push. If they went to work, fine. If they didn't, then the leader would quote something about the need for labor to ensure victory, with several witnesses present. If the person he was talking to still wouldn't work after that, then he would have him killed—probably just by pointing to him and quoting something about the need to eliminate the enemies of the populace.''

The Ascian said, ''The cries of the children are the cries of victory. Still, victory must learn wisdom.''

Foila interpreted for him. ''That means that although children are needed, what they say is meaningless. Most Ascians would consider us mute even if we learned their tongue, because groups of words that are not approved texts are without meaning for them. If they admitted—even to themselves—that such talk meant something, then it would be possible for them to hear disloyal remarks, and even to make them. That would be extremely dangerous. As long as they only understand and quote approved texts, no one can accuse them.''

I turned my head to look at the Ascian. It was clear that he had been listening attentively, but I could not be certain of what his expression meant beyond that. ''Those who write the approved texts,'' I told him, ''cannot themselves be quoting from approved texts as they write. Therefore even an approved text may contain elements of disloyalty.''

''Correct Thought is the thought of the populace. The populace cannot betray the populace or the Group of Seventeen.''

Foila called, ''Don't insult the populace or the Group of Seventeen. He might try to kill himself. Sometimes they do.''

''Will he ever be normal?''

''I've heard that some of them eventually come to talk more or less the way we do, if that's what you mean.''

I could think of nothing to say to that, and for some time we were quiet. There are long periods of silence, I found, in such a place, where almost everyone is ill. We knew that we had watch after watch to occupy; that if we did not say what we wished to say that afternoon there would be another opportunity that evening and another again the next morning. Indeed, anyone who talked as healthy people normally do—after a meal, for example—would have been intolerable.

But what had been said had set me thinking of the north, and I found I knew next to nothing about it. When I had been a boy, scrubbing floors and running errands in the Citadel, the war itself had seemed almost infinitely remote. I knew that most of the matrosses who manned the major batteries had taken part in it, but I knew it just as I knew that the sunlight that fell upon my hand had been to the sun. I would be a torturer, and as a torturer I would have no reason to enter the army and no reason to fear that I would be impressed into it. I never expected to see the war at the gates of Nessus (in fact, those gates themselves were hardly more than legends to me), and I never expected to leave the city, or even to leave that quarter of the city that held the Citadel.

The north, Ascia, was then inconceivably remote, a place as distant as the most distant galaxy, since both were forever out of reach. Mentally, I confused it with the dying belt of tropical vegetation that lay between our own land and theirs, although I would have distinguished the two without difficulty if Master Palaemon had asked me to in the classroom.

But of Ascia itself I had no idea. I did not know if it had great cities or none. I did not know if it was mountainous like the northern and eastern parts of our Commonwealth or as level as our pampas. I did have the impression (though I could not be sure it was correct) that it was a single land mass, and not a chain of islands like our south; and most distinct of all, I had the impression of an innumerable people—our Ascian's populace—an inexhaustible swarm that almost became a creature in itself, as a colony of ants does. To think of those millions upon millions without speech, or confined to parroting proverbial phrases that must surely have long ago lost most of their meaning, was nearly more than the mind could bear. Speaking almost to myself, I said, "It must surely be a trick, or a lie, or a mistake. Such a nation could not exist."

And the Ascian, his voice no louder than my own had been, and perhaps even softer, answered, "How shall the state be most vigorous? It shall be most vigorous when it is without conflict. How shall it be without conflict? When it is without disagreement. How shall disagreement be banished? By banishing the four causes of disagreement: lies, foolish talk, boastful talk, and talk which serves only to incite quarrels. How shall the four causes be banished? By speaking only Correct Thought. Then shall the state be without disagreement. Being without disagreement it shall be without conflict. Being without conflict it shall be vigorous, strong, and secure."

I had been answered, and doubly.

VI

Miles, Foila, Melito, and Hallvard

That evening I fell prey to a fear I had been trying to put from my mind for some time. Although I had seen nothing of the monsters Hethor had brought from beyond the stars since little Severian and I had escaped from the village of the sorcerers, I had not forgotten that he was searching for me. While I traveled in the wilderness or upon the waters of Lake Diuturna, I had not been much afraid he would overtake me. Now I was traveling no longer, and I could feel the weakness in my limbs, for despite the food I had eaten I was weaker than I had ever been while starving in the mountains.

Then too, I feared Agia almost more than Hethor's notules, his salamanders and slugs. I knew her courage, her cleverness, and her malice. Any one of the scarlet-clad priestesses of the Pelerines moving between the cots might easily be she, with a poisoned stiletto beneath her gown. I slept badly that night; but though I dreamed much, my dreams were indistinct, and I will not attempt to relate them here.

I woke feeling less than rested. My fever, of which I had hardly been conscious when I came to the lazaret, and which had seemed to subside on the day previous, returned. I felt its heat in every limb—it seemed to me that I must glow, that the very glaciers of the south would melt if I came among them. I took out the Claw and clasped it to me, and for a time even held it in my mouth. My fever sank again, but left me weak and dizzied.

That morning the soldier came to see me. He wore a white gown the Pelerines had given him in place of his armor, but he appeared wholly recovered, and told me he hoped to leave the next day. I said I would like to introduce him to the acquaintances I had made in this part of the lazaret and asked if he now recalled his name.

He shook his head. "I can remember very little. I am hoping that when I go among the units of the army I will find someone there who knows me."

I introduced him anyway, calling him Miles since I could think of nothing better. I did not know the Ascian's name either and discovered that no one did, not even Foila. When we asked him what it was, he only said, "I am Loyal to the Group of Seventeen."

For a time Foila, Melito, the soldier, and I chatted among ourselves. Melito seemed to like him very well, though perhaps only because of the similarity of the name I had given him to his own. Then the soldier helped me into a sitting posture, lowered his voice, and said, "Now I have to talk to you privately. As I said, I think I will leave here in the morning. From what I have seen of you, you won't be getting out for several days—maybe not for a couple of weeks. I may never see you again."

"Let us hope that isn't so."

"I hope not either. But if I can find my legion, I may be killed by the time you're well. And if I can't find it, I'll probably go into another to keep from being arrested as a deserter." He paused.

I smiled. "And I may die here, of the fever. You didn't want to say that. Do I look as bad as poor Melito?"

He shook his head. "Not as bad, no. I think you'll make it—"

"That's what the thrush sang while the lynx chased the hare around the bay tree."

Now it was his turn to smile. "You're right; I was about to say that."

"Is it a common expression in that part of the Commonwealth where you were brought up?"

The smile vanished. "I don't know. I can't remember where my home is, and that's part of the reason I have to talk to you now. I remember walking down a road with you at night—that's the only thing I *do* remember, before I came here. Where did you find me?"

"In a wood, I suppose about five or ten leagues south of here. Do you recall what I told you about the Claw as we walked?"

He shook his head. "I think I remember you mentioning such a thing, but not what you said."

"What do you remember? Tell me all of it, and I'll tell you what I know, and what I can guess."

"Walking with you. A lot of darkness . . . I fell, or maybe flew through it. Seeing my own face, multiplied again and again. A girl with hair like red gold and enormous eyes."

"A beautiful woman?"

He nodded. "The most beautiful in the world."

Raising my voice, I asked if anyone had a mirror he would lend us for a moment. Foila produced one from the possessions beneath her cot, and I held it up for the soldier. "Is this the face?"

He hesitated. "I think so."

"Blue eyes?"

". . . I can't be sure."

I returned the mirror to Foila. "I will tell you again what I told you on the road, and I wish we had a more private place in which to do it. Some time ago a talisman came into my hands. It came innocently, but it does not belong to me, and it is very valuable—sometimes, not always, but sometimes—it has the power to heal the sick, and even to revive the dead. Two days ago, as I was traveling north, I came across the body of a dead soldier. It was in a forest, away from the road. He had been dead less than a day; I would say it's likely he had died sometime during the preceding night. I was very hungry then, and I cut his pack straps and ate most of the food he had been carrying with him. Then I felt guilty about doing that and got out the talisman and tried to restore him to life. It has failed often before, and this time I thought for a while it was going to fail again. It didn't, although he returned to life slowly and for a long time did not seem to know where he was or what was happening to him."

"And I was that soldier?"

I nodded, looking into his honest blue eyes.

"May I see the talisman?"

I took it out and held it in the palm of my hand. He took it from me, examined both sides carefully, and tested the point against the ball of his finger. "It doesn't look magical," he said.

"I'm not sure *magical* is the right term for it. I've met magicians, and nothing they did reminded me of this or the way it acts. Sometimes it glows with light—it's very faint now, and I doubt if you can see it."

"I can't. There doesn't seem to be any writing on it."

"You mean spells or prayers. No, I've never noticed any, and I've carried it a long way. I don't really know anything about it except that it acts at times; but I think it is probably the kind of thing spells and prayers are made with, and not the kind that is made with them."

"You said it didn't belong to you."

I nodded again. "It belongs to the priestesses here, the Pelerines."

"You just came here. Two nights ago, when I did."

"I came looking for them, to give it back. It was taken from them—not by me—some time ago, in Nessus."

"And you're going to return it?" He looked at me as though he somehow doubted it.

"Yes, eventually."

He stood up, smoothing his robe with his hands.

I said, "You don't believe me, do you? Not about any of it."

"When I came here, you introduced me to the others nearby, the ones you'd talked with while you lay here on your cot." He spoke slowly, seeming to ponder every word. "Of course I've met some people too, where they put me. There's one who isn't really wounded very badly. He's just a boy, a youngster off some small holding a long way from here, and he mostly sits on his cot and looks at the floor."

"Homesick?" I asked.

The soldier shook his head. "He had an energy weapon. A korseke—that's what somebody told me. Are you familiar with them?"

"Not very."

"They project a beam straight forward, and at the same time two quartering beams, forward left and forward right. Their range isn't great, but they say they're very good for dealing with mass attacks, and I suppose they are."

He looked about for a moment to see if anyone was listening, but it is a point of honor in the lazaret to disregard completely any conversation not intended for oneself. If it were not so, the patients would soon be at each other's throats.

"His hundred was the target of one of those attacks. Most of the others broke and ran. He didn't, and they didn't get him. Another man told me there were three walls of bodies in front of him. He had dropped them until the Ascians were climbing up to the top and jumping down at him. Then he had backed away and piled them up again."

I said, "I suppose he got a medal and a promotion." I could not be sure if it was my fever returning or merely the heat of the day, but I felt sticky and somehow suffocated.

"No, they sent him here. I told you he was only a boy from the country. He had killed more people that day than he had ever seen up to the time a few months before when he went into the army. He still hasn't gotten over it, and maybe he never will."

"Yes?"

"It seems to me you might be like that."

"I don't understand you," I said.

"You talk as if you've just come here from the south, and I suppose that if you've left your legion that's the safest way to talk. Just the same, anybody can see it isn't true—people don't get cut up the way you are except where the fighting is. You were hit by rock splinters. That's what happened to you, and the Pelerine who spoke to us the first night we were here saw that right away. So I think you've been north longer than you'll admit, and maybe longer than you think yourself. If you've killed a lot of people, it might be nice for you to believe you have a way to bring them back.''

I tried to grin at him. ''And where does that leave you?''

''Where I am now. I'm not trying to say I owe you nothing. I had fever, and you found me. Maybe I was delirious. I think it's more likely I was unconscious, and that let you think I was dead. If you hadn't brought me here, I probably would have died.''

He started to stand up; I stopped him with a hand on his arm. ''There are some things I should tell you before you go,'' I said. ''About yourself.''

''You said you didn't know who I was.''

I shook my head. ''I didn't say that, not really. I said I found you in a wood two days ago. In the sense you mean, I *don't* know who you are—but in another sense I think I may. I think you're two people, and that I know one of them.''

''Nobody is two people.''

''I am. I'm two people already. Perhaps more people are two than we know. The first thing I want to tell you is much simpler, though. Now listen.'' I gave him detailed directions for finding the wood again, and when I was certain he understood them, I said, ''Your pack is probably still there, with the straps cut, so if you find the place you won't mistake it. There was a letter in your pack. I pulled it out and read a part of it. It didn't carry the name of the person you were writing to, but if you had finished it and were just waiting for a chance to send it off, it should have at least a part of your name at the end. I put it on the ground and it blew a little and caught against a tree. It may still be possible for you to find it.''

His face had tightened. ''You shouldn't have read it, and you shouldn't have thrown it away.''

''I thought you were dead, remember? Anyway, a good deal was going on at the time, mostly inside my head. Perhaps I was getting feverish—I don't know. Now here's the other part. You won't believe me, but it may be important that you listen. Will you hear me out?''

He nodded.

''Good. Have you heard of the mirrors of Father Inire? Do you know how they work?''

''I've heard of Father Inire's Mirror, but I couldn't tell you where I heard about it. You're supposed to be able to step into it, like you'd step into a doorway, and step out on a star. I don't think it's real.''

''The mirrors are real. I've seen them. Up until now I always thought of them in much the same way you did—as if they were a ship, but much faster. Now I'm not nearly so sure. Anyway, a certain friend of mine stepped between those mirrors and vanished. I was watching him. It was no trick and no superstition; he went wherever the mirrors take you. He went because he loved a certain woman, and he wasn't a whole man. Do you understand?''

''He'd had an accident?''

''An accident had had him, but never mind that. He told me he would come back. He said, 'I will come back for her when I have been repaired, when I am sane and whole.' I didn't quite know what to think when he said that, but now I believe he has come. It was I who revived you, and I had been wishing for his return—perhaps that had something to do with it.''

There was a pause. The soldier looked down at the trampled soil on which the cots had been set, then up again at me. ''Possibly whenever a man loses his friend and gets another, he feels the old friend is with him again.''

''Jonas—that was his name—had a habit of speech. Whenever he had to say something unpleasant, he softened it, made a joke of it, by attributing what he said to some comic situation. The first night we were here, when I asked you your name, you said, 'I lost it somewhere along the way. That's what the jaguar said, who had promised to guide the goat.' Do you recall that?''

He shook his head. ''I say a lot of foolish things.''

''It struck me as strange; because it was the kind of thing Jonas said, but he wouldn't have said it in that way unless he meant more by it than you seemed to. I think he would have said, 'That was the basket's story, that had been filled with water.' Something like that.''

I waited for him to speak, but he did not.

''The jaguar ate the goat, of course. Swallowed its flesh and cracked its bones, somewhere along the way.''

''Haven't you ever thought that it might be just the peculiarity of some town? Your friend might have come from the same place I do.''

I said, ''It was a time, I think, and not a place. Long ago, someone had to disarm fear—the fear that men of flesh and blood might feel when looking into a face of steel and glass. Jonas, I know you're listening. I don't blame you. The man was dead, and you were still alive. I understand that. But Jonas, Jolenta is gone—I watched her die, and I tried to bring her back with the Claw, but I failed. Perhaps she was too artificial, I don't know. You will have to find someone else.''

The soldier rose. His face was no longer angry, but empty as a somnambulist's. He turned and left without another word.

* * *

For perhaps a watch I lay on my cot with my hands behind my head, thinking of many things. Hallvard, Melito, and Foila were talking among themselves, but I did not attend to what they said. When one of the Pelerines brought the noon meal, Melito got my ear by rapping his platter with a fork and announced, "Severian, we have a favor to ask of you."

I was eager to put my speculations behind me, and told him I would help them in any way I could.

Foila, who had one of those radiant smiles Nature grants to some women, smiled at me now. "It's like this. These two have been bickering over me all morning. If they were well they could fight it out, but it will be a long time before they are, and I don't think I could stand it so long. Today I was thinking of my mother and father, and how they used to sit before the fire on long winter nights. If Hallvard and I marry, or Melito and I, someday we'll be doing that too. So I have decided to marry the best storyteller. Don't look at me as if I were mad—it's the only sensible thing I've done in my life. Both of them want me, both are very handsome, neither has any property, and if we don't settle this they'll kill each other or I'll kill them both. You're an educated man—we can tell by the way you talk. You listen and judge. Hallvard first, and the stories have to be original, not out of books."

Hallvard, who could walk a little, got up from his cot and came to sit on the foot of Melito's.

VII

Hallvard's Story—The Two Sealers

"This is a true story. I know many stories. Some are made up, though perhaps the made up ones were true in times everyone has forgotten. I also know many true ones, because many strange things happen in the isles of the south that you northern people never dream of. I chose this one because I was there myself and saw and heard as much of it as anyone did.

"I come from the easternmost of the southern isles, which is called Glacies. On our isle lived a man and a woman, my grandparents, who had three sons. Their names were Anskar, Hallvard, and Gundulf. Hallvard was my father, and when I grew large enough to help him on his boat, he no longer hunted and fished with his brothers. Instead, we two went out so that all we caught could be brought home to my mother, and my sisters and younger brother.

"My uncles never married, and so they continued to share a boat. What they caught they ate themselves or gave to my grandparents, who were no longer strong. In the summer they farmed my grandfather's land. He had the best on our isle, the only valley that never felt the ice wind. You could grow things there that would not ripen anywhere else on Glacies, because the growing season in this valley was two weeks longer.

"When my beard was starting to sprout, my grandfather called all the men of our family together—that was my father, my two uncles, and myself. When we got to his house, my grandmother was dead, and the priest from the big isle was there to lay out her body. Her sons wept, as I did myself.

"That night, when we sat at my grandfather's table, with him at one end and the priest at the other, he said, 'Now it is time that I dispose of my property. Bega is gone. Her family has no more claim on it, and I shall follow her shortly. Hallvard is married and has the portion that came to him from his wife. With that he provides for his family, and though they have little to spare, they do not go hungry. You, Anskar. And you, Gundulf. Will you ever marry?'

"Both my uncles shook their heads.

" 'Then this is my will. I call upon the Omnipotent to hear, and I call upon the servants of the Omnipotent also. When I die, all that I have shall go to Anskar and Gundulf. If one die, it shall go to the other. When both are dead, it shall go to Hallvard, or if Hallvard is dead, it shall be divided among his sons. You four—if you do not agree my will is just, speak now.'

"No one spoke, and thus it was decided.

"A year passed. A ship of Erebus came raiding out of the mists, and two ships put in for hides, sea ivory, and salt fish. My grandfather died, and my sister Fausta bore her girl. When the harvest was in, my uncles fished with the other men.

"When spring comes in the south, it is still too early to plant, for there will be many freezing nights to come. But when men see that the days are lengthening fast, they seek out the rookeries where the seals breed. These are on rocks far from any shore, there is much fog, and though they are growing longer, the days are still short. Often it is the men who die and not the seals.

"And so it was with my Uncle Anskar, for my Uncle Gundulf returned in their boat without him.

"Now you must know that when our men go sealing, or fishing, or hunting any other kind of sea game, they tie themselves to their boats. The rope is of braided walrus hide, and it is long enough to let the man move about in the boat as much as is needful, but not longer. The sea water is very cold and soon kills whoever remains in it, but our men dress in sealskin tight-sewn, and often a man's boat-mate can pull him back and in that way save his life.

"This is the tale my Uncle Gundulf told. They had gone far, seeking a rookery others had not visited, when Anskar saw a bull seal swimming in the water. He cast his harpoon; and when the seal sounded, a loop of the harpoon line had caught his ankle, so that he was dragged into the sea. He, Gundulf, had tried to pull him out, for he was a very strong man. But his pulling and the pulling of the seal on the harpoon line, which was tied to the base of the mast, had capsized their boat. Gundulf had saved himself by pulling himself hand over hand back to it and cutting the harpoon line with his knife. When the boat was righted he had tried to haul in Anskar, but the life rope had broken. He showed the frayed rope end. My Uncle Anskar was dead.

"Among my people, women die on land but men at sea, and therefore we call the kind of grave you make 'a woman's boat.' When a man dies as Uncle Anskar did, a hide is stretched and painted for him and hung in the house where the men meet to talk. It is never taken down until no man living can recall the man who was honored so. A hide like that was prepared for Anskar, and the painters began their work.

"Then one bright morning when my father and I were readying the tools to break ground for the new year's crop—well I remember it!—some children who had been sent to gather birds' eggs came running into the village. A seal, they said, lay on the shingle of the south bay. As everyone knows, no seal comes to land where men are. But it sometimes happens that a seal will die at sea or be injured in some fashion. Thinking of that, my father and I and many others ran to the beach, for the seal would belong to the first whose weapon pierced it.

"I was the swiftest of all, and I provided myself with an earth-fork. Such a thing does not throw well, but several other young men were at my heels, so when I was a hundred strides away I cast it. Straight and true it flew and buried its tines in the thing's back. Then followed such a moment as I hope never to see again. The weight of the fork's long handle overbalanced it, and it rolled until the handle rested on the ground.

"I saw the face of my Uncle Anskar, preserved by the cold sea brine. His beard was tangled with the dark green kelp, and his life rope of stout walrus hide had been cut only a few spans from his body.

"My Uncle Gundulf had not seen him, for he was gone to the big isle. My father took Anskar up, and I helped him, and we carried him to Gundulf's house and put the end of the rope upon his chest where Gundulf would see it, and with some other men of Glacies sat down to wait for him.

"He shouted when he saw his brother. It was not such a cry as a woman makes, but a bellow like the bull seal gives when he warns the other bulls from his herd. He ran in the dark. We set a guard on the boats and hunted him that night across the isle. The lights that spirits make in the ultimate south flamed all night, so we knew Anskar hunted with us. Brightest they flashed before they faded, when we found him among the rocks at Radbod's End."

Hallvard fell silent. Indeed, silence lay about us everywhere. All the sick within hearing had been listening to him. At last Melito said, "Did you kill him?"

"No. In the old days it was so, and a bad thing. Now the mainland law avenges bloodguilt, which is better. We bound his arms and legs and laid him in his house, and I sat with him while the older men readied the boats. He told me he had loved a woman on the big isle. I never saw her, but he said her name was Nennoc, and she was fair, and younger than he, but no man would have her because she had borne a child by a man who had died the winter before. In the boat, he had told Anskar he would carry Nennoc home, and Anskar called him *oath-breaker*. My Uncle Gundulf was strong. He seized Anskar and threw him out of the boat, then wrapped the life rope about his hands and snapped it as a woman who sews breaks her thread.

"He had stood then, he said, with one hand on the mast, as men do, and watched his brother in the water. He had seen the flash of the knife, but he thought only that Anskar sought to threaten him with it or to throw it."

Hallvard was silent again, and when I saw he would not speak, I said, "I don't understand. What did Anskar do?"

A smile, the very smallest smile, tugged at Hallvard's lips under his blond mustache. When I saw it, I felt I had seen the ice isles of the south, blue and bitterly cold. "He cut his life rope, the rope Gundulf had already broken. In that way, men who found his body would know that he had been murdered. Do you see?"

I saw, and for a while I said nothing more.

"So," Melito grunted to Foila, "the wonderful valley land went to Hallvard's father, and by this story he has managed to tell you that though he has no property, he has prospects of inheriting some. He has also told you, of course, that he comes of a murderous family."

"Melito believes me much cleverer than I am," the blond man rumbled. "I had no such thoughts. What matters now is not land or skins or gold, but who tells the best tale. And I, who know many, have told the best I know. It is true as he says that I might share my family's property when my father dies. But my unmarried sisters will have some part too for their marriage portions, and only what remained would be divided between my brother and myself. All that matters nothing, because I would not take Foila to the south, where life is so hard. Since I have carried a lance I have seen many better places."

Foila said, "I think your Uncle Gundulf must have loved Nennoc very much."

Hallvard nodded. "He said that too while he lay bound. But all the men of the south love their women. It is for them that they face the sea in winter, the storms and the freezing fogs. It is said that as a man pushes his boat out over the shingle, the sound the bottom makes grating on the stones is *my wife, my children, my children, my wife*."

I asked Melito if he wanted to begin his story then; but he shook his head and said that we were all full of Hallvard's, so he would wait and begin next day. Everyone then asked Hallvard questions about life in the south and compared what they had learned to the way their own people lived. Only the Ascian was silent. I was reminded of the floating islands of Lake Diuturna and told Hallvard and the others about them, though I did not describe the fight at Baldanders's castle. We talked in this way until it was time for the evening meal.

VIII

The Pelerine

By the time we had finished eating, it was beginning to get dark. We were always quieter then, not only because we lacked strength, but because we knew that those wounded who would die were more liable to do so after the sun set, and particularly in the deep of the night. It was the time when past battles called home their debts.

In other ways too, the night made us more aware of the war. Sometimes—and on that night I remember them particularly—the discharges of the great energy weapons blazed across the sky like heat lightning. One heard the sentries marching to their posts, so that the word *watch*, which we so often used with no meaning beyond that of a tenth part of the night, became an audible reality, an actuality of tramping feet and unintelligible commands.

There came a moment when no one spoke, that lengthened and lengthened, interrupted only by the murmurings of the well—the Pelerines and their male slaves—who came to ask the condition of this patient or that. One of the scarlet-clad priestesses came and sat by my cot, and my mind was so slow, so nearly sleeping, that it was some time before I realized that she must have carried a stool with her.

"You are Severian," she said, "the friend of Miles?"

"Yes."

"He has recalled his name. I thought you would like to know."

I asked her what it was.

"Why, Miles, of course. I told you."

"He will recall more than that, I think, as time goes by."

She nodded. She seemed to be a woman past middle age, with a kindly, austere face. "I am sure he will. His home and family."

"If he has them."

"Yes, some do not. Some lack even the ability to make a home."

"You're referring to me."

"No, not at all. Anyway, that lack is not something the person can do something about. But it is much better, particularly for men, if they have a home. Like the man your friend talked about, most men think they make their homes for their families, but the fact is that they make both homes and families for themselves."

"You were listening to Hallvard, then."

"Several of us were. It was a good story. A sister came and got me at the place where the patient's grandfather made his will. I heard all the rest. Do you know what the trouble was with the bad uncle? With Gundulf?"

"I suppose that he was in love."

"No, that was what was right with him. Every person, you see, is like a plant. There is a beautiful green part, often with flowers or fruit, that grows upward toward the sun, toward the Increate. There is also a dark part that grows away from it, tunneling where no light comes."

I said, "I have never studied the writings of the initiates, but even I am aware of the existence of good and evil in everyone."

"Was I speaking of good and evil? It is the roots that give the plant the strength to climb toward the sun, though they know nothing of it. Suppose that some scythe, whistling along the ground, should sever the stalk from its roots. The stalk would fall and die, but the roots might put up a new stalk."

"You are saying that evil is good."

"No. I am saying that the things we love in others and admire in ourselves spring from things we do not see and seldom think about. Gundulf, like other men, had the instinct to exercise authority. Its proper growth is the founding of a family—and women, too, have a similar instinct. In Gundulf that instinct had long been frustrated, as it is in so many of the soldiers we see here. The officers have their commands, but the soldiers who have no command suffer and do not know why they suffer. Some, of course, form bonds with others in the ranks. Sometimes several share a single woman, or a man who is like a woman. Some make pets of animals, and some befriend children left homeless by the struggle."

Remembering Casdoe's son, I said, "I can see why you object to that."

"We do not object—most certainly not to that, and not to things vastly less natural. I am only speaking of the instinct to exercise authority. In the bad uncle it made him love a woman, and specifically one who already possessed a child, so there would be a larger family for him as soon as there was a family for him at all. In that way, you see, he would have regained some part of the time he had lost.''

She paused, and I nodded.

''Too much time, however, had been lost already; the instinct broke out in another way. He saw himself as the rightful master of lands he only held in trust for one brother, and the master of the life of the other. That vision was delusive, was it not?''

''I suppose so.''

''Others can have visions equally deluding, though less dangerous.'' She smiled at me. ''Do you regard yourself as possessing any special authority?''

''I am a journeyman of the Seekers for Truth and Penitence, but that position carries no authority. We of the guild only do the will of judges.''

''I thought the torturers' guild abolished long ago. Has it become, then, a species of brotherhood for lictors?''

''It still exists,'' I told her.

''No doubt, but some centuries ago it was a true guild, like that of the silversmiths. At least so I have read in certain histories preserved by our order.''

As I heard her, I felt a moment of wild elation. It was not that I supposed her to be somehow correct. I am, perhaps, mad in certain respects, but I know what those respects are, and such self-deceptions are no part of them. Nevertheless, it seemed wonderful to me—if only for that moment—to exist in a world where such a belief was possible. I realized then, really for the first time, that there were millions of people in the Commonwealth who knew nothing of the higher forms of judicial punishment and nothing of the circles within circles of intrigue that ring the Autarch; and it was wine to me, or brandy rather, and left me reeling with giddy joy.

The Pelerine, seeing nothing of all this, said, ''Is there no other form of special authority that you believe yourself to possess?''

I shook my head.

''Miles told me that you believe yourself to possess the Claw of the Conciliator, and that you showed him a small black claw, such as might perhaps have come from an ocelot or a caracara, and that you told him you have raised many from the dead by means of it.''

The time had come then; the time when I would have to give it up. Ever since we had reached the lazaret, I had known it must come soon, but I had hoped to delay it until I was ready to depart. Now I took out the Claw, for the last time as I thought, and pressed it into the Pelerine's hand, saying, "With this you can save many. I did not steal it, and I have sought always to return it to your order."

"And with it," she asked gently, "you have revived numbers of the dead?"

"I myself would have died months ago without it," I told her, and I began to recount the story of my duel with Agilus.

"Wait," she said. "You must keep it." And she returned the Claw to me. "I am not a young woman any longer, as you see. Next year I will celebrate my thirtieth anniversary as a full member of our order. At each of the five superior feasts of the year, until this past spring, I saw the Claw of the Conciliator when it was elevated for our adoration. It was a great sapphire, as big around as an orichalk. It must have been worth more than many villas, and no doubt it was for that reason that the thieves took it."

I tried to interrupt her, but she silenced me with a gesture.

"As for its working miraculous cures and even restoring life to the dead, do you think our order would have any sick among us if it were so? We are few—far too few for the work we have to do. But if none of us had died before last spring, we would be much more numerous. Many whom I loved, my teachers and my friends, would be among us still. Ignorant people must have their wonders, even if they must scrape the mud from some epopt's boots to swallow. If, as we hope, it still exists and has not been cut to make smaller gems, the Claw of the Conciliator is the last relic we possess of the greatest of good men, and we treasured it because we still treasure his memory. If it had been the sort of thing you believe yourself to have, it would have been precious to everyone, and the autarchs would have wrested it from us long ago."

"It *is* a claw—" I began.

"That was only a flaw at the heart of the jewel. The Conciliator was a man, Severian the Lictor, and not a cat or a bird." She stood up.

"It was dashed against the rocks when the giant threw it from the parapet—"

"I had hoped to calm you, but I see that I am only exciting you," she said. Quite unexpectedly she smiled, leaned forward, and kissed me. "We meet many here who believe things that are not so. Not many have beliefs that do them as much credit as yours do you. You and I shall talk of this again some other time."

I watched her small, scarlet-clad figure until it was lost from sight in the darkness and silence of the rows of cots. While we talked, most of the sick had fallen asleep. A few groaned. Three slaves entered, two carrying a wounded man on a litter while the third held up a lamp so they could see their way. The light gleamed on their shaven heads, which were covered with sweat. They put the wounded man on a cot, arranged his limbs as though he were dead, and went away.

I looked at the Claw. It had been lifelessly black when the Pelerine saw it, but now muted sparks of white fire ran from its base to its point. I felt well—indeed, I found myself wondering how I had endured lying all day upon the narrow mattress; but when I tried to stand my legs would hardly hold me. Afraid at every moment that I would fall on one of the wounded, I staggered the twenty paces or so to the man I had just seen carried in.

It was Emilian, whom I had known as a gallant at the Autarch's court. I was so startled to see him here that I called him by name.

"Thecla," he murmured. "Thecla . . ."

"Yes. Thecla. You remember me, Emilian. Now be well." I touched him with the Claw.

He opened his eyes and screamed.

I fled, but fell when I was halfway to my own cot. I was so weak I don't believe I could have crawled the remaining distance then, but I managed to put away the Claw and roll beneath Hallvard's cot and so out of sight.

When the slaves came back, Emilian was sitting up and able to speak—though they could not, I think, make much sense of what he said. They gave him herbs, and one of them remained with him while he chewed them, then left silently.

I rolled from under the cot, and by holding on to the edge was able to pull myself erect. All was still again, but I knew that many of the wounded must have seen me before I had fallen. Emilian was not asleep, as I had supposed he would be, but he seemed dazed. "Thecla," he murmured. "I heard Thecla. They said she was dead. What voices are here from the lands of the dead?"

"None now," I told him. "You've been ill, but you'll be well soon."

I held the Claw overhead and tried to focus my thoughts on Melito and Foila as well as Emilian—on all the sick in the lazaret. It flickered and was dark.

IX

Melito's Story—The Cock, the Angel, and the Eagle

"Once not very long ago and not very far from the place where I was born, there was a fine farm. It was especially noted for its poultry: flocks of ducks white as snow, geese nearly as large as swans and so fat they could scarcely walk, and chickens that were as colorful as parrots. The farmer who had built up this place had a great many strange ideas about farming, but he had succeeded so much better with his strange ideas than any of his neighbors with their sensible ones, that few had the courage to tell him what a fool he was.

"One of his queer notions concerned the management of his chickens. Everyone knows that when chicks are observed to be little cocks they must be caponized. Only one cock is required in the barnyard, and two will fight.

"But this farmer saved himself all that trouble. 'Let them grow up,' he said. 'Let them fight, and let me tell you something, neighbor. The best and cockiest cock will win, and he is the one who will sire many more chicks to swell my flock. What's more, his chicks will be the hardiest, and the best suited to throwing off every disease—when your chickens are wiped out, you can come to me and I'll sell you some breeding stock at my own price. As for the beaten cocks, my family and I can eat them. There's no capon so tender as a cock that has been fought to death, just as the best beef comes from a bull that has died in the bull ring and the best venison from a stag the hounds have run all day. Besides, eating capons saps a man's virility.'

"This odd farmer also believed that it was his duty to select the worst bird from his flock whenever he wanted one for dinner. 'It is impious,' he said, 'for anyone to take the best. They should be left to prosper under the eye of the Pancreator, who made cocks and hens as well as men and women.' Perhaps because he felt as he did, his flock was so good that it seemed sometimes there was no worst among it.

"From all I have said, it will be clear that the cock of this flock was a very fine one. He was young, strong, and brave. His tail was as fine as the tails of many sorts of pheasants, and no doubt his comb would have been fine too, save that it had been torn to ribbons in the many desperate combats that had won him his place. His breast was of glowing scarlet—like the Pelerines' robes here—but the geese said it had been white before it was dyed in his own blood. His wings were so strong that he was a better flier than any of the white ducks, his spurs were longer than a man's middle finger, and his bill was as sharp as my sword.

"This fine cock had a thousand wives, but the darling of his heart was a hen as fine as he, the daughter of a noble race and the acknowledged queen of all the chickens for leagues around. How proudly they walked between the corner of the barn and the water of the duck pond! You could not hope to see anything finer, no, not if you saw the Autarch himself showing off his favorite at the Well of Orchids—the more so since the Autarch is a capon, as I hear it.

"Everything was bugs for breakfast for this happy pair until one night the cock was wakened by a terrible row. A great, eared owl had broken into the barn where the chickens roosted and was making his way among them as he sought for his dinner. Of course he seized upon the hen who was the particular favorite of the cock; and with her in his claws, he spread his wide, silent wings to sail away. Owls can see marvelously well in the dark, and so he must have seen the cock flying at him like a feathered fury. Who has ever seen an amazed expression on the face of an owl? Yet surely there was one on that owl in the barn that night. The cock's spurs shuffled faster than the feet of any dancer, and his bill struck for those round and shining eyes as the bill of a woodpecker hammers the trunk of a tree. The owl dropped the hen, flew from the barn, and was never seen again.

"No doubt the cock had a right to be proud, but he became too proud. Having defeated an owl in the dark, he felt he could defeat any bird, anywhere. He began to talk of rescuing the prey of hawks and bullying the teratornis, the largest and most terrible bird that flies. If he had surrounded himself with wise counselors, particularly the llama and the pig, those whom most princes choose to help guide their affairs, I feel sure his extravagances would soon have been effectively though courteously checked. Alas, he did not do so. He listened only to the hens, who were all infatuated with him, and to the geese and ducks, who felt that as his fellow barnyard fowl they shared to some extent in whatever glory he won. At last the day came, as it always does for those who show too much pride, when he went too far.

"It was sunrise, ever the most dangerous time for those who do not do well. The cock flew up and up and up, until he seemed about to pierce the sky, and at last, at the very apogee of his flight, perched himself atop the weathervane on the loftiest gable of the barn—the highest point in the entire farmyard. There as the sun drove out the shadows with lashes of crimson and gold, he screamed again and again that he was lord of all feathered things. Seven times he crowed so, and he might have got away with it, for seven is a lucky number. But he could not be content with that. An eighth time he made the same boast, and then flew down.

"He had not yet landed among his flock when there began a most marvelous phenomenon high in the air, directly above the barn. A hundred rays of sunlight seemed to tangle themselves as a kitten snarls a ball of wool, and to roll themselves together as a woman rolls up dough in a kneading pan. This collection of glorious light then put out legs, arms, a head, and at last wings, and swooped down upon the barnyard. It was an angel with wings of red and blue and green and gold, and though it seemed no bigger than the cock, he knew as soon as he had looked into its eyes that it was far larger on the inside than he.

" 'Now,' said the angel, 'hear justice. You claim that no feathered thing can stand against you. Here am I, plainly a feathered thing. All the mighty weapons of the armies of light I have left behind, and we will wrestle, we two.'

"At that the cock spread his wings and bowed so low that his tattered comb scraped the dust. 'I shall be honored to the end of my days to have been thought worthy of such a challenge,' he said, 'which no other bird has ever received before. It is with the most profound regret that I must tell you I cannot accept, and that for three reasons, the first of which is that though you have feathers on your wings, as you say, it is not against your wings that I would fight but against your head and breast. Thus you are not a feathered creature for the purposes of combat.'

"The angel closed his eyes and touched his hands to his own body, and when he drew them away the hair of his head had become feathers brighter than the feathers of the finest canary, and the linen of his robe had become feathers whiter than the feathers of the most brilliant dove.

" 'The second of which,' continued the cock, nothing daunted, 'is that you, having, as you so clearly do, the power to transform yourself, might choose during the course of our combat to change yourself into some creature that does not possess feathers—for example, a large snake. Thus if I were to fight you, I should have no guarantee of fair play.'

"At that, the angel tore open his breast, and displaying all the qualities therein to the assembled poultry, took out his ability to alter his shape. He handed it to the fattest goose to hold for the duration of the match, and the goose at once transformed himself, becoming a gray salt goose, such as stream from pole to pole. But he did not fly off, and he kept the angel's ability safe.

" 'The third of which,' continued the cock in desperation, 'is that you are clearly an officer in the Pancreator's service, and in prosecuting the cause of justice, as you do, are doing your duty. If I were to fight you as you ask, I should be committing a grave crime against the only ruler brave chickens acknowledge.'

" 'Very well,' said the angel. 'It is a strong legal position, and I suppose you think you've won your way free. The truth is that you have argued your way to your own death. I was only going to twist your wings back a bit and pull out your tail feathers.' Then he lifted his head and gave a strange, wild cry. Immediately an eagle dove from the sky and dropped like a thunderbolt into the barnyard.

"All around the barn they fought, and beside the duck pond, and across the pasture and back, for the eagle was very strong, but the cock was quick and brave. There was an old cart with a broken wheel leaning against one wall of the barn, and under it, where the eagle could not fly at him from above and he could cool himself somewhat in the shadow, the cock sought to make his final stand. He was bleeding so much, however, that before the eagle, who was almost as bloodied as he, could come at him there, he tottered, fell, tried to rise, and fell again.

" 'Now,' said the angel, addressing all the assembled birds, 'you have seen justice done. Be not proud! Be not boastful, for surely retribution will be visited upon you. You thought your champion invincible. There he lies, the victim not of this eagle but of pride, beaten and destroyed.'

"Then the cock, whom they had all thought dead, lifted his head. 'You are doubtless very wise, Angel,' he said. 'But you know nothing of the ways of cocks. A cock is not beaten until he turns tail and shows the white feather that lies beneath his tail feathers. My strength, which I made myself by flying and running, and in many battles, has failed me. My spirit, which I received from the hand of your master the Pancreator, has not failed me. Eagle, I ask no quarter from you. Come here and kill me now. But as you value your honor, never say that you have beaten me.'

"The eagle looked at the angel when he heard what the cock said, and the angel looked at the eagle. 'The Pancreator is infinitely far from us,' the angel said. 'And thus infinitely far from me, though I fly so much higher than you. I guess at his desires—no one can do otherwise.'

"He opened his chest once more and replaced the ability he had for a time surrendered. Then he and the eagle flew away, and for a time the salt goose followed them. That is the end of the story."

Melito had lain upon his back as he spoke, looking up at the canvas stretched overhead. I had the feeling he was too weak even to raise himself on one elbow. The rest of the wounded had been as quiet for his story as for Hallvard's.

At last I said, "That is a fine tale. It will be very hard for me to judge between the two, and if it is agreeable to you and Hallvard, and to Foila, I would like to give myself time to think about them both."

Foila, who was sitting up with her knees drawn under her chin, called, "Don't judge at all. The contest isn't over yet."

Everyone looked at her.

"I'll explain tomorrow," she said. "Just don't judge, Severian. But what did you think of that story?"

Hallvard rumbled, "I will tell you what I think. I think Melito is clever the way he claimed I was. He is not so well as I am, not so strong, and in this way he has drawn a woman's sympathy to himself. It was cunningly done, little cock."

Melito's voice seemed weaker than it had while he was recounting the battle of the birds. "It is the worst story I know."

"The worst?" I asked. We were all surprised.

"Yes, the worst. It is a foolish tale we tell our little children, who know nothing but the dust and the farm animals and the sky they see above them. Surely every word of it must make that clear."

Hallvard asked, "Don't you want to win, Melito?"

"Certainly I do. You don't love Foila as I love her. I would die to possess her, but I would sooner die than disappoint her. If the story I have just told can win, then I shall never disappoint her, at least with my stories. I have a thousand that are better than that."

Hallvard got up and came to sit on my cot as he had the day before, and I swung my legs over the edge to sit beside him. To me he said, "What Melito says is very clever. Everything he says is very clever. Still, you must judge us by the tales we told, and not by the ones we say we know but did not tell. I, too, know many other stories. Our winter nights are the longest in the Commonwealth."

I answered that according to Foila, who had originally thought of the contest and who was herself the prize, I was not yet to judge at all.

The Ascian said, "All who speak Correct Thought speak well. Where then is the superiority of some students to others? It is in the speaking. Intelligent students speak Correct Thought intelligently. The hearer knows by the intonation of their voices that they understand. By this superior speaking of intelligent students, Correct Thought is passed, like fire, from one to another."

I think that none of us had realized he was listening. We were all a trifle startled to hear him speak now. After a moment, Foila said, "He means you should not judge by the content of the stories, but by how well each was told. I'm not sure I agree with that—still, there may be something in it."

"I do not agree," Hallvard grumbled. "Those who listen soon tire of storyteller tricks. The best telling is the plainest."

Others joined in the argument, and we talked about it and about the little cock for a long time.

X

Ava

While I was ill I had never paid much attention to the people who brought our food, though when I reflected on it I was able to recall them clearly, as I recall everything. Once our server had been a Pelerine—she who had talked to me the night before. At other times they had been the shaven-headed male slaves, or postulants in brown. This evening, the evening of the day on which Melito had told his story, our suppers were carried in by a postulant I had not seen before, a slender, gray-eyed girl. I got up and helped her to pass around the trays.

When we were finished, she thanked me and said, ''You will not be here much longer.''

I told her I had something to do here, and nowhere else to go.

''You have your legion. If it has been destroyed, you will be assigned to a new one.''

''I am not a soldier. I came north with some thought of enlisting, but I fell sick before I got the opportunity.''

''You could have waited in your native town. I'm told that recruiting parties go to all the towns, twice a year at least.''

''My native town is Nessus, I'm afraid.'' I saw her smile. ''But I left it some time ago, and I wouldn't have wanted to sit around someplace else for half a year waiting. Anyway, I never thought of it. Are you from Nessus too?''

''You're having trouble standing up.''

''No, I'm fine.''

She touched my arm, a timid gesture that somehow reminded me of the tame deer in the Autarch's garden. ''You're swaying. Even if your fever is gone, you're no longer used to being on your feet. You have to realize that. You've been abed for several days. I want you to lie down again now."

"If I do that, there'll be no one to talk to except the people I've been talking with all day. The man on my right is an Ascian prisoner, and the man on my left comes from some village neither you nor I ever heard of."

"All right, if you'll lie down I'll sit and talk to you for a while. I've nothing more to do until the nocturne must be played anyway. What quarter of Nessus do you come from?"

As she escorted me to my cot, I told her that I did not want to talk, but to listen; and I asked her what quarter she herself called home.

"When you're with the Pelerines, that's your home—wherever the tents are set up. The order becomes your family and your friends, just as if all your friends had suddenly become your sisters too. But before I came here, I lived in the far northwestern part of the city, within easy sight of the Wall."

"Near the Sanguinary Field?"

"Yes, very near it. Do you know the place?"

"I fought there once."

Her eyes widened. "Did you, really? We used to go there and watch. We weren't supposed to, but we did anyway. Did you win?"

I had never thought about that and had to consider it. "No," I said after a moment. "I lost."

"But you lived. It's better, surely, to lose and live than to take another man's life."

I opened my robe and showed her the scar on my chest that Agilus's avern leaf had made.

"You were very lucky. Often they bring in soldiers with chest wounds like that, but we are seldom able to save them." Hesitantly she touched my chest. There was a sweetness in her face that I have not seen in the faces of other women. For a moment she stroked my skin, then she jerked her hand away. "It could not have been very deep."

"It wasn't," I told her.

"Once I saw a combat between an officer and an exultant in masquerade. They used poisoned plants for weapons—I suppose because the officer would have had an unfair advantage with the sword. The exultant was killed and I left, but afterward there was a great hullabaloo because the officer had run amok. He came dashing by me, striking out with his plant, but someone threw a cudgel at his legs and knocked him down. I think that was the most exciting fight I ever saw."

"Did they fight bravely?"

"Not really. There was a lot of argument about legalities—you know how men do when they don't want to begin."

" 'I shall be honored to the end of my days to have been thought worthy of such a challenge, which no other bird has ever received before. It is with the most profound regret that I must tell you I cannot accept, and that for three reasons, the first of which is that though you have feathers on your wings, as you say, it is not against your wings that I would fight.' Do you know that story?"

Smiling, she shook her head.

"It's a good one. I'll tell it to you some time. If you lived so near the Sanguinary Field, your family must have been an important one. Are you an armigette?"

"Practically all of us are armigettes or exultants. It's a rather aristocratic order, I'm afraid. Occasionally an optimate's daughter like me is admitted, when the optimate has been a longtime friend of the order, but there are only three of us. I'm told some optimates think all they have to do is make a large gift and their girls will be accepted, but it really isn't so—they have to help out in various ways, not just with money, and they have to have done it for a long time. The world, you see, is not really as corrupt as people like to believe."

I asked, "Do you think it is right to limit your order in that way? You serve the Conciliator. Did he ask the people he lifted out of death if they were armigers or exultants?"

She smiled again. "That's a question that has been debated many times in the order. But there are other orders that are quite open to optimates, and to the lower classes too, and by remaining as we are we get a great deal of money to use in our work and have a great deal of influence. If we nursed and fed only certain kinds of people, I would say you were right. But we don't; we even help animals when we can. Conexa Epicharis used to say we stopped at insects, but then she found one of us—I mean a postulant—trying to mend a butterfly's wing."

"Doesn't it bother you that these soldiers have been doing their best to kill Ascians?"

Her answer was very far from what I had expected. "Ascians are not human."

"I've already told you that the patient next to me is an Ascian. You're taking care of him, and as well as you take care of us, from what I've seen."

"And I've already told *you* that we take in animals when we can. Don't you know that human beings can lose their humanity?"

"You mean the zoanthropes. I've met some."

"Them, of course. They give up their humanity deliberately. There are others who lose theirs without intending to, often when they think they are enhancing it, or rising to some state higher than that to which we are born. Still others, like the Ascians, have it stripped from them.''

I thought of Baldanders, plunging from his castle wall into Lake Diuturna. ''Surely these . . . things deserve our sympathy.''

''Animals deserve our sympathy. That is why we of the order care for them. But it isn't murder for a man to kill one.''

I sat up and gripped her arm, feeling an excitement I could scarcely contain. ''Do you think that if something—some arm of the Conciliator, let us say—could cure human beings, it might nevertheless fail with those who are not human?''

''You mean the Claw. Close your mouth, please—you make me want to laugh when you leave it open like that, and we're not supposed to when people outside the order are around.''

''You know!''

''Your nurse told me. She said you were mad, but in a nice way, and that she didn't think you would ever hurt anyone. Then I asked her about it, and she told. You have the Claw, and sometimes you can cure the sick and even raise the dead.''

''Do you believe I'm mad?''

Still smiling, she nodded.

''Why? Never mind what the Pelerine told you. Have I said anything to you tonight to make you think so?''

''Or spellbound, perhaps. It isn't anything you've said at all. Or at least, not much. But you are not just one man.''

She paused after saying that. I think she was waiting for me to deny it, but I said nothing.

''It is in your face and the way you move—do you know that I don't even know your name? She didn't tell me.''

''Severian.''

''I'm Ava. Severian is one of those brother—sister names, isn't it? Severian and Severa. Do you have a sister?''

''I don't know. If I do, she's a witch.''

Ava let that pass. ''The other one. Does she have a name?''

''You know she's a woman then.''

''Uh huh. When I was serving the food, I thought for a moment that one of the exultant sisters had come to help me. Then I looked around and it was you. At first it seemed that it was just when I saw you from the corner of my eye, but sometimes, while we've been sitting here, I see her even when I'm looking right at you. When you glance to one side sometimes you vanish, and there's a tall, pale woman using your face. Please don't tell me I fast overmuch. That's what they all tell me, and it isn't true, and even if it were, this isn't that."

"Her name is Thecla. Do you remember what you were just saying about losing humanity? Were you trying to tell me about her?"

Ava shook her head. "I don't think so. But I wanted to ask you something. There was another patient here like you, and they told me he came with you."

"Miles, you mean. No, my case and his are quite different. I won't tell you about him. He should do it himself, or no one should. But I will tell you about myself. Do you know of the corpse-eaters?"

"You're not one of them. A few weeks ago we had three insurgent captives. I know what they're like."

"How do we differ?"

"With them . . ." She groped for words. "With them it's out of control. They talk to themselves—of course a lot of people do—and they look at things that aren't there. There's something lonely about it, and something selfish. You aren't one of them."

"But I am," I said. And I told her, without going into much detail, of Vodalus's banquet.

"They made you," she said when I was through. "If you had shown what you felt, they would have killed you."

"That doesn't matter. I drank the alzabo. I ate her flesh. And at first it was filthy, as you say, though I had loved her. She was in me, and I shared the life that had been hers, and yet she was dead. I could feel her rotting there. I had a wonderful dream of her on the first night; when I go back among my memories it is one of the things I treasure most. Afterward, there was something horrible, and sometimes I seemed to be dreaming while I was awake—that was the talking and staring you mentioned, I think. Now, and for a long time, she seems alive again, but inside me."

"I don't think the others are like that."

"I don't either," I said. "At least, not from what I've heard of them. There are a great many things I do not understand. What I have told you is one of the chief ones."

Ava was quiet for the space of two or three breaths, then her eyes opened wide. "The Claw, the thing you believe in. Did you have it then?"

"Yes, but I didn't know what it could do. It had not acted—or rather, it had acted, it had raised a woman called Dorcas, but I didn't know what had happened, where she had come from. If I had known, I might have saved Thecla, brought her back."

"But you had it? You had it with you?"

I nodded.

"Then don't you see? It *did* bring her back. You just said it could act without your even knowing it. You had it, and you had her, rotting, as you say, inside you."

"Without the body . . ."

"You're a materialist, like all ignorant people. But your materialism doesn't make materialism true. Don't you know that? In the final summing up, it is spirit and dream, thought and love and act that matter."

I was so stunned by the ideas that had come crowding in on me that I did not speak again for some time, but sat wrapped in my own speculations. When I came to myself again at last, I was surprised that Ava had not gone and tried to thank her.

"It was peaceful, sitting here with you, and if one of the sisters had come, I could have said I was waiting in case one of the sick should cry out."

"I haven't decided yet about what you said about Thecla. I'll have to think about it a long time, probably for many days. People tell me I am a rather stupid man."

She smiled, and the truth was that I had said what I had (though it was true) at least in part to make her smile. "I don't think so. A thorough man, rather."

"Anyway, I have another question. Often when I tried to sleep, or when I woke in the night, I have tried to connect my failures and my successes. I mean the times when I used the Claw and revived someone, and the times when I tried to but life did not return. It seems to me that it should be more than mere chance, though perhaps the link is something I cannot know."

"Do you think you've found it now?"

"What you said about people losing their humanity—that might be a part of it. There was a woman . . . I think she may have been like that, though she was very beautiful. And a man, my friend, who was only partly cured, only helped. If it's possible for someone to lose his humanity, surely it must be possible for something that once had none to find it. What one loses another finds, everywhere. He, I think, was like that. Then too, the effect always seems less when the deaths come by violence. . . ."

"I would expect that," Ava said softly.

"It cured the man-ape whose hand I had cut away. Perhaps that was because I had done it myself. And it helped Jonas, but I—Thecla—had used those whips."

"The powers of healing protect us from Nature. Why should the Increate protect us from ourselves? We might protect ourselves from ourselves. It may be that he will help us only when we come to regret what we have done."

Still thinking, I nodded.

"I am going to the chapel now. You're well enough to walk a short distance. Will you come with me?"

While I had been beneath that wide canvas roof, it had seemed the whole of the lazaret to me. Now I saw, though only dimly and by night, that there were many tents and pavilions. Most, like ours, had their walls gathered up for coolness, furled like the sails of a ship at anchor. We entered none of them but walked between them by winding paths that seemed long to me, until we reached one whose walls were down. It was of silk, not canvas, and shone scarlet because of the lights within.

"Once," Ava told me, "we had a great cathedral. It could hold ten thousand, yet be packed into a single wagon. Our Domnicellae had it burned just before I came to the order."

"I know," I said. "I saw it."

Inside the silken tent, we knelt before a simple altar heaped with flowers. Ava prayed. I, knowing no prayers, spoke without sound to someone who seemed at times within me and at times, as the angel had said, infinitely remote.

XI

Loyal to the Group of Seventeen's Story—The Just Man

The next morning, when we had eaten and everyone was awake, I ventured to ask Foila if it was now time for me to judge between Melito and Hallvard. She shook her head, but before she could speak, the Ascian announced, ''All must do their share in the service of the populace. The bullock draws the plow and the dog herds the sheep, but the cat catches mice in the granary. Thus men, women, and even children can serve the populace.''

Foila flashed that dazzling smile. ''Our friend wants to tell a story too.''

''What!'' For a moment I thought Melito was actually going to sit up. ''Are you going to let him—let one of them—consider—''

She gestured, and he sputtered to silence. ''Why yes.'' Something tugged at the corners of her lips. ''Yes, I think I shall. I'll have to interpret for the rest of you, of course. Will that be all right, Severian?''

''If you wish it,'' I said.

Hallvard rumbled, ''This was not in the original agreement. I recall each word.''

''So do I,'' Foila said. ''It isn't against it either, and in fact it's in accordance with the *spirit* of the agreement, which was that the rivals for my hand—neither very soft nor very fair now, I'm afraid, though it's becoming more so since I've been confined in this place—would compete. The Ascian would be my suitor if he thought he could; haven't you seen the way he looks at me?''

The Ascian recited, ''United, men and women are stronger; but a brave woman desires children, and not husbands.''

"He means that he would like to marry me, but he doesn't think his attentions would be acceptable. He's wrong." Foila looked from Melito to Hallvard, and her smile had become a grin. "Are you two really so frightened of him in a storytelling contest? You must have run like rabbits when you saw an Ascian on the battlefield."

Neither of them answered, and after a time, the Ascian began to speak: "In times past, loyalty to the cause of the populace was to be found everywhere. The will of the Group of Seventeen was the will of everyone."

Foila interpreted: *"Once upon a time . . ."*

"Let no one be idle. If one is idle, let him band together with others who are idle too, and let them look for idle land. Let everyone they meet direct them. It is better to walk a thousand leagues than to sit in the House of Starvation."

"There was a remote farm worked in partnership by people who were not related."

"One is strong, another beautiful, a third a cunning artificer. Which is best? He who serves the populace."

"On this farm lived a good man."

"Let the work be divided by a wise divider of work. Let the food be divided by a just divider of food. Let the pigs grow fat. Let rats starve."

"The others cheated him of his share."

"The people meeting in counsel may judge, but no one is to receive more than a hundred blows."

"He complained, and they beat him."

"How are the hands nourished? By the blood. How does the blood reach the hands? By the veins. If the veins are closed, the hands will rot away."

"He left that farm and took to the roads."

"Where the Group of Seventeen sit, there final justice is done."

"He went to the capital and complained of the way he had been treated."

"Let there be clean water for those who toil. Let there be hot food for them and a clean bed."

"He came back to the farm, tired and hungry after his journey."

"No one is to receive more than a hundred blows."

"They beat him again."

"Behind everything some further thing is found, forever; thus the tree behind the bird, stone beneath soil, the sun behind Urth. Behind our efforts, let there be found our efforts."

"The just man did not give up. He left the farm again to walk to the capital."?

"Can all petitioners be heard? No, for all cry together. Who, then, shall be heard—is it those who cry loudest? No, for all cry loudly. Those who cry longest shall be heard, and justice shall be done to them."

"Arriving at the capital, he camped upon the very doorstep of the Group of Seventeen and begged all who passed to listen to him. After a long time he was admitted to the palace, where those in authority heard his complaints with sympathy."

"So say the Group of Seventeen: From those who steal, take all they have, for nothing that they have is their own."

"They told him to go back to the farm and tell the bad men—in their name—that they must leave."

"As a good child to its mother, so is the citizen to the Group of Seventeen."

"He did just as they had said."

"What is foolish speech? It is wind. It has come in at the ears and goes out of the mouth. No one is to receive more than a hundred blows."

"They mocked him and beat him."

"Behind our efforts, let there be found our efforts."

"The just man did not give up. He returned to the capital once more."

"The citizen renders to the populace what is due to the populace. What is due to the populace? Everything."

"He was very tired. His clothes were in rags and his shoes worn out. He had no food and nothing to trade."

"It is better to be just than to be kind, but only good judges can be just; let those who cannot be just be kind."

"In the capital he lived by begging."

At this point I could not help but interrupt. I told Foila that I thought it was wonderful that she understood so well what each of the stock phrases the Ascian used meant in the context of his story, but that I could not understand how she did it—how she knew, for example, that the phrase about kindness and justice meant that the hero had become a beggar.

"Well, suppose that someone else—Melito, perhaps—were telling a story, and at some point in it he thrust out his hand and began to ask for alms. You'd know what that meant, wouldn't you?"

I agreed that I would.

"It's just the same here. Sometimes we find Ascian soldiers who are too hungry or too sick to keep up with the rest, and after they understand we aren't going to kill them, that business about kindness and justice is what they say. In Ascian, of course. It's what beggars say in Ascia."

"Those who cry longest shall be heard, and justice shall be done to them."

"This time he had to wait a long while before he was admitted to the palace, but at last they let him in and heard what he had to say."

"Those who will not serve the populace shall serve the populace."

"They said they would put the bad men in prison."

"Let there be clean water for those who toil. Let there be hot food for them, and a clean bed."

"He went back home."

"No one is to receive more than a hundred blows."

"He was beaten again."

"Behind our efforts, let there be found our efforts."

"But he did not give up. Once more he set off for the capital to complain."

"Those who fight for the populace fight with a thousand hearts. Those who fight against them with none."

"Now the bad men were afraid."

"Let no one oppose the decisions of the Group of Seventeen."

"They said to themselves, 'He has gone to the palace again and again, and each time he must have told the rulers there that we did not obey their earlier commands. Surely, this time they will send soldiers to kill us.' "

"If their wounds are in their backs, who shall stanch their blood?"

"The bad men ran away."

"Where are those who in times past have opposed the decisions of the Group of Seventeen?"

"They were never seen again."

"Let there be clean water for those who toil. Let there be hot food for them, and a clean bed. Then they will sing at their work, and their work will be light to them. Then they will sing at the harvest, and the harvest will be heavy."

"The just man returned home and lived happily ever after."

Everyone applauded this story, moved by the story itself, by the ingenuity of the Ascian prisoner, by the glimpse it had afforded us of life in Ascia, and most of all, I think, by the graciousness and wit Foila had brought to her translation.

I have no way of knowing whether you, who eventually will read this record, like stories or not. If you do not, no doubt you have turned these pages without attention. I confess that I love them. Indeed, it often seems to me that of all the good things in the world, the only ones humanity can claim for itself are stories and music; the rest, mercy, beauty, sleep, clean water and hot food (as the Ascian would have said) are all the work of the Increate. Thus, stories are small things indeed in the scheme of the universe, but it is hard not to love best what is our own—hard for me, at least.

From this story, though it was the shortest and the most simple too of all those I have recorded in this book, I feel that I learned several things of some importance. First of all, how much of our speech, which we think freshly minted in our own mouths, consists of set locutions. The Ascian seemed to speak only in sentences he had learned by rote, though until he used each for the first time we had never heard them. Foila seemed to speak as women commonly do, and if I had been asked whether she employed such tags, I would have said that she did not—but how often one might have predicted the ends of her sentences from their beginnings.

Second, I learned how difficult it is to eliminate the urge for expression. The people of Ascia were reduced to speaking only with their masters' voice; but they had made of it a new tongue, and I had no doubt, after hearing the Ascian, that by it he could express whatever thought he wished.

And third, I learned once again what a many-sided thing is the telling of any tale. None, surely, could be plainer than the Ascian's, yet what did it mean? Was it intended to praise the Group of Seventeen? The mere terror of their name had routed the evildoers. Was it intended to condemn them? They had heard the complaints of the just man, and yet they had done nothing for him beyond giving him their verbal support. There had been no indication they would ever do more.

But I had not learned those things I had most wished to learn as I listened to the Ascian and to Foila. What had been her motive in agreeing to allow the Ascian to compete? Mere mischief? From her laughing eyes I could easily believe it. Was she perhaps in truth attracted to him? I found that more difficult to credit, but it was surely not impossible. Who has not seen women attracted to men lacking every attractive quality? She had clearly had much to do with Ascians, and he was clearly no ordinary soldier, since he had been taught our language. Did she hope to wring some secret from him?

And what of him? Melito and Hallvard had accused each other of telling tales with an ulterior purpose. Had he done so as well? If he had, it had surely been to tell Foila—and the rest of us too—that he would never give up.

XII

Winnoc

That evening I had yet another visitor: one of the shaven-headed male slaves. I had been sitting up and attempting to talk with the Ascian, and he seated himself beside me. "Do you remember me, Lictor?" he asked. "My name is Winnoc."

I shook my head.

"It was I who bathed you and cared for you on the night you arrived," he told me. "I have been waiting until you were well enough to speak. I would have come last night, but you were deep in talk already with one of our postulants."

I asked what he wished to speak to me about.

"A moment ago I called you Lictor, and you did not deny it. Are you indeed a lictor? You were dressed as one that night."

"I have been a lictor," I said. "Those are the only clothes I own."

"But you are a lictor no longer?"

I shook my head. "I came north to enter the army."

"Ah," he said. For a moment he looked away.

"Surely others do the same."

"A few, yes. Most join in the south, or are made to join. A few come north like you, because they want some special unit where a friend or relation is already. A soldier's life . . ."

I waited for him to continue.

"It's a lot like a slave's, I think. I've never been a soldier myself, but I've talked to a lot of them."

"Is your life so miserable? I would have thought the Pelerines kind mistresses. Do they beat you?"

He smiled at that and turned until I could see his back. "You've been a lictor. What do you think of my scars?"

In the fading light I could scarcely make them out. I ran my fingers across them. "Only that they are very old and were made with the lash," I said.

"I got them before I was twenty, and I'm nearly fifty now. A man with black clothes like yours made them. Were you a lictor for long?"

"No, not long."

"Then you don't know much of the business?"

"Enough to practice it."

"And that's all? The man who whipped me told me he was from the guild of torturers. I thought maybe you might have heard of them."

"I have."

"Are they real? Some people have told me they died out a long time ago, but that isn't what the man who whipped me said."

I told him, "They still exist, so far as I'm aware. Do you happen to recall the name of the torturer who scourged you?"

"He called himself Journeyman Palaemon—ah, you know him!"

"Yes. He was my teacher for a time. He's an old man now."

"He's still alive, then? Will you ever see him again?"

"I don't think so."

"I'd like to see him myself. Maybe sometime I will. The Increate, after all, orders all things. You young men, you live wild lives—I know I did, at your age. Do you know yet that he shapes everything we do?"

"Perhaps."

"Believe me, it's so. I've seen much more than you. Since it is so, it may be that I'll never see Journeyman Palaemon again, and you've been brought here to be my messenger."

Just at that point, when I expected him to convey to me whatever message he had, he fell silent. The patients who had listened so attentively to the Ascian's story were talking among themselves now; but somewhere in the stack of soiled dishes the old slave had collected, one shifted its position with a faint clink, and I heard it.

"What do you know of the laws of slavery?" he asked me at last. "I mean, of the ways a man or a woman can become a slave under the law?"

"Very little," I said. "A certain friend of mine" (I was thinking of the green man) "was called a slave, but he was only an unlucky foreigner who'd been seized by some unscrupulous people. I knew that wasn't legal."

He nodded agreement. "Was he dark of skin?"

"You might say that, yes."

"In the olden times, or so I've heard, slavery was by skin color. The darker a man was, the more a slave they made him. That's hard to believe, I know. But we used to have a chatelaine in the order who knew a lot about history, and she told me. She was a truthful woman.''

''No doubt it originated because slaves must often toil in the sun,'' I observed. ''Many of the usages of the past now seem merely capricious to us.''

At that he became a trifle angry. ''Believe me, young man, I've lived in the old days and I've lived now, and I know a lot better than you which was the best.''

''So Master Palaemon used to say.''

As I had hoped it would, that restored him to the principal topic of his thought. ''There's only three ways a man can be a slave,'' he said. ''Though for a woman it's different, what with marriage and the like.

''If a man's brought—him being a slave—into the Commonwealth from foreign parts, a slave he remains, and the master that brought him here can sell him if he wants. That's one. Prisoners of war—like this Ascian here—are the slaves of the Autarch, the Master of Masters and the Slave of Slaves. The Autarch can sell them if he wants to. Often he does, and because most of these Ascians aren't much use except for tedious work, you often find them rowing on the upper rivers. That's two.

''Number three is that a man can sell himself into somebody's service, because a free man is the master of his own body—he's his own slave already, as it were.''

''Slaves,'' I remarked, ''are seldom beaten by torturers. What need of it, when they can be beaten by their own masters?''

''I wasn't a slave then. That's part of what I wanted to ask Journeyman Palaemon about. I was just a young fellow that had been caught stealing. Journeyman Palaemon came in to talk to me on the morning I was going to get my whipping. I thought it was a kindly thing for him to do, although it was then that he told me he was from the guild of torturers.''

''We always prepare a client, if we can,'' I said.

''He told me not to try to keep from yelling—it doesn't hurt quite so bad, is what he told me, if you yell out just as the whip comes down. He promised me there wouldn't be any hitting more than the number the judge said, so I could count them if I wanted to, and that way I'd know when it was about over. And he said he wouldn't hit harder than he had to, to cut the skin, and he wouldn't break any bones.''

I nodded.

''I asked him then if he'd do me a favor, and he said he would if he could. I wanted for him to come back afterward and talk to me again, and he said he would try to when I was a little recovered. Then a caloyer came in to read the prayer.

"They tied me to a post, with my hands over my head and the indictment tacked up above my hands. Probably you've done it yourself many times."

"Often enough," I told him.

"I doubt the way they did me was any different. I've got the scars of it still, but they've faded, just like you say. I've seen many a man with worse ones. The jailers, they dragged me back to my cell as the custom is, but I think I could have walked. It didn't hurt as much as losing an arm or a leg. Here I've helped the surgeons take off a good many."

"Were you thin in those days?" I asked him.

"Very thin. I think you could have counted every rib I had."

"That was much to your advantage, then. The lash cuts deep in a fat man's back, and he bleeds like a pig. People say the traders aren't punished enough for short weighing and the like, but those who speak so don't know how they suffer when they are."

Winnoc nodded to that. "The next day I felt almost as strong as ever, and Journeyman Palaemon came like he'd promised. I told him how it was with me—how I lived and all—and asked him a bit about himself. I guess it seems queer to you that I'd talk so to a man that had whipped me?"

"No. I've heard of similar things many times."

"He told me he'd done something against his guild. He wouldn't tell me what it was, but because of it he was exiled for a while. He told me how he felt about it and how lonesome he was. He said he'd tried to feel better by thinking how other people lived, by knowing they had no more guild than he did. But he could only feel sorry for them, and pretty soon he felt sorry for himself too. He told me that if I wanted to be happy, and not go through this kind of thing again, to find some sort of brotherhood for myself and join."

"Yes?" I asked.

"And I decided to do what he'd said. When I was let out, I spoke to the masters of a lot of guilds, picking and choosing them at first, then talking to any I thought might take me, like the butchers and the candlemakers. None of them would take on an apprentice as old as I was, or somebody that didn't have the fee, or somebody with a bad character—they looked at my back, you see, and decided I was a troublemaker.

"I thought about signing on a ship or joining the army, and since then I've often wished I'd gone ahead with one or the other, although maybe if I had I'd wish now I hadn't, or maybe not be living to wish at all. Then I got the notion of joining some religious order, I don't know why. I talked to a bunch of them, and two offered to take me, even when I told them I didn't have any money and showed them my back. But the more I heard about the way they were supposed to live in there, the less I felt like I could do it. I had been drunk a lot, and I liked the girls, and I didn't really want to change.

"Then one day when I was standing around on a corner I saw a man I took to belong to some order I hadn't talked to yet. By that time I was planning to sign aboard a certain ship, but it wasn't going to sail for almost a week, and a sailor had told me a lot of the hardest work came while they were getting ready, and I'd miss it if I waited until they were about to get up the anchor. That was all a lie, but I didn't know it then.

"Anyway, I followed this man I'd seen, and when he stopped—he'd been sent to buy vegetables, you see—I went up to him and asked him about his order. He told me he was a slave of the Pelerines and it was about the same as being in an order, but better. A man could have a drink or two and nobody'd object so long as he was sober when he came to his work. He could lie with the girls too, and there were good chances for that because the girls thought they were holy men, more or less, and they traveled all around.

"I asked if he thought they'd take me, and I said I couldn't believe the life was as good as he made it out to be. He said he was sure they would, and although he couldn't prove what he'd said about the girls right then and there, he'd prove what he'd said about drinking by splitting a bottle of red with me.

"We went to a tavern by the market and sat down, and he was as good as his word. He told me the life was a lot like a sailor's, because the best part of being a sailor was seeing various places, and they did that. It was like being a soldier too, because they carried weapons when the order journeyed in wild parts. Besides all of that, they paid you to sign. In an order, the order gets an offering from every man who takes their vow. If he decides to leave later, he gets some of it back, depending on how long he's been in. For us slaves, as he explained to me, all that went the other way. A slave got paid when he signed. If he left later he'd have to buy his way out, but if he stayed he could keep all the money.

"I had a mother, and even though I never went to see her I knew she didn't have an aes. While I was thinking about the religious orders, I'd got to be more religious myself, and I didn't see how I was going to minister to the Increate with her on my mind. I signed the paper—

naturally Goslin, the slave who'd brought me in, got a reward for it—and I took the money to my mother."

I said, "That made her happy, I'm sure, and you too."

"She thought it was some kind of trick, but I left it with her anyhow. I had to go back to the order right away, naturally, and they'd sent somebody with me. Now I've been here thirty years."

"You're to be congratulated, I hope."

"I don't know. It's been a hard life, but then all lives are hard, from what I've seen of them."

"I too," I said. To tell the truth, I was becoming sleepy and wished that he would go. "Thank you for telling me your story. I found it very interesting."

"I want to ask you something," he said, "and I want you to ask Journeyman Palaemon for me if you see him again."

I nodded, waiting.

"You said you thought the Pelerines would be kind mistresses, and I suppose you're right. I've had a lot of kindness from some of them, and I've never been whipped here—nothing worse than a few slaps. But you ought to know how they do it. Slaves that don't behave themselves get sold, that's all. Maybe you don't follow me."

"I don't think I do."

"A lot of men sell themselves to the order, thinking like I did that it'll be an easy life and an adventure. So it is, mostly, and it's a good feeling to help cure the sick and the wounded. But those who don't suit the Pelerines are sold off, and they get a lot more for them than they paid them. Do you see how it is now? This way, they don't have to beat anybody. About the worst punishment you get is scrubbing out the jakes. Only if you don't please them, you can find yourself getting driven down into a mine.

"What I've wanted to ask Journeyman Palaemon all these years . . ." Winnoc paused, gnawing at his lower lip. "He was a torturer, wasn't he? He said so, and so did you."

"Yes, he was. He still is."

"Then what I want to know is whether he told me what he did to torment me. Or was he giving me the best advice he could?" He looked away so that I would not see his expression. "Will you ask him that for me? Then maybe sometime I'll see you again."

I said, "He advised you as well as he could, I'm certain. If you'd stayed as you were, you might have been executed by him or another torturer long ago. Have you ever seen a man executed? But torturers don't know everything."

Winnoc stood up. "Neither do slaves. Thank you, young man."

I touched his arm to detain him for a moment. "May I ask you something now? I myself have been a torturer. If you've feared for so many years that Master Palaemon had said what he did only to give you pain, how do you know that I haven't done the same just now?"

"Because you would have said the other," he told me. "Good night, young man."

I thought for a time about what Winnoc had said, and about what Master Palaemon had said to him so long ago. He too had been a wanderer, then, perhaps ten years before I was born. And yet he had returned to the Citadel to become a master of the guild. I recalled the way Abdiesus (whom I had betrayed) had wished to have me made a Master. Surely, whatever crime Master Palaemon had committed had been hidden later by all the brothers of the guild. Now he was a master, though as I had seen all my life, being too accustomed to it to wonder at it, it was Master Gurloes who directed the guild's affairs despite his being so much younger. Outside the warm winds of the northern summer played among the tent ropes; but it seemed to me that I climbed the steep steps of the Matachin Tower again and heard the cold winds sing among the keeps of the Citadel.

At last, hoping to turn my mind to less painful matters, I stood and stretched and strolled to Foila's cot. She was awake, and I talked with her for a time, then asked if I might judge the stories now; but she said I would have to wait one more day at least.

XIII

Foila's Story—The Armiger's Daughter

"Hallvard and Melito and even the Ascian have had their chances. Don't you think I'm entitled to one too? Even a man who courts a maid thinking he has no rivals has one, and that one is herself. She may give herself to him, but she may also choose to keep herself for herself. He has to convince her that she will be happier with him than by herself, and though men convince maids of that often, it isn't often true. In this competition I will make my own entry, and win myself for myself if I can. If I marry for tales, should I marry someone who's a worse teller of them than I am myself?

"Each of the men has told a story of his own country. I will do the same. My land is the land of the far horizons, of the wide sky. It is the land of grass and wind and galloping hoofs. In summer the wind can be as hot as the breath of an oven, and when the pampas take fire, the line of smoke stretches a hundred leagues and the lions ride our cattle to escape it, looking like devils. The men of my country are brave as bulls and the women are fierce as hawks.

"When my grandmother was young, there was a villa in my country so remote that no one ever came there. It belonged to an armiger, a feudatory of the Liege of Pascua. The lands were rich, and it was a fine house, though the roof beams had been dragged by oxen all one summer to get them to the site. The walls were of earth, as the walls of all the houses in my country are, and they were three paces thick. People who live in woodlands scoff at such walls, but they are cool and make a fine appearance whitewashed and will not burn. There was a tower and a wide banqueting hall, and a contrivance of ropes and wheels and buckets by which two merychips, walking in a circle, watered the garden on the roof.

"The armiger was a gallant man and his wife a lovely woman, but of all their children only one lived beyond the first year. She was tall, brown as leather yet smooth as oil, with hair the color of the palest wine and eyes dark as thunderheads. Still, the villa where they dwelt was so remote that no one knew and no one came to seek her. Often she rode all day alone, hunting with her peregrine or dashing after her spotted hunting cats when they had started an antelope. Often too she sat alone in her bedchamber all the day, hearing the song of her lark in its cage and turning the pages of old books her mother had carried from her own home.

"At last her father determined that she must wed, for she was near the twentieth year, after which few would want her. Then he sent his servants everywhere for three hundred leagues around, crying her beauty and promising that on his death her husband should hold all that was his. Many fine riders came, with silver-mounted saddles and coral on the pommels of their swords. He entertained them all, and his daughter, with her hair in a man's hat and a long knife in a man's sash, mingled with them, feigning to be one of them, so that she might hear who boasted of many women and see who stole when he thought himself unobserved. Each night she went to her father and told him their names, and when she had gone he called them to him and told them of the stakes where no one goes, where men bound in rawhide die in the sun; and the next morning they saddled their mounts and rode away.

"Soon there remained but three. Then the armiger's daughter could go among them no more, for with so few she feared they would surely know her. She went to her bedchamber and let down her hair and brushed it, and took off her hunting clothes and bathed in scented water. She put rings on her fingers and bracelets on her arms and wide hoops of gold in her ears, and on her head that thin circlet of fine gold that an armiger's daughter is entitled to wear. In short, she did all she knew to make herself beautiful, and because her heart was brave, perhaps there was no maid anywhere more beautiful than she.

"When she was dressed as she wished, she sent her servant to call her father and the three suitors to her. 'Now behold me,' she said. 'You see a ring of gold about my brow, and smaller rings suspended from my ears. The arms that will embrace one of you are themselves embraced by rings smaller still, and rings yet smaller are on my fingers. My chest of jewels lies open before you, and there are no more rings to be found in it; but there is another ring still in this room—a ring I do not wear. Can one of you discover it and bring it to me?'

"The three suitors looked up and down, behind the arras, and beneath the bed. At last the youngest took the lark's cage from its hook and carried it to the armiger's daughter; and there, about the lark's right leg, was a tiny ring of gold. 'Now hear me,' she said. 'My husband shall be the man who shows me this little brown bird again.'

"And with that she opened the cage and thrust in her hand, then carrying the lark upon her finger took it to the window and tossed it in the air. For a moment the three suitors saw the gold ring glint in the sun. The lark rose until it was no more than a dot against the sky.

"Then the suitors rushed down the stair and out the door, calling for their mounts, the swift-footed friends that had carried them already so many leagues across the empty pampas. Their silver-mounted saddles they threw upon their backs, and in less than a moment all three were gone from the sight of the armiger and the armiger's daughter, and from each other's as well, for one rode north toward the jungles, and one east toward the mountains, and the youngest west toward the restless sea.

"When he who went north had ridden for some days, he came to a river too swift for swimming and rode along its bank, ever harkening to the songs of the birds who dwelt there, until he reached a ford. In that ford a rider in brown sat a brown destrier. His face was masked with a brown neckcloth, his cloak, his hat, and all his clothing were of brown, and about the ankle of his brown right boot was a ring of gold.

" 'Who are you?' called the suitor.

"The figure in brown answered not a word.

" 'There was among us at the armiger's house a certain young man who vanished on the day before the last day,' said the suitor, 'and I think that you are he. In some way you have learned of my quest, and now you seek to prevent me. Well, stand clear of my road, or die where you stand.'

"And with that he drew sword and spurred his destrier into the water. For some time they fought as the men of my country fight, with the sword in the right hand and the long knife in the left, for the suitor was strong and brave, and the rider in brown was quick and blade-crafty. But at last the latter fell, and his blood stained the water.

" 'I leave you your mount,' the suitor called, 'if your strength is sufficient to get you into the saddle again. For I am a merciful man.' And he rode away.

"When he who had ridden toward the mountains had ridden for some days also, he came to such a bridge as the mountain people build, a narrow affair of rope and bamboo, stretched across a chasm like the web of a spider. No man but a fool attempts to ride across such a contrivance, and so he dismounted and led his mount by the reins.

"When he began to cross it seemed to him that the bridge was all empty before him, but he had not come a quarter of the way when a figure appeared in the center. In form it was much like a man, but it was all of brown save for one flash of white, and it seemed to fold brown wings about itself. When the second suitor was closer still he saw that it wore a ring of gold about the ankle of one boot, and the brown wings now seemed no more than a cloak of that color.

"Then he traced a Sign in the air before him to protect him from those spirits that have forgotten their creator, and he called, 'Who are you? Name yourself!'

" 'You see me,' the figure answered him. 'Name me true, and your wish is my wish.'

" 'You are the spirit of the lark sent forth by the armiger's daughter,' said the second suitor. 'Your form you may change, but the ring marks you.'

"At that, the figure in brown drew sword and presented it hilt foremost to the second suitor. 'You have named me rightly,' it said. 'What would you have me do?'

" 'Return with me to the armiger's house,' said the suitor, 'so that I may show you to the armiger's daughter and so win her.'

" 'I will return with you gladly, if that is what you wish,' said the figure in brown. 'But I warn you now that if she sees me, she will not see in me what you see.'

" 'Nevertheless, come with me,' answered the suitor, for he did not know what else to say.

"On such a bridge as the mountain people build, a man may turn about without much difficulty, but a four-legged beast finds it nearly impossible to do so. Therefore, they were forced to continue to the farther side in order that the second suitor might face his mount toward the armiger's house once more. 'How tedious this is,' he thought as he walked the great catenary of the bridge, 'and yet, how difficult and dangerous. Cannot that be used to my benefit?' At last he called to the figure in brown, 'I must walk this bridge, and then walk it again. But must you do so as well? Why don't you fly to the other side and wait there for me?'

"At that, the figure in brown laughed, a wondrous trilling. 'Did you not see that one of my wings is bandaged? I fluttered too near one of your rivals, and he slashed at me with his sword.'

" 'Then you cannot fly far?' asked the second suitor.

" 'No indeed. As you approached this bridge I was perched on the brown walkway resting, and when I heard your tread I had scarcely strength to flutter up.'

" 'I see,' said the second suitor, and no more. But to himself he thought: 'If I were to cut this bridge, the lark would be forced to take bird-form again—yet it could not fly far, and I should surely kill it. Then I could carry it back, and the armiger's daughter would know it.'

"When they reached the farther side, he patted the neck of his mount and turned it about, thinking that it would die, but that the best such animal was a small price to set against the ownership of great herds. 'Follow us,' he said to the figure in brown, and led his mount onto the bridge again, so that over that windy and aching chasm he went first, and the destrier behind him, and the figure in brown last of all. 'The beast will rear as the bridge falls,' he thought, 'and the spirit of the lark will not be able to dash past, so it must resume its bird shape or perish.' His plans, you see, were themselves shaped by the beliefs of my land, where those who set store in shape-changers will tell you that like thoughts they will not change once they have been made prisoner.

"Down the long curve of the bridge again walked the three, and up the side from which the second suitor had come, and as soon as he set foot on the rock, he drew his sword, sharp as his labor could make it. Two handrails of rope the bridge had, and two cables of hemp to support the roadway. He ought to have cut those first, but he wasted a moment on the handrails, and the figure in brown sprang from behind into the destrier's saddle, drove spur to its flanks, and rode him down. Thus he died under the hoofs of his own mount.

"When the youngest suitor, who had gone toward the sea, had ridden some days as well, he reached its marge. There on the beach beside the unquiet sea he met someone cloaked in brown, with a brown hat, and a brown cloth across nose and mouth, and a gold ring about the ankle of a brown boot.

" 'You see me,' the person in brown called. 'Name me true, and your wish shall be my wish.'

" 'You are an angel,' replied the youngest suitor, 'sent to guide me to the lark I seek.'

"At that the brown angel drew a sword and presented it, hilt foremost, to the youngest suitor, saying, 'You have named me rightly. What would you have me do?'

" 'Never will I attempt to thwart the will of the Liege of Angels,' answered the youngest suitor. 'Since you are sent to guide me to the lark, my only wish is that you shall do so.'

" 'And so I shall,' said the angel. 'But would you go by the shortest road? Or the best?'

"At that the youngest suitor thought to himself, 'Here surely is some trick. Ever the empyrean powers rebuke the impatience of men, which they, being immortal, can easily afford to do. Doubtless the shortest way lies through the horrors of caverns underground, or something like.' Therefore he answered the angel, 'By the best. Would not it dishonor her whom I shall wed to travel any other?'

" 'Some say one thing and some another,' replied the angel. 'Now let me mount up behind you. Not far from here there is a goodly port, and there I have just sold two destriers as good as yours or better. We shall sell yours as well, and the gold ring that circles my boot.'

"In the port they did as the angel had indicated, and with their money purchased a ship, not large but swift and sound, and hired three knowing seamen to work her.

"On the third day out from port, the youngest suitor had such a dream by night as young men have. When he woke he touched the pillow near his head and found it warm, and when he lay down to sleep again, he winded some delicate perfume—the odor, it might have been, of the flowering grasses the women of my land dry in spring to braid in their hair.

"An isle they reached where no men come, and the youngest suitor went ashore to search for the lark. He found it not, but at the dying of the day stripped off his garments to cool himself in the surging sea. There, when the stars had brightened, another joined him. Together they swam, and together lay telling tales on the beach.

"One day while they were peering over the prow of their ship for another (for they traded at times and at times fought also) a great gust of wind came and the angel's hat was blown into the all-devouring sea, and soon the brown cloth that had covered her face went to join it.

"At last they grew weary of the unresting sea and thought of my land, where the lions ride our cattle in autumn when the grass burns, and the men are brave as bulls and the women fierce as hawks. Their ship they had called the *Lark*, and now the *Lark* flew across blue waters, each morn impaling the red sun upon her bowsprit. In the port where they had bought her they sold her and received three times the price, for she had become a famous vessel, renowned in song and story; and indeed, all who came to the port wondered at how small she was, a trim, brown craft hardly a score of paces from stem to rudderpost. Their loot they sold also, and the goods they had gained by trading. The people of my land keep the best destriers they breed for themselves, but it is to this port that they bring the best of those they sell, and there the youngest suitor and the angel bought good mounts and filled their saddlebags with gems and gold, and set out for the armiger's house that is so remote that no one ever comes there.

"Many a scrape did they have upon the way, and many a time bloody the swords that had been washed so often in the cleansing sea and wiped on sailcloth or sand. Yet at last come they did. There the angel was welcomed by the armiger, shouting, and by his wife, weeping, and by all the servants, talking. And there she doffed her brown clothing and became the armiger's daughter of old once more.

"A great wedding was planned. In my land such things take many days, for there are roasting pits to be dug anew, and cattle to be slaughtered, and messengers who must ride for days to fetch guests who must ride for days also. On the third day, as they waited, the armiger's daughter sent her servant to the youngest suitor, saying, 'My mistress will not hunt today. Rather, she invites you to her bedchamber, to talk of times past upon sea and land.'

"The youngest suitor dressed himself in the finest of the clothes he had bought when they had returned to port, and soon was at the door of the armiger's daughter.

"He found her sitting on a window seat, turning the pages of one of the old books her mother had carried from her own home and listening to the singing of a lark in a cage. To that cage he went, and saw that the lark had a ring of gold about one leg. Then he looked at the armiger's daughter, wondering.

" 'Did the angel you met upon the strand not promise you should be guided to this lark?' she said. 'And by the best road? Each morning I open his cage and cast him out upon the wind to exercise his wings. Soon he returns to it again, where there is food for him, clean water, and safety.'

"Some say the wedding of the youngest suitor and the armiger's daughter was the finest ever seen in my land."

XIV

Mannea

That night there was much talk of Foila's story, and this time it was I who postponed making any judgment among the tales. Indeed, I had formed a sort of horror of judging, the residue, perhaps, of my education among the torturers, who teach their apprentices from boyhood to execute the instructions of the judges appointed (as they themselves are not) by the officials of our Commonwealth.

In addition, I had something more pressing on my mind. I had hoped that our evening meal would be served by Ava, but when it was not, I rose anyway, dressed myself in my own clothes, and slipped off in the gathering dark.

It was a surprise—a very pleasant one—to find that my legs were strong again. I had been free of fever for several days, yet I had grown accustomed to thinking myself ill (just as I had earlier been accustomed to thinking myself well) and had lain in my cot without complaint. No doubt many a man who walks about and does his work is dying and ignorant of it, and many who lie abed all day are healthier than those who bring their food and wash them.

I tried to recall, as I followed the winding paths between the tents, when I had felt so well before. Not in the mountains or upon the lake—the hardships I had suffered there had gradually reduced my vitality until I fell prey to the fever. Not when I fled Thrax, for I was already worn out from my duties as lictor. Not when I had arrived at Thrax; Dorcas and I had undergone privations in the roadless country nearly as severe as I was to bear alone in the mountains. Not even when I had been at the House Absolute (a period that now seemed as remote as the reign of Ymar), because I had still been suffering the aftereffects of the alzabo and my ingestion of Thecla's dead memories.

At last it came to me: I felt now as I had on that memorable morning when Agia and I had set out for the Botanic Gardens, the first morning after I had left the Citadel. That morning, though I had not known it, I had acquired the Claw. For the first time I wondered if it had not been cursed as well as blessed. Or perhaps it was only that all the past months had been needed for me to recover fully from the leaf of the avern that had pierced me that same evening. I took out the Claw and stared at its silvery gleam, and when I raised my eyes, I saw the glowing scarlet of the Pelerines' chapel.

I could hear the chanting, and I knew it would be some time before the chapel would be empty, but I proceeded anyway, and at last slipped through the door and took a place in the back. Of the liturgy of the Pelerines, I will say nothing. Such things cannot always be well described, and even when they can, it is less than proper to do so. The guild called the Seekers for Truth and Penitence, to which I at one time belonged, has its own ceremonies, one of which I have described in some detail in another place. Certainly those ceremonies are peculiar to it, and perhaps those of the Pelerines were peculiar to them as well, though they may once have been universal.

Speaking in so far as I can as an unprejudiced observer, I would say that they were more beautiful than ours but less theatrical, and thus in the long run perhaps less moving. The costumes of the participants were ancient, I am sure, and striking. The chants possessed a queer attraction I have not encountered in other music. Our ceremonies were intended chiefly to impress the role of the guild upon the minds of our younger members. Possibly those of the Pelerines had a similar function. If not, then they were designed to engage the particular attention of the All-Seeing, and whether they did so I cannot say. In the event, the order received no special protection.

When the ceremony was over and the scarlet-clad priestesses filed out, I bowed my head and feigned to be deep in prayer. Very readily, I found, the pretense became the thing itself. I remained conscious of my kneeling body, but only as a peripheral burden. My mind was among the starry wastes, far from Urth and indeed far from Urth's archipelago of island worlds, and it seemed to me that that to which I spoke was farther still—I had come, as it were, to the walls of the universe, and now shouted through the walls to one who waited outside.

"Shouted," I said, but perhaps that is the wrong word. Rather I whispered, as Barnoch, perhaps, walled up in his house, might have whispered through some chink to a sympathetic passerby. I spoke of what I had been when I wore a ragged shirt and watched the beasts and birds through the narrow window of the mausoleum, and what I had become.

I spoke too, not of Vodalus and his struggle against the Autarch, but of the motives I had once foolishly attributed to him. I did not deceive myself with the thought that I had it in me to lead millions. I asked only that I might lead myself; and as I did so, I seemed to see, with a vision increasingly clear, through the chink in the universe to a new universe bathed in golden light, where my listener knelt to hear me. What had seemed a crevice in the world had expanded until I could see a face and folded hands, and the opening, like a tunnel, running deep into a human head that for a time seemed larger than the head of Typhon carved upon the mountain. I was whispering into my own ear, and when I realized it I flew into it like a bee and stood up.

Everyone was gone, and a silence as profound as any I have ever heard seemed to hang in the air with the incense. The altar rose before me, humble in comparison to that Agia and I had destroyed, yet beautiful with its lights and purity of line and panels of sunstone and lapis lazuli.

Now I came forward and knelt before it. I needed no scholar to tell me the Theologoumenon was no nearer now. Yet he seemed nearer, and I was able—for the final time—to take out the Claw, something I had feared I could not do. Forming the syllables only in my mind, I said, "I have carried you over many mountains, across rivers, and across the pampas. You have given Thecla life in me. You have given me Dorcas, and you have restored Jonas to this world. Surely I have no complaint of you, though you must have many of me. One I shall not deserve. It shall not be said that I did not do what I might to undo the harm I have done."

I knew the Claw would be swept away if I were to leave it openly on the altar. Mounting the dais, I searched among its furnishings for a place of concealment that should be secure and permanent, and at last noticed that the altar-stone itself was held from below with four clamps that had surely never been loosed since the altar was constructed, and seemed likely to remain in place so long as it stood. I have strong hands, and I was able to free them, though I do not think most men could. Beneath the stone some wood had been chiseled away so that it should be supported at the edges only and would not rock—it was more than I had dared to hope for. With Jonas's razor I cut a small square of cloth from the edge of my now-tattered guild cloak. In it I wrapped the Claw, then I laid it under the stone and retightened the clamps, bloodying my fingers in my effort to make sure they would not come loose by accident.

As I stepped away from the altar I felt a profound sorrow, but I had not gone halfway to the door of the chapel before I was seized with wild joy. The burden of life and death had been lifted from me. Now I was only a man again, and I was delirious with delight. I felt as I had felt as a child when the long lessons with Master Malrubius were over and I was free to play in the Old Yard or clamber across the broken curtain wall to run among the trees and mausoleums of our necropolis. I was disgraced and outcast and homeless, without friend and without money, and I had just given up the most valuable object in the world, which was, perhaps, in the end the only valuable object in the world. And yet I knew that all would be well. I had climbed to the bottom of existence and felt it with my hands, and I knew that there *was* a bottom, and that from this point onward I could only rise. I swirled my cloak about me as I had when I was an actor, for I knew that I was an actor and no torturer, though I had been a torturer. I leaped into the air and capered as the goats do on the mountainside, for I knew that I was a child, and that no man can be a man who is not.

Outside, the cool air seemed expressly made for me, a new creation and not the ancient atmosphere of Urth. I bathed in it, first spreading my cloak then raising my arms to the stars, filled my lungs as does one who has just escaped drowning in the fluids of birth.

All this took less time than it has required to describe it, and I was about to start back to the lazaret tent from which I had come when I became aware of a motionless figure watching me from the shadows of another tent some distance off. Ever since the boy and I had escaped the blindly questing creature that had destroyed the village of the magicians, I had been afraid that some of Hethor's servants might search me out again. I was about to flee when the figure stepped into the moonlight, and I saw it was only a Pelerine.

"Wait," she called. Then, coming nearer, "I am afraid I frightened you."

Her face was a smooth oval that seemed almost sexless. She was young, I thought, though not so young as Ava and a good two heads taller—a true exultant, as tall as Thecla had been.

I said, "When one has lived long with danger . . ."

"I understand. I know nothing of war, but much of the men and women who have seen it."

"And now how may I serve you, Chatelaine?"

"First I must know if you are well. Are you?"

"Yes," I said. "I will leave this place tomorrow."

"You were in the chapel giving thanks, then, for your recovery."

I hesitated. "I had much to say, Chatelaine. That was a part of it, yes."

"May I walk with you?"

"Of course, Chatelaine."

I have heard it said that a tall woman seems taller than any man, and perhaps it is true. This woman was far less in stature than Baldanders had been, yet walking beside her made me feel almost dwarfish. I recalled too how Thecla had bent over me when we embraced, and how I had kissed her breasts.

When we had taken two score steps or so, the Pelerine said, "You walk well. Your legs are long, and I think they have covered many leagues. You are not a cavalry trooper?"

"I have ridden a bit, but not with the cavalry. I came through the mountains on foot, if that's what you mean, Chatelaine."

"That is well, for I have no mount for you. But I do not believe I have told you my name. I am Mannea, mistress of the postulants of our order. Our Domnicellae is away, and so for the moment I am in charge of our people here."

"I am Severian of Nessus, a wanderer. I wish that I could give you a thousand chrisos to help carry out your good work, but I can only thank you for the kindness I have received here."

"When I spoke of a mount, Severian of Nessus, I was neither offering to sell you one nor offering to give you one in the hope of thus earning your gratitude. If we do not have your gratitude now, we shall not get it."

"You have it," I told her, "as I've said. As I've also said, I will not linger here presuming on your kindness."

Mannea looked down at me. "I did not think you would. This morning a postulant told me how one of the sick had gone to the chapel with her two nights ago and described him. This evening, when you remained behind after the rest left, I knew you were he. I have a task, you see, and no one to perform it. In calmer days I would send a party of our slaves, but they are trained in the care of the sick, and we have need of every one of them and more. Yet it is said, 'He sends the beggar a stick and to the hunter a spear.' "

"I have no wish to insult you, Chatelaine, but I think that if you trust me because I went to your chapel you trust me for a bad reason. For all you know, I could have been stealing gems from the altar."

"You mean that thieves and liars often come to pray. By the blessing of the Conciliator they do. Believe me, Severian, wanderer from Nessus, no one else does—in the order or out of it. But you molested nothing. We have not half the power ignorant people suppose—nevertheless, those who think us without power are more ignorant still. Will you go on an errand for me? I'll give you a safe-conduct so you will not be taken up as a deserter."

"If the errand is within my powers, Chatelaine."

She put her hand on my shoulder. It was the first time she had touched me, and I felt a slight shock, as though I had been brushed unexpectedly by the wing of a bird.

"About twenty leagues from here," she said, "is the hermitage of a certain wise and holy anchorite. Until now he has been safe, but all this summer the Autarch has been driven back, and soon the fury of the war will roll over that place. Someone must go to him and persuade him to come to us—or if he cannot be persuaded, force him to come. I believe the Conciliator has indicated that you are to be the messenger. Can you do it?"

"I'm no diplomatist," I told her. "But for the other business, I can honestly say I have received long training."

XV

The Last House

Mannea had given me a rough map showing the location of the anchorite's retreat, emphasizing that if I failed to follow the course indicated on it precisely, I would almost certainly be unable to locate it.

In what direction that house lay from the lazaret I cannot say. The distances shown on the map were in proportion to their difficulty, and turnings were adjusted to suit the dimensions of the paper. I began by walking east, but soon found that the route I followed had turned north, then west through a narrow canyon threaded by a rushing stream, and at last south.

On the earliest leg of my journey, I saw a great many soldiers—once a double column lining both sides of the road while mules carried back the wounded down the center. Twice I was stopped, but each time the display of my safe-conduct permitted me to proceed. It was written on cream-colored parchment, the finest I had then seen, and bore the narthex sigil of the order stamped in gold. It read:

To Those Who Serve—

The letter you read shall identify our servant Severian of Nessus, a young man dark of hair and eye, pale of face, thin, and well above the middle height. As you honor the memory we guard, and yourselves may wish in time for succor and if need be an honorable interment, we beg you not hinder this Severian as he prosecutes the business we have entrusted to him, but rather provide him such aid as he may require and you can supply.

For the Order of the Journeying Monials of the Conciliator, called *Pelerines*, I am

The Chatelaine Mannea
Instructress and
Directress

Once I had entered the narrow canyon, however, all the armies of the world seemed to vanish. I saw no more soldiers, and the rushing water drowned the distant thundering of the Autarch's sacars and culverins—if indeed they could have been heard in that place at all.

The anchorite's house had been described to me and the description augmented by a sketch on the map I carried; moreover, I had been told that two days would be required for me to reach it. I was considerably surprised, therefore, when, at sunset, I looked up and saw it perched atop the cliff looming over me.

There was no mistaking it. Mannea's sketch had captured perfectly that high, peaked gable with its air of lightness and strength. Already a lamp shone in one small window.

In the mountains I had climbed many cliffs; some had been much higher than this one, and some—at least in appearance—more sheer. I had by no means been looking forward to camping among the rocks, and as soon as I saw the anchorite's house, I decided I would sleep in it that night.

The first third of the climb was easy. I scaled the rock face like a cat and was more than halfway up the whole of it before the fading of the light.

I have always had good night vision; I told myself the moon would soon be out and continued. In that I was wrong. The old moon had died while I lay in the lazaret, and the new would not be born for several days. The stars shed some light, though they were crossed and recrossed by bands of hurrying clouds; but it was a deceptive light that seemed worse than none, save when I did not have it. I found myself recalling then how Agia had waited with her assassins for me to emerge from the underground realm of the man-apes. The skin of my back crawled as though in anticipation of the arbalests' blazing bolts.

Soon a worse difficulty overtook me: I lost my sense of balance. I do not mean that I was entirely at the mercy of vertigo. I knew, in a general way, that *down* was in the direction of my feet and *up* in the direction of the stars; but I could be no more precise than that, and because I could not, I could judge only poorly how far I might lean out to search for each new handhold.

Just when this feeling was at its worst, the hurrying clouds closed their ranks, and I was left in total darkness. Sometimes it seemed to me that the cliff face had assumed a more gentle slope, so that I might almost have stood erect and walked up it. Sometimes I felt that it was beetling out—I must cling to the underside or fall. Often I felt certain I had not been climbing at all, but edging long distances to the left or right. Once I found myself almost head downward.

At last I reached a ledge, and there I determined to stay until the light came again. I wrapped myself in my cloak, lay down, and shifted my body to bring my back firmly against the rock. No resistance met it. I shifted once more and still felt nothing. I grew afraid that my sense of direction had deserted me even as my sense of balance had, and that I had somehow turned myself about and was edging toward the drop. After feeling the rock to either side, I rolled on my back and extended my arms.

At that moment there came a flash of sulfurous light that dyed the belly of every cloud. Not far off, some great bombard had loosed its cargo of death, and in that hectic illumination I saw that I had gained the top of the cliff, and that the house I had seen there was nowhere to be found. I lay upon an empty expanse of rock and felt the first drops of the coming rain patter against my face.

Next morning, cold and miserable, I ate some of the food I had carried from the lazaret and made my way down the farther side of the high hill of which the cliff had formed a part. The slope there was easier, and it was my intention to double about the shoulder of the hill until I again reached the narrow valley indicated on my map.

I could not do so. It was not that my way was blocked, but rather that when, after long walking, I arrived at what should have been the location I sought, I found an entirely different place, a shallower valley and a broader stream. After several watches wasted searching there, I discovered the spot from which (as it seemed to me) I had seen the anchorite's house perched upon the cliff top. Needless to say, it was not there now, nor was the cliff so high nor so steep as I recalled it.

It was there that I took out the map again, and studying it noticed that Mannea had written, in a hand so fine that I could scarcely believe it had been done with the pen I had seen her use, the words *THE LAST HOUSE* beneath the image of the anchorite's dwelling. For some reason those words and the picture of the house itself atop its rock recalled to me the house Agia and I had seen in the Jungle Garden, where husband and wife had sat listening to the naked man called Isangoma. Agia, who had been wise in the ways of all the Botanic Gardens, had told me there that if I turned on the path and attempted to go back to the hut I should not find it. Reflecting upon that incident, I discovered that I did not now believe her, but that I had believed her at the time. It might be, of course, that my loss of credulity was only a reaction to her treachery, of which

I had by now had a sufficient sample. Or it might merely be that I was far more ingenuous then, when I was less than a day gone from the Citadel and the nurturing of the guild. But it was also possible—so it seemed to me now—that I had believed then because I had just seen the thing for myself, and that the sight of it, and the knowledge of those people, had carried its own conviction.

Father Inire was alleged to have built the Botanic Gardens. Might it not be that some part of the knowledge he commanded was shared by the anchorite? Father Inire, too, had built the secret room in the House Absolute that had appeared to be a painting. I had discovered it by accident but only because I had followed the instructions of the old picture cleaner, who had meant that I should. Now I was no longer following the instructions of Mannea.

I retraced my way around the shoulder of the hill and up the easy slope. The steep cliff I recalled dropped before me, and at its base rushed a narrow stream whose song filled all the strait valley. The position of the sun indicated that I had at most two watches of light remaining, but by that light the cliff was far easier to descend than it had been to climb by night. In less than a watch I was down, standing in the narrow valley I had left the evening before. I could see no lamp at any window, but the Last House stood where it had been, founded upon stone over which my boots had walked that day. I shook my head, turned away from it, and used the dying light to read the map Mannea had drawn for me.

Before I go further, I wish to make it clear that I am by no means certain there was anything preternatural in all that I have described. I saw the Last House thus twice, but on both occasions under similar lighting, the first time being by late twilight and the second by early twilight. It is surely possible that what I saw was no more than a creation of rocks and shadows, the illuminated window a star.

As to the vanishing of the narrow valley when I tried to come upon it from the other direction, there is no geographical feature more prone to disappear from sight than such a narrow declivity. The slightest unevenness in the ground conceals it. To protect themselves from marauders, some of the autochthonous peoples of the pampas go so far as to build their villages in that form, first digging a pit whose bottom can be reached by a ramp, then excavating houses and stables from the sides of it. As soon as the grass has covered the castout earth, which occurs very rapidly after the winter rains, one may ride to within half a chain of such a place without realizing it exists.

But though I may have been such a fool, I do not believe I was.

Master Palaemon used to say that the supernatural exists in order that we may not be humiliated at being frightened by the night wind; but I prefer to believe that there was some element truly uncanny surrounding that house. I believe it now more firmly than I did then.

However it may be, I followed the map I had been given from that time forward, and before the night was more than two watches old, found myself climbing a path that led to the door of the Last House, which stood at the edge of just such a cliff as I remembered. As Mannea had said, the trip had taken just two days.

XVI

The Anchorite

There was a porch. It was hardly higher than the stone upon which it stood, but it ran to either side of the house and around the corners, like those long porches one sometimes sees on the better sort of country houses, where there is little to fear and the owners like to sit in the cool of the evening and watch Urth fall below Lune. I rapped at the door, and then, when no one answered, walked around this porch, first right, then left, peering in the windows.

It was too dark inside for me to see anything, but I found that the porch circled the house as far as the edge of the cliff, and there ended without a railing. I knocked again as fruitlessly as before and had laid myself on the porch to sleep (for having a roof over it, it was a better place than any I was likely to find among the rocks) when I heard faint footsteps.

Somewhere high in that high house, a man was walking. His steps were but slow at first, so that I thought he must be an old man or a sick one. As they came nearer, however, they became firmer and more swift, until as they neared the door they seemed the regular tread of a man of purpose, such a one as might, perhaps, command a maniple, or an ile of cavalry.

I had stood again by then and dusted my cloak and made myself as presentable as I could, yet I was only poorly prepared for him I saw when the door swung back. He carried a candle as thick as my wrist, and by its light I beheld a face that was like the faces of the Hierodules I had met in Baldanders's castle, save that it was a human face—indeed, I felt that as the faces of the statues in the gardens of the House Absolute had imitated the faces of such beings as Famulimus, Barbatus, and Ossipago, so their faces were only imitations, in some alien medium, of such faces as the one I saw now. I have said often in this account that I remember everything, and so I do; but when I try to sketch that face beside these words of mine I find I cannot do so. No drawing that I make resembles it in the least. I can only say that the brows were heavy and straight, the eyes deep-set and deep blue, as Thecla's were. This man's skin was fine as a woman's too, but there was nothing womanish about him, and the beard that flowed to his waist was of darkest black. His robe seemed white, but there was a rainbow shimmering where it caught the candlelight.

I bowed as I had been taught in the Matachin Tower and told him my name and who had sent me. Then I said, "And are you, sieur, the anchorite of the Last House?"

He nodded. "I am the last man here. You may call me Ash."

He stood to one side, indicating that I should enter, then led me to a room at the rear of the house, where a wide window overlooked the valley from which I had climbed the night before. There were wooden chairs there and a wooden table. Metal chests, dully gleaming in the candlelight, rested in the corners and in the angles between floor and walls.

"You must pardon the poor appearance of this place," he said. "It is here that I receive company, but I have so little company that I have begun to use it as a storeroom."

"When one lives alone in such a lonely spot, it is well to seem poor, Master Ash. This room, however, does not."

I had not thought that face capable of smiling, yet he smiled. "You wish to see my treasures? Look." He rose and opened a chest, holding the candle so that it lit the interior. There were square loaves of hard bread and packages of pressed figs. Seeing my expression he asked, "Are you hungry? There is no spell upon this food, if you are fearful of such things."

I was ashamed, because I had carried food for the journey and still had some left for the return; but I said, "I would like some of that bread, if you can spare it."

He gave me half a loaf already cut (and with a very sharp knife), cheese wrapped in silver paper, and dry yellow wine.

"Mannea is a good woman," he told me. "And you, I think, are a good man of the kind who does not know himself to be one—some say that is the only kind. Does she think I can help you?"

"Rather she believes that I can help you, Master Ash. The armies of the Commonwealth are in retreat, and soon the battle will overwhelm all this part of the country, and after the battle, the Ascians."

He smiled again. "The men without shadows. It is one of those names, of which there are many, that are in error and yet perfectly correct. What would you think if an Ascian told you he really cast no shadow?"

"I don't know," I said. "I never heard of such a thing."

"It is an old story. Do you like old stories? Ah, I see a light in your eyes, and I wish I could tell it better. You call your enemies Ascians, which of course is not what they call themselves, because your fathers believed they came from the waist of Urth, where the sun is precisely overhead at noon. The truth is that their home is much farther north. Yet Ascians they are. In a fable made in the earliest morning of our race, a man sold his shadow and found himself driven out everywhere he went. No one would believe that he was human."

Sipping wine, I thought of the Ascian prisoner whose cot had stood beside my own. "Did this man ever regain his shadow, Master Ash?"

"No. But for a time he traveled with a man who had no reflection."

Master Ash fell silent. Then he said, "Mannea is a good woman; I wish that I could oblige you. But I cannot go, and the war will never reach me here, no matter how its columns march."

I said, "Perhaps it would be possible for you to come with me and reassure the Chatelaine."

"That I cannot do either."

I saw then that I would have to force him to accompany me, but there seemed to be no reason to resort to duress now; there would be plenty of opportunity in the morning. I shrugged my shoulders as though in resignation and asked, "May I then at least sleep here tonight? I will have to return and report your decision, but the distance is fifteen leagues or more, and I could not walk much farther now."

Again I saw his faint smile, just such a smile as a carving of ivory might make when the motion of a torch altered the shadow of its lips. "I had hoped to have some news of the world from you," he said. "But I see that you are weary. Come with me when you have finished eating. I will show you to your bed."

"I have no courtly manners, Master, but I am not so ill-bred as to sleep when my host still desires my conversation—though I'm afraid I have little enough news to give. From what I've learned from my fellow sufferers in the lazaret, the war proceeds and waxes hotter each day. We are reinforced with legions and half legions, they by whole armies sent down from the north. They have much artillery too, and therefore we must rely more upon our mounted lances, who can charge swiftly and engage the enemy closely before his heavy pieces can be pointed. They have more fliers also than they boasted last year, although we have destroyed many. The Autarch himself has come to command, bringing many of his household troops from the House Absolute. But . . ." Shrugging again, I paused to take a bite of bread and cheese.

"The study of war has always seemed to me the least interesting part of history. Even so, there are certain patterns. When one side in a long war shows sudden strength, it is usually for one of three reasons. The first is that it has formed some new alliance. Do the soldiers of these new armies differ in any way from those in the old?"

"Yes," I said. "I have heard that they are younger and on the whole less strong. And there are more women among them."

"No differences in tongue or dress?"

I shook my head.

"Then for the present at least we can dismiss an alliance. The second possibility would be the termination of another war, fought elsewhere. If that were so, the reinforcements would be veterans. You say they are not, thus only the third remains. For some reason your foes have need of an immediate victory and are straining every limb."

I had finished the bread, but I was truly curious by now. "Why should that be?"

"Without knowing more than I do, I cannot say. Perhaps their leaders fear their people, who have sickened of the war. Perhaps all the Ascians are only servants, and their masters now threaten to act for themselves."

"You extend hope at one moment and snatch it away at the next."

"Not I, but history. Have you yourself been at the front?"

I shook my head.

"That is well. In many respects, the more a man sees of war the less he knows of it. How stand the people of your Commonwealth? Are they united behind their Autarch? Or has the war so worn them that they shout for peace?"

I laughed at that, and all the old bitterness that had helped draw me to Vodalus came rushing back. "Unite? Shout? I know that you have isolated yourself, Master, to fix your mind on higher things, but I would not have thought any man could know so little of the land in which he lives. Carcerists, mercenaries, and young would-be adventurers fight the war. A hundred leagues south it is less than a rumor, outside the House Absolute."

Master Ash pursed his lips. "Your Commonwealth is stronger than I would have believed, then. No wonder your foes are in despair."

"If that is strength, may the All Merciful preserve us from weakness. Master Ash, the front may collapse at any time. It would be wise for you to come with me to a safer place."

He appeared not to have heard. "If Erebus and Abaia and the rest enter the field themselves, it will be a new struggle. If and when. Interesting. But you are tired. Come with me. I will show you your bed and the high matters that, as you said a moment ago, I came here to study.''

We ascended two flights and entered a room that must have been the one in which I had seen a light the evening before. It was a wide chamber of many windows, and it occupied the entire story. There were machines there, but they were smaller and fewer than those I had seen in Baldanders's castle, and there were tables too, and papers, and many books, and near the center a narrow bed.

''Here I nap,'' Master Ash explained, ''when my work will not let me retire. It is not large for a man of your frame, but I think you will find it comfortable.''

I had slept on stone the night before; it looked very appealing indeed.

After showing me where I could relieve myself and wash, he left. My last glimpse of him before he darkened the light caught the same perfect smile I had seen before.

An instant later, when my eyes had grown accustomed to the dark, I ceased to wonder about it, for outside all those many windows there shone an unbounded pearly radiance. ''We are above the clouds,'' I said to myself (I, too, half smiling), ''or rather, some low clouds have come to shroud this hilltop, unnoticed by me in the darkness but known in some fashion to him. Now I see the tops of those clouds, high matters surely, as I saw the tops of clouds from Typhon's eyes.'' And I laid myself down to sleep.

XVII

Ragnarok—The Final Winter

It seemed strange to wake without a weapon, though for some reason I cannot explain, that was the first morning on which I had felt so. After the destruction of *Terminus Est* I had slept at the sacking of Baldanders's castle without fear, and later journeyed north without fear. Only the night before, I had slept upon the bare rock of the cliff top weaponless and—perhaps only because I had been so tired—had not been afraid. I now think that during all those days, and indeed during all the days since I had left Thrax, I had been putting the guild behind me and coming to believe that I was what those who encountered me took me for—the sort of would-be adventurer I had mentioned the night before to Master Ash. As a torturer, I had not so much considered my sword a weapon as a tool and a badge of office. Now in retrospect it had become a weapon to me, and I had no weapon.

I thought about that as I lay upon my back on Master Ash's comfortable mattress, my hands behind my head. I would have to acquire another sword if I remained in the war-torn lands, and it would be wise to have one even if I turned south again. The question was whether to turn south or not. If I remained where I was, I risked being drawn into the fighting, where I might well be killed. But for me a return to the south would be even more dangerous. Abdiesus, the archon of Thrax, had no doubt posted a reward for my capture, and the guild would almost certainly procure my assassination if they learned I was anywhere near Nessus.

After vacillating over this decision for some time, as one does when only half-awake, I recalled Winnoc and what he had told me of the slaves of the Pelerines. Because it is a disgrace to us if our clients die after torment, we are taught a good deal of leech-craft in the guild; I thought I knew already at least as much as they. When I had cured the girl in the jacal, I had felt suddenly uplifted. The Chatelaine Mannea had a good opinion of me already and would have a better one when I returned with Master Ash.

A few moments before, I had been disturbed because I lacked a weapon. Now I felt I had one—resolution and a plan are better than a sword, because a man whets his own edges on them. I threw off the blankets, noticing then for the first time, I think, how soft they were. The big room was cold but filled with sunlight; it was almost as though there were suns on all four sides, as though all the walls were east walls. I walked naked to the nearest window and saw that undulating field of white I had vaguely noted the evening before.

It was not a mass of cloud but a plain of ice. The window would not open, or if it would, I could not solve the puzzle of its mechanism; but I put my face close to the glass and peered downward as well as I could. The Last House rose, as I had seen before, from a high hill of rock. Now this hilltop alone remained above the ice. I went from window to window, and the view from each was the same. Going back to the bed that had been mine, I pulled on my trousers and boots, and slung my cloak about my shoulders, hardly knowing what it was I did.

Master Ash appeared just as I finished dressing. "I hope I do not intrude," he said. "I heard you walking up here."

I shook my head.

"I did not want you to become disturbed."

Without my willing it, my hands had gone to my face. Now some foolish part of me became aware of my bristling beard. I said, "I meant to shave before putting on my cloak. That was stupid of me. I haven't shaved since I left the lazaret." It was as though my mind were trudging across the ice, leaving my tongue and lips to get along as best they might.

"There is hot water here, and soap."

"That's good," I said. And then, "If I go downstairs . . ."

That smile again. "Will it be the same? The ice? No. You are the first to have guessed. May I ask how you did it?"

"A long time ago—no, only a few months, actually, though it seems like such a long time now—I went to the Botanic Gardens in Nessus. There was a place called the Lake of Birds, where the bodies of the dead seemed to remain fresh forever. I was told it was some property of the water, but I wondered even then that there should be so much power in water. There was another place too, that they called the Jungle Garden, where the leaves were greener than I have ever known leaves to be—not a bright green but dark with greenness, as if the plants could never use all the energy the sun poured down. The people there seemed not of our time, though I could not say if they were of the past, or the future, or some third thing that is neither. They had a little house. It was much smaller than this, but this reminds me of it. I've thought often of the Botanic Gardens since I left them, and sometimes I've wondered if their secret were not that the time never changed in the Lake of Birds, and that one moved forward or backward—however it might be—when walking the path of the Jungle Garden. Am I perhaps speaking overmuch?"

Master Ash shook his head.

"Then when I was coming here, I saw your house at the top of this hill. But when I climbed to it, it was gone, and the valley below was not as I remembered it." I did not know what else to say, and fell silent.

"You are correct," Master Ash told me. "I have been put here to observe what you see about you now. The lower stories of my home, however, reach into older periods, of which yours is the oldest."

"That seems a great wonder."

He shook his head. "It is almost more wonderful that this spur of rock has been spared by the glaciers. The tops of peaks far higher are submerged. It is sheltered by a geographic pattern so subtle that it could only be achieved by accident."

"But it too will be covered at last?" I asked.

"Yes."

"And what then?"

"I shall leave. Or rather, I shall leave some time before it occurs."

I felt a surge of irrational anger, the same emotion I had sometimes known as a boy when I could not make Master Malrubius understand my questions. "I meant, what of Urth?"

He shrugged. "Nothing. What you see is the last glaciation. The surface of the sun is dull now; soon it will grow bright with heat, but the sun itself will shrink, giving less energy to its worlds. Eventually, should anyone come and stand upon the ice, he will see it only as a bright star. The ice he stands upon will not be that which you see but the atmosphere of this world. And so it will remain for a very long time. Perhaps until the close of the universal day."

I went to another window and looked out again on the expanse of ice. "Will this happen soon?"

"The scene you see is many thousands of years in your future."

"But before this, the ice must have come from the south."

Master Ash nodded. "And down from the mountaintops. Come with me."

We descended to the second level of the house, which I had scarcely noticed when I had come upstairs the night before. The windows were far fewer there, but Master Ash placed chairs before one and indicated that we would sit and look out. It was as he had said—ice, lovely in its purity, crept down the mountainsides to war with the pines. I asked if this too were far in the future, and he nodded once more. "You will not live to see it again."

"But so near that the life of a man will nearly reach it?"

He twitched his shoulders and smiled beneath his beard. "Let us say it is a thing of degree. You will not see this. Nor will your children, nor theirs. But the process has already begun. It began long before you were born."

I knew nothing of the south, but I found myself thinking of the island people of Hallvard's story, the precious little sheltered places with a growing season, the hunting of the seals. Those islands would not hold men and their families much longer. The boats would scrape over their stony beaches for the last time. *"My wife, my children, my children, my wife."*

"At this time, many of your people are already gone," Master Ash continued. "Those you call the cacogens have mercifully carried them to fairer worlds. Many more will leave before the final victory of the ice. I am myself, you see, descended from those refugees."

I asked if everyone would escape.

He shook his head. "No, not everyone. Some would not go, some could not be found. No home could be found for others."

For some time I sat looking out at the beleaguered valley and trying to order my thoughts. At last I said, "I have always found that men of religion tell comforting things that are not true, while men of science recount hideous truths. The Chatelaine Mannea said you were a holy man, but you appear to be a man of science, and you said your people had sent you to our dead Urth to study the ice."

"The distinction you mention no longer holds. Religion and science have always been matters of faith in something. It is the same something. You are yourself what you call a man of science, so I talk of science to you. If Mannea were here with her priestesses, I would talk differently."

I have so many memories that I often become lost among them. Now as I looked at the pines, waving in a wind I could not feel, I seemed to hear the beating of a drum. "I met another man who said he was from the future once," I said. "He was green—nearly as green as those trees—and he told me that his time was a time of brighter sun."

Master Ash nodded. "No doubt he spoke truly."

"But you tell me that what I see now is but a few lifetimes away, that it is part of a process already begun, and that this will be the last glaciation. Either you are a false prophet or he was."

"I am not a prophet," answered Master Ash, "nor was he. No one can know the future. We are speaking of the past."

I was angry again. "You told me this was only a few lifetimes away."

"I did. But you, and this scene, are past events for me."

"I am not a thing of the past! I belong to the present."

"From your own viewpoint you are correct. But you forget I cannot see you from your viewpoint. This is my house. It is through my windows that you have looked. My house strikes its roots into the past. Without that I should go mad here. As it is, I read these old centuries like books. I hear the voices of the long dead, yours among them. You think that time is a single thread. It is a weaving, a tapestry that extends forever in all directions. I follow a thread backward. You will trace a color forward, what color I cannot know. White may lead you to me, green to your green man."

Not knowing what to say, I could only mutter that I had conceived of time as a river.

"Yes—you came from Nessus, did you not? And that was a city built about a river. But it was once a city by the sea, and you would do better to think of time as a sea. The waves ebb and flow, and currents run beneath them."

"I would like to go downstairs," I said. "To return to my own time."

Master Ash said, "I understand."

"I wonder if you do. Your time, if I have heard you rightly, is that of this house's highest story, and you have a bed there, and other necessary things. Yet when you are not overwhelmed by your labors you sleep here, according to what you have told me. Yet you say this is nearer my time than your own."

He stood up. "I meant that I too flee the ice. Shall we go? You will want food before you begin the long trip back to Mannea."

"We both will," I said.

He turned to look at me before he started down the stair. "I told you I could not go with you. You have discovered for yourself how well hidden this house is. For all who do not walk the path correctly, even the lowest story stands in the future."

I caught both his arms behind him in a double lock and used my free hand to search him for weapons. There were none, and though he was strong, he was not as strong as I had feared he might be.

"You plan to carry me to Mannea. Is that correct?"

"Yes, Master, and we'll have a great deal less trouble if you will go willingly. Tell me where I can find some rope—I don't want to have to use the belt of your robe."

"There is none," he told me.

I bound his hands with his cincture, as I had first planned. "When we are some distance from here," I said, "I will loose you if you will give me your word to behave well."

"I made you welcome in my house. What harm have I done you?"

"Quite a bit, but that doesn't matter. I like you, Master Ash, and I respect you. I hope that you won't hold what I am doing to you against me any more than I hold what you have done to me against you. But the Pelerines sent me to fetch you, and I find I am a certain sort of man, if you understand what I mean. Now don't go down the steps too fast. If you fall, you won't be able to catch yourself."

I led him to the room to which he had first taken me and got some of the hard bread and a package of dried fruit. "I don't think of myself as one anymore," I continued, "but I was brought up as—" It was at my lips to say *torturer*, but I realized (then, I think, for the first time) that it was not quite the correct term for what the guild did and used the official one instead. "—as a Seeker for Truth and Penitence. We do what we have said we will do."

"I have duties to perform. In the upper level, where you slept."

"I am afraid they must go unperformed."

He was silent as we went out the door and onto the rocky hilltop. Then he said, "I will go with you, if I can. I have often wished to walk out of this door and never halt."

I told him that if he would swear upon his honor, I would untie him at once.

He shook his head. "You might think that I betrayed you."

I did not know what he meant.

"Perhaps somewhere there is the woman I have called Vine. But your world is your world. I can exist there only if the probability of my existence is high."

I said, "I existed in your house, didn't I?"

"Yes, but that was because your probability was complete. You are a part of the past from which my house and I have come. The question is whether I am the future to which you go."

I remembered the green man in Saltus, who had been solid enough. "Will you vanish like a soap bubble then?" I asked. "Or blow away like smoke?"

"I do not know," he said. "I do not know what will happen to me. Or where I will go when it does. I may cease to exist in any time. That was why I never left of my own will."

I took him by one arm, I suppose because I thought I could keep him with me in that way, and we walked on. I followed the route Mannea had drawn for me, and the Last House rose behind us as solidly as any other. My mind was busy with all the things he had told me and showed me, so that for a while, the space of twenty or thirty paces, perhaps, I did not look around at him. At last his remark about the tapestry suggested Valeria to me. The room where we had eaten cakes had been hung with them, and what he had said about tracing threads suggested the maze of tunnels through which I had run before encountering her. I started to tell him of it, but he was gone. My hand grasped empty air. For a moment I seemed to see the Last House afloat like a ship upon its ocean of ice. Then it merged into the dark hilltop on which it had stood; the ice was no more than what I had once taken it to be—a bank of cloud.

XVIII

Foila's Request

For another hundred paces or more, Master Ash was not entirely gone. I felt his presence, and sometimes even caught sight of him, walking beside me and half a step behind, when I did not try to look directly at him. How I saw him, how he could in some sense be present while in another absent, I do not know. Our eyes receive a rain of photons without mass or charge from swarming particles like a billion, billion suns—so Master Palaemon, who was nearly blind, had taught me. From the pattering of those photons we believe we see a man. Sometimes the man we believe we see may be as illusory as Master Ash, or more so.

His wisdom I felt with me too. It had been a melancholy wisdom, but a real one. I found myself wishing he had been able to accompany me, though I realized it would have meant the coming of the ice was certain. "I'm lonely, Master Ash," I said, not daring to look back. "How lonely I didn't realize until now. You were lonely also, I think. Who was the woman you called Vine?"

Perhaps I only imagined his voice. "*The first woman.*"

"Meschiane? Yes, I know her, and she is very lovely. My Meschiane was Dorcas, and I am lonely for her, but for all the others too. When Thecla became a part of me, I thought I would never be lonely again. But now she is so much a part that we're only one person, and I can be lonely for others. For Dorcas, for Pia the island girl, for little Severian and Drotte and Roche. If Eata were here, I could hug him.

"Most of all, I'd like to see Valeria. Jolenta was the most beautiful woman I've ever seen, but there was something in Valeria's face that tore my heart out. I was only a boy, I suppose, though I didn't think so then. I crawled up out of the dark and found myself in a place they called the Atrium of Time. Towers—the towers of Valeria's family—

rose on all sides of it. In the center was an obelisk covered with sundials, and though I remember its shadow on the snow, it couldn't have had sunlight there for more than two or three watches of each day; the towers must shade it most of the time. Your understanding is deeper than mine, Master Ash—can you tell me why they might have built it so?"

A wind that played among the rocks seized my cloak so that it billowed from my shoulders. I secured it again and pulled up my hood. "I was following a dog. I called him Triskele, and I said, even to myself, that he was mine, though I had no right to keep a dog. It was a winter day when I found him. We'd been doing laundry—washing the clients' bedclothes—and the drain plugged with rags and lint. I'd been shirking my work, and Drotte told me to go outside and ram a clothes prop up it. The wind was terribly cold. That was your ice coming, I suppose, though I didn't know it at the time—the winters getting a little worse each year. And of course when I got the drain open, a gush of filthy water would come out and wet my hands.

"I was angry because I was the oldest, except for Drotte and Roche, and I thought the younger apprentices ought to have to do the work. I was poking at the clog with my stick when I saw him across the Old Yard. The keepers in the Bear Tower had held a private fight, I suppose, the night before, and the dead beasts were lying outside their door waiting for the nacker. There was an arsinoither and a smilodon, and several dire wolves. The dog was lying on top. I suppose he had been the last to die, and from his wounds one of the dire wolves had killed him. Of course, he wasn't really dead, but he looked dead.

"I went over to see him—it was an excuse to stop what I was doing for a moment and blow on my fingers. He was as stiff and cold as . . . well, as anything I've ever seen. I killed a bull once with my sword, and when it was lying dead in its own blood it still looked quite a bit more living than Triskele did then. Anyway, I reached out and stroked his head. It was as big as a bear's, and they had cut off his ears, so that only two little points were left. When I touched him he opened his eyes. I dashed back across the Yard and rammed the stick up so hard it broke through at once, because I was afraid Drotte would send Roche down to see what I was doing.

"When I think back on it, it was as if I had the Claw already, more than a year before I got it. I can't describe how he looked when he rolled his eyes up to see me. He touched my heart. I never revived an animal when I had the Claw, but then I never tried. When I was among them, I was usually wishing I could kill one, because I wanted something to eat. Now I'm no longer sure that killing animals to eat is something we are meant to do. I noticed that you had no meat in your supplies—only bread and cheese, and wine and dried fruit. Do your people, on whatever world it is where people live in your time, feel so too?"

I paused, hoping for an answer, but none came. All the mountaintops had dropped below the sun now; I was no longer certain whether some thin presence of Master Ash followed me or only my shadow.

I said, "When I had the Claw I found that it would not revive those dead by human acts, though it seemed to heal the man-ape whose hand I had struck off. Dorcas thought it was because I had done it myself. I can't say—I never thought the Claw knew who held it, but perhaps it did."

A voice—not Master Ash's but a voice I had never heard before—called out, "A fine new year to you!"

I looked up and saw, perhaps forty paces off, just such an uhlan as Hethor's notules had killed on the green road to the House Absolute. Not knowing what else to do, I waved and shouted, "Is it New Year's Day, then?"

He touched spurs to his destrier and came galloping up. "Mid summer today, the beginning of the new year. A glorious one for our Autarch."

I tried to recall some of the phrases Jolenta had been so fond of. "Whose heart is the shrine of his subjects."

"Well said! I'm Ibar, of the Seventy-eighth Xenagie, patrolling the road until evening, worse luck."

"Surely it's lawful to use the road here."

"Entirely. Provided, of course, that you are prepared to identify yourself."

"Yes," I said. "Of course." I had almost forgotten the safe-conduct Mannea had written for me. Now I took it out and handed it to him.

When I had been stopped on my way to the Last House, I had by no means been sure that the soldiers who had questioned me could read. Each had stared wisely at the parchment, but it might well have been that they took in no more than the sigil of the order and Mannea's regular and vigorous, though slightly eccentric, penmanship. The uhlan unquestionably could. I could see his eyes traveling the lines of script, and even guess, I think, when they paused momentarily at "honorable interment."

He refolded the parchment carefully but retained it. "So you are a servant of the Pelerines."

"I have that honor, yes."

"You were praying, then. I thought you were talking to yourself when

I saw you. I don't hold with any religious nonsense. We have the standard of the xenagie near at hand and the Autarch at a distance, and that's all I need of reverence and mystery; but I have heard that they were good women."

I nodded. "I believe—perhaps somewhat more than you. But they are indeed."

"And you were sent on a task for them. How many days ago?"

"Three."

"Are you returning to the lazaret at Media Pars now?"

I nodded again. "I hope to reach it before nightfall."

He shook his head. "You won't. Take it easy, that's my advice to you." He held out the parchment.

I took it and returned it to my sabretache. "I was traveling with a companion, but we were separated. I wonder if you've seen him." I described Master Ash.

The uhlan shook his head. "I'll keep an eye out for him and tell him which way you went if I see him. Now—will you answer a question for me? It's not official, so you can tell me it's none of my affair if you want."

"I will if I can."

"What will you do when you leave the Pelerines?"

I was somewhat taken aback. "Why, I hadn't planned to leave at all. Someday, perhaps."

"Well, keep the light cavalry in mind. You look like a man of your hands, and we can always use one. You'll live half as long as you would in the infantry, and have twice as much fun."

He urged his mount forward, and I was left to ponder what he had said. I did not doubt that he had been serious in telling me to sleep on the road; but that very seriousness made me hurry forward all the faster. I have been blessed with long legs, so that when I need to I can walk as fast as most men can trot. I used them then, dropping all thoughts of Master Ash and my own troubled past. Perhaps some thin presence of Master Ash still accompanied me; perhaps it does so yet. But if it did, I was and remain unaware of it.

Urth had not yet turned her face from the sun when I came to that narrow road the dead soldier and I had taken only a little over a week before. There was blood in its dust still, much more than I had seen there previously. I had feared from what the uhlan had said that the Pelerines had been accused of some misdeed; now I felt sure that it was only that a great influx of wounded had been brought to the lazaret, and he had decided I deserved a night's rest before being set to work on them. That thought was a vast relief to me. A superabundance of the injured would give me an opportunity to show my skills and render it that much more likely that Mannea would accept me when I offered to sell myself to the order, if only I could contrive some tale to account for my failure at the Last House.

When I turned the final bend in the road, however, what I saw was entirely different.

Where the lazaret had stood, the ground seemed to have been plowed by a host of madmen, plowed and dug—its bottom already a small lake of shallow water. Shattered trees rimmed the circle.

Until darkness came, I walked back and forth across it. I was looking for some sign of my friends, and also for some trace of the altar that had held the Claw. I found a human hand, a man's hand, blown off at the wrist. It might have been Melito's, or Hallvard's, or the Ascian's, or Winnoc's. I could not tell.

I slept beside the road that night. When morning came I began my inquiries, and before evening I had located the survivors, some half dozen leagues from the original site. I went from cot to cot, but many were unconscious and so bandaged about the head that I could not have known them. It is possible that Ava, Mannea, and the Pelerine who had carried a stool to my bedside were among them, though I did not discover them there.

The only woman I recognized was Foila, and that only because she recognized me, calling "Severian!" as I walked among the wounded and dying. I went to her and tried to question her, but she was very weak and could tell me little. The attack had come without warning and shattered the lazaret like a thunderbolt; her memories were all of the aftermath, of hearing the screams that for a long time had brought no rescuers, and at last being dragged forth by soldiers who knew little of medicine. I kissed her as well as I could, and promised to come and see her again—a promise, I think, that both of us knew I would not be able to keep. She said, "Do you recall the time when all of us told stories? I thought of that."

I said I knew she had.

"I mean while they were carrying us here. Melito and Hallvard and the rest are dead, I think. You will be the only one who remembers, Severian."

I told her I would remember always.

"I want you to tell other people. On winter days, or a night when there is nothing else to do. Do you remember the stories?"

" 'My land is the land of far horizons, of the wide sky.' "

"Yes," she said, and seemed to sleep.

My second promise I have kept, first copying all the stories onto the blank pages at the close of the brown book, then giving them here, just as I heard them in the long, warm noons.

XIX

Guasacht

The next two days I spent in wandering. I will not say much of them here, for there is little to say. I might, I suppose, have enlisted in several units, but I was far from sure I wanted to enlist. I would have liked to return to the Last House, but I was too proud to cast myself on Master Ash's charity, assuming that Master Ash was again to be found there. I told myself I would gladly have returned to the post of Lictor of Thrax, yet if that had been possible, I am not certain I would have done so. I slept like an animal in wooded places and took what food I could, which was little.

On the third day I discovered a rusty falchion, dropped, as it appeared, in some campaign of the year before. I got out my little flask of oil and my broken whetstone (both of which I had retained, together with her hilt, when I had cast the wreck of *Terminus Est* into the water) and spent a happy watch in cleaning and sharpening it. When that was done, I trudged on, and soon struck a road.

With the protection of Mannea's safe-conduct effectively removed, I was more chary of showing myself than I had been on my way from Master Ash's. But it seemed probable that the dead soldier the Claw had raised, who now called himself Miles though I knew some part of him to be Jonas, had by now joined some unit. If so, he would be on a road or in camp near one, if he was not actually in battle; and I wished to speak to him. Like Dorcas, he had paused a time in the country of the dead. She had dwelt there longer, but I hoped that if I could question him before too much time had erased his memories of it, I might learn something that would—if not permit me to regain her—at least help reconcile me to her loss.

For I found I loved her now as I never had when we tramped cross-country to Thrax. Then my thoughts had been too much of Thecla; I had always been reaching inside myself to find her. Now it seemed, if only because she had been a part of me so long, that I had grasped her indeed, in an embrace more final than any coupling—or rather, that as the male's seed penetrates the female body to produce (if it be the will of Apeiron) a new human being, so she, entering my mouth, by my will had combined with the Severian that was to establish a new man: I who still call myself Severian but am conscious, as it were, of my double root.

Whether I could have learned what I sought from Miles-Jonas, I do not know. I have never found him, though I have persevered in the search from that day to this. By midafternoon I had entered a realm of broken trees, and from time to time I passed corpses in more or less advanced stages of decay. At first I tried to pillage them as I had the body of Miles-Jonas, but others had been there before me, and indeed the fennecs had come in the night with their sharp little teeth to loot the flesh.

Somewhat later, as my energies were beginning to flag, I paused at the smoldering remains of an empty supply wagon. The draft animals, which had not, it appeared, been dead long, lay in the road, with their driver pitched on his face between them; and it occurred to me that I might do worse than to cut as much meat as I wanted from their flanks and carry it to some isolated spot where I could kindle a fire. I had fleshed the point of the falchion in the haunch of one of these animals when I heard the drumming of hoofs, and supposing them to belong to the destrier of an estafette, moved to the edge of the road to let him pass.

It was instead a short, thick-bodied, energetic-looking man on a tall, ill-used mount. He reined up at the sight of me, but something in his expression told me there was no need for fight or flight. (If there had been, it would have been *fight*. His destrier would have done him little good among the stumps and fallen logs, and despite his haubergeon and brass-ringed buff cap, I thought I could best him.)

"Who are you?" he called. And when I told him, "Severian of Nessus, eh? You're civilized then, or half-civilized, but you don't look like you've been eating too well."

"On the contrary," I said. "Better than I've been accustomed to, recently." I did not want him to think me weak.

"But you could use some more—that's not Ascian blood on your sword. You're a schiavoni? An irregular?"

"My life has been pretty irregular of late, certainly."

"But you're attached to no formation?" With startling dexterity he vaulted from his saddle, threw the reins to the ground, and came striding over. He was slightly bowlegged and had one of those faces that appear to have been molded in clay and flattened from the top and bottom before firing, so that the forehead and chin are shallow but broad, the eyes slits, the mouth wide. Still I liked him at once for his verve, and because he took so little trouble to hide his dishonesty.

I said, "I'm attached to nothing and no one—memories excepted."

"Ahh!" He sighed, and for an instant rolled his eyes upward. "I know—I know. We have all had our difficulties, every one of us. What was it, a woman or the law?"

I had not previously viewed my troubles in that light, but after thinking for a moment I admitted it had been a bit of both.

"Well, you've come to the right place and you've met the right man. How'd you like a good meal tonight, a whole crowd of new friends, and a handful of orichalks tomorrow? Sound good? Good!"

He returned to his mount, and his hand darted out as quickly as a fencer's blade to grasp her bridle before she could shy away. When he had the reins again, he leaped into the saddle as readily as he had left it. "Now you get up behind me," he called. "It's not far, and she'll carry two easily enough."

I did as he told me, though with considerably more difficulty since I had no stirrup to assist me. The instant I was seated, the destrier struck like a bushmaster at my leg; but her master, who had clearly been anticipating the maneuver, clubbed her so hard with the brass pommel of his poniard that she stumbled and nearly fell.

"Pay no mind," he said. The shortness of his neck did not permit him to look over his shoulder, so he spoke out of the left side of his mouth to make it clear he was addressing me. "She's a fine animal and a plucky fighter, and she just wants to make sure you understand her value. A sort of initiation, you know. You know what an initiation is?"

I told him I thought myself familiar with the term.

"Anything that's worth belonging to has one, you'll find—I've found that out myself. I've never seen one that a plucky lad couldn't handle and laugh about afterwards."

With that cryptic encouragement he set his enormous spurs to the sides of his fine animal as if he meant to eviscerate her on the spot, and we went flying down the road, trailed by a cloud of dust.

Since the time I had ridden Vodalus's charger out of Saltus, I had supposed in my innocence that all mounts might be divided into two sorts: the highbred and swift, and the cold-blooded and slow. The better, I thought, ran with the graceful ease, almost, of a coursing cat; the worse moved so tardily that it hardly mattered how they did it. It used to be a maxim of one of Thecla's tutors that all two-valued systems are false, and I discovered on that ride a new respect for him. My benefactor's mount belonged to that third class (which I have since discovered is fairly extensive) comprising those animals that outrace the birds but seem to run with legs of iron upon a road of stone. Men have numberless advantages over women and for that reason are rightly charged to protect them, yet there is one great one women may boast over men: No woman has ever had her organs of generation crushed between her own pelvis and the bony spine of one of these galloping brutes. That happened to me twenty or thirty times before we reined up, and when I slid over the crupper at last and leaped aside to dodge a kick, I was in no very good mood.

We had halted in one of those little, lost fields one sometimes finds among the hills, an area more or less level and a hundred strides or so across. A tent the size of a cottage had been erected in the center, with a faded flag of black and green flapping before it. Several score hobbled mounts grazed at will over the field, and an equal number of ragged men, with a sprinkling of unkempt women, lounged about cleaning armor, sleeping, and gambling.

"Look here!" my benefactor shouted, dismounting to stand beside me. "Here's a new recruit!" To me he announced, "Severian of Nessus, you're standing in the presence of the Eighteenth Bacele of the Irregular Contarii, every one of us a fighter of dauntless courage whenever there's a speck of money to be made."

The ragged men and women were standing and drifting toward us, many of them frankly grinning. A tall and very thin man led the way.

"Comrades, I give you Severian of Nessus!

"Severian," my benefactor continued, "I'm your condottiere. Call me Guasacht. This fishing pole here, taller even than you are, is my second, Erblon. The rest will introduce themselves, I'm sure.

"Erblon, I want to talk to you. There'll be patrols tomorrow." He took the tall man by the arm and led him into the tent, leaving me with the crowd of troopers who had by now surrounded me.

One of the largest, an ursine man almost my height and at least twice my weight, gestured toward the falchion. "Don't you have a scabbard for that? Let's see it."

I surrendered it without argument; whatever might happen next, I felt certain it would not be an occasion for killing.

"So, you're a rider, are you?"

"No," I said. "I've ridden a bit, but I don't consider myself an expert."

"But you know how to manage them?"

"I know men and women better."

Everyone laughed at that, and the big man said, "Well, that's just fine, because you probably won't do much riding, but a good understanding of women—and destriers—will be a help to you."

As he spoke, I heard the sound of hoofs. Two men were leading up a piebald, muscular and wild-eyed. His reins had been divided and lengthened, permitting the men to stand at either side of his head, about three paces away. A trollop with fox-colored hair and a laughing face sat the saddle with ease, and in lieu of the reins held a riding whip in each hand. The troopers and their women cheered and clapped, and at the sound the piebald reared like a whirlwind and pawed the air, showing the three horny growths on each forefoot that we call hoofs for what they were—talons adapted almost as well to combat as to gripping turf. Their feints outsped my eyes.

The big man slapped me on the back. "He's not the best I ever had, but he's good enough, and I trained him myself. Mesrop and Lactan there are going to pass you those reins, and all you have to do is get up on him. If you can do it without knocking Daria off, you can have her until we run you down." He raised his voice: *"All right, let him go!"*

I had expected the two men to give me the reins. Instead they threw them at my face, and in snatching for them I missed them both. Someone goaded the piebald from behind, and the big man gave a peculiar, piercing whistle. The piebald had been taught to fight, like the destriers in the Bear Tower, and though his long teeth had not been augmented with metal, they had been left as nature made them and stood out from his mouth like knives.

I dodged a flashing forefoot and tried to grasp his halter; a blow from one of the whips caught me full across the face, and the piebald's rush knocked me sprawling.

The troopers must have held him back or I would have been trampled. Perhaps they also helped me to my feet—I cannot be sure. My throat was full of dust, and blood from my forehead trickled into my eyes.

I went for him again, circling to the right to keep clear of his hoofs, but he turned more quickly than I, and the girl called Daria snapped both lashes before my face to throw me off. More from anger than any plan I seized one. The thong of the whipstock was around her wrist; when I jerked the lash she came with it, falling into my arms. She bit my ear, but I got her by the back of the neck, spun her around, dug fingers into one firm buttock and lifted her. Kicking the air, her legs seemed to startle the piebald. I backed him through the crowd until one of his tormentors goaded him toward me, then stepped on his reins.

After that, it was easy. I dropped the girl, caught his halter, twisted his head, and kicked his forefeet from under him as we were taught to do with unruly clients. With a high-pitched, animal scream he came crashing down. I was in the saddle before he could get his legs beneath him, and from there I lashed his flanks with the long reins and sent him bolting through the crowd, then turned him and charged them again.

All my life I had heard of the excitement of this kind of fighting, though I had never experienced it. Now I found everything more than true. The troopers and their women were yelling and running, and a few flourished swords. They might have threatened a thunderstorm with more effect—I rode over half a dozen at a sweep. The girl's red hair flew like a banner as she fled, but no human legs could have outdistanced that steed. We flashed past her, and I caught her by that flaming banner and threw her over the arcione before me.

A twisting trail led to a dark ravine, and that ravine to another. Deer scattered ahead of us; in three bounds we overtook a buck in velvet and shouldered him out of the way. While I had been Lictor of Thrax, I had heard that the eclectics often raced game and leaped from their mounts to stab it. I believed those stories now—I could have cut the buck's throat with a butcher knife.

We left him behind, crested a new hill and dashed down into a silent, wooded valley. When the piebald had run himself out, I let him find his own path among the trees, which were the largest I had seen since leaving Saltus; and when he stopped to crop the sparse, tender grass that grew between their roots, I halted and threw the reins on the ground as I had seen Guasacht do, then dismounted and helped the red-haired girl off.

"Thanks," she said. And then, "You did it. I didn't think you could."

"Or you wouldn't have agreed to this? I had supposed they made you."

"I wouldn't have given you that cut with the whip. You'll want to repay me now, won't you? With the reins, I suppose."

"What makes you think that?" I was tired and sat down. Yellow flowers, each blossom no bigger than a drop of water, grew in the grass; I picked a few and found they smelled of calambac.

"You look the type. Besides, you carried me bottom up, and men who do that always want to hit it."

"I never knew that. It's an interesting thought."

"I have a lot of them—that kind." Quickly and gracefully she seated herself beside me and put a hand on my knee. "Listen, it was the initiation, that's all. We take turns, and it was my turn and I was supposed to hit you. Now it's over."

"I understand."

"Then you won't hurt me? That's wonderful. We can have a good time here, really. Whatever you want and as much as you want, and we won't go back until it's time to eat."

"I didn't say I wouldn't hurt you."

Her face, which had been wreathed with forced smiles, fell, and she looked at the ground. I suggested that she might run away.

"That would only make it more fun for you, and you'd hurt me more before we were through." Her hand crept up my thigh as she spoke. "You're nice looking, you know. And so tall." She made a sitting bow, pressing her face into my lap to give me a tingling kiss, then straightening up at once. "It could be nice. Really it could."

"Or you could kill yourself. Have you a knife?"

For an instant, her mouth formed a perfect little circle. "You're crazy, aren't you? I should have known." She leaped to her feet.

I caught her by one ankle and sent her sprawling to the soft forest floor. Her shift was rotten with wear—a pull and it fell away. "You said you wouldn't run."

She looked over her shoulder at me with large eyes.

I said, "You have no power over me, neither you nor they. I am not afraid of pain, or of death. There is only one living woman I desire, and no man but myself."

XX

Patrol

We held a perimeter no more than a couple of hundred paces across. For the most part, our enemies had only knives and axes—the axes and their ragged clothes recalled the volunteers I had helped Vodalus against in our necropolis—but there were hundreds of them already, and more coming.

The bacele had saddled up and left camp before dawn. The shadows were still long, somewhere along the shifting front, when a scout showed Guasacht the deep ruts of a coach traveling north. For three watches we tracked it.

The Ascian raiders who had captured it fought well, turning south to surprise us, then west, then north again like a writhing serpent; but always leaving a trail of dead, caught between our fire and that of the guards inside, who shot them through the loopholes. It was only toward the end, when the Ascians could no longer flee, that we grew aware of other hunters.

By noon, the little valley was surrounded. The gleaming steel coach with its dead and dying prisoners stood mired to the axles. Our Ascian prisoners squatted in front of it, guarded by our wounded. The Ascian officer spoke our tongue, and a watch earlier Guasacht had ordered him to free the coach and shot several Ascians when he had failed; thirty or more remained, nearly naked, listless and empty-eyed. Their weapons were piled some distance off, near our tethered mounts.

Now Guasacht was making the rounds, and I saw him pause at the stump that sheltered the trooper next to me. One of the enemy put her head from behind a clump of brush some way up the slope. My contus struck her with a bolt of flame; she leaped by reflex, then curled up as spiders do when someone tosses them among the coals of a campfire.

She had been white-faced beneath her red bandana, and I suddenly understood that she had been made to look—that there were those behind that brush who had disliked her, or at least not valued her, and who had forced her to look out. I fired again, slashing the green growth with the bolt and bringing a puff of acrid smoke that drifted toward me like her ghost.

"Don't waste those charges," Guasacht said at my elbow. More from habit, I think, than from fear, he had thrown himself flat beside me.

I asked if the charges would be exhausted before night if I fired six times a watch.

He shrugged, then shook his head.

"That's how fast I've been shooting this thing, as well as I can judge by the sun. And when night comes . . ."

I looked at him, and he could only shrug again.

"When night comes," I continued, "we won't be able to see them until they're only a few steps away. We'll fire more or less at random and kill a few score, then draw swords and stand back to back, and they'll kill us."

He said, "Help will arrive before then," and when he saw I did not believe him, he spat. "I wish I'd never looked at the damned thing's track. I wish I'd never heard of it."

It was my turn to shrug. "Give it back to the Ascians, and we'll break out."

"It's coin, I tell you! Gold to pay our troops. It's too heavy to be anything else."

"The armor must weigh a good deal."

"Not that much. I've seen these coaches before, and it's gold from Nessus or the House Absolute. But those things inside—who's ever seen such creatures?"

"I have."

Guasacht stared at me.

"When I went out through the Piteous Gate in the Wall of Nessus. They are man-beasts, contrived by the same lost arts that made our destriers faster than the road engines of old." I tried to recall what else Jonas had told me of them, and finished rather weakly by saying, "The Autarch employs them in duties too laborious for men, or for which men cannot be trusted."

"I suppose that might be right enough. They can't very well steal the money. Where would they go? Listen, I've had my eye on you."

"I know," I said. "I've felt it."

"I've had my eye on you, I say. Particularly since you made that piebald of yours go for the man that trained him. Up here in Orithyia we see a lot of strong men and a lot of brave ones—mostly when we step over their bodies. We see a lot of smart ones too, and nineteen out of twenty are too smart to be of use to anybody, including themselves. What's valuable are men, and sometimes women, who've got a kind of power, the power that makes other people want to do what they say. I don't mean to brag, but I've got it. You've got it too."

"It hasn't been overwhelmingly apparent in my life before this."

"Sometimes it takes the war to bring it out. That's one of the benefits of the war, and since it hasn't got many we ought to appreciate the ones it does. Severian, I want you to go down to the coach and treat with these man-animals. You say you know something about them. Get them to come out and help us fight. We're both on the same side, after all."

I nodded. "And if I can get them to open the doors, we can divide the money among us. Some of us, at least, may escape."

Guasacht shook his head in disgust. "What did I tell you just a moment ago about being too smart? If you were really smart, you wouldn't have ignored it. No, you tell them that even if there's only three or four of them, every fighter counts. Besides, there's at least a chance the sight of them will frighten these damn freebooters away. Let me have your contus, and I'll hold your position for you until you come back."

I handed over the long weapon. "Who are these people, anyway?"

"These? Camp followers. Sutlers and whores—men as well as women. Deserters. Every so often the Autarch or one of his generals has them rounded up and put to work, but they slip away before long. Slipping away's their specialty. They ought to be wiped out."

"I have your authority to treat with our prisoners in the coach? You'll back me up?"

"They're not prisoners—well, yes, I suppose they are. You tell them what I said and make the best deal you can. I'll back you."

I looked at him for a moment, trying to decide whether he meant it. Like so many middle-aged men, he carried the old man he would become in his face, soured and obscene, already muttering the objections and complaints that would be his in the final skirmish.

"You've got my word. Go on."

"All right." I rose. The armored coach resembled the carriages that had been used to bring important clients to our tower in the Citadel. Its windows were narrow and barred, its rear wheels as high as a man. The smooth steel sides suggested those lost arts I had mentioned to Guasacht, and I knew the man-beasts inside had better weapons than ours. I extended my hands to show I was unarmed and walked as steadily as I could toward them until a face showed at one window grill.

When one hears of such creatures, one imagines something stable, midway between beast and human; but when one actually sees them—as I now saw this man-beast, and as I had seen the manapes in the mine near Saltus—they are not like that at all. The best comparison I can make is to the flickering of a silver birch tossed by the wind. At one moment it seems a common tree, at the next, when the undersides of the leaves appear, a supernatural creation. So it is with the man-beasts. At first I thought a mastiff peered at me through the bars; then it seemed rather a man, nobly ugly, tawny-faced and amber-eyed. I raised my hands to the grill to give him my scent, thinking of Triskele.

"What do you want?" His voice was harsh but not unpleasant.

"I want to save your lives," I said. It was the wrong thing to say, and I knew it as soon as the words had left my mouth.

"We want to save our honor."

I nodded. "Honor is the higher life."

"If you can tell us how to save our honor, speak. We will listen. But we will never surrender our trust."

"You have already surrendered it," I said.

The wind died, and the mastiff was back in an instant, flashing teeth and blazing eyes.

"It was not to safeguard gold from the Ascians that you were put into this coach, but to safeguard it from those of our own Commonwealth who would steal it if they could. The Ascians are beaten—look at them. We are the Autarch's loyal humans. Those you were set to guard against will overwhelm us soon."

"They must kill me and my fellows before they can get the gold."

It *was* gold, then. I said, "They will do so. Come out and help us fight, while there is still a chance of victory."

He hesitated, and I was no longer sure that I had been entirely wrong to speak first of saving his life. "No," he said. "We cannot. What you say may be reason, I do not know. Our law is not the law of reason. Our law is honor and obedience. We stay."

"But you know that we are not your enemies?"

"Anyone seeking what we guard is our enemy."

"We're guarding it too. If these camp followers and deserters came within range of your weapons, would you fire on them?"

"Yes, of course."

I walked over to the spiritless cluster of Ascians and asked to speak with their commander. The man who stood was only slightly taller than the rest; the intelligence in his face was the kind one sometimes sees in cunning madmen. I told him Guasacht had sent me to treat in his stead because I had often spoken with Ascian prisoners and knew their ways.

This was, as I intended, overheard by his three wounded guards, who could see Guasacht manning my position on the perimeter.

"Greetings in the name of the Group of Seventeen," the Ascian said.

"In the name of the Group of Seventeen."

The Ascian looked startled but nodded.

"We are surrounded by the disloyal subjects of our Autarch, who are thus the enemies of both the Autarch and the Group of Seventeen. Our own commander, Guasacht, has devised a plan that will leave us all alive and free."

"The servants of the Group of Seventeen must not be expended without purpose."

"Precisely. Here is the plan. We will harness some of our destriers to the steel coach—as many as necessary to pull it free. You and your people must work to free it too. When it's free, we'll return your weapons and help you fight your way out of this cordon. Your soldiers and ours will go north, and you can keep the coach and the money inside to take to your superiors, just as you hoped when you captured it."

"The light of Correct Thought penetrates every darkness."

"No, we haven't gone over to the Group of Seventeen. You have to help us in return. In the first place, help get the coach out of the mud. In the second, help us fight our way out. In the third, provide us with an escort that will get us through your army and back to our own lines."

The Ascian officer glanced toward the gleaming coach. "No failure is permanent failure. But inevitable success may require new plans and greater strength."

"Then you approve of my new plan?" I had not been aware that I was perspiring, but now the sweat ran stinging into my eyes. I wiped my forehead with the edge of my cloak, just as Master Gurloes used to.

The Ascian officer nodded. "Study of Correct Thought eventually reveals the path of success."

"Yes," I said. "All right, I've studied it. Behind our efforts, let there be found our efforts."

When I returned to the coach, the same man-beast I had seen before came to the window again, not quite so hostile this time. I said, "The Ascians have agreed to try to push this thing out once more. We're going to have to unload it."

"That is impossible."

"If we don't, the gold will be lost with the sun. I'm not asking you to give it up—just take it out and mount guard over it. You'll have your weapons, and if any human bearing arms comes close to you, you can kill him. I'll be with you, unarmed. You can kill me too."

It took a great deal more talking, but eventually they did it. I got the wounded who had been watching the Ascians to lay down their conti and harness eight of our destriers to the coach, and got the Ascians positioned to pull on the harness and heave at the wheels. Then the door in the side of the steel coach swung open and the man-beasts carried out small metal chests, two working while the one I had spoken to stood guard. They were taller than I had expected and had fusils, with pistols in their belts to supplement them—the first pistols I had seen since I had watched the Hierodules use them to turn Baldanders's charges in the gardens of the House Absolute.

When all the chests were out and the three man-beasts were standing around them with their weapons at the ready, I shouted. The wounded troopers lashed every destrier in the new team, the Ascians heaved until their eyes started from their straining faces . . . and just when we all thought it would not, the steel coach lifted itself from the mud and lumbered half a chain before the wounded could bring it to a halt. Guasacht nearly got us both killed by running down from the perimeter waving my contus, but the man-beasts had just sense enough to see that he was merely excited and not dangerous.

He got a great deal more excited when he saw the man-beasts carry their gold inside again, and when he heard what I had promised the Ascians. I reminded him that he had given me leave to act in his name.

"When I act," he sputtered, "it's with the idea of winning."

I confessed I lacked his military experience, but told him I had found that in some situations winning consisted of disentangling oneself.

"Just the same, I had hoped you would work out something better."

Rising inexorably while we remained unaware of their motion, the mountain peaks to the west were already clawing for the lower edge of the sun; I pointed to it.

Suddenly, Guasacht smiled. "After all, these are the same Ascians we took it from before."

He called the Ascian officer over and told him our mounted troopers would lead the attack, and that his soldiers could follow the steel coach on foot. The Ascian agreed, but when his soldiers had rearmed themselves, he insisted on placing half a dozen on top of the coach and leading the attack himself with the rest. Guasacht agreed with an apparent bad grace that seemed to me entirely assumed. We put an armed trooper astride each of the eight destriers of the new team, and I saw Guasacht conversing earnestly with their cornet.

I had promised the Ascian we would break through the cordon of deserters to the north, but the ground in that direction proved to be unsuited to the steel coach, and in the end a route north by northwest was agreed upon. The Ascian infantry advanced at a pace not much short of a full run, firing as they came. The coach followed. The narrow, enduring bolts of the troopers' conti stabbed at the ragged mob who tried to close about it, and the Ascian arquebuses on its roof sent gouts of violet energy crashing among them. The man-beasts fired their fusils from the barred windows, slaughtering half a dozen with a single blast.

The remainder of our troops (I among them) followed the coach, having maintained our perimeter until it was gone. To save precious charges, many put their conti through the saddle rings, drew their swords, and rode down the straggling remnant the Ascians and the coach had left behind.

Then the enemy was past, and the ground clearer. At once the troopers whose mounts pulled the coach clapped spurs to them, and Guasacht, Erblon, and several others who were riding just behind it swept the Ascians from its top in a cloud of crimson flame and reeking smoke. Those on foot scattered, then turned to fire.

It was a fight I did not feel I could take part in. I reined up, and so saw—I believe, before any of the others—the first of the anpiels who dropped, like the angel in Melito's fable, from the sun-dyed clouds. They were fair to look upon, naked and having the slender bodies of young women; but their rainbow wings spread wider than any teratornis's, and each anpiel held a pistol in either hand.

Late that night, when we were back in camp and the wounded had been cared for, I asked Guasacht if he would do as he had again.

He thought for a moment. "I hadn't any way of knowing those flying girls would come. Looking at it from this end, it's natural enough—there must have been enough in that coach to pay half the army, and they wouldn't hesitate to send elite troops looking for it. But before it happened, would you have guessed it?"

I shook my head.

"Listen, Severian, I shouldn't be talking to you like this. But you did what you could, and you're the best leech I ever saw. Anyway, it came out all right in the end, didn't it? You saw how friendly their seraph was. What did she see, after all? Plucky lads trying to save the coach from the Ascians. We'll get a commendation, I should think. Maybe a reward."

I said, "You could have killed the man-beasts, and the Ascians too, when the gold was out of the coach. You didn't because I would have died with them. I think you deserve a commendation. From me, at least."

He rubbed his drawn face with both hands. "Well, I'm just as happy. It would have been the end of the Eighteenth; in another watch we'd have been killing each other for the money."

XXI

Deployment

Before the battle there were other patrols and days of idleness. Often enough we saw no Ascians, or saw only their dead. We were supposed to arrest deserters and drive from our area such peddlers and vagabonds as fatten on an army; but if they seemed to us such people as had surrounded the steel coach, we killed them, not executing them in any formal style but cutting them down from the saddle.

The moon waxed again nearly to the full, hanging like a green apple in the sky. Experienced troopers told me the worst fights always came at or near the full of the moon, which is said to breed madness. I suppose this is actually because its refulgence permits generals to bring up reinforcements by night.

On the day of the battle, the graisle's bray summoned us from our blankets at dawn. We formed a ragged double column in the mist, with Guasacht at our head and Erblon following him with our flag. I had supposed that the women would stay behind—as most had when we had gone on patrol—but more than half drew conti and came with us. Those who had helmets, I noticed, thrust their hair up into the bowl, and many wore corslets that flattened and concealed their breasts. I mentioned it to Mesrop, who rode opposite me.

"There might be trouble about the pay," he said. "Somebody with sharp eyes will be counting us, and the contracts usually call for men."

"Guasacht said there'd be more money today," I reminded him.

He cleared his throat and spat, the white phlegm vanishing into the clammy air as though Urth herself had swallowed it. "They won't pay until it's over. They never do."

Guasacht shouted and waved an arm; Erblon gestured with our flag, and we were off, the hoofbeats sounding like the thudding of a hundred muffled drums. I said, "I suppose that way they don't have to pay for those who are killed."

"They pay triple—once because he fought, once for blood money, and once for discharge money."

"Or she fought, I suppose."

Mesrop spat again.

We rode for some time, then halted at a spot that seemed no different from any other. As the column fell silent, I heard a humming or murmuring in the hills all around us. A scattered army, dispersed no doubt for sanitary reasons and to deprive the Ascian enemy of a concentrated target, was assembling now just as particles of dust in the stone town had come together in the bodies of its resuscitated dancers.

Not unnoticed. Even as birds of prey had once followed us before we reached that town, now five-armed shapes that spun like wheels pursued us above the scattered clouds that dimmed and melted in the level red light of dawn. At first, when they were highest, they seemed merely gray; but as we watched they dropped toward us, and I saw they were of a hue for which I can find no name but that stands to achroma as gold to yellow, or silver to white. The air groaned with their turning.

Another that we had not seen came leaping across our path, hardly higher than the treetops. Each spoke was the length of a tower, pierced with casements and ports. Though it lay flat upon the air, it seemed to stride along. Its wind whistled down upon us as if to blow away the trees. My piebald screamed and bolted, and so did many other destriers, often falling in that strange wind.

In the space of a heartbeat it was over. The leaves that had swirled about us like snow fell to earth. Guasacht shouted and Erblon sounded the graisle and brandished our flag. I got the piebald under control and cantered from one destrier to another, taking them by the nostrils until their riders could manage them again.

I rescued Daria, who I had not known was in the column, in this way. She looked very pretty and boyish dressed as a trooper, with a contus, and a slender sabre at either side of her saddle horn. I could not help thinking when I saw her of how other women I had known would appear in the same situation: Thea a theatrical warrior maid, beautiful and dramatic but essentially the figure of a figurehead; Thecla—now part of myself—a vengeful mimalone brandishing poisoned weapons; Agia astride a slender-legged sorrel, wearing a cuirass molded to her figure, while her hair, plaited with bowstrings, flew wild in the wind; Jolenta a floriate queen in armor spikey with thorns, her big breasts and fleshy thighs absurd at any gait faster than a walk, smiling dreamily at each halt and attempting to recline in the saddle; Dorcas a naiad riding, lifted momentarily like a fountain flashing with sunshine; Valeria, perhaps, an aristocratic Daria.

I had supposed, when I saw our people scatter, that it would be impossible to reassemble the column; but within a few moments of the time the pentadactyl air-strider had passed over us, we were together again. We galloped for a league or more—mostly, I suspect, to dissipate some of the nervous energy of our destriers—then halted by a brook and gave them just as much water as would wet their mouths without making them sluggish. When I had fought the piebald back from the bank, I rode to a clearing from which I could watch the sky. Soon Guasacht trotted over and asked me jocularly, "You looking for another one?"

I nodded and told him I had never seen such craft before.

"You wouldn't have, unless you've been close to the front. They'd never come back if they tried to go down south."

"Soldiers like us wouldn't stop them."

He grew suddenly serious, his tiny eyes mere slits in the sun-browned flesh. "No. But plucky lads can stop their raiding parties. The guns and air-galleys can't do that."

The piebald stirred and stamped with impatience. I said, "I come from a part of the city you've probably never heard of, the Citadel. There are guns there that look out over the whole quarter, but I've never known them to be fired except ceremonially." Still staring at the sky, I thought of the wheeling pentadactyls over Nessus, and a thousand blasts, issuing not just from the Barbican and the Great Keep, but from all the towers; and I wondered with what weapons the pentadactyls would reply.

"Come along," Guasacht said. "I know it's a temptation to keep a lookout for them, but it doesn't do any good."

I followed him back to the brook, where Erblon was lining up the column. "They didn't even fire at us. They must surely have guns in those fliers."

"We're pretty small fish." I could see that Guasacht wanted me to rejoin the column, though he hesitated to order me to do so directly.

For my part, I could feel fear grip me like a specter, strongest about my legs, but lifting cold tentacles into my bowels, touching my heart. I wanted to be silent, but I could not stop talking. "When we go onto the field of battle—" (I think I imagined this field like the shaven lawn of the Sanguinary Field, where I had fought Agilus.)

Guasacht laughed. "When we go into the fight, our gunners would be delighted to see them out after us." Before I understood what he was about to do, he struck the piebald with the flat of his blade and sent me cantering off.

Fear is like those diseases that disfigure the face with running sores. One becomes almost more afraid of their being seen than of their source, and comes to feel not only disgraced but defiled. When the piebald began to slow, I dug my heels into him and fell into line at the very end of the column.

Only a short time before I had been on the point of replacing Erblon; now I was demoted, not by Guasacht but by myself, to the lowest position. And yet when I had helped reassemble the scattered troopers, the thing I feared had already passed; so that the entire drama of my elevation had been played out after it had ended in debasement. It was as though one were to see a young man idling in a public garden stabbed—then watch him, all unknowing, strike up an acquaintance with the voluptuous wife of his murderer, and at last, having ascertained, as he thought, that her husband was in another part of the city, clasp her to him until she cried out from the pain of the dagger's hilt protruding from his chest.

When the column lurched forward, Daria detached herself from it and waited until she could fall in beside me. "You're afraid," she said. It was not a question but a statement, and not a reproach but almost a password, like the ridiculous phrases I had learned at Vodalus's banquet.

"Yes. You're about to remind me of the boast I made to you in the forest. I can only say that I did not know it to be an empty one when I made it. A certain wise man once tried to teach me that even after a client has mastered one excruciation, so that he can put it from his mind even while he screams and writhes, another quite different excruciation may be as effectual in breaking his will as in breaking a child's. I learned to explain all this when he asked me but never until now to apply it, as I should, to my own life. But if I am the client here, who is the torturer?"

"We're all more or less afraid," she said. "That was why— yes, I saw it—Guasacht sent you away. It was to keep you from making his own feeling worse. If it were worse, he wouldn't be able to lead. When the time comes, you'll do what you have to, and that's all any of them do."

"Hadn't we better go?" I asked. The end of the column was moving off in that surging way the tail of a long line always does.

"If we go now, a lot of them will know we're at the rear because we're afraid. If we wait just a little while longer, many of those who saw you talking with Guasacht will think he sent you back here to speed up stragglers, and that I came back to be with you."

"All right," I said.

Her hand, damp with sweat and as thin as Dorcas's, came sliding into mine.

Until that moment, I had been certain she had fought before. Now I asked her, "Is this your first time too?"

"I can fight better than most of them," she declared, "and I'm sick of being called a whore."

Together, we trotted after the column.

XXII

Battle

I saw them first as a scattering of colored dots on the farther side of the wide valley, skirmishers who seemed to move and mix, as bubbles do that dance upon the surface of a mug of cider. We were trotting through a grove of shattered trees whose white and naked wood was like the living bone of a compound fracture. Our column was much larger now, perhaps the whole of the irregular contarii. It had been under fire, in a more or less dilatory way, for about half a watch. Some troopers had been wounded (one, near me, quite badly) and several killed. The wounded cared for themselves and tried to help each other—if there were medical attendants for us they were too far behind us for me to be conscious of them.

From time to time we passed corpses among the trees; usually these were in little clusters of two or three, sometimes they were merely solitary individuals. I saw one who had contrived in dying to hook the collar of his brigandine jacket to a splinter protruding from one of the broken trunks, and I was struck by the horror of his situation, his being dead and yet unable to rest, and then by the thought that such was the plight of all those thousands of trees, trees that had been killed but could not fall.

At about the same time I became aware of the enemy, I realized that there were troops of our own army to either side. To our right a mixture, as it were, of mounted men and infantry, the riders helmetless and naked to the waist, with red and blue blanket rolls slung across their bronzed chests. They were better mounted, I thought, than most of us. They carried lancegays not much longer than the height of a man, many of them holding them aslant their saddle-bows. Each had a small copper shield bound to the upper part of his left arm. I had no idea from what part of the Commonwealth these men might come; but for some reason, perhaps only because of their long hair and bare chests, I felt sure they were savages.

If they were, the infantry that moved among them was something lower still, brown and stooped and shaggy-haired. I had only glimpses through the broken trees, but I thought they dropped to all fours at times. Occasionally one seemed to grasp the stirrup of some rider, as I had sometimes taken Jonas's when he rode his merychip; whenever that occurred, the rider struck at his companion's hand with the butt of his weapon.

A road ran through lower ground to our left; and down it, and to either side of it, there moved a force far more numerous than our column and the savage riders and their companions all combined: battalions of peltasts with blazing spears and big, transparent shields; hobilers on prancing mounts, with bows and arrow cases crossed over their backs; lightly armed cherkajis whose formations were seas of plumes and flags.

I could know nothing of the courage of all these strange soldiers who had suddenly become my comrades, but I unconsciously assumed it to be no greater than my own, and they seemed a slender defense indeed against the moving dots on the farther side. The fire to which we were subjected grew more intense, and so far as I could see, our enemies were under none at all.

Only a few weeks before (though it felt like at least a year now) I would have been terrified at the thought of being shot at with such a weapon as Vodalus had used on the foggy night in our necropolis with which I have begun this account. The bolts that struck all around us made that simple beam appear as childish as the shining slugs thrown from the hetman's archer's pellet bow.

I had no idea what sort of device was used to project these bolts, or even whether they were in fact pure energy or some type of missile; but as they landed among us, their nature was that of an explosion lengthened into something like a rod. And though they could not be seen until they struck, they whistled as they came, and by that whistled note, which endured no longer than the blink of an eye, I soon learned to tell how near they would hit and how powerful the extended detonation would be. If there was no change in the tone, so that it resembled the note a coryphaeus sounds on his pitch pipe, the strike would be some distance off. But if it rose quickly, as though a note first sounded for men had become one for women, its impact would be nearby; and though only the loudest of the monotonal bolts were dangerous, each that rose to a scream claimed at least one of us and often several.

It seemed madness to trot forward as we did. We should have scattered, or dismounted to take refuge among the trees; and if one of us had done it, I think all the rest would have followed him. With every bolt that fell, I was almost that one. But again and again, as if my mind were chained in some narrow circle, the memory of the fear I had shown earlier held me in my place. Let the rest run and I would run with them; but I would not run first.

Inevitably, a bolt struck parallel to our column. Six troopers flew apart as though they themselves had contained small bombs, the head of the first bursting in a gout of scarlet, the neck and shoulders of the second, the chest of the third, the bellies of the fourth and fifth, and the groin (or perhaps on the saddle and the back of his destrier) of the sixth, before the bolt struck the ground and sent up a geyser of dust and stones. The men and animals opposite those who were destroyed in this way were killed too, wracked by the force of the explosions and bombarded with the limbs and armor of the others.

Holding the piebald to a trot, and often to a walk, was the worst of it; if I could not run, I wanted to press forward, to get the fighting begun, to die if I was in fact to die. This hit gave me some opportunity to relieve my feelings. Waving to Daria to follow, I let the piebald lope past the little group of survivors who had been riding between us and the last trooper to die, and moved into the space in the column that had been the casualties'. Mesrop was there already, and he grinned at me. "Good thinking. Chances are there won't be another one here for quite a while." I forbore to disabuse him.

For a time it seemed he was correct anyway. Having hit us, the enemy gunners diverted their fire to the savages on our right. Their shambling infantry shrieked and gibbered as the bolts fell among them, but the riders reacted, so it appeared, by calling on magic to protect them. Often their chants sounded so clearly that I could make out the words, though they were in no language I had ever heard. Once one actually stood on his saddle like a performer in a riding exhibition, lifting a hand to the sun and extending the other toward the Ascians. Each rider seemed to have a personal spell; and it was easy to see, as I watched their numbers shrink under the bombardment, how such primitive minds come to believe in their charms, for the survivors could not but feel their thaumaturgy had saved them, and the rest could not complain of the failure of theirs.

Though we were advancing, for the most part, at the trot, we were not the first to engage the enemy. On the lower ground, the cherkajis had streaked across the valley, crashing against a square of foot soldiers like a wave of fire.

I had vaguely supposed that the enemy would be provided with weapons far superior to anything we had in the contarii—perhaps pistols and fusils, such as the man-beasts had carried—and that a hundred fighters so armed would easily destroy any quantity of cavalry. Nothing of the kind happened. Several rows of the square gave way, and I was close enough now to hear the riders' war cries, distant yet distinct, and see individual foot soldiers in flight. Some were casting aside immense shields, shields even larger than the glassy ones of the peltasts, though they shone with the luster of metal. Their offensive arms seemed to be splay-headed spears no more than three cubits long, weapons that could produce sheets of cleaving flame, but short in range.

A second infantry square emerged behind the first, then another and another, farther down the valley.

Just as I was sure we were about to ride to the assistance of the cherkajis, we received the order to halt. Looking to the right, I saw that the savages had already done so, stopping some distance behind us, and were now driving the hairy creatures that had accompanied them toward the side of their position farthest from us.

Guasacht called, "We're blocking! Sit easy, lads!"

I looked at Daria, who returned a look equally bewildered. Mesrop waved an arm toward the eastern end of the valley. "We're watching the flank. If nobody comes, we ought to have a good enough time of it today."

I said, "Except for the ones who've already died." The bombardment, which had been diminishing, now seemed to have stopped altogether. The silence of its absence lay all about us, almost more frightening than its screaming bolts had been.

"I suppose so." His shrug announced eloquently that we had lost a few dozen from a force of hundreds.

The cherkajis had recoiled, retreating behind a screen of hobilers who directed a shower of arrows at the leading edge of the Ascians' checkerboard battle line. Most seemed to glance off the shields, but a few must have buried their heads in the metal, which took fire from them and burned with a flame as bright as theirs and billowing white smoke.

When the arrows slackened, the squares of the checkerboard advanced again with a mechanical jerkiness. The cherkajis had continued to fall back and were now in the rear of a line of peltasts, very little in advance of us. I could see their dark faces clearly. They were all men and bearded, and numbered about two thousand; but they had among them a dozen or so bejeweled young women borne in gilded howdahs on the backs of caparisoned arsinoithers.

These women were dark-eyed and dark complexioned like the men, yet in their lush figures and languishing looks they reminded me of

Jolenta. I pointed them out to Daria and asked if she knew how they were armed, since I could see no weapons.

"You'd like one, would you? Or two. I'll bet they look good to you even from here."

Mesrop winked and said, "I wouldn't mind a couple myself."

Daria laughed. "They'd fight like alraunes if either of you tried to have anything to do with them. They're sacred and forbidden, the Daughters of War. Have you ever been around those animals they're riding?"

I shook my head.

"They charge easy and nothing stops them, but they always go the same way—straight at whatever it is that bothers them and past it for a chain or two. Then they stop and go back."

I watched. Arsinoithers have two big horns—not spreading horns like the horns of bulls, but horns that diverge about as much as a man's first and second fingers can. As I soon saw, they charge head down, with those horns level with the ground, and these did just as Daria had said. The cherkajis rallied and attacked again with their slender lances and forked swords. Trailing far behind that lightning dash, the arsinoithers lumbered forward, gray-black heads down and tails up, with the deep-bosomed, dark-faced maidens standing erect under their canopies and gripping the gilded poles. One could see from the way these women held themselves that their thighs were as full as the udders of milch cows and round as the trunks of trees.

The charge carried them through the swirling fight and deep—but not too deep—into the checkerboard. The Ascian foot soldiers blasted the sides of their beasts, which must have been like burning horn or *cuir boli*; they tried to mount their heads and were tossed into the air; they struggled to climb the gray flanks. The cherkajis came crashing to the rescue, and the checkerboard flowed and ebbed and lost a square.

Watching it from such a distance, I recalled my own thoughts of battle as a game of chess, and I felt that somewhere someone else had entertained the same thoughts and unconsciously allowed them to shape his plan.

"They're lovely," Daria continued, teasing me. "Chosen at twelve and fed on honey and pure oils. I've heard their flesh is so tender they can't lie on the ground without being bruised. Bags of feathers are carried about for them to sleep on. If those are lost, the girls have to lie in mud that shapes itself to support their bodies. The eunuchs who care for them mix it with wine warmed over a fire, so they will sleep and not be cold."

"We should dismount," Mesrop said. "It'll spare the animals."

But I wanted to watch the battle and would not get down, though soon only Guasacht and I remained in the saddle out of our entire bacele.

The cherkajis had been driven back once again, and now came under a withering bombardment from unseen artillery. The peltasts dropped to the ground, covering themselves with their shields. New squares of Ascian infantry emerged from the forest on the north side of the valley. There seemed to be no end to them; I felt we had been committed against an inexhaustible enemy.

The feeling grew stronger when the cherkajis charged a third time. A bolt struck an arsinoither, blowing it and the lovely woman it had carried to bloody ruin. The infantry was firing at those women now; one crumpled, and howdah and canopy vanished in a puff of flame. The infantry squares advanced over brightly clad corpses and dead destriers.

By each step in war the winner loses. The ground the checkerboard had won exposed the side of its leading square to us, and to my astonishment we were ordered to mount, spread into line, and wheeled against it, first trotting, then cantering, and at last, with the brass throats of all the graisles shouting, in a desperate rush that nearly blew the skin from our faces.

If the cherkajis were lightly armed, we were armed more lightly still. Yet there was a magic in the charge more powerful than the chants of our savage allies. The wildfire of our weapons played along the distant ranks as scythes attack a wheat field. I lashed the piebald with his reins to keep from being outdistanced by the roaring hoofs I heard behind me. Yet I was, and glimpsed Daria as she shot past, the flame of her hair flying free, her contus in one hand and a sabre in the other, her cheeks whiter than the foaming flanks of her destrier. I knew then how the custom of the cherkajis had begun, and I tried to charge faster still so that she should not die, though Thecla laughed through my lips at the thought.

Destriers do not run like common beasts—they skim the ground as arrows do air. For an instant, the fire of the Ascian infantry half a league away rose before us like a wall. A moment later we were among them, the legs of every mount bloody to the knee. The square that had seemed as solid as a building stone had become only a crowd of frantic soldiers with big shields and cropped heads, soldiers who often slew one another in their eagerness to slay us.

Fighting is a stupid business at best; but there are things to be learned about it, of which the first is that numbers tell only in time. The immediate struggle is always that of an individual against one or two others. In this our destriers gave us the upper hand—not only because of their height and weight, but because they bit and struck out with their forefeet, and the blows of their hoofs were more powerful than any man save Baldanders could have delivered with a mace.

Fire cut through my contus. I dropped it but continued to kill, slashing left, then right, then left again with the falchion and hardly noticing that the blast had laid open my leg.

I think I must have cut down half a dozen Ascians before I saw that they all looked the same—not that they all had the same face (as the men in some units of our own army do, who are indeed closer than brothers), but that the differences among them seemed accidental and trivial. I had observed this among our prisoners when we had retrieved the steel coach, but it had not really impressed itself upon my mind. In the madness of battle it did so, for it seemed a part of that madness. The frenzied figures were male and female: the women had small but pendulous breasts and were half a head shorter, but there was no other distinction. All had large, brilliant, wild eyes, hair clipped nearly to the skull, starved faces, screaming mouths, and prominent teeth.

We fought free as the cherkajis had; the square had been dented but not destroyed. While we let our mounts catch breath it reformed, the light, polished shields to the front. A spearman broke ranks and came running toward us waving his weapon. At first I thought it mere bluster; then, as he came nearer (for a normal man runs much less swiftly than a destrier), that he wished to surrender. At last, when he had almost reached our line, he fired, and a trooper shot him down. In his convulsions he threw his blazing spear into the air; I remember how it twisted against the dark blue sky.

Guasacht came trotting over. "You're bleeding bad. Can you ride when we charge them again?"

I felt as strong as I ever had in my life and told him so.

"Still, you'd better get a bandage on that leg."

The seared flesh had cracked; blood was oozing out. Daria, who had not been hurt at all, bound it up.

The charge for which I had been prepared never took place. Quite unexpectedly (at least as far as I was concerned) the order came to turn about, and we went trotting off to the northeast over open, rolling country whisperous with coarse grass.

The savages seemed to have vanished. A new force appeared in their place, on the flank that had now become our front. At first I thought they were cavalry on centaurs, creatures whose pictures I had encountered in the brown book. I could see the heads and shoulders of the riders above the human heads of their mounts, and both appeared to bear arms. When they drew nearer, I saw they were nothing so romantic:

merely small men—dwarfs, in fact—upon the shoulders of very tall ones.

Our directions of advance were nearly parallel but slowly converged. The dwarfs watched us with what seemed a sullen attention. The tall men did not look at us at all. At last, when our column was no more than a couple of chains from theirs, we halted and turned to face them. With a horror I had not felt before, I realized that these strange riders and strange steeds were Ascians; our maneuver had been intended to prevent them from taking the peltasts in the flank, and had now succeeded in that they would now have to make their attack, if they could, through us. There seemed to be about five thousand of them, however, and there were certainly many more than we had fit to fight.

Yet no attack came. We had halted and formed a tight line, stirrup to stirrup. Despite their numbers, they surged nervously up and down before it as though attracted first by the thought of passing it on the right, then on the left, then on the right again. It was clear, however, that they could not pass at all unless a part of their force engaged our front to prevent our striking the rest from behind. As if hoping to postpone the fight, we did not fire.

Now we saw repetitions of the behavior of the lone spearman who had left his square to attack us. One of the tall men dashed forward. In one hand he held a slender staff, hardly more than a switch; in the other, a sword of the kind called a *shotel*, which has a very long, double-edged blade whose forward half is curved into a semicircle. As he drew nearer he slowed, and I saw that his eyes were unfocused; that he was in fact blind. The dwarf on his shoulders had an arrow nocked to the string of a short, recurved bow.

When these two were within half a chain of us, Erblon detailed two men to drive them off. Before they could close with the blind man, he broke into a run as swift as any destrier's but eerily silent, and came flying toward us. Eight or ten troopers fired, but I saw then how difficult it is to hit a target moving at such speed. The arrow struck and burst in a blaze of orange light. A trooper tried to parry the blind man's wand—the shotel flashed down, and its hooked blade laid open the trooper's skull.

Then a group of three of the blind men with three riders detached itself from the mass of the enemy. Before they reached us, there were clusters of five or six coming. Far down the line, our hipparch raised his arm; Guasacht waved us forward and Erblon blew the charge, echoed to right and left—a bellowing note that seemed to have deep-mouthed bells in it.

Though I did not know it at the time, it is axiomatic that encounters purely between cavalry rapidly degenerate into mere skirmishes. So it was with ours. We rode at them, and though we lost twenty or thirty in doing so, we rode through them. At once we turned to engage them again, both to prevent their flanking the peltasts and to regain contact with our own army. They, of course, turned to face us; and in a short time neither we nor they had anything that could be called a front, or any tactics beyond those each fighter forged for himself.

My own were to veer away from any dwarf who looked ready to shoot and try to catch others from behind or from the side. They worked well enough when I could apply them, but I quickly found that though the dwarfs appeared almost helpless when the blind men they rode were killed under them, their tall steeds ran amok without their riders, attacking anything that stood in their path with frantic energy, so that they were more dangerous than ever.

Very soon the dwarfs' arrows and our conti had kindled scores of fires in the grass. The choking smoke rendered the confusion worse than ever. I had lost sight of Daria and Guasacht—of everyone I knew—sometime before. Through the acrid gray haze I could just make out a figure on a plunging destrier fighting off four Ascians. I went to him, and though one dwarf turned his blind steed and sent an arrow whizzing by my ear, I rode over them and heard the blind man's bones snap under the piebald's hoofs. A hairy figure rose from the smoldering grass behind the other pair and cut them down as a peon hews a tree—three or four strokes of his ax to the same spot until the blind man fell.

The mounted soldier I had come to rescue was not one of our troopers, but one of the savages who had been on our right earlier. He had been wounded, and when I saw the blood I recalled that I had been wounded too. My leg was stiff, my strength nearly gone. I would have ridden back toward the south crest of the valley and our own lines if I had known which way to go. As it was, I gave the piebald his head and a good slap from the reins, having heard that these animals will often return to the place where they last had water and rest. He broke into a canter that soon became a gallop. Once he jumped, nearly throwing me from the saddle, and I looked down to glimpse a dead destrier with Erblon dead beside him, and the brass graisle and the black and green flag lying on the burning turf. I would have turned the piebald and gone back for them, but by the time I pulled him up, I no longer knew the spot. To my right, a mounted line showed through the smoke, dark and almost formless, but serrated. Far behind it loomed a machine that flashed fire, a machine that was like a tower walking.

At one moment they were nearly invisible; at the next they were upon me like a torrent. I cannot say who the riders were or on what beasts they rode; not because I have forgotten (for I forget nothing) but because I saw nothing clearly. There was no question of fighting, only of seeking in some way to live. I parried a blow from a twisted weapon that was neither sword nor ax; the piebald reared, and I saw an arrow protruding from his chest like a horn of fire. A rider crashed against us, and we fell into the dark.

XXIII

The Pelagic Argosy Sights Land

When I regained consciousness, it was the pain in my leg that I felt first. It was pinned beneath the body of the piebald, and I struggled to free it almost before I knew who I was or how I found myself where I did. My hands and face, the very ground on which I lay, were crusted with blood.

And it was quiet—so quiet. I listened for the thudding of hoofs, the drum roll that makes Urth herself its drum. It was not there. The shouts of the cherkajis were no more, nor the shrill, mad cries that had come from the checkerboard of Ascian infantry. I tried to turn to push against the saddle, but I could not do so.

Somewhere far off, no doubt on one of the ridges that rimmed the valley, a dire wolf raised its maw to Lune. That inhuman howling, which Thecla had heard once or twice before when the court went to hunt near Silva, made me realize that the dimness of my sight was not due to the smoke of the grass fires that had burned earlier that day, or, as I had half feared, to some head injury. The land was twilit, though whether by dusk or dawn I could not say

I rested and perhaps I slept, then roused again at the sound of footsteps. It was darker than I remembered. The footsteps were slow, soft, and heavy. Not the sound of cavalry on the move, nor yet the measured tread of marching infantry—a walk heavier than Baldanders's and more slow. I opened my mouth to cry for help, then closed it again, thinking I might call upon myself something more terrible than that I had once waked in the mine of the man-apes. I lunged away from the dead piebald until it seemed I would wrench my leg from its socket. Another dire wolf, as frightful as the first and much closer, howled to the green isle overhead.

As a boy, I was often told I lacked imagination. If it were ever true, Thecla must have brought it to our nexus, for I could see the dire wolves in my mind, black and silent shapes, each as large as an onyger, pouring down into the valley; and I could hear them cracking the ribs of the dead. I called, and called again, before I knew what it was I did.

It seemed to me that the heavy footsteps paused. Certainly they moved toward me, whether they had been coming toward me before or not. I heard a rustling in the grass, and a little phenocod, striped like a melon, bounded out, terrified by something I still could not see. It shied at the sight of me and in a moment was gone.

I have said that Erblon's graisle was silenced. Another blew now, a deeper, longer, wilder note than I had ever heard. The outline of a bent orphicleide showed against the dusky sky. When its music was ended it fell, and in a moment more I saw the head of the player blotting out the brightening moon at three times the height of a mounted trooper's helmet—a domed head shaggy with hair.

The orphicleide sounded once more, deep as a waterfall, and this time I saw it rise, and the white, curling tusks that guarded it on each side, and I knew I lay in the path of the very symbol of dominion, the beast called Mammoth.

Guasacht had said I held some mastery over animals, even without the Claw. I strove to use it now, whispering I know not what, concentrating my thought until it seemed my temples would burst. The mammoth's trunk came questing toward me, its tip nearly a cubit across. Lightly as a child's hand it touched my face, flooding me with moist, hot breath sweet with hay. The corpse of the piebald was lifted away; I tried to stand but somehow fell. The mammoth caught me up, winding its trunk about my waist, and lifted me higher than its own head.

The first thing I saw was the muzzle of a trilhoen with a dark, bulging lens the size of a dinner plate. It was fitted with a seat for the operator, but no one sat there. The gunner had come down and stood upon the mammoth's neck as a sailor might upon the deck of a ship, with one hand on the barrel for balance. For a moment a light shone in my face, blinding me.

"It's you. Miracles converge on us." The voice was not truly either a man's or a woman's; it might almost have been a boy's. I was laid at the speaker's feet, and he said, "You're hurt. Can you stand on that leg?"

I managed to say I did not think I could.

"This is a poor place to lie, but a good one to fall from. There's a gondola farther back, but I'm afraid Mamillian can't reach it with his trunk. You'll have to sit up here, with your back against the swivel."

I felt his hands, small, soft, and moist, beneath my arms. Perhaps it was their touch that told me who he was: The androgyne I had met in the snow-covered House Azure, and later in that artfully foreshortened room that posed as a painting hanging in a corridor of the House Absolute.

The Autarch.

In Thecla's memories I saw him robed in jewels. Although he had said he recognized me, I could not believe in my dazed state that it was so, and I gave him the code phrase he had once given me, saying, "The pelagic argosy sights land."

"It does. It does indeed. Yet if you fall overboard now, I'm afraid Mamillian's not quite quick enough to catch you . . . despite his undoubted wisdom. Give him as much help as you can. I'm not as strong as I look."

I got some part of the trilhoen's mount in one hand and was able to pull myself around on the musty-smelling mat that was the mammoth's hide. "To speak the truth," I said, "you've never looked strong to me."

"You have the professional eye and ought to know, but I'm not even as strong as that. You, on the other hand, have always seemed to me a construction of horn and boiled leather. And you must be, or you'd be dead by now. What happened to your leg?"

"Burned, I think."

"We'll have to get you something for it." He raised his voice slightly. *"Home! Back home, Mamillian!"*

"May I ask what you're doing here?"

"Having a look at the field of battle. You fought here today, I take it."

I nodded, though I felt my head would tumble from my shoulders.

"I didn't . . . or rather, I did, but not personally. I ordered certain bodies of light auxiliaries into action, with a legion of peltasts in support. I suppose you must have been one of the auxiliaries. Were any of your friends killed?"

"I only had one. She was all right the last time I saw her."

His teeth flashed in the moonlight. "You maintain your interest in women. Was it the Dorcas you told me of?"

"No. It doesn't matter." I did not quite know how to phrase what I was about to say. (It is the worst of bad manners to state openly that one has penetrated an incognito.) At last I managed, "I can see you hold high rank in our Commonwealth. If it won't get me pushed from the back of this animal, can you tell me what someone who commands legions was doing conducting that place in the Algedonic Quarter?"

While I spoke, the night had grown rapidly darker, the stars winking out one after another like the tapers in a hall when the ball is over and footmen walk among them with snuffers like mitres of gold dangling from spidery rods. At a great distance I heard the androgyne say, "You know who we are. We are the thing itself, the self-ruler, the Autarch. We know more. We know who you are."

Master Malrubius was, as I realize now, a very sick man before he died. At the time I did not know it, because the thought of sickness was foreign to me. At least half our apprentices, and perhaps more than half, died before they were raised to journeyman; but it never occurred to me that our tower might be an unhealthy place, or that the lower reaches of Gyoll, where we so often swam, were little purer than a cesspool. Apprentices had always died, and when we living apprentices dug their graves we turned up small pelvises and skulls, which we, the succeeding generation, reburied again and again until they were so much injured by the spade that their chalky particles were lost in the tarlike soil. I, however, never suffered more than a sore throat and a running nose, forms of sickness that serve only to deceive healthy people into the belief that they know in what disease consists. Master Malrubius suffered real illness, which is to see death in shadows.

As he stood at his little table, one felt that he was conscious of someone standing behind him. He looked straight to the front, never turning his head and hardly moving a shoulder, and he spoke as much for that unknown listener as for us.

"I have done my best to teach you boys the rudiments of learning. They are the seeds of trees that should grow and blossom in your minds. Severian, look to your *Q*. It should be round and full like the face of a happy boy, but one of its cheeks is as fallen-in as your own. You have all, all you boys, seen how the spinal cord, lifting itself toward its culmination, expands and at last blossoms in the myriad pathways of the brain. And this one, one cheek round, the other seared and shriveled."

His trembling hand reached for the slate pencil, but it escaped his fingers and rolled over the edge of the table to clatter on the floor. He did not stoop to pick it up, fearful, I think, that in stooping he might glimpse the invisible presence.

"I have spent much of my life, boys, in trying to implant those seeds in the apprentices of our guild. I have had a few successes, but not many. There was a boy, but he—"

He went to the port and spat, and because I was sitting near it I saw the twisted shapes formed by the seeping blood and knew that the reason I could not see the dark figure (for death is of the color that is darker than fuligin) that accompanied him was that it stood within him.

Just as I had discovered that death in a new form, in the shape of war, could frighten me when it could no longer do so in its old ones, so I learned now that the weakness of my body could afflict me with the terror and despair my old teacher must have felt. Consciousness came and went.

Consciousness went and came like the errant winds of spring, and I, who so often have had difficulty in falling asleep among the besieging shades of memory, now fought to stay awake as a child struggles to lift a faltering kite by the string. At times I was oblivious to everything except my injured body. The wound in my leg, which I had hardly felt when I received it, and whose pain I had so effortlessly locked away when Daria had bandaged it, throbbed with an intensity that formed the background to all my thoughts, like the rumbling of the Drum Tower at the solstice. I turned from side to side, thinking always that I lay upon that leg.

I had hearing without sight and occasionally sight without hearing. I rolled my cheek from the matted hair of Mamillian and laid it on a pillow woven of the minute, downy feathers of hummingbirds.

Once I saw torches with dancing flames of scarlet and radiant gold held by solemn apes. A man with the horns and muzzled face of a bull bent over me, a constellation sprung to life. I spoke to him and found myself telling him that I was unsure of the precise date of my birth, that if his benign spirit of meadow and unfeigning force had governed my life I thanked him for it; then remembered that I knew the date, that my father had given a ball for me each year until his death, that it fell under the Swan. He listened intently, turning his head to watch me from one brown eye.

XXIV

The Flier

Sunlight in my face.

I tried to sit up, and in fact succeeded in getting one elbow beneath me. All about me shimmered an orb of color—purple and cyan, ruby and azure, with the orpiment of the sun piercing these enchanted tints like a sword to fall upon my eyes. Then it was blotted out, and its extinction revealed what its splendor had obscured: I lay in a domed pavilion of variegated silk, with an open door.

The rider of the mammoth was walking toward me. He was robed in saffron, as I had always seen him, and carried an ebony rod too light to be a weapon. "You have recovered," he said.

"I'd try and say yes, but I'm afraid the effort of speaking might kill me."

He smiled at that, though the smile was no more than a twitching of the mouth. "As you should know better than almost anyone, the sufferings we endure in this life make possible all the happy crimes and pleasant abominations we shall commit in the next . . . aren't you eager to collect?"

I shook my head and laid it on the pillow again. The softness smelled faintly of musk.

"That is just as well, because it will be some time before you do."

"Is that what your physician says?"

"I am my own, and I've been treating you myself. Shock was the principal problem . . . It sounds like a disorder for old women, as you are no doubt thinking at this moment. But it kills a great many men with wounds. If all of mine who die of it would only live, I would readily consent to the death of those who take a thrust in the heart."

"While you were being your own physician—and mine—were you telling the truth?"

He smiled more broadly at that. "I always do. In my position, I have to talk too much to keep a skein of lies in order; of course, you must realize that the truth . . . the little, ordinary truths that farm wives talk of, not the ultimate and universal Truth, which I'm no more capable of uttering than you . . . that truth is more deceptive."

"Before I lost consciousness, I heard you say you are the Autarch."

He threw himself down beside me like a child, his body making a distinct sound as it struck the piled carpets. "I did. I am. Are you impressed?"

"I would be more impressed," I said, "if I did not recall you so vividly from our meeting in the House Azure."

(That porch, covered with snow, heaped with snow that deadened our footsteps, stood in the silken pavilion like a specter. When the Autarch's blue eyes met mine, I felt that Roche stood beside me in the snow, both of us dressed in unfamiliar and none-too-well-fitting clothes. Inside, a woman who was not Thecla was transforming herself into Thecla as I was later to make myself Meschia, the first man. Who can say to what degree an actor assumes the spirit of the person he portrays? When I played the Familiar, it was nothing, because it was so close to what I was—or had at least believed myself to be—in life; but as Meschia I had sometimes had thoughts that could never have occurred to me otherwise, thoughts alien equally to Severian and to Thecla, thoughts of the beginnings of things and the morning of the world.)

"I never told you, you will recall, that I was *only* the Autarch."

"When I met you in the House Absolute, you appeared to be a minor official of the court. I admit you never told me that, and in fact I knew then who you were. But it was you, wasn't it, who gave the money to Dr. Talos?"

"I would have told you that without a blush. It is completely true. In fact, I am several of the minor officials of my court. . . . Why shouldn't I be? I have the authority to appoint such officials, and I can just as well appoint myself. An order from the Autarch is often too heavy an instrument, you see. You would never have tried to slit a nose with that big headsman's sword you carried. There is a time for a decree from the Autarch, and a time for a letter from the third bursar, and I am both and more besides."

"And in that house in the Algedonic Quarter—"

"I am also a criminal . . . just as you are."

There is no limit to stupidity. Space itself is said to be bounded by its own curvature, but stupidity continues beyond infinity. I, who had always thought myself, though not truly intelligent, at least prudent and quick to learn simple things, who had always counted myself the practical and foreseeing one when I had traveled with Jonas or Dorcas, had never until that instant connected the Autarch's position at the very apex of the structure of legality with his certain knowledge that I had penetrated the House Absolute as an emissary of Vodalus. At that moment, I would have leaped up and fled from the pavilion if I could, but my legs were like water.

"All of us are—all of us must be who must enforce the law. Do you think your guild brothers would have been so severe with you—and my agent reports that many of them wished to kill you—if they had themselves been guilty of something of the same kind? You were a danger to them unless you were terribly punished because they might otherwise someday be tempted. A judge or a jailer who has no crime of his own is a monster, alternately purloining the forgiveness that belongs to the Increate alone and practicing a deathly rigor that belongs to no one and nothing.

"So I became a criminal. The violent crimes offended my love of humanity, and I lack the quickness of hand and thought required of a thief. After blundering about for some time . . . that would be in about the year you were born, I suppose . . . I found my true profession. It takes care of certain emotional needs I cannot now satisfy otherwise . . . and I have, I really do have, a knowledge of human nature. I know just when to offer a bribe and how much to give, and, the most important thing, when not to. I know how to keep the girls who work for me happy enough with their careers to continue, and discontented enough with their fates. . . . They're khaibits, of course, grown from the body cells of exultant women so an exchange of blood will prolong the exultants' youth. I know how to make my clients feel that the encounters I arrange are unique experiences instead of something midway between dewy-eyed romance and solitary vice. You felt that you had a unique experience, didn't you?"

"That's what we call them too," I said. "*Clients.*" I had been listening as much to the tone of his voice as to his words. He was happy, as I thought he had not been on either of the other occasions on which I had encountered him, and to hear him was like hearing a thrush speak. He almost seemed to know it himself, lifting his face and extending his throat, the *R*s in *arrange* and *romance* trilled into the sunlight.

"It is useful too. It keeps me in touch with the underside of the population, so I know whether or not taxes are really being collected and whether they're thought fair, which elements are rising in society and which are going down."

I sensed that he was referring to me, though I had no idea what he meant. ''Those women from the court,'' I said. ''Why didn't you get the real ones to help you? One of them was pretending to be Thecla when Thecla was locked under our tower.''

He looked at me as though I had said something particularly stupid, as no doubt I had. ''Because I can't trust them, of course. A thing like that has to remain a secret. . . . Think of the opportunities for assassination. Do you believe that because all those gilded personages from ancient families bow so low in my presence, and smile, and whisper discreet jokes and lewd little invitations, they feel some loyalty to me? You will learn differently, you may be sure. There are few at my court I can trust, and none among the exultants.''

''You say I'll learn differently. Does that mean you don't intend to have me executed?'' I could feel the pulse in my neck and see the scarlet gout of blood.

''Because you know my secret now? No. We have other uses for you, as I told you when we talked in the room behind the picture.''

''Because I was sworn to Vodalus.''

At that his amusement mastered him. He threw back his head and laughed, a plump and happy child who had just discovered the secret of some clever toy. When the laughter subsided at last into a merry gulping, he clapped his hands. Soft though they looked, the sound was remarkably loud.

Two creatures with the bodies of women and the heads of cats entered. Their eyes were a span apart and as large as plums; they strode on their toes as dancers sometimes do, but more gracefully than any dancers I have ever seen, with something in their motions that told me it was their normal gait. I have said they had the bodies of women, but that was not quite true, for I saw the tips of claws sheathed in the short, soft fingers that dressed me. In wonder, I took the hand of one and pressed it as I have sometimes pressed the paw of a friendly cat, and saw the claws barred. My eyes brimmed with tears at the sight of them, because they were shaped like that claw that is the Claw, that once lay concealed in the gem that I, in my ignorance, called the Claw of the Conciliator. The Autarch saw I was weeping, and told the woman-cats they were hurting me and must put me down. I felt like an infant who has just learned he will never see his mother again.

''We do not harm him, Legion,'' one protested in such a voice as I had never heard before.

''Put him down, I said!''

''They have not so much as grazed my skin, Sieur,'' I told him.

*   *   *

With the woman-cats' support I was able to walk. It was morning, when all shadows flee the first sight of the sun; the light that had wakened me had been the earliest of the new day. Its freshness filled my lungs now, and the coarse grass over which we walked darkened my scuffed old boots with its dew; a breeze faint as the dim stars stirred my hair.

The Autarch's pavilion stood on the summit of a hill. All around lay the main bivouac of his army—tents of black and gray, and others like dead leaves; huts of turf and pits that led to shelters underground, from which streams of soldiers issued now like silver ants.

"We must be careful, you see," he said. "Though we are some distance behind the lines here, if this place were plainer it would invite attack from above."

"I used to wonder why your House Absolute lay beneath its own gardens, Sieur."

"The need has long passed now, but there was a time when they laid waste to Nessus."

Below us and all around us, the silver lips of trumpets sounded.

"Was it only the night?" I asked. "Or have I slept a whole day away?"

"No. Only the night. I gave you medicines to ease your pain and keep infection from your wound. I would not have roused you this morning, but I saw you were awake when I came in . . . and there is no more time."

I was not certain what he meant by that. Before I could ask, I caught sight of six nearly naked men hauling at a rope. My first impression was that they were bringing down some huge balloon, but it was a flier, and the sight of its black hull brought vivid memories of the Autarch's court.

"I was expecting—what was its name? Mamillian."

"No pets today. Mamillian is an excellent comrade, silent and wise and able to fight with a mind independent of my own, but when all is said and done, I ride him for pleasure. We will thieve a string from the Ascians' bow and use a mechanism today. They steal many from us."

"Is it true that it consumes their power to land? I think one of your aeronauts once told me that."

"When you were the Chatelaine Thecla, you mean. Thecla purely."

"Yes, of course. Would it be impolitic, Autarch, to ask why you had me killed? And how you know me now?"

"I know you because I see your face in the face of my young friend and hear your voice in his. Your nurses know you too. Look at them."

I did, and saw the woman-cats' faces twisted in snarls of fear and amazement.

"As to why you died, I will speak of that—to him—on board the flier . . . have we time. Now, go back. You find it easy to manifest yourself because he is weak and ill, but I must have him now, not you. If you will not go, there are means."

"Sieur—"

"Yes, Severian? Are you afraid? Have you entered such a contrivance before?"

"No," I said. "But I am not afraid."

"Do you recall your question about their power? It is true, in a sense. Their lift is supplied by the antimaterial equivalent of iron, held in a penning trap by magnetic fields. Since the anti-iron has a reversed magnetic structure, it is repelled by promagnetism. The builders of this flier have surrounded it with magnets, so that when it drifts from its position at the center it enters a stronger field and is forced back. On an antimaterial world, that iron would weigh as much as a boulder, but here on Urth it counters the weight of the promatter used in the construction of the flier. Do you follow me?"

"I believe so, Sieur."

"The trouble is that it is beyond our technology to seal the chamber hermetically. Some atmosphere—a few molecules—is always creeping in through porosities in the welds, or by penetrating the insulation of the magnetic wires. Each such molecule neutralizes its equivalent in anti-iron and produces heat, and each time one does so, the flier loses an infinitesimal amount of lift. The only solution anyone has found is to keep fliers as high as possible, where there is effectively no air pressure."

The flier was nosing down now, near enough for me to appreciate the beautiful sleekness of its lines. It had precisely the shape of a cherry leaf.

"I didn't understand all of that," I said. "But I would think the ropes would have to be immensely long to allow the fliers to float high enough to do any good, and that if the Ascian pentadactyls came over by night they would cut them and let the fliers drift away."

The woman-cats smiled at that with tiny, secretive twitchings of their lips.

"The rope is only for landing. Without it, our flier would require sufficient distance for its forward speed to drive it down. Now, knowing we're below, it drops its cable just as a man in a pond might extend his hand to someone who would pull him out. It has a mind of its own, you see. Not like Mamillian's—a mind we have made for it, but enough of a mind to permit it to stay out of difficulties and come down when it receives our signal."

The lower half of the flier was of opaque black metal, the upper half a dome so clear as to be nearly invisible—the same substance, I suppose, as the roof of the Botanic Gardens. A gun like the one the mammoth had carried thrust out from the stern, and another twice as large protruded from the bow.

The Autarch lifted one hand to his mouth and seemed to whisper into his palm. An aperture appeared in the dome (it was as if a hole had opened in a soap bubble) and a flight of silver steps, as thin and insubstantial looking as the web ladder of a spider, descended to us. The bare-chested men had left off pulling. "Do you think you can climb those?" the Autarch asked.

"If I can use my hands," I said.

He went before me, and I crawled up ignominiously after him, dragging my wounded leg. The seats, long benches that followed the curve of the hull on either side, were upholstered in fur; but even this fur felt colder than any ice. Behind me, the aperture narrowed and vanished.

"We will have surface pressure in here no matter how high we go. You don't have to worry about suffocating."

"I am afraid I am too ignorant to feel the fear, Sieur."

"Would you like to see your old bacele? They're far to the right, but I'll try to locate them for you."

The Autarch had seated himself at the controls. Almost the only machinery I had seen before had been Typhon's and Baldanders's, and that which Master Gurloes controlled in the Matachin Tower. It was of the machines, not of suffocation, that I was afraid; but I fought the fear down.

"When you rescued me last night, you indicated that you had not known I was in your army."

"I made inquiries while you slept."

"And it was you who ordered us forward?"

"In a sense . . . I issued the order that resulted in your movement, though I had nothing to do with your bacele directly. Do you resent what I did? When you joined, did you think you would never have to fight?"

We were soaring upward. Falling, as I had once feared to do, into the sky. But I remembered the smoke and the brassy shout of the graisle, the troopers blown to red paste by the whistling bolts, and all my terror turned to rage. "I knew nothing of war. How much do you know? Have you ever really been in a battle?"

He glanced over his shoulder at me, his blue eyes flashing. "I've been in a thousand. You are two, as people are usually counted. How many do you think I am?"

It was a long while before I answered him.

XXV

The Mercy of Agia

At first I thought there could be nothing stranger than to see the army stretch across the surface of Urth until it lay like a garland before us, coruscant with weapons and armor, many-hued; the winged anpiels soaring above it nearly as high as we, circling and rising on the dawn wind.

Then I beheld something stranger still. It was the army of the Ascians, an army of watery whites and grayish blacks, rigid as ours was fluid, deployed toward the northern horizon. I went forward to stare at it.

"I could show them to you more closely," the Autarch said. "Still, you would see only human faces."

I realized he was testing me, though I did not know how. "Let me see them," I said.

When I had ridden with the schiavoni and watched our troops go into action, I had been struck by their look of weakness in the mass, the cavalry all ebb and flow like a wave that crashes with great force—then drains away as mere water, too weak to bear the weight of a mouse, pale stuff a child might scoop up in his hands. Even the peltasts, with their serried ranks and crystal shields, had seemed hardly more formidable than toys on a tabletop. Now I saw how strong the rigid formations of our enemy appeared, rectangles that held machines as big as fortresses and a hundred thousand soldiers shoulder to shoulder.

But on a screen in the center of the control panel I looked under the visors of their helmets, and all that rigidity, all that strength, melted into a kind of horror. There were old people and children in the infantry files, and some who seemed idiots. Nearly all had the mad, famished faces I had observed the day before, and I recalled the man who had broken from his square and thrown his spear into the air as he died. I turned away.

The Autarch laughed. His laughter held no joy now; it was a flat sound, like the snapping of a flag in a high wind. "Did you see one kill himself?"

"No," I said.

"You were fortunate. I often do, when I look at them. They are not permitted arms until they are ready to engage us, and so many take advantage of the opportunity. The spearmen drive the butts of their weapons into soft ground, usually, then blast off their own heads. Once I saw two swordsmen—a man and a woman—who had made a compact. They stabbed each other in the belly, and I watched them counting first, moving their left hands . . . one . . . two . . . three, and dead."

"Who are they?" I asked.

He shot me a look I could not interpret. "What did you say?"

"I asked who they are, Sieur. I know they're our enemies, that they live to the north in the hot countries, and that they're said to be enslaved by Erebus. But who are they?"

"Up until now I doubt you knew you did not know. Did you?"

My throat felt parched, though I could not have told why. I said, "I suppose not. I'd never seen one until I came into the lazaret of the Pelerines. In the south, the war seems very remote."

He nodded. "We have driven them half as far to the north as they once drove us south, we autarchs. Who they are you will discover in due time. . . . What matters is that you wish to know." He paused. "Both could be ours. Both armies, not just the one to the south. . . . Would you advise me to take both?" As he spoke, he manipulated some control and the flier canted forward, its stern pointing at the sky and its bow to the green earth, as though he meant to pour us out upon the disputed ground.

"I don't understand what you mean," I told him.

"Half what you said of them was incorrect. They do not come from the hot countries of the north, but from the continent that lies across the equator. But you were right when you called them the slaves of Erebus. They think themselves the allies of those who wait in the deep. In truth, Erebus and his allies would give them to me if I would give our south to them. Give you and all the rest."

I had to grip the back of the seat to keep from falling toward him. "Why are you telling me this?"

The flier righted itself like a child's boat in a puddle, bobbing.

"Because it will soon be necessary for you to know that others have felt what you will feel."

I could not frame a question I dared to ask. At last I ventured, "You said you'd tell me here why you killed Thecla."

"Does she not live in Severian?"

A windowless wall in my mind fell to ruins. I shouted: *"I died!"* Not realizing what I had said until the words were past my lips.

The Autarch took a pistol from beneath the control panel, letting it lie across his thighs as he turned to face me.

"You won't need that, Sieur," I said. "I'm too weak."

"You have remarkable powers of recovery. . . . I have seen them already. Yes, the Chatelaine Thecla is gone, save as she endures in you, and though the two of you are always together, you are both lonely. Do you still seek for Dorcas? You told me of her, you remember, when we met in the Secret House."

"Why did you kill Thecla?"

"I did not. Your error lies in thinking I am at the bottom of everything. No one is. . . . Not I, or Erebus, or any other. As to the Chatelaine, you are she. Were you arrested openly?"

The memory came more vividly than I would have thought possible. I walked down a corridor whose walls were lined with sad masks of silver and entered one of the abandoned rooms, high-ceilinged and musty with ancient hangings. The courier I was to meet had not yet come. Because I knew the dusty divans would soil my gown, I took a chair, a spindly thing of gilt and ivory. The tapestry spilled from the wall behind me; I recalled looking up and seeing Destiny crowned in chains and Discontent with her staff and glass, all worked in colored wool, descending upon me.

The Autarch said, "You were taken by certain officers, who had learned that you were conveying information to your half sister's lover. Taken secretly, because your family has so much influence in the north, and conveyed to an almost forgotten prison. By the time I learned what had occurred, you were dead. Should I have punished those officers for acting in my absence? They are patriots, and you were a traitor."

"I, Severian, am a traitor too," I said, and I told him, then for the first time in detail, how I had once saved Vodalus, and of the banquet I had later shared with him.

When I had concluded, he nodded to himself. "Much of the loyalty you felt for Vodalus comes, surely, from the Chatelaine. Some she imparted to you while she was yet living, more after her death. Naive though you have been, I am certain you are not so naive as to think it a coincidence that it was she whose flesh was served to you by the corpse-eaters."

I protested, "Even if he had known of my connection with her, there was no time to bring her body from Nessus."

The Autarch smiled. "Have you forgotten that you told me a moment ago that when you had saved him, he fled in such a craft as this? From that forest, hardly a dozen leagues outside the City Wall, he could have flown to the center of Nessus, unearthed a corpse preserved by the chill soil of early spring, and returned in less than a watch. Actually, he need not have known so much or moved so swiftly. While you were imprisoned by your guild, he may have learned that the Chatelaine Thecla, who had been loyal to him even to death, was no more. By serving her flesh to his followers, he would strengthen them in his cause. He would require no additional motive to take her body, and no doubt he reinterred her in hoarded snow in some cellar, or in one of the abandoned mines with which that region abounds. You arrived, and wishing to bind you to him, he ordered her brought out."

Something passed too swiftly to be seen—an instant later the flier rocked with the violence of its motion. Sparks maneuvered on the screen.

Before the Autarch could take the controls again, we were scudding backward. There was a detonation so loud it seemed to paralyze me, and the reverberating sky opened in a blossom of yellow fire. I have seen a sparrow, struck by a stone from Eata's sling, reel in the air just as we did, and fall, like us, fluttering to one side.

I woke to darkness, pungent smoke, and the smell of fresh earth. For a moment or a watch I forgot my rescue and believed I lay on the field where Daria and I, with Guasacht, Erblon, and the rest, had fought the Ascians.

Someone lay near me—I heard the sigh of his breath, and the creakings and scrapings that betray movement—but at first I paid no heed to them, and later I came to believe that these sounds were made by foraging animals, and grew afraid; later still, I recalled what had happened and knew they were surely made by the Autarch, who must have survived the crash with me, and I called to him.

"So you still live, then." His voice was very weak. "I feared you would die . . . though I should have known better. I could not revive you, and your pulse was but faint."

"I have forgotten! Do you remember when we flew over the armies? For a time I forgot it! I know now what it is to forget."

There was pale laughter in his voice. "Which you will now remember always."

"I hope so, but it fades even as we speak. It vanishes like mist, which must itself be a forgetting. What was that weapon that brought us down?"

"I do not know. But listen. These are the most important words of my life. Listen. You have served Vodalus, and his dream of renewed empire. You still wish, do you not, that humankind should go again to the stars?''

I recalled something Vodalus had told me in the wood and said, ''Men of Urth, sailing between the stars, leaping from galaxy to galaxy, the masters of the daughters of the sun.''

''They were so once . . . and brought all the old wars of Urth with them, and in the young suns kindled new ones. Even they,'' (I could not see him, yet I knew by his tone that he had indicated the Ascians) ''understand it must not be so again. They wish the race to become a single individual . . . the same, duplicated to the end of number. We wish each to carry all the race and its longings within himself. Have you noticed the phial I wear at my neck?''

''Yes, often.''

''It contains a pharmacon like alzabo, already mixed and held in suspension. I am cold already below the waist. I will die soon. Before I die . . . you must use it.''

''I cannot see you,'' I said. ''And I can scarcely move.''

''Nevertheless, you will find a way. You remember everything, and so you must recall the night you came to my House Azure. That night someone else came to me. I was a servant once, in the House Absolute. . . . That is why they hate me. As they will hate you, for what you once were. Paeon, who trained me, who was honey-steward fifty years gone by. I knew what he was in truth, for I had met him before. He told me you were the one . . . the next. I did not think it would be quite so soon. . . .''

His voice fell away, and I began to grope for him, pulling myself along. My hand found his, and he whispered, ''Use the knife. We are behind the Ascian line, but I have called upon Vodalus to rescue you. . . . I hear the hoofs of his destriers.''

The words were so faint I could hardly hear, though my ear was within a span of his mouth. ''Rest,'' I said. Knowing that Vodalus hated him and sought to destroy him, I thought him delirious.

''I am his spy. That is another of my offices. He draws the traitors. . . . I learn who they are and what they do, what they think. That is one of his. Now I have told him the Autarch is trapped in this flier and given him our location. He has served me . . . as my bodyguard . . . before this.''

Now even I could hear the sound of feet on the ground outside. I reached up, searching for some means by which to signal; my hand touched fur, and I knew the flier had overturned, leaving us like hidden toads beneath it.

There was a snap and the scream of tearing metal. Moonlight, seeming bright as day but green as willow leaves, came flooding through a rent in the hull that gaped as I watched. I saw the Autarch, his thin white hair darkened with dried blood.

And above him silhouettes, green shades looking down upon us. Their faces were invisible; but I knew those gleaming eyes and narrow heads belonged to no followers of Vodalus. Frantically, I searched for the Autarch's pistol. My hands were seized. I was drawn up, and as I emerged I could not help thinking of the dead woman I had seen pulled from her grave in the necropolis, for the flier had fallen on soft ground and half buried itself. Where the Ascian bolt had struck it, its side was torn away, leaving a tangle of ruined wiring. The metal was twisted and burned.

I did not have much time to look at it. My captors turned me around and around as one after another took my face in his hands. My cloak was fingered as though they had never seen cloth. With their large eyes and hollow cheeks, these evzones seemed to me much like the infantry we had fought against, but though there were women among them, there were no old people and no children. They wore silvery caps and shirts in place of armor, and carried strangely shaped jezails, so long barreled that when their butt plates rested on the ground their muzzles were higher than their owners' heads. As I saw the Autarch lifted from the flier, I said, "Your message was intercepted, Sieur, I think."

"Nevertheless, it arrived." He was too weak to point, but I followed the direction of his eyes, and after a moment I saw flying shapes against the moon.

It almost seemed they slid down the beams to us, they came so quickly and so straight. Their heads were like the skulls of women, round and white, capped with miters of bone and stretched at the jaws into curved bills lined with pointed teeth. They were winged, the pinions so great they seemed to have no bodies at all. Twenty cubits at least these pinions stretched from tip to tip; when they beat they made no sound, but far below I felt the rush of air.

(Once I had imagined such creatures threshing the forests of Urth and beating flat her cities. Had my thought helped bring these?)

It seemed a long time before the Ascian evzones saw them. Then two or three fired at once, and the converging bolts caught one at their intersection and blew it to rags, then another and another. For an instant the light was blotted out, and something cold and flaccid struck my face, knocking me down.

When I could see again, half a dozen of the Ascians were gone, and the rest were firing into the air at targets almost imperceptible to me.

Something whitish fell from them. I thought it would explode and put my head down, but instead the hull of the wrecked flier rang like a cymbal. A body—a human body broken like a doll's—had struck it, but there was no blood.

One of the evzones jammed his weapon in my back and pushed me forward. Two more were supporting the Autarch much as the woman-cats had supported me. I discovered that I had lost all sense of direction. Though the moon still shone, masses of cloud veiled most of the stars. I looked in vain for the cross and for those three stars that are, for reasons no one understands, called *The Eight* and hang forever over the southern ice. Several of the evzones were still firing when there came blazing among us some arrow or spear that burst in a mass of blinding white sparks.

"That will do it," the Autarch whispered.

I was rubbing my eyes as I stumbled along, but I managed to ask what he meant.

"Can you see? No more can they. Our friends above . . . Vodalus's, I think . . . did not know our captors were so well armed. Now there will be no more good shooting, and as soon as that cloud drifts across the disc of Lune . . ."

I felt cold, as though a chill mountain wind had cut the tepid air around us. A few moments before I had been in despair to find myself among these gaunt soldiers. Now I would have given anything for some guarantee that I would remain among them.

The Autarch was to my left, hanging limp between two evzones who had slung their long-barreled jezails aslant their backs. As I watched, his head lolled to one side, and I knew he was unconscious or dead. "Legion" the woman-cats had called him, and it did not take great intellect to combine that name with what he had told me in the wrecked flier. Just as Thecla and Severian had joined in me, many personalities were surely united in him. Ever since the night I had first seen him, when Roche had brought me to the House Azure (whose odd name I was now, perhaps, beginning to grasp) I had sensed the complexity of his thought, as we sense, even in a bad light, the complexity of a mosaic, the myriad, infinitesimal chips that combine to produce the illuminated face and staring eyes of the New Sun.

He had said I was destined to succeed him, but for how long a reign? Preposterous as it was in a prisoner, and in a man so injured and so weak that a watch of rest on the coarse grass would have seemed like paradise, I was consumed with ambition. He had said I must eat his flesh and swallow the drug while he still lived; and, loving him, I would have torn my own from the grasp of my captors, if I had possessed the strength, to claim that luxury and pomp and power. I was Severian and Thecla united now, and perhaps the torturers' ragged apprentice had, without fully knowing it, longed for those things more than the young exultant held captive at court. I knew then what poor Cyriaca had felt in the gardens of the archon; yet if she had felt fully what I felt at that moment, it would have burst her heart.

An instant later I was unwilling. Some part of me treasured the privacy that not even Dorcas had entered. Deep inside the convolutions of my mind, in the embrace of the molecules, Thecla and I were twined together. For others—a dozen or a thousand, perhaps, if in absorbing the personality of the Autarch I was also to absorb those he had incorporated into himself—to come where we lay would be for the crowds of the bazaar to enter a bower. I clasped my heart's companion to me, and felt myself clasped. I felt myself clasped, and clasped my heart's companion to me.

The moon dimmed as a dark lantern does when one presses the lever that makes its plates iris closed until there remains no more than a point of light, then nothing. The Ascian evzones fired their jezails in a lattice of lilac and heliotrope, beams that diverged high in the atmosphere and at last pricked the clouds like colored pins; but without effect. There was a wind, hot and sudden, and what I can only call a flash of black. Then the Autarch was gone, and something huge rushed toward me. I threw myself down.

Perhaps I struck the ground, but I do not remember it. In an instant, it seemed, I was swooping through the air, turning, climbing surely, the world below no more than a darker night. An emaciated hand, hard as stone and three times human size, clutched me about the waist.

We ducked, turned, lurched, slipped sidewise down a slope of air, then, catching a rising wind, climbed till the cold stung and stiffened my skin. When I craned my neck to look upward, I could see the white, inhuman jaws of the creature that bore me. It was the nightmare I had known months earlier when I had shared Baldanders's bed, though in my dream I had ridden the thing's back. Why that difference between dream and truth should be, I cannot say. I cried out (I do not know what) and above me the thing opened its scimitar beak to hiss.

From above, too, I heard a woman's voice call, "Now I have repaid you for the mine—you are still alive."

XXVI

Above the Jungle

We landed by starlight. It was like awakening; I felt that it was not the sky but the country of nightmare I was leaving behind. Like a falling leaf, the immense creature settled in narrowing circles through regions of progressively warmer air until I could smell the odor of the Jungle Garden: the mingling of green life and rotting wood with the perfume of wide, waxen, unnamed blossoms.

A ziggurat lifted its dark head above the trees—yet carried the trees with it, for they sprouted from its crumbling walls like fungi from a dead tree. We settled on it weightlessly, and at once there came torches and excited voices. I was still faint from the thin and icy air I had been breathing only moments before.

Human hands replaced the claws that had grasped me for so long. We wound down ledges and stairways of broken stone until at last I stood before a fire and saw across it the handsome, unsmiling face of Vodalus and the heart-shaped one of his consort, Thea, our half sister.

"Who is this?" Vodalus asked.

I tried to lift my arms, but they were held. "Liege," I said, "you must know me."

From behind me, the voice I had heard in the air answered, "This is the man of the price, the killer of my brother. For him, I—and Hethor, who serves me—have served you."

"Then why do you bring him to me?" Vodalus asked. "He is yours. Did you think that when I had seen him, I would repent of our agreement?"

Perhaps I was stronger than I felt myself to be. Perhaps I only caught the man on my right off-balance; however it was, I succeeded in twisting about, jerking him into the fire, where his feet sent the red brands flying.

Agia stood behind me, naked to the waist, and Hethor behind her, showing all his rotten teeth as he cupped her breasts. I fought to escape. She slapped me with an open hand—there was a pull at my cheek, tearing pain, then the warm rush of blood.

Since then, I have learned that the weapon is called a *lucivee*, and that Agia had it because Vodalus had forbidden any but his own bodyguard to carry arms in his presence. It is no more than a small bar with rings for the thumb and fourth finger, and four or five curved blades that can be concealed in the palm; but few have survived its blow.

I was one of those few, and rose after two days to find myself shut in a bare room. Perhaps in each life one room must become better known than any other: for prisoners, it is always a cell. I, who had worked outside so many, thrusting in trays of food to the disfigured and demented, now knew again a cell of my own. What the ziggurat had once been, I never guessed. Perhaps a prison indeed; perhaps a temple, or the atelier of some forgotten art. My cell was about twice the size of the one I had occupied beneath the tower of the torturers, six paces wide and ten long. A door of ancient, gleaming alloy stood against the wall, useless to Vodalus's jailers because they could not lock it; a new one, roughly made of the ironlike timbers of some jungle tree, closed the doorway. A window I believe had never been meant for one, a circular opening hardly bigger than my arm, pierced the discolored wall high up and gave light to the cell.

Three days more passed before I was strong enough to jump and, gripping its lower edge with one hand, pull myself up to look out. When that day came, I saw a rolling green country dotted with butterflies—a place so foreign to what I had expected that I felt I might be mad and lost my hold upon the window in my astonishment. It was, as I eventually realized, the country of treetops, where ten-chain hardwoods spread a lawn of leaves, seldom seen save by the birds.

An old man with a knowledgeable, evil face had bandaged my cheek and changed the dressings on my leg. Later he brought a lad of about thirteen whose bloodstream he linked with mine until the boy's lips turned the hue of lead. I asked the old leech where he came from, and he, apparently thinking me a native of these parts, said, "From the big city in the south, in the valley of the river that drains the cold lands. It is a longer river than yours, is the Gyoll, though its flood is not so fierce."

"You have great skill," I said. "I've never heard of a physician who did as much. I feel well already, and wish you would stop before this boy dies."

The old man pinched his cheek. "He'll recover quickly—in time to warm my bed tonight. At his age they always do. Nay, it's not what you think. I only sleep beside him because the night-breath of the young acts as a restorative to those of my years. Youth, you see, is a disease, and we may hope to catch a mild case. How stands your wound?"

There was nothing—not even an admission, which might have been rooted in some perverse desire to maintain an appearance of potency—that could have convinced me so completely as his denial. I told him the truth, that my right cheek was numb save for a vague burning as irritating as an itch, and wondered which of his duties the miserable boy minded most.

The old man stripped away my bandages and gave my wounds a second coating of the foul-smelling brown salve he had used previously. "I'll be back tomorrow," he told me. "Although I don't think you'll need Mamas here again. You're coming along nicely. Her exultancy" (with a jerk of the head to show this was an ironical reference to Agia's stature) "will be most pleased."

I said, in what I sought to make an offhand way, that I hoped all his patients were doing as well.

"You mean the delator who was brought in with you? He's as well as can be expected." He turned aside as he spoke, so that I would not see his frightened expression.

On the chance that I might gain influence with him that would enable me to aid the Autarch, I praised his understanding of his craft extravagantly and ended by saying that I failed to comprehend why a physician of his ability consorted with these wicked people.

He looked at me narrowly, and his face grew serious. "For knowledge. There is nowhere a man in my profession can learn as I learn here."

"You mean the eating of the dead? I have shared in that too, though they may not have told you so."

"No, no. Learned men—particularly those of my profession—practice that everywhere, and usually with better effect, since we are more selective of our subjects and confine ourselves to the most retentive tissues. The knowledge I seek cannot be learned in that way, since none of the recently dead possessed it, and perhaps no one has ever possessed it."

He was leaning against the wall now, and seemed to be speaking as much to some invisible presence as to me. "The past's sterile science led to nothing but the exhaustion of the planet and the destruction of its races. It was founded in the mere desire to exploit the gross energies and material substances of the universe, without regard to their attractions, antipathies, and eventual destinies. Look!'' He thrust his hand into the beam of sunshine that was then issuing from my high, circular window. ''Here is light. You will say that it is not a living entity, but you miss the point that it is more, not less. Without occupying space, it fills the universe. It nourishes everything, yet itself feeds upon destruction. We claim to control it, but does it not perhaps cultivate us as a source of food? May it not be that all wood grows so that it can be set ablaze, and that men and women are born to kindle fires? Is it not possible that our claim to master light is as absurd as wheat's claiming to master us because we prepare the soil for it and attend its intercourse with Urth?''

''All that is well said,'' I told him. ''But nothing to the point. Why do you serve Vodalus?''

''Such knowledge is not gained without experiment.'' He smiled as he spoke, and touched the shoulder of the boy, and I had a vision of children in flames. I hope that I was wrong.

That had been two days before I pulled myself up to the window. The old leech did not come again; whether he had fallen from favor, or been dispatched to another place, or had merely decided no further attentions were necessary, I had no way of knowing.

Agia came once, and standing between two of Vodalus's armed women spat in my face as she described the torments she and Hethor had contrived for me when I was strong enough to endure them. When she finished, I told her quite truthfully that I had spent most of my life assisting at operations more terrible, and advised her to obtain trained assistance, at which she went away.

Thereafter for the better part of several days I was left alone. Each time I woke, I felt myself almost a different person, for in that solitude the isolation of my thoughts in the dark intervals of sleep was nearly sufficient to deprive me of my sense of personality. Yet all these Severians and Theclas sought freedom.

The retreat into memory was easy; we made it often, reliving those idyllic days when Dorcas and I had journeyed toward Thrax, the games played in the hedge-walled maze behind my father's villa and in the Old Yard, the long walk down the Adamnian Steps that Agia and I had taken before I knew her for my enemy.

But often too, I left memory and forced myself to think, sometimes limping up and down, sometimes only waiting for insects to enter the window so that I might for my amusement pluck them from the air. I planned escape, though until my circumstances altered there seemed no possibility of it; I pondered passages from the brown book and sought to match them to my own experiences in order to produce, insofar as possible, some general theory of human action that would be of benefit to me should I ever free myself.

For if the leech, who was an elderly man, could still pursue knowledge despite the certainty of imminent death, could not I whose death appeared more imminent still, take some comfort in the surety that it was less certain?

Thus I sifted the actions of the magicians, and of the man who had accosted me outside the jacal of the sick girl, and of many other men and women I had known, seeking for a key that would unlock all hearts.

I found none that could be expressed in few words: "Men and women do as they do because of thus and so. . . ." None of the ragged bits of metal fit—the desire for power, the lust of love, the need for reassurance, or the taste for seasoning life with romance. But I did find one principle, which I came to call that of Primitivity, that I believe is widely applicable, and which, if it does not initiate action, at least seems to influence the forms that action takes. I might state it this way: *Because the prehistoric cultures endured for so many chiliads, they have shaped our heritage in such a way as to cause us to behave as if their conditions obtained today.*

For example, the technology that once might have permitted Baldanders to observe all the actions of the hetman of the lakeside village has been dust now for thousands of years; but during the eons of its existence, it laid upon him a spell, as it were, by which it remained effective though no longer extant.

In the same way, we all have in us the ghosts of long-vanished things, of fallen cities and marvelous machines. The story I once read to Jonas when we were imprisoned (with how much less anxiety and how much more companionship) showed that clearly, and I read it over again in the ziggurat. The author, having need for some sea-born fiend like Erebus or Abaia, in a mythical setting, gave it a head like a ship—which was the whole of its visible body, the remainder being underwater—so that it was removed from protoplasmic reality and became the machine that the rhythms of his mind demanded.

While I amused myself with these speculations, I became increasingly aware of the impermanent nature of Vodalus's occupation of the ancient building. Though the leech came no more, as I have said, and Agia never visited me again, I frequently heard the sound of running feet in the corridor outside my door and occasionally a few shouted words.

Whenever such sounds came, I put my unbandaged ear to the planks; and in fact I often anticipated them, sitting that way for long periods in the hope of overhearing some snatch of conversation that would tell me something of Vodalus's plans. I could not help but think then, as I listened in vain, of the hundreds in our oubliette who must have listened to me when I carried their food to Drotte, and how they must have strained to overhear the fragments of conversation that drifted from Thecla's cell into the corridor, and thus into their own cells, when I visited her.

And what of the dead? I own that I thought of myself, at times, almost as dead. Are they not locked below ground in chambers smaller than mine was, in their millions of millions? There is no category of human activity in which the dead do not outnumber the living many times over. Most beautiful children are dead. Most soldiers, most cowards. The fairest women and the most learned men—all are dead. Their bodies repose in caskets, in sarcophagi, beneath arches of rude stone, everywhere under the earth. Their spirits haunt our minds, ears pressed to the bones of our foreheads. Who can say how intently they listen as we speak, or for what word?

XXVII

Before Vodalus

On the morning of the sixth day, two women came for me. I had slept very little the night before. One of the blood bats common in those northern jungles had entered my room by the window, and though I had succeeded in driving it out and staunching the blood, it had returned again and again, attracted, I suppose, by the odor of my wounds. Even now I cannot see the vague green darkness that is diffused moonlight without imagining I see the bat crawling there like a big spider, then springing into the air.

The women were as surprised to find me awake as I was to see them; it was just dawn. They made me stand, and one bound my hands while the other held her dirk to my throat. She asked how my cheek was healing, however, and added that she had been told I was a handsome fellow when I was brought in.

"I was almost as near to death then as I am now," I said to her. The truth was that though the concussion I had suffered when the flier crashed had healed, my leg, as well as my face, was still giving me considerable pain.

The women brought me to Vodalus; not, as I had more or less expected, somewhere in the ziggurat or on the ledge where he had sat in state with Thea, but in a clearing embraced on three sides by slow green water. It was a moment or two—I had to stand waiting while some other business was conducted—before I realized that the course of this river was fundamentally to the north and east, and that I had never seen northeastward-flowing water before; all streams, in my previous experience, ran south or southwest to join southwestern-flowing Gyoll.

At last Vodalus inclined his head toward me, and I was brought forward. When he saw that I could scarcely stand, he ordered my guards to seat me at his feet, then waved them back out of hearing distance. "Your entrance is somewhat less impressive than that you made in the forest beyond Nessus," he said.

I agreed. "But, Liege, I come now, as I did then, as your servant. Just as I was the first time you met me, when I saved your neck from the ax. If I appear before you in bloody rags and with bound hands, it is because you treat your servants so."

"Certainly I would agree that securing your wrists seems a trifle excessive in your condition." He smiled faintly. "Is it painful?"

"No. The feeling is gone."

"Still, the cords aren't needed." Vodalus stood and drew a slender blade, and leaning over me, flicked my bonds with the point.

I flexed my shoulders and the last strands parted. A thousand needles seemed to pierce my hands.

When he had taken his seat again, Vodalus asked if I were not going to thank him.

"You never thanked me, Liege. You gave me a coin instead. I think I have one here somewhere." I fumbled in my sabretache for the money I had been paid by Guasacht.

"You may keep your coin. I'm going to ask you for much more than that. Are you ready to tell me who you are?"

"I've always been ready to do that, Liege. I'm Severian, formerly a journeyman of the guild of torturers."

"But are you nothing else besides a former journeyman of that guild?"

"No."

Vodalus sighed and smiled, then leaned back in his chair and sighed again. "My servant Hildegrin always insisted you were important. When I asked him why, he had any number of speculations, none of which I found convincing. I thought he was trying to get silver from me for a little easy spying. Yet he was right."

"I have only been important once to you, Liege."

"Each time we meet, you remind me that you saved my life once. Did you know that Hildegrin once saved yours? It was he who shouted 'Run!' to your opponent when you dueled in the city. You had fallen, and he might have stabbed you."

"Is Agia here?" I asked. "She'll try to kill you if she hears that."

"No one can hear you but myself. You may tell her later, if you like. She will never believe you."

"You can't be sure of that."

He smiled more broadly. "Very well, I'll turn you over to her. You can then test your theory against mine."

"As you wish."

He brushed my acquiescence aside with an elegant motion of one hand. "You think you can stalemate me with your willingness to die. Actually you're offering me an easy exit from a dilemma. Your Agia came to me with a very valuable thaumaturgist in her train, and asked as the price of his service and her own only that you, Severian of the Order of the Seekers for Truth and Penitence, should be put into her hands. Now you say you are that Severian the Torturer and no one else, and it is with great embarrassment that I resist her demands."

"And whom do you wish me to be?" I asked.

"I have, or I should say I had, a most excellent servant in the House Absolute. You know him, of course, since it was to him that you gave my message." Vodalus paused and smiled again. "A week or so ago we received one from him. It was not, to be sure, openly addressed to me, but I had seen to it not long before that he was aware of our location, and we were not far from him. Do you know what he said?"

I shook my head.

"That's odd, because you must have been with him at the time. He said he was in a wrecked flier—and that the Autarch was in the flier with him. He would have been an idiot to have sent such a message in the ordinary course of things, because he gave his location—and he was behind our lines, as he must have known."

"You are a part of the Ascian army, then?"

"We serve them in certain scouting capacities, yes. I see you are troubled by the knowledge that Agia and the thaumaturgist killed a few of their soldiers to take you. You need not be. Their masters value them even less than I do, and it was not a time for negotiation."

"But they did not capture the Autarch." I am not a good liar, but I was too exhausted, I think, for Vodalus to read my face easily.

He leaned forward, and for a moment his eyes glowed as though candles burned in their depths. "He was there, then. How wonderful. You have seen him. You have ridden in the royal flier with him."

I nodded once more.

"You see, ridiculous though it sounds, I feared you were he. One never knows. An Autarch dies and another takes his place, and the new Autarch may be there for half a century or a fortnight. There were three of you then? No more?"

"No."

"What did the Autarch look like? Let me have every detail."

I did as he asked, describing Dr. Talos as he had appeared in the part.

"Did he escape both the thaumaturgist's creatures and the Ascians?

Or do the Ascians have him? Perhaps the woman and her paramour are holding him for themselves."

"I told you the Ascians did not take him."

Vodalus smiled again, but beneath his glowing eyes his twisted mouth suggested only pain. "You see," he repeated, "for a time I thought you might be the one. We have my servant, but he has suffered a head injury and is never conscious for more than a few moments. He will die very shortly, I'm afraid. But he has always told me the truth, and Agia says that you were the only one with him."

"You think that I am the Autarch? No."

"Yet you are changed from the man I met before."

"You yourself gave me the alzabo, and the life of the Chatelaine Thecla. I loved her. Did you think that to thus ingest her essence would leave me unaffected? She is with me always, so that I am two, in this single body. Yet I am not the Autarch, who in one body is a thousand."

Vodalus answered nothing, but half closed his eyes as though he were afraid I would see their fire. There was no sound but the lapping of the river water and the much-muted voices of the little knot of armed men and women, who talked among themselves a hundred paces off and glanced from time to time at us. A macaw shrieked, fluttering from one tree to another.

"I would still serve you," I told Vodalus, "if you would permit it." I was not certain it was a lie until the words had left my lips, and then I was bewildered in mind, seeking to understand how those words, which would have been true in the past for Thecla and for Severian too, were now false for me.

" 'The Autarch, who in one body is a thousand,' " Vodalus quoted me. "That is correct, but how few of us know it."

XXVIII

On the March

Today, this being the last before I am to leave the House Absolute, I participated in a solemn religious ceremony. Such rituals are divided into seven orders according to their importance, or as the heptarchs say, their "transcendence"—something I was quite ignorant of at the time of which I was writing a moment ago. At the lowest level, that of Aspiration, are the private pieties, including prayers pronounced privately, the casting of a stone upon a cairn, and so forth. The gatherings and public petitionings that I, as a boy, thought constituted the whole of organized religion, are actually at the second level, which is that of Integration. What we did today belonged to the seventh and highest, the level of Assimilation.

In accordance with the principle of circularity, most of the accretions gathered in the progression through the first six were now dispensed with. There was no music, and the rich vestments of Assurance were replaced by starched robes whose sculptural folds gave all of us something of the air of icons. It is no longer possible for us to carry out the ceremony, as once we did, wrapped in the shining belt of the galaxy; but to achieve the effect as nearly as possible, Urth's attractive field was excluded from the basilica. It was a novel sensation for me, and though I was unafraid, I was reminded again of that night I spent among the mountains when I felt myself on the point of falling off the world—something I will undergo in sober earnest tomorrow. At times the ceiling seemed a floor, or (what was to me far more disturbing) a wall became the ceiling, so that one looked upward through its open windows to see a mountainside of grass that lifted itself forever into the sky. Startling as it was, this vision was no less true than that we commonly see.

Each of us became a sun; the circling, ivory skulls were our planets.

I said we had dispensed with music, yet that was not entirely true, for as they swung about us there came a faint, sweet humming and whistling, caused by the flow of air through their eye sockets and teeth; those in nearly circular orbits maintained an almost steady note, varying only slightly as they rotated on their axes; the songs of those in elliptical orbits waxed and waned, rising as they approached me, sinking to a moan as they receded.

How foolish we are to see in those hollow eyes and marble calottes only death. How many friends are among them! The brown book, which I carried so far, the only one of the possessions I took from the Matachin Tower that still remains with me, was sewn and printed and composed by men and women with those bony faces; and we, engulfed by their voices, now on behalf of those who are the past, offered ourselves and the present to the fulgurant light of the New Sun.

Yet at that moment, surrounded by the most meaningful and magnificent symbolism, I could not but think how different the actuality had been when we had left the ziggurat on the day after my interview with Vodalus and had marched (I under the guard of six women, who were sometimes forced to carry me) for what must have been a week or more through pestilential jungle. I did not know—and still do not know—whether we were fleeing the armies of the Commonwealth or the Ascians who had been Vodalus's allies. Perhaps we were merely seeking to rejoin the major part of the insurgent force. My guards complained of the moisture that dripped from the trees to eat at their weapons and armor like acid, and of suffocating heat; I felt nothing of either. I remember looking down once at my thigh and noticing with surprise that the flesh had fallen away so that the muscles there stood out like cords and I could see the sliding parts of my knee as one sees the wheels and shafts of a mill.

The old leech was with us, and now visited me two or three times each day. At first he tried to keep dry bandages on my face; when he saw the effort was futile, he removed them all and contented himself with plastering the wounds there with his salve. After that, some of my women guards refused to look at me, and if they had reason to speak to me did so with downcast eyes. Others seemed to take pride in their ability to confront my torn face, standing straddle-legged (a pose they appeared to consider warlike) and resting their left hands upon the hilts of their weapons with studied casualness.

I talked with them as often as I could. Not because I desired them—the illness that had come with my wounds had taken all such desire from me—but because in the midst of the straggling column I was lonely in a way I had never been when I was alone in the war-torn north or even when I had been locked in my ancient, mold-streaked cell in the ziggurat, and because in some absurd corner of my mind I still hoped to escape. I questioned them about every subject of which they might conceivably have knowledge, and I was endlessly amazed to find how few were the points on which our minds coincided. Not one of the six had joined Vodalus because of an appreciation of the difference between the restoration of progress he sought to represent and the stagnation of the Commonwealth. Three had merely followed some man into the ranks; two had come in the hope of gaining revenge for some personal injustice, and one because she had been fleeing from a detested stepfather. All but the last now wished they had not joined. None knew with any precision where we had been or had the slightest idea where we were going.

For guides our column had three savages: a pair of young men who might have been brothers or even twins, and a much older one, twisted, I thought, by deformities as well as age, who perpetually wore a grotesque mask. Though the first two were younger and the third much older, all three of them recalled to me the naked man I had once seen in the Jungle Garden. They were as naked as he and had the same dark, metallic-looking skin and straight hair. The younger two carried cerbotanas longer than their outstretched arms and dart bags hand-knotted of wild cotton and dyed a burnt umber, doubtless with the juice of some plant. The old man had a staff as crooked as himself, topped with the dried head of a monkey.

A covered palanquin whose place in the column was considerably more advanced than my own bore the Autarch, whom my leech gave me to understand was still alive; and one night when my guards were chattering among themselves and I sat crouched over our little fire, I saw the old guide (his bent figure and the impression of an immense head conferred by his mask were unmistakable) approach this palanquin and slip beneath it. Some time passed before he scuttled away. This old man was said to be an *uturuncu*, a shaman capable of assuming the form of a tiger.

Within a few days of our leaving the ziggurat, without encountering anything that might be called a road or even a path, we struck a trail of corpses. They were Ascians, and they had been stripped of their clothing and equipment, so that their starved bodies seemed to have dropped from the air to the places where they lay. To me, they appeared to be about a week dead; but no doubt decay had been accelerated by the dampness and heat, and the actual time was much less. The cause of death was seldom apparent.

Until then we had seen few animals larger than the grotesque beetles that buzzed about our fires by night. Such birds as called from the treetops remained largely invisible, and if the blood-bats visited us, their inky wings were lost in the smothering dark. Now we moved, as it seemed, through an army of beasts drawn to the corpse trail as flies are to a dead sumpter. Hardly a watch passed without our hearing the sound of bones crushed by great jaws, and by night green and scarlet eyes, some of them two spans apart, shone outside our little circles of firelight. Though it was preposterous to suppose these carrion-gorged predators would molest us, my guards doubled their sentries; those who slept did so in their corslets, with curtelaxes in their hands.

With each new day the bodies were fresher, until at last not all were dead. A madwoman with cropped hair and staring eyes stumbled into the column just ahead of our party, shouted words no one could understand, and fled among the trees. We heard cries for help, screams, and ravings, but Vodalus permitted no one to turn aside, and on the afternoon of that day we plunged—much in the same sense we might earlier have been said to have plunged into the jungle—into the Ascian horde.

Our column consisted of the women and supplies, Vodalus himself and his household, and a few of his aides with their retinues. In all it surely amounted to no more than a fifth of his force; but if every insurgent he could have called to his banner had been there, and every fighter become a hundred, they would still have been among that multitude as a cupful of water in Gyoll.

Those we encountered first were infantry. I recalled that the Autarch had told me their weapons were kept from them until the time of battle; but if it were so, their officers must have thought that time to be at hand, or nearly. I saw thousands armed with the ransieur, so that at length I came to believe that all their infantry was equipped in that way; then, as night was falling, we overtook thousands more carrying demilunes.

Because we marched faster than they, we moved more deeply into their force; but we camped sooner than they (if they camped at all) and all that night, until at last I fell asleep, I heard their hoarse cries and the shuffling of their feet. In the morning we were again among their dead and dying, and it was a watch or more before we overtook the stumbling ranks.

These Ascian soldiers had a rigidity, a will-less attachment to order, that I have never seen elsewhere, and that appeared to me to have no roots in either spirit or discipline as I understand them. They seemed to obey because they could not conceive of any other course of action. Our soldiers nearly always carry several arms—at the very least an energy weapon and a long knife (among the schiavoni I was exceptional in not possessing such a knife in addition to my falchion). But I never saw an Ascian with more than one, and most of their officers bore no weapon at all, as if they regarded actual fighting with contempt.

XXIX

Autarch of the Commonwealth

By the middle of the day, we had again passed all those whom we had passed the afternoon before and came upon the baggage train. I think all of us were amazed to discover that the enormous force we had seen was no more than the rear guard of an army inconceivably greater.

The Ascians used uintathers and platybelodons as beasts of burden. Mixed with them were machines with six legs, machines apparently built to serve that purpose. So far as I could see, the drivers made no distinction between these devices and the animals; if a beast lay down and could not be made to rise again, or a machine fell and did not right itself, its load was distributed among those nearest to hand, and it was abandoned. There appeared to be no effort to slaughter the beasts for their meat or to repair or take parts from the machines.

Late in the afternoon some great excitement passed down our column, though neither I nor my guards could discover what it was. Vodalus himself and several of his lieutenants came hurrying by, and afterward there was much coming and going between the end of the column and its head. When dark came we did not camp, but continued to tramp through the night with the Ascians. Torches were passed back to us, and since I had no weapons to carry and was somewhat stronger than I had been, I carried them, feeling almost as though I commanded the six swords who surrounded me.

About midnight, as nearly as I could judge, we halted. My guards found sticks for a fire, which we kindled from a torch. Just as we were about to lie down, I saw a messenger rouse the palanquin bearers ahead of us and send them blundering forward in the dark. They were no sooner gone than he loped back to us and held a quick, whispered conversation with the sergeant of my guards. At once my hands were bound (as they had not been since Vodalus had cut them free) and we were hurrying after the palanquin. We passed the head of the column, marked by the Chatelaine Thea's little pavilion, without pausing, and were soon wandering among the myriad Ascian soldiers of the main body.

Their headquarters was a dome of metal. I suppose it must have folded or collapsed in some way as a tent does, but it appeared as permanent and solid as any building, black externally but glowing with a sourceless, pale light within when the side opened to admit us. Vodalus was there, stiff and deferential; beside him the palanquin stood with its curtains opened to show the immobile body of the Autarch. At the center of the dome, three women sat around a low table. Neither then nor later did they look at Vodalus, or the Autarch in his palanquin, or at me when I was brought forward, save for an occasional glance. There were stacks of papers before them, but they did not look at those at all—only at one another. In appearance they were much like the other Ascians I had seen, save that their eyes were saner and they were less starved looking.

"Here he is," Vodalus said. "Now you see them both before you."

One of the Ascians spoke to the other two in their own tongue. Both nodded and the one who had spoken said, "Only he who acts against the populace need hide his face."

There was a lengthy pause, then Vodalus hissed at me, "Answer her!"

"Answer what? There has been no question."

The Ascian said, "Who is the friend of the populace? He who aids the populace. Who is the enemy of the populace?"

Speaking very rapidly, Vodalus asked, "To the best of your knowledge are you, or is this unconscious man here, the leader of the peoples of the southern half of this hemisphere?"

"No," I said. It was an easy lie, since from what I had seen, the Autarch was the leader of very few in the Commonwealth. To Vodalus I added under my breath, "What kind of foolishness is this? Do they believe I would tell them if I were the Autarch?"

"All we say is being transmitted to the north."

One of the Ascians who had not spoken previously spoke now. Once she gestured in our direction. When she was finished, all three sat deathly still. I had the impression that they heard some voice inaudible to me, and that they did not dare move while it spoke; but that may have been mere imagination on my part. Vodalus fidgeted, I shifted my position to put a little less weight on my injured leg, and the Autarch's narrow chest heaved to the unsteady rhythm of his breathing, but the three of them remained as immobile as figures in a painting.

At last the one who had spoken first said, "All persons belong to the populace." At that the others seemed to relax.

"This man is ill," Vodalus said, looking toward the Autarch, "and he has been a useful servant to me, though I suppose his usefulness is now ended. The other I have promised to one of my followers."

"The merit of sacrifice falls on him who without thought to his own convenience offers what he has toward the service of the populace." The Ascian woman's tone made it clear that no further argument was possible.

Vodalus looked toward me and shrugged, then turned on his heel and strode out of the dome. Almost at once a file of Ascian officers entered carrying lashes.

We were imprisoned in an Ascian tent perhaps twice the size of my cell in the ziggurat. There was a fire there but no bedding, and the officers who had carried in the Autarch had merely dropped him on the ground beside it. After working my hands free, I tried to make him comfortable, turning him over on his back as he had been in the palanquin and arranging his arms at his sides.

About us the army lay quiet, or at least as quiet as an Ascian army ever is. From time to time someone far off cried out—in sleep, it seemed—but for the most part there was no sound but the slow pacing of the sentries outside. I cannot express the horror that the thought of going north to Ascia evoked in me then. To see only the Ascians' wild, starved faces and to encounter myself, no doubt for the remainder of my life, whatever it was that had driven them mad, seemed to me a more horrible fate than any the clients in the Matachin Tower were ever forced to endure. I tried to lift the skirt of the tent, thinking that the sentries could do nothing worse than take my life; but the edges were welded to the ground by some means I did not understand. All four walls were of a slick, tough substance I could not tear, and Miles's razor had been taken from me by my six female guards. I was about to rush out the door when the Autarch's well-remembered voice whispered, "Wait." I dropped to my knees beside him, suddenly afraid we would be overheard.

"I thought you were—sleeping."

"I suppose I have been in a coma most of the time. But when I was not, I feigned, so Vodalus would not question me. Are you going to escape?"

"Not without you, Sieur. Not now. I had given you up for dead."

"You were not far wrong . . . certainly not by so much as a day. Yes, I think that is best, you must escape. Father Inire is with the insurgents. He was to bring you what is necessary, then help you get away. But we are no longer there . . . are we? He may not be able to aid you. Open my robe. What you first require is thrust into my waistband."

I did as he asked; the flesh my fingers brushed was as cold as a corpse's. Near his left hip I saw a hilt of silvery metal no thicker than a woman's finger. I drew the weapon forth; the blade was not half a span in length, but thick and strong, and of that deadly sharpness I had not felt since Baldanders's mace had shattered *Terminus Est*.

"You must not go yet," the Autarch whispered.

"I will not leave you while you live," I said. "Do you doubt me?"

"We will both live, and both go. You know the abomination . . ." His hand closed on mine. "The eating of the dead, to devour their dead lives. But there is another way you do not know, and another drug. You must take it, and swallow the living cells of my forebrain."

I must have drawn away, for his hand gripped my own harder.

"When you lie with a woman, you thrust your life into hers so that perhaps there will be new life. When you do as I have commanded you, my life and the lives of all those who live in me will be continued in you. The cells will enter your own nervous system and multiply there. The drug is in the vial I wear at my neck, and that blade will split the bones of my skull like pine. I have had occasion to use it, and I promise it. Do you recall how you swore to serve me when I shut the book? Use the knife now, and go as quickly as you can."

I nodded and promised I would.

"The drug will be stronger than any you have known, and though all but mine will be faint, there will be hundreds of personalities. . . . We are many lives."

"I understand," I said.

"The Ascians march at dawn. Can there be more than a single watch remaining of the night?"

"I hope that you will live it out, Sieur, and many more. That you'll recover."

"You must kill me now, before Urth turns to face the sun. Then I will live in you . . . never die. I live by mere volition now. I am relinquishing my life as I speak."

To my utter surprise, my eyes were streaming with tears. "I've hated you since I was a boy, Sieur. I've done you no harm, but I would have harmed you if I could, and now I'm sorry."

His voice had faded until it was softer than the chirping of a cricket.

"You were right to hate me, Severian. I stand . . . as you will stand . . . for so much that is wrong."

"Why?" I asked. *"Why?"* I was on my knees beside him.

"Because all else is worse. Until the New Sun comes, we have but a choice of evils. All have been tried, and all have failed. Goods in common, the rule of the people . . . everything. You wish for progress? The Ascians have it. They are deafened by it, crazed by the death of Nature till they are ready to accept Erebus and the rest as gods. We hold humankind stationary . . . in barbarism. The Autarch protects the people from the exultants, and the exultants . . . shelter them from the Autarch. The religious comfort them. We have closed the roads to paralyze the social order. . . ."

His eyes fell shut. I put my hand upon his chest to feel the faint stirring of his heart.

"Until the New Sun . . ."

This was what I had sought to escape, not Agia or Vodalus or the Ascians. As gently as I could, I lifted the chain from his neck, unstoppered the vial and swallowed the drug. Then with that short, stiff blade I did what had to be done.

When it was over, I covered him from head to toe with his own saffron robe and hung the empty vial about my own neck. The effect of the drug was as violent as he had warned me it would be. You that read this, who have never, perhaps, possessed more than a single consciousness, cannot know what it is to have two or three, much less hundreds. They lived in me and were joyful, each in his own way, to find they had new life. The dead Autarch, whose face I had seen in scarlet ruin a few moments before, now lived again. My eyes and hands were his, I knew the work of the hives of the bees of the House Absolute and the sacredness of them, who steer by the sun and fetch gold of Urth's fertility. I knew his course to the Phoenix Throne, and to the stars, and back. His mind was mine and filled mine with lore whose existence I had never suspected and with the knowledge other minds had brought to his. The phenomenal world seemed dim and vague as a picture sketched in sand over which an errant wind veered and moaned. I could not have concentrated on it if I had wished to, and I had no such wish.

The black fabric of our prison tent faded to a pale dove-gray, and the angles of its top whirled like the prisms of a kaleidoscope. I had fallen without being aware of it and lay near the body of my predecessor, where my attempts to rise resulted in nothing more than the beating of my hands upon the ground.

* * *

How long I lay there I do not know. I had wiped the knife—now, still, *my* knife—and concealed it as he had. I could vividly picture a self of dozens of superposed images slitting the wall and slipping out into the night. Severian, Thecla, myriad others all escaping. So real was the thought that I often believed I had done it; but always, when I ought to have been running between the trees, avoiding the exhausted sleepers of the army of the Ascians, I found myself instead in the familiar tent, with the draped body not far from my own.

Hands clasped mine. I supposed that the officers had returned with their lashes, and tried to see and to rise so I would not be struck. But a hundred random memories intruded themselves like the pictures the owner holds up to us in rapid succession in a cheap gallery: a footrace, the towering pipes of an organ, a diagram with labeled angles, a woman riding in a cart.

Someone said, ''Are you all right? What's happened to you?'' I felt the spittle dribbling from my lips, but no words came.

XXX

The Corridors of Time

Something struck my face a tingling blow.

"What's happened? He's dead. Are you drugged?"

"Yes. Drugged." Someone else was speaking, and after a moment I knew who it was: Severian, the young torturer.

But who was I?

"Get up. We've got to get out."

"Sentry."

"Sentries," the voice corrected us. "There were three of them. We killed them."

I was walking down a stair white as salt, down to nenuphars and stagnant water. Beside me walked a suntanned girl with long and slanting eyes. Over her shoulder peered the sculptured face of one of the eponyms. The carver had worked in jade; the effect was that of a face of grass.

"Is he dying?"

"He sees us now. See his eyes."

I knew where I was. Soon the pitchman would thrust his head through the doorway of the tent to tell me to be gone. "Above ground," I said. "You told me I would see her above ground. But that was easy. She is here."

"We must go." The green man took my left arm and Agia my right, and they led me out.

We walked a long way, just as I had envisioned myself running, stepping sometimes over sleeping Ascians.

"They keep little guard," Agia whispered. "Vodalus told me their leaders are so well obeyed they can scarcely conceive of treacherous attack. In the war, our soldiers surprise them often."

I did not understand and repeated, " 'Our soldiers . . .' " like a child.

"Hethor and I will no longer fight for them. How could we, after we have seen them? My business is with you."

I was beginning to find myself again, the minds that made up *my* mind all falling into place. I had been told once that *autarch* meant "self-ruler," and I glimpsed the reason that title had come into being. I said, "You wanted to kill me. Now you are freeing me. You could have stabbed me." I saw a crooked dagger from Thrax quivering in Casdoe's shutter.

"I could have killed you more readily than that. Hethor's mirrors have given me a worm, no longer than your hand, that glows with white fire. I have only to fling it, and it kills and crawls back to me—one by one I slew the sentries so. But this green man would not permit it, and I would not wish it. Vodalus promised me your agony spread over weeks, and I will not have less."

"You're taking me back to him?"

She shook her head, and in the faint, gray dawn light that had crept through the leaves I saw her brown curls bounce on her shoulders as they had when I had watched her raise the gratings outside the rag shop. "Vodalus is dead. With the worm at my command, do you think I would let him cheat me and live? They would have taken you away. Now I will let you go free—because I have some inkling of where you will go—and in the end you will come into my hands again, as you did when our pteriopes took you from the evzones."

"You are rescuing me because you hate me then," I said, and she nodded. Vodalus, I suppose, had hated that part of me that had been the Autarch in the same way.

Or rather, he had hated his conception of the Autarch, for he had been loyal, in so far as he was capable of it, to the real Autarch, whom he supposed his servant. When I had been a boy in the kitchens of the House Absolute, there was a cook who so despised the armigers and exultants for whom he prepared food that, in order that he should never have to bear the indignity of their reproaches, he did everything with a feverish perfection. He was eventually made chief of the cooks of that wing. I thought of him, and while I did, Agia's touch on my arm, which had become almost imperceptible as we hastened along, vanished altogether. When I looked for her, she was gone; I was alone with the green man.

"How did you come to be here?" I asked him. "You nearly lost your life in these times, and I know you cannot thrive under our sun."

He smiled. Though his lips were green, his teeth were white; they gleamed in the faint light. "We are your children, and we are not less honest than you, though we do not kill to eat. You gave me half your stone, the stone that gnawed the iron and set me free. What did you think I would do when the chain no longer bound me?"

"I supposed you would return to your own day," I said. The spell of the drug had faded sufficiently for me to fear our talk would wake the Ascian soldiers. Yet I could see none—only the dark, towering boles of the jungle hardwoods.

"We requite our benefactors. I have been running up and down the corridors of Time, seeking for a moment in which you also were imprisoned, that I might free you."

When I heard that, I did not know what to say. At last I told him, "You cannot imagine how strange I feel now, knowing that someone has been searching my future, looking for an opportunity to do me good. But now, now that we are quits, surely you understand that I did not help you because I believed you could help me."

"You did—you desired my help in finding the woman who just left us, the woman whom since that occasion you have found several times. However, you ought to know that I was not alone: There are others questing there—I shall send two of them to you. And you and I are not yet at a balance, for although I found you captive here, the woman found you also and would have freed you without my help. So I shall see you again."

As he said these words, he let go of my arm and stepped in that direction I had never seen until I watched the ship vanish into it from the top of Baldanders's castle and could only see, it seemed, when there was something there. Immediately he turned and began to run, and despite the dimness of the dawn sky I could see his running figure for a long time, illuminated by intermittent but regular flashes. At last he faded to a point of darkness; but then, just when I expected that point to disappear utterly, it began to grow, so that I had the impression of something huge rushing toward me down that strangely angled tunnel.

It was not the ship I had seen but another and much smaller one. Still, it was so large that when it moved at last entirely into our field of consciousness, its gunwales touched several of the thick trunks at once. The hull dilated, and a pont, much shorter than the steps that had descended from the Autarch's flier, slid out to touch the ground.

Down it came Master Malrubius and my dog, Triskele.

At that moment I regained a command of my personality that I had not truly possessed since I had drunk alzabo with Vodalus and eaten Thecla's flesh. It was not that Thecla was gone (and indeed I could not wish her gone, though I knew that in many respects she had been a cruel and foolish woman) or that my predecessor and the hundred minds that had been enveloped in his had vanished. The old, simple structure of my single personality was no more; but the new, complex structure no longer dazzled and bewildered me. It was a maze, but I was the owner and even the builder of that maze, with the print of my thumb on every passageway. Malrubius touched me, and then taking my wondering hand in his laid it gently against his own cool cheek.

"You are real, then," I said.

"No. We are almost what you think us—powers from above the stage. Only not quite deities. You are an actor, I believe."

I shook my head. "Don't you know me, Master? You taught me when I was a boy, and I have become a journeyman of the guild."

"Yet you are an actor too. You have as much right to think of yourself in that way as the other. You had been performing when we spoke to you in the field near the Wall, and the next time we saw you, at the House Absolute, you were acting again. It was a good play; I should have liked to see the end."

"You were in our audience?"

Master Malrubius nodded. "As an actor, Severian, you surely know the phrase I hinted at a moment ago. It refers to some supernatural force, personified and brought onto the stage in the last act in order that the play may end well. None but poor playwrights do it, they say, but those who say so forget that it is better to have a power lowered on a rope, and a play that ends well, than to have nothing, and a play that ends badly. Here is our rope—many ropes, and a stout ship too. Will you come aboard?"

I said, "Is that why you are as you are? In order that I will trust you?"

"Yes, if you like." Master Malrubius nodded, and Triskele, who had been sitting at my feet and looking up into my face, ran with his bumping, three-legged gallop halfway up the pont and turned to look back at me, his stump tail wagging and his eyes pleading as a dog's eyes do.

"I know you can't be what you seem. Perhaps Triskele is, but I saw you buried, Master. Your face is no mask, but there's a mask somewhere, and under that mask you're what the common people call a cacogen, although Dr. Talos explained to me once that you prefer to be called Hierodules."

Again Malrubius laid his hand on mine. "We would not deceive you if we could. But I hope that you will deceive yourself, to your good and all Urth's. Some drug now dulls your mind—more than you realize—just as you were under the sway of sleep when we spoke to you in that meadow near the Wall. If you were undrugged now, perhaps you would lack the courage to come with us, even if you saw us, even if your reason convinced you that you should."

I said, "So far it hasn't convinced me of that, or of anything else. Where do you want to take me, and why do you want to take me there? Are you Master Malrubius or a Hierodule?" As I spoke I became more conscious of the trees, standing as soldiers stand while the officers of the staff discuss some point of strategy. Night was upon us still, but it had become a thinner darkness, even here.

"Do you know the meaning of that word *Hierodule* you use? I am Malrubius, and no Hierodule. Rather I serve those the Hierodules serve. *Hierodule* means *holy slave*. Do you think there can be slaves without masters?"

"And you take me—"

"To Ocean, to preserve your life." As if he had read my thought, he continued, "No, we do not take you to the paramours of Abaia, those who spared and succored you because you had been a torturer and would be Autarch. In any event, you have much worse to fear. Soon the slaves of Erebus, who held you captive here, will discover you have escaped; and Erebus would hurl that army, and many others like it, into the abyss to capture you. Come." He drew me onto the pont.

XXXI

The Sand Garden

That ship was worked by hands I could not see. I had supposed we would float up as the flier had or vanish like the green man down some corridor in time. Instead we rose so quickly I felt sick; alongside I heard the crashing of great limbs.

"You are the Autarch now," Malrubius told me. "Do you know it?" His voice seemed to blend with the whistle of the wind in the rigging.

"Yes. My predecessor, whose mind is now one of mine, came to office as I have. I know the secrets, the words of authority, though I haven't had time yet to think about them. Are you returning me to the House Absolute?"

He shook his head. "You are not ready. You believe that all the old Autarch knew is available to you now. You are correct—but it is not yet in your grasp, and when the tests come, you will encounter many who will slay you should you falter. You were nurtured in the Citadel of Nessus—what are the words for its castellan? How are the man-apes of the treasure mine to be commanded? What phrases unlock the vaults of the Secret House? You need not tell me, because these things are the arcana of your state, and I know them in any case. But do you yourself know them, without thinking long?"

The phrases I required were present in my mind, yet I failed when I sought to pronounce them to myself. Like little fish, they slipped aside, and in the end I could only lift my shoulders.

"And there is one thing more for you to do. One adventure more, beside the waters."

"What is it?"

"If I were to tell you, it would not come to pass. Do not be alarmed. It is a simple thing, over in a breath. But I must explain a great deal, and I have not much time in which to do it. Have you faith in the coming of the New Sun?''

As I had looked within myself for the words of command, so I looked within for my belief; and I could no more find it than I had found them. ''I have been taught so all my life,'' I said. ''But by teachers—the true Malrubius was one—who I think did not themselves believe. So I cannot now say whether I believe or not.''

''Who is the New Sun? A man? If a man, how can it be that every green thing is to grow darkly green again at his coming, and the granaries full?''

It was unpleasant to be drawn back to things half heard in childhood now, when I was just beginning to understand that I had inherited the Commonwealth. I said, ''He will be the Conciliator come again—his avatar, bringing justice and peace. In pictures he is shown with a shining face, like the sun. I was an apprentice of the torturers, not an acolyte, and that is all I can tell you.'' I drew my cloak about me for shelter from the cold wind. Triskele was huddled at my feet.

''And which does humanity need more? Justice and peace? Or a New Sun?''

At that I tried to smile. ''It has occurred to me that though you cannot possibly be my old teacher, you may incorporate his personality as I do the Chatelaine Thecla's. If that is so, you already know my answer. When a client is driven to the utmost extremity, it is warmth and food and ease from pain he wants. Peace and justice come afterward. Rain symbolizes mercy and sunlight charity, but rain and sunlight are better than mercy and charity. Otherwise they would degrade the things they symbolize.''

''To a large extent you are correct. The Master Malrubius you knew lives in me, and your old Triskele in this Triskele. But that is not important now. If there is time, you will understand before we go.'' Malrubius closed his eyes and scratched the gray hair on his chest, just as I remembered him doing when I was among the youngest of the apprentices. ''You were afraid to board this little ship, even when I told you it would not carry you away from Urth, or even to a continent other than your own. Suppose I were to tell you—I do *not* tell you, but suppose I did—that it would in fact take you from Urth, past the orbit of Phaleg, which you call Verthandi, past Bethor and Aratron, and at last into the outer dark, and across the dark to another place. Would you be frightened, now that you have sailed with us?''

''No man enjoys saying he is afraid. But yes, I would.''

''Afraid or not, would you go if it might bring the New Sun?''

It seemed then that some icy spirit from the gulf had already wrapped its hands about my heart. I was not deceived, nor, I think, did he mean I should be. To answer yes would be to undertake the journey. I hesitated, in silence except for the roar of my own blood in my ears.

"You need not answer now if you cannot. We will ask again. But I can tell you nothing more until you answer."

For a long time I stood on that strange deck, sometimes walking up and down, blowing on my fingers in the freezing wind while all my thoughts crowded around me. The stars watched us, and it seemed to me that Master Malrubius's eyes were two more such stars.

At last I returned to him and said, "I have long wanted . . . if it would bring the New Sun, I would go."

"I can give you no assurance. If it *might* bring the New Sun, would you then? Justice and peace, yes, but a New Sun—such an outpouring of warmth and energy upon Urth as she knew before the birth of the first man?"

Now came the strangest happening I have to tell in all this already overlong tale; yet there was no sound or sight associated with it, no speaking beast or gigantic woman. It was only that as I heard him I felt a pressure against my breastbone, as I had felt it in Thrax when I knew I should be going north with the Claw. I remembered the girl in the jacal. "Yes," I said. "If it might bring the New Sun, I would go."

"What if you were to stand trial there? You knew him who was autarch before you, and in the end you loved him. He lives in you. Was he a man?"

"He was a human being—as you, I think, are not, Master."

"That was not my question, as you know as well as I. Was he a man as you are a man? Half the dyad of man and woman?"

I shook my head.

"So you will become, should you fail the trial. Will you still go?"

Triskele laid his scarred head against my knee, the ambassador of all crippled things, of the Autarch who had carried a tray in the House Absolute and lain paralyzed in the palanquin waiting to pass to me the humming voices in his skull, of Thecla writhing under the Revolutionary, and of the woman even I, who had boasted I could forget nothing, had nearly forgotten, bleeding and dying beneath our tower. Perhaps after all it was my discovery of Triskele, which I have said changed nothing, that in the end changed everything. I did not have to answer this time; Master Malrubius saw my answer in my face.

"You know of the chasms of space, which some call the Black Pits, from which no speck of matter or gleam of light ever returns. But what you have not known until now is that these chasms have their counterparts in White Fountains, from which matter and energy rejected by a higher universe flow in endless cataract into this one. If you pass—if our race is judged ready to reenter the wide seas of space—such a white fountain will be created in the heart of our sun."

"But if I fail?"

"If you fail, your manhood will be taken from you, so that you cannot bequeath the Phoenix Throne to your descendants. Your predecessor also accepted the challenge."

"And failed. That is clear from what you said."

"Yes. Still, he was braver than many who are called heroes, the first to go in many reigns. Ymar, of whom you may have heard, was the last before him."

"Yet Ymar too must have been judged unfit. Are we going now? I can see only stars beyond the rail."

Master Malrubius shook his head. "You are not looking as carefully as you think. We are already near our destination."

Swaying, I walked to the railing. Some of my unsteadiness had its origin in the motion of the ship, I think; but some, too, came from the lingering effects of the drug.

Night still covered Urth, for we had flown swiftly to the west, and the faint dawn that had come to the Ascian army in the jungle had not yet appeared here. After a moment I saw that the stars over the side seemed to slip, and slide in their heaven, with an uneasy and wavering motion. Almost it seemed that something moved among the stars as the wind moves through wheat. Then I thought, *It is the sea* . . . and at that moment Master Malrubius said, "It is that great sea called Ocean."

"I have longed to visit it."

"In a short time you will be standing at its margin. You asked when you would leave this planet. Not until your rule here is secure. When the city and the House Absolute obey you and your armies have repelled the incursions of the slaves of Erebus. Within a few years, perhaps. But perhaps not for decades. We two will come for you."

"You are the second tonight to tell me I will see you again," I said. Just as I spoke, there was a slight shock, like the sensation one feels when a boat is brought skillfully to the dock. I walked down the pont and out upon sand, and Master Malrubius and Triskele followed me. I asked if they would not stay with me for a time to counsel me.

"For a short time only. If you have further questions, you must ask them now."

The silver tongue of the pont was already creeping back into the hull. It seemed that it had hardly come home before the ship lifted itself and scudded down the same aperture in reality into which the green man had run.

"You spoke of the peace and justice that the New Sun is to bring. Is there justice in his calling me so far? What is the test I must pass?"

"It is not he who calls you. Those who call hope to summon the New Sun to them," Master Malrubius said, but I did not understand him. Then he recounted to me in brief words the secret history of Time, which is the greatest of all secrets, and which I will set down here in the proper place. When he had finished, my mind reeled and I feared I would forget all he had said, because it seemed too great a thing for any living man to know, and because I had learned at last that the mists close for me as for other men.

"You will not forget, you above all. At Vodalus's banquet, you said you felt sure you would forget the foolish passwords he taught you in imitation of the words of authority. But you did not. You will remember everything. Remember too, not to be afraid. It may be that the epic penance of mankind is at an end. The old Autarch told you the truth—we will not go to the stars again until we go as a divinity, but that time may not be far off now. In you all the divergent tendencies of our race may have achieved synthesis."

Triskele stood on his hind legs for a moment as he used to, then spun around and galloped down the starlit beach, three paws scattering the little cat's-paw waves. When he was a hundred strides off he turned and looked back at me, as though he wished me to follow.

I took a few steps toward him, but Master Malrubius said, "You cannot go where he is going, Severian. I know you think us cacogens of a kind, and for a time I felt it would not be wise to wholly undeceive you, but I must do so now. We are aquastors, beings created and sustained by the power of the imagination and the concentration of thought."

"I have heard of such things," I told him. "But I have touched you."

"That is no test. We are as solid as most truly false things are—a dance of particles in space. Only the things no one can touch are true, as you should know by now. Once you met a woman named Cyriaca, who told you tales of the great thinking machines of the past. There is such a machine on the ship in which we sailed. It has the power to look into your mind."

I asked, "Are you that machine, then?" A feeling of loneliness and vague fear grew in me.

"I am Master Malrubius, and Triskele is Triskele. The machine looked among your memories and found us. Our lives in your mind are not so complete as those of Thecla and the old Autarch, but we are there nevertheless, and live while you live. But we are maintained in the physical world by the energies of the machine, and its range is but a few thousand years."

As he spoke these final words, his flesh was already fading into bright dust. For a moment it glinted in the cold starlight. Then it was gone. Triskele remained with me a few breaths longer, and when his yellow coat was already silvered and blowing away in the gentle breeze, I heard his bark.

Then I stood alone at the edge of the sea I had longed for so often; but though I was alone, I found it cheering, and breathed the air that is like no other, and smiled to hear the soft song of the little waves. Land—Nessus, the House Absolute, and all the rest—lay to the east; west lay the sea; I walked north because I was reluctant to leave it too soon, and because Triskele had run in that direction, along the margin of the sea. There great Abaia might wallow with his women, yet the sea was older far, and wiser than he; we human beings, like all the life of the land, had come from the sea; and because we could not conquer it, it was ours always. The old, red sun rose on my right and touched the waves with his fading beauty, and I heard the calling of the sea birds, the innumerable birds.

By the time the shadows were short, I was tired. My face and my wounded leg pained me; I had not eaten since noon of the previous day and had not slept save for my trance in the Ascian tent. I would have rested if I could, but the sun was warm, and the line of cliffs beyond the beach offered no shade. At last I followed the tracks of a two-wheeled cart and came to a clump of wild roses growing from a dune. There I halted, and seated myself in their shadow to take off my boots and pour out the sand that had entered their splitting seams.

A thorn caught my forearm and broke from its branch, remaining embedded in my skin, with a scarlet drop of blood, no bigger than a grain of millet, at its tip. I plucked it out—then fell to my knees.

It was the Claw.

The Claw perfect, shining black, just as I had placed it under the altar stone of the Pelerines. All that bush and all the other bushes growing with it were covered with white blossoms and these perfect Claws. The one in my palm flamed with transplendent light as I looked at it.

I had surrendered the Claw, but I had retained the little leather sack Dorcas had sewn for it. I took it from my sabretache and hung it about my neck in the old way, with the Claw once more inside. It was only when I had thus put it away that I recalled seeing just such a bush in the Botanic Gardens at the beginning of my journey.

* * *

No one can explain such things. Since I have come to the House Absolute, I have talked with the heptarch and with various acaryas; but they have been able to tell me very little save that the Increate has chosen before this to manifest himself in these plants.

At that time I did not think of it, being filled with wonder—but may it not be that we were guided to the unfinished Sand Garden? I carried the Claw even then, though I did not know it; Agia had already slipped it under the closure of my sabretache. Might it not be that we came to the unfinished garden so that the Claw, flying as it were against the wind of Time, might make its farewell? The idea is absurd. But then, all ideas are absurd.

What struck me on the beach—and it struck me indeed, so that I staggered as at a blow—was that if the Eternal Principle had rested in that curved thorn I had carried about my neck across so many leagues, and if it now rested in the new thorn (perhaps the same thorn) I had only now put there, then it might rest in anything, and in fact probably did rest in everything, in every thorn on every bush, in every drop of water in the sea. The thorn was a sacred Claw because all thorns were sacred Claws; the sand in my boots was sacred sand because it came from a beach of sacred sand. The cenobites treasured up the relics of the sannyasins because the sannyasins had approached the Pancreator. But everything had approached and even touched the Pancreator, because everything had dropped from his hand. Everything was a relic. All the world was a relic. I drew off my boots, that had traveled with me so far, and threw them into the waves that I might not walk shod on holy ground.

XXXII

The *Samru*

And I walked on as a mighty army, for I felt myself in the company of all those who walked in me. I was surrounded by a numerous guard; and I was the guard about the person of the monarch. There were women in my ranks, smiling and grim, and children who ran and laughed and, daring Erebus and Abaia, hurled seashells into the sea.

In half a day I came to the mouth of Gyoll, so wide that the farther shore was lost in distance. Three-sided isles lay in it, and through them vessels with billowing sails picked their way like clouds among the peaks of the mountains. I hailed one passing the point on which I stood and asked for passage to Nessus. A wild figure I must have appeared, with my scarred face and tattered cloak and every rib showing.

Her captain sent a boat for me nonetheless, a kindness I have not forgotten. I saw fear and awe in the eyes of the rowers. Perhaps it was only at the sight of my half-healed wounds; but they were men who had seen many wounds, and I recalled how I had felt when I first saw the face of the Autarch in the House Azure, though he was not a tall man, or even a man, truly.

Twenty days and nights the *Samru* made her way up Gyoll. We sailed when we could, and rowed, a dozen sweeps to a side, when we could not. It was a hard passage for the sailors, for though the current is almost imperceptibly slow, it runs day and night, and so long and so wide are the meanders of the channel that an oarsman often sees at evening the spot from which he labored when the beating of the drum first roused the watch.

For me it was as pleasant as a yachting expedition. Although I offered to make sail and row with the rest, they would not permit it. Then I told the captain, a sly-faced man who looked as though he lived by bargaining as much as by sailing, that I would pay him well when we reached Nessus; but he would not hear of it, and insisted (pulling at his mustache, which he did whenever he wished to show the greatest sincerity) that my presence was reward enough for him and his crew. I do not believe they guessed I was their Autarch, and for fear of such as Vodalus had been I was careful to drop no hints to them; but from my eyes and manner they seemed to feel I was an adept.

The incident of the captain's sword must have strengthened their superstition. It was a craquemarte, the heaviest of the sea swords, with a blade as wide as my palm, sharply curved and graven with stars and suns and other things the captain did not understand. He wore it when we were close enough to a riverbank village or another ship to make him feel the occasion demanded dignity; but for the most part he left it lying on the little quarterdeck. I found it there, and having nothing else to do but watch sticks and fruit skins bob in the green water, I took out my half stone and sharpened it. After a time he saw me testing the edge with my thumb and began to boast of his swordsmanship. Since the craquemarte was at least two-thirds the weight of *Terminus Est*, with a short grip, it was amusing to hear him; I listened with delight for half a watch or so. As it happened there was a hempen cable about the thickness of my wrist coiled nearby, and when he began to lose interest in his own inventions, I had him and the mate hold up three cubits or so between them. The craquemarte severed it like a hair; then before either of them could recover breath, I threw it flashing toward the sun and caught it by the hilt.

As I fear that incident shows too well, I was beginning to feel better. There is nothing to enthrall the reader in rest, fresh air, and plain food; but they can work wonders against wounds and exhaustion.

The captain would have given me his cabin if I had let him, but I slept on deck rolled in my cloak, and on our one night of rain found shelter under the boat, which was stowed bottom-up amidships. As I learned on board, it is the nature of breezes to die when Urth turns her back to the sun; so I went to sleep, on most nights, with the chant of the rowers in my ears. In the morning I woke to the rattle of the anchor chain.

Sometimes, though, I woke before morning, when we lay close to shore with only a sleepy lookout on deck. And sometimes the moonlight roused me to find us gliding forward under reefed sails, with the mate steering and the watch asleep beside the halyards. On one such night, shortly after we had passed through the Wall, I went aft and saw the phosphorescence of our wake like cold fire on the dark water and thought for a moment that the man-apes of the mine were coming to be cured by the Claw, or to gain an old revenge. That, of course, was not truly strange—only the foolish error of a mind still half in dream. What happened the next morning was not truly strange either, but it affected me deeply.

The oarsmen were rowing a slow beat to get us around a leagues-long bend to a point where we could catch what little wind there was. The sound of the drum and the hissing of the water falling from the long blades of the sweeps are hypnotic, I think because they are so similar to the beating of one's own heart in sleep and the sound the blood makes as it moves past the inner ear on its way to the brain.

I was standing by the rail looking at the shore, still marshy here where the plains of old have been flooded by silt-choked Gyoll; and it seemed to me that I saw forms in the hillocks and hummocks, as though all that vast, soft wilderness had a geometrical soul (as certain pictures do) that vanished when I stared at it, then reappeared when I took my eyes away. The captain came to stand beside me, and I told him I had heard that the ruins of the city extended far downriver and asked when we would sight them. He laughed and explained that we had been among them for the past two days, and loaned me his glass so I could see that what I had taken for a stump was in actuality a broken and tilted column covered with moss.

At once everything—walls, streets, monuments—seemed to spring from hiding, just as the stone town had reconstructed itself while we watched from the tomb roof with the two witches. No change had occurred outside my own mind, but I had been transported, far faster than Master Malrubius's ship could have taken me, from the desolate countryside to the midst of an ancient and immense ruin.

Even now I cannot help but wonder how much any of us see of what is before us. For weeks my friend Jonas had seemed to me only a man with a prosthetic hand, and when I was with Baldanders and Dr. Talos, I had overlooked a hundred clues that should have told me Baldanders was master. How impressed I was outside the Piteous Gate because Baldanders did not escape the doctor when he could.

As the day wore on, the ruins became plainer and plainer still. At each loop of the river, the green walls rose higher, from ever firmer ground. When I woke the next morning, some of the stronger buildings retained their upper stories. Not long afterward, I saw a little boat, newly built, tied to an ancient pier. I pointed it out to the captain, who smiled at my naivety and said, "There are families who live, grandson following grandsire, by sifting these ruins."

"So I've been told, but that cannot be one of their boats. It's too small to take much loot away in."

"Jewelry or coins. No one else goes ashore here. There's no law—the pillagers murder each other, and anyone else who lands."

"I must go there. Will you wait for me?"

He stared at me as though I were mad. "How long?"

"Until noon. No later."

"Look," he said, and pointed. "Ahead is the last big bend. Leave us here and meet us there, where the channel bows around again. It will be afternoon before we get there."

I agreed, and he had the *Samru*'s boat put into the water for me, and told four men to row me ashore. As we were about to cast off, he unbelted his craquemarte and handed it to me, saying solemnly, "It has stood by me in many a grim fight. Go for their heads, but be careful not to knick the edge on their belt buckles."

I accepted his sword with thanks, and told him I had always favored the neck. "That's good," he said, "if you don't have shipmates by that might be hurt when you swing it flat," and he pulled his mustache.

Sitting in the stern, I had ample opportunity to observe the faces of my rowers, and it was plain they were nearly as frightened of the shore as they were of me. They laid us alongside the small boat, then nearly capsized their own in their haste to be away. After determining that what I had seen from the rail was in fact what I had taken it to be, a wilted scarlet poppy left lying on the single seat, I watched them row back to the *Samru* and saw that though a light wind now favored the billowing mains'l, the sweeps had been brought out and were beating a quick-stroke. Presumably the captain planned to round the long meander as swiftly as he could; if I were not at the spot he had pointed out, he could proceed without me, telling himself (and others, should others inquire) that it was I who had failed our appointment and not he. By parting with the craquemarte he had further salved his conscience.

Stone steps very like those I had swum from as a boy had been cut into the sides of the pier. Its top was empty, nearly as lush as a lawn with the grass that had rooted between its stones. The ruined city, my own city of Nessus though it was the Nessus of a time now long past, lay quiet before me. A few birds wheeled overhead, but they were as silent as the sun-dimmed stars. Gyoll, whispering to itself in midstream, already seemed detached from me and the empty hulks of buildings among which I limped. As soon as I was out of sight of its waters, it fell silent, like some uncertain visitor who ceases to speak when we step into another room.

It seemed that this could hardly be the quarter from which (as Dorcas had told me) furniture and utensils were taken. At first I looked in often at doors and windows, but nothing had been left within but wrack and a few yellow leaves, drifted already from the young trees that were overturning the paving blocks. Nor did I see any sign of human pillagers, although there were animal droppings and a few feathers and scattered bones.

I do not know how far inland I walked. It seemed a league, though it may have been much less. Losing the transportation of the *Samru* did not much bother me. I had walked from Nessus most of the way to the mountain war, and although my steps were uneven still, my bare feet had been toughened on the deck. Because I had never really become accustomed to carrying a sword at my waist, I drew the craquemarte and put it on my shoulder, as I had often borne *Terminus Est.* The summer sunshine held that special, luxurious warmth it gains when a suggestion of chill has crept into the morning air. I enjoyed it, and would have enjoyed it more, and the silence and solitude too, if I had not been thinking of what I would say to Dorcas, if I found her, and what she might say to me.

Had I only known, I might have saved myself that concern; I came upon her sooner than I could reasonably have expected, and I did not speak to her—nor did she speak to me, or so far as I could judge, even see me.

The buildings, which had been large and solid near the river, had long since given way to lesser, fallen-in structures that must once have been houses and shops. I do not know what guided me to hers. There was no sound of weeping, though there may have been some small, unconscious noise, the creaking of a hinge or the scrape of a shoe. Perhaps it was no more than the perfume of the blossom she wore, because when I saw her she had an arum, freckled white and sweet as Dorcas herself had always been, thrust into her hair. No doubt she had brought it there for that purpose, and had taken out the wilted poppy and cast it down when she had tied up her boat. (But I have gotten ahead of my story.)

I tried to enter the building from the front, but the rotting floor was falling into the foundation in places as the arches under it collapsed. The storeroom at the rear was less open; the silent, shadowed walk, green with ferns, had been a dangerous alley once, and shopkeepers had put small windows there or none. Still, I found a narrow door hidden under ivy, a door whose iron had been eaten like sugar by the rain, whose oak was falling into mould. Stairs nearly sound led to the floor above.

She was kneeling with her back to me. She had always been slender; now her shoulders made me think of a wooden chair with a woman's jupe hung over it. Her hair, like the palest gold, was the same—unchanged since I had seen her first in the Garden of Endless Sleep. The body of the old man who had poled the skiff there lay on a bier before her, his back so straight, his face, in death, so youthful, that I hardly knew him. On the floor near her was a basket—not small yet not large either, and a corked water jar.

I said nothing, and when I had watched her for a time I went away. If she had been there long, I would have called to her and embraced her. But she had just arrived, and I saw that it was impossible. All the time I had spent in journeying from Thrax to Lake Diuturna, and from the lake to the war, and all the time I had spent as a prisoner of Vodalus, and in sailing up Gyoll, she had spent in returning here to her place, where she had lived forty years ago or more though it had now fallen into decay.

As I had myself, an ancient buzzing with antiquity as a corpse with flies. Not that the minds of Thecla and the old Autarch, or the hundred contained in his, had made me old. It was not their memories but my own that aged me, as I thought of Dorcas shivering beside me on the brown track of floating sedge, both of us cold and dripping, drinking together from Hildegrin's flask like two infants, which in fact we had been.

I paid no heed to where I walked after that. I went straight down a long street alive with silence, and when it ended at last I turned at random. After a time I reached Gyoll, and looking downstream saw the *Samru* riding at anchor at the meeting place. A basilosaur swimming up from the open sea would not have astounded me more.

In a few moments I was mobbed by smiling sailors. The captain wrung my hand, saying, "I was afraid we'd come too late. In my mind's eye I could see you struggling for your life in sight of the river, and us still half a league off."

The mate, a man so abysmally stupid that he thought the captain a leader, clapped me on the back and shouted, "He'd have given 'em a good fight!"

XXXIII

The Citadel of the Autarch

Though every league that separated me from Dorcas tore my heart, it was better than I can tell you to be back on the *Samru* again after seeing the empty, silent south.

Her decks were of the impure but lovely white of new-cut wood, scrubbed daily with a great mat called a *bear*—a sort of scouring pad woven from old cordage and weighed with the gross bodies of our two cooks, whom the crew had to drag over the last span of planking before breakfast. The crevices between the planks were sealed with pitch, so that the decks seemed terraces paved in a bold, fantastic design.

She was high in the bow, with a stem that curled back upon her. Eyes, each with a pupil as big as a plate and a sky-blue iris of the brightest obtainable paint, stared out across the green waters to help find her way; her left eye swept the anchor.

Forward of her stem, held there by a triangular wooden brace itself carved, pierced, gilded, and painted, was her figurehead, the bird of immortality. Its head was a woman's, the face long and aristocratic, the eyes tiny and black, its expressionlessness a magnificent commentary on the somber tranquillity of those who will never know death. Painted wooden feathers grew from its wooden scalp to clothe its shoulders and cup its hemispherical breasts; its arms were wings lifted up and back, their tips reaching higher than the termination of the stem and their gold and crimson primary feathers partially obscuring the triangular brace. I would have thought it a creature wholly fabulous—as no doubt the sailors did—had I not seen the Autarch's anpiels.

A long bowsprit passed to starboard of the stem, between the wings of the samru. The foremast, only slightly longer than this bowsprit, rose from the forecastle. It was raked forward to give the foresail room, as though it had been pulled out of true by the forestay and the laboring jib. The mainmast stood as straight as the pine it had once been, but the mizzenmast was raked back, so the mastheads of the three masts were considerably more separated than their bases. Each mast held a slanting yard made by lashing together two tapering spars that had once been entire saplings, and each of these yards carried a single, triangular, rust-colored sail.

The hull itself was painted white below the water and black above it, save for the figurehead and eyes I have already mentioned, and the quarterdeck rail, where scarlet had been used to symbolize both the captain's high state and his sanguinary background. This quarterdeck actually occupied no more than a sixth of the *Samru*'s length, but the wheel and the binnacle were there, and it was there that one had the finest view, short of that provided by the rigging. The ship's only real armament, a swivel gun not much larger than Mamillian's, was there, ready alike for freebooters and mutineers. Just aft of the sternrail, two iron posts as delicately curved as the horns of a cricket lifted many-faceted lanterns, one of palest red, the other viridescent as moonlight.

I was standing by these lanterns the next evening, listening to the thudding of the drum, the soft splashing of the sweepblades, and the rowers' chant, when I saw the first lights along the riverbank. Here was the dying edge of the city, the home of the poorest of the poorest of the poor—which only meant that the living edge of the city was here, that death's dominion ended here. Human beings were preparing to sleep here, perhaps still sharing the meal that marked the day's end. I saw a thousand kindnesses in each of those lights, and heard a thousand fireside stories. In some sense I was home again; and the same song that had urged me forth in the spring now bore me back:

Row, brothers, row!
The current is against us.
Row, brothers, row!
Yet God is for us.
Row, brothers, row!
The wind is against us.
Row, brothers, row!
Yet God is for us.

I could not help but wonder who was setting out that night.

Every long story, if it be told truly, will be found to contain all the elements that have contributed to the human drama since the first rude ship reached the strand of Lune: not only noble deeds and tender emotion, but grotesquerie, bathos, and so on. I have striven to set down the unembellished truth here, without the least worry that you, my reader, would find some parts improbable and others insipid; and if the mountain war was the scene of high deeds (belonging more to others than to me), and my imprisonment by Vodalus and the Ascians a time of horror, and my passage on the *Samru* an interlude of tranquillity, then we are come to the interval of comedy.

We approached that part of the city where the Citadel stands—which is southern but not the southernmost—under sail and by day. I watched the sun-gilt eastern bank with great care, and had the captain land me on those slimy steps where I had once swum and fought. I hoped to pass through the necropolis gate and so enter the Citadel through the breach in the curtain wall that was near the Matachin Tower; but the gate was closed and locked, and no convenient party of volunteers arrived to admit me. Thus I was forced instead to walk many chains along the margin of the necropolis, and several more along the curtain wall to the barbican.

There I encountered a numerous guard who carried me before their officer, who, when I told him I was a torturer, supposed me to be one of those wretches that, most often at the onset of winter, seek to gain admission to the guild. He decided (very properly, had he been correct) to have me whipped; and to prevent it I was forced to break the thumbs of two of his men, and then demand while I held him in the way called the *kitten and ball* that he take me to his superior, the castellan.

I admit I was somewhat awed at the thought of this official, whom I had seldom so much as seen in all the years I had been an apprentice in the fortress he commanded. I found him an old soldier, silver-haired and as lame as I. The officer stammered out his accusations while I stood by: I had assaulted and insulted (not true) his person, maimed two of his men, and so on. When he had finished, the castellan looked from me to him and back again, dismissed him, and offered me a seat.

"You are unarmed," he said. His voice was hoarse but soft, as though he had strained it shouting commands.

I admitted that I was.

"But you have seen fighting, and you have been in the jungle north of the mountains, where no battle has been since they turned our flank by crossing the Uroboros."

"That's true," I said. "But how can you know?"

"That wound in your thigh came from one of their spears. I've seen enough to recognize them. The beam flashed up through the muscle, reflected by the bone. You might have been up a tree and been stuck by a hastarus on the ground, I suppose, but the most likely thing is that you were mounted and charging infantry. Not a cataphract, or they wouldn't have got you so easily. The demilances?"

"Only the light irregulars."

"You'll have to tell me about that later, because you're a city man from your accent, and they're eclectics and suchlike for the most part. You have a double scar on your foot too, white and clean, with the marks half a span apart. That was a blood bat's bite, and they don't come that large except in the true jungle at the waist of the world. How did you get there?"

"Our flier crashed. I was taken prisoner."

"And escaped?"

In a moment more I would have been forced to talk of Agia and the green man, and of my journey from the jungle to the mouth of Gyoll, and those were high matters which I did not wish to disclose thus casually. Instead of an answer, I pronounced the words of authority applicable to the Citadel and its castellan.

Because he was lame, I would have had him remain seated if I could; but he sprang to his feet and saluted, then dropped to his knees to kiss my hand. He was thus, though he could not have known it, the first to pay me homage, a distinction that entitles him to a private audience once a year—an audience he has not yet requested and perhaps never will.

For me to proceed now, clothed as I was, was impossible. The old castellan would have died of a stroke had I demanded it, and he was so concerned for my safety that any incognito would have been accompanied by at least a platoon of lurking halberdiers. I soon found myself arrayed in lapis lazuli jazerant, cothurni, and a stephane, the whole set off by an ebony baculus and a voluminous damassin cape embroidered with rotting pearls. All these things were indescribably ancient, having been taken from a store preserved from the period when the Citadel was the residence of the autarchs.

Thus in place of entering our tower, as I had intended, in the same cloak in which I had left it, I returned as an unrecognizable being in ceremonial fancy dress, skeletally thin, lame, and hideously scarred. It was with this appearance that I entered Master Palaemon's study, and I am certain I must almost have frightened him to death, since he had been told only a few moments before that the Autarch was in the Citadel and wished to converse with him.

He seemed to me to have aged a great deal while I was gone. Perhaps it was simply that I recalled him not as he was when I was exiled, but as I had seen him in our little classroom when I was a boy. Still, I like to think he was concerned for me, and it is not really so unlikely that he was: I had always been his best pupil and his favorite; it was his vote, beyond doubt, that had countered Master Gurloes's and saved my life; he had given me his sword.

But whether he had worried much or little, his face seemed more deeply lined than it had been; and his scant hair, which I had thought gray, was now of that yellow hue seen in old ivory. He knelt and kissed my fingers, and was more than a little surprised when I helped him to rise and told him to seat himself behind his table again.

"You are too kind, Autarch," he said. Then, using an old formula, "Your mercy extends from sun to Sun."

"Do you not recall us?"

"Were you confined here?" He peered at me through the curious arrangement of lenses that alone permitted him to see at all, and I decided that his vision, exhausted long before I was born on the faded ink of the records of the guild, must have deteriorated further. "You have suffered torment, I see. But it is too crude, I hope, for our work."

"It was not your doing," I said, touching the scars on my cheek. "Nevertheless, we were confined for a time in the oubliette beneath this tower."

He sighed—an old man's shallow breath—and looked down at the gray litter of his papers. When he spoke I could not hear the words, and had to ask him to repeat them.

"It has come," he said. "I knew it would, but I hoped to be dead and forgotten. Will you dismiss us, Autarch? Or put us to some other task?"

"We have not yet decided what we will do with you and the guild you serve."

"It will not avail. If I offend you, Autarch, I ask your indulgence for my age . . . but still it will not avail. You will find in the end that you require men to do what we do. You may call it healing, if you wish. That has been done often. Or ritual, that has been done too. But you will find the thing itself grows more terrible in its disguise. Will you imprison those undeserving of death? You will find them a mighty army in chains. You will discover that you hold prisoners whose escape would be a catastrophe, and that you need servants who will wreak justice on those who have caused scores to die in agony. Who else will do that?"

"No one will wreak such justice as you. You say our mercy extends from sun to Sun, and we hope it is so. By our mercy we will grant even the foulest a quick death. Not because we pity them, but because it is intolerable that good men should spend a lifetime dispensing pain."

His head came up and the lenses flashed. For the only time in all the years I had known him, I was able to see the youth he had been. "It must be done by good men. You are badly advised, Autarch! What is intolerable is that it should be done by bad men."

I smiled. His face, as I had seen it then, had recalled something I had thrust from my mind months before. It was that this guild was my family, and all the home I should ever have. I would never find a friend in the world if I could not find friends here. "Between us, Master," I told him, "we have decided it should not be done at all."

He did not reply, and I saw from his expression that he had not even heard what I had said. He had been listening instead to my voice, and doubt and joy flickered over his worn, old face like shadow and firelight.

"Yes," I said. "It is Severian," and while he was struggling to regain possession of himself, I went to the door and got my sabretache, which I had ordered one of the officers of my guard to bring. I had wrapped it in what had been my fuligin guild cloak, now faded to mere rusty black. Spreading the cloak over Master Palaemon's table, I opened the sabretache and poured out its contents. "This is all we have brought back," I said.

He smiled as he used to in the schoolroom when he had caught me out in some minor matter. "That and the throne? Will you tell me about it?"

And so I did. It took a long while, and more than once my protectors rapped at the door to ascertain that I was unharmed, and at last I had a meal brought in to us; and when the pheasant was mere bones and the cakes were eaten and the wine drunk, we were still talking. It was then that I conceived the idea that has at last borne fruit in this record of my life. I had originally intended to begin it at the day I left our tower and to end it when I returned. But I soon saw that though such a construction would indeed supply the symmetry so valued by artists, it would be impossible for anyone to understand my adventures without knowing something of my adolescence. In the same way, some elements of my story would remain incomplete if I did not extend it (as I propose to do) a few days beyond my return. Perhaps I have contrived for someone *The Book of Gold*. Indeed, it may be that all my wanderings have been no more than a contrivance of the librarians to recruit their numbers; but perhaps even that is too much to hope.

XXXIV

The Key to the Universe

When he had heard everything, Master Palaemon went to my little heap of possessions and took up the grip, pommel, and silver guard that were all that remained of *Terminus Est*. "She was a good sword," he said. "Nearly I gave you your death, but she was a good sword."

"We were always proud to bear her, and never found reason to complain of her."

He sighed, and the breath seemed to catch in his throat. "She is gone. It is the blade that is the sword, not the sword furniture. The guild will preserve these somewhere, with your cloak and sabretache, because they have belonged to you. When you and I have been dead for centuries, old men like me will point them out to the apprentices. It's a pity we haven't the blade too. I used her for many years before you came to the guild, and never thought she would be destroyed fighting some diabolical weapon." He put down the opal pommel and frowned at me. "What's troubling you? I've seen men wince less when their eyes were torn out."

"There are many kinds of diabolical weapons, as you call them, that steel cannot withstand. We saw something of them when we were in Orithyia. And there are tens of thousands of our soldiers there holding them off with firework lances and javelins, and swords less well forged than *Terminus Est*. They succeed in so far as they do because the energy weapons of the Ascians are not numerous, and they are few because the Ascians lack the sources of power needed to produce them. What will happen if Urth is granted a New Sun? Won't the Ascians be better able to use its energy than we can?"

"Perhaps that may be," Master Palaemon acknowledged.

"We have been thinking with the autarchs who have gone before us—our guild brothers, as it were, in a new guild. Master Malrubius said that only our predecessor has dared the test in modern times. When we touch the minds of the others, we often find that they have refused it because they felt our enemies, who have retained so much more of the ancient sciences, would gain a greater advantage. Is it not possible they were right?''

Master Palaemon thought a long time before he answered. ''I cannot say. You believe me wise because I taught you once, but I have not been north, as you have. You have seen armies of Ascians, and I have never seen one. You flatter me by asking my opinion. Still—from all you've said, they are rigid, cast hard in their ways. I would guess that very few among them think much.''

I shrugged. ''That is true in any aggregate, Master. But as you say, it is possibly more true among them. And what you call their rigidity is terrible—a deadness that surpasses belief. Individually they seem men and women, but together they are like a machine of wood and stone.''

Master Palaemon rose and went to the port and looked out upon the thronging towers. ''We are too rigid here,'' he said. ''Too rigid in our guild, too rigid in the Citadel. It tells me a great deal that you, who were educated here, saw them as you did; they must be inflexible indeed. I think it may be that despite their science, which may amount to less than you suppose, the people of the Commonwealth will be better able to turn new circumstances to their benefit.''

''We are not flexible or inflexible,'' I said. ''Except for an unusually good memory, we are only an ordinary man.''

''No, no!'' Master Palaemon struck his table, and again the lenses flashed. ''You are an extraordinary man in an ordinary time. When you were a little apprentice, I beat you once or twice—you will recall that, I know. But even when I beat you, I knew you would become an extraordinary personage, the greatest master our guild would ever have. And you will be a master. Even if you destroy our guild, we will elect you!''

''We have already told you we mean to reform the guild, not destroy it. We're not even sure we're competent to do that. You respect us because we've moved to the highest place. But we reached it by chance, and know it. Our predecessor reached it by chance too, and the minds he brought to us, which we touch only faintly even now, are not, with one or two exceptions, those of genius. Most are only common men and women, sailors and artisans, farmwives and wantons. Most of the rest are eccentric second-rate scholars of the sort Thecla used to laugh at.''

''You have not just moved into the highest place,'' Master Palaemon said, ''you have become it. You are the state.''

"We are not. The state is everyone else—you, the castellan, those officers outside. We are the people, the Commonwealth." I had not known it myself until I spoke.

I picked up the brown book. "We are going to keep this. It was one of the good things, like your sword. The writing of books shall be encouraged again. There are no pockets in these clothes; but perhaps it will do good if we are seen to carry it when we leave."

"Carry it where?" Master Palaemon cocked his head like an old raven.

"To the House Absolute. We've been out of touch, or the Autarch has, if you wish to put it so, for over a month. We have to find out what's happening at the front, and perhaps dispatch reinforcements." I thought of Lomer and Nicarete, and the other prisoners in the antechamber. "We have other tasks there too," I said.

Master Palaemon stroked his chin. "Before you go, Severian—Autarch—would you like to tour the cells, for old times' sake? I doubt those fellows out there know of the door that opens to the western stair."

It is the least-used staircase in the tower, and perhaps the oldest. Certainly it is the one least altered from its original condition. The steps are narrow and steep, and wind down around a central column black with corrosion. The door to the room where I, as Thecla, had been subjected to the device called the Revolutionary stood half open, so that though we did not go inside, I nevertheless saw its ancient mechanisms: frightful, yet less hideous to me than the gleaming but far older things in Baldanders's castle.

Entering the oubliette meant returning to something I had, from the time I left for Thrax, assumed gone forever. Yet the metal corridors with their long rows of doors were unchanged, and when I peered through the tiny windows that pierced those doors I saw familiar faces, the faces of men and women I had fed and guarded as a journeyman.

"You are pale, Autarch," Master Palaemon said. "I feel your hand tremble." (I was supporting him a little with one hand on his arm.)

"You know that our memories never fade," I said. "For us the Chatelaine Thecla still sits in one of these cells, and the Journeyman Severian in another."

"I had forgotten. Yes, it must be terrible for you. I was going to take you to the Chatelaine's old one, but perhaps you would rather not see it."

I insisted that we visit it; but when we arrived, there was a new client inside, and the door was locked. I had Master Palaemon call the brother on duty to let us in, then stood for a moment looking at the cramped bed and the tiny table. At last I noticed the client, who sat upon the single chair, with wide eyes and an indescribable expression blended of hope and wonder. I asked him if he knew me.

"No, exultant."

"We are no exultant. We are your Autarch. Why are you here?"

He rose, then fell to his knees. "I am innocent! Believe me!"

"All right," I said. "We believe you. But we want you to tell us what you were accused of, and how you came to be convicted."

Shrilly, he began to pour forth one of the most complex and confused accounts I have ever heard. His sister-in-law had conspired with her mother against him. They said he had struck his wife, that he had neglected his ill wife, that he had stolen certain moneys from her that she had been entrusted with by her father, for purposes about which they disagreed. In explaining all this (and much more) he boasted of his own cleverness while decrying the frauds, tricks, and lies of the others that had sent him to the oubliette. He said that the gold in question had never existed, and also that his mother-in-law had used a part of it to bribe the judge. He said he had not known his wife was ill, and that he had procured the best physician he could afford for her.

When I left him, I went to the next cell and heard the client there, and then to the next and the next, until I had visited fourteen. Eleven clients protested their innocence, some better than the first, some even worse; but I found none whose protestations convinced me. Three admitted that they were guilty (though one swore, I think sincerely, that though he had committed most of the crimes with which he had been charged, he had also been charged with several he had not committed). Two of these promised earnestly to do nothing that would return them to the oubliette if only I would release them; which I did. The third—a woman who had stolen children and forced them to serve as articles of furniture in a room she had set aside for the purpose, in one instance nailing the hands of a little girl to the underside of a small tabletop so that she became in effect its pedestal—told me with apparently equal frankness that she felt sure she would return to what she called her sport because it was the only activity that really interested her. She did not ask to be released, only to have her sentence commuted to simple imprisonment. I felt certain she was mad; yet nothing in her conversation or her clear blue eyes indicated it, and she told me she had been examined prior to her trial and pronounced sane. I touched her forehead with the New Claw, but it was as inert as the old Claw had been when I had attempted to use it to help Jolenta and Baldanders.

* * *

I cannot escape the thought that the power manifested in both Claws is drawn from myself, and that it is for this reason that their radiance, said by others to be warm, has always seemed cold to me. This thought is the psychological equivalent of that aching abyss in the sky into which I feared to fall when I slept in the mountains. I reject and fear it because I desire so fervently that it be true; and I feel that if there were the least echo of truth in it, I would detect it within myself. I do not.

Furthermore, there are profound objections to it besides this lack of internal resonance, the most important, convincing, and apparently inescapable being that the Claw unquestionably reanimated Dorcas after many decades of death—and did so before I knew I carried it.

That argument appears conclusive; and still I am not sure that it is so. Did I in fact know? What is meant by *know*, in an appropriate sense? I have assumed I was unconscious when Agia slipped the Claw into my sabretache; but I may have been merely dazed, and in any case, many have long believed that unconscious persons are aware of their surroundings and respond internally to speech and music. How else explain the dreams dictated by external sounds? What portion of the brain is unconscious, after all? Not the whole of it, or the heart would not beat and the lungs no longer breathe. Much of the memory is chemical. All that, in fact, I have from Thecla and the former Autarch is fundamentally so—the drugs serving only to permit the complex compounds of thought to enter my own brain as information. May it not be that certain information derived from external phenomena are chemically impressed on our brains even when the electrical activity on which we depend for conscious thought has temporarily ceased?

Besides, if the energy has its origins in me, why should it have been necessary for me to be aware of the presence of the Claw for them to operate, any more than it would be necessary if they had their origin in the Claw itself? A strong suggestion of another kind might be equally effective, and certainly our careening invasion of the sacred precincts of the Pelerines and the way in which Agia and I emerged unhurt from the accident that killed the animals might have furnished such a suggestion. From the cathedral we had gone to the Botanic Gardens, and there, before we entered the Garden of Endless Sleep, I had seen a bush covered with Claws. At that time I believed the Claw to be a gem, but may not they have suggested it nonetheless? Our minds often play such punning tricks. In the yellow house we had met three persons who believed us supernatural presences.

If the supernatural power is mine (and yet clearly it is not mine), how did I come to have it? I have devised two explanations, both wildly improbable. Dorcas and I talked once of the symbolic significance of real-world things, which by the teachings of the philosophers stand for things higher than themselves, and in a lower order are themselves symbolized. To take an absurdly simple example, suppose an artist in a garret limning a peach. If we put the poor artist in the place of the Increate, we may say that his picture symbolizes the peach, and thus the fruits of the soil, while the glowing curve of the peach itself symbolizes the ripe beauty of womanhood. Were such a woman to enter the artist's garret (an improbability we must entertain for the sake of the explanation), she would doubtless remain unaware that the fullness of her hip and the hardness of her heart found their echoes in a basket on the table by the window, though perhaps the artist might be able to think of nothing else.

But if the Increate is in actual fact in place of the artist, is it not possible that such connections as these, many of which must always be unguessable by human beings, may have profound effects on the structure of the world, just as the artist's obsession may color his picture? If I am he who is to renew the youth of the sun with the White Fountain of which I have been told, may it not be that I have been given, almost unconsciously (if that expression may be used), the attributes of life and light that will belong to the renewed sun?

The other explanation I mentioned is hardly more than a speculation. But if, as Master Malrubius told me, those who will judge me among the stars will take my manhood should I fail their judgment, is it not possible also that they will confirm me in some gift of equal worth should I, as Humanity's representative, conform to their desires? It seems to me that justice demands it. If that is the case, may it not be that their gift transcends time, as they do themselves? The Hierodules I met in Baldanders's castle said they interested themselves in me because I would gain the throne—but would their interest have been so great if I were to be no more than the embattled ruler of some part of this continent, one of many embattled rulers in the long history of Urth?

On the whole, I think the first explanation the most probable; but the second is not wholly unlikely. Either would seem to indicate that the mission I am about to set out on will succeed. I will go with good heart.

And yet there is a third explanation. No human being or near-human being can conceive of such minds as those of Abaia, Erebus, and the rest. Their power surpasses understanding, and I know now that they could crush us in a day if it were not that they count only enslavement, and not annihilation, as victory. The great undine I saw was their creature, and less than their slave: their toy. It is possible that the power of the Claw, the Claw taken from a growing thing so near their sea, comes ultimately from them. They knew my destiny as well as Ossipago, Barbatus, and Famulimus, and they saved me when I was a boy so that I might fulfill it. After I departed from the Citadel they found me again, and thereafter my course was twisted by the Claw. Perhaps they hope to triumph by raising a torturer to the Autarchy, or to that position that is higher than the Autarch's.

Now I think that it is time to record what Master Malrubius explained to me. I cannot vouch for its truth, but I believe it to be true. I know no more than I set down here.

Just as a flower blooms, throws down its seed, dies, and rises from its seed to bloom again, so the universe we know diffuses itself to nullity in the infinitude of space, gathers its fragments (which because of the curvature of that space meet at last where they began) and from that seed blooms again. Each such cycle of flowering and decay marks a divine year.

As the flower that comes is like the flower from which it came, so the universe that comes repeats the one whose ruin was its origin; and this is as true of its finer features as of its grosser ones: The worlds that arise are not unlike the worlds that perished, and are peopled by similar races, though just as the flower evolves from summer to summer, all things advance by some minute step.

In a certain divine year (a time truly inconceivable to us, though that cycle of the universes was but one in an endless succession), a race was born that was so like to ours that Master Malrubius did not scruple to call it human. It expanded among the galaxies of its universe even as we are said to have done in the remote past, when Urth was, for a time, the center, or at least the home and symbol, of an empire.

These men encountered many beings on other worlds who had intelligence to some degree, or at least the potential for intelligence, and from them—that they might have comrades in the loneliness between the galaxies and allies among their swarming worlds—they formed beings like themselves.

It was not done swiftly or easily. Uncountable billions suffered and died under their guiding hands, leaving ineradicable memories of pain and blood. When their universe was old, and galaxy so far separated from galaxy that the nearest could not be seen even as faint stars, and the ships were steered thence by ancient records alone, the thing was done. Completed, the work was greater than those who began it could have guessed. What had been made was not a new race like Humanity's, but a race such as Humanity wished its own to be: united, compassionate, just.

I was not told what became of the Humanity of that cycle. Perhaps it survived until the implosion of the universe, then perished with it. Perhaps it evolved beyond our recognition. But the beings Humanity had shaped into what men and women wished to be escaped, opening a passage to Yesod, the universe higher than our own, where they created worlds suited to what they had become.

From that vantage point they look both forward and back, and in so looking they have discovered us. Perhaps we are no more than a race like that who shaped them. Perhaps it was we who shaped them—or our sons—or our fathers. Malrubius said he did not know, and I believe he told the truth. However it may be, they shape us now as they themselves were shaped; it is at once their repayment and their revenge.

The Hierodules they have found too, and formed more quickly, to serve them in this universe. On their instructions, the Hierodules construct such ships as the one that bore me from the jungle to the sea, so that aquastors like Malrubius and Triskele may serve them also. With these tongs, we are held in the forge.

The hammer they wield is their ability to draw their servants back, down the corridors of time, and to send them hurtling forward to the future. (This power is in essence the same as that which permitted them to evade the death of their universe—to enter the corridors of time is to leave the universe.) On Urth at least, their anvil is the necessity of life: our need in this age to fight against an ever-more-hostile world with the resources of the depleted continents. Because it is as cruel as the means by which they themselves were shaped, there is a conservation of justice; but when the New Sun appears, it will be a signal that at least the earliest operations of the shaping are complete.

XXXV

Father Inire's Letter

The quarters assigned to me were in the most ancient part of the Citadel. The rooms had been empty so long that the old castellan and the steward charged with maintaining them supposed the keys to have been lost, and offered, with many apologies and much reticence, to break the locks for me. I did not permit myself the luxury of watching their faces, but I heard their indrawn breath as I pronounced the simple words that controlled the doors.

It was fascinating, that evening, to see how much the fashions of the period in which those chambers were furnished differed from our own. They did without chairs as we know them, having for seats only complex cushions; and their tables lacked drawers and that symmetry we have come to consider essential. By our standards too, there was too much fabric and not enough wood, leather, stone, and bone; I found the effect at once sybaritic and uncomfortable.

Yet it was impossible that I should occupy a suite other than that anciently set aside for the autarchs; and impossible too that I should have it refurnished to a degree that would imply criticism of my predecessors. And if the furniture had more to recommend it to the mind than to the body, what a delight it was to discover the treasures those same predecessors had left behind: There were papers relating to matters now utterly forgotten and not always identifiable; mechanical devices ingenious and enigmatic; a microcosm that stirred to life at the warmth of my hands, and whose minute inhabitants seemed to grow larger and more human as I watched them; a laboratory containing the fabled "emerald bench" and many other things, the most interesting of which was a mandragora in spirits.

The cucurbit in which it floated was about seven spans in height and half as wide; the homuncule itself no more than two spans tall. When I tapped the glass, it turned eyes like clouded beads toward me, eyes blinder far in appearance than Master Palaemon's. I heard no sound when its lips twitched, yet I knew at once what words they shaped—and in some inexplicable sense I felt the pale fluid in which the mandragora was immersed had become my own blood-tinged urine.

''Why have you called me, Autarch, from the contemplation of your world?''

I asked, ''Is it truly mine? I know now that there are seven continents, and none but a part of this are obedient to the hallowed phrases.''

''You are the heir,'' the wizened thing said and turned, I could not tell if by accident or design, until it no longer faced me.

I tapped the cucurbit again. ''And who are you?''

''A being without parents, whose life is passed immersed in blood.''

''Why, such have I been! We should be friends then, you and I, as two of similar background usually are.''

''You *jest.*''

''Not at all. I feel a real sympathy for you, and I think we are more alike than you believe.''

The tiny figure turned again until its little face looked up into my own. *''I wish that I might credit you, Autarch.''*

''I mean it. No one has ever accused me of being an honest man, and I've told lies enough when I thought they would serve my turn, but I'm quite sincere. If I can do anything for you, tell me what it is.''

''Break the glass.''

I hesitated. ''Won't you die?''

''I have never lived. I will cease thinking. Break the glass.''

''You do live.''

''I neither grow, nor move, nor respond to any stimulus save thought, which is counted no response. I am incapable of propagating my kind, or any other. Break the glass.''

''If you are indeed unliving, I would rather find some way to stir you to life.''

''So much for brotherhood. When you were imprisoned here, Thecla, and that boy brought you the knife, why did not you look for more life then?''

The blood burned in my cheek, and I lifted the ebony baculus, but I did not strike. ''Alive or dead, you have a penetrating intelligence. Thecla is that part of me most prone to anger.''

''If you had inherited her glands with her memories, I would have succeeded.''

''And you know that. How can you know so much, who are blind?''

"The acts of coarse minds create minute vibrations that stir the waters of this bottle. I hear your thoughts."

"I notice that I hear yours. How is it that I can hear them, and not others?"

Looking now directly into the pinched face, which was lit by the sun's last shaft penetrating a dusty port, I could not be sure the lips moved at all. *"You hear yourself, as ever. You cannot hear others because your mind shrieks always, like an infant crying in a basket. Ah, I see you remember that."*

"I remember a time very long ago when I was cold and hungry. I lay upon my back, encircled by brown walls, and heard the sound of my own screams. Yes, I must have been an infant. Not old enough to crawl, I think. You are very clever. What am I thinking now?"

"That I am but an unconscious exercise of your own power, as the Claw was. It is true, of course. I was deformed, and died before birth, and have been kept here since in white brandy. Break the glass."

"I would question you first," I said.

"Brother, there is an old man with a letter at your door."

I listened. It was strange, after having listened only to his words in my mind, to hear real noises again—the calling of the sleepy blackbirds among the towers and the tapping at the door.

The messenger was old Rudesind, who had guided me to the picture-room of the House Absolute. I motioned him in (to the surprise, I think, of the sentries) because I wanted to talk to him and knew that with him I had no need to stand upon my dignity.

"Never been in here in all my years," he said. "How can I help you, Autarch?"

"We're served already, just by the sight of you. You know who we are, don't you? You recognized us when we met before."

"If I didn't know your face, Autarch, I'd know a couple dozen times over anyhow. I've been told that often. Nobody here talks about anything else, seems like. How you was licked to shape right here. How they seen you this time and that time. How you looked, and what you said to them. There ain't one cook that didn't treat you to a pastry often. All them soldiers told you stories. Been a while now since I met a woman didn't kiss you and sew up a hole in your pants. You had a dog—"

"That's true enough," I said. "We did."

"And a cat and a bird and a coti that stole apples. And you climbed every wall in this place. And jumped off after, or else swung on a rope, or else hid and pretended you'd jumped. You're every boy that's ever been here, and I've heard stories put on you that belong to men that was old when I was just a boy, and I've heard about things I did myself, seventy years ago.''

''We've already learned that the Autarch's face is always concealed behind the mask the people weave for him. No doubt it's a good thing; you can't become too proud once you understand how different you really are from the thing they bow to. But we want to hear about you. The old Autarch told us you were his sentinel in the House Absolute, and now we know you're a servant of Father Inire's.''

''I am,'' the old man said. ''I have that honor, and it's his letter I carry.'' He held up a small and somewhat smudged envelope.

''And we are Father Inire's master.''

He made a countrified bow. ''I know so, Autarch.''

''Then we order you to sit down, and rest yourself. We've questions to ask you, and we don't want to keep a man your age standing. When we were that boy you say everyone's talking of, or at least not much older, you directed us to Master Ultan's stacks. Why did you do that?''

''Not because I knew something others didn't. Not because my master ordered it, either, if that's what you're thinking. Won't you read his letter?''

''In a moment. After an honest answer, in a few words.''

The old man hung his head and pulled at his thin beard. I could see the dry skin of his face rise in hollow-sided, tiny cones as it sought to follow the white hairs. ''Autarch, you think I guessed at something back then. Perhaps some did. Perhaps my master did, I don't know.'' His rheumy eyes rolled up under his brows to look at me, then fell again. ''You were young, and seemed a likely-looking boy, so I wanted you to see.''

''To see what?''

''I'm an old man. An old man then, and an old man now. You've grown up since. I see it in your face. I'm hardly any older, because that much time isn't anything to me. If you counted all the time I've spent just going up and down my ladder, it'd be longer than that. I wanted you to see there has been a lot come before you. That there was thousands and thousands that lived and died before you was ever thought of, some better than you. I mean, Autarch, the way you was then. You'd think anybody growing up here in the old Citadel would be born knowing all that, but I've found they're not. Being around it all the time, they don't see it. But going down there to Master Ultan brings it home to the cleverer ones.''

''You are the advocate of the dead.''

The old man nodded. ''I am. People talk about being fair to this one and that one, but nobody I ever heard talks about doing right by them.

We take everything they had, which is all right. And spit, most often, on their opinions, which I suppose is all right too. But we ought to remember now and then how much of what we have we got from them. I figure while I'm still here I ought to put a word in for them. And now, if you don't mind, Autarch, I'll just lay the letter here on this funny table—''

''Rudesind . . .''

''Yes, Autarch?''

''Are you going to clean your paintings?''

He nodded again. ''That's one reason I'm eager to be gone, Autarch. I was at the House Absolute until my master—'' here he paused and seemed to swallow, as men do when they feel they have perhaps said too much ''—went away north. Got a Fechin to clean, and I'm behind.''

''Rudesind, we already know the answers to the question you think we are going to ask. We know your master is what the people call a cacogen, and that for whatever reason, he is one of those few who have chosen to cast their lots entirely with humanity, remaining on Urth as a human being. The Cumaean is another such, though perhaps you did not know that. We even know that your master was with us in the jungles of the north, where he tried until it was too late to rescue my predecessor. We only want to say that if a young man with an errand comes past again while you are on your ladder, you are to send him to Master Ultan. That is our order.''

When he had gone, I tore open the envelope. The sheet within was not large, but it was covered with tiny writing, as though a swarm of hatchling spiders had been pressed into its surface.

His servant Inire hails the bridegroom of the Urth, Master of Nessus and the House Absolute, Chief of his Race, Gold of his People, Messenger of Dawn, Helios, Hyperion, Surya, Savitar, and Autarch!

I hasten, and will reach you within two days.

It was a day and more ere I learned what had taken place. Much of my information came from the woman Agia, who at least by her own account was instrumental in freeing you. She told me also something of your past dealings with her, for I have, as you know, means of extracting information.

You will have learned from her that the Exultant Vodalus is dead by her act. His paramour, the Chatelaine Thea, at first attempted to gain control of those myrmidons who were about him at his death; but as she is by no means fitted to lead them, and still less to hold in check those in the south, I have contrived to set this woman Agia in her place. From your former mercy toward her, I trust that will meet with your approval. Certainly it is desirable to maintain in being a movement that has proved so useful in the past, and as long as the mirrors of the caller Hethor remain unbroken, she provides it with a plausible commander.

You will perhaps consider the ship I summoned to aid my master, the autarch of his day, inadequate—as for that matter do I—yet it was the best I could obtain, and I was hard pressed to get it. I myself have been forced to travel south otherwise, and much more slowly; the time may come soon when my cousins are ready to side not just with humankind but with *us*—but for the present they persist in viewing Urth as somewhat less significant than many of the colonized worlds, and ourselves on a par with the Ascians, and for that matter with the Xanthoderms and many others.

You will perhaps already have gained news both fresher and more precise than mine. On the chance that you have not: The war goes well and ill. Neither point of their envelopment penetrated far, and the southern thrust, particularly, suffered such losses that it may fairly be said to have been destroyed. I know the death of so many miserable slaves of Erebus will bring no joy to you, but at least our armies have a respite.

That they need badly. There is sedition among the Paralians, which must be rooted out. The Tarentines, your Antrustiones, and the city legions—the three groups that bore the brunt of the fighting—having suffered almost as badly as the enemy. There are cohorts among them that could not muster a hundred able soldiers.

I need not tell you we should obtain more small arms and, particularly, artillery, if my cousins can be persuaded to part with them at a price we can pay. In the meanwhile, what can be done to raise fresh troops must be done, and in time for the recruits to be trained by spring. Light units capable of skirmishing without scattering are the present need; but if the Ascians break out next year, we will require piquenaires and pilani by the hundreds of thousands, and it might be well to bring at least a part of them under arms now.

Any news you have of Abaia's incursions will be fresher than mine; I have had none since I left our lines. Hormisdas has gone into the South, I believe, but Olaguer may be able to inform you.

In haste and reverence,
INIRE

XXXVI

Of Bad Gold and Burning

Not much remains to be told. I knew I would have to leave the city in a few days, so all I hoped to do here would have to be done quickly. I had no friends in the guild I could be sure of beyond Master Palaemon, and he would be of little use in what I planned. I summoned Roche, knowing that he could not deceive me to my face for long. (I expected to see a man older than myself, but the red-haired journeyman who came at my command was hardly more than a boy; when he had gone, I studied my own face in a mirror, something I had not done before.)

He told me that he and several others who had been friends of mine more or less close had argued against my execution when the will of most of the guild was to kill me, and I believed him. He also admitted quite freely that he had proposed that I be maimed and expelled, though he said he had only done so because he had felt it to be the only way to save my life. I think he expected to be punished in some way—his cheeks and forehead, normally so ruddy, were white enough to make his freckles stand out like splatters of paint. His voice was steady, however, and he said nothing that seemed intended to excuse himself by throwing blame on someone else.

The fact was, of course, that I did intend to punish him, together with the rest of the guild. Not because I bore him or them any ill will, but because I felt that being locked below the tower for a time would arouse in them a sensitivity to that principle of justice of which Master Palaemon had spoken, and because it would be the best way to assure that the order forbidding torture I intended to issue would be carried out. Those who spend a few months in dread of that art are not likely to resent its being discontinued.

However, I said nothing about that to Roche but only asked him to bring me a journeyman's habit that evening, and to be ready with Drotte and Eata to aid me the next morning.

He returned with the clothing just after vespers. It was an indescribable pleasure to take off the stiff costume I had been wearing and put on fuligin again. By night, its dark embrace is the nearest approach to invisibility I know, and after I had slipped out of my chambers by one of the secret exits, I moved between tower and tower like a shadow until I reached the fallen section of the curtain wall.

Day had been warm; but the night was cool, and the necropolis filled with mist, just as it had been when I had come from behind the monument to save Vodalus. The mausoleum where I had played as a boy stood as I had left it, its jammed door three-quarters shut.

I had brought a candle, and I lit it when I was inside. The funeral brasses I had once kept polished were green again; drifted leaves lay uncrushed everywhere. A tree had flung a slender limb through the little, barred window.

Where I put you, there you lie,
Never let a stranger spy,
Like grass grow to any eye,
Not of me.

Here be safe, never leave it,
Should a hand come, deceive it,
Let strange eyes not believe it,
Till I see.

The stone was smaller and lighter than I remembered. The coin beneath it had grown dull with damp; but it was still there, and in a moment I held it again and recalled the boy I had been, walking shaken back to the torn wall through the fog.

Now I must ask you, you that have pardoned so many deviations and digressions from me, to excuse one more. It is the last.

A few days ago (which is to say, a long time after the real termination of the events I have set myself to narrate) I was told that a vagabond had come here to the House Absolute saying that he owed me money, and that he refused to pay it to anyone else. I suspected that I was about to see some old acquaintance, and told the chamberlain to bring him to me.

It was Dr. Talos. He appeared to be in funds, and he had dressed himself for the occasion in a capot of red velvet and a chechia of the same material. His face was still that of a stuffed fox; but it seemed to me at times that some hint of life crept into it, that something or someone now peered through the glass eyes.

"You have bettered yourself," he said, making such a low bow that the tassel of his cap swept the carpet. "You may recall that I invariably affirmed you would. Honesty, integrity, and intelligence cannot be kept down."

"We both know that nothing is easier to keep down," I said. "By my old guild, they were kept down every day. But it is good to see you again, even if you come as the emissary of your master."

For a moment the doctor looked blank. "Oh, Baldanders, you mean. No, he has dismissed me, I'm afraid. After the fight. After he dived into the lake."

"You believe he survived, then."

"Oh, I'm quite sure he survived. You didn't know him as I did, Severian. Breathing water would be nothing to him. Nothing! He had a marvelous mind. He was a supreme genius of a unique sort: everything turned inward. He combined the objectivity of the scholar with the self-absorption of the mystic."

I said, "By which you mean he carried out experiments on himself."

"Oh, no, not at all. He reversed that! Others experiment upon themselves in order to derive some rule they can apply to the world. Baldanders experimented on the world and spent the proceeds, if I can put it so bluntly, upon his person. They say—" here he looked about nervously to make sure no one but myself was in earshot "—they say I'm a monster, and so I am. But Baldanders was more monster than I. In some sense he was my father, but he had built himself. It's the law of nature, and of what is higher than nature, that each creature must have a creator. But Baldanders was his own creation; he stood behind himself, and cut himself off from the line linking the rest of us with the Increate. However, I stray from my subject." The doctor had a wallet of scarlet leather at his belt; he loosened the strings and began to rummage in it. I heard the chink of metal.

"Do you carry money now?" I asked. "You used to give everything to him."

His voice sank until I could hardly hear it. "Wouldn't you, in my present position, do the same thing? Now I leave coins, little stacks of aes and orichalks, near water." He spoke more loudly: "It does no harm, and reminds me of the great days. But I am honest, you see! He always demanded that of me. And he was honest too, after his fashion. Anyway, do you recall the morning before we came out the gate? I was handing round the receipts from the night before, and we were interrupted. There was a coin left, and it was to go to you. I saved it and meant to give it to you later, but I forgot, and then when you came to the castle. . . ." He gave me a sidelong glance. "But fair trade ends paid, as they say, and I have it here."

The coin was precisely like the one I had taken from under the stone. "You see now why I couldn't give it to your man—I'm sure he thought me mad."

I flipped the coin and caught it. It felt as though it had been lightly greased. "To tell the truth, Doctor, we don't."

"Because it's false, of course. I told you so that morning. How could I have told him I had come to pay the Autarch, and then given him a bad coin? They're terrified of you, and they'd have disemboweled me looking for a good one! Is it true you've an explosive that takes days to go up, so you can blow people apart slowly?"

I was looking at the two coins. They had the same brassy shine and appeared to have been struck in the same die.

But that little interview, as I have said, took place a long time after the proper close of my narrative. I returned to my chambers in the Flag Tower by the way I had come, and when I reached them again, took off the dripping cloak and hung it up. Master Gurloes used to say that not wearing a shirt was the hardest thing about belonging to the guild. Though he meant it ironically, it was in some sense true. I, who had gone through the mountains with a naked chest, had been softened sufficiently by a few days in the stifling autarchial vestments to shiver at a foggy autumn night.

There were fireplaces in all the rooms, and each was piled with wood so old and dry that I suspected it would fall to dust should I strike it against an andiron. I had never lit any of these fires; but I decided to do so now, and warm myself, and spread the clothes Roche had brought over the back of a chair to dry. When I looked for my firebox, however, I discovered that in my excitement I had left it in the mausoleum with the candle. Thinking vaguely that the autarch who had inhabited these rooms before me (a ruler far beyond the reach of my memory) must surely have kept some means of kindling his numerous fires close to hand, I began searching the drawers of the cabinets.

These were largely filled with the papers that had so fascinated me before; but instead of stopping to read them, as I had when I had made my original survey of the rooms, I lifted them from each drawer to see if there was not a steel, igniter, or syringe of amadou beneath them.

I found none; but instead, in the largest drawer of the largest cabinet, concealed under a filigree pen case, I discovered a small pistol.

I had seen such weapons before—the first time having been when

Vodalus had given me the false coin I had just reclaimed. Yet I had never held one in my own hands, and I found now that it was a very different thing from seeing them in the hands of others. Once when Dorcas and I were riding north toward Thrax we had fallen in with a caravan of tinkers and peddlers. We still had most of the money Dr. Talos had shared out when we met him in the forest north of the House Absolute; but we were uncertain how far it might carry us and how far we had to go, and so I was plying my trade with the rest, inquiring at each little town if there were not some malefactor to be mutilated or beheaded. The vagrants considered us two of themselves, and though some accorded us more or less exalted rank because I labored only for the authorities, others affected to despise us as the instruments of tyranny.

One evening, a grinder who had been friendlier than most and had done us several trifling favors offered to sharpen *Terminus Est* for me. I told him I kept her quite sharp enough for the work and invited him to test her edge with a finger. After he had cut himself slightly (as I had known he would) he grew quite taken with her, admiring not only her blade but her soft sheath, her carven guard, and so on. When I had answered innumerable questions regarding her making, history, and mode of use, he asked if I would permit him to hold her. I cautioned him about the weight of the blade and the danger of striking its fine edge against something that might injure it, then handed her over. He smiled and gripped the hilt as I had instructed him; but as he began to lift that long and shining instrument of death, his face went pale and his arms began to tremble so that I snatched her away from him before he dropped her. Afterward all he would say was *I've sharpened soldiers' swords often*, over and over.

Now I learned how he had felt. I laid the pistol on the table so quickly I nearly lost hold of it, then walked around and around it as though it had been a snake coiled to strike.

It was shorter than my hand, and so prettily made that it might have been a piece of jewelry; yet every line of it told of an origin beyond the nearer stars. Its silver had not yellowed with time, but might have come fresh from the buffing wheel. It was covered with decorations that were, perhaps, writing—I could not really tell which, and to eyes like mine, accustomed to patterns of straight lines and curves, they sometimes appeared to be no more than complex or shimmering reflections, save that they were reflections of something not present. The grips were encrusted with black stones whose name I did not know, gems like tourmalines but brighter. After a time I noticed that one, the smallest of all, seemed to vanish unless I looked at it straight on, when it sparkled with four-rayed brilliancy. Examining it more closely, I found it was not a gem at all, but a minute lens through which some inner fire shone. The pistol retained its charge then, after so many centuries.

Illogical though it might be, the knowledge reassured me. A weapon may be dangerous to its user in two ways: by wounding him by accident, or by failing him. The first remained; but when I saw the brightness of that point of light, I knew the second could be dismissed.

There was a sliding stud under the barrel that seemed likely to control the intensity of the discharge. My first thought was that whoever had last handled it would probably have set it to maximum intensity, and that by reversing the setting I would be able to experiment with some safety. But it was not so—the stud was positioned at the center of its range. At last I decided, by analogy with a bowstring, that the pistol was likely to be least dangerous when the stud was as far forward as possible. I put it there, pointed the weapon at the fireplace, and pulled the trigger.

The sound of a shot is the most horrible in the world. It is the scream of matter itself. Now the report was not loud, but threatening, like distant thunder. For an instant—so brief a time I might almost have believed I dreamed it—a narrow cone of violet flashed between the muzzle of the pistol and the heaped wood. Then it was gone, the wood was blazing, and slabs of burned and twisted metal fell with the noise of cracked bells from the back of the fireplace. A rivulet of silver ran out onto the hearth to scorch the mat and send up nauseous smoke.

I put the pistol into the sabretache of my new journeyman's habit.

XXXVII

Across the River Again

Before dawn, Roche was at my door, with Drotte and Eata. Drotte was the oldest of us, yet his face and flashing eyes made him seem younger than Roche. He was still the very picture of wiry strength, but I could not help but notice that I was now taller than he by the width of two fingers. I must surely have been so already when I left the Citadel, though I had not been conscious of it. Eata was still the smallest, and not yet even a journeyman—so I had only been away one summer, after all. He seemed a bit dazed when he greeted me, and I suppose he was having trouble believing I was now Autarch, particularly since he had not seen me again until now, when I was once more dressed in the habit of the guild.

I had told Roche that the three of them were to be armed; he and Drotte carried swords similar in form (though vastly inferior in workmanship) to *Terminus Est*, and Eata a clava I recalled having seen displayed at our Masking Day festivities. Before I had seen the fighting in the north, I would have thought them well-enough equipped; now all three, not only Eata, seemed like boys burdened with sticks and pine cones, ready to play at war.

For the last time we went out through the rent in the wall and threaded the paths of bone that wound among the cypresses and tombs. The death roses I had hesitated to pick for Thecla still showed a few autumnal blooms, and I found myself thinking of Morwenna, the only woman whose life I have ever taken, and of her enemy, Eusebia.

When we had passed the gate of the necropolis and entered the squalid city streets, my companions seemed to become almost lighthearted. I think they must have been subconsciously afraid they would be seen by Master Gurloes and punished in some way for having obeyed the Autarch.

"I hope you're not planning on going for a swim," Drotte said. "These choppers would sink us."

Roche chuckled. "Eata can float with his."

"We're going far to the north. We'll need a boat, but I think we'll be able to hire one if we walk along the embankment."

"If anybody will rent to us. And if we're not arrested. You know, Autarch—"

"Severian," I reminded him. "For as long as I wear these clothes."

"—Severian, we're only supposed to carry these things to the block, and it will take a lot of talking to make the peltasts think three of us are necessary. Will they know who you are? I don't—"

This time it was Eata who interrupted him, pointing toward the river. "Look, there's a boat!"

Roche bellowed, all three waved, and I held up one of the chrisos I had borrowed from the castellan, turning it so it would flash in the sunlight that was then just beginning to show over the towers behind us. The man at the tiller waved his cap, and what appeared to be a slender lad sprang forward to put the dipping lugsails on the other tack.

She was two-masted, rather narrow of beam and low of freeboard—an ideal craft, no doubt, for running untaxed merchandise past the patrol cutters that had suddenly become mine. The grizzled old moonraker of a steersman looked capable of much worse, and the slender "lad" was a girl with laughing eyes and a facility for looking from them sidelong.

"Well, this 'pears to be a day," the steersman said when he saw our habits. "I thought you was in mournin', I did, till I got up close. Eyes? I never heard of 'um, no more than a crow in court."

"We are," I told him as I got on board. It gave me a ridiculous pleasure to find I had not lost the sea legs I had acquired on the *Samru*, and to watch Drotte and Roche grab for the sheets when the lugger rocked beneath their weight.

"Mind if I've a look at that yellow boy? Just to see if he's good. I'll send him right home."

I tossed him the coin, which he rubbed and bit and at last surrendered with a respectful look.

"We may need your boat all day."

"For the yellow boy, you can have her all night too. We'll both be glad of the company, like the undertaker remarked to the ghost. There was things in the river up till first light, which I suppose might have something to do with you optimates being out on the water this mornin'?"

"Cast off," I said. "You can tell me, if you will, what these strange things were while we are under way."

Although he had broached the subject himself, the steersman seemed reluctant to go into much detail—perhaps only because he had difficulty in finding words to express what he had felt and to describe what he had seen and heard. There was a light west wind, so that with the lugger's batten-stiffened sails drawn taut we were able to run upstream handily. The brown girl had little to do but sit in the bow and trade glances with Eata. (It is possible she thought him, in his dirty gray shirt and trousers, only a paid attendant of ours.) The steersman, who called himself her uncle, kept a steady pressure on the tiller as he talked, to keep the lugger from flying off the wind.

"I'll tell you what I saw myself, like the carpenter did when he had the shutter up. We was eight or nine leagues north of where you hailed us. Clams was our cargo, you see, and there's no stoppin' with them, not when there's a chance of a warm afternoon. We goes down to the lower river and buys them off the diggers, do you see, then runs them up the channel quick so's they can be et before they goes bad. If they goes off you lose all, but you make double or better if you can sell them good.

"I've spent more nights on the river in my life than anywhere else—it's my bedroom, you might say, and this boat's my cradle, though I don't usually get to sleep until mornin'. But last night—sometimes I felt like I wasn't on old Gyoll at all, but on some other river, one that run up into the sky, or under the ground.

"I doubt you noticed unless you was out late, but it was a still night with just little breaths of wind that would blow for about as long as it takes a man to swear, then die down, then blow again. There was mist too, thick as cotton. It hung over the water the way mists always does, with about so much clear space as you could roll a keg through between it and the river. Most of the time we couldn't see the lights on either shore, just the mist. I used to have a horn I blowed for those that couldn't see our lights, but it went over the side last year, and being copper it sunk. So I shouted last night, whenever I felt like there was another boat or anything close by us.

"About a watch after the mist came I let Maxellindis go to sleep. Both sails was set, and when each puff of air come we would go up river a bit, and then I'd set out the anchor again. You maybe don't know it, optimates, but the rule of the river is that them that's goin' up keeps to the sides and them that's goin' down takes the middle. We was goin' up and ought to have been over to the east bank, but with the mist I couldn't tell.

"Then I heard sweeps. I looked in the mist, but I couldn't see lights, and I hollered so they'd sheer off. I leaned over the gunnel and put my ear close to the water so's to hear better. A mist soaks up noises, but the best hearin' you can ever have is when you gets your head under one, because the noise runs right along the water. Anyway, I did that, and she was a big one. You can't count how many sweeps there is with a good crew pullin', because they all go in and come up together, but when a big vessel goes fast you can hear water breakin' under her bow, and this was a big one. I got up on top of the deckhouse tryin' to see her, but there still wasn't any lights, though I knew she had to be close.

"Just when I was climbin' down I caught the sight of her—a galleass, four-masted and four-banked, no lights, comin' right up the channel, as near as I could judge. Pray for them that's comin' down, thinks I to myself, like the ox said when he fell out of the riggin'.

"Of course I only saw her for a minute before she was gone in the mist again, but I heard her a long while after. Seein' her like that made me feel so queer I yelled every once in a while even if no other craft was by. We had made another half league, I suppose, or maybe a little less, when I heard somebody yell back. Only it wasn't like answerin' my hail, but like somebody'd laid a rope end to him. I called again, and he called back regular, and it was a man I know named Trason what has his own boat just like I do. 'Is it you?' he called, and I said it was and asked if he was all right. 'Tie up!' he says.

"I told him I couldn't. I had clams, and even if the night was cool, I wanted to sell soon as I could. 'Tie up,' Trason calls again, 'tie up and go ashore.' So I call back, 'Why don't you?' Just then he come in sight, and there was more on his boat than I would've thought it would hold—pandours, I'd have said, but every pandour ever I saw had a face brown as mine or nearly, and these was white as the mist. They had scorpions and voulges—I could see the heads of them stickin' up over the crests of their helmets."

I interrupted him to ask if the soldiers he had seen were starved looking and if they had large eyes.

He shook his head, one corner of his mouth twisting up. "They was big men, bigger than you or me or anybody in this boat, a head taller than Trason. Anyway, they were gone in a moment, just like the galleass. That was the only other craft I saw till the mist lifted. But . . ."

I said, "But you saw something else. Or heard something."

He nodded. "I thought maybe you and your people here was out because of them. Yes, I saw and I heard things. There was things in this river *I* never saw before. Maxellindis, when she woke up and I told her about it, said it was the manatees. They're pale in moonlight and look human enough if you don't come too close. But I've seen 'em since I was a boy and never been fooled once. And there was women's voices, not loud but big. And something else. I couldn't understand what any of 'em was sayin', but I could hear the tone of it. You know how it is when you're listenin' to people over the water? They would say *so-and-so-and-so*. Then the deeper voice—I can't call it a man's because I don't think it was one—the deeper voice'd say *go-and-do-that-and-this-and-that*. I heard the women's voices three times and the other voice twice. You won't believe it, optimates, but sometimes it sounded like the voices was coming up out of the river."

With that he fell silent, looking out over the nenuphars. We were well above that part of Gyoll opposite the Citadel, but they were still packed more densely than wildflowers in any meadow this side of paradise.

The Citadel itself was visible now as a whole, and for all its vastness seemed a glittering flock fluttering upon the hill, its thousand metal towers ready to leap into the air at a word. Below them the necropolis spread an embroidery of mingled white and green. I know it is fashionable to speak in tones of faint disgust of the "unhealthy" growth of the lawns and trees in such places, but I have never observed that there is actually anything unhealthy about it. Green things die that men may live, and men die that green things may live, even that ignorant and innocent man I killed with his own ax there long ago. All our foliage is faded, so it is said, and no doubt it is so; and when the New Sun comes, his bride, the New Urth, will give glory to him with leaves like emeralds. But in the present day, the day of the old sun and old Urth, I have never seen any other green so deep as the great pines' in the necropolis when the wind swells their branches. They draw their strength from the departed generations of mankind, and the masts of argosies, that are built up of many trees, are not so high as they.

The Sanguinary Field stands far from the river. We four drew strange looks as we journeyed there, but no one halted us. The Inn of Lost Loves, which had ever seemed to me the least permanent of the houses of men, still stood as it had on the afternoon when I had come there with Agia and Dorcas. The fat innkeeper very nearly fainted when he saw us; I made him fetch Ouen, the waiter.

I had never really looked at him on that afternoon when he had carried in a tray for Dorcas, Agia, and me. I did so now. He was a balding man about as tall as Drotte, thin and somehow pinched looking; his eyes were deep blue, and there was a delicacy to the molding of his eyes and mouth that I recognized at once.

"Do you know who we are?" I asked him.

Slowly, he shook his head.

"Have you never had a torturer to serve?"

"Once this spring, sieur," he said. "And I know these two men in black are torturers. But you're no torturer, sieur, though you're dressed like one."

I let that pass. "You have never seen me?"

"No, sieur."

"Very well, perhaps you have not." (How strange it was to realize that I had changed so much.) "Ouen, since you do not know me, it might be well if I knew you. Tell me where you were born and who your parents were, and how you came to be employed at this inn."

"My father was a shopkeeper, sieur. We lived in Oldgate, on the west bank. When I was ten or so, I think, he sent me to an inn to be a potboy, and I've worked in one or another since."

"Your father was a shopkeeper. What of your mother?"

Ouen's face still held a waiter's deference, but his eyes were puzzled. "I never knew her, sieur. Cas they called her, but she died when I was young. In childbirth, my father said."

"But you know what she looked like."

He nodded. "My father had a locket with her likeness. Once when I was twenty or so I came to see him and found out he'd pledged it. I'd come into a bit of money then helping a certain optimate with his affairs—carrying messages to the ladies and standing watch outside doors and so on, and I went to the pawnbroker's and paid the pledge and took it. I still wear it, sieur. In a place like ours, where there's so many in 'n out all the time, it's best to keep your valuables about you."

He reached into his shirt and drew out a locket of cloisonné enamel. The pictures inside were of Dorcas in full face and profile, a Dorcas hardly younger than the Dorcas I had known.

"You say you became a potboy at ten, Ouen. But you can read and write."

"A bit, sieur." He looked embarrassed. "I've asked people, various times, what writing said. I don't forget much."

"You wrote something when the torturer was here this spring," I told him. "Do you recall what you wrote?"

Frightened, he shook his head. "Only a note to warn the girl."

"I do. It was, 'The woman with you has been here before. Do not trust her. Trudo says the man is a torturer. You are my mother come again.' "

Ouen tucked his locket under his shirt. "It was only that she was so much like her, sieur. When I was a younger man, I used to think that someday I'd find such a woman. I told myself, you know, that I was a better man than my father, and he had, after all. But I never did, and now I'm not so sure I'm a better man."

"At that time, you did not know what a torturer's habit looked like," I said. "But your friend Trudo, the ostler, knew. He knew a good deal more about torturers than you, and that was why he ran away."

"Yes, sieur. When he heard the torturer was asking for him, he did."

"But you saw the innocence of the girl and wanted to warn her against the torturer and the other woman. You were right about both of them, perhaps."

"If you say it, sieur."

"Do you know, Ouen, you look a bit like her."

The fat innkeeper had been listening more or less openly. Now he chuckled. "He looks more like you!"

I am afraid I turned to stare at him.

"No offense intended, sieur, but it's true. He's a bit older, but when you were talking I saw both your faces from the side, and there isn't a patch of difference."

I studied Ouen again. His hair and eyes were not dark like mine, but with that coloring aside, his face might almost have been my own.

"You said you never found a woman like Dorcas—like that one in your locket. Still you found a woman, I think."

His eyes would not meet mine. "Several, sieur."

"And fathered a child."

"No, sieur!" He was startled. "Never, sieur!"

"How interesting. Were you ever in difficulties with the law?"

"Several times, sieur."

"It is well to keep your voice low, but it need not be so low as that. And look at me when you speak to me. A woman you loved—or perhaps only one who loved you—a dark woman—was taken once?"

"Once, sieur," he said. "Yes, sieur. Catherine was her name. It's an old-fashioned name, they tell me." He paused and shrugged. "There was trouble, as you say, sieur. She'd run off from some order of monials. The law got her, and I never saw her again."

He did not want to come, but we brought him with us when we returned to the lugger.

When I had come upriver by night on the *Samru*, the line between the living and the dead city had been like that between the dark curve of the world and the celestial dome with its stars. Now, when there was so much more light, it had vanished. Half-ruinous structures lined the banks, but whether they were the homes of the most wretched of our citizens or mere deserted shells I could not determine until I saw a string on which three rags flapped.

"In the guild we have the ideal of poverty," I said to Drotte as we leaned on the gunnel. "But those people do not need the ideal; they have achieved it."

"I should think they'd need it most of all," he answered.

He was wrong. The Increate was there, a thing beyond the Hierodules and those they serve; even on the river, I could feel his presence as one feels that of the master of a great house, though he may be in an obscure room on another floor. When we went ashore, it seemed to me that if I were to step through any doorway there, I might surprise some shining figure; and that the commander of all such figures was everywhere invisible only because he was too large to be seen.

We found a man's sandal, worn but not old, lying in one of the grass-grown streets. I said, "I'm told there are looters wandering this place. That is one reason I asked you to come. If there were no one but myself involved, I would do it alone."

Roche nodded and drew his sword, but Drotte said, "There's no one here. You've become a great deal wiser than we are, Severian, but still, I think you've grown a little too accustomed to things that terrify ordinary people."

I asked what he meant.

"You knew what the boatman was talking about. I could see that in your face. You were afraid too, or at least concerned. But not frightened like he was in his boat last night, or like Roche or Ouen there or I would have been if we'd been close to the river and knew what was going on. The looters you're talking about were around last night, and they must keep a watch out for revenue boats. They won't be anywhere near water today, or for several days to come."

Eata touched my arm. "Do you think that girl—Maxellindis—is she in danger, back there on the boat?"

"She's not in as much danger as you are from her," I said. He did not know what I meant, but I did. His Maxellindis was not Thecla; his story could not be the same as my own. But I had seen the revolving corridors of Time behind the gamin face with the laughing brown eyes. Love is a long labor for torturers; and even if I were to dissolve the guild, Eata would become a torturer, as all men are, bound by the contempt for wealth without which a man is less than a man, inflicting pain by his nature, whether he willed it or not. I was sorry for him, and more sorry for Maxellindis the sailor girl.

* * *

Ouen and I went into the house, leaving Roche, Drotte, and Eata to keep watch from some distance away. As we stood at the door, I could hear the soft sound of Dorcas's steps inside.

"We will not tell you who you are," I said to Ouen. "And we cannot tell you what you may become. But we are your Autarch, and we tell you what you must do."

I had no words for him, but I discovered I did not need them. He knelt at once, as the castellan had.

"We brought the torturers with us so that you might know what was in store for you if you disobeyed us. But we do not wish you to disobey, and now, having met you, we doubt they were needed. There is a woman in this house. In a moment you will go in. You must tell her your story, as you told it to us, and you must remain with her and protect her, even if she tries to send you away."

"I will do my best, Autarch," Ouen said.

"When you can, you must persuade her to leave this city of death. Until then, we give you this." I took out the pistol and handed it to him. "It is worth a cartload of chrisos, but as long as you are here, it is far better for you to have than chrisos. When you and the woman are safe, we will buy it back from you, if you wish." I showed him how to operate the pistol and left him.

I was alone then, and I do not doubt that there are some who, reading this too-brief account of a summer more than normally turbulent, will say that I have usually been so. Jonas, my only real friend, was in his own eyes merely a machine; Dorcas, whom I yet love, is in her own eyes merely a kind of ghost.

I do not feel it is so. We choose—or choose not—to be alone when we decide whom we will accept as our fellows, and whom we will reject. Thus an eremite in a mountain cave is in company, because the birds and coneys, the initiates whose words live in his "forest books," and the winds—the messengers of the Increate— are his companions. Another man, living in the midst of millions, may be alone, because there are none but enemies and victims around him.

Agia, whom I might have loved, has chosen instead to become a female Vodalus, taking all that lives most fully in humanity as her opponent. I, who might have loved Agia, who loved Dorcas deeply but perhaps not deeply enough, was now alone because I had become a part of her past, which she loved better than she had ever (except, I think, at first) loved me.

XXXVIII

Resurrection

Almost nothing remains to be told. Dawn has come, the red sun like a bloody eye. The wind blows cold through the window. In a few moments, a footman will carry in a steaming tray; with him, no doubt, will be old, twisted Father Inire, eager to confer during the last few moments that remain; old Father Inire, alive so long beyond the span of his short-lived kind; old Father Inire, who will not, I fear, long survive the red sun. How upset he will be to find I have been sitting up writing all night here in the clerestory.

Soon I must don robes of argent, the color that is more pure than white. Never mind.

There will be long, slow days on the ship. I will read. I still have so much to learn. I will sleep, dozing in my berth, listening to the centuries wash against the hull. This manuscript I shall send to Master Ultan; but while I am on the ship, when I cannot sleep and have tired of reading, I shall write it out again—I who forget nothing—every word, just as I have written it here. I shall call it *The Book of the New Sun*, for that book, lost now for so many ages, is said to have predicted his coming. And when it is finished again, I shall seal that second copy in a coffer of lead and set it adrift on the seas of space and time.

Have I told you all I promised? I am aware that at various places in my narrative I have pledged that this or that should be made clear in the knitting up of the story. I remember them all, I am sure, but then I remember so much else. Before you assume that I have cheated you, read again, as I will write again.

Two things are clear to me. The first is that I am not the first Severian. Those who walk the corridors of Time saw him gain the Phoenix Throne, and thus it was that the Autarch, having been told of me, smiled in the House Azure, and the undine thrust me up when it seemed I must drown. (Yet surely the first Severian did not; something had already begun to reshape my life.) Let me guess now, though it is only a guess, at the story of that first Severian.

He too was reared by the torturers, I think. He too was sent forth to Thrax. He too fled Thrax, and though he did not carry the Claw of the Conciliator, he must have been drawn to the fighting in the north—no doubt he hoped to escape the archon by hiding himself among the army. How he encountered the Autarch there I cannot say; but encounter him he did, and so, even as I, he (who in the final sense was and is myself) became Autarch in turn and sailed beyond the candles of night. Then those who walk the corridors walked back to the time when he was young, and my own story—as I have given it here in so many pages—began.

The second thing is this. He was not returned to his own time but became himself a walker of the corridors. I know now the identity of the man called the Head of Day, and why Hildegrin, who was too near, perished when we met, and why the witches fled. I know too in whose mausoleum I tarried as a child, that little building of stone with its rose, its fountain, and its flying ship all graven. I have disturbed my own tomb, and now I go to lie in it.

When Drotte, Roche, Eata, and I returned to the Citadel, I received urgent messages from Father Inire and from the House Absolute, and yet I lingered. I asked the castellan for a map. After much searching he produced one, large and old, cracked in many places. It showed the curtain wall whole, but the names of the towers were not the names I knew—or that the castellan knew, for that matter—and there were towers on that map that are not in the Citadel, and towers in the Citadel that were not on that map.

I ordered a flier then, and for half a day soared among the towers. No doubt I saw the place I sought many times, but if so I did not recognize it.

At last, with a bright and unfailing lamp, I went down into our oubliette once more, down flight after flight of steps until I had reached the lowest level. What is it, I wonder, that has given so great a power to preserve the past to underground places? One of the bowls in which I had carried soup to Triskele was there still. (Triskele, who had stirred back to life beneath my hand two years before I bore the Claw.) I followed Triskele's footprints once more, as I had when still an apprentice, to the forgotten opening, and from there my own into the dark maze of tunnels.

Now in the steady light of my lamp I saw where I had lost the track, running straight on when Triskele had turned aside. I was tempted then to follow him instead of myself, so that I might see where he had emerged, and in that way perhaps discover who it was who had befriended him and to whom he used to return after greeting me, sometimes, in the byways of the Citadel. Possibly when I come back to Urth I shall do so, if indeed I do come back.

But once again, I did not turn aside. I followed the boy-man I had been, down a straight corridor floored with mud and pierced at rare intervals with forbidding vents and doors. The Severian I pursued wore ill-fitting shoes with run-down heels and worn soles; when I turned and flashed my light behind me, I observed that though the Severian who pursued him had excellent boots, his steps were of unequal length and the toe of one foot dragged at each. I thought, One Severian had good boots, the other good legs. And I laughed to myself, wondering who should come here in afteryears, and whether he would guess that the same feet left both tracks.

To what use these tunnels were once put, I cannot say. Several times I saw stairs that had once descended farther still, but always they led to dark, calm water. I found a skeleton, its bones scattered by the running feet of Severian, but it was only a skeleton, and told me nothing. In places there was writing on the walls, writing in faded orange or sturdy black; but it was in a character I could not read, as unintelligible as the scrawlings of the rats in Master Ultan's library. A few of the rooms into which I looked held walls in which there had once ticked a thousand or more clocks of various kinds, and though all were dead now, their chimes silenced and their hands corroded at hours that would never come again, I thought them good omens for one who sought the Atrium of Time.

And at last I found it. The little spot of sunshine was just as I had remembered it. No doubt I acted foolishly, but I extinguished my lamp and stood for a moment in the dark, looking at it. All was silence, and its bright, uneven square seemed at least as mysterious as it had before.

I had feared I would have difficulty in squeezing through its narrow crevice, but if the present Severian was somewhat larger of bone, he was also leaner, so that when I had worked my shoulders through the rest followed easily enough.

The snow I recalled was gone, but a chill had come into the air to say that it would soon return. A few dead leaves, which must have been carried in some updraft very high indeed, had come to rest here among the dying roses. The tilted dials still cast their crazy shadows, useless as the dead clocks beneath them, though not so unmoving. The carven animals stared at them, unwinking still.

I crossed to the door and tapped on it. The timorous old woman who had served us appeared, and I, stepping into that musty room in which I had warmed myself before, told her to bring Valeria to me. She hurried away, but before she was out of sight, something had wakened in the time-worn walls, its disembodied voices, hundred-tongued, demanding that Valeria report to some antiquely titled personage who I realized with a start must be myself.

Here my pen shall halt, reader, though I do not. I have carried you from gate to gate—from the locked and fog-shrouded gate of the necropolis of Nessus to that cloud-racked gate we call the sky, the gate that shall lead me, as I hope, beyond the nearer stars.

My pen halts, though I do not. Reader, you will walk no more with me. It is time we both take up our lives.

To this account, I, Severian the Lame, Autarch, do set my hand in what shall be called the last year of the old sun.

Appendix

The Arms of the Autarch and the Ships of the Hierodules

Nowhere are the manuscripts of *The Book of the New Sun* more obscure than in their treatment of weapons and military organization.

The confusion concerning the equipment of Severian's allies and adversaries appears to derive from two sources, of which the first is his marked tendency to label every variation in design or purpose with a separate name. In translating these, I have endeavored to bear in mind the radical meaning of the words employed as well as what I take to be the appearance and function of the weapons themselves. Thus *falchion, fuscina,* and many others. At one point I have put the *athame*, the warlock's sword, into Agia's hands.

The second source of difficulty seems to be that three quite different gradations of technology are involved. The lowest of these could be termed the smith level. The arms produced by it appear to consist of swords, knives, axes, and pikes, such as might have been forged by any skilled metalworker of, say, the fifteenth century. These appear to be readily obtained by the average citizen and to represent the technological ability of the society as a whole.

The second gradation might be called the Urth level. The long cavalry weapons I have chosen to call *lances, conti,* and so on undoubtedly belong to this group, as do the "spears" with which the hastarii menaced Severian outside the door of the antechamber and other arms used by infantry. How widely available such weapons were is not clear from the text, which at one point speaks of "arrows" and "long-shafted khetens" being offered for sale in Nessus. It seems certain that Guasacht's irregulars were issued their conti before battle and that these were collected and stored somewhere (possibly in his tent) afterward. Perhaps it should be noted that small arms were issued and collected in this way in the navies of the eighteenth and nineteenth centuries, although cutlasses and firearms could be freely purchased ashore. The arbalests used by Agia's assassins outside the mine are surely what I have called Urth weapons, but it is likely these men were deserters.

The Urth weapons, then, appear to represent the highest technology to be found on the planet, and perhaps in its solar system. How efficient they would be in comparison with our own arms is difficult to say. Armor appears to be not wholly ineffective against them, but precisely this is true with regard to our rifles, carbines, and submachine guns.

The third gradation I would call the stellar level. The pistol given Thea by Vodalus and the one given Ouen by Severian are unquestionably stellar weapons, but about many other arms mentioned in the manuscript we cannot be so sure. Some, or even all, of the artillery used in the mountain war may be stellar. The *fusils* and *jezails* carried by special troops on both sides may or may not belong to this gradation, though I am inclined to think they do.

It seems fairly clear that stellar weapons could not be produced on Urth and had to be obtained from the Hierodules at great cost. An interesting question—to which I can offer no certain answer—concerns the goods given in exchange. The Urth of the old sun seems, by our standards, destitute of raw materials; when Severian speaks of mining, he appears to mean what we should call archaeological pillaging, and the new continents said (in Dr. Talos's play) to be ready to rise with the coming of the New Sun have among their attractions "gold, silver, *iron*, and *copper* . . ." (Italics added.) Slaves—some slavery certainly exists in Severian's society—furs, meat and other foodstuffs, and labor-intensive items such as handmade jewelry would appear to be among the possibilities.

We would like to know more about almost everything mentioned in these manuscripts; but most of all, certainly, we would like to know more about the ships that sail between the stars, commanded by the Hierodules but sometimes crewed by human beings. (Two of the most enigmatic figures in the manuscripts, Jonas and Hethor, seem once to have been such crewmen.) But here the translator is forced against one of the most maddening of all his difficulties—Severian's failure to distinguish clearly between space-going and ocean-going craft.

Irritating though it is, it seems quite natural, given his circumstances. If a distant continent is as remote as the moon, then the moon is no more remote than a distant continent. Furthermore, the star-traveling ships appear to be propelled by light pressure on immense sails of metal foil, so that an applied science of masts, cables, and spars is common to ships of both kinds. Presumably, since many skills (and perhaps most of all that of enduring long periods of isolation) would be required equally on both types of craft, crewmen from vessels that would only excite our contempt may sign aboard others whose capabilities would astonish us. One notes that the captain of Severian's lugger shares some of Jonas's habits of speech.

And now, a final comment. In my translations and in these appendixes I have attached to them, I have attempted to eschew all speculations; it seems to me that now, near the close of seven years' labor, I may be permitted one. It is that the ability to traverse hours and aeons possessed by these ships may be no more than the natural consequence of their ability to penetrate interstellar and even intergalactic space, and to escape the death throes of the universe; and that to travel thus in time may not be so complex and difficult an affair as we are prone to suppose. It is possible that from the beginning Severian had some presentiment of his future.

G. W.